*The Wordsworth Collection of*

# *Classic Romance*

JANE AUSTEN

*Pride and Prejudice*

*Persuasion*

CHARLOTTE BRONTË

*Jane Eyre*

EMILY BRONTË

*Wuthering Heights*

THOMAS HARDY

*Tess of the d'Urbevilles*

*Wordsworth Editions*

Readers who are interested in other titles from
Wordsworth Editions are invited to visit out website at
www.wordsworth-editions.com

For our latest list and a full mail-order service contact
Bibliophile Books, 5 Thomas Road, London E14 7BN
Tel: +44 0207 515 9222 Fax: +44 0207 538 4115
e-mail: orders@bibliophilebooks.com

This edition published 2005 by Wordsworth Editions Limited
8B East Street, Ware, Hertfordshire SG12 9HJ

ISBN 1 84022 486 X



2 4 6 8 10 9 7 5 3 1



Typeset by Antony Gray
Printed in Great Britain by
Mackays of Chatham, Chatham, Kent

# CONTENTS

# PRIDE AND PREJUDICE

# Pride and Prejudice

JANE AUSTEN

*With illustrations by*

HUGH THOMSON

# *List of Illustrations*

## *Chapter 1*

It is a truth universally acknowledged, that a single man in possession of a good fortune, must be in want of a wife.

However little known the feelings or views of such a man may be on his first entering a neighbourhood, this truth is so well fixed in the minds of the surrounding families, that he is considered as the rightful property of some one or other of their daughters.

'My dear Mr Bennet,' said his lady to him one day, 'have you heard that Netherfield Park is let at last?'

Mr Bennet replied that he had not.

'But it is,' returned she; 'for Mrs Long has just been here, and she told me all about it.'

Mr Bennet made no answer.

'Do not you want to know who has taken it?' cried his wife impatiently.

'*You* want to tell me, and I have no objection to hearing it.'

This was invitation enough.

'Why, my dear, you must know, Mrs Long says that Netherfield is taken by a young man of large fortune from the north of England; that he came down on Monday in a chaise and four to see the place, and was so much delighted with it that he agreed with Mr Morris immediately; that he is to take possession before

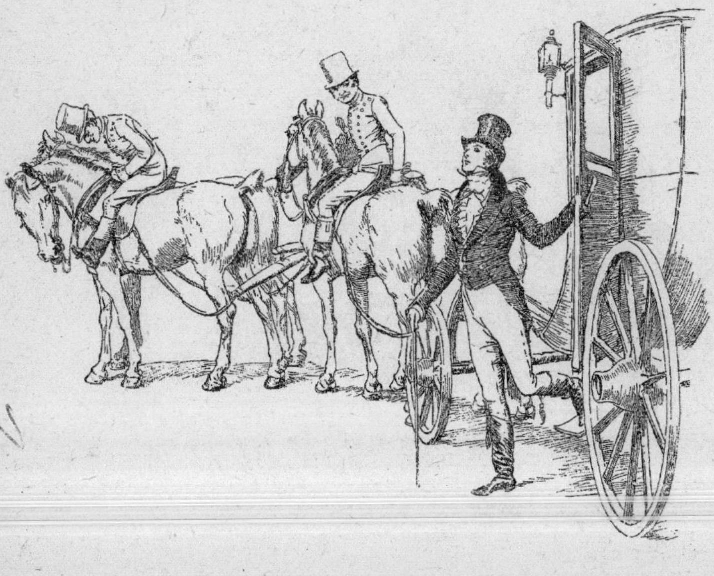

*He came down in a chaise and four to see the place*

Michaelmas, and some of his servants are to be in the house by the end of next week.'

'What is his name?'

'Bingley.'

'Is he married or single?'

'Oh! single, my dear, to be sure! A single man of large fortune; four or five thousand a year. What a fine thing for our girls!'

'How so? how can it affect them?'

'My dear Mr Bennet,' replied his wife, 'how can you be so tiresome! You must know that I am thinking of his marrying one of them.'

'Is that his design in settling here?'

'Design! nonsense, how can you talk so! But it is very likely that he *may* fall in love with one of them, and therefore you must visit him as soon as he comes.'

'I see no occasion for that. You and the girls may go, or you may send them by themselves, which perhaps will be still better, for as you are as handsome as any of them, Mr Bingley might like you the best of the party.'

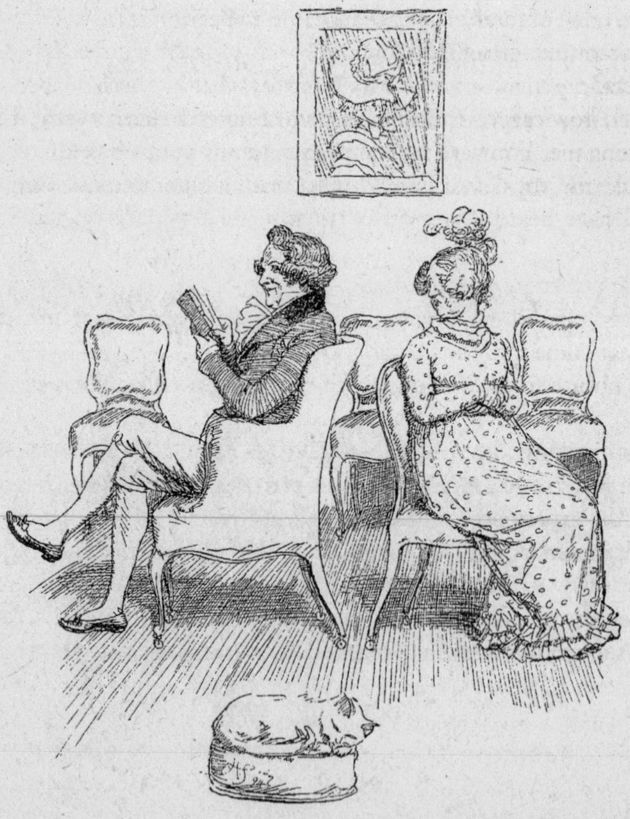

*Mr and Mrs Bennet*

'My dear, you flatter me. I certainly *have* had my share of beauty, but I do not pretend to be anything extraordinary now. When a woman has five grown-up daughters, she ought to give over thinking of her own beauty.'

'In such cases, a woman has not often much beauty to think of.'

'But, my dear, you must indeed go and see Mr Bingley when he comes into the neighbourhood.'

'It is more than I engage for, I assure you.'

'But consider your daughters. Only think what an establishment it would be for one of them. Sir William and Lady Lucas are determined to go, merely on that account, for in general you know they visit no newcomers. Indeed you must go, for it will be impossible for *us* to visit him, if you do not.'

'You are over-scrupulous surely. I dare say Mr Bingley will be very glad to see you; and I will send a few lines by you to assure him of my hearty consent to his marrying whichever he chooses of the girls; though I must throw in a good word for my little Lizzy.'

'I desire you will do no such thing. Lizzy is not a bit better than the others; and I am sure she is not half so handsome as Jane, nor half so good-humoured as Lydia. But you are always giving *her* the preference.'

'They have none of them much to recommend them,' replied he; 'they are all silly and ignorant like other girls; but Lizzy has something more of quickness than her sisters.'

'Mr Bennet, how can you abuse your own children in such a way? You take delight in vexing me. You have no compassion on my poor nerves.'

'You mistake me, my dear. I have a high respect for your nerves. They are my old friends. I have heard you mention them with consideration these twenty years at least.'

'Ah! you do not know what I suffer.'

'But I hope you will get over it, and live to see many young men of four thousand a year come into the neighbourhood.'

'It will be no use to us, if twenty such should come since you will not visit them.'

'Depend upon it, my dear, that when there are twenty, I will visit them all.'

Mr Bennet was so odd a mixture of quick parts, sarcastic humour, reserve, and caprice, that the experience of three and twenty years had been insufficient to make his wife understand his character. *Her* mind was less difficult to develop. She was a woman of mean understanding, little information, and uncertain temper. When she was discontented she fancied herself nervous. The business of her life was to get her daughters married; its solace was visiting and news.

# *Chapter 2*

Mr Bennet was among the earliest of those who waited on Mr Bingley. He had always intended to visit him, though to the last always assuring his wife that he should not go; and till the evening after the visit was paid, she had no knowledge of it. It was then disclosed in the following manner. Observing his second daughter employed in trimming a hat, he suddenly addressed her with, 'I hope Mr Bingley will like it Lizzy.'

'We are not in a way to know *what* Mr Bingley likes,' said her mother resentfully, 'since we are not to visit.'

'But you forget, mamma,' said Elizabeth, 'that we shall meet him at the assemblies, and that Mrs Long has promised to introduce him.'

'I do not believe Mrs Long will do any such thing. She has two nieces of her own. She is a selfish, hypocritical woman, and I have no opinion of her.'

'No more have I,' said Mr Bennet; 'and I am glad to find that you do not depend on her serving you.'

Mrs Bennet deigned not to make any reply; but unable to contain herself, began scolding one of her daughters.

'Don't keep coughing so, Kitty, for heaven's sake! Have a little compassion on my nerves. You tear them to pieces.'

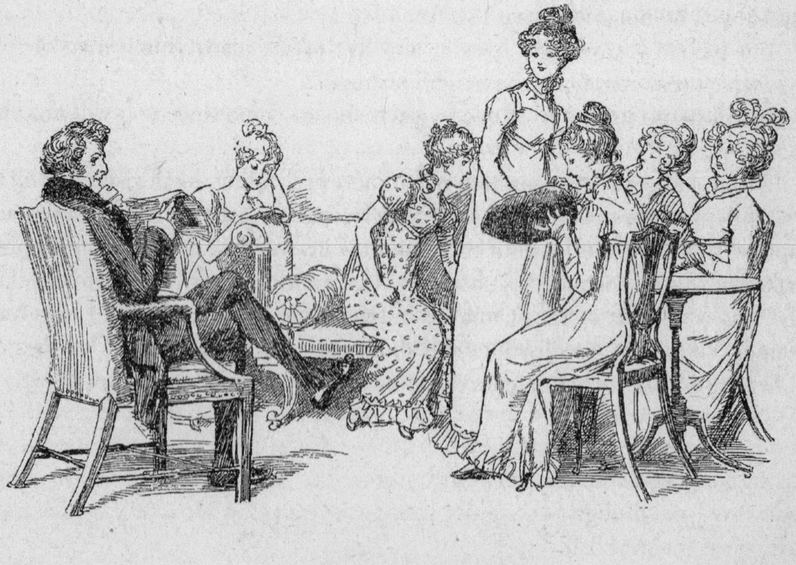

*I hope Mr Bingley will like it*

'Kitty has no discretion in her coughs,' said her father; 'she times them ill.'

'I do not cough for my own amusement,' replied Kitty fretfully.

'When is your next ball to be, Lizzy?'

'Tomorrow fortnight.'

'Aye, so it is,' cried her mother, 'and Mrs Long does not come back till the day before; so, it will be impossible for her to introduce him, for she will not know him herself.'

'Then, my dear, you may have the advantage of your friend, and introduce Mr Bingley to *her*.'

'Impossible, Mr Bennet, impossible, when I am not acquainted with him myself; how can you be so teasing?'

'I honour your circumspection. A fortnight's acquaintance is certainly very little. One cannot know what a man really is by the end of a fortnight. But if *we* do not venture, somebody else will; and after all, Mrs Long and her nieces must stand their chance; and therefore, as she will think it an act of kindness, if you decline the office, I will take it on myself.'

The girls stared at their father. Mrs Bennet said only, 'Nonsense, nonsense!'

'What can be the meaning of that emphatic exclamation?' cried he. 'Do you consider the forms of introduction, and the stress that is laid on them, as nonsense? I cannot quite agree with you *there*. What say you, Mary? for you are a young lady of deep reflection I know, and read great books, and make extracts.'

Mary wished to say something very sensible, but knew not how.

'While Mary is adjusting her ideas,' he continued, 'let us return to Mr Bingley.'

'I am sick of Mr Bingley,' cried his wife.

'I am sorry to hear *that*; but why did not you tell me so before? If I had known as much this morning, I certainly would not have called on him. It is very unlucky; but as I have actually paid the visit, we cannot escape the acquaintance now.'

The astonishment of the ladies was just what he wished; that of Mrs Bennet perhaps surpassing the rest; though when the first tumult of joy was over, she began to declare that it was what she had expected all the while.

'How good it was in you, my dear Mr Bennet! But I knew I should persuade you at last. I was sure you loved your girls too well to neglect such an acquaintance. Well, how pleased I am! and it is such a good joke, too, that you should have gone this morning, and never said a word about it till now.'

'Now, Kitty, you may cough as much as you choose,' said Mr Bennet; and, as he spoke, he left the room, fatigued with the raptures of his wife.

'What an excellent father you have, girls,' said she, when the door was shut. 'I do not know how you will ever make him amends for his kindness; or me either, for that matter. At our time of life, it is not so pleasant I can tell you, to be making new acquaintance every day; but for your sakes, we would do anything. Lydia, my love, though you *are* the youngest, I dare say Mr Bingley will dance with you at the next ball.'

'Oh!' said Lydia stoutly, 'I am not afraid; for though I *am* the youngest, I'm the tallest.'

The rest of the evening was spent in conjecturing how soon he would return Mr Bennet's visit, and determining when they should ask him to dinner.

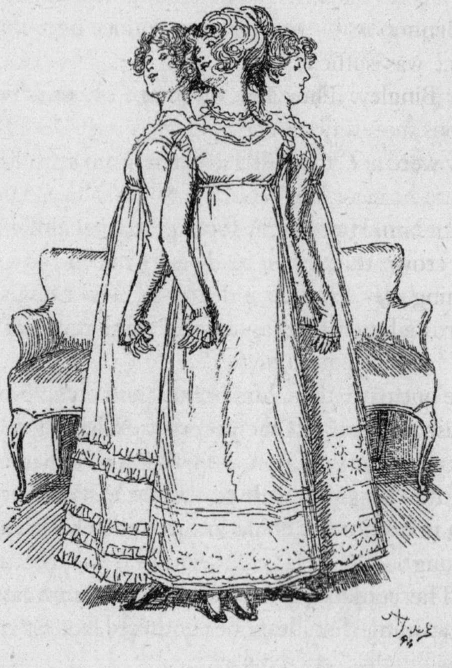

*Though I am the youngest, I'm the tallest*

## *Chapter 3*

Not all that Mrs Bennet, however, with the assistance of her five daughters, could ask on the subject was sufficient to draw from her husband any satisfactory description of Mr Bingley. They attacked him in various ways; with barefaced questions, ingenious suppositions, and distant surmises; but he eluded the skill of them all; and they were at last obliged to accept the second-hand intelligence of their neighbour Lady Lucas. Her report was highly favourable. Sir William had been delighted with him. He was quite young, wonderfully handsome, extremely agreeable, and to crown the whole, he meant to be at the next assembly with a large party. Nothing could be more delightful! To be fond of dancing was a certain step towards falling in love; and very lively hopes of Mr Bingley's heart were entertained.

'If I can but see one of my daughters happily settled at Netherfield,' said Mrs Bennet to her husband, 'and all the others equally well married, I shall have nothing to wish for.'

In a few days Mr Bingley returned Mr Bennet's visit, and sat about ten minutes with him in his library. He had entertained hopes of being admitted to a sight of the young ladies, of whose beauty he had heard much; but he saw only the father. The ladies were somewhat more fortunate, for they had the advantage of ascertaining from an upper window, that he wore a blue coat and rode a black horse.

An invitation to dinner was soon afterwards dispatched; and already had Mrs Bennet planned the courses that were to do credit to her housekeeping, when an answer arrived which deferred it all. Mr Bingley was obliged to be in town the following day, and consequently unable to accept the honour of their invitation, etc. Mrs Bennet was quite disconcerted. She could not imagine what business he could have in town so soon after his arrival in Hertfordshire; and she began to fear that he might be always flying about from one place to another, and never settled at Netherfield as he ought to be. Lady Lucas quieted her fears a little by starting the idea of his being gone to London only to get a large party for the ball; and a report soon followed that Mr Bingley was to bring twelve ladies and seven gentlemen with him to the assembly. The girls grieved over such a number of ladies; but were comforted the day before the ball by hearing, that instead of twelve, he had brought only six with him from London, his five sisters and a cousin. And when the party entered the assembly room, it consisted of only five altogether: Mr Bingley, his two sisters, the husband of the eldest, and another young man.

Mr Bingley was good looking and gentlemanlike; he had a pleasant countenance, and easy, unaffected manners. His sisters were fine women, with an air of decided fashion. His brother-in-law, Mr Hurst, merely looked the gentleman; but his friend Mr Darcy soon drew the attention of the room by his fine, tall person, handsome features, noble mien; and the report which was in general circulation within five minutes after his entrance, of his having ten thousand a year. The gentlemen pronounced him to be a fine figure of a man, the ladies declared he was much handsomer than Mr Bingley, and he was looked at with great admiration for about half the evening, till his manners gave a disgust which

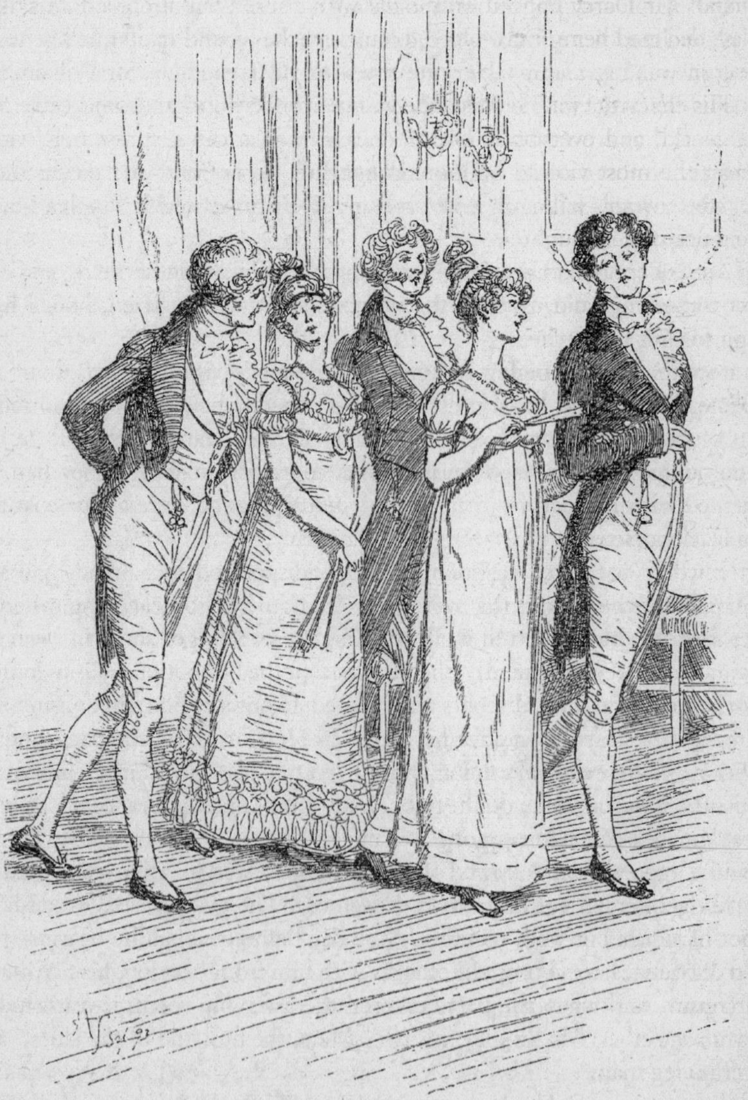

*When the party entered*

turned the tide of his popularity; for he was discovered to be proud, to be above his company, and above being pleased; and not all his large estate in Derbyshire could then save him from having a most forbidding, disagreeable countenance, and being unworthy to be compared with his friend.

Mr Bingley had soon made himself acquainted with all the principal people in the room; he was lively and unreserved, danced every dance, was angry that the ball closed so early, and talked of giving one himself at Netherfield. Such amiable qualities must speak for themselves. What a contrast between him and his friend! Mr Darcy danced only once with Mrs Hurst and once with Miss Bingley, declined being introduced to any other lady, and spent the rest of the evening in walking about the room, speaking occasionally to one of his own party. His character was decided. He was the proudest, most disagreeable man in the world, and everybody hoped that he would never come there again. Amongst the most violent against him was Mrs Bennet, whose dislike of his general behaviour, was sharpened into particular resentment, by his having slighted one of her daughters.

Elizabeth Bennet had been obliged, by the scarcity of gentlemen, to sit down for two dances; and during part of that time, Mr Darcy had been standing near enough for her to overhear a conversation between him and Mr Bingley, who came from the dance for a few minutes, to press his friend to join it.

'Come, Darcy,' said he, 'I must have you dance. I hate to see you standing about by yourself in this stupid manner. You had much better dance.'

'I certainly shall not. You know how I detest it, unless I am particularly acquainted with my partner. At such an assembly as this, it would be insupportable. Your sisters are engaged, and there is not another woman in the room, whom it would not be a punishment to me to stand up with.'

'I would not be so fastidious as you are,' cried Bingley, 'for a kingdom! Upon my honour, I never met with so many pleasant girls in my life, as I have this evening; and there are several of them you see uncommonly pretty.'

'*You* are dancing with the only handsome girl in the room,' said Mr Darcy, looking at the eldest Miss Bennet.

'Oh! she is the most beautiful creature I ever beheld! But there is one of her sisters sitting down just behind you, who is very pretty, and I dare say, very agreeable. Do let me ask my partner to introduce you.'

'Which do you mean?' and turning round, he looked for a moment at Elizabeth, till catching her eye, he withdrew his own and coldly said, 'She is tolerable; but not handsome enough to tempt *me*; and I am in no humour at present to give consequence to young ladies who are slighted by other men. You had better return to your partner and enjoy her smiles, for you are wasting your time with me.'

Mr Bingley followed his advice. Mr Darcy walked off; and Elizabeth remained with no very cordial feelings towards him. She told the story however with great spirit among her friends; for she had a lively, playful disposition, which delighted in anything ridiculous.

The evening altogether passed off pleasantly to the whole family. Mrs Bennet had seen her eldest daughter much admired by the Netherfield party. Mr Bingley had danced with her twice, and she had been distinguished by his sisters. Jane was as much gratified by this, as her mother could be, though in a quieter way. Elizabeth felt Jane's pleasure. Mary had heard herself mentioned to Miss Bingley as the most accomplished girl in the neighbourhood; and Catherine and Lydia had been fortunate enough to be never without partners, which was all that they had yet learnt to care for at a ball. They returned therefore in good spirits to Longbourn, the village where they lived, and of which they were the principal inhabitants. They found Mr Bennet still up. With a book he was regardless of time; and on the present occasion he had a good deal of curiosity as to the event of an evening which had raised such splendid expectations. He had rather hoped that all his wife's views on the stranger would be disappointed; but he soon found that he had a very different story to hear.

'Oh! my dear Mr Bennet,' as she entered the room, 'we have had a most delightful evening, a most excellent ball. I wish you had been there. Jane was so admired, nothing could be like it. Everybody said how well she looked; and Mr Bingley thought her quite beautiful, and danced with her twice. Only think of *that* my dear; he actually danced with her twice; and she was the only creature in the room that he asked a second time. First of all, he asked Miss Lucas. I was so vexed to see him stand up with her; but, however, he did not admire her at all: indeed, nobody can, you know; and he seemed quite struck with Jane as she was going down the dance. So, he enquired who she was, and got introduced, and asked her for the two next. Then, the two third he danced with Miss King, and the two fourth with Maria Lucas, and the two fifth with Jane again, and the two sixth with Lizzy, and the Boulanger – '

'If he had had any compassion for *me*,' cried her husband impatiently, 'he would not have danced half so much! For God's sake, say no more of his partners. Oh! that he had sprained his ankle in the first dance!'

'Oh! my dear,' continued Mrs Bennet, 'I am quite delighted with him. He is so excessively handsome! and his sisters are charming women. I never in my life saw anything more elegant than their dresses. I dare say the lace upon Mrs Hurst's gown – '

Here she was interrupted again. Mr Bennet protested against any description of finery. She was therefore obliged to seek another branch of the subject, and related, with much bitterness of spirit and some exaggeration, the shocking rudeness of Mr Darcy.

'But I can assure you,' she added, 'that Lizzy does not lose much by not suiting *his* fancy; for he is a most disagreeable, horrid man, not at all worth pleasing. So high and so conceited that there was no enduring him! He walked here, and he walked there, fancying himself so very great! Not handsome enough to dance with! I wish you had been there, my dear, to have given him one of your set downs. I quite detest the man.'

## *Chapter 4*

When Jane and Elizabeth were alone, the former, who had been cautious in her praise of Mr Bingley before, expressed to her sister how very much she admired him.

'He is just what a young man ought to be,' said she, 'sensible, good-humoured, lively; and I never saw such happy manners! – so much ease, with such perfect good breeding!'

'He is also handsome,' replied Elizabeth, 'which a young man ought likewise to be, if he possibly can. His character is thereby complete.'

'I was very much flattered by his asking me to dance a second time. I did not expect such a compliment.'

'Did not you? *I* did for you. But that is one great difference between us. Compliments always take *you* by surprise, and *me* never. What could be more natural than his asking you again? He could not help seeing that you were about five times as pretty as every other woman in the room. No thanks to his gallantry for that. Well, he certainly is very agreeable, and I give you leave to like him. You have liked many a stupider person.'

'Dear Lizzy!'

'Oh! you are a great deal too apt you know, to like people in general. You never see a fault in anybody. All the world are good and agreeable in your eyes. I never heard you speak ill of a human being in my life.'

'I would wish not to be hasty in censuring anyone; but I always speak what I think.'

'I know you do; and it is *that* which makes the wonder. With *your* good sense, to be so honestly blind to the follies and nonsense of others! Affectation of candour is common enough; – one meets it everywhere. But to be candid without ostentation or design – to take the good of everybody's character and make it still better, and say nothing of the bad – belongs to you alone. And so, you like this man's sisters too, do you? Their manners are not equal to his.'

'Certainly not; at first. But they are very pleasing women when you converse with them. Miss Bingley is to live with her brother and keep his house; and I am much mistaken if we shall not find a very charming neighbour in her.'

Elizabeth listened in silence, but was not convinced; their behaviour at the assembly had not been calculated to please in general; and with more quickness of observation and less pliancy of temper than her sister, and with a judgment too unassailed by any attention to herself, she was very little disposed to approve them. They were in fact very fine ladies; not deficient in good humour when they were pleased, nor in the power of being agreeable where they chose it; but proud and conceited. They were rather handsome, had been educated in one of the first private seminaries in town, had a fortune of twenty thousand pounds, were in the habit of spending more than they ought, and of associating with people of rank; and were therefore in every respect entitled to think well of themselves, and meanly of others. They were of a respectable family in the north of England; a circumstance more deeply impressed on their memories than that their brother's fortune and their own had been acquired by trade.

Mr Bingley inherited property to the amount of nearly a hundred thousand pounds from his father, who had intended to purchase an estate, but did not live to do it. Mr Bingley intended it likewise, and sometimes made choice of his county; but as he was now provided with a good house and the liberty of a manor, it was doubtful to many of those who best knew the easiness of his temper, whether he might not spend the remainder of his days at Netherfield, and leave the next generation to purchase.

His sisters were very anxious for his having an estate of his own; but though he was now established only as a tenant, Miss Bingley was by no means unwilling to preside at his table, nor was Mrs Hurst, who had married a man of more fashion than fortune, less disposed to consider his house as her home when it suited her. Mr Bingley had not been of age two years, when he was tempted by an accidental recommendation to look at Netherfield House. He did look at it and into it for half an hour, was pleased with the situation and the principal rooms, satisfied with what the owner said in its praise, and took it immediately.

Between him and Darcy there was a very steady friendship, in spite of a great opposition of character. Bingley was endeared to Darcy by the easiness, openness, ductility of his temper, though no disposition could offer a greater contrast to his own, and though with his own he never appeared dissatisfied. On the strength of Darcy's regard Bingley had the firmest reliance, and of his judgment the highest opinion. In understanding Darcy was the superior. Bingley was by no means deficient, but Darcy was clever. He was at the same time haughty, reserved, and fastidious, and his manners, though well bred, were not inviting. In that respect his friend had greatly the advantage. Bingley was sure of being liked wherever he appeared, Darcy was continually giving offence.

The manner in which they spoke of the Meryton assembly was sufficiently characteristic. Bingley had never met with pleasanter people or prettier girls in his life; everybody had been most kind and attentive to him, there had been no formality, no stiffness, he had soon felt acquainted with all the room; and as to Miss Bennet, he could not conceive an angel more beautiful. Darcy, on the contrary, had seen a collection of people in whom there was little beauty and no fashion, for none of whom he had felt the smallest interest, and from none received either attention or pleasure. Miss Bennet he acknowledged to be pretty, but she smiled too much.

Mrs Hurst and her sister allowed it to be so – but still they admired her and liked her, and pronounced her to be a sweet girl, and one whom they should not object to know more of. Miss Bennet was therefore established as a sweet girl, and their brother felt authorised by such commendation to think of her as he chose.

# *Chapter 5*

Within a short walk of Longbourn lived a family with whom the Bennets were particularly intimate. Sir William Lucas had been formerly in trade in Meryton, where he had made a tolerable fortune and risen to the honour of knighthood by an address to the King, during his mayoralty. The distinction had perhaps been felt too strongly. It had given him a disgust to his business and to his residence in a small market town; and quitting them both, he had removed with his family to a house about a mile from Meryton, denominated from that period Lucas Lodge, where he could think with pleasure of his own importance, and unshackled by business, occupy himself solely in being civil to all the world. For though elated by his rank, it did not render him supercilious; on the contrary, he was all attention to everybody. By nature inoffensive, friendly and obliging, his presentation at St James's had made him courteous.

Lady Lucas was a very good kind of woman, not too clever to be a valuable neighbour to Mrs Bennet. They had several children. The eldest of them, a sensible, intelligent young woman, about twenty-seven, was Elizabeth's intimate friend.

That the Miss Lucases and the Miss Bennets should meet to talk over a ball was absolutely necessary; and the morning after the assembly brought the former to Longbourn to hear and to communicate.

'*You* began the evening well, Charlotte,' said Mrs Bennet with civil self-command to Miss Lucas. '*You* were Mr Bingley's first choice.'

'Yes; – but he seemed to like his second better.'

'Oh! – you mean Jane, I suppose – because he danced with her twice. To be sure that *did* seem as if he admired her – indeed I rather believe he *did* – I heard something about it – but I hardly know what – something about Mr Robinson.'

'Perhaps you mean what I overheard between him and Mr Robinson; did not I mention it to you? Mr Robinson's asking him how he liked our Meryton assemblies, and whether he did not think there were a great many pretty women in the room, and *which* he thought the prettiest? and his answering immediately to the last question – Oh! the eldest Miss Bennet beyond a doubt, there cannot be two opinions on that point.'

'Upon my word! – Well, that was very decided indeed – that does seem as if – but however, it may all come to nothing you know.'

'*My* overhearings were more to the purpose than *yours*, Eliza,' said Charlotte. 'Mr Darcy is not so well worth listening to as his friend, is he? – Poor Eliza! – to be only just *tolerable*.'

'I beg you would not put it into Lizzy's head to be vexed by his ill-treatment; for he is such a disagreeable man that it would be quite a misfortune to be liked by him. Mrs Long told me last night that he sat close to her for half an hour without once opening his lips.'

'Are you quite sure, Ma'am? – is not there a little mistake?' said Jane. 'I certainly saw Mr Darcy speaking to her.'

'Aye – because she asked him at last how he liked Netherfield, and he could not help answering her; – but she said he seemed very angry at being spoke to.'

'Miss Bingley told me,' said Jane, 'that he never speaks much unless among his intimate acquaintance. With *them* he is remarkably agreeable.'

'I do not believe a word of it, my dear. If he had been so very agreeable he would have talked to Mrs Long. But I can guess how it was; everybody says that he is ate up with pride, and I dare say he had heard somehow that Mrs Long does not keep a carriage, and had come to the ball in a hack chaise.'

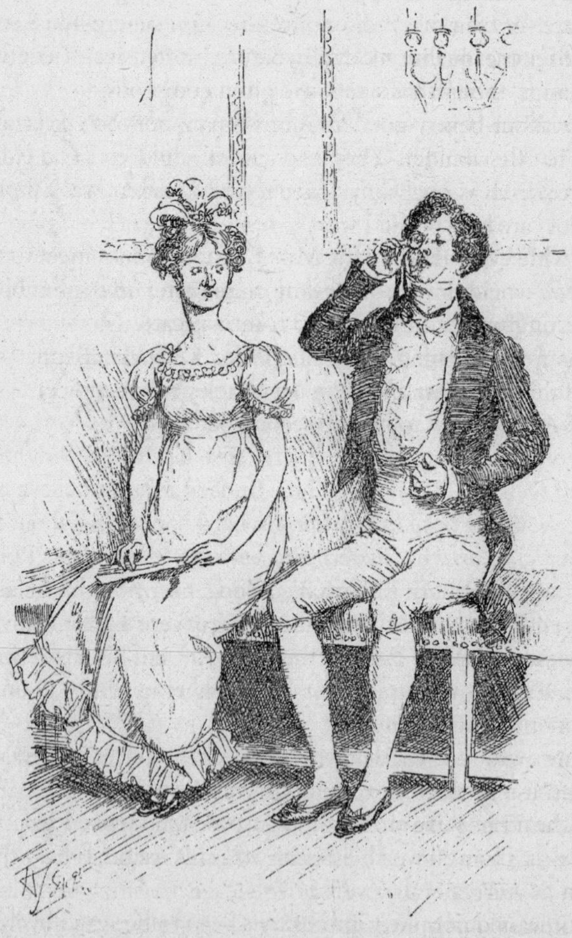

*He sat close to her for half an hour without once opening his lips*

'I do not mind his not talking to Mrs Long,' said Miss Lucas, 'but I wish he had danced with Eliza.'

'Another time, Lizzy,' said her mother, 'I would not dance with *him*, if I were you.'

'I believe, Ma'am, I may safely promise you *never* to dance with him.'

'His pride,' said Miss Lucas, 'does not offend *me* so much as pride often does, because there is an excuse for it. One cannot wonder that so very fine a young man, with family, fortune, everything in his favour, should think highly of himself. If I may so express it, he has a *right* to be proud.'

'That is very true,' replied Elizabeth, 'and I could easily forgive *his* pride, if he had not mortified *mine*.'

'Pride,' observed Mary, who piqued herself upon the solidity of her reflections, 'is a very common failing I believe. By all that I have ever read, I am convinced that it is very common indeed, that human nature is particularly prone to it, and that there are very few of us who do not cherish a feeling of self-complacency on the score of some quality or other, real or imaginary. Vanity and pride are different things, though the words are often used synonymously. A person may be proud without being vain. Pride relates more to our opinion of ourselves, vanity to what we would have others think of us.'

'If I were as rich as Mr Darcy,' cried a young Lucas who came with his sisters, 'I should not care how proud I was. I would keep a pack of foxhounds, and drink a bottle of wine every day.'

'Then you would drink a great deal more than you ought,' said Mrs Bennet; 'and if I were to see you at it I should take away your bottle directly.'

The boy protested that she should not; she continued to declare that she would, and the argument ended only with the visit.

## *Chapter 6*

The ladies of Longbourn soon waited on those of Netherfield. The visit was returned in due form. Miss Bennet's pleasing manners grew on the goodwill of Mrs Hurst and Miss Bingley; and though the mother was found to be intolerable and the younger sisters not worth speaking to, a wish of being better acquainted with *them*, was expressed towards the two eldest. By Jane this attention was received with the greatest pleasure; but Elizabeth still saw superciliousness in their treatment of everybody, hardly excepting even her sister, and could not like them; though their kindness to Jane, such as it was, had a value as arising in all probability from the influence of their brother's admiration. It was generally evident whenever they met, that he *did* admire her; and to *her* it was equally evident that Jane was yielding to the preference which she had begun to entertain for him from the first, and was in a way to be very much in love; but she considered with pleasure that it was not likely to be discovered by the world in general, since Jane united with great strength of feeling, a composure of temper and a uniform cheerfulness of manner, which would guard her from the suspicions of the impertinent. She mentioned this to her friend Miss Lucas.

'It may perhaps be pleasant,' replied Charlotte, 'to be able to impose on the public in such a case; but it is sometimes a disadvantage to be so very guarded. If a woman conceals her affection with the same skill from the object of it, she may lose the opportunity of fixing him; and it will then be but poor consolation to believe the world equally in the dark. There is so much of gratitude or vanity in almost every attachment, that it is not safe to leave any to itself. We can all *begin* freely – a slight preference is natural enough; but there are very few of us who have heart enough to be really in love without encouragement. In nine cases out of ten, a woman had better show *more* affection than she feels. Bingley likes your sister undoubtedly; but he may never do more than like her, if she does not help him on.'

'But she does help him on, as much as her nature will allow. If *I* can perceive her regard for him, he must be a simpleton indeed not to discover it too.'

'Remember, Eliza, that he does not know Jane's disposition as you do.'

'But if a woman is partial to a man, and does not endeavour to conceal it, he must find it out.'

'Perhaps he must, if he sees enough of her. But though Bingley and Jane meet tolerably often, it is never for many hours together; and as they always see each other in large mixed parties, it is impossible that every moment should be employed in conversing together. Jane should therefore make the most of every half-hour in which she can command his attention. When she is secure of him, there will be leisure for falling in love as much as she chooses.'

'Your plan is a good one,' replied Elizabeth, 'where nothing is in question but the desire of being well married; and if I were determined to get a rich husband, or any husband, I dare say I should adopt it. But these are not Jane's feelings; she is not acting by design. As yet, she cannot even be certain of the degree of her own regard, nor of its reasonableness. She has known him only a fortnight. She danced four dances with him at Meryton; she saw him one morning at his own house, and has since dined in company with him four times. This is not quite enough to make her understand his character.'

'Not as you represent it. Had she merely *dined* with him, she might only have discovered whether he had a good appetite; but you must remember that four evenings have been also spent together – and four evenings may do a great deal.'

'Yes; these four evenings have enabled them to ascertain that they both like vingt-un better than commerce; but with respect to any other leading characteristic, I do not imagine that much has been unfolded.'

'Well,' said Charlotte, 'I wish Jane success with all my heart; and if she were married to him tomorrow, I should think she had as good a chance of happiness, as if she were to be studying his character for a twelvemonth. Happiness in marriage is entirely a matter of chance. If the dispositions of the parties are ever so well known to each other, or ever so similar beforehand, it does not advance their felicity in the least. They always continue to grow sufficiently unlike afterwards to have their share of vexation; and it is better to know as little as possible of the defects of the person with whom you are to pass your life.'

'You make me laugh, Charlotte; but it is not sound. You know it is not sound, and that you would never act in this way yourself.'

Occupied in observing Mr Bingley's attentions to her sister, Elizabeth was far from suspecting that she was herself becoming an object of some interest in the eyes of his friend. Mr Darcy had at first scarcely allowed her to be pretty; he had looked at her without admiration at the ball; and when they next met, he looked at her only to criticise. But no sooner had he made it clear to himself and his friends that she had hardly a good feature in her face, than he began to find it was rendered uncommonly intelligent by the beautiful expression of her dark eyes. To this discovery succeeded some others equally mortifying. Though he had detected with a critical eye more than one failure of perfect symmetry in her form, he was forced to acknowledge her figure to be light and pleasing; and in spite of his asserting that her manners were not those of the fashionable world, he was caught by their easy playfulness. Of this she was perfectly unaware; – to her he was only the man who made himself agreeable nowhere, and who had not thought her handsome enough to dance with.

He began to wish to know more of her, and as a step towards conversing with her himself, attended to her conversation with others. His doing so drew her notice. It was at Sir William Lucas's, where a large party were assembled.

'What does Mr Darcy mean,' said she to Charlotte, 'by listening to my conversation with Colonel Forster?'

'That is a question which Mr Darcy only can answer.'

'But if he does it any more I shall certainly let him know that I see what he is about. He has a very satirical eye, and if I do not begin by being impertinent myself, I shall soon grow afraid of him.'

On his approaching them soon afterwards, though without seeming to have any intention of speaking, Miss Lucas defied her friend to mention such a subject to him, which immediately provoking Elizabeth to do it, she turned to him and said, 'Did not you think, Mr Darcy, that I expressed myself uncommonly well just now, when I was teasing Colonel Forster to give us a ball at Meryton?'

'With great energy; – but it is a subject which always makes a lady energetic.'

'You are severe on us.'

'It will be *her* turn soon to be teased,' said Miss Lucas. 'I am going to open the instrument, Eliza, and you know what follows.'

'You are a very strange creature by way of a friend! – always wanting me to play and sing before anybody and everybody! – If my vanity had taken a musical turn, you would have been invaluable, but as it is, I would really rather not sit down before those who must be in the habit of hearing the very best performers.' On Miss Lucas's persevering, however, she added, 'Very well; if it must be so, it must.' And gravely glancing at Mr Darcy, 'There is a fine old saying, which everybody here is of course familiar with – "Keep your breath to cool your porridge," – and I shall keep mine to swell my song.'

Her performance was pleasing, though by no means capital. After a song or two, and before she could reply to the entreaties of several that she would sing again, she was eagerly succeeded at the instrument by her sister Mary, who having, in consequence of being the only plain one in the family, worked hard for knowledge and accomplishments, was always impatient for display.

Mary had neither genius nor taste; and though vanity had given her application, it had given her likewise a pedantic air and conceited manner, which would have injured a higher degree of excellence than she had reached. Elizabeth, easy and unaffected, had been listened to with much more pleasure, though not playing half so well; and Mary, at the end of a long concerto, was glad to purchase praise and gratitude by Scotch and Irish airs, at the request of her younger sisters, who with some of the Lucases and two or three officers joined eagerly in dancing at one end of the room.

Mr Darcy stood near them in silent indignation at such a mode of passing the evening, to the exclusion of all conversation, and was too much engrossed by his own thoughts to perceive that Sir William Lucas was his neighbour, till Sir William thus began.

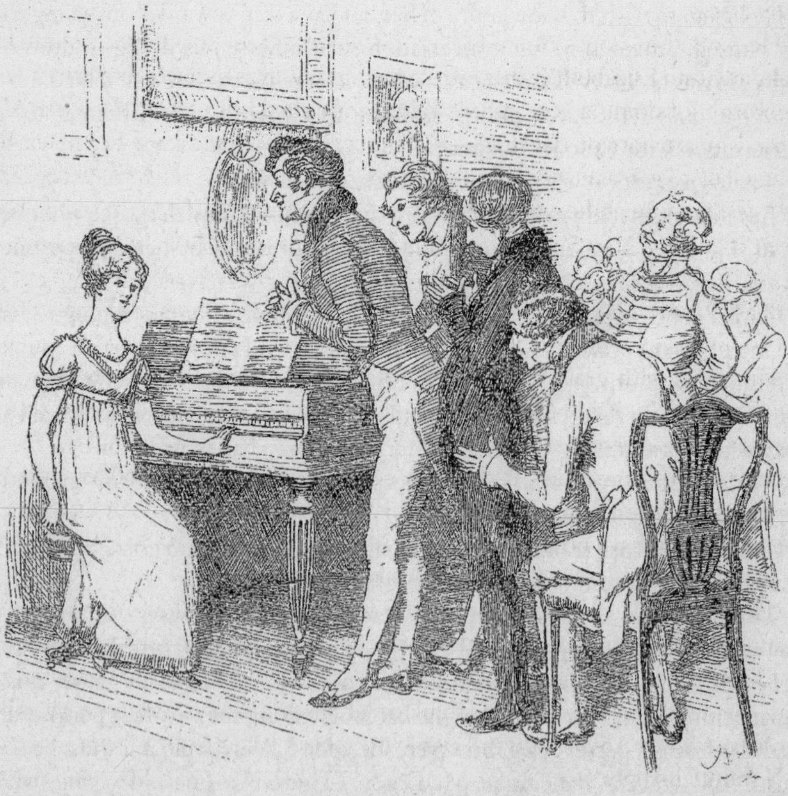

*The entreaties of several that she would sing again*

'What a charming amusement for young people this is, Mr Darcy! – There is nothing like dancing after all. – I consider it as one of the first refinements of polished societies.'

'Certainly, sir; – and it has the advantage also of being in vogue amongst the less polished societies of the world. – Every savage can dance.'

Sir William only smiled. 'Your friend performs delightfully;' he continued after a pause, on seeing Bingley join the group; – 'and I doubt not that you are an adept in the science yourself, Mr Darcy.'

'You saw me dance at Meryton, I believe, sir.'

'Yes, indeed, and received no inconsiderable pleasure from the sight. Do you often dance at St James's?'

'Never, sir.'

'Do you not think it would be a proper compliment to the place?'

'It is a compliment which I never pay to any place if I can avoid it.'

'You have a house in town, I conclude?'

Mr Darcy bowed.

'I had once some thoughts of fixing in town myself – for I am fond of superior society; but I did not feel quite certain that the air of London would agree with Lady Lucas.'

He paused in hopes of an answer; but his companion was not disposed to make any; and Elizabeth at that instant moving towards them, he was struck with the notion of doing a very gallant thing, and called out to her, 'My dear Miss Eliza, why are not you dancing? – Mr Darcy, you must allow me to present this young lady to you as a very desirable partner. – You cannot refuse to dance, I am sure, when so much beauty is before you.' And taking her hand, he would have given it to Mr Darcy, who, though extremely surprised, was not unwilling to receive it, when she instantly drew back, and said with some discomposure to Sir William, 'Indeed, sir, I have not the least intention of dancing. – I entreat you not to suppose that I moved this way in order to beg for a partner.'

Mr Darcy with grave propriety requested to be allowed the honour of her hand; but in vain. Elizabeth was determined; nor did Sir William at all shake her purpose by his attempt at persuasion.

'You excel so much in the dance, Miss Eliza, that it is cruel to deny me the happiness of seeing you; and though this gentleman dislikes the amusement in general, he can have no objection, I am sure, to oblige us for one half-hour.'

'Mr Darcy is all politeness,' said Elizabeth, smiling.

'He is indeed – but considering the inducement, my dear Miss Eliza, we cannot wonder at his complaisance; for who would object to such a partner?'

Elizabeth looked archly, and turned away. Her resistance had not injured her with the gentleman, and he was thinking of her with some complacency, when thus accosted by Miss Bingley, 'I can guess the subject of your reverie.'

'I should imagine not.'

'You are considering how insupportable it would be to pass many evenings in this manner – in such society; and indeed I am quite of your opinion. I was never more annoyed! The insipidity and yet the noise; the nothingness and yet the self-importance of all these people! – What would I give to hear your strictures on them!'

'Your conjecture is totally wrong, I assure you. My mind was more agreeably engaged. I have been meditating on the very great pleasure which a pair of fine eyes in the face of a pretty woman can bestow.'

Miss Bingley immediately fixed her eyes on his face, and desired he would tell her what lady had the credit of inspiring such reflections. Mr Darcy replied with great intrepidity, 'Miss Elizabeth Bennet.'

'Miss Elizabeth Bennet!' repeated Miss Bingley. 'I am all astonishment. How long has she been such a favourite? – and pray when am I to wish you joy?'

'That is exactly the question which I expected you to ask. A lady's imagination is very rapid; it jumps from admiration to love, from love to matrimony in a moment. I knew you would be wishing me joy.'

'Nay, if you are so serious about it, I shall consider the matter as absolutely settled. You will have a charming mother-in-law, indeed, and of course she will be always at Pemberley with you.'

He listened to her with perfect indifference, while she chose to entertain herself in this manner, and as his composure convinced her that all was safe, her wit flowed long.

## *Chapter 7*

Mr Bennet's property consisted almost entirely in an estate of two thousand a year, which, unfortunately for his daughters, was entailed in default of heirs male, on a distant relation; and their mother's fortune, though ample for her situation in life, could but ill supply the deficiency of his. Her father had been an attorney in Meryton, and had left her four thousand pounds.

She had a sister married to a Mr Philips, who had been a clerk to their father, and succeeded him in the business, and a brother settled in London in a respectable line of trade.

The village of Longbourn was only one mile from Meryton; a most convenient distance for the young ladies, who were usually tempted thither three or four times a week, to pay their duty to their aunt and to a milliner's shop just over the way. The two youngest of the family, Catherine and Lydia, were particularly frequent in these attentions; their minds were more vacant than their sisters', and when nothing better offered, a walk to Meryton was necessary to amuse their morning hours and furnish conversation for the evening; and however bare of news the country in general might be, they always contrived to learn some from their aunt. At present, indeed, they were well supplied both with news and happiness by the recent arrival of a militia regiment in the neighbourhood; it was to remain the whole winter, and Meryton was the headquarters.

Their visits to Mrs Philips were now productive of the most interesting intelligence. Every day added something to their knowledge of the officers' names and connections. Their lodgings were not long a secret, and at length they began to know the officers themselves. Mr Philips visited them all, and this opened to his nieces a source of felicity unknown before. They could talk of nothing but officers; and Mr Bingley's large fortune, the mention of which gave animation to their mother, was worthless in their eyes when opposed to the regimentals of an ensign.

After listening one morning to their effusions on this subject, Mr Bennet coolly observed, 'From all that I can collect by your manner of talking, you must be two of the silliest girls in the country. I have suspected it for some time, but I am now convinced.'

Catherine was disconcerted, and made no answer; but Lydia, with perfect indifference, continued to express her admiration of Captain Carter, and her hope of seeing him in the course of the day, as he was going the next morning to London.

'I am astonished, my dear,' said Mrs Bennet, 'that you should be so ready to think your own children silly. If I wished to think slightingly of anybody's children, it should not be of my own however.'

'If my children are silly I must hope to be always sensible of it.'

'Yes – but as it happens, they are all of them very clever.'

'This is the only point, I flatter myself, on which we do not agree. I had hoped that our sentiments coincided in every particular, but I must so far differ from you as to think our two youngest daughters uncommonly foolish.'

'My dear Mr Bennet, you must not expect such girls to have the sense of their father and mother. – When they get to our age I dare say they will not think about officers any more than we do. I remember the time when I liked a red coat myself very well – and indeed so I do still at my heart; and if a smart young colonel, with five or six thousand a year, should want one of my girls, I shall not say nay to him; and I thought Colonel Forster looked very becoming the other night at Sir William's in his regimentals.'

'Mamma,' cried Lydia, 'my aunt says that Colonel Forster and Captain Carter do not go so often to Miss Watson's as they did when they first came; she sees them now very often standing in Clarke's library.'

Mrs Bennet was prevented replying by the entrance of the footman with a note for Miss Bennet; it came from Netherfield, and the servant waited for an answer. Mrs Bennet's eyes sparkled with pleasure, and she was eagerly calling out, while her daughter read, 'Well, Jane, who is it from? what is it about? what does he say? Well, Jane, make haste and tell us; make haste, my love.'

'It is from Miss Bingley,' said Jane, and then read it aloud.

> 'My dear Friend – If you are not so compassionate as to dine today with Louisa and me, we shall be in danger of hating each other for the rest of our lives, for a whole day's tête-à-tête between two women can never end without a quarrel. Come as soon as you can on the receipt of this. My brother and the gentlemen are to dine with the officers. Yours ever,
>
> Caroline Bingley.'

'With the officers!' cried Lydia. 'I wonder my aunt did not tell us of *that.*'

'Dining out,' said Mrs Bennet, 'that is very unlucky.

'Can I have the carriage?' said Jane.

'No, my dear, you had better go on horseback, because it seems likely to rain; and then you must stay all night.'

'That would be a good scheme,' said Elizabeth, 'if you were sure that they would not offer to send her home.'

'Oh! but the gentlemen will have Mr Bingley's chaise to go to Meryton; and the Hursts have no horses to theirs.'

'I had much rather go in the coach.'

'But, my dear, your father cannot spare the horses, I am sure. They are wanted in the farm, Mr Bennet, are not they?'

'They are wanted in the farm much oftener that I can get them.'

'But if you have got them today,' said Elizabeth, 'my mother's purpose will be answered.'

She did at last extort from her father an acknowledgment that the horses were engaged. Jane was therefore obliged to go on horseback, and her mother

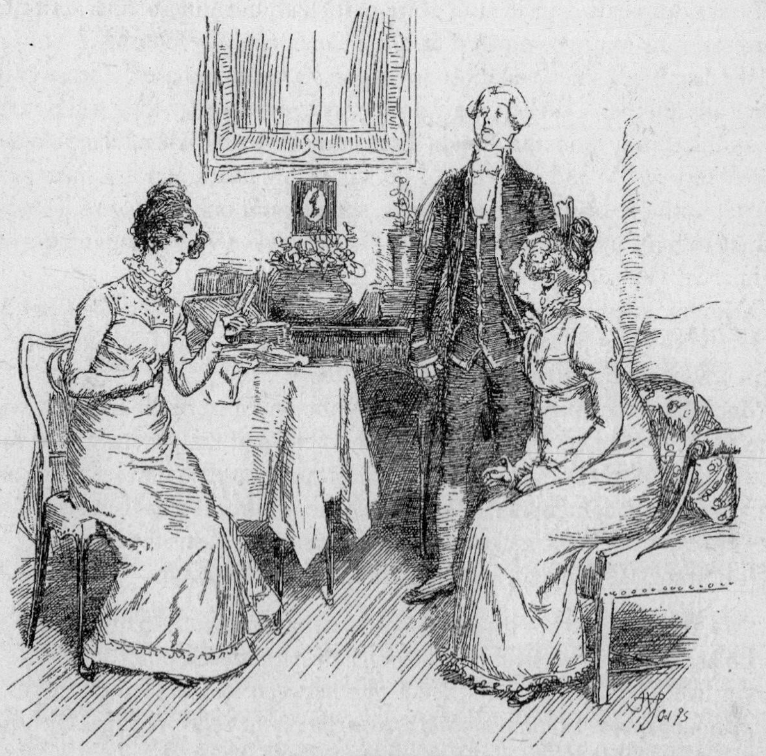

*A note for Miss Bennet*

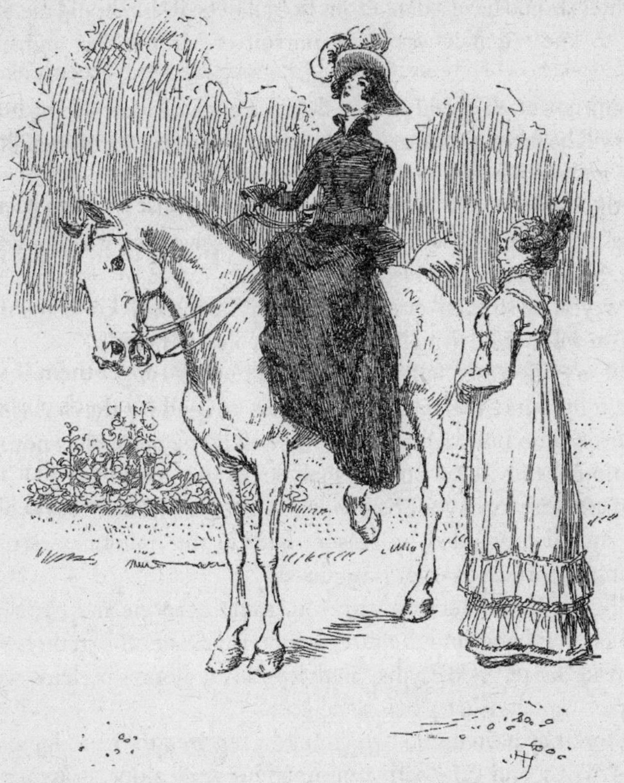

*With many cheerful prognostics of a bad day*

attended her to the door with many cheerful prognostics of a bad day. Her hopes were answered; Jane had not been gone long before it rained hard. Her sisters were uneasy for her, but her mother was delighted. The rain continued the whole evening without intermission; Jane certainly could not come back.

'This was a lucky idea of mine, indeed!' said Mrs Bennet, more than once, as if the credit of making it rain were all her own. Till the next morning, however, she was not aware of all the felicity of her contrivance. Breakfast was scarcely over when a servant from Netherfield brought the following note for Elizabeth:

> MY DEAREST LIZZY – I find myself very unwell this morning, which, I suppose, is to be imputed to my getting wet through yesterday. My kind friends will not hear of my returning home till I am better. They insist also on my seeing Mr Jones – therefore do not be alarmed if you should hear of his having been to me – and excepting a sore throat and headache there is not much the matter with me.
>
> Yours, &c.

'Well, my dear,' said Mr Bennet, when Elizabeth had read the note aloud, 'if your daughter should have a dangerous fit of illness, if she should die, it would be a comfort to know that it was all in pursuit of Mr Bingley, and under your orders.'

'Oh! I am not at all afraid of her dying. People do not die of little trifling colds. She will be taken good care of. As long as she stays there, it is all very well. I would go and see her, if I could have the carriage.'

Elizabeth, feeling really anxious, was determined to go to her, though the carriage was not to be had; and as she was no horsewoman, walking was her only alternative. She declared her resolution.

'How can you be so silly,' cried her mother, 'as to think of such a thing, in all this dirt! You will not be fit to be seen when you get there.'

'I shall be very fit to see Jane – which is all I want.'

'Is this a hint to me, Lizzy,' said her father, 'to send for the horses?'

'No, indeed. I do not wish to avoid the walk. The distance is nothing, when one has a motive; only three miles. I shall be back by dinner.'

'I admire the activity of your benevolence,' observed Mary, 'but every impulse of feeling should be guided by reason; and, in my opinion, exertion should always be in proportion to what is required.'

'We will go as far as Meryton with you,' said Catherine and Lydia. Elizabeth accepted their company, and the three young ladies set off together.

'If we make haste,' said Lydia, as they walked along, 'perhaps we may see something of Captain Carter before he goes.'

In Meryton they parted; the two youngest repaired to the lodgings of one of the officers' wives, and Elizabeth continued her walk alone, crossing field after field at a quick pace, jumping over stiles and springing over puddles with impatient activity, and finding herself at last within view of the house, with weary ankles, dirty stockings, and a face glowing with the warmth of exercise.

She was shown into the breakfast-parlour, where all but Jane were assembled, and where her appearance created a great deal of surprise. That she should have walked three miles so early in the day, in such dirty weather, and by herself, was almost incredible to Mrs Hurst and Miss Bingley; and Elizabeth was convinced that they held her in contempt for it. She was received, however, very politely by them; and in their brother's manners there was something better than politeness; there was good humour and kindness. – Mr Darcy said very little, and Mr Hurst nothing at all. The former was divided between admiration of the brilliancy which exercise had given to her complexion, and doubt as to the occasion's justifying her coming so far alone. The latter was thinking only of his breakfast.

Her enquiries after her sister were not very favourably answered. Miss Bennet had slept ill, and though up, was very feverish and not well enough to leave her room. Elizabeth was glad to be taken to her immediately; and Jane, who had only been withheld by the fear of giving alarm or inconvenience, from expressing in her note how much she longed for such a visit, was delighted at her entrance. She was not equal, however, to much conversation, and when

Miss Bingley left them together, could attempt little beside expressions of gratitude for the extraordinary kindness she was treated with. Elizabeth silently attended her.

When breakfast was over, they were joined by the sisters; and Elizabeth began to like them herself, when she saw how much affection and solicitude they showed for Jane. The apothecary came, and having examined his patient, said, as might be supposed, that she had caught a violent cold, and that they must endeavour to get the better of it; advised her to return to bed, and promised her some draughts. The advice was followed readily, for the feverish symptoms increased, and her head ached acutely. Elizabeth did not quit her room for a moment, nor were the other ladies often absent; the gentlemen being out, they had in fact nothing to do elsewhere.

When the clock struck three, Elizabeth felt that she must go; and very unwillingly said so. Miss Bingley offered her the carriage, and she only wanted a little pressing to accept it, when Jane testified such concern in parting with her, that Miss Bingley was obliged to convert the offer of the chaise into an invitation to remain at Netherfield for the present. Elizabeth most thankfully consented, and a servant was dispatched to Longbourn to acquaint the family with her stay, and bring back a supply of clothes.

## *Chapter 8*

At five o'clock the two ladies retired to dress, and at half-past six Elizabeth was summoned to dinner. To the civil enquiries which then poured in, and amongst which she had the pleasure of distinguishing the much superior solicitude of Mr Bingley's, she could not make a very favourable answer. Jane was by no means better. The sisters, on hearing this, repeated three or four times how much they were grieved, how shocking it was to have a bad cold, and how excessively they disliked being ill themselves; and then thought no more of the matter: and their indifference towards Jane when not immediately before them, restored Elizabeth to the enjoyment of all her original dislike.

Their brother, indeed, was the only one of the party whom she could regard with any complacency. His anxiety for Jane was evident, and his attentions to herself most pleasing, and they prevented her feeling herself so much an intruder as she believed she was considered by the others. She had very little notice from any but him. Miss Bingley was engrossed by Mr Darcy, her sister scarcely less so; and as for Mr Hurst, by whom Elizabeth sat, he was an indolent man, who lived only to eat, drink, and play at cards, who when he found her prefer a plain dish to a ragout, had nothing to say to her.

When dinner was over, she returned directly to Jane, and Miss Bingley began abusing her as soon as she was out of the room. Her manners were pronounced to be very bad indeed, a mixture of pride and impertinence; she had no conversation, no style, no taste, no beauty. Mrs Hurst thought the same, and added,

'She has nothing, in short, to recommend her, but being an excellent walker. I shall never forget her appearance this morning. She really looked almost wild.'

'She did indeed, Louisa. I could hardly keep my countenance. Very nonsensical to come at all! Why must *she* be scampering about the country, because her sister had a cold? Her hair so untidy, so blowsy!'

'Yes, and her petticoat; I hope you saw her petticoat, six inches deep in mud, I am absolutely certain; and the gown which had been let down to hide it, not doing its office.'

'Your picture may be very exact, Louisa,' said Bingley; 'but this was all lost upon me. I thought Miss Elizabeth Bennet looked remarkably well, when she came into the room this morning. Her dirty petticoat quite escaped my notice.'

'*You* observed it, Mr Darcy, I am sure,' said Miss Bingley; 'and I am inclined to think that you would not wish to see *your sister* make such an exhibition.'

'Certainly not.'

'To walk three miles, or four miles, or five miles, or whatever it is, above her ankles in dirt, and alone, quite alone! what could she mean by it? It seems to me to show an abominable sort of conceited independence, a most country town indifference to decorum.'

'It shows an affection for her sister that is very pleasing,' said Bingley.

'I am afraid, Mr Darcy,' observed Miss Bingley, in a half whisper, 'that this adventure has rather affected your admiration of her fine eyes.'

'Not at all,' he replied; 'they were brightened by the exercise.' – A short pause followed this speech, and Mrs Hurst began again.

'I have an excessive regard for Jane Bennet, she is really a very sweet girl, and I wish with all my heart she were well settled. But with such a father and mother, and such low connections, I am afraid there is no chance of it.'

'I think I have heard you say, that their uncle is an attorney in Meryton.'

'Yes; and they have another, who lives somewhere near Cheapside.'

'That is capital,' added her sister, and they both laughed heartily.

'If they had uncles enough to fill *all* Cheapside,' cried Bingley, 'it would not make them one jot less agreeable.'

'But it must very materially lessen their chance of marrying men of any consideration in the world,' replied Darcy.

To this speech Bingley made no answer; but his sisters gave it their hearty assent, and indulged their mirth for some time at the expense of their dear friend's vulgar relations.

With a renewal of tenderness, however, they repaired to her room on leaving the dining-parlour, and sat with her till summoned to coffee. She was still very poorly, and Elizabeth would not quit her at all, till late in the evening, when she had the comfort of seeing her asleep, and when it appeared to her rather right than pleasant that she should go downstairs herself. On entering the drawing-room she found the whole party at loo, and was immediately invited to join them; but suspecting them to be playing high she declined it, and making her sister the excuse, said she would amuse herself for the short time she could stay below with a book. Mr Hurst looked at her with astonishment.

'Do you prefer reading to cards?' said he; 'that is rather singular.'

'Miss Eliza Bennet,' said Miss Bingley, 'despises cards. She is a great reader and has no pleasure in anything else.'

'I deserve neither such praise nor such censure,' cried Elizabeth; 'I am *not* a great reader, and I have pleasure in many things.'

'In nursing your sister I am sure you have pleasure,' said Bingley; 'and I hope it will soon be increased by seeing her quite well.'

Elizabeth thanked him from her heart, and then walked towards a table where a few books were lying. He immediately offered to fetch her others; all that his library afforded.

'And I wish my collection were larger for your benefit and my own credit; but I am an idle fellow, and though I have not many, I have more than I ever look into.'

Elizabeth assured him that she could suit herself perfectly with those in the room.

'I am astonished,' said Miss Bingley, 'that my father should have left so small a collection of books. – What a delightful library you have at Pemberley, Mr Darcy!'

'It ought to be good,' he replied, 'it has been the work of many generations.'

'And then you have added so much to it yourself, you are always buying books.'

'I cannot comprehend the neglect of a family library in such days as these.'

'Neglect! I am sure you neglect nothing that can add to the beauties of that noble place. Charles, when you build *your* house, I wish it may be half as delightful as Pemberley.'

'I wish it may.'

'But I would really advise you to make your purchase in that neighbourhood, and take Pemberley for a kind of model. There is not a finer county in England than Derbyshire.'

'With all my heart; I will buy Pemberley itself if Darcy will sell it.'

'I am talking of possibilities, Charles.'

'Upon my word, Caroline, I should think it more possible to get Pemberley by purchase than by imitation.'

Elizabeth was so much caught by what passed, as to leave her very little attention for her book; and soon laying it wholly aside, she drew near the card-table, and stationed herself between Mr Bingley and his eldest sister to observe the game.

'Is Miss Darcy much grown since the spring?' said Miss Bingley; 'will she be as tall as I am?'

'I think she will. She is now about Miss Elizabeth Bennet's height, or rather taller.'

'How I long to see her again! I never met with anybody who delighted me so much. Such a countenance, such manners! and so extremely accomplished for her age! Her performance on the pianoforte is exquisite.'

'It is amazing to me,' said Bingley, 'how young ladies can have patience to be so very accomplished, as they all are.'

'All young ladies accomplished! My dear Charles, what do you mean?'

'Yes, all of them, I think. They all paint tables, cover screens and net purses. I scarcely know anyone who cannot do all this, and I am sure I never heard a young lady spoken of for the first time, without being informed that she was very accomplished.'

'Your list of the common extent of accomplishments,' said Darcy, 'has too much truth. The word is applied to many a woman who deserves it no otherwise than by netting a purse, or covering a screen. But I am very far from agreeing with you in your estimation of ladies in general. I cannot boast of knowing more than half a dozen, in the whole range of my acquaintance, that are really accomplished.'

'Nor I, I am sure,' said Miss Bingley.

'Then,' observed Elizabeth, 'you must comprehend a great deal in your idea of an accomplished woman.'

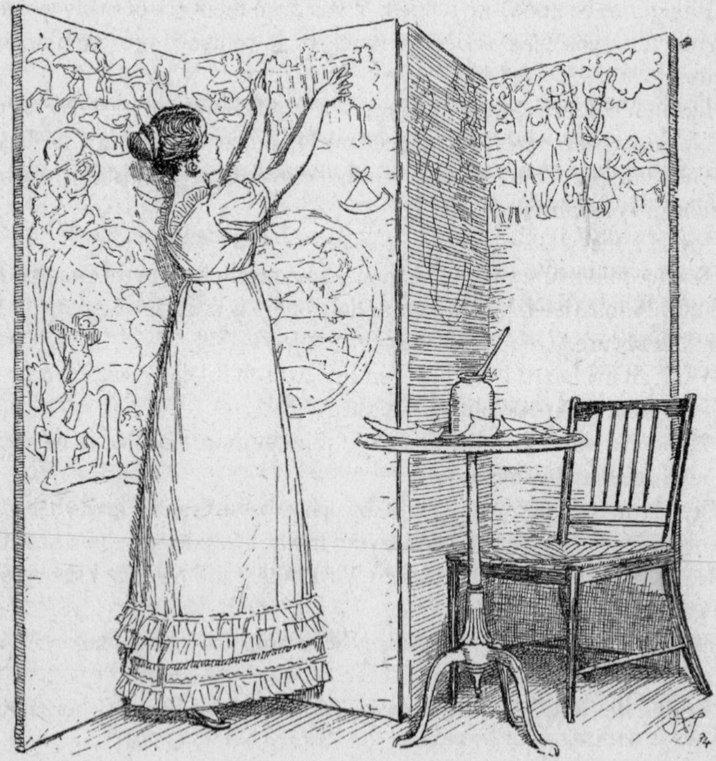

*They all paint tables, cover screens and net purses*

'Yes; I do comprehend a great deal in it.'

'Oh! certainly,' cried his faithful assistant, 'no one can be really esteemed accomplished, who does not greatly surpass what is usually met with. A woman must have a thorough knowledge of music, singing, drawing, dancing, and the modern languages, to deserve the word; and besides all this, she must possess a certain something in her air and manner of walking, the tone of her voice, her address and expressions, or the word will be but half deserved.'

'All this she must possess,' added Darcy, 'and to all this she must yet add something more substantial, in the improvement of her mind by extensive reading.'

'I am no longer surprised at your knowing *only* six accomplished women. I rather wonder now at your knowing *any*.'

'Are you so severe upon your own sex, as to doubt the possibility of all this?'

'*I* never saw such a woman. *I* never saw such capacity, and taste, and application, and elegance, as you describe, united.'

Mrs Hurst and Miss Bingley both cried out against the injustice of her implied doubt, and were both protesting that they knew many women who answered this description, when Mr Hurst called them to order, with bitter complaints of their inattention to what was going forward. As all conversation was thereby at an end, Elizabeth soon afterwards left the room.

'Eliza Bennet,' said Miss Bingley, when the door was closed on her, 'is one of those young ladies who seek to recommend themselves to the other sex, by undervaluing their own; and with many men, I dare say, it succeeds. But, in my opinion, it is a paltry device, a very mean art.'

'Undoubtedly,' replied Darcy, to whom this remark was chiefly addressed, 'there is meanness in *all* the arts which ladies sometimes condescend to employ for captivation. Whatever bears affinity to cunning is despicable.'

Miss Bingley was not so entirely satisfied with this reply as to continue the subject.

Elizabeth joined them again only to say that her sister was worse, and that she could not leave her. Bingley urged Mr Jones's being sent for immediately; while his sisters, convinced that no country advice could be of any service, recommended an express to town for one of the most eminent physicians. This, she would not hear of; but she was not so unwilling to comply with their brother's proposal; and it was settled that Mr Jones should be sent for early in the morning, if Miss Bennet were not decidedly better. Bingley was quite uncomfortable; his sisters declared that they were miserable. They solaced their wretchedness, however, by duets after supper, while he could find no better relief to his feelings than by giving his housekeeper directions that every possible attention might be paid to the sick lady and her sister.

## *Chapter 9*

Elizabeth passed the chief of the night in her sister's room, and in the morning had the pleasure of being able to send a tolerable answer to the enquiries which she very early received from Mr Bingley by a housemaid, and some time afterwards from the two elegant ladies who waited on his sisters. In spite of this amendment, however, she requested to have a note sent to Longbourn, desiring her mother to visit Jane, and form her own judgment of her situation. The note was immediately dispatched, and its contents as quickly complied with. Mrs Bennet, accompanied by her two youngest girls, reached Netherfield soon after the family breakfast.

Had she found Jane in any apparent danger, Mrs Bennet would have been very miserable; but being satisfied on seeing her that her illness was not alarming, she had no wish of her recovering immediately, as her restoration to health would probably remove her from Netherfield. She would not listen therefore to her

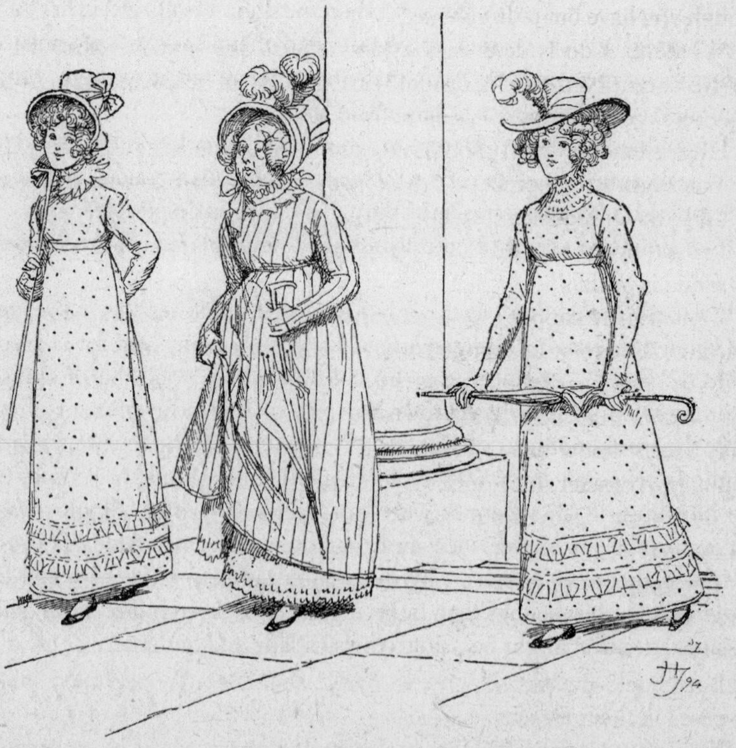

*Mrs Bennet, accompanied by her two youngest girls*

daughter's proposal of being carried home; neither did the apothecary, who arrived about the same time, think it at all advisable. After sitting a little while with Jane, on Miss Bingley's appearance and invitation, the mother and three daughters all attended her into the breakfast-parlour. Bingley met them with hopes that Mrs Bennet had not found Miss Bennet worse than she expected.

'Indeed I have, sir,' was her answer. 'She is a great deal too ill to be moved. Mr Jones says we must not think of moving her. We must trespass a little longer on your kindness.'

'Removed!' cried Bingley. 'It must not be thought of. My sister, I am sure, will not hear of her removal.'

'You may depend upon it, Madam,' said Miss Bingley, with cold civility, 'that Miss Bennet shall receive every possible attention while she remains with us.'

Mrs Bennet was profuse in her acknowledgments.

'I am sure,' she added, 'if it was not for such good friends I do not know what would become of her, for she is very ill indeed, and suffers a vast deal, though with the greatest patience in the world, which is always the way with her, for she has, without exception, the sweetest temper I ever met with. I often tell my other girls they are nothing to *her*. You have a sweet room here, Mr Bingley, and a charming prospect over that gravel walk. I do not know a place in the country that is equal to Netherfield. You will not think of quitting it in a hurry I hope, though you have but a short lease.'

'Whatever I do is done in a hurry,' replied he; 'and therefore if I should resolve to quit Netherfield, I should probably be off in five minutes. At present, however, I consider myself as quite fixed here.'

'That is exactly what I should have supposed of you,' said Elizabeth.

'You begin to comprehend me, do you?' cried he, turning towards her.

'Oh! yes – I understand you perfectly.'

'I wish I might take this for a compliment; but to be so easily seen through I am afraid is pitiful.'

'That is as it happens. It does not necessarily follow that a deep, intricate character is more or less estimable than such a one as yours.'

'Lizzy,' cried her mother, 'remember where you are, and do not run on in the wild manner that you are suffered to do at home.'

'I did not know before,' continued Bingley immediately, 'that you were a studier of character. It must be an amusing study.'

'Yes; but intricate characters are the *most* amusing. They have at least that advantage.'

'The country,' said Darcy, 'can in general supply but few subjects for such a study. In a country neighbourhood you move in a very confined and unvarying society.'

'But people themselves alter so much, that there is something new to be observed in them for ever.'

'Yes, indeed,' cried Mrs Bennet, offended by his manner of mentioning a country neighbourhood. 'I assure you there is quite as much of *that* going on in the country as in town.'

Everybody was surprised; and Darcy, after looking at her for a moment, turned silently away. Mrs Bennet, who fancied she had gained a complete victory over him, continued her triumph.

'I cannot see that London has any great advantage over the country for my part, except the shops and public places. The country is a vast deal pleasanter, is not it, Mr Bingley?'

'When I am in the country,' he replied, 'I never wish to leave it; and when I am in town it is pretty much the same. They have each their advantages, and I can be equally happy in either.'

'Aye – that is because you have the right disposition. But that gentleman,' looking at Darcy, 'seemed to think the country was nothing at all.'

'Indeed, Mamma, you are mistaken,' said Elizabeth, blushing for her mother. 'You quite mistook Mr Darcy. He only meant that there were not such a variety of people to be met with in the country as in town, which you must acknowledge to be true.'

'Certainly, my dear, nobody said there were; but as to not meeting with many people in this neighbourhood, I believe there are few neighbourhoods larger. I know we dine with four and twenty families.'

Nothing but concern for Elizabeth could enable Bingley to keep his countenance. His sister was less delicate, and directed her eye towards Mr Darcy with a very expressive smile. Elizabeth, for the sake of saying something that might turn her mother's thoughts, now asked her if Charlotte Lucas had been at Longbourn since *her* coming away.

'Yes, she called yesterday with her father. What an agreeable man Sir William is, Mr Bingley – is not he? so much the man of fashion! so genteel and so easy! – He has always something to say to everybody. – *That* is my idea of good breeding; and those persons who fancy themselves very important and never open their mouths, quite mistake the matter.'

'Did Charlotte dine with you?'

'No, she would go home. I fancy she was wanted about the mince pies. For my part, Mr Bingley, *I* always keep servants that can do their own work; *my* daughters are brought up differently. But everybody is to judge for themselves, and the Lucases are very good sort of girls, I assure you. It is a pity they are not handsome! Not that *I* think Charlotte so *very* plain – but then she is our particular friend.'

'She seems a very pleasant young woman,' said Bingley.

'Oh! dear, yes; – but you must own she is very plain. Lady Lucas herself has often said so, and envied me Jane's beauty. I do not like to boast of my own child, but to be sure, Jane – one does not often see anybody better looking. It is what everybody says. I do not trust my own partiality. When she was only fifteen, there was a gentleman at my brother Gardiner's in town, so much in love with her, that my sister-in-law was sure he would make her an offer before we came away. But however he did not. Perhaps he thought her too young. However, he wrote some verses on her, and very pretty they were.'

'And so ended his affection,' said Elizabeth impatiently. 'There has been many a one, I fancy, overcome in the same way. I wonder who first discovered the efficacy of poetry in driving away love!'

'I have been used to consider poetry as the *food* of love,' said Darcy.

'Of a fine, stout, healthy love it may. Everything nourishes what is strong already. But if it be only a slight, thin sort of inclination, I am convinced that one good sonnet will starve it entirely away.'

Darcy only smiled; and the general pause which ensued made Elizabeth tremble lest her mother should be exposing herself again. She longed to speak, but could think of nothing to say; and after a short silence Mrs Bennet began repeating her thanks to Mr Bingley for his kindness to Jane, with an apology for troubling him also with Lizzy. Mr Bingley was unaffectedly civil in his answer, and forced his younger sister to be civil also, and say what the occasion required. She performed her part indeed without much graciousness, but Mrs Bennet was satisfied, and soon afterwards ordered her carriage. Upon this signal, the youngest of her daughters put herself forward. The two girls had been whispering to each other during the whole visit, and the result of it was, that the youngest should tax Mr Bingley with having promised on his first coming into the country to give a ball at Netherfield.

Lydia was a stout, well-grown girl of fifteen, with a fine complexion and good-humoured countenance; a favourite with her mother, whose affection had brought her into public at an early age. She had high animal spirits, and a sort of natural self-consequence, which the attentions of the officers, to whom her uncle's good dinners and her own easy manners recommended her, had increased into assurance. She was very equal therefore to address Mr Bingley on the subject of the ball, and abruptly reminded him of his promise; adding, that it would be the most shameful thing in the world if he did not keep it. His answer to this sudden attack was delightful to their mother's ear.

'I am perfectly ready, I assure you, to keep my engagement; and when your sister is recovered, you shall if you please name the very day of the ball. But you would not wish to be dancing while she is ill.'

Lydia declared herself satisfied. 'Oh! yes – it would be much better to wait till Jane was well, and by that time most likely Captain Carter would be at Meryton again. And when you have given *your* ball,' she added, 'I shall insist on their giving one also. I shall tell Colonel Forster it will be quite a shame if he does not.'

Mrs Bennet and her daughters then departed, and Elizabeth returned instantly to Jane, leaving her own and her relations' behaviour to the remarks of the two ladies and Mr Darcy; the latter of whom, however, could not be prevailed on to join in their censure of *her*, in spite of all Miss Bingley's witticisms on *fine eyes*.

## *Chapter 10*

The day passed much as the day before had done. Mrs Hurst and Miss Bingley had spent some hours of the morning with the invalid, who continued, though slowly, to mend; and in the evening Elizabeth joined their party in the drawing-room. The loo table, however, did not appear. Mr Darcy was writing, and Miss Bingley, seated near him, was watching the progress of his letter, and repeatedly calling off his attention by messages to his sister. Mr Hurst and Mr Bingley were at piquet, and Mrs Hurst was observing their game.

Elizabeth took up some needlework, and was sufficiently amused in attending to what passed between Darcy and his companion. The perpetual commendations of the lady either on his handwriting, or on the evenness of his lines, or on the length of his letter, with the perfect unconcern with which her praises were received, formed a curious dialogue, and was exactly in unison with her opinion of each.

'How delighted Miss Darcy will be to receive such a letter!'

He made no answer.

'You write uncommonly fast.'

'You are mistaken. I write rather slowly.'

'How many letters you must have occasion to write in the course of the year! Letters of business too! How odious I should think them!'

'It is fortunate, then, that they fall to my lot instead of to yours.'

'Pray tell your sister that I long to see her.'

'I have already told her so once, by your desire.'

'I am afraid you do not like your pen. Let me mend it for you. I mend pens remarkably well.'

'Thank you – but I always mend my own.'

'How can you contrive to write so even?'

He was silent.

'Tell your sister I am delighted to hear of her improvement on the harp, and pray let her know that I am quite in raptures with her beautiful little design for a table, and I think it infinitely superior to Miss Grantley's.'

'Will you give me leave to defer your raptures till I write again? – At present I have not room to do them justice.'

'Oh! it is of no consequence. I shall see her in January. But do you always write such charming long letters to her, Mr Darcy?'

'They are generally long; but whether always charming, it is not for me to determine.'

'It is a rule with me, that a person who can write a long letter, with ease, cannot write ill.'

'That will not do for a compliment to Darcy, Caroline,' cried her brother – 'because he does *not* write with ease. He studies too much for words of four syllables. – Do not you, Darcy?'

'My style of writing is very different from yours.'

'Oh!' cried Miss Bingley, 'Charles writes in the most careless way imaginable. He leaves out half his words, and blots the rest.'

'My ideas flow so rapidly that I have not time to express them – by which means my letters sometimes convey no ideas at all to my correspondents.'

'Your humility, Mr Bingley,' said Elizabeth, 'must disarm reproof.'

'Nothing is more deceitful,' said Darcy, 'than the appearance of humility. It is often only carelessness of opinion, and sometimes an indirect boast.'

'And which of the two do you call *my* little recent piece of modesty?'

'The indirect boast; – for you are really proud of your defects in writing, because you consider them as proceeding from a rapidity of thought and carelessness of execution, which if not estimable, you think at least highly interesting. The power of doing anything with quickness is always much prized by the possessor, and often without any attention to the imperfection of the performance. When you told Mrs Bennet this morning that if you ever resolved on quitting Netherfield you should be gone in five minutes, you meant it to be a sort of panegyric, of compliment to yourself – and yet what is there so very laudable in a precipitance which must leave very necessary business undone, and can be of no real advantage to yourself or anyone else?'

'Nay,' cried Bingley, 'this is too much, to remember at night all the foolish things that were said in the morning. And yet, upon my honour, I believed what I said of myself to be true, and I believe it at this moment. At least, therefore, I did not assume the character of needless precipitance merely to show off before the ladies.'

'I dare say you believed it; but I am by no means convinced that you would be gone with such celerity. Your conduct would be quite as dependent on chance as that of any man I know; and if, as you were mounting your horse, a friend were to say, "Bingley, you had better stay till next week," you would probably do it, you would probably not go – and, at another word, might stay a month.'

'You have only proved by this,' cried Elizabeth, 'that Mr Bingley did not do justice to his own disposition. You have shown him off now much more than he did himself.'

'I am exceedingly gratified,' said Bingley, 'by your converting what my friend says into a compliment on the sweetness of my temper. But I am afraid you are giving it a turn which that gentleman did by no means intend; for he would certainly think the better of me, if under such a circumstance I were to give a flat denial, and ride off as fast as I could.'

'Would Mr Darcy then consider the rashness of your original intention as atoned for by your obstinacy in adhering to it?'

'Upon my word I cannot exactly explain the matter. Darcy must speak for himself.'

'You expect me to account for opinions which you choose to call mine, but which I have never acknowledged. Allowing the case, however, to stand according to your representation, you must remember, Miss Bennet, that the friend who is supposed to desire his return to the house, and the delay of his plan, has merely desired it, asked it without offering one argument in favour of its propriety.'

'To yield readily – easily – to the *persuasion* of a friend is no merit with you.'

'To yield without conviction is no compliment to the understanding of either.'

'You appear to me, Mr Darcy, to allow nothing for the influence of friendship and affection. A regard for the requester would often make one readily yield to a request, without waiting for arguments to reason one into it. I am not particularly speaking of such a case as you have supposed about Mr Bingley. We may as well wait, perhaps, till the circumstance occurs, before we discuss the discretion of his behaviour thereupon. But in general and ordinary cases between friend and friend, where one of them is desired by the other to change a resolution of no very great moment, should you think ill of that person for complying with the desire, without waiting to be argued into it?'

'Will it not be advisable, before we proceed on this subject, to arrange with rather more precision the degree of importance which is to appertain to this request, as well as the degree of intimacy subsisting between the parties?'

'By all means,' cried Bingley; 'let us hear all the particulars, not forgetting their comparative height and size; for that will have more weight in the argument, Miss Bennet, than you may be aware of. I assure you that if Darcy were not such a great tall fellow, in comparison with myself, I should not pay him half so much deference. I declare I do not know a more awful object than Darcy, on particular occasions, and in particular places; at his own house especially, and of a Sunday evening when he has nothing to do.'

Mr Darcy smiled; but Elizabeth thought she could perceive that he was rather offended; and therefore checked her laugh. Miss Bingley warmly resented the indignity he had received, in an expostulation with her brother for talking such nonsense.

'I see your design, Bingley,' said his friend. – 'You dislike an argument, and want to silence this.'

'Perhaps I do. Arguments are too much like disputes. If you and Miss Bennet will defer yours till I am out of the room, I shall be very thankful; and then you may say whatever you like of me.'

'What you ask,' said Elizabeth, 'is no sacrifice on my side; and Mr Darcy had much better finish his letter.'

Mr Darcy took her advice, and did finish his letter.

When that business was over, he applied to Miss Bingley and Elizabeth for the indulgence of some music. Miss Bingley moved with alacrity to the pianoforte, and after a polite request that Elizabeth would lead the way, which the other as politely and more earnestly negatived, she seated herself.

Mrs Hurst sang with her sister, and while they were thus employed Elizabeth could not help observing as she turned over some music books that lay on the instrument, how frequently Mr Darcy's eyes were fixed on her. She hardly knew how to suppose that she could be an object of admiration to so great a man; and yet that he should look at her because he disliked her, was still more strange. She could only imagine however at last, that she drew his notice because there was a something about her more wrong and reprehensible, according to his ideas of right, than in any other person present. The supposition did not pain her. She liked him too little to care for his approbation.

After playing some Italian songs, Miss Bingley varied the charm by a lively Scotch air; and soon afterwards Mr Darcy, drawing near Elizabeth, said to her, 'Do not you feel a great inclination, Miss Bennet, to seize such an opportunity of dancing a reel?'

She smiled, but made no answer. He repeated the question, with some surprise at her silence.

'Oh!' said she, 'I heard you before; but I could not immediately determine what to say in reply. You wanted me, I know, to say "Yes," that you might have the pleasure of despising my taste; but I always delight in overthrowing those kind of schemes, and cheating a person of their premeditated contempt. I have therefore made up my mind to tell you, that I do not want to dance a reel at all – and now despise me if you dare.'

'Indeed I do not dare.'

Elizabeth, having rather expected to affront him, was amazed at his gallantry; but there was a mixture of sweetness and archness in her manner which made it difficult for her to affront anybody; and Darcy had never been so bewitched by any woman as he was by her. He really believed, that were it not for the inferiority of her connections, he should be in some danger.

Miss Bingley saw, or suspected enough to be jealous; and her great anxiety for the recovery of her dear friend Jane, received some assistance from her desire of getting rid of Elizabeth.

She often tried to provoke Darcy into disliking her guest, by talking of their supposed marriage, and planning his happiness in such an alliance.

'I hope,' said she, as they were walking together in the shrubbery the next day, 'you will give your mother-in-law a few hints, when this desirable event takes place, as to the advantage of holding her tongue; and if you can compass it, do cure the younger girls of running after the officers. – And, if I may mention so delicate a subject, endeavour to check that little something, bordering on conceit and impertinence, which your lady possesses.'

'Have you anything else to propose for my domestic felicity?'

'Oh! yes. – Do let the portraits of your uncle and aunt Philips be placed in the gallery at Pemberley. Put them next to your great uncle the judge. They are in the same profession, you know; only in different lines. As for your Elizabeth's picture, you must not attempt to have it taken, for what painter could do justice to those beautiful eyes?'

'It would not be easy, indeed, to catch their expression, but their colour and shape, and the eyelashes, so remarkably fine, might be copied.'

At that moment they were met from another walk, by Mrs Hurst and Elizabeth herself.

'I did not know that you intended to walk,' said Miss Bingley, in some confusion, lest they had been overheard.

'You used us abominably ill,' answered Mrs Hurst, 'in running away without telling us that you were coming out.'

Then taking the disengaged arm of Mr Darcy, she left Elizabeth to walk by herself. The path just admitted three. Mr Darcy felt their rudeness and immediately said, 'This walk is not wide enough for our party. We had better go into the avenue.'

But Elizabeth, who had not the least inclination to remain with them, laughingly answered, 'No, no; stay where you are. – You are charmingly group'd, and appear to uncommon advantage. The picturesque would be spoilt by admitting a fourth. Goodbye.'

She then ran gaily off, rejoicing as she rambled about, in the hope of being at home again in a day or two. Jane was already so much recovered as to intend leaving her room for a couple of hours that evening.

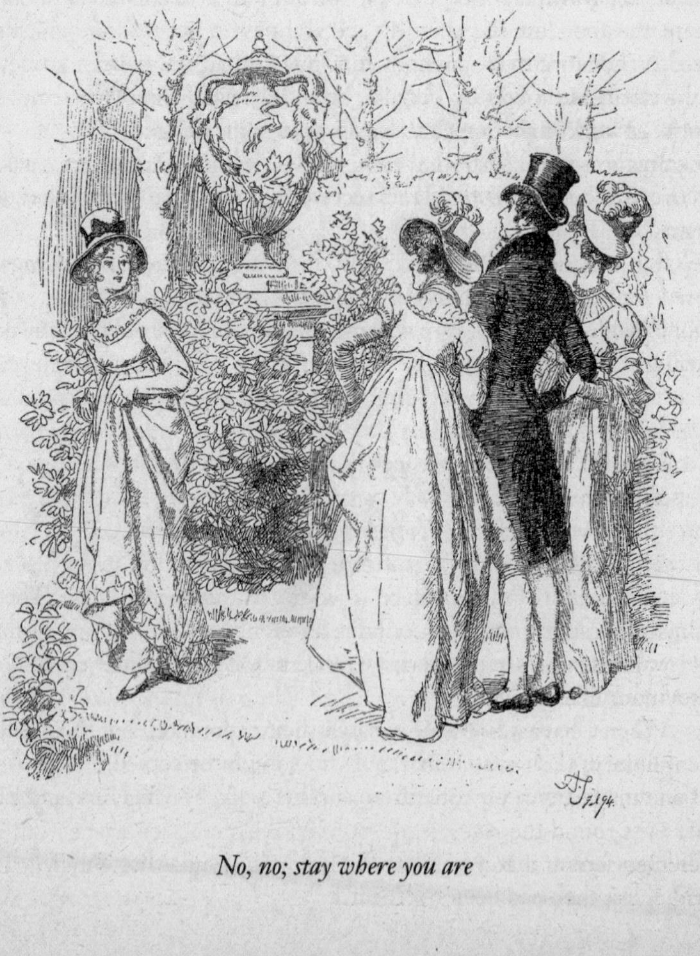

*No, no; stay where you are*

## *Chapter 11*

When the ladies removed after dinner, Elizabeth ran up to her sister, and seeing her well guarded from cold, attended her into the drawing-room; where she was welcomed by her two friends with many professions of pleasure; and Elizabeth had never seen them so agreeable as they were during the hour which passed before the gentlemen appeared. Their powers of conversation were considerable. They could describe an entertainment with accuracy, relate an anecdote with humour, and laugh at their acquaintance with spirit.

But when the gentlemen entered, Jane was no longer the first object. Miss Bingley's eyes were instantly turned towards Darcy, and she had something to say to him before he had advanced many steps. He addressed himself directly to Miss Bennet, with a polite congratulation; Mr Hurst also made her a slight bow, and said he was 'very glad'; but diffuseness and warmth remained for Bingley's salutation. He was full of joy and attention. The first half-hour was spent in piling up the fire, lest she should suffer from the change of room; and she removed at his desire to the other side of the fireplace, that she might be farther from the door. He then sat down by her, and talked scarcely to anyone else. Elizabeth, at work in the opposite corner, saw it all with great delight.

When tea was over, Mr Hurst reminded his sister-in-law of the card-table – but in vain. She had obtained private intelligence that Mr Darcy did not wish for cards; and Mr Hurst soon found even his open petition rejected. She assured him that no one intended to play, and the silence of the whole party on the subject, seemed to justify her. Mr Hurst had therefore nothing to do, but to stretch himself on one of the sofas and go to sleep. Darcy took up a book; Miss Bingley did the same; and Mrs Hurst, principally occupied in playing with her bracelets and rings, joined now and then in her brother's conversation with Miss Bennet.

Miss Bingley's attention was quite as much engaged in watching Mr Darcy's progress through *his* book, as in reading her own; and she was perpetually either making some enquiry, or looking at his page. She could not win him, however, to any conversation; he merely answered her question, and read on. At length, quite exhausted by the attempt to be amused with her own book, which she had only chosen because it was the second volume of his, she gave a great yawn and said, 'How pleasant it is to spend an evening in this way! I declare after all there is no enjoyment like reading! How much sooner one tires of anything than of a book! – When I have a house of my own, I shall be miserable if I have not an excellent library.'

No one made any reply. She then yawned again, threw aside her book, and cast her eyes round the room in quest of some amusement; when hearing her brother mentioning a ball to Miss Bennet, she turned suddenly towards him and said,

'By the by, Charles, are you really serious in meditating a dance at Netherfield? – I would advise you, before you determine on it, to consult the wishes of the present party; I am much mistaken if there are not some among us to whom a ball would be rather a punishment than a pleasure.'

'If you mean Darcy,' cried her brother, 'he may go to bed, if he chooses, before it begins – but as for the ball, it is quite a settled thing; and as soon as Nicholls has made white soup enough I shall send round my cards.'

'I should like balls infinitely better,' she replied, 'if they were carried on in a different manner; but there is something insufferably tedious in the usual process of such a meeting. It would surely be much more rational if conversation instead of dancing made the order of the day.'

'Much more rational, my dear Caroline, I dare say, but it would not be near so much like a ball.'

Miss Bingley made no answer; and soon afterwards got up and walked about the room. Her figure was elegant, and she walked well; – but Darcy, at whom it was all aimed, was still inflexibly studious. In the desperation of her feelings she resolved on one effort more; and, turning to Elizabeth, said, 'Miss Eliza Bennet, let me persuade you to follow my example, and take a turn about the room. – I assure you it is very refreshing after sitting so long in one attitude.'

Elizabeth was surprised, but agreed to it immediately. Miss Bingley succeeded

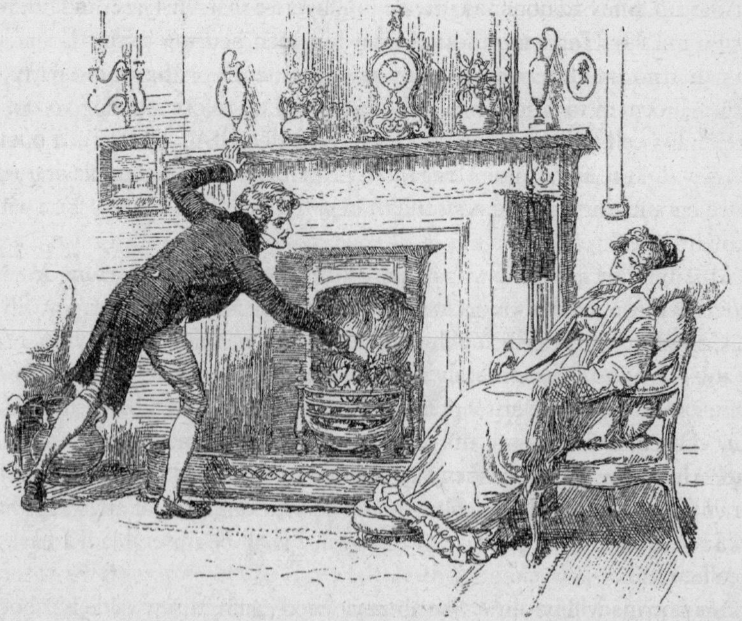

*The first half-hour was spent in piling up the fire*

no less in the real object of her civility; Mr Darcy looked up. He was as much awake to the novelty of attention in that quarter as Elizabeth herself could be, and unconsciously closed his book. He was directly invited to join their party, but he declined it, observing, that he could imagine but two motives for their choosing to walk up and down the room together, with either of which motives his joining them would interfere. 'What could he mean? She was dying to know what could be his meaning' – and asked Elizabeth whether she could at all understand him?

'Not at all,' was her answer; 'but depend upon it, he means to be severe on us, and our surest way of disappointing him, will be to ask nothing about it.'

Miss Bingley, however, was incapable of disappointing Mr Darcy in anything, and persevered therefore in requiring an explanation of his two motives.

'I have not the smallest objection to explaining them,' said he, as soon as she allowed him to speak. 'You either choose this method of passing the evening because you are in each other's confidence and have secret affairs to discuss, or because you are conscious that your figures appear to the greatest advantage in walking; – if the first, I should be completely in your way; – and if the second, I can admire you much better as I sit by the fire.'

'Oh! shocking!' cried Miss Bingley. 'I never heard anything so abominable. How shall we punish him for such a speech?'

'Nothing so easy, if you have but the inclination,' said Elizabeth. 'We can all plague and punish one another. Tease him – laugh at him. – Intimate as you are, you must know how it is to be done.'

'But upon my honour I do *not*. I do assure you that my intimacy has not yet taught me *that*. Tease calmness of temper and presence of mind! No, no – I feel he may defy us there. And as to laughter, we will not expose ourselves, if you please, by attempting to laugh without a subject. Mr Darcy may hug himself.'

'Mr Darcy is not to be laughed at!' cried Elizabeth. 'That is an uncommon advantage, and uncommon I hope it will continue, for it would be a great loss to *me* to have many such acquaintance. I dearly love a laugh.'

'Miss Bingley,' said he, 'has given me credit for more than can be. The wisest and the best of men, nay, the wisest and best of their actions, may be rendered ridiculous by a person whose first object in life is a joke.'

'Certainly,' replied Elizabeth – 'there are such people, but I hope I am not one of *them*. I hope I never ridicule what is wise or good. Follies and nonsense, whims and inconsistencies *do* divert me, I own, and I laugh at them whenever I can. – But these, I suppose, are precisely what you are without.'

'Perhaps that is not possible for anyone. But it has been the study of my life to avoid those weaknesses which often expose a strong understanding to ridicule.'

'Such as vanity and pride.'

'Yes, vanity is a weakness indeed. But pride – where there is a real superiority of mind, pride will be always under good regulation.'

Elizabeth turned away to hide a smile.

'Your examination of Mr Darcy is over, I presume,' said Miss Bingley; 'and pray what is the result?'

'I am perfectly convinced by it that Mr Darcy has no defect. He owns it himself without disguise.'

'No' – said Darcy, 'I have made no such pretension. I have faults enough, but they are not, I hope, of understanding. My temper I dare not vouch for. – It is I believe too little yielding – certainly too little for the convenience of the world. I cannot forget the follies and vices of others so soon as I ought, nor their offences against myself. My feelings are not puffed about with every attempt to move them. My temper would perhaps be called resentful. – My good opinion once lost is lost for ever.'

'*That* is a failing indeed!' – cried Elizabeth. 'Implacable resentment *is* a shade in a character. But you have chosen your fault well. – I really cannot *laugh* at it. You are safe from me.'

'There is, I believe, in every disposition a tendency to some particular evil, a natural defect, which not even the best education can overcome.'

'And *your* defect is a propensity to hate everybody.'

'And yours,' he replied with a smile, 'is wilfully to misunderstand them.'

'Do let us have a little music,' – cried Miss Bingley, tired of a conversation in which she had no share. – 'Louisa, you will not mind my waking Mr Hurst.'

Her sister made not the smallest objection, and the pianoforte was opened, and Darcy, after a few moments' recollection, was not sorry for it. He began to feel the danger of paying Elizabeth too much attention.

## *Chapter 12*

In consequence of an agreement between the sisters, Elizabeth wrote the next morning to her mother, to beg that the carriage might be sent for them in the course of the day. But Mrs Bennet, who had calculated on her daughters remaining at Netherfield till the following Tuesday, which would exactly finish Jane's week, could not bring herself to receive them with pleasure before. Her answer, therefore, was not propitious, at least not to Elizabeth's wishes, for she was impatient to get home. Mrs Bennet sent them word that they could not possibly have the carriage before Tuesday; and in her postscript it was added, that if Mr Bingley and his sister pressed them to stay longer, she could spare them very well. – Against staying longer, however, Elizabeth was positively resolved – nor did she much expect it would be asked; and fearful, on the contrary, as being considered as intruding themselves needlessly long, she urged Jane to borrow Mr Bingley's carriage immediately, and at length it was settled that their original design of leaving Netherfield that morning should be mentioned, and the request made.

The communication excited many professions of concern; and enough was said of wishing them to stay at least till the following day to work on Jane; and till the morrow, their going was deferred. Miss Bingley was then sorry that she had proposed the delay, for her jealousy and dislike of one sister much exceeded her affection for the other.

The master of the house heard with real sorrow that they were to go so soon, and repeatedly tried to persuade Miss Bennet that it would not be safe for her – that she was not enough recovered; but Jane was firm where she felt herself to be right.

To Mr Darcy it was welcome intelligence – Elizabeth had been at Netherfield long enough. She attracted him more than he liked – and Miss Bingley was uncivil to *her*, and more teasing than usual to himself. He wisely resolved to be particularly careful that no sign of admiration should *now* escape him, nothing that could elevate her with the hope of influencing his felicity; sensible that if such an idea had been suggested, his behaviour during the last day must have material weight in confirming or crushing it. Steady to his purpose, he scarcely spoke ten words to her through the whole of Saturday, and though they were at one time left by themselves for half an hour, he adhered most conscientiously to his book, and would not even look at her.

On Sunday, after morning service, the separation, so agreeable to almost all, took place. Miss Bingley's civility to Elizabeth increased at last very rapidly, as well as her affection for Jane; and when they parted, after assuring the latter of the pleasure it would always give her to see her either at Longbourn or Netherfield, and embracing her most tenderly, she even shook hands with the former. – Elizabeth took leave of the whole party in the liveliest spirits.

They were not welcomed home very cordially by their mother. Mrs Bennet wondered at their coming, and thought them very wrong to give so much trouble, and was sure Jane would have caught cold again. – But their father, though very laconic in his expressions of pleasure, was really glad to see them; he had felt their importance in the family circle. The evening conversation, when they were all assembled, had lost much of its animation, and almost all its sense, by the absence of Jane and Elizabeth.

They found Mary, as usual, deep in the study of thorough bass and human nature; and had some new extracts to admire, and some new observations of threadbare morality to listen to. Catherine and Lydia had information for them of a different sort. Much had been done, and much had been said in the regiment since the preceding Wednesday; several of the officers had dined lately with their uncle, a private had been flogged, and it had actually been hinted that Colonel Forster was going to be married.

## *Chapter 13*

'I hope, my dear,' said Mr Bennet to his wife, as they were at breakfast the next morning, 'that you have ordered a good dinner today, because I have reason to expect an addition to our family party.'

'Who do you mean, my dear? I know of nobody that is coming I am sure, unless Charlotte Lucas should happen to call in, and I hope *my* dinners are good enough for her. I do not believe she often sees such at home.'

'The person of whom I speak, is a gentleman and a stranger.' Mrs Bennet's eyes sparkled. – 'A gentleman and a stranger! It is Mr Bingley I am sure. Why Jane – you never dropped a word of this; you sly thing! Well, I am sure I shall be extremely glad to see Mr Bingley. – But – good lord! how unlucky! there is not a bit of fish to be got today. Lydia, my love, ring the bell. I must speak to Hill, this moment.'

'It is *not* Mr Bingley,' said her husband; 'it is a person whom I never saw in the whole course of my life.'

This roused a general astonishment; and he had the pleasure of being eagerly questioned by his wife and five daughters at once.

After amusing himself for some time with their curiosity, he thus explained. 'About a month ago I received this letter, and about a fortnight ago I answered it, for I thought it a case of some delicacy, and requiring early attention. It is from my cousin, Mr Collins, who, when I am dead, may turn you all out of this house as soon as he pleases.'

'Oh! my dear,' cried his wife, 'I cannot bear to hear that mentioned. Pray do not talk of that odious man. I do think it is the hardest thing in the world, that your estate should be entailed away from your own children; and I am sure if I had been you, I should have tried long ago to do something or other about it.'

Jane and Elizabeth attempted to explain to her the nature of an entail. They had often attempted it before, but it was a subject on which Mrs Bennet was beyond the reach of reason; and she continued to rail bitterly against the cruelty of settling an estate away from a family of five daughters, in favour of a man whom nobody cared anything about.

'It certainly is a most iniquitous affair,' said Mr Bennet, 'and nothing can clear Mr Collins from the guilt of inheriting Longbourn. But if you will listen to his letter, you may perhaps be a little softened by his manner of expressing himself.'

'No, that I am sure I shall not; and I think it was very impertinent of him to write to you at all, and very hypocritical. I hate such false friends. Why could not he keep on quarrelling with you, as his father did before him?'

'Why, indeed, he does seem to have had some filial scruples on that head, as you will hear.

*'Hunsford, near Westerham, Kent, 15th October.*

'DEAR SIR – The disagreement subsisting between yourself and my late honoured father, always gave me much uneasiness, and since I have had the misfortune to lose him, I have frequently wished to heal the breach; but for some time I was kept back by my own doubts, fearing lest it might seem disrespectful to his memory for me to be on good terms with anyone, with whom it had always pleased him to be at variance." There, Mrs Bennet. "My mind however is now made up on the subject, for having received ordination at Easter, I have been so fortunate as to be distinguished by the patronage of the Right Honourable Lady Catherine de Bourgh, widow of Sir Lewis de Bourgh, whose bounty and beneficence has preferred me to the valuable rectory of this parish, where it shall be my earnest endeavour to demean myself with grateful respect towards her ladyship, and be ever ready to perform those rites and ceremonies which are instituted by the Church of England. As a clergyman, moreover, I feel it my duty to promote and establish the blessing of peace in all families within the reach of my influence; and on these grounds I flatter myself that my present overtures of goodwill are highly commendable, and that the circumstance of my being next in the entail of Longbourn estate, will be kindly overlooked on your side, and not lead you to reject the offered olive branch. I cannot be otherwise than concerned at being the means of injuring your amiable daughters, and beg leave to apologise for it, as well as to assure you of my readiness to make them every possible amends, – but of this hereafter. If you should have no objection to receive me into your house, I propose myself the satisfaction of waiting on you and your family, Monday, November 18th, by four o'clock, and shall probably trespass on your hospitality till the Saturday se'night following, which I can do without any inconvenience, as Lady Catherine is far from objecting to my occasional absence on a Sunday, provided that some other clergyman is engaged to do the duty of the day. I remain, dear sir, with respectful compliments to your lady and daughters, your well-wisher and friend,

WILLIAM COLLINS.

'At four o'clock, therefore, we may expect this peace-making gentleman,' said Mr Bennet, as he folded up the letter. 'He seems to be a most conscientious and polite young man, upon my word; and I doubt not will prove a valuable acquaintance, especially if Lady Catherine should be so indulgent as to let him come to us again.'

'There is some sense in what he says about the girls however; and if he is disposed to make them any amends, I shall not be the person to discourage him.'

'Though it is difficult,' said Jane, 'to guess in what way he can mean to make us the atonement he thinks our due, the wish is certainly to his credit.'

Elizabeth was chiefly struck with his extraordinary deference for Lady Catherine, and his kind intention of christening, marrying, and burying his parishioners whenever it were required.

'He must be an oddity, I think,' said she. 'I cannot make him out. – There is something very pompous in his style. – And what can he mean by apologising for being next in the entail? – We cannot suppose he would help it, if he could. – Can he be a sensible man, sir?'

'No, my dear; I think not. I have great hopes of finding him quite the reverse. There is a mixture of servility and self-importance in his letter, which promises well. I am impatient to see him.'

'In point of composition,' said Mary, 'his letter does not seem defective. The idea of the olive branch perhaps is not wholly new, yet I think it is well expressed.'

To Catherine and Lydia, neither the letter nor its writer were in any degree interesting. It was next to impossible that their cousin should come in a scarlet coat, and it was now some weeks since they had received pleasure from the society of a man in any other colour. As for their mother, Mr Collins's letter had done away much of her ill-will, and she was preparing to see him with a degree of composure, which astonished her husband and daughters.

Mr Collins was punctual to his time, and was received with great politeness by the whole family. Mr Bennet indeed said little; but the ladies were ready enough to talk, and Mr Collins seemed neither in need of encouragement, nor inclined to be silent himself. He was a tall, heavy-looking young man of five and twenty. His air was grave and stately, and his manners were very formal. He had not been long seated before he complimented Mrs Bennet on having so fine a family of daughters, said he had heard much of their beauty, but that, in this instance, fame had fallen short of the truth; and added, that he did not doubt her seeing them all in due time well disposed of in marriage. This gallantry was not much to the taste of some of his hearers, but Mrs Bennet, who quarrelled with no compliments, answered most readily, 'You are very kind, sir, I am sure; and I wish with all my heart it may prove so; for else they will be destitute enough. Things are settled so oddly.'

'You allude perhaps to the entail of this estate.'

'Ah! sir, I do indeed. It is a grievous affair to my poor girls, you must confess. Not that I mean to find fault with *you*, for such things I know are all chance in this world. There is no knowing how estates will go when once they come to be entailed.'

'I am very sensible, madam, of the hardship to my fair cousins, – and could say much on the subject but that I am cautious of appearing forward and precipitate. But I can assure the young ladies that I come prepared to admire them. At present I will not say more, but perhaps when we are better acquainted – '

He was interrupted by a summons to dinner; and the girls smiled on each other. They were not the only objects of Mr Collins's admiration. The hall, the dining-room, and all its furniture were examined and praised; and his commendation of everything would have touched Mrs Bennet's heart, but for the mortifying supposition of his viewing it all as his own future property. The dinner too in its turn was highly admired; and he begged to know to which of his fair cousins, the excellence of its cookery was owing. But here he was set right by

Mrs Bennet, who assured him with some asperity that they were very well able to keep a good cook, and that her daughters had nothing to do in the kitchen. He begged pardon for having displeased her. In a softened tone she declared herself not at all offended; but he continued to apologise for about a quarter of an hour.

## *Chapter 14*

During dinner, Mr Bennet scarcely spoke at all; but when the servants were withdrawn, he thought it time to have some conversation with his guest, and therefore started a subject in which he expected him to shine, by observing that he seemed very fortunate in his patroness. Lady Catherine de Bourgh's attention to his wishes, and consideration for his comfort, appeared very remarkable. Mr Bennet could not have chosen better. Mr Collins was eloquent in her praise. The subject elevated him to more than usual solemnity of manner, and with a most important aspect he protested that he had never in his life witnessed such behaviour in a person of rank – such affability and condescension, as he had himself experienced from Lady Catherine. She had been graciously pleased to approve of both the discourses, which he had already had the honour of preaching before her. She had also asked him twice to dine at Rosings, and had sent for him only the Saturday before, to make up her pool of quadrille in the evening. Lady Catherine was reckoned proud by many people he knew, but *he* had never seen anything but affability in her. She had always spoken to him as she would to any other gentleman; she made not the smallest objection to his joining in the society of the neighbourhood, nor to his leaving his parish occasionally for a week or two, to visit his relations. She had even condescended to advise him to marry as soon as he could, provided he chose with discretion; and had once paid him a visit in his humble parsonage; where she had perfectly approved all the alterations he had been making, and had even vouchsafed to suggest some herself, – some shelves in the closets upstairs.

'That is all very proper and civil, I am sure,' said Mrs Bennet, 'and I dare say she is a very agreeable woman. It is a pity that great ladies in general are not more like her. Does she live near you, sir?'

'The garden in which stands my humble abode, is separated only by a lane from Rosings Park, her ladyship's residence.'

'I think you said she was a widow, sir. Has she any family?'

'She has one only daughter, the heiress of Rosings, and of very extensive property.'

'Ah!' cried Mrs Bennet, shaking her head, 'then she is better off than many girls. And what sort of young lady is she? Is she handsome?'

'She is a most charming young lady indeed. Lady Catherine herself says that in point of true beauty, Miss de Bourgh is far superior to the handsomest of her sex; because there is that in her features which marks the young woman of distinguished birth. She is unfortunately of a sickly constitution, which has prevented her making that progress in many accomplishments, which she could not otherwise have failed of; as I am informed by the lady who superintended her education, and who still resides with them. But she is perfectly amiable, and often condescends to drive by my humble abode in her little phaeton and ponies.'

'Has she been presented? I do not remember her name among the ladies at court.'

'Her indifferent state of health unhappily prevents her being in town; and by that means, as I told Lady Catherine myself one day, has deprived the British court of its brightest ornament. Her ladyship seemed pleased with the idea, and you may imagine that I am happy on every occasion to offer those little delicate compliments which are always acceptable to ladies. I have more than once observed to Lady Catherine, that her charming daughter seemed born to be a duchess, and that the most elevated rank, instead of giving her consequence, would be adorned by her. – These are the kind of little things which please her ladyship, and it is a sort of attention which I conceive myself peculiarly bound to pay.'

'You judge very properly,' said Mr Bennet, 'and it is happy for you that you possess the talent of flattering with delicacy. May I ask whether these pleasing attentions proceed from the impulse of the moment, or are the result of previous study?'

'They arise chiefly from what is passing at the time, and though I sometimes amuse myself with suggesting and arranging such little elegant compliments as may be adapted to ordinary occasions, I always wish to give them as unstudied an air as possible.'

Mr Bennet's expectations were fully answered. His cousin was as absurd as he had hoped, and he listened to him with the keenest enjoyment, maintaining at the same time the most resolute composure of countenance, and except in an occasional glance at Elizabeth, requiring no partner in his pleasure.

By tea-time however the dose had been enough, and Mr Bennet was glad to take his guest into the drawing-room again, and when tea was over, glad to invite him to read aloud to the ladies. Mr Collins readily assented, and a book was produced; but on beholding it, (for everything announced it to be from a circulating library,) he started back, and begging pardon, protested that he never read novels. – Kitty stared at him, and Lydia exclaimed. – Other books were produced, and after some deliberation he chose Fordyce's Sermons. Lydia gaped as he opened the volume, and before he had, with very monotonous solemnity, read three pages, she interrupted him with, 'Do you know, mamma, that my uncle Philips talks of turning away Richard, and if he does, Colonel Forster will hire him. My aunt told me so herself on Saturday. I shall walk to Meryton tomorrow to hear more about it, and to ask when Mr Denny comes back from town.'

Lydia was bid by her two eldest sisters to hold her tongue; but Mr Collins, much offended, laid aside his book, and said, 'I have often observed how little young ladies are interested by books of a serious stamp, though written solely for their benefit. It amazes me, I confess; – for certainly, there can be nothing so advantageous to them as instruction. But I will no longer importune my young cousin.'

Then turning to Mr Bennet, he offered himself as his antagonist at backgammon. Mr Bennet accepted the challenge, observing that he acted very wisely in leaving the girls to their own trifling amusements. Mrs Bennet and her daughters apologised most civilly for Lydia's interruption, and promised that it should not occur again, if he would resume his book; but Mr Collins, after assuring them that he bore his young cousin no ill will, and should never resent her behaviour as any affront, seated himself at another table with Mr Bennet, and prepared for backgammon.

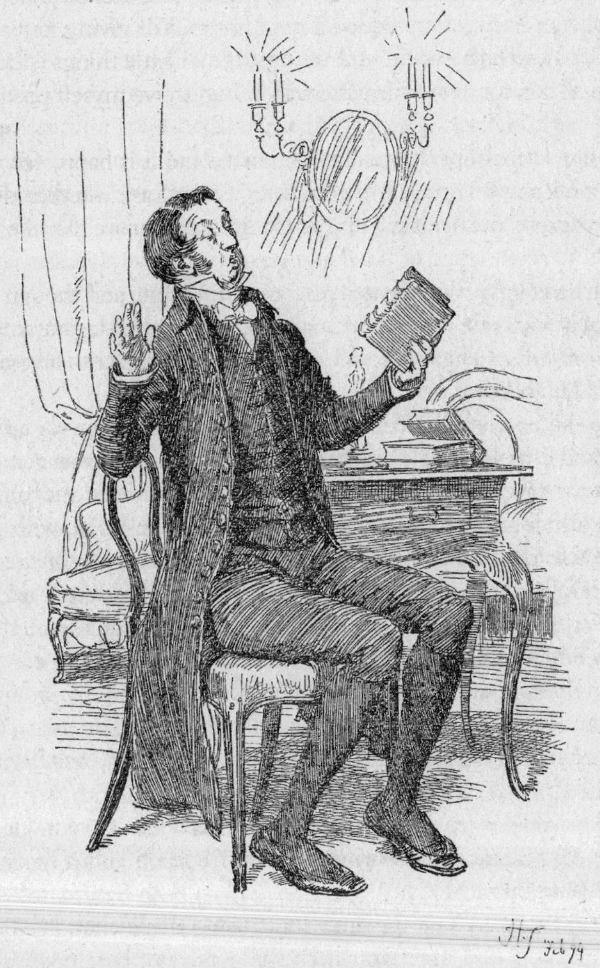

*He started back, and begging pardon, protested that he never read novels*

## *Chapter 15*

Mr Collins was not a sensible man, and the deficiency of nature had been but little assisted by education or society; the greatest part of his life having been spent under the guidance of an illiterate and miserly father; and though he belonged to one of the universities, he had merely kept the necessary terms, without forming at it any useful acquaintance. The subjection in which his father had brought him up, had given him originally great humility of manner, but it was now a good deal counteracted by the self-conceit of a weak head, living in retirement, and the consequential feelings of early and unexpected prosperity. A fortunate chance had recommended him to Lady Catherine de Bourgh when the living of Hunsford was vacant; and the respect which he felt for her high rank, and his veneration for her as his patroness, mingling with a very good opinion of himself, of his authority as a clergyman, and his rights as a rector, made him altogether a mixture of pride and obsequiousness, self-importance and humility.

Having now a good house and very sufficient income, he intended to marry; and in seeking a reconciliation with the Longbourn family he had a wife in view, as he meant to choose one of the daughters, if he found them as handsome and amiable as they were represented by common report. This was his plan of amends – of atonement – for inheriting their father's estate; and he thought it an excellent one, full of eligibility and suitableness, and excessively generous and disinterested on his own part.

His plan did not vary on seeing them. – Miss Bennet's lovely face confirmed his views, and established all his strictest notions of what was due to seniority; and for the first evening *she* was his settled choice. The next morning, however, made an alteration; for in a quarter of an hour's tête-à-tête with Mrs Bennet before breakfast, a conversation beginning with his parsonage-house, and leading naturally to the avowal of his hopes, that a mistress for it might be found at Longbourn, produced from her, amid very complaisant smiles and general encouragement, a caution against the very Jane he had fixed on. – 'As to her *younger* daughters she could not take upon her to say – she could not positively answer – but she did not *know* of any prepossession; – her *eldest* daughter, she must just mention – she felt it incumbent on her to hint, was likely to be very soon engaged.'

Mr Collins had only to change from Jane to Elizabeth – and it was soon done – done while Mrs Bennet was stirring the fire. Elizabeth, equally next to Jane in birth and beauty, succeeded her of course.

Mrs Bennet treasured up the hint, and trusted that she might soon have two daughters married; and the man whom she could not bear to speak of the day before, was now high in her good graces.

Lydia's intention of walking to Meryton was not forgotten; every sister except Mary agreed to go with her; and Mr Collins was to attend them, at the request of

Mr Bennet, who was most anxious to get rid of him, and have his library to himself; for thither Mr Collins had followed him after breakfast, and there he would continue, nominally engaged with one of the largest folios in the collection, but really talking to Mr Bennet, with little cessation, of his house and garden at Hunsford. Such doings discomposed Mr Bennet exceedingly. In his library he had been always sure of leisure and tranquillity; and though prepared, as he told Elizabeth, to meet with folly and conceit in every other room in the house, he was used to be free from them there; his civility, therefore, was most prompt in inviting Mr Collins to join his daughters in their walk; and Mr Collins, being in fact much better fitted for a walker than a reader, was extremely well pleased to close his large book, and go.

In pompous nothings on his side, and civil assents on that of his cousins, their time passed till they entered Meryton. The attention of the younger ones was then no longer to be gained by *him*. Their eyes were immediately wandering up in the street in quest of the officers, and nothing less than a very smart bonnet indeed, or a really new muslin in a shop window, could recall them.

But the attention of every lady was soon caught by a young man, whom they had never seen before, of most gentlemanlike appearance, walking with an officer on the other side of the way. The officer was the very Mr Denny, concerning whose return from London Lydia came to enquire, and he bowed as they passed. All were struck with the stranger's air, all wondered who he could be, and Kitty and Lydia, determined if possible to find out, led the way across the street, under pretence of wanting something in an opposite shop, and fortunately had just gained the pavement when the two gentlemen turning back had reached the same spot. Mr Denny addressed them directly, and entreated permission to introduce his friend, Mr Wickham, who had returned with him the day before from town, and he was happy to say had accepted a commission in their corps. This was exactly as it should be; for the young man wanted only regimentals to make him completely charming. His appearance was greatly in his favour; he had all the best part of beauty, a fine countenance, a good figure, and very pleasing address. The introduction was followed up on his side by a happy readiness of conversation – a readiness at the same time perfectly correct and unassuming; and the whole party were still standing and talking together very agreeably, when the sound of horses drew their notice, and Darcy and Bingley were seen riding down the street. On distinguishing the ladies of the group, the two gentlemen came directly towards them, and began the usual civilities. Bingley was the principal spokesman, and Miss Bennet the principal object. He was then, he said, on his way to Longbourn on purpose to enquire after her. Mr Darcy corroborated it with a bow, and was beginning to determine not to fix his eyes on Elizabeth, when they were suddenly arrested by the sight of the stranger, and Elizabeth happening to see the countenance of both as they looked at each other, was all astonishment at the effect of the meeting. Both changed colour, one looked white, the other red. Mr Wickham, after a few moments, touched his hat – a salutation which Mr Darcy just deigned to return. What could be the meaning of it? – It was impossible to imagine; it was impossible not to long to know.

In another minute Mr Bingley, but without seeming to have noticed what passed, took leave and rode on with his friend.

Mr Denny and Mr Wickham walked with the young ladies to the door of Mr Philips's house, and then made their bows, in spite of Miss Lydia's pressing entreaties that they would come in, and even in spite of Mrs Philips' throwing up the parlour window, and loudly seconding the invitation.

Mrs Philips was always glad to see her nieces, and the two eldest, from their recent absence, were particularly welcome, and she was eagerly expressing her surprise at their sudden return home, which, as their own carriage had not fetched them, she should have known nothing about, if she had not happened to see Mr Jones's shop boy in the street, who had told her that they were not to send any more draughts to Netherfield because the Miss Bennets were come away, when her civility was claimed towards Mr Collins by Jane's introduction of him. She received him with her very best politeness, which he returned with as much more, apologising for his intrusion, without any previous acquaintance with her, which he could not help flattering himself however might be justified by his relationship to the young ladies who introduced him to her notice. Mrs Philips was quite awed by such an excess of good breeding; but her contemplation of one stranger was soon put an end to by exclamations and inquiries about the other, of whom, however, she could only tell her nieces what they already knew, that Mr Denny had brought him from London, and that he was to have a lieutenant's commission in the —shire. She had been watching him the last hour, she said, as he walked up and down the street, and had Mr Wickham appeared Kitty and Lydia would certainly have continued the occupation, but unluckily no one passed the windows now except a few of the officers, who in comparison with the stranger, were become 'stupid, disagreeable fellows'. Some of them were to dine with the Philipses the next day, and their aunt promised to make her husband call on Mr Wickham, and give him an invitation also, if the family from Longbourn would come in the evening. This was agreed to, and Mrs Philips protested that they would have a nice comfortable noisy game of lottery tickets, and a little bit of hot supper afterwards. The prospect of such delights was very cheering, and they parted in mutual good spirits. Mr Collins repeated his apologies in quitting the room, and was assured with unwearying civility that they were perfectly needless.

As they walked home, Elizabeth related to Jane what she had seen pass between the two gentlemen; but though Jane would have defended either or both, had they appeared to be wrong, she could no more explain such behaviour than her sister.

Mr Collins on his return highly gratified Mrs Bennet by admiring Mrs Philips's manners and politeness. He protested that except Lady Catherine and her daughter, he had never seen a more elegant woman; for she had not only received him with the utmost civility, but had even pointedly included him in her invitation for the next evening, although utterly unknown to her before. Something he supposed might be attributed to his connection with them, but yet he had never met with so much attention in the whole course of his life.

## *Chapter 16*

As no objection was made to the young people's engagement with their aunt, and all Mr Collins's scruples of leaving Mr and Mrs Bennet for a single evening during his visit were most steadily resisted, the coach conveyed him and his five cousins at a suitable hour to Meryton; and the girls had the pleasure of hearing, as they entered the drawing-room, that Mr Wickham had accepted their uncle's invitation, and was then in the house.

When this information was given, and they had all taken their seats, Mr Collins was at leisure to look around him and admire, and he was so much struck with the size and furniture of the apartment, that he declared he might almost have supposed himself in the small summer breakfast-parlour at Rosings; a comparison that did not at first convey much gratification; but when Mrs Philips

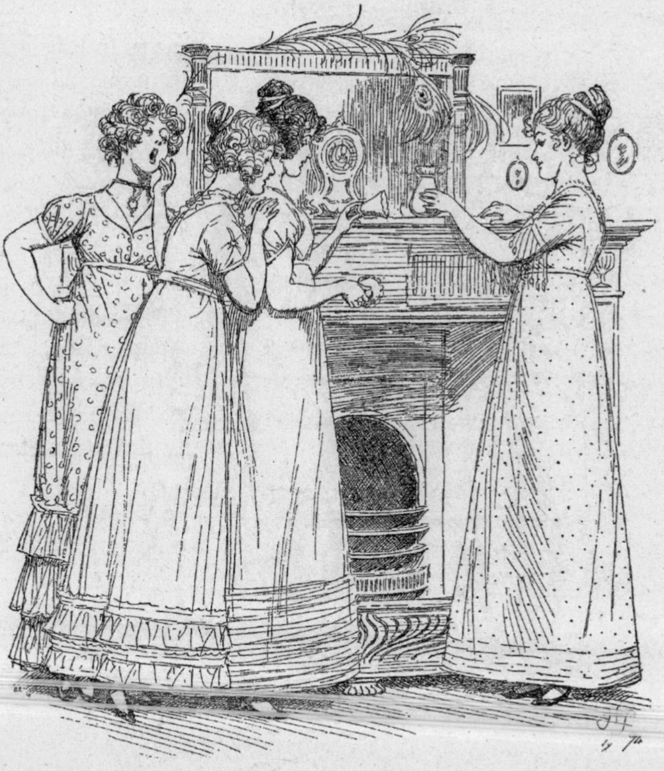

*To examine their own indifferent imitations of china on the mantelpiece*

understood from him what Rosings was, and who was its proprietor, when she had listened to the description of only one of Lady Catherine's drawing-rooms, and found that the chimney-piece alone had cost eight hundred pounds, she felt all the force of the compliment, and would hardly have resented a comparison with the housekeeper's room.

In describing to her all the grandeur of Lady Catherine and her mansion, with occasional digressions in praise of his own humble abode, and the improvements it was receiving, he was happily employed until the gentlemen joined them; and he found in Mrs Philips a very attentive listener, whose opinion of his consequence increased with what she heard, and who was resolving to retail it all among her neighbours as soon as she could. To the girls, who could not listen to their cousin, and who had nothing to do but to wish for an instrument, and examine their own indifferent imitations of china on the mantelpiece, the interval of waiting appeared very long. It was over at last however. The gentlemen did

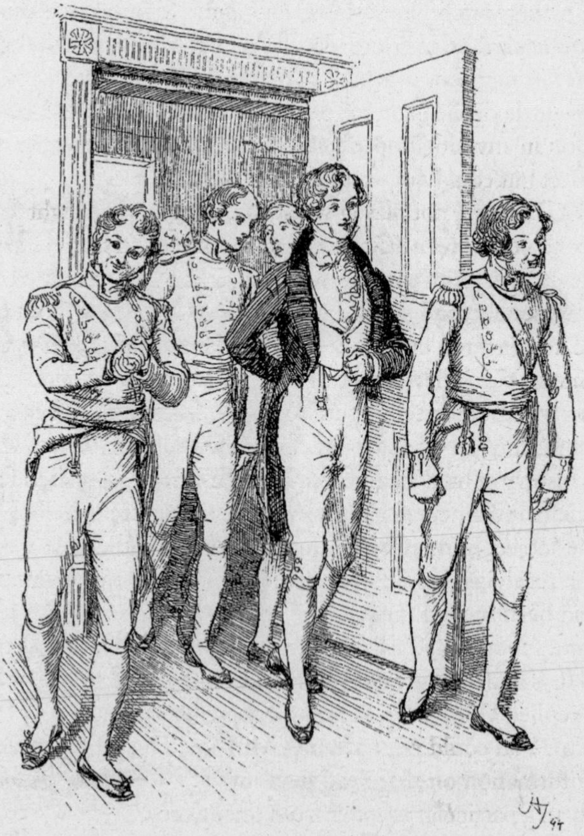

*The officers of the —shire were in general a very creditable, gentlemanlike set*

approach; and when Mr Wickham walked into the room, Elizabeth felt that she had neither been seeing him before, nor thinking of him since, with the smallest degree of unreasonable admiration. The officers of the —shire were in general a very creditable, gentlemanlike set, and the best of them were of the present party; but Mr Wickham was as far beyond them all in person, countenance, air, and walk, as *they* were superior to the broad-faced stuffy uncle Philips, breathing port wine, who followed them into the room.

Mr Wickham was the happy man towards whom almost every female eye was turned, and Elizabeth was the happy woman by whom he finally seated himself; and the agreeable manner in which he immediately fell into conversation, though it was only on its being a wet night, and on the probability of a rainy season, made her feel that the commonest, dullest, most threadbare topic might be rendered interesting by the skill of the speaker.

With such rivals for the notice of the fair, as Mr Wickham and the officers, Mr Collins seemed likely to sink into insignificance; to the young ladies he certainly was nothing; but he had still at intervals a kind listener in Mrs Philips, and was, by her watchfulness, most abundantly supplied with coffee and muffin.

When the card-tables were placed, he had an opportunity of obliging her in return, by sitting down to whist.

'I know little of the game, at present,' said he, 'but I shall be glad to improve myself, for in my situation of life – ' Mrs Philips was very thankful for his compliance, but could not wait for his reason.

Mr Wickham did not play at whist, and with ready delight was he received at the other table between Elizabeth and Lydia. At first there seemed danger of Lydia's engrossing him entirely, for she was a most determined talker; but being likewise extremely fond of lottery tickets, she soon grew too much interested in the game, too eager in making bets and exclaiming after prizes, to have attention for anyone in particular. Allowing for the common demands of the game, Mr Wickham was therefore at leisure to talk to Elizabeth, and she was very willing to hear him, though what she chiefly wished to hear she could not hope to be told, the history of his acquaintance with Mr Darcy. She dared not even mention that gentleman. Her curiosity however was unexpectedly relieved. Mr Wickham began the subject himself. He enquired how far Netherfield was from Meryton; and, after receiving her answer, asked in an hesitating manner how long Mr Darcy had been staying there.

'About a month,' said Elizabeth; and then, unwilling to let the subject drop, added, 'He is a man of very large property in Derbyshire, I understand.'

'Yes,' replied Wickham; – 'his estate there is a noble one. A clear ten thousand per annum. You could not have met with a person more capable of giving you certain information on that head than myself – for I have been connected with his family in a particular manner from my infancy.'

Elizabeth could not but look surprised.

'You may well be surprised, Miss Bennet, at such an assertion, after seeing, as you probably might, the very cold manner of our meeting yesterday. – Are you much acquainted with Mr Darcy?'

'As much as I ever wish to be,' cried Elizabeth warmly, – 'I have spent four days in the same house with him, and I think him very disagreeable.'

'I have no right to give *my* opinion,' said Wickham, 'as to his being agreeable or otherwise. I am not qualified to form one. I have known him too long and too well to be a fair judge. It is impossible for *me* to be impartial. But I believe your opinion of him would in general astonish – and perhaps you would not express it quite so strongly anywhere else. – Here you are in your own family.'

'Upon my word I say no more *here* than I might say in any house in the neighbourhood, except Netherfield. He is not at all liked in Hertfordshire. Everybody is disgusted with his pride. You will not find him more favourably spoken of by anyone.'

'I cannot pretend to be sorry,' said Wickham, after a short interruption, 'that he or that any man should not be estimated beyond their deserts; but with *him* I believe it does not often happen. The world is blinded by his fortune and consequence, or frightened by his high and imposing manners, and sees him only as he chooses to be seen.'

'I should take him, even on *my* slight acquaintance, to be an ill-tempered man.' Wickham only shook his head.

'I wonder,' said he, at the next opportunity of speaking, 'whether he is likely to be in this country much longer.'

'I do not at all know; but I *heard* nothing of his going away when I was at Netherfield. I hope your plans in favour of the —shire will not be affected by his being in the neighbourhood.'

'Oh! no – it is not for *me* to be driven away by Mr Darcy. If *he* wishes to avoid seeing *me*, he must go. We are not on friendly terms, and it always gives me pain to meet him, but I have no reason for avoiding *him* but what I might proclaim to all the world; a sense of very great ill-usage, and most painful regrets at his being what he is. His father, Miss Bennet, the late Mr Darcy, was one of the best men that ever breathed, and the truest friend I ever had; and I can never be in company with this Mr Darcy without being grieved to the soul by a thousand tender recollections. His behaviour to myself has been scandalous; but I verily believe I could forgive him anything and everything, rather than his disappointing the hopes and disgracing the memory of his father.'

Elizabeth found the interest of the subject increase, and listened with all her heart; but the delicacy of it prevented farther enquiry.

Mr Wickham began to speak on more general topics, Meryton, the neighbourhood, the society, appearing highly pleased with all that he had yet seen, and speaking of the latter especially, with gentle but very intelligible gallantry.

'It was the prospect of constant society, and good society,' he added, 'which was my chief inducement to enter the —shire. I knew it to be a most respectable, agreeable corps, and my friend Denny tempted me farther by his account of their present quarters, and the very great attentions and excellent acquaintance Meryton had procured them. Society, I own, is necessary to me. I have been a disappointed man, and my spirits will not bear solitude. I *must* have employment and society. A military life is not what I was intended for, but circumstances have now made it eligible. The church *ought* to have been my profession – I was brought up for the church, and I should at this time have been in possession of a most valuable living, had it pleased the gentleman we were speaking of just now.'

'Indeed!'

'Yes – the late Mr Darcy bequeathed me the next presentation of the best living in his gift. He was my godfather, and excessively attached to me. I cannot do justice to his kindness. He meant to provide for me amply, and thought he had done it; but when the living fell, it was given elsewhere.'

'Good heavens!' cried Elizabeth; 'but how could *that* be? – How could his will be disregarded? – Why did not you seek legal redress?'

'There was just such an informality in the terms of the bequest as to give me no hope from law. A man of honour could not have doubted the intention, but Mr Darcy chose to doubt it – or to treat it as a merely conditional recommendation, and to assert that I had forfeited all claim to it by extravagance, imprudence, in short anything or nothing. Certain it is, that the living became vacant two years ago, exactly as I was of an age to hold it, and that it was given to another man; and no less certain is it, that I cannot accuse myself of having really done anything to deserve to lose it. I have a warm, unguarded temper, and I may perhaps have sometimes spoken my opinion *of* him, and *to* him, too freely. I can recall nothing worse. But the fact is, that we are very different sort of men, and that he hates me.'

'This is quite shocking! – He deserves to be publicly disgraced.'

'Some time or other he *will* be – but it shall not be by *me*. Till I can forget his father, I can never defy or expose *him*.'

Elizabeth honoured him for such feelings, and thought him handsomer than ever as he expressed them.

'But what,' said she, after a pause, 'can have been his motive? – what can have induced him to behave so cruelly?'

'A thorough, determined dislike of me – a dislike which I cannot but attribute in some measure to jealousy. Had the late Mr Darcy liked me less, his son might have borne with me better; but his father's uncommon attachment to me, irritated him I believe very early in life. He had not a temper to bear the sort of competition in which we stood – the sort of preference which was often given me.'

'I had not thought Mr Darcy so bad as this – though I have never liked him, I had not thought so very ill of him – I had supposed him to be despising his fellow creatures in general, but did not suspect him of descending to such malicious revenge, such injustice, such inhumanity as this!'

After a few minutes' reflection, however, she continued, 'I *do* remember his boasting one day, at Netherfield, of the implacability of his resentments, of his having an unforgiving temper. His disposition must be dreadful.'

'I will not trust myself on the subject,' replied Wickham, '*I* can hardly be just to him.'

Elizabeth was again deep in thought, and after a time exclaimed, 'To treat in such a manner, the godson, the friend, the favourite of his father!' – She could have added, 'A young man too, like *you*, whose very countenance may vouch for your being amiable' – but she contented herself with, 'And one, too, who had probably been his own companion from childhood, connected together, as I think you said, in the closest manner!'

'We were born in the same parish, within the same park, the greatest part of our youth was passed together; inmates of the same house, sharing the same amusements, objects of the same parental care. *My* father began life in the profession which your uncle Mr Philips, appears to do so much credit to – but he gave up everything to be of use to the late Mr Darcy, and devoted all his time to the care of the Pemberley property. He was most highly esteemed by Mr Darcy, a most intimate, confidential friend. Mr Darcy often acknowledged himself to be under the greatest obligations to my father's active superintendance, and when immediately before my father's death, Mr Darcy gave him a voluntary promise of providing for me, I am convinced that he felt it to be as much a debt of gratitude to *him*, as of affection to myself.'

'How strange!' cried Elizabeth. 'How abominable! – I wonder that the very pride of this Mr Darcy has not made him just to you! – If from no better motive, that he should not have been too proud to be dishonest, – for dishonesty I must call it.'

'It *is* wonderful,' – replied Wickham, – 'for almost all his actions may be traced to pride; – and pride has often been his best friend. It has connected him nearer with virtue than any other feeling. But we are none of us consistent; and in his behaviour to me, there were stronger impulses even than pride.'

'Can such abominable pride as his, have ever done him good?'

'Yes. It has often led him to be liberal and generous, – to give his money freely, to display hospitality, to assist his tenants, and relieve the poor. Family pride, and *filial* pride, for he is very proud of what his father was, have done this. Not to appear to disgrace his family, to degenerate from the popular qualities, or lose the influence of the Pemberley House, is a powerful motive. He has also *brotherly* pride, which with *some* brotherly affection, makes him a very kind and careful guardian of his sister; and you will hear him generally cried up as the most attentive and best of brothers.'

'What sort of a girl is Miss Darcy?'

He shook his head. – 'I wish I could call her amiable. It gives me pain to speak ill of a Darcy. But she is too much like her brother, – very, very proud. – As a child, she was affectionate and pleasing, and extremely fond of me; and I have devoted hours and hours to her amusement. But she is nothing to me now. She is a handsome girl, about fifteen or sixteen, and I understand highly accomplished. Since her father's death, her home has been London, where a lady lives with her, and superintends her education.'

After many pauses and many trials of other subjects, Elizabeth could not help reverting once more to the first, and saying, 'I am astonished at his intimacy with Mr Bingley! How can Mr Bingley, who seems good humour itself, and is, I really believe, truly amiable, be in friendship with such a man? How can they suit each other? – Do you know Mr Bingley?'

'Not at all.'

'He is a sweet-tempered, amiable, charming man. He cannot know what Mr Darcy is.'

'Probably not; – but Mr Darcy can please where he chooses. He does not want abilities. He can be a conversible companion if he thinks it worth his while. Among those who are at all his equals in consequence, he is a very different man from what he is to the less prosperous. His pride never deserts him; but with the rich, he is liberal-minded, just, sincere, rational, honourable, and perhaps agreeable, – allowing something for fortune and figure.'

The whist party soon afterwards breaking up, the players gathered round the other table, and Mr Collins took his station between his cousin Elizabeth and Mrs Philips. – The usual inquiries as to his success were made by the latter. It had not been very great; he had lost every point; but when Mrs Philips began to express her concern thereupon, he assured her with much earnest gravity that it was not of the least importance, that he considered the money as a mere trifle, and begged she would not make herself uneasy.

'I know very well, madam,' said he, 'that when persons sit down to a card-table, they must take their chance of these things, – and happily I am not in such circumstances as to make five shillings any object. There are undoubtedly many who could not say the same, but thanks to Lady Catherine de Bourgh, I am removed far beyond the necessity of regarding little matters.'

Mr Wickham's attention was caught; and after observing Mr Collins for a few moments, he asked Elizabeth in a low voice whether her relations were very intimately acquainted with the family of de Bourgh.

'Lady Catherine de Bourgh,' she replied, 'has very lately given him a living. I hardly know how Mr Collins was first introduced to her notice, but he certainly has not known her long.'

'You know of course that Lady Catherine de Bourgh and Lady Anne Darcy were sisters; consequently that she is aunt to the present Mr Darcy.'

'No, indeed, I did not. – I knew nothing at all of Lady Catherine's connections. I never heard of her existence till the day before yesterday.'

'Her daughter, Miss de Bourgh, will have a very large fortune, and it is believed that she and her cousin will unite the two estates.'

This information made Elizabeth smile, as she thought of poor Miss Bingley. Vain indeed must be all her attentions, vain and useless her affection for his sister and her praise of himself, if he were already self-destined to another.

'Mr Collins,' said she, 'speaks highly both of Lady Catherine and her daughter; but from some particulars that he has related of her ladyship, I suspect his gratitude misleads him, and that in spite of her being his patroness, she is an arrogant, conceited woman.'

'I believe her to be both in a great degree,' replied Wickham; 'I have not seen her for many years, but I very well remember that I never liked her, and that her manners were dictatorial and insolent. She has the reputation of being remarkably sensible and clever; but I rather believe she derives part of her abilities from her rank and fortune, part from her authoritative manner, and the rest from the pride of her nephew, who chooses that everyone connected with him should have an understanding of the first class.'

Elizabeth allowed that he had given a very rational account of it, and they continued talking together with mutual satisfaction till supper put an end to cards; and gave the rest of the ladies their share of Mr Wickham's attentions. There could be no conversation in the noise of Mrs Philips's supper party, but his manners recommended him to everybody. Whatever he said, was said well; and whatever he did, done gracefully. Elizabeth went away with her head full of him. She could think of nothing but of Mr Wickham, and of what he had told her, all the way home; but there was not time for her even to mention his name as they went, for neither Lydia nor Mr Collins were once silent. Lydia talked incessantly of lottery tickets, of the fish she had lost and the fish she had won, and Mr Collins, in describing the civility of Mr and Mrs Philips, protesting that he did not in the least regard his losses at whist, enumerating all the dishes at supper, and repeatedly fearing that he crowded his cousins, had more to say than he could well manage before the carriage stopped at Longbourn House.

## *Chapter 17*

Elizabeth related to Jane the next day, what had passed between Mr Wickham and herself. Jane listened with astonishment and concern; – she knew not how to believe that Mr Darcy could be so unworthy of Mr Bingley's regard; and yet, it was not in her nature to question the veracity of a young man of such amiable appearance as Wickham. – The possibility of his having really endured such unkindness, was enough to interest all her tender feelings; and nothing therefore remained to be done, but to think well of them both, to defend the conduct of each, and throw into the account of accident or mistake, whatever could not be otherwise explained.

'They have both,' said she, 'been deceived, I dare say, in some way or other, of which we can form no idea. Interested people have perhaps misrepresented each to the other. It is, in short, impossible for us to conjecture the causes or circumstances which may have alienated them, without actual blame on either side.'

'Very true, indeed; – and now, my dear Jane, what have you got to say in behalf of the interested people who have probably been concerned in the business? – Do clear *them* too, or we shall be obliged to think ill of somebody.'

'Laugh as much as you choose, but you will not laugh me out of my opinion. My dearest Lizzy, do but consider in what a disgraceful light it places Mr Darcy, to be treating his father's favourite in such a manner, – one, whom his father had promised to provide for. – It is impossible. No man of common humanity, no man who had any value for his character, could be capable of it. Can his most intimate friends be so excessively deceived in him? Oh! no.'

'I can much more easily believe Mr Bingley's being imposed on, than that Mr Wickham should invent such a history of himself as he gave me last night;

names, facts, everything mentioned without ceremony. – If it be not so, let Mr Darcy contradict it. Besides, there was truth in his looks.'

'It is difficult indeed – it is distressing. – One does not know what to think.'

'I beg your pardon; – one knows exactly what to think.'

But Jane could think with certainty on only one point, – that Mr Bingley, if he *had been* imposed on, would have much to suffer when the affair became public.

The two young ladies were summoned from the shrubbery where this conversation passed, by the arrival of some of the very persons of whom they had been speaking; Mr Bingley and his sisters came to give their personal invitation for the long-expected ball at Netherfield, which was fixed for the following Tuesday. The two ladies were delighted to see their dear friend again, called it an age since they had met, and repeatedly asked what she had been doing with herself since their separation. To the rest of the family they paid little attention; avoiding Mrs Bennet as much as possible, saying not much to Elizabeth, and nothing at all to the others. They were soon gone again, rising from their seats with an activity which took their brother by surprise, and hurrying off as if eager to escape from Mrs Bennet's civilities.

The prospect of the Netherfield ball was extremely agreeable to every female of the family. Mrs Bennet chose to consider it as given in compliment to her

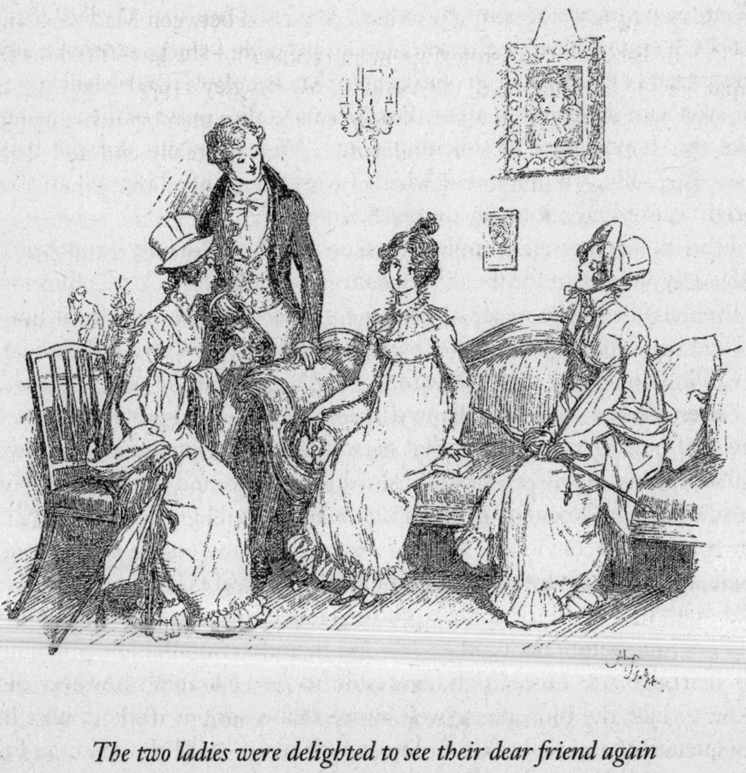

*The two ladies were delighted to see their dear friend again*

eldest daughter, and was particularly flattered by receiving the invitation from Mr Bingley himself, instead of a ceremonious card. Jane pictured to herself a happy evening in the society of her two friends, and the attentions of their brother; and Elizabeth thought with pleasure of dancing a great deal with Mr Wickham, and of seeing a confirmation of everything in Mr Darcy's looks and behaviour. The happiness anticipated by Catherine and Lydia, depended less on any single event, or any particular person, for though they each, like Elizabeth, meant to dance half the evening with Mr Wickham, he was by no means the only partner who could satisfy them, and a ball was at any rate, a ball. And even Mary could assure her family that she had no disinclination for it.

'While I can have my mornings to myself,' said she, 'it is enough. – I think it no sacrifice to join occasionally in evening engagements. Society has claims on us all; and I profess myself one of those who consider intervals of recreation and amusement as desirable for everybody.'

Elizabeth's spirits were so high on the occasion, that though she did not often speak unnecessarily to Mr Collins, she could not help asking him whether he intended to accept Mr Bingley's invitation, and if he did, whether he would think it proper to join in the evening's amusement; and she was rather surprised to find that he entertained no scruple whatever on that head, and was very far from dreading a rebuke either from the Archbishop, or Lady Catherine de Bourgh, by venturing to dance.

'I am by no means of opinion, I assure you,' said he, 'that a ball of this kind, given by a young man of character, to respectable people, can have any evil tendency; and I am so far from objecting to dancing myself that I shall hope to be honoured with the hands of all my fair cousins in the course of the evening, and I take this opportunity of soliciting yours, Miss Elizabeth, for the two first dances especially, – a preference which I trust my cousin Jane will attribute to the right cause, and not to any disrespect for her.'

Elizabeth felt herself completely taken in. She had fully proposed being engaged by Wickham for those very dances: – and to have Mr Collins instead! her liveliness had been never worse timed. There was no help for it however. Mr Wickham's happiness and her own was per force delayed a little longer, and Mr Collins's proposal accepted with as good a grace as she could. She was not the better pleased with his gallantry, from the idea it suggested of something more. – It now first struck her, that *she* was selected from among her sisters as worthy of being the mistress of Hunsford Parsonage, and of assisting to form a quadrille table at Rosings, in the absence of more eligible visitors. The idea soon reached to conviction, as she observed his increasing civilities toward herself, and heard his frequent attempt at a compliment on her wit and vivacity; and though more astonished than gratified herself, by this effect of her charms, it was not long before her mother gave her to understand that the probability of their marriage was exceedingly agreeable to *her*. Elizabeth however did not choose to take the hint, being well aware that a serious dispute must be the consequence of any reply. Mr Collins might never make the offer, and till he did, it was useless to quarrel about him.

If there had not been a Netherfield ball to prepare for and talk of, the younger Miss Bennets would have been in a pitiable state at this time, for from the day of the invitation, to the day of the ball, there was such a succession of rain as prevented their walking to Meryton once. No aunt, no officers, no news could be sought after; – the very shoe-roses for Netherfield were got by proxy. Even Elizabeth might have found some trial of her patience in weather, which totally suspended the improvement of her acquaintance with Mr Wickham; and nothing less than a dance on Tuesday, could have made such a Friday, Saturday, Sunday and Monday, endurable to Kitty and Lydia.

## *Chapter 18*

Till Elizabeth entered the drawing-room at Netherfield and looked in vain for Mr Wickham among the cluster of red coats there assembled, a doubt of his being present had never occurred to her. The certainty of meeting him had not been checked by any of those recollections that might not unreasonably have alarmed her. She had dressed with more than usual care, and prepared in the highest spirits for the conquest of all that remained unsubdued of his heart, trusting that it was not more than might be won in the course of the evening. But in an instant arose the dreadful suspicion of his being purposely omitted for Mr Darcy's pleasure in the Bingleys' invitation to the officers; and though this was not exactly the case, the absolute fact of his absence was pronounced by his friend Mr Denny, to whom Lydia eagerly applied, and who told them that Wickham had been obliged to go to town on business the day before, and was not yet returned; adding, with a significant smile, 'I do not imagine his business would have called him away just now, if he had not wished to avoid a certain gentleman here.'

This part of his intelligence, though unheard by Lydia, was caught by Elizabeth, and as it assured her that Darcy was not less answerable for Wickham's absence than if her first surmise had been just, every feeling of displeasure against the former was so sharpened by immediate disappointment, that she could hardly reply with tolerable civility to the polite inquiries which he directly afterwards approached to make. – Attention, forbearance, patience with Darcy, was injury to Wickham. She was resolved against any sort of conversation with him, and turned away with a degree of ill humour, which she could not wholly surmount even in speaking to Mr Bingley, whose blind partiality provoked her.

But Elizabeth was not formed for ill-humour; and though every prospect of her own was destroyed for the evening, it could not dwell long on her spirits; and having told all her griefs to Charlotte Lucas, whom she had not seen for a week, she was soon able to make a voluntary transition to the oddities of her cousin, and to point him out to her particular notice. The two first dances, however, brought a return of distress; they were dances of mortification. Mr Collins, awkward and solemn, apologising instead of attending, and often moving wrong without being aware of it, gave her all the shame and misery which a disagreeable partner for a couple of dances can give. The moment of her release from him was ecstasy.

She danced next with an officer, and had the refreshment of talking of Wickham, and of hearing that he was universally liked. When those dances were over she returned to Charlotte Lucas, and was in conversation with her, when she found herself suddenly addressed by Mr Darcy, who took her so much by surprise in his application for her hand, that, without knowing what she did, she accepted him. He walked away again immediately, and she was left to fret over her own want of presence of mind; Charlotte tried to console her.

'I dare say you will find him very agreeable.'

'Heaven forbid! – *That* would be the greatest misfortune of all! – To find a man agreeable whom one is determined to hate! – Do not wish me such an evil.'

When the dancing recommenced, however, and Darcy approached to claim her hand, Charlotte could not help cautioning her in a whisper not to be a simpleton and allow her fancy for Wickham to make her appear unpleasant in the eyes of a man of ten times his consequence. Elizabeth made no answer, and took her place in the set, amazed at the dignity to which she was arrived in being allowed to stand opposite to Mr Darcy, and reading in her neighbours' looks their equal amazement in beholding it. They stood for some time without speaking a word; and she began to imagine that their silence was to last through the two dances, and at first was resolved not to break it; till suddenly fancying that it would be the greater punishment to her partner to oblige him to talk, she made some slight observation on the dance. He replied, and was again silent. After a pause of some minutes she addressed him a second time with, 'It is *your* turn to say something now, Mr Darcy. – *I* talked about the dance, and *you* ought to make some kind of remark on the size of the room, or the number of couples.'

He smiled, and assured her that whatever she wished him to say should be said.

'Very well. – That reply will do for the present. – Perhaps by and by I may observe that private balls are much pleasanter than public ones. – But *now* we may be silent.'

'Do you talk by rule then, while you are dancing?'

'Sometimes. One must speak a little, you know. It would look odd to be entirely silent for half an hour together, and yet for the advantage of *some*, conversation ought to be so arranged as that they may have the trouble of saying as little as possible.'

'Are you consulting your own feelings in the present case, or do you imagine that you are gratifying mine?'

'Both,' replied Elizabeth archly; 'for I have always seen a great similarity in the turn of our minds. – We are each of an unsocial, taciturn disposition, unwilling to speak, unless we expect to say something that will amaze the whole room, and be handed down to posterity with all the éclat of a proverb.'

'This is no very striking resemblance of your own character, I am sure,' said he. 'How near it may be to *mine*, I cannot pretend to say. – *You* think it a faithful portrait undoubtedly.'

'I must not decide on my own performance.'

He made no answer, and they were again silent till they had gone down the dance, when he asked her if she and her sisters did not very often walk to Meryton. She answered in the affirmative, and, unable to resist the temptation, added, 'When you met us there the other day, we had just been forming a new acquaintance.'

The effect was immediate. A deeper shade of hauteur overspread his features, but he said not a word, and Elizabeth, though blaming herself for her own weakness, could not go on. At length Darcy spoke, and in a constrained manner said, 'Mr Wickham is blessed with such happy manners as may ensure his *making* friends – whether he may be equally capable of *retaining* them, is less certain.'

'He has been so unlucky as to lose *your* friendship,' replied Elizabeth with emphasis, 'and in a manner which he is likely to suffer from all his life.'

Darcy made no answer, and seemed desirous of changing the subject. At that moment Sir William Lucas appeared close to them, meaning to pass through the set to the other side of the room; but on perceiving Mr Darcy he stopped with a bow of superior courtesy to compliment him on his dancing and his partner.

'I have been most highly gratified indeed, my dear sir. Such very superior dancing is not often seen. It is evident that you belong to the first circles. Allow

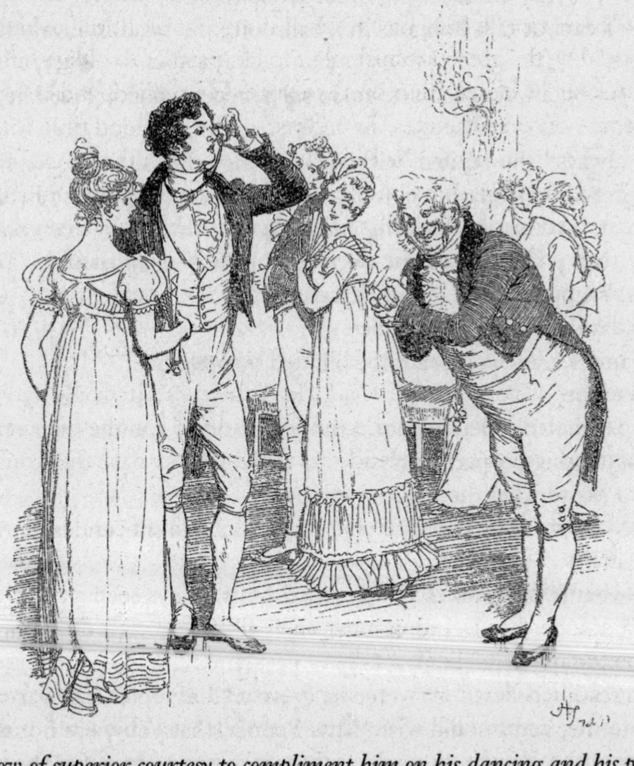

*With a bow of superior courtesy to compliment him on his dancing and his partner*

me to say, however, that your fair partner does not disgrace you, and that I must hope to have this pleasure often repeated, especially when a certain desirable event, my dear Miss Eliza, (glancing at her sister and Bingley,) shall take place. What congratulations will then flow in! I appeal to Mr Darcy – but let me not interrupt you, sir. – You will not thank me for detaining you from the bewitching converse of that young lady, whose bright eyes are also upbraiding me.'

The latter part of this address was scarcely heard by Darcy; but Sir William's allusion to his friend seemed to strike him forcibly, and his eyes were directed with a very serious expression towards Bingley and Jane, who were dancing together. Recovering himself, however, shortly, he turned to his partner, and said, 'Sir William's interruption has made me forget what we were talking of.'

'I do not think we were speaking at all. Sir William could not have interrupted any two people in the room who had less to say for themselves. – We have tried two or three subjects already without success, and what we are to talk of next I cannot imagine.'

'What think you of books?' said he, smiling.

'Books – Oh! no. – I am sure we never read the same, or not with the same feelings.'

'I am sorry you think so; but if that be the case, there can at least be no want of subject. – We may compare our different opinions.'

'No – I cannot talk of books in a ballroom; my head is always full of something else.'

'The *present* always occupies you in such scenes – does it?' said he, with a look of doubt.

'Yes, always,' she replied, without knowing what she said, for her thoughts had wandered far from the subject, as soon afterwards appeared by her suddenly exclaiming, 'I remember hearing you once say, Mr Darcy, that you hardly ever forgave, that your resentment once created was unappeasable. You are very cautious, I suppose, as to its *being created*.'

'I am,' said he, with a firm voice.

'And never allow yourself to be blinded by prejudice?'

'I hope not.'

'It is particularly incumbent on those who never change their opinion, to be secure of judging properly at first.'

'May I ask to what these questions tend?'

'Merely to the illustration of *your* character,' said she, endeavouring to shake off her gravity. 'I am trying to make it out.'

'And what is your success?'

She shook her head. 'I do not get on at all. I hear such different accounts of you as puzzle me exceedingly.'

'I can readily believe,' answered he gravely, 'that report may vary greatly with respect to me; and I could wish, Miss Bennet, that you were not to sketch my character at the present moment, as there is reason to fear that the performance would reflect no credit on either.'

'But if I do not take your likeness now, I may never have another opportunity.'

'I would by no means suspend any pleasure of yours,' he coldly replied. She said no more, and they went down the other dance and parted in silence; on each side dissatisfied, though not to an equal degree, for in Darcy's breast there was a tolerable powerful feeling towards her, which soon procured her pardon, and directed all his anger against another.

They had not long separated when Miss Bingley came towards her, and with an expression of civil disdain thus accosted her, 'So, Miss Eliza, I hear you are quite delighted with George Wickham! – Your sister has been talking to me about him, and asking me a thousand questions; and I find that the young man forgot to tell you, among his other communications, that he was the son of old Wickham, the late Mr Darcy's steward. Let me recommend you, however, as a friend, not to give implicit confidence to all his assertions; for as to Mr Darcy's using him ill, it is perfectly false; for, on the contrary, he has been always remarkably kind to him, though George Wickham has treated Mr Darcy in a most infamous manner. I do not know the particulars, but I know very well that Mr Darcy is not in the least to blame, that he cannot bear to hear George Wickham mentioned, and that though my brother thought he could not well avoid including him in his invitation to the officers, he was excessively glad to find that he had taken himself out of the way. His coming into the country at all, is a most insolent thing indeed, and I wonder how he could presume to do it. I pity you, Miss Eliza, for this discovery of your favourite's guilt; but really considering his descent, one could not expect much better.'

'His guilt and his descent appear by your account to be the same,' said Elizabeth angrily; 'for I have heard you accuse him of nothing worse than of being the son of Mr Darcy's steward, and of *that*, I can assure you, he informed me himself.'

'I beg your pardon,' replied Miss Bingley, turning away with a sneer. 'Excuse my interference. – It was kindly meant.'

'Insolent girl!' said Elizabeth to herself. – 'You are much mistaken if you expect to influence me by such a paltry attack as this. I see nothing in it but your own wilful ignorance and the malice of Mr Darcy.' She then sought her eldest sister, who had undertaken to make enquiries on the same subject of Bingley. Jane met her with a smile of such sweet complacency, a glow of such happy expression, as sufficiently marked how well she was satisfied with the occurrences of the evening. – Elizabeth instantly read her feelings, and at that moment solicitude for Wickham, resentment against his enemies, and everything else gave way before the hope of Jane's being in the fairest way for happiness.

'I want to know,' said she, with a countenance no less smiling than her sister's, 'what you have learnt about Mr Wickham. But perhaps you have been too pleasantly engaged to think of any third person, in which case you may be sure of my pardon.'

'No,' replied Jane, 'I have not forgotten him; but I have nothing satisfactory to tell you. Mr Bingley does not know the whole of his history, and is quite ignorant of the circumstances which have principally offended Mr Darcy; but he will vouch for the good conduct, the probity and honour of his friend, and is perfectly convinced that Mr Wickham has deserved much less attention from Mr Darcy than he has received; and I am sorry to say that by his account as well as his sister's, Mr Wickham is by no means a respectable young man. I am afraid he has been very imprudent, and has deserved to lose Mr Darcy's regard.'

'Mr Bingley does not know Mr Wickham himself?'

'No; he never saw him till the other morning at Meryton.'

'This account then is what he has received from Mr Darcy. I am perfectly satisfied. But what does he say of the living?'

'He does not exactly recollect the circumstances, though he has heard them from Mr Darcy more than once, but he believes that it was left to him *conditionally* only.'

'I have not a doubt of Mr Bingley's sincerity,' said Elizabeth warmly; 'but you must excuse my not being convinced by assurances only. Mr Bingley's defence of his friend was a very able one I dare say, but since he is unacquainted with several parts of the story, and has learnt the rest from that friend himself, I shall venture still to think of both gentlemen as I did before.'

She then changed the discourse to one more gratifying to each, and on which there could be no difference of sentiment. Elizabeth listened with delight to the happy, though modest hopes which Jane entertained of Bingley's regard, and said all in her power to heighten her confidence in it. On their being joined by Mr Bingley himself, Elizabeth withdrew to Miss Lucas; to whose enquiry after the pleasantness of her last partner she had scarcely replied, before Mr Collins came up to them and told her with great exultation that he had just been so fortunate as to make a most important discovery.

'I have found out,' said he, 'by a singular accident, that there is now in the room a near relation of my patroness. I happened to overhear the gentleman himself mentioning to the young lady who does the honours of this house the names of his cousin Miss de Bourgh, and of her mother Lady Catherine. How wonderfully these sort of things occur! Who would have thought of my meeting with – perhaps – a nephew of Lady Catherine de Bourgh in this assembly! – I am most thankful that the discovery is made in time for me to pay my respects to him, which I am now going to do, and trust he will excuse my not having done it before. My total ignorance of the connection must plead my apology.'

'You are not going to introduce yourself to Mr Darcy?'

'Indeed I am. I shall entreat his pardon for not having done it earlier. I believe him to be Lady Catherine's *nephew*. It will be in my power to assure him that her ladyship was quite well yesterday se'nnight.'

Elizabeth tried hard to dissuade him from such a scheme; assuring him that Mr Darcy would consider his addressing him without introduction as an impertinent freedom, rather than a compliment to his aunt; that it was not in the least necessary there should be any notice on either side, and that if it were, it must belong to Mr Darcy, the superior in consequence, to begin the acquaintance. – Mr Collins listened to her with the determined air of following his own inclination, and when she ceased speaking, replied thus, 'My dear Miss

Elizabeth, I have the highest opinion in the world of your excellent judgment in all matters within the scope of your understanding, but permit me to say that there must be a wide difference between the established forms of ceremony amongst the laity, and those which regulate the clergy; for give me leave to observe that I consider the clerical office as equal in point of dignity with the highest rank in the kingdom – provided that a proper humility of behaviour is at the same time maintained. You must therefore allow me to follow the dictates of my conscience on this occasion, which leads me to perform what I look on as a point of duty. Pardon me for neglecting to profit by your advice, which on every other subject shall be my constant guide, though in the case before us I consider myself more fitted by education and habitual study to decide on what is right than a young lady like yourself.' And with a low bow he left her to attack Mr Darcy, whose reception of his advances she eagerly watched, and whose astonishment at being so addressed was very evident. Her cousin prefaced his speech with a solemn bow, and though she could not hear a word of it, she felt as if hearing it all, and saw in the motion of his lips the words 'apology,' 'Hunsford', and 'Lady Catherine de Bourgh'. – It vexed her to see him expose himself to such a man. Mr Darcy was eyeing him with unrestrained wonder, and when at last Mr Collins allowed him time to speak, replied with an air of distant civility. Mr Collins, however, was not discouraged from speaking again, and Mr Darcy's contempt seemed abundantly increasing with the length of his second speech, and at the end of it he only made him a slight bow, and moved another way. Mr Collins then returned to Elizabeth.

'I have no reason, I assure you,' said he, 'to be dissatisfied with my reception. Mr Darcy seemed much pleased with the attention. He answered me with the utmost civility, and even paid me the compliment of saying, that he was so well convinced of Lady Catherine's discernment as to be certain she could never bestow a favour unworthily. It was really a very handsome thought. Upon the whole, I am much pleased with him.'

As Elizabeth had no longer any interest of her own to pursue, she turned her attention almost entirely on her sister and Mr Bingley, and the train of agreeable reflections which her observations gave birth to, made her perhaps almost as happy as Jane. She saw her in idea settled in that very house in all the felicity which a marriage of true affection could bestow; and she felt capable under such circumstances, of endeavouring even to like Bingley's two sisters. Her mother's thoughts she plainly saw were bent the same way, and she determined not to venture near her, lest she might hear too much. When they sat down to supper, therefore, she considered it a most unlucky perverseness which placed them within one of each other; and deeply was she vexed to find that her mother was talking to that one person (Lady Lucas) freely, openly, and of nothing else but of her expectation that Jane would be soon married to Mr Bingley. – It was an animating subject, and Mrs Bennet seemed incapable of fatigue while enumerating the advantages of the match. His being such a charming young man, and so rich, and living but three miles from them, were the first points of self-congratulation; and then it was such a comfort to think how fond the two sisters were of Jane, and to be certain that they must desire the connection as much as she could do. It was, moreover, such a promising thing for her younger daughters, as Jane's marrying so greatly must throw them in the way of other rich men; and lastly, it was so pleasant at her time of life to be able to consign her single daughters to the care of their sister, that she might not be obliged to go into company more than she liked. It was necessary to make this circumstance a matter of pleasure, because on such occasions it is the etiquette; but no one was less likely than Mrs Bennet to find comfort in staying at home at any period of her life. She concluded with many good wishes that Lady Lucas might soon be equally fortunate, though evidently and triumphantly believing there was no chance of it.

In vain did Elizabeth endeavour to check the rapidity of her mother's words, or persuade her to describe her felicity in a less audible whisper; for to her inexpressible vexation, she could perceive that the chief of it was overheard by Mr Darcy, who sat opposite to them. Her mother only scolded her for being nonsensical.

'What is Mr Darcy to me, pray, that I should be afraid of him? I am sure we owe him no such particular civility as to be obliged to say nothing *he* may not like to hear.'

'For heaven's sake, madam, speak lower. – What advantage can it be to you to offend Mr Darcy? – You will never recommend yourself to his friend by so doing.'

Nothing that she could say, however, had any influence. Her mother would talk of her views in the same intelligible tone. Elizabeth blushed and blushed again with shame and vexation. She could not help frequently glancing her eye at Mr Darcy, though every glance convinced her of what she dreaded; for though he was not always looking at her mother, she was convinced that his attention was invariably fixed by her. The expression of his face changed gradually from indignant contempt to a composed and steady gravity.

At length however Mrs Bennet had no more to say; and Lady Lucas, who had been long yawning at the repetition of delights which she saw no likelihood of sharing, was left to the comforts of cold ham and chicken. Elizabeth now began to revive. But not long was the interval of tranquillity; for when supper was over, singing was talked of, and she had the mortification of seeing Mary, after very little entreaty, preparing to oblige the company. By many significant looks and silent entreaties, did she endeavour to prevent such a proof of complaisance, – but in vain; Mary would not understand them; such an opportunity of exhibiting was delightful to her, and she began her song. Elizabeth's eyes were fixed on her with most painful sensations; and she watched her progress through the several stanzas with an impatience which was very ill rewarded at their close; for Mary, on receiving amongst the thanks of the table, the hint of a hope that she might be prevailed on to favour them again, after the pause of half a minute began another. Mary's powers were by no means fitted for such a display; her voice was weak, and her manner affected. – Elizabeth was in agonies. She looked at Jane, to see how she bore it; but Jane was very composedly talking to Bingley. She looked at his two sisters, and saw them making signs of derision at each other, and at Darcy, who continued however impenetrably grave. She looked at her father to entreat his interference, lest Mary should be singing all night. He took the hint, and when Mary had finished her second song, said aloud, 'That will do extremely well, child. You have delighted us long enough. Let the other young ladies have time to exhibit.'

Mary, though pretending not to hear, was somewhat disconcerted; and Elizabeth sorry for her, and sorry for her father's speech, was afraid her anxiety had done no good. – Others of the party were now applied to.

'If I,' said Mr Collins, 'were so fortunate as to be able to sing, I should have great pleasure, I am sure, in obliging the company with an air; for I consider music as a very innocent diversion, and perfectly compatible with the profession of a clergyman. – I do not mean however to assert that we can be justified in devoting too much of our time to music, for there are certainly other things to be attended to. The rector of a parish has much to do. – In the first place, he must make such an agreement for tithes as may be beneficial to himself and not offensive to his patron. He must write his own sermons; and the time that remains will not be too much for his parish duties, and the care and improvement of his dwelling, which he cannot be excused from making as comfortable as possible. And I do not think it of light importance that he should have attentive and conciliatory manners towards everybody, especially towards those to whom he owes his preferment. I cannot acquit him of that duty; nor could I think well of the man who should omit an occasion of testifying his respect towards anybody connected with the family.' And with a bow to Mr Darcy, he concluded his speech, which had been spoken so loud as to be heard by half the room. – Many stared. – Many smiled; but no one looked more amused than Mr Bennet himself, while his wife seriously commended Mr Collins for having spoken so sensibly, and observed in a half-whisper to Lady Lucas, that he was a remarkably clever, good kind of young man.

To Elizabeth it appeared, that had her family made an agreement to expose themselves as much as they could during the evening, it would have been impossible for them to play their parts with more spirit, or finer success; and happy did she think it for Bingley and her sister that some of the exhibition had escaped his notice, and that his feelings were not of a sort to be much distressed by the folly which he must have witnessed. That his two sisters and Mr Darcy, however, should have such an opportunity of ridiculing her relations was bad enough, and she could not determine whether the silent contempt of the gentleman, or the insolent smiles of the ladies, were more intolerable.

The rest of the evening brought her little amusement. She was teased by Mr Collins, who continued most perseveringly by her side, and though he could not prevail with her to dance with him again, put it out of her power to dance with others. In vain did she entreat him to stand up with somebody else, and offer to introduce him to any young lady in the room. He assured her that as to dancing, he was perfectly indifferent to it; that his chief object was by delicate attentions to recommend himself to her, and that he should therefore make a point of remaining close to her the whole evening. There was no arguing upon such a project. She owed her greatest relief to her friend Miss Lucas, who often joined them, and good-naturedly engaged Mr Collins's conversation to herself.

She was at least free from the offence of Mr Darcy's farther notice; though often standing within a very short distance of her, quite disengaged, he never came near enough to speak. She felt it to be the probable consequence of her allusions to Mr Wickham, and rejoiced in it.

The Longbourn party were the last of all the company to depart; and by a manoeuvre of Mrs Bennet had to wait for their carriages a quarter of an hour after everybody else was gone, which gave them time to see how heartily they were wished away by some of the family. Mrs Hurst and her sister scarcely opened their mouths except to complain of fatigue, and were evidently impatient to have the house to themselves. They repulsed every attempt of Mrs Bennet at conversation, and by so doing, threw a languor over the whole party, which was very little relieved by the long speeches of Mr Collins, who was complimenting Mr Bingley and his sisters on the elegance of their entertainment, and the hospitality and politeness which had marked their behaviour to their guests. Darcy said nothing at all. Mr Bennet, in equal silence, was enjoying the scene. Mr Bingley and Jane were standing together, a little detached from the rest, and talked only to each other. Elizabeth preserved as steady a silence as either Mrs Hurst or Miss Bingley; and even Lydia was too much fatigued to utter more than the occasional exclamation of 'Lord, how tired I am!' accompanied by a violent yawn.

When at length they arose to take leave, Mrs Bennet was most pressingly civil in her hope of seeing the whole family soon at Longbourn; and addressed herself particularly to Mr Bingley, to assure him how happy he would make them, by eating a family dinner with them at any time, without the ceremony of a formal invitation. Bingley was all grateful pleasure, and he readily engaged for taking the earliest opportunity of waiting on her, after his return from London, whither he was obliged to go the next day for a short time.

Mrs Bennet was perfectly satisfied; and quitted the house under the delightful persuasion that, allowing for the necessary preparations of settlements, new carriages and wedding clothes, she should undoubtedly see her daughter settled at Netherfield, in the course of three or four months. Of having another daughter married to Mr Collins, she thought with equal certainty, and with considerable, though not equal, pleasure. Elizabeth was the least dear to her of all her children; and though the man and the match were quite good enough for *her*, the worth of each was eclipsed by Mr Bingley and Netherfield.

## *Chapter 19*

The next day opened a new scene at Longbourn. Mr Collins made his declaration in form. Having resolved to do it without loss of time, as his leave of absence extended only to the following Saturday, and having no feelings of diffidence to make it distressing to himself even at the moment, he set about it in a very orderly manner, with all the observances which he supposed a regular part of the business. On finding Mrs Bennet, Elizabeth, and one of the younger girls together, soon after breakfast, he addressed the mother in these words, 'May I hope, Madam, for your interest with your fair daughter Elizabeth, when I solicit for the honour of a private audience with her in the course of this morning?'

Before Elizabeth had time for anything but a blush of surprise, Mrs Bennet instantly answered, 'Oh dear! – Yes – certainly. – I am sure Lizzy will be very happy – I am sure she can have no objection. – Come, Kitty, I want you upstairs.' And gathering her work together, she was hastening away, when Elizabeth called out, 'Dear Ma'am, do not go. – I beg you will not go. – Mr Collins must excuse me. – He can have nothing to say to me that anybody need not hear. I am going away myself.'

'No, no, nonsense, Lizzy. – I desire you will stay where you are.' – And upon Elizabeth's seeming really, with vexed and embarrassed looks, about to escape, she added, 'Lizzy, I *insist* upon your staying and hearing Mr Collins.'

Elizabeth would not oppose such an injunction – and a moment's consideration making her also sensible that it would be wisest to get it over as soon and as quietly as possible, she sat down again, and tried to conceal by incessant employment the feelings which were divided between distress and diversion. Mrs Bennet and Kitty walked off, and as soon as they were gone Mr Collins began.

'Believe me, my dear Miss Elizabeth, that your modesty, so far from doing you any disservice, rather adds to your other perfections. You would have been less amiable in my eyes had there *not* been this little unwillingness; but allow me to assure you that I have your respected mother's permission for this address. You can hardly doubt the purport of my discourse, however your natural delicacy may lead you to dissemble; my attentions have been too marked to be mistaken. Almost as soon as I entered the house I singled you out as the companion of my future life. But before I am run away with by my feelings on this subject, perhaps it will be advisable for me to state my reasons for marrying – and moreover for coming into Hertfordshire with the design of selecting a wife, as I certainly did.'

The idea of Mr Collins, with all his solemn composure, being run away with by his feelings, made Elizabeth so near laughing that she could not use the short pause he allowed in any attempt to stop him farther, and he continued:

'My reasons for marrying are, first, that I think it a right thing for every clergyman in easy circumstances (like myself) to set the example of matrimony in his parish. Secondly, that I am convinced it will add very greatly to my happiness;

and thirdly – which perhaps I ought to have mentioned earlier, that it is the particular advice and recommendation of the very noble lady whom I have the honour of calling patroness. Twice has she condescended to give me her opinion (unasked too!) on this subject; and it was but the very Saturday night before I left Hunsford – between our pools at quadrille, while Mrs Jenkinson was arranging Miss de Bourgh's footstool, that she said, "Mr Collins, you must marry. A clergyman like you must marry. – Choose properly, choose a gentlewoman for *my* sake; and for your *own*, let her be an active, useful sort of person, not brought up high, but able to make a small income go a good way. This is my advice. Find such a woman as soon as you can, bring her to Hunsford, and I will visit her." Allow me, by the way, to observe, my fair cousin, that I do not reckon the notice and kindness of Lady Catherine de Bourgh as among the least of the advantages in my power to offer. You will find her manners beyond anything I can describe; and your wit and vivacity I think must be acceptable to her, especially when tempered with the silence and respect which her rank will inevitably excite. Thus much for my general intention in favour of matrimony; it remains to be told why my views were directed to Longbourn instead of my own neighbourhood, where I assure you there are many amiable young women. But the fact is, that being, as I am, to inherit this estate after the death of your honoured father, (who, however, may live many years longer,) I could not satisfy myself without resolving to choose a wife from among his daughters, that the loss to them might be as little as possible, when the melancholy event takes place – which, however, as I have already said, may not be for several years. This has been my motive, my fair cousin, and I flatter myself it will not sink me in your esteem. And now nothing remains for me but to assure you in the most animated language of the violence of my affection. To fortune I am perfectly indifferent, and shall make no demand of that nature on your father, since I am well aware that it could not be complied with; and that one thousand pounds in the four per cents which will not be yours till after your mother's decease, is all that you may ever be entitled to. On that head, therefore, I shall be uniformly silent; and you may assure yourself that no ungenerous reproach shall ever pass my lips when we are married.'

It was absolutely necessary to interrupt him now.

'You are too hasty, sir,' she cried. 'You forget that I have made no answer. Let me do it without farther loss of time. Accept my thanks for the compliment you are paying me. I am very sensible of the honour of your proposals, but it is impossible for me to do otherwise than decline them.'

'I am not now to learn,' replied Mr Collins, with a formal wave of the hand, 'that it is usual with young ladies to reject the addresses of the man whom they secretly mean to accept, when he first applies for their favour; and that sometimes the refusal is repeated a second or even a third time. I am therefore by no means discouraged by what you have just said, and shall hope to lead you to the altar ere long.'

'Upon my word, sir,' cried Elizabeth, 'your hope is rather an extraordinary one after my declaration. I do assure you that I am not one of those young ladies (if such young ladies there are) who are so daring as to risk their happiness on the chance of being asked a second time. I am perfectly serious in my refusal. – You could not make *me* happy, and I am convinced that I am the last woman in the world who would make *you* so. – Nay, were your friend Lady Catherine to know me, I am persuaded she would find me in every respect ill qualified for the situation.'

'Were it certain that Lady Catherine would think so,' said Mr Collins very gravely – 'but I cannot imagine that her ladyship would at all disapprove of you. And you may be certain that when I have the honour of seeing her again I shall speak in the highest terms of your modesty, economy, and other amiable qualifications.'

'Indeed, Mr Collins, all praise of me will be unnecessary. You must give me leave to judge for myself, and pay me the compliment of believing what I say. I wish you very happy and very rich, and by refusing your hand, do all in my power to prevent your being otherwise. In making me the offer, you must have satisfied the delicacy of your feelings with regard to my family, and may take possession of Longbourn estate whenever it falls, without any self-reproach. This matter may be considered, therefore, as finally settled.' And rising as she

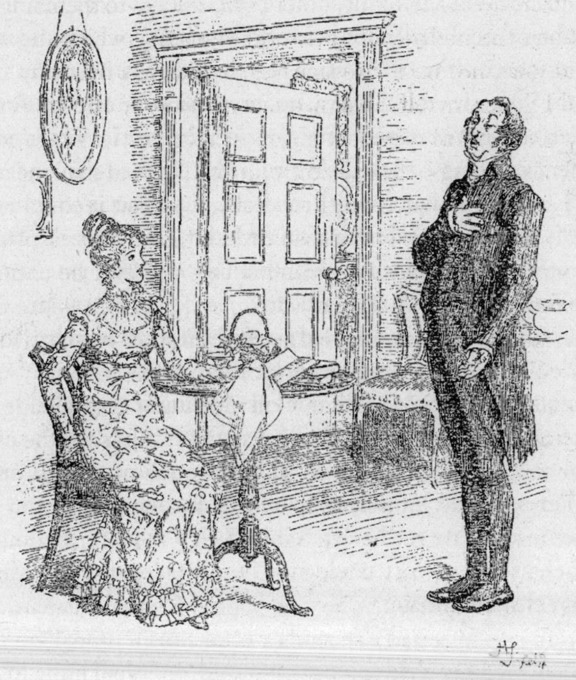

*To assure you in the most animated language*

thus spoke, she would have quitted the room, had not Mr Collins thus addressed her, 'When I do myself the honour of speaking to you next on this subject I shall hope to receive a more favourable answer than you have now given me; though I am far from accusing you of cruelty at present, because I know it to be the established custom of your sex to reject a man on the first application, and perhaps you have even now said as much to encourage my suit as would be consistent with the true delicacy of the female character.'

'Really, Mr Collins,' cried Elizabeth with some warmth, 'you puzzle me exceedingly. If what I have hitherto said can appear to you in the form of encouragement, I know not how to express my refusal in such a way as may convince you of its being one.'

'You must give me leave to flatter myself, my dear cousin, that your refusal of my addresses is merely words of course. My reasons for believing it are briefly these: – It does not appear to me that my hand is unworthy of your acceptance, or that the establishment I can offer would be any other than highly desirable. My situation in life, my connections with the family of de Bourgh, and my relationship to your own, are circumstances highly in my favour; and you should take it into farther consideration that in spite of your manifold attractions, it is by no means certain that another offer of marriage may ever be made you. Your portion is unhappily so small that it will in all likelihood undo the effects of your loveliness and amiable qualifications. As I must therefore conclude that you are not serious in your rejection of me, I shall choose to attribute it to your wish of increasing my love by suspense, according to the usual practice of elegant females.'

'I do assure you, sir, that I have no pretension whatever to that kind of elegance which consists in tormenting a respectable man. I would rather be paid the compliment of being believed sincere. I thank you again and again for the honour you have done me in your proposals, but to accept them is absolutely impossible. My feelings in every respect forbid it. Can I speak plainer? Do not consider me now as an elegant female intending to plague you, but as a rational creature speaking the truth from her heart.'

'You are uniformly charming!' cried he, with an air of awkward gallantry; 'and I am persuaded that when sanctioned by the express authority of both your excellent parents, my proposals will not fail of being acceptable.'

To such perseverance in wilful self-deception Elizabeth would make no reply, and immediately and in silence withdrew; determined, if he persisted in considering her repeated refusals as flattering encouragement, to apply to her father, whose negative might be uttered in such a manner as must be decisive, and whose behaviour at least could not be mistaken for the affectation and coquetry of an elegant female.

## *Chapter 20*

Mr Collins was not left long to the silent contemplation of his successful love; for Mrs Bennet, having dawdled about in the vestibule to watch for the end of the conference, no sooner saw Elizabeth open the door and with quick step pass her towards the staircase, than she entered the breakfast-room, and congratulated both him and herself in warm terms on the happy prospect of their nearer connection. Mr Collins received and returned these felicitations with equal pleasure, and then proceeded to relate the particulars of their interview, with the result of which he trusted he had every reason to be satisfied, since the refusal which his cousin had steadfastly given him would naturally flow from her bashful modesty and the genuine delicacy of her character.

This information, however, startled Mrs Bennet; – she would have been glad to be equally satisfied that her daughter had meant to encourage him by protesting against his proposals, but she dared not to believe it, and could not help saying so.

'But depend upon it, Mr Collins,' she added, 'that Lizzy shall be brought to reason. I will speak to her about it myself directly. She is a very headstrong foolish girl, and does not know her own interest; but I will *make* her know it.'

'Pardon me for interrupting you, Madam,' cried Mr Collins; 'but if she is really headstrong and foolish, I know not whether she would altogether be a very desirable wife to a man in my situation, who naturally looks for happiness in the marriage state. If therefore she actually persists in rejecting my suit, perhaps it were better not to force her into accepting me, because if liable to such defects of temper, she could not contribute much to my felicity.'

'Sir, you quite misunderstand me,' said Mrs Bennet, alarmed. 'Lizzy is only headstrong in such matters as these. In everything else she is as good-natured a girl as ever lived. I will go directly to Mr Bennet, and we shall very soon settle it with her, I am sure.'

She would not give him time to reply, but hurrying instantly to her husband, called out as she entered the library, 'Oh! Mr Bennet, you are wanted immediately; we are all in an uproar. You must come and make Lizzy marry Mr Collins, for she vows she will not have him, and if you do not make haste he will change his mind and not have *her*.'

Mr Bennet raised his eyes from his book as she entered, and fixed them on her face with a calm unconcern which was not in the least altered by her communication.

'I have not the pleasure of understanding you,' said he, when she had finished her speech. 'Of what are you talking?'

'Of Mr Collins and Lizzy. Lizzy declares she will not have Mr Collins, and Mr Collins begins to say that he will not have Lizzy.'

'And what am I to do on the occasion? – It seems an hopeless business.'

'Speak to Lizzy about it yourself. Tell her that you insist upon her marrying him.'

'Let her be called down. She shall hear my opinion.'

Mrs Bennet rang the bell, and Miss Elizabeth was summoned to the library.

'Come here, child,' cried her father as she appeared. 'I have sent for you on an affair of importance. I understand that Mr Collins has made you an offer of marriage. Is it true?' Elizabeth replied that it was. 'Very well – and this offer of marriage you have refused?'

'I have, sir.'

'Very well. We now come to the point. Your mother insists upon your accepting it. Is not it so, Mrs Bennet?'

'Yes, or I will never see her again.'

'An unhappy alternative is before you, Elizabeth. From this day you must be a stranger to one of your parents. – Your mother will never see you again if you do *not* marry Mr Collins, and I will never see you again if you *do*.'

Elizabeth could not but smile at such a conclusion of such a beginning; but Mrs Bennet, who had persuaded herself that her husband regarded the affair as she wished, was excessively disappointed.

'What do you mean, Mr Bennet, by talking in this way? You promised me to *insist* upon her marrying him.'

'My dear,' replied her husband, 'I have two small favours to request. First, that you will allow me the free use of my understanding on the present occasion; and secondly, of my room. I shall be glad to have the library to myself as soon as may be.'

Not yet, however, in spite of her disappointment in her husband, did Mrs Bennet give up the point. She talked to Elizabeth again and again; coaxed and threatened her by turns. She endeavoured to secure Jane in her interest, but Jane with all possible mildness declined interfering; – and Elizabeth sometimes with real earnestness and sometimes with playful gaiety replied to her attacks. Though her manner varied however, her determination never did.

Mr Collins, meanwhile, was meditating in solitude on what had passed. He thought too well of himself to comprehend on what motive his cousin could refuse him; and though his pride was hurt, he suffered in no other way. His regard for her was quite imaginary; and the possibility of her deserving her mother's reproach prevented his feeling any regret.

While the family were in this confusion, Charlotte Lucas came to spend the day with them. She was met in the vestibule by Lydia, who, flying to her, cried in a half-whisper, 'I am glad you are come, for there is such fun here! – What do you think has happened this morning? – Mr Collins has made an offer to Lizzy, and she will not have him.'

Charlotte had hardly time to answer, before they were joined by Kitty, who came to tell the same news, and no sooner had they entered the breakfast-room, where Mrs Bennet was alone, than she likewise began on the subject, calling on Miss Lucas for her compassion, and entreating her to persuade her friend Lizzy to comply with the wishes of all her family. 'Pray do, my dear Miss Lucas,' she added in a melancholy tone, 'for nobody is on my side, nobody takes part with me, I am cruelly used, nobody feels for my poor nerves.'

Charlotte's reply was spared by the entrance of Jane and Elizabeth.

'Aye, there she comes,' continued Mrs Bennet, 'looking as unconcerned as may be, and caring no more for us than if we were at York, provided she can have her own way. – But I tell you what, Miss Lizzy, if you take it into your head to go on refusing every offer of marriage in this way, you will never get a husband at all – and I am sure I do not know who is to maintain you when your father is dead. – *I* shall not be able to keep you – and so I warn you. – I have done with you from this very day. – I told you in the library, you know, that I should never speak to you again, and you will find me as good as my word. I have no pleasure in talking to undutiful children. – Not that I have much pleasure indeed in talking to anybody. People who suffer as I do from nervous complaints can have no great inclination for talking. Nobody can tell what I suffer! – But it is always so. Those who do not complain are never pitied.'

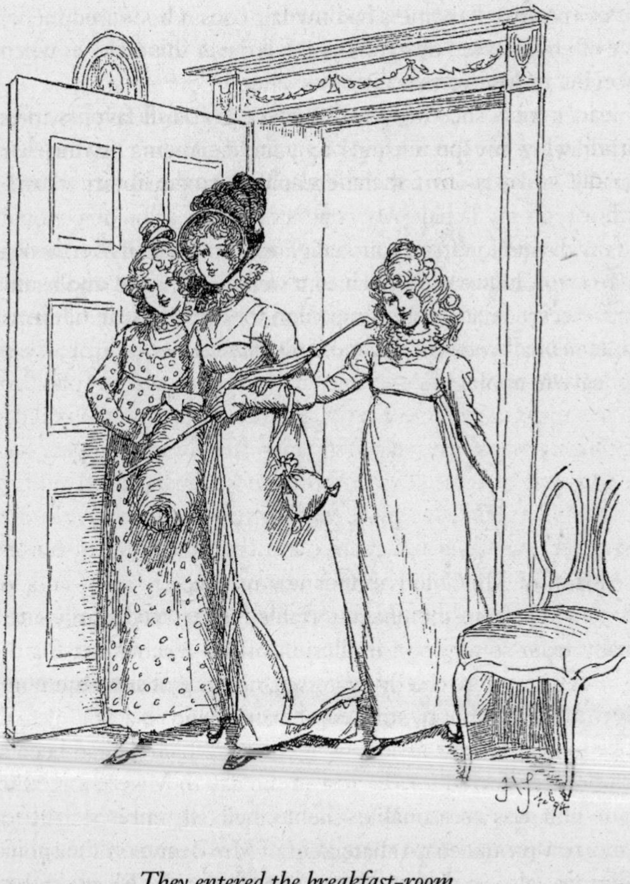

*They entered the breakfast-room*

Her daughters listened in silence to this effusion, sensible that any attempt to reason with or sooth her would only increase the irritation. She talked on, therefore, without interruption from any of them till they were joined by Mr Collins, who entered with an air more stately than usual, and on perceiving whom, she said to the girls, 'Now, I do insist upon it, that you, all of you, hold your tongues, and let Mr Collins and me have a little conversation together.'

Elizabeth passed quietly out of the room, Jane and Kitty followed, but Lydia stood her ground, determined to hear all she could; and Charlotte, detained first by the civility of Mr Collins, whose inquiries after herself and all her family were very minute, and then by a little curiosity, satisfied herself with walking to the window and pretending not to hear. In a doleful voice Mrs Bennet thus began the projected conversation. – 'Oh! Mr Collins! – '

'My dear Madam,' replied he, 'let us be for ever silent on this point. Far be it from me,' he presently continued in a voice that marked his displeasure, 'to resent the behaviour of your daughter. Resignation to inevitable evils is the duty of us all; the peculiar duty of a young man who has been so fortunate as I have been in early preferment; and I trust I am resigned. Perhaps not the less so from feeling a doubt of my positive happiness had my fair cousin honoured me with her hand; for I have often observed that resignation is never so perfect as when the blessing denied begins to lose somewhat of its value in our estimation. You will not, I hope, consider me as showing any disrespect to your family, my dear Madam, by thus withdrawing my pretensions to your daughter's favour, without having paid yourself and Mr Bennet the compliment of requesting you to interpose your authority in my behalf. My conduct may I fear be objectionable in having accepted my dismission from your daughter's lips instead of your own. But we are all liable to error. I have certainly meant well through the whole affair. My object has been to secure an amiable companion for myself, with due consideration for the advantage of all your family, and if my *manner* has been at all reprehensible, I here beg leave to apologise.'

## *Chapter 21*

The discussion of Mr Collins's offer was now nearly at an end, and Elizabeth had only to suffer from the uncomfortable feelings necessarily attending it, and occasionally from some peevish allusion of her mother. As for the gentleman himself, *his* feelings were chiefly expressed, not by embarrassment or dejection, or by trying to avoid her, but by stiffness of manner and resentful silence. He scarcely ever spoke to her, and the assiduous attentions which he had been so sensible of himself, were transferred for the rest of the day to Miss Lucas, whose civility in listening to him, was a seasonable relief to them all, and especially to her friend.

The morrow produced no abatement of Mrs Bennet's ill humour or ill health. Mr Collins was also in the same state of angry pride. Elizabeth had hoped that his resentment might shorten his visit, but his plan did not appear in the least affected by it. He was always to have gone on Saturday, and to Saturday he still meant to stay.

After breakfast, the girls walked to Meryton to enquire if Mr Wickham were returned, and to lament over his absence from the Netherfield ball. He joined them on their entering the town and attended them to their aunt's, where his regret and vexation, and the concern of everybody was well talked over. – To Elizabeth, however, he voluntarily acknowledged that the necessity of his absence *had* been self-imposed.

'I found,' said he, 'as the time drew near, that I had better not meet Mr Darcy; – that to be in the same room, the same party with him for so many hours together, might be more than I could bear, and that scenes might arise unpleasant to more than myself.'

She highly approved his forbearance, and they had leisure for a full discussion of it, and for all the commendation which they civilly bestowed on each other, as Wickham and another officer walked back with them to Longbourn, and during

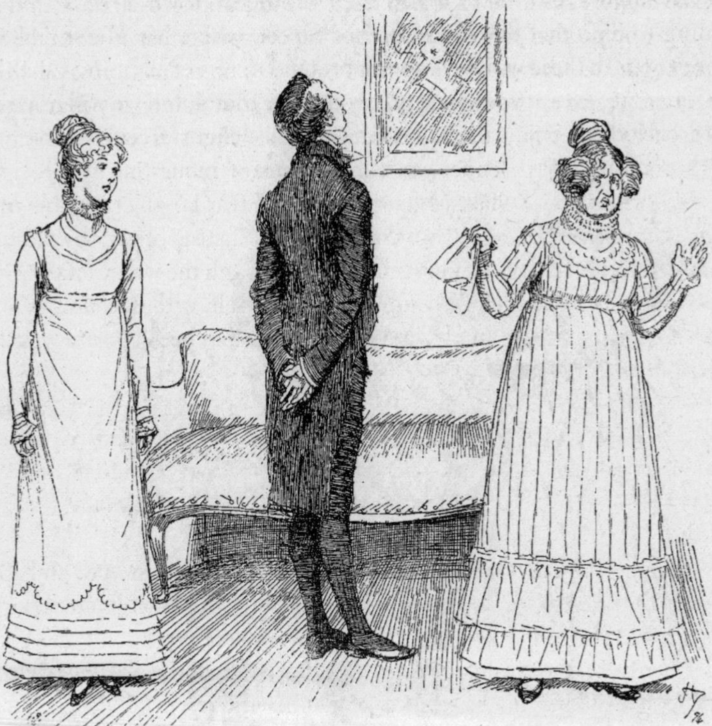

*The assiduous attentions which he had been so sensible of himself, were transferred for the rest of the day to Miss Lucas*

the walk, he particularly attended to her. His accompanying them was a double advantage; she felt all the compliment it offered to herself, and it was most acceptable as an occasion of introducing him to her father and mother.

Soon after their return, a letter was delivered to Miss Bennet; it came from Netherfield, and was opened immediately. The envelope contained a sheet of elegant, little, hot pressed paper, well covered with a lady's fair, flowing hand; and Elizabeth saw her sister's countenance change as she read it, and saw her dwelling intently on some particular passages. Jane recollected herself soon, and putting the letter away, tried to join with her usual cheerfulness in the general conversation; but Elizabeth felt an anxiety on the subject which drew off her attention even from Wickham; and no sooner had he and his companion taken leave, than a glance from Jane invited her to follow her upstairs. When they had gained their own room, Jane taking out the letter, said, 'This is from Caroline Bingley; what it contains, has surprised me a good deal. The whole party have left Netherfield by this time, and are on their way to town; and without any intention of coming back again. You shall hear what she says.'

She then read the first sentence aloud, which comprised the information of their having just resolved to follow their brother to town directly, and of their meaning to dine that day in Grosvenor Street, where Mr Hurst had a house. The next was in these words. 'I do not pretend to regret anything I shall leave in Hertfordshire, except your society, my dearest friend; but we will hope at some future period, to enjoy many returns of the delightful intercourse we have

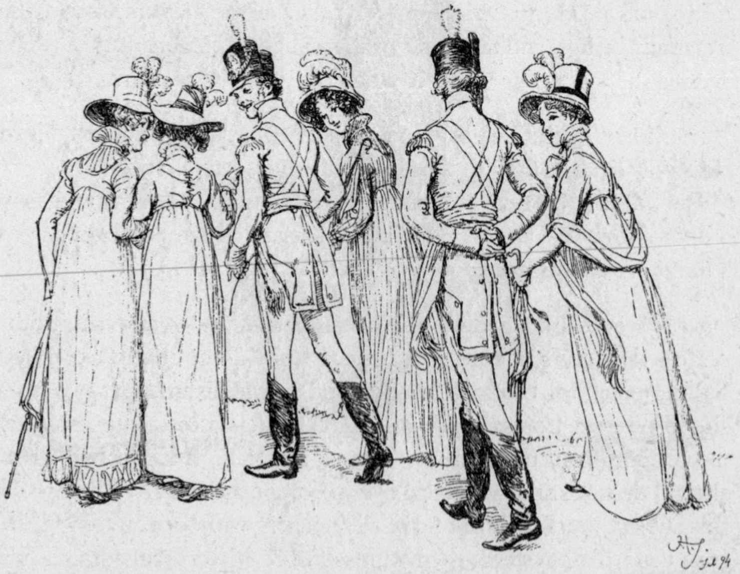

*Wickham and another officer walked back with them to Longbourn*

known, and in the meanwhile may lessen the pain of separation by a very frequent and most unreserved correspondence. I depend on you for that.' To these high-flown expressions, Elizabeth listened with all the insensibility of distrust; and though the suddenness of their removal surprised her, she saw nothing in it really to lament; it was not to be supposed that their absence from Netherfield would prevent Mr Bingley's being there; and as to the loss of their society, she was persuaded that Jane must soon cease to regard it, in the enjoyment of his.

'It is unlucky,' said she, after a short pause, 'that you should not be able to see your friends before they leave the country. But may we not hope that the period of future happiness to which Miss Bingley looks forward, may arrive earlier than she is aware, and that the delightful intercourse you have known as friends, will be renewed with yet greater satisfaction as sisters? – Mr Bingley will not be detained in London by them.'

'Caroline decidedly says that none of the party will return into Hertfordshire this winter. I will read it to you:

'When my brother left us yesterday, he imagined that the business which took him to London, might be concluded in three or four days, but as we are certain it cannot be so, and at the same time convinced that when Charles gets to town, he will be in no hurry to leave it again, we have determined on following him thither, that he may not be obliged to spend his vacant hours in a comfortless hotel. Many of my acquaintance are already there for the winter; I wish I could hear that you, my dearest friend, had any intention of making one in the crowd, but of that I despair. I sincerely hope your Christmas in Hertfordshire may abound in the gaieties which that season generally brings, and that your beaux will be so numerous as to prevent your feeling the loss of the three, of whom we shall deprive you.

'It is evident by this,' added Jane, 'that he comes back no more this winter.'

'It is only evident that Miss Bingley does not mean he *should*.'

'Why will you think so? It must be his own doing. – He is his own master. But you do not know *all*. I *will* read you the passage which particularly hurts me. I will have no reserves from *you*.

'Mr Darcy is impatient to see his sister, and to confess the truth, *we* are scarcely less eager to meet her again. I really do not think Georgiana Darcy has her equal for beauty, elegance, and accomplishments; and the affection she inspires in Louisa and myself, is heightened into something still more interesting, from the hope we dare to entertain of her being hereafter our sister. I do not know whether I ever before mentioned to you my feelings on this subject, but I will not leave the country without confiding them, and I trust you will not esteem them unreasonable. My brother admires her greatly already, he will have frequent opportunity now of seeing her on the most intimate footing, her relations all wish the connection as much as his own, and a sister's partiality is not misleading me, I think, when I call Charles most capable of engaging any woman's heart. With all these circumstances to favour an attachment and nothing to prevent it, am I wrong, my dearest Jane, in indulging the hope of an event which will secure the happiness of so many?

'What think you of *this* sentence, my dear Lizzy?' said Jane as she finished it.

'Is it not clear enough? – Does it not expressly declare that Caroline neither expects nor wishes me to be her sister; that she is perfectly convinced of her brother's indifference, and that if she suspects the nature of my feelings for him, she means (most kindly!) to put me on my guard? Can there be any other opinion on the subject?'

'Yes, there can; for mine is totally different. – Will you hear it?'

'Most willingly.'

'You shall have it in few words. Miss Bingley sees that her brother is in love with you, and wants him to marry Miss Darcy. She follows him to town in the hope of keeping him there, and tries to persuade you that he does not care about you.'

Jane shook her head.

'Indeed, Jane, you ought to believe me. – No one who has ever seen you together, can doubt his affection. Miss Bingley I am sure cannot. She is not such a simpleton. Could she have seen half as much love in Mr Darcy for herself, she would have ordered her wedding clothes. But the case is this. We are not rich enough, or grand enough for them; and she is the more anxious to get Miss Darcy for her brother, from the notion that when there has been *one* inter-marriage, she may have less trouble in achieving a second; in which there is certainly some ingenuity, and I dare say it would succeed, if Miss de Bourgh were out of the way. But, my dearest Jane, you cannot seriously imagine that because Miss Bingley tells you her brother greatly admires Miss Darcy, he is in the smallest degree less sensible of *your* merit than when he took leave of you on Tuesday, or that it will be in her power to persuade him that instead of being in love with you, he is very much in love with her friend.'

'If we thought alike of Miss Bingley,' replied Jane, 'your representation of all this, might make me quite easy. But I know the foundation is unjust. Caroline is incapable of wilfully deceiving anyone; and all that I can hope in this case is, that she is deceived herself.'

'That is right. – You could not have started a more happy idea, since you will not take comfort in mine. Believe her to be deceived by all means. You have now done your duty by her, and must fret no longer.'

'But, my dear sister, can I be happy, even supposing the best, in accepting a man whose sisters and friends are all wishing him to marry elsewhere?'

'You must decide for yourself,' said Elizabeth, 'and if upon mature deliberation, you find that the misery of disobliging his two sisters is more than equivalent to the happiness of being his wife, I advise you by all means to refuse him.'

'How can you talk so?' – said Jane faintly smiling, – 'You must know that though I should be exceedingly grieved at their disapprobation, I could not hesitate.'

'I did not think you would; – and that being the case, I cannot consider your situation with much compassion.'

'But if he returns no more this winter, my choice will never be required. A thousand things may arise in six months!'

The idea of his returning no more Elizabeth treated with the utmost contempt. It appeared to her merely the suggestion of Caroline's interested wishes, and she could not for a moment suppose that those wishes, however openly or artfully spoken, could influence a young man so totally independent of everyone.

She represented to her sister as forcibly as possible what she felt on the subject, and had soon the pleasure of seeing its happy effect. Jane's temper was not desponding, and she was gradually led to hope, though the diffidence of affection sometimes overcame the hope, that Bingley would return to Netherfield and answer every wish of her heart.

They agreed that Mrs Bennet should only hear of the departure of the family, without being alarmed on the score of the gentleman's conduct; but even this partial communication gave her a great deal of concern, and she bewailed it as exceedingly unlucky that the ladies should happen to go away, just as they were all getting so intimate together. After lamenting it however at some length, she had the consolation of thinking that Mr Bingley would be soon down again and soon dining at Longbourn, and the conclusion of all was the comfortable declaration that, though he had been invited only to a family dinner, she would take care to have two full courses.

## *Chapter* 22

The Bennets were engaged to dine with the Lucases, and again during the chief of the day, was Miss Lucas so kind as to listen to Mr Collins. Elizabeth took an opportunity of thanking her. 'It keeps him in good humour,' said she, 'and I am more obliged to you than I can express.' Charlotte assured her friend of her satisfaction in being useful, and that it amply repaid her for the little sacrifice of her time. This was very amiable, but Charlotte's kindness extended farther than Elizabeth had any conception of; – its object was nothing less, than to secure her from any return of Mr Collins's addresses, by engaging them towards herself. Such was Miss Lucas's scheme; and appearances were so favourable that when they parted at night, she would have felt almost sure of success if he had not been to leave Hertfordshire so very soon. But here, she did injustice to the fire and independence of his character, for it led him to escape out of Longbourn House the next morning with admirable slyness, and hasten to Lucas Lodge to throw himself at her feet. He was anxious to avoid the notice of his cousins, from a conviction that if they saw him depart, they could not fail to conjecture his design, and he was not willing to have the attempt known till its success could be known likewise; for though feeling almost secure, and with reason, for Charlotte had been tolerably encouraging, he was comparatively diffident since the adventure of Wednesday. His reception however was of the most flattering kind. Miss Lucas perceived him from an upper window as he walked towards the house, and instantly set out to meet him accidentally in the lane. But little had she dared to hope that so much love and eloquence awaited her there.

In as short a time as Mr Collins's long speeches would allow, everything was settled between them to the satisfaction of both; and as they entered the house, he earnestly entreated her to name the day that was to make him the happiest of men; and though such a solicitation must be waived for the present, the lady felt no inclination to trifle with his happiness. The stupidity with which he was favoured by nature, must guard his courtship from any charm that could make a woman wish for its continuance; and Miss Lucas, who accepted him solely from the pure and disinterested desire of an establishment, cared not how soon that establishment were gained.

Sir William and Lady Lucas were speedily applied to for their consent; and it was bestowed with a most joyful alacrity. Mr Collins's present circumstances made it a most eligible match for their daughter, to whom they could give little

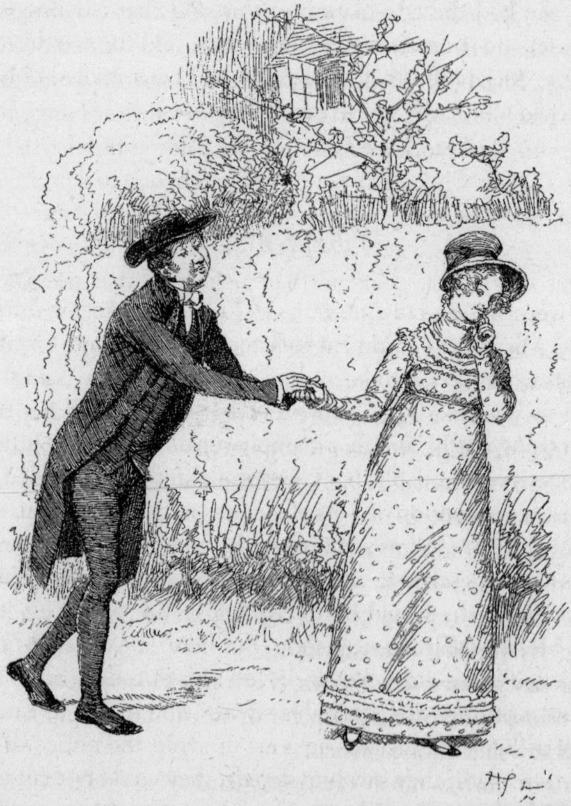

*So much love and eloquence*

fortune; and his prospects of future wealth were exceedingly fair. Lady Lucas began directly to calculate with more interest than the matter had ever excited before, how many years longer Mr Bennet was likely to live; and Sir William gave it as his decided opinion, that whenever Mr Collins should be in possession of the Longbourn estate, it would be highly expedient that both he and his wife should make their appearance at St James's. The whole family in short were properly overjoyed on the occasion. The younger girls formed hopes of *coming out* a year or two sooner than they might otherwise have done; and the boys were relieved from their apprehension of Charlotte's dying an old maid. Charlotte herself was tolerably composed. She had gained her point, and had time to consider of it. Her reflections were in general satisfactory. Mr Collins to be sure was neither sensible nor agreeable; his society was irksome, and his attachment to her must be imaginary. But still he would be her husband. – Without thinking highly either of men or of matrimony, marriage had always been her object; it was the only honourable provision for well-educated young women of small fortune, and however uncertain of giving happiness, must be their pleasantest preservative from want. This preservative she had now obtained; and at the age of twenty-seven, without having ever been handsome, she felt all the good luck of it. The least agreeable circumstance in the business, was the surprise it must occasion to Elizabeth Bennet, whose friendship she valued beyond that of any other person. Elizabeth would wonder, and probably would blame her; and though her resolution was not to be shaken, her feelings must be hurt by such disapprobation. She resolved to give her the information herself, and therefore charged Mr Collins when he returned to Longbourn to dinner, to drop no hint of what had passed before any of the family. A promise of secrecy was of course very dutifully given, but it could not be kept without difficulty; for the curiosity excited by his long absence, burst forth in such very direct questions on his return, as required some ingenuity to evade, and he was at the same time exercising great self-denial, for he was longing to publish his prosperous love.

As he was to begin his journey too early on the morrow to see any of the family, the ceremony of leave-taking was performed when the ladies moved for the night; and Mrs Bennet with great politeness and cordiality said how happy they should be to see him at Longbourn again, whenever his other engagements might allow him to visit them.

They were all astonished; and Mr Bennet, who could by no means wish for so speedy a return, immediately said, 'But is there not danger of Lady Catherine's disapprobation here, my good sir? – You had better neglect your relations, than run the risk of offending your patroness.'

'My dear sir,' replied Mr Collins, 'I am particularly obliged to you for this friendly caution, and you may depend upon my not taking so material a step without her ladyship's concurrence.'

'You cannot be too much on your guard. Risk anything rather than her displeasure; and if you find it likely to be raised by your coming to us again, which I should think exceedingly probable, stay quietly at home, and be satisfied that *we* shall take no offence.'

'Believe me, my dear sir, my gratitude is warmly excited by such affectionate attention; and depend upon it, you will speedily receive from me a letter of thanks for this, as well as for every other mark of your regard during my stay in Hertfordshire. As for my fair cousins, though my absence may not be long enough to render it necessary, I shall now take the liberty of wishing them health and happiness, not excepting my cousin Elizabeth.'

With proper civilities the ladies then withdrew; all of them equally surprised to find that he meditated a quick return. Mrs Bennet wished to understand by it that he thought of paying his addresses to one of her younger girls, and Mary might have been prevailed on to accept him. She rated his abilities much higher than any of the others; there was a solidity in his reflections which often struck her, and though by no means so clever as herself, she thought that if encouraged to read and improve himself by such an example as hers, he might become a very agreeable companion. But on the following morning, every hope of this kind was done away. Miss Lucas called soon after breakfast, and in a private conference with Elizabeth related the event of the day before.

The possibility of Mr Collins's fancying himself in love with her friend had once occurred to Elizabeth within the last day or two; but that Charlotte could encourage him, seemed almost as far from possibility as that she could encourage him herself, and her astonishment was consequently so great as to overcome at first the bounds of decorum, and she could not help crying out, 'Engaged to Mr Collins! my dear Charlotte, – impossible!'

The steady countenance which Miss Lucas had commanded in telling her story, gave way to a momentary confusion here on receiving so direct a reproach; though, as it was no more than she expected, she soon regained her composure, and calmly replied, 'Why should you be surprised, my dear Eliza? – Do you think it incredible that Mr Collins should be able to procure any woman's good opinion, because he was not so happy as to succeed with you?'

But Elizabeth had now recollected herself, and making a strong effort for it, was able to assure her with tolerable firmness that the prospect of their relationship was highly grateful to her, and that she wished her all imaginable happiness.

'I see what you are feeling,' replied Charlotte, – 'you must be surprised, very much surprised, – so lately as Mr Collins was wishing to marry you. But when you have had time to think it all over, I hope you will be satisfied with what I have done. I am not romantic you know. I never was. I ask only a comfortable home; and considering Mr Collins's character, connections, and situation in life, I am convinced that my chance of happiness with him is as fair, as most people can boast on entering the marriage state.'

Elizabeth quietly answered 'Undoubtedly;' – and after an awkward pause, they returned to the rest of the family. Charlotte did not stay much longer, and Elizabeth was then left to reflect on what she had heard. It was a long time before she became at all reconciled to the idea of so unsuitable a match. The strangeness of Mr Collins's making two offers of marriage within three days, was nothing in comparison of his being now accepted. She had always felt that Charlotte's opinion of matrimony was not exactly like her own, but she could not have supposed it possible that when called into action, she would have sacrificed every better feeling to worldly advantage. Charlotte the wife of Mr Collins, was a most humiliating picture! – And to the pang of a friend disgracing herself and sunk in her esteem, was added the distressing conviction that it was impossible for that friend to be tolerably happy in the lot she had chosen.

## *Chapter 23*

Elizabeth was sitting with her mother and sisters, reflecting on what she had heard, and doubting whether she were authorised to mention it, when Sir William Lucas himself appeared, sent by his daughter to announce her engagement to the family. With many compliments to them, and much self-congratulation on the prospect of a connection between the houses, he unfolded the matter, – to an audience not merely wondering, but incredulous; for Mrs Bennet, with more perseverance than politeness, protested he must be entirely mistaken, and Lydia, always unguarded and often uncivil, boisterously exclaimed, 'Good Lord! Sir William, how can you tell such a story? – Do not you know that Mr Collins wants to marry Lizzy?'

Nothing less than the complaisance of a courtier could have borne without anger such treatment; but Sir William's good breeding carried him through it

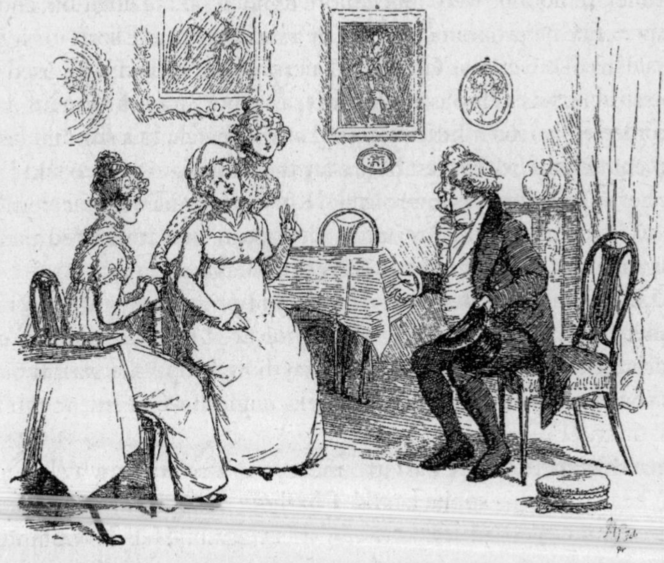

*Protested he must be entirely mistaken*

all; and though he begged leave to be positive as to the truth of his information, he listened to all their impertinence with the most forbearing courtesy.

Elizabeth, feeling it incumbent on her to relieve him from so unpleasant a situation, now put herself forward to confirm his account, by mentioning her prior knowledge of it from Charlotte herself; and endeavoured to put a stop to the exclamations of her mother and sisters, by the earnestness of her congratulations to Sir William, in which she was readily joined by Jane, and by making a variety of remarks on the happiness that might be expected from the match, the excellent character of Mr Collins, and the convenient distance of Hunsford from London.

Mrs Bennet was in fact too much overpowered to say a great deal while Sir William remained; but no sooner had he left them than her feelings found a rapid vent. In the first place, she persisted in disbelieving the whole of the matter; secondly, she was very sure that Mr Collins had been taken in; thirdly, she trusted that they would never be happy together; and fourthly, that the match might be broken off. Two inferences, however, were plainly deduced from the whole; one, that Elizabeth was the real cause of all the mischief; and the other, that she herself had been barbarously used by them all; and on these two points she principally dwelt during the rest of the day. Nothing could console and nothing appease her. – Nor did that day wear out her resentment. A week elapsed before she could see Elizabeth without scolding her, a month passed away before she could speak to Sir William or Lady Lucas without being rude, and many months were gone before she could at all forgive their daughter.

Mr Bennet's emotions were much more tranquil on the occasion, and such as he did experience he pronounced to be of a most agreeable sort; for it gratified him, he said, to discover that Charlotte Lucas, whom he had been used to think tolerably sensible, was as foolish as his wife, and more foolish than his daughter!

Jane confessed herself a little surprised at the match; but she said less of her astonishment than of her earnest desire for their happiness; nor could Elizabeth persuade her to consider it as improbable. Kitty and Lydia were far from envying Miss Lucas, for Mr Collins was only a clergyman; and it affected them in no other way than as a piece of news to spread at Meryton.

Lady Lucas could not be insensible of triumph on being able to retort on Mrs Bennet the comfort of having a daughter well married; and she called at Longbourn rather oftener than usual to say how happy she was, though Mrs Bennet's sour looks and ill-natured remarks might have been enough to drive happiness away.

Between Elizabeth and Charlotte there was a restraint which kept them mutually silent on the subject; and Elizabeth felt persuaded that no real confidence could ever subsist between them again. Her disappointment in Charlotte made her turn with fonder regard to her sister, of whose rectitude and delicacy she was sure her opinion could never be shaken, and for whose happiness she grew daily more anxious, as Bingley had now been gone a week, and nothing was heard of his return.

Jane had sent Caroline an early answer to her letter, and was counting the days till she might reasonably hope to hear again. The promised letter of thanks from Mr Collins arrived on Tuesday, addressed to their father, and written with all the solemnity of gratitude which a twelvemonth's abode in the family might have prompted. After discharging his conscience on that head, he proceeded to inform them, with many rapturous expressions, of his happiness in having obtained the affection of their amiable neighbour, Miss Lucas, and then explained that it was merely with the view of enjoying her society that he had been so ready to close with their kind wish of seeing him again at Longbourn, whither he hoped to be able to return on Monday fortnight; for Lady Catherine, he added, so heartily approved his marriage, that she wished it to take place as soon as possible, which he trusted would be an unanswerable argument with his amiable Charlotte to name an early day for making him the happiest of men.

Mr Collins's return into Hertfordshire was no longer a matter of pleasure to Mrs Bennet. On the contrary she was as much disposed to complain of it as her husband. – It was very strange that he should come to Longbourn instead of to Lucas Lodge; it was also very inconvenient and exceedingly troublesome. – She hated having visitors in the house while her health was so indifferent, and lovers were of all people the most disagreeable. Such were the gentle murmurs of Mrs Bennet, and they gave way only to the greater distress of Mr Bingley's continued absence.

Neither Jane nor Elizabeth were comfortable on this subject. Day after day passed away without bringing any other tidings of him than the report which shortly prevailed in Meryton of his coming no more to Netherfield the whole winter; a report which highly incensed Mrs Bennet, and which she never failed to contradict as a most scandalous falsehood.

Even Elizabeth began to fear – not that Bingley was indifferent – but that his sisters would be successful in keeping him away. Unwilling as she was to admit an idea so destructive to Jane's happiness, and so dishonourable to the stability of her lover, she could not prevent its frequently recurring. The united efforts of his two unfeeling sisters and of his overpowering friend, assisted by the attractions of Miss Darcy and the amusements of London, might be too much, she feared, for the strength of his attachment.

As for Jane, *her* anxiety under this suspense was, of course, more painful than Elizabeth's; but whatever she felt she was desirous of concealing, and between herself and Elizabeth, therefore, the subject was never alluded to. But as no such delicacy restrained her mother, an hour seldom passed in which she did not talk of Bingley, express her impatience for his arrival, or even require Jane to confess that if he did not come back, she should think herself very ill used. It needed all Jane's steady mildness to bear these attacks with tolerable tranquillity.

Mr Collins returned most punctually on the Monday fortnight, but his reception at Longbourn was not quite so gracious as it had been on his first introduction. He was too happy, however, to need much attention; and luckily for the others, the business of love-making relieved them from a great deal of his company. The chief of every day was spent by him at Lucas Lodge, and he sometimes returned to Longbourn only in time to make an apology for his absence before the family went to bed.

Mrs Bennet was really in a most pitiable state. The very mention of anything concerning the match threw her into an agony of ill-humour, and wherever she went she was sure of hearing it talked of. The sight of Miss Lucas was odious to her. As her successor in that house, she regarded her with jealous abhorrence. Whenever Charlotte came to see them she concluded her to be anticipating the hour of possession; and whenever she spoke in a low voice to Mr Collins, was convinced that they were talking of the Longbourn estate, and resolving to turn herself and her daughters out of the house, as soon as Mr Bennet were dead. She complained bitterly of all this to her husband.

'Indeed, Mr Bennet,' said she, 'it is very hard to think that Charlotte Lucas should ever be mistress of this house, that *I* should be forced to make way for *her*, and live to see her take my place in it!'

'My dear, do not give way to such gloomy thoughts. Let us hope for better things. Let us flatter ourselves that *I* may be the survivor.'

This was not very consoling to Mrs Bennet, and, therefore, instead of making

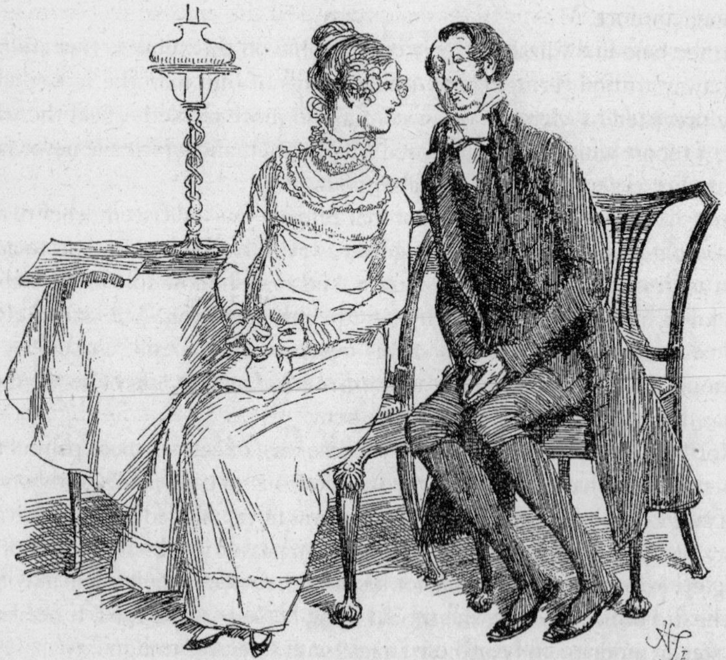

*Whenever she spoke in a low voice to Mr Collins*

any answer, she went on as before, 'I cannot bear to think that they should have all this estate. If it was not for the entail I should not mind it.'

'What should not you mind?'

'I should not mind anything at all.'

'Let us be thankful that you are preserved from a state of such insensibility.'

'I never can be thankful, Mr Bennet, for anything about the entail. How anyone could have the conscience to entail away an estate from one's own daughters I cannot understand; and all for the sake of Mr Collins too! – Why should *he* have it more than anybody else?'

'I leave it to yourself to determine,' said Mr Bennet.

## *Chapter 24*

Miss Bingley's letter arrived, and put an end to doubt. The very first sentence conveyed the assurance of their being all settled in London for the winter, and concluded with her brother's regret at not having had time to pay his respects to his friends in Hertfordshire before he left the country.

Hope was over, entirely over; and when Jane could attend to the rest of the letter, she found little, except the professed affection of the writer, that could give her any comfort. Miss Darcy's praise occupied the chief of it. Her many attractions were again dwelt on, and Caroline boasted joyfully of their increasing intimacy, and ventured to predict the accomplishment of the wishes which had been unfolded in her former letter. She wrote also with great pleasure of her brother's being an inmate of Mr Darcy's house, and mentioned with raptures, some plans of the latter with regard to new furniture.

Elizabeth, to whom Jane very soon communicated the chief of all this, heard it in silent indignation. Her heart was divided between concern for her sister, and resentment against all the others. To Caroline's assertion of her brother's being partial to Miss Darcy she paid no credit. That he was really fond of Jane, she doubted no more than she had ever done; and much as she had always been disposed to like him, she could not think without anger, hardly without contempt, on that easiness of temper, that want of proper resolution which now made him the slave of his designing friends, and led him to sacrifice his own happiness to the caprice of their inclinations. Had his own happiness, however, been the only sacrifice, he might have been allowed to sport with it in whatever manner he thought best; but her sister's was involved in it, as she thought he must be sensible himself. It was a subject, in short, on which reflection would be long indulged, and must be unavailing. She could think of nothing else, and yet whether Bingley's regard had really died away, or were suppressed by his friends' interference; whether he had been aware of Jane's attachment, or whether it had escaped his observation; whichever were the case, though her opinion of him must be materially affected by the difference, her sister's situation remained the same, her peace equally wounded.

A day or two passed before Jane had courage to speak of her feelings to Elizabeth; but at last on Mrs Bennet's leaving them together, after a longer irritation than usual about Netherfield and its master, she could not help saying, 'Oh! that my dear mother had more command over herself; she can have no idea of the pain she gives me by her continual reflections on him. But I will not repine. It cannot last long. He will be forgot, and we shall all be as we were before.'

Elizabeth looked at her sister with incredulous solicitude, but said nothing.

'You doubt me,' cried Jane, slightly colouring; 'indeed you have no reason. He may live in my memory as the most amiable man of my acquaintance, but that is all. I have nothing either to hope or fear, and nothing to reproach him with. Thank God! I have not *that* pain. A little time therefore. – I shall certainly try to get the better.'

With a stronger voice she soon added, 'I have this comfort immediately, that it has not been more than an error of fancy on my side, and that it has done no harm to anyone but myself.'

'My dear Jane!' exclaimed Elizabeth, 'you are too good. Your sweetness and disinterestedness are really angelic; I do not know what to say to you. I feel as if I had never done you justice, or loved you as you deserve.'

Miss Bennet eagerly disclaimed all extraordinary merit, and threw back the praise on her sister's warm affection.

'Nay,' said Elizabeth, 'this is not fair. *You* wish to think all the world respectable, and are hurt if I speak ill of anybody. *I* only want to think *you* perfect, and you set yourself against it. Do not be afraid of my running into any excess, of my encroaching on your privilege of universal goodwill. You need not. There are few people whom I really love, and still fewer of whom I think well. The more I see of the world, the more am I dissatisfied with it; and every day confirms my belief of the inconsistency of all human characters, and of the little dependence that can be placed on the appearance of either merit or sense. I have met with two instances lately; one I will not mention; the other is Charlotte's marriage. It is unaccountable! In every view it is unaccountable!'

'My dear Lizzy, do not give way to such feelings as these. They will ruin your happiness. You do not make allowance enough for difference of situation and temper. Consider Mr Collins's respectability, and Charlotte's prudent, steady character. Remember that she is one of a large family; that as to fortune, it is a most eligible match; and be ready to believe, for everybody's sake, that she may feel something like regard and esteem for our cousin.'

'To oblige you, I would try to believe almost anything, but no one else could be benefited by such a belief as this; for were I persuaded that Charlotte had any regard for him, I should only think worse of her understanding, than I now do of her heart. My dear Jane, Mr Collins is a conceited, pompous, narrow-minded, silly man; you know he is, as well as I do; and you must feel, as well as I do, that the woman who marries him, cannot have a proper way of thinking. You shall not defend her, though it is Charlotte Lucas. You shall not, for the sake of one individual, change the meaning of principle and integrity, nor endeavour to persuade yourself or me, that selfishness is prudence, and insensibility of danger, security for happiness.'

'I must think your language too strong in speaking of both,' replied Jane, 'and I hope you will be convinced of it, by seeing them happy together. But enough of this. You alluded to something else. You mentioned *two* instances. I cannot misunderstand you, but I entreat you, dear Lizzy, not to pain me by thinking *that person* to blame, and saying your opinion of him is sunk. We must not be so ready to fancy ourselves intentionally injured. We must not expect a lively young man to be always so guarded and circumspect. It is very often nothing but our own vanity that deceives us. Women fancy admiration means more than it does.'

'And men take care that they should.'

'If it is designedly done, they cannot be justified; but I have no idea of there being so much design in the world as some persons imagine.'

'I am far from attributing any part of Mr Bingley's conduct to design,' said Elizabeth; 'but without scheming to do wrong, or to make others unhappy, there may be error, and there may be misery. Thoughtlessness, want of attention to other people's feelings, and want of resolution, will do the business.'

'And do you impute it to either of those?'

'Yes; to the last. But if I go on, I shall displease you by saying what I think of persons you esteem. Stop me whilst you can.'

'You persist, then, in supposing his sisters influence him.'

'Yes, in conjunction with his friend.'

'I cannot believe it. Why should they try to influence him? They can only wish his happiness, and if he is attached to me, no other woman can secure it.'

'Your first position is false. They may wish many things besides his happiness; they may wish his increase of wealth and consequence; they may wish him to marry a girl who has all the importance of money, great connections, and pride.'

'Beyond a doubt, they *do* wish him to choose Miss Darcy,' replied Jane; 'but this may be from better feelings than you are supposing. They have known her much longer than they have known me; no wonder if they love her better. But, whatever may be their own wishes, it is very unlikely they should have opposed their brother's. What sister would think herself at liberty to do it, unless there were something very objectionable? If they believed him attached to me, they would not try to part us; if he were so, they could not succeed. By supposing such an affection, you make everybody acting unnaturally and wrong, and me most unhappy. Do not distress me by the idea. I am not ashamed of having been mistaken – or, at least, it is slight, it is nothing in comparison of what I should feel in thinking ill of him or his sisters. Let me take it in the best light, in the light in which it may be understood.'

Elizabeth could not oppose such a wish; and from this time Mr Bingley's name was scarcely ever mentioned between them.

Mrs Bennet still continued to wonder and repine at his returning no more, and though a day seldom passed in which Elizabeth did not account for it clearly, there seemed little chance of her ever considering it with less perplexity. Her daughter endeavoured to convince her of what she did not believe herself, that his attentions to Jane had been merely the effect of a common and transient liking, which ceased when he saw her no more; but though the probability of the statement was admitted at the time, she had the same story to repeat every day. Mrs Bennet's best comfort was, that Mr Bingley must be down again in the summer.

Mr Bennet treated the matter differently. 'So, Lizzy,' said he one day, 'your sister is crossed in love I find. I congratulate her. Next to being married, a girl likes to be crossed in love a little now and then. It is something to think of, and gives her a sort of distinction among her companions. When is your turn to come? You will hardly bear to be long outdone by Jane. Now is your time. Here are officers enough at Meryton to disappoint all the young ladies in the country. Let Wickham be *your* man. He is a pleasant fellow, and would jilt you creditably.'

'Thank you, sir, but a less agreeable man would satisfy me. We must not all expect Jane's good fortune.'

'True,' said Mr Bennet, 'but it is a comfort to think that, whatever of that kind may befall you, you have an affectionate mother who will always make the most of it.'

Mr Wickham's society was of material service in dispelling the gloom, which the late perverse occurrences had thrown on many of the Longbourn family. They saw him often, and to his other recommendations was now added that of general unreserve. The whole of what Elizabeth had already heard, his claims on Mr Darcy, and all that he had suffered from him, was now openly acknowledged and publicly canvassed; and everybody was pleased to think how much they had always disliked Mr Darcy before they had known anything of the matter.

Miss Bennet was the only creature who could suppose there might be any extenuating circumstances in the case, unknown to the society of Hertfordshire; her mild and steady candour always pleaded for allowances, and urged the possibility of mistakes – but by everybody else Mr Darcy was condemned as the worst of men.

## *Chapter 25*

After a week spent in professions of love and schemes of felicity, Mr Collins was called from his amiable Charlotte by the arrival of Saturday. The pain of separation, however, might be alleviated on his side, by preparations for the reception of his bride, as he had reason to hope, that shortly after his next return into Hertfordshire, the day would be fixed that was to make him the happiest of men. He took leave of his relations at Longbourn with as much solemnity as before; wished his fair cousins health and happiness again, and promised their father another letter of thanks.

On the following Monday, Mrs Bennet had the pleasure of receiving her brother and his wife, who came as usual to spend the Christmas at Longbourn. Mr Gardiner was a sensible, gentlemanlike man, greatly superior to his sister as well by nature as education. The Netherfield ladies would have had difficulty in believing that a man who lived by trade, and within view of his own warehouses, could have been so well bred and agreeable. Mrs Gardiner, who was several years younger than Mrs Bennet and Mrs Philips, was an amiable, intelligent, elegant woman, and a great favourite with all her Longbourn nieces. Between the two eldest and herself especially, there subsisted a very particular regard. They had frequently been staying with her in town.

The first part of Mrs Gardiner's business on her arrival, was to distribute her presents and describe the newest fashions. When this was done, she had a less active part to play. It became her turn to listen, Mrs Bennet had many grievances to relate, and much to complain of. They had all been very ill-used since she last saw her sister. Two of her girls had been on the point of marriage, and after all there was nothing in it.

'I do not blame Jane,' she continued, 'for Jane would have got Mr Bingley, if she could. But, Lizzy! Oh, sister! it is very hard to think that she might have been Mr Collins's wife by this time, had not it been for her own perverseness. He made her an offer in this very room, and she refused him. The consequence of it is, that Lady Lucas will have a daughter married before I have, and that Longbourn estate is just as much entailed as ever. The Lucases are very artful people indeed, sister. They are all for what they can get. I am sorry to say it of them, but so it is. It makes me very nervous and poorly, to be thwarted so in my own family, and to have neighbours who think of themselves before anybody else. However, your coming just at this time is the greatest of comforts, and I am very glad to hear what you tell us, of long sleeves.'

Mrs Gardiner, to whom the chief of this news had been given before, in the course of Jane and Elizabeth's correspondence with her, made her sister a slight answer, and in compassion to her nieces turned the conversation.

When alone with Elizabeth afterwards, she spoke more on the subject. 'It seems likely to have been a desirable match for Jane,' said she. 'I am sorry it went off. But these things happen so often! A young man, such as you describe Mr Bingley, so easily falls in love with a pretty girl for a few weeks, and when accident separates them, so easily forgets her, that these sort of inconstancies are very frequent.'

'An excellent consolation in its way,' said Elizabeth, 'but it will not do for *us*. We do not suffer by *accident*. It does not often happen that the interference of friends will persuade a young man of independent fortune to think no more of a girl, whom he was violently in love with only a few days before.'

'But that expression of "violently in love" is so hackneyed, so doubtful, so indefinite, that it gives me very little idea. It is as often applied to feelings which arise from an half-hour's acquaintance, as to a real, strong attachment. Pray, how *violent* was Mr Bingley's love?'

'I never saw a more promising inclination. He was growing quite inattentive to other people, and wholly engrossed by her. Every time they met, it was more decided and remarkable. At his own ball he offended two or three young ladies,

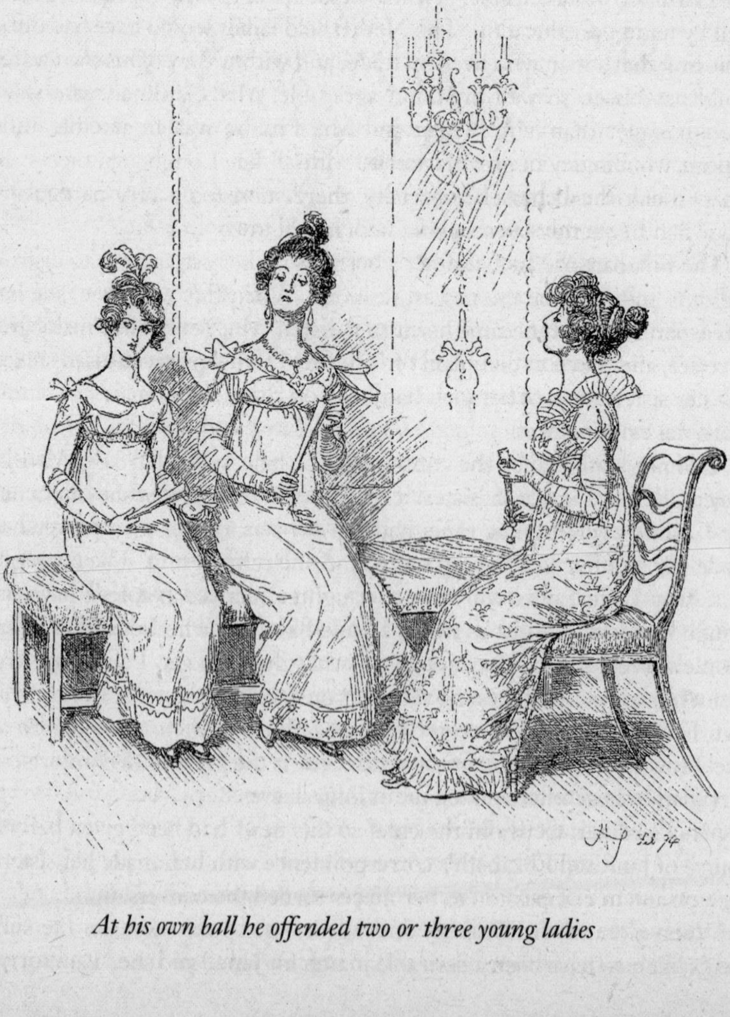

*At his own ball he offended two or three young ladies*

by not asking them to dance, and I spoke to him twice myself, without receiving an answer. Could there be finer symptoms? Is not general incivility the very essence of love?'

'Oh, yes! – of that kind of love which I suppose him to have felt. Poor Jane! I am sorry for her, because, with her disposition, she may not get over it immediately. It had better have happened to *you*, Lizzy; you would have laughed yourself out of it sooner. But do you think she would be prevailed on to go back with us? Change of scene might be of service – and perhaps a little relief from home, may be as useful as anything.'

Elizabeth was exceedingly pleased with this proposal, and felt persuaded of her sister's ready acquiescence.

'I hope,' added Mrs Gardiner, 'that no consideration with regard to this young man will influence her. We live in so different a part of town, all our connections are so different, and, as you well know, we go out so little, that it is very improbable they should meet at all, unless he really comes to see her.'

'And *that* is quite impossible; for he is now in the custody of his friend, and Mr Darcy would no more suffer him to call on Jane in such a part of London! My dear aunt, how could you think of it? Mr Darcy may perhaps have *heard* of such a place as Gracechurch Street, but he would hardly think a month's ablution enough to cleanse him from its impurities, were he once to enter it; and depend upon it, Mr Bingley never stirs without him.'

'So much the better. I hope they will not meet at all. But does not Jane correspond with the sister? *She* will not be able to help calling.'

'She will drop the acquaintance entirely.'

But in spite of the certainty in which Elizabeth affected to place this point, as well as the still more interesting one of Bingley's being withheld from seeing Jane, she felt a solicitude on the subject which convinced her, on examination, that she did not consider it entirely hopeless. It was possible, and sometimes she thought it probable, that his affection might be re-animated, and the influence of his friends successfully combated by the more natural influence of Jane's attractions.

Miss Bennet accepted her aunt's invitation with pleasure; and the Bingleys were no otherwise in her thoughts at the time, than as she hoped that, by Caroline's not living in the same house with her brother, she might occasionally spend a morning with her, without any danger of seeing him.

The Gardiners stayed a week at Longbourn; and what with the Philipses, the Lucases, and the officers, there was not a day without its engagement. Mrs Bennet had so carefully provided for the entertainment of her brother and sister, that they did not once sit down to a family dinner. When the engagement was for home, some of the officers always made part of it, of which officers Mr Wickham was sure to be one; and on these occasions, Mrs Gardiner, rendered suspicious by Elizabeth's warm commendation of him, narrowly observed them both. Without supposing them, from what she saw, to be very seriously in love, their preference of each other was plain enough to make her a little uneasy; and she resolved to speak to Elizabeth on the subject before she left Hertfordshire, and represent to her the imprudence of encouraging such an attachment.

To Mrs Gardiner, Wickham had one means of affording pleasure, unconnected with his general powers. About ten or a dozen years ago, before her marriage, she had spent a considerable time in that very part of Derbyshire, to which he belonged. They had, therefore, many acquaintance in common; and, though Wickham had been little there since the death of Darcy's father, five years before, it was yet in his power to give her fresher intelligence of her former friends, than she had been in the way of procuring.

Mrs Gardiner had seen Pemberley, and known the late Mr Darcy by character perfectly well. Here consequently was an inexhaustible subject of discourse. In comparing her recollection of Pemberley, with the minute description which Wickham could give, and in bestowing her tribute of praise on the character of its late possessor, she was delighting both him and herself. On being made acquainted with the present Mr Darcy's treatment of him, she tried to remember something of that gentleman's reputed disposition when quite a lad, which might agree with it, and was confident at last, that she recollected having heard Mr Fitzwilliam Darcy formerly spoken of as a very proud, ill-natured boy.

## *Chapter 26*

Mrs Gardiner's caution to Elizabeth was punctually and kindly given on the first favourable opportunity of speaking to her alone; after honestly telling her what she thought, she thus went on:

'You are too sensible a girl, Lizzy, to fall in love merely because you are warned against it; and, therefore, I am not afraid of speaking openly. Seriously, I would have you be on your guard. Do not involve yourself, or endeavour to involve him in an affection which the want of fortune would make so very imprudent. I have nothing to say against *him*; he is a most interesting young man; and if he had the fortune he ought to have, I should think you could not do better. But as it is – you must not let your fancy run away with you. You have sense, and we all expect you to use it. Your father would depend on *your* resolution and good conduct, I am sure. You must not disappoint your father.'

'My dear aunt, this is being serious indeed.'

'Yes, and I hope to engage you to be serious likewise.'

'Well, then, you need not be under any alarm. I will take care of myself, and of Mr Wickham too. He shall not be in love with me, if I can prevent it.'

'Elizabeth, you are not serious now.'

'I beg your pardon. I will try again. At present I am not in love with Mr Wickham; no, I certainly am not. But he is, beyond all comparison, the most agreeable man I ever saw – and if he becomes really attached to me – I believe it will be better that he should not. I see the imprudence of it. – Oh! *that* abominable Mr Darcy! – My father's opinion of me does me the greatest honour; and I should be miserable to forfeit it. My father, however, is partial to Mr Wickham. In short, my dear aunt, I should be very sorry to be the means of making any of you unhappy; but since we see every day that where there is affection, young people are seldom withheld by immediate want of fortune, from entering into engagements with each other, how can I promise to be wiser than so many of my fellow creatures if I am tempted, or how am I even to know that it would be wisdom to resist? All that I can promise you, therefore, is not to be in a hurry. I will not be in a hurry to believe myself his first object. When I am in company with him, I will not be wishing. In short, I will do my best.'

'Perhaps it will be as well, if you discourage his coming here so very often. At least, you should not *remind* your mother of inviting him.'

'As I did the other day,' said Elizabeth, with a conscious smile; 'very true, it will be wise in me to refrain from *that*. But do not imagine that he is always here so often. It is on your account that he has been so frequently invited this week. You know my mother's ideas as to the necessity of constant company for her friends. But really, and upon my honour, I will try to do what I think to be wisest; and now, I hope you are satisfied.'

Her aunt assured her that she was; and Elizabeth having thanked her for the kindness of her hints, they parted; a wonderful instance of advice being given on such a point, without being resented.

Mr Collins returned into Hertfordshire soon after it had been quitted by the Gardiners and Jane; but as he took up his abode with the Lucases, his arrival was no great inconvenience to Mrs Bennet. His marriage was now fast approaching, and she was at length so far resigned as to think it inevitable, and even repeatedly to say in an ill-natured tone that she '*wished* they might be happy'. Thursday was to be the wedding day, and on Wednesday Miss Lucas paid her farewell visit; and when she rose to take leave, Elizabeth, ashamed of her mother's ungracious and reluctant good wishes, and sincerely affected herself, accompanied her out of the room. As they went downstairs together, Charlotte said, 'I shall depend on hearing from you very often, Eliza.'

'*That* you certainly shall.'

'And I have another favour to ask. Will you come and see me?'

'We shall often meet, I hope, in Hertfordshire.'

'I am not likely to leave Kent for some time. Promise me, therefore, to come to Hunsford.'

Elizabeth could not refuse, though she foresaw little pleasure in the visit.

'My father and Maria are to come to me in March,' added Charlotte, 'and I hope you will consent to be of the party. Indeed, Eliza, you will be as welcome to me as either of them.'

The wedding took place; the bride and bridegroom set off for Kent from the church door, and everybody had as much to say or to hear on the subject as usual. Elizabeth soon heard from her friend; and their correspondence was as regular and frequent as it had ever been; that it should be equally unreserved was impossible. Elizabeth could never address her without feeling that all the comfort of intimacy was over, and, though determined not to slacken as a correspondent, it was for the sake of what had been, rather than what was. Charlotte's first letters were received with a good deal of eagerness; there could not but be curiosity to know how she would speak of her new home, how she would like Lady Catherine, and how happy she would dare pronounce herself to be; though, when the letters were read, Elizabeth felt that Charlotte expressed herself on every point exactly as she might have foreseen. She wrote cheerfully, seemed surrounded with comforts, and mentioned nothing which she could not praise. The house, furniture, neighbourhood, and roads, were all to her taste, and Lady Catherine's behaviour was most friendly and obliging. It was Mr Collins's picture of Hunsford and Rosings rationally softened; and Elizabeth perceived that she must wait for her own visit there, to know the rest.

Jane had already written a few lines to her sister to announce their safe arrival in London; and when she wrote again, Elizabeth hoped it would be in her power to say something of the Bingleys.

Her impatience for this second letter was as well rewarded as impatience generally is. Jane had been a week in town, without either seeing or hearing from Caroline. She accounted for it, however, by supposing that her last letter to her friend from Longbourn, had by some accident been lost.

'My aunt,' she continued, 'is going tomorrow into that part of the town, and I shall take the opportunity of calling in Grosvenor Street.'

She wrote again when the visit was paid, and she had seen Miss Bingley. 'I did

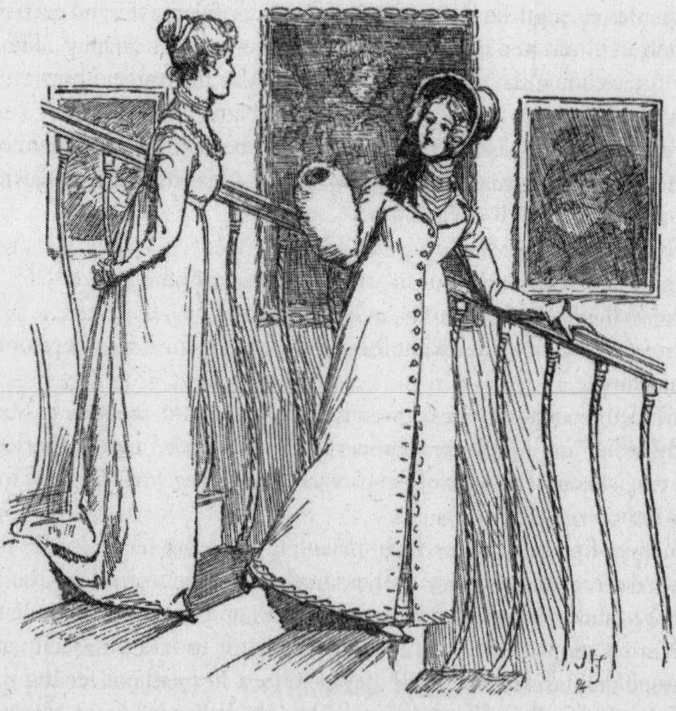

*Will you come and see me?*

not think Caroline in spirits,' were her words, 'but she was very glad to see me, and reproached me for giving her no notice of my coming to London. I was right, therefore; my last letter had never reached her. I enquired after their brother, of course. He was well, but so much engaged with Mr Darcy, that they scarcely ever saw him. I found that Miss Darcy was expected to dinner. I wish I could see her. My visit was not long, as Caroline and Mrs Hurst were going out. I dare say I shall soon see them here.'

Elizabeth shook her head over this letter. It convinced her, that accident only could discover to Mr Bingley her sister's being in town.

Four weeks passed away, and Jane saw nothing of him. She endeavoured to persuade herself that she did not regret it; but she could no longer be blind to Miss Bingley's inattention. After waiting at home every morning for a fortnight, and inventing every evening a fresh excuse for her, the visitor did at last appear; but the shortness of her stay, and yet more, the alteration of her manner, would allow Jane to deceive herself no longer. The letter which she wrote on this occasion to her sister, will prove what she felt.

My dearest Lizzy will, I am sure, be incapable of triumphing in her better judgment, at my expense, when I confess myself to have been entirely deceived in Miss Bingley's regard for me. But, my dear sister, though the event has proved you right, do not think me obstinate if I still assert, that, considering what her behaviour was, my confidence was as natural as your suspicion. I do not at all comprehend her reason for wishing to be intimate with me, but if the same circumstances were to happen again, I am sure I should be deceived again. Caroline did not return my visit till yesterday; and not a note, not a line, did I receive in the meantime. When she did come, it was very evident that she had no pleasure in it; she made a slight, formal, apology, for not calling before, said not a word of wishing to see me again, and was in every respect so altered a creature, that when she went away, I was perfectly resolved to continue the acquaintance no longer. I pity, though I cannot help blaming her. She was very wrong in singling me out as she did; I can safely say, that every advance to intimacy began on her side. But I pity her, because she must feel that she has been acting wrong, and because I am very sure that anxiety for her brother is the cause of it. I need not explain myself farther; and though *we* know this anxiety to be quite needless, yet if she feels it, it will easily account for her behaviour to me; and so deservedly dear as he is to his sister, whatever anxiety she may feel on his behalf, is natural and amiable. I cannot but wonder, however, at her having any such fears now, because, if he had at all cared about me, we must have met long, long ago. He knows of my being in town, I am certain, from something she said herself; and yet it should seem by her manner of talking, as if she wanted to persuade herself that he is really partial to Miss Darcy. I cannot understand it. If I were not afraid of judging harshly, I should be almost tempted to say, that there is a strong appearance of duplicity in all this. But I will endeavour to banish every painful thought, and think only of what will make me happy, your affection, and the invariable kindness of my dear uncle and aunt. Let me hear from you very soon. Miss Bingley said something of his never returning to Netherfield again, of giving up the house, but not with any certainty. We had better not mention it. I am extremely glad that you have such pleasant accounts from our friends at Hunsford. Pray go to see them, with Sir William and Maria. I am sure you will be very comfortable there.

Yours, &c.

This letter gave Elizabeth some pain; but her spirits returned as she considered that Jane would no longer be duped, by the sister at least. All expectation from the brother was now absolutely over. She would not even wish for any renewal of his attentions. His character sunk on every review of it; and as a punishment for him, as well as a possible advantage to Jane, she seriously hoped he might really soon marry Mr Darcy's sister, as, by Wickham's account, she would make him abundantly regret what he had thrown away.

Mrs Gardiner about this time reminded Elizabeth of her promise concerning that gentleman, and required information; and Elizabeth had such to send as might rather give contentment to her aunt than to herself. His apparent partiality had subsided, his attentions were over, he was the admirer of someone else. Elizabeth was watchful enough to see it all, but she could see it and write of it without material pain. Her heart had been but slightly touched, and her vanity was satisfied with believing that *she* would have been his only choice, had fortune permitted it. The sudden acquisition of ten thousand pounds was the most remarkable charm of the young lady, to whom he was now rendering himself agreeable; but Elizabeth, less clear-sighted perhaps in his case than in Charlotte's, did not quarrel with him for his wish of independence. Nothing, on the contrary, could be more natural; and while able to suppose that it cost him a few struggles to relinquish her, she was ready to allow it a wise and desirable measure for both, and could very sincerely wish him happy.

All this was acknowledged to Mrs Gardiner; and after relating the circumstances, she thus went on: – 'I am now convinced, my dear aunt, that I have never been much in love; for had I really experienced that pure and elevating passion, I should at present detest his very name, and wish him all manner of evil. But my feelings are not only cordial towards *him*; they are even impartial towards Miss King. I cannot find out that I hate her at all, or that I am in the least unwilling to think her a very good sort of girl. There can be no love in all this. My watchfulness has been effectual; and though I should certainly be a more interesting object to all my acquaintance, were I distractedly in love with him, I cannot say that I regret my comparative insignificance. Importance may sometimes be purchased too dearly. Kitty and Lydia take his defection much more to heart than I do. They are young in the ways of the world, and not yet open to the mortifying conviction that handsome young men must have something to live on, as well as the plain.'

## *Chapter 27*

With no greater events than these in the Longbourn family, and otherwise diversified by little beyond the walks to Meryton, sometimes dirty and sometimes cold, did January and February pass away. March was to take Elizabeth to Hunsford. She had not at first thought very seriously of going thither; but Charlotte, she soon found, was depending on the plan, and she gradually learned to consider it herself with greater pleasure as well as greater certainty. Absence had increased her desire of seeing Charlotte again, and weakened her disgust of Mr Collins. There was novelty in the scheme, and as, with such a mother and such uncompanionable sisters, home could not be faultless, a little change was not unwelcome for its own sake. The journey would moreover give her a peep at Jane; and, in short, as the time drew near, she would have been very sorry for any delay. Everything, however, went on smoothly, and was finally settled according to Charlotte's first sketch. She was to accompany Sir William and his second daughter. The improvement of spending a night in London was added in time, and the plan became perfect as plan could be.

The only pain was in leaving her father, who would certainly miss her, and who, when it came to the point, so little liked her going, that he told her to write to him, and almost promised to answer her letter.

The farewell between herself and Mr Wickham was perfectly friendly; on his side even more. His present pursuit could not make him forget that Elizabeth had been the first to excite and to deserve his attention, the first to listen and to pity, the first to be admired; and in his manner of bidding her adieu, wishing her every enjoyment, reminding her of what she was to expect in Lady Catherine de Bourgh, and trusting their opinion of her – their opinion of everybody – would always coincide, there was a solicitude, an interest which she felt must ever attach her to him with a most sincere regard; and she parted from him convinced, that whether married or single, he must always be her model of the amiable and pleasing.

Her fellow-travellers the next day, were not of a kind to make her think him less agreeable. Sir William Lucas, and his daughter Maria, a good-humoured girl, but as empty-headed as himself, had nothing to say that could be worth hearing, and were listened to with about as much delight as the rattle of the chaise. Elizabeth loved absurdities, but she had known Sir William's too long. He could tell her nothing new of the wonders of his presentation and knighthood; and his civilities were worn out like his information.

It was a journey of only twenty-four miles, and they began it so early as to be in Gracechurch Street by noon. As they drove to Mr Gardiner's door, Jane was at a drawing-room window watching their arrival; when they entered the passage she was there to welcome them, and Elizabeth, looking earnestly in her face, was pleased to see it healthful and lovely as ever. On the stairs were a troop of little boys and girls, whose eagerness for their cousin's appearance would not allow them to wait in the drawing-room, and whose shyness, as they had not seen her for a twelvemonth, prevented their coming lower. All was joy and kindness. The day passed most pleasantly away; the morning in bustle and shopping, and the evening at one of the theatres.

Elizabeth then contrived to sit by her aunt. Their first subject was her sister; and she was more grieved than astonished to hear, in reply to her minute enquiries, that though Jane always struggled to support her spirits, there were periods of dejection. It was reasonable, however, to hope, that they would not continue long. Mrs Gardiner gave her the particulars also of Miss Bingley's visit in Gracechurch Street, and repeated conversations occurring at different times between Jane and herself, which proved that the former had, from her heart, given up the acquaintance.

Mrs Gardiner then rallied her niece on Wickham's desertion, and complimented her on bearing it so well.

'But, my dear Elizabeth,' she added, 'what sort of girl is Miss King? I should be sorry to think our friend mercenary.'

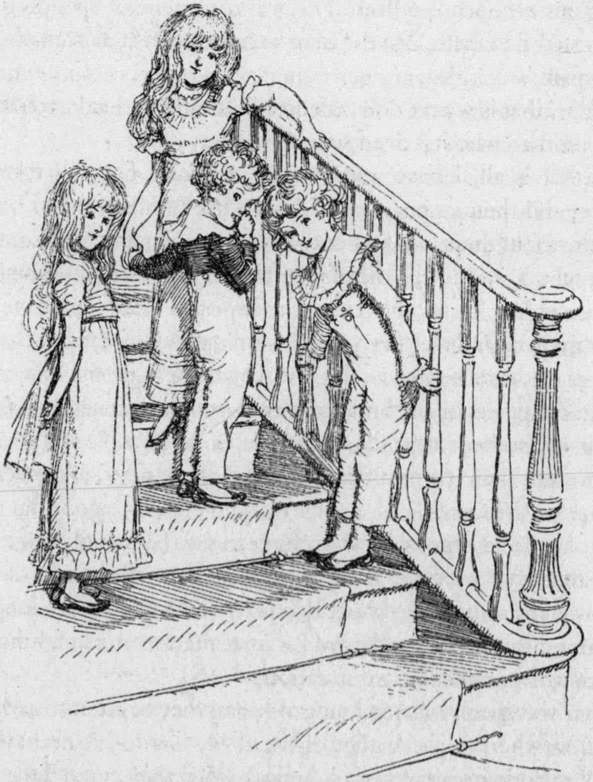

*On the stairs were a troop of little boys and girls*

'Pray, my dear aunt, what is the difference in matrimonial affairs, between the mercenary and the prudent motive? Where does discretion end, and avarice begin? Last Christmas you were afraid of his marrying me, because it would be imprudent; and now, because he is trying to get a girl with only ten thousand pounds, you want to find out that he is mercenary.'

'If you will only tell me what sort of girl Miss King is, I shall know what to think.'

'She is a very good kind of girl, I believe. I know no harm of her.'

'But he paid her not the smallest attention, till her grandfather's death made her mistress of this fortune.'

'No – why should he? If it was not allowable for him to gain *my* affections, because I had no money, what occasion could there be for making love to a girl whom he did not care about, and who was equally poor?'

'But there seems indelicacy in directing his attentions towards her, so soon after this event.'

'A man in distressed circumstances has not time for all those elegant decorums which other people may observe. If *she* does not object to it, why should *we*?'

'*Her* not objecting, does not justify *him*. It only shows her being deficient in something herself – sense or feeling.'

'Well,' cried Elizabeth, 'have it as you choose. *He* shall be mercenary, and *she* shall be foolish.'

'No, Lizzy, that is what I do *not* choose. I should be sorry, you know, to think ill of a young man who has lived so long in Derbyshire.'

'Oh! if that is all, I have a very poor opinion of young men who live in Derbyshire; and their intimate friends who live in Hertfordshire are not much better. I am sick of them all. Thank Heaven! I am going tomorrow where I shall find a man who has not one agreeable quality, who has neither manner nor sense to recommend him. Stupid men are the only ones worth knowing, after all.'

'Take care, Lizzy; that speech savours strongly of disappointment.'

Before they were separated by the conclusion of the play, she had the unexpected happiness of an invitation to accompany her uncle and aunt in a tour of pleasure which they proposed taking in the summer.

'We have not quite determined how far it shall carry us,' said Mrs Gardiner, 'but perhaps to the Lakes.'

No scheme could have been more agreeable to Elizabeth, and her acceptance of the invitation was most ready and grateful. 'My dear, dear aunt,' she rapturously cried, 'what delight! what felicity! You give me fresh life and vigour. Adieu to disappointment and spleen. What are men to rocks and mountains? Oh! what hours of transport we shall spend! And when we *do* return, it shall not be like other travellers, without being able to give one accurate idea of anything. We *will* know where we have gone – we *will* recollect what we have seen. Lakes, mountains, and rivers, shall not be jumbled together in our imaginations; nor, when we attempt to describe any particular scene, will we begin quarrelling about its relative situation. Let *our* first effusions be less insupportable than those of the generality of travellers.'

## *Chapter 28*

Every object in the next day's journey was new and interesting to Elizabeth; and her spirits were in a state for enjoyment; for she had seen her sister looking so well as to banish all fear for her health, and the prospect of her northern tour was a constant source of delight.

When they left the high road for the lane to Hunsford, every eye was in search of the Parsonage, and every turning expected to bring it in view. The paling of Rosings Park was their boundary on one side. Elizabeth smiled at the recollection of all that she had heard of its inhabitants.

At length the Parsonage was discernible. The garden sloping to the road, the house standing in it, the green pales and the laurel hedge, everything declared they were arriving. Mr Collins and Charlotte appeared at the door, and the carriage stopped at the small gate, which led by a short gravel walk to the house, amidst the nods and smiles of the whole party. In a moment they were all out of the chaise, rejoicing at the sight of each other. Mrs Collins welcomed her friend with the liveliest pleasure, and Elizabeth was more and more satisfied with coming, when she found herself so affectionately received. She saw instantly that her cousin's manners were not altered by his marriage; his formal civility was just what it had been, and he detained her some minutes at the gate to hear and satisfy his enquiries after all her family. They were then, with no other delay than his pointing out the neatness of the entrance, taken into the house; and as soon as they were in the parlour, he welcomed them a second time with ostentatious formality to his humble abode, and punctually repeated all his wife's offers of refreshment.

Elizabeth was prepared to see him in his glory; and he could not help fancying that in displaying the good proportion of the room, its aspect and its furniture, he addressed himself particularly to her, as if wishing to make her feel what she had lost in refusing him. But though everything seemed neat and comfortable, she was not able to gratify him by any sigh of repentance; and rather looked with wonder at her friend that she could have so cheerful an air, with such a companion. When Mr Collins said anything of which his wife might reasonably be ashamed, which certainly was not unseldom, she involuntarily turned her eye on Charlotte. Once or twice she could discern a faint blush; but in general Charlotte wisely did not hear. After sitting long enough to admire every article of furniture in the room, from the sideboard to the fender, to give an account of their journey and of all that had happened in London, Mr Collins invited them to take a stroll in the garden, which was large and well laid out, and to the cultivation of which he attended himself. To work in his garden was one of his most respectable pleasures; and Elizabeth admired the command of countenance with which Charlotte talked of the healthfulness of the exercise, and owned she encouraged it as much as possible. Here, leading the way through every walk and cross walk, and scarcely allowing them an interval to utter the praises he asked for, every view was pointed out with a minuteness which left beauty entirely behind. He could number the fields in every direction, and could tell how many trees there were in the most distant clump. But of all the views which his garden, or which the country, or the kingdom could boast, none were to be compared with the prospect of Rosings, afforded by an opening in the trees that bordered the park nearly opposite the front of his house. It was a handsome modern building, well situated on rising ground.

From his garden, Mr Collins would have led them round his two meadows, but the ladies not having shoes to encounter the remains of a white frost, turned back; and while Sir William accompanied him, Charlotte took her sister and friend over the house, extremely well pleased, probably, to have the opportunity of showing it without her husband's help. It was rather small, but well built and convenient; and everything was fitted up and arranged with a neatness and consistency of which Elizabeth gave Charlotte all the credit. When Mr Collins could be forgotten, there was really a great air of comfort throughout, and by Charlotte's evident enjoyment of it, Elizabeth supposed he must be often forgotten.

She had already learnt that Lady Catherine was still in the country. It was spoken of again while they were at dinner, when Mr Collins joining in, observed, 'Yes, Miss Elizabeth, you will have the honour of seeing Lady Catherine de Bourgh on the ensuing Sunday at church, and I need not say you will be delighted with her. She is all affability and condescension, and I doubt not but you will be honoured with some portion of her notice when service is over. I have scarcely any hesitation in saying that she will include you and my sister Maria in every invitation with which she honours us during your stay here. Her behaviour to my dear Charlotte is charming. We dine at Rosings twice every week, and are never allowed to walk home. Her ladyship's carriage is regularly ordered for us. I *should* say, one of her ladyship's carriages, for she has several.'

'Lady Catherine is a very respectable, sensible woman indeed,' added Charlotte, 'and a most attentive neighbour.'

'Very true, my dear, that is exactly what I say. She is the sort of woman whom one cannot regard with too much deference.'

The evening was spent chiefly in talking over Hertfordshire news, and telling again what had been already written; and when it closed, Elizabeth in the solitude of her chamber had to meditate upon Charlotte's degree of contentment, to understand her address in guiding, and composure in bearing with her husband, and to acknowledge that it was all done very well. She had also to anticipate how her visit would pass, the quiet tenor of their usual employments, the vexatious interruptions of Mr Collins, and the gaieties of their intercourse with Rosings. A lively imagination soon settled it all.

About the middle of the next day, as she was in her room getting ready for a walk, a sudden noise below seemed to speak the whole house in confusion; and after listening a moment, she heard somebody running upstairs in a violent hurry, and calling loudly after her. She opened the door, and met Maria in the landing place, who, breathless with agitation, cried out, 'Oh, my dear Eliza! pray make haste and come into the dining-room, for there is such a sight to be seen! I will not tell you what it is. Make haste, and come down this moment.'

Elizabeth asked questions in vain; Maria would tell her nothing more, and down they ran into the dining-room, which fronted the lane, in quest of this wonder; it was two ladies stopping in a low phaeton at the garden gate.

'And is this all?' cried Elizabeth. 'I expected at least that the pigs were got into the garden, and here is nothing but Lady Catherine and her daughter!'

'La! my dear,' said Maria quite shocked at the mistake, 'it is not Lady Catherine. The old lady is Mrs Jenkinson, who lives with them. The other is Miss de Bourgh. Only look at her. She is quite a little creature. Who would have thought she could be so thin and small!'

'She is abominably rude to keep Charlotte out of doors in all this wind. Why does she not come in?'

'Oh! Charlotte says, she hardly ever does. It is the greatest of favours when Miss de Bourgh comes in.'

'I like her appearance,' said Elizabeth, struck with other ideas. 'She looks sickly and cross. – Yes, she will do for him very well. She will make him a very proper wife.'

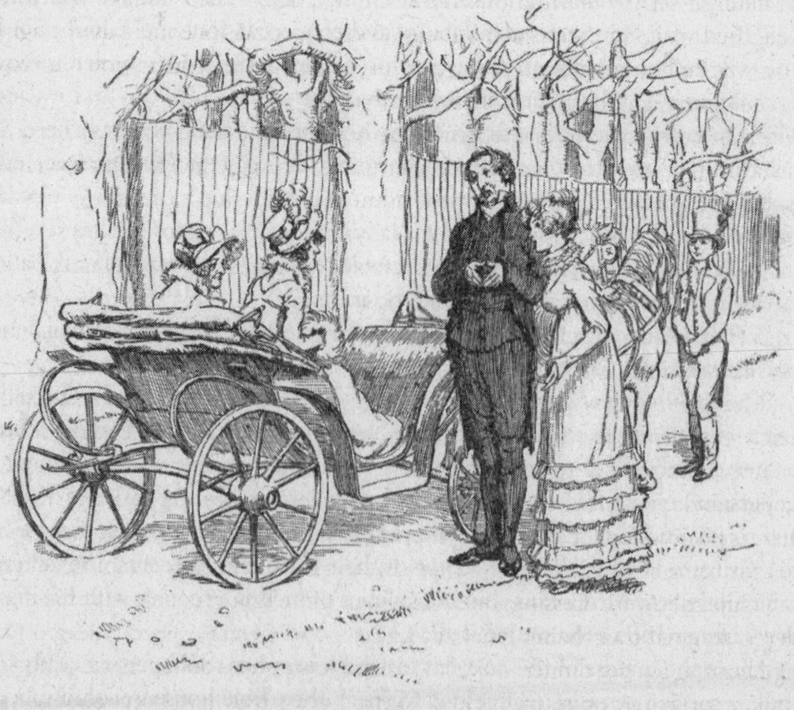

*In conversation with the ladies*

Mr Collins and Charlotte were both standing at the gate in conversation with the ladies; and Sir William, to Elizabeth's high diversion, was stationed in the doorway, in earnest contemplation of the greatness before him, and constantly bowing whenever Miss de Bourgh looked that way.

At length there was nothing more to be said; the ladies drove on, and the others returned into the house. Mr Collins no sooner saw the two girls than he began to congratulate them on their good fortune, which Charlotte explained by letting them know that the whole party was asked to dine at Rosings the next day.

## *Chapter 29*

Mr Collins's triumph in consequence of this invitation was complete. The power of displaying the grandeur of his patroness to his wondering visitors, and of letting them see her civility towards himself and his wife, was exactly what he had wished for; and that an opportunity of doing it should be given so soon, was such an instance of Lady Catherine's condescension as he knew not how to admire enough.

'I confess,' said he, 'that I should not have been at all surprised by her ladyship's asking us on Sunday to drink tea and spend the evening at Rosings. I rather expected, from my knowledge of her affability, that it would happen. But who could have foreseen such an attention as this? Who could have imagined that we should receive an invitation to dine there (an invitation moreover including the whole party) so immediately after your arrival!'

'I am the less surprised at what has happened,' replied Sir William, 'from that knowledge of what the manners of the great really are, which my situation in life has allowed me to acquire. About the Court, such instances of elegant breeding are not uncommon.'

Scarcely anything was talked of the whole day or next morning, but their visit to Rosings. Mr Collins was carefully instructing them in what they were to expect, that the sight of such rooms, so many servants, and so splendid a dinner might not wholly overpower them.

When the ladies were separating for the toilette, he said to Elizabeth, 'Do not make yourself uneasy, my dear cousin, about your apparel. Lady Catherine is far from requiring that elegance of dress in us, which becomes herself and daughter. I would advise you merely to put on whatever of your clothes is superior to the rest, there is no occasion for anything more. Lady Catherine will not think the worse of you for being simply dressed. She likes to have the distinction of rank preserved.'

While they were dressing, he came two or three times to their different doors, to recommend their being quick, as Lady Catherine very much objected to be kept waiting for her dinner. – Such formidable accounts of her ladyship, and her manner of living, quite frightened Maria Lucas, who had been little used to company, and she looked forward to her introduction at Rosings, with as much apprehension, as her father had done to his presentation at St James's.

As the weather was fine, they had a pleasant walk of about half a mile across the park. – Every park has its beauty and its prospects; and Elizabeth saw much to be pleased with, though she could not be in such raptures as Mr Collins expected the scene to inspire, and was but slightly affected by his enumeration of the windows in front of the house, and his relation of what the glazing altogether had originally cost Sir Lewis de Bourgh.

When they ascended the steps to the hall, Maria's alarm was every moment increasing, and even Sir William did not look perfectly calm. – Elizabeth's courage did not fail her. She had heard nothing of Lady Catherine that spoke her awful from any extraordinary talents or miraculous virtue, and the mere stateliness of money and rank, she thought she could witness without trepidation.

From the entrance hall, of which Mr Collins pointed out, with a rapturous air, the fine proportion and finished ornaments, they followed the servants through an antechamber, to the room where Lady Catherine, her daughter, and Mrs Jenkinson were sitting. – Her ladyship, with great condescension, arose to receive them; and as Mrs Collins had settled it with her husband that the office of introduction should be hers, it was performed in a proper manner, without any of those apologies and thanks which he would have thought necessary.

In spite of having been at St James's, Sir William was so completely awed, by the grandeur surrounding him, that he had but just courage enough to make a very low bow, and take his seat without saying a word; and his daughter, frightened almost out of her senses, sat on the edge of her chair, not knowing which way to look. Elizabeth found herself quite equal to the scene, and could observe the three ladies before her composedly. – Lady Catherine was a tall, large woman, with strongly-marked features, which might once have been handsome. Her air was not conciliating, nor was her manner of receiving them, such as to make her visitors forget their inferior rank. She was not rendered formidable by silence; but whatever she said, was spoken in so authoritative a tone, as marked her self-importance, and brought Mr Wickham immediately to Elizabeth's mind; and from the observation of the day altogether, she believed Lady Catherine to be exactly what he had represented.

When, after examining the mother, in whose countenance and deportment she soon found some resemblance of Mr Darcy, she turned her eyes on the daughter, she could almost have joined in Maria's astonishment, at her being so thin, and so small. There was neither in figure nor face, any likeness between the ladies. Miss de Bourgh was pale and sickly; her features, though not plain, were insignificant; and she spoke very little, except in a low voice, to Mrs Jenkinson, in whose appearance there was nothing remarkable, and who was entirely engaged in listening to what she said, and placing a screen in the proper direction before her eyes.

After sitting a few minutes, they were all sent to one of the windows, to admire the view, Mr Collins attending them to point out its beauties, and Lady Catherine kindly informing them that it was much better worth looking at in the summer.

The dinner was exceedingly handsome, and there were all the servants, and all the articles of plate which Mr Collins had promised; and, as he had likewise foretold, he took his seat at the bottom of the table, by her ladyship's desire, and looked as if he felt that life could furnish nothing greater. – He carved, and ate, and praised with delighted alacrity; and every dish was commended, first by him, and then by Sir William, who was now enough recovered to echo whatever his son-in-law said, in a manner which Elizabeth wondered Lady Catherine could bear. But Lady Catherine seemed gratified by their excessive admiration, and gave most gracious smiles, especially when any dish on the table proved a novelty to them. The party did not supply much conversation. Elizabeth was ready to speak whenever there was an opening, but she was seated between Charlotte and Miss de Bourgh – the former of whom was engaged in listening to Lady Catherine, and the latter said not a word to her all dinner time. Mrs Jenkinson was chiefly employed in watching how little Miss de Bourgh ate, pressing her to try some other dish, and fearing she were indisposed. Maria thought speaking out of the question, and the gentlemen did nothing but eat and admire.

When the ladies returned to the drawing-room, there was little to be done but to hear Lady Catherine talk, which she did without any intermission till coffee came in, delivering her opinion on every subject in so decisive a manner as proved that she was not used to have her judgment controverted. She enquired into Charlotte's domestic concerns familiarly and minutely, and gave her a great deal of advice, as to the management of them all; told her how everything ought to be regulated in so small a family as hers, and instructed her as to the care of her cows and her poultry. Elizabeth found that nothing was beneath this great lady's attention, which could furnish her with an occasion of dictating to others. In the intervals of her discourse with Mrs Collins, she addressed a variety of questions to Maria and Elizabeth, but especially to the latter, of whose connections she knew the least, and who she observed to Mrs Collins, was a very genteel, pretty kind of girl. She asked her at different times, how many sisters she had, whether they were older or younger than herself, whether any of them were likely to be married, whether they were handsome, where they had been educated, what carriage her father kept, and what had been her mother's maiden name? – Elizabeth felt all the impertinence of her questions, but answered them very composedly. – Lady Catherine then observed, 'Your father's estate is entailed on Mr Collins, I think. For your sake,' turning to Charlotte, 'I am glad of it; but otherwise I see no occasion for entailing estates from the female line. – It was not thought necessary in Sir Lewis de Bourgh's family. – Do you play and sing, Miss Bennet?'

'A little.'

'Oh! then – some time or other we shall be happy to hear you. Our instrument is a capital one, probably superior to – You shall try it someday. – Do your sisters play and sing?'

'One of them does.'

'Why did not you all learn? – You ought all to have learned. The Miss Webbs all play, and their father has not so good an income as yours. – Do you draw?'

'No, not at all.'

'What, none of you?'

'Not one.'

'That is very strange. But I suppose you had no opportunity. Your mother should have taken you to town every spring for the benefit of masters.'

'My mother would have had no objection, but my father hates London.'

'Has your governess left you?'

'We never had any governess.'

'No governess! How was that possible? Five daughters brought up at home without a governess! – I never heard of such a thing. Your mother must have been quite a slave to your education.'

Elizabeth could hardly help smiling, as she assured her that had not been the case.

'Then, who taught you? who attended to you? Without a governess you must have been neglected.'

'Compared with some families, I believe we were; but such of us as wished to learn, never wanted the means. We were always encouraged to read, and had all the masters that were necessary. Those who chose to be idle, certainly might.'

'Aye, no doubt; but that is what a governess will prevent, and if I had known your mother, I should have advised her most strenuously to engage one. I always say that nothing is to be done in education without steady and regular instruction, and nobody but a governess can give it. It is wonderful how many families I have been the means of supplying in that way. I am always glad to get a young person well placed out. Four nieces of Mrs Jenkinson are most delightfully situated through my means; and it was but the other day, that I recommended another young person, who was merely accidentally mentioned to me, and the family are quite delighted with her. Mrs Collins, did I tell you of Lady Metcalfe's calling yesterday to thank me? She finds Miss Pope a treasure. "Lady Catherine," said she, "you have given me a treasure." Are any of your younger sisters out, Miss Bennet?'

'Yes, Ma'am, all.'

'All! – What, all five out at once? Very odd! – And you only the second. – The younger ones out before the elder are married! – Your younger sisters must be very young?'

'Yes, my youngest is not sixteen. Perhaps *she* is full young to be much in company. But really, Ma'am, I think it would be very hard upon younger sisters, that they should not have their share of society and amusement because the elder may not have the means or inclination to marry early. – The last born has as good a right to the pleasures of youth, as the first. And to be kept back on *such* a motive! – I think it would not be very likely to promote sisterly affection or delicacy of mind.'

'Upon my word,' said her ladyship, 'you give your opinion very decidedly for so young a person. – Pray, what is your age?'

'With three younger sisters grown up,' replied Elizabeth smiling, 'your ladyship can hardly expect me to own it.'

Lady Catherine seemed quite astonished at not receiving a direct answer; and Elizabeth suspected herself to be the first creature who had ever dared to trifle with so much dignified impertinence.

'You cannot be more than twenty, I am sure, therefore you need not conceal your age.'

'I am not one and twenty.'

When the gentlemen had joined them, and tea was over, the card-tables were placed. Lady Catherine, Sir William, and Mr and Mrs Collins sat down to quadrille; and as Miss de Bourgh chose to play at casino, the two girls had the honour of assisting Mrs Jenkinson to make up her party. Their table was superlatively stupid. Scarcely a syllable was uttered that did not relate to the game, except when Mrs Jenkinson expressed her fears of Miss de Bourgh's being too hot or too cold, or having too much or too little light. A great deal more passed at the other table. Lady Catherine was generally speaking – stating the mistakes of the three others, or relating some anecdote of herself. Mr Collins was employed in agreeing to everything her ladyship said, thanking her for every fish he won, and apologising if he thought he won too many. Sir William did not say much. He was storing his memory with anecdotes and noble names.

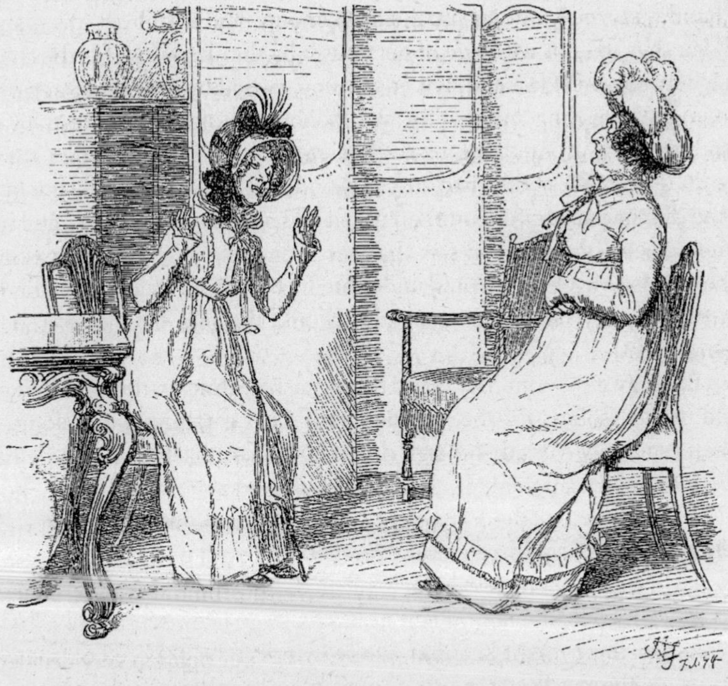

*'Lady Catherine,' said she, 'you have given me a treasure'*

When Lady Catherine and her daughter had played as long as they chose, the tables were broke up, the carriage was offered to Mrs Collins, gratefully accepted, and immediately ordered. The party then gathered round the fire to hear Lady Catherine determine what weather they were to have on the morrow. From these instructions they were summoned by the arrival of the coach, and with many speeches of thankfulness on Mr Collins's side, and as many bows on Sir William's, they departed. As soon as they had driven from the door, Elizabeth was called on by her cousin, to give her opinion of all that she had seen at Rosings, which, for Charlotte's sake, she made more favourable than it really was. But her commendation, though costing her some trouble, could by no means satisfy Mr Collins, and he was very soon obliged to take her ladyship's praise into his own hands.

## *Chapter 30*

Sir William stayed only a week at Hunsford; but his visit was long enough to convince him of his daughter's being most comfortably settled, and of her possessing such a husband and such a neighbour as were not often met with. While Sir William was with them, Mr Collins devoted his mornings to driving him out in his gig, and showing him the country; but when he went away, the whole family returned to their usual employments, and Elizabeth was thankful to find that they did not see more of her cousin by the alteration, for the chief of the time between breakfast and dinner was now passed by him either at work in the garden, or in reading and writing, and looking out of the window in his own book-room, which fronted the road. The room in which the ladies sat was backwards. Elizabeth at first had rather wondered that Charlotte should not prefer the dining-parlour for common use; it was a better-sized room, and had a pleasanter aspect; but she soon saw that her friend had an excellent reason for what she did, for Mr Collins would undoubtedly have been much less in his own apartment, had they sat in one equally lively; and she gave Charlotte credit for the arrangement.

From the drawing-room they could distinguish nothing in the lane, and were indebted to Mr Collins for the knowledge of what carriages went along, and how often especially Miss de Bourgh drove by in her phaeton, which he never failed coming to inform them of, though it happened almost every day. She not unfrequently stopped at the Parsonage, and had a few minutes' conversation with Charlotte, but was scarcely ever prevailed on to get out.

Very few days passed in which Mr Collins did not walk to Rosings, and not many in which his wife did not think it necessary to go likewise; and till Elizabeth recollected that there might be other family livings to be disposed of, she could not understand the sacrifice of so many hours. Now and then, they were honoured with a call from her ladyship, and nothing escaped her observation that was passing in the room during these visits. She examined into their employments, looked at their work, and advised them to do it differently; found fault with the arrangement of the furniture, or detected the housemaid in negligence; and if she accepted any refreshment, seemed to do it only for the sake of finding out that Mrs Collins's joints of meat were too large for her family.

Elizabeth soon perceived that though this great lady was not in the commission of the peace for the county, she was a most active magistrate in her own parish, the minutest concerns of which were carried to her by Mr Collins; and whenever any of the cottagers were disposed to be quarrelsome, discontented or too poor, she sallied forth into the village to settle their differences, silence their complaints, and scold them into harmony and plenty.

The entertainment of dining at Rosings was repeated about twice a week; and, allowing for the loss of Sir William, and there being only one card-table in the evening, every such entertainment was the counterpart of the first. Their other engagements were few; as the style of living of the neighbourhood in general, was beyond the Collinses' reach. This however was no evil to Elizabeth, and upon the whole she spent her time comfortably enough; there were half-

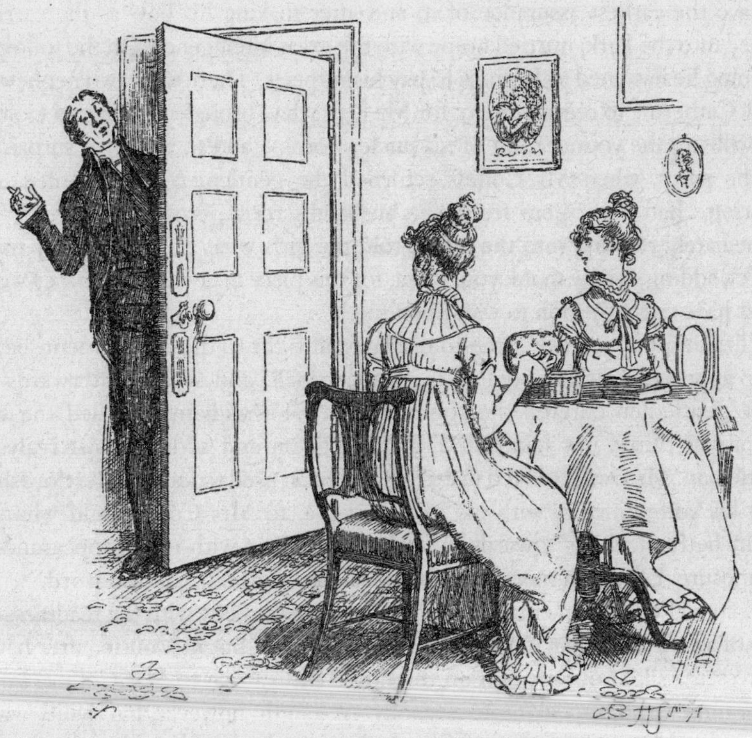

*He never failed coming to inform them*

hours of pleasant conversation with Charlotte, and the weather was so fine for the time of year, that she had often great enjoyment out of doors. Her favourite walk, and where she frequently went while the others were calling on Lady Catherine, was along the open grove which edged that side of the park, where there was a nice sheltered path, which no one seemed to value but herself, and where she felt beyond the reach of Lady Catherine's curiosity.

In this quiet way, the first fortnight of her visit soon passed away. Easter was approaching, and the week preceding it, was to bring an addition to the family at Rosings, which in so small a circle must be important. Elizabeth had heard soon after her arrival, that Mr Darcy was expected there in the course of a few weeks, and though there were not many of her acquaintance whom she did not prefer, his coming would furnish one comparatively new to look at in their Rosings parties, and she might be amused in seeing how hopeless Miss Bingley's designs on him were, by his behaviour to his cousin, for whom he was evidently destined by Lady Catherine; who talked of his coming with the greatest satisfaction, spoke of him in terms of the highest admiration, and seemed almost angry to find that he had already been frequently seen by Miss Lucas and herself.

His arrival was soon known at the Parsonage, for Mr Collins was walking the whole morning within view of the lodges opening into Hunsford Lane, in order to have the earliest assurance of it; and after making his bow as the carriage turned into the Park, hurried home with the great intelligence. On the following morning he hastened to Rosings to pay his respects. There were two nephews of Lady Catherine to require them, for Mr Darcy had brought with him a Colonel Fitzwilliam, the younger son of his uncle, Lord — and to the great surprise of all the party, when Mr Collins returned the gentlemen accompanied him. Charlotte had seen them from her husband's room, crossing the road, and immediately running into the other, told the girls what an honour they might expect, adding, 'I may thank you, Eliza, for this piece of civility. Mr Darcy would never have come so soon to wait upon me.'

Elizabeth had scarcely time to disclaim all right to the compliment, before their approach was announced by the doorbell, and shortly afterwards the three gentlemen entered the room. Colonel Fitzwilliam, who led the way, was about thirty, not handsome, but in person and address most truly the gentleman. Mr Darcy looked just as he had been used to look in Hertfordshire, paid his compliments, with his usual reserve, to Mrs Collins; and whatever might be his feelings towards her friend, met her with every appearance of composure. Elizabeth merely curtseyed to him, without saying a word.

Colonel Fitzwilliam entered into conversation directly with the readiness and ease of a well-bred man, and talked very pleasantly; but his cousin, after having addressed a slight observation on the house and garden to Mrs Collins, sat for some time without speaking to anybody. At length, however, his civility was so far awakened as to enquire of Elizabeth after the health of her family. She answered him in the usual way, and after a moment's pause, added, 'My eldest sister has been in town these three months. Have you never happened to see her there?'

She was perfectly sensible that he never had; but she wished to see whether he would betray any consciousness of what had passed between the Bingleys and Jane; and she thought he looked a little confused as he answered that he had never been so fortunate as to meet Miss Bennet. The subject was pursued no farther, and the gentlemen soon afterwards went away.

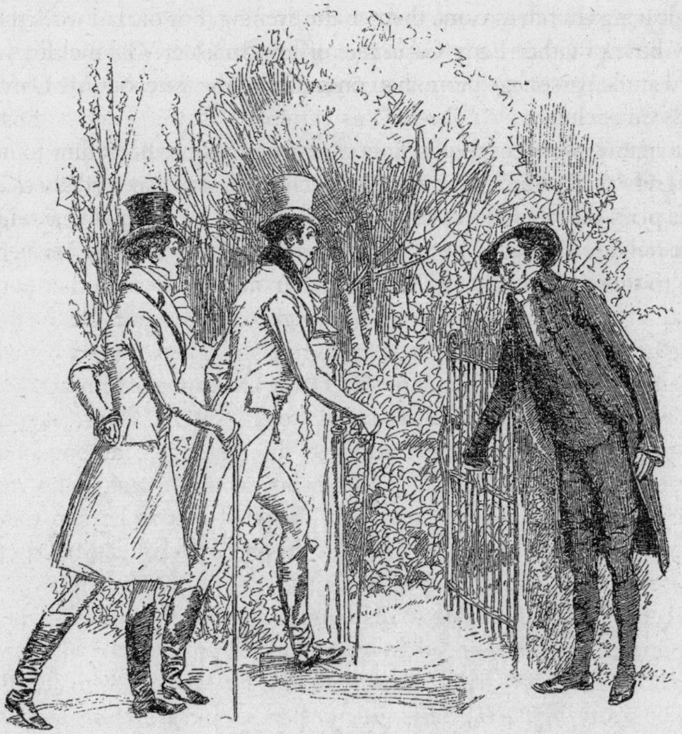

*The gentlemen accompanied him*

# *Chapter 31*

Colonel Fitzwilliam's manners were very much admired at the parsonage, and the ladies all felt that he must add considerably to the pleasure of their engagements at Rosings. It was some days, however, before they received any invitation thither, for while there were visitors in the house, they could not be necessary; and it was not till Easter Day, almost a week after the gentlemen's arrival, that they were honoured by such an attention, and then they were merely asked on leaving church to come there in the evening. For the last week they had seen very little of either Lady Catherine or her daughter. Colonel Fitzwilliam had called at the parsonage more than once during the time, but Mr Darcy they had only seen at church.

The invitation was accepted of course, and at a proper hour they joined the party in Lady Catherine's drawing-room. Her ladyship received them civilly, but it was plain that their company was by no means so acceptable as when she could get nobody else; and she was, in fact, almost engrossed by her nephews, speaking to them, especially to Darcy, much more than to any other person in the room.

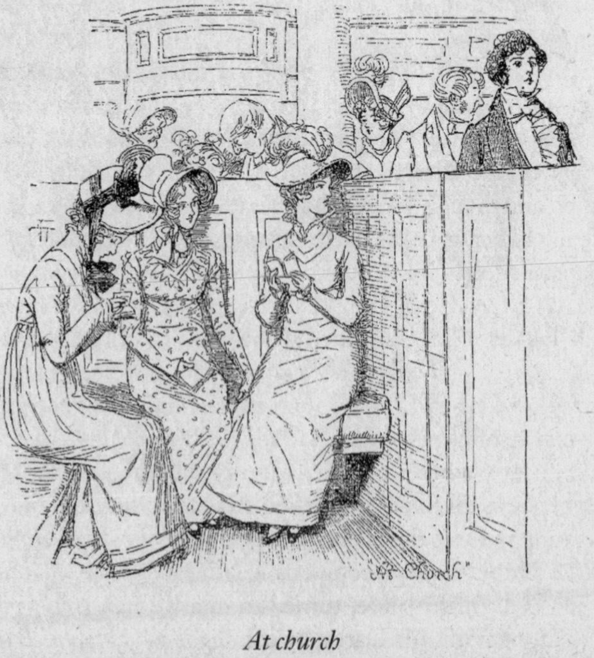


*At church*

Colonel Fitzwilliam seemed really glad to see them; anything was a welcome relief to him at Rosings; and Mrs Collins's pretty friend had moreover caught his fancy very much. He now seated himself by her, and talked so agreeably of Kent and Hertfordshire, of travelling and staying at home, of new books and music, that Elizabeth had never been half so well entertained in that room before; and they conversed with so much spirit and flow, as to draw the attention of Lady Catherine herself, as well as of Mr Darcy. *His* eyes had been soon and repeatedly turned towards them with a look of curiosity; and that her ladyship after a while shared the feeling, was more openly acknowledged, for she did not scruple to call out, 'What is that you are saying, Fitzwilliam? What is it you are talking of? What are you telling Miss Bennet? Let me hear what it is.'

'We are speaking of music, Madam,' said he, when no longer able to avoid a reply.

'Of music! Then pray speak aloud. It is of all subjects my delight. I must have my share in the conversation, if you are speaking of music. There are few people in England, I suppose, who have more true enjoyment of music than myself, or a better natural taste. If I had ever learnt, I should have been a great proficient. And so would Anne, if her health had allowed her to apply. I am confident that she would have performed delightfully. How does Georgiana get on, Darcy?'

Mr Darcy spoke with affectionate praise of his sister's proficiency.

'I am very glad to hear such a good account of her,' said Lady Catherine; 'and pray tell her from me, that she cannot expect to excel, if she does not practise a great deal.'

'I assure you, Madam,' he replied, 'that she does not need such advice. She practises very constantly.'

'So much the better. It cannot be done too much; and when I next write to her, I shall charge her not to neglect it on any account. I often tell young ladies, that no excellence in music is to be acquired, without constant practice. I have told Miss Bennet several times, that she will never play really well, unless she practises more; and though Mrs Collins has no instrument, she is very welcome, as I have often told her, to come to Rosings every day, and play on the pianoforte in Mrs Jenkinson's room. She would be in nobody's way, you know, in that part of the house.'

Mr Darcy looked a little ashamed of his aunt's ill breeding, and made no answer.

When coffee was over, Colonel Fitzwilliam reminded Elizabeth of having promised to play to him; and she sat down directly to the instrument. He drew a chair near her. Lady Catherine listened to half a song, and then talked, as before, to her other nephew; till the latter walked away from her, and moving with his usual deliberation towards the pianoforte, stationed himself so as to command a full view of the fair performer's countenance. Elizabeth saw what he was doing, and at the first convenient pause, turned to him with an arch smile, and said, 'You mean to frighten me, Mr Darcy, by coming in all this state to hear me? But I will not be alarmed though your sister *does* play so well. There is a stubbornness about me that never can bear to be frightened at the will of others. My courage always rises with every attempt to intimidate me.'

'I shall not say that you are mistaken,' he replied, 'because you could not really believe me to entertain any design of alarming you; and I have had the pleasure of your acquaintance long enough to know, that you find great enjoyment in occasionally professing opinions which in fact are not your own.'

Elizabeth laughed heartily at this picture of herself, and said to Colonel Fitzwilliam, 'Your cousin will give you a very pretty notion of me, and teach you not to believe a word I say. I am particularly unlucky in meeting with a person so well able to expose my real character, in a part of the world, where I had hoped to pass myself off with some degree of credit. Indeed, Mr Darcy, it is very ungenerous in you to mention all that you knew to my disadvantage in Hertfordshire – and, give me leave to say, very impolitic too – for it is provoking me to retaliate, and such things may come out, as will shock your relations to hear.'

'I am not afraid of you,' said he, smilingly.

'Pray let me hear what you have to accuse him of,' cried Colonel Fitzwilliam. 'I should like to know how he behaves among strangers.'

'You shall hear then – but prepare yourself for something very dreadful. The first time of my ever seeing him in Hertfordshire, you must know, was at a ball – and at this ball, what do you think he did? He danced only four dances! I am sorry to pain you – but so it was. He danced only four dances, though gentlemen were scarce; and, to my certain knowledge, more than one young lady was sitting down in want of a partner. Mr Darcy, you cannot deny the fact.'

'I had not at that time the honour of knowing any lady in the assembly beyond my own party.'

'True; and nobody can ever be introduced in a ballroom. Well, Colonel Fitzwilliam, what do I play next? My fingers wait your orders.'

'Perhaps,' said Darcy, 'I should have judged better, had I sought an introduction, but I am ill qualified to recommend myself to strangers.'

'Shall we ask your cousin the reason of this?' said Elizabeth, still addressing Colonel Fitzwilliam. 'Shall we ask him why a man of sense and education, and who has lived in the world, is ill qualified to recommend himself to strangers?'

'I can answer your question,' said Fitzwilliam, 'without applying to him. It is because he will not give himself the trouble.'

'I certainly have not the talent which some people possess,' said Darcy, 'of conversing easily with those I have never seen before. I cannot catch their tone of conversation, or appear interested in their concerns, as I often see done.'

'My fingers,' said Elizabeth, 'do not move over this instrument in the masterly manner which I see so many women's do. They have not the same force or rapidity, and do not produce the same expression. But then I have always supposed it to be my own fault – because I would not take the trouble of practising. It is not that I do not believe *my* fingers as capable as any other woman's of superior execution.'

Darcy smiled and said, 'You are perfectly right. You have employed your time much better. No one admitted to the privilege of hearing you, can think anything wanting. We neither of us perform to strangers.'

Here they were interrupted by Lady Catherine, who called out to know what they were talking of. Elizabeth immediately began playing again. Lady Catherine approached, and, after listening for a few minutes, said to Darcy, 'Miss Bennet would not play at all amiss, if she practised more, and could have the advantage of a London master. She has a very good notion of fingering, though her taste is not equal to Anne's. Anne would have been a delightful performer, had her health allowed her to learn.'

Elizabeth looked at Darcy to see how cordially he assented to his cousin's praise; but neither at that moment nor at any other could she discern any symptom of love; and from the whole of his behaviour to Miss de Bourgh she derived this comfort for Miss Bingley, that he might have been just as likely to marry *her*, had she been his relation.

Lady Catherine continued her remarks on Elizabeth's performance, mixing with them many instructions on execution and taste. Elizabeth received them with all the forbearance of civility; and at the request of the gentlemen remained at the instrument till her ladyship's carriage was ready to take them all home.

## *Chapter 32*

Elizabeth was sitting by herself the next morning, and writing to Jane, while Mrs Collins and Maria were gone on business into the village, when she was startled by a ring at the door, the certain signal of a visitor. As she had heard no carriage, she thought it not unlikely to be Lady Catherine, and under that apprehension was putting away her half-finished letter that she might escape all impertinent questions, when the door opened, and to her very great surprise, Mr Darcy, and Mr Darcy only, entered the room.

He seemed astonished too on finding her alone, and apologised for his intrusion, by letting her know that he had understood all the ladies to be within.

They then sat down, and when her enquiries after Rosings were made, seemed in danger of sinking into total silence. It was absolutely necessary, therefore, to think of something, and in this emergence recollecting *when* she had seen him last in Hertfordshire, and feeling curious to know what he would say on the subject of their hasty departure, she observed, 'How very suddenly you all quitted Netherfield last November, Mr Darcy! It must have been a most agreeable surprise to Mr Bingley to see you all after him so soon; for, if I recollect right, he went but the day before. He and his sisters were well, I hope, when you left London.'

'Perfectly so – I thank you.'

She found that she was to receive no other answer – and, after a short pause, added, 'I think I have understood that Mr Bingley has not much idea of ever returning to Netherfield again?'

'I have never heard him say so; but it is probable that he may spend very little of his time there in future. He has many friends, and he is at a time of life when friends and engagements are continually increasing.'

'If he means to be but little at Netherfield, it would be better for the neighbourhood that he should give up the place entirely, for then we might possibly get a settled family there. But perhaps Mr Bingley did not take the house so much for the convenience of the neighbourhood as for his own, and we must expect him to keep or quit it on the same principle.'

'I should not be surprised,' said Darcy, 'if he were to give it up, as soon as any eligible purchase offers.'

Elizabeth made no answer. She was afraid of talking longer of his friend; and, having nothing else to say, was now determined to leave the trouble of finding a subject to him.

He took the hint, and soon began with, 'This seems a very comfortable house. Lady Catherine, I believe, did a great deal to it when Mr Collins first came to Hunsford.'

'I believe she did – and I am sure she could not have bestowed her kindness on a more grateful object.'

'Mr Collins appears very fortunate in his choice of a wife.'

'Yes, indeed; his friends may well rejoice in his having met with one of the very few sensible women who would have accepted him, or have made him happy if they had. My friend has an excellent understanding – though I am not certain that I consider her marrying Mr Collins as the wisest thing she ever did. She seems perfectly happy, however, and in a prudential light, it is certainly a very good match for her.'

'It must be very agreeable to her to be settled within so easy a distance of her own family and friends.'

'An easy distance do you call it? It is nearly fifty miles.'

'And what is fifty miles of good road? Little more than half a day's journey. Yes, I call it a *very* easy distance.'

'I should never have considered the distance as one of the *advantages* of the match,' cried Elizabeth. 'I should never have said Mrs Collins was settled *near* her family.'

'It is a proof of your own attachment to Hertfordshire. Anything beyond the very neighbourhood of Longbourn, I suppose, would appear far.'

As he spoke there was a sort of smile, which Elizabeth fancied she understood; he must be supposing her to be thinking of Jane and Netherfield, and she blushed as she answered, 'I do not mean to say that a woman may not be settled too near her family. The far and the near must be relative, and depend on many varying circumstances. Where there is fortune to make the expense of travelling unimportant, distance becomes no evil. But that is not the case *here*. Mr and Mrs Collins have a comfortable income, but not such a one as will allow of frequent journeys – and I am persuaded my friend would not call herself *near* her family under less than *half* the present distance.'

Mr Darcy drew his chair a little towards her, and said, '*You* cannot have a right to such very strong local attachment. *You* cannot have been always at Longbourn.'

Elizabeth looked surprised. The gentleman experienced some change of feeling; he drew back his chair, took a newspaper from the table, and, glancing over it, said, in a colder voice, 'Are you pleased with Kent?'

A short dialogue on the subject of the country ensued, on either side calm and concise – and soon put an end to by the entrance of Charlotte and her sister, just returned from their walk. The tête-à-tête surprised them. Mr Darcy related the mistake which had occasioned his intruding on Miss Bennet, and after sitting a few minutes longer without saying much to anybody, went away.

'What can be the meaning of this!' said Charlotte, as soon as he was gone. 'My dear Eliza, he must be in love with you, or he would never have called on us in this familiar way.'

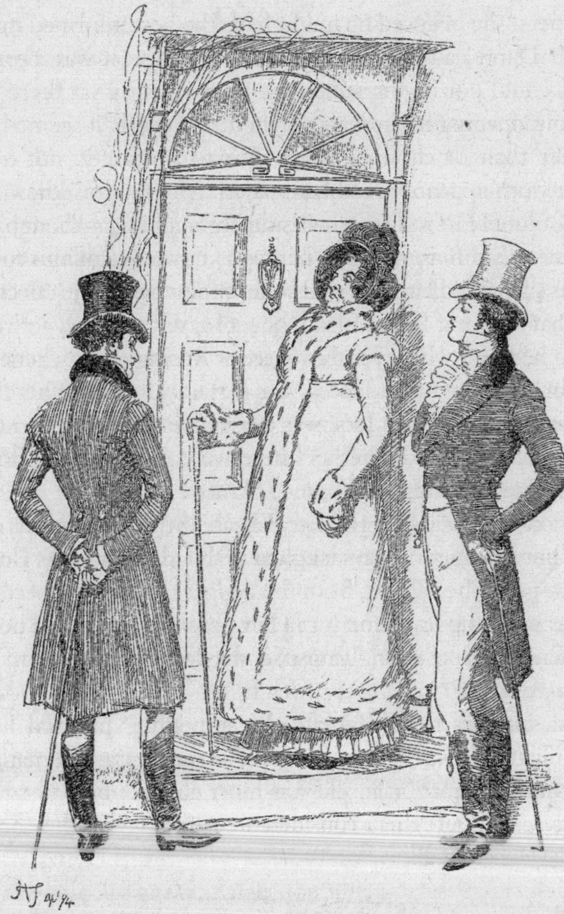

*Now and then accompanied by their aunt*

But when Elizabeth told of his silence, it did not seem very likely, even to Charlotte's wishes, to be the case; and after various conjectures, they could at last only suppose his visit to proceed from the difficulty of finding anything to do, which was the more probable from the time of year. All field sports were over. Within doors there was Lady Catherine, books, and a billiard-table, but gentlemen cannot be always within doors; and in the nearness of the Parsonage, or the pleasantness of the walk to it, or of the people who lived in it, the two cousins found a temptation from this period of walking thither almost every day. They called at various times of the morning, sometimes separately, sometimes together, and now and then accompanied by their aunt. It was plain to them all that Colonel Fitzwilliam came because he had pleasure in their society, a persuasion which of course recommended him still more; and Elizabeth was reminded by her own satisfaction in being with him, as well as by his evident admiration of her, of her former favourite George Wickham; and though, in comparing them, she saw there was less captivating softness in Colonel Fitzwilliam's manners, she believed he might have the best informed mind.

But why Mr Darcy came so often to the Parsonage, it was more difficult to understand. It could not be for society, as he frequently sat there ten minutes together without opening his lips; and when he did speak, it seemed the effect of necessity rather than of choice – a sacrifice to propriety, not a pleasure to himself. He seldom appeared really animated. Mrs Collins knew not what to make of him. Colonel Fitzwilliam's occasionally laughing at his stupidity, proved that he was generally different, which her own knowledge of him could not have told her; and as she would have liked to believe this change the effect of love, and the object of that love, her friend Eliza, she set herself seriously to work to find it out. – She watched him whenever they were at Rosings, and whenever he came to Hunsford; but without much success. He certainly looked at her friend a great deal, but the expression of that look was disputable. It was an earnest, steadfast gaze, but she often doubted whether there were much admiration in it, and sometimes it seemed nothing but absence of mind.

She had once or twice suggested to Elizabeth the possibility of his being partial to her, but Elizabeth always laughed at the idea; and Mrs Collins did not think it right to press the subject, from the danger of raising expectations which might only end in disappointment; for in her opinion it admitted not of a doubt, that all her friend's dislike would vanish, if she could suppose him to be in her power.

In her kind schemes for Elizabeth, she sometimes planned her marrying Colonel Fitzwilliam. He was beyond comparison the pleasantest man; he certainly admired her, and his situation in life was most eligible; but, to counterbalance these advantages, Mr Darcy had considerable patronage in the church, and his cousin could have none at all.

# Chapter 33

More than once did Elizabeth in her ramble within the Park, unexpectedly meet Mr Darcy. – She felt all the perverseness of the mischance that should bring him where no one else was brought; and to prevent its ever happening again, took care to inform him at first, that it was a favourite haunt of hers. – How it could occur a second time therefore was very odd! – Yet it did, and even a third. It seemed like wilful ill-nature, or a voluntary penance, for on these occasions it was not merely a few formal enquiries and an awkward pause and then away, but he actually thought it necessary to turn back and walk with her. He never said a great deal, nor did she give herself the trouble of talking or of listening much; but it struck her in the course of their third rencontre that he was asking some odd unconnected questions – about her pleasure in being at Hunsford, her love of solitary walks, and her opinion of Mr and Mrs Collins's happiness; and that in speaking of Rosings and her not perfectly understanding the house, he seemed to expect that whenever she came into Kent again she would be staying *there* too. His words seemed to imply it. Could he have Colonel Fitzwilliam in his thoughts? She supposed, if he meant anything, he must mean an allusion to what might arise in that quarter. It distressed her a little, and she was quite glad to find herself at the gate in the pales opposite the Parsonage.

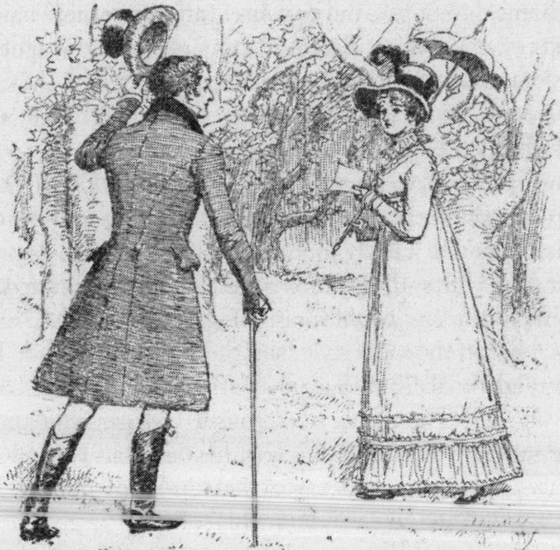

*She saw on looking up that Colonel Fitzwilliam was meeting her*

She was engaged one day as she walked, in reperusing Jane's last letter, and dwelling on some passages which proved that Jane had not written in spirits, when, instead of being again surprised by Mr Darcy, she saw on looking up that Colonel Fitzwilliam was meeting her. Putting away the letter immediately and forcing a smile, she said, 'I did not know before that you ever walked this way.'

'I have been making the tour of the Park,' he replied, 'as I generally do every year, and intend to close it with a call at the Parsonage. Are you going much farther?'

'No, I should have turned in a moment.'

And accordingly she did turn, and they walked towards the Parsonage together.

'Do you certainly leave Kent on Saturday?' said she.

'Yes – if Darcy does not put it off again. But I am at his disposal. He arranges the business just as he pleases.'

'And if not able to please himself in the arrangement, he has at least great pleasure in the power of choice. I do not know anybody who seems more to enjoy the power of doing what he likes than Mr Darcy.'

'He likes to have his own way very well,' replied Colonel Fitzwilliam. 'But so we all do. It is only that he has better means of having it than many others, because he is rich, and many others are poor. I speak feelingly. A younger son, you know, must be inured to self-denial and dependence.'

'In my opinion, the younger son of an Earl can know very little of either. Now, seriously, what have you ever known of self-denial and dependence? When have you been prevented by want of money from going wherever you chose, or procuring anything you had a fancy for?'

'These are home questions – and perhaps I cannot say that I have experienced many hardships of that nature. But in matters of greater weight, I may suffer from the want of money. Younger sons cannot marry where they like.'

'Unless where they like women of fortune, which I think they very often do.'

'Our habits of expense make us too dependant, and there are not many in my rank of life who can afford to marry without some attention to money.'

'Is this,' thought Elizabeth, 'meant for me?' and she coloured at the idea; but, recovering herself, said in a lively tone, 'And pray, what is the usual price of an Earl's younger son? Unless the elder brother is very sickly, I suppose you would not ask above fifty thousand pounds.'

He answered her in the same style, and the subject dropped. To interrupt a silence which might make him fancy her affected with what had passed, she soon afterwards said, 'I imagine your cousin brought you down with him chiefly for the sake of having somebody at his disposal. I wonder he does not marry, to secure a lasting convenience of that kind. But, perhaps his sister does as well for the present, and, as she is under his sole care, he may do what he likes with her.'

'No,' said Colonel Fitzwilliam, 'that is an advantage which he must divide with me. I am joined with him in the guardianship of Miss Darcy.'

'Are you, indeed? And pray what sort of guardians do you make? Does your charge give you much trouble? Young ladies of her age, are sometimes a little difficult to manage, and if she has the true Darcy spirit, she may like to have her own way.'

As she spoke, she observed him looking at her earnestly, and the manner in which he immediately asked her why she supposed Miss Darcy likely to give them any uneasiness, convinced her that she had somehow or other got pretty near the truth. She directly replied, 'You need not be frightened. I never heard any harm of her; and I dare say she is one of the most tractable creatures in the world. She is a very great favourite with some ladies of my acquaintance, Mrs Hurst and Miss Bingley. I think I have heard you say that you know them.'

'I know them a little. Their brother is a pleasant gentlemanlike man – he is a great friend of Darcy's.'

'Oh! yes,' said Elizabeth drily – 'Mr Darcy is uncommonly kind to Mr Bingley, and takes a prodigious deal of care of him.'

'Care of him! – Yes, I really believe Darcy *does* take care of him in those points where he most wants care. From something that he told me in our journey hither, I have reason to think Bingley very much indebted to him. But I ought to beg his pardon, for I have no right to suppose that Bingley was the person meant. It was all conjecture.'

'What is it you mean?'

'It is a circumstance which Darcy of course would not wish to be generally known, because if it were to get round to the lady's family, it would be an unpleasant thing.'

'You may depend upon my not mentioning it.'

'And remember that I have not much reason for supposing it to be Bingley. What he told me was merely this; that he congratulated himself on having lately saved a friend from the inconveniences of a most imprudent marriage, but without mentioning names or any other particulars, and I only suspected it to be Bingley from believing him the kind of young man to get into a scrape of that sort, and from knowing them to have been together the whole of last summer.'

'Did Mr Darcy give you his reasons for this interference?'

'I understood that there were some very strong objections against the lady.'

'And what arts did he use to separate them?'

'He did not talk to me of his own arts,' said Fitzwilliam smiling. 'He only told me, what I have now told you.'

Elizabeth made no answer, and walked on, her heart swelling with indignation. After watching her a little, Fitzwilliam asked her why she was so thoughtful.

'I am thinking of what you have been telling me,' said she. 'Your cousin's conduct does not suit my feelings. Why was he to be the judge?'

'You are rather disposed to call his interference officious?'

'I do not see what right Mr Darcy had to decide on the propriety of his friend's inclination, or why, upon his own judgment alone, he was to determine and direct in what manner that friend was to be happy.' 'But,' she continued, recollecting herself, 'as we know none of the particulars, it is not fair to condemn him. It is not to be supposed that there was much affection in the case.'

'That is not an unnatural surmise,' said Fitzwilliam, 'but it is lessening the honour of my cousin's triumph very sadly.'

This was spoken jestingly, but it appeared to her so just a picture of Mr Darcy, that she would not trust herself with an answer; and, therefore, abruptly changing the conversation, talked on indifferent matters till they reached the parsonage. There, shut into her own room, as soon as their visitor left them, she could think without interruption of all that she had heard. It was not to be supposed that any other people could be meant than those with whom she was connected. There could not exist in the world *two* men, over whom Mr Darcy could have such boundless influence. That he had been concerned in the measures taken to separate Mr Bingley and Jane, she had never doubted; but she had always attributed to Miss Bingley the principal design and arrangement of them. If his own vanity, however, did not mislead him, *he* was the cause, his pride and caprice were the cause of all that Jane had suffered, and still continued to suffer. He had ruined for a while every hope of happiness for the most affectionate, generous heart in the world; and no one could say how lasting an evil he might have inflicted.

'There were some very strong objections against the lady,' were Colonel Fitzwilliam's words, and these strong objections probably were, her having one uncle who was a country attorney, and another who was in business in London.

'To Jane herself,' she exclaimed, 'there could be no possibility of objection. All loveliness and goodness as she is! Her understanding excellent, her mind improved, and her manners captivating. Neither could anything be urged against my father, who, though with some peculiarities, has abilities which Mr Darcy himself need not disdain, and respectability which he will probably never reach.' When she thought of her mother indeed, her confidence gave way a little, but she would not allow that any objections *there* had material weight with Mr Darcy, whose pride, she was convinced, would receive a deeper wound from the want of importance in his friend's connections, than from their want of sense; and she was quite decided at last, that he had been partly governed by this worst kind of pride, and partly by the wish of retaining Mr Bingley for his sister.

The agitation and tears which the subject occasioned, brought on a headache; and it grew so much worse towards the evening that, added to her unwillingness to see Mr Darcy, it determined her not to attend her cousins to Rosings, where they were engaged to drink tea. Mrs Collins, seeing that she was really unwell, did not press her to go, and as much as possible prevented her husband from pressing her, but Mr Collins could not conceal his apprehension of Lady Catherine's being rather displeased by her staying at home.

## *Chapter 34*

When they were gone, Elizabeth, as if intending to exasperate herself as much as possible against Mr Darcy, chose for her employment the examination of all the letters which Jane had written to her since her being in Kent. They contained no actual complaint, nor was there any revival of past occurrences, or any communication of present suffering. But in all, and in almost every line of each, there was a want of that cheerfulness which had been used to characterise her style, and which, proceeding from the serenity of a mind at ease with itself, and kindly

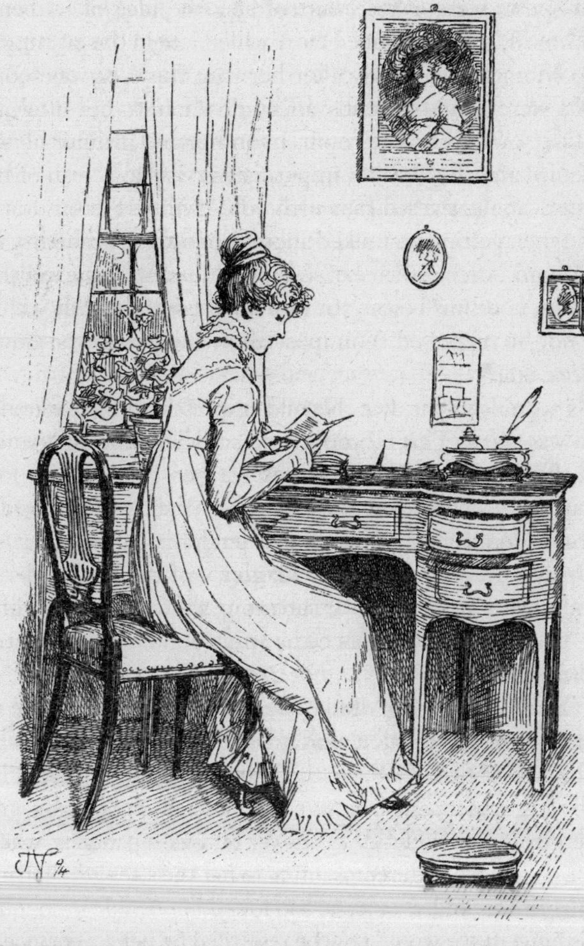

*Elizabeth chose for her employment the examination of all the letters which Jane had written to her since her being in Kent*

disposed towards everyone, had been scarcely ever clouded. Elizabeth noticed every sentence conveying the idea of uneasiness, with an attention which it had hardly received on the first perusal. Mr Darcy's shameful boast of what misery he had been able to inflict, gave her a keener sense of her sister's sufferings. It was some consolation to think that his visit to Rosings was to end on the day after the next, and a still greater, that in less than a fortnight she should herself be with Jane again, and enabled to contribute to the recovery of her spirits, by all that affection could do.

She could not think of Darcy's leaving Kent, without remembering that his cousin was to go with him; but Colonel Fitzwilliam had made it clear that he had no intentions at all, and agreeable as he was, she did not mean to be unhappy about him.

While settling this point, she was suddenly roused by the sound of the door bell, and her spirits were a little fluttered by the idea of its being Colonel Fitzwilliam himself, who had once before called late in the evening, and might now come to enquire particularly after her. But this idea was soon banished, and her spirits were very differently affected, when, to her utter amazement, she saw Mr Darcy walk into the room. In an hurried manner he immediately began an enquiry after her health, imputing his visit to a wish of hearing that she were better. She answered him with cold civility. He sat down for a few moments, and then getting up walked about the room. Elizabeth was surprised, but said not a word. After a silence of several minutes he came towards her in an agitated manner, and thus began, 'In vain have I struggled. It will not do. My feelings will not be repressed. You must allow me to tell you how ardently I admire and love you.'

Elizabeth's astonishment was beyond expression. She stared, coloured, doubted, and was silent. This he considered sufficient encouragement, and the avowal of all that he felt and had long felt for her, immediately followed. He spoke well, but there were feelings besides those of the heart to be detailed, and he was not more eloquent on the subject of tenderness than of pride. His sense of her inferiority – of its being a degradation – of the family obstacles which judgment had always opposed to inclination, were dwelt on with a warmth which seemed due to the consequence he was wounding, but was very unlikely to recommend his suit.

In spite of her deeply-rooted dislike, she could not be insensible to the compliment of such a man's affection, and though her intentions did not vary for an instant, she was at first sorry for the pain he was to receive; till, roused to resentment by his subsequent language, she lost all compassion in anger. She tried, however, to compose herself to answer him with patience, when he should have done. He concluded with representing to her the strength of that attachment which, in spite of all his endeavours, he had found impossible to conquer; and with expressing his hope that it would now be rewarded by her acceptance of his hand. As he said this, she could easily see that he had no doubt of a favourable answer. He *spoke* of apprehension and anxiety, but his countenance expressed real security. Such a circumstance could only exasperate farther, and when he ceased, the colour rose into her cheeks, and she said, 'In such cases as this, it is, I believe, the established mode to express a sense of obligation for the sentiments avowed, however unequally they may be returned. It is natural that obligation should be felt, and if I could *feel* gratitude, I would now thank you. But I cannot – I have never desired your good opinion, and you have certainly bestowed it most unwillingly. I am sorry to have occasioned pain to anyone. It has been most unconsciously done, however, and I hope will be of short duration. The feelings which, you tell me, have long prevented the acknowledgment of your regard, can have little difficulty in overcoming it after this explanation.'

Mr Darcy, who was leaning against the mantelpiece with his eyes fixed on her face, seemed to catch her words with no less resentment than surprise. His complexion became pale with anger, and the disturbance of his mind was visible in every feature. He was struggling for the appearance of composure, and would not open his lips, till he believed himself to have attained it. The pause was to Elizabeth's feelings dreadful. At length, in a voice of forced calmness, he said, 'And this is all the reply which I am to have the honour of expecting! I might, perhaps, wish to be informed why, with so little *endeavour* at civility, I am thus rejected. But it is of small importance.'

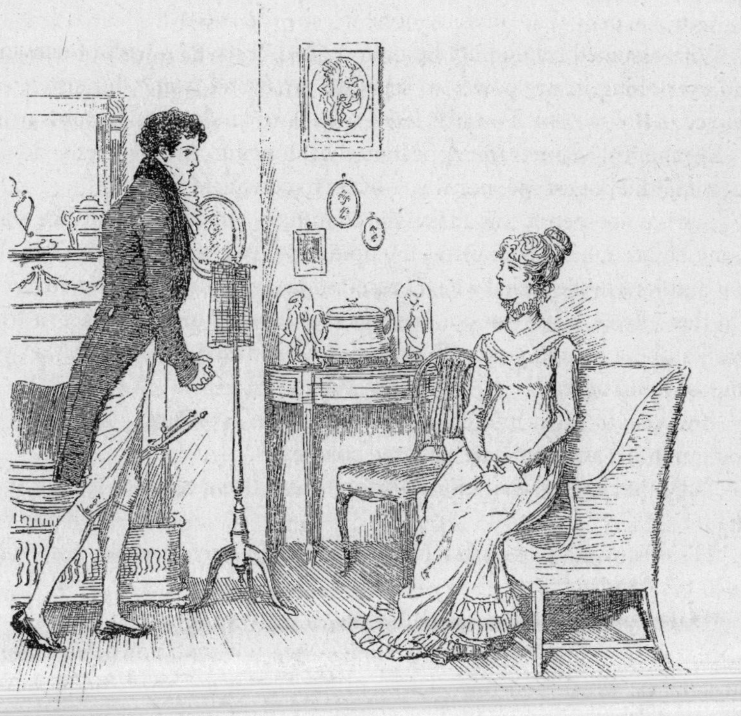

*'You must allow me to tell you how ardently I admire and love you'*

'I might as well enquire,' replied she, 'why with so evident a design of offending and insulting me, you chose to tell me that you liked me against your will, against your reason, and even against your character? Was not this some excuse for incivility, if I *was* uncivil? But I have other provocations. You know I have. Had not my own feelings decided against you, had they been indifferent, or had they even been favourable, do you think that any consideration would tempt me to accept the man, who has been the means of ruining, perhaps for ever, the happiness of a most beloved sister?'

As she pronounced these words, Mr Darcy changed colour; but the emotion was short, and he listened without attempting to interrupt her while she continued.

'I have every reason in the world to think ill of you. No motive can excuse the unjust and ungenerous part you acted *there*. You dare not, you cannot deny that you have been the principal, if not the only means of dividing them from each other, of exposing one to the censure of the world for caprice and instability, the other to its derision for disappointed hopes, and involving them both in misery of the acutest kind.'

She paused, and saw with no slight indignation that he was listening with an air which proved him wholly unmoved by any feeling of remorse. He even looked at her with a smile of affected incredulity.

'Can you deny that you have done it?' she repeated.

With assumed tranquillity he then replied, 'I have no wish of denying that I did everything in my power to separate my friend from your sister, or that I rejoice in my success. Towards *him* I have been kinder than towards myself.'

Elizabeth disdained the appearance of noticing this civil reflection, but its meaning did not escape, nor was it likely to conciliate her.

'But it is not merely this affair,' she continued, 'on which my dislike is founded. Long before it had taken place, my opinion of you was decided. Your character was unfolded in the recital which I received many months ago from Mr Wickham. On this subject, what can you have to say? In what imaginary act of friendship can you here defend yourself? or under what misrepresentation, can you here impose upon others?'

'You take an eager interest in that gentleman's concerns,' said Darcy in a less tranquil tone, and with a heightened colour.

'Who that knows what his misfortunes have been, can help feeling an interest in him?'

'His misfortunes!' repeated Darcy contemptuously; 'yes, his misfortunes have been great indeed.'

'And of your infliction,' cried Elizabeth with energy. 'You have reduced him to his present state of poverty, comparative poverty. You have withheld the advantages, which you must know to have been designed for him. You have deprived the best years of his life, of that independence which was no less his due than his desert. You have done all this! and yet you can treat the mention of his misfortunes with contempt and ridicule.'

'And this,' cried Darcy, as he walked with quick steps across the room, 'is your opinion of me! This is the estimation in which you hold me! I thank you for explaining it so fully. My faults, according to this calculation, are heavy indeed! But perhaps,' added he, stopping in his walk, and turning towards her, 'these offences might have been overlooked, had not your pride been hurt by my honest confession of the scruples that had long prevented my forming any serious design. These bitter accusations might have been suppressed, had I with greater policy concealed my struggles, and flattered you into the belief of my being impelled by unqualified, unalloyed inclination; by reason, by reflection, by everything. But disguise of every sort is my abhorrence. Nor am I ashamed of the feelings I related. They were natural and just. Could you expect me to rejoice in the inferiority of your connections? To congratulate myself on the hope of relations, whose condition in life is so decidedly beneath my own?'

Elizabeth felt herself growing more angry every moment; yet she tried to the utmost to speak with composure when she said, 'You are mistaken, Mr Darcy, if you suppose that the mode of your declaration affected me in any other way, than as it spared me the concern which I might have felt in refusing you, had you behaved in a more gentlemanlike manner.'

She saw him start at this, but he said nothing, and she continued, 'You could not have made me the offer of your hand in any possible way that would have tempted me to accept it.'

Again his astonishment was obvious; and he looked at her with an expression of mingled incredulity and mortification. She went on.

'From the very beginning, from the first moment I may almost say, of my acquaintance with you, your manners impressing me with the fullest belief of your arrogance, your conceit, and your selfish disdain of the feelings of others, were such as to form that groundwork of disapprobation, on which succeeding events have built so immoveable a dislike; and I had not known you a month before I felt that you were the last man in the world whom I could ever be prevailed on to marry.'

'You have said quite enough, madam. I perfectly comprehend your feelings, and have now only to be ashamed of what my own have been. Forgive me for having taken up so much of your time, and accept my best wishes for your health and happiness.'

And with these words he hastily left the room, and Elizabeth heard him the next moment open the front door and quit the house.

The tumult of her mind was now painfully great. She knew not how to support herself, and from actual weakness sat down and cried for half an hour. Her astonishment, as she reflected on what had passed, was increased by every review of it. That she should receive an offer of marriage from Mr Darcy! that he should have been in love with her for so many months! so much in love as to wish to marry her in spite of all the objections which had made him prevent his friend's marrying her sister, and which must appear at least with equal force in his own case, was almost incredible! It was gratifying to have inspired unconsciously so strong an affection. But his pride, his abominable pride, his shameless avowal of what he had done with respect to Jane, his unpardonable assurance in acknowledging, though he could not justify it, and the unfeeling manner in which he had mentioned Mr Wickham, his cruelty towards whom he had not attempted to deny, soon overcame the pity which the consideration of his attachment had for a moment excited.

She continued in very agitating reflections till the sound of Lady Catherine's carriage made her feel how unequal she was to encounter Charlotte's observation, and hurried her away to her room.

## *Chapter 35*

Elizabeth awoke the next morning to the same thoughts and meditations which had at length closed her eyes. She could not yet recover from the surprise of what had happened; it was impossible to think of anything else, and totally indisposed for employment, she resolved soon after breakfast to indulge herself in air and exercise. She was proceeding directly to her favourite walk, when the recollection of Mr Darcy's sometimes coming there stopped her, and instead of entering the park, she turned up the lane, which led her farther from the turnpike road. The park paling was still the boundary on one side, and she soon passed one of the gates into the ground.

After walking two or three times along that part of the lane, she was tempted, by the pleasantness of the morning, to stop at the gates and look into the park. The five weeks which she had now passed in Kent, had made a great difference in the country, and every day was adding to the verdure of the early trees. She was on the point of continuing her walk, when she caught a glimpse of a gentleman within the sort of grove which edged the park; he was moving that way; and fearful of its being Mr Darcy, she was directly retreating. But the person who advanced, was now near enough to see her, and stepping forward with eagerness, pronounced her name. She had turned away, but on hearing herself called, though in a voice which proved it to be Mr Darcy, she moved again towards the gate. He had by that time reached it also, and holding out a letter, which she instinctively took, said with a look of haughty composure, 'I have been walking in the grove for some time in the hope of meeting you. Will you do me the honour of reading that letter?' – And then, with a slight bow, turned again into the plantation, and was soon out of sight.

With no expectation of pleasure, but with the strongest curiosity, Elizabeth opened the letter, and to her still increasing wonder, perceived an envelope containing two sheets of letter paper, written quite through, in a very close hand. – The envelope itself was likewise full. – Pursuing her way along the lane, she then began it. It was dated from Rosings, at eight o'clock in the morning, and was as follows:

> Be not alarmed, Madam, on receiving this letter, by the apprehension of its containing any repetition of those sentiments, or renewal of those offers,

which were last night so disgusting to you. I write without any intention of paining you, or humbling myself, by dwelling on wishes, which, for the happiness of both, cannot be too soon forgotten; and the effort which the formation, and the perusal of this letter must occasion, should have been spared, had not my character required it to be written and read. You must, therefore, pardon the freedom with which I demand your attention; your feelings, I know, will bestow it unwillingly, but I demand it of your justice.

Two offences of a very different nature, and by no means of equal magnitude, you last night laid to my charge. The first mentioned was, that, regardless of the sentiments of either, I had detached Mr Bingley from your sister, – and the other, that I had, in defiance of various claims, in defiance of honour and humanity, ruined the immediate prosperity, and blasted the prospects of Mr Wickham. – Wilfully and wantonly to have thrown off the companion of my youth, the acknowledged favourite of my father, a young man who had scarcely any other dependence than on our patronage, and who had been brought up to expect its exertion, would be a depravity, to which the separation of two young persons, whose affection could be the growth of only

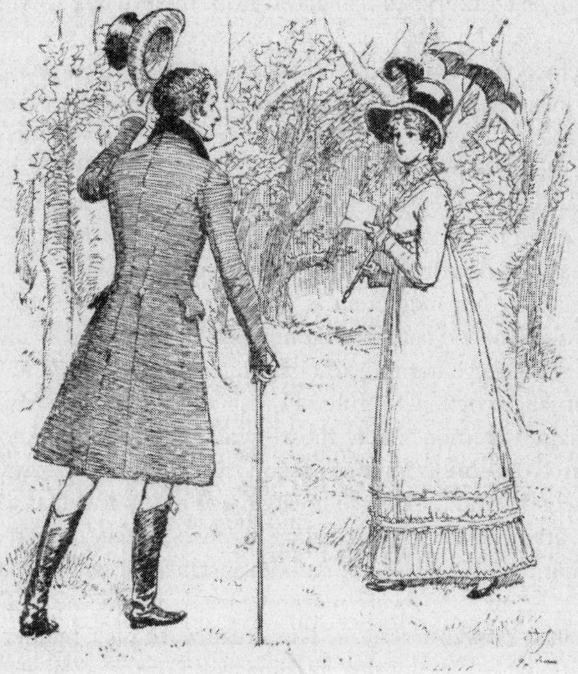

*Hearing herself called, though in a voice which proved it to be Mr Darcy, she moved again towards the gate*

a few weeks, could bear no comparison. – But from the severity of that blame which was last night so liberally bestowed, respecting each circumstance, I shall hope to be in future secured, when the following account of my actions and their motives has been read. – If, in the explanation of them which is due to myself, I am under the necessity of relating feelings which may be offensive to yours, I can only say that I am sorry. – The necessity must be obeyed – and farther apology would be absurd. – I had not been long in Hertfordshire, before I saw, in common with others, that Bingley preferred your eldest sister, to any other young woman in the country. – But it was not till the evening of the dance at Netherfield that I had any apprehension of his feeling a serious attachment. – I had often seen him in love before. – At that ball, while I had the honour of dancing with you, I was first made acquainted, by Sir William Lucas's accidental information, that Bingley's attentions to your sister had given rise to a general expectation of their marriage. He spoke of it as a certain event, of which the time alone could be undecided. From that moment I observed my friend's behaviour attentively; and I could then perceive that his partiality for Miss Bennet was beyond what I had ever witnessed in him. Your sister I also watched. – Her look and manners were open, cheerful and engaging as ever, but without any symptom of peculiar regard, and I remained convinced from the evening's scrutiny, that though she received his attentions with pleasure, she did not invite them by any participation of sentiment. – If *you* have not been mistaken here, *I* must have been in an error. Your superior knowledge of your sister must make the latter probable. – If it be so, if I have been misled by such error, to inflict pain on her, your resentment has not been unreasonable. But I shall not scruple to assert, that the serenity of your sister's countenance and air was such, as might have given the most acute observer, a conviction that, however amiable her temper, her heart was not likely to be easily touched. – That I was desirous of believing her indifferent is certain – but I will venture to say that my investigations and decisions are not usually influenced by my hopes or fears. – I did not believe her to be indifferent because I wished it; – I believed it on impartial conviction, as truly as I wished it in reason. – My objections to the marriage were not merely those, which I last night acknowledged to have required the utmost force of passion to put aside, in my own case; the want of connection could not be so great an evil to my friend as to me. – But there were other causes of repugnance; – causes which, though still existing, and existing to an equal degree in both instances, I had myself endeavoured to forget, because they were not immediately before me. – These causes must be stated, though briefly. – The situation of your mother's family, though objectionable, was nothing in comparison of that total want of propriety so frequently, so almost uniformly betrayed by herself, by your three younger sisters, and occasionally even by your father. – Pardon me. – It pains me to offend you. But amidst your concern for the defects of your nearest relations, and your displeasure at this representation of them, let it give you consolation to consider that, to have conducted yourselves so as to avoid any share of the like censure, is praise no less generally bestowed on you and your eldest sister, than it is honourable to the sense and disposition of both. – I will only say farther, that from what passed that evening, my opinion of all parties was confirmed, and every inducement heightened, which could have led me before, to preserve my friend from what I esteemed a most unhappy connection. – He left Netherfield for London, on the day following, as you, I am certain, remember, with the design of soon returning. – The part which I acted, is now to be explained. – His sisters' uneasiness had been equally excited with my own; our coincidence of feeling was soon discovered; and, alike sensible that no time was to be lost in detaching their brother, we shortly resolved on joining him directly in London. – We accordingly went – and there I readily engaged in the office of pointing out to my friend, the certain evils of such a choice. – I described, and enforced them earnestly. – But, however this remonstrance might have staggered or delayed his determination, I do not suppose that it would ultimately have prevented the marriage, had it not been seconded by the assurance which I hesitated not in giving, of your sister's indifference. He had before believed her to return his affection with sincere, if not with equal regard. – But Bingley has great natural modesty, with a stronger dependence on my judgment than on his own. – To convince him, therefore, that he had deceived himself, was no very difficult point. To persuade him against returning into Hertfordshire, when that conviction had been given, was scarcely the work of a moment. – I cannot blame myself for having done thus much. There is but one part of my conduct in the whole affair, on which I do not reflect with satisfaction; it is that I condescended to adopt the measures of art so far as to conceal from him your sister's being in town. I knew it myself, as it was known to Miss Bingley, but her brother is even yet ignorant of it. – That they might have met without ill consequence, is perhaps probable; – but his regard did not appear to me enough extinguished for him to see her without some danger. – Perhaps this concealment, this disguise, was beneath me. – It is done, however, and it was done for the best. – On this subject I have nothing more to say, no other apology to offer. If I have wounded your sister's feelings, it was unknowingly done; and though the motives which governed me may to you very naturally appear insufficient, I have not yet learnt to condemn them. – With respect to that other, more weighty accusation, of having injured Mr Wickham, I can only refute it by laying before you the whole of his connection with my family. Of what he has *particularly* accused me I am ignorant; but of the truth of what I shall relate, I can summon more than one witness of undoubted veracity. Mr Wickham is the son of a very respectable man, who had for many years the management of all the Pemberley estates; and whose good conduct in the discharge of his trust, naturally inclined my father to be of service to him, and on George Wickham, who was his godson, his kindness was therefore liberally bestowed. My father supported him at school, and afterwards at Cambridge; – most important assistance, as his own father, always poor from the extravagance of his wife, would have been unable to give him a gentleman's education. My father was not only fond of this young man's society, whose manners were always engaging; he had also the highest opinion of him, and hoping the church would be his profession, intended to provide him in it. As for myself, it is many, many years since I first began to think of him in a very different manner. The vicious propensities – the want of principle which he was careful to guard from the knowledge of his best friend, could not escape the observation of a young man of nearly the same age with himself, and who had opportunities of seeing him in unguarded moments, which Mr Darcy could not have. Here again I shall give you pain – to what degree you only can tell. But whatever may be the sentiments which Mr Wickham has created, a suspicion of their nature shall not prevent me from unfolding his real character. It adds even another motive. My excellent father died about five years ago; and his attachment to Mr Wickham was to the last so steady, that in his will he particularly recommended it to me, to promote his advancement in the best manner that his profession might allow, and if he took orders, desired that a valuable family living might be his as soon as it became vacant. There was also a legacy of one thousand pounds. His own father did not long survive mine, and within half a year from these events, Mr Wickham wrote to inform me that, having finally resolved against taking orders, he hoped I should not think it unreasonable for him to expect some more immediate pecuniary advantage, in lieu of the preferment, by which he could not be benefited. He had some intention, he added, of studying the law, and I must be aware that the interest of one thousand pounds would be a very insufficient support therein. I rather wished, than believed him to be sincere; but at any rate, was perfectly ready to accede to his proposal. I knew that Mr Wickham ought not to be a clergyman. The business was therefore soon settled. He resigned all claim to assistance in the church, were it possible that he could ever be in a situation to receive it, and accepted in return three thousand pounds. All connection between us seemed now dissolved. I thought too ill of him, to invite him to Pemberley, or admit his society in town. In town I believe he chiefly lived, but his studying the law was a mere pretence, and being now free from all restraint, his life was a life of idleness and dissipation. For about three years I heard little of him; but on the decease of the incumbent of the living which had been designed for him, he applied to me again by letter for the presentation. His circumstances, he assured me, and I had no difficulty in believing it, were exceedingly bad. He had found the law a most unprofitable study, and was now absolutely resolved on being ordained, if I would present him to the living in question – of which he trusted there could be little doubt, as he was well assured that I had no other person to provide for, and I could not have forgotten my revered father's intentions. You will hardly blame me for refusing to comply with this entreaty, or for resisting every repetition of it. His resentment was in proportion to the distress of his circumstances – and he was doubtless as violent in his abuse of me to others, as in his reproaches to myself. After this period, every appearance of acquaintance was dropped. How he lived I know not. But last summer he was again most painfully obtruded on my notice. I must now mention a circumstance which I would wish to forget myself, and which no obligation less than the present should induce me to unfold to any human being. Having said thus much, I feel no doubt of your secrecy. My sister, who is more than ten years my junior, was left to the guardianship of my mother's nephew, Colonel Fitzwilliam, and myself.About a year ago, she was taken from school, and an establishment formed for her in London; and last summer she went with the lady who presided over it, to Ramsgate; and thither also went Mr Wickham, undoubtedly by design; for there proved to have been a prior acquaintance between him and Mrs Younge, in whose character we were most unhappily deceived; and by her connivance and aid, he so far recommended himself to Georgiana, whose affectionate heart retained a strong impression of his kindness to her as a child, that she was persuaded to believe herself in love, and to consent to an elopement. She was then but fifteen, which must be her excuse; and after stating her imprudence, I am happy to add, that I owed the knowledge of it to herself. I joined them unexpectedly a day or two before the intended elopement, and then Georgiana, unable to support the idea of grieving and offending a brother whom she almost looked up to as a father, acknowledged the whole to me. You may imagine what I felt and how I acted. Regard for my sister's credit and feelings prevented any public exposure, but I wrote to Mr Wickham, who left the place immediately, and Mrs Younge was of course removed from her charge. Mr Wickham's chief object was unquestionably my sister's fortune, which is thirty thousand pounds; but I cannot help supposing that the hope of revenging himself on me, was a strong inducement. His revenge would have been complete indeed. This, madam, is a faithful narrative of every event in which we have been concerned together; and if you do not absolutely reject it as false, you will, I hope, acquit me henceforth of cruelty towards Mr Wickham. I know not in what manner, under what form of falsehood he has imposed on you; but his success is not perhaps to be wondered at. Ignorant as you previously were of everything concerning either, detection could not be in your power, and suspicion certainly not in your inclination. You may possibly wonder why all this was not told you last night. But I was not then master enough of myself to know what could or ought to be revealed. For the truth of everything here related, I can appeal more particularly to the testimony of Colonel Fitzwilliam, who from our near relationship and constant intimacy, and still more as one of the executors of my father's will, has been unavoidably acquainted with every particular of these transactions. If your abhorrence of *me* should make *my* assertions valueless, you cannot be prevented by the same cause from confiding in my cousin; and that there may be the possibility of consulting him, I shall endeavour to find some opportunity of putting this letter in your hands in the course of the morning. I will only add, God bless you.

FITZWILLIAM DARCY.'

## *Chapter 36*

If Elizabeth, when Mr Darcy gave her the letter, did not expect it to contain a renewal of his offers, she had formed no expectation at all of its contents. But such as they were, it may be well supposed how eagerly she went through them, and what a contrariety of emotion they excited. Her feelings as she read were scarcely to be defined. With amazement did she first understand that he believed any apology to be in his power; and steadfastly was she persuaded that he could have no explanation to give, which a just sense of shame would not conceal. With a strong prejudice against everything he might say, she began his account of what had happened at Netherfield. She read, with an eagerness which hardly left her power of comprehension, and from impatience of knowing what the next sentence might bring, was incapable of attending to the sense of the one before her eyes. His belief of her sister's insensibility, she instantly resolved to be false, and his account of the real, the worst objections to the match, made her too angry to have any wish of doing him justice. He expressed no regret for what he had done which satisfied her; his style was not penitent, but haughty. It was all pride and insolence.

But when this subject was succeeded by his account of Mr Wickham, when she read with somewhat clearer attention, a relation of events, which, if true, must overthrow every cherished opinion of his worth, and which bore so alarming an affinity to his own history of himself, her feelings were yet more acutely painful and more difficult of definition. Astonishment, apprehension, and even horror, oppressed her. She wished to discredit it entirely, repeatedly exclaiming, 'This must be false! This cannot be! This must be the grossest falsehood!' – and when she had gone through the whole letter, though scarcely knowing anything of the last page or two, put it hastily away, protesting that she would not regard it, that she would never look in it again.

In this perturbed state of mind, with thoughts that could rest on nothing, she walked on; but it would not do; in half a minute the letter was unfolded again, and collecting herself as well as she could, she again began the mortifying perusal of all that related to Wickham, and commanded herself so far as to examine the meaning of every sentence. The account of his connection with the Pemberley family, was exactly what he had related himself; and the kindness of the late Mr Darcy, though she had not before known its extent, agreed equally well with his own words. So far each recital confirmed the other: but when she came to the will, the difference was great. What Wickham had said of the living was fresh in her memory, and as she recalled his very words, it was impossible not to feel that there was gross duplicity on one side or the other; and, for a few moments, she flattered herself that her wishes did not err. But when she read, and reread with the closest attention, the particulars immediately following of Wickham's resigning all pretensions to the living, of his receiving in lieu, so considerable a sum as three thousand pounds, again was she forced to hesitate. She put down the letter, weighed every circumstance with what she meant to be impartiality – deliberated on the probability of each statement – but with little success. On both sides it was only assertion. Again she read on. But every line proved more clearly that the affair, which she had believed it impossible that any contrivance could so represent, as to render Mr Darcy's conduct in it less than infamous, was capable of a turn which must make him entirely blameless throughout the whole.

The extravagance and general profligacy which he scrupled not to lay to Mr Wickham's charge, exceedingly shocked her; the more so, as she could bring no proof of its injustice. She had never heard of him before his entrance into the —shire Militia, in which he had engaged at the persuasion of the young man, who, on meeting him accidentally in town, had there renewed a slight acquaintance. Of his former way of life, nothing had been known in Hertfordshire but what he told himself. As to his real character, had information been in her power, she had never felt a wish of enquiring. His countenance, voice, and manner, had established him at once in the possession of every virtue. She tried to recollect some instance of goodness, some distinguished trait of integrity or benevolence, that might rescue him from the attacks of Mr Darcy; or at least, by the predominance of virtue, atone for those casual errors, under which she would endeavour to class, what Mr Darcy had described as the idleness and vice of

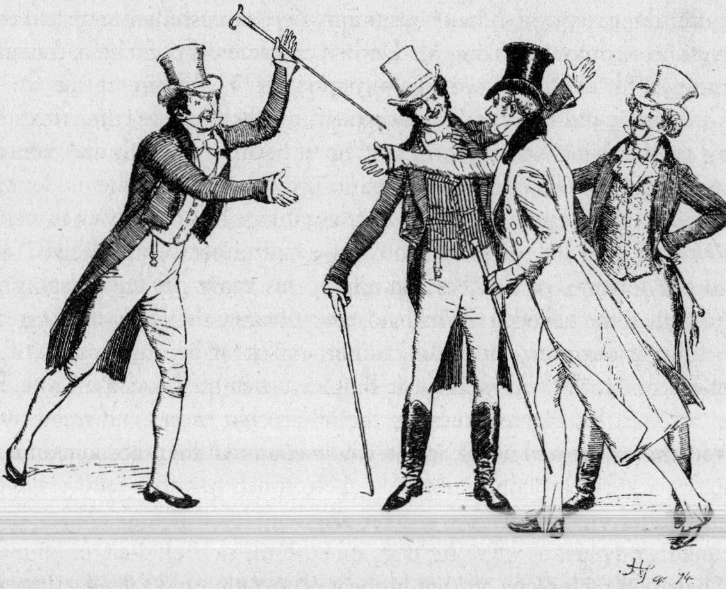

*Meeting him accidentally in town*

many years' continuance. But no such recollection befriended her. She could see him instantly before her, in every charm of air and address; but she could remember no more substantial good than the general approbation of the neighbourhood, and the regard which his social powers had gained him in the mess. After pausing on this point a considerable while, she once more continued to read. But, alas! the story which followed of his designs on Miss Darcy, received some confirmation from what had passed between Colonel Fitzwilliam and herself only the morning before; and at last she was referred for the truth of every particular to Colonel Fitzwilliam himself – from whom she had previously received the information of his near concern in all his cousin's affairs, and whose character she had no reason to question. At one time she had almost resolved on applying to him, but the idea was checked by the awkwardness of the application, and at length wholly banished by the conviction that Mr Darcy would never have hazarded such a proposal, if he had not been well assured of his cousin's corroboration.

She perfectly remembered everything that had passed in conversation between Wickham and herself, in their first evening at Mr Philips's. Many of his expressions were still fresh in her memory. She was *now* struck with the impropriety of such communications to a stranger, and wondered it had escaped her before. She saw the indelicacy of putting himself forward as he had done, and the inconsistency of his professions with his conduct. She remembered that he had boasted of having no fear of seeing Mr Darcy – that Mr Darcy might leave the country, but that *he* should stand his ground; yet he had avoided the Netherfield ball the very next week. She remembered also, that till the Netherfield family had quitted the country, he had told his story to no one but herself; but that after their removal, it had been everywhere discussed; that he had then no reserves, no scruples in sinking Mr Darcy's character, though he had assured her that respect for the father, would always prevent his exposing the son.

How differently did everything now appear in which he was concerned! His attentions to Miss King were now the consequence of views solely and hatefully mercenary; and the mediocrity of her fortune proved no longer the moderation of his wishes, but his eagerness to grasp at anything. His behaviour to herself could now have had no tolerable motive; he had either been deceived with regard to her fortune, or had been gratifying his vanity by encouraging the preference which she believed she had most incautiously shown. Every lingering struggle in his favour grew fainter and fainter; and in farther justification of Mr Darcy, she could not but allow that Mr Bingley, when questioned by Jane, had long ago asserted his blamelessness in the affair; that proud and repulsive as were his manners, she had never, in the whole course of their acquaintance, an acquaintance which had latterly brought them much together, and given her a sort of intimacy with his ways, seen anything that betrayed him to be unprincipled or unjust – anything that spoke him of irreligious or immoral habits. That among his own connections he was esteemed and valued – that even Wickham had allowed him merit as a brother, and that she had often heard him speak so affectionately of his sister as to prove him capable of *some* amiable feeling. That had his actions been what Wickham represented them, so gross a violation of everything right could hardly have been concealed from the world; and that friendship between a person capable of it, and such an amiable man as Mr Bingley, was incomprehensible.

She grew absolutely ashamed of herself. – Of neither Darcy nor Wickham could she think, without feeling that she had been blind, partial, prejudiced, absurd.

'How despicably have I acted!' she cried. – 'I, who have prided myself on my discernment! – I, who have valued myself on my abilities! who have often disdained the generous candour of my sister, and gratified my vanity, in useless or blameable distrust. – How humiliating is this discovery! – Yet, how just a humiliation! – Had I been in love, I could not have been more wretchedly blind. But vanity, not love, has been my folly. – Pleased with the preference of one, and offended by the neglect of the other, on the very beginning of our acquaintance, I have courted prepossession and ignorance, and driven reason away, where either were concerned. Till this moment, I never knew myself.'

From herself to Jane – from Jane to Bingley, her thoughts were in a line which soon brought to her recollection that Mr Darcy's explanation *there*, had appeared very insufficient; and she read it again. Widely different was the effect of a second perusal. – How could she deny that credit to his assertions, in one instance, which she had been obliged to give in the other? – He declared himself to have been totally unsuspicious of her sister's attachment; – and she could not help remembering what Charlotte's opinion had always been. – Neither could she deny the justice of his description of Jane. – She felt that Jane's feelings, though fervent, were little displayed, and that there was a constant complacency in her air and manner, not often united with great sensibility.

When she came to that part of the letter in which her family were mentioned, in terms of such mortifying, yet merited reproach, her sense of shame was severe. The justice of the charge struck her too forcibly for denial, and the circumstances to which he particularly alluded, as having passed at the Netherfield ball, and as confirming all his first disapprobation, could not have made a stronger impression on his mind than on hers.

The compliment to herself and her sister, was not unfelt. It soothed, but it could not console her for the contempt which had been thus self-attracted by the rest of her family; – and as she considered that Jane's disappointment had in fact been the work of her nearest relations, and reflected how materially the credit of both must be hurt by such impropriety of conduct, she felt depressed beyond anything she had ever known before.

After wandering along the lane for two hours, giving way to every variety of thought; reconsidering events, determining probabilities, and reconciling herself as well as she could, to a change so sudden and so important, fatigue, and a recollection of her long absence, made her at length return home; and she entered the house with the wish of appearing cheerful as usual, and the resolution of repressing such reflections as must make her unfit for conversation.

She was immediately told, that the two gentlemen from Rosings had each called during her absence; Mr Darcy, only for a few minutes to take leave, but that Colonel Fitzwilliam had been sitting with them at least an hour, hoping for her return, and almost resolving to walk after her till she could be found. – Elizabeth could but just *affect* concern in missing him; she really rejoiced at it. Colonel Fitzwilliam was no longer an object. She could think only of her letter.

## *Chapter 37*

The two gentlemen left Rosings the next morning; and Mr Collins having been in waiting near the lodges, to make them his parting obeisance, was able to bring home the pleasing intelligence, of their appearing in very good health, and in as tolerable spirits as could be expected, after the melancholy scene so lately gone through at Rosings. To Rosings he then hastened to console Lady Catherine, and her daughter; and on his return, brought back, with great satisfaction, a message from her ladyship, importing that she felt herself so dull as to make her very desirous of having them all to dine with her.

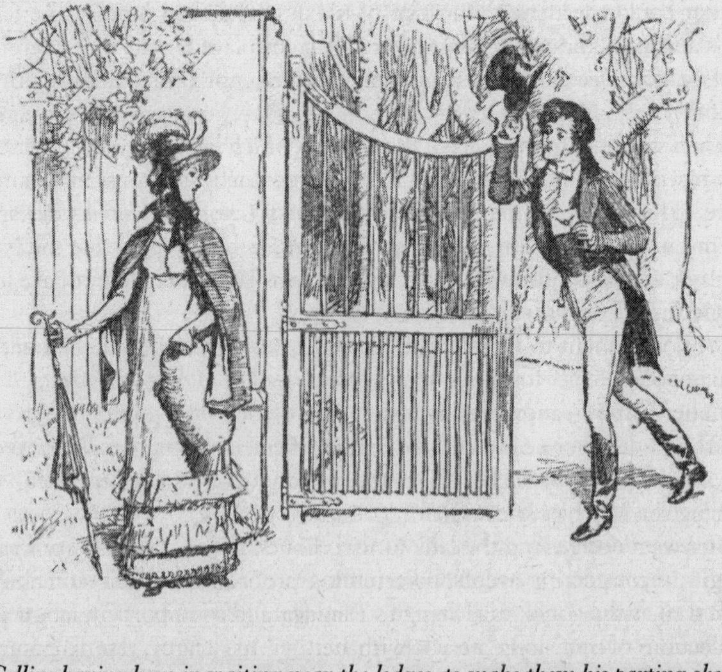

*Mr Collins having been in waiting near the lodges, to make them his parting obeisance*

Elizabeth could not see Lady Catherine without recollecting, that had she chosen it, she might by this time have been presented to her, as her future niece; nor could she think, without a smile, of what her ladyship's indignation would have been. 'What would she have said? – how would she have behaved?' were questions with which she amused herself.

Their first subject was the diminution of the Rosings party. – 'I assure you, I feel it exceedingly,' said Lady Catherine; 'I believe nobody feels the loss of friends so much as I do. But I am particularly attached to these young men; and know them to be so much attached to me! – They were excessively sorry to go! But so they always are. The dear colonel rallied his spirits tolerably till just at last; but Darcy seemed to feel it most acutely, more I think than last year. His attachment to Rosings, certainly increases.'

Mr Collins had a compliment, and an allusion to throw in here, which were kindly smiled on by the mother and daughter.

Lady Catherine observed, after dinner, that Miss Bennet seemed out of spirits, and immediately accounting for it herself, by supposing that she did not like to go home again so soon, she added, 'But if that is the case, you must write to your mother to beg that you may stay a little longer. Mrs Collins will be very glad of your company, I am sure.'

'I am much obliged to your ladyship for your kind invitation,' replied Elizabeth, 'but it is not in my power to accept it. – I must be in town next Saturday.'

'Why, at that rate, you will have been here only six weeks. I expected you to stay two months. I told Mrs Collins so before you came. There can be no occasion for your going so soon. Mrs Bennet could certainly spare you for another fortnight.'

'But my father cannot. – He wrote last week to hurry my return.'

'Oh! your father of course may spare you, if your mother can. – Daughters are never of so much consequence to a father. And if you will stay another *month* complete, it will be in my power to take one of you as far as London, for I am going there early in June, for a week; and as Dawson does not object to the Barouche box, there will be very good room for one of you – and indeed, if the weather should happen to be cool, I should not object to taking you both, as you are neither of you large.'

'You are all kindness, Madam; but I believe we must abide by our original plan.'

Lady Catherine seemed resigned.

'Mrs Collins, you must send a servant with them. You know I always speak my mind, and I cannot bear the idea of two young women travelling post by themselves. It is highly improper. You must contrive to send somebody. I have the greatest dislike in the world to that sort of thing. – Young women should always be properly guarded and attended, according to their situation in life. When my niece Georgiana went to Ramsgate last summer, I made a point of her having two menservants go with her. – Miss Darcy, the daughter of Mr Darcy, of Pemberley, and Lady Anne, could not have appeared with propriety in a different manner. – I am excessively attentive to all those things. You must send John with the young ladies, Mrs Collins. I am glad it occurred to me to mention it; for it would really be discreditable to *you* to let them go alone.'

'My uncle is to send a servant for us.'

'Oh! – Your uncle! – He keeps a manservant, does he? – I am very glad you have somebody who thinks of those things. Where shall you change horses? – Oh! Bromley, of course. – If you mention my name at the Bell, you will be attended to.'

Lady Catherine had many other questions to ask respecting their journey, and as she did not answer them all herself, attention was necessary, which Elizabeth believed to be lucky for her; or, with a mind so occupied, she might have forgotten where she was. Reflection must be reserved for solitary hours; whenever she was alone, she gave way to it as the greatest relief; and not a day went by without a solitary walk, in which she might indulge in all the delight of unpleasant recollections.

Mr Darcy's letter, she was in a fair way of soon knowing by heart. She studied every sentence: and her feelings towards its writer were at times widely different. When she remembered the style of his address, she was still full of indignation; but when she considered how unjustly she had condemned and upbraided him, her anger was turned against herself; and his disappointed feelings became the object of compassion. His attachment excited gratitude, his general character respect; but she could not approve him; nor could she for a moment repent her refusal, or feel the slightest inclination ever to see him again. In her own past behaviour, there was a constant source of vexation and regret; and in the unhappy defects of her family a subject of yet heavier chagrin. They were hopeless of remedy. Her father, contented with laughing at them, would never exert himself to restrain the wild giddiness of his youngest daughters; and her mother, with manners so far from right herself, was entirely insensible of the evil. Elizabeth had frequently united with Jane in an endeavour to check the imprudence of Catherine and Lydia; but while they were supported by their mother's indulgence, what chance could there be of improvement? Catherine, weak-spirited, irritable, and completely under Lydia's guidance, had been always affronted by their advice; and Lydia, self-willed and careless, would scarcely give them a hearing. They were ignorant, idle, and vain. While there was an officer in Meryton, they would flirt with him; and while Meryton was within a walk of Longbourn, they would be going there for ever.

Anxiety on Jane's behalf, was another prevailing concern, and Mr Darcy's explanation, by restoring Bingley to all her former good opinion, heightened the sense of what Jane had lost. His affection was proved to have been sincere, and his conduct cleared of all blame, unless any could attach to the implicitness of his confidence in his friend. How grievous then was the thought that, of a situation so desirable in every respect, so replete with advantage, so promising for happiness, Jane had been deprived, by the folly and indecorum of her own family!

When to these recollections was added the development of Wickham's character, it may be easily believed that the happy spirits which had seldom been depressed before, were now so much affected as to make it almost impossible for her to appear tolerably cheerful.

Their engagements at Rosings were as frequent during the last week of her stay, as they had been at first. The very last evening was spent there; and her ladyship again enquired minutely into the particulars of their journey, gave them directions as to the best method of packing, and was so urgent on the necessity of placing gowns in the only right way, that Maria thought herself obliged, on her return, to undo all the work of the morning, and pack her trunk afresh.

When they parted, Lady Catherine, with great condescension, wished them a good journey, and invited them to come to Hunsford again next year; and Miss de Bourgh exerted herself so far as to curtsey and hold out her hand to both.

## *Chapter 38*

On Saturday morning Elizabeth and Mr Collins met for breakfast a few minutes before the others appeared; and he took the opportunity of paying the parting civilities which he deemed indispensably necessary.

'I know not, Miss Elizabeth,' said he, 'whether Mrs Collins has yet expressed her sense of your kindness in coming to us, but I am very certain you will not leave the house without receiving her thanks for it. The favour of your company has been much felt, I assure you. We know how little there is to tempt anyone to our humble abode. Our plain manner of living, our small rooms, and few domestics, and the little we see of the world, must make Hunsford extremely dull to a young lady like yourself; but I hope you will believe us grateful for the condescension, and that we have done everything in our power to prevent your spending your time unpleasantly.'

Elizabeth was eager with her thanks and assurances of happiness. She had spent six weeks with great enjoyment; and the pleasure of being with Charlotte, and the kind attentions she had received, must make *her* feel the obliged. Mr Collins was gratified; and with a more smiling solemnity replied, 'It gives me the greatest pleasure to hear that you have passed your time not disagreeably. We have certainly done our best; and most fortunately having it in our power to introduce you to very superior society, and from our connection with Rosings, the frequent means of varying the humble home scene, I think we may flatter ourselves that your Hunsford visit cannot have been entirely irksome. Our situation with regard to Lady Catherine's family is indeed the sort of extraordinary advantage and blessing which few can boast. You see on what a footing we are. You see how continually we are engaged there. In truth I must acknowledge that, with all the disadvantages of this humble parsonage, I should not think anyone abiding in it an object of compassion, while they are sharers of our intimacy at Rosings.'

Words were insufficient for the elevation of his feelings; and he was obliged to walk about the room, while Elizabeth tried to unite civility and truth in a few short sentences.

'You may, in fact, carry a very favourable report of us into Hertfordshire, my dear cousin. I flatter myself at least that you will be able to do so. Lady Catherine's great attentions to Mrs Collins you have been a daily witness of; and altogether I trust it does not appear that your friend has drawn an unfortunate – but on this point it will be as well to be silent. Only let me assure you, my dear Miss Elizabeth, that I can from my heart most cordially wish you equal felicity in marriage. My dear Charlotte and I have but one mind and one way of thinking. There is in everything a most remarkable resemblance of character and ideas between us. We seem to have been designed for each other.'

Elizabeth could safely say that it was a great happiness where that was the case, and with equal sincerity could add that she firmly believed and rejoiced in his domestic comforts. She was not sorry, however, to have the recital of them interrupted by the entrance of the lady from whom they sprung. Poor Charlotte! – it was melancholy to leave her to such society! – But she had chosen it with her eyes open; and though evidently regretting that her visitors were to go, she did not seem to ask for compassion. Her home and her housekeeping, her parish and her poultry, and all their dependent concerns, had not yet lost their charms.

At length the chaise arrived, the trunks were fastened on, the parcels placed within, and it was pronounced to be ready. After an affectionate parting between the friends, Elizabeth was attended to the carriage by Mr Collins, and as they

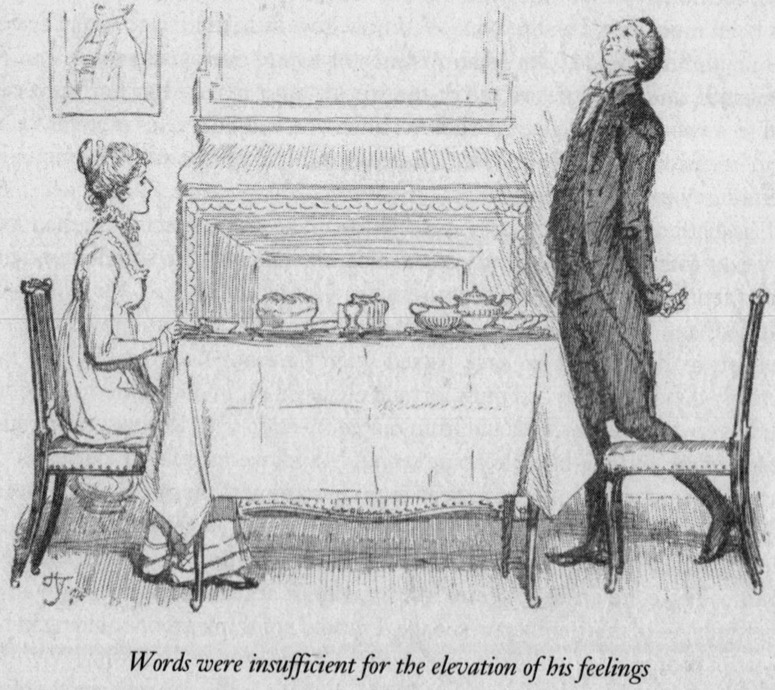

*Words were insufficient for the elevation of his feelings*

walked down the garden, he was commissioning her with his best respects to all her family, not forgetting his thanks for the kindness he had received at Longbourn in the winter, and his compliments to Mr and Mrs Gardiner, though unknown. He then handed her in, Maria followed, and the door was on the point of being closed, when he suddenly reminded them, with some consternation, that they had hitherto forgotten to leave any message for the ladies of Rosings.

'But,' he added, 'you will of course wish to have your humble respects delivered to them, with your grateful thanks for their kindness to you while you have been here.'

Elizabeth made no objection; – the door was then allowed to be shut, and the carriage drove off.

'Good gracious!' cried Maria, after a few minutes' silence, 'it seems but a day or two since we first came! – and yet how many things have happened!'

'A great many indeed,' said her companion with a sigh.

'We have dined nine times at Rosings, besides drinking tea there twice! – How much I shall have to tell!'

Elizabeth privately added, 'And how much I shall have to conceal.'

Their journey was performed without much conversation, or any alarm; and within four hours of their leaving Hunsford, they reached Mr Gardiner's house, where they were to remain a few days.

Jane looked well, and Elizabeth had little opportunity of studying her spirits, amidst the various engagements which the kindness of her aunt had reserved for them. But Jane was to go home with her, and at Longbourn there would be leisure enough for observation.

It was not without an effort meanwhile that she could wait even for Longbourn, before she told her sister of Mr Darcy's proposals. To know that she had the power of revealing what would so exceedingly astonish Jane, and must, at the same time, so highly gratify whatever of her own vanity she had not yet been able to reason away, was such a temptation to openness as nothing could have conquered but the state of indecision in which she remained, as to the extent of what she should communicate; and her fear, if she once entered on the subject, of being hurried into repeating something of Bingley, which might only grieve her sister farther.

## *Chapter 39*

It was the second week in May, in which the three young ladies set out together from Gracechurch Street, for the town of — in Hertfordshire; and, as they drew near the appointed inn where Mr Bennet's carriage was to meet them, they quickly perceived, in token of the coachman's punctuality, both Kitty and Lydia looking out of a dining-room upstairs. These two girls had been above an hour in the place, happily employed in visiting an opposite milliner, watching the sentinel on guard, and dressing a salad and cucumber.

After welcoming their sisters, they triumphantly displayed a table set out with such cold meat as an inn larder usually affords, exclaiming, 'Is not this nice? Is not this an agreeable surprise?'

'And we mean to treat you all,' added Lydia; 'but you must lend us the money, for we have just spent ours at the shop out there.' Then showing her purchases: 'Look here, I have bought this bonnet. I do not think it is very pretty; but I thought I might as well buy it as not. I shall pull it to pieces as soon as I get home, and see if I can make it up any better.'

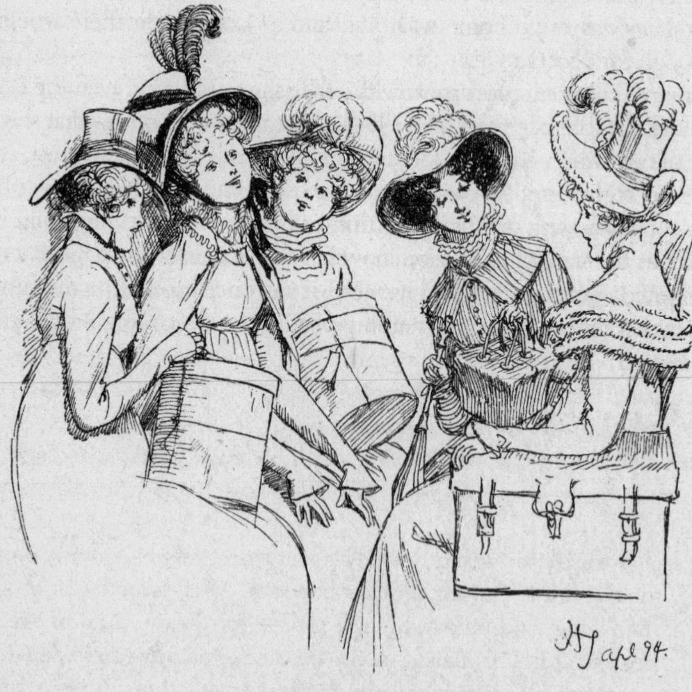


*How nicely we are crammed in!*

And when her sisters abused it as ugly, she added, with perfect unconcern, 'Oh! but there were two or three much uglier in the shop; and when I have bought some prettier-coloured satin to trim it with fresh, I think it will be very tolerable. Besides, it will not much signify what one wears this summer, after the —shire have left Meryton, and they are going in a fortnight.'

'Are they indeed?' cried Elizabeth, with the greatest satisfaction.

'They are going to be encamped near Brighton; and I do so want papa to take us all there for the summer! It would be such a delicious scheme, and I dare say would hardly cost anything at all. Mamma would like to go too of all things! Only think what a miserable summer else we shall have!'

'Yes,' thought Elizabeth, '*that* would be a delightful scheme, indeed, and completely do for us at once. Good Heaven! Brighton, and a whole campful of soldiers, to us, who have been overset already by one poor regiment of militia, and the monthly balls of Meryton.'

'Now I have got some news for you,' said Lydia, as they sat down to table. 'What do you think? It is excellent news, capital news, and about a certain person that we all like.'

Jane and Elizabeth looked at each other, and the waiter was told that he need not stay. Lydia laughed, and said, 'Aye, that is just like your formality and discretion. You thought the waiter must not hear, as if he cared! I dare say he often hears worse things said than I am going to say. But he is an ugly fellow! I am glad he is gone. I never saw such a long chin in my life. Well, but now for my news: it is about dear Wickham; too good for the waiter, is not it? There is no danger of Wickham's marrying Mary King. There's for you! She is gone down to her uncle at Liverpool; gone to stay. Wickham is safe.'

'And Mary King is safe!' added Elizabeth; 'safe from a connection imprudent as to fortune.'

'She is a great fool for going away, if she liked him.'

'But I hope there is no strong attachment on either side,' said Jane.

'I am sure there is not on *his*. I will answer for it he never cared three straws about her. Who *could* about such a nasty little freckled thing?'

Elizabeth was shocked to think that, however incapable of such coarseness of *expression* herself, the coarseness of the *sentiment* was little other than her own breast had formerly harboured and fancied liberal!

As soon as all had ate, and the elder ones paid, the carriage was ordered; and after some contrivance, the whole party, with all their boxes, workbags, and parcels, and the unwelcome addition of Kitty's and Lydia's purchases, were seated in it.

'How nicely we are crammed in!' cried Lydia. 'I am glad I bought my bonnet, if it is only for the fun of having another bandbox! Well, now let us be quite comfortable and snug, and talk and laugh all the way home. And in the first place, let us hear what has happened to you all, since you went away. Have you seen any pleasant men? Have you had any flirting? I was in great hopes that one of you would have got a husband before you came back. Jane will be quite an old maid soon, I declare. She is almost three and twenty! Lord, how ashamed I should be of not being married before three and twenty! My aunt Philips wants you so to get husbands, you can't think. She says Lizzy had better have taken Mr Collins; but *I* do not think there would have been any fun in it. Lord! how I should like to be married before any of you; and then I would chaperon you about to all the balls. Dear me! we had such a good piece of fun the other day at Colonel Forster's. Kitty and me were to spend the day there, and Mrs Forster promised to have a little dance in the evening; (by the by, Mrs Forster and me are *such* friends!) and so she asked the two Harringtons to come, but Harriet was ill, and so Pen was forced to come by herself; and then, what do you think we did? We dressed up Chamberlayne in woman's clothes, on purpose to pass for a lady, – only think what fun! Not a soul knew of it, but Colonel and Mrs Forster, and Kitty and me, except my aunt, for we were forced to borrow one of her gowns; and you cannot imagine how well he looked! When Denny, and Wickham, and Pratt, and two or three more of the men came in, they did not know him in the least. Lord! how I laughed! and so did Mrs Forster. I thought I should have died. And *that* made the men suspect something, and then they soon found out what was the matter.'

With such kind of histories of their parties and good jokes, did Lydia, assisted by Kitty's hints and additions, endeavour to amuse her companions all the way to Longbourn. Elizabeth listened as little as she could, but there was no escaping the frequent mention of Wickham's name.

Their reception at home was most kind. Mrs Bennet rejoiced to see Jane in undiminished beauty; and more than once during dinner did Mr Bennet say voluntarily to Elizabeth, 'I am glad you are come back, Lizzy.'

Their party in the dining-room was large, for almost all the Lucases came to meet Maria and hear the news: and various were the subjects which occupied them; Lady Lucas was enquiring of Maria across the table, after the welfare and poultry of her eldest daughter; Mrs Bennet was doubly engaged, on one hand collecting an account of the present fashions from Jane, who sat some way below her, and on the other, retailing them all to the younger Miss Lucases; and Lydia, in a voice rather louder than any other person's, was enumerating the various pleasures of the morning to anybody who would hear her.

'Oh! Mary,' said she, 'I wish you had gone with us, for we had such fun! as we went along, Kitty and me drew up all the blinds, and pretended there was nobody in the coach; and I should have gone so all the way, if Kitty had not been sick; and when we got to the George, I do think we behaved very handsomely, for we treated the other three with the nicest cold luncheon in the world, and if you would have gone, we would have treated you too. And then when we came away it was such fun! I thought we never should have got into the coach. I was ready to die of laughter. And then we were so merry all the way home! we talked and laughed so loud, that anybody might have heard us ten miles off!'

To this, Mary very gravely replied, 'Far be it from me, my dear sister, to depreciate such pleasures. They would doubtless be congenial with the generality of female minds. But I confess they would have no charms for *me*. I should infinitely prefer a book.'

But of this answer Lydia heard not a word. She seldom listened to anybody for more than half a minute, and never attended to Mary at all.

In the afternoon Lydia was urgent with the rest of the girls to walk to Meryton and see how everybody went on; but Elizabeth steadily opposed the scheme. It should not be said, that the Miss Bennets could not be at home half a day before they were in pursuit of the officers. There was another reason too for her opposition. She dreaded seeing Wickham again, and was resolved to avoid it as long as possible. The comfort to *her*, of the regiment's approaching removal, was indeed beyond expression. In a fortnight they were to go, and once gone, she hoped there could be nothing more to plague her on his account.

She had not been many hours at home, before she found that the Brighton scheme, of which Lydia had given them a hint at the inn, was under frequent discussion between her parents. Elizabeth saw directly that her father had not the smallest intention of yielding; but his answers were at the same time so vague and equivocal, that her mother, though often disheartened, had never yet despaired of succeeding at last.

## *Chapter 40*

Elizabeth's impatience to acquaint Jane with what had happened could no longer be overcome; and at length resolving to suppress every particular in which her sister was concerned, and preparing her to be surprised, she related to her the next morning the chief of the scene between Mr Darcy and herself.

Miss Bennet's astonishment was soon lessened by the strong sisterly partiality which made any admiration of Elizabeth appear perfectly natural; and all surprise was shortly lost in other feelings. She was sorry that Mr Darcy should have delivered his sentiments in a manner so little suited to recommend them; but still more was she grieved for the unhappiness which her sister's refusal must have given him.

'His being so sure of succeeding, was wrong,' said she; 'and certainly ought not to have appeared; but consider how much it must increase his disappointment.'

'Indeed,' replied Elizabeth, 'I am heartily sorry for him; but he has other feelings which will probably soon drive away his regard for me. You do not blame me, however, for refusing him?'

'Blame you! Oh, no.'

'But you blame me for having spoken so warmly of Wickham.'

'No – I do not know that you were wrong in saying what you did.'

'But you *will* know it, when I have told you what happened the very next day.'

She then spoke of the letter, repeating the whole of its contents as far as they concerned George Wickham. What a stroke was this for poor Jane! who would willingly have gone through the world without believing that so much wickedness existed in the whole race of mankind, as was here collected in one individual. Nor was Darcy's vindication, though grateful to her feelings, capable of consoling her for such discovery. Most earnestly did she labour to prove the probability of error, and seek to clear one, without involving the other.

'This will not do,' said Elizabeth. 'You never will be able to make both of them good for anything. Take your choice, but you must be satisfied with only one. There is but such a quantity of merit between them; just enough to make one good sort of man; and of late it has been shifting about pretty much. For my part, I am inclined to believe it all Mr Darcy's, but you shall do as you choose.'

It was some time, however, before a smile could be extorted from Jane.

'I do not know when I have been more shocked,' said she. 'Wickham so very bad! It is almost past belief. And poor Mr Darcy! dear Lizzy, only consider what he must have suffered. Such a disappointment! and with the knowledge of your ill opinion too! and having to relate such a thing of his sister! It is really too distressing. I am sure you must feel it so.'

'Oh! no, my regret and compassion are all done away by seeing you so full of both. I know you will do him such ample justice, that I am growing every moment more unconcerned and indifferent. Your profusion makes me saving; and if you lament over him much longer, my heart will be as light as a feather.'

'Poor Wickham; there is such an expression of goodness in his countenance! such an openness and gentleness in his manner.'

'There certainly was some great mismanagement in the education of those two young men. One has got all the goodness, and the other all the appearance of it.'

'I never thought Mr Darcy so deficient in the *appearance* of it as you used to do.'

'And yet I meant to be uncommonly clever in taking so decided a dislike to him, without any reason. It is such a spur to one's genius, such an opening for wit to have a dislike of that kind. One may be continually abusive without saying anything just; but one cannot be always laughing at a man without now and then stumbling on something witty.'

'Lizzy, when you first read that letter, I am sure you could not treat the matter as you do now.'

'Indeed I could not. I was uncomfortable enough. I was very uncomfortable, I may say unhappy. And with no one to speak to, of what I felt, no Jane to comfort me and say that I had not been so very weak and vain and nonsensical as I knew I had! Oh! how I wanted you!'

'How unfortunate that you should have used such very strong expressions in speaking of Wickham to Mr Darcy, for now they *do* appear wholly undeserved.'

'Certainly. But the misfortune of speaking with bitterness, is a most natural consequence of the prejudices I had been encouraging. There is one point, on which I want your advice. I want to be told whether I ought, or ought not to make our acquaintance in general understand Wickham's character.'

Miss Bennet paused a little and then replied, 'Surely there can be no occasion for exposing him so dreadfully. What is your own opinion?'

'That it ought not to be attempted. Mr Darcy has not authorised me to make his communication public. On the contrary every particular relative to his sister, was meant to be kept as much as possible to myself; and if I endeavour to undeceive people as to the rest of his conduct, who will believe me? The general prejudice against Mr Darcy is so violent, that it would be the death of half the good people in Meryton, to attempt to place him in an amiable light. I am not equal to it. Wickham will soon be gone; and therefore it will not signify to anybody here, what he really is. Sometime hence it will be all found out, and then we may laugh at their stupidity in not knowing it before. At present I will say nothing about it.'

'You are quite right. To have his errors made public might ruin him for ever. He is now perhaps sorry for what he has done, and anxious to re-establish a character. We must not make him desperate.'

The tumult of Elizabeth's mind was allayed by this conversation. She had got rid of two of the secrets which had weighed on her for a fortnight, and was certain of a willing listener in Jane, whenever she might wish to talk again of either. But there was still something lurking behind, of which prudence forbad the disclosure. She dared not relate the other half of Mr Darcy's letter, nor explain to her sister how sincerely she had been valued by his friend. Here was knowledge in which no one could partake; and she was sensible that nothing less than a perfect understanding between the parties could justify her in throwing off this last encumbrance of mystery. 'And then,' said she, 'if that very improbable event should ever take place, I shall merely be able to tell what Bingley may tell in a much more agreeable manner himself. The liberty of communication cannot be mine till it has lost all its value!'

She was now, on being settled at home, at leisure to observe the real state of her sister's spirits. Jane was not happy. She still cherished a very tender affection for Bingley. Having never even fancied herself in love before, her regard had all the warmth of first attachment, and from her age and disposition, greater steadiness than first attachments often boast; and so fervently did she value his remembrance, and prefer him to every other man, that all her good sense, and all her attention to the feelings of her friends, were requisite to check the indulgence of those regrets, which must have been injurious to her own health and their tranquillity.

'Well, Lizzy,' said Mrs Bennet one day, 'what is your opinion *now* of this sad business of Jane's? For my part, I am determined never to speak of it again to anybody. I told my sister Philips so the other day. But I cannot find out that Jane saw anything of him in London. Well, he is a very undeserving young man – and I do not suppose there is the least chance in the world of her ever getting him now. There is no talk of his coming to Netherfield again in the summer; and I have enquired of everybody too, who is likely to know.'

'I do not believe that he will ever live at Netherfield any more.'

'Oh, well! it is just as he chooses. Nobody wants him to come. Though I shall always say that he used my daughter extremely ill; and if I was her, I would not have put up with it. Well, my comfort is, I am sure Jane will die of a broken heart, and then he will be sorry for what he has done.'

But as Elizabeth could not receive comfort from any such expectation, she made no answer.

'Well, Lizzy,' continued her mother soon afterwards, 'and so the Collinses live very comfortable, do they? Well, well, I only hope it will last. And what sort of table do they keep? Charlotte is an excellent manager, I dare say. If she is half as sharp as her mother, she is saving enough. There is nothing extravagant in *their* housekeeping, I dare say.'

'No, nothing at all.'

'A great deal of good management, depend upon it. Yes, yes. *They* will take care not to outrun their income. *They* will never be distressed for money. Well, much good may it do them! And so, I suppose, they often talk of having Longbourn when your father is dead. They look upon it quite as their own, I dare say, whenever that happens.'

'It was a subject which they could not mention before me.'

'No. It would have been strange if they had. But I make no doubt, they often talk of it between themselves. Well, if they can be easy with an estate that is not lawfully their own, so much the better. *I* should be ashamed of having one that was only entailed on me.'

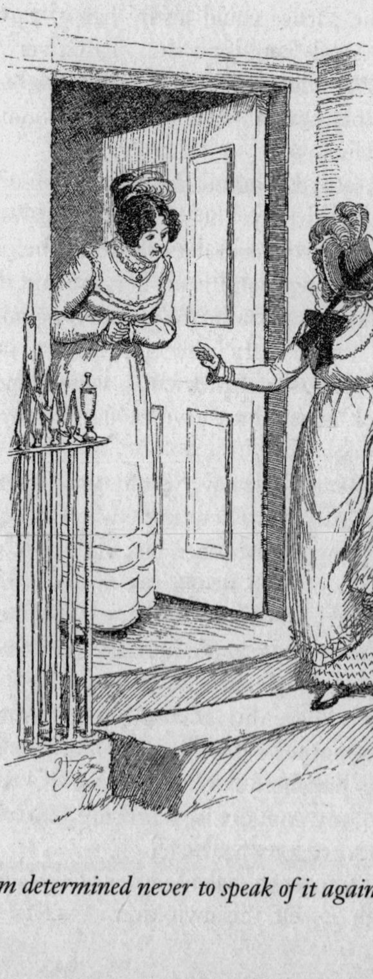

*I am determined never to speak of it again to anybody*

# *Chapter 41*

The first week of their return was soon gone. The second began. It was the last of the regiment's stay in Meryton, and all the young ladies in the neighbourhood were drooping apace. The dejection was almost universal. The elder Miss Bennets alone were still able to eat, drink, and sleep, and pursue the usual course of their employments. Very frequently were they reproached for this insensibility by Kitty and Lydia, whose own misery was extreme, and who could not comprehend such hard-heartedness in any of the family.

'Good Heaven! What is to become of us! What are we to do!' would they often exclaim in the bitterness of woe. 'How can you be smiling so, Lizzy?'

Their affectionate mother shared all their grief; she remembered what she had herself endured on a similar occasion, five and twenty years ago.

'I am sure,' said she, 'I cried for two days together when Colonel Millar's regiment went away. I thought I should have broke my heart.'

'I am sure I shall break *mine*,' said Lydia.

'If one could but go to Brighton!' observed Mrs Bennet.

'Oh, yes! – if one could but go to Brighton! But papa is so disagreeable.'

'A little sea-bathing would set me up for ever.'

'And my aunt Philips is sure it would do *me* a great deal of good,' added Kitty.

Such were the kind of lamentations resounding perpetually through Longbourn House. Elizabeth tried to be diverted by them; but all sense of pleasure was lost in shame. She felt anew the justice of Mr Darcy's objections; and never had she before been so much disposed to pardon his interference in the views of his friend.

But the gloom of Lydia's prospect was shortly cleared away; for she received an invitation from Mrs Forster, the wife of the colonel of the regiment, to accompany her to Brighton. This invaluable friend was a very young woman, and very lately married. A resemblance in good humour and good spirits had recommended her and Lydia to each other, and out of their *three* months' acquaintance they had been intimate *two*.

The rapture of Lydia on this occasion, her adoration of Mrs Forster, the delight of Mrs Bennet, and the mortification of Kitty, are scarcely to be described. Wholly inattentive to her sister's feelings, Lydia flew about the house in restless ecstasy, calling for everyone's congratulations, and laughing and talking with more violence than ever; whilst the luckless Kitty continued in the parlour repining at her fate in terms as unreasonable as her accent was peevish.

'I cannot see why Mrs Forster should not ask *me* as well as Lydia,' said she, 'though I am *not* her particular friend. I have just as much right to be asked as she has, and more too, for I am two years older.'

In vain did Elizabeth attempt to make her reasonable, and Jane to make her resigned. As for Elizabeth herself, this invitation was so far from exciting in her the same feelings as in her mother and Lydia, that she considered it as the death-warrant of all possibility of common sense for the latter; and detestable as such a step must make her were it known, she could not help secretly advising her father not to let her go. She represented to him all the improprieties of Lydia's general behaviour, the little advantage she could derive from the friendship of such a woman as Mrs Forster, and the probability of her being yet more imprudent with such a companion at Brighton, where the temptations must be greater than at home. He heard her attentively, and then said, 'Lydia will never be easy till she has exposed herself in some public place or other, and we can never expect her to do it with so little expense or inconvenience to her family as under the present circumstances.'

'If you were aware,' said Elizabeth, 'of the very great disadvantage to us all, which must arise from the public notice of Lydia's unguarded and imprudent manner; nay, which has already arisen from it, I am sure you would judge differently in the affair.'

'Already arisen!' repeated Mr Bennet. 'What, has she frightened away some of your lovers? Poor little Lizzy! But do not be cast down. Such squeamish youths as cannot bear to be connected with a little absurdity, are not worth a regret. Come, let me see the list of the pitiful fellows who have been kept aloof by Lydia's folly.'

'Indeed you are mistaken. I have no such injuries to resent. It is not of peculiar, but of general evils, which I am now complaining. Our importance, our respectability in the world, must be affected by the wild volatility, the assurance and disdain of all restraint which mark Lydia's character. Excuse me – for I must speak plainly. If you, my dear father, will not take the trouble of checking her exuberant spirits, and of teaching her that her present pursuits are not to be the business of her life, she will soon be beyond the reach of amendment. Her character will be fixed, and she will, at sixteen, be the most determined flirt that ever made herself and her family ridiculous. A flirt too, in the worst and meanest degree of flirtation; without any attraction beyond youth and a tolerable person; and from the ignorance and emptiness of her mind, wholly unable to ward off any portion of that universal contempt which her rage for admiration will excite. In this danger Kitty is also comprehended. She will follow wherever Lydia leads. Vain, ignorant, idle, and absolutely uncontrolled! Oh! my dear father, can you suppose it possible that they will not be censured and despised wherever they are known, and that their sisters will not be often involved in the disgrace?'

Mr Bennet saw that her whole heart was in the subject; and affectionately taking her hand, said in reply, 'Do not make yourself uneasy, my love. Wherever you and Jane are known, you must be respected and valued; and you will not appear to less advantage for having a couple of – or I may say, three very silly sisters. We shall have no peace at Longbourn if Lydia does not go to Brighton. Let her go then. Colonel Forster is a sensible man, and will keep her out of any real mischief; and she is luckily too poor to be an object of prey to anybody. At Brighton she will be of less importance even as a common flirt than she has been here. The officers will find women better worth their notice. Let us hope, therefore, that her being there may teach her her own insignificance. At any rate, she cannot grow many degrees worse, without authorising us to lock her up for the rest of her life.'

With this answer Elizabeth was forced to be content; but her own opinion continued the same, and she left him disappointed and sorry. It was not in her nature, however, to increase her vexations, by dwelling on them. She was confident of having performed her duty, and to fret over unavoidable evils, or augment them by anxiety, was no part of her disposition.

Had Lydia and her mother known the substance of her conference with her father, their indignation would hardly have found expression in their united volubility. In Lydia's imagination, a visit to Brighton comprised every possibility of earthly happiness. She saw with the creative eye of fancy, the streets of that gay bathing place covered with officers. She saw herself the object of attention, to tens and to scores of them at present unknown. She saw all the glories of the camp; its tents stretched forth in beauteous uniformity of lines, crowded with the young and the gay, and dazzling with scarlet; and to complete the view, she saw herself seated beneath a tent, tenderly flirting with at least six officers at once.

Had she known that her sister sought to tear her from such prospects and such realities as these, what would have been her sensations? They could have been understood only by her mother, who might have felt nearly the same. Lydia's going to Brighton was all that consoled her for the melancholy conviction of her husband's never intending to go there himself.

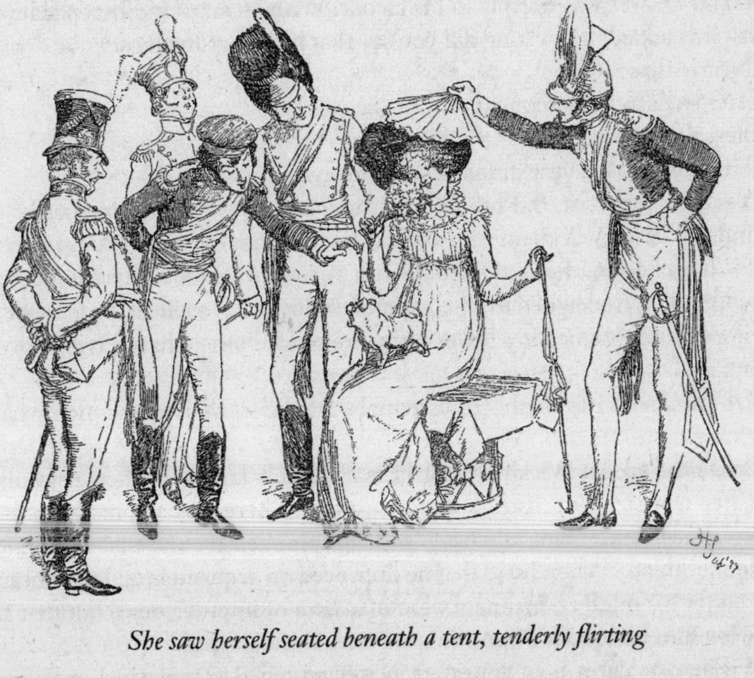

*She saw herself seated beneath a tent, tenderly flirting*

But they were entirely ignorant of what had passed; and their raptures continued with little intermission to the very day of Lydia's leaving home.

Elizabeth was now to see Mr Wickham for the last time. Having been frequently in company with him since her return, agitation was pretty well over; the agitations of former partiality entirely so. She had even learnt to detect, in the very gentleness which had first delighted her, an affectation and a sameness to disgust and weary. In his present behaviour to herself, moreover, she had a fresh source of displeasure, for the inclination he soon testified of renewing those attentions which had marked the early part of their acquaintance, could only serve, after what had since passed, to provoke her. She lost all concern for him in finding herself thus selected as the object of such idle and frivolous gallantry; and while she steadily repressed it, could not but feel the reproof contained in his believing, that however long, and for whatever cause, his attentions had been withdrawn, her vanity would be gratified and her preference secured at any time by their renewal.

On the very last day of the regiment's remaining in Meryton, he dined with others of the officers at Longbourn; and so little was Elizabeth disposed to part from him in good humour, that on his making some enquiry as to the manner in which her time had passed at Hunsford, she mentioned Colonel Fitzwilliam's and Mr Darcy's having both spent three weeks at Rosings, and asked him if he were acquainted with the former.

He looked surprised, displeased, alarmed; but with a moment's recollection and a returning smile, replied, that he had formerly seen him often; and after observing that he was a very gentlemanlike man, asked her how she had liked him. Her answer was warmly in his favour. With an air of indifference he soon afterwards added, 'How long did you say that he was at Rosings?'

'Nearly three weeks.'

'And you saw him frequently?'

'Yes, almost every day.'

'His manners are very different from his cousin's.'

'Yes, very different. But I think Mr Darcy improves on acquaintance.'

'Indeed!' cried Wickham with a look which did not escape her. 'And pray may I ask?' but checking himself, he added in a gayer tone, 'Is it in address that he improves? Has he deigned to add ought of civility to his ordinary style? for I dare not hope,' he continued in a lower and more serious tone, 'that he is improved in essentials.'

'Oh, no!' said Elizabeth. 'In essentials, I believe, he is very much what he ever was.'

While she spoke, Wickham looked as if scarcely knowing whether to rejoice over her words, or to distrust their meaning. There was a something in her countenance which made him listen with an apprehensive and anxious attention, while she added, 'When I said that he improved on acquaintance, I did not mean that either his mind or manners were in a state of improvement, but that from knowing him better, his disposition was better understood.'

Wickham's alarm now appeared in a heightened complexion and agitated look; for a few minutes he was silent; till, shaking off his embarrassment, he turned to her again, and said in the gentlest of accents, 'You, who so well know my feelings towards Mr Darcy, will readily comprehend how sincerely I must rejoice that he is wise enough to assume even the *appearance* of what is right. His pride, in that direction, may be of service, if not to himself, to many others, for it must deter him from such foul misconduct as I have suffered by. I only fear that the sort of cautiousness, to which you, I imagine, have been alluding, is merely adopted on his visits to his aunt, of whose good opinion and judgment he stands much in awe. His fear of her, has always operated, I know, when they were together; and a good deal is to be imputed to his wish of forwarding the match with Miss de Bourgh, which I am certain he has very much at heart.'

Elizabeth could not repress a smile at this, but she answered only by a slight inclination of the head. She saw that he wanted to engage her on the old subject of his grievances, and she was in no humour to indulge him. The rest of the evening passed with the *appearance*, on his side, of usual cheerfulness, but with no farther attempt to distinguish Elizabeth; and they parted at last with mutual civility, and possibly a mutual desire of never meeting again.

When the party broke up, Lydia returned with Mrs Forster to Meryton, from whence they were to set out early the next morning. The separation between her and her family was rather noisy than pathetic. Kitty was the only one who shed tears; but she did weep from vexation and envy. Mrs Bennet was diffuse in her good wishes for the felicity of her daughter, and impressive in her injunctions that she would not miss the opportunity of enjoying herself as much as possible; advice, which there was every reason to believe would be attended to; and in the clamorous happiness of Lydia herself in bidding farewell, the more gentle adieus of her sisters were uttered without being heard.

## *Chapter 42*

Had Elizabeth's opinion been all drawn from her own family, she could not have formed a very pleasing picture of conjugal felicity or domestic comfort. Her father, captivated by youth and beauty, and that appearance of good humour, which youth and beauty generally give, had married a woman whose weak understanding and illiberal mind, had very early in their marriage put an end to all real affection for her. Respect, esteem, and confidence, had vanished for ever; and all his views of domestic happiness were overthrown. But Mr Bennet was not of a disposition to seek comfort for the disappointment which his own imprudence had brought on, in any of those pleasures which too often console the unfortunate for their folly or their vice. He was fond of the country and of books; and from these tastes had arisen his principal enjoyments. To his wife he was very little otherwise indebted, than as her ignorance and folly had contributed to his amusement. This is not the sort of happiness which a man would in general wish to owe to his wife; but where other powers of entertainment are wanting, the true philosopher will derive benefit from such as are given.

Elizabeth, however, had never been blind to the impropriety of her father's behaviour as a husband. She had always seen it with pain; but respecting his abilities, and grateful for his affectionate treatment of herself, she endeavoured to forget what she could not overlook, and to banish from her thoughts that continual breach of conjugal obligation and decorum which, in exposing his wife to the contempt of her own children, was so highly reprehensible. But she had never felt so strongly as now, the disadvantages which must attend the children of so unsuitable a marriage, nor ever been so fully aware of the evils arising from so ill-judged a direction of talents; talents which rightly used, might at least have preserved the respectability of his daughters, even if incapable of enlarging the mind of his wife.

When Elizabeth had rejoiced over Wickham's departure, she found little other cause for satisfaction in the loss of the regiment. Their parties abroad were less varied than before; and at home she had a mother and sister whose constant repinings at the dullness of everything around them, threw a real gloom over their domestic circle; and, though Kitty might in time regain her natural degree of sense, since the disturbers of her brain were removed, her other sister, from whose disposition greater evil might be apprehended, was likely to be hardened in all her folly and assurance, by a situation of such double danger as a watering place and a camp. Upon the whole, therefore, she found, what has been sometimes found before, that an event to which she had looked forward with impatient desire, did not in taking place, bring all the satisfaction she had promised herself. It was consequently necessary to name some other period for the commencement of actual felicity; to have some other point on which her wishes and hopes might be fixed, and by again enjoying the pleasure of anticipation, console herself for the present, and prepare for another disappointment. Her tour to the Lakes was now the object of her happiest thoughts; it was her best consolation for all the uncomfortable hours, which the discontentedness of her mother and Kitty made inevitable; and could she have included Jane in the scheme, every part of it would have been perfect.

'But it is fortunate,' thought she, 'that I have something to wish for. Were the whole arrangement complete, my disappointment would be certain. But here, by carrying with me one ceaseless source of regret in my sister's absence, I may reasonably hope to have all my expectations of pleasure realised. A scheme of which every part promises delight, can never be successful; and general disappointment is only warded off by the defence of some little peculiar vexation.'

When Lydia went away, she promised to write very often and very minutely to her mother and Kitty; but her letters were always long expected, and always very short. Those to her mother, contained little else, than that they were just returned from the library, where such and such officers had attended them, and where she had seen such beautiful ornaments as made her quite wild; that she had a new gown, or a new parasol, which she would have described more fully, but was obliged to leave off in a violent hurry, as Mrs Forster called her, and they were going to the camp; – and from her correspondence with her sister, there was still less to be learnt – for her letters to Kitty, though rather longer, were much too full of lines under the words to be made public.

After the first fortnight or three weeks of her absence, health, good humour and cheerfulness began to re-appear at Longbourn. Everything wore a happier aspect. The families who had been in town for the winter came back again, and summer finery and summer engagements arose. Mrs Bennet was restored to her usual querulous serenity, and by the middle of June Kitty was so much recovered as to be able to enter Meryton without tears; an event of such happy promise as to make Elizabeth hope, that by the following Christmas, she might be so tolerably reasonable as not to mention an officer above once a day, unless by some cruel and malicious arrangement at the War Office, another regiment should be quartered in Meryton.

The time fixed for the beginning of their Northern tour was now fast approaching; and a fortnight only was wanting of it, when a letter arrived from Mrs Gardiner, which at once delayed its commencement and curtailed its extent. Mr Gardiner would be prevented by business from setting out till a fortnight later in July, and must be in London again within a month; and as that left too short a period for them to go so far, and see so much as they had proposed, or at least to see it with the leisure and comfort they had built on, they were obliged to give up the Lakes, and substitute a more contracted tour; and, according to the present plan, were to go no farther northward than Derbyshire. In that county, there was enough to be seen, to occupy the chief of their three weeks; and to Mrs Gardiner it had a peculiarly strong attraction. The town where she had formerly passed some years of her life, and where they were now to spend a few days, was probably as great an object of her curiosity, as all the celebrated beauties of Matlock, Chatsworth, Dovedale, or the Peak.

Elizabeth was excessively disappointed; she had set her heart on seeing the Lakes; and still thought there might have been time enough. But it was her business to be satisfied – and certainly her temper to be happy; and all was soon right again.

With the mention of Derbyshire, there were many ideas connected. It was impossible for her to see the word without thinking of Pemberley and its owner. 'But surely,' said she, 'I may enter his county with impunity, and rob it of a few petrified spars without his perceiving me.'

The period of expectation was now doubled. Four weeks were to pass away before her uncle and aunt's arrival. But they did pass away, and Mr and Mrs Gardiner, with their four children, did at length appear at Longbourn. The children, two girls of six and eight years old, and two younger boys, were to be left under the particular care of their cousin Jane, who was the general favourite, and whose steady sense and sweetness of temper exactly adapted her for attending to them in every way – teaching them, playing with them, and loving them.

The Gardiners stayed only one night at Longbourn, and set off the next morning with Elizabeth in pursuit of novelty and amusement. One enjoyment was certain – that of suitableness as companions; a suitableness which comprehended health and temper to bear inconveniences – cheerfulness to enhance every pleasure – and affection and intelligence, which might supply it among themselves if there were disappointments abroad.

It is not the object of this work to give a description of Derbyshire, nor of any of the remarkable places through which their route thither lay; Oxford, Blenheim, Warwick, Kenilworth, Birmingham, etc. are sufficiently known. A small part of Derbyshire is all the present concern. To the little town of Lambton, the scene of Mrs Gardiner's former residence, and where she had lately learned that some acquaintance still remained, they bent their steps, after having seen all the principal wonders of the country; and within five miles of Lambton, Elizabeth found from her aunt, that Pemberley was situated. It was not in their direct road, nor more than a mile or two out of it. In talking over their route the evening before, Mrs Gardiner expressed an inclination to see the place again. Mr Gardiner declared his willingness, and Elizabeth was applied to for her approbation.

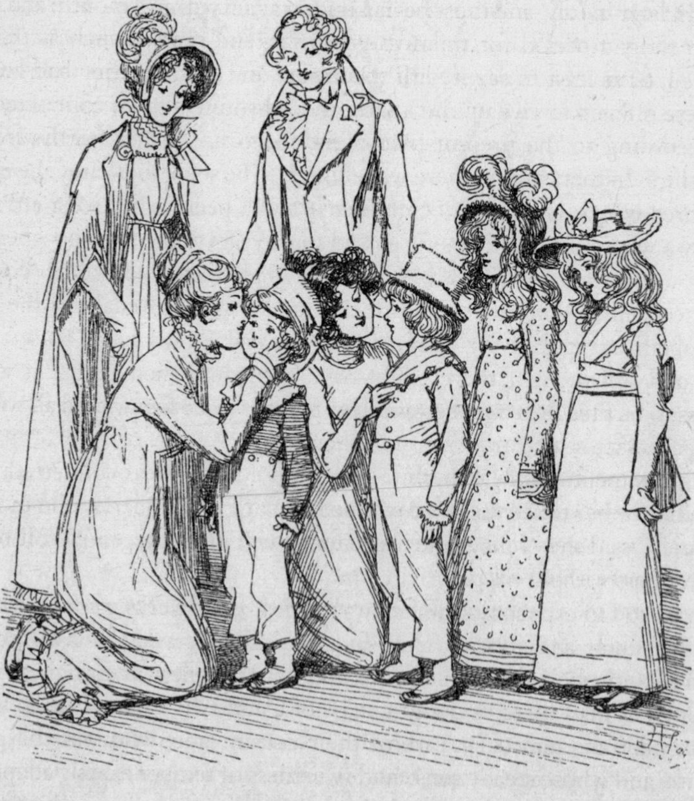

*Mr and Mrs Gardiner, with their four children*

'My love, should not you like to see a place of which you have heard so much?' said her aunt. 'A place too, with which so many of your acquaintance are connected. Wickham passed all his youth there, you know.'

Elizabeth was distressed. She felt that she had no business at Pemberley, and was obliged to assume a disinclination for seeing it. She must own that she was tired of great houses; after going over so many, she really had no pleasure in fine carpets or satin curtains.

Mrs Gardiner abused her stupidity. 'If it were merely a fine house richly furnished,' said she, 'I should not care about it myself; but the grounds are delightful. They have some of the finest woods in the country.'

Elizabeth said no more – but her mind could not acquiesce. The possibility of meeting Mr Darcy, while viewing the place, instantly occurred. It would be dreadful! She blushed at the very idea; and thought it would be better to speak openly to her aunt, than to run such a risk. But against this, there were objections; and she finally resolved that it could be the last resource, if her private enquiries as to the absence of the family, were unfavourably answered.

Accordingly, when she retired at night, she asked the chambermaid whether Pemberley were not a very fine place, what was the name of its proprietor, and with no little alarm, whether the family were down for the summer. A most welcome negative followed the last question – and her alarms being now removed, she was at leisure to feel a great deal of curiosity to see the house herself; and when the subject was revived the next morning, and she was again applied to, could readily answer, and with a proper air of indifference, that she had not really any dislike to the scheme.

To Pemberley, therefore, they were to go.

## *Chapter 43*

Elizabeth, as they drove along, watched for the first appearance of Pemberley Woods with some perturbation; and when at length they turned in at the lodge, her spirits were in a high flutter.

The park was very large, and contained great variety of ground. They entered it in one of its lowest points, and drove for some time through a beautiful wood, stretching over a wide extent.

Elizabeth's mind was too full for conversation, but she saw and admired every remarkable spot and point of view. They gradually ascended for half a mile, and then found themselves at the top of a considerable eminence, where the wood ceased, and the eye was instantly caught by Pemberley House, situated on the opposite side of a valley, into which the road with some abruptness wound. It was a large, handsome, stone building, standing well on rising ground, and backed by a ridge of high woody hills; – and in front, a stream of some natural importance was swelled into greater, but without any artificial appearance. Its banks were neither formal, nor falsely adorned. Elizabeth was delighted. She had never seen a place for which nature had done more, or where natural beauty had been so little counteracted by an awkward taste. They were all of them warm in their admiration; and at that moment she felt, that to be mistress of Pemberley might be something!

They descended the hill, crossed the bridge, and drove to the door; and, while examining the nearer aspect of the house, all her apprehensions of meeting its owner returned. She dreaded lest the chambermaid had been mistaken. On applying to see the place, they were admitted into the hall; and Elizabeth, as they waited for the housekeeper, had leisure to wonder at her being where she was.

The housekeeper came; a respectable-looking, elderly woman, much less fine, and more civil, than she had any notion of finding her. They followed her into the dining-parlour. It was a large, well-proportioned room, handsomely fitted up. Elizabeth, after slightly surveying it, went to a window to enjoy its prospect. The hill, crowned with wood, from which they had descended, receiving increased abruptness from the distance, was a beautiful object. Every disposition of the ground was good; and she looked on the whole scene, the river, the trees scattered on its banks, and the winding of the valley, as far as she could trace it, with delight. As they passed into other rooms, these objects were taking different positions; but from every window there were beauties to be seen. The rooms were lofty and handsome, and their furniture suitable to the fortune of their proprietor; but Elizabeth saw, with admiration of his taste, that it was neither gaudy nor uselessly fine; with less of splendour, and more real elegance, than the furniture of Rosings.

'And of this place,' thought she, 'I might have been mistress! With these rooms I might now have been familiarly acquainted! Instead of viewing them as a stranger, I might have rejoiced in them as my own, and welcomed to them as visitors my uncle and aunt. – But no,' – recollecting herself, – 'that could never be: my uncle and aunt would have been lost to me: I should not have been allowed to invite them.'

This was a lucky recollection – it saved her from something like regret.

She longed to enquire of the housekeeper, whether her master were really absent, but had not courage for it. At length, however, the question was asked by her uncle; and she turned away with alarm, while Mrs Reynolds replied, that he was, adding, 'but we expect him tomorrow, with a large party of friends.' How rejoiced was Elizabeth that their own journey had not by any circumstance been delayed a day!

Her aunt now called her to look at a picture. She approached, and saw the likeness of Mr Wickham suspended, amongst several other miniatures, over the mantelpiece. Her aunt asked her, smilingly, how she liked it. The housekeeper came forward, and told them it was the picture of a young gentleman, the son of her late master's steward, who had been brought up by him at his own expense. – 'He is now gone into the army,' she added, 'but I am afraid he has turned out very wild.'

Mrs Gardiner looked at her niece with a smile, but Elizabeth could not return it.

'And that,' said Mrs Reynolds, pointing to another of the miniatures, 'is my master – and very like him. It was drawn at the same time as the other – about eight years ago.'

'I have heard much of your master's fine person,' said Mrs Gardiner, looking at the picture; 'it is a handsome face. But, Lizzy, you can tell us whether it is like or not.'

Mrs Reynolds's respect for Elizabeth seemed to increase on this intimation of her knowing her master.

'Does that young lady know Mr Darcy?'

Elizabeth coloured, and said – 'A little.'

'And do not you think him a very handsome gentleman, Ma'am?'

'Yes, very handsome.'

'I am sure *I* know none so handsome; but in the gallery upstairs you will see a finer, larger picture of him than this. This room was my late master's favourite room, and these miniatures are just as they used to be then. He was very fond of them.'

This accounted to Elizabeth for Mr Wickham's being among them.

Mrs Reynolds then directed their attention to one of Miss Darcy, drawn when she was only eight years old.

'And is Miss Darcy as handsome as her brother?' said Mr Gardiner.

'Oh! yes – the handsomest young lady that ever was seen; and so accomplished! – She plays and sings all day long. In the next room is a new instrument just come down for her – a present from my master; she comes here tomorrow with him.'

Mr Gardiner, whose manners were easy and pleasant, encouraged her communicativeness by his questions and remarks; Mrs Reynolds, either from pride or attachment, had evidently great pleasure in talking of her master and his sister.

'Is your master much at Pemberley in the course of the year?'

'Not so much as I could wish, sir; but I dare say he may spend half his time here; and Miss Darcy is always down for the summer months.'

'Except,' thought Elizabeth, 'when she goes to Ramsgate.'

'If your master would marry, you might see more of him.'

'Yes, sir; but I do not know when *that* will be. I do not know who is good enough for him.'

Mr and Mrs Gardiner smiled. Elizabeth could not help saying, 'It is very much to his credit, I am sure, that you should think so.'

'I say no more than the truth, and what everybody will say that knows him,' replied the other. Elizabeth thought this was going pretty far; and she listened with increasing astonishment as the housekeeper added, 'I have never had a cross word from him in my life, and I have known him ever since he was four years old.'

This was praise, of all others most extraordinary, most opposite to her ideas. That he was not a good-tempered man, had been her firmest opinion. Her keenest attention was awakened; she longed to hear more, and was grateful to her uncle for saying, 'There are very few people of whom so much can be said. You are lucky in having such a master.'

'Yes, sir, I know I am. If I was to go through the world, I could not meet with a better. But I have always observed, that they who are good-natured when children, are good-natured when they grow up; and he was always the sweetest-tempered, most generous-hearted, boy in the world.'

Elizabeth almost stared at her. – 'Can this be Mr Darcy!' thought she.

'His father was an excellent man,' said Mrs Gardiner.

'Yes, Ma'am, that he was indeed; and his son will be just like him – just as affable to the poor.'

Elizabeth listened, wondered, doubted, and was impatient for more. Mrs Reynolds could interest her on no other point. She related the subject of the pictures, the dimensions of the rooms, and the price of the furniture, in vain. Mr Gardiner, highly amused by the kind of family prejudice, to which he attributed her excessive commendation of her master, soon led again to the subject; and she dwelt with energy on his many merits, as they proceeded together up the great staircase.

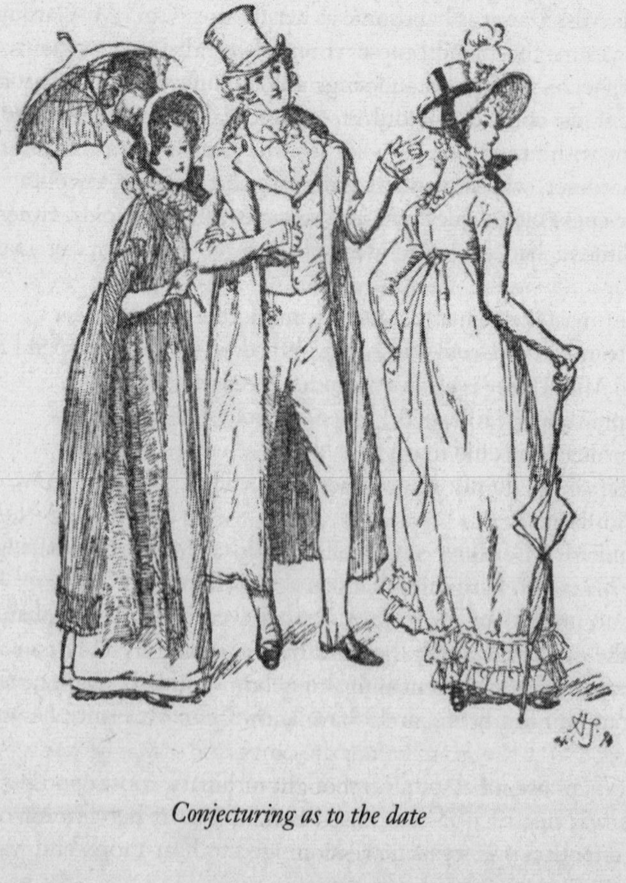

*Conjecturing as to the date*

'He is the best landlord, and the best master,' said she, 'that ever lived. Not like the wild young men nowadays, who think of nothing but themselves. There is not one of his tenants or servants but what will give him a good name. Some people call him proud; but I am sure I never saw anything of it. To my fancy, it is only because he does not rattle away like other young men.'

'In what an amiable light does this place him!' thought Elizabeth.

'This fine account of him,' whispered her aunt, as they walked, 'is not quite consistent with his behaviour to our poor friend.'

'Perhaps we might be deceived.'

'That is not very likely; our authority was too good.'

On reaching the spacious lobby above, they were shown into a very pretty sitting-room, lately fitted up with greater elegance and lightness than the apartments below; and were informed that it was but just done, to give pleasure to Miss Darcy, who had taken a liking to the room, when last at Pemberley.

'He is certainly a good brother,' said Elizabeth, as she walked towards one of the windows.

Mrs Reynolds anticipated Miss Darcy's delight, when she should enter the room. 'And this is always the way with him,' she added. – 'Whatever can give his sister any pleasure, is sure to be done in a moment. There is nothing he would not do for her.'

The picture gallery, and two or three of the principal bedrooms, were all that remained to be shown. In the former were many good paintings; but Elizabeth knew nothing of the art; and from such as had been already visible below, she had willingly turned to look at some drawings of Miss Darcy's, in crayons, whose subjects were usually more interesting, and also more intelligible.

In the gallery there were many family portraits, but they could have little to fix the attention of a stranger. Elizabeth walked on in quest of the only face whose features would be known to her. At last it arrested her – and she beheld a striking resemblance of Mr Darcy, with such a smile over the face, as she remembered to have sometimes seen, when he looked at her. She stood several minutes before the picture in earnest contemplation, and returned to it again before they quitted the gallery. Mrs Reynolds informed them, that it had been taken in his father's life time.

There was certainly at this moment, in Elizabeth's mind, a more gentle sensation towards the original, than she had ever felt in the height of their acquaintance. The commendation bestowed on him by Mrs Reynolds was of no trifling nature. What praise is more valuable than the praise of an intelligent servant? As a brother, a landlord, a master, she considered how many people's happiness were in his guardianship! – How much of pleasure or pain it was in his power to bestow! – How much of good or evil must be done by him! Every idea that had been brought forward by the housekeeper was favourable to his character, and as she stood before the canvas, on which he was represented, and fixed his eyes upon herself, she thought of his regard with a deeper sentiment of gratitude than it had ever raised before; she remembered its warmth, and softened its impropriety of expression.

When all of the house that was open to general inspection had been seen, they returned downstairs, and taking leave of the housekeeper, were consigned over to the gardener, who met them at the hall door.

As they walked across the lawn towards the river, Elizabeth turned back to look again; her uncle and aunt stopped also, and while the former was conjecturing as to the date of the building, the owner of it himself suddenly came forward from the road, which led behind it to the stables.

They were within twenty yards of each other, and so abrupt was his appearance, that it was impossible to avoid his sight. Their eyes instantly met, and the cheeks of each were overspread with the deepest blush. He absolutely started, and for a moment seemed immoveable from surprise; but shortly recovering himself, advanced towards the party, and spoke to Elizabeth, if not in terms of perfect composure, at least of perfect civility.

She had instinctively turned away; but, stopping on his approach, received his compliments with an embarrassment impossible to be overcome. Had his first appearance, or his resemblance to the picture they had just been examining, been insufficient to assure the other two that they now saw Mr Darcy, the gardener's expression of surprise, on beholding his master, must immediately have told it. They stood a little aloof while he was talking to their niece, who, astonished and confused, scarcely dared lift her eyes to his face, and knew not what answer she returned to his civil enquiries after her family. Amazed at the alteration in his manner since they last parted, every sentence that he uttered was increasing her embarrassment; and every idea of the impropriety of her being found there, recurring to her mind, the few minutes in which they continued together, were some of the most uncomfortable of her life. Nor did he seem much more at ease; when he spoke, his accent had none of its usual sedateness; and he repeated his enquiries as to the time of her having left Longbourn, and of her stay in Derbyshire, so often, and in so hurried a way, as plainly spoke the distraction of his thoughts.

At length, every idea seemed to fail him; and, after standing a few moments without saying a word, he suddenly recollected himself, and took leave.

The others then joined her, and expressed their admiration of his figure; but Elizabeth heard not a word, and, wholly engrossed by her own feelings, followed them in silence. She was overpowered by shame and vexation. Her coming there was the most unfortunate, the most ill-judged thing in the world! How strange must it appear to him! In what a disgraceful light might it not strike so vain a man! It might seem as if she had purposely thrown herself in his way again! Oh! why did she come? or, why did he thus come a day before he was expected? Had they been only ten minutes sooner, they should have been beyond the reach of his discrimination, for it was plain that he was that moment arrived, that moment alighted from his horse or his carriage. She blushed again and again over the perverseness of the meeting. And his behaviour, so strikingly altered, – what could it mean? That he should even speak to her was amazing! – but to speak with such civility, to enquire after her family! Never in her life had she seen his manners so little dignified, never had he spoken with such gentleness as on this unexpected meeting. What a contrast did it offer to his last address in Rosing's Park, when he put his letter into her hand! She knew not what to think, nor how to account for it.

They had now entered a beautiful walk by the side of the water, and every step was bringing forward a nobler fall of ground, or a finer reach of the woods to which they were approaching; but it was some time before Elizabeth was sensible of any of it; and, though she answered mechanically to the repeated appeals of her uncle and aunt, and seemed to direct her eyes to such objects as they pointed out, she distinguished no part of the scene. Her thoughts were all fixed on that one spot of Pemberley House, whichever it might be, where Mr Darcy then was. She longed to know what at that moment was passing in his mind; in what manner he thought of her, and whether, in defiance of everything, she was still dear to him. Perhaps he had been civil, only because he felt himself at ease; yet there had been *that* in his voice, which was not like ease. Whether he had felt more of pain or of pleasure in seeing her, she could not tell, but he certainly had not seen her with composure.

At length, however, the remarks of her companions on her absence of mind roused her, and she felt the necessity of appearing more like herself.

They entered the woods, and bidding adieu to the river for a while, ascended some of the higher grounds; whence, in spots where the opening of the trees gave the eye power to wander, were many charming views of the valley, the opposite hills, with the long range of woods overspreading many, and occasionally part of the stream. Mr Gardiner expressed a wish of going round the whole Park, but feared it might be beyond a walk. With a triumphant smile, they were told, that it was ten miles round. It settled the matter; and they pursued the accustomed circuit; which brought them again, after some time, in a descent among hanging woods, to the edge of the water, in one of its narrowest parts. They crossed it by a simple bridge, in character with the general air of the scene; it was a spot less adorned than any they had yet visited; and the valley, here contracted into a glen, allowed room only for the stream, and a narrow walk amidst the rough coppice-wood which bordered it. Elizabeth longed to explore its windings; but when they had crossed the bridge, and perceived their distance from the house, Mrs Gardiner, who was not a great walker, could go no farther, and thought only of returning to the carriage as quickly as possible. Her niece was, therefore, obliged to submit, and they took their way towards the house on the opposite side of the river, in the nearest direction; but their progress was slow, for Mr Gardiner, though seldom able to indulge the taste, was very fond of fishing, and was so much engaged in watching the occasional appearance of some trout in the water, and talking to the man about them, that he advanced but little. Whilst wandering on in this slow manner, they were again surprised, and Elizabeth's astonishment was quite equal to what it had been at first, by the sight of Mr Darcy approaching them, and at no great distance. The walk being here less sheltered than on the other side, allowed them to see him before they met. Elizabeth, however astonished, was at least more prepared for an interview than before, and resolved to appear and to speak with calmness, if he really intended to meet them. For a few moments, indeed, she felt that he would probably strike into some other path. This idea lasted while a turning in the walk concealed him from their view; the turning passed, he was immediately before them. With a glance she saw, that he had lost none of his recent civility; and, to imitate his politeness, she began, as they met, to admire the beauty of the place; but she had not got beyond the words 'delightful', and 'charming', when some unlucky recollections obtruded, and she fancied that praise of Pemberley from her, might be mischievously construed. Her colour changed, and she said no more.

Mrs Gardiner was standing a little behind; and on her pausing, he asked her, if she would do him the honour of introducing him to her friends. This was a stroke of civility for which she was quite unprepared; and she could hardly suppress a smile, at his being now seeking the acquaintance of some of those very people, against whom his pride had revolted, in his offer to herself. 'What will be his surprise,' thought she, 'when he knows who they are! He takes them now for people of fashion.'

The introduction, however, was immediately made; and as she named their relationship to herself, she stole a sly look at him, to see how he bore it; and was not without the expectation of his decamping as fast as he could from such disgraceful companions. That he was *surprised* by the connection was evident; he sustained it however with fortitude, and so far from going away, turned back with them, and entered into conversation with Mr Gardiner. Elizabeth could not but be pleased, could not but triumph. It was consoling, that he should know she had some relations for whom there was no need to blush. She listened most attentively to all that passed between them, and gloried in every expression, every sentence of her uncle, which marked his intelligence, his taste, or his good manners.

The conversation soon turned upon fishing, and she heard Mr Darcy invite him, with the greatest civility, to fish there as often as he chose, while he continued in the neighbourhood, offering at the same time to supply him with fishing tackle, and pointing out those parts of the stream where there was usually most sport. Mrs Gardiner, who was walking arm in arm with Elizabeth, gave her a look expressive of her wonder. Elizabeth said nothing, but it gratified her exceedingly; the compliment must be all for herself. Her astonishment, however, was extreme; and continually was she repeating, 'Why is he so altered? From what can it proceed? It cannot be for *me*, it cannot be for *my* sake that his manners are thus softened. My reproofs at Hunsford could not work such a change as this. It is impossible that he should still love me.'

After walking for some time in this way, the two ladies in front, the two gentlemen behind, on resuming their places, after descending to the brink of the river for the better inspection of some curious water-plant, there chanced to be a little alteration. It originated in Mrs Gardiner, who, fatigued by the exercise of the morning, found Elizabeth's arm inadequate to her support, and consequently preferred her husband's. Mr Darcy took her place by her niece, and they walked on together. After a short silence, the lady first spoke. She wished him to know that she had been assured of his absence before she came to the place, and accordingly began by observing, that his arrival had been very unexpected – 'for your housekeeper,' she added, 'informed us that you would certainly not be here till tomorrow; and indeed, before we left Bakewell, we understood that you were not immediately expected in the country.' He acknowledged the truth of it all; and said that business with his steward had occasioned his coming forward a few hours before the rest of the party with whom he had been travelling. 'They will join me early tomorrow,' he continued, 'and among them are some who will claim an acquaintance with you, – Mr Bingley and his sisters.'

Elizabeth answered only by a slight bow. Her thoughts were instantly driven back to the time when Mr Bingley's name had been last mentioned between them; and if she might judge from his complexion, *his* mind was not very differently engaged.

'There is also one other person in the party,' he continued after a pause, 'who more particularly wishes to be known to you. – Will you allow me, or do I ask too much, to introduce my sister to your acquaintance during your stay at Lambton?'

The surprise of such an application was great indeed; it was too great for her to know in what manner she acceded to it. She immediately felt that whatever desire Miss Darcy might have of being acquainted with her, must be the work of her brother, and without looking farther, it was satisfactory; it was gratifying to know that his resentment had not made him think really ill of her.

They now walked on in silence; each of them deep in thought. Elizabeth was not comfortable; that was impossible; but she was flattered and pleased. His wish of introducing his sister to her, was a compliment of the highest kind. They soon outstripped the others, and when they had reached the carriage, Mr and Mrs Gardiner were half a quarter of a mile behind.

He then asked her to walk into the house – but she declared herself not tired, and they stood together on the lawn. At such a time, much might have been said, and silence was very awkward. She wanted to talk, but there seemed an embargo on every subject. At last she recollected that she had been travelling, and they talked of Matlock and Dove Dale with great perseverance. Yet time and her aunt moved slowly – and her patience and her ideas were nearly worn out before the tête-à-tête was over. On Mr and Mrs Gardiner's coming up, they were all pressed to go into the house and take some refreshment; but this was declined, and they parted on each side with the utmost politeness. Mr Darcy handed the ladies into the carriage, and when it drove off, Elizabeth saw him walking slowly towards the house.

The observations of her uncle and aunt now began; and each of them pronounced him to be infinitely superior to anything they had expected. 'He is perfectly well behaved, polite, and unassuming,' said her uncle.

'There *is* something a little stately in him to be sure,' replied her aunt, 'but it is confined to his air, and is not unbecoming. I can now say with the housekeeper, that though some people may call him proud, *I* have seen nothing of it.'

'I was never more surprised than by his behaviour to us. It was more than civil; it was really attentive; and there was no necessity for such attention. His acquaintance with Elizabeth was very trifling.'

'To be sure, Lizzy,' said her aunt, 'he is not so handsome as Wickham; or rather he has not Wickham's countenance, for his features are perfectly good. But how came you to tell us that he was so disagreeable?'

Elizabeth excused herself as well as she could; said that she had liked him better when they met in Kent than before, and that she had never seen him so pleasant as this morning.

'But perhaps he may be a little whimsical in his civilities,' replied her uncle. 'Your great men often are; and therefore I shall not take him at his word about fishing, as he might change his mind another day, and warn me off his grounds.'

Elizabeth felt that they had entirely mistaken his character, but said nothing.

'From what we have seen of him,' continued Mrs Gardiner, 'I really should not have thought that he could have behaved in so cruel a way by anybody, as he has done by poor Wickham. He has not an ill-natured look. On the contrary, there is something pleasing about his mouth when he speaks. And there is something of dignity in his countenance, that would not give one an unfavourable idea of his heart. But to be sure, the good lady who showed us the house, did give him a most flaming character! I could hardly help laughing aloud sometimes. But he is a liberal master, I suppose, and *that* in the eye of a servant comprehends every virtue.'

Elizabeth here felt herself called on to say something in vindication of his behaviour to Wickham; and therefore gave them to understand, in as guarded a manner as she could, that by what she had heard from his relations in Kent, his actions were capable of a very different construction; and that his character was by no means so faulty, nor Wickham's so amiable, as they had been considered in Hertfordshire. In confirmation of this, she related the particulars of all the pecuniary transactions in which they had been connected, without actually naming her authority, but stating it to be such as might be relied on.

Mrs Gardiner was surprised and concerned; but as they were now approaching the scene of her former pleasures, every idea gave way to the charm of recollection; and she was too much engaged in pointing out to her husband all the interesting spots in its environs, to think of anything else. Fatigued as she had been by the morning's walk, they had no sooner dined than she set off again in quest of her former acquaintance, and the evening was spent in the satisfactions of an intercourse renewed after many years' discontinuance.

The occurrences of the day were too full of interest to leave Elizabeth much attention for any of these new friends; and she could do nothing but think, and think with wonder, of Mr Darcy's civility, and above all, of his wishing her to be acquainted with his sister.

# Chapter 44

Elizabeth had settled it that Mr Darcy would bring his sister to visit her, the very day after her reaching Pemberley; and was consequently resolved not to be out of sight of the inn the whole of that morning. But her conclusion was false; for on the very morning after their own arrival at Lambton, these visitors came. They had been walking about the place with some of their new friends, and were just returned to the inn to dress themselves for dining with the same family, when the sound of a carriage drew them to the window, and they saw a gentleman and lady in a curricle, driving up the street. Elizabeth immediately recognising the livery, guessed what it meant, and imparted no small degree of surprise to her relations, by acquainting them with the honour which she expected. Her uncle and aunt were all amazement; and the embarrassment of her manner as she spoke, joined to the circumstance itself, and many of the circumstances of the preceding day, opened to them a new idea on the business. Nothing had ever suggested it before, but they now felt that there was no other way of accounting for such attentions from such a quarter, than by supposing a partiality for their niece. While these newly-born notions were passing in their heads, the perturbation of Elizabeth's feelings was every moment increasing.

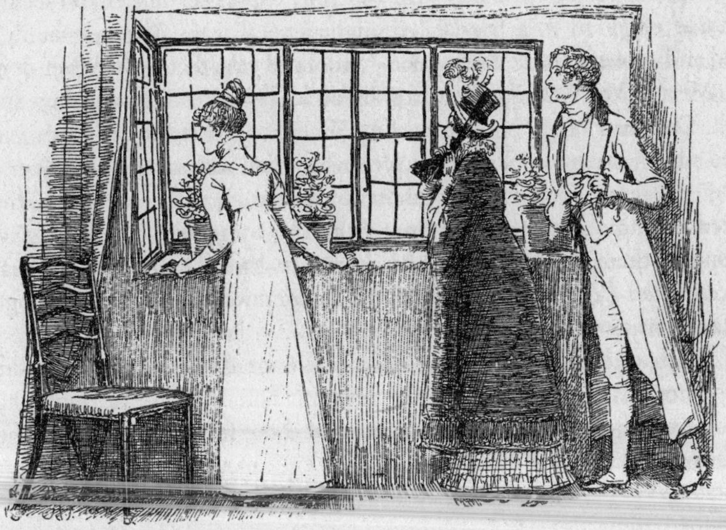

*The sound of a carriage drew them to the window*

She was quite amazed at her own discomposure; but amongst other causes of disquiet, she dreaded lest the partiality of the brother should have said too much in her favour; and more than commonly anxious to please, she naturally suspected that every power of pleasing would fail her.

She retreated from the window, fearful of being seen; and as she walked up and down the room, endeavouring to compose herself, saw such looks of enquiring surprise in her uncle and aunt, as made everything worse.

Miss Darcy and her brother appeared, and this formidable introduction took place. With astonishment did Elizabeth see, that her new acquaintance was at least as much embarrassed as herself. Since her being at Lambton, she had heard that Miss Darcy was exceedingly proud; but the observation of a very few minutes convinced her, that she was only exceedingly shy. She found it difficult to obtain even a word from her beyond a monosyllable.

Miss Darcy was tall, and on a larger scale than Elizabeth; and, though little more than sixteen, her figure was formed, and her appearance womanly and graceful. She was less handsome than her brother, but there was sense and good humour in her face, and her manners were perfectly unassuming and gentle. Elizabeth, who had expected to find in her as acute and unembarrassed an observer as ever Mr Darcy had been, was much relieved by discerning such different feelings.

They had not been long together, before Darcy told her that Bingley was also coming to wait on her; and she had barely time to express her satisfaction, and prepare for such a visitor, when Bingley's quick step was heard on the stairs, and in a moment he entered the room. All Elizabeth's anger against him had been long done away; but, had she still felt any, it could hardly have stood its ground against the unaffected cordiality with which he expressed himself, on seeing her again. He enquired in a friendly, though general way, after her family, and looked and spoke with the same good-humoured ease that he had ever done.

To Mr and Mrs Gardiner he was scarcely a less interesting personage than to herself. They had long wished to see him. The whole party before them, indeed, excited a lively attention. The suspicions which had just arisen of Mr Darcy and their niece, directed their observation towards each with an earnest, though guarded, enquiry; and they soon drew from those enquiries the full conviction that one of them at least knew what it was to love. Of the lady's sensations they remained a little in doubt; but that the gentleman was overflowing with admiration was evident enough.

Elizabeth, on her side, had much to do. She wanted to ascertain the feelings of each of her visitors, she wanted to compose her own, and to make herself agreeable to all; and in the latter object, where she feared most to fail, she was most sure of success, for those to whom she endeavoured to give pleasure were prepossessed in her favour. Bingley was ready, Georgiana was eager, and Darcy determined, to be pleased.

In seeing Bingley, her thoughts naturally flew to her sister; and oh! how ardently did she long to know, whether any of his were directed in a like manner. Sometimes she could fancy, that he talked less than on former occasions, and once or twice pleased herself with the notion that as he looked at her, he was trying to trace a resemblance. But, though this might be imaginary, she could not be deceived as to his behaviour to Miss Darcy, who had been set up as a rival of Jane. No look appeared on either side that spoke particular regard. Nothing occurred between them that could justify the hopes of his sister. On this point she was soon satisfied; and two or three little circumstances occurred ere they parted, which, in her anxious interpretation, denoted a recollection of Jane, not untinctured by tenderness, and a wish of saying more that might lead to the mention of her, had he dared. He observed to her, at a moment when the others were talking together, and in a tone which had something of real regret, that it 'was a very long time since he had had the pleasure of seeing her'; and, before she could reply, he added, 'It is above eight months. We have not met since the 26th of November, when we were all dancing together at Netherfield.'

Elizabeth was pleased to find his memory so exact; and he afterwards took occasion to ask her, when unattended to by any of the rest, whether *all* her sisters were at Longbourn. There was not much in the question, nor in the preceding remark, but there was a look and a manner which gave them meaning.

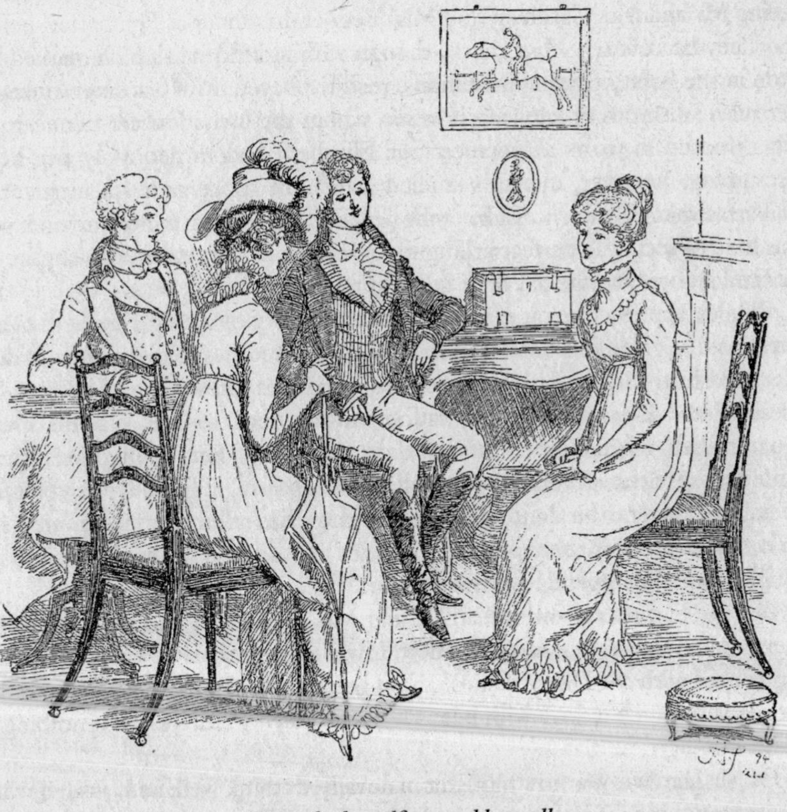

*To make herself agreeable to all*

It was not often that she could turn her eyes on Mr Darcy himself; but, whenever she did catch a glimpse, she saw an expression of general complaisance, and in all that he said, she heard an accent so far removed from hauteur or disdain of his companions, as convinced her that the improvement of manners which she had yesterday witnessed, however temporary its existence might prove, had at least outlived one day. When she saw him thus seeking the acquaintance, and courting the good opinion of people, with whom any intercourse a few months ago would have been a disgrace; when she saw him thus civil, not only to herself, but to the very relations whom he had openly disdained, and recollected their last lively scene in Hunsford Parsonage, the difference, the change was so great, and struck so forcibly on her mind, that she could hardly restrain her astonishment from being visible. Never, even in the company of his dear friends at Netherfield, or his dignified relations at Rosings, had she seen him so desirous to please, so free from self-consequence, or unbending reserve as now, when no importance could result from the success of his endeavours, and when even the acquaintance of those to whom his attentions were addressed, would draw down the ridicule and censure of the ladies both of Netherfield and Rosings.

Their visitors stayed with them above half an hour, and when they arose to depart, Mr Darcy called on his sister to join him in expressing their wish of seeing Mr and Mrs Gardiner, and Miss Bennet, to dinner at Pemberley, before they left the country. Miss Darcy, though with a diffidence which marked her little in the habit of giving invitations, readily obeyed. Mrs Gardiner looked at her niece, desirous of knowing how *she*, whom the invitation most concerned, felt disposed as to its acceptance, but Elizabeth had turned away her head. Presuming, however, that this studied avoidance spoke rather a momentary embarrassment, than any dislike of the proposal, and seeing in her husband, who was fond of society, a perfect willingness to accept it, she ventured to engage for her attendance, and the day after the next was fixed on.

Bingley expressed great pleasure in the certainty of seeing Elizabeth again, having still a great deal to say to her, and many enquiries to make after all their Hertfordshire friends. Elizabeth, construing all this into a wish of hearing her speak of her sister, was pleased; and on this account, as well as some others, found herself, when their visitors left them, capable of considering the last half-hour with some satisfaction, though while it was passing, the enjoyment of it had been little. Eager to be alone, and fearful of enquiries or hints from her uncle and aunt, she stayed with them only long enough to hear their favourable opinion of Bingley, and then hurried away to dress.

But she had no reason to fear Mr and Mrs Gardiner's curiosity; it was not their wish to force her communication. It was evident that she was much better acquainted with Mr Darcy than they had before any idea of; it was evident that he was very much in love with her. They saw much to interest, but nothing to justify enquiry.

Of Mr Darcy it was now a matter of anxiety to think well; and, as far as their acquaintance reached, there was no fault to find. They could not be untouched by his politeness, and had they drawn his character from their own feelings, and his servant's report, without any reference to any other account, the circle in Hertfordshire to which he was known, would not have recognised it for Mr Darcy. There was now an interest, however, in believing the housekeeper; and they soon became sensible, that the authority of a servant who had known him since he was four years old, and whose own manners indicated respectability, was not to be hastily rejected. Neither had anything occurred in the intelligence of their Lambton friends, that could materially lessen its weight. They had nothing to accuse him of but pride; pride he probably had, and if not, it would certainly be imputed by the inhabitants of a small market-town, where the family did not visit. It was acknowledged, however, that he was a liberal man, and did much good among the poor.

With respect to Wickham, the travellers soon found that he was not held there in much estimation; for though the chief of his concerns, with the son of his patron, were imperfectly understood, it was yet a well known fact that, on his quitting Derbyshire, he had left many debts behind him, which Mr Darcy afterwards discharged.

As for Elizabeth, her thoughts were at Pemberley this evening more than the last; and the evening, though as it passed it seemed long, was not long enough to determine her feelings towards *one* in that mansion; and she lay awake two whole hours, endeavouring to make them out. She certainly did not hate him. No; hatred had vanished long ago, and she had almost as long been ashamed of ever feeling a dislike against him, that could be so called. The respect created by the conviction of his valuable qualities, though at first unwillingly admitted, had for some time ceased to be repugnant to her feelings; and it was now heightened into somewhat of a friendlier nature, by the testimony so highly in his favour, and bringing forward his disposition in so amiable a light, which yesterday had produced. But above all, above respect and esteem, there was a motive within her of goodwill which could not be overlooked. It was gratitude. – Gratitude, not merely for having once loved her, but for loving her still well enough, to forgive all the petulance and acrimony of her manner in rejecting him, and all the unjust accusations accompanying her rejection. He who, she had been persuaded, would avoid her as his greatest enemy, seemed, on this accidental meeting, most eager to preserve the acquaintance, and without any indelicate display of regard, or any peculiarity of manner, where their two selves only were concerned, was soliciting the good opinion of her friends, and bent on making her known to his sister. Such a change in a man of so much pride, excited not only astonishment but gratitude – for to love, ardent love, it must be attributed; and as such its impression on her was of a sort to be encouraged, as by no means unpleasing, though it could not be exactly defined. She respected, she esteemed, she was grateful to him, she felt a real interest in his welfare; and she only wanted to know how far she wished that welfare to depend upon herself, and how far it would be for the happiness of both that she should employ the power, which her fancy told her she still possessed, of bringing on the renewal of his addresses.

It had been settled in the evening, between the aunt and niece, that such a striking civility as Miss Darcy's, in coming to them on the very day of her arrival at Pemberley, for she had reached it only to a late breakfast, ought to be imitated, though it could not be equalled, by some exertion of politeness on their side; and, consequently, that it would be highly expedient to wait on her at Pemberley the following morning. They were, therefore, to go. – Elizabeth was pleased, though, when she asked herself the reason, she had very little to say in reply.

Mr Gardiner left them soon after breakfast. The fishing scheme had been renewed the day before, and a positive engagement made of his meeting some of the gentlemen at Pemberley by noon.

## *Chapter 45*

Convinced as Elizabeth now was that Miss Bingley's dislike of her had originated in jealousy, she could not help feeling how very unwelcome her appearance at Pemberley must be to her, and was curious to know with how much civility on that lady's side, the acquaintance would now be renewed.

On reaching the house, they were shown through the hall into the saloon, whose northern aspect rendered it delightful for summer. Its windows opening to the ground, admitted a most refreshing view of the high woody hills behind the house, and of the beautiful oaks and Spanish chestnuts which were scattered over the intermediate lawn.

In this room they were received by Miss Darcy, who was sitting there with Mrs Hurst and Miss Bingley, and the lady with whom she lived in London. Georgiana's reception of them was very civil; but attended with all that embarrassment which, though proceeding from shyness and the fear of doing wrong, would easily give to those who felt themselves inferior, the belief of her being proud and reserved. Mrs Gardiner and her niece, however, did her justice, and pitied her.

By Mrs Hurst and Miss Bingley, they were noticed only by a curtsey; and on their being seated, a pause, awkward as such pauses must always be, succeeded for a few moments. It was first broken by Mrs Annesley, a genteel, agreeable-looking woman, whose endeavour to introduce some kind of discourse, proved her to be more truly well bred than either of the others; and between her and Mrs Gardiner, with occasional help from Elizabeth, the conversation was carried on. Miss Darcy looked as if she wished for courage enough to join in it; and sometimes did venture a short sentence, when there was least danger of its being heard.

Elizabeth soon saw that she was herself closely watched by Miss Bingley, and that she could not speak a word, especially to Miss Darcy, without calling her attention. This observation would not have prevented her from trying to talk to the latter, had they not been seated at an inconvenient distance; but she was not sorry to be spared the necessity of saying much. Her own thoughts were employing her. She expected every moment that some of the gentlemen would enter the room. She wished, she feared that the master of the house might be amongst them; and whether she wished or feared it most, she could scarcely determine. After sitting in this manner a quarter of an hour, without hearing Miss Bingley's voice, Elizabeth was roused by receiving from her a cold enquiry after the health of her family. She answered with equal indifference and brevity, and the other said no more.

The next variation which their visit afforded was produced by the entrance of servants with cold meat, cake, and a variety of all the finest fruits in season; but this did not take place till after many a significant look and smile from Mrs Annesley to Miss Darcy had been given, to remind her of her post. There was now employment for the whole party; for though they could not all talk, they could all eat; and the beautiful pyramids of grapes, nectarines, and peaches, soon collected them round the table.

While thus engaged, Elizabeth had a fair opportunity of deciding whether she most feared or wished for the appearance of Mr Darcy, by the feelings which prevailed on his entering the room; and then, though but a moment before she had believed her wishes to predominate, she began to regret that he came.

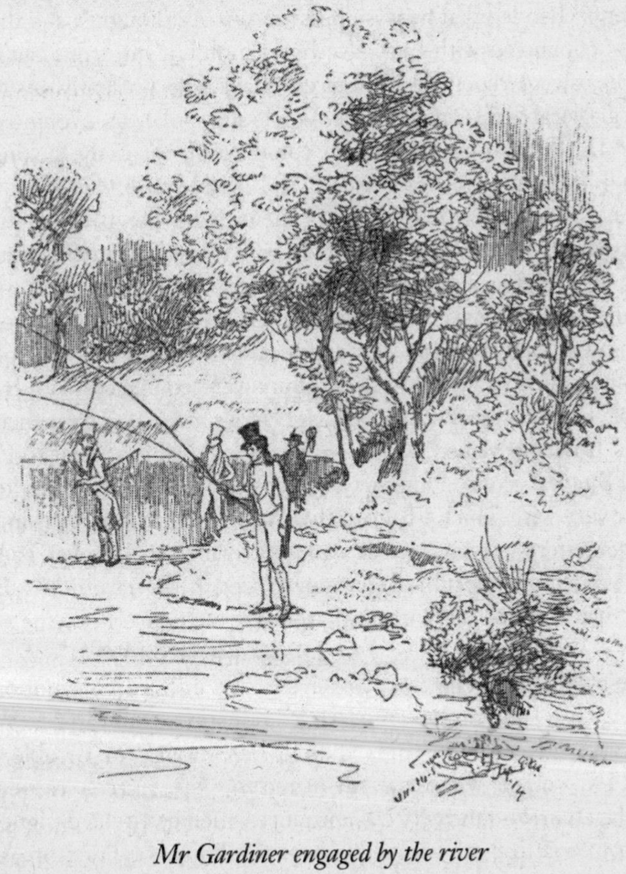

*Mr Gardiner engaged by the river*

He had been for some time with Mr Gardiner, who, with two or three other gentlemen from the house, was engaged by the river, and had left him only on learning that the ladies of the family intended a visit to Georgiana that morning. No sooner did he appear, than Elizabeth wisely resolved to be perfectly easy and unembarrassed; – a resolution the more necessary to be made, but perhaps not the more easily kept, because she saw that the suspicions of the whole party were awakened against them, and that there was scarcely an eye which did not watch his behaviour when he first came into the room. In no countenance was attentive curiosity so strongly marked as in Miss Bingley's, in spite of the smiles which overspread her face whenever she spoke to one of its objects; for jealousy had not yet made her desperate, and her attentions to Mr Darcy were by no means over. Miss Darcy, on her brother's entrance, exerted herself much more to talk; and Elizabeth saw that he was anxious for his sister and herself to get acquainted, and forwarded, as much as possible, every attempt at conversation on either side. Miss Bingley saw all this likewise; and, in the imprudence of anger, took the first opportunity of saying, with sneering civility, 'Pray, Miss Eliza, are not the —shire militia removed from Meryton? They must be a great loss to *your* family.'

In Darcy's presence she dared not mention Wickham's name; but Elizabeth instantly comprehended that he was uppermost in her thoughts; and the various recollections connected with him gave her a moment's distress; but, exerting herself vigorously to repel the ill-natured attack, she presently answered the question in a tolerably disengaged tone. While she spoke, an involuntary glance showed her Darcy with an heightened complexion, earnestly looking at her, and his sister overcome with confusion, and unable to lift up her eyes. Had Miss Bingley known what pain she was then giving her beloved friend, she undoubtedly would have refrained from the hint; but she had merely intended to discompose Elizabeth, by bringing forward the idea of a man to whom she believed her partial, to make her betray a sensibility which might injure her in Darcy's opinion, and perhaps to remind the latter of all the follies and absurdities, by which some part of her family were connected with that corps. Not a syllable had ever reached her of Miss Darcy's meditated elopement. To no creature had it been revealed, where secrecy was possible, except to Elizabeth; and from all Bingley's connections her brother was particularly anxious to conceal it, from that very wish which Elizabeth had long ago attributed to him, of their becoming hereafter her own. He had certainly formed such a plan, and without meaning that it should affect his endeavour to separate him from Miss Bennet, it is probable that it might add something to his lively concern for the welfare of his friend.

Elizabeth's collected behaviour, however, soon quieted his emotion; and as Miss Bingley, vexed and disappointed, dared not approach nearer to Wickham, Georgiana also recovered in time, though not enough to be able to speak any more. Her brother, whose eye she feared to meet, scarcely recollected her interest in the affair, and the very circumstance which had been designed to turn his thoughts from Elizabeth, seemed to have fixed them on her more, and more cheerfully.

Their visit did not continue long after the question and answer above-mentioned; and while Mr Darcy was attending them to their carriage, Miss Bingley was venting her feelings in criticisms on Elizabeth's person, behaviour, and dress. But Georgiana would not join her. Her brother's recommendation was enough to ensure her favour: his judgment could not err, and he had spoken in such terms of Elizabeth, as to leave Georgiana without the power of finding her otherwise than lovely and amiable. When Darcy returned to the saloon, Miss Bingley could not help repeating to him some part of what she had been saying to his sister.

'How very ill Eliza Bennet looks this morning, Mr Darcy,' she cried; 'I never in my life saw anyone so much altered as she is since the winter. She is grown so brown and coarse! Louisa and I were agreeing that we should not have known her again.'

However little Mr Darcy might have liked such an address, he contented himself with coolly replying, that he perceived no other alteration than her being rather tanned, – no miraculous consequence of travelling in the summer.

'For my own part,' she rejoined, 'I must confess that I never could see any beauty in her. Her face is too thin; her complexion has no brilliancy; and her features are not at all handsome. Her nose wants character; there is nothing marked in its lines. Her teeth are tolerable, but not out of the common way; and as for her eyes, which have sometimes been called so fine, I never could perceive anything extraordinary in them. They have a sharp, shrewish look, which I do not like at all; and in her air altogether, there is a self-sufficiency without fashion, which is intolerable.'

Persuaded as Miss Bingley was that Darcy admired Elizabeth, this was not the best method of recommending herself; but angry people are not always wise; and in seeing him at last look somewhat nettled, she had all the success she expected. He was resolutely silent however; and, from a determination of making him speak, she continued, 'I remember, when we first knew her in Hertfordshire, how amazed we all were to find that she was a reputed beauty; and I particularly recollect your saying one night, after they had been dining at Netherfield, "*She* a beauty! – I should as soon call her mother a wit." But afterwards she seemed to improve on you, and I believe you thought her rather pretty at one time.'

'Yes,' replied Darcy, who could contain himself no longer, 'but *that* was only when I first knew her, for it is many months since I have considered her as one of the handsomest women of my acquaintance.'

He then went away, and Miss Bingley was left to all the satisfaction of having forced him to say what gave no one any pain but herself.

Mrs Gardiner and Elizabeth talked of all that had occurred, during their visit, as they returned, except what had particularly interested them both. The looks and behaviour of everybody they had seen were discussed, except of the person who had mostly engaged their attention. They talked of his sister, his friends, his house, his fruit, of everything but himself; yet Elizabeth was longing to know what Mrs Gardiner thought of him, and Mrs Gardiner would have been highly gratified by her niece's beginning the subject.

## *Chapter 46*

Elizabeth had been a good deal disappointed in not finding a letter from Jane, on their first arrival at Lambton; and this disappointment had been renewed on each of the mornings that had now been spent there; but on the third, her repining was over, and her sister justified by the receipt of two letters from her at once, on one of which was marked that it had been mis-sent elsewhere. Elizabeth was not surprised at it, as Jane had written the direction remarkably ill.

They had just been preparing to walk as the letters came in; and her uncle and aunt, leaving her to enjoy them in quiet, set off by themselves. The one mis-sent must be first attended to; it had been written five days ago. The beginning contained an account of all their little parties and engagements, with such news as the country afforded; but the latter half, which was dated a day later, and written in evident agitation, gave more important intelligence. It was to this effect:

> Since writing the above, dearest Lizzy, something has occurred of a most unexpected and serious nature; but I am afraid of alarming you – be assured that we are all well. What I have to say relates to poor Lydia. An express came at twelve last night, just as we were all gone to bed, from Colonel Forster, to inform us that she was gone off to Scotland with one of his officers; to own the truth, with Wickham! – Imagine our surprise. To Kitty, however, it does not seem so wholly unexpected. I am very, very sorry. So imprudent a match on both sides! – But I am willing to hope the best, and that his character has been misunderstood. Thoughtless and indiscreet I can easily believe him, but this step (and let us rejoice over it) marks nothing bad at heart. His choice is disinterested at least, for he must know my father can give her nothing. Our poor mother is sadly grieved. My father bears it better. How thankful am I, that we never let them know what has been said against him; we must forget it ourselves. They were off Saturday night about twelve, as is conjectured, but were not missed till yesterday morning at eight. The express was sent off directly. My dear Lizzy, they must have passed within ten miles of us. Colonel Forster gives us reason to expect him here soon. Lydia left a few lines for his wife, informing her of their intention. I must conclude, for I cannot be long from my poor mother. I am afraid you will not be able to make it out, but I hardly know what I have written.'

Without allowing herself time for consideration, and scarcely knowing what she felt, Elizabeth on finishing this letter, instantly seized the other, and opening it with the utmost impatience, read as follows: it had been written a day later than the conclusion of the first.

'By this time, my dearest sister, you have received my hurried letter; I wish this may be more intelligible, but though not confined for time, my head is so bewildered that I cannot answer for being coherent. Dearest Lizzy, I hardly know what I would write, but I have bad news for you, and it cannot be delayed. Imprudent as a marriage between Mr Wickham and our poor Lydia would be, we are now anxious to be assured it has taken place, for there is but too much reason to fear they are not gone to Scotland. Colonel Forster came yesterday, having left Brighton the day before, not many hours after the express. Though Lydia's short letter to Mrs F. gave them to understand that they were going to Gretna Green, something was dropped by Denny expressing his belief that W. never intended to go there, or to marry Lydia at all, which was repeated to Colonel F. who instantly taking the alarm, set off from B. intending to trace their route. He did trace them easily to Clapham, but no farther; for on entering that place they removed into a hackney-coach and dismissed the chaise that brought them from Epsom. All that is known after this is, that they were seen to continue the London road. I know not what to think. After making every possible enquiry on that side London, Colonel F. came on into Hertfordshire, anxiously renewing them at all the turnpikes, and at the inns in Barnet and Hatfield, but without any success, no such people had been seen to pass through. With the kindest concern he came on to Longbourn, and broke his apprehensions to us in a manner most creditable to his heart. I am sincerely grieved for him and Mrs F. but no one can throw any blame on them. Our distress, my dear Lizzy, is very great. My father and mother believe the worst, but I cannot think so ill of him. Many circumstances might make it more eligible for them to be married privately in town than to pursue their first plan; and even if *he* could form such a design against a young woman of Lydia's connections, which is not likely, can I suppose her so lost to everything? – Impossible. I grieve to find, however, that Colonel F. is not disposed to depend upon their marriage; he shook his head when I expressed my hopes, and said he feared W. was not a man to be trusted. My poor mother is really ill and keeps her room. Could she exert herself it would be better, but this is not to be expected; and as to my father, I never in my life saw him so affected. Poor Kitty has anger for having concealed their attachment; but as it was a matter of confidence one cannot wonder. I am truly glad, dearest Lizzy, that you have been spared something of these distressing scenes; but now as the first shock is over, shall I own that I long for your return? I am not so selfish, however, as to press for it, if inconvenient. Adieu. I take up my pen again to do, what I have just told you I would not, but circumstances are such, that I cannot help earnestly begging you all to come here, as soon as possible. I know my dear uncle and aunt so well, that I am not afraid of requesting it, though I have still something more to ask of the former. My father is going to London with Colonel Forster instantly, to try to discover her. What he means to do, I am sure I know not; but his excessive distress will not allow him to pursue any measure in the best and safest way, and Colonel Forster is obliged to be at Brighton again tomorrow evening. In such an exigence my uncle's advice and assistance would be everything in the world; he will immediately comprehend what I must feel, and I rely upon his goodness.'

'Oh! where, where is my uncle?' cried Elizabeth, darting from her seat as she finished the letter, in eagerness to follow him, without losing a moment of the time so precious; but as she reached the door, it was opened by a servant, and Mr Darcy appeared. Her pale face and impetuous manner made him start, and before he could recover himself enough to speak, she, in whose mind every idea was superseded by Lydia's situation, hastily exclaimed, 'I beg your pardon, but I must leave you. I must find Mr Gardiner this moment, on business that cannot be delayed; I have not an instant to lose.'

'Good God! what is the matter?' cried he, with more feeling than politeness; then recollecting himself, 'I will not detain you a minute, but let me, or let the servant, go after Mr and Mrs Gardiner. You are not well enough; – you cannot go yourself.'

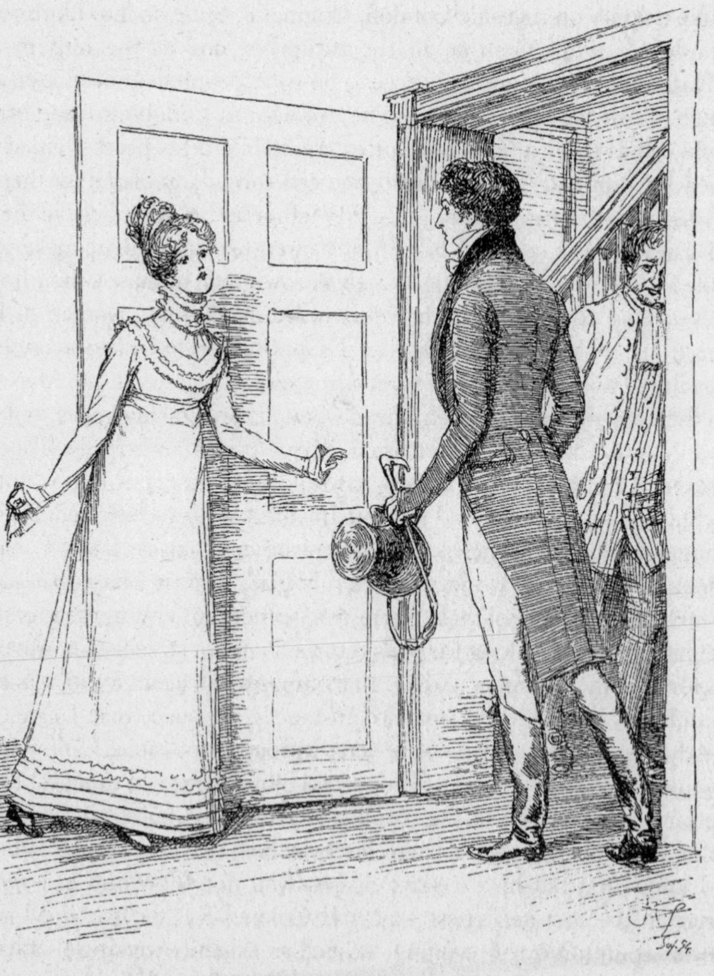

*I have not an instant to lose*

Elizabeth hesitated, but her knees trembled under her, and she felt how little would be gained by her attempting to pursue them. Calling back the servant, therefore, she commissioned him, though in so breathless an accent as made her almost unintelligible, to fetch his master and mistress home, instantly.

On his quitting the room, she sat down, unable to support herself, and looking so miserably ill, that it was impossible for Darcy to leave her, or to refrain from saying, in a tone of gentleness and commiseration, 'Let me call your maid. Is there nothing you could take, to give you present relief? – A glass of wine; – shall I get you one? – You are very ill.'

'No, I thank you;' she replied, endeavouring to recover herself. 'There is nothing the matter with me. I am quite well. I am only distressed by some dreadful news which I have just received from Longbourn.'

She burst into tears as she alluded to it, and for a few minutes could not speak another word. Darcy, in wretched suspense, could only say something indistinctly of his concern, and observe her in compassionate silence. At length, she spoke again. 'I have just had a letter from Jane, with such dreadful news. It cannot be concealed from anyone. My youngest sister has left all her friends – has eloped; – has thrown herself into the power of – of Mr Wickham. They are gone off together from Brighton. *You* know him too well to doubt the rest. She has no money, no connections, nothing that can tempt him to – she is lost for ever.'

Darcy was fixed in astonishment. 'When I consider,' she added, in a yet more agitated voice, 'that *I* might have prevented it! – *I* who knew what he was. Had I but explained some part of it only – some part of what I learnt, to my own family! Had his character been known, this could not have happened. But it is all, all too late now.'

'I am grieved, indeed,' cried Darcy; 'grieved – shocked. But is it certain, absolutely certain?'

'Oh yes! – They left Brighton together on Sunday night, and were traced almost to London, but not beyond; they are certainly not gone to Scotland.'

'And what has been done, what has been attempted, to recover her?'

'My father is gone to London, and Jane has written to beg my uncle's immediate assistance, and we shall be off, I hope, in half an hour. But nothing can be done; I know very well that nothing can be done. How is such a man to be worked on? How are they even to be discovered? I have not the smallest hope. It is every way horrible!'

Darcy shook his head in silent acquiescence.

'When *my* eyes were opened to his real character. – Oh! had I known what I ought, what I dared, to do! But I knew not – I was afraid of doing too much. Wretched, wretched, mistake!'

Darcy made no answer. He seemed scarcely to hear her, and was walking up and down the room in earnest meditation; his brow contracted, his air gloomy. Elizabeth soon observed, and instantly understood it. Her power was sinking; everything *must* sink under such a proof of family weakness, such an assurance of the deepest disgrace. She could neither wonder nor condemn, but the belief of his self-conquest brought nothing consolatory to her bosom, afforded no palliation of her distress. It was, on the contrary, exactly calculated to make her understand her own wishes; and never had she so honestly felt that she could have loved him, as now, when all love must be vain.

But self, though it would intrude, could not engross her. Lydia – the humiliation, the misery, she was bringing on them all, soon swallowed up every private care; and covering her face with her handkerchief, Elizabeth was soon lost to everything else; and, after a pause of several minutes, was only recalled to a sense of her situation by the voice of her companion, who, in a manner, which though it spoke compassion, spoke likewise restraint, said, 'I am afraid you have been long desiring my absence, nor have I anything to plead in excuse of my stay, but real, though unavailing, concern. Would to heaven that anything could be either said or done on my part, that might offer consolation to such distress. – But I will not torment you with vain wishes, which may seem purposely to ask for your thanks. This unfortunate affair will, I fear, prevent my sister's having the pleasure of seeing you at Pemberley today.'

'Oh, yes. Be so kind as to apologise for us to Miss Darcy. Say that urgent business calls us home immediately. Conceal the unhappy truth as long as it is possible. – I know it cannot be long.'

He readily assured her of his secrecy – again expressed his sorrow for her distress, wished it a happier conclusion than there was at present reason to hope, and leaving his compliments for her relations, with only one serious, parting look, went away.

As he quitted the room, Elizabeth felt how improbable it was that they should ever see each other again on such terms of cordiality as had marked their several meetings in Derbyshire; and as she threw a retrospective glance over the whole of their acquaintance, so full of contradictions and varieties, sighed at the perverseness of those feelings which would now have promoted its continuance, and would formerly have rejoiced in its termination.

If gratitude and esteem are good foundations of affection, Elizabeth's change of sentiment will be neither improbable nor faulty. But if otherwise, if the regard springing from such sources is unreasonable or unnatural, in comparison of what is so often described as arising on a first interview with its object, and even before two words have been exchanged, nothing can be said in her defence, except that she had given somewhat of a trial to the latter method, in her partiality for Wickham, and that its ill-success might perhaps authorise her to seek the other less interesting mode of attachment. Be that as it may, she saw him go with regret; and in this early example of what Lydia's infamy must produce, found additional anguish as she reflected on that wretched business. Never, since reading Jane's second letter, had she entertained a hope of Wickham's meaning to marry her. No one but Jane, she thought, could flatter herself with such an expectation. Surprise was the least of her feelings on this development. While the contents of the first letter remained on her mind, she was all surprise – all astonishment that Wickham should marry a girl, whom it was impossible he could marry for money; and how Lydia could ever have attached him, had appeared incomprehensible. But now it was all too natural. For such an attachment as this, she might have sufficient charms; and though she did not suppose Lydia to be deliberately engaging in an elopement, without the intention of marriage, she had no difficulty in believing that neither her virtue nor her understanding would preserve her from falling an easy prey.

She had never perceived, while the regiment was in Hertfordshire, that Lydia had any partiality for him, but she was convinced that Lydia had wanted only encouragement to attach herself to anybody. Sometimes one officer, sometimes another had been her favourite, as their attentions raised them in her opinion. Her affections had been continually fluctuating, but never without an object. The mischief of neglect and mistaken indulgence towards such a girl. – Oh! how acutely did she now feel it.

She was wild to be at home – to hear, to see, to be upon the spot, to share with Jane in the cares that must now fall wholly upon her, in a family so deranged; a father absent, a mother incapable of exertion, and requiring constant attendance; and though almost persuaded that nothing could be done for Lydia, her uncle's interference seemed of the utmost importance, and till he entered the room, the misery of her impatience was severe. Mr and Mrs Gardiner had hurried back in alarm, supposing, by the servant's account, that their niece was taken suddenly ill; – but satisfying them instantly on that head, she eagerly communicated the cause of their summons, reading the two letters aloud, and dwelling on the postscript of the last, with trembling energy. – Though Lydia had never been a favourite with them, Mr and Mrs Gardiner could not but be deeply affected. Not Lydia only, but all were concerned in it; and after the first exclamations of surprise and horror, Mr Gardiner readily promised every assistance in his power. – Elizabeth, though expecting no less, thanked him with tears of gratitude; and all three being actuated by one spirit, everything relating to their journey was speedily settled. They were to be off as soon as possible. 'But what is to be done about Pemberley?' cried Mrs Gardiner. 'John told us Mr Darcy was here when you sent for us; – was it so?'

'Yes; and I told him we should not be able to keep our engagement. *That* is all settled.'

'That is all settled;' repeated the other, as she ran into her room to prepare. 'And are they upon such terms as for her to disclose the real truth! Oh, that I knew how it was!'

But wishes were vain; or at best could serve only to amuse her in the hurry and confusion of the following hour. Had Elizabeth been at leisure to be idle, she would have remained certain that all employment was impossible to one so wretched as herself; but she had her share of business as well as her aunt, and amongst the rest there were notes to be written to all their friends in Lambton, with false excuses for their sudden departure. An hour, however, saw the whole completed; and Mr Gardiner meanwhile having settled his account at the inn, nothing remained to be done but to go; and Elizabeth, after all the misery of the morning, found herself, in a shorter space of time than she could have supposed, seated in the carriage, and on the road to Longbourn.

## *Chapter 47*

'I have been thinking it over again, Elizabeth,' said her uncle, as they drove from the town; 'and really, upon serious consideration, I am much more inclined than I was to judge as your eldest sister does of the matter. It appears to me so very unlikely, that any young man should form such a design against a girl who is by no means unprotected or friendless, and who was actually staying in his colonel's family, that I am strongly inclined to hope the best. Could he expect that her friends would not step forward? Could he expect to be noticed again by the regiment, after such an affront to Colonel Forster? His temptation is not adequate to the risk.'

'Do you really think so?' cried Elizabeth, brightening up for a moment.

'Upon my word,' said Mrs Gardiner, 'I begin to be of your uncle's opinion. It is really too great a violation of decency, honour, and interest, for him to be guilty of it. I cannot think so very ill of Wickham. Can you, yourself, Lizzy, so wholly give him up, as to believe him capable of it?'

'Not perhaps of neglecting his own interest. But of every other neglect I can believe him capable. If, indeed, it should be so! But I dare not hope it. Why should they not go on to Scotland, if that had been the case?'

'In the first place,' replied Mr Gardiner, 'there is no absolute proof that they are not gone to Scotland.'

'Oh! but their removing from the chaise into an hackney coach is such a presumption! And, besides, no traces of them were to be found on the Barnet road.'

'Well, then – supposing them to be in London. They may be there, though for the purpose of concealment, for no more exceptionable purpose. It is not likely that money should be very abundant on either side; and it might strike them that they could be more economically, though less expeditiously, married in London, than in Scotland.'

'But why all this secrecy? Why any fear of detection? Why must their marriage be private? Oh! no, no, this is not likely. His most particular friend, you see by Jane's account, was persuaded of his never intending to marry her. Wickham will never marry a woman without some money. He cannot afford it. And what claims has Lydia, what attractions has she beyond youth, health, and good humour, that could make him for her sake, forego every chance of benefiting himself by marrying well? As to what restraint the apprehension of disgrace in the corps might throw on a dishonourable elopement with her, I am not able to judge; for I know nothing of the effects that such a step might produce. But as to your other objection, I am afraid it will hardly hold good. Lydia has no brothers to step forward; and he might imagine, from my father's behaviour, from his indolence and the little attention he has ever seemed to give to what was going forward in his family, that *he* would do as little, and think as little about it, as any father could do, in such a matter.'

'But can you think that Lydia is so lost to everything but love of him, as to consent to live with him on any other terms than marriage?'

'It does seem, and it is most shocking indeed,' replied Elizabeth, with tears in her eyes, 'that a sister's sense of decency and virtue in such a point should admit of doubt. But, really, I know not what to say. Perhaps I am not doing her justice. But she is very young; she has never been taught to think on serious subjects; and for the last half-year, nay, for a twelvemonth, she has been given up to nothing but amusement and vanity. She has been allowed to dispose of her time in the most idle and frivolous manner, and to adopt any opinions that came in her way. Since the —shire were first quartered in Meryton, nothing but love, flirtation, and officers, have been in her head. She has been doing everything in her power by thinking and talking on the subject, to give greater – what shall I call it? susceptibility to her feelings; which are naturally lively enough. And we all know that Wickham has every charm of person and address that can captivate a woman.'

'But you see that Jane,' said her aunt, 'does not think so ill of Wickham, as to believe him capable of the attempt.'

'Of whom does Jane ever think ill? And who is there, whatever might be their former conduct, that she would believe capable of such an attempt, till it were proved against them? But Jane knows, as well as I do, what Wickham really is. We both know that he has been profligate in every sense of the word. That he has neither integrity nor honour. That he is as false and deceitful, as he is insinuating.'

'And do you really know all this?' cried Mrs Gardiner, whose curiosity as to the mode of her intelligence was all alive.

'I do, indeed,' replied Elizabeth, colouring. 'I told you the other day, of his infamous behaviour to Mr Darcy; and you, yourself, when last at Longbourn, heard in what manner he spoke of the man, who had behaved with such forbearance and liberality towards him. And there are other circumstances which I am not at liberty – which it is not worthwhile to relate; but his lies about the whole Pemberley family are endless. From what he said of Miss Darcy, I was thoroughly prepared to see a proud, reserved, disagreeable girl. Yet he knew to the contrary himself. He must know that she was as amiable and unpretending as we have found her.'

'But does Lydia know nothing of this? Can she be ignorant of what you and Jane seem so well to understand?'

'Oh, yes! – that, that is the worst of all. Till I was in Kent, and saw so much both of Mr Darcy and his relation, Colonel Fitzwilliam, I was ignorant of the truth myself. And when I returned home, the —shire was to leave Meryton in a week or fortnight's time. As that was the case, neither Jane, to whom I related the whole, nor I, thought it necessary to make our knowledge public; for of what use could it apparently be to anyone, that the good opinion which all the neighbourhood had of him, should then be overthrown? And even when it was settled that Lydia should go with Mrs Forster, the necessity of opening her eyes to his character never occurred to me. That *she* could be in any danger from the deception never entered my head. That such a consequence as *this* should ensue, you may easily believe was far enough from my thoughts.'

'When they all removed to Brighton, therefore, you had no reason, I suppose, to believe them fond of each other.'

'Not the slightest. I can remember no symptom of affection on either side; and had anything of the kind been perceptible, you must be aware that ours is not a family, on which it could be thrown away. When first he entered the corps, she was ready enough to admire him; but so we all were. Every girl in, or near Meryton, was out of her senses about him for the first two months; but he never distinguished *her* by any particular attention, and, consequently, after a moderate period of extravagant and wild admiration, her fancy for him gave way, and others of the regiment, who treated her with more distinction, again became her favourites.'

It may be easily believed, that however little of novelty could be added to their fears, hopes, and conjectures, on this interesting subject, by its repeated discussion, no other could detain them from it long, during the whole of the journey. From Elizabeth's thoughts it was never absent. Fixed there by the keenest of all anguish, self-reproach, she could find no interval of ease or forgetfulness.

They travelled as expeditiously as possible; and sleeping one night on the road, reached Longbourn by dinner-time the next day. It was a comfort to Elizabeth to consider that Jane could not have been wearied by long expectations.

The little Gardiners, attracted by the sight of a chaise, were standing on the steps of the house, as they entered the paddock; and when the carriage drove up to the door, the joyful surprise that lighted up their faces, and displayed itself over their whole bodies, in a variety of capers and frisks, was the first pleasing earnest of their welcome.

Elizabeth jumped out; and, after giving each of them an hasty kiss, hurried into the vestibule, where Jane, who came running downstairs from her mother's apartment, immediately met her.

Elizabeth, as she affectionately embraced her, whilst tears filled the eyes of both, lost not a moment in asking whether anything had been heard of the fugitives.

'Not yet,' replied Jane. 'But now that my dear uncle is come, I hope everything will be well.'

'Is my father in town?'

'Yes, he went on Tuesday as I wrote you word.'

'And have you heard from him often?'

'We have heard only once. He wrote me a few lines on Wednesday, to say that he had arrived in safety, and to give me his directions, which I particularly begged him to do. He merely added, that he should not write again, till he had something of importance to mention.'

'And my mother – How is she? How are you all?'

'My mother is tolerably well, I trust; though her spirits are greatly shaken.

She is upstairs, and will have great satisfaction in seeing you all. She does not yet leave her dressing-room. Mary and Kitty, thank Heaven! are quite well.'

'But you – How are you?' cried Elizabeth. 'You look pale. How much you must have gone through!'

Her sister, however, assured her, of her being perfectly well; and their conversation, which had been passing while Mr and Mrs Gardiner were engaged with their children, was now put an end to, by the approach of the whole party. Jane ran to her uncle and aunt, and welcomed and thanked them both, with alternate smiles and tears.

When they were all in the drawing-room, the questions which Elizabeth had already asked, were of course repeated by the others, and they soon found that Jane had no intelligence to give. The sanguine hope of good, however, which the benevolence of her heart suggested, had not yet deserted her; she still expected that it would all end well, and that every morning would bring some letter, either from Lydia or her father, to explain their proceedings, and perhaps announce the marriage.

Mrs Bennet, to whose apartment they all repaired, after a few minutes' conversation together, received them exactly as might be expected; with tears and lamentations of regret, invectives against the villainous conduct of Wickham, and complaints of her own sufferings and ill-usage; blaming everybody but the person to whose ill-judging indulgence the errors of her daughter must be principally owing.

'If I had been able,' said she, 'to carry my point of going to Brighton, with all my family, *this* would not have happened; but poor dear Lydia had nobody to

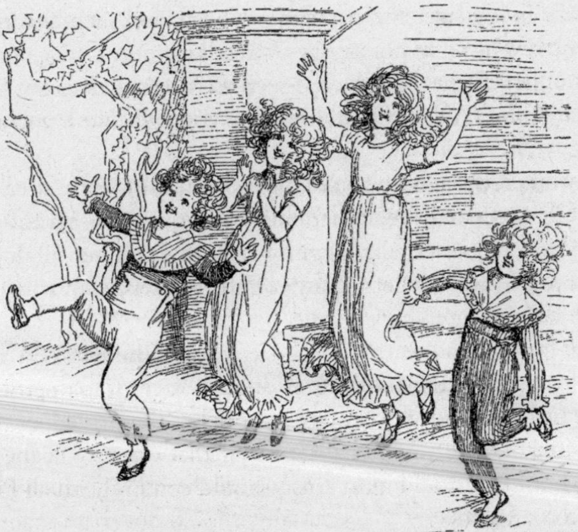

*The first pleasing earnest of their welcome*

take care of her. Why did the Forsters ever let her go out of their sight? I am sure there was some great neglect or other on their side, for she is not the kind of girl to do such a thing, if she had been well looked after. I always thought they were very unfit to have the charge of her; but I was overruled, as I always am. Poor dear child! And now here's Mr Bennet gone away, and I know he will fight Wickham, wherever he meets him, and then he will be killed, and what is to become of us all? The Collinses will turn us out, before he is cold in his grave; and if you are not kind to us, brother, I do not know what we shall do.'

They all exclaimed against such terrific ideas; and Mr Gardiner, after general assurances of his affection for her and all her family, told her that he meant to be in London the very next day, and would assist Mr Bennet in every endeavour for recovering Lydia.

'Do not give way to useless alarm,' added he, 'though it is right to be prepared for the worst, there is no occasion to look on it as certain. It is not quite a week since they left Brighton. In a few days more, we may gain some news of them, and till we know that they are not married, and have no design of marrying, do not let us give the matter over as lost. As soon as I get to town, I shall go to my brother, and make him come home with me to Gracechurch Street, and then we may consult together as to what is to be done.'

'Oh! my dear brother,' replied Mrs Bennet, 'that is exactly what I could most wish for. And now do, when you get to town, find them out, wherever they may be; and if they are not married already, *make* them marry. And as for wedding clothes, do not let them wait for that, but tell Lydia she shall have as much money as she chooses, to buy them, after they are married. And, above all things, keep Mr Bennet from fighting. Tell him what a dreadful state I am in, – that I am frightened out of my wits; and have such tremblings, such flutterings, all over me, such spasms in my side, and pains in my head, and such beatings at heart, that I can get no rest by night nor by day. And tell my dear Lydia, not to give any directions about her clothes, till she has seen me, for she does not know which are the best warehouses. Oh, brother, how kind you are! I know you will contrive it all.'

But Mr Gardiner, though he assured her again of his earnest endeavours in the cause, could not avoid recommending moderation to her, as well in her hopes as her fears; and, after talking with her in this manner till dinner was on table, they left her to vent all her feelings on the housekeeper, who attended, in the absence of her daughters.

Though her brother and sister were persuaded that there was no real occasion for such a seclusion from the family, they did not attempt to oppose it, for they knew that she had not prudence enough to hold her tongue before the servants, while they waited at table, and judged it better that *one* only of the household, and the one whom they could most trust, should comprehend all her fears and solicitude on the subject.

In the dining-room they were soon joined by Mary and Kitty, who had been too busily engaged in their separate apartments, to make their appearance before. One came from her books, and the other from her toilette. The faces of both, however, were tolerably calm; and no change was visible in either, except that the loss of her favourite sister, or the anger which she had herself incurred in the business, had given something more of fretfulness than usual, to the accents of Kitty. As for Mary, she was mistress enough of herself to whisper to Elizabeth with a countenance of grave reflection, soon after they were seated at table.

'This is a most unfortunate affair; and will probably be much talked of. But we must stem the tide of malice, and pour into the wounded bosoms of each other, the balm of sisterly consolation.'

Then, perceiving in Elizabeth no inclination of replying, she added, 'Unhappy as the event must be for Lydia, we may draw from it this useful lesson; that loss of virtue in a female is irretrievable – that one false step involves her in endless ruin – that her reputation is no less brittle than it is beautiful, – and that she cannot be too much guarded in her behaviour towards the undeserving of the other sex.'

Elizabeth lifted up her eyes in amazement, but was too much oppressed to make any reply. Mary, however, continued to console herself with such kind of moral extractions from the evil before them.

In the afternoon, the two elder Miss Bennets were able to be for half an hour by themselves; and Elizabeth instantly availed herself of the opportunity of making any enquiries, which Jane was equally eager to satisfy. After joining in general lamentations over the dreadful sequel of this event, which Elizabeth considered as all but certain, and Miss Bennet could not assert to be wholly impossible; the former continued the subject, by saying, 'But tell me all and everything about it, which I have not already heard. Give me farther particulars. What did Colonel Forster say? Had they no apprehension of anything before the elopement took place? They must have seen them together for ever.'

'Colonel Forster did own that he had often suspected some partiality, especially on Lydia's side, but nothing to give him any alarm. I am so grieved for him. His behaviour was attentive and kind to the utmost. He *was* coming to us, in order to assure us of his concern, before he had any idea of their not being gone to Scotland: when that apprehension first got abroad, it hastened his journey.'

'And was Denny convinced that Wickham would not marry? Did he know of their intending to go off? Had Colonel Forster seen Denny himself?'

'Yes; but when questioned by *him* Denny denied knowing anything of their plan, and would not give his real opinion about it. He did not repeat his persuasion of their not marrying – and from *that*, I am inclined to hope, he might have been misunderstood before.'

'And till Colonel Forster came himself, not one of you entertained a doubt, I suppose, of their being really married?'

'How was it possible that such an idea should enter our brains! I felt a little uneasy – a little fearful of my sister's happiness with him in marriage, because I knew that his conduct had not been always quite right. My father and mother knew nothing of that, they only felt how imprudent a match it must be. Kitty then owned, with a very natural triumph on knowing more than the rest of us, that in Lydia's last letter, she had prepared her for such a step. She had known, it seems, of their being in love with each other, many weeks.'

'But not before they went to Brighton?'

'No, I believe not.'

'And did Colonel Forster appear to think ill of Wickham himself? Does he know his real character?'

'I must confess that he did not speak so well of Wickham as he formerly did. He believed him to be imprudent and extravagant. And since this sad affair has taken place, it is said, that he left Meryton greatly in debt; but I hope this may be false.'

'Oh, Jane, had we been less secret, had we told what we knew of him, this could not have happened!'

'Perhaps it would have been better;' replied her sister. 'But to expose the former faults of any person, without knowing what their present feelings were, seemed unjustifiable. We acted with the best intentions.'

'Could Colonel Forster repeat the particulars of Lydia's note to his wife?'

'He brought it with him for us to see.'

Jane then took it from her pocketbook, and gave it to Elizabeth. These were the contents:

> MY DEAR HARRIET – You will laugh when you know where I am gone, and I cannot help laughing myself at your surprise tomorrow morning, as soon as I am missed. I am going to Gretna Green, and if you cannot guess with who, I shall think you a simpleton, for there is but one man in the world I love, and he is an angel. I should never be happy without him, so think it no harm to be off. You need not send them word at Longbourn of my going, if you do not like it, for it will make the surprise the greater, when I write to them, and sign my name Lydia Wickham. What a good joke it will be! I can hardly write for laughing. Pray make my excuses to Pratt, for not keeping my engagement, and dancing with him tonight. Tell him I hope he will excuse me when he knows all, and tell him I will dance with him at the next ball we meet, with great pleasure. I shall send for my clothes when I get to Longbourn; but I wish you would tell Sally to mend a great slit in my worked muslin gown, before they are packed up. Goodbye. Give my love to Colonel Forster, I hope you will drink to our good journey.
>
> Your affectionate friend,
>
> LYDIA BENNET.

'Oh! thoughtless, thoughtless Lydia!' cried Elizabeth when she had finished it. 'What a letter is this, to be written at such a moment. But at least it shows, that *she* was serious in the object of her journey. Whatever he might afterwards persuade her to, it was not on her side a *scheme* of infamy. My poor father! how he must have felt it!'

'I never saw anyone so shocked. He could not speak a word for full ten minutes. My mother was taken ill immediately, and the whole house in such confusion!'

'Oh! Jane,' cried Elizabeth, 'was there a servant belonging to it, who did not know the whole story before the end of the day?'

'I do not know. – I hope there was. – But to be guarded at such a time, is very difficult. My mother was in hysterics, and though I endeavoured to give her every assistance in my power, I am afraid I did not do so much as I might have done! But the horror of what might possibly happen, almost took from me my faculties.'

'Your attendance upon her has been too much for you. You do not look well. Oh! that I had been with you, you have had every care and anxiety upon yourself alone.'

'Mary and Kitty have been very kind, and would have shared in every fatigue, I am sure, but I did not think it right for either of them. Kitty is slight and delicate, and Mary studies so much, that her hours of repose should not be broken in on. My aunt Philips came to Longbourn on Tuesday, after my father went away; and was so good as to stay till Thursday with me. She was of great use and comfort to us all, and Lady Lucas has been very kind; she walked here on Wednesday morning to condole with us, and offered her services, or any of her daughters, if they could be of use to us.'

'She had better have stayed at home,' cried Elizabeth; 'perhaps she *meant* well, but, under such a misfortune as this, one cannot see too little of one's neighbours. Assistance is impossible; condolence, insufferable. Let them triumph over us at a distance, and be satisfied.'

She then proceeded to enquire into the measures which her father had intended to pursue, while in town, for the recovery of his daughter.

'He meant, I believe,' replied Jane, 'to go to Epsom, the place where they last changed horses, see the postilions, and try if anything could be made out from them. His principal object must be, to discover the number of the hackney coach which took them from Clapham. It had come with a fare from London; and as he thought the circumstance of a gentleman and lady's removing from one carriage into another, might be remarked, he meant to make enquiries at Clapham. If he could anyhow discover at what house the coachman had before set down his fare, he determined to make enquiries there, and hoped it might not be impossible to find out the stand and number of the coach. I do not know of any other designs that he had formed: but he was in such a hurry to be gone, and his spirits so greatly discomposed, that I had difficulty in finding out even so much as this.'

# *Chapter 48*

The whole party were in hopes of a letter from Mr Bennet the next morning, but the post came in without bringing a single line from him. His family knew him to be on all common occasions, a most negligent and dilatory correspondent, but at such a time, they had hoped for exertion. They were forced to conclude, that he had no pleasing intelligence to send, but even of *that* they would have been glad to be certain. Mr Gardiner had waited only for the letters before he set off.

When he was gone, they were certain at least of receiving constant information of what was going on, and their uncle promised, at parting, to prevail on Mr Bennet to return to Longbourn, as soon as he could, to the great consolation of his sister, who considered it as the only security for her husband's not being killed in a duel.

Mrs Gardiner and the children were to remain in Hertfordshire a few days longer, as the former thought her presence might be serviceable to her nieces. She shared in their attendance on Mrs Bennet, and was a great comfort to them, in their hours of freedom. Their other aunt also visited them frequently, and always, as she said, with the design of cheering and heartening them up, though as she never came without reporting some fresh instance of Wickham's extravagance or irregularity, she seldom went away without leaving them more dispirited than she found them.

All Meryton seemed striving to blacken the man, who, but three months before, had been almost an angel of light. He was declared to be in debt to every tradesman in the place, and his intrigues, all honoured with the title of seduction, had been extended into every tradesman's family. Everybody declared that he was the wickedest young man in the world; and everybody began to find out, that they had always distrusted the appearance of his goodness. Elizabeth, though she did not credit above half of what was said, believed enough to make her former assurance of her sister's ruin still more certain; and even Jane, who believed still less of it, became almost hopeless, more especially as the time was now come, when if they had gone to Scotland, which she had never before entirely despaired of, they must in all probability have gained some news of them.

Mr Gardiner left Longbourn on Sunday; on Tuesday, his wife received a letter from him; it told them, that on his arrival, he had immediately found out his brother, and persuaded him to come to Gracechurch Street. That Mr Bennet had been to Epsom and Clapham, before his arrival, but without gaining any satisfactory information; and that he was now determined to enquire at all the principal hotels in town, as Mr Bennet thought it possible they might have gone to one of them, on their first coming to London, before they procured lodgings. Mr Gardiner himself did not expect any success from this measure, but as his brother was eager in it, he meant to assist him in pursuing it. He added, that Mr Bennet seemed wholly disinclined at present, to leave

London, and promised to write again very soon. There was also a postscript to this effect.

'I have written to Colonel Forster to desire him to find out, if possible, from some of the young man's intimates in the regiment, whether Wickham has any relations or connections, who would be likely to know in what part of the town he has now concealed himself. If there were anyone, that one could apply to, with a probability of gaining such a clue as that, it might be of essential consequence. At present we have nothing to guide us. Colonel Forster will, I dare say, do everything in his power to satisfy us on this head. But, on second thoughts, perhaps Lizzy could tell us, what relations he has now living, better than any other person.'

Elizabeth was at no loss to understand from whence this deference for her authority proceeded; but it was not in her power to give any information of so satisfactory a nature, as the compliment deserved.

She had never heard of his having had any relations, except a father and mother, both of whom had been dead many years. It was possible, however, that some of his companions in the —shire, might be able to give more information; and, though she was not very sanguine in expecting it, the application was a something to look forward to.

Every day at Longbourn was now a day of anxiety; but the most anxious part of each was when the post was expected. The arrival of letters was the first grand object of every morning's impatience. Through letters, whatever of good or bad was to be told, would be communicated, and every succeeding day was expected to bring some news of importance.

But before they heard again from Mr Gardiner, a letter arrived for their father, from a different quarter, from Mr Collins; which, as Jane had received directions to open all that came for him in his absence, she accordingly read; and Elizabeth, who knew what curiosities his letters always were, looked over her, and read it likewise. It was as follows:

> My dear Sir – I feel myself called upon, by our relationship, and my situation in life, to condole with you on the grievous affliction you are now suffering under, of which we were yesterday informed by a letter from Hertfordshire. Be assured, my dear sir, that Mrs Collins and myself sincerely sympathise with you, and all your respectable family, in your present distress, which must be of the bitterest kind, because proceeding from a cause which no time can remove. No arguments shall be wanting on my part, that can alleviate so severe a misfortune; or that may comfort you, under a circumstance that must be of all others most afflicting to a parent's mind. The death of your daughter would have been a blessing in comparison of this. And it is the more to be lamented, because there is reason to suppose, as my dear Charlotte informs me, that this licentiousness of behaviour in your daughter, has proceeded from a faulty degree of indulgence, though, at the same time, for the consolation of yourself and Mrs Bennet, I am inclined to think that her own disposition must be naturally bad, or she could not be guilty of such

an enormity, at so early an age. Howsoever that may be, you are grievously to be pitied, in which opinion I am not only joined by Mrs Collins, but likewise by Lady Catherine and her daughter, to whom I have related the affair. They agree with me in apprehending that this false step in one daughter, will be injurious to the fortunes of all the others, for who, as Lady Catherine herself condescendingly says, will connect themselves with such a family. And this consideration leads me moreover to reflect with augmented satisfaction on a certain event of last November, for had it been otherwise, I must have been involved in all your sorrow and disgrace. Let me advise you then, my dear Sir, to console yourself as much as possible, to throw off your unworthy child from your affection for ever, and leave her to reap the fruits of her own heinous offence,

I am, dear Sir, &c. &c.

Mr Gardiner did not write again, till he had received an answer from Colonel Forster; and then he had nothing of a pleasant nature to send. It was not known that Wickham had a single relation, with whom he kept up any connection, and

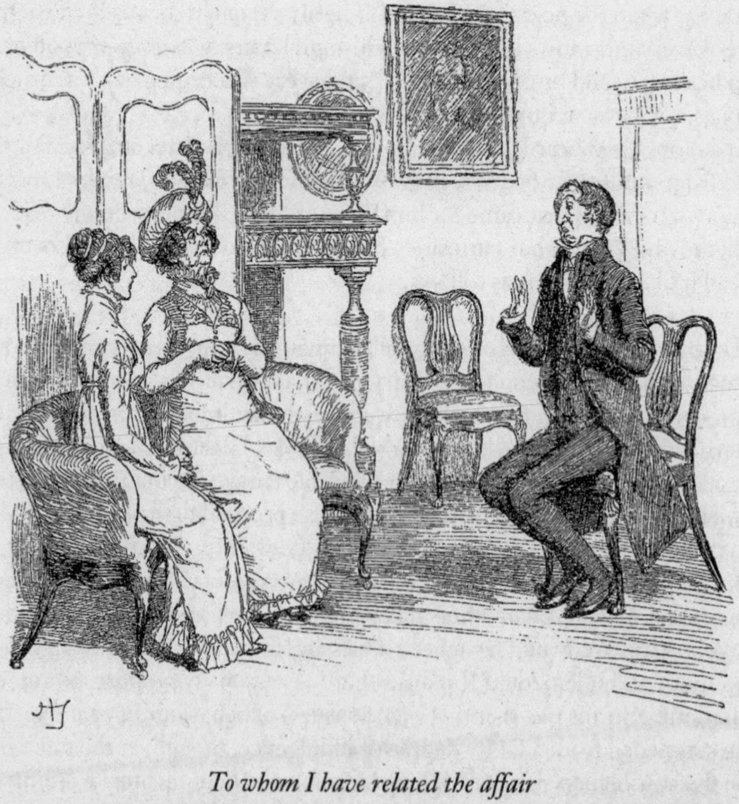

*To whom I have related the affair*

it was certain that he had no near one living. His former acquaintance had been numerous; but since he had been in the militia, it did not appear that he was on terms of particular friendship with any of them. There was no one therefore who could be pointed out, as likely to give any news of him. And in the wretched state of his own finances, there was a very powerful motive for secrecy, in addition to his fear of discovery by Lydia's relations, for it had just transpired that he had left gaming debts behind him, to a very considerable amount. Colonel Forster believed that more than a thousand pounds would be necessary to clear his expenses at Brighton. He owed a good deal in the town, but his debts of honour were still more formidable. Mr Gardiner did not attempt to conceal these particulars from the Longbourn family; Jane heard them with horror. 'A gamester!' she cried. 'This is wholly unexpected. I had not an idea of it.'

Mr Gardiner added in his letter, that they might expect to see their father at home on the following day, which was Saturday. Rendered spiritless by the ill-success of all their endeavours, he had yielded to his brother-in-law's entreaty that he would return to his family, and leave it to him to do, whatever occasion might suggest to be advisable for continuing their pursuit. When Mrs Bennet was told of this, she did not express so much satisfaction as her children expected, considering what her anxiety for his life had been before.

'What, is he coming home, and without poor Lydia!' she cried. 'Sure he will not leave London before he has found them. Who is to fight Wickham, and make him marry her, if he comes away?'

As Mrs Gardiner began to wish to be at home, it was settled that she and her children should go to London, at the same time that Mr Bennet came from it. The coach, therefore, took them the first stage of their journey, and brought its master back to Longbourn.

Mrs Gardiner went away in all the perplexity about Elizabeth and her Derbyshire friend, that had attended her from that part of the world. His name had never been voluntarily mentioned before them by her niece; and the kind of half-expectation which Mrs Gardiner had formed, of their being followed by a letter from him, had ended in nothing. Elizabeth had received none since her return, that could come from Pemberley.

The present unhappy state of the family, rendered any other excuse for the lowness of her spirits unnecessary; nothing, therefore, could be fairly conjectured from *that*, though Elizabeth, who was by this time tolerably well acquainted with her own feelings, was perfectly aware, that, had she known nothing of Darcy, she could have borne the dread of Lydia's infamy somewhat better. It would have spared her, she thought, one sleepless night out of two.

When Mr Bennet arrived, he had all the appearance of his usual philosophic composure. He said as little as he had ever been in the habit of saying; made no mention of the business that had taken him away, and it was some time before his daughters had courage to speak of it.

It was not till the afternoon, when he joined them at tea, that Elizabeth ventured to introduce the subject; and then, on her briefly expressing her sorrow for what he must have endured, he replied, 'Say nothing of that. Who should suffer but myself? It has been my own doing, and I ought to feel it.'

'You must not be too severe upon yourself,' replied Elizabeth.

'You may well warn me against such an evil. Human nature is so prone to fall into it! No, Lizzy, let me once in my life feel how much I have been to blame. I am not afraid of being overpowered by the impression. It will pass away soon enough.'

'Do you suppose them to be in London?'

'Yes; where else can they be so well concealed?'

'And Lydia used to want to go to London,' added Kitty.

'She is happy, then,' said her father, drily; 'and her residence there will probably be of some duration.'

Then, after a short silence, he continued, 'Lizzy, I bear you no ill will for being justified in your advice to me last May, which, considering the event, shows some greatness of mind.'

They were interrupted by Miss Bennet, who came to fetch her mother's tea.

'This is a parade,' cried he, 'which does one good; it gives such an elegance to misfortune! Another day I will do the same; I will sit in my library, in my night cap and powdering gown, and give as much trouble as I can, – or, perhaps, I may defer it, till Kitty runs away.'

'I am not going to run away, Papa,' said Kitty, fretfully; 'if I should ever go to Brighton, I would behave better than Lydia.'

'*You* go to Brighton! – I would not trust you so near it as Eastbourne, for fifty pounds! No, Kitty, I have at last learnt to be cautious, and you will feel the effects of it. No officer is ever to enter my house again, nor even to pass through the village. Balls will be absolutely prohibited, unless you stand up with one of your sisters. And you are never to stir out of doors, till you can prove, that you have spent ten minutes of every day in a rational manner.'

Kitty, who took all these threats in a serious light, began to cry.

'Well, well,' said he, 'do not make yourself unhappy. If you are a good girl for the next ten years, I will take you to a review at the end of them.'

## *Chapter 49*

Two days after Mr Bennet's return, as Jane and Elizabeth were walking together in the shrubbery behind the house, they saw the housekeeper coming towards them, and, concluding that she came to call them to their mother, went forward to meet her; but, instead of the expected summons, when they approached her, she said to Miss Bennet, 'I beg your pardon, madam, for interrupting you, but I was in hopes you might have got some good news from town, so I took the liberty of coming to ask.'

'What do you mean, Hill? We have heard nothing from town.'

'Dear madam,' cried Mrs Hill, in great astonishment, 'don't you know there is an express come for master from Mr Gardiner? He has been here this half-hour, and master has had a letter.'

Away ran the girls, too eager to get in to have time for speech. They ran through the vestibule into the breakfast-room; from thence to the library; – their father was in neither; and they were on the point of seeking him upstairs with their mother, when they were met by the butler, who said, 'If you are looking for my master, ma'am, he is walking towards the little copse.'

Upon this information, they instantly passed through the hall once more, and ran across the lawn after their father, who was deliberately pursuing his way towards a small wood on one side of the paddock.

Jane, who was not so light, nor so much in the habit of running as Elizabeth, soon lagged behind, while her sister, panting for breath, came up with him, and eagerly cried out, 'Oh, Papa, what news? what news? have you heard from my uncle?'

'Yes, I have had a letter from him by express.'

'Well, and what news does it bring? good or bad?'

'What is there of good to be expected?' said he, taking the letter from his pocket; 'but perhaps you would like to read it.'

Elizabeth impatiently caught it from his hand. Jane now came up.

'Read it aloud,' said their father, 'for I hardly know myself what it is about.'

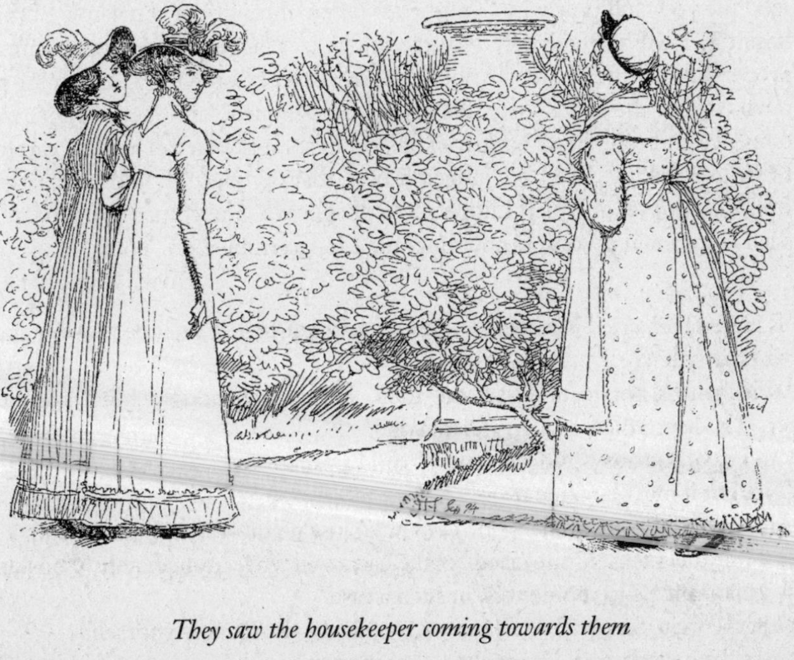

*They saw the housekeeper coming towards them*

*'Gracechurch Street, Monday, August 2*

'My dear Brother – At last I am able to send you some tidings of my niece, and such as, upon the whole, I hope will give you satisfaction. Soon after you left me on Saturday, I was fortunate enough to find out in what part of London they were. The particulars, I reserve till we meet. It is enough to know they are discovered, I have seen them both – '

'Then it is, as I always hoped,' cried Jane; 'they are married!'
Elizabeth read on:

'I have seen them both. They are not married, nor can I find there was any intention of being so; but if you are willing to perform the engagements which I have ventured to make on your side, I hope it will not be long before they are. All that is required of you is, to assure to your daughter, by settlement, her equal share of the five thousand pounds, secured among your children after the decease of yourself and my sister; and, moreover, to enter into an engagement of allowing her, during your life, one hundred pounds per annum. These are conditions, which, considering everything, I had no hesitation in complying with, as far as I thought myself privileged, for you. I shall send this by express, that no time may be lost in bringing me your answer. You will easily comprehend, from these particulars, that Mr Wickham's circumstances are not so hopeless as they are generally believed to be. The world has been deceived in that respect; and I am happy to say, there will be some little money, even when all his debts are discharged, to settle on my niece, in addition to her own fortune. If, as I conclude will be the case, you send me your full powers to act in your name, throughout the whole of this business, I will immediately give directions to Haggerston for preparing a proper settlement. There will not be the smallest occasion for your coming to town again; therefore, stay quietly at Longbourn, and depend on my diligence and care. Send back your answer as soon as you can, and be careful to write explicitly. We have judged it best, that my niece should be married from this house, of which I hope you will approve. She comes to us today. I shall write again as soon as anything more is determined on. Yours, &c.

'Edw. Gardiner.'

'Is it possible!' cried Elizabeth, when she had finished. 'Can it be possible that he will marry her?'

'Wickham is not so undeserving, then, as we have thought him;' said her sister. 'My dear father, I congratulate you.'

'And have you answered the letter?' said Elizabeth.

'No; but it must be done soon.'

Most earnestly did she then entreat him to lose no more time before he wrote.

'Oh! my dear father,' she cried, 'come back, and write immediately. Consider how important every moment is, in such a case.'

'Let me write for you,' said Jane, 'if you dislike the trouble yourself.'

'I dislike it very much,' he replied; 'but it must be done.'

And so saying, he turned back with them, and walked towards the house.

'And may I ask?' said Elizabeth, 'but the terms, I suppose, must be complied with.'

'Complied with! I am only ashamed of his asking so little.'

'And they *must* marry! Yet he is *such* a man!'

'Yes, yes, they must marry. There is nothing else to be done. But there are two things that I want very much to know: – one is, how much money your uncle has laid down, to bring it about; and the other, how I am ever to pay him.'

'Money! my uncle!' cried Jane, 'what do you mean, sir?'

'I mean, that no man in his senses, would marry Lydia on so slight a temptation as one hundred a year during my life, and fifty after I am gone.'

'That is very true,' said Elizabeth; 'though it had not occurred to me before. His debts to be discharged, and something still to remain! Oh! it must be my uncle's doings! Generous, good man, I am afraid he has distressed himself. A small sum could not do all this.'

'No,' said her father, 'Wickham's a fool, if he takes her with a farthing less than ten thousand pounds. I should be sorry to think so ill of him, in the very beginning of our relationship.'

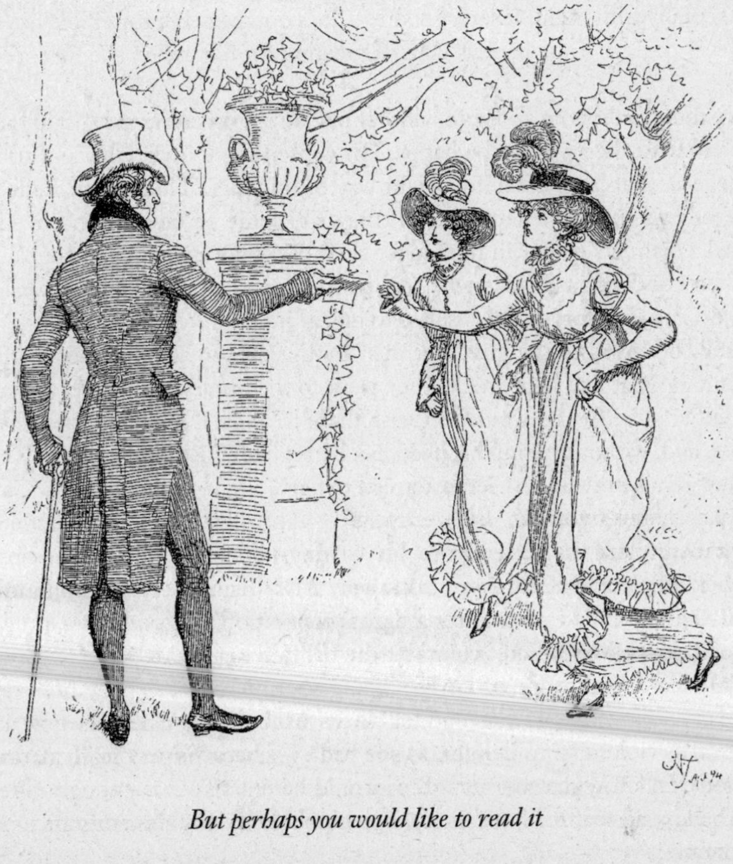

*But perhaps you would like to read it*

'Ten thousand pounds! Heaven forbid! How is half such a sum to be repaid?'

Mr Bennet made no answer, and each of them, deep in thought, continued silent till they reached the house. Their father then went to the library to write, and the girls walked into the breakfast-room.

'And they are really to be married!' cried Elizabeth, as soon as they were by themselves. 'How strange this is! And for *this* we are to be thankful. That they should marry, small as is their chance of happiness, and wretched as is his character, we are forced to rejoice! Oh, Lydia!'

'I comfort myself with thinking,' replied Jane, 'that he certainly would not marry Lydia, if he had not a real regard for her. Though our kind uncle has done something towards clearing him, I cannot believe that ten thousand pounds, or anything like it, has been advanced. He has children of his own, and may have more. How could he spare half ten thousand pounds?'

'If we are ever able to learn what Wickham's debts have been,' said Elizabeth, 'and how much is settled on his side on our sister, we shall exactly know what Mr Gardiner has done for them, because Wickham has not sixpence of his own. The kindness of my uncle and aunt can never be requited. Their taking her home, and affording her their personal protection and countenance, is such a sacrifice to her advantage, as years of gratitude cannot enough acknowledge. By this time she is actually with them! If such goodness does not make her miserable now, she will never deserve to be happy! What a meeting for her, when she first sees my aunt!'

'We must endeavour to forget all that has passed on either side,' said Jane: 'I hope and trust they will yet be happy. His consenting to marry her is a proof, I will believe, that he is come to a right way of thinking. Their mutual affection will steady them; and I flatter myself they will settle so quietly, and live in so rational a manner, as may in time make their past imprudence forgotten.'

'Their conduct has been such,' replied Elizabeth, 'as neither you, nor I, nor anybody, can ever forget. It is useless to talk of it.'

It now occurred to the girls that their mother was in all likelihood perfectly ignorant of what had happened. They went to the library, therefore, and asked their father, whether he would not wish them to make it known to her. He was writing, and, without raising his head, coolly replied, 'Just as you please.'

'May we take my uncle's letter to read to her?'

'Take whatever you like, and get away.'

Elizabeth took the letter from his writing-table, and they went upstairs together. Mary and Kitty were both with Mrs Bennet: one communication would, therefore, do for all. After a slight preparation for good news, the letter was read aloud. Mrs Bennet could hardly contain herself. As soon as Jane had read Mr Gardiner's hope of Lydia's being soon married, her joy burst forth, and every following sentence added to its exuberance. She was now in an irritation as violent from delight, as she had ever been fidgety from alarm and vexation. To know that her daughter would be married was enough. She was disturbed by no fear for her felicity, nor humbled by any remembrance of her misconduct.

'My dear, dear Lydia!' she cried: 'This is delightful indeed! – She will be married! – I shall see her again! – She will be married at sixteen! – My good, kind brother! – I knew how it would be – I knew he would manage everything. How I long to see her! and to see dear Wickham too! But the clothes, the wedding clothes! I will write to my sister Gardiner about them directly. Lizzy, my dear, run down to your father, and ask him how much he will give her. Stay, stay, I will go myself. Ring the bell, Kitty, for Hill. I will put on my things in a moment. My dear, dear Lydia! How merry we shall be together when we meet!'

Her eldest daughter endeavoured to give some relief to the violence of these transports, by leading her thoughts to the obligations which Mr Gardiner's behaviour laid them all under.

'For we must attribute this happy conclusion,' she added, 'in a great measure, to his kindness. We are persuaded that he has pledged himself to assist Mr Wickham with money.'

'Well,' cried her mother, 'it is all very right; who should do it but her own uncle? If he had not had a family of his own, I and my children must have had all his money you know, and it is the first time we have ever had anything from him, except a few presents. Well! I am so happy. In a short time, I shall have a daughter married. Mrs Wickham! How well it sounds. And she was only sixteen last June. My dear Jane, I am in such a flutter, that I am sure I can't write; so I will dictate, and you write for me. We will settle with your father about the money afterwards; but the things should be ordered immediately.'

She was then proceeding to all the particulars of calico, muslin, and cambric, and would shortly have dictated some very plentiful orders, had not Jane, though with some difficulty, persuaded her to wait, till her father was at leisure to be consulted. One day's delay she observed, would be of small importance; and her mother was too happy, to be quite so obstinate as usual. Other schemes too came into her head.

'I will go to Meryton,' said she, 'as soon as I am dressed, and tell the good, good news to my sister Philips. And as I come back, I can call on Lady Lucas and Mrs Long. Kitty, run down and order the carriage. An airing would do me a great deal of good, I am sure. Girls, can I do anything for you in Meryton? Oh! here comes Hill. My dear Hill, have you heard the good news? Miss Lydia is going to be married; and you shall all have a bowl of punch, to make merry at her wedding.'

Mrs Hill began instantly to express her joy. Elizabeth received her congratulations amongst the rest, and then, sick of this folly, took refuge in her own room, that she might think with freedom.

Poor Lydia's situation must, at best, be bad enough; but that it was no worse, she had need to be thankful. She felt it so; and though, in looking forward, neither rational happiness nor worldly prosperity, could be justly expected for her sister; in looking back to what they had feared, only two hours ago, she felt all the advantages of what they had gained.

## *Chapter 50*

Mr Bennet had very often wished, before this period of his life, that, instead of spending his whole income, he had laid by an annual sum, for the better provision of his children, and of his wife, if she survived him. He now wished it more than ever. Had he done his duty in that respect, Lydia need not have been indebted to her uncle, for whatever of honour or credit could now be purchased for her. The satisfaction of prevailing on one of the most worthless young men in Great Britain to be her husband, might then have rested in its proper place.

He was seriously concerned, that a cause of so little advantage to anyone, should be forwarded at the sole expense of his brother-in-law, and he was determined, if possible, to find out the extent of his assistance, and to discharge the obligation as soon as he could.

When first Mr Bennet had married, economy was held to be perfectly useless; for, of course, they were to have a son. This son was to join in cutting off the entail, as soon as he should be of age, and the widow and younger children would by that means be provided for. Five daughters successively entered the world, but yet the son was to come; and Mrs Bennet, for many years after Lydia's birth, had been certain that he would. This event had at last been despaired of, but it was then too late to be saving. Mrs Bennet had no turn for economy, and her husband's love of independence had alone prevented their exceeding their income.

Five thousand pounds was settled by marriage articles on Mrs Bennet and the children. But in what proportions it should be divided amongst the latter, depended on the will of the parents. This was one point, with regard to Lydia at least, which was now to be settled, and Mr Bennet could have no hesitation in acceding to the proposal before him. In terms of grateful acknowledgment for the kindness of his brother, though expressed most concisely, he then delivered on paper his perfect approbation of all that was done, and his willingness to fulfil the engagements that had been made for him. He had never before supposed that, could Wickham be prevailed on to marry his daughter, it would be done with so little inconvenience to himself, as by the present arrangement. He would scarcely be ten pounds a year the loser, by the hundred that was to be paid them; for, what with her board and pocket allowance, and the continual presents in money, which passed to her, through her mother's hands, Lydia's expenses had been very little within that sum.

That it would be done with such trifling exertion on his side, too, was another very welcome surprise; for his chief wish at present, was to have as little trouble in the business as possible. When the first transports of rage which had produced his activity in seeking her were over, he naturally returned to all his former indolence. His letter was soon dispatched; for though dilatory in undertaking business, he was quick in its execution. He begged to know farther particulars of what he was indebted to his brother; but was too angry with Lydia, to send any message to her.

The good news quickly spread through the house; and with proportionate speed through the neighbourhood. It was borne in the latter with decent philosophy. To be sure it would have been more for the advantage of conversation, had Miss Lydia Bennet come upon the town; or, as the happiest alternative, been secluded from the world, in some distant farmhouse. But there was much to be talked of, in marrying her; and the good-natured wishes for her well-doing, which had proceeded before, from all the spiteful old ladies in Meryton, lost but little of their spirit in this change of circumstances, because with such an husband, her misery was considered certain.

It was a fortnight since Mrs Bennet had been downstairs, but on this happy day, she again took her seat at the head of her table, and in spirits oppressively high. No sentiment of shame gave a damp to her triumph. The marriage of a

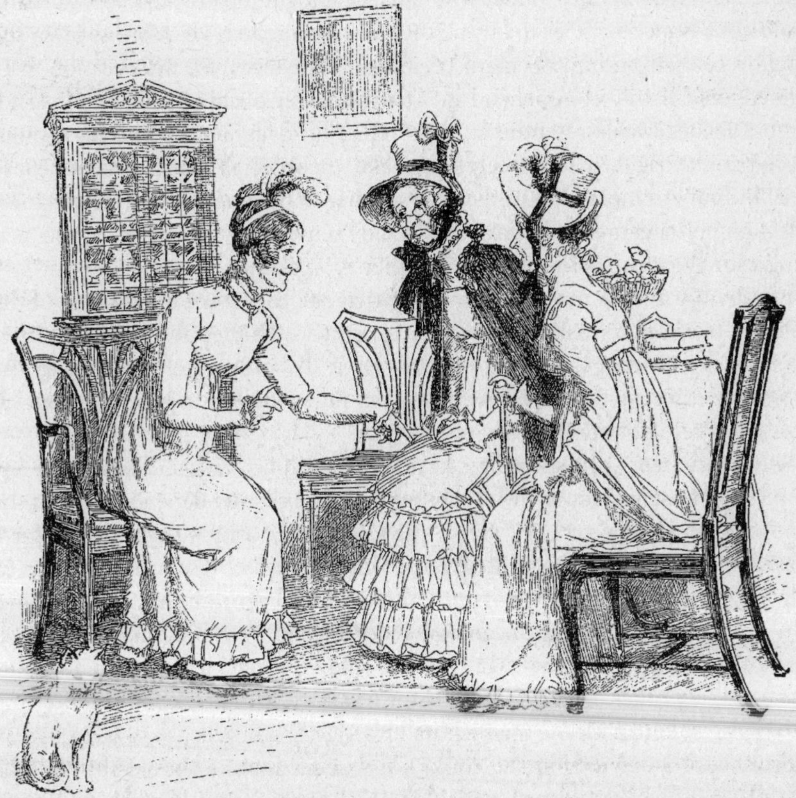

*The spiteful old ladies in Meryton*

daughter, which had been the first object of her wishes, since Jane was sixteen, was now on the point of accomplishment, and her thoughts and her words ran wholly on those attendants of elegant nuptials, fine muslins, new carriages, and servants. She was busily searching through the neighbourhood for a proper situation for her daughter, and, without knowing or considering what their income might be, rejected many as deficient in size and importance.

'Haye Park might do,' said she, 'if the Gouldings would quit it, or the great house at Stoke, if the drawing-room were larger; but Ashworth is too far off! I could not bear to have her ten miles from me; and as for Purvis Lodge, the attics are dreadful.'

Her husband allowed her to talk on without interruption, while the servants remained. But when they had withdrawn, he said to her, 'Mrs Bennet, before you take any, or all of these houses, for your son and daughter, let us come to a right understanding. Into *one* house in this neighbourhood, they shall never have admittance. I will not encourage the impudence of either, by receiving them at Longbourn.'

A long dispute followed this declaration; but Mr Bennet was firm: it soon led to another; and Mrs Bennet found, with amazement and horror, that her husband would not advance a guinea to buy clothes for his daughter. He protested that she should receive from him no mark of affection whatever, on the occasion. Mrs Bennet could hardly comprehend it. That his anger could be carried to such a point of inconceivable resentment, as to refuse his daughter a privilege, without which her marriage would scarcely seem valid, exceeded all that she could believe possible. She was more alive to the disgrace, which the want of new clothes must reflect on her daughter's nuptials, than to any sense of shame at her eloping and living with Wickham, a fortnight before they took place.

Elizabeth was now most heartily sorry that she had, from the distress of the moment, been led to make Mr Darcy acquainted with their fears for her sister; for since her marriage would so shortly give the proper termination to the elopement, they might hope to conceal its unfavourable beginning, from all those who were not immediately on the spot.

She had no fear of its spreading farther, through his means. There were few people on whose secrecy she would have more confidently depended; but at the same time, there was no one, whose knowledge of a sister's frailty would have mortified her so much. Not, however, from any fear of disadvantage from it, individually to herself; for at any rate, there seemed a gulf impassable between them. Had Lydia's marriage been concluded on the most honourable terms, it was not to be supposed that Mr Darcy would connect himself with a family, where to every other objection would now be added, an alliance and relationship of the nearest kind with the man whom he so justly scorned.

From such a connection she could not wonder that he should shrink. The wish of procuring her regard, which she had assured herself of his feeling in Derbyshire, could not in rational expectation survive such a blow as this. She was humbled, she was grieved; she repented, though she hardly knew of what. She became jealous of his esteem, when she could no longer hope to be benefited by it. She wanted to hear of him, when there seemed the least chance of gaining intelligence. She was convinced that she could have been happy with him; when it was no longer likely they should meet.

What a triumph for him, as she often thought, could he know that the proposals which she had proudly spurned only four months ago, would now have been gladly and gratefully received! He was as generous, she doubted not, as the most generous of his sex. But while he was mortal, there must be a triumph.

She began now to comprehend that he was exactly the man, who, in disposition and talents, would most suit her. His understanding and temper, though unlike her own, would have answered all her wishes. It was an union that must have been to the advantage of both; by her ease and liveliness, his mind might have been softened, his manners improved, and from his judgment, information, and knowledge of the world, she must have received benefit of greater importance.

But no such happy marriage could now teach the admiring multitude what connubial felicity really was. An union of a different tendency, and precluding the possibility of the other, was soon to be formed in their family.

How Wickham and Lydia were to be supported in tolerable independence, she could not imagine. But how little of permanent happiness could belong to a couple who were only brought together because their passions were stronger than their virtue, she could easily conjecture.

Mr Gardiner soon wrote again to his brother. To Mr Bennet's acknowledgments he briefly replied, with assurances of his eagerness to promote the welfare of any of his family; and concluded with entreaties that the subject might never be mentioned to him again. The principal purport of his letter was to inform them, that Mr Wickham had resolved on quitting the Militia.

> It was greatly my wish that he should do so,' he added, 'as soon as his marriage was fixed on. And I think you will agree with me, in considering a removal from that corps as highly advisable, both on his account and my niece's. It is Mr Wickham's intention to go into the regulars; and, among his former friends, there are still some who are able and willing to assist him in the army. He has the promise of an ensigncy in General —'s regiment, now quartered in the North. It is an advantage to have it so far from this part of the kingdom. He promises fairly, and I hope among different people, where they may each have a character to preserve, they will both be more prudent. I have written to Colonel Forster, to inform him of our present arrangements, and to request that he will satisfy the various creditors of Mr Wickham in and near Brighton, with assurances of speedy payment, for which I have pledged myself. And will you give yourself the trouble of carrying similar assurances to his creditors in Meryton, of whom I shall subjoin a list, according to his information. He has given in all his debts; I hope at least he has not deceived us. Haggerston has our directions, and all will be completed in a week. They will then join his regiment, unless they are first invited to Longbourn; and I understand from

Mrs Gardiner, that my niece is very desirous of seeing you all, before she leaves the South. She is well, and begs to be dutifully remembered to you and her mother. – Yours, &c.

E. Gardiner

Mr Bennet and his daughters saw all the advantages of Wickham's removal from the —shire, as clearly as Mr Gardiner could do. But Mrs Bennet, was not so well pleased with it. Lydia's being settled in the North, just when she had expected most pleasure and pride in her company, for she had by no means given up her plan of their residing in Hertfordshire, was a severe disappointment; and besides, it was such a pity that Lydia should be taken from a regiment where she was acquainted with everybody, and had so many favourites.

'She is so fond of Mrs Forster,' said she, 'it will be quite shocking to send her away! And there are several of the young men, too, that she likes very much. The officers may not be so pleasant in General —'s regiment.'

His daughter's request, for such it might be considered, of being admitted into her family again, before she set off for the North, received at first an absolute negative. But Jane and Elizabeth, who agreed in wishing, for the sake of their sister's feelings and consequence, that she should be noticed on her marriage by her parents, urged him so earnestly, yet so rationally and so mildly, to receive her and her husband at Longbourn, as soon as they were married, that he was prevailed on to think as they thought, and act as they wished. And their mother had the satisfaction of knowing, that she should be able to show her married daughter in the neighbourhood, before she was banished to the North. When Mr Bennet wrote again to his brother, therefore, he sent his permission for them to come; and it was settled, that as soon as the ceremony was over, they should proceed to Longbourn. Elizabeth was surprised, however, that Wickham should consent to such a scheme, and, had she consulted only her own inclination, any meeting with him would have been the last object of her wishes.

## *Chapter 51*

Their sister's wedding day arrived; and Jane and Elizabeth felt for her probably more than she felt for herself. The carriage was sent to meet them at —, and they were to return in it, by dinner-time. Their arrival was dreaded by the elder Miss Bennets; and Jane more especially, who gave Lydia the feelings which would have attended herself, had *she* been the culprit, was wretched in the thought of what her sister must endure.

They came. The family were assembled in the breakfast-room, to receive them. Smiles decked the face of Mrs Bennet, as the carriage drove up to the door; her husband looked impenetrably grave; her daughters, alarmed, anxious, uneasy.

Lydia's voice was heard in the vestibule; the door was thrown open, and she ran into the room. Her mother stepped forwards, embraced her, and welcomed her with rapture; gave her hand with an affectionate smile to Wickham, who followed his lady, and wished them both joy, with an alacrity which showed no doubt of their happiness.

Their reception from Mr Bennet, to whom they then turned, was not quite so cordial. His countenance rather gained in austerity; and he scarcely opened his lips. The easy assurance of the young couple, indeed, was enough to provoke him. Elizabeth was disgusted, and even Miss Bennet was shocked. Lydia was Lydia still; untamed, unabashed, wild, noisy, and fearless. She turned from sister to sister, demanding their congratulations, and when at length they all sat down, looked eagerly round the room, took notice of some little alteration in it, and observed, with a laugh, that it was a great while since she had been there.

Wickham was not at all more distressed then herself, but his manners were always so pleasing, that had his character and his marriage been exactly what they ought, his smiles and his easy address, while he claimed their relationship,

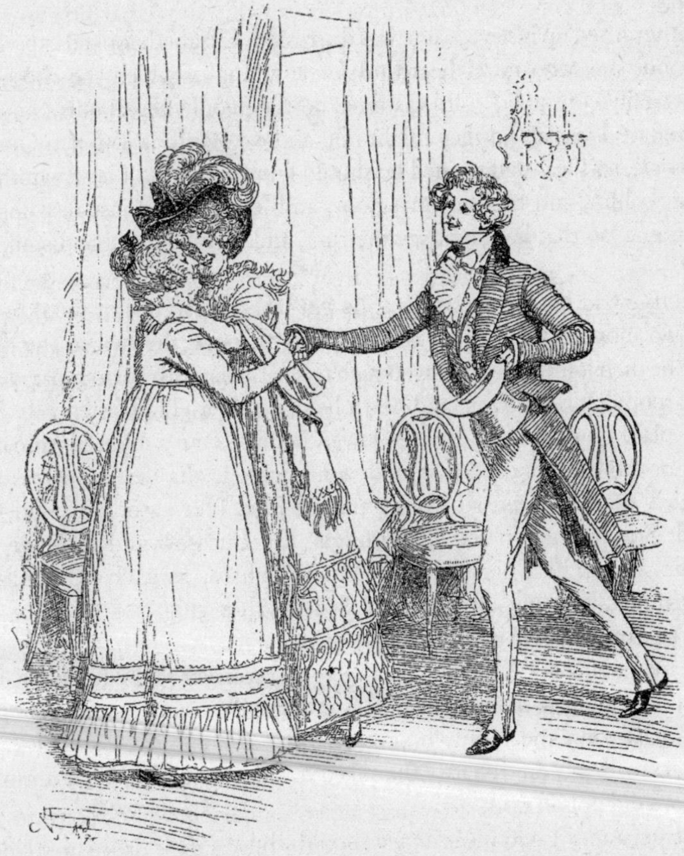

*With an affectionate smile*

would have delighted them all. Elizabeth had not before believed him quite equal to such assurance; but she sat down, resolving within herself, to draw no limits in future to the impudence of an impudent man. *She* blushed, and Jane blushed; but the cheeks of the two who caused their confusion, suffered no variation of colour.

There was no want of discourse. The bride and her mother could neither of them talk fast enough; and Wickham, who happened to sit near Elizabeth, began enquiring after his acquaintance in that neighbourhood, with a good-humoured ease, which she felt very unable to equal in her replies. They seemed each of them to have the happiest memories in the world. Nothing of the past was recollected with pain; and Lydia led voluntarily to subjects, which her sisters would not have alluded to for the world.

'Only think of its being three months,' she cried, 'since I went away; it seems but a fortnight I declare; and yet there have been things enough happened in the time. Good gracious! when I went away, I am sure I had no more idea of being married till I came back again! though I thought it would be very good fun if I was.'

Her father lifted up his eyes. Jane was distressed. Elizabeth looked expressively at Lydia; but she, who never heard or saw anything of which she chose to be insensible, gaily continued, 'Oh! mamma, do the people hereabouts know I am married today? I was afraid they might not; and we overtook William Goulding in his curricle, so I was determined he should know it, and so I let down the side glass next to him, and took off my glove, and let my hand just rest upon the window frame, so that he might see the ring, and then I bowed and smiled like anything.'

Elizabeth could bear it no longer. She got up, and ran out of the room; and returned no more, till she heard them passing through the hall to the dining-parlour. She then joined them soon enough to see Lydia, with anxious parade, walk up to her mother's right hand, and heard her say to her eldest sister, 'Ah! Jane, I take your place now, and you must go lower, because I am a married woman.'

It was not to be supposed that time would give Lydia that embarrassment, from which she had been so wholly free at first. Her ease and good spirits increased. She longed to see Mrs Philips, the Lucases, and all their other neighbours, and to hear herself called 'Mrs Wickham,' by each of them; and in the meantime, she went after dinner to show her ring and boast of being married, to Mrs Hill and the two housemaids.

'Well, mamma,' said she, when they were all returned to the breakfast-room, 'and what do you think of my husband? Is not he a charming man? I am sure my sisters must all envy me. I only hope they may have half my good luck. They must all go to Brighton. That is the place to get husbands. What a pity it is, mamma, we did not all go.'

'Very true; and if I had my will, we should. But my dear Lydia, I don't at all like your going such a way off. Must it be so?'

'Oh, lord! yes; – there is nothing in that. I shall like it of all things. You and papa, and my sisters, must come down and see us. We shall be at Newcastle all the winter, and I dare say there will be some balls, and I will take care to get good partners for them all.'

'I should like it beyond anything!' said her mother.

'And then when you go away, you may leave one or two of my sisters behind you; and I dare say I shall get husbands for them before the winter is over.'

'I thank you for my share of the favour,' said Elizabeth; 'but I do not particularly like your way of getting husbands.'

Their visitors were not to remain above ten days with them. Mr Wickham had received his commission before he left London, and he was to join his regiment at the end of a fortnight.

No one but Mrs Bennet, regretted that their stay would be so short; and she made the most of the time, by visiting about with her daughter, and having very frequent parties at home. These parties were acceptable to all; to avoid a family circle was even more desirable to such as did think, than such as did not.

Wickham's affection for Lydia, was just what Elizabeth had expected to find it; not equal to Lydia's for him. She had scarcely needed her present observation to be satisfied, from the reason of things, that their elopement had been brought on by the strength of her love, rather than by his; and she would have wondered why, without violently caring for her, he chose to elope with her at all, had she not felt certain that his flight was rendered necessary by distress of circumstances; and if that were the case, he was not the young man to resist an opportunity of having a companion.

Lydia was exceedingly fond of him. He was her dear Wickham on every occasion; no one was to be put in competition with him. He did everything best in the world; and she was sure he would kill more birds on the first of September, than anybody else in the country.

One morning, soon after their arrival, as she was sitting with her two elder sisters, she said to Elizabeth, 'Lizzy, I never gave *you* an account of my wedding, I believe. You were not by, when I told mamma, and the others, all about it. Are not you curious to hear how it was managed?'

'No really,' replied Elizabeth; 'I think there cannot be too little said on the subject.'

'La! You are so strange! But I must tell you how it went off. We were married, you know, at St Clement's, because Wickham's lodgings were in that parish. And it was settled that we should all be there by eleven o'clock. My uncle and aunt and I were to go together; and the others were to meet us at the church. Well, Monday morning came, and I was in such a fuss! I was so afraid you know that something would happen to put it off, and then I should have gone quite distracted. And there was my aunt, all the time I was dressing, preaching and talking away just as if she was reading a sermon. However, I did not hear above one word in ten, for I was thinking, you may suppose, of my dear Wickham. I longed to know whether he would be married in his blue coat.

'Well, and so we breakfasted at ten as usual; I thought it would never be over; for, by the by, you are to understand, that my uncle and aunt were horrid unpleasant all the time I was with them. If you'll believe me, I did not once put my foot out of doors, though I was there a fortnight. Not one party, or scheme, or anything. To be sure London was rather thin, but however the little Theatre was open. Well, and so just as the carriage came to the door, my uncle was called away upon business to that horrid man Mr Stone. And then, you know, when once they get together, there is no end of it. Well, I was so frightened I did not know what to do, for my uncle was to give me away; and if we were beyond the hour, we could not be married all day. But, luckily, he came back again in ten minutes' time, and then we all set out. However, I recollected afterwards, that if he *had* been prevented going, the wedding need not be put off, for Mr Darcy might have done as well.'

'Mr Darcy!' repeated Elizabeth, in utter amazement.

'Oh, yes! – he was to come there with Wickham, you know. But gracious me! I quite forgot! I ought not to have said a word about it. I promised them so faithfully! What will Wickham say? It was to be such a secret!'

'If it was to be secret,' said Jane, 'say not another word on the subject. You may depend upon my seeking no further.'

'Oh! certainly,' said Elizabeth, though burning with curiosity; 'we will ask you no questions.'

'Thank you,' said Lydia, 'for if you did, I should certainly tell you all, and then Wickham would be angry.'

On such encouragement to ask, Elizabeth was forced to put it out of her power, by running away.

But to live in ignorance on such a point was impossible; or at least it was impossible not to try for information. Mr Darcy had been at her sister's wedding. It was exactly a scene, and exactly among people, where he had apparently least to do, and least temptation to go. Conjectures as to the meaning of it, rapid and wild, hurried into her brain; but she was satisfied with none. Those that best pleased her, as placing his conduct in the noblest light, seemed most improbable. She could not bear such suspense; and hastily seizing a sheet of paper, wrote a short letter to her aunt, to request an explanation of what Lydia had dropped, if it were compatible with the secrecy which had been intended.

'You may readily comprehend,' she added, 'what my curiosity must be to know how a person unconnected with any of us, and (comparatively speaking) a stranger to our family, should have been amongst you at such a time. Pray write instantly, and let me understand it – unless it is, for very cogent reasons, to remain in the secrecy which Lydia seems to think necessary; and then I must endeavour to be satisfied with ignorance.'

'Not that I *shall* though,' she added to herself, as she finished the letter; 'and my dear aunt, if you do not tell me in an honourable manner, I shall certainly be reduced to tricks and stratagems to find it out.'

Jane's delicate sense of honour would not allow her to speak to Elizabeth privately of what Lydia had let fall; Elizabeth was glad of it; – till it appeared whether her enquiries would receive any satisfaction, she had rather be without a confidante.

# *Chapter 52*

Elizabeth had the satisfaction of receiving an answer to her letter, as soon as she possibly could. She was no sooner in possession of it, than hurrying into the little copse, where she was least likely to be interrupted, she sat down on one of the benches, and prepared to be happy; for the length of the letter convinced her that it did not contain a denial.

*Gracechurch Street, September 6*

My dear niece – I have just received your letter, and shall devote this whole morning to answering it, as I foresee that a *little* writing will not comprise what I have to tell you. I must confess myself surprised by your application; I did not expect it from *you*. Don't think me angry, however, for I only mean to let you know, that I had not imagined such enquiries to be necessary on *your* side. If you do not choose to understand me, forgive my impertinence. Your uncle is as much surprised as I am – and nothing but the belief of your being a party concerned, would have allowed him to act as he has done. But if you are really innocent and ignorant, I must be more explicit. On the very day of my coming home from Longbourn, your uncle had a most unexpected visitor. Mr Darcy called, and was shut up with him several hours. It was all over before I arrived; so my curiosity was not so dreadfully racked as *yours* seems to have been. He came to tell Mr Gardiner that he had found out where your sister and Mr Wickham were, and that he had seen and talked with them both, Wickham repeatedly, Lydia once. From what I can collect, he left Derbyshire only one day after ourselves, and came to town with the resolution of hunting for them. The motive professed, was his conviction of its being owing to himself that Wickham's worthlessness had not been so well known, as to make it impossible for any young woman of character, to love or confide in him. He generously imputed the whole to his mistaken pride, and confessed that he had before thought it beneath him, to lay his private actions open to the world. His character was to speak for itself. He called it, therefore, his duty to step forward, and endeavour to remedy an evil, which had been brought on by himself. If he *had another* motive, I am sure it would never disgrace him. He had been some days in town, before he was able to discover them; but he had something to direct his search, which was more than *we* had; and the consciousness of this, was another reason for his resolving to follow us. There is a lady, it seems, a Mrs Younge, who was some time ago governess to Miss Darcy, and was dismissed from her charge on some cause of disapprobation, though he did not say what. She then took a large house in Edward Street, and has since maintained herself by letting lodgings. This Mrs Younge was, he knew, intimately acquainted with Wickham; and he went to her for intelligence of him, as soon as he got to town. But it was two or three days before he could get from her what he wanted. She would not betray her trust, I suppose, without bribery and corruption, for she really did know where her friend was to be found. Wickham indeed had gone to her, on their first arrival in London, and had she been able to receive them into her house, they would have taken up their abode with her. At length, however, our kind friend procured the wished-for direction. They were in — Street. He saw Wickham, and afterwards insisted on seeing Lydia. His first object with her, he acknowledged, had been to persuade her to quit her present disgraceful situation, and return to her friends as soon as they could be prevailed on to receive her, offering his assistance, as far as it would go. But he found Lydia absolutely resolved on remaining where she was. She cared for none of her friends, she wanted no help of his, she would not hear of leaving Wickham. She was sure they should be married some time or other, and it did not much signify when. Since such were her feelings, it only remained, he thought, to secure and expedite a marriage, which, in his very first conversation with Wickham, he easily learnt, had never been *his* design. He confessed himself obliged to leave the regiment, on account of some debts of honour, which were very pressing; and scrupled not to lay all the ill-consequences of Lydia's flight, on her own folly alone. He meant to resign his commission immediately; and as to his future situation, he could conjecture very little about it. He must go somewhere, but he did not know where, and he knew he should have nothing to live on. Mr Darcy asked him why he had not married your sister at once. Though Mr Bennet was not imagined to be very rich, he would have been able to do something for him, and his situation must have been benefited by marriage. But he found, in reply to this question, that Wickham still cherished the hope of more effectually making his fortune by marriage, in some other country. Under such circumstances, however, he was not likely to be proof against the temptation of immediate relief. They met several times, for there was much to be discussed. Wickham of course wanted more than he could get; but at length was reduced to be reasonable. Everything being settled between *them*, Mr Darcy's next step was to make your uncle acquainted with it, and he first called in Gracechurch Street the evening before I came home. But Mr Gardiner could not be seen, and Mr Darcy found, on further enquiry, that your father was still with him, but would quit town the next morning. He did not judge your father to be a person whom he could so properly consult as your uncle, and therefore readily postponed seeing him, till after the departure of the former. He did not leave his name, and till the next day, it was only known that a gentleman had called on business. On Saturday he came again. Your father was gone, your uncle at home, and, as I said before, they had a great deal of talk together. They met again on Sunday, and then *I* saw him too. It was not all settled before Monday: as soon as it was, the express was sent off to Longbourn. But our visitor was very obstinate! I fancy, Lizzy, that obstinacy is the real defect of his character after all. He has been accused of many faults at different times;

but *this* is the true one. Nothing was to be done that he did not do himself; though I am sure (and I do not speak it to be thanked, therefore say nothing about it,) your uncle would most readily have settled the whole. They battled it together for a long time, which was more than either the gentleman or lady concerned in it deserved. But at last your uncle was forced to yield, and instead of being allowed to be of use to his niece, was forced to put up with only having the probable credit of it, which went sorely against the grain; and I really believe your letter this morning gave him great pleasure, because it required an explanation that would rob him of his borrowed feathers, and give the praise where it was due. But, Lizzy, this must go no farther than yourself, or Jane at most. You know pretty well, I suppose, what has been done for the young people. His debts are to be paid, amounting, I believe, to considerably more than a thousand pounds, another thousand in addition to her own settled upon *her*, and his commission purchased. The reason why all this was to be done by him alone, was such as I have given above. It was owing to him, to his reserve, and want of proper consideration, that Wickham's character had been so misunderstood, and consequently that he had been received and noticed as he was. Perhaps there was some truth in this; though I doubt whether *his* reserve, or *anybody's* reserve, can be answerable for the event. But in spite of all this fine talking, my dear Lizzy, you may rest perfectly assured, that your uncle would never have yielded, if we had not given him credit for *another interest* in the affair. When all this was resolved on, he returned again to his friends, who were still staying at Pemberley; but it was agreed that he should be in London once more when the wedding took place, and all money matters were then to receive the last finish. I believe I have now told you everything. It is a relation which you tell me is to give you great surprise; I hope at least it will not afford you any displeasure. Lydia came to us; and Wickham had constant admission to the house. *He* was exactly what he had been, when I knew him in Hertfordshire; but I would not tell you how little I was satisfied with *her* behaviour while she stayed with us, if I had not perceived, by Jane's letter last Wednesday, that her conduct on coming home was exactly of a piece with it, and therefore what I now tell you, can give you no fresh pain. I talked to her repeatedly in the most serious manner, representing to her all the wickedness of what she had done, and all the unhappiness she had brought on her family. If she heard me, it was by good luck, for I am sure she did not listen. I was sometimes quite provoked, but then I recollected my dear Elizabeth and Jane, and for their sakes had patience with her. Mr Darcy was punctual in his return, and as Lydia informed you, attended the wedding. He dined with us the next day, and was to leave town again on Wednesday or Thursday. Will you be very angry with me, my dear Lizzy, if I take this opportunity of saying (what I was never bold enough to say before) how much I like him. His behaviour to us has, in every respect, been as pleasing as when we were in Derbyshire. His understanding and opinions all please me; he wants nothing but a little more liveliness, and *that*, if he marry *prudently*, his wife may teach him. I thought him very sly; – he hardly ever mentioned your name. But slyness seems the fashion. Pray forgive me, if I have been very presuming, or at least do not punish me so far, as to exclude me from P. I shall never be quite happy till I have been all round the park. A low phaeton, with a nice little pair of ponies, would be the very thing. But I must write no more. The children have been wanting me this half-hour. Yours, very sincerely,

M. Gardiner.

The contents of this letter threw Elizabeth into a flutter of spirits, in which it was difficult to determine whether pleasure or pain bore the greatest share. The vague and unsettled suspicions which uncertainty had produced of what Mr Darcy might have been doing to forward her sister's match, which she had feared to encourage, as an exertion of goodness too great to be probable, and at the same time dreaded to be just, from the pain of obligation, were proved beyond their greatest extent to be true! He had followed them purposely to town, he had taken on himself all the trouble and mortification attendant on such a research; in which supplication had been necessary to a woman whom he must abominate

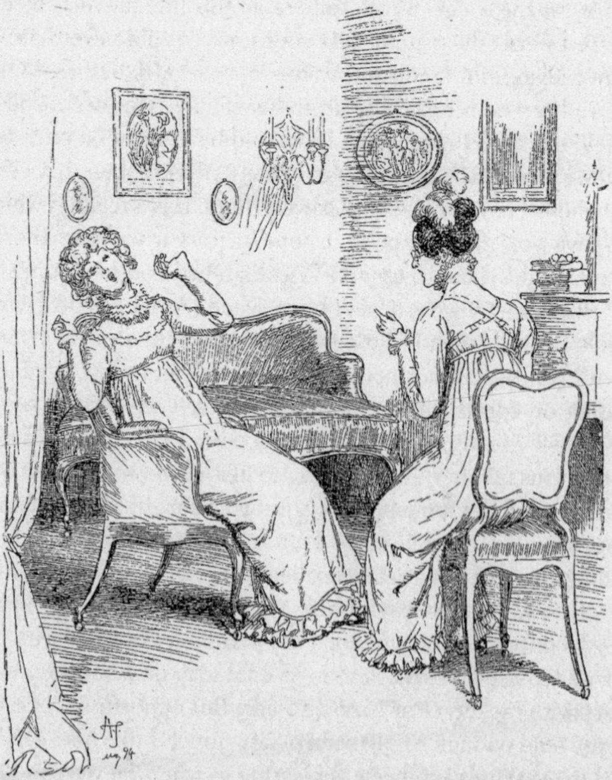

*I am sure she did not listen*

and despise, and where he was reduced to meet, frequently meet, reason with, persuade, and finally bribe, the man whom he always most wished to avoid, and whose very name it was punishment to him to pronounce. He had done all this for a girl whom he could neither regard nor esteem. Her heart did whisper, that he had done it for her. But it was a hope shortly checked by other considerations, and she soon felt that even her vanity was insufficient, when required to depend on his affection for her, for a woman who had already refused him, as able to overcome a sentiment so natural as abhorrence against relationship with Wickham. Brother-in-law of Wickham! Every kind of pride must revolt from the connection. He had to be sure done much. She was ashamed to think how much. But he had given a reason for his interference, which asked no extraordinary stretch of belief. It was reasonable that he should feel he had been wrong; he had liberality, and he had the means of exercising it; and though she would not place herself as his principal inducement, she could, perhaps, believe, that remaining partiality for her, might assist his endeavours in a cause where her peace of mind must be materially concerned. It was painful, exceedingly painful, to know that they were under obligations to a person who could never receive a return. They owed the restoration of Lydia, her character, everything to him. Oh! how heartily did she grieve over every ungracious sensation she had ever encouraged, every saucy speech she had ever directed towards him. For herself she was humbled; but she was proud of him. Proud that in a cause of compassion and honour, he had been able to get the better of himself. She read over her aunt's commendation of him again and again. It was hardly enough; but it pleased her. She was even sensible of some pleasure, though mixed with regret, on finding how steadfastly both she and her uncle had been persuaded that affection and confidence subsisted between Mr Darcy and herself.

She was roused from her seat, and her reflections, by someone's approach; and before she could strike into another path, she was overtaken by Wickham.

'I am afraid I interrupt your solitary ramble, my dear sister?' said he, as he joined her.

'You certainly do,' she replied with a smile; 'but it does not follow that the interruption must be unwelcome.'

'I should be sorry indeed, if it were. *We* were always good friends; and now we are better.'

'True. Are the others coming out?'

'I do not know. Mrs Bennet and Lydia are going in the carriage to Meryton. And so, my dear sister, I find from our uncle and aunt, that you have actually seen Pemberley.'

She replied in the affirmative.

'I almost envy you the pleasure, and yet I believe it would be too much for me, or else I could take it in my way to Newcastle. And you saw the old housekeeper, I suppose? Poor Reynolds, she was always very fond of me. But of course she did not mention my name to you.'

'Yes, she did.'

'And what did she say?'

'That you were gone into the army, and she was afraid had – not turned out well. At such a distance as *that*, you know, things are strangely misrepresented.'

'Certainly,' he replied, biting his lips. Elizabeth hoped she had silenced him; but he soon afterwards said, 'I was surprised to see Darcy in town last month. We passed each other several times. I wonder what he can be doing there.'

'Perhaps preparing for his marriage with Miss de Bourgh,' said Elizabeth. 'It must be something particular, to take him there at this time of year.'

'Undoubtedly. Did you see him while you were at Lambton? I thought I understood from the Gardiners that you had.'

'Yes; he introduced us to his sister.'

'And do you like her?'

'Very much.'

'I have heard, indeed, that she is uncommonly improved within this year or two. When I last saw her, she was not very promising. I am very glad you liked her. I hope she will turn out well.'

'I dare say she will; she has got over the most trying age.'

'Did you go by the village of Kympton?'

'I do not recollect that we did.'

'I mention it, because it is the living which I ought to have had. A most delightful place! – Excellent Parsonage House! It would have suited me in every respect.'

'How should you have liked making sermons?'

'Exceedingly well. I should have considered it as part of my duty, and the exertion would soon have been nothing. One ought not to repine; – but, to be sure, it would have been such a thing for me! The quiet, the retirement of such a life, would have answered all my ideas of happiness! But it was not to be. Did you ever hear Darcy mention the circumstance, when you were in Kent?'

'I *have* heard from authority, which I thought *as good*, that it was left you conditionally only, and at the will of the present patron.'

'You have. Yes, there was something in *that*, I told you so from the first, you may remember.'

'I *did* hear, too, that there was a time, when sermon-making was not so palatable to you as it seems to be at present; that you actually declared your resolution of never taking orders, and that the business had been compromised accordingly.'

'You did! and it was not wholly without foundation. You may remember what I told you on that point, when first we talked of it.'

They were now almost at the door of the house, for she had walked fast to get rid of him; and unwilling for her sister's sake, to provoke him, she only said in reply, with a good-humoured smile, 'Come, Mr Wickham, we are brother and sister, you know. Do not let us quarrel about the past. In future, I hope we shall be always of one mind.'

She held out her hand; he kissed it with affectionate gallantry, though he hardly knew how to look, and they entered the house.

## *Chapter 53*

Mr Wickham was so perfectly satisfied with this conversation, that he never again distressed himself, or provoked his dear sister Elizabeth, by introducing the subject of it; and she was pleased to find that she had said enough to keep him quiet.

The day of his and Lydia's departure soon came, and Mrs Bennet was forced to submit to a separation, which, as her husband by no means entered into her scheme of their all going to Newcastle, was likely to continue at least a twelve-month.

'Oh! my dear Lydia,' she cried, 'when shall we meet again?'

'Oh, lord! I don't know. Not these two or three years perhaps.'

'Write to me very often, my dear.'

'As often as I can. But you know married women have never much time for writing. My sisters may write to *me*. They will have nothing else to do.'

Mr Wickham's adieus were much more affectionate than his wife's. He smiled, looked handsome, and said many pretty things.

'He is as fine a fellow,' said Mr Bennet, as soon as they were out of the house, 'as ever I saw. He simpers, and smirks, and makes love to us all. I am prodigiously proud of him. I defy even Sir William Lucas himself, to produce a more valuable son-in-law.'

The loss of her daughter made Mrs Bennet very dull for several days.

'I often think,' said she, 'that there is nothing so bad as parting with one's friends. One seems so forlorn without them.'

'This is the consequence you see, Madam, of marrying a daughter,' said Elizabeth. 'It must make you better satisfied that your other four are single.'

'It is no such thing. Lydia does not leave me because she is married; but only because her husband's regiment happens to be so far off. If that had been nearer, she would not have gone so soon.'

But the spiritless condition which this event threw her into, was shortly relieved, and her mind opened again to the agitation of hope, by an article of news, which then began to be in circulation. The housekeeper at Netherfield had received orders to prepare for the arrival of her master, who was coming down in a day or two, to shoot there for several weeks. Mrs Bennet was quite in the fidgets. She looked at Jane, and smiled, and shook her head by turns.

'Well, well, and so Mr Bingley is coming down, sister,' (for Mrs Philips first brought her the news.) 'Well, so much the better. Not that I care about it, though. He is nothing to us, you know, and I am sure *I* never want to see him again. But, however, he is very welcome to come to Netherfield, if he likes it. And who knows what *may* happen? But that is nothing to us. You know, sister, we agreed long ago never to mention a word about it. And so, is it quite certain he is coming?'

'You may depend on it,' replied the other, 'for Mrs Nicholls was in Meryton last night; I saw her passing by, and went out myself on purpose to know the truth of it; and she told me that it was certain true. He comes down on Thursday at the latest, very likely on Wednesday. She was going to the butcher's, she told me, on purpose to order in some meat on Wednesday, and she has got three couple of ducks, just fit to be killed.'

Miss Bennet had not been able to hear of his coming, without changing colour. It was many months since she had mentioned his name to Elizabeth; but now, as soon as they were alone together, she said, 'I saw you look at me today, Lizzy, when my aunt told us of the present report; and I know I appeared distressed. But don't imagine it was from any silly cause. I was only confused for the moment, because I felt that I *should* be looked at. I do assure you, that the news does not affect me either with pleasure or pain. I am glad of one thing, that he comes alone; because we shall see the less of him. Not that I am afraid of *myself*, but I dread other people's remarks.'

Elizabeth did not know what to make of it. Had she not seen him in Derbyshire, she might have supposed him capable of coming there, with no other view than what was acknowledged; but she still thought him partial to Jane, and she wavered as to the greater probability of his coming there *with* his friend's permission, or being bold enough to come without it.

'Yet it is hard,' she sometimes thought, 'that this poor man cannot come to a house, which he has legally hired, without raising all this speculation! I *will* leave him to himself.'

In spite of what her sister declared, and really believed to be her feelings, in the expectation of his arrival, Elizabeth could easily perceive that her spirits were affected by it. They were more disturbed, more unequal, than she had often seen them.

The subject which had been so warmly canvassed between their parents, about a twelvemonth ago, was now brought forward again.

'As soon as ever Mr Bingley comes, my dear,' said Mrs Bennet, 'you will wait on him of course.'

'No, no. You forced me into visiting him last year, and promised if I went to see him, he should marry one of my daughters. But it ended in nothing, and I will not be sent on a fool's errand again.'

His wife represented to him how absolutely necessary such an attention would be from all the neighbouring gentlemen, on his returning to Netherfield.

' 'Tis an etiquette I despise,' said he. 'If he wants our society, let him seek it. He knows where we live. I will not spend *my* hours in running after my neighbours every time they go away, and come back again.'

'Well, all I know is, that it will be abominably rude if you do not wait on him. But, however, that shan't prevent my asking him to dine here, I am determined. We must have Mrs Long and the Gouldings soon. That will make thirteen with ourselves, so there will be just room at table for him.'

Consoled by this resolution, she was the better able to bear her husband's incivility; though it was very mortifying to know that her neighbours might all see Mr Bingley in consequence of it, before *they* did. As the day of his arrival drew near, 'I begin to be sorry that he comes at all,' said Jane to her sister. 'It would be nothing; I could see him with perfect indifference, but I can hardly bear to hear it thus perpetually talked of. My mother means well; but she does not know, no one can know how much I suffer from what she says. Happy shall I be, when his stay at Netherfield is over!'

'I wish I could say anything to comfort you,' replied Elizabeth; 'but it is wholly out of my power. You must feel it; and the usual satisfaction of preaching patience to a sufferer is denied me, because you have always so much.'

Mr Bingley arrived. Mrs Bennet, through the assistance of servants, contrived to have the earliest tidings of it, that the period of anxiety and fretfulness on her side, might be as long as it could. She counted the days that must intervene before their invitation could be sent; hopeless of seeing him before. But on the third morning after his arrival in Hertfordshire, she saw him from her dressing-room window, enter the paddock, and ride towards the house.

Her daughters were eagerly called to partake of her joy. Jane resolutely kept her place at the table; but Elizabeth, to satisfy her mother, went to the window – she looked, – she saw Mr Darcy with him, and sat down again by her sister.

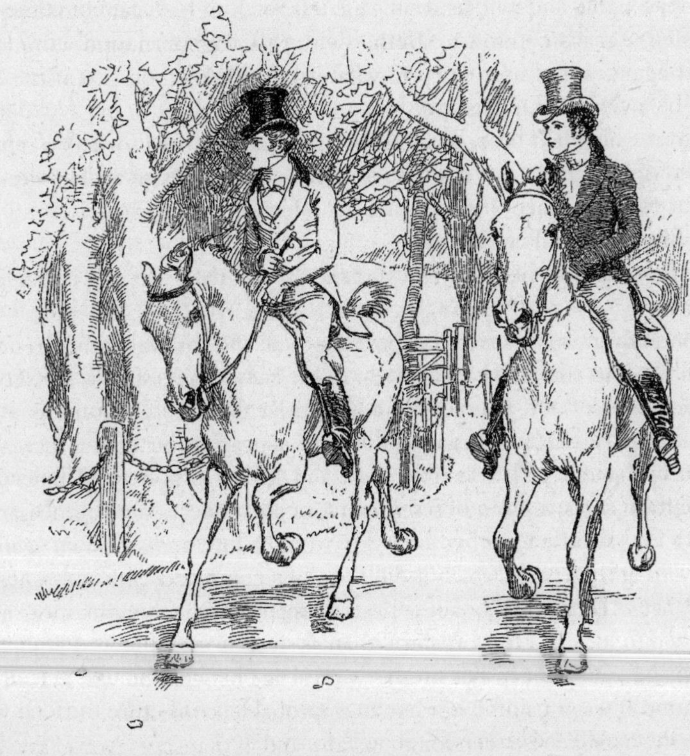

*She saw Mr Darcy with him*

'There is a gentleman with him, mamma,' said Kitty; 'who can it be?'

'Some acquaintance or other, my dear, I suppose; I am sure I do not know.'

'La!' replied Kitty, 'it looks just like that man that used to be with him before. Mr what's his name. That tall, proud man.'

'Good gracious! Mr Darcy! – and so it does I vow. Well, any friend of Mr Bingley's will always be welcome here to be sure; but else I must say that I hate the very sight of him.'

Jane looked at Elizabeth with surprise and concern. She knew but little of their meeting in Derbyshire, and therefore felt for the awkwardness which must attend her sister, in seeing him almost for the first time after receiving his explanatory letter. Both sisters were uncomfortable enough. Each felt for the other, and of course for themselves; and their mother talked on, of her dislike of Mr Darcy, and her resolution to be civil to him only as Mr Bingley's friend, without being heard by either of them. But Elizabeth had sources of uneasiness which could not be suspected by Jane, to whom she had never yet had courage to show Mrs Gardiner's letter, or to relate her own change of sentiment towards him. To Jane, he could be only a man whose proposals she had refused, and whose merit she had undervalued; but to her own more extensive information, he was the person, to whom the whole family were indebted for the first of benefits, and whom she regarded herself with an interest, if not quite so tender, at least as reasonable and just, as what Jane felt for Bingley. Her astonishment at his coming – at his coming to Netherfield, to Longbourn, and voluntarily seeking her again, was almost equal to what she had known on first witnessing his altered behaviour in Derbyshire.

The colour which had been driven from her face, returned for half a minute with an additional glow, and a smile of delight added lustre to her eyes, as she thought for that space of time, that his affection and wishes must still be unshaken. But she would not be secure.

'Let me first see how he behaves;' said she; 'it will then be early enough for expectation.'

She sat intently at work, striving to be composed, and without daring to lift up her eyes, till anxious curiosity carried them to the face of her sister, as the servant was approaching the door. Jane looked a little paler than usual, but more sedate than Elizabeth had expected. On the gentlemen's appearing, her colour increased; yet she received them with tolerable ease, and with a propriety of behaviour equally free from any symptom of resentment, or any unnecessary complaisance.

Elizabeth said as little to either as civility would allow, and sat down again to her work, with an eagerness which it did not often command. She had ventured only one glance at Darcy. He looked serious as usual; and she thought, more as he had been used to look in Hertfordshire, than as she had seen him at Pemberley. But, perhaps he could not in her mother's presence be what he was before her uncle and aunt. It was a painful, but not an improbable, conjecture.

Bingley, she had likewise seen for an instant, and in that short period saw him looking both pleased and embarrassed. He was received by Mrs Bennet with a degree of civility, which made her two daughters ashamed, especially when contrasted with the cold and ceremonious politeness of her curtsey and address to his friend.

Elizabeth particularly, who knew that her mother owed to the latter the preservation of her favourite daughter from irremediable infamy, was hurt and distressed to a most painful degree by a distinction so ill applied.

Darcy, after enquiring of her how Mr and Mrs Gardiner did, a question which she could not answer without confusion, said scarcely anything. He was not seated by her; perhaps that was the reason of his silence; but it had not been so in Derbyshire. There he had talked to her friends, when he could not to herself. But now several minutes elapsed, without bringing the sound of his voice; and when occasionally, unable to resist the impulse of curiosity, she raised her eyes to his face, she as often found him looking at Jane, as at herself, and frequently on no object but the ground. More thoughtfulness, and less anxiety to please than when they last met, were plainly expressed. She was disappointed, and angry with herself for being so.

'Could I expect it to be otherwise!' said she. 'Yet why did he come?'

She was in no humour for conversation with anyone but himself; and to him she had hardly courage to speak.

She enquired after his sister, but could do no more.

'It is a long time, Mr Bingley, since you went away,' said Mrs Bennet.

He readily agreed to it.

'I began to be afraid you would never come back again. People *did* say, you meant to quit the place entirely at Michaelmas; but, however, I hope it is not true. A great many changes have happened in the neighbourhood, since you went away. Miss Lucas is married and settled. And one of my own daughters. I suppose you have heard of it; indeed, you must have seen it in the papers. It was in the Times and the Courier, I know; though it was not put in as it ought to be. It was only said, "Lately, George Wickham, Esq. to Miss Lydia Bennet," without there being a syllable said of her father, or the place where she lived, or anything. It was my brother Gardiner's drawing up too, and I wonder how he came to make such an awkward business of it. Did you see it?'

Bingley replied that he did, and made his congratulations. Elizabeth dared not lift up her eyes. How Mr Darcy looked, therefore, she could not tell.

'It is a delightful thing, to be sure, to have a daughter well married,' continued her mother, 'but at the same time, Mr Bingley, it is very hard to have her taken such a way from me. They are gone down to Newcastle, a place quite northward, it seems, and there they are to stay, I do not know how long. His regiment is there; for I suppose you have heard of his leaving the —shire, and of his being gone into the regulars. Thank Heaven! he has *some* friends, though perhaps not so many as he deserves.'

Elizabeth, who knew this to be levelled at Mr Darcy, was in such misery of shame, that she could hardly keep her seat. It drew from her, however, the exertion of speaking, which nothing else had so effectually done before; and she asked Bingley, whether he meant to make any stay in the country at present. A few weeks, he believed.

'When you have killed all your own birds, Mr Bingley,' said her mother, 'I beg you will come here, and shoot as many as you please, on Mr Bennet's manor. I am sure he will be vastly happy to oblige you, and will save all the best of the covies for you.'

Elizabeth's misery increased, at such unnecessary, such officious attention! Were the same fair prospect to arise at present, as had flattered them a year ago, everything, she was persuaded, would be hastening to the same vexatious conclusion. At that instant she felt, that years of happiness could not make Jane or herself amends, for moments of such painful confusion.

'The first wish of my heart,' said she to herself, 'is never more to be in company with either of them. Their society can afford no pleasure, that will atone for such wretchedness as this! Let me never see either one or the other again!'

Yet the misery, for which years of happiness were to offer no compensation, received soon afterwards material relief, from observing how much the beauty of her sister rekindled the admiration of her former lover. When first he came in, he had spoken to her but little; but every five minutes seemed to be giving her more of his attention. He found her as handsome as she had been last year; as good-natured, and as unaffected, though not quite so chatty. Jane was anxious that no difference should be perceived in her at all, and was really persuaded that she talked as much as ever. But her mind was so busily engaged, that she did not always know when she was silent.

When the gentlemen rose to go away, Mrs Bennet was mindful of her intended civility, and they were invited and engaged to dine at Longbourn in a few days' time.

'You are quite a visit in my debt, Mr Bingley,' she added, 'for when you went to town last winter, you promised to take a family dinner with us, as soon as you returned. I have not forgot, you see; and I assure you, I was very much disappointed that you did not come back and keep your engagement.'

Bingley looked a little silly at this reflection, and said something of his concern, at having been prevented by business. They then went away.

Mrs Bennet had been strongly inclined to ask them to stay and dine there, that day; but, though she always kept a very good table, she did not think anything less than two courses, could be good enough for a man, on whom she had such anxious designs, or satisfy the appetite and pride of one who had ten thousand a year.

## *Chapter 54*

As soon as they were gone, Elizabeth walked out to recover her spirits; or in other words, to dwell without interruption on those subjects that must deaden them more. Mr Darcy's behaviour astonished and vexed her.

'Why, if he came only to be silent, grave, and indifferent,' said she, 'did he come at all?'

She could settle it in no way that gave her pleasure.

'He could be still amiable, still pleasing, to my uncle and aunt, when he was in town; and why not to me? If he fears me, why come hither? If he no longer cares for me, why silent? Teasing, teasing, man! I will think no more about him.'

Her resolution was for a short time involuntarily kept by the approach of her sister, who joined her with a cheerful look, which showed her better satisfied with their visitors, than Elizabeth.

'Now,' said she, 'that this first meeting is over, I feel perfectly easy. I know my own strength, and I shall never be embarrassed again by his coming. I am glad he dines here on Tuesday. It will then be publicly seen, that on both sides, we meet only as common and indifferent acquaintance.'

'Yes, very indifferent indeed,' said Elizabeth, laughingly. 'Oh, Jane, take care.'

'My dear Lizzy, you cannot think me so weak, as to be in danger now.'

'I think you are in very great danger of making him as much in love with you as ever.'

They did not see the gentlemen again till Tuesday; and Mrs Bennet, in the meanwhile, was giving way to all the happy schemes, which the good humour, and common politeness of Bingley, in half an hour's visit, had revived.

On Tuesday there was a large party assembled at Longbourn; and the two, who were most anxiously expected, to the credit of their punctuality as sportsmen, were in very good time. When they repaired to the dining-room, Elizabeth eagerly watched to see whether Bingley would take the place, which, in all their former parties, had belonged to him, by her sister. Her prudent mother, occupied by the same ideas, forbore to invite him to sit by herself. On entering the room, he seemed to hesitate; but Jane happened to look round, and happened to smile: it was decided. He placed himself by her.

Elizabeth, with a triumphant sensation, looked towards his friend. He bore it with noble indifference, and she would have imagined that Bingley had received his sanction to be happy, had she not seen his eyes likewise turned towards Mr Darcy, with an expression of half-laughing alarm.

His behaviour to her sister was such, during dinner time, as showed an admiration of her, which, though more guarded than formerly, persuaded Elizabeth, that if left wholly to himself, Jane's happiness, and his own, would be speedily secured. Though she dared not depend upon the consequence, she yet received pleasure from observing his behaviour. It gave her all the animation that her spirits could boast; for she was in no cheerful humour. Mr Darcy was almost as far from her, as the table could divide them. He was on one side of her mother. She knew how little such a situation would give pleasure to either, or make either appear to advantage. She was not near enough to hear any of their discourse, but she could see how seldom they spoke to each other, and how formal and cold was their manner, whenever they did. Her mother's ungraciousness, made the sense of what they owed him more painful to Elizabeth's mind; and she would, at times, have given anything to be privileged to tell him, that his kindness was neither unknown nor unfelt by the whole of the family.

She was in hopes that the evening would afford some opportunity of bringing them together; that the whole of the visit would not pass away without enabling them to enter into something more of conversation, than the mere ceremonious salutation attending his entrance. Anxious and uneasy, the period which passed in the drawing-room, before the gentlemen came, was wearisome and dull to a degree, that almost made her uncivil. She looked forward to their entrance, as the point on which all her chance of pleasure for the evening must depend.

'If he does not come to me, *then*,' said she, 'I shall give him up for ever.'

The gentlemen came; and she thought he looked as if he would have answered her hopes; but, alas! the ladies had crowded round the table, where Miss Bennet was making tea, and Elizabeth pouring out the coffee, in so close a confederacy, that there was not a single vacancy near her, which would admit of a chair. And on the gentlemen's approaching, one of the girls moved closer to her than ever, and said, in a whisper, 'The men shan't come and part us, I am determined. We want none of them; do we?'

Darcy had walked away to another part of the room. She followed him with her eyes, envied everyone to whom he spoke, had scarcely patience enough to help anybody to coffee; and then was enraged against herself for being so silly!

'A man who has once been refused! How could I ever be foolish enough to expect a renewal of his love? Is there one among the sex, who would not protest against such a weakness as a second proposal to the same woman? There is no indignity so abhorrent to their feelings!'

She was a little revived, however, by his bringing back his coffee cup himself; and she seized the opportunity of saying, 'Is your sister at Pemberley still?'

'Yes, she will remain there till Christmas.'

'And quite alone? Have all her friends left her?'

'Mrs Annesley is with her. The others have been gone on to Scarborough, these three weeks.'

She could think of nothing more to say; but if he wished to converse with her, he might have better success. He stood by her, however, for some minutes, in silence; and, at last, on the young lady's whispering to Elizabeth again, he walked away.

When the tea things were removed, and the card-tables placed, the ladies all rose, and Elizabeth was then hoping to be soon joined by him, when all her views were overthrown, by seeing him fall a victim to her mother's rapacity for whist players, and in a few moments after seated with the rest of the party. She now lost every expectation of pleasure. They were confined for the evening at different tables, and she had nothing to hope, but that his eyes were so often turned towards her side of the room, as to make him play as unsuccessfully as herself.

Mrs Bennet had designed to keep the two Netherfield gentlemen to supper; but their carriage was unluckily ordered before any of the others, and she had no opportunity of detaining them.

'Well girls,' said she, as soon as they were left to themselves, 'What say you to the day? I think everything has passed off uncommonly well, I assure you. The dinner was as well dressed as any I ever saw. The venison was roasted to a turn – and everybody said, they never saw so fat a haunch. The soup was fifty times better than what we had at the Lucas's last week; and even Mr Darcy acknowledged, that the partridges were remarkably well done; and I suppose he has two or three French cooks at least. And, my dear Jane, I never saw you look in greater beauty. Mrs Long said so too, for I asked her whether you did not. And what do you think she said besides? "Ah! Mrs Bennet, we shall have her at

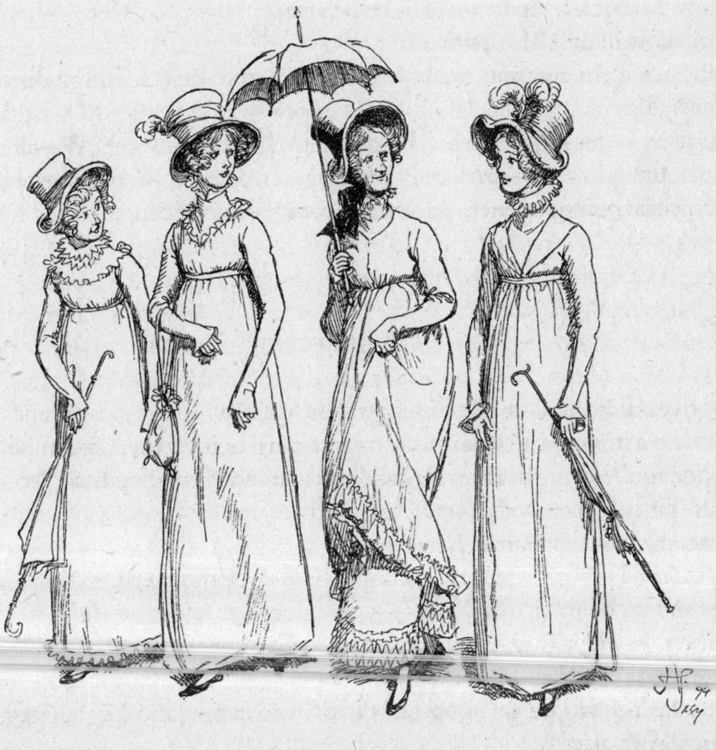

*Mrs Long and her nieces*

Netherfield at last." She did indeed. I do think Mrs Long is as good a creature as ever lived – and her nieces are very pretty behaved girls, and not at all handsome: I like them prodigiously.'

Mrs Bennet, in short, was in very great spirits; she had seen enough of Bingley's behaviour to Jane, to be convinced that she would get him at last; and her expectations of advantage to her family, when in a happy humour, were so far beyond reason, that she was quite disappointed at not seeing him there again the next day, to make his proposals.

'It has been a very agreeable day,' said Miss Bennet to Elizabeth. 'The party seemed so well selected, so suitable one with the other. I hope we may often meet again.'

Elizabeth smiled.

'Lizzy, you must not do so. You must not suspect me. It mortifies me. I assure you that I have now learnt to enjoy his conversation as an agreeable and sensible young man, without having a wish beyond it. I am perfectly satisfied from what his manners now are, that he never had any design of engaging my affection. It is only that he is blessed with greater sweetness of address, and a stronger desire of generally pleasing than any other man.'

'You are very cruel,' said her sister, 'you will not let me smile, and are provoking me to it every moment.'

'How hard it is in some cases to be believed!'

'And how impossible in others!'

'But why should you wish to persuade me that I feel more than I acknowledge?'

'That is a question which I hardly know how to answer. We all love to instruct, though we can teach only what is not worth knowing. Forgive me; and if you persist in indifference, do not make *me* your confidante.'

## *Chapter 55*

A few days after this visit, Mr Bingley called again, and alone. His friend had left him that morning for London, but was to return home in ten days' time. He sat with them above an hour, and was in remarkably good spirits. Mrs Bennet invited him to dine with them; but, with many expressions of concern, he confessed himself engaged elsewhere.

'Next time you call,' said she, 'I hope we shall be more lucky.'

He should be particularly happy at any time, etc. etc.; and if she would give him leave, would take an early opportunity of waiting on them.

'Can you come tomorrow?'

Yes, he had no engagement at all for tomorrow; and her invitation was accepted with alacrity.

He came, and in such very good time, that the ladies were none of them dressed. In ran Mrs Bennet to her daughter's room, in her dressing gown, and with her hair half-finished, crying out, 'My dear Jane, make haste and hurry down. He is come – Mr Bingley is come. – He is, indeed. Make haste, make haste. Here, Sarah, come to Miss Bennet this moment, and help her on with her gown. Never mind Miss Lizzy's hair.'

'We will be down as soon as we can,' said Jane; 'but I dare say Kitty is forwarder than either of us, for she went upstairs half an hour ago.'

'Oh! hang Kitty! what has she to do with it? Come, be quick, be quick! where is your sash my dear?'

But when her mother was gone, Jane would not be prevailed on to go down without one of her sisters.

The same anxiety to get them by themselves, was visible again in the evening. After tea, Mr Bennet retired to the library, as was his custom, and Mary went upstairs to her instrument. Two obstacles of the five being thus removed, Mrs Bennet sat looking and winking at Elizabeth and Catherine for a considerable

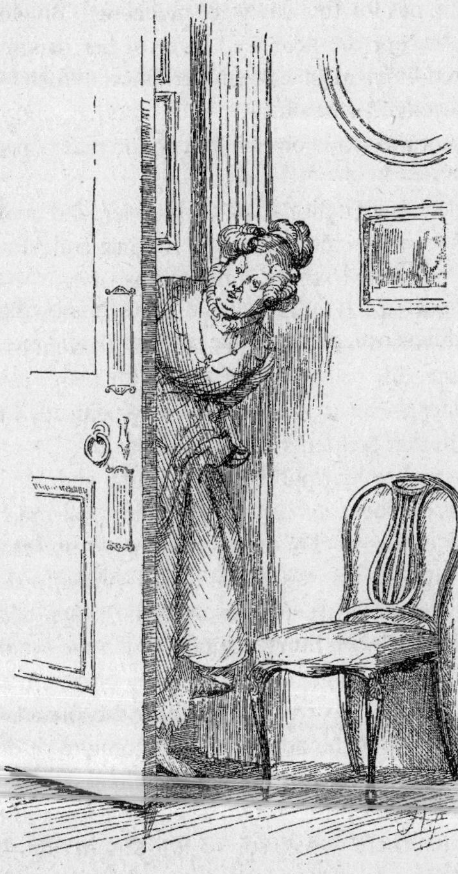

*Come here, my love, I want to speak to you*

time, without making any impression on them. Elizabeth would not observe her; and when at last Kitty did, she very innocently said, 'What is the matter mamma? What do you keep winking at me for? What am I to do?'

'Nothing child, nothing. I did not wink at you.' She then sat still five minutes longer; but unable to waste such a precious occasion, she suddenly got up, and saying to Kitty, 'Come here, my love, I want to speak to you,' took her out of the room. Jane instantly gave a look at Elizabeth, which spoke her distress at such premeditation, and her entreaty that *she* would not give in to it. In a few minutes, Mrs Bennet half opened the door and called out, 'Lizzy, my dear, I want to speak with you.'

Elizabeth was forced to go.

'We may as well leave them by themselves you know;' said her mother as soon as she was in the hall. 'Kitty and I are going upstairs to sit in my dressing-room.'

Elizabeth made no attempt to reason with her mother, but remained quietly in the hall, till she and Kitty were out of sight, then returned into the drawing-room.

Mrs Bennet's schemes for this day were ineffectual. Bingley was everything that was charming, except the professed lover of her daughter. His ease and cheerfulness rendered him a most agreeable addition to their evening party; and he bore with the ill-judged officiousness of the mother, and heard all her silly remarks with a forbearance and command of countenance, particularly grateful to the daughter.

He scarcely needed an invitation to stay to supper; and before he went away, an engagement was formed, chiefly through his own and Mrs Bennet's means, for his coming next morning to shoot with her husband.

After this day, Jane said no more of her indifference. Not a word passed between the sisters concerning Bingley; but Elizabeth went to bed in the happy belief that all must speedily be concluded, unless Mr Darcy returned within the stated time. Seriously, however, she felt tolerably persuaded that all this must have taken place with that gentleman's concurrence.

Bingley was punctual to his appointment; and he and Mr Bennet spent the morning together, as had been agreed on. The latter was much more agreeable than his companion expected. There was nothing of presumption or folly in Bingley, that could provoke his ridicule, or disgust him into silence; and he was more communicative, and less eccentric than the other had ever seen him. Bingley of course returned with him to dinner; and in the evening Mrs Bennet's invention was again at work to get everybody away from him and her daughter. Elizabeth, who had a letter to write, went into the breakfast-room for that purpose soon after tea; for as the others were all going to sit down to cards, she could not be wanted to counteract her mother's schemes.

But on returning to the drawing-room, when her letter was finished, she saw, to her infinite surprise, there was reason to fear that her mother had been too ingenious for her. On opening the door, she perceived her sister and Bingley standing together over the hearth, as if engaged in earnest conversation; and had this led to no suspicion, the faces of both as they hastily turned round, and moved away from each other, would have told it all. *Their* situation was awkward enough; but *hers* she thought was still worse. Not a syllable was uttered by either; and Elizabeth was on the point of going away again, when Bingley, who as well as the other had sat down, suddenly rose, and whispering a few words to her sister, ran out of the room.

Jane could have no reserves from Elizabeth, where confidence would give pleasure; and instantly embracing her, acknowledged, with the liveliest emotion, that she was the happiest creature in the world.

' 'Tis too much!' she added, 'by far too much. I do not deserve it. Oh! why is not everybody as happy?'

Elizabeth's congratulations were given with a sincerity, a warmth, a delight, which words could but poorly express. Every sentence of kindness was a fresh source of happiness to Jane. But she would not allow herself to stay with her sister, or say half that remained to be said, for the present.

'I must go instantly to my mother;' she cried. 'I would not on any account trifle with her affectionate solicitude; or allow her to hear it from anyone but myself. He is gone to my father already. Oh! Lizzy, to know that what I have to relate will give such pleasure to all my dear family! how shall I bear so much happiness!'

She then hastened away to her mother, who had purposely broken up the card party, and was sitting upstairs with Kitty.

Elizabeth, who was left by herself, now smiled at the rapidity and ease with which an affair was finally settled, that had given them so many previous months of suspense and vexation.

'And this,' said she, 'is the end of all his friend's anxious circumspection! of all his sister's falsehood and contrivance! the happiest, wisest, most reasonable end!'

In a few minutes she was joined by Bingley, whose conference with her father had been short and to the purpose.

'Where is your sister?' said he hastily, as he opened the door.

'With my mother upstairs. She will be down in a moment I dare say.'

He then shut the door, and coming up to her, claimed the good wishes and affection of a sister. Elizabeth honestly and heartily expressed her delight in the prospect of their relationship. They shook hands with great cordiality; and then till her sister came down, she had to listen to all he had to say, of his own happiness, and of Jane's perfections; and in spite of his being a lover, Elizabeth really believed all his expectations of felicity, to be rationally founded, because they had for basis the excellent understanding, and super-excellent disposition of Jane, and a general similarity of feeling and taste between her and himself.

It was an evening of no common delight to them all; the satisfaction of Miss Bennet's mind gave a glow of such sweet animation to her face, as made her look handsomer than ever. Kitty simpered and smiled, and hoped her turn was coming soon. Mrs Bennet could not give her consent, or speak her approbation in terms warm enough to satisfy her feelings, though she talked to Bingley of nothing else, for half an hour; and when Mr Bennet joined them at supper, his voice and manner plainly showed how really happy he was.

Not a word, however, passed his lips in allusion to it, till their visitor took his leave for the night; but as soon as he was gone, he turned to his daughter and said, 'Jane, I congratulate you. You will be a very happy woman.'

Jane went to him instantly, kissed him, and thanked him for his goodness.

'You are a good girl;' he replied, 'and I have great pleasure in thinking you will be so happily settled. I have not a doubt of your doing very well together. Your tempers are by no means unlike. You are each of you so complying, that nothing will ever be resolved on; so easy, that every servant will cheat you; and so generous, that you will always exceed your income.'

'I hope not so. Imprudence or thoughtlessness in money matters, would be unpardonable in *me*.'

'Exceed their income! My dear Mr Bennet,' cried his wife, 'what are you talking of? Why, he has four or five thousand a year, and very likely more.' Then addressing her daughter, 'Oh! my dear, dear Jane, I am so happy! I am sure I shan't get a wink of sleep all night. I knew how it would be. I always said it must be so, at last. I was sure you could not be so beautiful for nothing! I remember, as soon as ever I saw him, when he first came into Hertfordshire last year, I thought how likely it was that you should come together. Oh! he is the handsomest young man that ever was seen!'

Wickham, Lydia, were all forgotten. Jane was beyond competition her favourite child. At that moment, she cared for no other. Her younger sisters soon began to make interest with her for objects of happiness which she might in future be able to dispense.

Mary petitioned for the use of the library at Netherfield; and Kitty begged very hard for a few balls there every winter.

Bingley, from this time, was of course a daily visitor at Longbourn; coming frequently before breakfast, and always remaining till after supper; unless when some barbarous neighbour, who could not be enough detested, had given him an invitation to dinner, which he thought himself obliged to accept.

Elizabeth had now but little time for conversation with her sister; for while he was present, Jane had no attention to bestow on anyone else; but she found herself considerably useful to both of them, in those hours of separation that must sometimes occur. In the absence of Jane, he always attached himself to Elizabeth, for the pleasure of talking to her; and when Bingley was gone, Jane constantly sought the same means of relief.

'He has made me so happy,' said she, one evening, 'by telling me, that he was totally ignorant of my being in town last spring! I had not believed it possible.'

'I suspected as much,' replied Elizabeth. 'But how did he account for it?'

'It must have been his sister's doing. They were certainly no friends to his acquaintance with me, which I cannot wonder at, since he might have chosen so much more advantageously in many respects. But when they see, as I trust they will, that their brother is happy with me, they will learn to be contented, and we shall be on good terms again; though we can never be what we once were to each other.'

'That is the most unforgiving speech,' said Elizabeth, 'that I ever heard you utter. Good girl! It would vex me, indeed, to see you again the dupe of Miss Bingley's pretended regard.'

'Would you believe it, Lizzy, that when he went to town last November, he really loved me, and nothing but a persuasion of *my* being indifferent, would have prevented his coming down again!'

'He made a little mistake to be sure; but it is to the credit of his modesty.'

This naturally introduced a panegyric from Jane on his diffidence, and the little value he put on his own good qualities.

Elizabeth was pleased to find, that he had not betrayed the interference of his friend, for, though Jane had the most generous and forgiving heart in the world, she knew it was a circumstance which must prejudice her against him.

'I am certainly the most fortunate creature that ever existed!' cried Jane. 'Oh! Lizzy, why am I thus singled from my family, and blessed above them all! If I could but see *you* as happy! If there *were* but such another man for you!'

'If you were to give me forty such men, I never could be so happy as you. Till I have your disposition, your goodness, I never can have your happiness. No, no, let me shift for myself; and, perhaps, if I have very good luck, I may meet with another Mr Collins in time.'

The situation of affairs in the Longbourn family could not be long a secret. Mrs Bennet was privileged to whisper it to Mrs Philips, and *she* ventured, without any permission, to do the same by all her neighbours in Meryton.

The Bennets were speedily pronounced to be the luckiest family in the world, though only a few weeks before, when Lydia had first run away, they had been generally proved to be marked out for misfortune.

## *Chapter 56*

One morning, about a week after Bingley's engagement with Jane had been formed, as he and the females of the family were sitting together in the dining-room, their attention was suddenly drawn to the window, by the sound of a carriage; and they perceived a chaise and four driving up the lawn. It was too early in the morning for visitors, and besides, the equipage did not answer to that of any of their neighbours. The horses were post; and neither the carriage, nor the livery of the servant who preceded it, were familiar to them. As it was certain, however, that somebody was coming, Bingley instantly prevailed on Miss Bennet to avoid the confinement of such an intrusion, and walk away with him into the shrubbery. They both set off, and the conjectures of the remaining three continued, though with little satisfaction, till the door was thrown open, and their visitor entered. It was Lady Catherine de Bourgh.

They were of course all intending to be surprised; but their astonishment was beyond their expectation; and on the part of Mrs Bennet and Kitty, though she was perfectly unknown to them, even inferior to what Elizabeth felt.

She entered the room with an air more than usually ungracious, made no other reply to Elizabeth's salutation, than a slight inclination of the head, and sat down without saying a word. Elizabeth had mentioned her name to her mother, on her ladyship's entrance, though no request of introduction had been made.

Mrs Bennet all amazement, though flattered by having a guest of such high importance, received her with the utmost politeness. After sitting for a moment in silence, she said very stiffly to Elizabeth, 'I hope you are well, Miss Bennet. That lady I suppose is your mother.'

Elizabeth replied very concisely that she was.

'And *that* I suppose is one of your sisters.'

'Yes, madam,' said Mrs Bennet, delighted to speak to a Lady Catherine. 'She is my youngest girl but one. My youngest of all, is lately married, and my eldest is somewhere about the grounds, walking with a young man, who I believe will soon become a part of the family.'

'You have a very small park here,' returned Lady Catherine after a short silence.

'It is nothing in comparison of Rosings, my lady, I dare say; but I assure you it is much larger than Sir William Lucas's.'

'This must be a most inconvenient sitting-room for the evening, in summer; the windows are full west.'

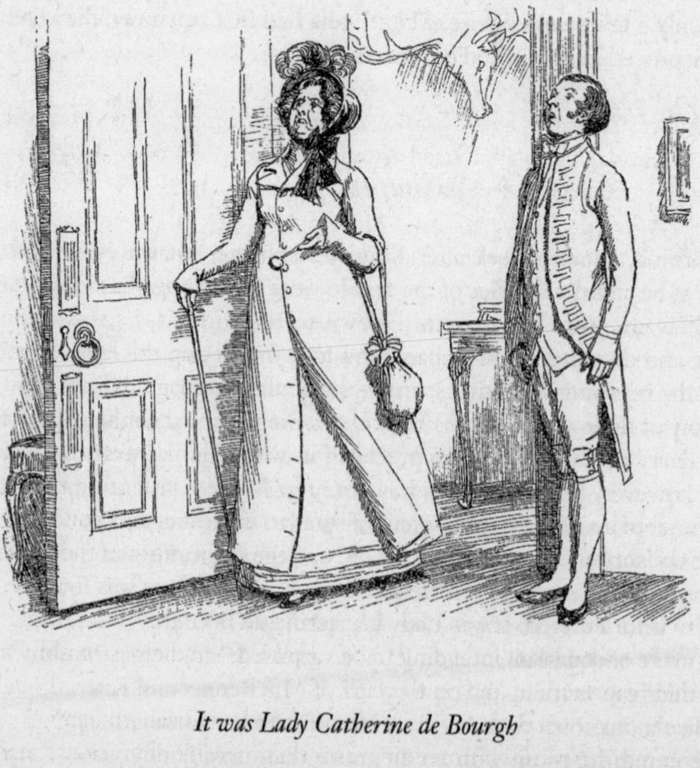

*It was Lady Catherine de Bourgh*

Mrs Bennet assured her that they never sat there after dinner; and then added, 'May I take the liberty of asking your ladyship whether you left Mr and Mrs Collins well.'

'Yes, very well. I saw them the night before last.'

Elizabeth now expected that she would produce a letter for her from Charlotte, as it seemed the only probable motive for her calling. But no letter appeared, and she was completely puzzled.

Mrs Bennet, with great civility, begged her ladyship to take some refreshment; but Lady Catherine very resolutely, and not very politely, declined eating anything; and then rising up, said to Elizabeth, 'Miss Bennet, there seemed to be a prettyish kind of a little wilderness on one side of your lawn. I should be glad to take a turn in it, if you will favour me with your company.'

'Go, my dear,' cried her mother, 'and show her ladyship about the different walks. I think she will be pleased with the hermitage.'

Elizabeth obeyed, and running into her own room for her parasol, attended her noble guest downstairs. As they passed through the hall, Lady Catherine opened the doors into the dining-parlour and drawing-room, and pronouncing them, after a short survey, to be decent-looking rooms, walked on.

Her carriage remained at the door, and Elizabeth saw that her waiting-woman was in it. They proceeded in silence along the gravel walk that led to the copse; Elizabeth was determined to make no effort for conversation with a woman, who was now more than usually insolent and disagreeable.

'How could I ever think her like her nephew?' said she, as she looked in her face.

As soon as they entered the copse, Lady Catherine began in the following manner: 'You can be at no loss, Miss Bennet, to understand the reason of my journey hither. Your own heart, your own conscience, must tell you why I come.'

Elizabeth looked with unaffected astonishment.

'Indeed, you are mistaken, Madam. I have not been at all able to account for the honour of seeing you here.'

'Miss Bennet,' replied her ladyship, in an angry tone, 'you ought to know, that I am not to be trifled with. But however insincere *you* may choose to be, you shall not find *me* so. My character has ever been celebrated for its sincerity and frankness, and in a cause of such moment as this, I shall certainly not depart from it. A report of a most alarming nature, reached me two days ago. I was told, that not only your sister was on the point of being most advantageously married, but that *you*, that Miss Elizabeth Bennet, would, in all likelihood, be soon afterwards united to my nephew, my own nephew, Mr Darcy. Though I *know* it must be a scandalous falsehood; though I would not injure him so much as to suppose the truth of it possible, I instantly resolved on setting off for this place, that I might make my sentiments known to you.'

'If you believed it impossible to be true,' said Elizabeth, colouring with astonishment and disdain, 'I wonder you took the trouble of coming so far. What could your ladyship propose by it?'

'At once to insist upon having such a report universally contradicted.'

'Your coming to Longbourn, to see me and my family,' said Elizabeth, coolly, 'will be rather a confirmation of it; if, indeed, such a report is in existence.'

'If! Do you then pretend to be ignorant of it? Has it not been industriously circulated by yourselves? Do you not know that such a report is spread abroad?'

'I never heard that it was.'

'And can you likewise declare, that there is no *foundation* for it?'

'I do not pretend to possess equal frankness with your ladyship. *You* may ask questions, which *I* shall not choose to answer.'

'This is not to be borne. Miss Bennet, I insist on being satisfied. Has he, has my nephew, made you an offer of marriage?'

'Your ladyship has declared it to be impossible.'

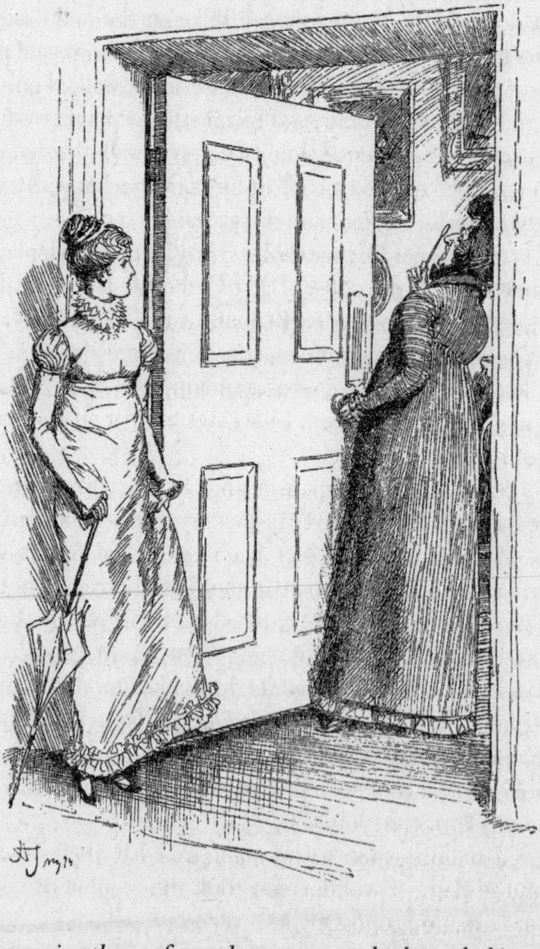

*Pronouncing them, after a short survey, to be decent looking rooms*

'It ought to be so; it must be so, while he retains the use of his reason. But *your* arts and allurements may, in a moment of infatuation, have made him forget what he owes to himself and to all his family. You may have drawn him in.'

'If I have, I shall be the last person to confess it.'

'Miss Bennet, do you know who I am? I have not been accustomed to such language as this. I am almost the nearest relation he has in the world, and am entitled to know all his dearest concerns.'

'But you are not entitled to know *mine*; nor will such behaviour as this, ever induce me to be explicit.'

'Let me be rightly understood. This match, to which you have the presumption to aspire, can never take place. No, never. Mr Darcy is engaged to *my daughter*. Now what have you to say?'

'Only this; that if he is so, you can have no reason to suppose he will make an offer to me.'

Lady Catherine hesitated for a moment, and then replied, 'The engagement between them is of a peculiar kind. From their infancy, they have been intended for each other. It was the favourite wish of *his* mother, as well as of hers. While in their cradles, we planned the union: and now, at the moment when the wishes of both sisters would be accomplished, in their marriage, to be prevented by a young woman of inferior birth, of no importance in the world, and wholly unallied to the family! Do you pay no regard to the wishes of his friends? To his tacit engagement with Miss de Bourgh? Are you lost to every feeling of propriety and delicacy? Have you not heard me say, that from his earliest hours he was destined for his cousin?'

'Yes, and I had heard it before. But what is that to me? If there is no other objection to my marrying your nephew, I shall certainly not be kept from it, by knowing that his mother and aunt wished him to marry Miss de Bourgh. You both did as much as you could, in planning the marriage. Its completion depended on others. If Mr Darcy is neither by honour nor inclination confined to his cousin, why is not he to make another choice? And if I am that choice, why may not I accept him?'

'Because honour, decorum, prudence, nay, interest, forbid it. Yes, Miss Bennet, interest; for do not expect to be noticed by his family or friends, if you wilfully act against the inclinations of all. You will be censured, slighted, and despised, by everyone connected with him. Your alliance will be a disgrace; your name will never even be mentioned by any of us.'

'These are heavy misfortunes,' replied Elizabeth. 'But the wife of Mr Darcy must have such extraordinary sources of happiness necessarily attached to her situation, that she could, upon the whole, have no cause to repine.'

'Obstinate, headstrong girl! I am ashamed of you! Is this your gratitude for my attentions to you last spring? Is nothing due to me on that score?

'Let us sit down. You are to understand, Miss Bennet, that I came here with the determined resolution of carrying my purpose; nor will I be dissuaded from it. I have not been used to submit to any person's whims. I have not been in the habit of brooking disappointment.'

'*That* will make your ladyship's situation at present more pitiable; but it will have no effect on *me.*'

'I will not be interrupted. Hear me in silence. My daughter and my nephew are formed for each other. They are descended on the maternal side, from the same noble line; and, on the father's, from respectable, honourable, and ancient, though untitled families. Their fortune on both sides is splendid. They are destined for each other by the voice of every member of their respective houses; and what is to divide them? The upstart pretensions of a young woman without family, connections, or fortune. Is this to be endured! But it must not, shall not be. If you were sensible of your own good, you would not wish to quit the sphere, in which you have been brought up.'

'In marrying your nephew, I should not consider myself as quitting that sphere. He is a gentleman; I am a gentleman's daughter; so far we are equal.'

'True. You *are* a gentleman's daughter. But who was your mother? Who are your uncles and aunts? Do not imagine me ignorant of their condition.'

'Whatever my connections may be,' said Elizabeth, 'if your nephew does not object to them, they can be nothing to *you*.'

'Tell me once for all, are you engaged to him?'

Though Elizabeth would not, for the mere purpose of obliging Lady Catherine, have answered this question, she could not but say, after a moment's deliberation, 'I am not.'

Lady Catherine seemed pleased.

'And will you promise me, never to enter into such an engagement?'

'I will make no promise of the kind.'

'Miss Bennet, I am shocked and astonished. I expected to find a more reasonable young woman. But do not deceive yourself into a belief that I will ever recede. I shall not go away, till you have given me the assurance I require.'

'And I certainly *never* shall give it. I am not to be intimidated into anything so wholly unreasonable. Your ladyship wants Mr Darcy to marry your daughter; but would my giving you the wished-for promise, make *their* marriage at all more probable? Supposing him to be attached to me, would *my* refusing to accept his hand, make him wish to bestow it on his cousin? Allow me to say, Lady Catherine, that the arguments with which you have supported this extraordinary application, have been as frivolous as the application was ill-judged. You have widely mistaken my character, if you think I can be worked on by such persuasions as these. How far your nephew might approve of your interference in *his* affairs, I cannot tell; but you have certainly no right to concern yourself in mine. I must beg, therefore, to be importuned no farther on the subject.'

'Not so hasty, if you please. I have by no means done. To all the objections I have already urged, I have still another to add. I am no stranger to the particulars of your youngest sister's infamous elopement. I know it all; that the young man's marrying her, was a patched-up business, at the expense of your father and uncles. And is *such* a girl to be my nephew's sister? Is *her* husband, is the son of his late father's steward, to be his brother? Heaven and earth! – of what are you thinking? Are the shades of Pemberley to be thus polluted?'

'You can *now* have nothing farther to say,' she resentfully answered. 'You have insulted me, in every possible method. I must beg to return to the house.'

And she rose as she spoke. Lady Catherine rose also, and they turned back. Her ladyship was highly incensed.

'You have no regard, then, for the honour and credit of my nephew! Unfeeling, selfish girl! Do you not consider that a connection with you, must disgrace him in the eyes of everybody?'

'Lady Catherine, I have nothing farther to say. You know my sentiments.'

'You are then resolved to have him?'

'I have said no such thing. I am only resolved to act in that manner, which will, in my own opinion, constitute my happiness, without reference to *you*, or to any person so wholly unconnected with me.'

'It is well. You refuse, then, to oblige me. You refuse to obey the claims of duty, honour, and gratitude. You are determined to ruin him in the opinion of all his friends, and make him the contempt of the world.'

'Neither duty, nor honour, nor gratitude,' replied Elizabeth, 'have any possible claim on me, in the present instance. No principle of either, would be violated by my marriage with Mr Darcy. And with regard to the resentment of his family, or the indignation of the world, if the former *were* excited by his marrying me, it would not give me one moment's concern – and the world in general would have too much sense to join in the scorn.'

'And this is your real opinion! This is your final resolve! Very well. I shall now know how to act. Do not imagine, Miss Bennet, that your ambition will ever be gratified. I came to try you. I hoped to find you reasonable; but depend upon it I will carry my point.'

In this manner Lady Catherine talked on, till they were at the door of the carriage, when turning hastily round, she added, 'I take no leave of you, Miss Bennet. I send no compliments to your mother. You deserve no such attention. I am most seriously displeased.'

Elizabeth made no answer; and without attempting to persuade her ladyship to return into the house, walked quietly into it herself. She heard the carriage drive away as she proceeded upstairs. Her mother impatiently met her at the door of the dressing-room, to ask why Lady Catherine would not come in again and rest herself.

'She did not choose it,' said her daughter, 'she would go.'

'She is a very fine-looking woman! and her calling here was prodigiously civil! for she only came, I suppose, to tell us the Collinses were well. She is on her road somewhere, I dare say, and so passing through Meryton, thought she might as well call on you. I suppose she had nothing particular to say to you, Lizzy?'

Elizabeth was forced to give in to a little falsehood here; for to acknowledge the substance of their conversation was impossible.

## *Chapter 57*

The discomposure of spirits, which this extraordinary visit threw Elizabeth into, could not be easily overcome; nor could she for many hours, learn to think of it less than incessantly. Lady Catherine it appeared, had actually taken the trouble of this journey from Rosings, for the sole purpose of breaking off her supposed engagement with Mr Darcy. It was a rational scheme to be sure! but from what the report of their engagement could originate, Elizabeth was at a loss to imagine; till she recollected that *his* being the intimate friend of Bingley, and *her* being the sister of Jane, was enough, at a time when the expectation of one wedding, made everybody eager for another, to supply the idea. She had not herself forgotten to feel that the marriage of her sister must bring them more frequently together. And her neighbours at Lucas Lodge, therefore, (for through their communication with the Collinses, the report she concluded had reached Lady Catherine) had only set *that* down, as almost certain and immediate, which *she* had looked forward to as possible, at some future time.

In revolving Lady Catherine's expressions, however, she could not help feeling some uneasiness as to the possible consequence of her persisting in this interference. From what she had said of her resolution to prevent their marriage, it occurred to Elizabeth that she must meditate an application to her nephew; and how *he* might take a similar representation of the evils attached to a connection with her, she dared not pronounce. She knew not the exact degree of his affection for his aunt, or his dependence on her judgment, but it was natural to suppose that he thought much higher of her ladyship than *she* could do; and it was certain, that in enumerating the miseries of a marriage with *one*, whose immediate connections were so unequal to his own, his aunt would address him on his weakest side. With his notions of dignity, he would probably feel that the arguments, which to Elizabeth had appeared weak and ridiculous, contained much good sense and solid reasoning.

If he had been wavering before, as to what he should do, which had often seemed likely, the advice and entreaty of so near a relation might settle every doubt, and determine him at once to be as happy, as dignity unblemished could make him. In that case he would return no more. Lady Catherine might see him in her way through town; and his engagement to Bingley of coming again to Netherfield must give way.

'If, therefore, an excuse for not keeping his promise, should come to his friend within a few days,' she added, 'I shall know how to understand it. I shall then give over every expectation, every wish of his constancy. If he is satisfied with only regretting me, when he might have obtained my affections and hand, I shall soon cease to regret him at all.'

The surprise of the rest of the family, on hearing who their visitor had been, was very great; but they obligingly satisfied it, with the same kind of supposition, which had appeased Mrs Bennet's curiosity; and Elizabeth was spared from much teasing on the subject.

The next morning, as she was going downstairs, she was met by her father, who came out of his library with a letter in his hand.

'Lizzy,' said he, 'I was going to look for you; come into my room.'

She followed him hither; and her curiosity to know what he had to tell her, was heightened by the supposition of its being in some manner connected with the letter he held. It suddenly struck her that it might be from Lady Catherine; and she anticipated with dismay all the consequent explanations.

She followed her father to the fireplace, and they both sat down. He then said, 'I have received a letter this morning that has astonished me exceedingly. As it principally concerns yourself, you ought to know its contents. I did not know before, that I had *two* daughters on the brink of matrimony. Let me congratulate you, on a very important conquest.'

The colour now rushed into Elizabeth's cheeks in the instantaneous conviction of its being a letter from the nephew, instead of the aunt; and she was undetermined whether most to be pleased that he explained himself at all, or offended that his letter was not rather addressed to herself; when her father continued, 'You look conscious. Young ladies have great penetration in such matters as these; but I think I may defy even *your* sagacity, to discover the name of your admirer. This letter is from Mr Collins.'

'From Mr Collins! and what can *he* have to say?'

'Something very much to the purpose of course. He begins with congratulations on the approaching nuptials of my eldest daughter, of which it seems he has been told, by some of the good-natured, gossiping Lucases. I shall not sport with your impatience, by reading what he says on that point. What relates to yourself, is as follows. "Having thus offered you the sincere congratulations of Mrs Collins and myself on this happy event, let me now add a short hint on the subject of another; of which we have been advertised by the same authority. Your daughter Elizabeth, it is presumed, will not long bear the name of Bennet, after her elder sister has resigned it, and the chosen partner of her fate, may be reasonably looked up to, as one of the most illustrious personages in this land."

'Can you possibly guess, Lizzy, who is meant by this? "This young gentleman is blessed in a peculiar way, with everything the heart of mortal can most desire, – splendid property, noble kindred, and extensive patronage. Yet in spite of all these temptations, let me warn my cousin Elizabeth, and yourself, of what evils you may incur, by a precipitate closure with this gentleman's proposals, which, of course, you will be inclined to take immediate advantage of."

'Have you any idea, Lizzy, who this gentleman is? But now it comes out.

' "My motive for cautioning you, is as follows. We have reason to imagine that his aunt, Lady Catherine de Bourgh, does not look on the match with a friendly eye."

'*Mr Darcy*, you see, is the man! Now, Lizzy, I think I *have* surprised you.

Could he, or the Lucases, have pitched on any man, within the circle of our acquaintance, whose name would have given the lie more effectually to what they related? Mr Darcy, who never looks at any woman but to see a blemish, and who probably never looked at *you* in his life! It is admirable!'

Elizabeth tried to join in her father's pleasantry, but could only force one most reluctant smile. Never had his wit been directed in a manner so little agreeable to her.

'Are you not diverted?'

'Oh! yes. Pray read on.'

' "After mentioning the likelihood of this marriage to her ladyship last night, she immediately, with her usual condescension, expressed what she felt on the occasion; when it became apparent, that on the score of some family objections on the part of my cousin, she would never give her consent to what she termed so disgraceful a match. I thought it my duty to give the speediest intelligence of this to my cousin, that she and her noble admirer may be aware of what they are about, and not run hastily into a marriage which has not been properly sanctioned." Mr Collins moreover adds, "I am truly rejoiced that my cousin Lydia's sad business has been so well hushed up, and am only concerned that their living together before the marriage took place, should be so generally known. I must not, however, neglect the duties of my station, or refrain from declaring my amazement, at hearing that you received the young couple into your house as soon as they were married. It was an encouragement of vice; and had I been the rector of Longbourn, I should very strenuously have opposed it. You ought certainly to forgive them as a Christian, but never to admit them in your sight, or allow their names to be mentioned in your hearing." *That* is his

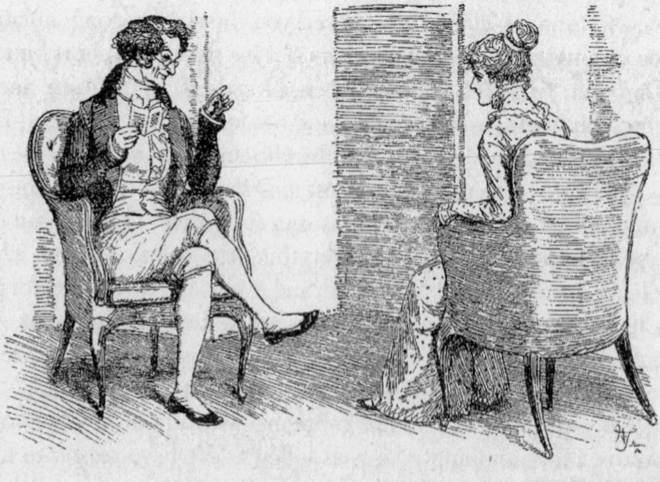

*But now it comes out*

notion of Christian forgiveness! The rest of his letter is only about his dear Charlotte's situation, and his expectation of a young olive-branch. But, Lizzy, you look as if you did not enjoy it. You are not going to be *Missish*, I hope, and pretend to be affronted at an idle report. For what do we live, but to make sport for our neighbours, and laugh at them in our turn?'

'Oh!' cried Elizabeth, 'I am excessively diverted. But it is so strange!'

'Yes – *that* is what makes it amusing. Had they fixed on any other man it would have been nothing; but *his* perfect indifference, and *your* pointed dislike, make it so delightfully absurd! Much as I abominate writing, I would not give up Mr Collins's correspondence for any consideration. Nay, when I read a letter of his, I cannot help giving him the preference even over Wickham, much as I value the impudence and hypocrisy of my son-in-law. And pray, Lizzy, what said Lady Catherine about this report? Did she call to refuse her consent?'

To this question his daughter replied only with a laugh; and as it had been asked without the least suspicion, she was not distressed by his repeating it. Elizabeth had never been more at a loss to make her feelings appear what they were not. It was necessary to laugh, when she would rather have cried. Her father had most cruelly mortified her, by what he said of Mr Darcy's indifference, and she could do nothing but wonder at such a want of penetration, or fear that perhaps, instead of his seeing too *little*, she might have fancied too *much*.

## *Chapter 58*

Instead of receiving any such letter of excuse from his friend, as Elizabeth half expected Mr Bingley to do, he was able to bring Darcy with him to Longbourn before many days had passed after Lady Catherine's visit. The gentlemen arrived early; and, before Mrs Bennet had time to tell him of their having seen his aunt, of which her daughter sat in momentary dread, Bingley, who wanted to be alone with Jane, proposed their all walking out. It was agreed to. Mrs Bennet was not in the habit of walking, Mary could never spare time, but the remaining five set off together. Bingley and Jane, however, soon allowed the others to outstrip them. They lagged behind, while Elizabeth, Kitty, and Darcy, were to entertain each other. Very little was said by either; Kitty was too much afraid of him to talk; Elizabeth was secretly forming a desperate resolution; and perhaps he might be doing the same.

They walked towards the Lucases, because Kitty wished to call upon Maria; and as Elizabeth saw no occasion for making it a general concern, when Kitty left them, she went boldly on with him alone. Now was the moment for her resolution to be executed, and, while her courage was high, she immediately said, 'Mr Darcy, I am a very selfish creature; and, for the sake of giving relief to my own feelings, care not how much I may be wounding yours. I can no longer help thanking you for your unexampled kindness to my poor sister. Ever since I have known it, I have been most anxious to acknowledge to you how gratefully

I feel it. Were it known to the rest of my family, I should not have merely my own gratitude to express.'

'I am sorry, exceedingly sorry,' replied Darcy, in a tone of surprise and emotion, 'that you have ever been informed of what may, in a mistaken light, have given you uneasiness. I did not think Mrs Gardiner was so little to be trusted.'

'You must not blame my aunt. Lydia's thoughtlessness first betrayed to me that you had been concerned in the matter; and, of course, I could not rest till I knew the particulars. Let me thank you again and again, in the name of all my family, for that generous compassion which induced you to take so much trouble, and bear so many mortifications, for the sake of discovering them.'

'If you *will* thank me,' he replied, 'let it be for yourself alone. That the wish of giving happiness to you, might add force to the other inducements which led me on, I shall not attempt to deny. But your *family* owe me nothing. Much as I respect them, I believe, I thought only of *you*.'

Elizabeth was too much embarrassed to say a word. After a short pause, her companion added, 'You are too generous to trifle with me. If your feelings are still what they were last April, tell me so at once. *My* affections and wishes are unchanged, but one word from you will silence me on this subject for ever.'

Elizabeth feeling all the more than common awkwardness and anxiety of his situation, now forced herself to speak; and immediately, though not very fluently, gave him to understand, that her sentiments had undergone so material a change, since the period to which he alluded, as to make her receive with gratitude and pleasure, his present assurances. The happiness which this reply produced, was such as he had probably never felt before; and he expressed himself on the occasion as sensibly and as warmly as a man violently in love can be supposed to do. Had Elizabeth been able to encounter his eye, she might have seen how well the expression of heartfelt delight, diffused over his face, became him; but, though she could not look, she could listen, and he told her of feelings, which, in proving of what importance she was to him, made his affection every moment more valuable.

They walked on, without knowing in what direction. There was too much to be thought, and felt, and said, for attention to any other objects. She soon learnt that they were indebted for their present good understanding to the efforts of his aunt, who *did* call on him in her return through London, and there relate her journey to Longbourn, its motive, and the substance of her conversation with Elizabeth; dwelling emphatically on every expression of the latter, which, in her ladyship's apprehension, peculiarly denoted her perverseness and assurance, in the belief that such a relation must assist her endeavours to obtain that promise from her nephew, which *she* had refused to give. But, unluckily for her ladyship, its effect had been exactly contrariwise.

'It taught me to hope,' said he, 'as I had scarcely ever allowed myself to hope before. I knew enough of your disposition to be certain, that, had you been absolutely, irrevocably decided against me, you would have acknowledged it to Lady Catherine, frankly and openly.'

Elizabeth coloured and laughed as she replied, 'Yes, you know enough of my *frankness* to believe me capable of *that*. After abusing you so abominably to your face, I could have no scruple in abusing you to all your relations.'

'What did you say of me, that I did not deserve? For, though your accusations were ill-founded, formed on mistaken premises, my behaviour to you at the time, had merited the severest reproof. It was unpardonable. I cannot think of it without abhorrence.'

'We will not quarrel for the greater share of blame annexed to that evening,' said Elizabeth. 'The conduct of neither, if strictly examined, will be irreproachable; but since then, we have both, I hope, improved in civility.'

'I cannot be so easily reconciled to myself. The recollection of what I then said, of my conduct, my manners, my expressions during the whole of it, is now, and has been many months, inexpressibly painful to me. Your reproof, so well applied, I shall never forget: "had you behaved in a more gentlemanlike manner." Those were your words. You know not, you can scarcely conceive, how they have tortured me; – though it was some time, I confess, before I was reasonable enough to allow their justice.'

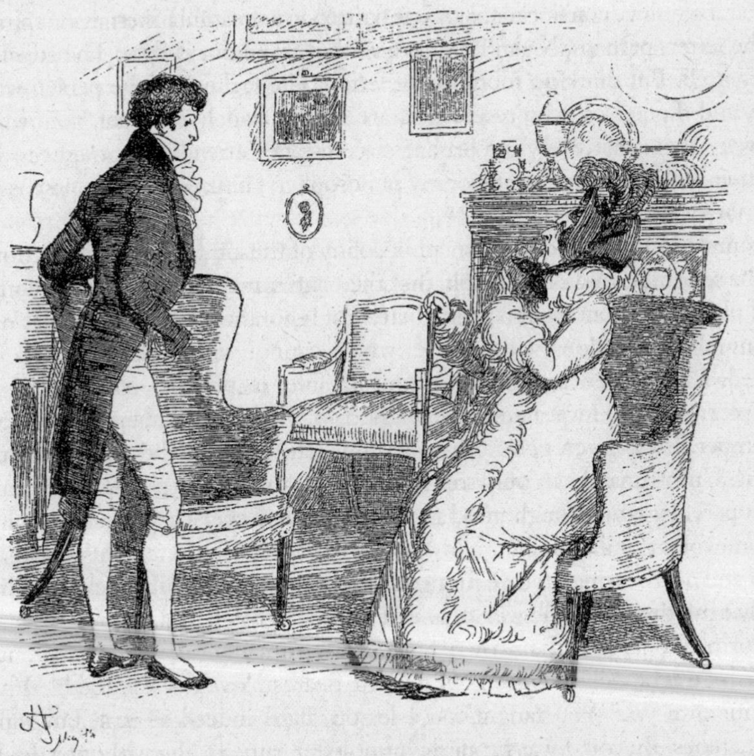

*The efforts of his aunt*

'I was certainly very far from expecting them to make so strong an impression. I had not the smallest idea of their being ever felt in such a way.'

'I can easily believe it. You thought me then devoid of every proper feeling, I am sure you did. The turn of your countenance I shall never forget, as you said that I could not have addressed you in any possible way; that would induce you to accept me.'

'Oh! do not repeat what I then said. These recollections will not do at all. I assure you, that I have long been most heartily ashamed of it.'

Darcy mentioned his letter. 'Did it,' said he, 'did it *soon* make you think better of me? Did you, on reading it, give any credit to its contents?'

She explained what its effect on her had been, and how gradually all her former prejudices had been removed.

'I knew,' said he, 'that what I wrote must give you pain, but it was necessary. I hope you have destroyed the letter. There was one part especially, the opening of it, which I should dread your having the power of reading again. I can remember some expressions which might justly make you hate me.'

'The letter shall certainly be burnt, if you believe it essential to the preservation of my regard; but, though we have both reason to think my opinions not entirely unalterable, they are not, I hope, quite so easily changed as that implies.'

'When I wrote that letter,' replied Darcy, 'I believed myself perfectly calm and cool, but I am since convinced that it was written in a dreadful bitterness of spirit.'

'The letter, perhaps, began in bitterness, but it did not end so. The adieu is charity itself. But think no more of the letter. The feelings of the person who wrote, and the person who received it, are now so widely different from what they were then, that every unpleasant circumstance attending it, ought to be forgotten. You must learn some of my philosophy. Think only of the past as its remembrance gives you pleasure.'

'I cannot give you credit for any philosophy of the kind. *Your* retrospections must be so totally void of reproach, that the contentment arising from them, is not of philosophy, but what is much better, of ignorance. But with *me*, it is not so. Painful recollections will intrude, which cannot, which ought not to be repelled. I have been a selfish being all my life, in practice, though not in principle. As a child I was taught what was *right*, but I was not taught to correct my temper. I was given good principles, but left to follow them in pride and conceit. Unfortunately an only son (for many years an only *child*), I was spoilt by my parents, who though good themselves (my father particularly, all that was benevolent and amiable), allowed, encouraged, almost taught me to be selfish and overbearing, to care for none beyond my own family circle, to think meanly of all the rest of the world, to *wish* at least to think meanly of their sense and worth compared with my own. Such I was, from eight to eight and twenty; and such I might still have been but for you, dearest, loveliest Elizabeth! What do I not owe you! You taught me a lesson, hard indeed at first, but most advantageous. By you, I was properly humbled. I came to you without a doubt of my reception. You showed me how insufficient were all my pretensions to please a woman worthy of being pleased.'

'Had you then persuaded yourself that I should?'

'Indeed I had. What will you think of my vanity? I believed you to be wishing, expecting my addresses.'

'My manners must have been in fault, but not intentionally I assure you. I never meant to deceive you, but my spirits might often lead me wrong. How you must have hated me after *that* evening?'

'Hate you! I was angry perhaps at first, but my anger soon began to take a proper direction.'

'I am almost afraid of asking what you thought of me, when we met at Pemberley. You blamed me for coming?'

'No indeed; I felt nothing but surprise.'

'Your surprise could not be greater than *mine* in being noticed by you. My conscience told me that I deserved no extraordinary politeness, and I confess that I did not expect to receive *more* than my due.'

'My object *then*,' replied Darcy, 'was to show you, by every civility in my power, that I was not so mean as to resent the past; and I hoped to obtain your forgiveness, to lessen your ill opinion, by letting you see that your reproofs had been attended to. How soon any other wishes introduced themselves I can hardly tell, but I believe in about half an hour after I had seen you.'

He then told her of Georgiana's delight in her acquaintance, and of her disappointment at its sudden interruption; which naturally leading to the cause of that interruption, she soon learnt that his resolution of following her from Derbyshire in quest of her sister, had been formed before he quitted the inn, and that his gravity and thoughtfulness there, had arisen from no other struggles than what such a purpose must comprehend.

She expressed her gratitude again, but it was too painful a subject to each, to be dwelt on farther.

After walking several miles in a leisurely manner, and too busy to know anything about it, they found at last, on examining their watches, that it was time to be at home.

'What could become of Mr Bingley and Jane!' was a wonder which introduced the discussion of *their* affairs. Darcy was delighted with their engagement; his friend had given him the earliest information of it.

'I must ask whether you were surprised?' said Elizabeth.

'Not at all. When I went away, I felt that it would soon happen.'

'That is to say, you had given your permission. I guessed as much.' And though he exclaimed at the term, she found that it had been pretty much the case.

'On the evening before my going to London,' said he 'I made a confession to him, which I believe I ought to have made long ago. I told him of all that had occurred to make my former interference in his affairs, absurd and impertinent. His surprise was great. He had never had the slightest suspicion. I told him, moreover, that I believed myself mistaken in supposing, as I had done, that your sister was indifferent to him; and as I could easily perceive that his attachment to her was unabated, I felt no doubt of their happiness together.'

Elizabeth could not help smiling at his easy manner of directing his friend.

'Did you speak from your own observation,' said she, 'when you told him that my sister loved him, or merely from my information last spring?'

'From the former. I had narrowly observed her during the two visits which I had lately made her here; and I was convinced of her affection.'

'And your assurance of it, I suppose, carried immediate conviction to him.'

'It did. Bingley is most unaffectedly modest. His diffidence had prevented his depending on his own judgment in so anxious a case, but his reliance on mine, made everything easy. I was obliged to confess one thing, which for a time, and not unjustly, offended him. I could not allow myself to conceal that your sister had been in town three months last winter, that I had known it, and purposely kept it from him. He was angry. But his anger, I am persuaded, lasted no longer than he remained in any doubt of your sister's sentiments. He has heartily forgiven me now.'

Elizabeth longed to observe that Mr Bingley had been a most delightful friend; so easily guided that his worth was invaluable; but she checked herself. She remembered that he had yet to learn to be laughed at, and it was rather too early to begin. In anticipating the happiness of Bingley, which of course was to be inferior only to his own, he continued the conversation till they reached the house. In the hall they parted.

## *Chapter 59*

'My dear Lizzy, where can you have been walking to?' was a question which Elizabeth received from Jane as soon as she entered the room, and from all the others when they sat down to table. She had only to say in reply, that they had wandered about, till she was beyond her own knowledge. She coloured as she spoke; but neither that, nor anything else, awakened a suspicion of the truth.

The evening passed quietly, unmarked by anything extraordinary. The acknowledged lovers talked and laughed, the unacknowledged were silent. Darcy was not of a disposition in which happiness overflows in mirth; and Elizabeth, agitated and confused, rather *knew* that she was happy, than *felt* herself to be so; for, besides the immediate embarrassment, there were other evils before her. She anticipated what would be felt in the family when her situation became known; she was aware that no one liked him but Jane; and even feared that with the others it was a *dislike* which not all his fortune and consequence might do away.

At night she opened her heart to Jane. Though suspicion was very far from Miss Bennet's general habits, she was absolutely incredulous here.

'You are joking, Lizzy. This cannot be! – engaged to Mr Darcy! No, no, you shall not deceive me. I know it to be impossible.'

'This is a wretched beginning indeed! My sole dependence was on you; and I am sure nobody else will believe me, if you do not. Yet, indeed, I am in earnest. I speak nothing but the truth. He still loves me, and we are engaged.'

Jane looked at her doubtingly. 'Oh, Lizzy! it cannot be. I know how much you dislike him.'

'You know nothing of the matter. *That* is all to be forgot. Perhaps I did not always love him so well as I do now. But in such cases as these, a good memory is unpardonable. This is the last time I shall ever remember it myself.'

Miss Bennet still looked all amazement. Elizabeth again, and more seriously assured her of its truth.

'Good Heaven! can it be really so! Yet now I must believe you,' cried Jane. 'My dear, dear Lizzy, I would – I do congratulate you – but are you certain? Forgive the question – are you quite certain that you can be happy with him?'

'There can be no doubt of that. It is settled between us already, that we are to be the happiest couple in the world. But are you pleased, Jane? Shall you like to have such a brother?'

'Very, very much. Nothing could give either Bingley or myself more delight. But we considered it, we talked of it as impossible. And do you really love him quite well enough? Oh, Lizzy! do anything rather than marry without affection. Are you quite sure that you feel what you ought to do?'

'Oh, yes! You will only think I feel more than I ought to do, when I tell you all.'

'What do you mean?'

'Why, I must confess, that I love him better than I do Bingley. I am afraid you will be angry.'

'My dearest sister, now *be* serious. I want to talk very seriously. Let me know everything that I am to know, without delay. Will you tell me how long you have loved him?'

'It has been coming on so gradually, that I hardly know when it began. But I believe I must date it from my first seeing his beautiful grounds at Pemberley.'

Another entreaty that she would be serious, however, produced the desired effect; and she soon satisfied Jane by her solemn assurances of attachment. When convinced on that article, Miss Bennet had nothing farther to wish.

'Now I am quite happy,' said she, 'for you will be as happy as myself. I always had a value for him. Were it for nothing but his love of you, I must always have esteemed him; but now, as Bingley's friend and your husband, there can be only Bingley and yourself more dear to me. But Lizzy, you have been very sly, very reserved with me. How little did you tell me of what passed at Pemberley and Lambton! I owe all that I know of it, to another, not to you.'

Elizabeth told her the motives of her secrecy. She had been unwilling to mention Bingley; and the unsettled state of her own feelings had made her equally avoid the name of his friend. But now she would no longer conceal from her, his share in Lydia's marriage. All was acknowledged, and half the night spent in conversation.

'Good gracious!' cried Mrs Bennet, as she stood at a window the next morning, 'if that disagreeable Mr Darcy is not coming here again with our dear Bingley! What can he mean by being so tiresome as to be always coming here? I had no notion but he would go a shooting, or something or other, and not disturb us with his company. What shall we do with him? Lizzy, you must walk out with him again, that he may not be in Bingley's way.'

Elizabeth could hardly help laughing at so convenient a proposal; yet was really vexed that her mother should be always giving him such an epithet.

As soon as they entered, Bingley looked at her so expressively, and shook hands with such warmth, as left no doubt of his good information; and he soon afterwards said aloud, 'Mr Bennet, have you no more lanes hereabouts in which Lizzy may lose her way again today?'

'I advise Mr Darcy, and Lizzy, and Kitty,' said Mrs Bennet, 'to walk to Oakham Mount this morning. It is a nice long walk, and Mr Darcy has never seen the view.'

'It may do very well for the others,' replied Mr Bingley; 'but I am sure it will be too much for Kitty. Won't it, Kitty?'

Kitty owned that she had rather stay at home. Darcy professed a great curiosity to see the view from the Mount, and Elizabeth silently consented. As she went upstairs to get ready, Mrs Bennet followed her, saying, 'I am quite sorry, Lizzy, that you should be forced to have that disagreeable man all to yourself. But I hope you will not mind it: it is all for Jane's sake, you know; and there is no occasion for talking to him, except just now and then. So, do not put yourself to inconvenience.'

During their walk, it was resolved that Mr Bennet's consent should be asked in the course of the evening. Elizabeth reserved to herself the application for her mother's. She could not determine how her mother would take it; sometimes doubting whether all his wealth and grandeur would be enough to overcome her abhorrence of the man. But whether she were violently set against the match, or violently delighted with it, it was certain that her manner would be equally ill-adapted to do credit to her sense; and she could no more bear that Mr Darcy should hear the first raptures of her joy, than the first vehemence of her disapprobation.

In the evening, soon after Mr Bennet withdrew to the library, she saw Mr Darcy rise also and follow him, and her agitation on seeing it was extreme. She did not fear her father's opposition, but he was going to be made unhappy, and that it should be through her means, that *she*, his favourite child, should be distressing him by her choice, should be filling him with fears and regrets in disposing of her, was a wretched reflection, and she sat in misery till Mr Darcy appeared again, when, looking at him, she was a little relieved by his smile. In a few minutes he approached the table where she was sitting with Kitty; and, while pretending to admire her work, said in a whisper, 'Go to your father, he wants you in the library.' She was gone directly.

Her father was walking about the room, looking grave and anxious. 'Lizzy,' said he, 'what are you doing? Are you out of your senses, to be accepting this man? Have not you always hated him?'

How earnestly did she then wish that her former opinions had been more reasonable, her expressions more moderate! It would have spared her from explanations and professions which it was exceedingly awkward to give; but they were now necessary, and she assured him with some confusion, of her attachment to Mr Darcy.

'Or in other words, you are determined to have him. He is rich, to be sure, and you may have more fine clothes and fine carriages than Jane. But will they make you happy?'

'Have you any other objection,' said Elizabeth, 'than your belief of my indifference?'

'None at all. We all know him to be a proud, unpleasant sort of man; but this would be nothing if you really liked him.'

'I do, I do like him,' she replied, with tears in her eyes, 'I love him. Indeed he has no improper pride. He is perfectly amiable. You do not know what he really is; then pray do not pain me by speaking of him in such terms.'

'Lizzy,' said her father, 'I have given him my consent. He is the kind of man, indeed, to whom I should never dare refuse anything, which he condescended to ask. I now give it to *you*, if you are resolved on having him. But let me advise you to think better of it. I know your disposition, Lizzy. I know that you could be neither happy nor respectable, unless you truly esteemed your husband; unless you looked up to him as a superior. Your lively talents would place you in the greatest danger in an unequal marriage. You could scarcely escape discredit and misery. My child, let me not have the grief of seeing *you* unable to respect your partner in life. You know not what you are about.'

Elizabeth, still more affected, was earnest and solemn in her reply; and at length, by repeated assurances that Mr Darcy was really the object of her choice, by explaining the gradual change which her estimation of him had undergone, relating her absolute certainty that his affection was not the work of a day, but had stood the test of many months' suspense, and enumerating with energy all his good qualities, she did conquer her father's incredulity, and reconcile him to the match.

'Well, my dear,' said he, when she ceased speaking, 'I have no more to say. If this be the case, he deserves you. I could not have parted with you, my Lizzy, to anyone less worthy.'

To complete the favourable impression, she then told him what Mr Darcy had voluntarily done for Lydia. He heard her with astonishment.

'This is an evening of wonders, indeed! And so, Darcy did everything; made up the match, gave the money, paid the fellow's debts, and got him his commission! So much the better. It will save me a world of trouble and economy. Had it been your uncle's doing, I must and *would* have paid him; but these violent young lovers carry everything their own way. I shall offer to pay him tomorrow; he will rant and storm about his love for you, and there will be an end of the matter.'

He then recollected her embarrassment a few days before, on his reading Mr Collins's letter; and after laughing at her for some time, allowed her at last to go – saying, as she quitted the room, 'If any young men come for Mary or Kitty, send them in, for I am quite at leisure.'

Elizabeth's mind was now relieved from a very heavy weight; and, after half an hour's quiet reflection in her own room, she was able to join the others with tolerable composure. Everything was too recent for gaiety, but the evening passed tranquilly away; there was no longer anything material to be dreaded, and the comfort of ease and familiarity would come in time.

When her mother went up to her dressing-room at night, she followed her, and made the important communication. Its effect was most extraordinary; for on first hearing it, Mrs Bennet sat quite still, and unable to utter a syllable. Nor was it under many, many minutes, that she could comprehend what she heard; though not in general backward to credit what was for the advantage of her family, or that came in the shape of a lover to any of them. She began at length to recover, to fidget about in her chair, get up, sit down again, wonder, and bless herself.

'Good gracious! Lord bless me! only think! dear me! Mr Darcy! Who would have thought it! And is it really true? Oh! my sweetest Lizzy! how rich and how great you will be! What pin money, what jewels, what carriages you will have! Jane's is nothing to it – nothing at all. I am so pleased – so happy. Such a charming man! – so handsome! so tall! – Oh, my dear Lizzy! pray apologise for

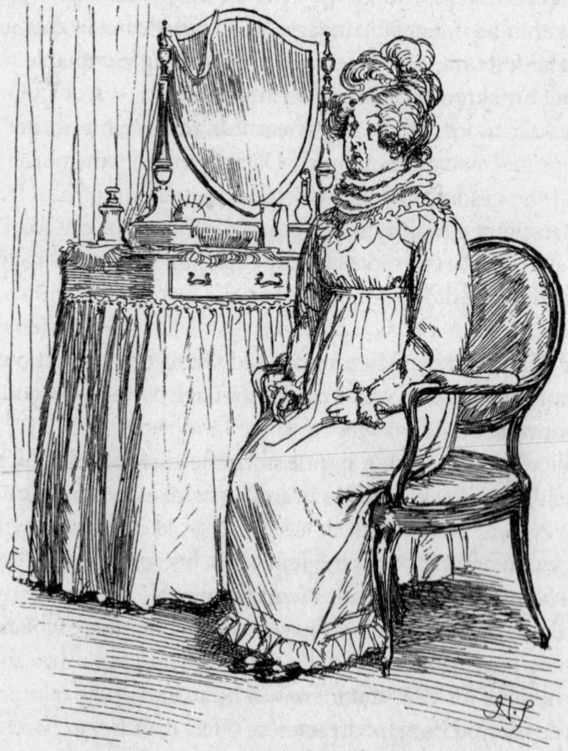

*Unable to utter a syllable*

my having disliked him so much before. I hope he will overlook it. Dear, dear Lizzy. A house in town! Everything that is charming! Three daughters married! Ten thousand a year! Oh, Lord! What will become of me. I shall go distracted.'

This was enough to prove that her approbation need not be doubted: and Elizabeth, rejoicing that such an effusion was heard only by herself, soon went away. But before she had been three minutes in her own room, her mother followed her.

'My dearest child,' she cried, 'I can think of nothing else! Ten thousand a year, and very likely more! 'Tis as good as a Lord! And a special licence. You must and shall be married by a special licence. But my dearest love, tell me what dish Mr Darcy is particularly fond of, that I may have it tomorrow.'

This was a sad omen of what her mother's behaviour to the gentleman himself might be; and Elizabeth found, that though in the certain possession of his warmest affection, and secure of her relations' consent, there was still something to be wished for. But the morrow passed off much better than she expected; for Mrs Bennet luckily stood in such awe of her intended son-in-law, that she ventured not to speak to him, unless it was in her power to offer him any attention, or mark her deference for his opinion.

Elizabeth had the satisfaction of seeing her father taking pains to get acquainted with him; and Mr Bennet soon assured her that he was rising every hour in his esteem.

'I admire all my three sons-in-law highly,' said he. 'Wickham, perhaps, is my favourite; but I think I shall like *your* husband quite as well as Jane's.'

## *Chapter 60*

Elizabeth's spirits soon rising to playfulness again, she wanted Mr Darcy to account for his having ever fallen in love with her. 'How could you begin?' said she. 'I can comprehend your going on charmingly, when you had once made a beginning; but what could set you off in the first place?'

'I cannot fix on the hour, or the spot, or the look, or the words, which laid the foundation. It is too long ago. I was in the middle before I knew that I *had* begun.'

'My beauty you had early withstood, and as for my manners – my behaviour to *you* was at least always bordering on the uncivil, and I never spoke to you without rather wishing to give you pain than not. Now be sincere; did you admire me for my impertinence?'

'For the liveliness of your mind, I did.'

'You may as well call it impertinence at once. It was very little less. The fact is, that you were sick of civility, of deference, of officious attention. You were disgusted with the women who were always speaking and looking, and thinking for *your* approbation alone. I roused, and interested you, because I was so unlike *them*. Had you not been really amiable you would have hated me for it;

but in spite of the pains you took to disguise yourself, your feelings were always noble and just; and in your heart, you thoroughly despised the persons who so assiduously courted you. There – I have saved you the trouble of accounting for it; and really, all things considered, I begin to think it perfectly reasonable. To be sure, you knew no actual good of me – but nobody thinks of *that* when they fall in love.'

'Was there no good in your affectionate behaviour to Jane, while she was ill at Netherfield?'

'Dearest Jane! who could have done less for her? But make a virtue of it by all means. My good qualities are under your protection, and you are to exaggerate them as much as possible; and, in return, it belongs to me to find occasions for teasing and quarrelling with you as often as may be; and I shall begin directly by asking you what made you so unwilling to come to the point at last. What made you so shy of me, when you first called, and afterwards dined here? Why, especially, when you called, did you look as if you did not care about me?'

'Because you were grave and silent, and gave me no encouragement.'

'But I was embarrassed.'

'And so was I.'

'You might have talked to me more when you came to dinner.'

'A man who had felt less, might.'

'How unlucky that you should have a reasonable answer to give, and that I should be so reasonable as to admit it! But I wonder how long you *would* have gone on, if you had been left to yourself. I wonder when you *would* have spoken, if I had not asked you! My resolution of thanking you for your kindness to Lydia had certainly great effect. *Too much*, I am afraid; for what becomes of the moral, if our comfort springs from a breach of promise, for I ought not to have mentioned the subject? This will never do.'

'You need not distress yourself. The moral will be perfectly fair. Lady Catherine's unjustifiable endeavours to separate us, were the means of removing all my doubts. I am not indebted for my present happiness to your eager desire of expressing your gratitude. I was not in a humour to wait for any opening of yours. My aunt's intelligence had given me hope, and I was determined at once to know everything.'

'Lady Catherine has been of infinite use, which ought to make her happy, for she loves to be of use. But tell me, what did you come down to Netherfield for? Was it merely to ride to Longbourn and be embarrassed? or had you intended any more serious consequence?'

'My real purpose was to see *you*, and to judge, if I could, whether I might ever hope to make you love me. My avowed one, or what I avowed to myself, was to see whether your sister were still partial to Bingley, and if she were, to make the confession to him which I have since made.'

'Shall you ever have courage to announce to Lady Catherine, what is to befall her?'

'I am more likely to want time than courage, Elizabeth. But it ought to be done, and if you will give me a sheet of paper, it shall be done directly.'

'And if I had not a letter to write myself, I might sit by you, and admire the evenness of your writing, as another young lady once did. But I have an aunt, too, who must not be longer neglected.'

From an unwillingness to confess how much her intimacy with Mr Darcy had been overrated, Elizabeth had never yet answered Mrs Gardiner's long letter, but now, having *that* to communicate which she knew would be most welcome, she was almost ashamed to find, that her uncle and aunt had already lost three days of happiness, and immediately wrote as follows:

> I would have thanked you before, my dear aunt, as I ought to have done, for your long, kind, satisfactory, detail of particulars; but to say the truth, I was too cross to write. You supposed more than really existed. But *now* suppose as much as you choose; give a loose to your fancy, indulge your imagination in every possible flight which the subject will afford, and unless you believe me actually married, you cannot greatly err. You must write again very soon, and praise him a great deal more than you did in your last. I thank you, again and again, for not going to the Lakes. How could I be so silly as to wish it! Your idea of the ponies is delightful. We will go round the Park every day. I am the happiest creature in the world. Perhaps other people have said so before, but not one with such justice. I am happier even than Jane; she only smiles, I laugh. Mr Darcy sends you all the love in the world, that he can spare from me. You are all to come to Pemberley at Christmas. Yours, etc.

Mr Darcy's letter to Lady Catherine, was in a different style; and still different from either, was what Mr Bennet sent to Mr Collins, in reply to his last.

> DEAR SIR – I must trouble you once more for congratulations. Elizabeth will soon be the wife of Mr Darcy. Console Lady Catherine as well as you can. But, if I were you, I would stand by the nephew. He has more to give.
>
> Yours sincerely, etc.

Miss Bingley's congratulations to her brother, on his approaching marriage, were all that was affectionate and insincere. She wrote even to Jane on the occasion, to express her delight, and repeat all her former professions of regard. Jane was not deceived, but she was affected; and though feeling no reliance on her, could not help writing her a much kinder answer than she knew was deserved.

The joy which Miss Darcy expressed on receiving similar information, was as sincere as her brother's in sending it. Four sides of paper were insufficient to contain all her delight, and all her earnest desire of being loved by her sister.

Before any answer could arrive from Mr Collins, or any congratulations to Elizabeth, from his wife, the Longbourn family heard that the Collinses were come themselves to Lucas Lodge. The reason of this sudden removal was soon evident. Lady Catherine had been rendered so exceedingly angry by the contents of her nephew's letter, that Charlotte, really rejoicing in the match, was anxious to get away till the storm was blown over. At such a moment, the arrival of her friend was a sincere pleasure to Elizabeth, though in the course of their meetings she must sometimes think the pleasure dearly bought, when she saw Mr Darcy exposed to all the parading and obsequious civility of her husband. He bore it however with admirable calmness. He could even listen to Sir William Lucas, when he complimented him on carrying away the brightest jewel of the country, and expressed his hopes of their all meeting frequently at St James's, with very decent composure. If he did shrug his shoulders, it was not till Sir William was out of sight.

Mrs Philips's vulgarity was another, and perhaps a greater tax on his forbearance; and though Mrs Philips, as well as her sister, stood in too much awe of him to speak with the familiarity which Bingley's good humour encouraged, yet, whenever she *did* speak, she must be vulgar. Nor was her respect for him, though it made her more quiet, at all likely to make her more elegant. Elizabeth did all

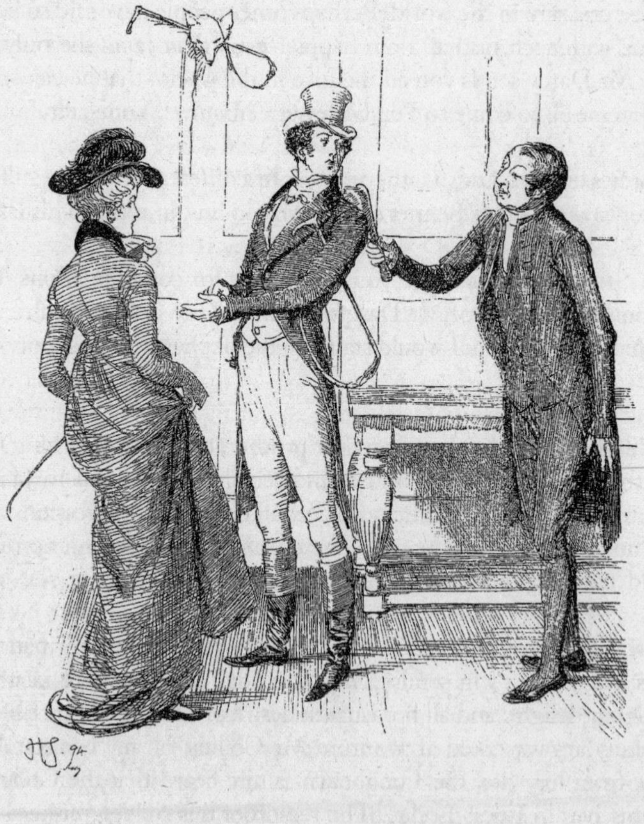

*Obsequious civility of her husband*

she could, to shield him from the frequent notice of either, and was ever anxious to keep him to herself, and to those of her family with whom he might converse without mortification; and though the uncomfortable feelings arising from all this took from the season of courtship much of its pleasure, it added to the hope of the future; and she looked forward with delight to the time when they should be removed from society so little pleasing to either, to all the comfort and elegance of their family party at Pemberley.

## *Chapter 61*

Happy for all her maternal feelings was the day on which Mrs Bennet got rid of her two most deserving daughters. With what delighted pride she afterwards visited Mrs Bingley and talked of Mrs Darcy may be guessed. I wish I could say, for the sake of her family, that the accomplishment of her earnest desire in the establishment of so many of her children, produced so happy an effect as to make her a sensible, amiable, well-informed woman for the rest of her life; though perhaps it was lucky for her husband, who might not have relished domestic felicity in so unusual a form, that she still was occasionally nervous and invariably silly.

Mr Bennet missed his second daughter exceedingly; his affection for her drew him oftener from home than anything else could do. He delighted in going to Pemberley, especially when he was least expected.

Mr Bingley and Jane remained at Netherfield only a twelvemonth. So near a vicinity to her mother and Meryton relations was not desirable even to *his* easy temper, or *her* affectionate heart. The darling wish of his sisters was then gratified; he bought an estate in a neighbouring county to Derbyshire, and Jane and Elizabeth, in addition to every other source of happiness, were within thirty miles of each other.

Kitty, to her very material advantage, spent the chief of her time with her two elder sisters. In society so superior to what she had generally known, her improvement was great. She was not of so ungovernable a temper as Lydia, and, removed from the influence of Lydia's example, she became, by proper attention and management, less irritable, less ignorant, and less insipid. From the farther disadvantage of Lydia's society she was of course carefully kept, and though Mrs Wickham frequently invited her to come and stay with her, with the promise of balls and young men, her father would never consent to her going.

Mary was the only daughter who remained at home; and she was necessarily drawn from the pursuit of accomplishments by Mrs Bennet's being quite unable to sit alone. Mary was obliged to mix more with the world, but she could still moralise over every morning visit; and as she was no longer mortified by comparisons between her sisters' beauty and her own, it was suspected by her father that she submitted to the change without much reluctance.

As for Wickham and Lydia, their characters suffered no revolution from the marriage of her sisters. He bore with philosophy the conviction that Elizabeth must now become acquainted with whatever of his ingratitude and falsehood had before been unknown to her; and in spite of everything, was not wholly without hope that Darcy might yet be prevailed on to make his fortune. The congratulatory letter which Elizabeth received from Lydia on her marriage, explained to her that, by his wife at least, if not by himself, such a hope was cherished. The letter was to this effect:

> My dear Lizzy – I wish you joy. If you love Mr Darcy half as well as I do my dear Wickham, you must be very happy. It is a great comfort to have you so rich, and when you have nothing else to do, I hope you will think of us. I am sure Wickham would like a place at court very much, and I do not think we shall have quite money enough to live upon without some help. Any place would do, of about three or four hundred a year; but, however, do not speak to Mr Darcy about it, if you had rather not.
>
> Yours, etc.

As it happened that Elizabeth had *much* rather not, she endeavoured in her answer to put an end to every entreaty and expectation of the kind. Such relief, however, as it was in her power to afford, by the practice of what might be called economy in her own private expenses, she frequently sent them. It had always been evident to her that such an income as theirs, under the direction of two persons so extravagant in their wants, and heedless of the future, must be very insufficient to their support; and whenever they changed their quarters, either Jane or herself were sure of being applied to, for some little assistance towards discharging their bills. Their manner of living, even when the restoration of peace dismissed them to a home, was unsettled in the extreme. They were always moving from place to place in quest of a cheap situation, and always spending more than they ought. His affection for her soon sunk into indifference; hers lasted a little longer; and in spite of her youth and her manners, she retained all the claims to reputation which her marriage had given her.

Though Darcy could never receive *him* at Pemberley, yet, for Elizabeth's sake, he assisted him farther in his profession. Lydia was occasionally a visitor there, when her husband was gone to enjoy himself in London or Bath; and with the Bingleys they both of them frequently stayed so long, that even Bingley's good humour was overcome, and he proceeded so far as to *talk* of giving them a hint to be gone.

Miss Bingley was very deeply mortified by Darcy's marriage; but as she thought it advisable to retain the right of visiting at Pemberley, she dropped all her resentment; was fonder than ever of Georgiana, almost as attentive to Darcy as heretofore, and paid off every arrear of civility to Elizabeth.

Pemberley was now Georgiana's home; and the attachment of the sisters was exactly what Darcy had hoped to see. They were able to love each other, even as well as they intended. Georgiana had the highest opinion in the world of Elizabeth; though at first she often listened with an astonishment bordering on alarm, at her lively, sportive, manner of talking to her brother. He, who had always inspired in herself a respect which almost overcame her affection, she now saw the object of open pleasantry. Her mind received knowledge which had never before fallen in her way. By Elizabeth's instructions she began to comprehend that a woman may take liberties with her husband, which a brother will not always allow in a sister more than ten years younger than himself.

Lady Catherine was extremely indignant on the marriage of her nephew; and as she gave way to all the genuine frankness of her character, in her reply to the letter which announced its arrangement, she sent him language so very abusive, especially of Elizabeth, that for some time all intercourse was at an end. But at length, by Elizabeth's persuasion, he was prevailed on to overlook the offence, and seek a reconciliation; and, after a little farther resistance on the part of his aunt, her resentment gave way, either to her affection for him, or her curiosity to see how his wife conducted herself; and she condescended to wait on them at Pemberley, in spite of that pollution which its woods had received, not merely from the presence of such a mistress, but the visits of her uncle and aunt from the city.

With the Gardiners, they were always on the most intimate terms. Darcy, as well as Elizabeth, really loved them; and they were both ever sensible of the warmest gratitude towards the persons who, by bringing her into Derbyshire, had been the means of uniting them.

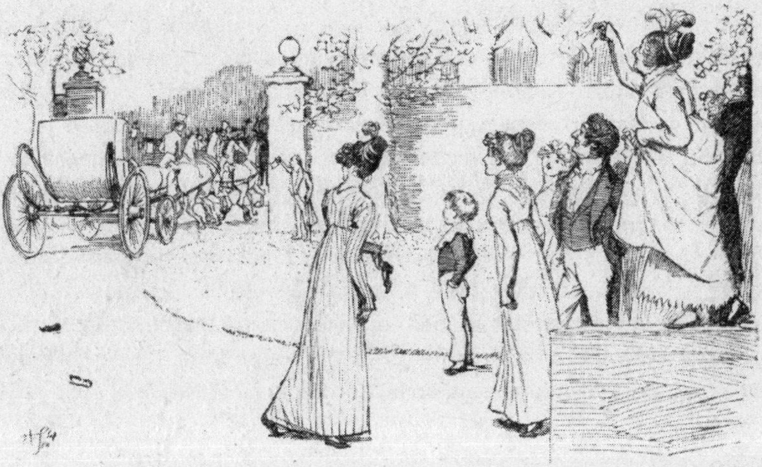

# PERSUASION

# Persuasion

JANE AUSTEN

## *List of Illustrations*

## VOLUME I

# *Chapter 1*

Sir Walter Elliot, of Kellynch Hall, in Somersetshire, was a man who, for his own amusement, never took up any book but the Baronetage; there he found occupation for an idle hour, and consolation in a distressed one; there his faculties were roused into admiration and respect, by contemplating the limited remnant of the earliest patents; there any unwelcome sensations, arising from domestic affairs, changed naturally into pity and contempt. As he turned over the almost endless creations of the last century – and there, if every other leaf were powerless, he could read his own history with an interest which never failed – this was the page at which the favourite volume always opened:

ELLIOT OF KELLYNCH HALL.

Walter Elliot, born March 1, 1760, married, July 15, 1784, Elizabeth, daughter of James Stevenson, Esq. of South Park, in the county of Gloucester; by which lady (who died 1800) he has issue Elizabeth, born June 1, 1785; Anne, born August 9, 1787; a stillborn son, Nov. 5, 1789; Mary, born Nov. 20, 1791.

Precisely such had the paragraph originally stood from the printer's hands; but Sir Walter had improved it by adding, for the information of himself and his family, these words, after the date of Mary's birth – 'married, Dec. 16, 1810, Charles, son and heir of Charles Musgrove, Esq. of Uppercross, in the county of Somerset' – and by inserting most accurately the day of the month on which he had lost his wife.

Then followed the history and rise of the ancient and respectable family, in the usual terms: how it had been first settled in Cheshire, how mentioned in Dugdale – serving the office of high sheriff, representing a borough in three successive parliaments, exertions of loyalty, and dignity of baronet, in the first year of Charles II., with all the Marys and Elizabeths they had married; forming altogether two handsome duodecimo pages, and concluding with the arms and motto: 'Principal seat, Kellynch Hall, in the county of Somerset,' and Sir Walter's handwriting again in this finale:

Heir presumptive, William Walter Elliot, Esq., great grandson of the second Sir Walter.

Vanity was the beginning and the end of Sir Walter Elliot's character; vanity of person and of situation. He had been remarkably handsome in his youth; and, at fifty-four, was still a very fine man. Few women could think more of their personal appearance than he did; nor could the valet of any new-made lord be more delighted with the place he held in society. He considered the blessing of beauty as inferior only to the blessing of a baronetcy; and the Sir Walter Elliot, who united these gifts, was the constant object of his warmest respect and devotion.

His good looks and his rank had one fair claim on his attachment; since to them he must have owed a wife of very superior character to anything deserved by his own. Lady Elliot had been an excellent woman, sensible and amiable; whose judgment and conduct, if they might be pardoned the youthful infatuation which made her Lady Elliot, had never required indulgence afterwards. – She had humoured, or softened, or concealed his failings, and promoted his real respectability for seventeen years; and though not the very happiest being in the world herself, had found enough in her duties, her friends, and her children, to attach her to life, and make it no matter of indifference to her when she was called on to quit them. – Three girls, the two eldest sixteen and fourteen, was an awful legacy for a mother to bequeath; an awful charge rather, to confide to the authority and guidance of a conceited, silly father. She had, however, one very intimate friend, a sensible, deserving woman, who had been brought, by strong attachment to herself, to settle close by her, in the village of Kellynch; and on her kindness and advice, Lady Elliot mainly relied for the best help and maintenance of the good principles and instruction which she had been anxiously giving her daughters.

This friend, and Sir Walter, did *not* marry, whatever might have been anticipated on that head by their acquaintance. – Thirteen years had passed away since Lady Elliot's death, and they were still near neighbours and intimate friends; and one remained a widower, the other a widow.

That Lady Russell, of steady age and character, and extremely well provided for, should have no thought of a second marriage, needs no apology to the public, which is rather apt to be unreasonably discontented when a woman *does* marry again, than when she does *not;* but Sir Walter's continuing in singleness requires explanation. – Be it known, then, that Sir Walter, like a good father (having met with one or two private disappointments in very unreasonable applications), prided himself on remaining single for his dear daughter's sake. For one daughter, his eldest, he would really have given up anything, which he had not been very much tempted to do. Elizabeth had succeeded, at sixteen, to all that was possible, of her mother's rights and consequence, and being very handsome, and very like himself, her influence had always been great, and they had gone on together most happily. His two other children were of very inferior value. Mary had acquired a little artificial importance, by becoming Mrs Charles Musgrove; but Anne, with an elegance of mind and sweetness of character, which must have placed her high with any people of real understanding, was nobody with either father or sister: her word had no weight; her convenience was always to give way – she was only Anne.

To Lady Russell, indeed, she was a most dear and highly valued goddaughter, favourite and friend. Lady Russell loved them all; but it was only in Anne that she could fancy the mother to revive again.

A few years before, Anne Elliot had been a very pretty girl, but her bloom had vanished early; and as even in its height, her father had found little to admire in her (so totally different were her delicate features and mild dark eyes from his own), there could be nothing in them, now that she was faded and thin, to excite his esteem. He had never indulged much hope, he had now none, of ever reading her name in any other page of his favourite work. All equality of alliance must rest with Elizabeth: for Mary had merely connected herself with an old country family of respectability and large fortune, and had therefore *given* all the honour, and received none; Elizabeth would, one day or other, marry suitably.

It sometimes happens, that a woman is handsomer at twenty-nine than she was ten years before; and, generally speaking, if there has been neither ill health nor anxiety, it is a time of life at which scarcely any charm is lost. It was so with Elizabeth; still the same handsome Miss Elliot that she had begun to be thirteen years ago; and Sir Walter might be excused, therefore, in forgetting her age, or, at least, be deemed only half a fool, for thinking himself and Elizabeth as blooming as ever, amidst the wreck of the good looks of everybody else; for he could plainly see how old all the rest of his family and acquaintance were growing. Anne haggard, Mary coarse, every face in the neighbourhood worsting; and the rapid increase of the crow's foot about Lady Russell's temples had long been a distress to him.

Elizabeth did not quite equal her father in personal contentment. Thirteen years had seen her mistress of Kellynch Hall, presiding and directing with a self-possession and decision which could never have given the idea of her being younger than she was. For thirteen years had she been doing the honours, and laying down the domestic law at home, and leading the way to the chaise and four, and walking immediately after Lady Russell out of all the drawing-rooms and dining-rooms in the country. Thirteen winters' revolving frosts had seen her opening every ball of credit which a scanty neighbourhood afforded; and thirteen springs shown their blossoms, as she travelled up to London with her father, for a few weeks annual enjoyment of the great world. She had the remembrance of all this; she had the consciousness of being nine-and-twenty, to give her some regrets and some apprehensions. She was fully satisfied of being still quite as handsome as ever; but she felt her approach to the years of danger, and would have rejoiced to be certain of being properly solicited by baronet blood within the next twelvemonth or two. Then might she again take up the book of books with as much enjoyment as in her early youth; but now she liked it not. Always to be presented with the date of her own birth, and see no marriage follow but that of a youngest sister, made the book an evil; and more than once, when her father had left it open on the table near her, had she closed it, with averted eyes, and pushed it away.

She had had a disappointment, moreover, which that book, and especially the history of her own family, must ever present the remembrance of. The heir presumptive, the very William Walter Elliot, Esq. whose rights had been so generously supported by her father, had disappointed her.

She had, while a very young girl, as soon as she had known him to be, in the event of her having no brother, the future baronet, meant to marry him; and her father had always meant that she should. He had not been known to them as a boy, but soon after Lady Elliot's death Sir Walter had sought the acquaintance, and though his overtures had not been met with any warmth, he had persevered in seeking it, making allowance for the modest drawing back of youth; and in one of their spring excursions to London, when Elizabeth was in her first bloom, Mr Elliot had been forced into the introduction.

He was at that time a very young man, just engaged in the study of the law; and Elizabeth found him extremely agreeable, and every plan in his favour was confirmed. He was invited to Kellynch Hall; he was talked of and expected all the rest of the year; but he never came. The following spring he was seen again in town, found equally agreeable, again encouraged, invited and expected, and again he did not come; and the next tidings were that he was married. Instead of pushing his fortune in the line marked out for the heir of the house of Elliot, he had purchased independence by uniting himself to a rich woman of inferior birth.

Sir Walter had resented it. As the head of the house, he felt that he ought to have been consulted, especially after taking the young man so publicly by the hand: 'For they must have been seen together,' he observed, 'once at Tattersal's, and twice in the lobby of the House of Commons.' His disapprobation was expressed, but apparently very little regarded. Mr Elliot had attempted no apology, and shown himself as unsolicitous of being longer noticed by the family as Sir Walter considered him unworthy of it; all acquaintance between them had ceased.

This very awkward history of Mr Elliot, was still, after an interval of several years, felt with anger by Elizabeth, who had liked the man for himself, and still more for being her father's heir, and whose strong family pride could see only in *him* a proper match for Sir Walter Elliot's eldest daughter. There was not a baronet from A to Z, whom her feelings could have so willingly acknowledged as an equal. Yet so miserably had he conducted himself that though she was at this present time (the summer of 1814) wearing black ribbons for his wife, she could not admit him to be worth thinking of again. The disgrace of his first marriage might, perhaps, as there was no reason to suppose it perpetuated by offspring, have been got over, had he not done worse; but he had, as by the accustomary intervention of kind friends they had been informed, spoken most disrespectfully of them all, most slightingly and contemptuously of the very blood he belonged to, and the honours which were hereafter to be his own. This could not be pardoned.

Such were Elizabeth Elliot's sentiments and sensations; such the cares to alloy, the agitations to vary, the sameness and the elegance, the prosperity and the nothingness, of her scene of life – such the feelings to give interest to a long, uneventful residence in one country circle, to fill the vacancies which there were no habits of utility abroad, no talents or accomplishments for home, to occupy.

But now, another occupation and solicitude of mind was beginning to be added to these. Her father was growing distressed for money. She knew, that when he now took up the Baronetage, it was to drive the heavy bills of his tradespeople, and the unwelcome hints of Mr Shepherd, his agent, from his thoughts. The Kellynch property was good, but not equal to Sir Walter's apprehension of the state required in its possessor. While Lady Elliot lived, there had been method, moderation, and economy, which had just kept him within his income; but with her had died all such right mindedness, and from that period he had been constantly exceeding it. It had not been possible for him to spend less; he had done nothing but what Sir Walter Elliot was imperiously called on to do; but blameless as he was, he was not only growing dreadfully in debt, but was hearing of it so often that it became vain to attempt concealing it longer, even partially, from his daughter. He had given her some hints of it the last spring in town; he had gone so far even as to say, 'Can we retrench? does it occur to you that there is any one article in which we can retrench?' – and Elizabeth, to do her justice, had, in the first ardour of female alarm, set seriously to think what could be done, and had finally proposed these two branches of economy: to cut off some unnecessary charities, and to refrain from new-furnishing the drawing-room; to which expedients she afterwards added the happy thought of their taking no present down to Anne, as had been the usual yearly custom. But these measures, however good in themselves, were insufficient for the real extent of the evil, the whole of which Sir Walter found himself obliged to confess to her soon afterwards. Elizabeth had nothing to propose of deeper efficacy. She felt herself ill-used and unfortunate, as did her father; and they were neither of them able to devise any means of lessening their expenses without compromising their dignity, or relinquishing their comforts in a way not to be borne.

There was only a small part of his estate that Sir Walter could dispose of; but had every acre been alienable, it would have made no difference. He had condescended to mortgage as far as he had the power, but he would never condescend to sell. No; he would never disgrace his name so far. The Kellynch estate should be transmitted whole and entire, as he had received it.

Their two confidential friends, Mr Shepherd, who lived in the neighbouring market town, and Lady Russell, were called on to advise them; and both father and daughter seemed to expect that something should be struck out by one or the other to remove their embarrassments and reduce their expenditure, without involving the loss of any indulgence of taste or pride.

## *Chapter 2*

Mr Shepherd, a civil, cautious lawyer, who, whatever might be his hold or his views on Sir Walter, would rather have the *disagreeable* prompted by anybody else, excused himself from offering the slightest hint, and only begged leave to recommend an implicit reference to the excellent judgment of Lady Russell, – from whose known good sense he fully expected to have just such resolute measures advised as he meant to see finally adopted.

Lady Russell was most anxiously zealous on the subject, and gave it much serious consideration. She was a woman rather of sound than of quick abilities, whose difficulties in coming to any decision in this instance were great, from the opposition of two leading principles. She was of strict integrity herself, with a delicate sense of honour; but she was as desirous of saving Sir Walter's feelings, as solicitous for the credit of the family, as aristocratic in her ideas of what was due to them, as anybody of sense and honesty could well be. She was a benevolent, charitable, good woman, and capable of strong attachments; most correct in her conduct, strict in her notions of decorum, and with manners that were held a standard of good breeding. She had a cultivated mind, and was, generally speaking, rational and consistent – but she had prejudices on the side of ancestry; she had a value for rank and consequence, which blinded her a little to the faults of those who possessed them. Herself, the widow of only a knight, she gave the dignity of a baronet all its due; and Sir Walter, independent of his claims as an old acquaintance, an attentive neighbour, an obliging landlord, the husband of her very dear friend, the father of Anne and her sisters, was, as being Sir Walter, in her apprehension entitled to a great deal of compassion and consideration under his present difficulties.

They must retrench; that did not admit of a doubt. But she was very anxious to have it done with the least possible pain to him and Elizabeth. She drew up plans of economy, she made exact calculations, and she did what nobody else thought of doing: she consulted Anne, who never seemed considered by the others as having any interest in the question. She consulted, and in a degree was influenced by her, in marking out the scheme of retrenchment, which was at last submitted to Sir Walter. Every emendation of Anne's had been on the side of honesty against importance. She wanted more vigorous measures, a more complete reformation, a quicker release from debt, a much higher tone of indifference for everything but justice and equity.

'If we can persuade your father to all this,' said Lady Russell, looking over her paper, 'much may be done. If he will adopt these regulations, in seven years he will be clear; and I hope we may be able to convince him and Elizabeth, that Kellynch Hall has a respectability in itself, which cannot be affected by these reductions; and that the true dignity of Sir Walter Elliot will be very far from lessened, in the eyes of sensible people, by his acting like a man of principle. What will he be doing, in fact, but what very many of our first families have done, – or ought to do? – There will be nothing singular in his case; and it is singularity which often makes the worst part of our suffering, as it always does of our conduct. I have great hope of our prevailing. We must be serious and decided – for, after all, the person who has contracted debts must pay them; and though a great deal is due to the feelings of the gentleman, and the head of a house, like your father, there is still more due to the character of an honest man.'

This was the principle on which Anne wanted her father to be proceeding, his friends to be urging him. She considered it as an act of indispensable duty to clear away the claims of creditors, with all the expedition which the most comprehensive retrenchments could secure, and saw no dignity in anything short of it. She wanted it to be prescribed, and felt as a duty. She rated Lady Russell's influence highly, and as to the severe degree of self-denial, which her own conscience prompted, she believed there might be little more difficulty in persuading them to a complete, than to half a reformation. Her knowledge of her father and Elizabeth inclined her to think that the sacrifice of one pair of horses would be hardly less painful than of both, and so on, through the whole list of Lady Russell's too gentle reductions.

How Anne's more rigid requisitions might have been taken is of little consequence. Lady Russell's had no success at all – could not be put up with – were not to be borne. 'What! Every comfort of life knocked off! Journeys, London, servants, horses, table – contractions and restrictions everywhere. To live no longer with the decencies even of a private gentleman! No, he would sooner quit Kellynch Hall at once, than remain in it on such disgraceful terms.'

'Quit Kellynch Hall.' The hint was immediately taken up by Mr Shepherd, whose interest was involved in the reality of Sir Walter's retrenching, and who was perfectly persuaded that nothing would be done without a change of abode. – 'Since the idea had been started in the very quarter which ought to dictate, he had no scruple,' he said, 'in confessing his judgment to be entirely on that side. It did not appear to him that Sir Walter could materially alter his style of living in a house which had such a character of hospitality and ancient dignity to support. – In any other place, Sir Walter might judge for himself; and would be looked up to, as regulating the modes of life, in whatever way he might choose to model his household.'

Sir Walter would quit Kellynch Hall – and after a very few days more of doubt and indecision, the great question of whither he should go was settled, and the first outline of this important change made out.

There had been three alternatives, London, Bath, or another house in the country. All Anne's wishes had been for the latter. A small house in their own neighbourhood, where they might still have Lady Russell's society, still be near Mary, and still have the pleasure of sometimes seeing the lawns and groves of Kellynch, was the object of her ambition. But the usual fate of Anne attended her, in having something very opposite from her inclination fixed on. She disliked Bath, and did not think it agreed with her – and Bath was to be her home.

Sir Walter had at first thought more of London, but Mr Shepherd felt that he could not be trusted in London, and had been skilful enough to dissuade him from it, and make Bath preferred. It was a much safer place for a gentleman in his predicament – he might there be important at comparatively little expense. Two material advantages of Bath over London had of course been given all their weight; its more convenient distance from Kellynch, only fifty miles, and Lady Russell's spending some part of every winter there; and to the very great satisfaction of Lady Russell, whose first views on the projected change had been for Bath, Sir Walter and Elizabeth were induced to believe that they should lose neither consequence nor enjoyment by settling there.

Lady Russell felt obliged to oppose her dear Anne's known wishes. It would be too much to expect Sir Walter to descend into a small house in his own neighbourhood. Anne herself would have found the mortifications of it more than she foresaw, and to Sir Walter's feelings they must have been dreadful. And with regard to Anne's dislike of Bath, she considered it as a prejudice and mistake, arising first from the circumstance of her having been three years at school there, after her mother's death, and, secondly, from her happening to be not in perfectly good spirits the only winter which she had afterwards spent there with herself.

Lady Russell was fond of Bath in short, and disposed to think it must suit them all; and as to her young friend's health, by passing all the warm months with her at Kellynch Lodge, every danger would be avoided; and it was, in fact, a change which must do both health and spirits good. Anne had been too little from home, too little seen. Her spirits were not high. A larger society would improve them. She wanted her to be more known.

The undesirableness of any other house in the same neighbourhood for Sir Walter was certainly much strengthened by one part, and a very material part of the scheme, which had been happily engrafted on the beginning. He was not only to quit his home, but to see it in the hands of others; a trial of fortitude, which stronger heads than Sir Walter's have found too much. – Kellynch Hall was to be let. This, however, was a profound secret; not to be breathed beyond their own circle.

Sir Walter could not have borne the degradation of being known to design letting his house. – Mr Shepherd had once mentioned the word, 'advertise' – but never dared approach it again; Sir Walter spurned the idea of its being offered in any manner; forbad the slightest hint being dropped of his having such an intention; and it was only on the supposition of his being spontaneously solicited by some most unexceptionable applicant, on his own terms, and as a great favour, that he would let it at all.

How quick come the reasons for approving what we like! – Lady Russell had another excellent one at hand, for being extremely glad that Sir Walter and his family were to remove from the country. Elizabeth had been lately forming an intimacy, which she wished to see interrupted. It was with a daughter of Mr Shepherd, who had returned, after an unprosperous marriage, to her father's house, with the additional burden of two children. She was a clever young woman, who understood the art of pleasing; the art of pleasing, at least, at Kellynch Hall; and who had made herself so acceptable to Miss Elliot as to have been already staying there more than once, in spite of all that Lady Russell, who thought it a friendship quite out of place, could hint of caution and reserve.

Lady Russell, indeed, had scarcely any influence with Elizabeth, and seemed to love her, rather because she would love her, than because Elizabeth deserved it. She had never received from her more than outward attention, nothing beyond the observances of complaisance; had never succeeded in any point which she wanted to carry, against previous inclination. She had been repeatedly very earnest in trying to get Anne included in the visit to London, sensibly open to all the injustice and all the discredit of the selfish arrangements which shut her out, and on many lesser occasions had endeavoured to give Elizabeth the advantage of her own better judgment and experience – but always in vain; Elizabeth would go her own way – and never had she pursued it in more decided opposition to Lady Russell than in this selection of Mrs Clay; turning from the society of so deserving a sister to bestow her affection and confidence on one who ought to have been nothing to her but the object of distant civility.

From situation, Mrs Clay was, in Lady Russell's estimate, a very unequal, and in her character she believed a very dangerous companion – and a removal that would leave Mrs Clay behind, and bring a choice of more suitable intimates within Miss Elliot's reach, was therefore an object of first-rate importance.

## *Chapter 3*

'I must take leave to observe, Sir Walter,' said Mr Shepherd one morning at Kellynch Hall, as he laid down the newspaper, 'that the present juncture is much in our favour. This peace will be turning all our rich navy officers ashore. They will be all wanting a home. Could not be a better time, Sir Walter, for having a choice of tenants, very responsible tenants. Many a noble fortune has been made during the war. If a rich Admiral were to come in our way, Sir Walter – '

'He would be a very lucky man, Shepherd,' replied Sir Walter, 'that's all I have to remark. A prize indeed would Kellynch Hall be to him; rather the greatest prize of all, let him have taken ever so many before – hey, Shepherd?'

Mr Shepherd laughed, as he knew he must, at this wit, and then added,

'I presume to observe, Sir Walter, that, in the way of business, gentlemen of the navy are well to deal with. I have had a little knowledge of their methods of doing business, and I am free to confess that they have very liberal notions, and are as likely to make desirable tenants as any set of people one should meet with. Therefore, Sir Walter, what I would take leave to suggest is, that if in consequence of any rumours getting abroad of your intention – which must be contemplated as a possible thing, because we know how difficult it is to keep the actions and designs of one part of the world from the notice and curiosity of the other – consequence has its tax – I, John Shepherd, might conceal any family matters that I chose, for nobody would think it worth their while to observe me, but Sir Walter Elliot has eyes upon him which it may be very difficult to elude – and therefore, thus much I venture upon, that it will not greatly surprise me if, with all our caution, some rumour of the truth should get abroad – in the supposition of which, as I was going to observe, since applications will unquestionably follow, I should think any from our wealthy naval commanders particularly worth attending to – and beg leave to add, that two hours will bring me over at any time, to save you the trouble of replying.'

Sir Walter only nodded. But soon afterwards, rising and pacing the room, he observed sarcastically,

'There are few among the gentlemen of the navy, I imagine, who would not be surprised to find themselves in a house of this description.'

'They would look around them, no doubt, and bless their good fortune,' said Mrs Clay, for Mrs Clay was present; her father had driven her over, nothing being of so much use to Mrs Clay's health as a drive to Kellynch: 'but I quite agree with my father in thinking a sailor might be a very desirable tenant. I have known a good deal of the profession; and besides their liberality, they are so neat and careful in all their ways! These valuable pictures of yours, Sir Walter, if you chose to leave them, would be perfectly safe. Everything in and about the house would be taken such excellent care of! the gardens and shrubberies would be kept in almost as high order as they are now. You need not be afraid, Miss Elliot, of your own sweet flower-garden's being neglected.'

'As to all that,' rejoined Sir Walter coolly, 'supposing I were induced to let my house, I have by no means made up my mind as to the privileges to be annexed to it. I am not particularly disposed to favour a tenant. The park would be open to him of course, and few navy officers, or men of any other description, can have had such a range; but what restrictions I might impose on the use of the pleasure-grounds, is another thing. I am not fond of the idea of my shrubberies being always approachable; and I should recommend Miss Elliot to be on her guard with respect to her flower-garden. I am very little disposed to grant a tenant of Kellynch Hall any extraordinary favour, I assure you, be he sailor or soldier.'

After a short pause, Mr Shepherd presumed to say, 'In all these cases, there are established usages which make everything plain and easy between landlord and tenant. Your interest, Sir Walter, is in pretty safe hands. Depend upon me for taking care that no tenant has more than his just rights. I venture to hint, that Sir Walter Elliot cannot be half so jealous for his own, as John Shepherd will be for him.'

Here Anne spoke –

'The navy, I think, who have done so much for us, have at least an equal claim with any other set of men, for all the comforts and all the privileges which any home can give. Sailors work hard enough for their comforts, we must all allow.'

'Very true, very true. What Miss Anne says, is very true,' was Mr Shepherd's rejoinder, and 'Oh! certainly' was his daughter's; but Sir Walter's remark was, soon afterwards –

'The profession has its utility, but I should be sorry to see any friend of mine belonging to it.'

'Indeed!' was the reply, and with a look of surprise.

'Yes; it is in two points offensive to me; I have two strong grounds of objection to it. First, as being the means of bringing persons of obscure birth into undue distinction, and raising men to honours which their fathers and grandfathers never dreamt of; and secondly, as it cuts up a man's youth and vigour most horribly; a sailor grows old sooner than any other man; I have observed it all my life. A man is in greater danger in the navy of being insulted by the rise of one whose father, his father might have disdained to speak to, and of becoming prematurely an object of disgust himself, than in any other line. One day last spring, in town, I was in company with two men, striking instances of what I am talking of, Lord St Ives, whose father we all know to have been a country curate, without bread to eat; I was to give place to Lord St Ives, and a certain Admiral Baldwin, the most deplorable looking personage you can imagine, his face the colour of mahogany, rough and rugged to the last degree, all lines and wrinkles, nine grey hairs of a side, and nothing but a dab of powder at top. – "In the name of heaven, who is that old fellow?" said I, to a friend of mine who was standing near (Sir Basil Moreley). "Old fellow!" cried Sir Basil, "it is Admiral Baldwin. What do you take his age to be?" "Sixty," said I, "or perhaps sixty-two." "Forty," replied Sir Basil, "forty, and no more." Picture to yourselves

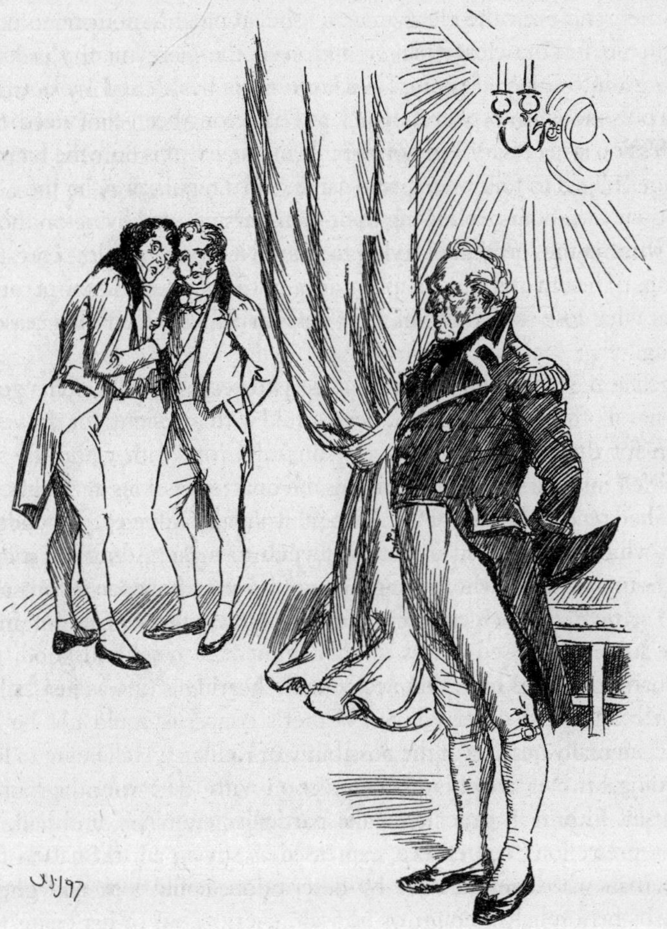

*'In the name of heaven, who is that old fellow?'*

my amazement; I shall not easily forget Admiral Baldwin. I never saw quite so wretched an example of what a seafaring life can do; but to a degree, I know it is the same with them all: they are all knocked about, and exposed to every climate, and every weather, till they are not fit to be seen. It is a pity they are not knocked on the head at once, before they reach Admiral Baldwin's age.'

'Nay, Sir Walter,' cried Mrs Clay, 'this is being severe indeed. Have a little mercy on the poor men. We are not all born to be handsome. The sea is no beautifier, certainly; sailors do grow old betimes; I have often observed it; they soon lose the look of youth. But then, is not it the same with many other professions, perhaps most other? Soldiers, in active service, are not at all better off; and even in the quieter professions, there is a toil and a labour of the mind, if not of the body, which seldom leaves a man's looks to the natural effect of time. The lawyer plods, quite careworn; the physician is up at all hours, and travelling in all weather; and even the clergyman – ' she stopped a moment to consider what might do for the clergyman – 'and even the clergyman, you know, is obliged to go into infected rooms, and expose his health and looks to all the injury of a poisonous atmosphere. In fact, as I have long been convinced, though every profession is necessary and honourable in its turn, it is only the lot of those who are not obliged to follow any, who can live in a regular way, in the country, choosing their own hours, following their own pursuits, and living on their own property, without the torment of trying for more; it is only *their* lot, I say, to hold the blessings of health and a good appearance to the utmost: I know no other set of men but what lose something of their personableness when they cease to be quite young.'

It seemed as if Mr Shepherd, in this anxiety to bespeak Sir Walter's goodwill towards a naval officer as tenant, had been gifted with foresight; for the very first application for the house was from an Admiral Croft, with whom he shortly afterwards fell into company in attending the quarter sessions at Taunton; and indeed, he had received a hint of the Admiral from a London correspondent. By the report which he hastened over to Kellynch to make, Admiral Croft was a native of Somersetshire, who having acquired a very handsome fortune, was wishing to settle in his own country, and had come down to Taunton in order to look at some advertised places in that immediate neighbourhood, which, however, had not suited him; that accidentally hearing – (it was just as he had foretold, Mr Shepherd observed, Sir Walter's concerns could not be kept a secret) – accidentally hearing of the possibility of Kellynch Hall being to let, and understanding his (Mr Shepherd's) connection with the owner, he had introduced himself to him in order to make particular enquiries, and had, in the course of a pretty long conference, expressed as strong an inclination for the place as a man who knew it only by description, could feel; and given Mr Shepherd, in his explicit account of himself, every proof of his being a most responsible, eligible tenant.

'And who is Admiral Croft?' was Sir Walter's cold suspicious enquiry.

Mr Shepherd answered for his being of a gentleman's family, and mentioned a place; and Anne, after the little pause which followed, added –

'He is Rear-Admiral of the White. He was in the Trafalgar action, and has been in the East Indies since; he has been stationed there, I believe, several years.'

'Then I take it for granted,' observed Sir Walter, 'that his face is about as orange as the cuffs and capes of my livery.'

Mr Shepherd hastened to assure him, that Admiral Croft was a very hale, hearty, well-looking man, a little weather-beaten, to be sure, but not much; and quite the gentleman in all his notions and behaviour – not likely to make the smallest difficulty about terms – only wanted a comfortable home, and to get into it as soon as possible – knew he must pay for his convenience – knew what rent a ready-furnished house of that consequence might fetch – should not have been surprised if Sir Walter had asked more – had enquired about the manor – would be glad of the deputation, certainly, but made no great point of it – said he sometimes took out a gun, but never killed – quite the gentleman.

Mr Shepherd was eloquent on the subject, pointing out all the circumstances of the admiral's family, which made him peculiarly desirable as a tenant. He was a married man, and without children; the very state to be wished for. A house was never taken good care of, Mr Shepherd observed, without a lady: he did not know, whether furniture might not be in danger of suffering as much where there was no lady, as where there were many children. A lady, without a family, was the very best preserver of furniture in the world. He had seen Mrs Croft, too; she was at Taunton with the Admiral, and had been present almost all the time they were talking the matter over.

'And a very well-spoken, genteel, shrewd lady, she seemed to be,' continued he; 'asked more questions about the house, and terms, and taxes, than the Admiral himself, and seemed more conversant with business. And moreover, Sir Walter, I found she was not quite unconnected in this country, any more than her husband; that is to say, she is sister to a gentleman who did live amongst us once; she told me so herself; sister to the gentleman who lived a few years back, at Monkford. Bless me! what was his name? At this moment I cannot recollect his name, though I have heard it so lately. Penelope, my dear, can you help me to the name of the gentleman who lived at Monkford – Mrs Croft's brother?'

But Mrs Clay was talking so eagerly with Miss Elliot that she did not hear the appeal.

'I have no conception whom you can mean, Shepherd; I remember no gentleman resident at Monkford since the time of old Governor Trent.'

'Bless me! how very odd! I shall forget my own name soon, I suppose. A name that I am so very well acquainted with; knew the gentleman so well by sight; seen him a hundred times; came to consult me once, I remember, about a trespass of one of his neighbours; farmer's man breaking into his orchard – wall torn down – apples stolen – caught in the fact; and afterwards, contrary to my judgement, submitted to an amicable compromise. Very odd indeed!'

After waiting another moment –

'You mean Mr Wentworth, I suppose,' said Anne.

Mr Shepherd was all gratitude.

'Wentworth was the very name! Mr Wentworth was the very man. He had the curacy of Monkford, you know, Sir Walter, some time back, for two or three years. Came there about the year —5, I take it. You remember him, I am sure.'

'Wentworth? Oh! ay – Mr Wentworth, the curate of Monkford. You misled me by the term *gentleman*. I thought you were speaking of some man of property: Mr Wentworth was nobody, I remember; quite unconnected; nothing to do with the Strafford family. One wonders how the names of many of our nobility become so common.'

As Mr Shepherd perceived that this connection of the Crofts did them no service with Sir Walter, he mentioned it no more, returning, with all his zeal, to dwell on the circumstances more indisputably in their favour; their age, and number, and fortune; the high idea they had formed of Kellynch Hall, and extreme solicitude for the advantage of renting it; making it appear as if they ranked nothing beyond the happiness of being the tenants of Sir Walter Elliot: an extraordinary taste, certainly, could they have been supposed in the secret of Sir Walter's estimate of the dues of a tenant.

It succeeded, however; and though Sir Walter must ever look with an evil eye on anyone intending to inhabit that house, and think them infinitely too well off in being permitted to rent it on the highest terms, he was talked into allowing Mr Shepherd to proceed in the treaty, and authorising him to wait on Admiral Croft, who still remained at Taunton, and fix a day for the house being seen.

Sir Walter was not very wise; but still he had experience enough of the world to feel that a more unobjectionable tenant, in all essentials, than Admiral Croft bid fair to be, could hardly offer. So far went his understanding; and his vanity supplied a little additional soothing, in the Admiral's situation in life, which was just high enough, and not too high. 'I have let my house to Admiral Croft,' would sound extremely well; very much better than to any mere *Mr* —; a *Mr* (save, perhaps, some half-dozen in the nation) always needs a note of explanation. An admiral speaks his own consequence, and, at the same time can never make a baronet look small. In all their dealings and intercourse, Sir Walter Elliot must ever have the precedence.

Nothing could be done without a reference to Elizabeth; but her inclination was growing so strong for a removal that she was happy to have it fixed and expedited by a tenant at hand; and not a word to suspend decision was uttered by her.

Mr Shepherd was completely empowered to act; and no sooner had such an end been reached, than Anne, who had been a most attentive listener to the whole, left the room, to seek the comfort of cool air for her flushed cheeks; and as she walked along a favourite grove, said, with a gentle sigh, 'a few months more, and *he*, perhaps, may be walking here.'

## *Chapter 4*

He was not Mr Wentworth, the former curate of Monkford, however suspicious appearances may be, but a captain Frederick Wentworth, his brother, who being made commander in consequence of the action off St Domingo, and not immediately employed, had come into Somersetshire, in the summer of 1806; and having no parent living, found a home for half a year, at Monkford. He was, at that time, a remarkably fine young man, with a great deal of intelligence, spirit, and brilliancy; and Anne an extremely pretty girl, with gentleness, modesty, taste, and feeling. – Half the sum of attraction on either side, might have been enough, for he had nothing to do, and she had hardly anybody to love; but the encounter of such lavish recommendations could not fail. They were gradually acquainted, and when acquainted, rapidly and deeply in love. It would be difficult to say which had seen highest perfection in the other, or which had been the happiest; she, in receiving his declarations and proposals, or he in having them accepted.

A short period of exquisite felicity followed, and but a short one. – Troubles soon arose. Sir Walter, on being applied to, without actually withholding his consent, or saying it should never be, gave it all the negative of great astonishment, great coldness, great silence, and a professed resolution of doing nothing for his daughter. He thought it a very degrading alliance; and Lady Russell, though with more tempered and pardonable pride, received it as a most unfortunate one.

Anne Elliot, with all her claims of birth, beauty, and mind, to throw herself away at nineteen; involve herself at nineteen in an engagement with a young man, who had nothing but himself to recommend him, and no hopes of attaining affluence, but in the chances of a most uncertain profession, and no connections to secure even his farther rise in that profession; would be, indeed, a throwing away, which she grieved to think of ! Anne Elliot, so young; known to so few, to be snatched off by a stranger without alliance or fortune; or rather sunk by him into a state of most wearing, anxious, youth-killing dependence! It must not be, if by any fair interference of friendship, any representations from one who had almost a mother's love, and mother's rights, it would be prevented.

Captain Wentworth had no fortune. He had been lucky in his profession, but spending freely what had come freely, had realised nothing. But, he was confident that he should soon be rich – full of life and ardour, he knew that he should soon have a ship, and soon be on a station that would lead to everything he wanted. He had always been lucky; he knew he should be so still. – Such confidence, powerful in its own warmth, and bewitching the wit which often expressed it, must have been enough for Anne; but Lady Russell saw it very differently. – His sanguine temper, and fearlessness of mind, operated very differently on her. She saw in it but an aggravation of the evil. It only added a dangerous character to himself. He was brilliant, he was headstrong. – Lady Russell had little taste for wit; and of anything approaching to imprudence a horror. She deprecated the connection in every light.

Such opposition as these feelings produced was more than Anne could combat. Young and gentle as she was, it might yet have been possible to withstand her father's ill will, though unsoftened by one kind word or look on the part of her sister – but Lady Russell, whom she had always loved and relied on, could not, with such steadiness of opinion, and such tenderness of manner, be continually advising her in vain. She was persuaded to believe the engagement a wrong thing – indiscreet, improper, hardly capable of success, and not deserving it. But it was not a merely selfish caution, under which she acted, in putting an end to it. Had she not imagined herself consulting his good, even more than her own, she could hardly have given him up. – The belief of being prudent, and self-denying principally for *his* advantage, was her chief consolation, under the misery of a parting – a final parting; and every consolation was required, for she had to encounter all the additional pain of opinions, on his side, totally unconvinced and unbending, and of his feeling himself ill-used by so forced a relinquishment. He had left the country in consequence.

A few months had seen the beginning and the end of their acquaintance; but, not with a few months ended Anne's share of suffering from it. Her attachment and regrets had, for a long time, clouded every enjoyment of youth; and an early loss of bloom and spirits had been their lasting effect.

More than seven years were gone since this little history of sorrowful interest had reached its close; and time had softened down much, perhaps nearly all of peculiar attachment to him – but she had been too dependent on time alone; no aid had been given in change of place (except in one visit to Bath soon after the rupture) or in any novelty or enlargement of society. – No one had ever come within the Kellynch circle, who could bear a comparison with Frederick Wentworth, as he stood in her memory. No second attachment, the only thoroughly natural, happy, and sufficient cure, at her time of life, had been possible to the nice tone of her mind, the fastidiousness of her taste, in the small limits of the society around them. She had been solicited, when about two-and-twenty, to change her name, by the young man, who not long afterwards found a more willing mind in her younger sister; and Lady Russell had lamented her refusal; for Charles Musgrove was the eldest son of a man, whose landed property and general importance, were second, in that country, only to Sir Walter's, and of good character and appearance; and however Lady Russell might have asked yet for something more, while Anne was nineteen, she would have rejoiced to see her at twenty-two, so respectably removed from the partialities and injustice of her father's house, and settled so permanently near herself. But in this case, Anne had left nothing for advice to do; and though Lady Russell, as satisfied as ever with her own discretion, never wished the past undone, she began now to have the anxiety which borders on hopelessness for Anne's being tempted, by some man of talents and independence, to enter a state for which she held her to be peculiarly fitted by her warm affections and domestic habits.

They knew not each other's opinion, either its constancy or its change, on the one leading point of Anne's conduct, for the subject was never alluded to – but Anne, at seven-and-twenty, thought very differently from what she had been made to think at nineteen. – She did not blame Lady Russell, she did not blame herself for having been guided by her; but she felt that were any young person, in similar circumstances, to apply to her for counsel, they would never receive any of such certain immediate wretchedness, such uncertain future good. – She was persuaded that under every disadvantage of disapprobation at home, and every anxiety attending his profession, all their probable fears, delays and disappointments, she should yet have been a happier woman in maintaining the engagement than she had been in the sacrifice of it; and this, she fully believed, had the usual share, had even more than a usual share of all such solicitudes and suspense been theirs, without reference to the actual results of their case, which, as it happened, would have bestowed earlier prosperity than could be reasonably calculated on. All his sanguine expectations, all his confidence had been justified. His genius and ardour had seemed to foresee and to command his prosperous path. He had, very soon after their engagement ceased, got employ; and all that he had told her would follow had taken place. He had distinguished himself, and early gained the other step in rank – and must now, by successive captures, have made a handsome fortune. She had only navy lists and newspapers for her authority, but she could not doubt his being rich – and, in favour of his constancy, she had no reason to believe him married.

How eloquent could Anne Elliot have been – how eloquent, at least, were her wishes on the side of early warm attachment, and a cheerful confidence in futurity, against that over anxious caution which seems to insult exertion and distrust Providence! She had been forced into prudence in her youth, she learned romance as she grew older – the natural sequel of an unnatural beginning.

With all these circumstances, recollections and feelings she could not hear that Captain Wentworth's sister was likely to live at Kellynch, without a revival of former pain; and many a stroll and many a sigh were necessary to dispel the agitation of the idea. She often told herself it was folly before she could harden her nerves sufficiently to feel the continual discussion of the Crofts and their business no evil. She was assisted, however, by that perfect indifference and apparent unconsciousness, among the only three of her own friends in the secret of the past, which seemed almost to deny any recollection of it. She could do justice to the superiority of Lady Russell's motives in this, over those of her father and Elizabeth; she could honour all the better feelings of her calmness – but the general air of oblivion among them was highly important from whatever it sprung; and in the event of Admiral Croft's really taking Kellynch Hall, she rejoiced anew over the conviction which had always been most grateful to her, of the past being known to those three only among her connections, by whom no syllable, she believed, would ever be whispered, and in the trust that among his, the brother only with whom he had been residing, had received any information of their short-lived engagement. – That brother had been long removed from the country – and being a sensible man, and, moreover, a single man at the time, she had a fond dependence on no human creature's having heard of it from him.

The sister, Mrs Croft, had then been out of England, accompanying her husband on a foreign station, and her own sister, Mary, had been at school while it all occurred and never admitted by the pride of some, and the delicacy of others, to the smallest knowledge of it afterwards.

With these supports, she hoped that the acquaintance between herself and the Crofts, which, with Lady Russell, still resident in Kellynch, and Mary fixed only three miles off, must be anticipated, need not involve any particular awkwardness.

## *Chapter 5*

On the morning appointed for Admiral and Mrs Croft's seeing Kellynch Hall, Anne found it most natural to take her almost daily walk to Lady Russell's, and keep out of the way till all was over; when she found it most natural to be sorry that she had missed the opportunity of seeing them.

This meeting of the two parties proved highly satisfactory, and decided the whole business at once. Each lady was previously well disposed for an agreement, and saw nothing, therefore, but good manners in the other; and, with regard to the gentlemen, there was such an hearty good humour, such an open, trusting liberality on the Admiral's side, as could not but influence Sir Walter, who had besides been flattered into his very best and most polished behaviour by Mr Shepherd's assurances of his being known, by report, to the Admiral, as a model of good breeding.

The house and grounds, and furniture, were approved, the Crofts were approved, terms, time, everything, and everybody, was right; and Mr Shepherd's clerks were set to work, without there having been a single preliminary difference to modify of all that 'This indenture showeth'.

Sir Walter, without hesitation, declared the Admiral to be the best-looking sailor he had ever met with, and went so far as to say that, if his own man might have had the arranging of his hair, he should not be ashamed of being seen with him anywhere; and the Admiral, with sympathetic cordiality, observed to his wife as they drove back through the Park, 'I thought we should soon come to a deal, my dear, in spite of what they told us at Taunton. The Baronet will never set the Thames on fire, but there seems no harm in him': reciprocal compliments, which would have been esteemed about equal.

The Crofts were to have possession at Michaelmas, and as Sir Walter proposed removing to Bath in the course of the preceding month, there was no time to be lost in making every dependent arrangement.

Lady Russell, convinced that Anne would not be allowed to be of any use, or any importance, in the choice of the house which they were going to secure, was very unwilling to have her hurried away so soon, and wanted to make it possible for her to stay behind till she might convey her to Bath herself after Christmas; but having engagements of her own, which must take her from Kellynch for several weeks, she was unable to give the full invitation she wished; and Anne, though dreading the possible heats of September in all the white glare of Bath, and grieving to forgo all the influence so sweet and so sad of the autumnal months in the country, did not think that, everything considered, she wished to remain. It would be most right, and most wise, and, therefore, must involve least suffering, to go with the others.

Something occurred, however, to give her a different duty. Mary, often a little unwell, and always thinking a great deal of her own complaints, and always in the habit of claiming Anne when anything was the matter, was indisposed; and foreseeing that she should not have a day's health all the autumn, entreated, or rather required her, for it was hardly entreaty, to come to Uppercross Cottage, and bear her company as long as she should want her, instead of going to Bath.

'I cannot possibly do without Anne,' was Mary's reasoning; and Elizabeth's reply was, 'Then I am sure Anne had better stay, for nobody will want her in Bath.'

To be claimed as a good, though in an improper style, is at least better than being rejected as no good at all; and Anne, glad to be thought of some use, glad to have anything marked out as a duty, and certainly not sorry to have the scene of it in the country, and her own dear country, readily agreed to stay.

This invitation of Mary's removed all Lady Russell's difficulties, and it was consequently soon settled that Anne should not go to Bath till Lady Russell took her, and that all the intervening time should be divided between Uppercross Cottage and Kellynch Lodge.

So far all was perfectly right; but Lady Russell was almost startled by the wrong of one part of the Kellynch Hall plan, when it burst on her, which was, Mrs Clay's being engaged to go to Bath with Sir Walter and Elizabeth, as a most important and valuable assistant to the latter in all the business before her. Lady Russell was extremely sorry that such a measure should have been resorted to at all – wondered, grieved, and feared – and the affront it contained to Anne, in Mrs Clay's being of so much use, while Anne could be of none, was a very sore aggravation.

Anne herself was become hardened to such affronts; but she felt the imprudence of the arrangement quite as keenly as Lady Russell. With a great deal of quiet observation, and a knowledge, which she often wished less, of her father's character, she was sensible that results the most serious to his family from the intimacy were more than possible. She did not imagine that her father had at present an idea of the kind. Mrs Clay had freckles; and a projecting tooth, and a clumsy wrist, which he was continually making severe remarks upon, in her absence; but she was young, and certainly altogether well looking, and possessed, in an acute mind and assiduous pleasing manners, infinitely more dangerous attractions than any merely personal might have been. Anne was so impressed by the degree of their danger that she could not excuse herself from trying to make it perceptible to her sister. She had little hope of success; but Elizabeth, who in the event of such a reverse would be so much more to be pitied than herself, should never, she thought, have reason to reproach her for giving no warning.

She spoke, and seemed only to offend. Elizabeth could not conceive how such an absurd suspicion should occur to her; and indignantly answered for each party's perfectly knowing their situation.

'Mrs Clay,' said she warmly, 'never forgets who she is; and as I am rather better acquainted with her sentiments than you can be, I can assure you, that upon the subject of marriage they are particularly nice; and that she reprobates all inequality of condition and rank more strongly than most people. And as to my father, I really should not have thought that he, who has kept himself single so long for our sakes, need be suspected now. If Mrs Clay were a very beautiful woman, I grant you, it might be wrong to have her so much with me; not that anything in the world, I am sure, would induce my father to make a degrading match; but he might be rendered unhappy. But poor Mrs Clay, who, with all her merits, can never have been reckoned tolerably pretty! I really think poor Mrs Clay may be staying here in perfect safety. One would imagine you had never heard my father speak of her personal misfortunes, though I know you must fifty times. That tooth of hers! and those freckles! Freckles do not disgust me so very much as they do him: I have known a face not materially disfigured by a few, but he abominates them. You must have heard him notice Mrs Clay's freckles.'

'There is hardly any personal defect,' replied Anne, 'which an agreeable manner might not gradually reconcile one to.'

'I think very differently,' answered Elizabeth, shortly; 'an agreeable manner may set off handsome features, but can never alter plain ones. However, at any rate, as I have a great deal more at stake on this point than anybody else can have, I think it rather unnecessary in you to be advising me.'

Anne had done – glad that it was over, and not absolutely hopeless of doing good. Elizabeth, though resenting the suspicion, might yet be made observant by it.

The last office of the four carriage-horses was to draw Sir Walter, Miss Elliot, and Mrs Clay to Bath. The party drove off in very good spirits; Sir Walter prepared with condescending bows for all the afflicted tenantry and cottagers who might have had a hint to show themselves; and Anne walked up at the same time, in a sort of desolate tranquillity, to the Lodge, where she was to spend the first week.

Her friend was not in better spirits than herself. Lady Russell felt this break-up of the family exceedingly. Their respectability was as dear to her as her own; and a daily intercourse had become precious by habit. It was painful to look upon their deserted grounds, and still worse to anticipate the new hands they were to fall into; and to escape the solitariness and the melancholy of so altered a village, and be out of the way when Admiral and Mrs Croft first arrived, she had determined to make her own absence from home begin when she must give up Anne. Accordingly their removal was made together, and Anne was set down at Uppercross Cottage, in the first stage of Lady Russell's journey.

Uppercross was a moderate-sized village, which a few years back had been completely in the old English style, containing only two houses superior in appearance to those of the yeomen and labourers – the mansion of the squire with its high walls, great gates, and old trees, substantial and unmodernised – and the compact, tight parsonage enclosed in its own neat garden, with a vine and a pear tree trained round its casements; but upon the marriage of the young squire, it had received the improvement of a farmhouse elevated into a cottage for his residence; and Uppercross Cottage, with its veranda, French windows, and other prettinesses, was quite as likely to catch the traveller's eye as the more consistent and considerable aspect and premises of the Great House, about a quarter of a mile farther on.

Here Anne had often been staying. She knew the ways of Uppercross as well as those of Kellynch. The two families were so continually meeting, so much in the habit of running in and out of each other's house at all hours, that it was rather a surprise to her to find Mary alone; but being alone, her being unwell and out of spirits, was almost a matter of course. Though better endowed than the elder sister, Mary had not Anne's understanding or temper. While well, and happy, and properly attended to, she had great good humour and excellent spirits; but any indisposition sunk her completely; she had no resources for solitude; and, inheriting a considerable share of the Elliot self-importance, was very prone to add to every other distress that of fancying herself neglected and ill-used. In person, she was inferior to both sisters, and had, even in her bloom, only reached the dignity of being 'a fine girl'. She was now lying on the faded sofa of the pretty little drawing-room, the once elegant furniture of which had been gradually growing shabby, under the influence of four summers and two children; and, on Anne's appearing, greeted her with, 'So, you are come at last! I began to think I should never see you. I am so ill I can hardly speak. I have not seen a creature the whole morning!'

'I am sorry to find you unwell,' replied Anne. 'You sent me such a good account of yourself on Thursday!'

'Yes, I made the best of it; I always do; but I was very far from well at the time; and I do not think I ever was so ill in my life as I have been all this morning – very unfit to be left alone, I am sure. Suppose I were to be seized of a sudden in some dreadful way, and not able to ring the bell! So, Lady Russell would not get out. I do not think she has been in this house three times this summer.'

Anne said what was proper, and enquired after her husband. 'Oh! Charles is out shooting. I have not seen him since seven o'clock. He would go, though I told him how ill I was. He said he should not stay out long; but he has never come back, and now it is almost one. I assure you, I have not seen a soul this whole long morning.'

'You have had your little boys with you?'

'Yes, as long as I could bear their noise; but they are so unmanageable that they do me more harm than good. Little Charles does not mind a word I say, and Walter is growing quite as bad.'

'Well, you will soon be better now,' replied Anne, cheerfully. 'You know I always cure you when I come. How are your neighbours at the Great House?'

'I can give you no account of them. I have not seen one of them today, except Mr Musgrove, who just stopped and spoke through the window, but without getting off his horse; and though I told him how ill I was, not one of them have been near me. It did not happen to suit the Miss Musgroves, I suppose, and they never put themselves out of their way.'

'You will see them yet, perhaps, before the morning is gone. It is early.'

'I never want them, I assure you. They talk and laugh a great deal too much for me. Oh! Anne, I am so very unwell! It was quite unkind of you not to come on Thursday.'

'My dear Mary, recollect what a comfortable account you sent me of yourself! You wrote in the cheerfullest manner, and said you were perfectly well, and in no hurry for me; and that being the case, you must be aware that my wish would be to remain with Lady Russell to the last; and besides what I felt on her account, I have really been so busy, have had so much to do, that I could not very conveniently have left Kellynch sooner.'

'Dear me! What can *you* possibly have to do?'

'A great many things, I assure you. More than I can recollect in a moment; but I can tell you some. I have been making a duplicate of the catalogue of my father's books and pictures. I have been several times in the garden with Mackenzie, trying to understand, and make him understand, which of Elizabeth's plants are for Lady Russell. I have had all my own little concerns to arrange – books and music to divide, and all my trunks to repack, from not having understood in time what was intended as to the waggons. And one thing I have had to do, Mary, of a more trying nature: going to almost every house in the parish, as a sort of take-leave. I was told that they wished it. But all these things took up a great deal of time.'

'Oh! well' – and after a moment's pause, 'But you have never asked me one word about our dinner at the Pooles yesterday.'

'Did you go then? I have made no enquiries, because I concluded you must have been obliged to give up the party.'

'Oh! yes, I went. I was very well yesterday; nothing at all the matter with me till this morning. It would have been strange if I had not gone.'

'I am very glad you were well enough, and I hope you had a pleasant party.'

'Nothing remarkable. One always knows beforehand what the dinner will be, and who will be there. And it is so very uncomfortable, not having a carriage of one's own. Mr and Mrs Musgrove took me, and we were so crowded! They are both so very large, and take up so much room! And Mr Musgrove always sits forward. So, there was I, crowded into the back seat with Henrietta and Louisa. And I think it very likely that my illness today may be owing to it.'

A little farther perseverance in patience, and forced cheerfulness on Anne's side, produced nearly a cure on Mary's. She could soon sit upright on the sofa, and began to hope she might be able to leave it by dinner-time. Then, forgetting to think of it, she was at the other end of the room, beautifying a nosegay; then, she ate her cold meat; and then she was well enough to propose a little walk.

'Where shall we go?' said she, when they were ready. 'I suppose you will not like to call at the Great House before they have been to see you?'

'I have not the smallest objection on that account,' replied Anne. 'I should never think of standing on such ceremony with people I know so well as Mrs and the Miss Musgroves.'

'Oh! but they ought to call upon you as soon as possible. They ought to feel what is due to you as *my* sister. However, we may as well go and sit with them a little while, and when we have got that over, we can enjoy our walk.'

Anne had always thought such a style of intercourse highly imprudent; but she had ceased to endeavour to check it, from believing that, though there were on each side continual subjects of offence, neither family could now do without it. To the Great House accordingly they went, to sit the full half-hour in the old-fashioned square parlour, with a small carpet and shining floor, to which the present daughters of the house were gradually giving the proper air of confusion by a grand pianoforte and a harp, flower-stands and little tables placed in every direction. Oh! could the originals of the portraits against the wainscot, could the gentlemen in brown velvet and the ladies in blue satin have seen what was going on, have been conscious of such an overthrow of all order and neatness! The portraits themselves seemed to be staring in astonishment.

The Musgroves, like their houses, were in a state of alteration, perhaps of improvement. The father and mother were in the old English style, and the young people in the new. Mr and Mrs Musgrove were a very good sort of people; friendly and hospitable, not much educated, and not at all elegant. Their children had more modern minds and manners. There was a numerous family; but the only two grown up, excepting Charles, were Henrietta and Louisa, young ladies of nineteen and twenty, who had brought from a school at Exeter all the usual stock of accomplishments, and were now, like thousands of other young ladies, living to be fashionable, happy, and merry. Their dress had every advantage, their faces were rather pretty, their spirits extremely good, their manners unembarrassed and pleasant; they were of consequence at home, and favourites abroad. Anne always contemplated them as some of the happiest creatures of her acquaintance; but still, saved as we all are by some comfortable feeling of superiority from wishing for the possibility of exchange, she would not have given up her own more elegant and cultivated mind for all their enjoyments; and envied them nothing but that seemingly perfect good understanding and agreement together, that good-humoured mutual affection, of which she had known so little herself with either of her sisters.

They were received with great cordiality. Nothing seemed amiss on the side of the Great House family, which was generally, as Anne very well knew, the least to blame. The half-hour was chatted away pleasantly enough; and she was not at all surprised, at the end of it, to have their walking party joined by both the Miss Musgroves, at Mary's particular invitation.

# *Chapter 6*

Anne had not wanted this visit to Uppercross to learn that a removal from one set of people to another, though at a distance of only three miles, will often include a total change of conversation, opinion, and idea. She had never been staying there before, without being struck by it, or without wishing that other Elliots could have her advantage in seeing how unknown, or unconsidered there, were the affairs which at Kellynch Hall were treated as of such general publicity and pervading interest; yet, with all this experience, she believed she must now submit to feel that another lesson, in the art of knowing our own nothingness beyond our own circle, was become necessary for her – for certainly, coming as she did, with a heart full of the subject which had been completely occupying both houses in Kellynch for many weeks, she had expected rather more curiosity and sympathy than she found in the separate, but very similar remark of Mr and Mrs Musgrove: 'So, Miss Anne, Sir Walter and your sister are gone; and what part of Bath do you think they will settle in?' and this, without much waiting for an answer – or in the young ladies' addition of, 'I hope *we* shall be in Bath in the winter; but remember, papa, if we do go, we must be in a good situation – none of your Queen Squares for us!' or in the anxious supplement from Mary, of 'Upon my word, I shall be pretty well off, when you are all gone away to be happy at Bath!'

She could only resolve to avoid such self-delusion in future, and think with heightened gratitude of the extraordinary blessing of having one such truly sympathising friend as Lady Russell.

The Mr Musgroves had their own game to guard, and to destroy; their own horses, dogs, and newspapers to engage them; and the females were fully occupied in all the other common subjects of housekeeping, neighbours, dress, dancing, and music. She acknowledged it to be very fitting that every little social commonwealth should dictate its own matters of discourse; and hoped, ere long, to become a not unworthy member of the one she was now transplanted into. – With the prospect of spending at least two months at Uppercross, it was highly incumbent on her to clothe her imagination, her memory, and all her ideas in as much of Uppercross as possible.

She had no dread of these two months. Mary was not so repulsive and unsisterly as Elizabeth, nor so inaccessible to all influence of hers; neither was there anything among the other component parts of the cottage inimical to comfort. – She was always on friendly terms with her brother-in-law; and in the children, who loved her nearly as well, and respected her a great deal more than their mother, she had an object of interest, amusement, and wholesome exertion.

Charles Musgrove was civil and agreeable; in sense and temper he was undoubtedly superior to his wife; but not of powers, or conversation, or grace to make the past, as they were connected together, at all a dangerous contemplation; though, at the same time, Anne could believe, with Lady Russell, that a more equal match might have greatly improved him; and that a woman of real understanding might have given more consequence to his character, and more usefulness, rationality, and elegance to his habits and pursuits. As it was, he did nothing with much zeal, but sport; and his time was otherwise trifled away, without benefit from books, or anything else. He had very good spirits, which never seemed much affected by his wife's occasional lowness; bore with her unreasonableness sometimes to Anne's admiration; and, upon the whole, though there was very often a little disagreement (in which she had sometimes more share than she wished, being appealed to by both parties), they might pass for a happy couple. They were always perfectly agreed in the want of more money, and a strong inclination for a handsome present from his father; but here, as on most topics, he had the superiority, for while Mary thought it a great shame that such a present was not made, he always contended for his father's having many other uses for his money, and a right to spend it as he liked.

As to the management of their children, his theory was much better than his wife's and his practice not so bad. – 'I could manage them very well, if it were not for Mary's interference,' was what Anne often heard him say, and had a good deal of faith in; but when listening in turn to Mary's reproach of 'Charles spoils the children so that I cannot get them into any order,' she never had the smallest temptation to say, 'Very true.'

One of the least agreeable circumstances of her residence there, was her being treated with too much confidence by all parties, and being too much in the secret of the complaints of each house. Known to have some influence with her sister, she was continually requested, or at least receiving hints to exert it, beyond what was practicable. 'I wish you could persuade Mary not to be always fancying herself ill,' was Charles's language; and, in an unhappy mood, thus spoke Mary: 'I do believe if Charles were to see me dying, he would not think there was anything the matter with me. I am sure, Anne, if you would, you might persuade him that I really am very ill – a great deal worse than I ever own.'

Mary's declaration was, 'I hate sending the children to the Great House, though their grandmamma is always wanting to see them, for she humours and indulges them to such a degree, and gives them so much trash and sweet things, that they are sure to come back sick and cross for the rest of the day.' And Mrs Musgrove took the first opportunity of being alone with Anne, to say, 'Oh! Miss Anne, I cannot help wishing Mrs Charles had a little of your method with those children. They are quite different creatures with you! But to be sure, in general they are so spoiled! It is a pity you cannot put your sister in the way of managing them. They are as fine healthy children as ever were seen, poor little dears, without partiality; but Mrs Charles knows no more how they should be treated! – Bless me, how troublesome they are sometimes! – I assure you, Miss Anne, it prevents my wishing to see them at our house so often as I otherwise should. I believe Mrs Charles is not quite pleased with my not inviting them oftener; but you know it is very bad to have children with one, that one is obliged to be checking every moment – "don't do this, and don't do that" – or that one can only keep in tolerable order by more cake than is good for them.'

She had this communication, moreover, from Mary. 'Mrs Musgrove thinks all her servants so steady that it would be high treason to call it in question, but I am sure, without exaggeration, that her upper housemaid and laundrymaid, instead of being in their business, are gadding about the village, all day long. I meet them wherever I go; and I declare I never go twice into my nursery without seeing something of them. If Jemima were not the trustiest, steadiest creature in the world, it would be enough to spoil her; for she tells me they are always tempting her to take a walk with them.' And on Mrs Musgrove's side, it was, 'I make a rule of never interfering in any of my daughter-in-law's concerns, for I know it would not do; but I shall tell *you* Miss Anne, because you may be able to set things to rights, that I have no very good opinion of Mrs Charles's nurserymaid: I hear strange stories of her; she is always upon the gad; and from my own knowledge, I can declare, she is such a fine-dressing lady that she is enough to ruin any servants she comes near. Mrs Charles quite swears by her, I know; but I just give you this hint, that you may be upon the watch; because, if you see anything amiss, you need not be afraid of mentioning it.'

Again; it was Mary's complaint, that Mrs Musgrove was very apt not to give her the precedence that was her due when they dined at the Great House with other families; and she did not see any reason why she was to be considered so much at home as to lose her place. And one day, when Anne was walking with only the Miss Musgroves, one of them, after talking of rank, people of rank, and jealousy of rank, said, 'I have no scruple of observing to *you*, how nonsensical some persons are about their place, because, all the world knows how easy and indifferent you are about it; but I wish anybody could give Mary a hint that it would be a great deal better if she were not so very tenacious; especially, if she would not be always putting herself forward to take place of mamma. Nobody doubts her right to have precedence of mamma, but it would be more becoming in her not to be always insisting on it. It is not that mamma cares about it the least in the world, but I know it is taken notice of by many persons.'

How was Anne to set all these matters to rights? She could do little more than listen patiently, soften every grievance, and excuse each to the other; give them all hints of the forbearance necessary between such near neighbours, and make those hints broadest which were meant for her sister's benefit.

In all other respects, her visit began and proceeded very well. Her own spirits improved by change of place and subject, by being removed three miles from Kellynch; Mary's ailments lessened by having a constant companion; and their daily intercourse with the other family, since there was neither superior affection, confidence, nor employment in the cottage to be interrupted by it, was rather an advantage. It was certainly carried nearly as far as possible, for they met every morning, and hardly ever spent an evening asunder; but she believed they should not have done so well without the sight of Mr and Mrs Musgrove's respectable forms in the usual places, or without the talking, laughing, and singing of their daughters.

She played a great deal better than either of the Miss Musgroves; but having no voice, no knowledge of the harp, and no fond parents to sit by and fancy themselves delighted, her performance was little thought of, only out of civility, or to refresh the others, as she was well aware. She knew that when she played she was giving pleasure only to herself; but this was no new sensation: excepting one short period of her life, she had never, since the age of fourteen, never since the loss of her dear mother, known the happiness of being listened to, or

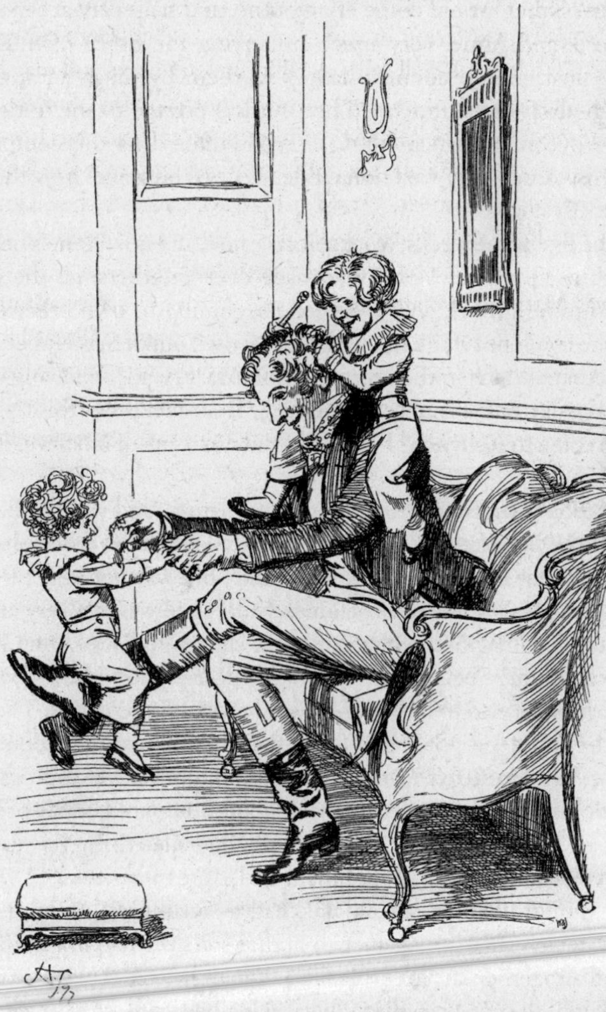

*'Charles spoils the children so'*

encouraged by any just appreciation or real taste. In music she had been always used to feel alone in the world; and Mr and Mrs Musgrove's fond partiality for their own daughters' performance, and total indifference to any other person's, gave her much more pleasure for their sakes than mortification for her own.

The party at the Great House was sometimes increased by other company. The neighbourhood was not large, but the Musgroves were visited by everybody, and had more dinner parties, and more callers, more visitors by invitation and by chance, than any other family. They were more completely popular.

The girls were wild for dancing; and the evenings ended, occasionally, in an unpremeditated little ball. There was a family of cousins within a walk of Uppercross, in less affluent circumstances, who depended on the Musgroves for all their pleasures; they would come at any time, and help play at anything, or dance anywhere; and Anne, very much preferring the office of musician to a more active post, played country-dances to them by the hour together; a kindness which always recommended her musical powers to the notice of Mr and Mrs Musgrove more than anything else, and often drew this compliment – 'Well done, Miss Anne! very well done indeed! Lord bless me! how those little fingers of yours fly about!'

So passed the first three weeks. Michaelmas came; and now Anne's heart must be in Kellynch again. A beloved home made over to others; all the precious rooms and furniture, groves, and prospects, beginning to own other eyes and other limbs! She could not think of much else on the 29th of September; and she had this sympathetic touch in the evening, from Mary, who, on having occasion to note down the day of the month, exclaimed, 'Dear me! is not this the day the Crofts were to come to Kellynch? I am glad I did not think of it before. How low it makes me!'

The Crofts took possession with true naval alertness, and were to be visited. Mary deplored the necessity for herself. 'Nobody knew how much she should suffer. She should put it off as long as she could'; but was not easy till she had talked Charles into driving her over on an early day; and was in a very animated, comfortable state of imaginary agitation when she came back. Anne had very sincerely rejoiced in there being no means of her going. She wished, however, to see the Crofts, and was glad to be within when the visit was returned. They came; the master of the house was not at home, but the two sisters were together; and as it chanced that Mrs Croft fell to the share of Anne, while the Admiral sat by Mary, and made himself very agreeable by his good-humoured notice of her little boys, she was well able to watch for a likeness, and if it failed her in the features, to catch it in the voice, or the turn of sentiment and expression.

Mrs Croft, though neither tall nor fat, had a squareness, uprightness, and vigour of form, which gave importance to her person. She had bright dark eyes, good teeth, and altogether an agreeable face; though her reddened and weather-beaten complexion, the consequence of her having been almost as much at sea as her husband, made her seem to have lived some years longer in the world than her real eight-and-thirty. Her manners were open, easy, and decided, like one who had no distrust of herself, and no doubts of what to do; without any approach to coarseness, however, or any want of good humour. Anne gave her credit, indeed, for feelings of great consideration towards herself, in all that related to Kellynch; and it pleased her – especially, as she had satisfied herself in the very first half-minute, in the instant even of introduction, that there was not the smallest symptom of any knowledge or suspicion on Mrs Croft's side to give a bias of any sort. She was quite easy on that head, and consequently full of strength and courage, till for a moment electrified by Mrs Croft's suddenly saying,

'It was you, and not your sister, I find, that my brother had the pleasure of being acquainted with, when he was in this country.'

Anne hoped she had outlived the age of blushing; but the age of emotion she certainly had not.

'Perhaps you may not have heard that he is married,' added Mrs Croft.

She could now answer as she ought and was happy to feel, when Mrs Croft's next words explained it to be Mr Wentworth of whom she spoke, that she had said nothing which might not do for either brother. She immediately felt how reasonable it was that Mrs Croft should be thinking and speaking of Edward, and not of Frederick; and, with shame at her own forgetfulness, applied herself to the knowledge of their former neighbour's present state, with proper interest.

The rest was all tranquillity; till just as they were moving, she heard the Admiral say to Mary,

'We are expecting a brother of Mrs Croft's here soon; I dare say you know him by name.'

He was cut short by the eager attacks of the little boys, clinging to him like an old friend, and declaring he should not go; and being too much engrossed by proposals of carrying them away in his coat-pocket, etc., to have another moment for finishing or recollecting what he had begun, Anne was left to persuade herself, as well as she could, that the same brother must still be in question. She could not, however, reach such a degree of certainty as not to be anxious to hear whether anything had been said on the subject at the other house, where the Crofts had previously been calling.

The folks of Great House were to spend the evening of this day at the Cottage; and it being now too late in the year for such visits to be made on foot, the coach was beginning to be listened for, when the youngest Miss Musgrove walked in. That she was coming to apologise, and that they should have to spend the evening by themselves, was the first black idea; and Mary was quite ready to be affronted, when Louisa made all right by saying that she only came on foot to leave more room for the harp, which she was bringing in the carriage.

'And I will tell you our reason,' she added, 'and all about it. I am come on to give you notice, that papa and mamma are out of spirits this evening, especially mamma; she is thinking so much of poor Richard! And we agreed it would be best to have the harp, for it seems to amuse her more than the pianoforte. I will tell you why she is out of spirits. When the Crofts called this morning (they called here afterwards, did not they?), they happened to say that her brother, Captain Wentworth, is just returned to England, or paid off, or something, and is coming to see them almost directly; and most unluckily it came into mamma's head, when they were gone, that Wentworth, or something very like it, was the name of poor Richard's captain, at one time, I do not know when or where, but a great while before he died, poor fellow! And upon looking over his letters and things, she found it was so; and is perfectly sure that this must be the very man, and her head is quite full of it, and of poor Richard! So we must all be as merry as we can, that she may not be dwelling upon such gloomy things.'

The real circumstances of this pathetic piece of family history were that the Musgroves had had the ill fortune of a very troublesome, hopeless son; and the good fortune to lose him before he reached his twentieth year; that he had been sent to sea, because he was stupid and unmanageable on shore; that he had been very little cared for at any time by his family, though quite as much as he deserved; seldom heard of, and scarcely at all regretted, when the intelligence of his death abroad had worked its way to Uppercross, two years before.

He had, in fact, though his sisters were now doing all they could for him, by

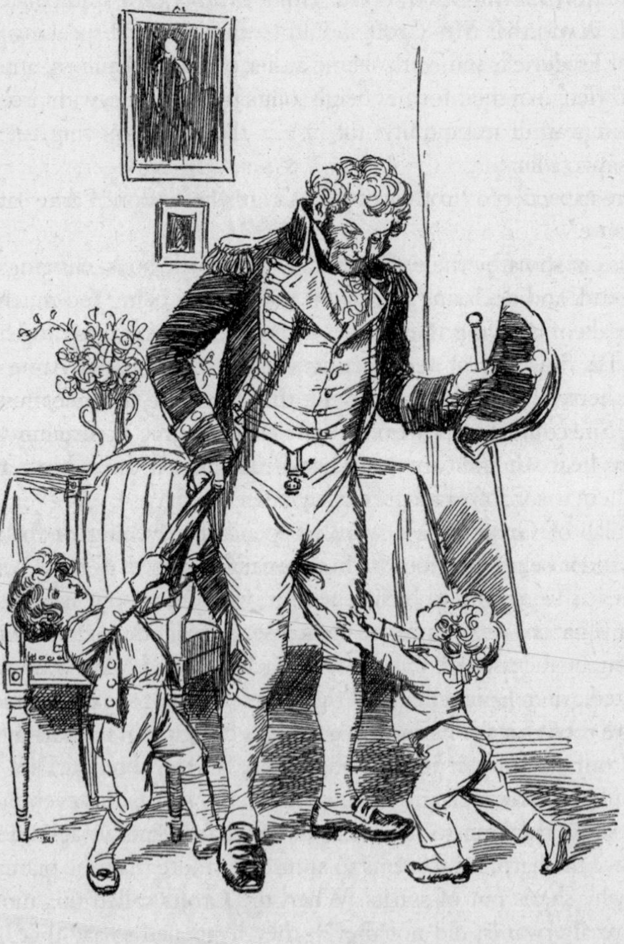

*Declaring he should not go*

calling him 'poor Richard', been nothing better than a thick headed, unfeeling, unprofitable Dick Musgrove, who had never done anything to entitle himself to more than the abbreviation of his name, living or dead.

He had been several years at sea, and had, in the course of those removals to which all midshipmen are liable, and especially such midshipmen as every captain wishes to get rid of, been six months on board Captain Frederick Wentworth's frigate, the *Laconia*; and from the *Laconia* he had, under the influence of his captain, written the only two letters which his father and mother had ever received from him during the whole of his absence; that is to say, the only two disinterested letters; all the rest had been mere applications for money.

In each letter he had spoken well of his captain; but yet, so little were they in the habit of attending to such matters, so unobservant and incurious were they as to the names of men or ships, that it had made scarcely any impression at the time; and that Mrs Musgrove should have been suddenly struck, this very day, with a recollection of the name of Wentworth, as connected with her son, seemed one of those extraordinary bursts of mind which do sometimes occur.

She had gone to her letters, and found it all as she supposed; and the reperusal of these letters, after so long an interval, her poor son gone forever, and all the strength of his faults forgotten, had affected her spirits exceedingly, and thrown her into greater grief for him than she had known on first hearing of his death. Mr Musgrove was, in a lesser degree, affected likewise; and when they reached the Cottage, they were evidently in want, first, of being listened to anew on this subject, and afterwards, of all the relief which cheerful companions could give.

To hear them talking so much of Captain Wentworth, repeating his name so often, puzzling over past years, and at last ascertaining that it *might*, that it probably *would*, turn out to be the very same Captain Wentworth whom they recollected meeting, once or twice, after their coming back from Clifton – a very fine young man; but they could not say whether it was seven or eight years ago – was a new sort of trial to Anne's nerves. She found, however, that it was one to which she must inure herself. Since he actually was expected in the country, she must teach herself to be insensible on such points. And not only did it appear that he was expected, and speedily, but the Musgroves, in their warm gratitude for the kindness he had shown poor Dick, and very high respect for his character, stamped as it was by poor Dick's having been six months under his care, and mentioning him in strong, though not perfectly well-spelled praise, as 'a fine dashing felow, only two perticular about the schoolmaster', were bent on introducing themselves, and seeking his acquaintance, as soon as they could hear of his arrival.

The resolution of doing so helped to form the comfort of their evening.

## Chapter 7

A very few days more, and Captain Wentworth was known to be at Kellynch, and Mr Musgrove had called on him, and come back warm in his praise, and he was engaged with the Crofts to dine at Uppercross by the end of another week. It had been a great disappointment to Mr Musgrove to find that no earlier day could be fixed, so impatient was he to show his gratitude, by seeing Captain Wentworth under his own roof, and welcoming him to all that was strongest and best in his cellars. But a week must pass; only a week, in Anne's reckoning, and then, she supposed, they must meet; and soon she began to wish that she could feel secure even for a week.

Captain Wentworth made a very early return to Mr Musgrove's civility, and she was all but calling there in the same half-hour! – She and Mary were actually setting forward for the Great House, where, as she afterwards learned, they must inevitably have found him, when they were stopped by the eldest boy's being at that moment brought home in consequence of a bad fall. The child's situation put the visit entirely aside, but she could not hear of her escape with indifference, even in the midst of the serious anxiety which they afterwards felt on his account.

His collarbone was found to be dislocated, and such injury received in the back as roused the most alarming ideas. It was an afternoon of distress, and Anne had everything to do at once – the apothecary to send for – the father to have pursued and informed – the mother to support and keep from hysterics – the servants to control – the youngest child to banish, and the poor suffering one to attend and soothe – besides sending, as soon as she recollected it, proper notice to the other house, which brought her an accession rather of frightened, enquiring companions than of very useful assistants.

Her brother's return was the first comfort – he could take best care of his wife – and the second blessing was the arrival of the apothecary. Till he came and had examined the child, their apprehensions were the worse for being vague; they suspected great injury, but knew not where; but now the collarbone was soon replaced and though Mr Robinson felt and felt, and rubbed, and looked grave, and spoke low words both to the father and the aunt, still they were all to hope for the best, and to be able to part and eat their dinner in tolerable ease of mind; and then it was, just before they parted, that the two young aunts were able so far to disgress from their nephew's state as to give the information of Captain Wentworth's visit – staying five minutes behind their father and mother, to endeavour to express how perfectly delighted they were with him, how much handsomer, how infinitely more agreeable they thought him than any individual among their male acquaintance, who had been at all a favourite before – how glad they had been to hear papa invite him to stay for dinner – how sorry when he said it was quite out of his power – and how glad again, when he had promised to reply to papa and mamma's farther pressing invitations to come and dine with them on the morrow, actually on the morrow! – And he had promised it in so pleasant a manner, as if he felt all the motive of their attention just as he ought! – And, in short, he had looked and said everything with such exquisite grace that they could assure them all, their heads were both turned by him! – And off they ran, quite as full of glee as of love, and apparently more full of Captain Wentworth than of little Charles.

The same story and the same raptures were repeated, when the two girls came with their father, through the gloom of the evening, to make enquiries; and Mr Musgrove, no longer under the first uneasiness about his heir, could add his confirmation and praise, and hope there would be now no occasion for putting Captain Wentworth off, and only be sorry to think that the Cottage party, probably, would not like to leave the little boy, to give him the meeting. 'Oh, no! as to leaving the little boy!' both father and mother were in much too strong and recent alarm to bear the thought; and Anne, in the joy of the escape, could not help adding her warm protestations to theirs.

Charles Musgrove, indeed, afterwards showed more of inclination: 'the child was going on so well – and he wished so much to be introduced to Captain Wentworth that, perhaps, he might join them in the evening; he would not dine from home, but he might walk in for half an hour'. But in this he was eagerly opposed by his wife, with 'Oh, no! indeed, Charles, I cannot bear to have you go away. Only think, if anything should happen!'

The child had a good night, and was going on well the next day. It must be a work of time to ascertain that no injury had been done to the spine, but Mr Robinson found nothing to increase alarm, and Charles Musgrove began consequently to feel no necessity for longer confinement. The child was to be kept in bed, and amused as quietly as possible; but what was there for a father to do? This was quite a female case, and it would be highly absurd in him, who could be of no use at home, to shut himself up. His father very much wished him to meet Captain Wentworth, and there being no sufficient reason against it, he ought to go; and it ended in his making a bold public declaration, when he came in from shooting, of his meaning to dress directly, and dine at the other house.

'Nothing can be going on better than the child,' said he, 'so I told my father just now that I would come, and he thought me quite right. Your sister being with you, my love, I have no scruple at all. You would not like to leave him yourself, but you see I can be of no use. Anne will send for me if anything is the matter.'

Husbands and wives generally understand when opposition will be vain. Mary knew, from Charles's manner of speaking, that he was quite determined on going, and that it would be of no use to tease him. She said nothing, therefore, till he was out of the room, but as soon as there was only Anne to hear,

'So! You and I are to be left to shift by ourselves, with this poor sick child – and not a creature coming near us all the evening! I knew how it would be. This is always my luck! If there is anything disagreeable going on, men are always sure to get out of it, and Charles is as bad as any of them. Very unfeeling! I must say it is very unfeeling of him, to be running away from his poor little boy, talks of his being going on so well! How does he know that he is going on well, or that there may not be a sudden change half an hour hence? I did not think Charles would have been so unfeeling. So, here he is to go away and enjoy himself, and because I am the poor mother, I am not to be allowed to stir – and yet, I am sure, I am more unfit than anybody else to be about the child. My being the mother is the very reason why my feelings should not be tried. I am not at all equal to it. You saw how hysterical I was yesterday.'

'But that was only the effect of the suddenness of your alarm – of the shock. You will not be hysterical again. I dare say we shall have nothing to distress us. I perfectly understand Mr Robinson's directions, and have no fears; and indeed, Mary, I cannot wonder at your husband. Nursing does not belong to a man, it is not his province. A sick child is always the mother's property, her own feelings generally make it so.'

'I hope I am as fond of my child as any mother – but I do not know that I am of any more use in the sickroom than Charles, for I cannot be always scolding and teasing a poor child when it is ill; and you saw, this morning, that if I told him to keep quiet, he was sure to begin kicking about. I have not nerves for the sort of thing.'

'But, could you be comfortable yourself, to be spending the whole evening away from the poor boy?'

'Yes; you see his papa can, and why should not I? – Jemima is so careful! And she could send us word every hour how he was. I really think Charles might as well have told his father we would all come. I am not more alarmed about little Charles now than he is. I was dreadfully alarmed yesterday, but the case is very different today.'

'Well – if you do not think it too late to give notice for yourself, suppose you were to go, as well as your husband. Leave little Charles to my care. Mr and Mrs Musgrove cannot think it wrong while I remain with him.'

'Are you serious?' cried Mary, her eyes brightening. 'Dear me! that's a very good thought, very good indeed. To be sure I may just as well go as not, for I am of no use at home – am I? and it only harasses me. You, who have not a mother's feelings, are a great deal the properest person. You can make little Charles do anything; he always minds you at a word. It will be a great deal better than leaving him with only Jemima. Oh! I will certainly go; I am sure I ought if I can quite as much as Charles, for they want me excessively to be acquainted with Captain Wentworth, and I know you do not mind being left alone. An excellent thought of yours, indeed, Anne! I will go and tell Charles, and get ready directly. You can send for us, you know, at a moment's notice, if anything is the matter; but I dare say there will be nothing to alarm you. I should not go, you may be sure, if I did not feel quite at ease about my dear child.'

The next moment she was tapping at her husband's dressing-room door, and, as Anne followed her upstairs, she was in time for the whole conversation, which began with Mary's saying, in a tone of great exultation,

'I mean to go with you, Charles, for I am of no more use at home than you are. If I were to shut myself up forever with the child, I should not be able to persuade him to do anything he did not like. Anne will stay; Anne undertakes to stay at home and take care of him. It is Anne's own proposal, and so I shall go with you, which will be a great deal better, for I have not dined at the other house since Tuesday.'

'This is very kind of Anne,' was her husband's answer, 'and I should be very glad to have you go; but it seems rather hard that she should be left at home by herself, to nurse our sick child.'

Anne was now at hand to take up her own cause, and the sincerity of her manner being soon sufficient to convince him, where conviction was at least very agreeable, he had no farther scruples as to her being left to dine alone, though he still wanted her to join them in the evening, when the child might be at rest for the night, and kindly urged her to let him come and fetch her; but she was quite unpersuadable; and this being the case, she had ere long the pleasure of seeing them set off together in high spirits. They were gone, she hoped, to be happy, however oddly constructed such happiness might seem; as for herself, she was left with as many sensations of comfort, as were, perhaps, ever likely to be hers. She knew herself to be of the first utility to the child; and what was it to her if Frederick Wentworth were only half a mile distant, making himself agreeable to others!

She would have liked to know how he felt as to a meeting. Perhaps indifferent, if indifference could exist under such circumstances. He must be either indifferent or unwilling. Had he wished ever to see her again, he need not have waited till this time; he would have done what she could not but believe that in his place she should have done long ago, when events had been early giving him the independence which alone had been wanting.

Her brother and sister came back delighted with their new acquaintance, and their visit in general. There had been music, singing, talking, laughing, all that that was most agreeable; charming manners in Captain Wentworth, no shyness or reserve; they seemed all to know each other perfectly, and he was coming the very next morning to shoot with Charles. He was to come to breakfast, but not at the Cottage, though that had been proposed at first; but then he had been pressed to come to the Great House instead, and he seemed afraid of being in Mrs Charles Musgrove's way, on account of the child; and therefore, somehow, they hardly knew how, it ended in Charles's being to meet him to breakfast at his father's.

Anne understood it. He wished to avoid seeing her. He had enquired after her, she found, slightly, as might suit a former slight acquaintance, seeming to acknowledge such as she had acknowledged, actuated, perhaps, by the same view of escaping introduction when they were to meet.

The morning hours of the Cottage were always later than those of the other house; and on the morrow the difference was so great that Mary and Anne were not more than beginning breakfast when Charles came in to say that they were just setting off, that he was come for his dogs, that his sisters were following with Captain Wentworth, his sisters meaning to visit Mary and the child, and Captain Wentworth proposing also to wait on her for a few minutes, if not inconvenient; and though Charles had answered for the child's being in no such state as could make it inconvenient, Captain Wentworth would not be satisfied without his running on to give notice.

Mary, very much gratified by this attention, was delighted to receive him; while a thousand feelings rushed on Anne, of which this was the most consoling, that it would soon be over. And it was soon over. In two minutes after Charles's preparation, the others appeared; they were in the drawing-room. Her eye half met Captain Wentworth's; a bow, a curtsey passed; she heard his voice – he talked to Mary; said all that was right; said something to the Miss Musgroves, enough to mark an easy footing; the room seemed full – full of persons and voices – but a few minutes ended it. Charles showed himself at the window, all was ready, their visitor had bowed and was gone; the Miss Musgroves were gone too, suddenly resolving to walk to the end of the village with the sportsmen; the room was cleared, and Anne might finish her breakfast as she could.

'It is over! it is over!' she repeated to herself again, and again, in nervous gratitude. 'The worst is over!'

Mary talked, but she could not attend. She had seen him. They had met. They had been once more in the same room!

Soon, however, she began to reason with herself, and try to be feeling less. Eight years, almost eight years had passed, since all had been given up. How absurd to be resuming the agitation which such an interval had banished into distance and indistinctness! What might not eight years do? Events of every description, changes, alienations, removals – all, all must be comprised in it; and oblivion of the past – how natural, how certain too! It included nearly a third part of her own life.

Alas! with all her reasonings, she found that to retentive feelings eight years may be little more than nothing.

Now, how were his sentiments to be read? Was this like wishing to avoid her? And the next moment she was hating herself for the folly which asked the question.

On one other question, which perhaps her utmost wisdom might not have prevented, she was soon spared all suspense; for after the Miss Musgroves had returned and finished their visit at the Cottage, she had this spontaneous information from Mary:

'Captain Wentworth is not very gallant by you, Anne, though he was so attentive to me. Henrietta asked him what he thought of you, when they went away; and he said, 'You were so altered he should not have known you again.'

Mary had no feelings to make her respect her sisters in a common way; but she was perfectly unsuspicious of inflicting any peculiar wound.

'Altered beyond his knowledge!' Anne fully submitted, in silent, deep mortification. Doubtless it was so; and she could take no revenge, for he was not altered, or not for the worse. She had already acknowledged it to herself, and she could not think differently, let him think of her as he would. No; the years which had destroyed her youth and bloom had only given him a more glowing, manly, open look, in no respect lessening his personal advantages. She had seen the same Frederick Wentworth.

'So altered that he should not have known her again!' These were words which could not but dwell with her. Yet she soon began to rejoice that she had heard them. They were of sobering tendency; they allayed agitation; they composed, and consequently must make her happier.

Frederick Wentworth had used such words, or something like them, but without an idea that they would be carried round to her. He had thought her wretchedly altered, and, in the first moment of appeal, had spoken as he felt. He had not forgiven Anne Elliot. She had used him ill; deserted and disappointed him; and worse, she had shown a feebleness of character in doing so, which his own decided, confident temper could not endure. She had given him up to oblige others. It had been the effect of overpersuasion. It had been weakness and timidity.

He had been most warmly attached to her, and had never seen a woman since whom he thought her equal; but, except from some natural sensation of curiosity, he had no desire of meeting her again. Her power with him was gone forever.

It was now his object to marry. He was rich, and being turned on shore, fully intended to settle as soon as he could be properly tempted; actually looking round, ready to fall in love with all the speed which a clear head and quick taste could allow. He had a heart for either of the Miss Musgroves, if they could catch it; a heart, in short, for any pleasing young woman who came in his way, excepting Anne Elliot. This was his only secret exception, when he said to his sister, in answer to her suppositions,

'Yes, here I am, Sophia, quite ready to make a foolish match. Anybody between fifteen and thirty may have me for asking. A little beauty, and a few smiles, and a few compliments to the navy, and I am a lost man. Should not this be enough for a sailor, who has had no society among women to make him nice?'

He said it, she knew, to be contradicted. His bright, proud eye spoke the happy conviction that he was nice; and Anne Elliot was not out of his thoughts when he more seriously described the woman he should wish to meet with. 'A strong mind, with sweetness of manner,' made the first and the last of the description.

'This is the woman I want,' said he. 'Something a little inferior I shall of course put up with, but it must not be much. If I am a fool I shall be a fool indeed, for I have thought on the subject more than most men.'

## *Chapter 8*

From this time Captain Wentworth and Anne Elliot were repeatedly in the same circle. They were soon dining in company together at Mr Musgrove's, for the little boy's state could no longer supply his aunt with a pretence for absenting herself; and this was but the beginning of other dinings and other meetings.

Whether former feelings were to be renewed must be brought to the proof; former times must undoubtedly be brought to the recollection of each; *they* could not but be reverted to; the year of their engagement could not but be named by him, in the little narratives or descriptions which conversation called forth. His profession qualified him, his disposition led him, to talk; and '*That* was in the year six'; '*That* happened before I went to sea in the year six' occurred in the course of the first evening they spent together; and though his voice did not falter, and though she had no reason to suppose his eye wandering towards her while he spoke, Anne felt the utter impossibility, from her knowledge of his mind, that he could be unvisited by remembrance any more than herself. There must be the same immediate association of thought, though she was very far from conceiving it to be of equal pain.

They had no conversation together, no intercourse but what the commonest civility required. Once so much to each other! Now nothing! There *had* been a time, when of all the large party now filling the drawing-room at Uppercross, they would have found it most difficult to cease to speak to one another. With the exception, perhaps, of Admiral and Mrs Croft, who seemed particularly attached and happy (Anne could allow no other exception even among the married couples), there could have been no two hearts so open, no tastes so similar, no feelings so in unison, no countenances so beloved. Now they were as strangers; nay, worse than strangers, for they could never become acquainted. It was a perpetual estrangement.

When he talked, she heard the same voice, and discerned the same mind. There was a very general ignorance of all naval matters throughout the party; and he was very much questioned, and especially by the two Miss Musgroves, who seemed hardly to have any eyes but for him, as to the manner of living on board, daily regulations, food, hours, etc.; and their surprise at his accounts, at learning the degree of accommodation and arrangement which was practicable, drew from him some pleasant ridicule, which reminded Anne of the early days when she too had been ignorant, and she too had been accused of supposing sailors to be living on board without anything to eat, or any cook to dress it if there were, or any servant to wait, or any knife and fork to use.

From thus listening and thinking, she was roused by a whisper of Mrs Musgrove's, who, overcome by fond regrets, could not help saying,

'Ah! Miss Anne, if it had pleased Heaven to spare my poor son, I dare say he would have been just such another by this time.'

Anne suppressed a smile, and listened kindly, while Mrs Musgrove relieved her heart a little more; and for a few minutes, therefore, could not keep pace with the conversation of the others. – When she could let her attention take its natural course again, she found the Miss Musgroves just fetching the navy list (their own navy list, the first that had ever been at Uppercross); and sitting down together to pore over it, with the professed view of finding out the ships which Captain Wentworth had commanded.

'Your first was the *Asp*, I remember; we will look for the *Asp*.'

'You will not find her there. – Quite worn out and broken up. I was the last man who commanded her. – Hardly fit for service then. – Reported fit for home service for a year or two – and so I was sent off to the West Indies.'

The girls looked all amazement.

'The admiralty,' he continued, 'entertain themselves now and then, with sending a few hundred men to sea, in a ship not fit to be employed. But they have a great many to provide for; and among the thousands that may just as well go to the bottom as not, it is impossible for them to distinguish the very set who may be least missed.'

'Phoo! phoo!' cried the Admiral, 'what stuff these young fellows talk! Never was a better sloop than the *Asp* in her day. – For an old built sloop, you would not see her equal. Lucky fellow to get her! – He knows there must have been twenty better men than himself applying for her at the same time. Lucky fellow to get anything so soon, with no more interest than his.'

'I felt my luck, Admiral, I assure you;' replied Captain Wentworth, seriously. 'I was as well satisfied with my appointment as you can desire. It was a great object with me, at that time, to be at sea – a very great object. I wanted to be doing something.'

'To be sure you did. – What should a young fellow, like you, do ashore, for half a year together? – If a man has not a wife, he soon wants to be afloat again.'

'But, Captain Wentworth,' cried Louisa, 'how vexed you must have been when you came to the *Asp*, to see what an old thing they had given you.'

'I knew pretty well what she was, before that day,' said he, smiling. 'I had no more discoveries to make than you would have as to the fashion and strength of any old pelisse, which you had seen lent about among half your acquaintance, ever since you could remember, and which at last, on some very wet day, is lent to yourself. – Ah! she was a dear old *Asp* to me. She did all that I wanted. I knew she would – I knew that we should either go to the bottom together, or that she would be the making of me; and I never had two days of foul weather all the time I was at sea in her; and after taking privateers enough to be very entertaining, I had the good luck, in my passage home the next autumn, to fall in with the very French frigate I wanted. – I brought her into Plymouth; and here was another instance of luck. We had not been six hours in the Sound, when a gale came on, which lasted four days and nights, and which would have done for poor old *Asp*, in half the time; our touch with the Great Nation not having much improved our condition. Four-and-twenty hours later, and I should only have been a gallant Captain Wentworth, in a small paragraph at one corner of the newspapers; and being lost in only a sloop, nobody would have thought about me.'

Anne's shudderings were to herself, alone; but the Miss Musgroves could be as open as they were sincere, in their exclamations of pity and horror.

'And so then, I suppose,' said Mrs Musgrove, in a low voice, as if thinking aloud, 'so then he went away to the *Laconia*, and there he met with our poor boy. – Charles, my dear,' (beckoning him to her), 'do ask Captain Wentworth where it was he first met with your poor brother. I always forget.'

'It was at Gibraltar, mother, I know. Dick had been left ill at Gibraltar, with a recommendation from his former captain to Captain Wentworth.'

'Oh! – but, Charles, tell Captain Wentworth, he need not be afraid of mentioning poor Dick before me, for it would be rather a pleasure to hear him talked of, by such a good friend.'

Charles, being somewhat more mindful of the probabilities of the case, only nodded in reply, and walked away.

The girls were now hunting for the *Laconia*; and Captain Wentworth could not deny himself the pleasure of taking the precious volume into his own hands to save them the trouble, and once more read aloud the little statement of her name and rate, and present non-commissioned class, observing over it that she too had been one of the best friends man ever had.

'Ah! those were pleasant days when I had the *Laconia*! How fast I made money in her. – A friend of mine, and I, had such a lovely cruise together off the Western Islands – Poor Harville, sister! You know how much he wanted money – worse than myself. He had a wife. – Excellent fellow! I shall never forget his happiness. He felt it all, so much for her sake. – I wished for him again the next summer, when I had still the same luck in the Mediterranean.'

'And I am sure, sir,' said Mrs Musgrove, 'it was a lucky day for *us*, when you were put captain into that ship. *We* shall never forget what you did.'

Her feelings made her speak low; and Captain Wentworth, hearing only in part, and probably not having Dick Musgrove at all near his thoughts, looked rather in suspense, and as if waiting for more.

'My brother,' whispered one of the girls; 'mamma is thinking of poor Richard.'

'Poor dear fellow!' continued Mrs Musgrove; 'he was grown so steady, and such an excellent correspondent, while he was under your care! Ah! it would have been a happy thing, if he had never left you. I assure you, Captain Wentworth, we are very sorry he ever left you.'

There was a momentary expression in Captain Wentworth's face at this speech, a certain glance of his bright eye, and curl of his handsome mouth, which convinced Anne that instead of sharing in Mrs Musgrove's kind wishes, as to her son, he had probably been at some pains to get rid of him; but it was too transient an indulgence of self-amusement to be detected by any who understood him less than herself; in another moment he was perfectly collected and serious; and almost instantly afterwards coming up to the sofa, on which she and Mrs Musgrove were sitting, took a place by the latter, and entered into conversation with her, in a low voice, about her son, doing it with so much sympathy and natural grace as showed the kindest consideration for all that was real and unabsurd in the parent's feelings.

They were actually on the same sofa, for Mrs Musgrove had most readily made room for him – they were divided only by Mrs Musgrove. It was no insignificant barrier indeed. Mrs Musgrove was of a comfortable substantial size, infinitely more fitted by nature to express good cheer and good humour than tenderness and sentiment; and while the agitations of Anne's slender form, and pensive face, may be considered as very completely screened, Captain Wentworth should be allowed some credit for the self-command with which he attended to her large, fat sighings over the destiny of a son, whom alive nobody had cared for.

Personal size and mental sorrow have certainly no necessary proportions. A large bulky figure has as good a right to be in deep affliction as the most graceful

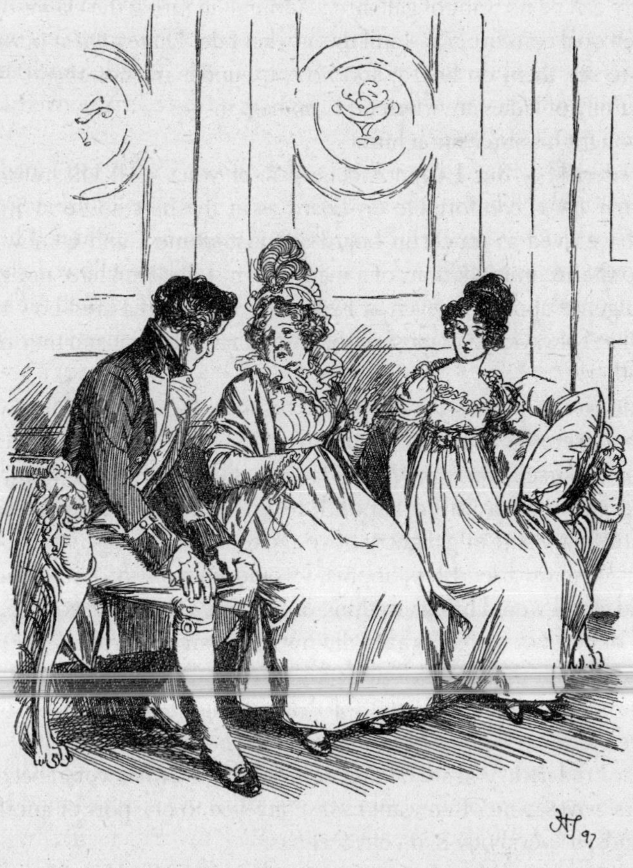

*He attended to her large, fat sighings*

set of limbs in the world. But, fair or not fair, there are unbecoming conjunctions, which reason will patronise in vain – which taste cannot tolerate – which ridicule will seize.

The Admiral, after taking two or three refreshing turns about the room with his hands behind him, being called to order by his wife, now came up to Captain Wentworth, and without any observation of what he might be interrupting, thinking only of his own thoughts, began with,

'If you had been a week later at Lisbon, last spring, Frederick, you would have been asked to give a passage to Lady Mary Grierson and her daughters.'

'Should I? I am glad I was not a week later then.'

The Admiral abused him for his want of gallantry. He defended himself; though professing that he would never willingly admit any ladies on board a ship of his, excepting for a ball, or a visit, which a few hours might comprehend.

'But, if I know myself,' said he, 'this is from no want of gallantry towards them. It is rather from feeling how impossible it is, with all one's efforts, and all one's sacrifices, to make the accommodations on board, such as women ought to have. There can be no want of gallantry, Admiral, in rating the claims of women to every personal comfort *high* – and this is what I do. I hate to hear of women on board, or to see them on board; and no ship, under my command, shall ever convey a family of ladies anywhere, if I can help it.'

This brought his sister upon him.

'Oh Frederick! – But I cannot believe it of you. – All idle refinement! – Women may be as comfortable on board as in the best house in England. I believe I have lived as much on board as most women, and I know nothing superior to the accommodations of a man-of-war. I declare I have not a comfort or an indulgence about me, even at Kellynch Hall' (with a kind bow to Anne), 'beyond what I always had in most of the ships I have lived in; and they have been five altogether.'

'Nothing to the purpose,' replied her brother. 'You were living with your husband; and were the only woman on board.'

'But you, yourself, brought Mrs Harville, her sister, her cousin, and the three children round from Portsmouth to Plymouth. Where was this superfine, extraordinary sort of gallantry of yours, then?'

'All merged in my friendship, Sophia. I would assist any brother-officer's wife that I could, and I would bring anything of Harville's from the world's end, if he wanted it. But do not imagine that I did not feel it an evil in itself.'

'Depend upon it they were all perfectly comfortable.'

'I might not like them the better for that, perhaps. Such a number of women and children have no *right* to be comfortable on board.'

'My dear Frederick, you are talking quite idly. Pray, what would become of us poor sailors' wives, who often want to be conveyed to one port or another, after our husbands, if everybody had your feelings?'

'My feelings, you see, did not prevent my taking Mrs Harville, and all her family, to Plymouth.'

'But I hate to hear you talking so, like a fine gentleman, and as if women were all fine ladies, instead of rational creatures. We none of us expect to be in smooth water all our days.'

'Ah! my dear,' said the Admiral, 'when he has got a wife, he will sing a different tune. When he is married, if we have the good luck to live to another war, we shall see him do as you and I, and a great many others, have done. We shall have him very thankful to anybody that will bring him his wife.'

'Ay, that we shall.'

'Now I have done,' cried Captain Wentworth. 'When once married people begin to attack me with, "Oh! you will think very differently, when you are married," I can only say, "No, I shall not;" and then they say again, "Yes, you will," and there is an end of it.'

He got up and moved away.

'What a great traveller you must have been, ma'am!' said Mrs Musgrove to Mrs Croft.

'Pretty well, ma'am, in the fifteen years of my marriage; though many women have done more. I have crossed the Atlantic four times, and have been once to the East Indies, and back again; and only once, besides being in different places about home – Cork, and Lisbon, and Gibraltar. But I never went beyond the Streights – and never was in the West Indies. We do not call Bermuda or Bahama, you know, the West Indies.'

Mrs Musgrove had not a word to say in dissent, she could not accuse herself of having ever called them anything in the whole course of her life.

'And I do assure you, ma'am,' pursued Mrs Croft, 'that nothing can exceed the accommodations of a man-of-war; I speak, you know, of the higher rates. When you come to a frigate, of course, you are more confined – though any reasonable woman may be perfectly happy in one of them; and I can safely say, that the happiest part of my life has been spent on board a ship. While we were together, you know, there was nothing to be feared. Thank God! I have always been blessed with excellent health, and no climate disagrees with me. A little disordered always the first twenty-four hours of going to sea, but never knew what sickness was afterwards. The only time that I ever really suffered in body or mind, the only time that I ever fancied myself unwell, or had any ideas of danger, was the winter that I passed by myself at Deal, when the Admiral (*Captain* Croft then) was in the North Seas. I lived in perpetual fright at that time, and had all manner of imaginary complaints from not knowing what to do with myself, or when I should hear from him next; but as long as we could be together, nothing ever ailed me, and I never met with the smallest inconvenience.'

'Ay, to be sure. – Yes, indeed, oh yes, I am quite of your opinion, Mrs Croft,' was Mrs Musgrove's hearty answer. 'There is nothing so bad as a separation. I am quite of your opinion. *I* know what it is, for Mr Musgrove always attends the assizes, and I am so glad when they are over, and he is safe back again.'

The evening ended with dancing. On its being proposed, Anne offered her services, as usual, and though her eyes would sometimes fill with tears as she sat at the instrument, she was extremely glad to be employed, and desired nothing in return but to be unobserved.

It was a merry, joyous party, and no one seemed in higher spirits than Captain Wentworth. She felt that he had everything to elevate him, which general attention and deference, and especially the attention of all the young women could do. The Miss Hayters, the females of the family of cousins already mentioned, were apparently admitted to the honour of being in love with him; and as for Henrietta and Louisa, they both seemed so entirely occupied by him that nothing but the continued appearance of the most perfect goodwill between themselves could have made it credible that they were not decided rivals. If he were a little spoiled by such universal, such eager admiration, who could wonder?

These were some of the thoughts which occupied Anne, while her fingers were mechanically at work, proceeding for half an hour together, equally without error, and without consciousness. *Once* she felt that he was looking at herself – observing her altered features, perhaps, trying to trace in them the ruins of the face which had once charmed him; and *once* she knew that he must have spoken of her; – she was hardly aware of it, till she heard the answer; but then she was sure of his having asked his partner whether Miss Elliot never danced? The answer was, 'Oh! no, never; she has quite given up dancing. She had rather play. She is never tired of playing.' Once, too, he spoke to her. She had left the instrument on the dancing being over, and he had sat down to try to make out an air which he wished to give the Miss Musgroves an idea of. Unintentionally she returned to that part of the room; he saw her, and, instantly rising, said, with studied politeness,

'I beg your pardon, madam, this is your seat;' and though she immediately drew back with a decided negative, he was not to be induced to sit down again.

Anne did not wish for more of such looks and speeches. His cold politeness, his ceremonious grace, were worse than anything.

## *Chapter 9*

Captain Wentworth was come to Kellynch as to a home, to stay as long as he liked, being as thoroughly the object of the Admiral's fraternal kindness as of his wife's. He had intended, on first arriving, to proceed very soon into Shropshire, and visit the brother settled in that county, but the attractions of Uppercross induced him to put this off. There was so much of friendliness, and of flattery, and of everything most bewitching in his reception there; the old were so hospitable, the young so agreeable, that he could not but resolve to remain where he was, and take all the charms and perfections of Edward's wife upon credit a little longer.

It was soon Uppercross with him almost every day. The Musgroves could hardly be more ready to invite than he to come, particularly in the morning, when he had no companion at home, for the Admiral and Mrs Croft were generally out-of-doors together, interesting themselves in their new possessions, their grass, and their sheep, and dawdling about in a way not endurable to a third person, or driving out in a gig, lately added to their establishment.

Hitherto there had been but one opinion of Captain Wentworth, among the Musgroves and their dependencies. It was unvarying, warm admiration everywhere. But this intimate footing was not more than established, when a certain Charles Hayter returned among them, to be a good deal disturbed by it, and to think Captain Wentworth very much in the way.

Charles Hayter was the eldest of all the cousins, and a very amiable, pleasing young man, between whom and Henrietta there had been a considerable appearance of attachment previous to Captain Wentworth's introduction. He was in orders, and having a curacy in the neighbourhood where residence was not required, lived at his father's house, only two miles from Uppercross. A short absence from home had left his fair one unguarded by his attentions at this critical period, and when he came back he had the pain of finding very altered manners, and of seeing Captain Wentworth.

Mrs Musgrove and Mrs Hayter were sisters. They had each had money, but their marriages had made a material difference in their degree of consequence. Mr Hayter had some property of his own, but it was insignificant compared with Mr Musgrove's; and while the Musgroves were in the first class of society in the country, the young Hayters would, from their parents' inferior, retired, and unpolished way of living, and their own defective education, have been hardly in any class at all, but for their connection with Uppercross; this eldest son of course excepted, who had chosen to be a scholar and a gentleman, and who was very superior in cultivation and manners to all the rest.

The two families had always been on excellent terms, there being no pride on one side, and no envy on the other, and only such a consciousness of superiority in the Miss Musgroves, as made them pleased to improve their cousins. Charles's attentions to Henrietta had been observed by her father and mother without any disapprobation. 'It would not be a great match for her; but if Henrietta liked him,' – and Henrietta *did* seem to like him.

Henrietta fully thought so herself, before Captain Wentworth came; but from that time Cousin Charles had been very much forgotten.

Which of the two sisters was preferred by Captain Wentworth was as yet quite doubtful, as far as Anne's observation reached. Henrietta was perhaps the prettiest, Louisa had the higher spirits, and she knew not *now*, whether the more gentle or the more lively character were most likely to attract him.

Mr and Mrs Musgrove, either from seeing little, or from an entire confidence in the discretion of both their daughters, and of all the young men who came near them, seemed to leave everything to take its chance. There was not the smallest appearance of solicitude or remark about them, in the Mansion House; but it was different at the Cottage: the young couple there were more disposed to speculate and wonder; and Captain Wentworth had not been above four or five times in the Miss Musgroves' company, and Charles Hayter had but just reappeared, when Anne had to listen to the opinions of her brother and sister, as to *which* was the one liked best. Charles gave it for Louisa, Mary for

Henrietta, but quite agreeing that to have him marry either would be extremely delightful.

Charles 'had never seen a pleasanter man in his life; and, from what he had once heard Captain Wentworth himself say, was very sure that he had not made less than twenty thousand pounds by the war. Here was a fortune at once; besides which, there would be the chance of what might be done in any future war; and he was sure Captain Wentworth was as likely a man to distinguish himself as any officer in the navy. Oh! it would be a capital match for either of his sisters.'

'Upon my word it would,' replied Mary. 'Dear me! If he should rise to any very great honours! If he should ever be made a baronet! "Lady Wentworth" sounds very well. That would be a noble thing, indeed, for Henrietta! She would take place of me then, and Henrietta would not dislike that. Sir Frederick and Lady Wentworth! It would be but a new creation, however, and I never think much of your new creations.'

It suited Mary best to think Henrietta the one preferred, on the very account of Charles Hayter, whose pretensions she wished to see put an end to. She looked down very decidedly upon the Hayters, and thought it would be quite a misfortune to have the existing connection between the families renewed – very sad for herself and her children.

'You know,' said she, 'I cannot think him at all a fit match for Henrietta; and considering the alliances which the Musgroves have made, she has no right to throw herself away. I do not think any young woman has a right to make a choice that may be disagreeable and inconvenient to the *principal* part of her family, and be giving bad connections to those who have not been used to them. And, pray, who is Charles Hayter? Nothing but a country curate. A most improper match for Miss Musgrove, of Uppercross.'

Her husband, however, would not agree with her here; for besides having a regard for his cousin, Charles Hayter was an eldest son, and he saw things as an eldest son himself.

'Now you are talking nonsense, Mary,' was therefore his answer. 'It would not be a *great* match for Henrietta, but Charles has a very fair chance, through the Spicers, of getting something from the Bishop in the course of a year or two; and you will please to remember that he is the eldest son; whenever my uncle dies, he steps into very pretty property. The estate at Winthrop is not less than two hundred and fifty acres, besides the farm near Taunton, which is some of the best land in the country. I grant you, that any of them but Charles would be a very shocking match for Henrietta, and indeed it could not be; he is the only one that could be possible; but he is a very good-natured, good sort of a fellow; and whenever Winthrop comes into his hands, he will make a different sort of place of it, and live in a very different sort of way; and with that property, he will never be a contemptible man. Good, freehold property. No, no; Henrietta might do worse than marry Charles Hayter; and if she has him, and Louisa can get Captain Wentworth, I shall be very well satisfied.'

'Charles may say what he pleases,' cried Mary to Anne, as soon as he was out of the room, 'but it would be shocking to have Henrietta marry Charles Hayter; a very bad thing for *her*, and still worse for *me*; and therefore it is very much to be wished that Captain Wentworth may soon put him quite out of her head, and I have very little doubt that he has. She took hardly any notice of Charles Hayter yesterday. I wish you had been there to see her behaviour. And as to Captain Wentworth's liking Louisa as well as Henrietta, it is nonsense to say so; for he certainly *does* like Henrietta a great deal the best. But Charles is so positive! I wish you had been with us yesterday, for then you might have decided between us; and I am sure you would have thought as I did, unless you had been determined to give it against me.'

A dinner at Mr Musgrove's had been the occasion when all these things should have been seen by Anne; but she had stayed at home, under the mixed plea of a headache of her own, and some return of indisposition in little Charles. She had thought only of avoiding Captain Wentworth; but an escape from being appealed to as umpire was now added to the advantages of a quiet evening.

As to Captain Wentworth's views, she deemed it of more consequence that he should know his own mind, early enough not to be endangering the happiness of either sister, or impeaching his own honour, than that he should prefer Henrietta to Louisa, or Louisa to Henrietta. Either of them would, in all probability, make him an affectionate, good-humoured wife. With regard to Charles Hayter, she had delicacy which must be pained by any lightness of conduct in a well-meaning young woman, and a heart to sympathise in any of the sufferings it occasioned; but if Henrietta found herself mistaken in the nature of her feelings, the alteration could not be understood too soon.

Charles Hayter had met with much to disquiet and mortify him in his cousin's behaviour. She had too old a regard for him to be so wholly estranged as might in two meetings extinguish every past hope, and leave him nothing to do but to keep away from Uppercross; but there was such a change as became very alarming when such a man as Captain Wentworth was to be regarded as the probable cause. He had been absent only two Sundays; and when they parted, had left her interested, even to the height of his wishes, in his prospect of soon quitting his present curacy, and obtaining that of Uppercross instead. It had then seemed the object nearest her heart that Dr Shirley, the rector, who for more than forty years had been zealously discharging all the duties of his office, but was now growing too infirm for many of them, should be quite fixed on engaging a curate; should make his curacy quite as good as he could afford, and should give Charles Hayter the promise of it. The advantage of his having to come only to Uppercross, instead of going six miles another way; of his having in every respect, a better curacy; of his belonging to their dear Dr Shirley, and of dear, good Dr Shirley's being relieved from the duty which he could no longer get through without most injurious fatigue, had been a great deal, even to Louisa, but had been almost everything to Henrietta. When he came back, alas! the zeal of the business was gone by. Louisa could not listen at all to his account of a conversation which he had just held with Dr Shirley: she was at the window, looking out for Captain Wentworth; and even Henrietta had at best only a divided attention to give, and seemed to have forgotten all the former doubt and solicitude of the negotiation.

'Well, I am very glad indeed, but I always thought you would have it; I always thought you sure. It did not appear to me that – in short, you know, Dr Shirley *must* have a curate, and you had secured his promise. Is he coming, Louisa?'

One morning, very soon after the dinner at the Musgroves, at which Anne had not been present, Captain Wentworth walked into the drawing-room at the Cottage, where were only herself and the little invalid Charles, who was lying on the sofa.

The surprise of finding himself almost alone with Anne Elliot deprived his manners of their usual composure: he started, and could only say, 'I thought the Miss Musgroves had been here – Mrs Musgrove told me I should find them here,' before he walked to the window to recollect himself, and feel how he ought to behave.

'They are upstairs with my sister – they will be down in a few moments, I dare say,' had been Anne's reply, in all the confusion that was natural; and if the child had not called her to come and do something for him, she would have been out of the room the next moment, and released Captain Wentworth as well as herself.

He continued at the window; and after calmly and politely saying, 'I hope the little boy is better,' was silent. She was obliged to kneel down by the sofa, and remain there to satisfy her patient; and thus they continued a few minutes, when, to her very great satisfaction, she heard some other person crossing the little vestibule. She hoped, on turning her head, to see the master of the house; but it proved to be one much less calculated for making matters easy – Charles Hayter, probably not at all better pleased by the sight of Captain Wentworth than Captain Wentworth had been by the sight of Anne.

She only attempted to say, 'How do you do? Will not you sit down? The others will be here presently.'

Captain Wentworth, however, came from his window, apparently not ill-disposed for conversation; but Charles Hayter soon put an end to his attempts by seating himself near the table, and taking up the newspaper; and Captain Wentworth returned to his window.

Another minute brought another addition. The younger boy, a remarkable stout, forward child, of two years old, having got the door opened for him by someone without, made his determined appearance among them, and went straight to the sofa to see what was going on, and put in his claim to anything good that might be giving away.

There being nothing to be eat, he could only have some play; and as his aunt would not let him tease his sick brother, he began to fasten himself upon her, as she knelt, in such a way that, busy as she was about Charles, she could not shake him off. She spoke to him – ordered, entreated, and insisted in vain. Once she did contrive to push him away, but the boy had the greater pleasure in getting upon her back again directly.

'Walter,' said she, 'get down this moment. You are extremely troublesome. I am very angry with you.'

'Walter,' cried Charles Hayter, 'why do you not do as you are bid? Do not you hear your aunt speak? Come to me, Walter, come to Cousin Charles.'

But not a bit did Walter stir.

In another moment, however, she found herself in the state of being released from him; someone was taking him from her, though he had bent down her head so much that his little sturdy hands were unfastened from around her neck, and he was resolutely borne away before she knew that Captain Wentworth had done it.

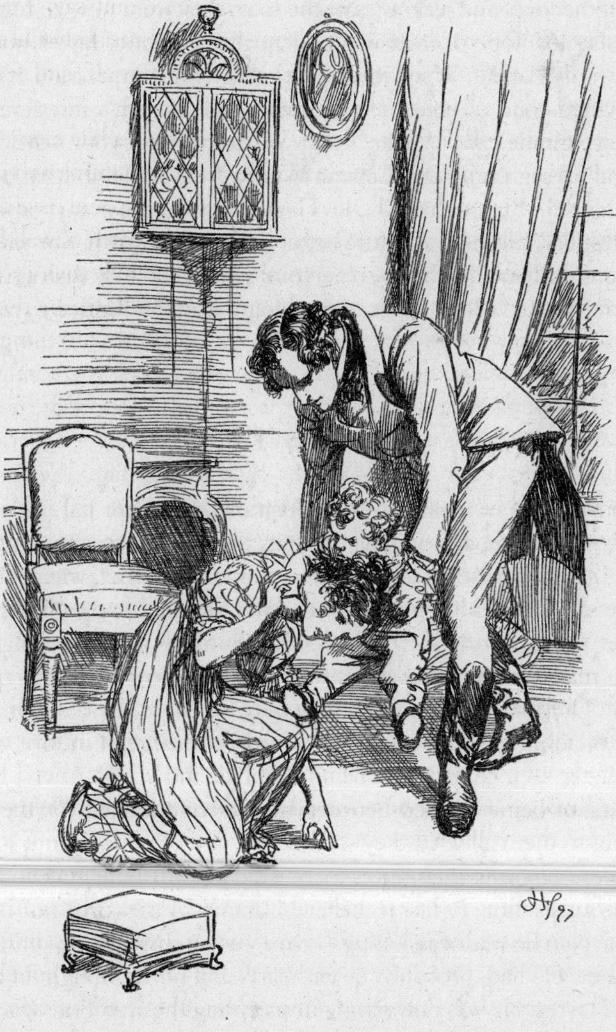

*Someone was taking him from her*

Her sensations on the discovery made her perfectly speechless. She could not even thank him. She could only hang over little Charles, with most disordered feelings. His kindness in stepping forward to her relief – the manner – the silence in which it had passed – the little particulars of the circumstance – with the conviction soon forced on her, by the noise he was studiously making with the child, that he meant to avoid hearing her thanks, and rather sought to testify that her conversation was the last of his wants, produced such a confusion of varying, but very painful agitation, as she could not recover from, till enabled by the entrance of Mary and the Miss Musgroves to make over her little patient to their cares, and leave the room. She could not stay. It might have been an opportunity of watching the loves and jealousies of the four; they were now all together, but she could stay for none of it. It was evident that Charles Hayter was not well inclined towards Captain Wentworth. She had a strong impression of his having said, in a vexed tone of voice, after Captain Wentworth's interference, 'You ought to have minded *me*, Walter; I told you not to tease your aunt;' and could comprehend his regretting that Captain Wentworth should do what he ought to have done himself. But neither Charles Hayter's feelings, nor anybody's feelings, could interest her, till she had a little better arranged her own. She was ashamed of herself, quite ashamed of being so nervous, so overcome by such a trifle; but so it was; and it required a long application of solitude and reflection to recover her.

## *Chapter 10*

Other opportunities of making her observations could not fail to occur. Anne had soon been in company with all the four together often enough to have an opinion, though too wise to acknowledge as much at home, where she knew it would have satisfied neither husband nor wife; for while she considered Louisa to be rather the favourite, she could not but think, as far as she might dare to judge from memory and experience, that Captain Wentworth was not in love with either. They were more in love with him; yet there it was not love. It was a little fever of admiration; but it might, probably must, end in love with some. Charles Hayter seemed aware of being slighted, and yet Henrietta had sometimes the air of being divided between them. Anne longed for the power of representing to them all what they were about, and of pointing out some of the evils they were exposing themselves to. She did not attribute guile to any. It was the highest satisfaction to her to believe Captain Wentworth not in the least aware of the pain he was occasioning. There was no triumph, no pitiful triumph in his manner. He had, probably, never heard, and never thought of any claims of Charles Hayter. He was only wrong in accepting the attentions (for accepting must be the word) of two young women at once.

After a short struggle, however, Charles Hayter seemed to quit the field. Three days had passed without his coming once to Uppercross; a most decided change. He had even refused one regular invitation to dinner; and having been found on the occasion by Mr Musgrove with some large books before him, Mr and Mrs Musgrove were sure all could not be right, and talked, with grave faces, of his studying himself to death. It was Mary's hope and belief that he had received a positive dismissal from Henrietta, and her husband lived under the constant dependence of seeing him tomorrow. Anne could only feel that Charles Hayter was wise.

One morning, about this time, Charles Musgrove and Captain Wentworth being gone a-shooting together, as the sisters in the Cottage were sitting quietly at work, they were visited at the window by the sisters from the Mansion House.

It was a very fine November day, and the Miss Musgroves came through the little grounds, and stopped for no other purpose than to say that they were going to take a *long* walk, and, therefore, concluded Mary could not like to go with them; and when Mary immediately replied, with some jealousy, at not being supposed a good walker, 'Oh, yes, I should like to join you very much, I am very fond of a long walk,' Anne felt persuaded, by the looks of the two girls, that it was precisely what they did not wish, and admired again the sort of necessity which the family habits seemed to produce, of everything being to be communicated, and everything being to be done together, however undesired and inconvenient. She tried to dissuade Mary from going, but in vain; and that being the case, thought it best to accept the Miss Musgroves' much more cordial invitation to herself to go likewise, as she might be useful in turning back with her sister, and lessening the interference in any plan of their own.

'I cannot imagine why they should suppose I should not like a long walk!' said Mary, as she went upstairs. 'Everybody is always supposing that I am not a good walker! And yet they would not have been pleased, if we had refused to join them. When people come in this manner on purpose to ask us, how can one say no?'

Just as they were setting off, the gentlemen returned. They had taken out a young dog, who had spoiled their sport, and sent them back early. Their time and strength, and spirits, were, therefore, exactly ready for this walk, and they entered into it with pleasure. Could Anne have foreseen such a junction, she would have stayed at home; but, from some feelings of interest and curiosity, she fancied now that it was too late to retract, and the whole six set forward together in the direction chosen by the Miss Musgroves, who evidently considered the walk as under their guidance.

Anne's object was not to be in the way of anybody, and where the narrow paths across the fields made many separations necessary, to keep with her brother and sister. Her *pleasure* in the walk must arise from the exercise and the day, from the view of the last smiles of the year upon the tawny leaves and withered hedges, and from repeating to herself some few of the thousand poetical descriptions extant of autumn, that season of peculiar and inexhaustible influence on the mind of taste and tenderness, that season which has drawn from every poet, worthy of being read, some attempt at description, or some lines of feeling. She occupied her mind as much as possible in such like musings and quotations; but it was not possible that when within reach of Captain Wentworth's conversation with either of the Miss Musgroves, she should not try to hear it; yet she caught little very remarkable. It was mere lively chat – such as any young persons, on an intimate footing, might fall into. He was more engaged with Louisa than with Henrietta. Louisa certainly put more forward for his notice than her sister. This distinction appeared to increase, and there was one speech of Louisa's which struck her. After one of the many praises of the day, which were continually bursting forth, Captain Wentworth added,

'What glorious weather for the Admiral and my sister! They meant to take a long drive this morning; perhaps we may hail them from some of these hills. They talked of coming into this side of the country. I wonder whereabouts they will upset today. Oh! it does happen very often, I assure you – but my sister makes nothing of it – she would as lieve be tossed out as not.'

'Ah! You make the most of it, I know,' cried Louisa, 'but if it were really so, I should do just the same in her place. If I loved a man, as she loves the Admiral, I would be always with him, nothing should ever separate us, and I would rather be overturned by him than driven safely by anybody else.'

It was spoken with enthusiasm.

'Had you?' cried he, catching the same tone; 'I honour you!' And there was silence between them for a little while.

Anne could not immediately fall into a quotation again. The sweet scenes of autumn were for a while put by – unless some tender sonnet, fraught with the apt analogy of the declining year, with declining happiness, and the images of youth and hope, and spring, all gone together, blessed her memory. She roused herself to say, as they struck by order into another path, 'Is not this one of the ways to Winthrop?' But nobody heard, or, at least, nobody answered her.

Winthrop, however, or its environs – for young men are, sometimes, to be met with, strolling about near home – was their destination; and after another half-mile of gradual ascent through large enclosures, where the ploughs at work, and the fresh-made path spoke the farmer, counteracting the sweets of poetical despondence, and meaning to have spring again, they gained the summit of the most considerable hill, which parted Uppercross and Winthrop, and soon commanded a full view of the latter, at the foot of the hill on the other side.

Winthrop, without beauty and without dignity, was stretched before them; an indifferent house, standing low, and hemmed in by the barns and buildings of a farmyard.

Mary exclaimed, 'Bless me! here is Winthrop – I declare I had no idea! – well, now I think we had better turn back; I am excessively tired.'

Henrietta, conscious and ashamed, and seeing no Cousin Charles walking along any path, or leaning against any gate, was ready to do as Mary wished; but 'No,' said Charles Musgrove, 'And no, no,' cried Louisa more eagerly, and taking her sister aside, seemed to be arguing the matter warmly.

Charles, in the meanwhile, was very decidedly declaring his resolution of calling on his aunt, now that he was so near; and very evidently, though more fearfully, trying to induce his wife to go too. But this was one of the points on which the lady showed her strength, and when he recommended the advantage of resting herself a quarter of an hour at Winthrop, as she felt so tired, she resolutely answered, 'Oh! no, indeed! – walking up that hill again would do her more harm than any sitting down could do her good;' and, in short, her look and manner declared, that go she would not.

After a little succession of these sort of debates and consultations, it was settled between Charles and his two sisters, that he, and Henrietta, should just run down for a few minutes, to see their aunt and cousins, while the rest of the party waited for them at the top of the hill. Louisa seemed the principal arranger of the plan; and, as she went a little way with them, down the hill, still talking to Henrietta, Mary took the opportunity of looking scornfully around her, and saying to Captain Wentworth,

'It is very unpleasant, having such connections! But I assure you, I have never been in the house above twice in my life.'

She received no other answer, than an artificial, assenting smile, followed by a contemptuous glance, as he turned away, which Anne perfectly knew the meaning of.

The brow of the hill, where they remained, was a cheerful spot; Louisa returned, and Mary, finding a comfortable seat for herself, on the step of a stile, was very well satisfied so long as the others all stood about her; but when Louisa drew Captain Wentworth away, to try for a gleaning of nuts in an adjoining hedgerow, and they were gone by degrees quite out of sight and sound, Mary was happy no longer; she quarrelled with her own seat – was sure Louisa had got a much better somewhere – and nothing could prevent her from going to look for a better also. She turned through the same gate – but could not see them. – Anne found a nice seat for her, on a dry sunny bank, under the hedgerow, in which she had no doubt of their still being – in some spot or other. Mary sat down for a moment, but it would not do; she was sure Louisa had found a better seat somewhere else, and she would go on, till she overtook her.

Anne, really tired herself, was glad to sit down; and she very soon heard Captain Wentworth and Louisa in the hedgerow, behind her, as if making their way back, along the rough, wild sort of channel, down the centre. They were speaking as they drew near. Louisa's voice was the first distinguished. She seemed to be in the middle of some eager speech. What Anne first heard was,

'And so, I made her go. I could not bear that she should be frightened from the visit by such nonsense. What! – would I be turned back from doing a thing that I had determined to do, and that I knew to be right, by the airs and interference of such a person? – or, of any person I may say. No – I have no idea of being so easily persuaded. When I have made up my mind, I have made it. And Henrietta seemed entirely to have made up hers to call at Winthrop today – and yet, she was as near giving it up, out of nonsensical complaisance!'

'She would have turned back then, but for you?'

'She would indeed. I am almost ashamed to say it.'

'Happy for her, to have such a mind as yours at hand! – After the hints you gave just now, which did but confirm my own observations, the last time I was in company with him, I need not affect to have no comprehension of what is going on. I see that more than a mere dutiful morning visit to your aunt was in question – and woe betide him, and her too, when it comes to things of consequence, when they are placed in circumstances, requiring fortitude and strength of mind, if she have not resolution enough to resist idle interference in such a trifle as this. Your sister is an amiable creature; but *yours* is the character of decision and firmness, I see. If you value her conduct or happiness, infuse as much of your own spirit into her as you can. But this, no doubt, you have been always doing. It is the worst evil of too yielding and indecisive a character, that no influence over it can be depended on. – You are never sure of a good impression being durable. Everybody may sway it; let those who would be happy be firm. – Here is a nut,' said he, catching one down from an upper bough. 'To exemplify – a beautiful glossy nut, which, blessed with original strength, has outlived all the storms of autumn. Not a puncture, not a weak spot anywhere. – This nut,' he continued, with playful solemnity, 'while so many of its brethren have fallen and been trodden under foot, is still in possession of all the happiness that a hazelnut can be supposed capable of.' Then, returning to his former earnest tone: 'My first wish for all whom I am interested in, is that they should be firm. If Louisa Musgrove would be beautiful and happy in her November of life, she will cherish all her present powers of mind.'

He had done – and was unanswered. It would have surprised Anne if Louisa could have readily answered such a speech – words of such interest, spoken with such serious warmth! – she could imagine what Louisa was feeling. For herself – she feared to move, lest she should be seen. While she remained, a bush of low rambling holly protected her, and they were moving on. Before they were beyond her hearing, however, Louisa spoke again.

'Mary is good-natured enough in many respects,' said she; 'but she does sometimes provoke me excessively, by her nonsense and her pride; the Elliot pride. She has a great deal too much of the Elliot pride. – We do so wish that Charles had married Anne instead. – I suppose you know he wanted to marry Anne?'

After a moment's pause, Captain Wentworth said,

'Do you mean that she refused him?'

'Oh! yes, certainly.'

'When did that happen?'

'I do not exactly know, for Henrietta and I were at school at the time; but I believe about a year before he married Mary. I wish she had accepted him. We should all have liked her a great deal better; and papa and mamma always think it was her great friend Lady Russell's doing, that she did not. – They think Charles might not be learned and bookish enough to please Lady Russell, and that, therefore, she persuaded Anne to refuse him.'

The sounds were retreating, and Anne distinguished no more. Her own emotions still kept her fixed. She had much to recover from before she could move. The listener's proverbial fate was not absolutely hers; she had heard no evil of herself – but she had heard a great deal of very painful import. She saw how her own character was considered by Captain Wentworth; and there had been just that degree of feeling and curiosity about her in his manner which must give her extreme agitation.

As soon as she could, she went after Mary, and having found, and walked back with her to their former station, by the stile, felt some comfort in their whole party being immediately afterwards collected, and once more in motion together. Her spirits wanted the solitude and silence which only numbers could give.

Charles and Henrietta returned, bringing, as may be conjectured, Charles Hayter with them. The minutiae of the business Anne could not attempt to understand; even Captain Wentworth did not seem admitted to perfect confidence here; but that there had been a withdrawing on the gentleman's side, and a relenting on the lady's, and that they were now very glad to be together again, did not admit a doubt. Henrietta looked a little ashamed, but very well pleased – Charles Hayter exceedingly happy, and they were devoted to each other almost from the first instant of their all setting forward for Uppercross.

Everything now marked out Louisa for Captain Wentworth; nothing could be plainer; and where many divisions were necessary, or even where they were not, they walked side by side, nearly as much as the other two. In a long strip of meadow land, where there was ample space for all, they were thus divided – forming three distinct parties; and to that party of the three which boasted least animation, and least complaisance, Anne necessarily belonged. She joined Charles and Mary, and was tired enough to be very glad of Charles's other arm – but Charles, though in very good humour with her, was out of temper with his wife. Mary had shown herself disobliging to him, and was now to reap the consequence, which consequence was his dropping her arm almost every moment, to cut off the heads of some nettles in the hedge with his switch; and when Mary began to complain of it, and lament her being ill-used, according to custom, in being on the hedge side, while Anne was never incommoded on the other, he dropped the arms of both to hunt after a weasel which he had a momentary glance of; and they could hardly get him along at all.

This long meadow bordered a lane, which their footpath, at the end of it, was to cross; and when the party had all reached the gate of exit, the carriage advancing in the same direction, which had been some time heard, was just coming up, and proved to be Admiral Croft's gig. – He and his wife had taken their intended drive, and were returning home. Upon hearing how long a walk the young people had engaged in, they kindly offered a seat to any lady who might be particularly tired; it would save her full a mile, and they were going through Uppercross. The invitation was general, and generally declined. The Miss Musgroves were not at all tired, and Mary was either offended, by not being asked before any of the others, or what Louisa called the Elliot pride could not endure to make a third in a one-horse chaise.

The walking-party had crossed the lane and were surmounting an opposite stile; and the Admiral was putting his horse into motion again, when Captain Wentworth cleared the hedge in a moment to say something to his sister. – The something might be guessed by its effects.

'Miss Elliot, I am sure *you* are tired,' cried Mrs Croft. 'Do let us have the pleasure of taking you home. Here is excellent room for three, I assure you. If we were all like you, I believe we might sit four. – You must, indeed, you must.'

Anne was still in the lane; and though instinctively beginning to decline, she was not allowed to proceed. The Admiral's kind urgency came in support of his wife's; they would not be refused; they compressed themselves into the smallest possible space to leave her a corner, and Captain Wentworth, without saying a word, turned to her, and quietly obliged her to be assisted into the carriage.

Yes – he had done it. She was in the carriage, and felt that he had placed her there, that his will and his hands had done it, that she owed it to his perception of her fatigue, and his resolution to give her rest. She was very much affected by the view of his disposition towards her which all these things made apparent. This little circumstance seemed the completion of all that had gone before. She understood him. He could not forgive her – but he could not be unfeeling. Though condemning her for the past, and considering it with high and unjust resentment, though perfectly careless of her, and though becoming attached to another, still he could not see her suffer without the desire of giving her relief. It was a remainder of former sentiment; it was an impulse of pure, though unacknowledged friendship; it was a proof of his own warm and amiable heart, which she could not contemplate without emotions so compounded of pleasure and pain that she knew not which prevailed.

Her answers to the kindness and the remarks of her companions were at first unconsciously given. They had travelled half their way along the rough lane before she was quite awake to what they said. She then found them talking of 'Frederick'.

'He certainly means to have one or other of those two girls, Sophy,' said the Admiral; 'but there is no saying which. He has been running after them, too, long enough, one would think, to make up his mind. Ay, this comes of the peace. If it were war, now, he would have settled it long ago. – We sailors, Miss Elliot, cannot afford to make long courtships in time of war. How many days was it, my dear, between the first time of my seeing you, and our sitting down together in our lodgings at North Yarmouth?'

'We had better not talk about it, my dear,' replied Mrs Croft, pleasantly; 'for if Miss Elliot were to hear how soon we came to an understanding, she would never be persuaded that we could be happy together. I had known you by character, however, long before.'

'Well, and I had heard of you as a very pretty girl; and what were we to wait for besides? – I do not like having such things so long in hand. I wish Frederick would spread a little more canvas, and bring us home one of these young ladies to Kellynch. Then, there would always be company for them. – And very nice young ladies they both are; I hardly know one from the other.'

'Very good-humoured, unaffected girls, indeed,' said Mrs Croft, in a tone of calmer praise, such as made Anne suspect that her keener powers might not consider either of them as quite worthy of her brother; 'and a very respectable family. One could not be connected with better people – My dear Admiral, that post! – we shall certainly take that post.'

But by coolly giving the reins a better direction herself they happily passed the danger; and by once afterwards judiciously putting out her hand they neither fell into a rut, or ran foul of a dung-cart; and Anne, with some amusement at their style of driving, which she imagined no bad representation of the general guidance of their affairs, found herself safely deposited by them at the Cottage.

## Chapter *11*

The time now approached for Lady Russell's return; the day was even fixed, and Anne, being engaged to join her as soon as she was resettled, was looking forward to an early removal to Kellynch, and beginning to think how her own comfort was likely to be affected by it.

It would place her in the same village with Captain Wentworth, within half a mile of him; they would have to frequent the same church, and there must be intercourse between the two families. This was against her; but, on the other hand, he spent so much of his time at Uppercross that in removing thence she might be considered rather as leaving him behind, than as going towards him; and, upon the whole, she believed she must, on this interesting question, be the gainer, almost as certainly as in her change of domestic society, in leaving poor Mary for Lady Russell.

She wished it might be possible for her to avoid ever seeing Captain Wentworth at the Hall – those rooms had witnessed former meetings which would be brought too painfully before her; but she was yet more anxious for the possibility of Lady Russell and Captain Wentworth never meeting anywhere. They did not like each other, and no renewal of acquaintance now could do any good; and were Lady Russell to see them together, she might think that he had too much self-possession, and she too little.

These points formed her chief solicitude in anticipating her removal from Uppercross, where she felt she had been stationed quite long enough. Her usefulness to little Charles would always give some sweetness to the memory of her two months' visit there, but he was gaining strength apace, and she had nothing else to stay for.

The conclusion of her visit, however, was diversified in a way which she had not at all imagined. Captain Wentworth, after being unseen and unheard of at Uppercross for two whole days, appeared again among them to justify himself by a relation of what had kept him away.

A letter from his friend, Captain Harville, having found him out at last, had brought intelligence of Captain Harville's being settled with his family at Lyme for the winter; of their being, therefore, quite unknowingly, within twenty miles of each other. Captain Harville had never been in good health since a severe wound which he received two years before, and Captain Wentworth's anxiety to see him had determined him to go immediately to Lyme. He had been there for four-and-twenty hours. His acquittal was complete, his friendship warmly honoured, a lively interest excited for his friend, and his description of the fine country about Lyme so feelingly attended to by the party, that an earnest desire to see Lyme themselves, and a project for going thither was the consequence.

The young people were all wild to see Lyme. Captain Wentworth talked of going there again himself; it was only seventeen miles from Uppercross; though November, the weather was by no means bad; and, in short, Louisa, who was the most eager of the eager, having formed the resolution to go, and besides the pleasure of doing as she liked, being now armed with the idea of merit in maintaining her own way, bore down all the wishes of her father and mother for putting it off till summer; and to Lyme they were to go – Charles, Mary, Anne, Henrietta, Louisa, and Captain Wentworth.

The first heedless scheme had been to go in the morning and return at night, but to this Mr Musgrove, for the sake of his horses, would not consent; and when it came to be rationally considered, a day in the middle of November would not leave much time for seeing a new place, after deducting seven hours, as the nature of the country required, for going and returning. They were consequently to stay the night there, and not to be expected back till the next day's dinner. This was felt to be a considerable amendment; and though they all met at the Great House at rather an early breakfast hour, and set off very punctually, it was so much past noon before the two carriages, Mr Musgrove's coach containing the four ladies, and Charles's curricle, in which he drove Captain Wentworth, were descending the long hill into Lyme, and entering upon the still steeper street of the town itself, that it was very evident they would not have more than time for looking about them, before the light and warmth of the day were gone.

After securing accommodations, and ordering a dinner at one of the inns, the next thing to be done was unquestionably to walk directly down to the sea. They were come too late in the year for any amusement or variety which Lyme, as a public place, might offer: the rooms were shut up, the lodgers almost all gone, scarcely any family but of the residents left. – And, as there is nothing to admire in the buildings themselves, the remarkable situation of the town, the principal street almost hurrying into the water, the walk to the Cobb, skirting round the pleasant little bay, which in the season is animated with bathing machines and company; the Cobb itself, its old wonders and new improvements, with the very beautiful line of cliffs stretching out to the east of the town, are what the stranger's eye will seek; and a very strange stranger it must be, who does not see charms in the immediate environs of Lyme, to make him wish to know it better. The scenes in its neighbourhood, Charmouth, with its high grounds and extensive sweeps of country, and still more its sweet retired bay, backed by dark cliffs, where fragments of low rock among the sands make it the happiest spot for watching the flow of the tide, for sitting in unwearied contemplation; the woody varieties of the cheerful village of Up

Lyme; and, above all, Pinny, with its green chasms between romantic rocks, where the scattered forest trees and orchards of luxuriant growth declare that many a generation must have passed away since the first partial falling of the cliff prepared the ground for such a state, where a scene so wonderful and so lovely is exhibited, as may more than equal any of the resembling scenes of the far-famed Isle of Wight: these places must be visited, and visited again, to make the worth of Lyme understood.

The party from Uppercross passing down by the now deserted – and melancholy-looking rooms, and still descending, soon found themselves on the seashore, and lingering only, as all must linger and gaze on a first return to the sea, who ever deserve to look on it at all, proceeded towards the Cobb, equally their object in itself and on Captain Wentworth's account; for in a small house, near the foot of an old pier of unknown date, were the Harvilles settled. Captain Wentworth turned in to call on his friend; the others walked on, and he was to join them on the Cobb.

They were by no means tired of wondering and admiring; and not even Louisa seemed to feel that they had parted with Captain Wentworth long, when they saw him coming after them, with three companions, all well known already by description to be Captain and Mrs Harville, and a Captain Benwick, who was staying with them.

Captain Benwick had some time ago been first lieutenant of the *Laconia*; and the account which Captain Wentworth had given of him, on his return from Lyme before; his warm praise of him as an excellent young man and an officer, whom he had always valued highly, which must have stamped him well in the esteem of every listener, had been followed by a little history of his private life, which rendered him perfectly interesting in the eyes of all the ladies. He had been engaged to Captain Harville's sister, and was now mourning her loss. They had been a year or two waiting for fortune and promotion. Fortune came, his prize-money as lieutenant being great – promotion, too, came at last; but Fanny Harville did not live to know it. She had died the preceding summer, while he was at sea. Captain Wentworth believed it impossible for man to be more attached to woman than poor Benwick had been to Fanny Harville, or to be more deeply afflicted under the dreadful change. He considered his disposition as of the sort which must suffer heavily, uniting very strong feelings with quiet, serious, and retiring manners, and a decided taste for reading, and sedentary pursuits. To finish the interest of the story, the friendship between him and the Harvilles seemed, if possible, augmented by the event which closed all their views of alliance, and Captain Benwick was now living with them entirely. Captain Harville had taken his present house for half a year, his taste, and his health, and his fortune all directing him to a residence unexpensive, and by the sea; and the grandeur of the country, and the retirement of Lyme in the winter, appeared exactly adapted to Captain Benwick's state of mind. The sympathy and goodwill excited towards Captain Benwick was very great.

'And yet,' said Anne to herself, as they now moved forward to meet the party, 'he has not, perhaps, a more sorrowing heart than I have. I cannot believe his prospects so blighted forever. He is younger than I am; younger in feeling, if not in fact; younger as a man. He will rally again, and be happy with another.'

They all met, and were introduced. Captain Harville was a tall, dark man, with a sensible, benevolent countenance; a little lame; and from strong features, and want of health, looking much older than Captain Wentworth. Captain Benwick looked and was the youngest of the three, and, compared with either of them, a little man. He had a pleasing face and a melancholy air, just as he ought to have, and drew back from conversation.

Captain Harville, though not equalling Captain Wentworth in manners, was a perfect gentleman, unaffected, warm, and obliging. Mrs Harville, a degree less polished than her husband, seemed however to have the same good feelings; and nothing could be more pleasant than their desire of considering the whole party as friends of their own, because the friends of Captain Wentworth, or more kindly hospitable than their entreaties for their all promising to dine with them. The dinner, already ordered at the inn, was at last, though unwillingly, accepted as an excuse; but they seemed almost hurt that Captain Wentworth should have brought any such party to Lyme, without considering it as a thing of course that they should dine with them.

There was so much attachment to Captain Wentworth in all this, and such a bewitching charm in a degree of hospitality so uncommon, so unlike the usual style of give-and-take invitations, and dinners of formality and display, that Anne felt her spirits not likely to be benefited by an increasing acquaintance among his brother-officers. 'These would have been all my friends,' was her thought; and she had to struggle against a great tendency to lowness.

On quitting the Cobb, they all went indoors with their new friends, and found rooms so small as none but those who invite from the heart could think capable of accommodating so many. Anne had a moment's astonishment on the subject herself; but it was soon lost in the pleasanter feelings which sprang from the sight of all the ingenious contrivances and nice arrangements of Captain Harville, to turn the actual space to the best possible account, to supply the deficiencies of lodging-house furniture, and defend the windows and doors against the winter storms to be expected. The varieties in the fitting up of the rooms, where the common necessaries provided by the owner, in the common indifferent plight, were contrasted with some few articles of a rare species of wood, excellently worked up, and with something curious and valuable from all the distant countries Captain Harville had visited, were more than amusing to Anne: connected as it all was with his profession, the fruit of its labours, the effect of its influence on his habits, the picture of repose and domestic happiness it presented, made it to her a something more, or less, than gratification.

Captain Harville was no reader; but he had contrived excellent accommodations, and fashioned very pretty shelves, for a tolerable collection of well-bound volumes, the property of Captain Benwick. His lameness prevented him from taking much exercise; but a mind of usefulness and ingenuity seemed to furnish him with constant employment within. He drew, he varnished, he carpentered, he glued; he made toys for the children, he fashioned new netting-

situation, she was emboldened to go on; and feeling in herself the right of seniority of mind, she ventured to recommend a larger allowance of prose in his daily study; and, on being requested to particularise, mentioned such works of our best moralists, such collections of the finest letters, such memoirs of characters of worth and suffering, as occurred to her at the moment as calculated to rouse and fortify the mind by the highest precepts, and the strongest examples of moral and religious endurances.

Captain Benwick listened attentively, and seemed grateful for the interest implied; and though with a shake of the head, and sighs which declared his little faith in the efficacy of any books on grief like his, noted down the names of those she recommended, and promised to procure and read them.

When the evening was over, Anne could not but be amused at the idea of her coming to Lyme to preach patience and resignation to a young man whom she had never seen before; nor could she help fearing, on more serious reflection, that, like many other great moralists and preachers, she had been eloquent on a point in which her own conduct would ill bear examination.

## *Chapter 12*

Anne and Henrietta, finding themselves the earliest of the party the next morning, agreed to stroll down to the sea before breakfast. – They went to the sands, to watch the flowing of the tide, which a fine south-easterly breeze was bringing in with all the grandeur which so flat a shore admitted. They praised the morning; gloried in the sea; sympathised in the delight of the fresh-feeling breeze and were silent; till Henrietta suddenly began again, with,

'Oh! yes – I am quite convinced that, with very few exceptions, the sea air always does good. There can be no doubt of its having been of the greatest service to Dr Shirley, after his illness, last spring twelvemonth. He declares himself, that coming to Lyme for a month did him more good than all the medicine he took; and, that being by the sea always makes him feel young again. Now, I cannot help thinking it a pity that he does not live entirely by the sea. I do think he had better leave Uppercross entirely, and fix at Lyme. – Do not you, Anne? – Do not you agree with me, that it is the best thing he could do, both for himself and Mrs Shirley? – She has cousins here, you know, and many acquaintance, which would make it cheerful for her and I am sure she would be glad to get to a place where she could have medical attendance at hand, in case of his having another seizure. Indeed I think it quite melancholy to have such excellent people as Dr and Mrs Shirley, who have been doing good all their lives, wearing out their last days in a place like Uppercross, where, excepting our family, they seem shut out from all the world. I wish his friends would propose it to him. I really think they ought. And, as to procuring a dispensation, there could be no difficulty at his time of life, and with his character. My only doubt is, whether anything could persuade him to leave his parish. He is so very strict and scrupulous in his notions; overscrupulous, I must say. Do not you think, Anne, it is being overscrupulous? Do not you think it is quite a mistaken point of conscience, when a clergyman sacrifices his health for the sake of duties, which may be just as well performed by another person? – And at Lyme too only seventeen miles off – he would be near enough to hear, if people thought there was anything to complain of.'

Anne smiled more than once to herself during this speech, and entered into the subject, as ready to do good by entering into the feelings of a young lady as of a young man though here it was good of a lower standard, for what could be offered but general acquiescence? – She said all that was reasonable and proper on the business; felt the claims of Dr Shirley to repose, as she ought; saw how very desirable it was that he should have some active, respectable young man, as a resident curate, and was even courteous enough to hint at the advantage of such resident curate's being married.

'I wish,' said Henrietta, very well pleased with her companion, 'I wish Lady Russell lived at Uppercross, and were intimate with Dr Shirley. I have always heard of Lady Russell as a woman of the greatest influence with everybody! I always look upon her as able to persuade a person to anything! I am afraid of her, as I have told you before, quite afraid of her, because she is so very clever; but I respect her amazingly, and wish we had such a neighbour at Uppercross.'

Anne was amused by Henrietta's manner of being grateful, and amused also that the course of events and the new interests of Henrietta's views should have placed her friend at all in favour with any of the Musgrove family; she had only time, however, for a general answer, and a wish that such another woman were at Uppercross, before all subjects suddenly ceased on seeing Louisa and Captain Wentworth coming towards them. They came also for a stroll till breakfast was likely to be ready; but Louisa recollecting, immediately afterwards, that she had something to procure at a shop, invited them all to go back with her into the town. They were all at her disposal.

When they came to the steps, leading upwards from the beach, a gentleman, at the same moment preparing to come down, politely drew back, and stopped to give them way. They ascended and passed him; and as they passed, Anne's face caught his eye, and he looked at her with a degree of earnest admiration which she could not be insensible of. She was looking remarkably well; her very regular, very pretty features, having the bloom and freshness of youth restored by the fine wind which had been blowing on her complexion, and by the animation of eye which it had also produced. It was evident that the gentleman (completely a gentleman in manner), admired her exceedingly. Captain Wentworth looked round at her instantly in a way which showed his noticing of it. He gave her a momentary glance – a glance of brightness, which seemed to say, 'That man is struck with you – and even I, at this moment, see something like Anne Elliot again.'

After attending Louisa through her business, and loitering about a little longer, they returned to the inn; and Anne, in passing afterwards quickly from her own chamber to their dining-room, had nearly run against the very same gentleman, as he came out of an adjoining apartment. She had before conjectured him to be a stranger like themselves, and determined that a well-looking groom, who was strolling about near the two inns as they came back, should be his servant. Both master and man being in mourning assisted the idea. It was now proved that he belonged to the same inn as themselves; and this second meeting, short as it was, also proved again by the gentleman's looks that he thought hers very lovely, and by the readiness and propriety of his apologies that he was a man of exceedingly good manners. He seemed about thirty, and, though not handsome, had an agreeable person. Anne felt that she should like to know who he was.

They had nearly done breakfast, when the sound of a carriage (almost the first they had heard since entering Lyme), drew half the party to the window. 'It was a gentleman's carriage – a curricle – but only coming round from the stable-yard to the front door. – Somebody must be going away. – It was driven by a servant in mourning.'

The word curricle made Charles Musgrove jump up, that he might compare it with his own, the servant in mourning roused Anne's curiosity, and the whole six were collected to look by the time the owner of the curricle was to be seen

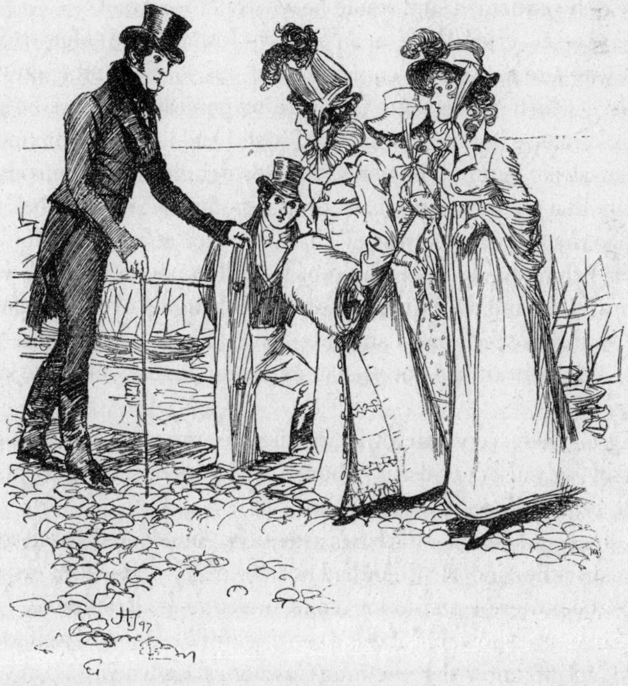

*A gentleman politely drew back*

issuing from the door amidst the bows and civilities of the household, and taking his seat, to drive off.

'Ah!' cried Captain Wentworth, instantly, and with half a glance at Anne; 'it is the very man we passed.'

The Miss Musgroves agreed to it; and having all kindly watched him as far up the hill as they could, they returned to the breakfast-table. The waiter came into the room soon afterwards.

'Pray,' said Captain Wentworth, immediately, 'can you tell us the name of the gentleman who is just gone away?'

'Yes, sir, a Mr Elliot; a gentleman of large fortune – came in last night from Sidmouth – dare say you heard the carriage, sir, while you were at dinner, and going on now for Crewkherne, in his way to Bath and London.'

'Elliot!' – Many had looked on each other, and many had repeated the name, before all this had been got through, even by the smart rapidity of a waiter.

'Bless me!' cried Mary; 'it must be our cousin – it must be our Mr Elliot it must, indeed! – Charles, Anne, must not it? In mourning, you see, just as our Mr Elliot must be. How very extraordinary! In the very same inn with us! Anne, must not it be our Mr Elliot; my father's next heir? Pray, sir,' turning to the waiter, 'did not you hear – did not his servant say whether he belonged to the Kellynch family?'

'No, ma'am – he did not mention no particular family, but he said his master was a very rich gentleman, and would be a baronet someday.'

'There! you see' cried Mary, in an ecstasy, 'Just as I said! Heir to Sir Walter Elliot! – I was sure that would come out, if it was so. Depend upon it, that is a circumstance which his servants take care to publish wherever he goes. But, Anne, only conceive how extraordinary! I wish I had looked at him more. I wish we had been aware in time who it was, that he might have been introduced to us. What a pity that we should not have been introduced to each other! – Do you think he had the Elliot countenance? I hardly looked at him, I was looking at the horses; but I think he had something of the Elliot countenance. I wonder the arms did not strike me! Oh! – the greatcoat was hanging over the panel, and hid the arms; so it did, otherwise, I am sure, I should have observed them, and the livery too; if the servant had not been in mourning, one should have known him by the livery.'

'Putting all these very extraordinary circumstances together,' said Captain Wentworth, 'we must consider it to be the arrangement of Providence that you should not be introduced to your cousin.'

When she could command Mary's attention, Anne quietly tried to convince her that their father and Mr Elliot had not, for many years, been on such terms as to make the power of attempting an introduction at all desirable.

At the same time, however, it was a secret gratification to herself to have seen her cousin, and to know that the future owner of Kellynch was undoubtedly a gentleman, and had an air of good sense. She would not, upon any account, mention her having met with him the second time; luckily Mary did not much attend to their having passed close by him in their early walk, but she would have felt quite ill-used by Anne's having actually run against him in the passage, and received his very polite excuses, while she had never been near him at all; no, that cousinly little interview must remain a perfect secret.

'Of course,' said Mary, 'you will mention our seeing Mr Elliot the next time you write to Bath. I think my father certainly ought to hear of it; do mention all about him.'

Anne avoided a direct reply, but it was just the circumstance which she considered as not merely unnecessary to be communicated, but as what ought to be suppressed. The offence which had been given her father, many years back, she knew; Elizabeth's particular share in it she suspected; and that Mr Elliot's idea always produced irritation in both was beyond a doubt. Mary never wrote to Bath herself; all the toil of keeping up a slow and unsatisfactory correspondence with Elizabeth fell on Anne.

Breakfast had not been long over, when they were joined by Captain and Mrs Harville, and Captain Benwick, with whom they had appointed to take their last walk about Lyme. They ought to be setting off for Uppercross by one, and in the meanwhile were to be all together, and out-of-doors as long as they could.

Anne found Captain Benwick getting near her as soon as they were all fairly in the street. Their conversation, the preceding evening, did not disincline him to seek her again; and they walked together some time, talking as before of Mr Scott and Lord Byron, and still as unable, as before, and as unable as any other two readers, to think exactly alike of the merits of either, till something occasioned an almost general change amongst their party, and instead of Captain Benwick, she had Captain Harville by her side.

'Miss Elliot,' said he, speaking rather low, 'you have done a good deed in making that poor fellow talk so much. I wish he could have such company oftener. It is bad for him, I know, to be shut up as he is; but what can we do? we cannot part.'

'No,' said Anne, 'that I can easily believe to be impossible; but in time, perhaps – we know what time does in every case of affliction, and you must remember, Captain Harville, that your friend may yet be called a young mourner. – Only last summer, I understand.'

'Ay, true enough,' (with a deep sigh) 'only June.'

'And not known to him, perhaps, so soon.'

'Not till the first week in August, when he came home from the Cape – just made into the *Grappler*. I was at Plymouth, dreading to hear of him; he sent in letters, but the *Grappler* was under orders for Portsmouth. There the news must follow him, but who was to tell it? not I. I would as soon have been run up to the yardarm. Nobody could do it but that good fellow,' pointing to Captain Wentworth. 'The *Laconia* had come into Plymouth the week before; no danger of her being sent to sea again. He stood his chance for the rest – wrote up for leave of absence, but without waiting the return, travelled night and day till he got to Portsmouth, rowed off to the *Grappler* that instant, and never left the poor fellow for a week; that's what he did, and nobody else could have saved poor James. You may think, Miss Elliot, whether he is dear to us!'

Anne did think on the question with perfect decision, and said as much in reply as her own feelings could accomplish, or as his seemed able to bear, for he was too much affected to renew the subject – and when he spoke again, it was of something totally different.

Mrs Harville's giving it as her opinion that her husband would have quite walking enough by the time he reached home, determined the direction of all the party in what was to be their last walk; they would accompany them to their door, and then return and set off themselves. By all their calculations there was just time for this; but as they drew near the Cobb, there was such a general wish to walk along it once more, all were so inclined, and Louisa soon grew so determined, that the difference of a quarter of an hour, it was found, would be no difference at all, so with all the kind leave-taking, and all the kind interchange of invitations and promises which may be imagined, they parted from Captain and Mrs Harville at their own door, and still accompanied by Captain Benwick, who seemed to cling to them to the last, proceeded to make the proper adieus to the Cobb.

Anne found Captain Benwick again drawing near her. Lord Byron's 'dark blue seas' could not fail of being brought forward by their present view, and she gladly gave him all her attention as long as attention was possible. It was soon drawn perforce another way.

There was too much wind to make the high part of the new Cobb pleasant for the ladies, and they agreed to get down the steps to the lower, and all were contented to pass quietly and carefully down the steep flight, excepting Louisa; she must be jumped down them by Captain Wentworth. In all their walks, he had had to jump her from the stiles; the sensation was delightful to her. The hardness of the pavement for her feet, made him less willing upon the present occasion; he did it, however; she was safely down, and instantly, to show her enjoyment, ran up the steps to be jumped down again. He advised her against it, thought the jar too great; but no, he reasoned and talked in vain; she smiled and said, 'I am determined I will:' he put out his hands; she was too precipitate by half a second, she fell on the pavement on the lower Cobb, and was taken up lifeless!

There was no wound, no blood, no visible bruise; but her eyes were closed, she breathed not, her face was like death. – The horror of that moment to all who stood around!

Captain Wentworth, who had caught her up, knelt with her in his arms, looking on her with a face as pallid as her own, in an agony of silence. 'She is dead! she is dead!' screamed Mary, catching hold of her husband, and contributing with his own horror to make him immovable; and in another moment, Henrietta, sinking under the conviction, lost her senses too, and would have fallen on the steps, but for Captain Benwick and Anne, who caught and supported her between them.

'Is there no one to help me?' were the first words which burst from Captain Wentworth, in a tone of despair, and as if all his own strength were gone.

'Go to him, go to him,' cried Anne, 'for heaven's sake go to him. I can support her myself. Leave me, and go to him. Rub her hands, rub her temples; here are salts – take them, take them.'

Captain Benwick obeyed, and Charles at the same moment, disengaging himself from his wife, they were both with him; and Louisa was raised up and supported more firmly between them, and everything was done that Anne had prompted, but in vain; while Captain Wentworth, staggering against the wall for his support, exclaimed in the bitterest agony,

'Oh God! her father and mother!'

'A surgeon!' said Anne.

He caught the word; it seemed to rouse him at once, and saying only 'True, true, a surgeon this instant,' was darting away, when Anne eagerly suggested,

'Captain Benwick, would not it be better for Captain Benwick? He knows where a surgeon is to be found.'

Everyone capable of thinking felt the advantage of the idea, and in a moment (it was all done in rapid moments), Captain Benwick had resigned the poor

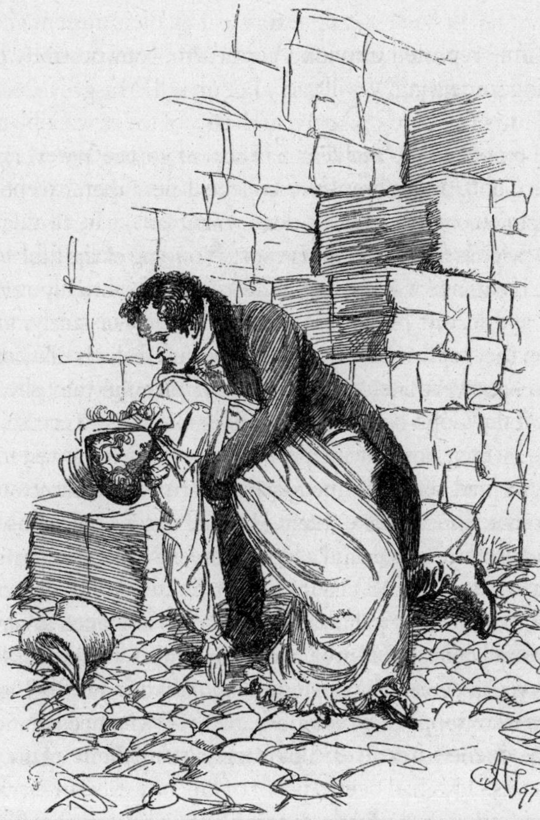

*Looking on her with a face as pallid as her own*

corpse-like figure entirely to the brother's care, and was off for the town with the utmost rapidity.

As to the wretched party left behind, it could scarcely be said which of the three, who were completely rational, was suffering most: Captain Wentworth, Anne, or Charles, who, really a very affectionate brother, hung over Louisa with sobs of grief, and could only turn his eyes from one sister, to see the other in a state as insensible, or to witness the hysterical agitations of his wife, calling on him for help which he could not give.

Anne, attending with all the strength and zeal, and thought, which instinct supplied, to Henrietta, still tried, at intervals, to suggest comfort to the others, tried to quiet Mary, to animate Charles, to assuage the feelings of Captain Wentworth. Both seemed to look to her for directions.

'Anne, Anne,' cried Charles, 'what is to be done next? What, in heaven's name, is to be done next?'

Captain Wentworth's eyes were also turned towards her.

'Had not she better be carried to the inn? Yes, I am sure, carry her gently to the inn.'

'Yes, yes, to the inn,' repeated Captain Wentworth, comparatively collected, and eager to be doing something. 'I will carry her myself. Musgrove, take care of the others.'

By this time the report of the accident had spread among the workmen and boatmen about the Cobb, and many were collected near them, to be useful if wanted; at any rate, to enjoy the sight of a dead young lady, nay, two dead young ladies, for it proved twice as fine as the first report. To some of the best-looking of these good people Henrietta was consigned, for, though partially revived, she was quite helpless; and in this manner, Anne walking by her side, and Charles attending to his wife, they set forward, treading back with feelings unutterable, the ground which so lately, so very lately, and so light of heart, they had passed along.

They were not off the Cobb before the Harvilles met them. Captain Benwick had been seen flying by their house, with a countenance which showed something to be wrong; and they had set off immediately, informed and directed, as they passed, towards the spot. Shocked as Captain Harville was, he brought senses and nerves that could be instantly useful; and a look between him and his wife decided what was to be done. She must be taken to their house – all must go to their house – and wait the surgeon's arrival there. They would not listen to scruples: he was obeyed; they were all beneath his roof; and while Louisa, under Mrs Harville's direction, was conveyed upstairs, and given possession of her own bed, assistance, cordials, restoratives were supplied by her husband to all who needed them.

Louisa had once opened her eyes, but soon closed them again, without apparent consciousness. This had been a proof of life, however, of service to her sister; and Henrietta, though perfectly incapable of being in the same room with Louisa, was kept, by the agitation of hope and fear, from a return of her own insensibility. Mary, too, was growing calmer.

The surgeon was with them almost before it had seemed possible. They were sick with horror while he examined; but he was not hopeless. The head had received a severe contusion, but he had seen greater injuries recovered from: he was by no means hopeless; he spoke cheerfully.

That he did not regard it as a desperate case – that he did not say a few hours must end it – was at first felt beyond the hope of most; and the ecstasy of such a reprieve, the rejoicing, deep and silent, after a few fervent ejaculations of gratitude to Heaven had been offered, may be conceived.

The tone, the look, with which 'Thank God!' was uttered by Captain Wentworth, Anne was sure could never be forgotten by her; nor the sight of him afterwards, as he sat near a table, leaning over it with folded arms, and face concealed, as if overpowered by the various feelings of his soul, and trying by prayer and reflection to calm them.

Louisa's limbs had escaped. There was no injury but to the head.

It now became necessary for the party to consider what was best to be done, as to their general situation. They were now able to speak to each other, and consult. That Louisa must remain where she was, however distressing to her friends to be involving the Harvilles in such trouble, did not admit a doubt. Her removal was impossible. The Harvilles silenced all scruples; and, as much as they could, all gratitude. They had looked forward and arranged everything before the others began to reflect. Captain Benwick must give up his room to them, and get a bed elsewhere – and the whole was settled. They were only concerned that the house could accommodate no more; and yet perhaps by 'putting the children away in the maid's room, or swinging a cot somewhere', they could hardly bear to think of not finding room for two or three besides, supposing they might wish to stay; though, with regard to any attendance on Miss Musgrove, there need not be the least uneasiness in leaving her to Mrs Harville's care entirely. Mrs Harville was a very experienced nurse; and her nurserymaid, who had lived with her long and gone about with her everywhere, was just such another. Between those two, she could want no possible attendance by day or night. And all this was said with a truth and sincerity of feeling irresistible.

Charles, Henrietta, and Captain Wentworth were the three in consultation, and for a little while it was only an interchange of perplexity and terror. 'Uppercross – the necessity of someone's going to Uppercross – the news to be conveyed – how it could be broken to Mr and Mrs Musgrove – the lateness of the morning – an hour already gone since they ought to have been off – the impossibility of being in tolerable time. At first, they were capable of nothing more to the purpose than such exclamations; but, after a while, Captain Wentworth, exerting himself, said,

'We must be decided, and without the loss of another minute. Every minute is valuable. Some must resolve on being off for Uppercross instantly. Musgrove, either you or I must go.'

Charles agreed; but declared his resolution of not going away. He would be as little incumbrance as possible to Captain and Mrs Harville, but as to leaving his sister in such a state, he neither ought, nor would. So far it was decided; and Henrietta at first declared the same. She, however, was soon persuaded to think differently. The usefulness of her staying! – She, who had not been able to remain in Louisa's room, or to look at her, without sufferings which made her worse than helpless! She was forced to acknowledge that she could do no good; yet was still unwilling to be away, till touched by the thought of her father and mother, she gave it up, she consented, she was anxious to be at home.

The plan had reached this point, when Anne, coming quietly down from Louisa's room, could not but hear what followed, for the parlour-door was open.

'Then it is settled, Musgrove,' cried Captain Wentworth, 'that you stay, and that I take care of your sister home. But as to the rest – as to the others. – If one stays to assist Mrs Harville, I think it need be only one. – Mrs Charles Musgrove will, of course, wish to get back to her children; but, if Anne will stay, no one so proper, so capable as Anne!'

She paused a moment to recover from the emotion of hearing herself so spoken of. The other two warmly agreed to what he said, and she then appeared.

'You will stay, I am sure; you will stay and nurse her,' cried he, turning to her and speaking with a glow, and yet a gentleness, which seemed almost restoring the past. – She coloured deeply; and he recollected himself, and moved away. – She expressed herself most willing, ready, happy to remain. 'It was what she had been thinking of and wishing to be allowed to do. – A bed on the floor in Louisa's room would be sufficient for her, if Mrs Harville would but think so.'

One thing more, and all seemed arranged. Though it was rather desirable that Mr and Mrs Musgrove should be previously alarmed by some share of delay; yet the time required by the Uppercross horses to take them back would be a dreadful extension of suspense; and Captain Wentworth proposed, and Charles Musgrove agreed, that it would be much better for him to take a chaise from the inn, and leave Mr Musgrove's carriage and horses to be sent home the next morning early, when there would be the farther advantage of sending an account of Louisa's night.

Captain Wentworth now hurried off to get everything ready on his part, and to be soon followed by the two ladies. When the plan was made known to Mary, however, there was an end of all peace in it. She was so wretched, and so vehement, complained so much of injustice in being expected to go away, instead of Anne – Anne, who was nothing to Louisa, while she was her sister, and had the best right to stay in Henrietta's stead! Why was not she to be as useful as Anne? And to go home without Charles, too – without her husband! No, it was too unkind! And, in short, she said more than her husband could long withstand; and as none of the others could oppose when he gave way, there was no help for it: the change of Mary for Anne was inevitable.

Anne had never submitted more reluctantly to the jealous and ill-judging claims of Mary; but so it must be, and they set off for the town, Charles taking care of his sister, and Captain Benwick attending to her. She gave a moment's recollection, as they hurried along, to the little circumstances which the same spots had witnessed earlier in the morning. There she had listened to Henrietta's schemes for Dr Shirley's leaving Uppercross; farther on, she had first seen Mr Elliot; a moment seemed all that could now be given to anyone but Louisa, or those who were wrapped up in her welfare.

Captain Benwick was most considerately attentive to her; and, united as they all seemed by the distress of the day, she felt an increasing degree of goodwill towards him, and a pleasure even in thinking that it might, perhaps, be the occasion of continuing their acquaintance.

Captain Wentworth was on the watch for them, and a chaise and four in waiting, stationed for their convenience in the lowest part of the street; but his evident surprise and vexation at the substitution of one sister for the other – the change of his countenance – the astonishment – the expressions begun and suppressed, with which Charles was listened to, made but a mortifying reception of Anne; or must at least convince her that she was valued only as she could be useful to Louisa.

She endeavoured to be composed, and to be just. Without emulating the feelings of an Emma towards her Henry, she would have attended on Louisa with a zeal above the common claims of regard, for his sake- and she hoped he would not long be so unjust as to suppose she would shrink unnecessarily from the office of a friend.

In the meanwhile she was in the carriage. He had handed them both in, and placed himself between them; and in this manner, under these circumstances full of astonishment and emotion to Anne, she quitted Lyme. How the long stage would pass; how it was to affect their manners; what was to be their sort of intercourse, she could not foresee. It was all quite natural, however. He was devoted to Henrietta; always turning towards her; and when he spoke at all, always with the view of supporting her hopes and raising her spirits. In general, his voice and manner were studiously calm. To spare Henrietta from agitation seemed the governing principle. Once only, when she had been grieving over the last ill-judged, ill-fated walk to the Cobb, bitterly lamenting that it ever had been thought of, he burst forth, as if wholly overcome –

'Don't talk of it, don't talk of it,' he cried. 'Oh God! that I had not given way to her at the fatal moment! Had I done as I ought! But so eager and so resolute! Dear, sweet Louisa!'

Anne wondered whether it ever occurred to him, now, to question the justness of his own previous opinion as to the universal felicity and advantage of firmness of character; and whether it might not strike him, that, like all other qualities of the mind, it should have its proportions and limits. She thought it could scarcely escape him to feel that a persuadable temper might sometimes be as much in favour of happiness as a very resolute character.

They got on fast. Anne was astonished to recognise the same hills and the same objects so soon. Their actual speed, heightened by some dread of the conclusion, made the road appear but half as long as on the day before. It was growing quite dusk, however, before they were in the neighbourhood of Uppercross, and there had been total silence among them for some time, Henrietta leaning back in the corner, with a shawl over her face, giving the hope of her having cried herself to sleep; when, as they were going up their last hill, Anne found herself all at once addressed by Captain Wentworth. In a low, cautious voice, he said,

'I have been considering what we had best do. She must not appear at first.

She could not stand it. I have been thinking whether you had not better remain in the carriage with her, while I go in and break it to Mr and Mrs Musgrove. Do you think this a good plan?'

She did; he was satisfied and said no more. But the remembrance of the appeal remained a pleasure to her – as a proof of friendship, and of deference for her judgment, a great pleasure; and when it became a sort of parting proof, its value did not lessen.

When the distressing communication at Uppercross was over, and he had seen the father and mother quite as composed as could be hoped, and the daughter all the better for being with them, he announced his intention of returning in the same carriage to Lyme; and when the horses were baited, he was off.

## VOLUME II

# *Chapter 1*

The remainder of Anne's time at Uppercross, comprehending only two days, was spent entirely at the Mansion House, and she had the satisfaction of knowing herself extremely useful there, both as an immediate companion, and as assisting in all those arrangements for the future, which, in Mr and Mrs Musgrove's distressed state of spirits, would have been difficulties.

They had an early account from Lyme the next morning. Louisa was much the same. No symptoms worse than before had appeared. Charles came a few hours afterwards to bring a later and more particular account. He was tolerably cheerful. A speedy cure must not be hoped, but everything was going on as well as the nature of the case admitted. In speaking of the Harvilles, he seemed unable to satisfy his own sense of their kindness, especially of Mrs Harville's exertions as a nurse. 'She really left nothing for Mary to do. He and Mary had been persuaded to go early to their inn last night. Mary had been hysterical again this morning. When he came away, she was going to walk out with Captain Benwick, which, he hoped, would do her good. He almost wished she had been prevailed on to come home the day before; but the truth was that Mrs Harville left nothing for anybody to do.'

Charles was to return to Lyme the same afternoon, and his father had at first half a mind to go with him but the ladies could not consent. It would be going only to multiply trouble to the others, and increase his own distress; and a much better scheme followed and was acted upon. A chaise was sent for from Crewkherne, and Charles conveyed back a far more useful person in the old nurserymaid of the family, one who having brought up all the children, and seen the very last, the lingering and long-petted master Harry, sent to school after his brothers, was now living in her deserted nursery to mend stockings, and dress all the blains and bruises she could get near her, and who, consequently, was only too happy in being allowed to go and help nurse dear Miss Louisa. Vague wishes of getting Sarah thither had occurred before to Mrs Musgrove and Henrietta; but without Anne, it would hardly have been resolved on, and found practicable so soon.

They were indebted, the next day, to Charles Hayter for all the minute knowledge of Louisa, which it was so essential to obtain every twenty-four hours. He made it his business to go to Lyme, and his account was still encouraging. The intervals of sense and consciousness were believed to be stronger. Every report agreed in Captain Wentworth's appearing fixed in Lyme.

Anne was to leave them on the morrow, an event which they all dreaded. 'What should they do without her? They were wretched comforters for one another!' And so much was said in this way that Anne thought she could not do better than impart among them the general inclination to which she was privy, and persuade them all to go to Lyme at once. She had little difficulty; it was soon determined that they would go, go tomorrow, fix themselves at the inn, or get into lodgings, as it suited, and there remain till dear Louisa could be moved. They must be taking off some trouble from the good people she was with; they might at least relieve Mrs Harville from the care of her own children; and in short they were so happy in the decision that Anne was delighted with what she had done, and felt that she could not spend her last morning at Uppercross better than in assisting their preparations, and sending them off at an early hour, though her being left to the solitary range of the house was the consequence.

She was the last, excepting the little boys at the Cottage, she was the very last, the only remaining one of all that had filled and animated both houses, of all that had given Uppercross its cheerful character. A few days had made a change indeed!

If Louisa recovered, it would all be well again. More than former happiness would be restored. There could not be a doubt, to her mind there was none, of what would follow her recovery. A few months hence, and the room now so deserted, occupied but by her silent, pensive self, might be filled again with all that was happy and gay, all that was glowing and bright in prosperous love, all that was most unlike Anne Elliot!

An hour's complete leisure for such reflections as these, on a dark November day, a small thick rain almost blotting out the very few objects ever to be discerned from the windows, was enough to make the sound of Lady Russell's carriage exceedingly welcome; and yet, though desirous to be gone, she could not quit the Mansion House, or look an adieu to the Cottage, with its black, dripping, and comfortless veranda, or even notice through the misty glasses the last humble tenements of the village, without a saddened heart. – Scenes had passed in Uppercross which made it precious. It stood the record of many sensations of pain, once severe, but now softened; and of some instances of relenting feeling, some breathings of friendship and reconciliation, which could never be looked for again, and which could never cease to be dear. She left it all behind her; all but the recollection that such things had been.

Anne had never entered Kellynch since her quitting Lady Russell's house, in September. It had not been necessary, and the few occasions of its being possible for her to go to the Hall she had contrived to evade and escape from. Her first return was to resume her place in the modern and elegant apartments of the Lodge, and to gladden the eyes of its mistress.

There was some anxiety mixed with Lady Russell's joy in meeting her. She knew who had been frequenting Uppercross. But happily, either Anne was improved in plumpness and looks, or Lady Russell fancied her so; and Anne, in receiving her compliments on the occasion; had the amusement of connecting them with the silent admiration of her cousin, and of hoping that she was to be blessed with a second spring of youth and beauty.

When they came to converse, she was soon sensible of some mental change. The subjects of which her heart had been full on leaving Kellynch, and which she had felt slighted, and been compelled to smother among the Musgroves, were now become but of secondary interest. She had lately lost sight even of her father and sister and Bath. Their concerns had been sunk under those of Uppercross, and when Lady Russell reverted to their former hopes and fears, and spoke her satisfaction in the house in Camden Place which had been taken, and her regret that Mrs Clay should still be with them, Anne would have been ashamed to have it known how much more she was thinking of Lyme, and Louisa Musgrove, and all her acquaintance there; how much more interesting to her was the home and the friendship of the Harvilles and Captain Benwick than her own father's house in Camden Place, or her own sister's intimacy with Mrs Clay. She was actually forced to exert herself to meet Lady Russell with anything like the appearance of equal solicitude, on topics which had by nature the first claim on her.

There was a little awkwardness at first in their discourse on another subject. They must speak of the accident at Lyme. Lady Russell had not been arrived five minutes the day before, when a full account of the whole had burst on her; but still it must be talked of, she must make enquiries, she must regret the imprudence, lament the result, and Captain Wentworth's name must be mentioned by both. Anne was conscious of not doing it so well as Lady Russell. She could not speak the name, and look straight forward to Lady Russell's eye, till she had adopted the expedient of telling her briefly what she thought of the attachment between him and Louisa. When this was told, his name distressed her no longer.

Lady Russell had only to listen composedly, and wish them happy; but internally her heart revelled in angry pleasure, in pleased contempt, that the man who at twenty-three had seemed to understand somewhat of the value of an Anne Elliot, should, eight years afterwards, be charmed by a Louisa Musgrove.

The first three or four days passed most quietly, with no circumstance to mark them excepting the receipt of a note or two from Lyme, which found their way to Anne, she could not tell how, and brought a rather improving account of Louisa. At the end of that period, Lady Russell's politeness could repose no longer, and the fainter self-threatenings of the past became in a decided tone, 'I must call on Mrs Croft; I really must call upon her soon. Anne, have you courage to go with me, and pay a visit in that house? It will be some trial to us both.'

Anne did not shrink from it; on the contrary, she truly felt as she said, in observing,

'I think you are very likely to suffer the most of the two; your feelings are less reconciled to the change than mine. By remaining in the neighbourhood, I am become inured to it.'

She could have said more on the subject; for she had in fact so high an opinion of the Crofts, and considered her father so very fortunate in his tenants, felt the parish to be so sure of a good example, and the poor of the best attention and relief, that however sorry and ashamed for the necessity of the removal, she could not but in conscience feel that they were gone who deserved not to stay, and that Kellynch Hall had passed into better hands than its owners. These convictions must unquestionably have their own pain, and severe was its kind; but they precluded that pain which Lady Russell would suffer in entering the house again, and returning through the well-known apartments.

In such moments Anne had no power of saying to herself, 'These rooms ought to belong only to us. Oh, how fallen in their destination! How unworthily occupied! An ancient family to be so driven away! Strangers filling their place!' No, except when she thought of her mother, and remembered where she had been used to sit and preside, she had no sigh of that description to heave.

Mrs Croft always met her with a kindness which gave her the pleasure of fancying herself a favourite; and on the present occasion, receiving her in that house, there was particular attention.

The sad accident at Lyme was soon the prevailing topic; and on comparing their latest accounts of the invalid, it appeared that each lady dated her intelligence from the same hour of yestermorn, that Captain Wentworth had been in Kellynch yesterday (the first time since the accident), had brought Anne the last note, which she had not been able to trace the exact steps of, had stayed a few hours and then returned again to Lyme – and without any present intention of quitting it any more. – He had enquired after her, she found, particularly – had expressed his hope of Miss Elliot's not being the worse for her exertions, and had spoken of those exertions as great. – This was handsome – and gave her more pleasure than almost anything else could have done.

As to the sad catastrophe itself, it could be canvassed only in one style by a couple of steady, sensible women, whose judgements had to work on ascertained events; and it was perfectly decided that it had been the consequence of much thoughtlessness and much imprudence; that its effects were most alarming, and that it was frightful to think how long Miss Musgrove's recovery might yet be doubtful, and how liable she would still remain to suffer from the concussion hereafter! – The Admiral wound it all up summarily by exclaiming,

'Ay, a very bad business indeed. – A new sort of way this, for a young fellow to be making love, by breaking his mistress's head! – is not it, Miss Elliot? – This is breaking a head and giving a plaister truly!'

Admiral Croft's manners were not quite of the tone to suit Lady Russell, but they delighted Anne. His goodness of heart and simplicity of character were irresistible.

'Now, this must be very bad for you,' said he, suddenly rousing from a little reverie, 'to be coming and finding us here – I had not recollected it before, I declare – but it must be very bad. – But now, do not stand upon ceremony. – Get up and go over all the rooms in the house if you like it.'

'Another time, sir, I thank you, not now.'

'Well, whenever it suits you. – You can slip in from the shrubbery at any time. And there you will find we keep our umbrellas, hanging up by that door. A good place, is not it? But' (checking himself) 'you will not think it a good place, for yours were always kept in the butler's room. Ay, so it always is, I believe. One man's ways may be as good as another's, but we all like our own best. And so you must judge for yourself whether it would be better for you to go about the house or not.'

Anne, finding she might decline it, did so, very gratefully.

'We have made very few changes either!' continued the Admiral, after thinking a moment. 'Very few. – We told you about the laundry-door, at Uppercross. That has been a very great improvement. The wonder was, how any family upon earth could bear with the inconvenience of its opening as it did, so long! – You will tell Sir Walter what we have done, and that Mr Shepherd thinks it the greatest improvement the house ever had. Indeed, I must do ourselves the justice to say, that the few alterations we have made have been all very much for the better. My wife should have the credit of them, however. I have done very little besides sending away some of the large looking-glasses from my dressing-room, which was your father's. A very good man, and very much the gentleman I am sure – but I should think, Miss Elliot' (looking with serious reflection ) 'I should think he must be rather a dressy man for his time of life. – Such a number of looking-glasses! Oh Lord! there was no getting away from oneself. So I got Sophy to lend me a hand, and we soon shifted their quarters; and now I am quite snug, with my little shaving-glass in one corner, and another great thing that I never go near.'

Anne, amused in spite of herself, was rather distressed for an answer, and the Admiral, fearing he might not have been civil enough, took up the subject again, to say,

'The next time you write to your good father, Miss Elliot, pray give my compliments and Mrs Croft's, and say that we are settled here quite to our liking, and have no fault at all to find with the place. The breakfast-room chimney smokes a little, I grant you, but it is only when the wind is due north and blows hard, which may not happen three times a winter. And take it altogether, now that we have been into most of the houses hereabouts and can judge, there is not one that we like better than this. Pray say so, with my compliments. He will be glad to hear it.'

Lady Russell and Mrs Croft were very well pleased with each other; but the acquaintance which this visit began was fated not to proceed far at present; for when it was returned, the Crofts announced themselves to be going away for a few weeks, to visit their connections in the north of the county, and probably might not be at home again before Lady Russell would be removing to Bath.

So ended all danger to Anne of meeting Captain Wentworth at Kellynch Hall, or of seeing him in company with her friend. Everything was safe enough and she smiled over the many anxious feelings she had wasted on the subject.

## *Chapter 2*

Though Charles and Mary had remained at Lyme much longer after Mr and Mrs Musgrove's going than Anne conceived they could have been at all wanted, they were yet the first of the family to be at home again, and as soon as possible after their return to Uppercross, they drove over to the Lodge. – They had left Louisa beginning to sit up; but her head, though clear, was exceedingly weak, and her nerves susceptible to the highest extreme of tenderness; and though she might be pronounced to be altogether doing very well, it was still impossible to say when she might be able to bear the removal home; and her father and mother, who must return in time to receive their younger children for the Christmas holidays, had hardly a hope of being allowed to bring her with them.

They had been all in lodgings together. Mrs Musgrove had got Mrs Harville's children away as much as she could, every possible supply from Uppercross had been furnished, to lighten the inconvenience to the Harvilles, while the Harvilles had been wanting them to come to dinner everyday; and, in short, it seemed to have been only a struggle on each side as to which should be most disinterested and hospitable.

Mary had had her evils; but upon the whole, as was evident by her staying so long, she had found more to enjoy than to suffer. – Charles Hayter had been at Lyme oftener than suited her, and when they dined with the Harvilles there had been only a maidservant to wait, and at first, Mrs Harville had always given Mrs Musgrove precedence; but then, she had received so very handsome an apology from her on finding out whose daughter she was, and there had been so much going on everyday, there had been so many walks between their lodgings and the Harvilles, and she had got books from the library and changed them so often, that the balance had certainly been much in favour of Lyme. She had been taken to Charmouth too, and she had bathed, and she had gone to church, and there were a great many more people to look at in the church at Lyme than at Uppercross – and all this, joined to the sense of being so very useful, had made really an agreeable fortnight.

Anne enquired after Captain Benwick. Mary's face was clouded directly. Charles laughed.

'Oh! Captain Benwick is very well, I believe, but he is a very odd young man. I do not know what he would be at. We asked him to come home with us for a day or two; Charles undertook to give him some shooting, and he seemed quite delighted, and for my part, I thought it was all settled; when behold! on Tuesday night, he made a very awkward sort of excuse; "he never shot" and he had "been quite misunderstood", and he had promised this and he had promised that, and the end of it was, I found, that he did not mean to come. I suppose he was afraid of finding it dull; but upon my word I should have thought we were lively enough at the Cottage for such a heartbroken man as Captain Benwick.'

Charles laughed again and said, 'Now Mary, you know very well how it really was. – It was all your doing' (turning to Anne). 'He fancied that if he went with us, he should find you close by; he fancied everybody to be living in Uppercross; and when he discovered that Lady Russell lived three miles off, his heart failed him, and he had not courage to come. That is the fact, upon my honour. Mary knows it is.'

But Mary did not give in to it very graciously; whether from not considering Captain Benwick entitled by birth and situation to be in love with an Elliot, or from not wanting to believe Anne a greater attraction to Uppercross than herself, must be left to be guessed. Anne's goodwill, however, was not to be lessened by what she heard. She boldly acknowledged herself flattered, and continued her enquiries.

'Oh! he talks of you,' cried Charles, 'in such terms – ' Mary interrupted him: 'I declare, Charles, I never heard him mention Anne twice all the time I was there. I declare, Anne, he never talks of you at all.'

'No,' admitted Charles, 'I do not know that he ever does, in a general way – but, however, it is a very clear thing that he admires you exceedingly. – His head is full of some books that he is reading upon your recommendation, and he wants to talk to you about them; he has found out something or other in one of them which he thinks – Oh! I cannot pretend to remember it, but it was something very fine – I overheard him telling Henrietta all about it – and then "Miss Elliot" was spoken of in the highest terms! – Now Mary, I declare it was so, I heard it myself, and you were in the other room: "Elegance, sweetness, beauty." Oh! there was no end of Miss Elliot's charms.'

'And I am sure,' cried Mary warmly, 'it was very little to his credit, if he did. Miss Harville only died last June. Such a heart is very little worth having; is it, Lady Russell? I am sure you will agree with me.'

'I must see Captain Benwick before I decide,' said Lady Russell, smiling.

'And that you are very likely to do very soon, I can tell you, ma'am,' said Charles. 'Though he had not nerves for coming away with us and setting off again afterwards to pay a formal visit here, he will make his way over to Kellynch one day by himself, you may depend on it. I told him the distance and the road, and I told him of the church's being so very well worth seeing, for as he has a taste for those sort of things, I thought that would be a good excuse, and he listened with all his understanding and soul; and I am sure from his manner that you will have him calling here soon. So, I give you notice, Lady Russell.'

'Any acquaintance of Anne's will always be welcome to me,' was Lady Russell's kind answer.

'Oh! as to being Anne's acquaintance,' said Mary, 'I think he is rather my acquaintance, for I have been seeing him everyday this last fortnight.'

'Well, as your joint acquaintance, then, I shall be very happy to see Captain Benwick.'

'You will not find anything very agreeable in him, I assure you, ma'am. He is one of the dullest young men that ever lived. He has walked with me, sometimes, from one end of the sands to the other, without saying a word. He is not at all a well-bred young man. I am sure you will not like him.'

'There we differ, Mary,' said Anne. 'I think Lady Russell would like him. I think she would be so much pleased with his mind that she would very soon see no deficiency in his manner.'

'So do I, Anne,' said Charles. 'I am sure Lady Russell would like him. He is just Lady Russell's sort. Give him a book, and he will read all day long.'

'Yes, that he will!' exclaimed Mary, tauntingly. 'He will sit poring over his book, and not know when a person speaks to him, or when one drops one's scissors, or anything that happens. Do you think Lady Russell would like that?'

Lady Russell could not help laughing. 'Upon my word,' said she, 'I should not have supposed that my opinion of anyone could have admitted of such difference of conjecture, steady and matter of fact as I may call myself. I have really a curiosity to see the person who can give occasion to such directly opposite notions. I wish he may be induced to call here. And when he does, Mary, you may depend upon hearing my opinion; but I am determined not to judge him beforehand.'

'You will not like him, I will answer for it.'

Lady Russell began talking of something else. Mary spoke with animation of their meeting with, or rather missing, Mr Elliot so extraordinarily.

'He is a man,' said Lady Russell, 'whom I have no wish to see. His declining to be on cordial terms with the head of his family has left a very strong impression in his disfavour with me.'

This decision checked Mary's eagerness, and stopped her short in the midst of the Elliot countenance.

With regard to Captain Wentworth, though Anne hazarded no enquiries there was voluntary communication sufficient. His spirits had been greatly recovering lately, as might be expected. As Louisa improved, he had improved; and he was now quite a different creature from what he had been the first week. He had not seen Louisa; and was so extremely fearful of any ill consequence to her from an interview that he did not press for it at all; and, on the contrary, seemed to have a plan of going away for a week or ten days, till her head were stronger. He had talked of going down to Plymouth for a week, and wanted to persuade Captain Benwick to go with him; but, as Charles maintained to the last, Captain Benwick seemed much more disposed to ride over to Kellynch.

There can be no doubt that Lady Russell and Anne were both occasionally thinking of Captain Benwick, from this time. Lady Russell could not hear the doorbell without feeling that it might be his herald; nor could Anne return from any stroll of solitary indulgence in her father's grounds, or any visit of charity in the village, without wondering whether she might see him or hear of him. Captain Benwick came not, however. He was either less disposed for it than Charles had imagined, or he was too shy; and after giving him a week's indulgence, Lady Russell determined him to be unworthy of the interest which he had been beginning to excite.

The Musgroves came back to receive their happy boys and girls from school, bringing with them Mrs Harville's little children, to improve the noise of Uppercross, and lessen that of Lyme. Henrietta remained with Louisa; but all the rest of the family were again in their usual quarters.

Lady Russell and Anne paid their compliments to them once, when Anne could not but feel that Uppercross was already quite alive again. Though neither Henrietta, nor Louisa, nor Charles Hayter, nor Captain Wentworth were there, the room presented as strong a contrast as could be wished to the last state she had seen it in.

Immediately surrounding Mrs Musgrove were the little Harvilles, whom she was sedulously guarding from the tyranny of the two children from the Cottage, expressly arrived to amuse them. On one side was a table, occupied by some chattering girls, cutting up silk and gold paper; and on the other were tressels and trays, bending under the weight of brawn and cold pies, where riotous boys were holding high revel; the whole completed by a roaring Christmas fire, which seemed determined to be heard, in spite of all the noise of the others. Charles and Mary also came in, of course, during their visit; and Mr Musgrove made a point of paying his respects to Lady Russell, and sat down close to her for ten minutes, talking with a very raised voice, but, from the clamour of the children on his knees, generally in vain. It was a fine family-piece.

Anne, judging from her own temperament, would have deemed such a

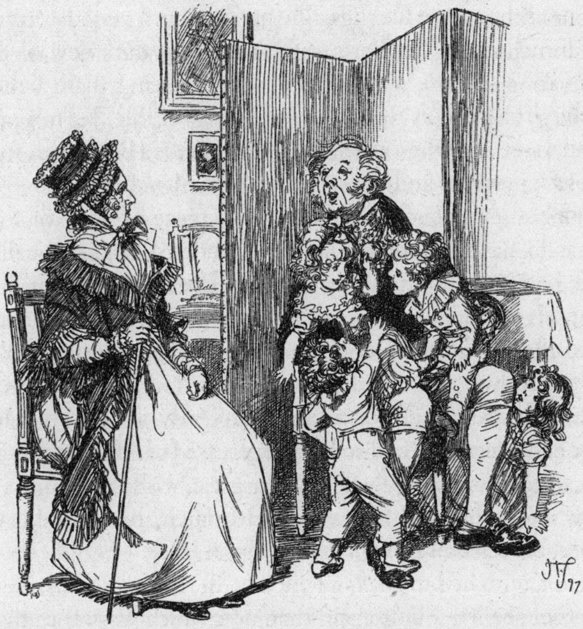

*Talking with a very raised voice*

domestic hurricane a bad restorative of the nerves, which Louisa's illness must have so greatly shaken; but Mrs Musgrove, who got Anne near her on purpose to thank her most cordially, again and again, for all her attentions to them, concluded a short recapitulation of what she had suffered herself by observing, with a happy glance round the room, that after all she had gone through, nothing was so likely to do her good as a little quiet cheerfulness at home.

Louisa was now recovering apace. Her mother could even think of her being able to join their party at home before her brothers and sisters went to school again. The Harvilles had promised to come with her and stay at Uppercross, whenever she returned. Captain Wentworth was gone, for the present, to see his brother in Shropshire.

'I hope I shall remember, in future,' said Lady Russell, as soon as they were reseated in the carriage, 'not to call at Uppercross in the Christmas holidays.'

Everybody has their taste in noises as well as in other matters; and sounds are quite innoxious, or most distressing, by their sort rather than their quantity. When Lady Russell, not long afterwards, was entering Bath on a wet afternoon, and driving through the long course of streets from the Old Bridge to Camden Place, amidst the dash of other carriages, the heavy rumble of carts and drays, the bawling of newsmen, muffin-men, and milkmen, and the ceaseless clink of pattens, she made no complaint. No, these were noises which belonged to the winter pleasures; her spirits rose under their influence; and, like Mrs Musgrove, she was feeling, though not saying that, after being long in the country, nothing could be so good for her as a little quiet cheerfulness.

Anne did not share these feelings. She persisted in a very determined, though very silent, disinclination for Bath; caught the first dim view of the extensive buildings, smoking in rain, without any wish of seeing them better; felt their progress through the streets to be, however disagreeable, yet too rapid; for who would be glad to see her when she arrived? And looked back, with fond regret, to the bustles of Uppercross and the seclusion of Kellynch.

Elizabeth's last letter had communicated a piece of news of some interest. Mr Elliot was in Bath. He had called in Camden Place; had called a second time, a third; had been pointedly attentive: if Elizabeth and her father did not deceive themselves, had been taking as much pains to seek the acquaintance, and proclaim the value of the connection, as he had formerly taken pains to show neglect. This was very wonderful, if it were true; and Lady Russell was in a state of very agreeable curiosity and perplexity about Mr Elliot, already recanting the sentiment she had so lately expressed to Mary, of his being 'a man whom she had no wish to see'. She had a great wish to see him. If he really sought to reconcile himself like a dutiful branch, he must be forgiven for having dismembered himself from the paternal tree.

Anne was not animated to an equal pitch by the circumstance; but she felt that she would rather see Mr Elliot again than not, which was more than she could say for many other persons in Bath.

She was put down in Camden Place; and Lady Russell then drove to her own lodgings, in Rivers Street.

## *Chapter 3*

Sir Walter had taken a very good house in Camden Place, a lofty, dignified situation, such as becomes a man of consequence; and both he and Elizabeth were settled there, much to their satisfaction.

Anne entered it with a sinking heart, anticipating an imprisonment of many months, and anxiously saying to herself, 'Oh! when shall I leave you again?' A degree of unexpected cordiality, however, in the welcome she received, did her good. Her father and sister were glad to see her, for the sake of showing her the house and furniture, and met her with kindness. Her making a fourth, when they sat down to dinner, was noticed as an advantage.

Mrs Clay was very pleasant, and very smiling; but her courtesies and smiles were more a matter of course. Anne had always felt that she would pretend what was proper on her arrival; but the complaisance of the others was unlooked for. They were evidently in excellent spirits, and she was soon to listen to the causes. They had no inclination to listen to her. After laying out for some compliments of being deeply regretted in their old neighbourhood, which Anne could not pay, they had only a few faint enquiries to make before the talk must be all their own. Uppercross excited no interest, Kellynch very little, it was all Bath.

They had the pleasure of assuring her that Bath more than answered their expectations in every respect. Their house µwas undoubtedly the best in Camden Place; their drawing-rooms had many decided advantages over all the others which they had either seen or heard of; and the superiority was not less in the style of the fitting up, or the taste of the furniture. Their acquaintance was exceedingly sought after. Everybody was wanting to visit them. They had drawn back from many introductions, and still were perpetually having cards left by people of whom they knew nothing.

Here were funds of enjoyment! Could Anne wonder that her father and sister were happy? She might not wonder, but she must sigh that her father should feel no degradation in his change; should see nothing to regret in the duties and dignity of the resident landholder; should find so much to be vain of in the littlenesses of a town; and she must sigh, and smile, and wonder too, as Elizabeth threw open the folding doors, and walked with exultation from one drawing-room to the other, boasting of their space, at the possibility of that woman, who had been mistress of Kellynch Hall, finding extent to be proud of between two walls, perhaps thirty feet asunder.

But this was not all which they had to make them happy. They had Mr Elliot, too. Anne had a great deal to hear of Mr Elliot. He was not only pardoned, they were delighted with him. He had been in Bath about a fortnight (he had passed through Bath in November, in his way to London, when the intelligence of Sir Walter's being settled there had of course reached him, though only twenty-four hours in the place, but he had not been able to avail himself of it); but he had now been a fortnight in Bath, and his first object, on arriving, had been to leave his card in Camden Place, following it up by such assiduous endeavours to meet, and, when they did meet, by such great openness of conduct, such readiness to apologise for the past, such solicitude to be received as a relation again that their former good understanding was completely re-established.

They had not a fault to find in him. He had explained away all the appearance of neglect on his own side. It had originated in misapprehension entirely. He had never had an idea of throwing himself off; he had feared that he was thrown off, but knew not why; and delicacy had kept him silent. Upon the hint of having spoken disrespectfully or carelessly of the family, and the family honours, he was quite indignant. He who had ever boasted of being an Elliot, and whose feelings, as to connection, were only too strict to suit the unfeudal tone of the present day! He was astonished, indeed! But his character and general conduct must refute it. He could refer Sir Walter to all who knew him; and, certainly, the pains he had been taking on this, the first opportunity of reconciliation, to be restored to the footing of a relation and heir-presumptive was a strong proof of his opinions on the subject.

The circumstances of his marriage too were found to admit of much extenuation. This was an article not to be entered on by himself; but a very intimate friend of his, a Colonel Wallis, a highly respectable man, perfectly the gentleman (and not an ill-looking man, Sir Walter added), who was living in very good style in Marlborough Buildings, and had, at his own particular request, been admitted to their acquaintance through Mr Elliot, had mentioned one or two things relative to the marriage, which made a material difference in the discredit of it.

Colonel Wallis had known Mr Elliot long, had been well acquainted also with his wife, had perfectly understood the whole story. She was certainly not a woman of family, but well educated, accomplished, rich, and excessively in love with his friend. There had been the charm. She had sought him. Without that attraction, not all her money would have tempted Elliot, and Sir Walter was, moreover, assured of her having been a very fine woman. Here was a great deal to soften the business. A very fine woman, with a large fortune, in love with him! Sir Walter seemed to admit it as complete apology, and though Elizabeth could not see the circumstance in quite so favourable a light, she allowed it be a great extenuation.

Mr Elliot had called repeatedly, had dined with them once, evidently delighted by the distinction of being asked, for they gave no dinners in general; delighted, in short, by every proof of cousinly notice, and placing his whole happiness in being on intimate terms in Camden Place.

Anne listened, but without quite understanding it. Allowances, large allowances, she knew, must be made for the ideas of those who spoke. She heard it all under embellishment. All that sounded extravagant or irrational in the progress of the reconciliation might have no origin but in the language of the relators. Still, however, she had the sensation of there being something more than immediately appeared, in Mr Elliot's wishing, after an interval of so many years, to be well received by them. In a worldly view, he had nothing to gain by being on terms with Sir Walter, nothing to risk by a state of variance. In all probability he was already the richer of the two, and the Kellynch estate would as surely be his hereafter as the title. A sensible man! and he had looked like a *very* sensible man, why should it be an object to him? She could only offer one solution; it was, perhaps, for Elizabeth's sake. There might really have been a liking formerly, though convenience and accident had drawn him a different way, and now that he could afford to please himself, he might mean to pay his addresses to her. Elizabeth was certainly very handsome, with well-bred, elegant manners, and her character might never have been penetrated by Mr Elliot, knowing her but in public, and when very young himself. How her temper and understanding might bear the investigation of his present keener time of life was another concern, and rather a fearful one. Most earnestly did she wish that he might not be too nice, or too observant, if Elizabeth were his object; and that Elizabeth was disposed to believe herself so, and that her friend Mrs Clay was encouraging the idea, seemed apparent by a glance or two between them while Mr Elliot's frequent visits were talked of.

Anne mentioned the glimpses she had had of him at Lyme, but without being much attended to. 'Oh! yes, perhaps, it had been Mr Elliot. They did not know. It might be him, perhaps.' They could not listen to her description of him. They were describing him themselves; Sir Walter especially. He did justice to his very gentlemanlike appearance, his air of elegance and fashion, his good-shaped face, his sensible eye, but, at the same time, 'must lament his being very much under-hung, a defect which time seemed to have increased; nor could he pretend to say that ten years had not altered almost every feature for the worse. Mr Elliot appeared to think that he (Sir Walter) was looking exactly as he had done when they last parted'; but Sir Walter had 'not been able to return the compliment entirely, which had embarrassed him. He did not mean to complain, however. Mr Elliot was better to look at than most men, and he had no objection to being seen with him anywhere'.

Mr Elliot, and his friends in Marlborough Buildings were talked of the whole evening. 'Colonel Wallis had been so impatient to be introduced to them! and Mr Elliot so anxious that he should!' And there was a Mrs Wallis, at present only known to them by description, as she was in daily expectation of her confinement; but Mr Elliot spoke of her as 'a most charming woman, quite worthy of being known in Camden Place', and as soon as she recovered, they were to be acquainted. Sir Walter thought much of Mrs Wallis; she was said to be an excessively pretty woman, beautiful. 'He longed to see her. He hoped she might make some amends for the many very plain faces he was continually passing in the streets. The worst of Bath was the number of its plain women. He did not mean to say that there were no pretty women, but the number of the plain was out of all proportion. He had frequently observed, as he walked, that one handsome face would be followed by thirty, or five-and-thirty frights; and once, as he had stood in a shop in Bond Street, he had counted eighty-seven women go by, one after another, without there being a tolerable face among them. It had been a frosty morning, to be sure, a sharp frost, which hardly one woman in a thousand could stand the test of. But still, there certainly were a dreadful multitude of ugly women in Bath; and as for the men! they were infinitely worse. Such scarecrows as the streets were full of! It was evident how little the women were used to the sight of anything tolerable, by the effect which a man of decent appearance produced. He had never walked anywhere arm in arm with Colonel Wallis (who was a fine military figure, though sandy-haired), without observing that every woman's eye was upon him; every woman's eye was sure to be upon Colonel Wallis.' Modest Sir Walter! He was not allowed to escape, however. His daughter and Mrs Clay united in hinting that Colonel Wallis' companion might have as good a figure as Colonel Wallis, and certainly was not sandy-haired.

'How is Mary looking?' said Sir Walter, in the height of his good humour. 'The last time I saw her, she had a red nose, but I hope that may not happen everyday.'

'Oh! no, that must have been quite accidental. In general she has been in very good health, and very good looks since Michaelmas.'

'If I thought it would not tempt her to go out in sharp winds, and grow coarse, I would send her a new hat and pelisse.'

Anne was considering whether she should venture to suggest that a gown, or a cap, would not be liable to any such misuse, when a knock at the door suspended everything. 'A knock at the door! and so late! It was ten o'clock. Could it be Mr Elliot? They knew he was to dine in Lansdown Crescent. It was possible that he might stop in his way home to ask them how they did. They could think of no one else. Mrs Clay decidedly thought it Mr Elliot's knock.' Mrs Clay was right. With all the state which a butler and footboy could give, Mr Elliot was ushered into the room.

It was the same, the very same man, with no difference but of dress. Anne drew a little back, while the others received his compliments, and her sister his apologies for calling at so unusual an hour, but 'he could not be so near without wishing to know that neither she nor her friend had taken cold the day before, etc., etc.', which was all as politely done, and as politely taken as possible, but her part must follow then. Sir Walter talked of his youngest daughter; 'Mr Elliot must give him leave to present him to his youngest daughter' (there was no occasion for remembering Mary), and Anne, smiling and blushing, very becomingly showed to Mr Elliot the pretty features which he had by no means forgotten, and instantly saw, with amusement at his little start of surprise, that he had not been at all aware of who she was. He looked completely astonished, but not more astonished than pleased; his eyes brightened, and with the most perfect alacrity he welcomed the relationship, alluded to the past, and entreated to be received as an acquaintance already. He was quite as good-looking as he had appeared at Lyme, his countenance improved by speaking, and his manners were so exactly what they ought to be, so polished, so easy, so particularly agreeable, that she could compare them in excellence to only one person's manners. They were not the same, but they were, perhaps, equally good.

He sat down with them, and improved their conversation very much. There could be no doubt of his being a sensible man. Ten minutes were enough to certify that. His tone, his expressions, his choice of subject, his knowing where to stop – it was all the operation of a sensible, discerning mind. As soon as he could, he began to talk to her of Lyme, wanting to compare opinions respecting the place, but especially wanting to speak of the circumstance of their happening to be guests in the same inn at the same time; to give his own route, understand something of hers, and regret that he should have lost such an opportunity of paying his respects to her. She gave him a short account of her party, and business at Lyme. His regret increased as he listened. He had spent his whole solitary evening in the room adjoining theirs; had heard voices – mirth continually; thought they must be a most delightful set of people – longed to be with them; but certainly without the smallest suspicion of his possessing the shadow of a right to introduce himself. If he had but asked who the party were! The name of Musgrove would have told him enough. 'Well, it would serve to cure him of an absurd practice of never asking a question at an inn, which he had adopted, when quite a young man, on the principle of its being very ungenteel to be curious.

'The notions of a young man of one- or two-and-twenty,' said he, 'as to what is necessary in manners to make him quite the thing are more absurd, I believe, than those of any other set of beings in the world. The folly of the means they often employ is only to be equalled by the folly of what they have in view.'

But he must not be addressing his reflections to Anne alone, he knew it; he was soon diffused again among the others, and it was only at intervals that he could return to Lyme.

His enquiries, however, produced at length an account of the scene she had been engaged in there, soon after his leaving the place. Having alluded to 'an accident', he must hear the whole. When he questioned, Sir Walter and Elizabeth began to question also; but the difference in their manner of doing it could not be unfelt. She could only compare Mr Elliot to Lady Russell, in the wish of really comprehending what had passed, and in the degree of concern for what she must have suffered in witnessing it.

He stayed an hour with them. The elegant little clock on the mantelpiece had struck 'eleven with its silver sounds' and the watchman was beginning to be heard at a distance telling the same tale before Mr Elliot or any of them seemed to feel that he had been there long.

Anne could not have supposed it possible that her first evening in Camden Place could have passed so well!

## *Chapter 4*

There was one point which Anne, on returning to her family, would have been more thankful to ascertain even than Mr Elliot's being in love with Elizabeth, which was, her father's not being in love with Mrs Clay; and she was very far from easy about it, when she had been at home a few hours. On going down to breakfast the next morning, she found there had just been a decent pretence on the lady's side of meaning to leave them. She could imagine Mrs Clay to have said, that 'now Miss Anne was come, she could not suppose herself at all wanted'; for Elizabeth was replying, in a sort of whisper, 'That must not be any reason, indeed. I assure you I feel it none. She is nothing to me, compared with you;' and she was in full time to hear her father say, 'My dear madam, this must not be. As yet, you have seen nothing of Bath. You have been here only to be useful. You must not run away from us now. You must stay to be acquainted with Mrs Wallis, the beautiful Mrs Wallis. To your fine mind, I well know the sight of beauty is a real gratification.'

He spoke and looked so much in earnest that Anne was not surprised to see Mrs Clay stealing a glance at Elizabeth and herself. Her countenance, perhaps, might express some watchfulness; but the praise of the fine mind did not appear to excite a thought in her sister. The lady could not but yield to such joint entreaties, and promise to stay.

In the course of the same morning, Anne and her father chancing to be alone together, he began to compliment her on her improved looks – he thought her 'less thin in her person, in her cheeks; her skin, her complexion, greatly improved – clearer, fresher. Had she been using anything in particular?' 'No, nothing.' 'Merely Gowland,' he supposed. 'No, nothing at all.' 'Ha! he was surprised at that'; and added, 'Certainly you cannot do better than continue as you are; you cannot be better than well; or I should recommend Gowland, the constant use of Gowland, during the spring months. Mrs Clay has been using it at my recommendation, and you see what it has done for her. You see how it has carried away her freckles.'

If Elizabeth could but have heard this! Such personal praise might have struck her, especially as it did not appear to Anne that the freckles were at all lessened. But everything must take its chance. The evil of the marriage would be much diminished if Elizabeth were also to marry. As for herself, she might always command a home with Lady Russell.

Lady Russell's composed mind and polite manners were put to some trial on this point, in her intercourse in Camden Place. The sight of Mrs Clay in such favour, and of Anne so overlooked, was a perpetual provocation to her there; and vexed her as much when she was away as a person in Bath who drinks the water, gets all the new publications, and has a very large acquaintance, has time to be vexed.

As Mr Elliot became known to her, she grew more charitable, or more indifferent, towards the others. His manners were an immediate recommendation; and on conversing with him she found the solid so fully supporting the superficial, that she was at first, as she told Anne, almost ready to exclaim, 'Can this be Mr Elliot?' and could not seriously picture to herself a more agreeable or estimable man. Everything united in him: good understanding, correct opinions, knowledge of the world, and a warm heart. He had strong feelings of family attachment and family honour, without pride or weakness; he lived with the liberality of a man of fortune, without display; he judged for himself in everything essential, without defying public opinion in any point of worldly decorum. He was steady, observant, moderate, candid;

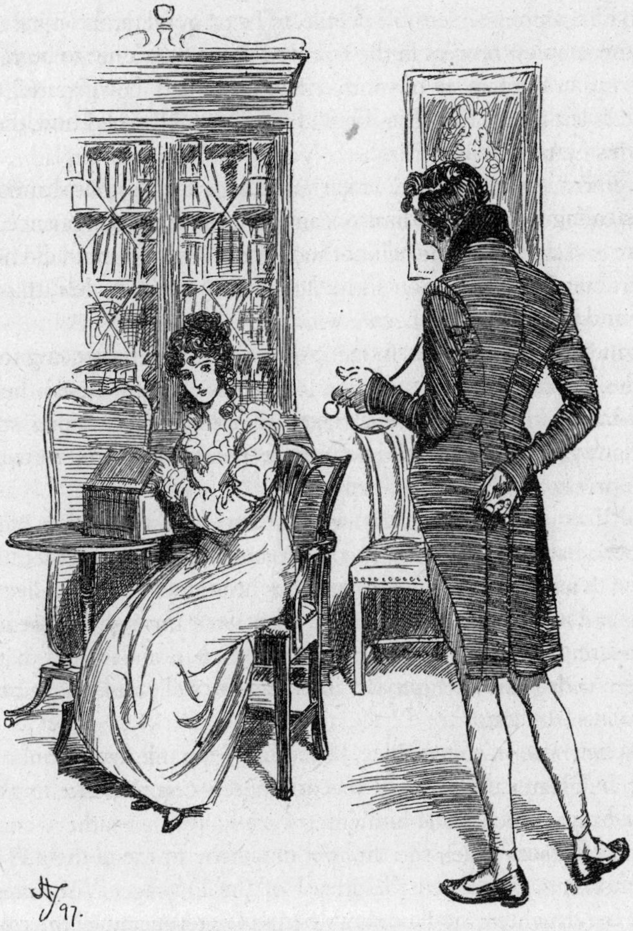

*He began to compliment her on her improved looks*

never run away with by spirits or by selfishness, which fancied itself strong feeling; and yet, with a sensibility to what was amiable and lovely, and a value for all the felicities of domestic life, which characters of fancied enthusiasm and violent agitation seldom really possess. She was sure that he had not been happy in marriage. Colonel Wallis said it, and Lady Russell saw it; but it had been no unhappiness to sour his mind, nor (she began pretty soon to suspect) to prevent his thinking of a second choice. Her satisfaction in Mr Elliot outweighed all the plague of Mrs Clay.

It was now some years since Anne had begun to learn that she and her excellent friend could sometimes think differently; and it did not surprise her, therefore, that Lady Russell should see nothing suspicious or inconsistent, nothing to require more motives than appeared in Mr Elliot's great desire of a reconciliation. In Lady Russell's view, it was perfectly natural that Mr Elliot at a mature time of life, should feel it a most desirable object, and what would very generally recommend him, among all sensible people, to be on good terms with the head of his family; the simplest process in the world of time upon a head naturally clear, and only erring in the heyday of youth. Anne presumed, however, still to smile about it; and at last to mention 'Elizabeth'. Lady Russell listened, and looked, and made only this cautious reply: 'Elizabeth! Very well. Time will explain.'

It was a reference to the future, which Anne, after a little observation, felt she must submit to. She could determine nothing at present. In that house Elizabeth must be first; and she was in the habit of such general observance as 'Miss Elliot' that any particularity of attention seemed almost impossible. Mr Elliot, too, it must be remembered, had not been a widower seven months. A little delay on his side might be very excusable. In fact, Anne could never see the crape round his hat, without fearing that she was the inexcusable one, in attributing to him such imaginations; for though his marriage had not been very happy, still it had existed so many years that she could not comprehend a very rapid recovery from the awful impression of its being dissolved.

However it might end, he was without any question their pleasantest acquaintance in Bath; she saw nobody equal to him; and it was a great indulgence now and then to talk to him about Lyme, which he seemed to have as lively a wish to see again, and to see more of, as herself. They went through the particulars of their first meeting a great many times. He gave her to understand that he had looked at her with some earnestness. She knew it well; and she remembered another person's look also.

They did not always think alike. His value for rank and connection she perceived to be greater than hers. It was not merely complaisance, it must be a liking to the cause, which made him enter warmly into her father's and sister's solicitudes on a subject which she thought unworthy to excite them. The Bath paper one morning announced the arrival of the Dowager Viscountess Dalrymple, and her daughter, the Honourable Miss Carteret; and all the comfort of No. —, Camden Place was swept away for many days; for the Dalrymples (in Anne's opinion, most unfortunately) were cousins of the Elliot's; and the agony was, how to introduce themselves properly.

Anne had never seen her father and sister before in contact with nobility, and she must acknowledge herself disappointed. She had hoped better things from their high ideas of their own situation in life, and was reduced to form a wish which she had never foreseen – a wish that they had more pride; for 'our cousins Lady Dalrymple and Miss Carteret'; 'our cousins the Dalrymples' sounded in her ears all day long.

Sir Walter had once been in company with the late Viscount, but had never seen any of the rest of the family, and the difficulties of the case arose from there having been a suspension of all intercourse by letters of ceremony, ever since the death of that said late Viscount, when, in consequence of a dangerous illness of Sir Walter's at the same time, there had been an unlucky omission at Kellynch. No letter of condolence had been sent to Ireland. The neglect had been visited on the head of the sinner, for when poor Lady Elliot died herself, no letter of condolence was received at Kellynch, and, consequently, there was but too much reason to apprehend that the Dalrymples considered the relationship as closed. How to have this anxious business set to rights, and be admitted as cousins again, was the question; and it was a question which, in a more rational manner, neither Lady Russell nor Mr Elliot thought unimportant. 'Family connections were always worth preserving, good company always worth seeking; Lady Dalrymple had taken a house, for three months, in Laura Place, and would be living in style. She had been at Bath the year before, and Lady Russell had heard her spoken of as a charming woman. It was very desirable that the connection should be renewed, if it could be done without any compromise of propriety on the side of the Elliots.'

Sir Walter, however, would choose his own means, and at last wrote a very fine letter of ample explanation, regret and entreaty, to his right honourable cousin. Neither Lady Russell nor Mr Elliot could admire the letter; but it did all that was wanted in bringing three lines of scrawl from the Dowager Viscountess. 'She was very much honoured, and should be happy in their acquaintance'. The toils of the business were over, the sweets began. They visited in Laura Place, they had the cards of Dowager Viscountess Dalrymple, and the Honourable Miss Carteret, to be arranged wherever they might be most visible- and 'Our cousins in Laura Place' – 'Our cousins, Lady Dalrymple and Miss Carteret' were talked of to everybody.

Anne was ashamed. Had Lady Dalrymple and her daughter even been very agreeable, she would still have been ashamed of the agitation they created, but they were nothing. There was no superiority of manner, accomplishment, or understanding. Lady Dalrymple had acquired the name of 'a charming woman', because she had a smile and a civil answer for everybody. Miss Carteret, with still less to say, was so plain and so awkward that she would never have been tolerated in Camden Place but for her birth.

Lady Russell confessed that she had expected something better; but yet 'it was an acquaintance worth having', and when Anne ventured to speak her opinion of them to Mr Elliot, he agreed to their being nothing in themselves, but still maintained that as a family connection, as good company, as those who would collect good company around them, they had their value. Anne smiled and said,

'My idea of good company, Mr Elliot, is the company of clever, well-informed people, who have a great deal of conversation; that is what I call good company.'

'You are mistaken,' said he gently, 'that is not good company, that is the best. Good company requires only birth, education and manners, and with regard to education is not very nice. Birth and good manners are essential; but a little learning is by no means a dangerous thing in good company; on the contrary, it will do very well. My cousin, Anne, shakes her head. She is not satisfied. She is fastidious. My dear cousin,' (sitting down by her) 'you have a better right to be fastidious than almost any other woman I know; but will it answer? Will it make you happy? Will it not be wiser to accept the society of these good ladies in Laura Place, and enjoy all the advantages of the connection as far as possible? You may depend upon it, that they will move in the first set in Bath this winter, and as rank is rank, your being known to be related to them will have its use in fixing your family (our family let me say), in that degree of consideration which we must all wish for.'

'Yes,' sighed Anne, 'we shall, indeed, be known to be related to them!' – then recollecting herself, and not wishing to be answered, she added, 'I certainly do think there has been by far too much trouble taken to procure the acquaintance. I suppose' (smiling) 'I have more pride than any of you; but I confess it does vex me, that we should be so solicitous to have the relationship acknowledged, which we may be very sure is a matter of perfect indifference to them.'

'Pardon me, my dear cousin, you are unjust to your own claims. In London, perhaps, in your present quiet style of living, it might be as you say; but in Bath, Sir Walter Elliot and his family will always be worth knowing, always acceptable as acquaintance.'

'Well,' said Anne, 'I certainly am proud, too proud to enjoy a welcome which depends so entirely upon place.'

'I love your indignation,' said he; 'it is very natural. But here you are in Bath, and the object is to be established here with all the credit and dignity which ought to belong to Sir Walter Elliot. You talk of being proud, I am called proud I know, and I shall not wish to believe myself otherwise, for our pride, if investigated, would have the same object, I have no doubt, though the kind may seem a little different. In one point, I am sure, my dear cousin.' (he continued, speaking lower, though there was no one else in the room), 'in one point, I am sure, we must feel alike. We must feel that every addition to your father's society, among his equals or superiors, may be of use in diverting his thoughts from those who are beneath him.'

He looked, as he spoke, to the seat which Mrs Clay had been lately occupying, a sufficient explanation of what he particularly meant; and though Anne could not believe in their having the same sort of pride, she was pleased with him for not liking Mrs Clay; and her conscience admitted that his wishing to promote her father's getting great acquaintance was more than excusable in the view of defeating her.

## *Chapter 5*

While Sir Walter and Elizabeth were assiduously pushing their good fortune in Laura Place, Anne was renewing an acquaintance of a very different description.

She had called on her former governess, and had heard from her of there being an old schoolfellow in Bath, who had the two strong claims on her attention, of past kindness and present suffering. Miss Hamilton, now Mrs Smith, had shown her kindness in one of those periods of her life when it had been most valuable. Anne had gone unhappy to school, grieving for the loss of a mother whom she had dearly loved, feeling her separation from home, and suffering as a girl of fourteen, of strong sensibility and not high spirits, must suffer at such a time; and Miss Hamilton, three years older than herself, but still from the want of near relations and a settled home, remaining another year at school, had been useful and good to her in a way which had considerably lessened her misery, and could never be remembered with indifference.

Miss Hamilton had left school, had married not long afterwards, was said to have married a man of fortune, and this was all that Anne had known of her, till now that their governess's account brought her situation forward in a more decided but very different form.

She was a widow, and poor. Her husband had been extravagant; and at his death, about two years before, had left his affairs dreadfully involved. She had had difficulties of every sort to contend with, and in addition to these distresses, had been afflicted with a severe rheumatic fever, which finally settling in her legs, had made her for the present a cripple. She had come to Bath on that account, and was now in lodgings near the hot baths living in a very humble way, unable even to afford herself the comfort of a servant, and of course almost excluded from society.

Their mutual friend answered for the satisfaction which a visit from Miss Elliot would give Mrs Smith, and Anne therefore lost no time in going. She mentioned nothing of what she had heard, or what she intended, at home. It would excite no proper interest there. She only consulted Lady Russell, who entered thoroughly into her sentiments, and was most happy to convey her as near to Mrs Smith's lodgings in Westgate Buildings, as Anne chose to be taken.

The visit was paid, their acquaintance re-established, their interest in each other more than rekindled. The first ten minutes had its awkwardness and its emotion. Twelve years were gone since they had parted, and each presented a somewhat different person from what the other had imagined. Twelve years had changed Anne from the blooming, silent, unformed girl of fifteen to the elegant little woman of seven-and-twenty, with every beauty excepting bloom, and with manners as consciously right as they were invariably gentle; and twelve years had transformed the fine-looking, well-grown Miss Hamilton, in all the glow of health and confidence of superiority, into a poor, infirm, helpless widow, receiving the visit of her former protégée as a favour; but all that was uncomfortable in the meeting had soon passed away, and left only the interesting charm of remembering former partialities and talking over old times.

Anne found in Mrs Smith the good sense and agreeable manners which she had almost ventured to depend on, and a disposition to converse and be cheerful beyond her expectation. Neither the dissipations of the past – and she had lived very much in the world – nor the restrictions of the present; neither sickness nor sorrow seemed to have closed her heart or ruined her spirits.

In the course of a second visit she talked with great openness, and Anne's astonishment increased. She could scarcely imagine a more cheerless situation in itself than Mrs Smith's. She had been very fond of her husband – she had buried him. She had been used to affluence – it was gone. She had no child to connect her with life and happiness again, no relations to assist in the arrangement of perplexed affairs, no health to make all the rest supportable. Her accommodations were limited to a noisy parlour, and a dark bedroom behind, with no possibility of moving from one to the other without assistance, which there was only one servant in the house to afford, and she never quitted the house but to be conveyed into the warm bath. – Yet, in spite of all this, Anne had reason to believe that she had moments only of languor and depression to hours of occupation and enjoyment. How could it be? She watched – observed – reflected – and finally determined that this was not a case of fortitude or of resignation only. – A submissive spirit might be patient, a strong understanding would supply resolution, but here was something more; here was that elasticity of mind, that disposition to be comforted, that power of turning readily from evil to good, and of finding employment which carried her out of herself, which was from nature alone. It was the choicest gift of Heaven; and Anne viewed her friend as one of those instances in which, by a merciful appointment, it seems designed to counterbalance almost every other want.

There had been a time, Mrs Smith told her, when her spirits had nearly failed. She could not call herself an invalid now, compared with her state on first reaching Bath. Then, she had indeed been a pitiable object – for she had caught cold on the journey, and had hardly taken possession of her lodgings before she was again confined to her bed, and suffering under severe and constant pain; and all this among strangers – with the absolute necessity of having a regular nurse, and finances at that moment particularly unfit to meet any extraordinary expense. She had weathered it however, and could truly say that it had done her good. It had increased her comforts by making her feel herself to be in good hands. She had seen too much of the world, to expect sudden or disinterested attachment anywhere, but her illness had proved to her that her landlady had a character to preserve, and would not use her ill; and she had been particularly fortunate in her nurse, as a sister of her landlady, a nurse by profession, and who had always a home in that house when unemployed, chanced to be at liberty just in time to attend her. 'And she,' said Mrs Smith, 'besides nursing me most admirably, has really proved an invaluable acquaintance. – As soon as I could use my hands, she taught me to knit, which has been a great amusement; and she put me in the way of making these little thread-cases, pincushions and card-racks, which you always find me so busy about, and which supply me with the means of doing a little good to one or two very poor families in this neighbourhood. She has a large acquaintance, of course professionally, among those who can afford to buy, and she disposes of my merchandise. She always takes the right time for applying. Everybody's heart is open, you know, when they have recently escaped from severe pain, or are recovering the blessing of health, and nurse Rooke thoroughly understands when to speak. She is a shrewd, intelligent, sensible woman. Hers is a line for seeing human nature; and she has a fund of good sense and observation which, as a companion, make her infinitely superior to thousands of those who, having only received "the best education in the world" know nothing worth attending to. Call it gossip if you will; but when nurse Rooke has half an hour's leisure to bestow on me, she is sure to have something to relate that is entertaining and profitable, something that makes one know one's species better. One likes to hear what is going on, to be *au fait* as to the newest modes of being trifling and silly. To me, who live so much alone, her conversation I assure you is a treat.'

Anne, far from wishing to cavil at the pleasure, replied, 'I can easily believe it. Women of that class have great opportunities, and if they are intelligent may be well worth listening to. Such varieties of human nature as they are in the habit of witnessing! And it is not merely in its follies that they are well read; for they see it occasionally under every circumstance that can be most interesting or affecting. What instances must pass before them of ardent, disinterested, self-denying attachment, of heroism, fortitude, patience, resignation – of all the conflicts and all the sacrifices that ennoble us most. A sick-chamber may often furnish the worth of volumes.'

'Yes,' said Mrs Smith more doubtingly, 'sometimes it may, though I fear its lessons are not often in the elevated style you describe. Here and there, human nature may be great in times of trial, but generally speaking it is its weakness and not its strength that appears in a sick-chamber; it is selfishness and impatience rather than generosity and fortitude, that one hears of. There is so little real friendship in the world! – and unfortunately' (speaking low and tremulously), 'there are so many who forget to think seriously till it is almost too late.'

Anne saw the misery of such feelings. The husband had not been what he ought, and the wife had been led among that part of mankind which made her think worse of the world than she hoped it deserved. It was but a passing emotion, however, with Mrs Smith; she shook it off, and soon added in a different tone,

'I do not suppose the situation my friend Mrs Rooke is in at present will furnish much either to interest or edify me. – She is only nursing Mrs Wallis of Marlborough Buildings – a mere pretty, silly, expensive, fashionable woman, I believe – and of course will have nothing to report but of lace and finery. – I mean to make my profit of Mrs Wallis, however. She has plenty of money, and I intend she shall buy all the high-priced things I have in hand now.'

Anne had called several times on her friend before the existence of such a person was known in Camden Place. At last, it became necessary to speak of her. – Sir Walter, Elizabeth, and Mrs Clay returned one morning from Laura Place, with a sudden invitation from Lady Dalrymple for the same evening, and Anne was already engaged to spend that evening in Westgate Buildings. She was not sorry for the excuse. They were only asked, she was sure, because Lady Dalrymple, being kept at home by a bad cold, was glad to make use of the relationship which had been so pressed on her – and she declined on her own account with great alacrity – 'She was engaged to spend the evening with an old schoolfellow'. They were not much interested in anything relative to Anne, but still there were questions enough asked to make it understood what this old schoolfellow was; and Elizabeth was disdainful, and Sir Walter severe.

'Westgate Buildings!' said he; 'and who is Miss Anne Elliot to be visiting in Westgate Buildings? – A Mrs Smith. A widow Mrs Smith – and who was her husband? One of the five thousand Mr Smiths whose names are to be met with everywhere. And what is her attraction? That she is old and sickly. – Upon my word, Miss Anne Elliot, you have the most extraordinary taste! Everything that revolts other people, low company, paltry rooms, foul air, disgusting associations are inviting to you. But surely you may put off this old lady till tomorrow. She is not so near her end, I presume, but that she may hope to see another day. What is her age? Forty?'

'No, sir, she is not one-and-thirty; but I do not think I can put off my engagement, because it is the only evening for some time which will at once suit her and myself. – She goes into the warm bath tomorrow, and for the rest of the week you know we are engaged.'

'But what does Lady Russell think of this acquaintance?' asked Elizabeth.

'She sees nothing to blame in it,' replied Anne; 'on the contrary, she approves it; and has generally taken me, when I have called on Mrs Smith.'

'Westgate Buildings must have been rather surprised by the appearance of a carriage drawn up near its pavement!' observed Sir Walter. 'Sir Henry Russell's widow, indeed, has no honours to distinguish her arms; but, still, it is a handsome equipage, and no doubt is well known to convey a Miss Elliot. – A widow Mrs Smith, lodging in Westgate Buildings! – A poor widow, barely able to live, between thirty and forty – a mere Mrs Smith, an everyday Mrs Smith, of all people and all names in the world, to be the chosen friend of Miss Anne Elliot, and to be preferred by her, to her own family connections among the nobility of England and Ireland! Mrs Smith, such a name!'

Mrs Clay, who had been present while all this passed, now thought it advisable to leave the room, and Anne could have said much and did long to say a little, in defence of *her* friend's not very dissimilar claims to theirs, but her sense of personal respect to her father prevented her. She made no reply. She left it to himself to recollect that Mrs Smith was not the only widow in Bath between thirty and forty, with little to live on, and no surname of dignity.

Anne kept her appointment; the others kept theirs, and of course she heard the next morning that they had had a delightful evening. – She had been the only one of the set absent; for Sir Walter and Elizabeth had not only been quite at her ladyship's service themselves, but had actually been happy to be employed by her in collecting others, and had been at the trouble of inviting both Lady Russell and Mr Elliot; and Mr Elliot had made a point of leaving Colonel Wallis early, and Lady Russell had fresh arranged all her evening engagements in order to wait on her. Anne had the whole history of all that such an evening could supply from Lady Russell. To her, its greatest interest must be in having been very much talked of between her friend and Mr Elliot, in having been wished for, regretted, and at the same time honoured for staying away in such a cause. – Her kind, compassionate visits to this old schoolfellow, sick and reduced, seemed to have quite delighted Mr Elliot. He thought her a most extraordinary young woman; in her temper, manners, mind, a model of female excellence. He could meet even Lady Russell in a discussion of her merits; and Anne could not be given to understand so much by her friend, could not know herself to be so highly rated by a sensible man, without many of those agreeable sensations which her friend meant to create.

Lady Russell was now perfectly decided in her opinion of Mr Elliot. She was as much convinced of his meaning to gain Anne in time as of his deserving her; and was beginning to calculate the number of weeks which would free him from all the remaining restraints of widowhood, and leave him at liberty to exert his most open powers of pleasing. She would not speak to Anne with half the certainty she felt on the subject, she would venture on little more than hints of what might be hereafter, of a possible attachment on his side, of the desirableness of the alliance, supposing such attachment to be real, and returned. Anne heard her, and made no violent exclamations. She only smiled, blushed, and gently shook her head.

'I am no matchmaker, as you well know,' said Lady Russell, 'being much too well aware of the uncertainty of all human events and calculations. I only mean that if Mr Elliot should some time hence pay his addresses to you, and if you should be disposed to accept him, I think there would be every possibility of your being happy together. A most suitable connection everybody must consider it – but I think it might be a very happy one.'

'Mr Elliot is an exceedingly agreeable man, and in many respects I think highly of him,' said Anne; 'but we should not suit.'

Lady Russell let this pass, and only said in rejoinder, 'I own that to be able to regard you as the future mistress of Kellynch, the future Lady Elliot – to look forward and see you occupying your dear mother's place succeeding to all her rights, and all her popularity, as well as to all her virtues, would be the highest possible gratification to me. – You are your mother's self in countenance and disposition; and if I might be allowed to fancy you such as she was, in situation, and name, and home, presiding and blessing in the same spot, and only superior to her in being more highly valued! My dearest Anne, it would give me more delight than is often felt at my time of life!'

Anne was obliged to turn away, to rise, to walk to a distant table, and, leaning there in pretended employment, try to subdue the feelings this picture excited. For a few moments her imagination and her heart were bewitched. The idea of becoming what her mother had been; of having the precious name of 'Lady Elliot' first revived in herself; of being restored to Kellynch, calling it her home again, her home forever, was a charm which she could not immediately resist. Lady Russell said not another word, willing to leave the matter to its own operation; and believing that, could Mr Elliot at that moment with propriety have spoken for himself! – She believed, in short, what Anne did not believe. The same image of Mr Elliot speaking for himself brought Anne to composure again. The charm of Kellynch and of 'Lady Elliot' all faded away. She never could accept him. And it was not only that her feelings were still adverse to any man save one; her judgement, on a serious consideration of the possibilities of such a case, was against Mr Elliot.

Though they had now been acquainted a month, she could not be satisfied that she really knew his character. That he was a sensible man, an agreeable man – that he talked well, professed good opinions, seemed to judge properly and as a man of principle – this was all clear enough. He certainly knew what was right, nor could she fix on any one article of moral duty evidently transgressed; but yet she would have been afraid to answer for his conduct. She distrusted the past, if not the present. The names which occasionally dropped of former associates, the allusions to former practices and pursuits, suggested suspicions not favourable of what he had been. She saw that there had been bad habits; that Sunday travelling had been a common thing; that there had been a period of his life (and probably not a short one) when he had been, at least, careless on all serious matters; and, though he might now think very differently, who could answer for the true sentiments of a clever, cautious man, grown old enough to appreciate a fair character? How could it ever be ascertained that his mind was truly cleansed?

Mr Elliot was rational, discreet, polished – but he was not open. There was never any burst of feeling, any warmth of indignation or delight, at the evil or good of others. This, to Anne, was a decided imperfection. Her early impressions were incurable. She prized the frank, the open-hearted, the eager character beyond all others. Warmth and enthusiasm did captivate her still. She felt that she could so much more depend upon the sincerity of those who sometimes looked or said a careless or a hasty thing, than of those whose presence of mind never varied, whose tongue never slipped.

Mr Elliot was too generally agreeable. Various were the tempers in her father's house, he pleased them all. He endured too well – stood too well with everybody. He had spoken to her with some degree of openness of Mrs Clay; had appeared completely to see what Mrs Clay was about, and to hold her in contempt; and yet Mrs Clay found him as agreeable as anybody.

Lady Russell saw either less or more than her young friend, for she saw nothing to excite distrust. She could not imagine a man more exactly what he ought to be than Mr Elliot; nor did she ever enjoy a sweeter feeling than the hope of seeing him receive the hand of her beloved Anne in Kellynch church, in the course of the following autumn.

## *Chapter 6*

It was the beginning of February; and Anne, having been a month in Bath, was growing very eager for news from Uppercross and Lyme. She wanted to hear much more than Mary communicated. It was three weeks since she had heard at all. She only knew that Henrietta was at home again; and that Louisa, though considered to be recovering fast, was still at Lyme; and she was thinking of them all very intently one evening, when a thicker letter than usual from Mary was delivered to her, and, to quicken the pleasure and surprise, with Admiral and Mrs Croft's compliments.

The Crofts must be in Bath! A circumstance to interest her. They were people whom her heart turned to very naturally.

'What is this?' cried Sir Walter. 'The Crofts arrived in Bath? The Crofts who rent Kellynch? What have they brought you?'

'A letter from Uppercross Cottage, sir.'

'Oh! those letters are convenient passports. They secure an introduction. I should have visited Admiral Croft, however, at any rate. I know what is due to my tenant.'

Anne could listen no longer; she could not even have told how the poor Admiral's complexion escaped; her letter engrossed her. It had been begun several days back.

February 1st, —

My Dear Anne – I make no apology for my silence, because I know how little people think of letters in such a place as Bath. You must be a great deal too happy to care for Uppercross, which, as you well know, affords little to write about. We have had a very dull Christmas; Mr and Mrs Musgrove have not had one dinner-party all the holidays. I do not reckon the Hayters as anybody. The holidays, however, are over at last: I believe no children ever had such long ones. I am sure I had not. The house was cleared yesterday, except of the little Harvilles; but you will be surprised to hear that they have never gone home. Mrs Harville must be an odd mother to part with them so long. I do not understand it. They are not at all nice children, in my opinion; but Mrs Musgrove seems to like them quite as well, if not better, than her grandchildren. What dreadful weather we have had! It may not be felt in Bath, with your nice pavements; but in the country it is of some consequence. I have not had a creature call on me since the second week in January, except Charles Hayter, who has been calling much oftener than was welcome. Between ourselves, I think it a great pity Henrietta did not remain at Lyme as long as Louisa; it would have kept her a little out of his way. The carriage is gone today, to bring Louisa and the Harvilles tomorrow. We are not asked to dine with them, however, till the day after, Mrs Musgrove is so afraid of her being fatigued by the journey, which is not very likely, considering the care that will be taken of her; and it would be much more convenient to me to dine there tomorrow. I am glad you find Mr Elliot so agreeable, and wish I could be acquainted with him too; but I have my usual luck, I am always out of the way when anything desirable is going on; always the last of my family to be noticed. What an immense time Mrs Clay has been staying with Elizabeth! Does she never mean to go away? But perhaps if she were to leave the room vacant we might not be invited. Let me know what you think of this. I do not expect my children to be asked, you know. I can leave them at the Great House very well, for a month or six weeks. I have this moment heard that the Crofts are going to Bath almost immediately; they think the Admiral gouty. Charles heard it quite by chance: they have not had the civility to give me any notice, or offer to take anything. I do not think they improve at all as neighbours. We see nothing of them, and this is really an instance of gross inattention. Charles joins me in love, and everything proper. Yours, affectionately,

MARY M—

I am sorry to say that I am very far from well; and Jemima has just told me that the butcher says there is a bad sore-throat very much about. I dare say I shall catch it; and my sore-throats, you know, are always worse than anybody's.

So ended the first part, which had been afterwards put into an envelope containing nearly as much more.

I kept my letter open, that I might send you word how Louisa bore her journey, and now I am extremely glad I did, having a great deal to add. In the first place, I had a note from Mrs Croft yesterday, offering to convey anything to you; a very kind, friendly note indeed, addressed to me, just as it ought; I shall therefore be able to make my letter as long as I like. The Admiral does not seem very ill, and I sincerely hope Bath will do him all the good he wants. I shall be truly glad to have them back again. Our neighbourhood cannot spare such a pleasant family. But now for Louisa. I have something to communicate that will astonish you not a little. She and the Harvilles came on Tuesday very safely, and in the evening we went to ask her how she did, when we were rather surprised not to find Captain Benwick of the party, for he had been invited as well as the Harvilles; and what do you think was the reason? Neither more nor less than his being in love with Louisa, and not choosing to venture to Uppercross till he had had an answer from Mr Musgrove; for it was all settled between him and her before she came away, and he had written to her father by Captain Harville. True, upon my honour. Are not you astonished? I shall be surprised at least if you ever received a hint of it, for I never did. Mrs Musgrove protests solemnly that she knew nothing of the matter. We are all very well pleased, however; for though it is not equal to her marrying Captain Wentworth, it is infinitely better than Charles Hayter; and Mr Musgrove has written his consent, and Captain Benwick is expected today. Mrs Harville says her husband feels a good deal on his poor sister's account, but, however, Louisa is a great favourite with both. Indeed Mrs Harville and I quite agree that we love her the better for having nursed her. Charles wonders what Captain Wentworth will say; but, if you remember, I never thought him attached to Louisa; I never could see anything of it. And this is the end, you see, of Captain Benwick's being supposed to be an admirer of yours. How Charles could take such a thing into his head was always incomprehensible to me. I hope he will be more agreeable now. Certainly not a great match for Louisa Musgrove; but a million times better than marrying among the Hayters.

Mary need not have feared her sister's being in any degree prepared for the news. She had never in her life been more astonished. Captain Benwick and Louisa Musgrove! It was almost too wonderful for belief; and it was with the greatest effort that she could remain in the room, preserve an air of calmness, and answer the common questions of the moment. Happily for her, they were not many. Sir Walter wanted to know whether the Crofts travelled with four horses, and whether they were likely to be situated in such a part of Bath as it might suit Miss Elliot and himself to visit in; but had little curiosity beyond.

'How is Mary?' said Elizabeth; and without waiting for an answer, 'And pray what brings the Crofts to Bath?'

'They come on the Admiral's account. He is thought to be gouty.'

'Gout and decrepitude!' said Sir Walter. 'Poor old gentleman.'

'Have they any acquaintance here?' asked Elizabeth.

'I do not know; but I can hardly suppose that, at Admiral Croft's time of life, and in his profession, he should not have many acquaintances in such a place as this.'

'I suspect,' said Sir Walter coolly, 'that Admiral Croft will be best known in Bath as the renter of Kellynch Hall. Elizabeth, may we venture to present him and his wife in Laura Place?'

'Oh! no, I think not. Situated as we are with Lady Dalrymple, cousins, we ought to be very careful not to embarrass her with acquaintance she might not approve. If we were not related, it would not signify; but as cousins, she would feel scrupulous as to any proposal of ours. We had better leave the Crofts to find their own level. There are several odd-looking men walking about here, who, I am told, are sailors. The Crofts will associate with them!'

This was Sir Walter and Elizabeth's share of interest in the letter; when Mrs Clay had paid her tribute of more decent attention, in an enquiry after Mrs Charles Musgrove, and her fine little boys, Anne was at liberty.

In her own room she tried to comprehend it. Well might Charles wonder how Captain Wentworth would feel! Perhaps he had quitted the field, had given Louisa up, had ceased to love, had found he did not love her. She could not endure the idea of treachery or levity, or anything akin to ill usage between him and his friend. She could not endure that such a friendship as theirs should be severed unfairly.

Captain Benwick and Louisa Musgrove! The high spirited, joyous-talking

Louisa Musgrove, and the dejected, thinking, feeling, reading Captain Benwick, seemed each of them everything that would not suit the other. Their minds most dissimilar! Where could have been the attraction? The answer soon presented itself. It had been in situation. They had been thrown together several weeks; they had been living in the same small family-party; since Henrietta's coming away, they must have been depending almost entirely on each other, and Louisa, just recovering from illness, had been in an interesting state, and Captain Benwick was not inconsolable. That was a point which Anne had not been able to avoid suspecting before; and instead of drawing the same conclusion as Mary, from the present course of events, they served only to confirm the idea of his having felt some dawning of tenderness toward herself. She did not mean, however, to derive much more from it to gratify her vanity than Mary might have allowed. She was persuaded that any tolerably pleasing young woman who had listened and seemed to feel for him would have received the same compliment. He had an affectionate heart. He must love somebody.

She saw no reason against their being happy. Louisa had fine naval fervour to begin with, and they would soon grow more alike. He would gain cheerfulness, and she would learn to be an enthusiast for Scott and Lord Byron; nay, that was probably learned already; of course they had fallen in love over poetry. The idea of Louisa Musgrove turned into a person of literary taste, and sentimental reflection, was amusing, but she had no doubt of its being so. The day at Lyme, the fall from the Cobb, might influence her health, her nerves, her courage, her character to the end of her life, as thoroughly as it appeared to have influenced her fate.

The conclusion of the whole was that if the woman who had been sensible of Captain Wentworth's merits could be allowed to prefer another man, there was nothing in the engagement to excite lasting wonder; and if Captain Wentworth lost no friend by it, certainly nothing to be regretted. No, it was not regret which made Anne's heart beat in spite of herself, and brought the colour into her cheeks when she thought of Captain Wentworth unshackled and free. She had some feelings which she was ashamed to investigate. They were too much like joy, senseless joy!

She longed to see the Crofts, but when the meeting took place, it was evident that no rumour of the news had yet reached them. The visit of ceremony was paid and returned, and Louisa Musgrove was mentioned, and Captain Benwick too, without even half a smile.

The Crofts had placed themselves in lodgings in Gay Street, perfectly to Sir Walter's satisfaction. He was not at all ashamed of the acquaintance, and did, in fact, think and talk a great deal more about the Admiral than the Admiral ever thought or talked about him.

The Crofts knew quite as many people in Bath as they wished for, and considered their intercourse with the Elliots as a mere matter of form, and not in the least likely to afford them any pleasure. They brought with them their country habit of being almost always together. He was ordered to walk, to keep off the gout, and Mrs Croft seemed to go shares with him in everything, and to walk for her life, to do him good. Anne saw them wherever she went. Lady Russell took her out in her carriage almost every morning, and she never failed to think of them, and never failed to see them. Knowing their feelings as she did, it was a most attractive picture of happiness to her. She always watched them as long as she could; delighted to fancy she understood what they might be talking of, as they walked along in happy independence, or equally delighted to see the Admiral's hearty shake of the hand when he encountered an old friend, and observe their eagerness of conversation when occasionally forming into a little knot of the navy, Mrs Croft looking as intelligent and keen as any of the officers around her.

Anne was too much engaged with Lady Russell to be often walking herself, but it so happened that one morning, about a week or ten days after the Crofts' arrival, it suited her best to leave her friend, or her friend's carriage, in the lower part of the town, and return alone to Camden Place; and in walking up Milsom Street, she had the good fortune to meet with the Admiral. He was standing by himself, at a print-shop window, with his hands behind him, in earnest

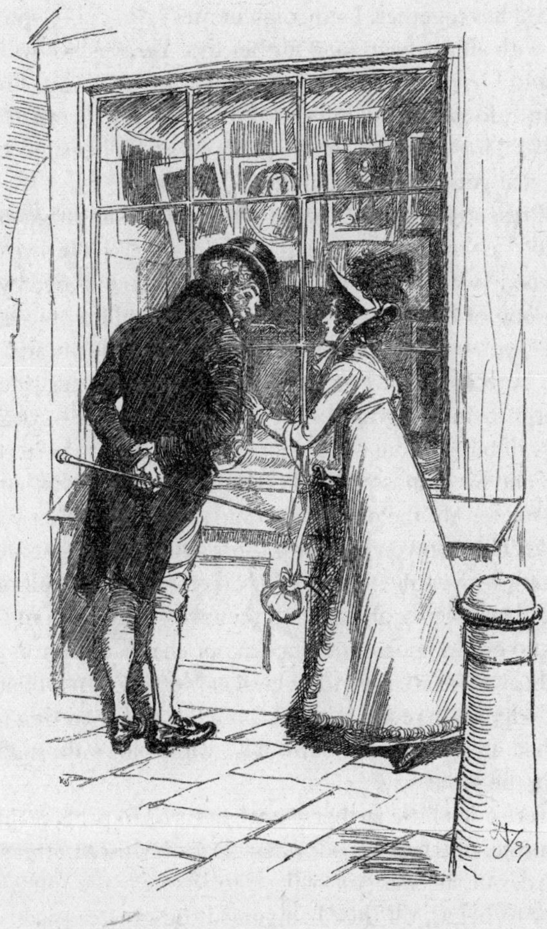

*Obliged to touch him before she could catch his notice*

contemplation of some print, and she not only might have passed him unseen, but was obliged to touch as well as address him before she could catch his notice. When he did perceive and acknowledge her, however, it was done with all his usual frankness and good humour. 'Ha! is it you? Thank you, thank you. This is treating me like a friend. Here I am, you see, staring at a picture. I can never get by this shop without stopping. But what a thing here is, by way of a boat. Do look at it. Did you ever see the like? What queer fellows your fine painters must be, to think that anybody would venture their lives in such a shapeless old cockleshell as that. And yet, here are two gentlemen stuck up in it mightily at their ease, and looking about them at the rocks and mountains, as if they were not to be upset the next moment, which they certainly must be. I wonder where that boat was built!' (laughing heartily) 'I would not venture over a horse-pond in it. Well,' (turning away) 'now, where are you bound? Can I go anywhere for you, or with you? Can I be of any use?'

'None, I thank you, unless you will give me the pleasure of your company the little way our road lies together. I am going home.'

'That I will, with all my heart, and farther too. Yes, yes, we will have a snug walk together; and I have something to tell you as we go along. There, take my arm; that's right; I do not feel comfortable if I have not a woman there. Lord! what a boat it is!' taking a last look at the picture, as they began to be in motion.

'Did you say that you had something to tell me, sir?'

'Yes, I have. Presently. But here comes a friend, Captain Brigden; I shall only say, "How d'ye do" as we pass, however. I shall not stop. "How d'ye do." Brigden stares to see anybody with me but my wife. She, poor soul, is tied by the leg. She has a blister on one of her heels, as large as a three-shilling piece. If you look across the street, you will see Admiral Brand coming down and his brother. Shabby fellows, both of them! I am glad they are not on this side of the way. Sophy cannot bear them. They played me a pitiful trick once – got away some of my best men. I will tell you the whole story another time. There comes old Sir Archibald Drew and his grandson. Look, he sees us; he kisses his hand to you; he takes you for my wife. Ah! the peace has come too soon for that younker. Poor old Sir Archibald! How do you like Bath, Miss Elliot? It suits us very well. We are always meeting with some old friend or other; the streets full of them every morning; sure to have plenty of chat; and then we get away from them all, and shut ourselves into our lodgings, and draw in our chairs, and are as snug as if we were at Kellynch, ay, or as we used to be even at North Yarmouth and Deal. We do not like our lodgings here the worse, I can tell you, for putting us in mind of those we first had at North Yarmouth. The wind blows through one of the cupboards just in the same way.'

When they were got a little farther, Anne ventured to press again for what he had to communicate. She had hoped, when clear of Milsom Street, to have her curiosity gratified; but she was still obliged to wait, for the Admiral had made up his mind not to begin, till they had gained the greater space and quiet of Belmont, and as she was not really Mrs Croft, she must let him have his own way.

As soon as they were fairly ascending Belmont, he began, 'Well, now you shall hear something that will surprise you. But first of all, you must tell me the name of the young lady I am going to talk about. That young lady you know, that we have all been so concerned for. The Miss Musgrove that all this has been happening to. Her Christian name – I always forget her Christian name.'

Anne had been ashamed to appear to comprehend so soon as she really did; but now she could safely suggest the name of 'Louisa'.

'Ay, ay, Miss Louisa Musgrove, that is the name. I wish young ladies had not such a number of fine christian names. I should never be out, if they were all Sophys, or something of that sort. Well, this Miss Louisa, we all thought, you know, was to marry Frederick. He was courting her week after week. The only

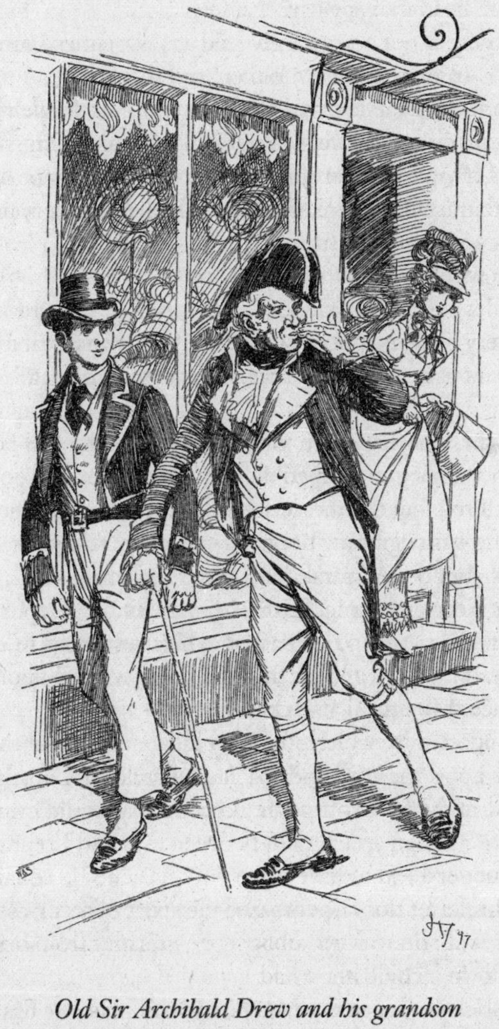

*Old Sir Archibald Drew and his grandson*

wonder was, what they could be waiting for, till the business at Lyme came; then, indeed, it was clear enough that they must wait till her brain was set to right. But even then, there was something odd in their way of going on. Instead of staying at Lyme, he went off to Plymouth, and then he went off to see Edward. When we came back from Minehead, he was gone down to Edward's, and there he has been ever since. We have seen nothing of him since November. Even Sophy could not understand it. But now, the matter has taken the strangest turn of all; for this young lady, this same Miss Musgrove, instead of being to marry Frederick, is to marry James Benwick. You know James Benwick.'

'A little. I am a little acquainted with Captain Benwick.'

'Well, she is to marry him. Nay, most likely they are married already, for I do not know what they should wait for.'

'I thought Captain Benwick a very pleasing young man,' said Anne, 'and I understand that he bears an excellent character.'

'Oh! yes, yes, there is not a word to be said against James Benwick. He is only a commander, it is true, made last summer, and these are bad times for getting on, but he has not another fault that I know of. An excellent, good-hearted fellow, I assure you; a very active, zealous officer too, which is more than you would think for, perhaps, for that soft sort of manner does not do him justice.'

'Indeed you are mistaken there, sir. I should never augur want of spirit from Captain Benwick's manners. I thought them particularly pleasing, and I will answer for it they would generally please.'

'Well, well, ladies are the best judges; but James Benwick is rather too piano for me, and though very likely it is all our partiality, Sophy and I cannot help thinking Frederick's manners better than his. There is something about Frederick more to our taste.'

Anne was caught. She had only meant to oppose the too-common idea of spirit and gentleness being incompatible with each other, not at all to represent Captain Benwick's manners as the very best that could possibly be, and, after a little hesitation, she was beginning to say, 'I was not entering into any comparison of the two friends,' but the Admiral interrupted her with,

'And the thing is certainly true. It is not a mere bit of gossip. We have it from Frederick himself. His sister had a letter from him yesterday, in which he tells us of it, and he had just had it in a letter from Harville, written upon the spot, from Uppercross. I fancy they are all at Uppercross.'

This was an opportunity which Anne could not resist; she said, therefore, 'I hope, Admiral, I hope there is nothing in the style of Captain Wentworth's letter to make you and Mrs Croft particularly uneasy. It did certainly seem, last autumn, as if there were an attachment between him and Louisa Musgrove; but I hope it may be understood to have worn out on each side equally, and without violence. I hope his letter does not breathe the spirit of an ill-used man.'

'Not at all, not at all; there is not an oath or a murmur from beginning to end.'

Anne looked down to hide her smile.

'No, no; Frederick is not a man to whine and complain; he has too much spirit for that. If the girl likes another man better, it is very fit she should have him.'

'Certainly. But what I mean is, that I hope there is nothing in Captain Wentworth's manner of writing to make you suppose he thinks himself ill-used by his friend, which might appear, you know, without its being absolutely said. I should be very sorry that such a friendship as has subsisted between him and Captain Benwick should be destroyed, or even wounded, by a circumstance of this sort.'

'Yes, yes, I understand you. But there is nothing at all of that nature in the letter. He does not give the least fling at Benwick; does not so much as say, "I wonder at it, I have a reason of my own for wondering at it." No, you would not guess, from his way of writing, that he had ever thought of this Miss (what's her name?) for himself. He very handsomely hopes they will be happy together, and there is nothing very unforgiving in that, I think.'

Anne did not receive the perfect conviction which the Admiral meant to convey, but it would have been useless to press the enquiry farther. She, therefore, satisfied herself with commonplace remarks or quiet attention, and the Admiral had it all his own way.

'Poor Frederick!' said he at last. 'Now he must begin all over again with somebody else. I think we must get him to Bath. Sophy must write, and beg him to come to Bath. Here are pretty girls enough, I am sure. It would be of no use to go to Uppercross again, for that other Miss Musgrove, I find, is bespoke by her cousin, the young parson. Do not you think, Miss Elliot, we had better try to get him to Bath?'

## *Chapter 7*

While Admiral Croft was taking this walk with Anne, and expressing his wish of getting Captain Wentworth to Bath, Captain Wentworth was already on his way thither. Before Mrs Croft had written, he was arrived; and the very next time Anne walked out, she saw him.

Mr Elliot was attending his two cousins and Mrs Clay. They were in Milsom Street. It began to rain, not much, but enough to make shelter desirable for women, and quite enough to make it very desirable for Miss Elliot to have the advantage of being conveyed home in Lady Dalrymple's carriage, which was seen waiting at a little distance; she, Anne, and Mrs Clay, therefore, turned into Molland's, while Mr Elliot stepped to Lady Dalrymple, to request her assistance. He soon joined them again, successful, of course; Lady Dalrymple would be most happy to take them home, and would call for them in a few minutes.

Her ladyship's carriage was a barouche, and did not hold more than four with any comfort. Miss Carteret was with her mother; consequently it was not reasonable to expect accommodation for all the three Camden Place ladies. There could be no doubt as to Miss Elliot. Whoever suffered inconvenience, she must suffer none, but it occupied a little time to settle the point of civility between the other two. The rain was a mere trifle, and Anne was most sincere in preferring a walk with Mr Elliot. But the rain was also a mere trifle to Mrs Clay; she would hardly allow it even to drop at all, and her boots were so thick! much thicker than Miss Anne's – and, in short, her civility rendered her quite as anxious to be left to walk with Mr Elliot as Anne could be, and it was discussed between them with a generosity so polite and so determined that the others were obliged to settle it for them. Miss Elliot maintaining that Mrs Clay had a little cold already, and Mr Elliot deciding on appeal that his cousin Anne's boots were rather the thickest.

It was fixed accordingly that Mrs Clay should be of the party in the carriage; and they had just reached this point when Anne, as she sat near the window, descried most decidedly and distinctly, Captain Wentworth walking down the street.

Her start was perceptible only to herself; but she instantly felt that she was the greatest simpleton in the world, the most unaccountable and absurd! For a few minutes she saw nothing before her. It was all confusion. She was lost; and when she had scolded back her senses, she found the others still waiting for the carriage, and Mr Elliot (always obliging), just setting off for Union Street on a commission of Mrs Clay's.

She now felt a great inclination to go to the outer door; she wanted to see if it rained. Why was she to suspect herself of another motive? Captain Wentworth must be out of sight. She left her seat, she would go, one half of her should not be always so much wiser than the other half, or always suspecting the other of being worse than it was. She would see if it rained. She was sent back, however, in a moment by the entrance of Captain Wentworth himself, among a party of gentlemen and ladies, evidently his acquaintance, and whom he must have joined a little below Milsom Street. He was more obviously struck and confused by the sight of her than she had ever observed before; he looked quite red. For the first time, since their renewed acquaintance, she felt that she was betraying the least sensibility of the two. She had the advantage of him, in the preparation of the last few moments. All the overpowering, blinding, bewildering, first effects of strong surprise were over with her. Still, however, she had enough to feel! It was agitation, pain, pleasure, a something between delight and misery.

He spoke to her, and then turned away. The character of his manner was embarrassment. She could not have called it either cold or friendly, or anything so certainly as embarrassed.

After a short interval, however, he came towards her and spoke again. Mutual enquiries on common subjects passed; neither of them, probably, much the wiser for what they heard, and Anne continuing fully sensible of his being less at ease than formerly. They had, by dint of being so very much together, got to speak to each other with a considerable portion of apparent indifference and calmness; but he could not do it now. Time had changed him, or Louisa had changed him. There was consciousness of some sort or other. He looked very well, not as if he had been suffering in health or spirits, and he talked of Uppercross, of the Musgroves, nay, even of Louisa, and had even a momentary look of his own arch significance as he named her; but yet it was Captain Wentworth not comfortable, not easy, not able to feign that he was.

It did not surprise, but it grieved Anne to observe that Elizabeth would not know him. She saw that he saw Elizabeth, that Elizabeth saw him, that there was complete internal recognition on each side; she was convinced that he was ready to be acknowledged as an acquaintance, expecting it, and she had the pain of seeing her sister turn away with unalterable coldness.

Lady Dalrymple's carriage, for which Miss Elliot was growing very impatient, now drew up; the servant came in to announce it. It was beginning to rain again, and altogether there was a delay, and a bustle, and a talking, which must make all the little crowd in the shop understand that Lady Dalrymple was calling to convey Miss Elliot. At last Miss Elliot and her friend, unattended but by the servant (for there was no cousin returned), were walking off; and Captain Wentworth, watching them, turned again to Anne, and by manner, rather than words, was offering his services to her.

'I am much obliged to you,' was her answer, 'but I am not going with them. The carriage would not accommodate so many. I walk. I prefer walking.'

'But it rains.'

'Oh! very little. Nothing that I regard.'

After a moment's pause he said, 'Though I came only yesterday, I have equipped myself properly for Bath already, you see,' (pointing to a new umbrella) 'I wish you would make use of it, if you are determined to walk; though, I think, it would be more prudent to let me get you a chair.'

She was very much obliged to him, but declined it all, repeating her conviction, that the rain would come to nothing at present, and adding, 'I am only waiting for Mr Elliot. He will be here in a moment, I am sure.'

She had hardly spoken the words, when Mr Elliot walked in. Captain Wentworth recollected him perfectly. There was no difference between him and the man who had stood on the steps at Lyme, admiring Anne as she passed, except in the air and look and manner of the privileged relation and friend. He came in with eagerness, appeared to see and think only of her, apologised for his stay, was grieved to have kept her waiting, and anxious to get her away without further loss of time, and before the rain increased; and in another moment they walked off together, her arm under his, a gentle and embarrassed glance, and a 'good-morning to you', being all that she had time for, as she passed away.

As soon as they were out of sight, the ladies of Captain Wentworth's party began talking of them.

'Mr Elliot does not dislike his cousin, I fancy?'

'Oh! no, that is clear enough. One can guess what will happen there. He is always with them; half lives in the family, I believe. What a very good-looking man!'

'Yes, and Miss Atkinson, who dined with him once at the Wallises', says he is the most agreeable man she ever was in company with.'

'She is pretty, I think, Anne Elliot; very pretty, when one comes to look at her. It is not the fashion to say so, but I confess I admire her more than her sister.'

'Oh! so do I.'

'And so do I. No comparison. But the men are all wild after Miss Elliot. Anne is too delicate for them.'

Anne would have been particularly obliged to her cousin, if he would have walked by her side all the way to Camden Place, without saying a word. She had never found it so difficult to listen to him, though nothing could exceed his solicitude and care, and though his subjects were principally such as were wont to be always interesting – praise, warm, just, and discriminating, of Lady Russell, and insinuations highly rational against Mrs Clay. But just now she could think only of Captain Wentworth. She could not understand his present feelings, whether he were really suffering much from disappointment or not; and till that point were settled, she could not be quite herself.

She hoped to be wise and reasonable in time; but alas! alas! she must confess to herself that she was not wise yet.

Another circumstance very essential for her to know was how long he meant to be in Bath; he had not mentioned it, or she could not recollect it. He might be only passing through. But it was more probable that he should be come to stay. In that case, so liable as everybody was to meet everybody in Bath, Lady Russell would in all likelihood see him somewhere. – Would she recollect him? How would it all be?

She had already been obliged to tell Lady Russell that Louisa Musgrove was to marry Captain Benwick. It had cost her something to encounter Lady Russell's surprise; and now, if she were by any chance to be thrown into company with Captain Wentworth, her imperfect knowledge of the matter might add another shade of prejudice against him.

The following morning Anne was out with her friend, and for the first hour, in an incessant and fearful sort of watch for him in vain; but at last, in returning down Pulteney Street, she distinguished him on the right-hand pavement at such a distance as to have him in view the greater part of the street. There were many other men about him, many groups walking the same way, but there was no mistaking him. She looked instinctively at Lady Russell; but not from any mad idea of her recognising him so soon as she did herself. No, it was not to be supposed that Lady Russell would perceive him till they were nearly opposite. She looked at her however, from time to time, anxiously; and when the moment approached which must point him out, though not daring to look again (for her own countenance she knew was unfit to be seen), she was yet perfectly conscious of Lady Russell's eyes being turned exactly in the direction for him, of her being in short intently observing him. She could thoroughly comprehend the sort of fascination he must possess over Lady Russell's mind, the difficulty it must be for her to withdraw her eyes, the astonishment she must be feeling that eight or nine years should have passed over him, and in foreign climes and in active service too, without robbing him of one personal grace!

At last, Lady Russell drew back her head. 'Now, how would she speak of him?'

'You will wonder,' said she, 'what has been fixing my eye so long; but I was looking after some window-curtains, which Lady Alicia and Mrs Frankland were telling me of last night. They described the drawing-room window-curtains of one of the houses on this side of the way, and this part of the street, as being the handsomest and best hung of any in Bath, but could not recollect the exact number, and I have been trying to find out which it could be; but I confess I can see no curtains hereabouts that answer their description.'

Anne sighed and blushed and smiled, in pity and disdain, either at her friend or herself. – The part which provoked her most, was that in all this waste of foresight and caution, she should have lost the right moment for seeing whether he saw them.

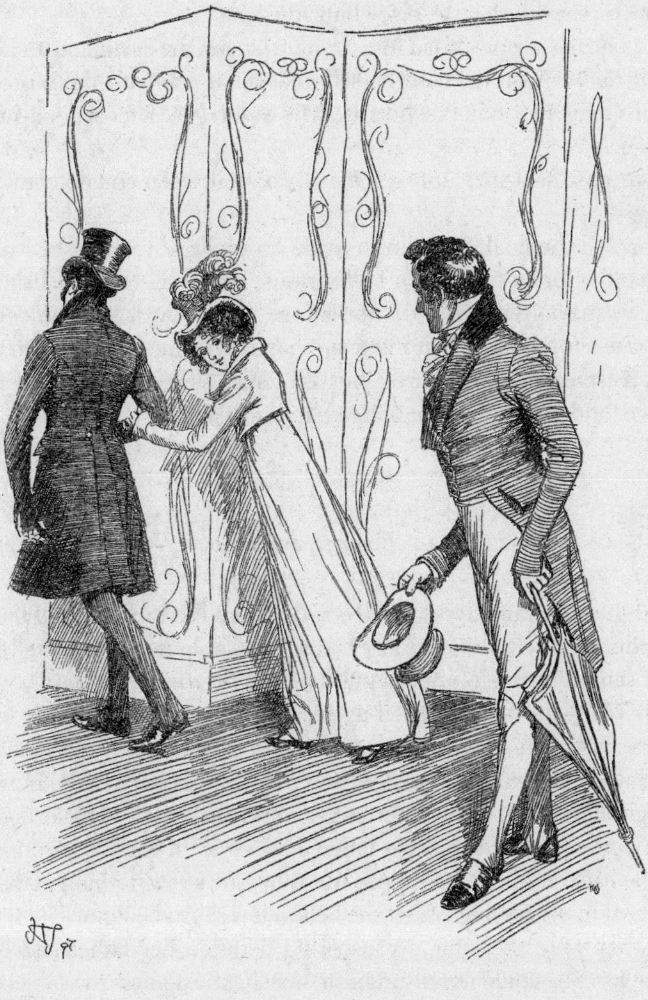

*And in another moment they walked off together*

A day or two passed without producing anything. The theatre or the rooms, where he was most likely to be, were not fashionable enough for the Elliots, whose evening amusements were solely in the elegant stupidity of private parties, in which they were getting more and more engaged; and Anne, wearied of such a state of stagnation, sick of knowing nothing, and fancying herself stronger because her strength was not tried, was quite impatient for the concert evening. It was a concert for the benefit of a person patronised by Lady Dalrymple. Of course they must attend. It was really expected to be a good one, and Captain Wentworth was very fond of music. If she could only have a few minutes' conversation with him again, she fancied she should be satisfied; and as to the power of addressing him she felt all over courage if the opportunity occurred. Elizabeth had turned from him, Lady Russell overlooked him; her nerves were strengthened by these circumstances; she felt that she owed him attention.

She had once partly promised Mrs Smith to spend the evening with her; but in a short hurried call she excused herself and put it off, with the more decided promise of a longer visit on the morrow. Mrs Smith gave a most good-humoured acquiescence.

'By all means,' said she; 'only tell me all about it when you do come. Who is your party?'

Anne named them all. Mrs Smith made no reply; but when she was leaving her, said, and with an expression half serious, half arch, 'Well, I heartily wish your concert may answer; and do not fail me tomorrow if you can come; for I begin to have a foreboding that I may not have many more visits from you.'

Anne was startled and confused, but after standing in a moment's suspense, was obliged, and not sorry to be obliged, to hurry away.

## *Chapter 8*

Sir Walter, his two daughters, and Mrs Clay, were the earliest of all their party, at the rooms in the evening; and as Lady Dalrymple must be waited for, they took their station by one of the fires in the octagon room. But hardly were they so settled, when the door opened again, and Captain Wentworth walked in alone. Anne was the nearest to him, and making yet a little advance, she instantly spoke. He was preparing only to bow and pass on, but her gentle 'How do you do?' brought him out of the straight line to stand near her, and make enquiries in return, in spite of the formidable father and sister in the background. Their being in the background was a support to Anne; she knew nothing of their looks, and felt equal to everything which she believed right to be done.

While they were speaking, a whispering between her father and Elizabeth caught her ear. She could not distinguish, but she must guess the subject; and on Captain Wentworth's making a distant bow, she comprehended that her father had judged so well as to give him that simple acknowledgment of acquaintance, and she was just in time by a side-glance to see a slight curtsey from Elizabeth herself. This, though late and reluctant and ungracious, was yet better than nothing, and her spirits improved.

After talking, however, of the weather and Bath and the concert, their conversation began to flag, and so little was said at last that she was expecting him to go every moment; but he did not; he seemed in no hurry to leave her; and presently with renewed spirit, with a little smile, a little glow, he said,

'I have hardly seen you since our day at Lyme. I am afraid you must have suffered from the shock, and the more from its not overpowering you at the time.'

She assured him that she had not.

'It was a frightful hour,' said he, 'a frightful day!' and he passed his hand across his eyes, as if the remembrance were still too painful; but in a moment half smiling again, added, 'The day has produced some effects, however – has had some consequences which must be considered as the very reverse of frightful. – When you had the presence of mind to suggest that Benwick would be the properest person to fetch a surgeon, you could have little idea of his being eventually one of those most concerned in her recovery.'

'Certainly I could have none. But it appears – I should hope it would be a very happy match. There are on both sides good principles and good temper.'

'Yes,' said he, looking not exactly forward, 'but there I think ends the resemblance. With all my soul I wish them happy, and rejoice over every circumstance in favour of it. They have no difficulties to contend with at home, no opposition, no caprice, no delays. – The Musgroves are behaving like themselves, most honourably and kindly, only anxious with true parental hearts to promote their daughter's comfort. All this is much, very much in favour of their happiness; more than perhaps – '

He stopped. A sudden recollection seemed to occur, and to give him some taste of that emotion which was reddening Anne's cheeks and fixing her eyes on the ground. – After clearing his throat, however, he proceeded thus,

'I confess that I do think there is a disparity, too great a disparity, and in a point no less essential than mind. – I regard Louisa Musgrove as a very amiable, sweet-tempered girl, and not deficient in understanding; but Benwick is something more. He is a clever man, a reading man – and I confess that I do consider his attaching himself to her with some surprise. Had it been the effect of gratitude, had he learned to love her, because he believed her to be preferring him, it would have been another thing. But I have no reason to suppose it so. It seems, on the contrary, to have been a perfectly spontaneous, untaught feeling on his side, and this surprises me. A man like him, in his situation! With a heart pierced, wounded, almost broken! Fanny Harville was a very superior creature; and his attachment to her was indeed attachment. A man does not recover from such a devotion of the heart to such a woman! – He ought not – he does not.'

Either from the consciousness, however, that his friend had recovered, or from some other consciousness, he went no farther; and Anne, who, in spite of the agitated voice in which the latter part had been uttered, and in spite of all the various noises of the room, the almost ceaseless slam of the door, and ceaseless buzz of persons walking through, had distinguished every word, was struck, gratified, confused, and beginning to breathe very quick, and feel an hundred things in a moment. It was impossible for her to enter on such a subject; and yet, after a pause, feeling the necessity of speaking, and having not the smallest wish for a total change, she only deviated so far as to say,

'You were a good while at Lyme, I think?'

'About a fortnight. I could not leave it till Louisa's doing well was quite ascertained. I had been too deeply concerned in the mischief to be soon at peace. It had been my doing – solely mine. She would not have been obstinate if I had not been weak. The country round Lyme is very fine. I walked and rode a great deal; and the more I saw, the more I found to admire.'

'I should very much like to see Lyme again,' said Anne.

'Indeed! I should not have supposed that you could have found anything in Lyme to inspire such a feeling. The horror and distress you were involved in – the stretch of mind, the wear of spirits! – I should have thought your last impressions of Lyme must have been strong disgust.'

'The last few hours were certainly very painful,' replied Anne: 'but when pain is over, the remembrance of it often becomes a pleasure. One does not love a place the less for having suffered in it, unless it has been all suffering, nothing but suffering – which was by no means the case at Lyme. We were only in anxiety and distress during the last two hours; and, previously, there had been a great deal of enjoyment. So much novelty and beauty! I have travelled so little that every fresh place would be interesting to me – but there is real beauty at Lyme; and in short' (with a faint blush at some recollections) 'altogether my impressions of the place are very agreeable.'

As she ceased, the entrance door opened again, and the very party appeared for whom they were waiting. 'Lady Dalrymple, Lady Dalrymple,' was the rejoicing sound; and with all the eagerness compatible with anxious elegance, Sir Walter and his two ladies stepped forward to meet her. Lady Dalrymple and Miss Carteret, escorted by Mr Elliot and Colonel Wallis, who had happened to arrive nearly at the same instant, advanced into the room. The others joined them, and it was a group in which Anne found herself also necessarily included. She was divided from Captain Wentworth. Their interesting, almost too interesting conversation must be broken up for a time; but slight was the penance compared with the happiness which brought it on! She had learned, in the last ten minutes, more of his feelings towards Louisa, more of all his feelings, than she dared to think of! and she gave herself up to the demands of the party, to the needful civilities of the moment, with exquisite, though agitated sensations. She was in good humour with all. She had received ideas which disposed her to be courteous and kind to all, and to pity everyone, as being less happy than herself.

The delightful emotions were a little subdued, when, on stepping back from the group, to be joined again by Captain Wentworth, she saw that he was gone. She was just in time to see him turn into the concert room. He was gone – he had disappeared; she felt a moment's regret. But 'they should meet again. He would look for her – he would find her out long before the evening were over – and at present, perhaps, it was as well to be asunder. She was in need of a little interval for recollection'.

Upon Lady Russell's appearance soon afterwards, the whole party was collected, and all that remained was to marshal themselves, and proceed into the concert room; and be of all the consequence in their power, draw as many eyes, excite as many whispers, and disturb as many people as they could.

Very, very happy were both Elizabeth and Anne Elliot as they walked in. Elizabeth, arm in arm with Miss Carteret, and looking on the broad back of the dowager Viscountess Dalrymple before her, had nothing to wish for which did not seem within her reach, and Anne – but it would be an insult to the nature of Anne's felicity to draw any comparison between it and her sister's; the origin of one all selfish vanity, of the other all generous attachment.

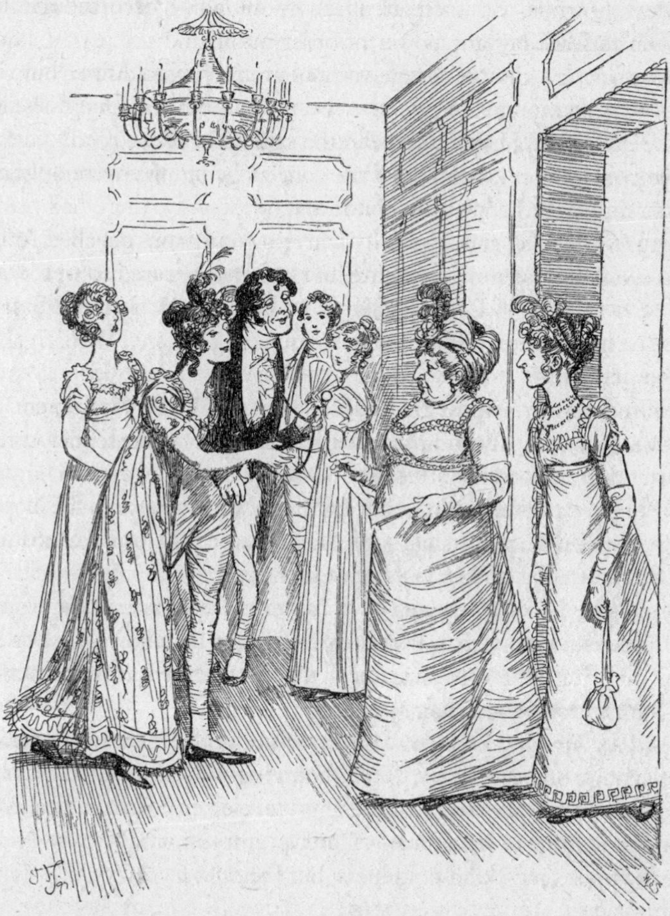

*With all the eagerness compatible with anxious elegance*

Anne saw nothing, thought nothing of the brilliancy of the room. Her happiness was from within. Her eyes were bright, and her cheeks glowed – but she knew nothing about it. She was thinking only of the last half-hour, and as they passed to their seats, her mind took a hasty range over it. His choice of subjects, his expressions, and still more his manner and look, had been such as she could see in only one light. His opinion of Louisa Musgrove's inferiority, an opinion which he had seemed solicitous to give, his wonder at Captain Benwick, his feelings as to a first, strong attachment – sentences begun which he could not finish – his half-averted eyes, and more than half-expressive glance – all, all declared that he had a heart returning to her at least; that anger, resentment, avoidance, were no more; and that they were succeeded, not merely by friendship and regard, but by the tenderness of the past; yes, some share of the tenderness of the past. She could not contemplate the change as implying less. – He must love her.

These were thoughts, with their attendant visions, which occupied and flurried her too much to leave her any power of observation; and she passed along the room without having a glimpse of him, without even trying to discern him. When their places were determined on, and they were all properly arranged, she looked round to see if he should happen to be in the same part of the room, but he was not, her eye could not reach him; and the concert being just opening, she must consent for a time to be happy in an humbler way.

The party was divided, and disposed of on two contiguous benches: Anne was among those on the foremost, and Mr Elliot had manoeuvred so well, with the assistance of his friend Colonel Wallis, as to have a seat by her. Miss Elliot, surrounded by her cousins, and the principal object of Colonel Wallis' gallantry, was quite contented.

Anne's mind was in a most favourable state for the entertainment of the evening; it was just occupation enough: she had feelings for the tender, spirits for the gay, attention for the scientific, and patience for the wearisome; and had never liked a concert better, at least during the first act. Towards the close of it, in the interval succeeding an Italian song, she explained the words of the song to Mr Elliot. – They had a concert bill between them.

'This,' said she, 'is nearly the sense, or rather the meaning of the words, for certainly the sense of an Italian love-song must not be talked of – but it is as nearly the meaning as I can give; for I do not pretend to understand the language. I am a very poor Italian scholar.'

'Yes, yes, I see you are. I see you know nothing of the matter. You have only knowledge enough of the language to translate at sight these inverted, transposed, curtailed Italian lines, into clear, comprehensible, elegant English. You need not say anything more of your ignorance. – Here is complete proof.'

'I will not oppose such kind politeness; but I should be sorry to be examined by a real proficient.'

'I have not had the pleasure of visiting in Camden Place so long,' replied he, 'without knowing something of Miss Anne Elliot; and I do regard her as one who is too modest for the world in general to be aware of half her accomplishments, and too highly accomplished for modesty to be natural in any other woman.'

'For shame! for shame! – this is too much of flattery. I forget what we are to have next,' turning to the bill.

'Perhaps,' said Mr Elliot, speaking low, 'I have had a longer acquaintance with your character than you are aware of.'

'Indeed! – How so? You can have been acquainted with it only since I came to Bath, excepting as you might hear me previously spoken of in my own family.'

'I knew you by report long before you came to Bath. I had heard you described by those who knew you intimately. I have been acquainted with you by character many years. Your person, your disposition, accomplishments, manner – they were all described, they were all present to me.'

Mr Elliot was not disappointed in the interest he hoped to raise. No one can withstand the charm of such a mystery. To have been described long ago to a recent acquaintance, by nameless people, is irresistible; and Anne was all curiosity. She wondered, and questioned him eagerly – but in vain. He delighted in being asked, but he would not tell.

'No, no – sometime or other perhaps, but not now. He would mention no names now; but such, he could assure her, had been the fact. He had many years ago received such a description of Miss Anne Elliot as had inspired him with the highest idea of her merit, and excited the warmest curiosity to know her.'

Anne could think of no one so likely to have spoken with partiality of her many years ago as the Mr Wentworth, of Monkford, Captain Wentworth's brother. He might have been in Mr Elliot's company, but she had not courage to ask the question.

'The name of Anne Elliot,' said he, 'has long had an interesting sound to me. Very long has it possessed a charm over my fancy; and, if I dared, I would breathe my wishes that the name might never change.'

Such she believed were his words; but scarcely had she received their sound than her attention was caught by other sounds immediately behind her, which rendered everything else trivial. Her father and Lady Dalrymple were speaking.

'A well-looking man,' said Sir Walter, 'a very well-looking man.'

'A very fine young man indeed!' said Lady Dalrymple. 'More air than one often sees in Bath. – Irish, I dare say.'

'No, I just know his name. A bowing acquaintance. Wentworth – Captain Wentworth of the navy. His sister married my tenant in Somersetshire – the Croft, who rents Kellynch.'

Before Sir Walter had reached this point, Anne's eyes had caught the right direction, and distinguished Captain Wentworth, standing among a cluster of men at a little distance. As her eyes fell on him, his seemed to be withdrawn from her. It had that appearance. It seemed as if she had been one moment too late; and as long as she dared observe, he did not look again; but the performance was recommencing, and she was forced to seem to restore her attention to the orchestra, and look straight forward.

When she could give another glance, he had moved away. He could not have come nearer to her if he would; she was so surrounded and shut in; but she would rather have caught his eye.

Mr Elliot's speech too distressed her. She had no longer any inclination to talk to him. She wished him not so near her.

The first act was over. Now she hoped for some beneficial change; and, after a period of nothing-saying amongst the party, some of them did decide on going in quest of tea. Anne was one of the few who did not choose to move. She remained in her seat, and so did Lady Russell; but she had the pleasure of getting rid of Mr Elliot; and she did not mean, whatever she might feel on Lady Russell's account, to shrink from conversation with Captain Wentworth, if he gave her the opportunity. She was persuaded by Lady Russell's countenance that she had seen him.

He did not come, however. Anne sometimes fancied she discerned him at a distance, but he never came. The anxious interval wore away unproductively. The others returned, the room filled again, benches were reclaimed and repossessed, and another hour of pleasure or of penance was to be set out, another hour of music was to give delight or the gapes, as real or affected taste for it prevailed. To Anne, it chiefly wore the prospect of an hour of agitation. She could not quit that room in peace without seeing Captain Wentworth once more, without the interchange of one friendly look.

In resettling themselves, there were now many changes, the result of which was favourable for her. Colonel Wallis declined sitting down again, and Mr Elliot was invited by Elizabeth and Miss Carteret, in a manner not to be refused, to sit between them; and by some other removals, and a little scheming of her own, Anne was enabled to place herself much nearer the end of the bench than she had been before, much more within reach of a passer-by. She could not do so, without comparing herself with Miss Larolles, the inimitable Miss Larolles – but still she did it, and not with much happier effect; though by what seemed prosperity in the shape of an early abdication in her next neighbours, she found herself at the very end of the bench before the concert closed.

Such was her situation, with a vacant space at hand, when Captain Wentworth was again in sight. She saw him not far off. He saw her too; yet he looked grave, and seemed irresolute, and only by very slow degrees came at last near enough to speak to her. She felt that something must be the matter. The change was indubitable. The difference between his present air and what it had been in the octagon room was strikingly great. – Why was it? She thought of her father – of Lady Russell. Could there have been any unpleasant glances? He began by speaking of the concert, gravely; more like the Captain Wentworth of Uppercross; owned himself disappointed, had expected better singing; and, in short, must confess that he should not be sorry when it was over. Anne replied, and spoke in defence of the performance so well, and yet in allowance for his feelings, so pleasantly, that his countenance improved, and he replied again with almost a smile. They talked for a few minutes more; the improvement held; he even looked down towards the bench, as if he saw a place on it well worth occupying; when, at that moment, a touch on her shoulder obliged Anne to turn round. – It came from Mr Elliot. He begged her pardon, but she must be applied to, to explain Italian again. Miss Carteret was very anxious to have a general idea of what was next to be sung. Anne could not refuse; but never had she sacrificed to politeness with a more suffering spirit.

A few minutes, though as few as possible, were inevitably consumed; and when her own mistress again, when able to turn and look as she had done before, she found herself accosted by Captain Wentworth, in a reserved yet hurried sort of farewell. 'He must wish her good-night. He was going – he should get home as fast as he could.'

'Is not this song worth staying for?' said Anne, suddenly struck by an idea which made her yet more anxious to be encouraging.

'No!' he replied impressively, 'there is nothing worth my staying for;' and he was gone directly.

Jealousy of Mr Elliot! It was the only intelligible motive. Captain Wentworth jealous of her affection! Could she have believed it a week ago – three hours ago! For a moment the gratification was exquisite. But alas! there were very different thoughts to succeed. How was such jealousy to be quieted? How was the truth to reach him? How, in all the peculiar disadvantages of their respective situations, would he ever learn her real sentiments? It was misery to think of Mr Elliot's attentions. – Their evil was incalculable.

## *Chapter 9*

Anne recollected with pleasure the next morning her promise of going to Mrs Smith; meaning that it should engage her from home at the time when Mr Elliot would be most likely to call; for to avoid Mr Elliot was almost a first object.

She felt a great deal of goodwill towards him. In spite of the mischief of his attentions, she owed him gratitude and regard, perhaps compassion. She could not help thinking much of the extraordinary circumstances attending their acquaintance; of the right which he seemed to have to interest her, by everything in situation, by his own sentiments, by his early prepossession. It was altogether very extraordinary. – Flattering, but painful. There was much to regret. How she might have felt, had there been no Captain Wentworth in the case, was not worth enquiry; for there was a Captain Wentworth; and be the conclusion of the present suspense good or bad, her affection would be his forever. Their union, she believed, could not divide her more from other men than their final separation.

Prettier musings of high-wrought love and eternal constancy could never have passed along the streets of Bath than Anne was sporting with from Camden Place to Westgate Buildings. It was almost enough to spread purification and perfume all the way.

She was sure of a pleasant reception; and her friend seemed this morning particularly obliged to her for coming, seemed hardly to have expected her, though it had been an appointment.

An account of the concert was immediately claimed; and Anne's recollections of the concert were quite happy enough to animate her features, and make her rejoice to talk of it. All that she could tell, she told most gladly; but the all was little for one who had been there, and unsatisfactory for such an enquirer as Mrs Smith, who had already heard, through the short cut of a laundress and a waiter, rather more of the general success and produce of the evening than Anne could relate; and who now asked in vain for several particulars of the company. Everybody of any consequence or notoriety in Bath was well known by name to Mrs Smith.

'The little Durands were there, I conclude,' said she, 'with their mouths open to catch the music; like unfledged sparrows ready to be fed. They never miss a concert.'

'Yes. I did not see them myself, but I heard Mr Elliot say they were in the room.'

'The Ibbotsons – were they there? and the two new beauties, with the tall Irish officer, who is talked of for one of them.'

'I do not know. – I do not think they were.'

'Old Lady Mary Maclean? I need not ask after her. She never misses, I know; and you must have seen her. She must have been in your own circle, for as you went with Lady Dalrymple you were in the seats of grandeur; round the orchestra, of course.'

'No, that was what I dreaded. It would have been very unpleasant to me in every respect. But happily Lady Dalrymple always chooses to be farther off; and we were exceedingly well placed – that is for hearing; I must not say for seeing, because I appear to have seen very little.'

'Oh! you saw enough for your own amusement – I can understand. There is a sort of domestic enjoyment to be known even in a crowd, and this you had. You were a large party in yourselves, and you wanted nothing beyond.'

'But I ought to have looked about me more,' said Anne, conscious while she spoke that there had in fact been no want of looking about; that the object only had been deficient.

'No, no – you were better employed. You need not tell me that you had a pleasant evening. I see it in your eye. I perfectly see how the hours passed – that you had always something agreeable to listen to. In the intervals of the concert, it was conversation.'

Anne half smiled and said, 'Do you see that in my eye?'

'Yes, I do. Your countenance perfectly informs me that you were in company last night with the person whom you think the most agreeable in the world, the person who interests you at this present time more than all the rest of the world put together.'

A blush overspread Anne's cheeks. She could say nothing.

'And such being the case,' continued Mrs Smith after a short pause, 'I hope you believe that I do know how to value your kindness in coming to me this morning. It is really very good of you to come and sit with me when you must have so many pleasanter demands upon your time.'

Anne heard nothing of this. She was still in the astonishment and confusion excited by her friend's penetration, unable to imagine how any report of Captain Wentworth could have reached her. After another short silence –

'Pray,' said Mrs Smith, 'is Mr Elliot aware of your acquaintance with me? Does he know that I am in Bath?'

'Mr Elliot!' repeated Anne, looking up surprised. A moment's reflection showed her the mistake she had been under. She caught it instantaneously; and, recovering courage with the feeling of safety, soon added, more composedly, 'are you acquainted with Mr Elliot?'

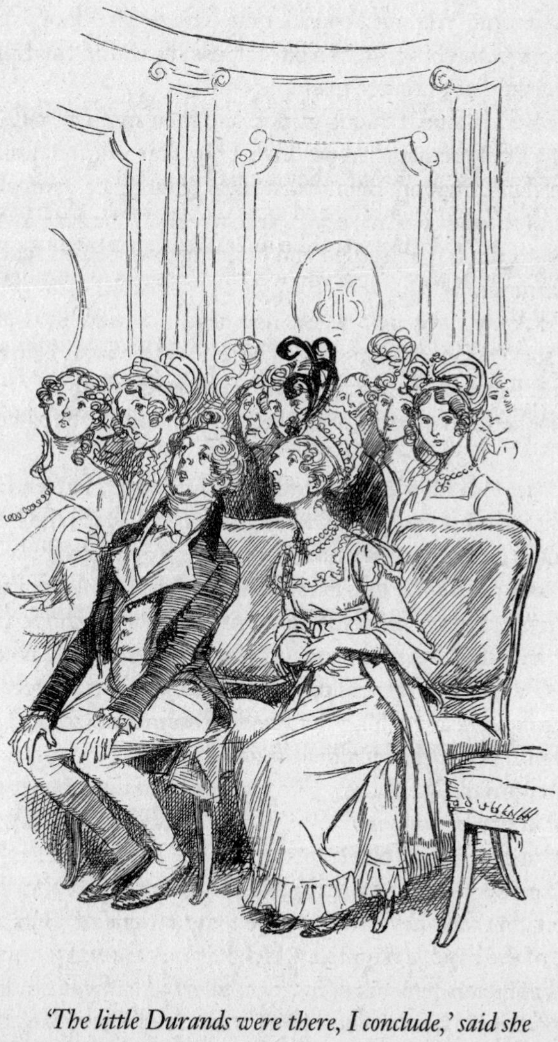

*'The little Durands were there, I conclude,' said she*

'I have been a good deal acquainted with him,' replied Mrs Smith, gravely, 'but it seems worn out now. It is a great while since we met.'

'I was not at all aware of this. You never mentioned it before. Had I known it, I would have had the pleasure of talking to him about you.'

'To confess the truth,' said Mrs Smith, assuming her usual air of cheerfulness, 'that is exactly the pleasure I want you to have. I want you to talk about me to Mr Elliot. I want your interest with him. He can be of essential service to me; and if you would have the goodness, my dear Miss Elliot, to make it an object to yourself, of course it is done.'

'I should be extremely happy – I hope you cannot doubt my willingness to be of even the slightest use to you,' replied Anne; 'but I suspect that you are considering me as having a higher claim on Mr Elliot – a greater right to influence him than is really the case. I am sure you have, somehow or other, imbibed such a notion. You must consider me only as Mr Elliot's relation. If in that light, if there is anything which you suppose his cousin might fairly ask of him, I beg you would not hesitate to employ me.'

Mrs Smith gave her a penetrating glance, and then smiling, said,

'I have been a little premature, I perceive. I beg your pardon. I ought to have waited for official information. But now, my dear Miss Elliot, as an old friend, do give me a hint as to when I may speak. Next week? To be sure by next week I may be allowed to think it all settled and build my own selfish schemes on Mr Elliot's good fortune.'

'No,' replied Anne, 'nor next week, nor next, nor next. I assure you that nothing of the sort you are thinking of will be settled any week. I am not going to marry Mr Elliot. I should like to know why you imagine I am.'

Mrs Smith looked at her again, looked earnestly, smiled, shook her head, and exclaimed,

'Now, how I do wish I understood you! How I do wish I knew what you were at! I have a great idea that you do not design to be cruel, when the right moment comes. Till it does come, you know, we women never mean to have anybody. It is a thing of course among us, that every man is refused – till he offers. But why should you be cruel? Let me plead for my – present friend I cannot call him – but for my former friend. Where can you look for a more suitable match? Where could you expect a more gentlemanlike, agreeable man? Let me recommend Mr Elliot. I am sure you hear nothing but good of him from Colonel Wallis; and who can know him better than Colonel Wallis?'

'My dear Mrs Smith, Mr Elliot's wife has not been dead much above half a year. He ought not to be supposed to be paying his addresses to anyone.'

'Oh! if these are your only objections,' cried Mrs Smith, archly, 'Mr Elliot is safe, and I shall give myself no more trouble about him. Do not forget me when you are married, that's all. Let him know me to be a friend of yours, and then he will think little of the trouble required, which it is very natural for him now, with so many affairs and engagements of his own, to avoid and get rid of as he can – very natural, perhaps. Ninety-nine out of a hundred would do the same. Of course, he cannot be aware of the importance to me. Well, my dear Miss Elliot,

I hope and trust you will be very happy. Mr Elliot has sense to understand the value of such a woman. Your peace will not be shipwrecked as mine has been. You are safe in all worldly matters, and safe in his character. He will not be led astray, he will not be misled by others to his ruin.'

'No,' said Anne, 'I can readily believe all that of my cousin. He seems to have a calm, decided temper, not at all open to dangerous impressions. I consider him with great respect. I have no reason, from anything that has fallen within my observation, to do otherwise. But I have not known him long; and he is not a man, I think, to be known intimately soon. Will not this manner of speaking of him, Mrs Smith, convince you that he is nothing to me? Surely, this must be calm enough. And, upon my word, he is nothing to me. Should he ever propose to me (which I have very little reason to imagine he has any thought of doing), I shall not accept him. I assure you I shall not. I assure you Mr Elliot had not the share which you have been supposing, in whatever pleasure the concert of last night might afford – not Mr Elliot; it is not Mr Elliot that – '

She stopped, regretting with a deep blush that she had implied so much; but less would hardly have been sufficient. Mrs Smith would hardly have believed so soon in Mr Elliot's failure, but from the perception of there being a somebody else. As it was, she instantly submitted, and with all the semblance of seeing nothing beyond; and Anne, eager to escape farther notice, was impatient to know why Mrs Smith should have fancied she was to marry Mr Elliot, where she could have received the idea, or from whom she could have heard it.

'Do tell me how it first came into your head.'

'It first came into my head,' replied Mrs Smith, 'upon finding how much you were together, and feeling it to be the most probable thing in the world to be wished for by everybody belonging to either of you; and you may depend upon it that all your acquaintance have disposed of you in the same way. But I never heard it spoken of till two days ago.'

'And has it indeed been spoken of?'

'Did you observe the woman who opened the door to you, when you called yesterday?'

'No. Was not it Mrs Speed, as usual, or the maid? I observed no one in particular.'

'It was my friend, Mrs Rooke – Nurse Rooke, who, by the by, had a great curiosity to see you, and was delighted to be in the way to let you in. She came away from Marlborough Buildings only on Sunday; and she it was who told me you were to marry Mr Elliot. She had had it from Mrs Wallis herself, which did not seem bad authority. She sat an hour with me on Monday evening, and gave me the whole history.'

'The whole history!' repeated Anne, laughing. 'She could not make a very long history, I think, of one such little article of unfounded news.'

Mrs Smith said nothing.

'But,' continued Anne, presently, 'though there is no truth in my having this claim on Mr Elliot, I should be extremely happy to be of use to you, in any way that I could. Shall I mention to him your being in Bath? Shall I take any message?'

'No, I thank you; no, certainly not. In the warmth of the moment, and under a mistaken impression, I might, perhaps, have endeavoured to interest you in some circumstances. But not now; no, I thank you, I have nothing to trouble you with.'

'I think you spoke of having known Mr Elliot many years?'

'I did.'

'Not before he married, I suppose?'

'Yes; he was not married when I knew him first.'

'And – were you much acquainted?'

'Intimately.'

'Indeed! Then do tell me what he was at that time of life. I have a great curiosity to know what Mr Elliot was as a very young man. Was he at all such as he appears now?'

'I have not seen Mr Elliot these three years,' was Mrs Smith's answer, given so gravely that it was impossible to pursue the subject farther; and Anne felt that she had gained nothing but an increase of curiosity. They were both silent – Mrs Smith very thoughtful. At last,

'I beg your pardon, my dear Miss Elliot,' she cried, in her natural tone of cordiality, 'I beg your pardon for the short answers I have been giving you, but I have been uncertain what I ought to do. I have been doubting and considering as to what I ought to tell you. There were many things to be taken into the account. One hates to be officious, to be giving bad impressions, making mischief. Even the smooth surface of family-union seems worth preserving, though there may be nothing durable beneath. However, I have determined; I think I am right; I think you ought to be made acquainted with Mr Elliot's real character. Though I fully believe that, at present, you have not the smallest intention of accepting him, there is no saying what may happen. You might, sometime or other, be differently affected towards him. Hear the truth, therefore, now, while you are unprejudiced. Mr Elliot is a man without heart or conscience; a designing, wary, cold-blooded being, who thinks only of himself; who, for his own interest or ease, would be guilty of any cruelty, or any treachery, that could be perpetrated without risk of his general character. He has no feeling for others. Those whom he has been the chief cause of leading into ruin, he can neglect and desert without the smallest compunction. He is totally beyond the reach of any sentiment of justice or compassion. Oh! he is black at heart, hollow and black!'

Anne's astonished air, and exclamation of wonder, made her pause, and in a calmer manner she added,

'My expressions startle you. You must allow for an injured, angry woman. But I will try to command myself. I will not abuse him. I will only tell you what I have found him. Facts shall speak. He was the intimate friend of my dear husband, who trusted and loved him, and thought him as good as himself. The intimacy had been formed before our marriage. I found them most intimate friends; and I, too, became excessively pleased with Mr Elliot, and entertained the highest opinion of him. At nineteen, you know, one does not think very seriously, but Mr Elliot appeared to me quite as good as others, and much more agreeable than most others, and we were almost always together. We were principally in town, living in very good style. He was then the inferior in circumstances, he was then the poor one; he had chambers in the Temple, and it was as much as he could do to support the appearance of a gentleman. He had always a home with us whenever he chose it; he was always welcome; he was like a brother. My poor Charles, who had the finest, most generous spirit in the world, would have divided his last farthing with him; and I know that his purse was open to him; I know that he often assisted him.'

'This must have been about that very period of Mr Elliot's life,' said Anne, 'which has always excited my particular curiosity. It must have been about the same time that he became known to my father and sister. I never knew him myself, I only heard of him, but there was a something in his conduct then with regard to my father and sister, and afterwards in the circumstances of his marriage, which I never could quite reconcile with present times. It seemed to announce a different sort of man.'

'I know it all, I know it all,' cried Mrs Smith. 'He had been introduced to Sir Walter and your sister before I was acquainted with him, but I heard him speak of them forever. I know he was invited and encouraged, and I know he did not choose to go. I can satisfy you, perhaps on points which you would little expect; and as to his marriage, I knew all about it at the time. I was privy to all the fors and against, I was the friend to whom he confided his hopes and plans, and though I did not know his wife previously (her inferior situation in society, indeed, rendered that impossible), yet I knew her all her life afterwards, or, at least, till within the last two years of her life, and can answer any question you wish to put.'

'Nay,' said Anne, 'I have no particular enquiry to make about her. I have always understood they were not a happy couple. But I should like to know why, at that time of his life, he should slight my father's acquaintance as he did. My father was certainly disposed to take very kind and proper notice of him. Why did Mr Elliot draw back?'

'Mr Elliot,' replied Mrs Smith, 'at that period of his life, had one object in view – to make his fortune, and by a rather quicker process than the law. He was determined to make it by marriage. He was determined, at least, not to mar it by an imprudent marriage; and I know it was his belief (whether justly or not, of course I cannot decide), that your father and sister, in their civilities and invitations, were designing a match between the heir and the young lady; and it was impossible that such a match should have answered his ideas of wealth and independence. That was his motive for drawing back, I can assure you. He told me the whole story. He had no concealments with me. It was curious, that having just left you behind me in Bath, my first and principal acquaintance on marrying should be your cousin; and that, through him, I should be continually hearing of your father and sister. He described one Miss Elliot, and I thought very affectionately of the other.'

'Perhaps,' cried Anne, struck by a sudden idea, 'you sometimes spoke of me to Mr Elliot?'

'To be sure I did, very often. I used to boast of my own Anne Elliot, and vouch for your being a very different creature from – '

She checked herself just in time.

'This accounts for something which Mr Elliot said last night,' cried Anne. 'This explains it. I found he had been used to hear of me. I could not comprehend how. What wild imaginations one forms, where dear self is concerned! How sure to be mistaken! But I beg your pardon; I have interrupted you. Mr Elliot married, then, completely for money? The circumstance, probably, which first opened your eyes to his character.'

Mrs Smith hesitated a little here. 'Oh! those things are too common. When one lives in the world, a man or woman's marrying for money is too common to strike one as it ought. I was very young, and associated only with the young and we were a thoughtless, gay set, without any strict rules of conduct. We lived for enjoyment. I think differently now; time and sickness, and sorrow, have given me other notions; but, at that period I must own I saw nothing reprehensible in what Mr Elliot was doing. "To do the best for himself", passed as a duty.'

'But was not she a very low woman?'

'Yes, which I objected to, but he would not regard. Money, money, was all that he wanted. Her father was a grazier, her grandfather had been a butcher, but that was all nothing. She was a fine woman, had had a decent education, was brought forward by some cousins, thrown by chance into Mr Elliot's company, and fell in love with him; and not a difficulty or a scruple was there on his side, with respect to her birth. All his caution was spent in being secured of the real amount of her fortune before he committed himself. Depend upon it, whatever esteem Mr Elliot may have for his own situation in life now, as a young man he had not the smallest value for it. His chance of the Kellynch estate was something, but all the honour of the family he held as cheap as dirt. I have often heard him declare, that if baronetcies were saleable, anybody should have his for fifty pounds, arms and motto, name and livery included; but I will not pretend to repeat half that I used to hear him say on that subject. It would not be fair. And yet you ought to have proof, for what is all this but assertion? and you shall have proof.'

'Indeed, my dear Mrs Smith, I want none,' cried Anne, 'You have asserted nothing contradictory to what Mr Elliot appeared to be some years ago. This is all in confirmation, rather, of what we used to hear and believe. I am more curious to know why he should be so different now?'

'But for my satisfaction; if you will have the goodness to ring for Mary – stay, I am sure you will have the still greater goodness of going yourself into my bedroom and bringing me the small inlaid box which you will find on the upper shelf of the closet.'

Anne, seeing her friend to be earnestly bent on it, did as she was desired. The box was brought and placed before her, and Mrs Smith, sighing over it as she unlocked it, said,

'This is full of papers belonging to him, to my husband, a small portion only of what I had to look over when I lost him. The letter I am looking for was one written by Mr Elliot to him before our marriage, and happened to be saved; why, one can hardly imagine. But he was careless and immethodical, like other men, about those things; and when I came to examine his papers, I found it with others still more trivial from different people scattered here and there, while many letters and memorandums of real importance had been destroyed. Here it is. I would not burn it, because being even then very little satisfied with Mr Elliot, I was determined to preserve every document of former intimacy. I have now another motive for being glad that I can produce it.'

This was the letter, directed to 'Charles Smith, Esq. Tunbridge Wells', and dated from London, as far back as July, 1803:

> DEAR SMITH – I have received yours. Your kindness almost overpowers me. I wish nature had made such hearts as yours more common, but I have lived three-and-twenty years in the world, and have seen none like it. At present, believe me, I have no need of your services, being in cash again. Give me joy: I have got rid of Sir Walter and Miss. They are gone back to Kellynch, and almost made me swear to visit them this summer, but my first visit to Kellynch will be with a surveyor, to tell me how to bring it with best advantage to the hammer. The Baronet, nevertheless, is not unlikely to marry again; he is quite fool enough. If he does, however, they will leave me in peace, which may be a decent equivalent for the reversion. He is worse than last year.
>
> I wish I had any name but Elliot. I am sick of it. The name of Walter I can drop, thank God! and I desire you will never insult me with my second W. again, meaning, for the rest of my life, to be only yours truly,
>
> WM ELLIOT.

Such a letter could not be read without putting Anne in a glow; and Mrs Smith, observing the high colour in her face, said,

'The language, I know, is highly disrespectful. Though I have forgot the exact terms, I have a perfect impression of the general meaning. But it shows you the man. Mark his professions to my poor husband. Can anything be stronger?'

Anne could not immediately get over the shock and mortification of finding such words applied to her father. She was obliged to recollect that her seeing the letter was a violation of the laws of honour, that no one ought to be judged or to be known by such testimonies, that no private correspondence could bear the eye of others, before she could recover calmness enough to return the letter which she had been meditating over, and say,

'Thank you. This is full proof undoubtedly, proof of everything you were saying. But why be acquainted with us now?'

'I can explain this too,' cried Mrs Smith, smiling.

'Can you really?'

'Yes. I have shown you Mr Elliot, as he was a dozen years ago, and I will show him as he is now. I cannot produce written proof again, but I can give as authentic oral testimony as you can desire of what he is now wanting, and what he is now doing. He is no hypocrite now. He truly wants to marry you. His present attentions to your family are very sincere, quite from the heart. I will give you my authority: his friend Colonel Wallis.'

'Colonel Wallis! are you acquainted with him?'

'No. It does not come to me in quite so direct a line as that; it takes a bend or two, but nothing of consequence. The stream is as good as at first; the little rubbish it collects in the turnings is easily moved away. Mr Elliot talks unreservedly to Colonel Wallis of his views on you – which said Colonel Wallis I imagine to be in himself a sensible, careful, discerning sort of character; but Colonel Wallis has a very pretty silly wife, to whom he tells things which he had better not, and he repeats it all to her. She, in the overflowing spirits of her recovery, repeats it all to her nurse; and the nurse, knowing my acquaintance with you, very naturally brings it all to me. On Monday evening my good friend Mrs Rooke let me thus much into the secrets of Marlborough Buildings. When I talked of a whole history, therefore, you see I was not romancing so much as you supposed.'

'My dear Mrs Smith, your authority is deficient. This will not do. Mr Elliot's having any views on me will not in the least account for the efforts he made towards a reconciliation with my father. That was all prior to my coming to Bath. I found them on the most friendly terms when I arrived.'

'I know you did; I know it all perfectly, but – '

'Indeed, Mrs Smith, we must not expect to get real information in such a line. Facts or opinions which are to pass through the hands of so many, to be misconceived by folly in one, and ignorance in another, can hardly have much truth left.'

'Only give me a hearing. You will soon be able to judge of the general credit due, by listening to some particulars which you can yourself immediately contradict or confirm. Nobody supposes that you were his first inducement. He had seen you indeed before he came to Bath and admired you, but without knowing it to be you. So says my historian at least. Is this true? Did he see you last summer or autumn, "somewhere down in the west" to use her own words, without knowing it to be you?'

'He certainly did. So far it is very true. At Lyme; I happened to be at Lyme.'

'Well,' continued Mrs Smith triumphantly, 'grant my friend the credit due to the establishment of the first point asserted. He saw you then at Lyme, and liked you so well as to be exceedingly pleased to meet with you again in Camden Place, as Miss Anne Elliot, and from that moment, I have no doubt, had a double motive in his visits there. But there was another, and an earlier; which I will now explain. If there is anything in my story which you know to be either false or improbable, stop me. My account states, that your sister's friend, the lady now staying with you, whom I have heard you mention, came to Bath with Miss Elliot and Sir Walter as long ago as September (in short when they first came themselves), and has been staying there ever since; that she is a clever, insinuating, handsome woman, poor and plausible, and altogether such in situation and manner as to give a general idea among Sir Walter's acquaintance of her meaning to be Lady

Elliot, and as general a surprise that Miss Elliot should be apparently blind to the danger.'

Here Mrs Smith paused a moment; but Anne had not a word to say, and she continued,

'This was the light in which it appeared to those who knew the family, long before your return to it; and Colonel Wallis had his eye upon your father enough to be sensible of it, though he did not then visit in Camden Place; but his regard for Mr Elliot gave him an interest in watching all that was going on there, and when Mr Elliot came to Bath for a day or two, as he happened to do a little before Christmas, Colonel Wallis made him acquainted with the appearance of things, and the reports beginning to prevail – Now you are to understand that time had worked a very material change in Mr Elliot's opinions as to the value of a baronetcy. Upon all points of blood and connection, he is a completely altered man. Having long had as much money as he could spend, nothing to wish for on the side of avarice or indulgence, he has been gradually learning to pin his happiness upon the consequence he is heir to. I thought it coming on before our acquaintance ceased, but it is now a confirmed feeling. He cannot bear the idea of not being Sir William. You may guess therefore that the news he heard from his friend could not be very agreeable, and you may guess what it produced; the resolution of coming back to Bath as soon as possible, and of fixing himself here for a time, with the view of renewing his former acquaintance and recovering such a footing in the family as might give him the means of ascertaining the degree of his danger, and of circumventing the lady if he found it material. This was agreed upon between the two friends as the only thing to be done; and Colonel Wallis was to assist in every way that he could. He was to be introduced, and Mrs Wallis was to be introduced, and everybody was to be introduced. Mr Elliot came back accordingly; and on application was forgiven, as you know, and readmitted into the family; and there it was his constant object, and his only object (till your arrival added another motive) to watch Sir Walter and Mrs Clay. He omitted no opportunity of being with them, threw himself in their way, called at all hours – but I need not be particular on this subject. You can imagine what an artful man would do; and with this guide, perhaps, may recollect what you have seen him do.'

'Yes,' said Anne, 'you tell me nothing which does not accord with what I have known, or could imagine. There is always something offensive in the details of cunning. The manoeuvres of selfishness and duplicity must ever be revolting, but I have heard nothing which really surprises me. I know those who would be shocked by such a representation of Mr Elliot, who would have difficulty in believing it; but I have never been satisfied. I have always wanted some other motive for his conduct than appeared. – I should like to know his present opinion, as to the probability of the event he has been in dread of; whether he considers the danger to be lessening or not.'

'Lessening, I understand,' replied Mrs Smith. 'He thinks Mrs Clay afraid of him, aware that he sees through her, and not daring to proceed as she might do in his absence. But since he must be absent sometime or other, I do not perceive how he can ever be secure, while she holds her present influence. Mrs Wallis has an amusing idea, as nurse tells me, that it is to be put into the marriage articles when you and Mr Elliot marry, that your father is not to marry Mrs Clay. A scheme worthy of Mrs Wallis' understanding, by all accounts; but my sensible nurse Rooke sees the absurdity of it. – "Why, to be sure, ma'am," said she, "it would not prevent his marrying anybody else." And indeed, to own the truth, I do not think nurse in her heart is a very strenuous opposer of Sir Walter's making a second match. She must be allowed to be a favourer of matrimony you know, and (since self will intrude) who can say that she may not have some flying visions of attending the next Lady Elliot, through Mrs Wallis' recommendation?'

'I am very glad to know all this,' said Anne, after a little thoughtfulness. 'It will be more painful to me in some respects to be in company with him, but I shall know better what to do. My line of conduct will be more direct. Mr Elliot is evidently a disingenuous, artificial, worldly man, who has never had any better principle to guide him than selfishness.'

But Mr Elliot was not yet done with. Mrs Smith had been carried away from her first direction, and Anne had forgotten, in the interest of her own family concerns, how much had been originally implied against him; but her attention was now called to the explanation of those first hints, and she listened to a recital which, if it did not perfectly justify the unqualified bitterness of Mrs Smith, proved him to have been very unfeeling in his conduct towards her, very deficient both in justice and compassion.

She learned that (the intimacy between them continuing unimpaired by Mr Elliot's marriage), they had been as before always together, and Mr Elliot had led his friend into expenses much beyond his fortune. Mrs Smith did not want to take blame to herself, and was most tender of throwing any on her husband; but Anne could collect that their income had never been equal to their style of living, and that from the first, there had been a great deal of general and joint extravagance. From his wife's account of him, she could discern Mr Smith to have been a man of warm feelings, easy temper, careless habits, and not strong understanding, much more amiable than his friend, and very unlike him – led by him, and probably despised by him. Mr Elliot, raised by his marriage to great affluence, and disposed to every gratification of pleasure and vanity which could be commanded without involving himself (for with all his self-indulgence he had become a prudent man), and beginning to be rich, just as his friend ought to have found himself to be poor, seemed to have had no concern at all for that friend's probable finances, but, on the contrary, had been prompting and encouraging expenses which could end only in ruin. And the Smiths accordingly had been ruined.

The husband had died just in time to be spared the full knowledge of it. They had previously known embarrassments enough to try the friendship of their friends, and to prove that Mr Elliot's had better not be tried; but it was not till his death that the wretched state of his affairs was fully known. With a confidence in Mr Elliot's regard more creditable to his feelings than his judgment, Mr Smith had appointed him the executor of his will; but Mr Elliot would not act, and the difficulties and distresses which this refusal had heaped on her, in addition to the inevitable sufferings of her situation, had been such as could not be related without anguish of spirit, or listened to without corresponding indignation.

Anne was shown some letters of his on the occasion, answers to urgent applications from Mrs Smith, which all breathed the same stern resolution of not engaging in a fruitless trouble, and, under a cold civility, the same hard-hearted indifference to any of the evils it might bring on her. It was a dreadful picture of ingratitude and inhumanity; and Anne felt at some moments that no flagrant open crime could have been worse. She had a great deal to listen to; all the particulars of past sad scenes, all the minutiae of distress upon distress, which in former conversations had been merely hinted at, were dwelled on now with a natural indulgence. Anne could perfectly comprehend the exquisite relief, and was only the more inclined to wonder at the composure of her friend's usual state of mind.

There was one circumstance in the history of her grievances of particular irritation. She had good reason to believe that some property of her husband in the West Indies, which had been for many years under a sort of sequestration for the payment of its own incumbrances, might be recoverable by proper measures; and this property, though not large, would be enough to make her comparatively rich. But there was nobody to stir in it. Mr Elliot would do nothing, and she could do nothing herself, equally disabled from personal exertion by her state of bodily weakness, and from employing others by her want of money. She had no natural connections to assist her even with their counsel, and she could not afford to purchase the assistance of the law. This was a cruel aggravation of actually straitened means. To feel that she ought to be in better circumstances, that a little trouble in the right place might do it, and to fear that delay might be even weakening her claims, was hard to bear!

It was on this point that she had hoped to engage Anne's good offices with Mr Elliot. She had previously, in the anticipation of their marriage, been very apprehensive of losing her friend by it; but on being assured that he could have made no attempt of that nature, since he did not even know her to be in Bath, it immediately occurred that something might be done in her favour by the influence of the woman he loved, and she had been hastily preparing to interest Anne's feelings, as far as the observances due to Mr Elliot's character would allow, when Anne's refutation of the supposed engagement changed the face of everything, and while it took from her the new-formed hope of succeeding in the object of her first anxiety, left her at least the comfort of telling the whole story her own way.

After listening to this full description of Mr Elliot, Anne could not but express some surprise at Mrs Smith's having spoken of him so favourably in the beginning of their conversation. 'She had seemed to recommend and praise him!'

'My dear,' was Mrs Smith's reply, 'there was nothing else to be done. I considered your marrying him as certain, though he might not yet have made the offer, and I could no more speak the truth of him than if he had been your husband. My heart bled for you, as I talked of happiness. And yet, he is sensible, he is agreeable, and with such a woman as you, it was not absolutely hopeless. He was very unkind to his first wife. They were wretched together. But she was too ignorant and giddy for respect, and he had never loved her. I was willing to hope that you must fare better.'

Anne could just acknowledge within herself such a possibility of having been induced to marry him as made her shudder at the idea of the misery which must have followed. It was just possible that she might have been persuaded by Lady Russell! And under such a supposition, which would have been most miserable, when time had disclosed all, too late?

It was very desirable that Lady Russell should be no longer deceived; and one of the concluding arrangements of this important conference, which carried them through the greater part of the morning, was that Anne had full liberty to communicate to her friend everything relative to Mrs Smith in which his conduct was involved.

## *Chapter 10*

Anne went home to think over all that she had heard. In one point, her feelings were relieved by this knowledge of Mr Elliot. There was no longer anything of tenderness due to him. He stood, as opposed to Captain Wentworth, in all his own unwelcome obtrusiveness; and the evil of his attentions last night, the irremediable mischief he might have done, was considered with sensations unqualified, unperplexed. – Pity for him was all over. But this was the only point of relief. In every other respect, in looking around her, or penetrating forward, she saw more to distrust and to apprehend. She was concerned for the disappointment and pain Lady Russell would be feeling, for the mortifications which must be hanging over her father and sister, and had all the distress of foreseeing many evils, without knowing how to avert any one of them. – She was most thankful for her own knowledge of him. She had never considered herself as entitled to reward for not slighting an old friend like Mrs Smith, but here was a reward indeed springing from it! – Mrs Smith had been able to tell her what no one else could have done. Could the knowledge have been extended through her family! – But this was a vain idea. She must talk to Lady Russell, tell her, consult with her, and having done her best, wait the event with as much composure as possible; and after all, her greatest want of composure would be in that quarter of the mind which could not be opened to Lady Russell, in that flow of anxieties and fears which must be all to herself.

She found, on reaching home, that she had, as she intended, escaped seeing Mr Elliot; that he had called and paid them a long morning visit; but hardly had she congratulated herself, and felt safe till tomorrow, when she heard that he was coming again in the evening.

'I had not the smallest intention of asking him,' said Elizabeth, with affected carelessness, 'but he gave so many hints; so Mrs Clay says, at least.'

'Indeed I do say it. I never saw anybody in my life spell harder for an invitation. Poor man! I was really in pain for him; for your hard-hearted sister, Miss Anne, seems bent on cruelty.'

'Oh!' cried Elizabeth, 'I have been rather too much used to the game to be soon overcome by a gentleman's hints. However, when I found how excessively he was regretting that he should miss my father this morning, I gave way immediately, for I would never really omit an opportunity of bringing him and Sir Walter together. They appear to so much advantage in company with each other! Each behaving so pleasantly! Mr Elliot looking up with so much respect!'

'Quite delightful!' cried Mrs Clay, not daring, however, to turn her eyes towards Anne. 'Exactly like father and son! Dear Miss Elliot, may I not say father and son?'

'Oh! I lay no embargo on anybody's words. If you will have such ideas! But, upon my word, I am scarcely sensible of his attentions being beyond those of other men.'

'My dear Miss Elliot!' exclaimed Mrs Clay, lifting up her hands and eyes, and sinking all the rest of her astonishment in a convenient silence.

'Well, my dear Penelope, you need not be so alarmed about him. I did invite him, you know. I sent him away with smiles. When I found he was really going to his friends at Thornberry Park for the whole day tomorrow, I had compassion on him.'

Anne admired the good acting of the friend in being able to show such pleasure as she did in the expectation, and in the actual arrival of the very person whose presence must really be interfering with her prime object. It was impossible but that Mrs Clay must hate the sight of Mr Elliot; and yet she could assume a most obliging, placid look, and appear quite satisfied with the curtailed license of devoting herself only half as much to Sir Walter as she would have done otherwise.

To Anne herself it was most distressing to see Mr Elliot enter the room; and quite painful to have him approach and speak to her. She had been used before to feel that he could not be always quite sincere, but now she saw insincerity in everything. His attentive deference to her father, contrasted with his former language, was odious; and when she thought of his cruel conduct towards Mrs Smith, she could hardly bear the sight of his present smiles and mildness, or the sound of his artificial good sentiments. She meant to avoid any such alteration of manners as might provoke a remonstrance on his side. It was a great object with her to escape all enquiry or éclat; but it was her intention to be as decidedly cool to him as might be compatible with their relationship, and to retrace, as quietly as she could, the few steps of unnecessary intimacy she had been gradually led along. She was accordingly more guarded, and more cool, than she had been the night before.

He wanted to animate her curiosity again as to how and where he could have heard her formerly praised; wanted very much to be gratified by more solicitation; but the charm was broken: he found that the heat and animation of a public room were necessary to kindle his modest cousin's vanity; he found, at least, that it was not to be done now, by any of those attempts which he could hazard among the too-commanding claims of the others. He little surmised that it was a subject acting now exactly against his interest, bringing immediately into her thoughts all those parts of his conduct which were least excusable.

She had some satisfaction in finding that he was really going out of Bath the next morning, going early, and that he would be gone the greater part of two days. He was invited again to Camden Place the very evening of his return; but from Thursday to Saturday evening his absence was certain. It was bad enough that a Mrs Clay should be always before her; but that a deeper hypocrite should be added to their party seemed the destruction of everything like peace and comfort. It was so humiliating to reflect on the constant deception practised on her father and Elizabeth; to consider the various sources of mortification preparing for them! Mrs Clay's selfishness was not so complicated nor so revolting as his; and Anne would have compounded for the marriage at once, with all its evils, to be clear of Mr Elliot's subtleties, in endeavouring to prevent it.

On Friday morning she meant to go very early to Lady Russell, and accomplish the necessary communication; and she would have gone directly after breakfast but that Mrs Clay was also going out on some obliging purpose of saving her sister trouble, which determined her to wait till she might be safe from such a companion. She saw Mrs Clay fairly off, therefore, before she began to talk of spending the morning in Rivers Street.

'Very well,' said Elizabeth, 'I have nothing to send but my love. Oh! you may as well take back that tiresome book she would lend me, and pretend I have read it through. I really cannot be plaguing myself for ever with all the new poems and states of the nation that come out. Lady Russell quite bores one with her new publications. You need not tell her so, but I thought her dress hideous the other night. I used to think she had some taste in dress, but I was ashamed of her at the concert. Something so formal and *arrangé* in her air! and she sits so upright! My best love, of course.'

'And mine,' added Sir Walter. 'Kindest regards. And you may say, that I mean to call upon her soon. Make a civil message. But I shall only leave my card. Morning visits are never fair by women at her time of life, who make themselves up so little. If she would only wear rouge, she would not be afraid of being seen; but last time I called, I observed the blinds were let down immediately.'

While her father spoke, there was a knock at the door. Who could it be? Anne, remembering the preconcerted visits, at all hours, of Mr Elliot, would have expected him, but for his known engagement seven miles off. After the usual period of suspense, the usual sounds of approach were heard, and 'Mr and Mrs Charles Musgrove' were ushered into the room.

Surprise was the strongest emotion raised by their appearance; but Anne was really glad to see them, and the others were not so sorry but that they could put on a decent air of welcome; and as soon as it became clear that these, their nearest relations, were not arrived with any views of accommodation in that house, Sir Walter and Elizabeth were able to rise in cordiality, and do the honours of it very well. They were come to Bath for a few days with Mrs Musgrove, and were at the White Hart. So much was pretty soon understood; but till Sir Walter and Elizabeth were walking Mary into the other drawing-room, and regaling themselves with her admiration, Anne could not draw upon Charles's brain for a regular history of their coming, or an explanation of some smiling hints of particular business, which had been ostentatiously dropped by Mary, as well as of some apparent confusion as to whom their party consisted of.

She then found that it consisted of Mrs Musgrove, Henrietta, and Captain Harville, beside their two selves. He gave her a very plain, intelligible account of the whole; a narration in which she saw a great deal of most characteristic proceeding. The scheme had received its first impulse by Captain Harville's wanting to come to Bath on business. He had begun to talk of it a week ago; and by way of doing something, as shooting was over, Charles had proposed coming with him, and Mrs Harville had seemed to like the idea of it very much, as an advantage to her husband; but Mary could not bear to be left, and had made herself so unhappy about it that, for a day or two, everything seemed to be in suspense, or at an end. But then, it had been taken up by his father and mother. His mother had some old friends in Bath, whom she wanted to see; it was thought a good opportunity for Henrietta to come and buy wedding-clothes for herself and her sister; and, in short, it ended in being his mother's party, that everything might be comfortable and easy to Captain Harville; and he and Mary were included in it, by way of general convenience. They had arrived late the night before. Mrs Harville, her children, and Captain Benwick, remained with Mr Musgrove and Louisa at Uppercross.

Anne's only surprise was that affairs should be in forwardness enough for Henrietta's wedding-clothes to be talked of: she had imagined such difficulties of fortune to exist there as must prevent the marriage from being near at hand; but she learned from Charles that, very recently (since Mary's last letter to herself), Charles Hayter had been applied to by a friend to hold a living for a youth who could not possibly claim it under many years; and that, on the strength of this present income, with almost a certainty of something more permanent long before the term in question, the two families had consented to the young people's wishes, and that their marriage was likely to take place in a few months, quite as soon as Louisa's. 'And a very good living it was,' Charles added, 'only five-and-twenty miles from Uppercross, and in a very fine country – fine part of Dorsetshire. In the centre of some of the best preserves in the kingdom, surrounded by three great proprietors, each more careful and jealous than the other; and to two of the three, at least, Charles Hayter might get a special recommendation. Not that he will value it as he ought,' he observed, 'Charles is too cool about sporting. That's the worst of him.'

'I am extremely glad, indeed,' cried Anne, 'particularly glad that this should happen; and that of two sisters, who both deserve equally well, and who have always been such good friends, the pleasant prospects of one should not be dimming those of the other – that they should be so equal in their prosperity and comfort. I hope your father and mother are quite happy with regard to both.'

'Oh! yes. My father would be as well pleased if the gentlemen were richer, but he has no other fault to find. Money, you know, coming down with money – two daughters at once – it cannot be a very agreeable operation, and it straitens him as to many things. However, I do not mean to say they have not a right to it. It is very fit they should have daughters' shares; and I am sure he has always been a very kind, liberal father to me. Mary does not above half like Henrietta's match. She never did, you know. But she does not do him justice, nor think enough about Winthrop. I cannot make her attend to the value of the property. It is a very fair match, as times go; and I have liked Charles Hayter all my life, and I shall not leave off now.'

'Such excellent parents as Mr and Mrs Musgrove,' exclaimed Anne, 'should be happy in their children's marriages. They do everything to confer happiness, I am sure. What a blessing to young people to be in such hands! Your father and mother seem so totally free from all those ambitious feelings which have led to so much misconduct and misery, both in young and old! I hope you think Louisa perfectly recovered now?'

He answered rather hesitatingly, 'Yes, I believe I do – very much recovered; but she is altered: there is no running or jumping about, no laughing or dancing; it is quite different. If one happens only to shut the door a little hard, she starts and wriggles like a young dabchick in the water; and Benwick sits at her elbow, reading verses, or whispering to her, all day long.'

Anne could not help laughing. 'That cannot be much to your taste, I know, said she; 'but I do believe him to be an excellent young man.'

'To be sure he is. Nobody doubts it; and I hope you do not think I am so illiberal as to want every man to have the same objects and pleasures as myself. I have a great value for Benwick; and when one can but get him to talk, he has plenty to say. His reading has done him no harm, for he has fought as well as read. He is a brave fellow. I got more acquainted with him last Monday than ever I did before. We had a famous set-to at rat-hunting all the morning, in my father's great barns; and he played his part so well that I have liked him the better ever since.'

Here they were interrupted by the absolute necessity of Charles's following the others to admire mirrors and china; but Anne had heard enough to understand the present state of Uppercross, and rejoice in its happiness; and though she sighed as she rejoiced, her sigh had none of the ill will of envy in it. She would certainly have risen to their blessings if she could, but she did not want to lessen theirs.

The visit passed off altogether in high good humour. Mary was in excellent spirits, enjoying the gaiety and the change; and so well satisfied with the journey in her mother-in-law's carriage with four horses, and with her own complete independence of Camden Place, that she was exactly in a temper to admire everything as she ought, and enter most readily into all the superiorities of the house, as they were detailed to her. She had no demands on her father or sister, and her consequence was just enough increased by their handsome drawing-rooms.

Elizabeth was, for a short time, suffering a good deal. She felt that Mrs Musgrove and all her party ought to be asked to dine with them, but she could not bear to have the difference of style, the reduction of servants which a dinner must betray, witnessed by those who had been always so inferior to the Elliots of Kellynch. It was a struggle between propriety and vanity; but vanity got the better, and then Elizabeth was happy again. These were her internal persuasions: 'Old-fashioned notions – country hospitality – we do not profess to give dinners – few people in Bath do – Lady Alicia never does; did not even ask her own sister's family, though they were here a month; and I dare say it would be very inconvenient to Mrs Musgrove – put her quite out of her way. I am sure she would rather not come – she cannot feel easy with us. I will ask

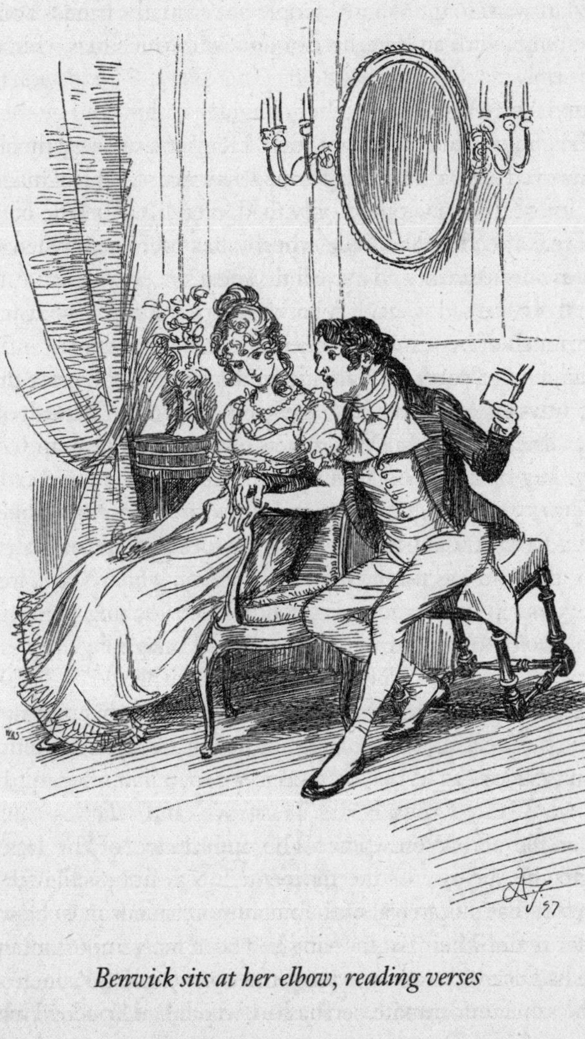

*Benwick sits at her elbow, reading verses*

them all for an evening; that will be much better – that will be a novelty and a treat. They have not seen two such drawing-rooms before. They will be delighted to come tomorrow evening. It shall be a regular party – small, but most elegant.' And this satisfied Elizabeth; and when the invitation was given to the two present, and promised for the absent, Mary was as completely satisfied. She was particularly asked to meet Mr Elliot, and be introduced to Lady Dalrymple and Miss Carteret, who were fortunately already engaged to come; and she could not have received a more gratifying attention. Miss Elliot was to have the honour of calling on Mrs Musgrove in the course of the morning, and Anne walked off with Charles and Mary, to go and see her and Henrietta directly.

Her plan of sitting with Lady Russell must give way for the present. They all three called in Rivers Street for a couple of minutes; but Anne convinced herself that a day's delay of the intended communication could be of no consequence, and hastened forward to the White Hart, to see again the friends and companions of the last autumn, with an eagerness of goodwill which many associations contributed to form.

They found Mrs Musgrove and her daughter within, and by themselves, and Anne had the kindest welcome from each. Henrietta was exactly in that state of recently improved views, of fresh-formed happiness, which made her full of regard and interest for everybody she had ever liked before at all; and Mrs Musgrove's real affection had been won by her usefulness when they were in distress. It was a heartiness, and a warmth, and a sincerity which Anne delighted in the more from the sad want of such blessings at home. She was entreated to give them as much of her time as possible, invited for everyday and all day long, or rather claimed as a part of the family; and in return, she naturally fell into all her wonted ways of attention and assistance, and on Charles's leaving them together, was listening to Mrs Musgrove's history of Louisa, and to Henrietta's of herself, giving opinions on business, and recommendations to shops; with intervals of every help which Mary required, from altering her ribbon to settling her accounts, from finding her keys, and assorting her trinkets, to trying to convince her that she was not ill-used by anybody; which Mary, well amused as she generally was in her station at a window overlooking the entrance to the pump-room, could not but have her moments of imagining.

A morning of thorough confusion was to be expected. A large party in an hotel ensured a quick-changing, unsettled scene. One five minutes brought a note, the next a parcel, and Anne had not been there half an hour, when their dining-room, spacious as it was, seemed more than half filled: a party of steady old friends were seated round Mrs Musgrove, and Charles came back with Captains Harville and Wentworth. The appearance of the latter could not be more than the surprise of the moment. It was impossible for her to have forgotten to feel that this arrival of their common friends must be soon bringing them together again. Their last meeting had been most important in opening his feelings; she had derived from it a delightful conviction; but she feared from his looks that the same unfortunate persuasion, which had hastened him away from the concert room, still governed. He did not seem to want to be near enough for conversation.

She tried to be calm, and leave things to take their course; and tried to dwell much on this argument of rational dependence – 'Surely, if there be constant attachment on each side, our hearts must understand each other ere long. We are not boy and girl, to be captiously irritable, misled by every moment's inadvertence, and wantonly playing with our own happiness.' And yet, a few minutes afterwards, she felt as if their being in company with each other, under their present circumstances, could only be exposing them to inadvertencies and misconstructions of the most mischievous kind.

'Anne,' cried Mary, still at her window, 'there is Mrs Clay, I am sure, standing under the colonnade, and a gentleman with her. I saw them turn the corner from Bath Street just now. They seem deep in talk. Who is it? – Come, and tell me. Good heavens! I recollect. – It is Mr Elliot himself.'

'No,' cried Anne quickly, 'it cannot be Mr Elliot, I assure you. He was to leave Bath at nine this morning, and does not come back till tomorrow.'

As she spoke, she felt that Captain Wentworth was looking at her; the consciousness of which vexed and embarrassed her, and made her regret that she had said so much, simple as it was.

Mary, resenting that she should be supposed not to know her own cousin, began talking very warmly about the family features, and protesting still more positively that it was Mr Elliot, calling again upon Anne to come and look herself; but Anne did not mean to stir, and tried to be cool and unconcerned. Her distress returned, however, on perceiving smiles and intelligent glances pass between two or three of the lady visitors, as if they believed themselves quite in the secret. It was evident that the report concerning her had spread; and a short pause succeeded, which seemed to ensure that it would now spread farther.

'Do come, Anne,' cried Mary, 'come and look yourself. You will be too late, if you do not make haste. They are parting, they are shaking hands. He is turning away. Not know Mr Elliot, indeed! – You seem to have forgot all about Lyme.'

To pacify Mary, and perhaps screen her own embarrassment, Anne did move quietly to the window. She was just in time to ascertain that it really was Mr Elliot (which she had never believed), before he disappeared on one side, as Mrs Clay walked quickly off on the other; and checking the surprise which she could not but feel at such an appearance of friendly conference between two persons of totally opposite interests, she calmly said, 'Yes, it is Mr Elliot certainly. He has changed his hour of going, I suppose, that is all – or I may be mistaken; I might not attend;' and walked back to her chair, recomposed, and with the comfortable hope of having acquitted herself well.

The visitors took their leave; and Charles, having civilly seen them off, and then made a face at them, and abused them for coming, began with –

'Well, mother, I have done something for you that you will like. I have been to the theatre, and secured a box for tomorrow night. An't I a good boy? I know you love a play; and there is room for us all. It holds nine. I have engaged

Captain Wentworth. Anne will not be sorry to join us, I am sure. We all like a play. Have not I done well, mother?'

Mrs Musgrove was good humouredly beginning to express her perfect readiness for the play, if Henrietta and all the others liked it, when Mary eagerly interrupted her by exclaiming,

'Good heavens, Charles! how can you think of such a thing? Take a box for tomorrow night! Have you forgot that we are engaged to Camden Place tomorrow night? and that we were most particularly asked on purpose to meet Lady Dalrymple and her daughter, and Mr Elliot – all the principal family connections – on purpose to be introduced to them? How can you be so forgetful?'

'Phoo! phoo!' replied Charles, 'what's an evening party? Never worth remembering. Your father might have asked us to dinner, I think, if he had wanted to see us. You may do as you like, but I shall go to the play.'

'Oh! Charles, I declare it will be too abominable if you do! when you promised to go.'

'No, I did not promise. I only smirked and bowed and said the word "happy". There was no promise.'

'But you must go, Charles. It would be unpardonable to fail. We were asked on purpose to be introduced. There was always such a great connection between the Dalrymples and ourselves. Nothing ever happened on either side that was not announced immediately. We are quite near relations, you know; and Mr Elliot too, whom you ought so particularly to be acquainted with! Every attention is due to Mr Elliot. Consider, my father's heir – the future representative of the family.'

'Don't talk to me about heirs and representatives,' cried Charles. 'I am not one of those who neglect the reigning power to bow to the rising sun. If I would not go for the sake of your father, I should think it scandalous to go for the sake of his heir. What is Mr Elliot to me?'

The careless expression was life to Anne, who saw that Captain Wentworth was all attention, looking and listening with his whole soul; and that the last words brought his enquiring eyes from Charles to herself.

Charles and Mary still talked on in the same style; he, half serious and half jesting, maintaining the scheme for the play; and she, invariably serious, most warmly opposing it, and not omitting to make it known that however determined to go to Camden Place herself, she should not think herself very well used, if they went to the play without her. Mrs Musgrove interposed.

'We had better put it off. Charles, you had much better go back, and change the box for Tuesday. It would be a pity to be divided, and we should be losing Miss Anne too, if there is a party at her father's; and I am sure neither Henrietta nor I should care at all for the play if Miss Anne could not be with us.'

Anne felt truly obliged to her for such kindness; and quite as much so, moreover, for the opportunity it gave her of decidedly saying –

'If it depended only on my inclination, ma'am, the party at home (excepting on Mary's account) would not be the smallest impediment. I have no pleasure in the sort of meeting, and should be too happy to change it for a play, and with you. But it had better not be attempted, perhaps.'

She had spoken it; but she trembled when it was done, conscious that her words were listened to, and daring not even to try to observe their effect.

It was soon generally agreed that Tuesday should be the day, Charles only reserving the advantage of still teasing his wife, by persisting that he would go to the play tomorrow, if nobody else would.

Captain Wentworth left his seat, and walked to the fireplace; probably for the sake of walking away from it soon afterwards, and taking a station, with less barefaced design, by Anne.

'You have not been long enough in Bath,' said he, 'to enjoy the evening-parties of the place.'

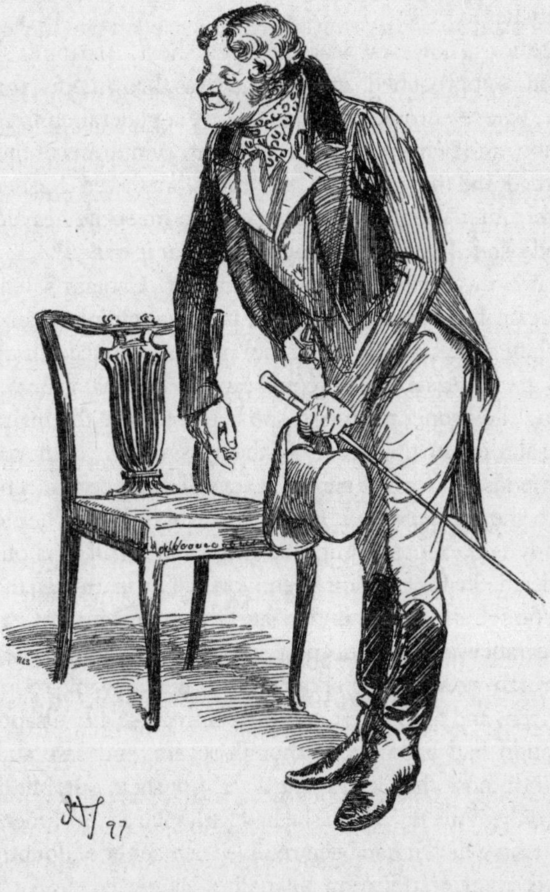

*'I only smirked and bowed'*

'Oh! no. The usual character of them has nothing for me. I am no card-player.'

'You were not formerly, I know. You did not use to like cards; but time makes many changes.'

'I am not yet so much changed,' cried Anne, and stopped, fearing she hardly knew what misconstruction. After waiting a few moments he said – and as if it were the result of immediate feeling – 'It is a period, indeed! Eight years and a half is a period!'

Whether he would have proceeded farther was left to Anne's imagination to ponder over in a calmer hour; for while still hearing the sounds he had uttered, she was startled to other subjects by Henrietta, eager to make use of the present leisure for getting out, and calling on her companions to lose no time, lest somebody else should come in.

They were obliged to move. Anne talked of being perfectly ready, and tried to look it; but she felt that could Henrietta have known the regret and reluctance of her heart in quitting that chair, in preparing to quit the room, she would have found in all her own sensations for her cousin, in the very security of his affection, wherewith to pity her.

Their preparations, however, were stopped short. Alarming sounds were heard; other visitors approached, and the door was thrown open for Sir Walter and Miss Elliot, whose entrance seemed to give a general chill. Anne felt an instant oppression, and, wherever she looked, saw symptoms of the same. The comfort, the freedom, the gaiety of the room was over, hushed into cold composure, determined silence, or insipid talk, to meet the heartless elegance of her father and sister. How mortifying to feel that it was so!

Her jealous eye was satisfied in one particular. Captain Wentworth was acknowledged again by each, by Elizabeth more graciously than before. She even addressed him once, and looked at him more than once. Elizabeth was, in fact, revolving a great measure. The sequel explained it. After the waste of a few minutes in saying the proper nothings, she began to give the invitation which was to comprise all the remaining dues of the Musgroves. 'Tomorrow evening, to meet a few friends, no formal party.' It was all said very gracefully and the cards with which she had provided herself, the 'Miss Elliot at home', were laid on the table, with a courteous, comprehensive smile to all, and one smile and one card more decidedly for Captain Wentworth. The truth was, that Elizabeth had been long enough in Bath to understand the importance of a man of such an air and appearance as his. The past was nothing. The present was that Captain Wentworth would move about well in her drawing-room. The card was pointedly given, and Sir Walter and Elizabeth arose and disappeared.

The interruption had been short, though severe; and ease and animation returned to most of those they left, as the door shut them out, but not to Anne. She could think only of the invitation she had with such astonishment witnessed; and of the manner in which it had been received, a manner of doubtful meaning, of surprise rather than gratification, of polite acknowledgement rather than acceptance. She knew him; she saw disdain in his eye, and could not venture to believe that he had determined to accept such an offering as atonement for all the insolence of the past. Her spirits sank. He held the card in his hand after they were gone, as if deeply considering it.

'Only think of Elizabeth's including everybody!' whispered Mary very audibly. 'I do not wonder Captain Wentworth is delighted! You see he cannot put the card out of his hand.'

Anne caught his eye, saw his cheeks glow, and his mouth form itself into a momentary expression of contempt, and turned away, that she might neither see nor hear more to vex her.

The party separated. The gentlemen had their own pursuits, the ladies proceeded on their own business, and they met no more while Anne belonged to them. She was earnestly begged to return and dine, and give them all the rest of the day; but her spirits had been so long exerted that at present she felt unequal to move, and fit only for home, where she might be sure of being as silent as she chose.

Promising to be with them the whole of the following morning, therefore, she closed the fatigues of the present by a toilsome walk to Camden Place, there to spend the evening chiefly in listening to the busy arrangements of Elizabeth and Mrs Clay for the morrow's party, the frequent enumeration of the persons invited, and the continually improving detail of all the embellishments which were to make it the most completely elegant of its kind in Bath, while harassing herself in secret with the never-ending question of whether Captain Wentworth would come or not. They were reckoning him as certain, but, with her, it was a gnawing solicitude never appeased for five minutes together. She generally thought he would come, because she generally thought he ought; but it was a case which she could not so shape into any positive act of duty or discretion as inevitably to defy the suggestions of very opposite feelings.

She only roused herself from the broodings of this restless agitation to let Mrs Clay know that she had been seen with Mr Elliot three hours after his being supposed to be out of Bath; for having watched in vain for some intimation of the interview from the lady herself, she determined to mention it, and it seemed to her that there was guilt in Mrs Clay's face as she listened. It was transient, cleared away in an instant, but Anne could imagine she read there the consciousness of having, by some complication of mutual trick, or some overbearing authority of his, been obliged to attend (perhaps for half an hour) to his lectures and restrictions on her designs on Sir Walter. She exclaimed, however, with a very tolerable imitation of nature,

'Oh dear! very true. Only think, Miss Elliot, to my great surprise I met with Mr Elliot in Bath Street! I was never more astonished. He turned back and walked with me to the Pump Yard. He had been prevented setting off for Thornberry, but I really forget by what – for I was in a hurry, and could not much attend, and I can only answer for his being determined not to be delayed in his return. He wanted to know how early he might be admitted tomorrow. He was full of "tomorrow"; and it is very evident that I have been full of it too ever since I entered the house, and learned the extension of your plan, and all that had happened, or my seeing him could never have gone so entirely out of my head.'

## *Chapter 11*

One day only had passed since Anne's conversation with Mrs Smith; but a keener interest had succeeded, and she was now so little touched by Mr Elliot's conduct, except by its effects in one quarter, that it became a matter of course the next morning, still to defer her explanatory visit in Rivers Street. She had promised to be with the Musgroves from breakfast to dinner. Her faith was plighted, and Mr Elliot's character, like the Sultaness Scheherazade's head, must live another day.

She could not keep her appointment punctually, however; the weather was unfavourable, and she had grieved over the rain on her friend's account, and felt it very much on her own, before she was able to attempt the walk. When she reached the White Hart, and made her way to the proper apartment, she found herself neither arriving quite in time, nor the first to arrive. The party before her were Mrs Musgrove, talking to Mrs Croft, and Captain Harville to Captain Wentworth, and she immediately heard that Mary and Henrietta, too impatient to wait, had gone out the moment it had cleared, but would be back again soon, and that the strictest injunctions had been left with Mrs Musgrove to keep her there till they returned. She had only to submit, sit down, be outwardly composed, and feel herself plunged at once in all the agitations which she had merely laid her account of tasting a little before the morning closed. There was no delay, no waste of time. She was deep in the happiness of such misery, or the misery of such happiness, instantly. Two minutes after her entering the room, Captain Wentworth said,

'We will write the letter we were talking of, Harville, now, if you will give me materials.'

Materials were all at hand, on a separate table; he went to it, and nearly turning his back on them all, was engrossed by writing.

Mrs Musgrove was giving Mrs Croft the history of her eldest daughter's engagement, and just in that inconvenient tone of voice which was perfectly audible while it pretended to be a whisper. Anne felt that she did not belong to the conversation, and yet, as Captain Harville seemed thoughtful and not disposed to talk, she could not avoid hearing many undesirable particulars, such as 'how Mr Musgrove and my brother Hayter had met again and again to talk it over; what my brother Hayter had said one day, and what Mr Musgrove had proposed the next, and what had occurred to my sister Hayter, and what the young people had wished, and what I said at first I never could consent to, but was afterwards persuaded to think might do very well', and a great deal in the same style of open-hearted communication – minutiae which, even with every advantage of taste and delicacy which good Mrs Musgrove could not give, could be properly interesting only to the principals. Mrs Croft was attending with great good humour, and whenever she spoke at all, it was very sensibly. Anne hoped the gentlemen might each be too much self-occupied to hear.

'And so, ma'am, all these things considered,' said Mrs Musgrove in her powerful whisper, 'though we could have wished it different, yet altogether we did not think it fair to stand out any longer; for Charles Hayter was quite wild about it, and Henrietta was pretty near as bad; and so we thought they had better marry at once, and make the best of it, as many others have done before them. At any rate, said I, it will be better than a long engagement.'

'That is precisely what I was going to observe,' cried Mrs Croft, 'I would rather have young people settle on a small income at once, and have to struggle with a few difficulties together, than be involved in a long engagement. I always think that no mutual – '

'Oh! dear Mrs Croft,' cried Mrs Musgrove, unable to let her finish her speech, 'there is nothing I so abominate for young people as a long engagement. It is what I always protested against for my children. It is all very well, I used to say, for young people to be engaged, if there is a certainty of their being able to marry in six months, or even in twelve, but a long engagement!'

'Yes, dear ma'am,' said Mrs Croft, 'or an uncertain engagement; an engagement which may be long. To begin without knowing that at such a time there will be the means of marrying I hold to be very unsafe and unwise, and what, I think, all parents should prevent as far as they can.'

Anne found an unexpected interest here. She felt its application to herself, felt it in a nervous thrill all over her, and at the same moment that her eyes instinctively glanced towards the distant table, Captain Wentworth's pen ceased to move, his head was raised, pausing, listening, and he turned round the next instant to give a look – one quick, conscious look at her.

The two ladies continued to talk, to re-urge the same admitted truths, and enforce them with such examples of the ill effect of a contrary practice as had fallen within their observation, but Anne heard nothing distinctly; it was only a buzz of words in her ear, her mind was in confusion.

Captain Harville, who had in truth been hearing none of it, now left his seat, and moved to a window; and Anne seeming to watch him, though it was from thorough absence of mind, became gradually sensible that he was inviting her to join him where he stood. He looked at her with a smile, and a little motion of the head, which expressed, 'Come to me, I have something to say;' and the unaffected, easy kindness of manner which denoted the feelings of an older acquaintance than he really was strongly enforced the invitation. She roused herself and went to him. The window at which he stood was at the other end of the room from where the two ladies were sitting, and though nearer to Captain Wentworth's table, not very near. As she joined him, Captain Harville's countenance reassumed the serious, thoughtful expression which seemed its natural character.

'Look here,' said he, unfolding a parcel in his hand, and displaying a small miniature painting, 'do you know who that is?'

'Certainly, Captain Benwick.'

'Yes, and you may guess who it is for. But' (in a deep tone) 'it was not done for her. Miss Elliot, do you remember our walking together at Lyme, and grieving for him? I little thought then – but no matter. This was drawn at the Cape. He met with a clever young German artist at the Cape, and in compliance with a promise to my poor sister, sat to him, and was bringing it home for her. And I have now the charge of getting it properly set for another! It was a commission to me! But who else was there to employ? I hope I can allow for him. I am not sorry, indeed, to make it over to another. He undertakes it;' (looking towards Captain Wentworth) 'he is writing about it now.' And with a quivering lip he wound up the whole by adding, 'Poor Fanny! she would not have forgotten him so soon!'

'No,' replied Anne, in a low feeling voice. 'That, I can easily believe.'

'It was not in her nature. She doted on him.'

'It would not be the nature of any woman who truly loved.'

Captain Harville smiled, as much as to say, 'Do you claim that for your sex?' and she answered the question, smiling also, 'Yes. We certainly do not forget you so soon as you forget us. It is, perhaps, our fate rather than our merit. We cannot help ourselves. We live at home, quiet, confined, and our feelings prey upon us. You are forced on exertion. You have always a profession, pursuits, business of some sort or other, to take you back into the world immediately, and continual occupation and change soon weaken impressions.'

'Granting your assertion that the world does all this so soon for men (which, however, I do not think I shall grant), it does not apply to Benwick. He has not been forced upon any exertion. The peace turned him on shore at the very moment, and he has been living with us, in our little family-circle, ever since.'

'True,' said Anne, 'very true; I did not recollect; but what shall we say now, Captain Harville? If the change be not from outward circumstances, it must be from within; it must be nature, man's nature, which has done the business for Captain Benwick.'

'No, no, it is not man's nature. I will not allow it to be more man's nature than woman's to be inconstant and forget those they do love, or have loved. I believe the reverse. I believe in a true analogy between our bodily frames and our mental; and that as our bodies are the strongest, so are our feelings; capable of bearing most rough usage, and riding out the heaviest weather.'

'Your feelings may be the strongest,' replied Anne, 'but the same spirit of analogy will authorise me to assert that ours are the most tender. Man is more robust than woman, but he is not longer-lived; which exactly explains my view of the nature of their attachments. Nay, it would be too hard upon you if it were otherwise. You have difficulties, and privations, and dangers enough to struggle with. You are always labouring and toiling, exposed to every risk and hardship. Your home, country, friends, all quitted. Neither time, nor health, nor life, to be called your own. It would be too hard indeed' (with a faltering voice), 'if woman's feelings were to be added to all this.'

'We shall never agree upon this question,' Captain Harville was beginning to say, when a slight noise called their attention to Captain Wentworth's hitherto perfectly quiet division of the room. It was nothing more than that his pen had fallen down, but Anne was startled at finding him nearer than she had supposed, and half inclined to suspect that the pen had only fallen, because he had been occupied by them, striving to catch sounds, which yet she did not think he could have caught.

'Have you finished your letter?' said Captain Harville.

'Not quite, a few lines more. I shall have done in five minutes.'

'There is no hurry on my side. I am only ready whenever you are. – I am in a very good anchorage here' (smiling at Anne), 'well supplied, and want for nothing. – No hurry for a signal at all. – Well, Miss Elliot' (lowering his voice), 'as I was saying, we shall never agree I suppose upon this point. No man and woman would, probably. But let me observe that all histories are against you, all stories, prose and verse. If I had such a memory as Benwick, I could bring you fifty quotations in a moment on my side the argument, and I do not think I ever opened a book in my life which had not something to say upon woman's inconstancy. Songs and proverbs all talk of woman's fickleness. But perhaps you will say, these were all written by men.'

'Perhaps I shall. – Yes, yes, if you please, no reference to examples in books. Men have had every advantage of us in telling their own story. Education has been theirs in so much higher a degree; the pen has been in their hands. I will not allow books to prove anything.'

'But how shall we prove anything?'

'We never shall. We never can expect to prove anything upon such a point. It is a difference of opinion which does not admit of proof. We each begin probably with a little bias towards our own sex, and upon that bias build every circumstance in favour of it which has occurred within our own circle; many of which circumstances (perhaps those very cases which strike us the most) may be precisely such as cannot be brought forward without betraying a confidence, or in some respect saying what should not be said.'

'Ah!' cried Captain Harville, in a tone of strong feeling, 'if I could but make you comprehend what a man suffers when he takes a last look at his wife and children, and watches the boat that he has sent them off in, as long as it is in sight, and then turns away and says, "God knows whether we ever meet again!" And then, if I could convey to you the glow of his soul when he does see them again; when, coming back after a twelvemonth's absence perhaps, and obliged to put into another port, he calculates how soon it be possible to get them there, pretending to deceive himself, and saying, "They cannot be here till such a day," but all the while hoping for them twelve hours sooner, and seeing them arrive at last, as if Heaven had given them wings, by many hours sooner still! If I could explain to you all this, and all that a man can bear and do, and glories to do for the sake of these treasures of his existence! I speak, you know, only of such men as have hearts!' pressing his own with emotion.

'Oh!' cried Anne eagerly, 'I hope I do justice to all that is felt by you, and by those who resemble you. God forbid that I should undervalue the warm and faithful feelings of any of my fellow-creatures. I should deserve utter contempt if I dared to suppose that true attachment and constancy were known only by woman. No, I believe you capable of everything great and good in your married lives. I believe you equal to every important exertion, and to every domestic forbearance, so long as – if I may be allowed the expression, so long as you have an object. I mean, while the woman you love lives, and lives for you. All the privilege I claim for my own sex (it is not a very enviable one, you need not covet it), is that of loving longest, when existence or when hope is gone.'

She could not immediately have uttered another sentence; her heart was too full, her breath too much oppressed.

'You are a good soul,' cried Captain Harville, putting his hand on her arm quite affectionately. 'There is no quarrelling with you. – And when I think of Benwick, my tongue is tied.'

Their attention was called towards the others. – Mrs Croft was taking leave.

'Here, Frederick, you and I part company, I believe,' said she. 'I am going home, and you have an engagement with your friend. – To-night we may have the pleasure of all meeting again, at your party' (turning to Anne). 'We had your sister's card yesterday, and I understood Frederick had a card too, though I did not see it – and you are disengaged, Frederick, are you not, as well as ourselves?'

Captain Wentworth was folding up a letter in great haste, and either could not or would not answer fully.

'Yes,' said he, 'very true; here we separate, but Harville and I shall soon be after you, that is, Harville, if you are ready, I am in half a minute. I know you will not be sorry to be off. I shall be at your service in half a minute.'

Mrs Croft left them, and Captain Wentworth, having sealed his letter with great rapidity, was indeed ready, and had even a hurried, agitated air, which showed impatience to be gone. Anne knew not how to understand it. She had the kindest 'Good-morning, God bless you,' from Captain Harville, but from him not a word nor a look. He had passed out of the room without a look!

She had only time, however, to move closer to the table where he had been writing, when footsteps were heard returning; the door opened; it was himself. He begged their pardon, but he had forgotten his gloves, and instantly crossing the room to the writing-table, and standing with his back towards Mrs Musgrove, he drew out a letter from under the scattered paper, placed it before Anne with eyes of glowing entreaty fixed on her for a moment, and hastily collecting his gloves, was again out of the room, almost before Mrs Musgrove was aware of his being in it – the work of an instant!

The revolution which one instant had made in Anne was almost beyond expression. The letter, with a direction hardly legible, to 'Miss A. E—' was evidently the one which he had been folding so hastily. While supposed to be writing only to Captain Benwick, he had been also addressing her! On the contents of that letter depended all which this world could do for her! Anything was possible, anything might be defied rather than suspense. Mrs Musgrove had little arrangements of her own at her own table; to their protection she must trust, and sinking into the chair which he had occupied, succeeding to the very spot where he had leaned and written, her eyes devoured the following words:

I can listen no longer in silence. I must speak to you by such means as are within my reach. You pierce my soul. I am half agony, half hope. Tell me not that I am too late, that such precious feelings are gone forever. I offer myself to you again with a heart even more your own than when you almost broke it eight years and a half ago. Dare not say that man forgets sooner than woman, that his love has an earlier death. I have loved none but you. Unjust I may have been, weak and resentful I have been, but never inconstant. You alone have brought me to Bath. For you alone I think and plan. – Have you not seen this? Can you fail to have understood my wishes? – I had not waited even these ten days, could I have read your feelings, as I think you must have penetrated mine. I can hardly write. I am every instant hearing something which overpowers me. You sink your voice, but I can distinguish the tones of that voice, when they would be lost on others. – Too good, too excellent creature! You do us justice indeed. You do believe that there is true attachment and constancy among men. Believe it to be most fervent, most undeviating in

F. W.

I must go, uncertain of my fate; but I shall return hither, or follow your party, as soon as possible. A word, a look will be enough to decide whether I enter your father's house this evening, or never.

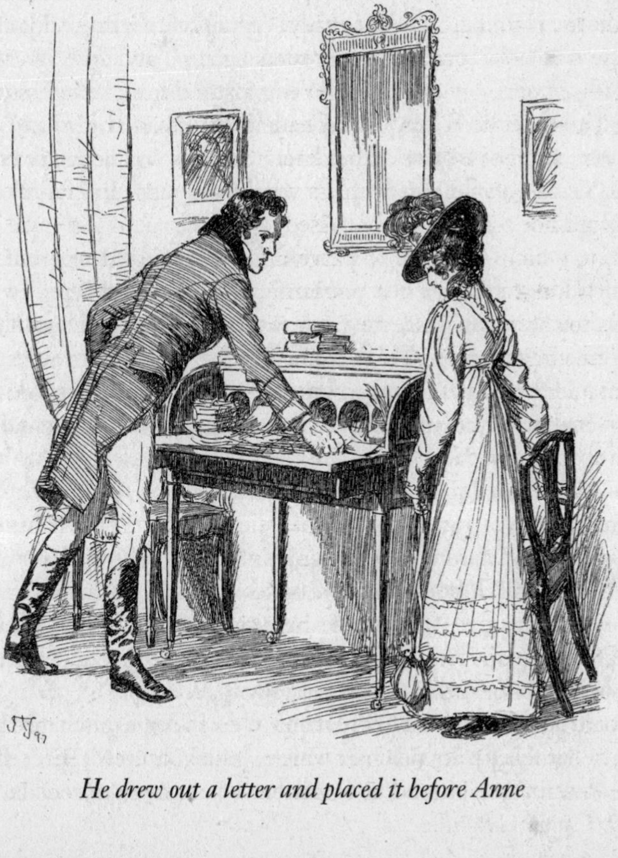

*He drew out a letter and placed it before Anne*

Such a letter was not to be soon recovered from. Half an hour's solitude and reflection might have tranquillised her; but the ten minutes only, which now passed before she was interrupted, with all the restraints of her situation, could do nothing towards tranquillity. Every moment rather brought fresh agitation. It was an overpowering happiness. And before she was beyond the first stage of full sensation, Charles, Mary, and Henrietta all came in.

The absolute necessity of seeming like herself produced then an immediate struggle; but after a while she could do no more. She began not to understand a word they said, and was obliged to plead indisposition and excuse herself. They could then see that she looked very ill – were shocked and concerned – and would not stir without her for the world. This was dreadful! Would they only have gone away, and left her in the quiet possession of that room, it would have been her cure; but to have them all standing or waiting around her was distracting, and, in desperation, she said she would go home.

'By all means, my dear,' cried Mrs Musgrove, 'go home directly and take care of yourself, that you may be fit for the evening. I wish Sarah was here to doctor you, but I am no doctor myself. Charles, ring and order a chair. She must not walk.'

But the chair would never do. Worse than all! To lose the possibility of speaking two words to Captain Wentworth in the course of her quiet, solitary progress up the town (and she felt almost certain of meeting him) could not be borne. The chair was earnestly protested against; and Mrs Musgrove, who thought only of one sort of illness, having assured herself, with some anxiety, that there had been no fall in the case; that Anne had not, at any time lately, slipped down, and got a blow on her head; that she was perfectly convinced of having had no fall, could part with her cheerfully, and depend on finding her better at night.

Anxious to omit no possible precaution, Anne struggled, and said,

'I am afraid, ma'am, that it is not perfectly understood. Pray be so good as to mention to the other gentlemen that we hope to see your whole party this evening. I am afraid there has been some mistake; and I wish you particularly to assure Captain Harville, and Captain Wentworth, that we hope to see them both.'

'Oh! my dear, it is quite understood, I give you my word. Captain Harville has no thought but of going.'

'Do you think so? But I am afraid; and I should be so very sorry! Will you promise me to mention it, when you see them again? You will see them both again this morning, I dare say. Do promise me.'

'To be sure I will, if you wish it. Charles, if you see Captain Harville anywhere, remember to give Miss Anne's message. But indeed, my dear, you need not be uneasy. Captain Harville holds himself quite engaged, I'll answer for it; and Captain Wentworth the same, I dare say.'

Anne could do no more; but her heart prophesied some mischance to damp the perfection of her felicity. It could not be very lasting, however. Even if he did not come to Camden Place himself, it would be in her power to send an intelligible sentence by Captain Harville.

Another momentary vexation occurred. Charles, in his real concern and good nature, would go home with her; there was no preventing him. This was almost cruel! But she could not be long ungrateful; he was sacrificing an engagement at a gunsmith's to be of use to her; and she set off with him, with no feeling but gratitude apparent.

They were in Union Street, when a quicker step behind, a something of familiar sound, gave her two moments preparation for the sight of Captain Wentworth. He joined them; but, as if irresolute whether to join or to pass on, said nothing – only looked. Anne could command herself enough to receive that look, and not repulsively. The cheeks which had been pale now glowed, and the movements which had hesitated were decided. He walked by her side. Presently, struck by a sudden thought, Charles said,

'Captain Wentworth, which way are you going? only to Gay Street, or farther up the town?'

'I hardly know,' replied Captain Wentworth, surprised.

'Are you going as high as Belmont? Are you going near Camden Place? Because if you are, I shall have no scruple in asking you to take my place, and give Anne your arm to her father's door. She is rather done for this morning, and must not go so far without help. And I ought to be at that fellow's in the marketplace. He promised me the sight of a capital gun he is just going to send off; said he would keep it unpacked to the last possible moment, that I might see it; and if I do not turn back now, I have no chance. By his description, a good deal like the second-sized double-barrel of mine, which you shot with one day, round Winthrop.'

There could not be an objection. There could be only a most proper alacrity, a most obliging compliance for public view; and smiles reined in and spirits dancing in private rapture. In half a minute, Charles was at the bottom of Union Street again, and the other two proceeding together; and soon words enough had passed between them to decide their direction towards the comparatively quiet and retired gravel-walk, where the power of conversation would make the present hour a blessing indeed; and prepare it for all the immortality which the happiest recollections of their own future lives could bestow. There they exchanged again those feelings and those promises which had once before seemed to secure everything, but which had been followed by so many, many years of division and estrangement. There they returned again into the past, more exquisitely happy, perhaps, in their reunion than when it had been first projected; more tender, more tried, more fixed in a knowledge of each other's character, truth, and attachment; more equal to act, more justified in acting. And there, as they slowly paced the gradual ascent, heedless of every group around them, seeing neither sauntering politicians, bustling housekeepers, flirting girls, nor nurserymaids and children, they could indulge in those retrospections and acknowledgements, and especially in those explanations of what had directly preceded the present moment, which were so poignant and so ceaseless in interest. All the little variations of the last week were gone through; and of yesterday and today there could scarcely be an end.

She had not mistaken him. Jealousy of Mr Elliot had been the retarding weight, the doubt, the torment. That had begun to operate in the very hour of first meeting her in Bath; that had returned, after a short suspension, to ruin the concert; and that had influenced him in everything he had said and done, or omitted to say and do, in the last four-and-twenty hours. It had been gradually yielding to the better hopes which her looks, or words, or actions occasionally encouraged; it had been vanquished at last by those sentiments and those tones which had reached him while she talked with Captain Harville; and under the irresistible governance of which he had seized a sheet of paper, and poured out his feelings.

Of what he had then written, nothing was to be retracted or qualified. He persisted in having loved none but her. She had never been supplanted. He never even believed himself to see her equal. Thus much indeed he was obliged to acknowledge – that he had been constant unconsciously, nay unintentionally; that he had meant to forget her, and believed it to be done. He had imagined himself indifferent, when he had only been angry; and he had been unjust to her merits, because he had been a sufferer from them. Her character was now fixed on his mind as perfection itself, maintaining the loveliest medium of fortitude and gentleness; but he was obliged to acknowledge that only at Uppercross had he learned to do her justice, and only at Lyme had he begun to understand himself.

At Lyme, he had received lessons of more than one sort. The passing admiration of Mr Elliot had at least roused him, and the scenes on the Cobb, and at Captain Harville's, had fixed her superiority.

In his preceding attempts to attach himself to Louisa Musgrove (the attempts of angry pride), he protested that he had forever felt it to be impossible; that he had not cared, could not care for Louisa; though, till that day, till the leisure for reflection which followed it, he had not understood the perfect excellence of the mind with which Louisa's could so ill bear a comparison; or the perfect, unrivalled hold it possessed over his own. There, he had learnt to distinguish between the steadiness of principle and the obstinacy of self-will, between the darings of heedlessness and the resolution of a collected mind. There, he had seen everything to exalt in his estimation the woman he had lost, and there begun to deplore the pride, the folly, the madness of resentment which had kept him from trying to regain her when thrown in his way.

From that period his penance had become severe. He had no sooner been free from the horror and remorse attending the first few days of Louisa's accident, no sooner begun to feel himself alive again, than he had began to feel himself, though alive, not at liberty.

'I found,' said he, 'that I was considered by Harville an engaged man! That neither Harville nor his wife entertained a doubt of our mutual attachment. I was startled and shocked. To a degree, I could contradict this instantly; but, when I began to reflect that others might have felt the same – her own family, nay, perhaps herself, I was no longer at my own disposal. I was hers; in honour if she wished it. I had been unguarded. I had not thought seriously on this subject before. I had not considered that my excessive intimacy must have its danger of ill consequence in many ways; and that I had no right to be trying whether I could attach myself to either of the girls, at the risk of raising even an unpleasant report, were there no other ill effects. I had been grossly wrong, and must abide the consequences.'

He found too late, in short, that he had entangled himself; and that precisely as he became fully satisfied of his not caring for Louisa at all, he must regard himself as bound to her, if her sentiments for him were what the Harvilles supposed. It determined him to leave Lyme, and await her complete recovery elsewhere. He would gladly weaken, by any fair means, whatever feelings or speculations concerning him might exist; and he went, therefore, to his brother's, meaning after a while to return to Kellynch, and act as circumstances might require.

'I was six weeks with Edward,' said he, 'and saw him happy. I could have no other pleasure. I deserved none. He enquired after you very particularly; asked even if you were personally altered, little suspecting that to my eye you could never alter.'

Anne smiled, and let it pass. It was too pleasing a blunder for a reproach. It is something for a woman to be assured, in her eight-and-twentieth year, that she has not lost one charm of earlier youth; but the value of such homage was inexpressibly increased to Anne by comparing it with former words, and feeling it to be the result, not the cause of a revival of his warm attachment.

He had remained in Shropshire, lamenting the blindness of his own pride, and the blunders of his own calculations, till at once released from Louisa by the astonishing and felicitous intelligence of her engagement with Benwick.

'Here,' said he, 'ended the worst of my state; for now I could at least put myself in the way of happiness, I could exert myself, I could do something. But to be waiting so long in inaction, and waiting only for evil, had been dreadful. Within the first five minutes I said, "I will be at Bath on Wednesday," and I was. Was it unpardonable to think it worth my while to come? and to arrive with some degree of hope? You were single. It was possible that you might retain the feelings of the past, as I did; and one encouragement happened to be mine. I could never doubt that you would be loved and sought by others, but I knew to a certainty that you had refused one man at least, of better pretensions than myself; and I could not help often saying, "Was this for me?" '

Their first meeting in Milsom Street afforded much to be said, but the concert still more. That evening seemed to be made up of exquisite moments. The moment of her stepping forward in the octagon room to speak to him, the moment of Mr Elliot's appearing and tearing her away, and one or two subsequent moments, marked by returning hope or increasing despondence, were dwelled on with energy.

'To see you,' cried he, 'in the midst of those who could not be my well-wishers, to see your cousin close by you, conversing and smiling, and feel all the horrible eligibilities and proprieties of the match! To consider it as the certain wish of every being who could hope to influence you! Even, if your own feelings were reluctant or indifferent, to consider what powerful supports would be his! Was it not enough to make the fool of me which I appeared? How could I look on without agony? Was not the very sight of the friend who sat behind you, was not the recollection of what had been, the knowledge of her influence, the indelible, immovable impression of what persuasion had once done – was it not all against me?'

'You should have distinguished,' replied Anne. 'You should not have suspected me now; the case so different, and my age so different. If I was wrong in yielding to persuasion once, remember that it was to persuasion exerted on the side of safety, not of risk. When I yielded, I thought it was to duty; but no duty could be called in aid here. In marrying a man indifferent to me, all risk would have been incurred, and all duty violated.'

'Perhaps I ought to have reasoned thus,' he replied, 'but I could not. I could not derive benefit from the late knowledge I had acquired of your character. I could not bring it into play; it was overwhelmed, buried, lost in those earlier feelings which I had been smarting under year after year. I could think of you only as one who had yielded, who had given me up, who had been influenced by anyone rather than by me. I saw you with the very person who had guided you in that year of misery. I had no reason to believe her of less authority now. – The force of habit was to be added.'

'I should have thought,' said Anne, 'that my manner to yourself might have spared you much or all of this.'

'No, no! your manner might be only the ease which your engagement to another man would give. I left you in this belief; and yet – I was determined to see you again. My spirits rallied with the morning, and I felt that I had still a motive for remaining here.'

At last Anne was at home again, and happier than anyone in that house could have conceived. All the surprise and suspense, and every other painful part of the morning dissipated by this conversation, she re-entered the house so happy as to be obliged to find an alloy in some momentary apprehensions of its being impossible to last. An interval of meditation, serious and grateful, was the best corrective of everything dangerous in such high-wrought felicity; and she went to her room, and grew steadfast and fearless in the thankfulness of her enjoyment.

The evening came, the drawing-rooms were lighted up, the company assembled. It was but a card-party, it was but a mixture of those who had never met before, and those who met too often – a commonplace business, too numerous for intimacy, too small for variety; but Anne had never found an evening shorter. Glowing and lovely in sensibility and happiness, and more generally admired than she thought about or cared for, she had cheerful or forbearing feelings for every creature around her. Mr Elliot was there; she avoided, but she could pity him. The Wallises; she had amusement in understanding them. Lady Dalrymple and Miss Carteret; they would soon be innoxious cousins to her. She cared not for Mrs Clay, and had nothing to blush for in the public manners of her father and sister. With the Musgroves, there was the happy chat of perfect ease; with Captain Harville, the kind-hearted intercourse of brother and sister; with Lady Russell, attempts at conversation, which a delicious consciousness cut short; with Admiral and Mrs Croft, everything of peculiar cordiality and fervent interest, which the same consciousness sought to conceal – and with Captain Wentworth, some moments of communication continually occurring, and always the hope of more, and always the knowledge of his being there!

It was in one of these short meetings, each apparently occupied in admiring a fine display of greenhouse plants, that she said –

'I have been thinking over the past, and trying impartially to judge of the right and wrong, I mean with regard to myself; and I must believe that I was right, much as I suffered from it, that I was perfectly right in being guided by the friend whom you will love better than you do now. To me, she was in the place of a parent. Do not mistake me, however. I am not saying that she did not err in her advice. It was, perhaps, one of those cases in which advice is good or bad only as the event decides; and for myself, I certainly never should, in any circumstance of tolerable similarity, give such advice. But I mean that I was right in submitting to her, and that if I had done otherwise, I should have suffered more in continuing the engagement than I did even in giving it up, because I should have suffered in my conscience. I have now, as far as such a sentiment is allowable in human nature, nothing to reproach myself with; and if I mistake not, a strong sense of duty is no bad part of a woman's portion.'

He looked at her, looked at Lady Russell, and looking again at her, replied, as if in cool deliberation,

'Not yet. But there are hopes of her being forgiven in time. I trust to being in charity with her soon. But I too have been thinking over the past, and a question has suggested itself, whether there may not have been one person more my enemy even than that lady? My own self. Tell me if, when I returned to England in the year eight, with a few thousand pounds, and was posted into the *Laconia*, if I had then written to you, would you have answered my letter? would you, in short, have renewed the engagement then?'

'Would I!' was all her answer; but the accent was decisive enough.

'Good God!' he cried, 'you would! It is not that I did not think of it, or desire it as what could alone crown all my other success. But I was proud, too proud to ask again. I did not understand you. I shut my eyes, and would not understand you, or do you justice. This is a recollection which ought to make me forgive everyone sooner than myself. Six years of separation and suffering might have been spared. It is a sort of pain, too, which is new to me. I have been used to the gratification of believing myself to earn every blessing that I enjoyed. I have valued myself on honourable toils and just rewards. Like other great men under reverses,' he added with a smile, 'I must endeavour to subdue my mind to my fortune. I must learn to brook being happier than I deserve.'

## *Chapter 12*

Who can be in doubt of what followed? When any two young people take it into their heads to marry, they are pretty sure by perseverance to carry their point, be they ever so poor, or ever so imprudent, or ever so little likely to be necessary to each other's ultimate comfort. This may be bad morality to conclude with, but I believe it to be truth; and if such parties succeed, how should a Captain Wentworth and an Anne Elliot, with the advantage of maturity of mind, consciousness of right, and one independent fortune between them, fail of bearing down every opposition? They might in fact have borne down a great deal more than they met with, for there was little to distress them beyond the want of graciousness and warmth. – Sir Walter made no objection, and Elizabeth did nothing worse than look cold and unconcerned. Captain Wentworth, with five-and-twenty thousand pounds, and as high in his profession as merit and activity could place him, was no longer nobody. He was now esteemed quite worthy to address the daughter of a foolish, spendthrift baronet, who had not had principle or sense enough to maintain himself in the situation in which Providence had placed him, and who could give his daughter at present but a small part of the share of ten thousand pounds which must be hers hereafter.

Sir Walter indeed, though he had no affection for Anne, and no vanity flattered, to make him really happy on the occasion, was very far from thinking it a bad match for her. On the contrary, when he saw more of Captain Wentworth, saw him repeatedly by daylight and eyed him well, he was very much struck by his personal claims, and felt that his superiority of appearance might be not unfairly balanced against her superiority of rank; and all this, assisted by his well-sounding name, enabled Sir Walter at last to prepare his pen with a very good grace for the insertion of the marriage in the volume of honour.

The only one among them, whose opposition of feeling could excite any serious anxiety, was Lady Russell. Anne knew that Lady Russell must be suffering some pain in understanding and relinquishing Mr Elliot, and be making some struggles to become truly acquainted with, and do justice to Captain Wentworth. This however was what Lady Russell had now to do. She must learn to feel that she had been mistaken with regard to both; that she had been unfairly influenced by appearances in each; that because Captain Wentworth's manners had not suited her own ideas, she had been too quick in suspecting them to indicate a character of dangerous impetuosity; and that because Mr Elliot's manners had precisely pleased her in their propriety and correctness, their general politeness and suavity, she had been too quick in receiving them as the certain result of the most correct opinions and well-regulated mind. There was nothing less for Lady Russell to do than to admit that she had been pretty completely wrong, and to take up a new set of opinions and of hopes.

There is a quickness of perception in some, a nicety in the discernment of character, a natural penetration, in short, which no experience in others can equal, and Lady Russell had been less gifted in this part of understanding than her young friend. But she was a very good woman, and if her second object was to be sensible and well judging, her first was to see Anne happy. She loved Anne better than she loved her own abilities; and when the awkwardness of the beginning was over, found little hardship in attaching herself as a mother to the man who was securing the happiness of her other child.

Of all the family, Mary was probably the one most immediately gratified by the circumstance. It was creditable to have a sister married, and she might flatter herself with having been greatly instrumental to the connection, by keeping Anne with her in the autumn; and as her own sister must be better than her

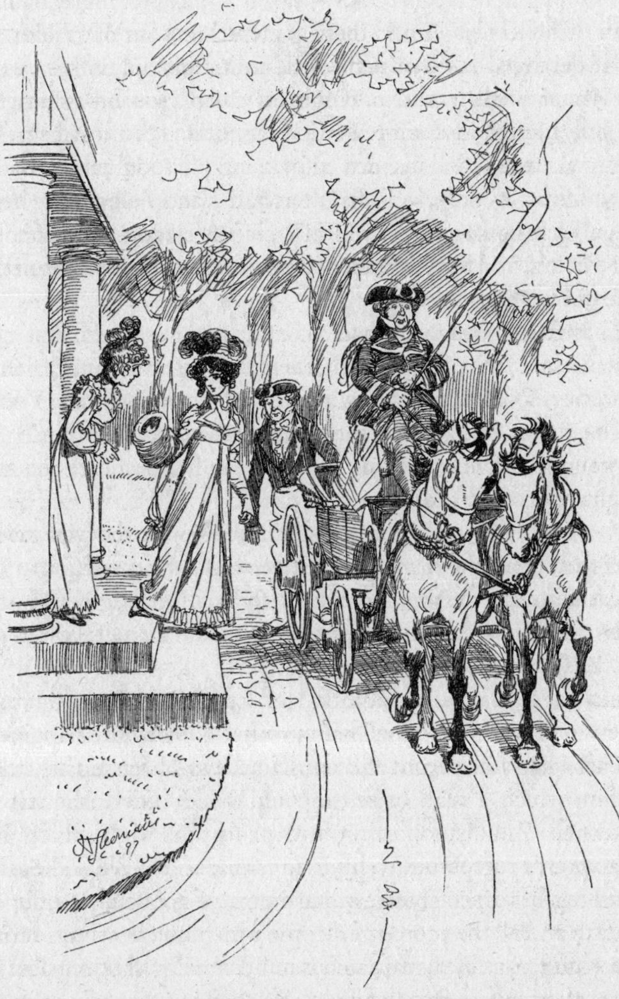

*The mistress of a very pretty landaulette*

husband's sisters, it was very agreeable that Captain Wentworth should be a richer man than either Captain Benwick or Charles Hayter. – She had something to suffer perhaps when they came into contact again, in seeing Anne restored to the rights of seniority, and the mistress of a very pretty landaulette; but she had a future to look forward to, of powerful consolation. Anne had no Uppercross Hall before her, no landed estate, no headship of a family; and if they could but keep Captain Wentworth from being made a baronet, she would not change situations with Anne.

It would be well for the eldest sister if she were equally satisfied with her situation, for a change is not very probable there. She had soon the mortification of seeing Mr Elliot withdraw; and no one of proper condition has since presented himself to raise even the unfounded hopes which sunk with him.

The news of his cousin Anne's engagement burst on Mr Elliot most unexpectedly. It deranged his best plan of domestic happiness, his best hope of keeping Sir Walter single by the watchfulness which a son-in-law's rights would have given. But, though discomfited and disappointed, he could still do something for his own interest and his own enjoyment. He soon quitted Bath; and on Mrs Clay's quitting it likewise soon afterwards, and being next heard of as established under his protection in London, it was evident how double a game he had been playing, and how determined he was to save himself from being cut out by one artful woman, at least.

Mrs Clay's affections had overpowered her interest, and she had sacrificed, for the young man's sake, the possibility of scheming longer for Sir Walter. She has abilities, however, as well as affections; and it is now a doubtful point whether his cunning, or hers, may finally carry the day; whether, after preventing her from being the wife of Sir Walter, he may not be wheedled and caressed at last into making her the wife of Sir William.

It cannot be doubted that Sir Walter and Elizabeth were shocked and mortified by the loss of their companion, and the discovery of their deception in her. They had their great cousins, to be sure, to resort to for comfort; but they must long feel that to flatter and follow others, without being flattered and followed in turn, is but a state of half-enjoyment.

Anne, satisfied at a very early period of Lady Russell's meaning to love Captain Wentworth as she ought, had no other alloy to the happiness of her prospects than what arose from the consciousness of having no relations to bestow on him which a man of sense could value. There she felt her own inferiority keenly. The disproportion in their fortune was nothing; it did not give her a moment's regret; but to have no family to receive and estimate him properly; nothing of respectability, of harmony, of goodwill to offer in return for all the worth and all the prompt welcome which met her in his brothers and sisters, was a source of as lively pain as her mind could well be sensible of, under circumstances of otherwise strong felicity. She had but two friends in the world to add to his list, Lady Russell and Mrs Smith. To those, however, he was very well disposed to attach himself. Lady Russell, in spite of all her former transgressions, he could now value from his heart. While he was not obliged to say that he believed her to have been right in originally dividing them, he was ready to say almost everything else in her favour; and as for Mrs Smith, she had claims of various kinds to recommend her quickly and permanently.

Her recent good offices by Anne had been enough in themselves; and their marriage, instead of depriving her of one friend, secured her two. She was their earliest visitor in their settled life; and Captain Wentworth, by putting her in the way of recovering her husband's property in the West Indies; by writing for her, acting for her, and seeing her through all the petty difficulties of the case, with the activity and exertion of a fearless man and a determined friend, fully requited the services which she had rendered, or ever meant to render, to his wife.

Mrs Smith's enjoyments were not spoiled by this improvement of income, with some improvement of health, and the acquisition of such friends to be often with, for her cheerfulness and mental alacrity did not fail her; and while these prime supplies of good remained, she might have bid defiance even to greater accessions of worldly prosperity. She might have been absolutely rich and perfectly healthy, and yet be happy. Her spring of felicity was in the glow of her spirits, as her friend Anne's was in the warmth of her heart. Anne was tenderness itself, and she had the full worth of it in Captain Wentworth's affection. His profession was all that could ever make her friends wish that tenderness less; the dread of a future war all that could dim her sunshine. She gloried in being a sailor's wife, but she must pay the tax of quick alarm for belonging to that profession which is, if possible, more distinguished in its domestic virtues than in its national importance.

# JANE EYRE

# Jane Eyre

CHARLOTTE BRONTË

TO

W. M. THACKERAY, ESQ.

THIS WORK IS

RESPECTFULLY INSCRIBED

BY THE AUTHOR

# *Chapter 1*

There was no possibility of taking a walk that day. We had been wandering, indeed, in the leafless shrubbery an hour in the morning; but since dinner (Mrs Reed, when there was no company, dined early) the cold winter wind had brought with it clouds so sombre, and a rain so penetrating, that further outdoor exercise was now out of the question.

I was glad of it: I never liked long walks, especially on chilly afternoons: dreadful to me was the coming home in the raw twilight, with nipped fingers and toes, and a heart saddened by the chidings of Bessie, the nurse, and humbled by the consciousness of my physical inferiority to Eliza, John, and Georgiana Reed.

The said Eliza, John, and Georgiana were now clustered round their mama in the drawing-room: she lay reclined on a sofa by the fireside, and with her darlings about her (for the time neither quarrelling nor crying) looked perfectly happy. Me, she had dispensed from joining the group; saying, 'She regretted to be under the necessity of keeping me at a distance; but that until she heard from Bessie, and could discover by her own observation, that I was endeavouring in good earnest to acquire a more sociable and childlike disposition, a more attractive and sprightly manner – something lighter, franker, more natural, as it were – she really must exclude me from privileges intended only for contented, happy, little children.'

'What does Bessie say I have done?' I asked.

'Jane, I don't like cavillers or questioners; besides, there is something truly forbidding in a child taking up her elders in that manner. Be seated somewhere; and until you can speak pleasantly, remain silent.'

A small breakfast-room adjoined the drawing-room, I slipped in there. It contained a bookcase: I soon possessed myself of a volume, taking care that it should be one stored with pictures. I mounted into the window-seat: gathering up my feet, I sat cross-legged, like a Turk; and, having drawn the red moreen curtain nearly close, I was shrined in double retirement.

Folds of scarlet drapery shut in my view to the right hand; to the left were the clear panes of glass, protecting, but not separating me from the drear November day. At intervals, while turning over the leaves of my book, I studied the aspect of that winter afternoon. Afar, it offered a pale blank of mist and cloud; near a scene of wet lawn and storm-beat shrub, with ceaseless rain sweeping away wildly before a long and lamentable blast.

I returned to my book – Bewick's *History of British Birds*: the letterpress thereof I cared little for, generally speaking; and yet there were certain introductory pages that, child as I was, I could not pass quite as a blank. They were those which treat of the haunts of sea-fowl; of 'the solitary rocks and promontories' by them only inhabited; of the coast of Norway, studded with isles from its southern extremity, the Lindeness, or Naze, to the North Cape –

Where the Northern Ocean, in vast whirls,
Boils round the naked, melancholy isles
Of farthest Thule; and the Atlantic surge
Pours in among the stormy Hebrides.

Nor could I pass unnoticed the suggestion of the bleak shores of Lapland, Siberia, Spitzbergen, Nova Zembla, Iceland, Greenland, with 'the vast sweep of the Arctic Zone, and those forlorn regions of dreary space, that reservoir of frost and snow, where firm fields of ice, the accumulation of centuries of winters, glazed in Alpine heights above heights, surround the pole and concentre the multiplied rigours of extreme cold.' Of these death-white realms I formed an idea of my own: shadowy, like all the half-comprehended notions that float dim through children's brains, but strangely impressive. The words in these introductory pages connected themselves with the succeeding vignettes, and gave significance to the rock standing up alone in a sea of billow and spray; to the broken boat stranded on a desolate coast; to the cold and ghastly moon glancing through bars of cloud at a wreck just sinking.

I cannot tell what sentiment haunted the quite solitary churchyard, with its inscribed headstone; its gate, its two trees, its low horizon, girdled by a broken wall, and its newly-risen crescent, attesting the hour of eventide.

The two ships becalmed on a torpid sea, I believed to be marine phantoms.

The fiend pinning down the thief's pack behind him, I passed over quickly: it was an object of terror.

So was the black horned thing seated aloof on a rock, surveying a distant crowd surrounding a gallows.

Each picture told a story; mysterious often to my undeveloped understanding and imperfect feelings, yet ever profoundly interesting: as interesting as the tales Bessie sometimes narrated on winter evenings, when she chanced to be in good humour; and when, having brought her ironing-table to the nursery hearth, she allowed us to sit about it, and while she got up Mrs Reed's lace frills, and crimped her nightcap borders, fed our eager attention with passages of love and adventure taken from old fairy tales and other ballads; or (as at a later period I discovered) from the pages of *Pamela*, and *Henry, Earl of Moreland*.

With Bewick on my knee, I was then happy: happy at least in my way. I feared nothing but interruption, and that came too soon. The breakfast-room door opened.

'Boh! Madam Mope!' cried the voice of John Reed; then he paused: he found the room apparently empty.

'Where the dickens is she!' he continued. 'Lizzy! Georgy!' (calling to his sisters) 'Joan is not here: tell mama she is run out into the rain – bad animal!'

'It is well I drew the curtain,' thought I; and I wished fervently he might not discover my hiding place: nor would John Reed have found it out himself; he was not quick either of vision or conception; but Eliza just put her head in at the door, and said at once – 'She is in the window-seat, to be sure, Jack.'

And I came out immediately, for I trembled at the idea of being dragged forth by the said Jack.

'What do you want?' I asked, with awkward diffidence.

'Say, "What do you want, Master Reed?" ' was the answer. 'I want you to come here;' and seating himself in an armchair, he intimated by a gesture that I was to approach and stand before him.

John Reed was a schoolboy of fourteen years old; four years older than I, for I was but ten: large and stout for his age, with a dingy and unwholesome skin; thick lineaments in a spacious visage, heavy limbs and large extremities. He gorged himself habitually at table, which made him bilious, and gave him a dim and bleared eye and flabby cheeks. He ought now to have been at school; but his mama had taken him home for a month or two, 'on account of his delicate health.' Mr Miles, the master, affirmed that he would do very well if he had fewer cakes and sweetmeats sent him from home; but the mother's heart turned from an opinion so harsh, and inclined rather to the more refined idea that John's sallowness was owing to over-application and, perhaps, to pining after home.

John had not much affection for his mother and sisters, and an antipathy to me. He bullied and punished me; not two or three times in the week, nor once or twice in the day, but continually: every nerve I had feared him, and every morsel of flesh in my bones shrank when he came near. There were moments when I was bewildered by the terror he inspired, because I had no appeal whatever against either his menaces or his inflictions; the servants did not like to offend their young master by taking my part against him, and Mrs Reed was blind and deaf on the subject: she never saw him strike or heard him abuse me, though he did both now and then in her very presence, more frequently, however, behind her back.

Habitually obedient to John, I came up to his chair: he spent some three minutes in thrusting out his tongue at me as far as he could without damaging the roots: I knew he would soon strike, and while dreading the blow, I mused on the disgusting and ugly appearance of him who would presently deal it. I wonder if he read that notion in my face; for, all at once, without speaking, he struck suddenly and strongly. I tottered, and on regaining my equilibrium retired back a step or two from his chair.

'That is for your impudence in answering mama awhile since,' said he, 'and for your sneaking way of getting behind curtains, and for the look you had in your eyes two minutes since, you rat!'

Accustomed to John Reed's abuse, I never had an idea of replying to it; my care was how to endure the blow which would certainly follow the insult.

'What were you doing behind the curtain?' he asked.

'I was reading.'

'Show the book.'

I returned to the window and fetched it thence.

'You have no business to take our books; you are a dependant, mama says; you have no money; your father left you none; you ought to beg, and not to live here with gentlemen's children like us, and eat the same meals we do, and wear clothes at our mama's expense. Now, I'll teach you to rummage my bookshelves:

for they *are* mine; all the house belongs to me, or will do in a few years. Go and stand by the door, out of the way of the mirror and the windows.'

I did so, not at first aware what was his intention; but when I saw him lift and poise the book and stand in act to hurl it, I instinctively started aside with a cry of alarm: not soon enough, however; the volume was flung, it hit me, and I fell, striking my head against the door and cutting it. The cut bled, the pain was sharp: my terror had passed its climax; other feelings succeeded.

'Wicked and cruel boy!' I said. 'You are like a murderer – you are like a slave-driver – you are like the Roman emperors!'

I had read Goldsmith's *History of Rome*, and had formed my opinion of Nero, Caligula, etc. Also I had drawn parallels in silence, which I never thought thus to have declared aloud.

'What! what!' he cried. 'Did she say that to me? Did you hear her, Eliza and Georgiana? Won't I tell mama? but first – '

He ran headlong at me: I felt him grasp my hair and my shoulder: he had closed with a desperate thing. I really saw in him a tyrant, a murderer. I felt a drop or two of blood from my head trickle down my neck, and was sensible of somewhat pungent suffering: these sensations for the time predominated over fear, and I received him in frantic sort. I don't very well know what I did with my hands, but he called me 'Rat! Rat!' and bellowed out aloud. Aid was near him: Eliza and Georgiana had run for Mrs Reed, who was gone upstairs: she now came upon the scene, followed by Bessie and her maid Abbot. We were parted: I heard the words – 'Dear! dear! What a fury to fly at Master John!'

'Did ever anybody see such a picture of passion!'

Then Mrs Reed subjoined – 'Take her away to the red-room, and lock her in there.' Four hands were immediately laid upon me, and I was borne upstairs.

## *Chapter 2*

I resisted all the way: a new thing for me, and a circumstance which greatly strengthened the bad opinion Bessie and Miss Abbot were disposed to entertain of me. The fact is, I was a trifle beside myself; or rather *out* of myself, as the French would say: I was conscious that a moment's mutiny had already rendered me liable to strange penalties, and, like any other rebel slave, I felt resolved, in my desperation, to go all lengths.

'Hold her arms, Miss Abbot: she's like a mad cat.'

'For shame! for shame!' cried the lady's-maid. 'What shocking conduct, Miss Eyre, to strike a young gentleman, your benefactress's son! Your young master.'

'Master! How is he my master? Am I a servant?'

'No; you are less than a servant, for you do nothing for your keep. There, sit down, and think over your wickedness.'

They had got me by this time into the apartment indicated by Mrs Reed, and had thrust me upon a stool: my impulse was to rise from it like a spring; their two pair of hands arrested me instantly.

'If you don't sit still, you must be tied down,' said Bessie. 'Miss Abbot, lend me your garters; she would break mine directly.'

Miss Abbot turned to divest a stout leg of the necessary ligature. This preparation for bonds, and the additional ignominy it inferred, took a little of the excitement out of me.

'Don't take them off,' I cried; 'I will not stir.'

In guarantee whereof, I attached myself to my seat by my hands.

'Mind you don't,' said Bessie; and when she had ascertained that I was really subsiding, she loosened her hold of me; then she and Miss Abbot stood with folded arms, looking darkly and doubtfully on my face, as incredulous of my sanity.

'She never did so before,' at last said Bessie, turning to the Abigail.

'But it was always in her,' was the reply. 'I've told Missis often my opinion about the child, and Missis agreed with me. She's an underhand little thing: I never saw a girl of her age with so much cover.'

Bessie answered not; but ere long, addressing me, she said – 'You ought to be aware, Miss, that you are under obligations to Mrs Reed: she keeps you: if she were to turn you off, you would have to go to the poor-house.'

I had nothing to say to these words: they were not new to me: my very first recollections of existence included hints of the same kind. This reproach of my dependence had become a vague singsong in my ear: very painful and crushing, but only half intelligible. Miss Abbot joined in – 'And you ought not to think yourself on an equality with the Misses Reed and Master Reed, because Missis kindly allows you to be brought up with them. They will have a great deal of money, and you will have none: it is your place to be humble, and to try to make yourself agreeable to them.'

'What we tell you is for your good,' added Bessie, in no harsh voice; 'you should try to be useful and pleasant, then, perhaps, you would have a home here; but if you become passionate and rude, Missis will send you away, I am sure.'

'Besides,' said Miss Abbot, 'God will punish her: He might strike her dead in the midst of her tantrums, and then where would she go? Come, Bessie, we will leave her: I wouldn't have her heart for anything. Say your prayers, Miss Eyre, when you are by yourself; for if you don't repent, something bad might be permitted to come down the chimney and fetch you away.'

They went, shutting the door, and locking it behind them.

The red-room was a square chamber, very seldom slept in, I might say never, indeed, unless when a chance influx of visitors at Gateshead Hall rendered it necessary to turn to account all the accommodation it contained: yet it was one of the largest and stateliest chambers in the mansion. A bed supported on massive pillars of mahogany, hung with curtains of deep red damask, stood out like a tabernacle in the centre; the two large windows, with their blinds always drawn down, were half shrouded in festoons and falls of similar drapery; the carpet was red; the table at the foot of the bed was covered with a crimson cloth; the walls were a soft fawn colour with a blush of pink in it; the wardrobe, the toilet-table, the chairs were of darkly polished old mahogany. Out of these deep surrounding shades rose high, and glared white, the piled-up mattresses and pillows of the bed, spread with a snowy Marseilles counterpane. Scarcely less prominent was an ample cushioned easy-chair near the head of the bed, also white, with a footstool before it; and looking, as I thought, like a pale throne.

This room was chill, because it seldom had a fire; it was silent, because remote from the nursery and kitchen; solemn, because it was known to be so seldom entered. The housemaid alone came here on Saturdays, to wipe from the mirrors and the furniture a week's quiet dust: and Mrs Reed herself, at far intervals, visited it to review the contents of a certain secret drawer in the wardrobe, where were stored divers parchments, her jewel-casket, and a miniature of her deceased husband; and in those last words lies the secret of the red-room – the spell which kept it so lonely in spite of its grandeur.

Mr Reed had been dead nine years: it was in this chamber he breathed his last; here he lay in state; hence his coffin was borne by the undertaker's men; and, since that day, a sense of dreary consecration had guarded it from frequent intrusion.

My seat, to which Bessie and the bitter Miss Abbot had left me riveted, was a low ottoman near the marble chimney-piece; the bed rose before me; to my right hand there was the high, dark wardrobe, with subdued, broken reflections varying the gloss of its panels; to my left were the muffled windows; a great looking-glass between them repeated the vacant majesty of the bed and room. I was not quite sure whether they had locked the door; and when I dared move, I got up and went to see. Alas! yes: no jail was ever more secure. Returning, I had to cross before the looking-glass; my fascinated glance involuntarily explored the depth it revealed. All looked colder and darker in that visionary hollow than in reality: and the strange little figure there gazing at me, with a white face and arms specking the gloom, and glittering eyes of fear moving where all else was still, had the effect of a real spirit: I thought it like one of the tiny phantoms, half fairy, half imp, Bessie's evening stories represented as coming out of lone, ferny dells in moors, and appearing before the eyes of belated travellers. I returned to my stool.

Superstition was with me at that moment; but it was not yet her hour for complete victory: my blood was still warm; the mood of the revolted slave was still bracing me with its bitter vigour; I had to stem a rapid rush of retrospective thought before I quailed to the dismal present.

All John Reed's violent tyrannies, all his sisters' proud indifference, all his mother's aversion, all the servants' partiality, turned up in my disturbed mind like a dark deposit in a turbid well. Why was I always suffering, always browbeaten, always accused, for ever condemned? Why could I never please? Why was it useless to try to win anyone's favour? Eliza, who was headstrong and selfish, was respected. Georgiana, who had a spoiled temper, a very acrid spite, a captious and insolent carriage, was universally indulged. Her beauty, her pink cheeks and golden curls, seemed to give delight to all who looked at her, and to purchase indemnity for every fault. John no one thwarted, much less punished;

though he twisted the necks of the pigeons, killed the little pea-chicks, set the dogs at the sheep, stripped the hothouse vines of their fruit, and broke the buds off the choicest plants in the conservatory: he called his mother "old girl", too; sometimes reviled her for her dark skin, similar to his own; bluntly disregarded her wishes; not unfrequently tore and spoiled her silk attire; and he was still 'her own darling'. I dared commit no fault: I strove to fulfil every duty; and I was termed naughty and tiresome, sullen and sneaking, from morning to noon, and from noon to night.

My head still ached and bled with the blow and fall I had received: no one had reproved John for wantonly striking me; and because I had turned against him to avert farther irrational violence, I was loaded with general opprobrium.

'Unjust! – unjust!' said my reason, forced by the agonising stimulus into precocious though transitory power: and Resolve, equally wrought up, instigated some strange expedient to achieve escape from insupportable oppression – as running away, or, if that could not be effected, never eating or drinking more, and letting myself die.

What a consternation of soul was mine that dreary afternoon! How all my brain was in tumult, and all my heart in insurrection! Yet in what darkness, what dense ignorance, was the mental battle fought! I could not answer the ceaseless inward question – *why* I thus suffered; now, at the distance of – I will not say how many years, I see it clearly.

I was a discord in Gateshead Hall: I was like nobody there; I had nothing in harmony with Mrs Reed or her children, or her chosen vassalage. If they did not love me, in fact, as little did I love them. They were not bound to regard with affection a thing that could not sympathise with one amongst them; a heterogeneous thing, opposed to them in temperament, in capacity, in propensities; a useless thing, incapable of serving their interest, or adding to their pleasure; a noxious thing, cherishing the germs of indignation at their treatment, of contempt of their judgement. I know that had I been a sanguine, brilliant, careless, exacting, handsome, romping child – though equally dependent and friendless – Mrs Reed would have endured my presence more complacently; her children would have entertained for me more of the cordiality of fellow-feeling; the servants would have been less prone to make me the scapegoat of the nursery.

Daylight began to forsake the red-room; it was past four o'clock, and the beclouded afternoon was tending to drear twilight. I heard the rain still beating continuously on the staircase window, and the wind howling in the grove behind the hall; I grew by degrees cold as a stone, and then my courage sank. My habitual mood of humiliation, self-doubt, forlorn depression, fell damp on the embers of my decaying ire. All said I was wicked, and perhaps I might be so; what thought had I been but just conceiving of starving myself to death? That certainly was a crime: and was I fit to die? Or was the vault under the chancel of Gateshead Church an inviting bourne? In such vault I had been told did Mr Reed lie buried; and led by this thought to recall his idea, I dwelt on it with gathering dread. I could not remember him; but I knew that he was my own uncle – my mother's brother – that he had taken me when a parentless infant to his house; and that in his last moments he had required a promise of Mrs Reed that she would rear and maintain me as one of her own children. Mrs Reed probably considered she had kept this promise; and so she had, I dare say, as well as her nature would permit her; but how could she really like an interloper not of her race, and unconnected with her, after her husband's death, by any tie? It must have been most irksome to find herself bound by a hard-wrung pledge to stand in the stead of a parent to a strange child she could not love, and to see an uncongenial alien permanently intruded on her own family group.

A singular notion dawned upon me. I doubted not – never doubted – that if Mr Reed had been alive he would have treated me kindly; and now, as I sat looking at the white bed and overshadowed walls – occasionally also turning a fascinated eye towards the dimly gleaming mirror – I began to recall what I had heard of dead men, troubled in their graves by the violation of their last wishes, revisiting the earth to punish the perjured and avenge the oppressed; and I thought Mr Reed's spirit, harassed by the wrongs of his sister's child, might quit its abode – whether in the church vault or in the unknown world of the departed – and rise before me in this chamber. I wiped my tears and hushed my sobs, fearful lest any sign of violent grief might waken a preternatural voice to comfort me, or elicit from the gloom some haloed face, bending over me with strange pity. This idea, consolatory in theory, I felt would be terrible if realised: with all my might I endeavoured to stifle it – I endeavoured to be firm. Shaking my hair from my eyes, I lifted my head and tried to look boldly round the dark room; at this moment a light gleamed on the wall. Was it, I asked myself, a ray from the moon penetrating some aperture in the blind? No; moonlight was still, and this stirred; while I gazed, it glided up to the ceiling and quivered over my head. I can now conjecture readily that this streak of light was, in all likelihood, a gleam from a lantern carried by someone across the lawn: but then, prepared as my mind was for horror, shaken as my nerves were by agitation, I thought the swift darting beam was a herald of some coming vision from another world. My heart beat thick, my head grew hot; a sound filled my ears, which I deemed the rushing of wings; something seemed near me; I was oppressed, suffocated: endurance broke down; I rushed to the door and shook the lock in desperate effort. Steps came running along the outer passage; the key turned, Bessie and Abbot entered.

'Miss Eyre, are you ill?' said Bessie.

'What a dreadful noise! it went quite through me!' exclaimed Abbot.

'Take me out! Let me go into the nursery!' was my cry.

'What for? Are you hurt? Have you seen something?' again demanded Bessie.

'Oh! I saw a light, and I thought a ghost would come.' I had now got hold of Bessie's hand, and she did not snatch it from me.

'She has screamed out on purpose,' declared Abbot, in some disgust. 'And what a scream! If she had been in great pain one would have excused it, but she only wanted to bring us all here: I know her naughty tricks.'

'What is all this?' demanded another voice peremptorily; and Mrs Reed came along the corridor, her cap flying wide, her gown rustling stormily. 'Abbot and Bessie, I believe I gave orders that Jane Eyre should be left in the red-room till I came to her myself.'

'Miss Jane screamed so loud, ma'am,' pleaded Bessie.

'Let her go,' was the only answer. 'Loose Bessie's hand, child: you cannot succeed in getting out by these means, be assured. I abhor artifice, particularly in children; it is my duty to show you that tricks will not answer: you will now stay here an hour longer, and it is only on condition of perfect submission and stillness that I shall liberate you then.'

'O aunt! have pity! Forgive me! I cannot endure it – let me be punished some other way! I shall be killed if – '

'Silence! This violence is all most repulsive:' and so, no doubt, she felt it. I was a precocious actress in her eyes; she sincerely looked on me as a compound of virulent passions, mean spirit, and dangerous duplicity.

Bessie and Abbot having retreated, Mrs Reed, impatient of my now frantic anguish and wild sobs, abruptly thrust me back and locked me in, without farther parley. I heard her sweeping away; and soon after she was gone, I suppose I had a species of fit: unconsciousness closed the scene.

## *Chapter 3*

The next thing I remember is, waking up with a feeling as if I had had a frightful nightmare, and seeing before me a terrible red glare, crossed with thick black bars. I heard voices, too, speaking with a hollow sound, and as if muffled by a rush of wind or water: agitation, uncertainty, and an all-predominating sense of terror confused my faculties. Ere long, I became aware that someone was handling me; lifting me up and supporting me in a sitting posture, and that more tenderly than I had ever been raised or upheld before. I rested my head against a pillow or an arm, and felt easy.

In five minutes more the cloud of bewilderment dissolved: I knew quite well that I was in my own bed, and that the red glare was the nursery fire. It was night: a candle burnt on the table; Bessie stood at the bed-foot with a basin in her hand, and a gentleman sat in a chair near my pillow, leaning over me.

I felt an inexpressible relief, a soothing conviction of protection and security, when I knew that there was a stranger in the room, an individual not belonging to Gateshead, and not related to Mrs Reed. Turning from Bessie (though her presence was far less obnoxious to me than that of Abbot, for instance, would have been), I scrutinised the face of the gentleman: I knew him; it was Mr Lloyd, an apothecary, sometimes called in by Mrs Reed when the servants were ailing: for herself and the children she employed a physician.

'Well, who am I?' he asked.

I pronounced his name, offering him at the same time my hand: he took it, smiling and saying, 'We shall do very well by and by.' Then he laid me down, and addressing Bessie, charged her to be very careful that I was not disturbed during the night. Having given some further directions, and intimated that he should call again the next day, he departed; to my grief. I felt so sheltered and befriended while he sat in the chair near my pillow; and as he closed the door after him, all the room darkened and my heart again sank: inexpressible sadness weighed it down.

'Do you feel as if you should sleep, Miss?' asked Bessie, rather softly.

Scarcely dared I answer her; for I feared the next sentence might be rough. 'I will try.'

'Would you like to drink, or could you eat anything?'

'No, thank you; Bessie.'

'Then I think I shall go to bed, for it is past twelve o'clock; but you may call me if you want anything in the night.'

Wonderful civility this! It emboldened me to ask a question.

'Bessie, what is the matter with me? Am I ill?'

'You fell sick, I suppose, in the red-room with crying; you'll be better soon, no doubt.'

Bessie went into the housemaid's apartment, which was near. I heard her say – 'Sarah, come and sleep with me in the nursery; I daren't for my life be alone with that poor child tonight: she might die; it's such a strange thing she should have that fit: I wonder if she saw anything. Missis was rather too hard.'

Sarah came back with her; they both went to bed; they were whispering together for half an hour before they fell asleep. I caught scraps of their conversation, from which I was able only too distinctly to infer the main subject discussed.

'Something passed her, all dressed in white, and vanished' – 'A great black dog behind him' – 'Three loud raps on the chamber door' – 'A light in the churchyard just over his grave,' etc., etc.

At last both slept: the fire and the candle went out. For me, the watches of that long night passed in ghastly wakefulness; ear, eye, and mind were alike strained by dread: such dread as children only can feel.

No severe or prolonged bodily illness followed this incident of the red-room; it only gave my nerves a shock of which I feel the reverberation to this day. Yes, Mrs Reed, to you I owe some fearful pangs of mental suffering, but I ought to forgive you, for you knew not what you did: while rending my heartstrings, you thought you were only uprooting my bad propensities.

Next day, by noon, I was up and dressed, and sat wrapped in a shawl by the nursery hearth. I felt physically weak and broken down: but my worse ailment was an unutterable wretchedness of mind: a wretchedness which kept drawing from me silent tears; no sooner had I wiped one salt drop from my cheek than another followed. Yet, I thought, I ought to have been happy, for none of the Reeds were there, they were all gone out in the carriage with their mama. Abbot, too, was sewing in another room, and Bessie, as she moved hither and thither, putting away toys and arranging drawers, addressed to me every now and then a word of unwonted kindness. This state of things should have been to me a paradise of peace, accustomed as I was to a life of ceaseless reprimand and thankless fagging; but, in fact, my racked nerves were now in such a state that no calm could soothe, and no pleasure excite them agreeably.

Bessie had been down into the kitchen, and she brought up with her a tart on a certain brightly painted china plate, whose bird of paradise, nestling in a wreath of convolvuli and rosebuds, had been wont to stir in me a most enthusiastic sense of admiration; and which plate I had often petitioned to be allowed to take in my hand in order to examine it more closely, but had always hitherto been deemed unworthy of such a privilege. This precious vessel was now placed on my knee, and I was cordially invited to eat the circlet of delicate pastry upon it. Vain favour! coming, like most other favours long deferred and often wished for too late! I could not eat the tart; and the plumage of the bird, the tints of the flowers, seemed strangely faded: I put both plate and tart away. Bessie asked if I would have a book: the word *book* acted as a transient stimulus, and I begged her to fetch *Gulliver's Travels* from the library. This book I had again and again perused with delight. I considered it a narrative of facts, and discovered in it a vein of interest deeper than what I found in fairy tales: for as to the elves, having sought them in vain among foxglove leaves and bells, under mushrooms and beneath the ground-ivy mantling old wall-nooks, I had at length made up my mind to the sad truth, that they were all gone out of England to some savage country where the woods were wilder and thicker, and the population more scant; whereas, Lilliput and Brobdingnag being, in my creed, solid parts of the earth's surface, I doubted not that I might one day, by taking a long voyage, see with my own eyes the little fields, houses, and trees, the diminutive people, the tiny cows, sheep, and birds of the one realm; and the cornfields, forest-high, the mighty mastiffs, the monster cats, the tower-like men and women, of the other. Yet, when this cherished volume was now placed in my hand – when I turned over its leaves, and sought in its marvellous pictures the charm I had, till now, never failed to find – all was eerie and dreary; the giants were gaunt goblins, the pigmies malevolent and fearful imps, Gulliver a most desolate wanderer in most dread and dangerous regions. I closed the book, which I dared no longer peruse, and put it on the table, beside the untasted tart.

Bessie had now finished dusting and tidying the room, and having washed her hands, she opened a certain little drawer, full of splendid shreds of silk and satin, and began making a new bonnet for Georgiana's doll. Meantime she sang: her song was –

'In the days when we went gypsying,
A long time ago.'

I had often heard the song before, and always with lively delight; for Bessie had a sweet voice, at least, I thought so. But now, though her voice was still sweet, I found in its melody an indescribable sadness. Sometimes, preoccupied with her work, she sang the refrain very low, very lingeringly; 'A long time ago' came out like the saddest cadence of a funeral hymn. She passed into another ballad, this time a really doleful one.

'My feet they are sore, and my limbs they are weary;
Long is the way, and the mountains are wild;
Soon will the twilight close moonless and dreary
Over the path of the poor orphan child.

Why did they send me so far and so lonely,
Up where the moors spread and grey rocks are piled?
Men are hard-hearted, and kind angels only
Watch o'er the steps of a poor orphan child.

Yet distant and soft the night breeze is blowing,
Clouds there are none, and clear stars beam mild,
God, in His mercy, protection is showing,
Comfort and hope to the poor orphan child.

Ev'n should I fall o'er the broken bridge passing,
Or stray in the marshes, by false lights beguiled,
Still will my Father, with promise and blessing,
Take to His bosom the poor orphan child.

There is a thought that for strength should avail me,
Though both of shelter and kindred despoiled;
Heaven is a home, and a rest will not fail me;
God is a friend to the poor orphan child.'

'Come, Miss Jane, don't cry,' said Bessie as she finished. She might as well have said to the fire, 'don't burn!' but how could she divine the morbid suffering to which I was a prey? In the course of the morning Mr Lloyd came again.

'What, already up!' said he, as he entered the nursery. 'Well, nurse, how is she?'

Bessie answered that I was doing very well.

'Then she ought to look more cheerful. Come here, Miss Jane: your name is Jane, is it not?'

'Yes, sir, Jane Eyre.'

'Well, you have been crying, Miss Jane Eyre; can you tell me what about? Have you any pain?'

'No, sir.'

'Oh! I dare say she is crying because she could not go out with Missis in the carriage,' interposed Bessie.

'Surely not! why, she is too old for such pettishness.'

I thought so too; and my self-esteem being wounded by the false charge, I answered promptly, 'I never cried for such a thing in my life: I hate going out in the carriage. I cry because I am miserable.'

'Oh fie, Miss!' said Bessie.

The good apothecary appeared a little puzzled. I was standing before him; he fixed his eyes on me very steadily: his eyes were small and grey; not very bright, but I dare say I should think them shrewd now: he had a hard-featured yet good-natured looking face. Having considered me at leisure, he said – 'What made you ill yesterday?'

'She had a fall,' said Bessie, again putting in her word.

'Fall! why, that is like a baby again! Can't she manage to walk at her age? She must be eight or nine years old.'

'I was knocked down,' was the blunt explanation, jerked out of me by another pang of mortified pride; 'but that did not make me ill,' I added; while Mr Lloyd helped himself to a pinch of snuff.

As he was returning the box to his waistcoat pocket, a loud bell rang for the servants' dinner; he knew what it was. 'That's for you, nurse,' said he; 'you can go down; I'll give Miss Jane a lecture till you come back.'

Bessie would rather have stayed, but she was obliged to go, because punctuality at meals was rigidly enforced at Gateshead Hall.

'The fall did not make you ill; what did, then?' pursued Mr Lloyd when Bessie was gone.

'I was shut up in a room where there is a ghost till after dark.'

I saw Mr Lloyd smile and frown at the same time. 'Ghost! What, you are a baby after all! You are afraid of ghosts?'

'Of Mr Reed's ghost I am: he died in that room, and was laid out there. Neither Bessie nor anyone else will go into it at night, if they can help it; and it was cruel to shut me up alone without a candle, so cruel that I think I shall never forget it.'

'Nonsense! And is it that makes you so miserable? Are you afraid now in daylight?'

'No: but night will come again before long: and besides, I am unhappy, very unhappy, for other things.'

'What other things? Can you tell me some of them?'

How much I wished to reply fully to this question! How difficult it was to frame any answer! Children can feel, but they cannot analyse their feelings; and if the analysis is partially effected in thought, they know not how to express the result of the process in words. Fearful, however, of losing this first and only opportunity of relieving my grief by imparting it, I, after a disturbed pause, contrived to frame a meagre, though, as far as it went, true response.

'For one thing, I have no father or mother, brothers or sisters.'

'You have a kind aunt and cousins.'

Again I paused; then bunglingly enounced – 'But John Reed knocked me down, and my aunt shut me up in the red-room.'

Mr Lloyd a second time produced his snuff-box.

'Don't you think Gateshead Hall a very beautiful house?' asked he. 'Are you not very thankful to have such a fine place to live at?'

'It is not my house, sir; and Abbot says I have less right to be here than a servant.'

'Pooh! you can't be silly enough to wish to leave such a splendid place?'

'If I had anywhere else to go, I should be glad to leave it; but I can never get away from Gateshead till I am a woman.'

'Perhaps you may – who knows? Have you any relations besides Mrs Reed?'

'I think not, sir.'

'None belonging to your father?'

'I don't know: I asked Aunt Reed once, and she said possibly I might have some poor, low relations called Eyre, but she knew nothing about them.'

'If you had such, would you like to go to them?'

I reflected. Poverty looks grim to grown people; still more so to children: they have not much idea of industrious, working, respectable poverty; they think of the word only as connected with ragged clothes, scanty food, fireless grates, rude manners, and debasing vices: poverty for me was synonymous with degradation.

'No; I should not like to belong to poor people,' was my reply.

'Not even if they were kind to you?'

I shook my head: I could not see how poor people had the means of being kind; and then to learn to speak like them, to adopt their manners, to be uneducated, to grow up like one of the poor women I saw sometimes nursing their children or washing their clothes at the cottage doors of the village of Gateshead: no, I was not heroic enough to purchase liberty at the price of caste.

'But are your relatives so very poor? Are they working people?'

'I cannot tell; Aunt Reed says if I have any, they must be a beggarly set: I should not like to go a-begging.'

'Would you like to go to school?'

Again I reflected: I scarcely knew what school was: Bessie sometimes spoke of it as a place where young ladies sat in the stocks, wore backboards, and were expected to be exceedingly genteel and precise: John Reed hated his school, and abused his master; but John Reed's tastes were no rule for mine, and if Bessie's accounts of school-discipline (gathered from the young ladies of a family where she had lived before coming to Gateshead) were somewhat appalling, her details of certain accomplishments attained by these same young ladies were, I thought, equally attractive. She boasted of beautiful paintings of landscapes and flowers by them executed; of songs they could sing and pieces they could play, of purses they could net, of French books they could translate; till my spirit was moved to emulation as I listened. Besides, school would be a complete change: it implied a long journey, an entire separation from Gateshead, an entrance into a new life.

'I should indeed like to go to school,' was the audible conclusion of my musings.

'Well, well! who knows what may happen?' said Mr Lloyd, as he got up. 'The child ought to have change of air and scene,' he added, speaking to himself; 'nerves not in a good state.'

Bessie now returned; at the same moment the carriage was heard rolling up the gravel-walk.

'Is that your mistress, nurse?' asked Mr Lloyd. 'I should like to speak to her before I go.'

Bessie invited him to walk into the breakfast-room, and led the way out. In the interview which followed between him and Mrs Reed, I presume, from after-occurrences, that the apothecary ventured to recommend my being sent to school; and the recommendation was no doubt readily enough adopted; for as Abbot said, in discussing the subject with Bessie when both sat sewing in the nursery one night, after I was in bed, and, as they thought, asleep, 'Missis was, she dared say, glad enough to get rid of such a tiresome, ill-conditioned child, who always looked as if she were watching everybody, and scheming plots underhand.' Abbot, I think, gave me credit for being a sort of infantine Guy Fawkes.

On that same occasion I learned, for the first time, from Miss Abbot's communications to Bessie, that my father had been a poor clergyman; that my mother had married him against the wishes of her friends, who considered the match beneath her; that my grandfather Reed was so irritated at her disobedience, he cut her off without a shilling; that after my mother and father had been married a year, the latter caught the typhus fever while visiting among the poor of a large manufacturing town where his curacy was situated, and where that disease was then prevalent: that my mother took the infection from him, and both died within a month of each other.

Bessie, when she heard this narrative, sighed and said, 'Poor Miss Jane is to be pitied too, Abbot.'

'Yes,' responded Abbot; 'if she were a nice, pretty child, one might compassionate her forlornness; but one really cannot care for such a little toad as that.'

'Not a great deal, to be sure,' agreed Bessie: 'at any rate, a beauty like Miss Georgiana would be more moving in the same condition.'

'Yes, I dote on Miss Georgiana!' cried the fervent Abbot. 'Little darling! – with her long curls and her blue eyes, and such a sweet colour as she has; just as if she were painted! – Bessie, I could fancy a Welsh rabbit for supper.'

'So could I – with a roast onion. Come, we'll go down.' They went.

## *Chapter 4*

From my discourse with Mr Lloyd, and from the above reported conference between Bessie and Abbot, I gathered enough of hope to suffice as a motive for wishing to get well: a change seemed near, I desired and waited it in silence. It tarried, however: days and weeks passed: I had regained my normal state of health, but no new allusion was made to the subject over which I brooded. Mrs Reed surveyed me at times with a severe eye, but seldom addressed me: since my illness, she had drawn a more marked line of separation than ever between me and her own children; appointing me a small closet to sleep in by myself, condemning me to take my meals alone, and pass all my time in the nursery, while my cousins were constantly in the drawing-room. Not a hint, however, did she drop about sending me to school: still I felt an instinctive certainty that she would not long endure me under the same roof with her; for her glance, now more than ever, when turned on me, expressed an insuperable and rooted aversion.

Eliza and Georgiana, evidently acting according to orders, spoke to me as little as possible: John thrust his tongue in his cheek whenever he saw me, and once attempted chastisement; but as I instantly turned against him, roused by the same sentiment of deep ire and desperate revolt which had stirred my corruption before, he thought it better to desist, and ran from me uttering execrations, and vowing I had burst his nose. I had indeed levelled at that prominent feature as hard a blow as my knuckles could inflict; and when I saw that either that or my look daunted him, I had the greatest inclination to follow up my advantage to purpose; but he was already with his mama. I heard him in a blubbering tone commence the tale of how 'that nasty Jane Eyre' had flown at him like a mad cat: he was stopped rather harshly – 'Don't talk to me about her, John: I told you not to go near her; she is not worthy of notice; I do not choose that either you or your sisters should associate with her.'

Here, leaning over the banister, I cried out suddenly, and without at all deliberating on my words – 'They are not fit to associate with me.'

Mrs Reed was rather a stout woman; but, on hearing this strange and audacious declaration, she ran nimbly up the stair, swept me like a whirlwind into the nursery, and crushing me down on the edge of my crib, dared me in an emphatic voice to rise from that place, or utter one syllable during the remainder of the day.

'What would Uncle Reed say to you, if he were alive?' was my scarcely voluntary demand. I say scarcely voluntary, for it seemed as if my tongue pronounced words without my will consenting to their utterance: something spoke out of me over which I had no control.

'What?' said Mrs Reed under her breath: her usually cold composed grey eye became troubled with a look like fear; she took her hand from my arm, and gazed at me as if she really did not know whether I were child or fiend. I was now in for it.

'My Uncle Reed is in heaven, and can see all you do and think; and so can papa and mama: they know how you shut me up all day long, and how you wish me dead.'

Mrs Reed soon rallied her spirits: she shook me most soundly, she boxed both my ears, and then left me without a word. Bessie supplied the hiatus by a homily of an hour's length, in which she proved beyond a doubt that I was the most wicked and abandoned child ever reared under a roof. I half believed her; for I felt indeed only bad feelings surging in my breast.

November, December, and half of January passed away. Christmas and the New Year had been celebrated at Gateshead with the usual festive cheer; presents had been interchanged, dinners and evening parties given. From every enjoyment I was, of course excluded: my share of the gaiety consisted in witnessing the daily apparelling of Eliza and Georgiana, and seeing them descend to the drawing-room, dressed out in thin muslin frocks and scarlet sashes, with hair elaborately ringleted; and afterwards, in listening to the sound of the piano or the harp played below, to the passing to and fro of the butler and footman, to the jingling of glass and china as refreshments were handed, to the broken hum of conversation as the drawing-room door opened and closed. When tired of this occupation, I would retire from the stairhead to the solitary and silent nursery: there, though somewhat sad, I was not miserable. To speak truth, I had not the least wish to go into company, for in company I was very rarely noticed; and if Bessie had but been kind and companionable, I should have deemed it a treat to spend the evenings quietly with her, instead of passing them under the formidable eye of Mrs Reed, in a room full of ladies and gentlemen. But Bessie, as soon as she had dressed her young ladies, used to take herself off to the lively regions of the kitchen and housekeeper's room, generally bearing the candle along with her. I then sat with my doll on my knee till the fire got low, glancing round occasionally to make sure that nothing worse than myself haunted the shadowy room; and when the embers sank to a dull red, I undressed hastily, tugging at knots and strings as I best might, and sought shelter from cold and darkness in my crib. To this crib I always took my doll; human beings must love something, and, in the dearth of worthier objects of affection, I contrived to find a pleasure in loving and cherishing a faded graven image, shabby as a miniature scarecrow. It puzzles me now to remember with what absurd sincerity I doted on this little toy, half fancying it alive and capable of sensation. I could not sleep unless it was folded in my nightgown; and when it lay there safe and warm, I was comparatively happy, believing it to be happy likewise.

Long did the hours seem while I waited the departure of the company, and listened for the sound of Bessie's step on the stairs: sometimes she would come up in the interval to seek her thimble or her scissors, or perhaps to bring me something by way of supper – a bun or a cheesecake – then she would sit on the bed while I ate it, and when I had finished, she would tuck the clothes round me, and twice she kissed me, and said, 'Good-night, Miss Jane.' When thus gentle, Bessie seemed to me the best, prettiest, kindest being in the world; and I wished most intensely that she would always be so pleasant and amiable, and never push me about, or scold, or task me unreasonably, as she was too often wont to do. Bessie Lee must, I think, have been a girl of good natural capacity, for she was smart in all she did, and had a remarkable knack of narrative; so, at least, I judge from the impression made on me by her nursery tales. She was pretty too, if my recollections of her face and person are correct. I remember her as a slim young woman, with black hair, dark eyes, very nice features, and good, clear complexion; but she had a capricious and hasty temper, and indifferent ideas of principle or justice: still, such as she was, I preferred her to anyone else at Gateshead Hall.

It was the fifteenth of January, about nine o'clock in the morning: Bessie was gone down to breakfast; my cousins had not yet been summoned to their mama; Eliza was putting on her bonnet and warm garden-coat to go and feed her poultry, an occupation of which she was fond: and not less so of selling the eggs to the housekeeper and hoarding up the money she thus obtained. She had a turn for traffic, and a marked propensity for saving; shown not only in the vending of eggs and chickens, but also in driving hard bargains with the gardener about flower-roots, seeds, and slips of plants; that functionary having orders from Mrs Reed to buy of his young lady all the products of her parterre she wished to sell:

and Eliza would have sold the hair off her head if she could have made a handsome profit thereby. As to her money, she first secreted it in odd corners, wrapped in a rag or an old curl-paper; but some of these hoards having been discovered by the housemaid, Eliza, fearful of one day losing her valued treasure, consented to entrust it to her mother, at a usurious rate of interest – fifty or sixty per cent.; which interest she exacted every quarter, keeping her accounts in a little book with anxious accuracy.

Georgiana sat on a high stool, dressing her hair at the glass, and interweaving her curls with artificial flowers and faded feathers, of which she had found a store in a drawer in the attic. I was making my bed, having received strict orders from Bessie to get it arranged before she returned (for Bessie now frequently employed me as a sort of under-nurserymaid, to tidy the room, dust the chairs, etc.). Having spread the quilt and folded my nightdress, I went to the window-seat to put in order some picture-books and doll's house furniture scattered there; an abrupt command from Georgiana to let her playthings alone (for the tiny chairs and mirrors, the fairy plates and cups, were her property) stopped my proceedings; and then, for lack of other occupation, I fell to breathing on the frost-flowers with which the window was fretted, and thus clearing a space in the glass through which I might look out on the grounds, where all was still and petrified under the influence of a hard frost.

From this window were visible the porter's lodge and the carriage-road, and just as I had dissolved so much of the silver-white foliage veiling the panes as left room to look out, I saw the gates thrown open and a carriage roll through. I watched it ascending the drive with indifference; carriages often came to Gateshead, but none ever brought visitors in whom I was interested; it stopped in front of the house, the doorbell rang loudly, the newcomer was admitted. All this being nothing to me, my vacant attention soon found livelier attraction in the spectacle of a little hungry robin, which came and chirruped on the twigs of the leafless cherry tree nailed against the wall near the casement. The remains of my breakfast of bread and milk stood on the table, and having crumbled a morsel of roll, I was tugging at the sash to put out the crumbs on the window-sill, when Bessie came running upstairs into the nursery.

'Miss Jane, take off your pinafore; what are you doing there? Have you washed your hands and face this morning?' I gave another tug before I answered, for I wanted the bird to be secure of its bread: the sash yielded; I scattered the crumbs, some on the stone sill, some on the cherry-tree bough, then, closing the window, I replied – 'No, Bessie; I have only just finished dusting.'

'Troublesome, careless child! and what are you doing now? You look quite red, as if you have been about some mischief: what were you opening the window for?'

I was spared the trouble of answering, for Bessie seemed in too great a hurry to listen to explanations; she hauled me to the washstand, inflicted a merciless, but happily brief scrub on my face and hands with soap, water, and a coarse towel; disciplined my head with a bristly brush, denuded me of my pinafore, and then hurrying me to the top of the stairs, bid me go down directly, as I was wanted in the breakfast-room.

I would have asked who wanted me: I would have demanded if Mrs Reed was there; but Bessie was already gone, and had closed the nursery-door upon me. I slowly descended. For nearly three months, I had never been called to Mrs Reed's presence; restricted so long to the nursery, the breakfast, dining, and drawing-rooms were become for me awful regions, on which it dismayed me to intrude.

I now stood in the empty hall; before me was the breakfast-room door, and I stopped, intimidated and trembling. What a miserable little poltroon had fear, engendered of unjust punishment, made of me in those days! I feared to return to the nursery, and feared to go forward to the parlour; ten minutes I stood in agitated hesitation; the vehement ringing of the breakfast-room bell decided me; I *must* enter.

'Who could want me?' I asked inwardly, as with both hands I turned the stiff door-handle, which, for a second or two, resisted my efforts. 'What should I see besides Aunt Reed in the apartment? – a man or a woman?' The handle turned, the door unclosed, and passing through and curtseying low, I looked up at – a black pillar! – such, at least, appeared to me, at first sight, the straight, narrow, sable-clad shape standing erect on the rug: the grim face at the top was like a carved mask, placed above the shaft by way of capital.

Mrs Reed occupied her usual seat by the fireside; she made a signal to me to approach; I did so, and she introduced me to the stony stranger with the words: 'This is the little girl respecting whom I applied to you.'

*He*, for it was a man, turned his head slowly towards where I stood, and having examined me with the two inquisitive-looking grey eyes which twinkled under a pair of bushy brows, said solemnly, and in a bass voice, 'Her size is small: what is her age?'

'Ten years.'

'So much?' was the doubtful answer; and he prolonged his scrutiny for some minutes. Presently he addressed me – 'Your name, little girl?'

'Jane Eyre, sir.'

In uttering these words I looked up: he seemed to me a tall gentleman; but then I was very little; his features were large, and they and all the lines of his frame were equally harsh and prim.

'Well, Jane Eyre, and are you a good child?'

Impossible to reply to this in the affirmative: my little world held a contrary opinion: I was silent. Mrs Reed answered for me by an expressive shake of the head, adding soon, 'Perhaps the less said on that subject the better, Mr Brocklehurst.'

'Sorry indeed to hear it! she and I must have some talk;' and bending from the perpendicular, he installed his person in the armchair opposite Mrs Reed's. 'Come here,' he said.

I stepped across the rug; he placed me square and straight before him. What a face he had, now that it was almost on a level with mine! what a great nose! and what a mouth! and what large prominent teeth!

'No sight so sad as that of a naughty child,' he began, 'especially a naughty little girl. Do you know where the wicked go after death?'

'They go to hell,' was my ready and orthodox answer.

'And what is hell? Can you tell me that?'

'A pit full of fire.'

'And should you like to fall into that pit, and to be burning there for ever?'

'No, sir.'

'What must you do to avoid it?'

I deliberated a moment; my answer, when it did come, was objectionable: 'I must keep in good health, and not die.'

'How can you keep in good health? Children younger than you die daily. I buried a little child of five years old only a day or two since, a good little child, whose soul is now in heaven. It is to be feared the same could not be said of you were you to be called hence.'

Not being in a condition to remove his doubt, I only cast my eyes down on the two large feet planted on the rug, and sighed, wishing myself far enough away.

'I hope that sigh is from the heart, and that you repent of ever having been the occasion of discomfort to your excellent benefactress.'

'Benefactress! benefactress!' said I inwardly: 'they all call Mrs Reed my benefactress; if so, a benefactress is a disagreeable thing.'

'Do you say your prayers night and morning?' continued my interrogator.

'Yes, sir.'

'Do you read your Bible?'

'Sometimes.'

'With pleasure? Are you fond of it?

'I like Revelations, and the book of Daniel, and Genesis and Samuel, and a little bit of Exodus, and some parts of Kings and Chronicles, and Job and Jonah.'

'And the Psalms? I hope you like them?'

'No, sir.'

'No? oh, shocking! I have a little boy, younger than you, who knows six Psalms by heart: and when you ask him which he would rather have, a gingerbread-nut to eat or a verse of a Psalm to learn, he says: "Oh! the verse of a Psalm! angels sing Psalms;" says he, "I wish to be a little angel here below;" he then gets two nuts in recompense for his infant piety.'

'Psalms are not interesting,' I remarked.

'That proves you have a wicked heart; and you must pray to God to change it: to give you a new and clean one: to take away your heart of stone and give you a heart of flesh.'

I was about to propound a question, touching the manner in which that operation of changing my heart was to be performed, when Mrs Reed interposed, telling me to sit down; she then proceeded to carry on the conversation herself.

'Mr Brocklehurst, I believe I intimated in the letter which I wrote to you three weeks ago, that this little girl has not quite the character and disposition I could wish: should you admit her into Lowood School I should be glad if the superintendent and teachers were requested to keep a strict eye on her, and, above all, to guard against her worst fault, a tendency to deceit. I mention this in your hearing, Jane, that you may not attempt to impose on Mr Brocklehurst.'

Well might I dread, well might I dislike Mrs Reed; for it was her nature to wound me cruelly; never was I happy in her presence; however carefully I obeyed, however strenuously I strove to please her, my efforts were still repulsed and repaid by such sentences as the above. Now, uttered before a stranger, the accusation cut me to the heart; I dimly perceived that she was already obliterating hope from the new phase of existence which she destined me to enter; I felt, though I could not have expressed the feeling, that she was sowing aversion and unkindness along my future path; I saw myself transformed under Mr Brocklehurst's eye into an artful, noxious child, and what could I do to remedy the injury?

'Nothing, indeed,' thought I, as I struggled to repress a sob, and hastily wiped away some tears, the impotent evidences of my anguish.

'Deceit is, indeed, a sad fault in a child,' said Mr Brocklehurst; 'it is akin to falsehood, and all liars will have their portion in the lake burning with fire and brimstone; she shall, however, be watched, Mrs Reed. I will speak to Miss Temple and the teachers.'

'I should wish her to be brought up in a manner suiting her prospects,' continued my benefactress; 'to be made useful, to be kept humble: as for the vacations, she will, with your permission, spend them always at Lowood.'

'Your decisions are perfectly judicious, madam,' returned Mr Brocklehurst. 'Humility is a Christian grace, and one peculiarly appropriate to the pupils of Lowood; I, therefore, direct that especial care shall be bestowed on its cultivation amongst them. I have studied how best to mortify in them the worldly sentiment of pride; and, only the other day, I had a pleasing proof of my success. My second daughter, Augusta, went with her mama to visit the school, and on her return she exclaimed: "Oh, dear papa, how quiet and plain all the girls at Lowood look, with their hair combed behind their ears, and their long pinafores, and those little holland pockets outside their frocks – they are almost like poor people's children! and," said she, "they looked at my dress and mama's, as if they had never seen a silk gown before." '

'This is the state of things I quite approve,' returned Mrs Reed; 'had I sought all England over, I could scarcely have found a system more exactly fitting a child like Jane Eyre. Consistency, my dear Mr Brocklehurst; I advocate consistency in all things.'

'Consistency, madam, is the first of Christian duties; and it has been observed in every arrangement connected with the establishment of Lowood: plain fare, simple attire, unsophisticated accommodations, hardy and active habits; such is the order of the day in the house and its inhabitants.'

'Quite right, sir. I may then depend upon this child being received as a pupil at Lowood, and there being trained in conformity to her position and prospects?'

'Madam, you may: she shall be placed in that nursery of chosen plants, and I trust she will show herself grateful for the inestimable privilege of her election.'

'I will send her, then, as soon as possible, Mr Brocklehurst; for, I assure you, I feel anxious to be relieved of a responsibility that was becoming too irksome.'

'No doubt, no doubt, madam; and now I wish you good-morning. I shall return to Brocklehurst Hall in the course of a week or two: my good friend, the Archdeacon, will not permit me to leave him sooner. I shall send Miss Temple notice that she is to expect a new girl, so that there will be no difficulty about receiving her. Goodbye.'

'Goodbye, Mr Brocklehurst; remember me to Mrs and Miss Brocklehurst, and to Augusta and Theodore, and Master Broughton Brocklehurst.'

'I will, madam. Little girl, here is a book entitled the *Child's Guide;* read it with prayer, especially that part containing "An account of the awfully sudden death of Martha G—, a naughty child addicted to falsehood and deceit." '

With these words Mr Brocklehurst put into my hand a thin pamphlet sewn in a cover, and having rung for his carriage, he departed.

Mrs Reed and I were left alone: some minutes passed in silence; she was sewing, I was watching her. Mrs Reed might be at that time some six or seven and thirty; she was a woman of robust frame, square-shouldered and strong-limbed, not tall, and, though stout, not obese: she had a somewhat large face, the under jaw being much developed and very solid; her brow was low, her chin large and prominent, mouth and nose sufficiently regular; under her light eyebrows glimmered an eye devoid of ruth; her skin was dark and opaque, her hair nearly flaxen; her constitution was sound as a bell – illness never came near her; she was an exact, clever manager; her household and tenantry were thoroughly under her control; her children only at times defied her authority and laughed it to scorn; she dressed well, and had a presence and port calculated to set off handsome attire.

Sitting on a low stool, a few yards from her armchair, I examined her figure; I perused her features. In my hand I held the tract containing the sudden death of the Liar, to which narrative my attention had been pointed as to an appropriate warning. What had just passed; what Mrs Reed had said concerning me to Mr Brocklehurst; the whole tenor of their conversation, was recent, raw, and stinging in my mind; I had felt every word as acutely as I had heard it plainly, and a passion of resentment fomented now within me.

Mrs Reed looked up from her work; her eye settled on mine, her fingers at the same time suspended their nimble movements.

'Go out of the room; return to the nursery,' was her mandate. My look or something else must have struck her as offensive, for she spoke with extreme though suppressed irritation. I got up, I went to the door; I came back again; I walked to the window, across the room, then close up to her.

*Speak* I must: I had been trodden on severely, and *must* turn: but how? What strength had I to dart retaliation at my antagonist? I gathered my energies and launched them in this blunt sentence – 'I am not deceitful: if I were, I should say I loved *you*; but I declare I do not love you: I dislike you the worst of anybody in the world except John Reed; and this book about the liar, you may give to your girl, Georgiana, for it is she who tells lies, and not I.'

Mrs Reed's hands still lay on her work inactive: her eye of ice continued to dwell freezingly on mine.

'What more have you to say?' she asked, rather in the tone in which a person might address an opponent of adult age than such as is ordinarily used to a child.

That eye of hers, that voice stirred every antipathy I had. Shaking from head to foot, thrilled with ungovernable excitement, I continued – 'I am glad you are no relation of mine: I will never call you aunt again so long as I live. I will never come to see you when I am grown up; and if anyone asks me how I liked you, and how you treated me, I will say the very thought of you makes me sick, and that you treated me with miserable cruelty.'

'How dare you affirm that, Jane Eyre?'

'How dare I, Mrs Reed? How dare I? Because it is the *truth*. You think I have no feelings, and that I can do without one bit of love or kindness; but I cannot live so: and you have no pity. I shall remember how you thrust me back – roughly and violently thrust me back – into the red-room, and locked me up there, to my dying day; though I was in agony; though I cried out, while suffocating with distress, "Have mercy! Have mercy, Aunt Reed!" And that punishment you made me suffer because your wicked boy struck me – knocked me down for nothing. I will tell anybody who asks me questions, this exact tale. People think you a good woman, but you are bad, hardhearted. *You* are deceitful!'

Ere I had finished this reply, my soul began to expand, to exult, with the strangest sense of freedom, of triumph, I ever felt. It seemed as if an invisible bond had burst, and that I had struggled out into unhoped-for liberty. Not without cause was this sentiment: Mrs Reed looked frightened; her work had slipped from her knee; she was lifting up her hands, rocking herself to and fro, and even twisting her face as if she would cry.

'Jane, you are under a mistake: what is the matter with you? Why do you tremble so violently? Would you like to drink some water?'

'No, Mrs Reed.'

'Is there anything else you wish for, Jane? I assure you, I desire to be your friend.'

'Not you. You told Mr Brocklehurst I had a bad character, a deceitful disposition; and I'll let everybody at Lowood know what you are, and what you have done.'

'Jane, you don't understand these things: children must be corrected for their faults.'

'Deceit is not my fault!' I cried out in a savage, high voice.

'But you are passionate, Jane, that you must allow: and now return to the nursery – there's a dear – and lie down a little.'

'I am not your dear; I cannot lie down: send me to school soon, Mrs Reed, for I hate to live here.'

'I will indeed send her to school soon,' murmured Mrs Reed *sotto voce*; and gathering up her work, she abruptly quitted the apartment.

I was left there alone – winner of the field. It was the hardest battle I had fought, and the first victory I had gained: I stood awhile on the rug, where Mr Brocklehurst had stood, and I enjoyed my conqueror's solitude. First, I smiled to myself and felt elate; but this fierce pleasure subsided in me as fast as did the accelerated throb of my pulses. A child cannot quarrel with its elders, as I had done; cannot give its furious feelings uncontrolled play, as I had given mine, without experiencing afterwards the pang of remorse and the chill of reaction. A ridge of lighted heath, alive, glancing, devouring, would have been a meet emblem of my mind when I accused and menaced Mrs Reed: the same ridge, black and blasted after the flames are dead, would have represented as meetly my subsequent condition, when half an hour's silence and reflection had shown me the madness of my conduct, and the dreariness of my hated and hating position.

Something of vengeance I had tasted for the first time; as aromatic wine it seemed, on swallowing, warm and racy: its after-flavour, metallic and corroding, gave me a sensation as if I had been poisoned. Willingly would I now have gone and asked Mrs Reed's pardon; but I knew, partly from experience and partly from instinct, that was the way to make her repulse me with double scorn, thereby re-exciting every turbulent impulse of my nature.

I would fain exercise some better faculty than that of fierce speaking; fain find nourishment for some less fiendish feeling than that of sombre indignation. I took a book – some Arabian tales; I sat down and endeavoured to read. I could make no sense of the subject; my own thoughts swam always between me and the page I had usually found fascinating. I opened the glass-door in the breakfast-room: the shrubbery was quite still: the black frost reigned, unbroken by sun or breeze, through the grounds. I covered my head and arms with the skirt of my frock, and went out to walk in a part of the plantation which was quite sequestered; but I found no pleasure in the silent trees, the falling fir-cones, the congealed relics of autumn, russet leaves, swept by past winds in heaps, and now stiffened together. I leaned against a gate, and looked into an empty field where no sheep were feeding, where the short grass was nipped and blanched. It was a very grey day; a most opaque sky, 'onding on snaw', canopied all; thence flakes fell at intervals, which settled on the hard path and on the hoary lea without melting. I stood, a wretched child enough, whispering to myself over and over again, 'What shall I do? – what shall I do?'

All at once I heard a clear voice call, 'Miss Jane! where are you? Come to lunch!'

It was Bessie, I knew well enough; but I did not stir; her light step came tripping down the path.

'You naughty little thing!' she said. 'Why don't you come when you are called?'

Bessie's presence, compared with the thoughts over which I had been brooding, seemed cheerful; even though, as usual, she was somewhat cross. The fact is, after my conflict with and victory over Mrs Reed, I was not disposed to care much for the nursemaid's transitory anger; and I *was* disposed to bask in her youthful lightness of heart. I just put my two arms round her and said, 'Come, Bessie! don't scold.'

The action was more frank and fearless than any I was habituated to indulge in: somehow it pleased her.

'You are a strange child, Miss Jane,' she said, as she looked down at me; 'a little roving, solitary thing: and you are going to school, I suppose?'

I nodded.

'And won't you be sorry to leave poor Bessie?'

'What does Bessie care for me? She is always scolding me.'

'Because you're such a queer, frightened, shy little thing. You should be bolder.'

'What! to get more knocks?'

'Nonsense! But you are rather put upon, that's certain. My mother said, when she came to see me last week, that she would not like a little one of her own to be in your place. Now, come in, and I've some good news for you.'

'I don't think you have, Bessie.'

'Child! what do you mean? What sorrowful eyes you fix on me! Well, but Missis and the young ladies and Master John are going out to tea this afternoon, and you shall have tea with me. I'll ask cook to bake you a little cake, and then you shall help me to look over your drawers; for I am soon to pack your trunk. Missis intends you to leave Gateshead in a day or two, and you shall choose what toys you like to take with you.'

'Bessie, you must promise not to scold me any more till I go.'

'Well, I will; but mind you are a very good girl, and don't be afraid of me. Don't start when I chance to speak rather sharply; it's so provoking.'

'I don't think I shall ever be afraid of you again Bessie, because I have got used to you, and I shall soon have another set of people to dread.'

'If you dread them they'll dislike you.'

'As you do, Bessie?'

'I don't dislike you, Miss: I believe I am fonder of you than of all the others.'

'You don't show it.'

'You little sharp thing! you've got quite a new way of talking. What makes you so venturesome and hardy?'

'Why, I shall soon be away from you, and besides' – I was going to say something about what had passed between me and Mrs Reed, but on second thoughts I considered it better to remain silent on that head.

'And so you're glad to leave me?'

'Not at all, Bessie; indeed, just now I'm rather sorry.'

'Just now! and rather! How coolly my little lady says it! I dare say now if I were to ask you for a kiss you wouldn't give it me: you'd say you'd *rather* not.'

'I'll kiss you and welcome: bend your head down.' Bessie stooped; we mutually embraced, and I followed her into the house quite comforted. That afternoon lapsed in peace and harmony; and in the evening Bessie told me some of her most enchanting stories, and sang me some of her sweetest songs. Even for me life had its gleams of sunshine.

## *Chapter 5*

Five o'clock had hardly struck on the morning of the 19th of January, when Bessie brought a candle into my closet and found me already up and nearly dressed. I had risen half an hour before her entrance, and had washed my face, and put on my clothes by the light of a half-moon just setting, whose rays streamed through the narrow window near my crib. I was to leave Gateshead that day by a coach which passed the lodge gates at six a.m. Bessie was the only person yet risen; she had lit a fire in the nursery, where she now proceeded to make my breakfast. Few children can eat when excited with the thoughts of a journey; nor could I. Bessie, having pressed me in vain to take a few spoonfuls of the boiled milk and bread she had prepared for me, wrapped up some biscuits in a paper and put them into my bag; then she helped me on with my pelisse and bonnet, and wrapping herself in a shawl, she and I left the nursery. As we passed Mrs Reed's bedroom, she said, 'Will you go in and bid Missis goodbye?'

'No, Bessie: she came to my crib last night when you were gone down to supper, and said I need not disturb her in the morning, or my cousins either; and she told me to remember that she had always been my best friend, and to speak of her and be grateful to her accordingly.'

'What did you say, Miss?'

'Nothing: I covered my face with the bedclothes, and turned from her to the wall.'

'That was wrong, Miss Jane.'

'It was quite right, Bessie. Your Missis has not been my friend: she has been my foe.'

'O Miss Jane! don't say so!'

'Goodbye to Gateshead!' cried I, as we passed through the hall and went out at the front door.

The moon was set, and it was very dark; Bessie carried a lantern, whose light glanced on wet steps and gravel road sodden by a recent thaw. Raw and chill was the winter morning: my teeth chattered as I hastened down the drive. There was a light in the porter's lodge: when we reached it, we found the porter's wife just kindling her fire: my trunk, which had been carried down the evening before, stood corded at the door. It wanted but a few minutes of six, and shortly after that hour had struck, the distant roll of wheels announced the coming coach; I went to the door and watched its lamps approach rapidly through the gloom.

'Is she going by herself?' asked the porter's wife.

'Yes.'

'And how far is it?'

'Fifty miles.'

'What a long way! I wonder Mrs Reed is not afraid to trust her so far alone.'

The coach drew up; there it was at the gates with its four horses and its top laden with passengers: the guard and coachman loudly urged haste; my trunk was hoisted up; I was taken from Bessie's neck, to which I clung with kisses.

'Be sure and take good care of her,' cried she to the guard, as he lifted me into the inside.

'Ay, ay!' was the answer: the door was slapped to, a voice exclaimed 'All right,' and on we drove. Thus was I severed from Bessie and Gateshead; thus whirled away to unknown, and, as I then deemed, remote and mysterious regions.

I remember but little of the journey; I only know that the day seemed to me of a preternatural length, and that we appeared to travel over hundreds of miles of road. We passed through several towns, and in one, a very large one, the coach stopped; the horses were taken out, and the passengers alighted to dine. I was carried into an inn, where the guard wanted me to have some dinner; but, as I had no appetite, he left me in an immense room with a fireplace at each end, a chandelier pendent from the ceiling, and a little red gallery high up against the wall filled with musical instruments. Here I walked about for a long time, feeling very strange and mortally apprehensive of someone coming in and kidnapping me; for I believed in kidnappers, their exploits having frequently figured in Bessie's fireside chronicles. At last the guard returned; once more I was stowed away in the coach, my protector mounted his own seat, sounded his hollow horn, and away we rattled over the 'stony street' of L—.

The afternoon came on wet and somewhat misty: as it waned into dusk, I began to feel that we were getting very far indeed from Gateshead: we ceased to pass through towns; the country changed; great grey hills heaved up round the horizon: as twilight deepened, we descended a valley, dark with wood, and long after night had overclouded the prospect, I heard a wild wind rushing amongst trees.

Lulled by the sound, I at last dropped asleep; I had not long slumbered when the sudden cessation of motion awoke me; the coach-door was open, and a person like a servant was standing at it: I saw her face and dress by the light of the lamps.

'Is there a little girl called Jane Eyre here?' she asked. I answered 'Yes', and was then lifted out; my trunk was handed down, and the coach instantly drove away.

I was stiff with long sitting, and bewildered with the noise and motion of the coach: gathering my faculties, I looked about me. Rain, wind, and darkness filled the air; nevertheless, I dimly discerned a wall before me and a door open in it; through this door I passed with my new guide: she shut and locked it behind her. There was now visible a house or houses – for the building spread far – with many windows, and lights burning in some; we went up a broad pebbly path, splashing wet, and were admitted at a door; then the servant led me through a passage into a room with a fire, where she left me alone.

I stood and warmed my numbed fingers over the blaze, then I looked round; there was no candle, but the uncertain light from the hearth showed, by intervals, papered walls, carpet, curtains, shining mahogany furniture: it was a parlour, not so spacious or splendid as the drawing-room at Gateshead, but comfortable enough. I was puzzling to make out the subject of a picture on the wall, when the door opened, and an individual carrying a light entered; another followed close behind.

The first was a tall lady with dark hair, dark eyes, and a pale and large forehead; her figure was partly enveloped in a shawl, her countenance was grave, her bearing erect.

'The child is very young to be sent alone,' said she, putting her candle down on the table. She considered me attentively for a minute or two, then further added – 'She had better be put to bed soon; she looks tired: are you tired?' she asked, placing her hand on my shoulder.

'A little, ma'am.'

'And hungry too, no doubt: let her have some supper before she goes to bed, Miss Miller. Is this the first time you have left your parents to come to school, my little girl?'

I explained to her that I had no parents. She enquired how long they had been dead: then how old I was, what was my name, whether I could read, write, and sew a little: then she touched my cheek gently with her forefinger, and saying, 'She hoped I should be a good child,' dismissed me along with Miss Miller.

The lady I had left might be about twenty-nine; the one who went with me appeared some years younger: the first impressed me by her voice, look, and air. Miss Miller was more ordinary; ruddy in complexion, though of a careworn countenance; hurried in gait and action, like one who had always a multiplicity of tasks on hand: she looked, indeed, what I afterwards found she really was, an under-teacher. Led by her, I passed from compartment to compartment, from passage to passage, of a large and irregular building; till, emerging from the total and somewhat dreary silence pervading that portion of the house we had traversed, we came upon the hum of many voices, and presently entered a wide, long room, with great deal tables, two at each end, on each of which burnt a pair of candles, and seated all round on benches, a congregation of girls of every age, from nine or ten to twenty. Seen by the dim light of the dips, their number to me appeared countless, though not in reality exceeding eighty; they were uniformly dressed in brown stuff frocks of quaint fashion, and long holland pinafores. It was the hour of study; they were engaged in conning over their tomorrow's task, and the hum I had heard was the combined result of their whispered repetitions.

Miss Miller signed to me to sit on a bench near the door, then walking up to the top of the long room she cried out – 'Monitors, collect the lesson-books and put them away!'

Four tall girls arose from different tables, and going round, gathered the books and removed them. Miss Miller again gave the word of command – 'Monitors, fetch the supper-trays!'

The tall girls went out and returned presently, each bearing a tray, with portions of something, I knew not what, arranged thereon, and a pitcher of water and mug in the middle of each tray. The portions were handed round; those who liked took a draught of the water, the mug being common to all.

When it came to my turn, I drank, for I was thirsty, but did not touch the food, excitement and fatigue rendering me incapable of eating; I now saw, however, that it was a thin oaten cake shared into fragments.

The meal over, prayers were read by Miss Miller, and the classes filed off, two and two, upstairs. Overpowered by this time with weariness, I scarcely noticed what sort of a place the bedroom was, except that, like the schoolroom, I saw it was very long. Tonight I was to be Miss Miller's bedfellow; she helped me to undress: when laid down I glanced at the long rows of beds, each of which was quickly filled with two occupants; in ten minutes the single light was extinguished, and amidst silence and complete darkness I fell asleep.

The night passed rapidly: I was too tired even to dream; I only once awoke to hear the wind rave in furious gusts, and the rain fall in torrents, and to be sensible that Miss Miller had taken her place by my side. When I again unclosed my eyes, a loud bell was ringing; the girls were up and dressing; day had not yet begun to dawn, and a rushlight or two burned in the room. I too rose reluctantly; it was bitter cold, and I dressed as well as I could for shivering, and washed when there was a basin at liberty, which did not occur soon, as there was but one basin to six girls, on the stands down the middle of the room. Again the bell rang; all formed in file, two and two, and in that order descended the stairs and entered the cold and dimly lit schoolroom: here prayers were read by Miss Miller; afterwards she called out – 'Form classes!'

A great tumult succeeded for some minutes, during which Miss Miller repeatedly exclaimed, 'Silence!' and 'Order!' When it subsided, I saw them all drawn up in four semicircles, before four chairs, placed at the four tables; all held books in their hands, and a great book, like a Bible, lay on each table, before the vacant seat. A pause of some seconds succeeded, filled up by the low, vague hum of numbers; Miss Miller walked from class to class, hushing this indefinite sound.

A distant bell tinkled: immediately three ladies entered the room, each walked to a table and took her seat; Miss Miller assumed the fourth vacant chair, which was that nearest the door, and around which the smallest of the children were assembled: to this inferior class I was called, and placed at the bottom of it.

Business now began: the day's Collect was repeated, then certain texts of Scripture were said, and to these succeeded a protracted reading of chapters in the Bible, which lasted an hour. By the time that exercise was terminated, day had fully dawned. The indefatigable bell now sounded for the fourth time: the classes were marshalled and marched into another room to breakfast: how glad I was to behold a prospect of getting something to eat! I was now nearly sick from inanition, having taken so little the day before.

The refectory was a great, low-ceiled, gloomy room; on two long tables smoked basins of something hot, which, however, to my dismay, sent forth an odour far from inviting. I saw a universal manifestation of discontent when the fumes of the repast met the nostrils of those destined to swallow it; from the van of the procession, the tall girls of the first class, rose the whispered words – 'Disgusting! The porridge is burnt again!'

'Silence!' ejaculated a voice; not that of Miss Miller, but one of the upper teachers, a little and dark personage, smartly dressed, but of somewhat morose aspect, who installed herself at the top of one table, while a more buxom lady presided at the other. I looked in vain for her I had first seen the night before; she was not visible: Miss Miller occupied the foot of the table where I sat, and a strange, foreign-looking, elderly lady, the French teacher, as I afterwards found, took the corresponding seat at the other board. A long grace was said and a hymn sung; then a servant brought in some tea for the teachers, and the meal began.

Ravenous, and now very faint, I devoured a spoonful or two of my portion without thinking of its taste; but the first edge of hunger blunted, I perceived I had got in hand a nauseous mess; burnt porridge is almost as bad as rotten potatoes; famine itself soon sickens over it. The spoons were moved slowly: I saw each girl taste her food and try to swallow it; but in most cases the effort was soon relinquished. Breakfast was over, and none had breakfasted. Thanks being returned for what we had not got, and a second hymn chanted, the refectory was evacuated for the schoolroom. I was one of the last to go out, and in passing the tables, I saw one teacher take a basin of the porridge and taste it; she looked at the others; all their countenances expressed displeasure, and one of them, the stout one, whispered – 'Abominable stuff! How shameful!'

A quarter of an hour passed before lessons again began, during which the schoolroom was in a glorious tumult; for that space of time it seemed to be permitted to talk loud and more freely, and they used their privilege. The whole conversation ran on the breakfast, which one and all abused roundly. Poor things! it was the sole consolation they had; Miss Miller was now the only teacher in the room: a group of great girls standing about her spoke with serious and sullen gestures. I heard the name of Mr Brocklehurst pronounced by some lips; at which Miss Miller shook her head disapprovingly; but she made no great effort to check the general wrath; doubtless she shared in it.

A clock in the schoolroom struck nine; Miss Miller left her circle, and standing in the middle of the room, cried – 'Silence! To your seats!'

Discipline prevailed: in five minutes the confused throng was resolved into order, and comparative silence quelled the Babel clamour of tongues. The upper teachers now punctually resumed their posts: but still, all seemed to wait. Ranged on benches down the sides of the room, the eighty girls sat motionless and erect; a quaint assemblage they appeared, all with plain locks combed from their faces, not a curl visible; in brown dresses, made high and surrounded by a narrow tucker about the throat, with little pockets of holland (shaped something like a Highlander's purse) tied in front of their frocks, and destined to serve the purpose of a work-bag: all, too, wearing woollen stockings and country-made shoes, fastened with brass buckles. Above twenty of those clad in this costume were full-grown girls, or rather young women; it suited them ill, and gave an air of oddity even to the prettiest.

I was still looking at them, and also at intervals examining the teachers – none of whom precisely pleased me; for the stout one was a little coarse, the dark one not a little fierce, the foreigner harsh and grotesque, and Miss Miller, poor thing! looked purple, weather-beaten, and overworked – when, as my eye wandered from face to face, the whole school rose simultaneously, as if moved by a common spring.

What was the matter? I had heard no order given: I was puzzled. Ere I had gathered my wits, the classes were again seated: but as all eyes were now turned to one point, mine followed the general direction, and encountered the personage who had received me last night. She stood at the bottom of the long room, on the hearth; for there was a fire at each end; she surveyed the two rows of girls silently and gravely. Miss Miller, approaching, seemed to ask her a question, and having received her answer, went back to her place, and said aloud – 'Monitor of the first class, fetch the globes!'

While the direction was being executed, the lady consulted moved slowly up the room. I suppose I have a considerable organ of veneration, for I retain yet the sense of admiring awe with which my eyes traced her steps. Seen now, in broad daylight, she looked tall, fair, and shapely; brown eyes with a benignant light in their irids, and a fine pencilling of long lashes round, relieved the whiteness of her large front; on each of her temples her hair, of a very dark brown, was clustered in round curls, according to the fashion of those times, when neither smooth bands nor long ringlets were in vogue; her dress, also in the mode of the day, was of purple cloth, relieved by a sort of Spanish trimming of black velvet; a gold watch (watches were not so common then as now) shone at her girdle. Let the reader add, to complete the picture, refined features; a complexion, if pale, clear; and a stately air and carriage, and he will have, at least, as clearly as words can give it, a correct idea of the exterior of Miss Temple – Maria Temple, as I afterwards saw the name written in a prayer-book entrusted to me to carry to church.

The superintendent of Lowood (for such was this lady) having taken her seat before a pair of globes placed on one of the tables, summoned the first class round her, and commenced giving a lesson on geography; the lower classes were called by the teachers: repetitions in history, grammar, etc., went on for an hour; writing and arithmetic succeeded, and music lessons were given by Miss Temple to some of the elder girls. The duration of each lesson was measured by the clock, which at last struck twelve. The superintendent rose – 'I have a word to address to the pupils,' said she.

The tumult of cessation from lessons was already breaking forth, but it sank at her voice. She went on – 'You had this morning a breakfast which you could not eat; you must be hungry: I have ordered that a lunch of bread and cheese shall be served to all.'

The teachers looked at her with a sort of surprise.

'It is to be done on my responsibility,' she added, in an explanatory tone to them, and immediately afterwards left the room.

The bread and cheese was presently brought in and distributed, to the high delight and refreshment of the whole school. The order was now given 'To the garden!' Each put on a coarse straw bonnet, with strings of coloured calico, and a cloak of grey frieze, I was similarly equipped, and, following the stream, I made my way into the open air.

The garden was a wide enclosure, surrounded with walls so high as to exclude every glimpse of prospect; a covered verandah ran down one side, and broad walks bordered a middle space divided into scores of little beds: these beds were assigned as gardens for the pupils to cultivate, and each bed had an owner. When full of flowers they would doubtless look pretty; but now, at the latter end of January, all was wintry blight and brown decay. I shuddered as I stood and looked round me: it was an inclement day for outdoor exercise; not positively rainy, but darkened by a drizzling yellow fog; all under foot was still soaking –wet with the floods of yesterday. The stronger among the girls ran about and engaged in active games, but sundry pale and thin ones herded together for shelter and warmth in the verandah; and amongst these, as the dense mist penetrated to their shivering frames, I heard frequently the sound of a hollow cough.

As yet I had spoken to no one, nor did anybody seem to take notice of me; I stood lonely enough: but to that feeling of isolation I was accustomed; it did not oppress me much. I leant against a pillar of the verandah, drew my grey mantle close about me, and, trying to forget the cold which nipped me without, and the unsatisfied hunger which gnawed me within, delivered myself up to the employment of watching and thinking. My reflections were too undefined and fragmentary to merit record: I hardly yet knew where I was; Gateshead and my past life seemed floated away to an immeasurable distance; the present was vague and strange, and of the future I could form no conjecture. I looked round the convent-like garden, and then up at the house – a large building, half of which seemed grey and old, the other half quite new. The new part, containing the schoolroom and dormitory, was lit by mullioned and latticed windows, which gave it a church-like aspect; a stone tablet over the door bore this inscription: 'Lowood Institution. This portion was rebuilt AD —, by Naomi Brocklehurst, of Brocklehurst Hall, in this county. "Let your light so shine before men, that they may see your good works, and glorify your Father which is in heaven." – St Matthew, 5:16.'

I read these words over and over again: I felt that an explanation belonged to them, and was unable fully to penetrate their import. I was still pondering the signification of 'Institution', and endeavouring to make out a connection between the first words and the verse of Scripture, when the sound of a cough close behind me made me turn my head. I saw a girl sitting on a stone bench near; she was bent over a book, on the perusal of which she seemed intent: from where I stood I could see the title – it was *Rasselas*; a name that struck me as strange, and consequently attractive. In turning a leaf she happened to look up, and I said to her directly – 'Is your book interesting?' I had already formed the intention of asking her to lend it to me someday. 'I like it,' she answered, after a pause of a second or two, during which she examined me.

'What is it about?' I continued. I hardly know where I found the hardihood thus to open a conversation with a stranger; the step was contrary to my nature and habits: but I think her occupation touched a chord of sympathy somewhere; for I too liked reading, though of a frivolous and childish kind; I could not digest or comprehend the serious or substantial.

'You may look at it,' replied the girl, offering me the book.

I did so; a brief examination convinced me that the contents were less taking than the title: *Rasselas* looked dull to my trifling taste; I saw nothing about fairies, nothing about genii; no bright variety seemed spread over the closely-printed pages. I returned it to her; she received it quietly, and without saying anything she was about to relapse into her former studious mood: again I ventured to disturb her – 'Can you tell me what the writing on that stone over the door means? What is Lowood Institution?'

'This house where you are come to live.'

'And why do they call it Institution? Is it in any way different from other schools?'

'It is partly a charity-school: you and I, and all the rest of us, are charity children. I suppose you are an orphan: are not either your father or your mother dead?'

'Both died before I can remember.'

'Well, all the girls here have lost either one or both parents, and this is called an institution for educating orphans.'

'Do we pay no money? Do they keep us for nothing?'

'We pay, or our friends pay, fifteen pounds a year for each.'

'Then why do they call us charity-children?'

'Because fifteen pounds is not enough for board and teaching, and the deficiency is supplied by subscription.'

'Who subscribes?'

'Different benevolent-minded ladies and gentlemen in this neighbourhood and in London.'

'Who was Naomi Brocklehurst?'

'The lady who built the new part of this house as that tablet records, and whose son overlooks and directs everything here.'

'Why?'

'Because he is treasurer and manager of the establishment.'

'Then this house does not belong to that tall lady who wears a watch, and who said we were to have some bread and cheese?'

'To Miss Temple? Oh, no! I wish it did: she has to answer to Mr Brocklehurst for all she does. Mr Brocklehurst buys all our food and all our clothes.'

'Does he live here?'

'No – two miles off, at a large hall.'

'Is he a good man?'

'He is a clergyman, and is said to do a great deal of good.'

'Did you say that tall lady was called Miss Temple?'

'Yes.'

'And what are the other teachers called?'

'The one with red cheeks is called Miss Smith; she attends to the work, and cuts out – for we make our own clothes, our frocks, and pelisses, and everything; the little one with black hair is Miss Scatcherd; she teaches history and grammar, and hears the second class repetitions; and the one who wears a shawl, and has a pocket-handkerchief tied to her side with a yellow ribband, is Mme Pierrot: she comes from Lisle, in France, and teaches French.'

'Do you like the teachers?'

'Well enough.'

'Do you like the little black one, and the Madame — ? I cannot pronounce her name as you do.'

'Miss Scatcherd is hasty – you must take care not to offend her; Mme Pierrot is not a bad sort of person.'

'But Miss Temple is the best – isn't she?'

'Miss Temple is very good and very clever; she is above the rest, because she knows far more than they do.'

'Have you been long here?'

'Two years.'

'Are you an orphan?'

'My mother is dead.'

'Are you happy here?'

'You ask rather too many questions. I have given you answers enough for the present: now I want to read.'

But at that moment the summons sounded for dinner; all re-entered the house. The odour which now filled the refectory was scarcely more appetising than that which had regaled our nostrils at breakfast: the dinner was served in two huge tin-plated vessels, whence rose a strong steam redolent of rancid fat. I found the mess to consist of indifferent potatoes and strange shreds of rusty meat, mixed and cooked together. Of this preparation a tolerably abundant plateful was apportioned to each pupil. I ate what I could, and wondered within myself whether every day's fare would be like this.

After dinner, we immediately adjourned to the schoolroom: lessons recommenced, and were continued till five o'clock.

The only marked event of the afternoon was, that I saw the girl with whom I had conversed in the verandah dismissed in disgrace by Miss Scatcherd from a history class, and sent to stand in the middle of the large schoolroom. The punishment seemed to me in a high degree ignominious, especially for so great a girl – she looked thirteen or upwards. I expected she would show signs of great distress and shame; but to my surprise she neither wept nor blushed: composed, though grave, she stood, the central mark of all eyes. 'How can she bear it so quietly – so firmly?' I asked of myself. 'Were I in her place, it seems to me I should wish the earth to open and swallow me up. She looks as if she were thinking of something beyond her punishment – beyond her situation: of something not round her nor before her. I have heard of day-dreams – is she in a day-dream now? Her eyes are fixed on the floor, but I am sure they do not see it – her sight seems turned in, gone down into her heart: she is looking at what she can remember, I believe; not at what is really present. I wonder what sort of a girl she is – whether good or naughty.'

Soon after five p.m. we had another meal, consisting of a small mug of coffee, and half a slice of brown bread. I devoured my bread and drank my coffee with relish; but I should have been glad of as much more – I was still hungry. Half an hour's recreation succeeded, then study; then the glass of water and the piece of oatcake, prayers, and bed. Such was my first day at Lowood.

## *Chapter 6*

The next day commenced as before, getting up and dressing by rushlight; but this morning we were obliged to dispense with the ceremony of washing; the water in the pitchers was frozen. A change had taken place in the weather the preceding evening, and a keen north-east wind, whistling through the crevices of our bedroom windows all night long, had made us shiver in our beds, and turned the contents of the ewers to ice.

Before the long hour and a half of prayers and Bible-reading was over, I felt ready to perish with cold. Breakfast-time came at last, and this morning the porridge was not burnt; the quality was eatable, the quantity small. How small my portion seemed! I wished it had been doubled.

In the course of the day I was enrolled a member of the fourth class, and regular tasks and occupations were assigned me: hitherto, I had only been a spectator of the proceedings at Lowood; I was now to become an actor therein. At first, being little accustomed to learn by heart, the lessons appeared to me both long and difficult; the frequent change from task to task, too, bewildered me; and I was glad when, about three o'clock in the afternoon, Miss Smith put into my hands a border of muslin two yards long, together with needle, thimble, etc., and sent me to sit in a quiet corner of the schoolroom, with directions to hem the same. At that hour most of the others were sewing likewise; but one class still stood round Miss Scatcherd's chair reading, and as all was quiet, the subject of their lessons could be heard, together with the manner in which each girl acquitted herself, and the animadversions or commendations of Miss Scatcherd on the performance. It was English history; among the readers I observed my acquaintance of the verandah: at the commencement of the lesson, her place had been at the top of the class, but for some error of pronunciation, or some inattention to stops, she was suddenly sent to the very bottom. Even in that obscure position, Miss Scatcherd continued to make her an object of constant notice; she was continually addressing to her such phrases as the following: 'Burns' (such it seems was her name: the girls here were all called by their surnames, as boys are elsewhere), 'Burns, you are standing on the side of your shoe; turn your toes out immediately.' 'Burns, you poke your chin most unpleasantly; draw it in.' 'Burns, I insist on your holding your head up; I will not have you before me in that attitude,' etc. etc.

A chapter having been read through twice, the books were closed and the girls examined. The lesson had comprised part of the reign of Charles I, and there were sundry questions about tonnage and poundage and ship-money, which most of them appeared unable to answer; still, every little difficulty was solved instantly when it reached Burns: her memory seemed to have retained the substance of the whole lesson, and she was ready with answers on every point. I kept expecting that Miss Scatcherd would praise her attention; but, instead of that, she suddenly cried out – 'You dirty, disagreeable girl! you have never cleaned your nails this morning!'

Burns made no answer: I wondered at her silence.

'Why,' thought I, 'does she not explain that she could neither clean her nails nor wash her face, as the water was frozen?'

My attention was now called off by Miss Smith desiring me to hold a skein of thread: while she was winding it, she talked to me from time to time, asking whether I had ever been at school before, whether I could mark, stitch, knit, etc.; till she dismissed me, I could not pursue my observations on Miss Scatcherd's movements. When I returned to my seat, that lady was just delivering an order of which I did not catch the import; but Burns immediately left the class, and going into the small inner room where the books were kept, returned in half a minute, carrying in her hand a bundle of twigs tied together at one end. This ominous tool she presented to Miss Scatcherd with a respectful curtsey; then she quietly, and without being told, unloosed her pinafore, and the teacher instantly and sharply inflicted on her neck a dozen strokes with the bunch of twigs. Not a tear rose to Burns' eye; and, while I paused from my sewing, because my fingers quivered at this spectacle with a sentiment of unavailing and impotent anger, not a feature of her pensive face altered its ordinary expression.

'Hardened girl!' exclaimed Miss Scatcherd; 'nothing can correct you of your slatternly habits: carry the rod away.'

Burns obeyed: I looked at her narrowly as she emerged from the book-closet; she was just putting back her handkerchief into her pocket, and the trace of a tear glistened on her thin cheek.

The play-hour in the evening I thought the pleasantest fraction of the day at Lowood: the bit of bread, the draught of coffee swallowed at five o'clock had revived vitality, if it had not satisfied hunger: the long restraint of the day was slackened; the schoolroom felt warmer than in the morning – its fires being allowed to burn a little more brightly, to supply, in some measure, the place of candles, not yet introduced: the ruddy gloaming, the licensed uproar, the confusion of many voices gave one a welcome sense of liberty.

On the evening of the day on which I had seen Miss Scatcherd flog her pupil, Burns, I wandered as usual among the forms and tables and laughing groups without a companion, yet not feeling lonely: when I passed the windows, I now and then lifted a blind, and looked out; it snowed fast, a drift was already forming against the lower panes; putting my ear close to the window, I could distinguish from the gleeful tumult within, the disconsolate moan of the wind outside.

Probably, if I had lately left a good home and kind parents, this would have been the hour when I should most keenly have regretted the separation; that wind would then have saddened my heart; this obscure chaos would have disturbed my peace! as it was, I derived from both a strange excitement, and reckless and feverish, I wished the wind to howl more wildly, the gloom to deepen to darkness, and the confusion to rise to clamour.

Jumping over forms, and creeping under tables, I made my way to one of the fireplaces; there, kneeling by the high wire fender, I found Burns, absorbed, silent, abstracted from all round her by the companionship of a book, which she read by the dim glare of the embers.

'Is it still *Rasselas*?' I asked, coming behind her.

'Yes,' she said, 'and I have just finished it.'

And in five minutes more she shut it up. I was glad of this.

'Now,' thought I, 'I can perhaps get her to talk.' I sat down by her on the floor.

'What is your name besides Burns?'

'Helen.'

'Do you come a long way from here?'

'I come from a place farther north, quite on the borders of Scotland.'

'Will you ever go back?'

'I hope so; but nobody can be sure of the future.'

'You must wish to leave Lowood?'

'No! why should I? I was sent to Lowood to get an education; and it would be of no use going away until I have attained that object.'

'But that teacher, Miss Scatcherd, is so cruel to you?'

'Cruel? Not at all! She is severe: she dislikes my faults.'

'And if I were in your place I should dislike her; I should resist her. If she struck me with that rod, I should get it from her hand; I should break it under her nose.'

'Probably you would do nothing of the sort: but if you did, Mr Brocklehurst would expel you from the school; that would be a great grief to your relations. It is far better to endure patiently a smart which nobody feels but yourself, than to commit a hasty action whose evil consequences will extend to all connected with you; and besides, the Bible bids us return good for evil.'

'But then it seems disgraceful to be flogged, and to be sent to stand in the middle of a room full of people; and you are such a great girl: I am far younger than you, and I could not bear it.'

'Yet it would be your duty to bear it, if you could not avoid it: it is weak and silly to say you *cannot bear* what it is your fate to be required to bear.'

I heard her with wonder: I could not comprehend this doctrine of endurance; and still less could I understand or sympathise with the forbearance she expressed for her chastiser. Still I felt that Helen Burns considered things by a light invisible to my eyes. I suspected she might be right and I wrong; but I would not ponder the matter deeply; like Felix, I put it off to a more convenient season.

'You say you have faults, Helen: what are they? To me you seem very good.'

'Then learn from me, not to judge by appearances: I am, as Miss Scatcherd said, slatternly; I seldom put, and never keep, things in order; I am careless; I forget rules; I read when I should learn my lessons; I have no method; and sometimes I say, like you, I cannot *bear* to be subjected to systematic arrangements. This is all very provoking to Miss Scatcherd, who is naturally neat, punctual, and particular.'

'And cross and cruel,' I added; but Helen Burns would not admit my addition: she kept silence.

'Is Miss Temple as severe to you as Miss Scatcherd?'

At the utterance of Miss Temple's name, a soft smile flitted over her grave face.

'Miss Temple is full of goodness; it pains her to be severe to anyone, even the worst in the school: she sees my errors, and tells me of them gently; and if I do anything worthy of praise, she gives me my meed liberally. One strong proof of my wretchedly defective nature is, that even her expostulations, so mild, so rational, have not influence to cure me of my faults; and even her praise, though I value it most highly, cannot stimulate me to continued care and foresight.'

'That is curious,' said I, 'it is so easy to be careful.'

'For *you* I have no doubt it is. I observed you in your class this morning, and saw you were closely attentive: your thoughts never seemed to wander while Miss Miller explained the lesson and questioned you. Now, mine continually rove away; when I should be listening to Miss Scatcherd, and collecting all she says with assiduity, often I lose the very sound of her voice; I fall into a sort of dream. Sometimes I think I am in Northumberland, and that the noises I hear round me are the bubbling of a little brook which runs through Deepden, near our house; then, when it comes to my turn to reply, I have to be awakened; and having heard nothing of what was read for listening to the visionary brook, I have no answer ready.'

'Yet how well you replied this afternoon.'

'It was mere chance; the subject on which we had been reading had interested me. This afternoon, instead of dreaming of Deepden, I was wondering how a man who wished to do right could act so unjustly and unwisely as Charles the First sometimes did; and I thought what a pity it was that, with his integrity and conscientiousness, he could see no farther than the prerogatives of the crown. If he had but been able to look to a distance, and see how what they call the spirit of the age was tending! Still, I like Charles – I respect him – I pity him, poor murdered king! Yes, his enemies were the worst: they shed blood they had no right to shed. How dared they kill him!'

Helen was talking to herself now: she had forgotten I could not very well understand her – that I was ignorant, or nearly so, of the subject she discussed. I recalled her to my level.

'And when Miss Temple teaches you, do your thoughts wander then?'

'No, certainly, not often: because Miss Temple has generally something to say which is newer than my own reflections; her language is singularly agreeable to me, and the information she communicates is often just what I wished to gain.'

'Well, then, with Miss Temple you are good?'

'Yes, in a passive way: I make no effort, I follow as inclination guides me. There is no merit in such goodness.'

'A great deal: you are good to those who are good to you. It is all I ever desire to be. If people were always kind and obedient to those who are cruel and unjust, the wicked people would have it all their own way: they would never feel afraid, and so they would never alter, but would grow worse and worse. When we are struck at without a reason, we should strike back again very hard; I am sure we should – so hard as to teach the person who struck us never to do it again.'

'You will change your mind, I hope, when you grow older: as yet you are but a little untaught girl.'

'But I feel this, Helen; I must dislike those who whatever I do to please them, persist in disliking me, I must resist those who punish me unjustly. It is as natural as that I should love those who show me affection, or submit to punishment when I feel it is deserved.'

'Heathens and savage tribes hold that doctrine, but Christians and civilised nations disown it.'

'How? I don't understand.'

'It is not violence that best overcomes hate – nor vengeance that most certainly heals injury.'

'What then?'

'Read the New Testament, and observe what Christ says, and how He acts; make His word your rule, and His conduct your example.'

'What does He say?'

'Love your enemies; bless them that curse you; do good to them that hate you and despitefully use you.'

'Then I should love Mrs Reed, which I cannot do; I should bless her son John, which is impossible.'

In her turn, Helen Burns asked me to explain, and I proceeded forthwith to pour out, in my own way, the tale of my sufferings and resentments. Bitter and truculent when excited, I spoke as I felt, without reserve or softening.

Helen heard me patiently to the end: I expected she would then make a remark, but she said nothing.

'Well,' I asked impatiently, 'is not Mrs Reed a hard-hearted, bad woman?'

'She has been unkind to you, no doubt; because you see, she dislikes your cast of character, as Miss Scatcherd does mine; but how minutely you remember all she has done and said to you! What a singularly deep impression her injustice seems to have made on your heart! No ill-usage so brands its record on my feelings. Would you not be happier if you tried to forget her severity, together with the passionate emotions it excited? Life appears to me too short to be spent in nursing animosity or registering wrongs. We are, and must be, one and all, burdened with faults in this world: but the time will soon come when, I trust, we shall put them off in putting off our corruptible bodies; when debasement and sin will fall from us with this cumbrous frame of flesh, and only the spark of the spirit will remain, the impalpable principle of light and thought, pure as when it left the Creator to inspire the creature: whence it came it will return; perhaps again to be communicated to some being higher than man – perhaps to pass through gradations of glory, from the pale human soul to brighten to the seraph! Surely it will never, on the contrary, be suffered to degenerate from man to fiend? No; I cannot believe that: I hold another creed: which no one ever taught me, and which I seldom mention; but in which I delight, and to which I cling: for it extends hope to all: it makes Eternity a rest – a mighty home, not a terror and an abyss. Besides, with this creed, I can so clearly distinguish between the criminal and his crime; I can so sincerely forgive the first while I abhor the last: with this creed revenge never worries my heart, degradation never too deeply disgusts me, injustice never crushes me too low: I live in calm, looking to the end.'

Helen's head, always drooping, sank a little lower as she finished this sentence. I saw by her look she wished no longer to talk to me, but rather to converse with her own thoughts. She was not allowed much time for meditation: a monitor, a great rough girl presently came up, exclaiming in a strong Cumberland accent – 'Helen Burns, if you don't go and put your drawer in order, and fold up your work this minute, I'll tell Miss Scatcherd to come and look at it!'

Helen sighed as her reverie fled, and getting up, obeyed the monitor without reply as without delay.

## *Chapter 7*

My first quarter at Lowood seemed an age; and not the golden age either; it comprised an irksome struggle with difficulties in habituating myself to new rules and unwonted tasks. The fear of failure in these points harassed me worse than the physical hardships of my lot; though these were no trifles.

During January, February, and part of March, the deep snows, and, after their melting, the almost impassable roads, prevented our stirring beyond the garden walls, except to go to church; but within these limits we had to pass an hour every day in the open air. Our clothing was insufficient to protect us from the severe cold: we had no boots, the snow got into our shoes and melted there: our ungloved hands became numbed and covered with chilblains, as were our feet: I remember well the distracting irritation I endured from this cause every evening, when my feet inflamed; and the torture of thrusting the swelled, raw, and stiff toes into my shoes in the morning. Then the scanty supply of food was distressing: with the keen appetites of growing children, we had scarcely sufficient to keep alive a delicate invalid. From this deficiency of nourishment resulted an abuse, which pressed hardly on the younger pupils: whenever the famished great girls had an opportunity, they would coax or menace the little ones out of their portion. Many a time I have shared between two claimants the precious morsel of brown bread distributed at teatime; and after relinquishing to a third half the contents of my mug of coffee, I have swallowed the remainder with an accompaniment of secret tears, forced from me by the exigency of hunger.

Sundays were dreary days in that wintry season. We had to walk two miles to Brocklebridge Church, where our patron officiated. We set out cold, we arrived at church colder: during the morning service we became almost paralysed. It was too far to return to dinner, and an allowance of cold meat and bread, in the same penurious proportion observed in our ordinary meals, was served round between the services.

At the close of the afternoon service we returned by an exposed and hilly road, where the bitter winter wind, blowing over a range of snowy summits to the north, almost flayed the skin from our faces.

I can remember Miss Temple walking lightly and rapidly along our drooping line, her plaid cloak, which the frosty wind fluttered, gathered close about her, and encouraging us, by precept and example, to keep up our spirits, and march forward, as she said, 'like stalwart soldiers.' The other teachers, poor things, were generally themselves too much dejected to attempt the task of cheering others.

How we longed for the light and heat of a blazing fire when we got back! But, to the little ones at least, this was denied: each hearth in the schoolroom was immediately surrounded by a double row of great girls, and behind them the younger children crouched in groups, wrapping their starved arms in their pinafores.

A little solace came at tea-time, in the shape of a double ration of bread – a whole, instead of a half, slice – with the delicious addition of a thin scrape of butter: it was the hebdomadal treat to which we all looked forward from Sabbath to Sabbath. I generally contrived to reserve a moiety of this bounteous repast for myself; but the remainder I was invariably obliged to part with.

The Sunday evening was spent in repeating, by heart, the Church Catechism, and the fifth, sixth, and seventh chapters of St Matthew; and in listening to a long sermon, read by Miss Miller, whose irrepressible yawns attested her weariness. A frequent interlude of these performances was the enactment of the part of Eutychus by some half-dozen of little girls, who, overpowered with sleep, would fall down, if not out of the third loft, yet off the fourth form, and be taken up half dead. The remedy was, to thrust them forward into the centre of the schoolroom, and oblige them to stand there till the sermon was finished. Sometimes their feet failed them, and they sank together in a heap; they were then propped up with the monitors' high stools.

I have not yet alluded to the visits of Mr Brocklehurst; and indeed that gentleman was from home during the greater part of the first month after my arrival; perhaps prolonging his stay with his friend the archdeacon: his absence was a relief to me. I need not say that I had my own reasons for dreading his coming: but come he did at last.

One afternoon (I had then been three weeks at Lowood), as I was sitting with a slate in my hand, puzzling over a sum in long division, my eyes, raised in abstraction to the window, caught sight of a figure just passing: I recognised almost instinctively that gaunt outline; and when, two minutes after, all the school, teachers included, rose *en masse*, it was not necessary for me to look up in order to ascertain whose entrance they thus greeted. A long stride measured the schoolroom, and presently beside Miss Temple, who herself had risen, stood the same black column which had frowned on me so ominously from the hearthrug of Gateshead. I now glanced sideways at this piece of architecture. Yes, I was right: it was Mr Brocklehurst, buttoned up in a surtout, and looking longer, narrower, and more rigid than ever.

I had my own reasons for being dismayed at this apparition; too well I remembered the perfidious hints given by Mrs Reed about my disposition, etc.; the promise pledged by Mr Brocklehurst to apprise Miss Temple and the teachers of my vicious nature. All along I had been dreading the fulfilment of this promise, I had been looking out daily for the 'Coming Man', whose information respecting my past life and conversation was to brand me as a bad child for ever: now there he was.

He stood at Miss Temple's side; he was speaking low in her ear: I did not doubt he was making disclosures of my villainy; and I watched her eye with painful anxiety, expecting every moment to see its dark orb turn on me a glance of repugnance and contempt. I listened too; and as I happened to be seated quite at the top of the room, I caught most of what he said: its import relieved me from immediate apprehension.

'I suppose, Miss Temple, the thread I bought at Lowton will do; it struck me that it would be just of the quality for the calico chemises, and I sorted the needles to match. You may tell Miss Smith that I forgot to make a memorandum of the darning needles, but she shall have some papers sent in next week; and she is not, on any account, to give out more than one at a time to each pupil: if they have more, they are apt to be careless and lose them. And, O ma'am! I wish the woollen stockings were better looked to! – when I was here last, I went into the kitchen-garden and examined the clothes drying on the line; there was a quantity of black hose in a very bad state of repair: from the size of the holes in them I was sure they had not been well mended from time to time.'

He paused.

'Your directions shall be attended to, sir,' said Miss Temple.

'And, ma'am,' he continued, 'the laundress tells me some of the girls have two clean tuckers in the week: it is too much; the rules limit them to one.'

'I think I can explain that circumstance, sir. Agnes and Catherine Johnstone were invited to take tea with some friends at Lowton last Thursday, and I gave them leave to put on clean tuckers for the occasion.'

Mr Brocklehurst nodded.

'Well, for once it may pass; but please not to let the circumstance occur too often. And there is another thing which surprised me; I find, in settling accounts with the housekeeper, that a lunch, consisting of bread and cheese, has twice been served out to the girls during the past fortnight. How is this? I looked over the regulations, and I find no such meal as lunch mentioned. Who introduced this innovation? and by what authority?'

'I must be responsible for the circumstance, sir,' replied Miss Temple: 'the breakfast was so ill prepared that the pupils could not possibly eat it; and I dared not allow them to remain fasting till dinner-time.'

'Madam, allow me an instant. You are aware that my plan in bringing up these girls is, not to accustom them to habits of luxury and indulgence, but to render them hardy, patient, self-denying. Should any little accidental disappointment of the appetite occur, such as the spoiling of a meal, the under or the over dressing of a dish, the incident ought not to be neutralised by replacing with something more delicate the comfort lost, thus pampering the body and obviating the aim of this institution; it ought to be improved to the spiritual edification of the pupils, by encouraging them to evince fortitude under the temporary privation. A brief address on those occasions would not be mistimed, wherein a judicious instructor would take the opportunity of referring to the sufferings of the primitive Christians; to the torments of martyrs; to the exhortations of our blessed Lord Himself, calling upon His disciples to take up their cross and follow Him; to His warnings that man shall not live by bread alone, but by every word that proceedeth out of the mouth of God; to His divine consolations, "If ye suffer hunger or thirst for My sake, happy are ye." Oh, madam, when you put bread and cheese, instead of burnt porridge, into these children's mouths, you may indeed feed their vile bodies, but you little think how you starve their immortal souls!'

Mr Brocklehurst again paused – perhaps overcome by his feelings. Miss Temple had looked down when he first began to speak to her; but she now gazed straight before her, and her face, naturally pale as marble, appeared to be assuming also the coldness and fixity of that material; especially her mouth, closed as if it would have required a sculptor's chisel to open it, and her brow settled gradually into petrified severity.

Meantime, Mr Brocklehurst, standing on the hearth with his hands behind his back, majestically surveyed the whole school. Suddenly his eye gave a blink, as if it had met something that either dazzled or shocked its pupil; turning, he said in more rapid accents than he had hitherto used – 'Miss Temple, Miss Temple, what – *what* is that girl with curled hair? Red hair, ma'am, curled – curled all over?' And extending his cane he pointed to the awful object, his hand shaking as he did so.

'It is Julia Severn,' replied Miss Temple, very quietly.

'Julia Severn, ma'am! And why has she, or any other, curled hair? Why, in defiance of every precept and principle of this house, does she conform to the world so openly – here in an evangelical, charitable establishment – as to wear her hair one mass of curls?'

'Julia's hair curls naturally,' returned Miss Temple, still more quietly.

'Naturally! Yes, but we are not to conform to nature; I wish these girls to be the children of Grace: and why that abundance? I have again and again intimated that I desire the hair to be arranged closely, modestly, plainly. Miss Temple, that girl's hair must be cut off entirely; I will send a barber tomorrow: and I see others who have far too much of the excrescence – that tall girl, tell her to turn round. Tell all the first form to rise up and direct their faces to the wall.'

Miss Temple passed her handkerchief over her lips, as if to smooth away the involuntary smile that curled them; she gave the order, however, and when the first class could take in what was required of them, they obeyed. Leaning a little back on my bench, I could see the looks and grimaces with which they commented on this manoeuvre: it was a pity Mr Brocklehurst could not see them too; he would perhaps have felt that, whatever he might do with the outside of the cup and platter, the inside was further beyond his interference than he imagined.

He scrutinised the reverse of these living medals some five minutes, then pronounced sentence. These words fell like the knell of doom – 'All those topknots must be cut off.'

Miss Temple seemed to remonstrate.

'Madam,' he pursued, 'I have a Master to serve whose kingdom is not of this world: my mission is to mortify in these girls the lusts of the flesh; to teach them to clothe themselves with shamefacedness and sobriety, not with braided hair and costly apparel; and each of the young persons before us has a string of hair twisted in plaits which vanity itself might have woven; these, I repeat, must be cut off; think of the time wasted, of – '

Mr Brocklehurst was here interrupted: three other visitors, ladies, now entered the room. They ought to have come a little sooner to have heard his lecture on dress, for they were splendidly attired in velvet, silk, and furs. The two younger of the trio (fine girls of sixteen and seventeen) had grey beaver hats, then in fashion, shaded with ostrich plumes, and from under the brim of this graceful head-dress fell a profusion of light tresses, elaborately curled; the elder lady was enveloped in a costly velvet shawl, trimmed with ermine, and she wore a false front of French curls.

These ladies were deferentially received by Miss Temple, as Mrs and the Misses Brocklehurst, and conducted to seats of honour at the top of the room. It seems they had come in the carriage with their reverend relative, and had been conducting a rummaging scrutiny of the room upstairs, while he transacted business with the housekeeper, questioned the laundress, and lectured the superintendent. They now proceeded to address divers remarks and reproofs to Miss Smith, who was charged with the care of the linen and the inspection of the dormitories: but I had no time to listen to what they said; other matters called off and enchained my attention.

Hitherto, while gathering up the discourse of Mr Brocklehurst and Miss Temple, I had not, at the same time, neglected precautions to secure my personal safety; which I thought would be effected, if I could only elude observation. To this end, I had sat well back on the form, and while seeming to be busy with my sum, had held my slate in such a manner as to conceal my face: I might have escaped notice, had not my treacherous slate somehow happened to slip from my hand, and falling with an obtrusive crash, directly drawn every eye upon me; I knew it was all over now, and, as I stooped to pick up the two fragments of slate, I rallied my forces for the worst. It came.

'A careless girl!' said Mr Brocklehurst, and immediately after – 'It is the new pupil, I perceive.' And before I could draw breath, 'I must not forget I have a word to say respecting her.' Then aloud: how loud it seemed to me! 'Let the child who broke her slate come forward!'

Of my own accord I could not have stirred; I was paralysed: but the two great girls who sat on each side of me, set me on my legs and pushed me towards the dread judge, and then Miss Temple gently assisted me to his very feet, and I caught her whispered counsel – 'Don't be afraid, Jane, I saw it was an accident; you shall not be punished.'

The kind whisper went to my heart like a dagger. 'Another minute, and she will despise me for a hypocrite,' thought I; and an impulse of fury against Reed, Brocklehurst, and Co. bounded in my pulses at the conviction. I was no Helen Burns.

'Fetch that stool,' said Mr Brocklehurst, pointing to a very high one from which a monitor had just risen: it was brought.

'Place the child upon it.'

And I was placed there, by whom I don't know: I was in no condition to note particulars; I was only aware that they had hoisted me up to the height of Mr Brocklehurst's nose, that he was within a yard of me, and that a spread of shot orange and purple silk pelisses and a cloud of silvery plumage extended and waved below me.

Mr Brocklehurst hemmed.

'Ladies,' said he, turning to his family, 'Miss Temple, teachers, and children, you all see this girl?' Of course they did; for I felt their eyes directed like burning-glasses against my scorched skin.

'You see she is yet young; you observe she possesses the ordinary form of childhood; God has graciously given her the shape that He has given to all of us; no signal deformity points her out as a marked character. Who would think that the Evil One had already found a servant and agent in her? Yet such, I grieve to say, is the case.'

A pause – in which I began to steady the palsy of my nerves, and to feel that the Rubicon was passed; and that the trial, no longer to be shirked, must be firmly sustained.

'My dear children,' pursued the black marble clergyman, with pathos, 'this is a sad, a melancholy occasion; for it becomes my duty to warn you, that this girl, who might be one of God's own lambs, is a little castaway: not a member of the true flock, but evidently an interloper and an alien. You must be on your guard against her; you must shun her example; if necessary, avoid her company, exclude her from your sports, and shut her out from your converse. Teachers, you must watch her: keep your eyes on her movements, weigh well her words, scrutinise her actions, punish her body to save her soul: if, indeed, such salvation be possible, for (my tongue falters while I tell it) this girl, this child, the native of a Christian land, worse than many a little heathen who says its prayers to Brahma and kneels before Juggernaut – this girl is – a liar!'

Now came a pause of ten minutes, during which I, by this time in perfect possession of my wits, observed all the female Brocklehursts produce their pocket-handkerchiefs and apply them to their optics, while the elderly lady swayed herself to and fro, and the two younger ones whispered, 'How shocking!'

Mr Brocklehurst resumed.

'This I learned from her benefactress; from the pious and charitable lady who adopted her in her orphan state, reared her as her own daughter, and whose kindness, whose generosity the unhappy girl repaid by an ingratitude so bad, so dreadful, that at last her excellent patroness was obliged to separate her from her own young ones, fearful lest her vicious example should contaminate their purity: she has sent her here to be healed, even as the Jews of old sent their diseased to the troubled pool of Bethesda; and, teachers, superintendent, I beg of you not to allow the waters to stagnate round her.'

With this sublime conclusion, Mr Brocklehurst adjusted the top button of his surtout, muttered something to his family, who rose, bowed to Miss Temple, and then all the great people sailed in state from the room. Turning at the door, my judge said – 'Let her stand half an hour longer on that stool, and let no one speak to her during the remainder of the day.'

There was I, then, mounted aloft; I, who had said I could not bear the shame of standing on my natural feet in the middle of the room, was now exposed to general view on a pedestal of infamy. What my sensations were, no language can describe; but just as they all rose, stifling my breath and constricting my throat, a girl came up and passed me: in passing, she lifted her eyes. What a strange light inspired them! What an extraordinary sensation that ray sent through me! How the new feeling bore me up! It was as if a martyr, a hero, had passed a slave or victim, and imparted strength in the transit. I mastered the rising hysteria, lifted up my head, and took a firm stand on the stool. Helen Burns asked some slight question about her work of Miss Smith, was chidden for the triviality of the enquiry, returned to her place, and smiled at me as she again went by. What a smile! I remember it now, and I know that it was the effluence of fine intellect, of true courage; it lit up her marked lineaments, her thin face, her sunken grey eye, like a reflection from the aspect of an angel. Yet at that moment Helen Burns wore on her arm 'the untidy badge;' scarcely an hour ago I had heard her condemned by Miss Scatcherd to a dinner of bread and water on the morrow because she had blotted an exercise in copying it out. Such is the imperfect nature of man! such spots are there on the disc of the dearest planet; and eyes like Miss Scatcherd's can only see those minute defects, and are blind to the full brightness of the orb.

## *Chapter 8*

Ere the half-hour ended, five o'clock struck; school was dismissed, and all were gone into the refectory to tea. I now ventured to descend: it was deep dusk; I retired into a corner and sat down on the floor. The spell by which I had been so far supported began to dissolve; reaction took place, and soon, so overwhelming was the grief that seized me, I sank prostrate with my face to the ground. Now I wept: Helen Burns was not here; nothing sustained me; left to myself I abandoned myself, and my tears watered the boards. I had meant to be so good, and to do so much at Lowood: to make so many friends, to earn respect and win affection. Already I had made visible progress: that very morning I had reached the head of my class; Miss Miller had praised me warmly; Miss Temple had smiled approbation; she had promised to teach me drawing, and to let me learn French, if I continued to make similar improvement two months longer: and then I was well received by my fellow-pupils; treated as an equal by those of my own age, and not molested by any; now, here I lay again crushed and trodden on; and could I ever rise more?

'Never,' I thought; and ardently I wished to die. While sobbing out this wish in broken accents, someone approached: I started up – again Helen Burns was near me; the fading fires just showed her coming up the long, vacant room; she brought my coffee and bread.

'Come, eat something,' she said; but I put both away from me, feeling as if a drop or a crumb would have choked me in my present condition. Helen regarded me, probably with surprise: I could not now abate my agitation, though I tried hard; I continued to weep aloud. She sat down on the ground near me, embraced her knees with her arms, and rested her head upon them; in that attitude she remained silent as an Indian. I was the first who spoke – 'Helen, why do you stay with a girl whom everybody believes to be a liar?'

'Everybody, Jane? Why, there are only eighty people who have heard you called so, and the world contains hundreds of millions.'

'But what have I to do with millions? The eighty, I know, despise me.'

'Jane, you are mistaken: probably not one in the school either despises or dislikes you: many, I am sure, pity you much.'

'How can they pity me after what Mr Brocklehurst has said?'

'Mr Brocklehurst is not a god: nor is he even a great and admired man; he is little liked here; he never took steps to make himself liked. Had he treated you as an especial favourite, you would have found enemies, declared or covert, all around you; as it is, the greater number would offer you sympathy if they dared. Teachers and pupils may look coldly on you for a day or two, but friendly feelings are concealed in their hearts; and if you persevere in doing well, these feelings will ere long appear so much the more evidently for their temporary suppression. Besides, Jane' – she paused.

'Well, Helen?' said I, putting my hand into hers: she chafed my fingers gently to warm them, and went on – 'If all the world hated you, and believed you wicked, while your own conscience approved you, and absolved you from guilt, you would not be without friends.'

'No; I know I should think well of myself; but that is not enough: if others don't love me I would rather die than live – I cannot bear to be solitary and hated, Helen. Look here; to gain some real affection from you, or Miss Temple, or any other whom I truly love, I would willingly submit to have the bone of my arm broken, or to let a bull toss me, or to stand behind a kicking horse, and let it dash its hoof at my chest – '

'Hush, Jane! you think too much of the love of human beings; you are too impulsive, too vehement; the sovereign hand that created your frame, and put life into it, has provided you with other resources than your feeble self, or than creatures feeble as you. Besides this earth, and besides the race of men, there is an invisible world and a kingdom of spirits: that world is round us, for it is everywhere; and those spirits watch us, for they are commissioned to guard us; and if we were dying in pain and shame, if scorn smote us on all sides, and hatred crushed us, angels see our tortures, recognise our innocence (if innocent we be: as I know you are of this charge which Mr Brocklehurst has weakly and pompously repeated at second-hand from Mrs Reed; for I read a sincere nature in your ardent eyes and on your clear front), and God waits only the separation of spirit from flesh to crown us with a full reward. Why, then, should we ever sink overwhelmed with distress, when life is so soon over, and death is so certain an entrance to happiness – to glory?'

I was silent; Helen had calmed me; but in the tranquillity she imparted there was an alloy of inexpressible sadness. I felt the impression of woe as she spoke, but I could not tell whence it came; and when, having done speaking, she breathed a little fast and coughed a short cough, I momentarily forgot my own sorrows to yield to a vague concern for her.

Resting my head on Helen's shoulder, I put my arms round her waist; she drew me to her, and we reposed in silence. We had not sat long thus, when another person came in. Some heavy clouds, swept from the sky by a rising wind, had left the moon bare; and her light, streaming in through a window near, shone full both on us and on the approaching figure, which we at once recognised as Miss Temple.

'I came on purpose to find you, Jane Eyre,' said she; 'I want you in my room; and as Helen Burns is with you, she may come too.'

We went; following the superintendent's guidance, we had to thread some intricate passages, and mount a staircase before we reached her apartment; it contained a good fire, and looked cheerful. Miss Temple told Helen Burns to be seated in a low armchair on one side of the hearth, and herself taking another, she called me to her side.

'Is it all over?' she asked, looking down at my face. 'Have you cried your grief away?'

'I am afraid I never shall do that.'

'Why?'

'Because I have been wrongly accused; and you, ma'am, and everybody else, will now think me wicked.'

'We shall think you what you prove yourself to be, my child. Continue to act as a good girl, and you will satisfy us.'

'Shall I, Miss Temple?'

'You will,' said she, passing her arm round me. 'And now tell me who is the lady whom Mr Brocklehurst called your benefactress?'

'Mrs Reed, my uncle's wife. My uncle is dead, and he left me to her care.'

'Did she not, then, adopt you of her own accord?'

'No, ma'am; she was sorry to have to do it: but my uncle, as I have often heard the servants say, got her to promise before he died that she would always keep me.'

'Well now, Jane, you know, or at least I will tell you, that when a criminal is accused, he is always allowed to speak in his own defence. You have been charged with falsehood; defend yourself to me as well as you can. Say whatever your memory suggests as true; but add nothing and exaggerate nothing.'

I resolved, in the depth of my heart, that I would be most moderate – most correct; and, having reflected a few minutes in order to arrange coherently what I had to say, I told her all the story of my sad childhood. Exhausted by emotion, my language was more subdued than it generally was when it developed that sad theme; and mindful of Helen's warnings against the indulgence of resentment, I infused into the narrative far less of gall and wormwood than ordinary. Thus restrained and simplified, it sounded more credible: I felt as I went on that Miss Temple fully believed me.

In the course of the tale I had mentioned Mr Lloyd as having come to see me after the fit: for I never forgot the, to me, frightful episode of the red-room: in detailing which, my excitement was sure, in some degree, to break bounds; for nothing could soften in my recollection the spasm of agony which clutched my heart when Mrs Reed spurned my wild supplication for pardon, and locked me a second time in the dark and haunted chamber.

I had finished: Miss Temple regarded me a few minutes in silence; she then said – 'I know something of Mr Lloyd; I shall write to him; if his reply agrees with your statement, you shall be publicly cleared from every imputation; to me, Jane, you are clear now.'

She kissed me, and still keeping me at her side (where I was well contented to stand, for I derived a child's pleasure from the contemplation of her face, her dress, her one or two ornaments, her white forehead, her clustered and shining curls, and beaming dark eyes), she proceeded to address Helen Burns.

'How are you tonight, Helen? Have you coughed much today?'

'Not quite so much, I think, ma'am.'

'And the pain in your chest?'

'It is a little better.

Miss Temple got up, took her hand and examined her pulse; then she returned to her own seat: as she resumed it, I heard her sigh low. She was pensive a few minutes, then rousing herself, she said cheerfully – 'But you two are my visitors tonight; I must treat you as such.' She rang her bell.

'Barbara,' she said to the servant who answered it, 'I have not yet had tea; bring the tray and place cups for these two young ladies.'

And a tray was soon brought. How pretty, to my eyes, did the china cups and bright teapot look, placed on the little round table near the fire! How fragrant was the steam of the beverage, and the scent of the toast! of which, however, I, to my dismay (for I was beginning to be hungry), discerned only a very small portion: Miss Temple discerned it too.

'Barbara,' said she, 'can you not bring a little more bread and butter? There is not enough for three.'

Barbara went out: she returned soon – 'Madam, Mrs Harden says she has sent up the usual quantity.'

Mrs Harden, be it observed, was the housekeeper: a woman after Mr Brocklehurst's own heart, made up of equal parts of whalebone and iron.

'Oh, very well!' returned Miss Temple; 'we must make it do, Barbara, I suppose.' And as the girl withdrew she added, smiling, 'Fortunately, I have it in my power to supply deficiencies for this once.'

Having invited Helen and me to approach the table and placed before each of us a cup of tea with one delicious but thin morsel of toast, she got up, unlocked a drawer, and taking from it a parcel wrapped in paper, disclosed presently to our eyes a good-sized seed-cake.

'I meant to give each of you some of this to take with you,' said she, 'but as there is so little toast, you must have it now,' and she proceeded to cut slices with a generous hand.

We feasted that evening as on nectar and ambrosia; and not the least delight of the entertainment was the smile of gratification with which our hostess regarded us, as we satisfied our famished appetites on the delicate fare she liberally supplied.

Tea over and the tray removed, she again summoned us to the fire; we sat one on each side of her, and now a conversation followed between her and Helen, which it was indeed a privilege to be admitted to hear.

Miss Temple had always something of serenity in her air, of state in her mien, of refined propriety in her language, which precluded deviation into the ardent, the excited, the eager: something which chastened the pleasure of those who looked on her and listened to her, by a controlling sense of awe; and such was my feeling now: but as to Helen Burns, I was struck with wonder.

The refreshing meal, the brilliant fire, the presence and kindness of her beloved instructress, or, perhaps, more than all these, something in her own unique mind, had roused her powers within her. They woke, they kindled: first, they glowed in the bright tint of her cheek, which till this hour I had never seen but pale and bloodless; then they shone in the liquid lustre of her eyes, which had suddenly acquired a beauty more singular than that of Miss Temple's – a beauty neither of fine colour nor long eyelash, nor pencilled brow, but of meaning, of movement, of radiance. Then her soul sat on her lips, and language flowed, from what source I cannot tell. Has a girl of fourteen a heart large enough, vigorous enough, to hold the swelling spring of pure, full, fervid eloquence? Such was the characteristic of Helen's discourse on that, to me, memorable evening; her spirit seemed hastening to live within a very brief span as much as many live during a protracted existence.

They conversed of things I had never heard of; of nations and times past; of countries far away; of secrets of nature discovered or guessed at: they spoke of books: how many they had read! What stores of knowledge they possessed! Then they seemed so familiar with French names and French authors: but my amazement reached its climax when Miss Temple asked Helen if she sometimes snatched a moment to recall the Latin her father had taught her, and taking a book from a shelf, bade her read and construe a page of Virgil; and Helen obeyed, my organ of veneration expanding at every sounding line. She had scarcely finished ere the bell announced bedtime! no delay could be admitted; Miss Temple embraced us both, saying, as she drew us to her heart – 'God bless you, my children!'

Helen she held a little longer than me: she let her go more reluctantly; it was Helen her eye followed to the door; it was for her she a second time breathed a sad sigh; for her she wiped a tear from her cheek.

On reaching the bedroom, we heard the voice of Miss Scatcherd: she was examining drawers; she had just pulled out Helen Burns's, and when we entered Helen was greeted with a sharp reprimand, and told that tomorrow she should have half a dozen of untidily folded articles pinned to her shoulder.

'My things were indeed in shameful disorder,' murmured Helen to me, in a low voice: 'I intended to have arranged them, but I forgot.'

Next morning, Miss Scatcherd wrote in conspicuous characters on a piece of pasteboard the word 'Slattern,' and bound it like a phylactery round Helen's large, mild, intelligent, and benign-looking forehead. She wore it till evening, patient, unresentful, regarding it as a deserved punishment. The moment Miss Scatcherd withdrew after afternoon school, I ran to Helen, tore it off, and thrust it into the fire: the fury of which she was incapable had been burning in my soul all day, and tears, hot and large, had continually been scalding my cheek; for the spectacle of her sad resignation gave me an intolerable pain at the heart.

About a week subsequently to the incidents above narrated, Miss Temple, who had written to Mr Lloyd, received his answer: it appeared that what he said went to corroborate my account. Miss Temple, having assembled the whole school, announced that enquiry had been made into the charges alleged against Jane Eyre, and that she was most happy to be able to pronounce her completely cleared from every imputation. The teachers then shook hands with me and kissed me, and a murmur of pleasure ran through the ranks of my companions.

Thus relieved of a grievous load, I from that hour set to work afresh, resolved to pioneer my way through every difficulty: I toiled hard, and my success was proportionate to my efforts; my memory, not naturally tenacious, improved with practice; exercise sharpened my wits; in a few weeks I was promoted to a higher class; in less than two months I was allowed to commence French and drawing. I learned the first two tenses of the verb *etre*, and sketched my first cottage (whose walls, by the by, outrivalled in slope those of the leaning tower of Pisa), on the same day. That night, on going to bed, I forgot to prepare in imagination the Barmecide supper of hot roast potatoes, or white bread and new milk, with which I was wont to amuse my inward cravings: I feasted instead on the spectacle of ideal drawings, which I saw in the dark; all the work of my own hands: freely pencilled houses and trees, picturesque rocks and ruins, Cuyp-like groups of cattle, sweet paintings of butterflies hovering over unblown roses, of birds picking at ripe cherries, of wrens' nests enclosing pearl-like eggs, wreathed about with young ivy sprays. I examined, too, in thought, the possibility of my ever being able to translate currently a certain little French story which Mme Pierrot had that day shown me; nor was that problem solved to my satisfaction ere I fell sweetly asleep.

Well has Solomon said – 'Better is a dinner of herbs where love is, than a stalled ox and hatred therewith.'

I would not now have exchanged Lowood with all its privations for Gateshead and its daily luxuries.

## *Chapter 9*

But the privations, or rather the hardships, of Lowood lessened. Spring drew on: she was indeed already come; the frosts of winter had ceased; its snows were melted, its cutting winds ameliorated. My wretched feet, flayed and swollen to lameness by the sharp air of January, began to heal and subside under the gentler breathings of April; the nights and mornings no longer by their Canadian temperature froze the very blood in our veins; we could now endure the play-hour passed in the garden: sometimes on a sunny day it began even to be pleasant and genial, and a greenness grew over those brown beds, which, freshening daily, suggested the thought that Hope traversed them at night, and left each morning brighter traces of her steps. Flowers peeped out amongst the leaves; snowdrops, crocuses, purple auriculas, and golden-eyed pansies. On Thursday afternoons (half-holidays) we now took walks, and found still sweeter flowers opening by the wayside, under the hedges.

I discovered, too, that a great pleasure, an enjoyment which the horizon only bounded, lay all outside the high and spike-guarded walls of our garden: this pleasure consisted in prospect of noble summits girdling a great hill-hollow, rich in verdure and shadow; in a bright beck, full of dark stones and sparkling eddies. How different had this scene looked when I viewed it laid out beneath the iron sky of winter, stiffened in frost, shrouded with snow! – when mists as chill as death wandered to the impulse of east winds along those purple peaks, and rolled down 'ing' and holm till they blended with the frozen fog of the beck! That beck itself was then a torrent, turbid and curbless: it tore asunder the wood, and sent a raving sound through the air, often thickened with wild rain or whirling sleet; and for the forest on its banks, *that* showed only ranks of skeletons.

April advanced to May: a bright, serene May it was; days of blue sky, placid sunshine, and soft western or southern gales filled up its duration. And now vegetation matured with vigour; Lowood shook loose its tresses; it became all green, all flowery; its great elm, ash, and oak skeletons were restored to majestic life; woodland plants sprang up profusely in its recesses; unnumbered varieties of moss filled its hollows, and it made a strange ground-sunshine out of the wealth of its wild primrose plants: I have seen their pale gold gleam in overshadowed spots like scatterings of the sweetest lustre. All this I enjoyed often and fully, free, unwatched, and almost alone: for this unwonted liberty and pleasure there was a cause, to which it now becomes my task to advert.

Have I not described a pleasant site for a dwelling, when I speak of it as bosomed in hill and wood, and rising from the verge of a stream? Assuredly, pleasant enough: but whether healthy or not is another question.

That forest-dell, where Lowood lay, was the cradle of fog and fog-bred pestilence; which, quickening with the quickening spring, crept into the Orphan

Asylum, breathed typhus through its crowded schoolroom and dormitory, and, ere May arrived, transformed the seminary into an hospital.

Semi-starvation and neglected colds had predisposed most of the pupils to receive infection: forty-five out of the eighty girls lay ill at one time. Classes were broken up, rules relaxed. The few who continued well were allowed almost unlimited license; because the medical attendant insisted on the necessity of frequent exercise to keep them in health: and had it been otherwise, no one had leisure to watch or restrain them. Miss Temple's whole attention was absorbed by the patients: she lived in the sickroom, never quitting it except to snatch a few hours' rest at night. The teachers were fully occupied with packing up and making other necessary preparations for the departure of those girls who were fortunate enough to have friends and relations able and willing to remove them from the seat of contagion. Many, already smitten, went home only to die: some died at the school, and were buried quietly and quickly, the nature of the malady forbidding delay.

While disease had thus become an inhabitant of Lowood, and death its frequent visitor; while there was gloom and fear within its walls; while its rooms and passages steamed with hospital smells, the drug and the pastille striving vainly to overcome the effluvia of mortality, that bright May shone unclouded over the bold hills and beautiful woodland out of doors. Its garden, too, glowed with flowers: hollyhocks had sprung up tall as trees, lilies had opened, tulips and roses were in bloom; the borders of the little beds were gay with pink thrift and crimson double daisies; the sweetbriars gave out, morning and evening, their scent of spice and apples; and these fragrant treasures were all useless for most of the inmates of Lowood, except to furnish now and then a handful of herbs and blossoms to put in a coffin.

But I, and the rest who continued well, enjoyed fully the beauties of the scene and season; they let us ramble in the wood, like gypsies, from morning till night; we did what we liked, went where we liked: we lived better too. Mr Brocklehurst and his family never came near Lowood now: household matters were not scrutinised into; the cross housekeeper was gone, driven away by the fear of infection; her successor, who had been matron at the Lowton Dispensary, unused to the ways of her new abode, provided with comparative liberality. Besides, there were fewer to feed; the sick could eat little; our breakfast-basins were better filled; when there was no time to prepare a regular dinner, which often happened, she would give us a large piece of cold pie, or a thick slice of bread and cheese, and this we carried away with us to the wood, where we each chose the spot we liked best, and dined sumptuously.

My favourite seat was a smooth and broad stone, rising white and dry from the very middle of the beck, and only to be got at by wading through the water; a feat I accomplished barefoot. The stone was just broad enough to accommodate, comfortably, another girl and me, at that time my chosen comrade – one Mary Ann Wilson; a shrewd, observant personage, whose society I took pleasure in, partly because she was witty and original, and partly because she had a manner which set me at my ease. Some years older than I, she knew more of the world, and could tell me many things I liked to hear: with her my curiosity found gratification: to my faults also she gave ample indulgence, never imposing curb or rein on anything I said. She had a turn for narrative, I for analysis; she liked to inform, I to question; so we got on swimmingly together, deriving much entertainment, if not much improvement, from our mutual intercourse.

And where, meantime, was Helen Burns? Why did I not spend these sweet days of liberty with her? Had I forgotten her? or was I so worthless as to have grown tired of her pure society? Surely the Mary Ann Wilson I have mentioned was inferior to my first acquaintance: she could only tell me amusing stories, and reciprocate any racy and pungent gossip I chose to indulge in; while, if I have spoken truth of Helen, she was qualified to give those who enjoyed the privilege of her converse a taste of far higher things.

True, reader; and I knew and felt this: and though I am a defective being, with many faults and few redeeming points, yet I never tired of Helen Burns; nor ever ceased to cherish for her a sentiment of attachment, as strong, tender, and respectful as any that ever animated my heart. How could it be otherwise, when Helen, at all times and under all circumstances, evinced for me a quiet and faithful friendship, which ill-humour never soured, nor irritation never troubled? But Helen was ill at present: for some weeks she had been removed from my sight to I knew not what room upstairs. She was not, I was told, in the hospital portion of the house with the fever patients; for her complaint was consumption, not typhus: and by consumption I, in my ignorance, understood something mild, which time and care would be sure to alleviate.

I was confirmed in this idea by the fact of her once or twice coming downstairs on very warm sunny afternoons, and being taken by Miss Temple into the garden; but, on these occasions, I was not allowed to go and speak to her; I only saw her from the schoolroom window, and then not distinctly; for she was much wrapped up, and sat at a distance under the verandah.

One evening, in the beginning of June, I had stayed out very late with Mary Ann in the wood; we had, as usual, separated ourselves from the others, and had wandered far; so far that we lost our way, and had to ask it at a lonely cottage, where a man and woman lived, who looked after a herd of half-wild swine that fed on the mast in the wood. When we got back, it was after moonrise: a pony, which we knew to be the surgeon's, was standing at the garden door. Mary Ann remarked that she supposed someone must be very ill, as Mr Bates had been sent for at that time of the evening. She went into the house; I stayed behind a few minutes to plant in my garden a handful of roots I had dug up in the forest, and which I feared would wither if I left them till the morning. This done, I lingered yet a little longer: the flowers smelt so sweet as the dew fell; it was such a pleasant evening, so serene, so warm; the still glowing west promised so fairly another fine day on the morrow; the moon rose with such majesty in the grave east. I was noting these things and enjoying them as a child might, when it entered my mind as it had never done before: 'How sad to be lying now on a sick bed, and to be in danger of dying! This world is pleasant – it would be dreary to be called from it, and to have to go who knows where?'

And then my mind made its first earnest effort to comprehend what had been infused into it concerning heaven and hell; and for the first time it recoiled, baffled; and for the first time glancing behind, on each side, and before it, it saw all round an unfathomed gulf: it felt the one point where it stood – the present; all the rest was formless cloud and vacant depth; and it shuddered at the thought of tottering, and plunging amid that chaos. While pondering this new idea, I heard the front door open; Mr Bates came out, and with him was a nurse. After she had seen him mount his horse and depart, she was about to close the door, but I ran up to her.

'How is Helen Burns?'

'Very poorly,' was the answer.

'Is it her Mr Bates has been to see?'

'Yes.'

'And what does he say about her?'

'He says she'll not be here long.'

This phrase, uttered in my hearing yesterday, would have only conveyed the notion that she was about to be removed to Northumberland, to her own home. I should not have suspected that it meant she was dying; but I knew instantly now! It opened clear on my comprehension that Helen Burns was numbering her last days in this world, and that she was going to be taken to the region of spirits, if such region there were. I experienced a shock of horror, then a strong thrill of grief, then a desire – a necessity to see her; and I asked in what room she lay.

'She is in Miss Temple's room,' said the nurse.

'May I go up and speak to her?'

'Oh no, child! It is not likely; and now it is time for you to come in; you'll catch the fever if you stop out when the dew is falling.'

The nurse closed the front door; I went in by the side entrance which led to the schoolroom: I was just in time; it was nine o'clock, and Miss Miller was calling the pupils to go to bed.

It might be two hours later, probably near eleven, when I – not having been able to fall asleep, and deeming, from the perfect silence of the dormitory, that my companions were all wrapped in profound repose – rose softly, put on my frock over my nightdress, and, without shoes, crept from the apartment, and set off in quest of Miss Temple's room. It was quite at the other end of the house; but I knew my way; and the light of the unclouded summer moon, entering here and there at passage windows, enabled me to find it without difficulty. An odour of camphor and burnt vinegar warned me when I came near the fever room: and I passed its door quickly, fearful lest the nurse who sat up all night should hear me. I dreaded being discovered and sent back; for I *must* see Helen, I must embrace her before she died, I must give her one last kiss, exchange with her one last word.

Having descended a staircase, traversed a portion of the house below, and succeeded in opening and shutting, without noise, two doors, I reached another flight of steps; these I mounted, and then just opposite to me was

Miss Temple's room. A light shone through the keyhole and from under the door; a profound stillness pervaded the vicinity. Coming near, I found the door slightly ajar; probably to admit some fresh air into the close abode of sickness. Indisposed to hesitate, and full of impatient impulses – soul and senses quivering with keen throes – I put it back and looked in. My eye sought Helen, and feared to find death.

Close by Miss Temple's bed, and half covered with its white curtains, there stood a little crib. I saw the outline of a form under the clothes, but the face was hid by the hangings: the nurse I had spoken to in the garden sat in an easy-chair asleep; an unsnuffed candle burnt dimly on the table. Miss Temple was not to be seen: I knew afterwards that she had been called to a delirious patient in the fever-room. I advanced; then paused by the crib side: my hand was on the curtain, but I preferred speaking before I withdrew it. I still recoiled at the dread of seeing a corpse.

'Helen!' I whispered softly, 'are you awake?'

She stirred herself, put back the curtain, and I saw her face, pale, wasted, but quite composed: she looked so little changed that my fear was instantly dissipated.

'Can it be you, Jane?' she asked, in her own gentle voice.

'Oh!' I thought, 'she is not going to die; they are mistaken: she could not speak and look so calmly if she were.'

I got on to her crib and kissed her: her forehead was cold, and her cheek both cold and thin, and so were her hand and wrist; but she smiled as of old.

'Why are you come here, Jane? It is past eleven o'clock: I heard it strike some minutes since.'

'I came to see you, Helen: I heard you were very ill, and I could not sleep till I had spoken to you.'

'You came to bid me goodbye, then: you are just in time probably.'

'Are you going somewhere, Helen? Are you going home?'

'Yes; to my long home – my last home.'

'No, no, Helen!' I stopped, distressed. While I tried to devour my tears, a fit of coughing seized Helen; it did not, however, wake the nurse; when it was over, she lay some minutes exhausted; then she whispered – 'Jane, your little feet are bare; lie down and cover yourself with my quilt.'

I did so: she put her arm over me, and I nestled close to her. After a long silence, she resumed, still whispering – 'I am very happy, Jane; and when you hear that I am dead, you must be sure and not grieve: there is nothing to grieve about. We all must die one day, and the illness which is removing me is not painful; it is gentle and gradual: my mind is at rest. I leave no one to regret me much: I have only a father; and he is lately married, and will not miss me. By dying young, I shall escape great sufferings. I had not qualities or talents to make my way very well in the world: I should have been continually at fault.'

'But where are you going to, Helen? Can you see? Do you know?'

'I believe; I have faith: I am going to God.'

'Where is God? What is God?'

'My Maker and yours, who will never destroy what He created. I rely implicitly on His power, and confide wholly in His goodness: I count the hours till that eventful one arrives which shall restore me to Him, reveal Him to me.'

'You are sure, then, Helen, that there is such a place as heaven, and that our souls can get to it when we die?'

'I am sure there is a future state; I believe God is good; I can resign my immortal part to Him without any misgiving. God is my father; God is my friend: I love Him; I believe He loves me.'

'And shall I see you again, Helen, when I die?'

'You will come to the same region of happiness: be received by the same mighty, universal Parent, no doubt, dear Jane.'

Again I questioned, but this time only in thought. 'Where is that region? Does it exist?' And I clasped my arms closer round Helen; she seemed dearer to me than ever; I felt as if I could not let her go; I lay with my face hidden on her neck. Presently she said, in the sweetest tone – 'How comfortable I am! That last fit of coughing has tired me a little; I feel as if I could sleep: but don't leave me, Jane; I like to have you near me.'

'I'll stay with you, *dear* Helen: no one shall take me away.'

'Are you warm, darling?'

'Yes.'

'Good-night, Jane.'

'Good-night, Helen.'

She kissed me, and I her, and we both soon slumbered.

When I awoke it was day: an unusual movement roused me; I looked up; I was in somebody's arms; the nurse held me; she was carrying me through the passage back to the dormitory. I was not reprimanded for leaving my bed; people had something else to think about; no explanation was afforded then to my many questions; but a day or two afterwards I learned that Miss Temple, on returning to her own room at dawn, had found me laid in the little crib; my face against Helen Burns's shoulder, my arms round her neck. I was asleep, and Helen was – dead.

Her grave is in Brocklebridge churchyard: for fifteen years after her death it was only covered by a grassy mound; but now a grey marble tablet marks the spot, inscribed with her name, and the word 'Resurgam'.

## *Chapter 10*

Hitherto I have recorded in detail the events of my insignificant existence: to the first ten years of my life I have given almost as many chapters. But this is not to be a regular autobiography: I am only bound to invoke Memory where I know her responses will possess some degree of interest; therefore I now pass a space of eight years almost in silence: a few lines only are necessary to keep up the links of connection.

When the typhus fever had fulfilled its mission of devastation at Lowood, it gradually disappeared from thence; but not till its virulence and the number of its victims had drawn public attention on the school. Enquiry was made into the origin of the scourge, and by degrees various facts came out which excited public indignation in a high degree. The unhealthy nature of the site; the quantity and quality of the children's food; the brackish, fetid water used in its preparation; the pupils' wretched clothing and accommodations – all these things were discovered, and the discovery produced a result mortifying to Mr Brocklehurst, but beneficial to the institution.

Several wealthy and benevolent individuals in the county subscribed largely for the erection of a more convenient building in a better situation; new regulations were made; improvements in diet and clothing introduced; the funds of the school were entrusted to the management of a committee. Mr Brocklehurst, who, from his wealth and family connections, could not be overlooked, still retained the post of treasurer; but he was aided in the discharge of his duties by gentlemen of rather more enlarged and sympathising minds: his office of inspector, too, was shared by those who knew how to combine reason with strictness, comfort with economy, compassion with uprightness. The school, thus improved, became in time a truly useful and noble institution. I remained an inmate of its walls, after its regeneration, for eight years: six as pupil, and two as teacher; and in both capacities I bear my testimony to its value and importance.

During these eight years my life was uniform: but not unhappy, because it was not inactive. I had the means of an excellent education placed within my reach; a fondness for some of my studies, and a desire to excel in all, together with a great delight in pleasing my teachers, especially such as I loved, urged me on: I availed myself fully of the advantages offered me. In time I rose to be the first girl of the first class; then I was invested with the office of teacher; which I discharged with zeal for two years: but at the end of that time I altered.

Miss Temple, through all changes, had thus far continued superintendent of the seminary: to her instruction I owed the best part of my acquirements; her friendship and society had been my continual solace; she had stood me in the stead of mother, governess, and, latterly, companion. At this period she married, removed with her husband (a clergyman, an excellent man, almost worthy of such a wife) to a distant county, and consequently was lost to me.

From the day she left I was no longer the same: with her was gone every settled feeling, every association that had made Lowood in some degree a home to me. I had imbibed from her something of her nature and much of her habits: more harmonious thoughts: what seemed better regulated feelings had become the inmates of my mind. I had given in allegiance to duty and order; I was quiet; I believed I was content: to the eyes of others, usually even to my own, I appeared a disciplined and subdued character.

But destiny, in the shape of the Revd Mr Nasmyth, came between me and Miss Temple: I saw her in her travelling dress step into a post-chaise, shortly after the marriage ceremony; I watched the chaise mount the hill and disappear beyond its brow; and then retired to my own room, and there spent in solitude the greatest part of the half-holiday granted in honour of the occasion.

I walked about the chamber most of the time. I imagined myself only to be regretting my loss, and thinking how to repair it; but when my reflections were concluded, and I looked up and found that the afternoon was gone, and evening far advanced, another discovery dawned on me, namely, that in the interval I had undergone a transforming process; that my mind had put off all it had borrowed of Miss Temple – or rather that she had taken with her the serene atmosphere I had been breathing in her vicinity – and that now I was left in my natural element, and beginning to feel the stirring of old emotions. It did not seem as if a prop were withdrawn, but rather as if a motive were gone: it was not the power to be tranquil which had failed me, but the reason for tranquillity was no more. My world had for some years been in Lowood: my experience had been of its rules and systems; now I remembered that the real world was wide, and that a varied field of hopes and fears, of sensations and excitements, awaited those who had courage to go forth into its expanse, to seek real knowledge of life amidst its perils.

I went to my window, opened it, and looked out. There were the two wings of the building; there was the garden; there were the skirts of Lowood; there was the hilly horizon. My eye passed all other objects to rest on those most remote, the blue peaks; it was those I longed to surmount; all within their boundary of rock and heath seemed prison-ground, exile limits. I traced the white road winding round the base of one mountain, and vanishing in a gorge between two; how I longed to follow it farther! I recalled the time when I had travelled that very road in a coach; I remembered descending that hill at twilight; an age seemed to have elapsed since the day which brought me first to Lowood, and I had never quitted it since. My vacations had all been spent at school: Mrs Reed had never sent for me to Gateshead; neither she nor any of her family had ever been to visit me. I had had no communication by letter or message with the outer world: school-rules, school-duties, school-habits and notions, and voices, and faces, and phrases, and costumes, and preferences, and antipathies – such was what I knew of existence. And now I felt that it was not enough; I tired of the routine of eight years in one afternoon. I desired liberty; for liberty I gasped; for liberty I uttered a prayer; it seemed scattered on the wind then faintly blowing. I abandoned it and framed a humbler supplication; for change, stimulus: that petition, too, seemed swept off into vague space: 'Then,' I cried, half desperate, 'grant me at least a new servitude!'

Here a bell, ringing the hour of supper, called me downstairs.

I was not free to resume the interrupted chain of my reflections till bedtime: even then a teacher who occupied the same room with me kept me from the subject to which I longed to recur, by a prolonged effusion of small talk. How I wished sleep would silence her. It seemed as if, could I but go back to the idea which had last entered my mind as I stood at the window, some inventive suggestion would rise for my relief.

Miss Gryce snored at last; she was a heavy Welshwoman, and till now her habitual nasal strains had never been regarded by me in any other light than as a nuisance; tonight I hailed the first deep notes with satisfaction; I was debarrassed of interruption; my half-effaced thought instantly revived.

'A new servitude! There is something in that,' I soliloquised (mentally, be it understood; I did not talk aloud). 'I know there is, because it does not sound too sweet; it is not like such words as Liberty, Excitement, Enjoyment: delightful sounds truly; but no more than sounds for me; and so hollow and fleeting that it is mere waste of time to listen to them. But Servitude! That must be matter of fact. Anyone may serve: I have served here eight years; now all I want is to serve elsewhere. Can I not get so much of my own will? Is not the thing feasible? Yes – yes – the end is not so difficult; if I had only a brain active enough to ferret out the means of attaining it.'

I sat up in bed by way of arousing this said brain: it was a chilly night; I covered my shoulders with a shawl, and then I proceeded *to think* again with all my might.

'What do I want? A new place, in a new house, amongst new faces, under new circumstances: I want this because it is of no use wanting anything better. How do people do to get a new place? They apply to friends, I suppose: I have no friends. There are many others who have no friends, who must look about for themselves and be their own helpers; and what is their resource?'

I could not tell: nothing answered me; I then ordered my brain to find a response, and quickly. It worked and worked faster: I felt the pulses throb in my head and temples; but for nearly an hour it worked in chaos; and no result came of its efforts. Feverish with vain labour, I got up and took a turn in the room; undrew the curtain, noted a star or two, shivered with cold, and again crept to bed.

A kind fairy, in my absence, had surely dropped the required suggestion on my pillow; for as I lay down, it came quietly and naturally to my mind: 'Those who want situations advertise; you must advertise in the *—shire Herald*.'

'How? I know nothing about advertising.'

Replies rose smooth and prompt now: 'You must enclose the advertisement and the money to pay for it under a cover directed to the editor of the *Herald*; you must put it, the first opportunity you have, into the post at Lowton; answers must be addressed to J. E., at the post-office there; you can go and enquire in about a week after you send your letter, if any are come, and act accordingly.'

This scheme I went over twice, thrice; it was then digested in my mind; I had it in a clear practical form: I felt satisfied, and fell asleep.

With earliest day, I was up: I had my advertisement written, enclosed, and directed before the bell rang to rouse the school; it ran thus: 'A young lady accustomed to tuition' (had I not been a teacher two years?) 'is desirous of meeting with a situation in a private family where the children are under fourteen (I thought that as I was barely eighteen, it would not do to undertake the guidance of pupils nearer my own age). She is qualified to teach the usual branches of a good English education, together with French, Drawing, and Music' (in those days, reader, this now narrow catalogue of accomplishments would have been held tolerably comprehensive). 'Address, J. E., Post-office, Lowton, —shire.' This document remained locked in my drawer all day: after tea, I asked leave of the new superintendent to go to Lowton, in order to perform some small commissions for myself and one or two of my fellow-teachers; permission was readily granted; I went. It was a walk of two miles, and the evening was wet, but the days were still long; I visited a shop or two, slipped the letter into the post-office, and came back through heavy rain, with streaming garments, but with a relieved heart.

The succeeding week seemed long: it came to an end at last, however, like all sublunary things, and once more, towards the close of a pleasant autumn day, I found myself afoot on the road to Lowton. A picturesque track it was, by the way; lying along the side of the beck and through the sweetest curves of the dale: but that day I thought more of the letters, that might or might not be awaiting me at the little burgh whither I was bound, than of the charms of lea and water.

My ostensible errand on this occasion was to get measured for a pair of shoes; so I discharged that business first, and when it was done, I stepped across the clean and quiet little street from the shoemaker's to the post-office: it was kept by an old dame, who wore horn spectacles on her nose, and black mittens on her hands.

'Are there any letters for J. E.?' I asked.

She peered at me over her spectacles, and then she opened a drawer and fumbled among its contents for a long time, so long that my hopes began to falter. At last, having held a document before her glasses for nearly five minutes, she presented it across the counter, accompanying the act by another inquisitive and mistrustful glance – it was for J. E.

'Is there only one?' I demanded.

'There are no more,' said she; and I put it in my pocket and turned my face homeward: I could not open it then; rules obliged me to be back by eight, and it was already half-past seven.

Various duties awaited me on my arrival: I had to sit with the girls during their hour of study; then it was my turn to read prayers; to see them to bed: afterwards I supped with the other teachers. Even when we finally retired for the night, the inevitable Miss Gryce was still my companion: we had only a short end of candle in our candlestick, and I dreaded lest she should talk till it was all burnt out; fortunately, however, the heavy supper she had eaten produced a soporific effect: she was already snoring before I had finished undressing. There still remained an inch of candle: I now took out my letter; the seal was an initial F.; I broke it; the contents were brief.

> If J. E., who advertised in the *—shire Herald* of last Thursday, possesses the acquirements mentioned, and if she is in a position to give satisfactory references as to character and competency, a situation can be offered her where there is but one pupil, a little girl, under ten years of age; and where the salary is thirty pounds per annum. J. E. is requested to send references, name, address, and all particulars to the direction: 'Mrs Fairfax, Thornfield, near Millcote, —shire.'

I examined the document long: the writing was old-fashioned and rather uncertain, like that of an elderly lady. This circumstance was satisfactory: a private fear had haunted me, that in thus acting for myself, and by my own guidance, I ran the risk of getting into some scrape; and, above all things, I wished the result of my endeavours to be respectable, proper, *en règle*. I now felt that an elderly lady was no bad ingredient in the business I had on hand. Mrs Fairfax! I saw her in a black gown and widow's cap; frigid, perhaps, but not uncivil: a model of elderly English respectability. Thornfield! that, doubtless, was the name of her house: a neat orderly spot, I was sure; though I failed in my efforts to conceive a correct plan of the premises. Millcote, —shire; I brushed up my recollections of the map of England; yes, I saw it; both the shire and the town. —shire was seventy miles nearer London than the remote county where I now resided: that was a recommendation to me. I longed to go where there was life and movement: Millcote was a large manufacturing town on the banks of the A—; a busy place enough, doubtless: so much the better; it would be a complete change at least. Not that my fancy was much captivated by the idea of long chimneys and clouds of smoke – 'but,' I argued, 'Thornfield will, probably, be a good way from the town.'

Here the socket of the candle dropped, and the wick went out.

Next day new steps were to be taken; my plans could no longer be confined to my own breast; I must impart them in order to achieve their success. Having sought and obtained an audience of the superintendent during the noontide recreation, I told her I had a prospect of getting a new situation where the salary would be double what I now received (for at Lowood I only got £15 per annum); and requested she would break the matter for me to Mr Brocklehurst, or some of the committee, and ascertain whether they would permit me to mention them as references. She obligingly consented to act as mediatrix in the matter. The next day she laid the affair before Mr Brocklehurst, who said that Mrs Reed must be written to, as she was my natural guardian. A note was accordingly addressed to that lady, who returned for answer, that 'I might do as I pleased: she had long relinquished all interference in my affairs.' This note went the round of the committee, and at last, after what appeared to me most tedious delay, formal leave was given me to better my condition if I could; and an assurance added, that as I had always conducted myself well, both as teacher and pupil, at Lowood, a testimonial of character and capacity, signed by the inspectors of that institution, should forthwith be furnished me.

This testimonial I accordingly received in about a month, forwarded a copy of it to Mrs Fairfax, and got that lady's reply, stating that she was satisfied, and fixing that day fortnight as the period for my assuming the post of governess in her house.

I now busied myself in preparations: the fortnight passed rapidly. I had not a very large wardrobe, though it was adequate to my wants; and the last day sufficed to pack my trunk, the same I had brought with me eight years ago from Gateshead.

The box was corded, the card nailed on. In half an hour the carrier was to call for it to take it to Lowton, whither I myself was to repair at an early hour the next morning to meet the coach. I had brushed my black stuff travelling-dress, prepared my bonnet, gloves, and muff; sought in all my drawers to see that no article was left behind; and now having nothing more to do, I sat down and tried to rest. I could not; though I had been on foot all day, I could not now repose an instant; I was too much excited. A phase of my life was closing tonight, a new one opening tomorrow: impossible to slumber in the interval; I must watch feverishly while the change was being accomplished.

'Miss,' said a servant who met me in the lobby, where I was wandering like a troubled spirit, 'a person below wishes to see you.'

'The carrier, no doubt,' I thought, and ran downstairs without enquiry. I was passing the back-parlour or teachers' sitting-room, the door of which was half open, to go to the kitchen, when someone ran out – 'It's her, I am sure! – I could have told her anywhere!' cried the individual who stopped my progress and took my hand.

I looked: I saw a woman attired like a well-dressed servant, matronly, yet still young; very good-looking, with black hair and eyes, and lively complexion.

'Well, who is it?' she asked, in a voice and with a smile I half recognised; 'you've not quite forgotten me, I think, Miss Jane?'

In another second I was embracing and kissing her rapturously: 'Bessie! Bessie! Bessie!' that was all I said; whereat she half laughed, half cried, and we both went into the parlour. By the fire stood a little fellow of three years old, in plaid frock and trousers.

'That is my little boy,' said Bessie directly.

'Then you are married, Bessie?'

'Yes; nearly five years since to Robert Leaven, the coachman; and I've a little girl besides Bobby there, that I've christened Jane.'

'And you don't live at Gateshead?'

'I live at the lodge: the old porter has left.'

'Well, and how do they all get on? Tell me everything about them, Bessie: but sit down first; and, Bobby, come and sit on my knee, will you?' but Bobby preferred sidling over to his mother.

'You're not grown so very tall, Miss Jane, nor so very stout,' continued Mrs Leaven. 'I dare say they've not kept you too well at school: Miss Reed is the head and shoulders taller than you are; and Miss Georgiana would make two of you in breadth.'

'Georgiana is handsome, I suppose, Bessie?'

'Very. She went up to London last winter with her mama, and there everybody admired her, and a young lord fell in love with her: but his relations were against the match; and – what do you think? – he and Miss Georgiana made it up to run away; but they were found out and stopped. It was Miss Reed that found them out: I believe she was envious; and now she and her sister lead a cat and dog life together; they are always quarrelling.'

'Well, and what of John Reed?'

'Oh, he is not doing so well as his mama could wish. He went to college, and he got – plucked, I think they call it: and then his uncles wanted him to be a barrister, and study the law: but he is such a dissipated young man, they will never make much of him, I think.'

'What does he look like?'

'He is very tall: some people call him a fine-looking young man; but he has such thick lips.'

'And Mrs Reed?

'Missis looks stout and well enough in the face, but I think she's not quite easy in her mind: Mr John's conduct does not please her – he spends a deal of money.'

'Did she send you here, Bessie?'

'No, indeed: but I have long wanted to see you, and when I heard that there had been a letter from you, and that you were going to another part of the country, I thought I'd just set off, and get a look at you before you were quite out of my reach.'

'I am afraid you are disappointed in me, Bessie.' I said this laughing: I perceived that Bessie's glance, though it expressed regard, did in no shape denote admiration.

'No, Miss Jane, not exactly: you are genteel enough; your look like a lady, and it is as much as ever I expected of you: you were no beauty as a child.'

I smiled at Bessie's frank answer: I felt that it was correct, but I confess I was not quite indifferent to its import: at eighteen most people wish to please, and the conviction that they have not an exterior likely to second that desire brings anything but gratification.

'I dare say you are clever, though,' continued Bessie, by way of solace. 'What can you do? Can you play on the piano?'

'A little.'

There was one in the room; Bessie went and opened it, and then asked me to sit down and give her a tune: I played a waltz or two, and she was charmed.

'The Miss Reeds could not play as well!' said she exultingly. 'I always said you would surpass them in learning: and can you draw?'

'That is one of my paintings over the chimney-piece.' It was a landscape in water colours, of which I had made a present to the superintendent, in acknowledgement of her obliging mediation with the committee on my behalf, and which she had framed and glazed.

'Well, that is beautiful. Miss Jane! It is as fine a picture as any Miss Reed's drawing-master could paint, let alone the young ladies themselves, who could not come near it: and have you learnt French?'

'Yes, Bessie, I can both read it and speak it.'

'And you can work on muslin and canvas?'

'I can.'

'Oh, you are quite a lady, Miss Jane! I knew you would be: you will get on whether your relations notice you or not. There was something I wanted to ask you. Have you ever heard anything from your father's kinsfolk, the Eyres?'

'Never in my life.'

'Well, you know Missis always said they were poor and quite despicable: and they may be poor; but I believe they are as much gentry as the Reeds are; for one day, nearly seven years ago, a Mr Eyre came to Gateshead and wanted to see you; Missis said you were at school fifty miles off; he seemed so much disappointed, for he could not stay: he was going on a voyage to a foreign country, and the ship was to sail from London in a day or two. He looked quite a gentleman, and I believe he was your father's brother.'

'What foreign country was he going to, Bessie?'

'An island thousands of miles off, where they make wine – the butler did tell me – '

'Madeira?' I suggested.

'Yes, that is it – that is the very word.'

'So he went?'

'Yes; he did not stay many minutes in the house: Missis was very high with him; she called him afterwards a "sneaking tradesman". My Robert believes he was a wine-merchant.'

'Very likely,' I returned; 'or perhaps clerk or agent to a wine-merchant.'

Bessie and I conversed about old times an hour longer, and then she was obliged to leave me: I saw her again for a few minutes the next morning at Lowton, while I was waiting for the coach. We parted finally at the door of the Brocklehurst Arms there; each went her separate way; she set off for the brow of Lowood Fell to meet the conveyance which was to take her back to Gateshead, I mounted the vehicle which was to bear me to new duties and a new life in the unknown environs of Millcote.

## *Chapter 11*

A new chapter in a novel is something like a new scene in a play; and when I draw up the curtain this time, reader, you must fancy you see a room in the George Inn at Millcote, with such large figured papering on the walls as inn rooms have; such a carpet, such furniture, such ornaments on the mantelpiece, such prints, including a portrait of George the Third, and another of the Prince of Wales, and a representation of the death of Wolfe. All this is visible to you by the light of an oil lamp hanging from the ceiling, and by that of an excellent fire, near which I sit in my cloak and bonnet; my muff and umbrella lie on the table, and I am warming away the numbness and chill contracted by sixteen hours' exposure to the rawness of an October day: I left Lowton at four o'clock p.m., and the Millcote town clock is now just striking eight.

Reader, though I look comfortably accommodated, I am not very tranquil in my mind. I thought when the coach stopped here there would be someone to meet me; I looked anxiously round as I descended the wooden steps the 'boots' placed for my convenience, expecting to hear my name pronounced, and to see some description of carriage waiting to convey me to Thornfield. Nothing of the sort was visible; and when I asked a waiter if anyone had been to enquire after a Miss Eyre, I was answered in the negative: so I had no resource but to request to be shown into a private room: and here I am waiting, while all sorts of doubts and fears are troubling my thoughts.

It is a very strange sensation to inexperienced youth to feel itself quite alone in the world, cut adrift from every connection, uncertain whether the port to which it is bound can be reached, and prevented by many impediments from returning to that it has quitted. The charm of adventure sweetens that sensation, the glow of pride warms it; but then the throb of fear disturbs it; and fear with me became predominant when half an hour elapsed and still I was alone. I bethought myself to ring the bell.

'Is there a place in this neighbourhood called Thornfield?' I asked of the waiter who answered the summons.

'Thornfield? I don't know, ma'am; I'll enquire at the bar.' He vanished, but reappeared instantly – 'Is your name Eyre, Miss?'

'Yes.'

'Person here waiting for you.'

I jumped up, took my muff and umbrella, and hastened into the inn-passage: a man was standing by the open door, and in the lamp-lit street I dimly saw a one-horse conveyance.

'This will be your luggage, I suppose?' said the man rather abruptly when he saw me, pointing to my trunk in the passage.

'Yes.' He hoisted it on to the vehicle, which was a sort of car, and then I got in; before he shut me up, I asked him how far it was to Thornfield.

'A matter of six miles.'

'How long shall we be before we get there?'

'Happen an hour and a half.'

He fastened the car door, climbed to his own seat outside, and we set off. Our progress was leisurely, and gave me ample time to reflect; I was content to be at length so near the end of my journey; and as I leaned back in the comfortable though not elegant conveyance, I meditated much at my ease.

'I suppose,' thought I, 'judging from the plainness of the servant and carriage, Mrs Fairfax is not a very dashing person: so much the better; I never lived amongst fine people but once, and I was very miserable with them. I wonder if she lives alone except this little girl; if so, and if she is in any degree amiable, I shall surely be able to get on with her; I will do my best; it is a pity that doing one's best does not always answer. At Lowood, indeed, I took that resolution, kept it, and succeeded in pleasing; but with Mrs Reed, I remember my best was always spurned with scorn. I pray God Mrs Fairfax may not turn out a second Mrs Reed; but if she does, I am not bound to stay with her! let the worst come to the worst, I can advertise again. How far are we on our road now, I wonder?'

I let down the window and looked out; Millcote was behind us; judging by the number of its lights, it seemed a place of considerable magnitude, much larger than Lowton. We were now, as far as I could see, on a sort of common; but there were houses scattered all over the district; I felt we were in a different region to Lowood, more populous, less picturesque; more stirring, less romantic.

The roads were heavy, the night misty; my conductor let his horse walk all the way, and the hour and a half extended, I verily believe, to two hours; at last he turned in his seat and said – 'You're noan so far fro' Thornfield now.'

Again I looked out: we were passing a church; I saw its low broad tower against the sky, and its bell was tolling a quarter; I saw a narrow galaxy of lights too, on a hillside, marking a village or hamlet. About ten minutes after, the driver got down and opened a pair of gates: we passed through, and they clashed to behind us. We now slowly ascended a drive, and came upon the long front of a house: candlelight gleamed from one curtained bow-window; all the rest were dark. The car stopped at the front door; it was opened by a maidservant; I alighted and went in.

'Will you walk this way, ma'am?' said the girl; and I followed her across a square hall with high doors all round: she ushered me into a room whose double illumination of fire and candle at first dazzled me, contrasting as it did with the darkness to which my eyes had been for two hours inured; when I could see, however, a cosy and agreeable picture presented itself to my view.

A snug small room; a round table by a cheerful fire; an armchair high-backed and old-fashioned, wherein sat the neatest imaginable little elderly lady, in widow's cap, black silk gown, and snowy muslin apron; exactly like what I had fancied Mrs Fairfax, only less stately and milder looking. She was occupied in knitting; a large cat sat demurely at her feet; nothing in short was wanting to complete the beau-ideal of domestic comfort. A more reassuring introduction for a new governess could scarcely be conceived; there was no grandeur to overwhelm, no stateliness to embarrass; and then, as I entered, the old lady got up and promptly and kindly came forward to meet me.

'How do you do, my dear? I am afraid you have had a tedious ride; John drives so slowly; you must be cold, come to the fire.'

'Mrs Fairfax, I suppose?' said I.

'Yes, you are right: do sit down.'

She conducted me to her own chair, and then began to remove my shawl and untie my bonnet-strings; I begged she would not give herself so much trouble.

'Oh, it is no trouble; I dare say your own hands are almost numbed with cold. Leah, make a little hot negus and cut a sandwich or two: here are the keys of the storeroom.'

And she produced from her pocket a most housewifely bunch of keys, and delivered them to the servant.

'Now, then, draw nearer to the fire,' she continued. 'You've brought your luggage with you, haven't you, my dear?'

'Yes, ma'am.'

'I'll see it carried into your room,' she said, and bustled out.

'She treats me like a visitor,' thought I. 'I little expected such a reception; I anticipated only coldness and stiffness: this is not like what I have heard of the treatment of governesses; but I must not exult too soon.'

She returned; with her own hands cleared her knitting apparatus and a book or two from the table, to make room for the tray which Leah now brought, and then herself handed me the refreshments. I felt rather confused at being the object of more attention than I had ever before received, and, that too, shown by my employer and superior; but as she did not herself seem to consider she was doing anything out of her place, I thought it better to take her civilities quietly.

'Shall I have the pleasure of seeing Miss Fairfax tonight?' I asked, when I had partaken of what she offered me.

'What did you say, my dear? I am a little deaf,' returned the good lady, approaching her ear to my mouth.

I repeated the question more distinctly.

'Miss Fairfax? Oh, you mean Miss Varens! Varens is the name of your future pupil.'

'Indeed! Then she is not your daughter?'

'No, I have no family.'

I should have followed up my first enquiry, by asking in what way Miss Varens was connected with her; but I recollected it was not polite to ask too many questions: besides, I was sure to hear in time.

'I am so glad,' she continued, as she sat down opposite to me, and took the cat on her knee; 'I am so glad you are come; it will be quite pleasant living here now with a companion. To be sure it is pleasant at any time; for Thornfield is a fine old hall, rather neglected of late years perhaps, but still it is a respectable place; yet you know in winter-time one feels dreary quite alone in the best quarters. I say alone – Leah is a nice girl to be sure, and John and his wife are very decent people; but then you see they are only servants, and one can't converse with them on terms of equality: one must keep them at due distance, for fear of losing one's authority. I'm sure last winter (it was a very severe one, if you recollect, and when it did not snow, it rained and blew), not a creature but the butcher and postman came to the house, from November till February; and I really got quite melancholy with sitting night after night alone; I had Leah in to read to me sometimes; but I don't think the poor girl liked the task much: she felt it confining. In spring and summer one got on better: sunshine and long days make such a difference; and then, just at the commencement of this autumn, little Adela Varens came and her nurse: a child makes a house alive all at once; and now you are here I shall be quite gay.'

My heart really warmed to the worthy lady as I heard her talk; and I drew my chair a little nearer to her, and expressed my sincere wish that she might find my company as agreeable as she anticipated.

'But I'll not keep you sitting up late tonight,' said she; 'it is on the stroke of twelve now, and you have been travelling all day: you must feel tired. If you have got your feet well warmed, I'll show you your bedroom. I've had the room next to mine prepared for you; it is only a small apartment, but I thought you would like it better than one of the large front chambers: to be sure they have finer furniture, but they are so dreary and solitary, I never sleep in them myself.'

I thanked her for her considerate choice, and as I really felt fatigued with my long journey, expressed my readiness to retire. She took her candle, and I followed her from the room. First she went to see if the hall-door was fastened; having taken the key from the lock, she led the way upstairs. The steps and banisters were of oak; the staircase window was high and latticed; both it and the long gallery into which the bedroom doors opened looked as if they belonged to a church rather than a house. A very chill and vaultlike air pervaded the stairs and gallery, suggesting cheerless ideas of space and solitude; and I was glad, when finally ushered into my chamber, to find it of small dimensions, and furnished in ordinary, modern style.

When Mrs Fairfax had bidden me a kind good-night, and I had fastened my door, gazed leisurely round, and in some measure effaced the eerie impression made by that wide hall, that dark and spacious staircase, and that long, cold gallery, by the livelier aspect of my little room, I remembered that, after a day of bodily fatigue and mental anxiety, I was now at last in safe haven. The impulse of gratitude swelled my heart, and I knelt down at the bedside, and offered up thanks where thanks were due; not forgetting, ere I rose, to implore aid on my further path, and the power of meriting the kindness which seemed so frankly offered me before it was earned. My couch had no thorns in it that night; my solitary room no fears. At once weary and content, I slept soon and soundly: when I awoke it was broad day.

The chamber looked such a bright little place to me as the sun shone in between the gay blue chintz window curtains, showing papered walls and a carpeted floor, so unlike the bare planks and stained plaster of Lowood, that my spirits rose at the view. Externals have a great effect on the young: I thought that a fairer era of life was beginning for me – one that was to have its flowers and pleasures, as well as its thorns and toils. My faculties, roused by the change of scene, the new field offered to hope, seemed all astir. I cannot precisely define what they expected, but it was something pleasant: not perhaps that day or that month, but at an indefinite future period.

I rose; I dressed myself with care: obliged to be plain – for I had no article of attire that was not made with extreme simplicity – I was still by nature solicitous to be neat. It was not my habit to be disregardful of appearance or careless of the impression I made: on the contrary, I ever wished to look as well as I could, and to please as much as my want of beauty would permit. I sometimes regretted that I was not handsomer; I sometimes wished to have rosy cheeks, a straight nose, and small cherry mouth; I desired to be tall, stately, and finely developed in figure; I felt it a misfortune that I was so little, so pale, and had features so irregular and so marked. And why had I these aspirations and these regrets? It would be difficult to say: I could not then distinctly say it to myself; yet I had a reason, and a logical, natural reason too. However, when I had brushed my hair very smooth, and put on my black frock – which, Quakerlike as it was, at least had the merit of fitting to a nicety – and adjusted my clean white tucker, I thought I should do respectably enough to appear before Mrs Fairfax, and that my new pupil would not at least recoil from me with antipathy. Having opened my chamber window, and seen that I left all things straight and neat on the toilet table, I ventured forth.

Traversing the long and matted gallery, I descended the slippery steps of oak; then I gained the hall: I halted there a minute; I looked at some pictures on the walls (one, I remember, represented a grim man in a cuirass, and one a lady with powdered hair and a pearl necklace), at a bronze lamp pendent from the ceiling, at a great clock whose case was of oak curiously carved, and ebon black with time and rubbing. Everything appeared very stately and imposing to me; but then I was so little accustomed to grandeur. The hall-door, which was half of glass, stood open; I stepped over the threshold. It was a fine autumn morning; the early sun shone serenely on embrowned groves and still green fields; advancing on to the lawn, I looked up and surveyed the front of the mansion. It was three storeys high, of proportions not vast, though considerable: a gentleman's manor-house, not a nobleman's seat: battlements round the top gave it a picturesque look. Its grey front stood out well from the background of a rookery, whose cawing tenants were now on the wing: they flew over the lawn and grounds to alight in a great meadow, from which these were separated by a sunk fence, and where an array of mighty old thorn trees, strong, knotty, and broad as oaks, at once explained the etymology of the mansion's designation. Farther off were hills: not so lofty as those round Lowood, nor so craggy, nor so like barriers of separation from the living world; but yet quiet and lonely hills enough, and seeming to embrace Thornfield with a seclusion I had not expected to find existent so near the stirring locality of Millcote. A little hamlet, whose roofs, were blended with trees, straggled up the side of one of these hills; the church of the district stood nearer Thornfield: its old tower-top looked over a knoll between the house and gates.

I was yet enjoying the calm prospect and pleasant fresh air, yet listening with delight to the cawing of the rooks, yet surveying the wide, hoary front of the hall, and thinking what a great place it was for one lonely little dame like Mrs Fairfax to inhabit, when that lady appeared at the door.

'What! out already?' said she. 'I see you are an early riser.' I went up to her, and was received with an affable kiss and shake of the hand.

'How do you like Thornfield?' she asked. I told her I liked it very much.

'Yes,' she said, 'it is a pretty place; but I fear it will be getting out of order, unless Mr Rochester should take it into his head to come and reside here permanently; or, at least, visit it rather oftener: great houses and fine grounds require the presence of the proprietor.'

'Mr Rochester!' I exclaimed. 'Who is he?'

'The owner of Thornfield,' she responded quietly. 'Did you not know he was called Rochester?'

Of course I did not – I had never heard of him before; but the old lady seemed to regard his existence as a universally understood fact, with which everybody must be acquainted by instinct.

'I thought,' I continued, 'Thornfield belonged to you.'

'To me? Bless you, child; what an idea! To me! I am only the housekeeper – the manager. To be sure I am distantly related to the Rochesters by the mother's side, or at least my husband was; he was a clergyman, incumbent of Hay – that little village yonder on the hill – and that church near the gates was his. The present Mr Rochester's mother was a Fairfax, and second cousin to my husband: but I never presume on the connection – in fact, it is nothing to me; I consider myself quite in the light of an ordinary housekeeper: my employer is always civil, and I expect nothing more.'

'And the little girl – my pupil!'

'She is Mr Rochester's ward; he commissioned me to find a governess for her. He intended to have her brought up in —shire, I believe. Here she comes, with her "bonne", as she calls her nurse.' The enigma then was explained: this affable and kind little widow was no great dame; but a dependant like myself. I did not like her the worse for that; on the contrary, I felt better pleased than ever. The equality between her and me was real; not the mere result of condescension on her part: so much the better – my position was all the freer.

As I was meditating on this discovery, a little girl, followed by her attendant, came running up the lawn. I looked at my pupil, who did not at first appear to notice me: she was quite a child, perhaps seven or eight years old, slightly built, with a pale, small-featured face, and a redundancy of hair falling in curls to her waist.

'Good-morning, Miss Adela,' said Mrs Fairfax. 'Come and speak to the lady who is to teach you, and to make you a clever woman someday.' She approached.

'C'est là ma gouvernante?' said she, pointing to me, and addressing her nurse; who answered – 'Mais oui, certainement.'

'Are they foreigners?' I enquired, amazed at hearing the French language.

'The nurse is a foreigner, and Adela was born on the Continent; and, I believe, never left it till within six months ago. When she first came here she could speak no English; now she can make shift to talk it a little: I don't understand her, she mixes it so with French; but you will make out her meaning very well, I dare say.'

Fortunately I had had the advantage of being taught French by a French lady; and as I had always made a point of conversing with Mme Pierrot as often as I could, and had besides, during the last seven years, learnt a portion of French by heart daily – applying myself to take pains with my accent, and imitating as closely as possible the pronunciation of my teacher, I had acquired a certain degree of readiness and correctness in the language, and was not likely to be much at a loss with Mlle Adela. She came and shook hands with me when she heard that I was her governess; and as I led her in to breakfast, I addressed some phrases to her in her own tongue: she replied briefly at first, but after we were seated at the table, and she had examined me some ten minutes with her large hazel eyes, she suddenly commenced chattering fluently.

'Ah!' cried she, in French, 'you speak my language as well as Mr Rochester does: I can talk to you as I can to him, and so can Sophie. She will be glad: nobody here understands her: Mme Fairfax is all English. Sophie is my nurse; she came with me over the sea in a great ship with a chimney that smoked – how it did smoke! – and I was sick, and so was Sophie, and so was Mr Rochester. Mr Rochester lay down on a sofa in a pretty room called the salon, and Sophie and I had little beds in another place. I nearly fell out of mine; it was like a shelf. And Mademoiselle what is your name?'

'Eyre – Jane Eyre.'

'Aire? Bah! I cannot say it. Well, our ship stopped in the morning, before it was quite daylight, at a great city – a huge city, with very dark houses and all smoky; not at all like the pretty clean town I came from; and Mr Rochester carried me in his arms over a plank to the land, and Sophie came after, and we all got into a coach, which took us to a beautiful large house, larger than this and finer, called an hotel. We stayed there nearly a week: I and Sophie used to walk every day in a great green place full of trees, called the Park; and there were many children there besides me, and a pond with beautiful birds in it, that I fed with crumbs.'

'Can you understand her when she runs on so fast?' asked Mrs Fairfax.

I understood her very well, for I had been accustomed to the fluent tongue of Mme Pierrot.

'I wish,' continued the good lady, 'you would ask her a question or two about her parents: I wonder if she remembers them?'

'Adèle,' I enquired, 'with whom did you live when you were in that pretty clean town you spoke of?'

'I lived long ago with mama; but she is gone to the Holy Virgin. Mama used to teach me to dance and sing, and to say verses. A great many gentlemen and ladies came to see mama, and I used to dance before them, or to sit on their knees and sing to them: I liked it. Shall I let you hear me sing now?'

She had finished her breakfast, so I permitted her to give a specimen of her accomplishments. Descending from her chair, she came and placed herself on my knee; then, folding her little hands demurely before her, shaking back her curls and lifting her eyes to the ceiling, she commenced singing a song from some opera. It was the strain of a forsaken lady, who, after bewailing the perfidy of her lover, calls pride to her aid; desires her attendant to deck her in her brightest jewels and richest robes, and resolves to meet the false one that night at a ball, and prove to him, by the gaiety of her demeanour, how little his desertion has affected her.

The subject seemed strangely chosen for an infant singer; but I suppose the point of the exhibition lay in hearing the notes of love and jealousy warbled with the lisp of childhood; and in very bad taste that point was: at least I thought so.

Adèle sang the canzonette tunefully enough, and with the *naïveté* of her age. This achieved, she jumped from my knee and said, 'Now, Mademoiselle, I will repeat you some poetry.'

Assuming an attitude, she began 'La Ligue des Rats: fable de La Fontaine.' She then declaimed the little piece with an attention to punctuation and emphasis, a flexibility of voice and an appropriateness of gesture, very unusual indeed at her age, and which proved she had been carefully trained.

'Was it your mama who taught you that piece?' I asked.

'Yes, and she just used to say it in this way: "Qu'avez vous donc? lui dit un de ces rats; parlez!"; She made me lift my hand – so – to remind me to raise my voice at the question. Now shall I dance for you?'

'No, that will do: but after your mama went to the Holy Virgin, as you say, with whom did you live then?'

'With Mme Frédéric and her husband: she took care of me, but she is nothing related to me. I think she is poor, for she had not so fine a house as mama. I was not long there. Mr Rochester asked me if I would like to go and live with him in England, and I said yes; for I knew Mr Rochester before I knew Mme Frédéric, and he was always kind to me and gave me pretty dresses and toys: but you see he has not kept his word, for he has brought me to England, and now he is gone back again himself, and I never see him.'

After breakfast, Adèle and I withdrew to the library, which room, it appears, Mr Rochester had directed should be used as the schoolroom. Most of the books were locked up behind glass doors; but there was one bookcase left open containing everything that could be needed in the way of elementary works, and several volumes of light literature, poetry, biography, travels, a few romances, etc. I suppose he had considered that these were all the governess would require for her private perusal; and, indeed, they contented me amply for the present; compared with the scanty pickings I had now and then been able to glean at Lowood, they seemed to offer an abundant harvest of entertainment and information. In this room, too, there was a cabinet piano, quite new and of superior tone; also an easel for painting and a pair of globes.

I found my pupil sufficiently docile, though disinclined to apply: she had not been used to regular occupation of any kind. I felt it would be injudicious to confine her too much at first; so, when I had talked to her a great deal, and got her to learn a little, and when the morning had advanced to noon, I allowed her to return to her nurse. I then proposed to occupy myself till dinner-time in drawing some little sketches for her use.

As I was going upstairs to fetch my portfolio and pencils, Mrs Fairfax called to me: 'Your morning school-hours are over now, I suppose,' said she. She was in a room the folding-doors of which stood open: I went in when she addressed me. It was a large, stately apartment, with purple chairs and curtains, a Turkey carpet, walnut-panelled walls, one vast window rich in stained glass, and a lofty ceiling, nobly moulded. Mrs Fairfax was dusting some vases of fine purple spar, which stood on a sideboard.

'What a beautiful room!' I exclaimed, as I looked round; for I had never before seen any half so imposing.

'Yes; this is the dining-room. I have just opened the window, to let in a little air and sunshine; for everything gets so damp in apartments that are seldom inhabited; the drawing-room yonder feels like a vault.'

She pointed to a wide arch corresponding to the window, and hung like it with a Tyrian-dyed curtain, now looped up. Mounting to it by two broad steps, and looking through, I thought I caught a glimpse of a fairy place, so bright to my novice-eyes appeared the view beyond. Yet it was merely a very pretty drawing-room, and within it a boudoir, both spread with white carpets, on which seemed laid brilliant garlands of flowers; both ceiled with snowy mouldings of white grapes and vine-leaves, beneath which glowed in rich contrast crimson couches and ottomans; while the ornaments on the pale Parian mantelpiece were of sparkling Bohemian glass, ruby red; and between the windows large mirrors repeated the general blending of snow and fire.

'In what order you keep these rooms, Mrs Fairfax!' said I. 'No dust, no canvas coverings: except that the air feels chilly, one would think they were inhabited daily.'

'Why, Miss Eyre, though Mr Rochester's visits here are rare, they are always sudden and unexpected; and as I observed that it put him out to find everything swathed up, and to have a bustle of arrangement on his arrival, I thought it best to keep the rooms in readiness.'

'Is Mr Rochester an exacting, fastidious sort of man?'

'Not particularly so; but he has a gentleman's tastes and habits, and he expects to have things managed in conformity to them.'

'Do you like him? Is he generally liked?'

'Oh, yes; the family have always been respected here. Almost all the land in this neighbourhood, as far as you can see, has belonged to the Rochesters time out of mind.'

'Well, but, leaving his land out of the question, do you like him? Is he liked for himself?'

'*I* have no cause to do otherwise than like him; and I believe he is considered a just and liberal landlord by his tenants: but he has never lived much amongst them.'

'But has he no peculiarities? What, in short, is his character?'

'Oh! his character is unimpeachable, I suppose. He is rather peculiar, perhaps: he has travelled a great deal, and seen a great deal of the world, I should think. I dare say he is clever, but I never had much conversation with him.'

'In what way is he peculiar?'

'I don't know – it is not easy to describe – nothing striking, but you feel it when he speaks to you; you cannot be always sure whether he is in jest or earnest, whether he is pleased or the contrary; you don't thoroughly understand him, in short – at least, I don't: but it is of no consequence, he is a very good master.'

This was all the account I got from Mrs Fairfax of her employer and mine. There are people who seem to have no notion of sketching a character, or observing and describing salient points, either in persons or things: the good lady evidently belonged to this class; my queries puzzled, but did not draw her out. Mr Rochester was Mr Rochester in her eyes; a gentleman, a landed proprietor – nothing more: she enquired and searched no further, and evidently wondered at my wish to gain a more definite notion of his identity.

When we left the dining-room, she proposed to show me over the rest of the house; and I followed her upstairs and downstairs, admiring as I went; for all was well arranged and handsome. The large front chambers I thought especially grand: and some of the third-storey rooms, though dark and low, were interesting from their air of antiquity. The furniture once appropriated to the lower apartments had from time to time been removed here, as fashions changed: and the imperfect light entering by their narrow casement showed bedsteads of a hundred years old; chests in oak or walnut, looking, with their strange carvings of palm branches and cherubs' heads, like types of the Hebrew ark; rows of venerable chairs, high-backed and narrow; stools still more antiquated, on whose cushioned tops were yet apparent traces of half-effaced embroideries, wrought by fingers that for two generations had been coffin-dust. All these relics gave to the third storey of Thornfield Hall the aspect of a home of the past: a shrine of memory. I liked the hush, the gloom, the quaintness of these retreats in the day; but I by no means coveted a night's repose on one of those wide and heavy beds: shut in, some of them, with doors of oak; shaded, others, with wrought old English hangings crusted with thick work, portraying effigies of strange flowers, and stranger birds, and strangest human beings, all which would have looked strange, indeed, by the pallid gleam of moonlight.

'Do the servants sleep in these rooms?' I asked.

'No; they occupy a range of smaller apartments to the back; no one ever sleeps here: one would almost say that, if there were a ghost at Thornfield Hall, this would be its haunt.'

'So I think: you have no ghost, then?'

'None that I ever heard of,' returned Mrs Fairfax, smiling.

'Nor any traditions of one? no legends or ghost stories?'

'I believe not. And yet it is said the Rochesters have been rather a violent than a quiet race in their time: perhaps, though, that is the reason they rest tranquilly in their graves now.'

'Yes – "after life's fitful fever they sleep well," ' I muttered. 'Where are you going now, Mrs Fairfax?' for she was moving away.

'On to the leads; will you come and see the view from thence?' I followed still, up a very narrow staircase to the attics, and thence by a ladder and through a trap-door to the roof of the hall. I was now on a level with the crow colony, and could see into their nests. Leaning over the battlements and looking far down, I surveyed the grounds laid out like a map: the bright and velvet lawn closely girdling the grey base of the mansion; the field, wide as a park, dotted with its ancient timber; the wood, dun and sere, divided by a path visibly overgrown, greener with moss than the trees were with foliage; the church at the gates, the road, the tranquil hills, all reposing in the autumn day's sun; the horizon bounded by a propitious sky, azure, marbled with pearly white. No feature in the scene was extraordinary, but all was pleasing. When I turned from it and repassed the trap-door, I could scarcely see my way down the ladder; the attic seemed black as a vault compared with that arch of blue air to which I had been looking up, and to that sunlit scene of grove, pasture, and green hill, of which the hall was the centre, and over which I had been gazing with delight.

Mrs Fairfax stayed behind a moment to fasten the trap-door; I, by dint of groping, found the outlet from the attic, and proceeded to descend the narrow garret staircase. I lingered in the long passage to which this led, separating the front and back rooms of the third storey: narrow, low, and dim, with only one little window at the far end, and looking, with its two rows of small black doors all shut, like a corridor in some Bluebeard's castle.

While I paced softly on, the last sound I expected to hear in so still a region, a laugh, struck my ear. It was a curious laugh; distinct, formal, mirthless. I stopped: the sound ceased, only for an instant; it began again, louder: for at first, though distinct, it was very low. It passed off in a clamorous peal that seemed to wake an echo in every lonely chamber; though it originated but in one, and I could have pointed out the door whence the accents issued.

'Mrs Fairfax!' I called out: for I now heard her descending the great stairs. 'Did you hear that loud laugh? Who is it?'

'Some of the servants, very likely,' she answered: 'perhaps Grace Poole.'

'Did you hear it?' I again enquired.

'Yes, plainly: I often hear her: she sews in one of these rooms. Sometimes Leah is with her; they are frequently noisy together.'

The laugh was repeated in its low, syllabic tone, and terminated in an odd murmur.

'Grace!' exclaimed Mrs Fairfax.

I really did not expect any Grace to answer; for the laugh was as tragic, as preternatural a laugh as any I ever heard; and, but that it was high noon, and that no circumstance of ghostliness accompanied the curious cachinnation; but that neither scene nor season favoured fear, I should have been superstitiously afraid. However, the event showed me I was a fool for entertaining a sense even of surprise.

The door nearest me opened, and a servant came out, a woman of between thirty and forty; a set, square-made figure, red-haired, and with a hard, plain face: any apparition less romantic or less ghostly could scarcely be conceived.

'Too much noise, Grace,' said Mrs Fairfax. 'Remember directions!' Grace curtseyed silently and went in.

'She is a person we have to sew and assist Leah in her housemaid's work,' continued the widow; 'not altogether unobjectionable in some points, but she does well enough. By the by, how have you got on with your new pupil this morning?'

The conversation, thus turned on Adèle, continued till we reached the light and cheerful region below. Adèle came running to meet us in the hall, exclaiming – 'Mesdames, vous êtes servies!' adding, 'J'ai bien faim, moi!'

We found dinner ready, and waiting for us in Mrs Fairfax's room.

## *Chapter 12*

The promise of a smooth career, which my first calm introduction to Thornfield Hall seemed to pledge, was not belied on a longer acquaintance with the place and its inmates. Mrs Fairfax turned out to be what she appeared, a placid-tempered, kind-natured woman, of competent education and average intelligence. My pupil was a lively child, who had been spoilt and indulged, and therefore was sometimes wayward; but as she was committed entirely to my care, and no injudicious interference from any quarter ever thwarted my plans for her improvement, she soon forgot her little freaks, and became obedient and teachable. She had no great talents, no marked traits of character, no peculiar development of feeling or taste which raised her one inch above the ordinary level of childhood; but neither had she any deficiency or vice which sunk her below it. She made reasonable progress, entertained for me a vivacious, though perhaps not very profound, affection; and by her simplicity, gay prattle, and efforts to please, inspired me, in return, with a degree of attachment sufficient to make us both content in each other's society.

This, *par parenthèse*, will be thought cool language by persons who entertain solemn doctrines about the angelic nature of children, and the duty of those charged with their education to conceive for them an idolatrous devotion: but I am not writing to flatter parental egotism, to echo cant, or prop up humbug; I am merely telling the truth. I felt a conscientious solicitude for Adèle's welfare and progress, and a quiet liking for her little self: just as I cherished towards Mrs Fairfax a thankfulness for her kindness, and a pleasure in her society proportionate to the tranquil regard she had for me, and the moderation of her mind and character.

Anybody may blame me who likes, when I add further, that, now and then, when I took a walk by myself in the grounds; when I went down to the gates and looked through them along the road; or when, while Adèle played with her nurse, and Mrs Fairfax made jellies in the storeroom, I climbed the three staircases, raised the trap-door of the attic, and having reached the leads, looked out afar over sequestered field and hill, and along dim skyline – that then I longed for a power of vision which might overpass that limit; which might reach the busy world, towns, regions full of life I had heard of but never seen – that then I desired more of practical experience than I possessed; more of intercourse with my kind, of acquaintance with variety of character, than was here within my reach. I valued what was good in Mrs Fairfax, and what was good in Adèle; but I believed in the existence of other and more vivid kinds of goodness, and what I believed in I wished to behold.

Who blames me? Many, no doubt; and I shall be called discontented. I could not help it: the restlessness was in my nature; it agitated me to pain sometimes. Then my sole relief was to walk along the corridor of the third storey, backwards and forwards, safe in the silence and solitude of the spot, and allow my mind's eye to dwell on whatever bright visions rose before it – and, certainly, they were many and glowing; to let my heart be heaved by the exultant movement, which, while it swelled it in trouble, expanded it with life; and, best of all, to open my inward ear to a tale that was never ended – a tale my imagination created, and narrated continuously; quickened with all of incident, life, fire, feeling, that I desired and had not in my actual existence.

It is in vain to say human beings ought to be satisfied with tranquillity: they must have action; and they will make it if they cannot find it. Millions are condemned to a stiller doom than mine, and millions are in silent revolt against their lot. Nobody knows how many rebellions besides political rebellions ferment in the masses of life which people earth. Women are supposed to be very calm generally: but women feel just as men feel; they need exercise for their faculties, and a field for their efforts, as much as their brothers do; they suffer from too rigid a restraint, too absolute a stagnation, precisely as men would suffer; and it is narrow-minded in their more privileged fellow-creatures to say that they ought to confine themselves to making puddings and knitting stockings, to playing on the piano and embroidering bags. It is thoughtless to condemn them, or laugh at them, if they seek to do more or learn more than custom has pronounced necessary for their sex.

When thus alone, I not unfrequently heard Grace Poole's laugh: the same peal, the same low, slow ha! ha! which, when first heard, had thrilled me: I heard, too, her eccentric murmurs; stranger than her laugh. There were days when she was quite silent; but there were others when I could not account for the sounds she made. Sometimes I saw her: she would come out of her room with a basin, or a plate, or a tray in her hand, go down to the kitchen and shortly return, generally (oh, romantic reader, forgive me for telling the plain truth!) bearing a pot of porter. Her appearance always acted as a damper to the curiosity raised by her oral oddities: hard-featured and staid, she had no point to which interest could attach. I made some attempts to draw her into conversation, but she seemed a person of few words: a monosyllabic reply usually cut short every effort of that sort.

The other members of the household, viz., John and his wife, Leah the housemaid, and Sophie the French nurse, were decent people; but in no respect remarkable; with Sophie I used to talk French, and sometimes I asked her questions about her native country; but she was not of a descriptive or narrative turn, and generally gave such vapid and confused answers as were calculated rather to check than encourage enquiry.

October, November, December passed away. One afternoon in January, Mrs Fairfax had begged a holiday for Adèle, because she had a cold; and, as Adèle seconded the request with an ardour that reminded me how precious occasional holidays had been to me in my own childhood, I accorded it, deeming that I did well in showing pliability on the point. It was a fine, calm day, though very cold; I was tired of sitting still in the library through a whole long morning: Mrs Fairfax had just written a letter which was waiting to be posted, so I put on my bonnet and cloak and volunteered to carry it to Hay; the distance, two miles, would be a pleasant winter afternoon walk. Having seen Adèle comfortably seated in her little chair by Mrs Fairfax's parlour fireside, and given her her best wax doll (which I usually kept enveloped in silver paper in a drawer) to play with, and a storybook for change of amusement; and having replied to her 'Revenez bientôt, ma bonne amie, ma chère Mlle Jeannette,' with a kiss I set out.

The ground was hard, the air was still, my road was lonely; I walked fast till I got warm, and then I walked slowly to enjoy and analyse the species of pleasure brooding for me in the hour and situation. It was three o'clock; the church bell tolled as I passed under the belfry: the charm of the hour lay in its approaching dimness, in the low-gliding and pale-beaming sun. I was a mile from Thornfield, in a lane noted for wild roses in summer, for nuts and blackberries in autumn, and even now possessing a few coral treasures in hips and haws, but whose best winter delight lay in its utter solitude and leafless repose. If a breath of air stirred, it made no sound here; for there was not a holly, not an evergreen to rustle, and the stripped hawthorn and hazel bushes were as still as the white, worn stones which causewayed the middle of the path. Far and wide, on each side, there were only fields, where no cattle now browsed; and the little brown birds, which stirred occasionally in the hedge, looked like single russet leaves that had forgotten to drop.

This lane inclined uphill all the way to Hay; having reached the middle, I sat down on a stile which led thence into a field. Gathering my mantle about me, and sheltering my hands in my muff, I did not feel the cold, though it froze keenly; as was attested by a sheet of ice covering the causeway, where a little brooklet, now congealed, had overflowed after a rapid thaw some days since. From my seat I could look down on Thornfield: the grey and battlemented hall was the principal object in the vale below me; its woods and dark rookery rose against the west. I lingered till the sun went down amongst the trees, and sank crimson and clear behind them. I then turned eastward.

On the hilltop above me sat the rising moon; pale yet as a cloud, but brightening momentarily, she looked over Hay, which, half lost in trees, sent up a blue smoke from its few chimneys: it was yet a mile distant, but in the absolute hush I could hear plainly its thin murmurs of life. My ear, too, felt the flow of currents; in what dales and depths I could not tell: but there were many hills beyond Hay, and doubtless many becks threading their passes. That evening calm betrayed alike the tinkle of the nearest streams, the sough of the most remote.

A rude noise broke on these fine ripplings and whisperings, at once so far away and so clear: a positive tramp, tramp, a metallic clatter, which effaced the soft wave-wanderings; as, in a picture, the solid mass of a crag, or the rough boles of a great oak, drawn in dark and strong on the foreground, efface the aerial distance of azure hill, sunny horizon, and blended clouds where tint melts into tint.

The din was on the causeway: a horse was coming; the windings of the lane yet hid it, but it approached. I was just leaving the stile; yet, as the path was narrow, I sat still to let it go by. In those days I was young, and all sorts of fancies bright and dark tenanted my mind: the memories of nursery stories were there amongst other rubbish; and when they recurred, maturing youth added to them a vigour and vividness beyond what childhood could give. As this horse approached, and as I watched for it to appear through the dusk, I remembered certain of Bessie's tales, wherein figured a North-of-England spirit called a 'Gytrash', which, in the form of horse, mule, or large dog, haunted solitary ways, and sometimes came upon belated travellers, as this horse was now coming upon me.

It was very near, but not yet in sight; when, in addition to the tramp, tramp, I heard a rush under the hedge, and close down by the hazel stems glided a great dog, whose black and white colour made him a distinct object against the trees. It was exactly one form of Bessie's Gytrash – a lion-like creature with long hair and a huge head: it passed me, however, quietly enough; not staying to look up, with strange pretercanine eyes, in my face, as I half expected it would. The horse followed, a tall steed, and on its back a rider. The man, the human being, broke the spell at once. Nothing ever rode the Gytrash: it was always alone; and goblins, to my notions, though they might tenant the dumb carcasses of beasts, could scarce covet shelter in the commonplace human form. No Gytrash was this, only a traveller taking the short cut to Millcote. He passed, and I went on; a few steps, and I turned: a sliding sound and an exclamation of 'What the deuce is to do now?' and a clattering tumble, arrested my attention. Man and horse were down; they had slipped on the sheet of ice which glazed the causeway. The dog came bounding back, and seeing his master in a predicament, and hearing the horse groan, barked till the evening hills echoed the sound, which was deep in proportion to his magnitude. He snuffed round the prostrate group, and then he ran up to me; it was all he could do, there was no other help at hand to summon. I obeyed him, and walked down to the traveller, by this time struggling himself free of his steed. His efforts were so vigorous, I thought he could not be much hurt; but I asked him the question – 'Are you injured, sir?'

I think he was swearing, but am not certain; however, he was pronouncing some formula which prevented him from replying to me directly.

'Can I do anything?' I asked again.

'You must just stand on one side,' he answered as he rose, first to his knees, and then to his feet. I did; whereupon began a heaving, stamping, clattering process, accompanied by a barking and baying which removed me effectually some yards' distance; but I would not be driven quite away till I saw the event. This was finally fortunate; the horse was re-established, and the dog was silenced with a 'Down, Pilot!' The traveller now, stooping, felt his foot and leg, as if trying whether they were sound; apparently something ailed them, for he halted to the stile whence I had just risen, and sat down.

I was in the mood for being useful, or at least officious, I think, for I now drew near him again.

'If you are hurt, and want help, sir, I can fetch someone either from Thornfield Hall or from Hay.'

'Thank you: I shall do: I have no broken bones, only a sprain;' and again he stood up and tried his foot, but the result extorted an involuntary 'Ugh!'

Something of daylight still lingered, and the moon was waxing bright: I could see him plainly. His figure was enveloped in a riding cloak, fur collared and steel clasped; its details were not apparent, but I traced the general points of middle height and considerable breadth of chest. He had a dark face, with stern features and a heavy brow; his eyes and gathered eyebrows looked ireful and thwarted just now; he was past youth, but had not reached middle-age; perhaps he might be thirty-five. I felt no fear of him and but little shyness. Had he been a handsome, heroic-looking young gentleman, I should not have dared to stand thus questioning him against his will, and offering my services unasked. I had hardly ever seen a handsome youth; never in my life spoken to one. I had a theoretical reverence and homage for beauty, elegance, gallantry, fascination; but had I met those qualities incarnate in masculine shape, I should have known instinctively that they neither had nor could have sympathy with anything in me, and should have shunned them as one would fire, lightning, or anything else that is bright but antipathetic.

If even this stranger had smiled and been good-humoured to me when I addressed him; if he had put off my offer of assistance gaily and with thanks, I should have gone on my way and not felt any vocation to renew enquiries: but the frown, the roughness of the traveller, set me at my ease: I retained my station when he waved to me to go, and announced – 'I cannot think of leaving you, sir, at so late an hour, in this solitary lane, till I see you are fit to mount your horse.'

He looked at me when I said this; he had hardly turned his eyes in my direction before.

'I should think you ought to be at home yourself,' said he, 'if you have a home in this neighbourhood: where do you come from?'

'From just below; and I am not at all afraid of being out late when it is moonlight: I will run over to Hay for you with pleasure, if you wish it: indeed, I am going there to post a letter.'

'You live just below – do you mean at that house with the battlements?' pointing to Thornfield Hall, on which the moon cast a hoary gleam, bringing it out distinct and pale from the woods, that, by contrast with the western sky, now seemed one mass of shadow.

'Yes, sir.'

'Whose house is it?'

'Mr Rochester's.'

'Do you know Mr Rochester?'

'No, I have never seen him.'

'He is not resident, then?'

'No.'

'Can you tell me where he is?'

'I cannot.'

'You are not a servant at the hall, of course. You are – ' He stopped, ran his eye over my dress, which, as usual, was quite simple: a black merino cloak, a black beaver bonnet; neither of them half fine enough for a lady's-maid. He seemed puzzled to decide what I was; I helped him.

'I am the governess.'

'Ah, the governess!' he repeated; 'deuce take me, if I had not forgotten! The governess!' and again my raiment underwent scrutiny. In two minutes he rose from the stile: his face expressed pain when he tried to move.

'I cannot commission you to fetch help,' he said; 'but you may help me a little yourself, if you will be so kind.'

'Yes, sir.'

'You have not an umbrella that I can use as a stick?'

'No.'

'Try to get hold of my horse's bridle and lead him to me: you are not afraid?'

I should have been afraid to touch a horse when alone, but when told to do it, I was disposed to obey. I put down my muff on the stile, and went up to the tall steed; I endeavoured to catch the bridle, but it was a spirited thing, and would not let me come near its head; I made effort on effort, though in vain: meantime, I was mortally afraid of its trampling forefeet. The traveller waited and watched for some time, and at last he laughed.

'I see,' he said, 'the mountain will never be brought to Muhammad, so all you can do is to aid Muhammad to go to the mountain; I must beg of you to come here.'

I came. 'Excuse me,' he continued: 'necessity compels me to make you useful.' He laid a heavy hand on my shoulder, and leaning on me with some stress, limped to his horse. Having once caught the bridle, he mastered it directly and sprang to his saddle; grimacing grimly as he made the effort, for it wrenched his sprain.

'Now,' said he, releasing his under lip from a hard bite, 'just hand me my whip; it lies there under the hedge.'

I sought it and found it.

'Thank you; now make haste with the letter to Hay, and return as fast as you can.'

A touch of a spurred heel made his horse first start and rear, and then bound away; the dog rushed in his traces; all three vanished,

Like heath that, in the wilderness,
The wild wind whirls away.

I took up my muff and walked on. The incident had occurred and was gone for me: it was an incident of no moment, no romance, no interest in a sense; yet it marked with change one single hour of a monotonous life. My help had been needed and claimed; I had given it: I was pleased to have done something; trivial, transitory though the deed was, it was yet an active thing, and I was weary of an existence all passive. The new face, too, was like a new picture introduced to the gallery of memory; and it was dissimilar to all the others hanging there: firstly, because it was masculine; and, secondly, because it was dark, strong, and stern. I had it still before me when I entered Hay, and slipped the letter into the post-office; I saw it as I walked fast downhill all the way home. When I came to the stile, I stopped a minute, looked round and listened, with an idea that a horse's hoofs might ring on the causeway again, and that a rider in a cloak, and a Gytrash-like Newfoundland dog, might be again apparent: I saw only the hedge and a pollard willow before me, rising up still and straight to meet the moon-beams; I heard only the faintest waft of wind roaming fitful among the trees round Thornfield, a mile distant; and when I glanced down in the direction of the murmur, my eye, traversing the hall-front, caught a light kindling in a window: it reminded me that I was late, and I hurried on.

I did not like re-entering Thornfield. To pass its threshold was to return to stagnation; to cross the silent hall, to ascend the darksome staircase, to seek my own lonely little room, and then to meet tranquil Mrs Fairfax, and spend the long winter evening with her, and her only, was to quell wholly the faint excitement wakened by my walk, to slip again over my faculties the viewless fetters of an uniform and too still existence; of an existence whose very privileges of security and ease I was becoming incapable of appreciating. What good it would have done me at that time to have been tossed in the storms of an uncertain struggling life, and to have been taught by rough and bitter experience to long for the calm amidst which I now repined! Yes, just as much good as it would do a man tired of sitting still in a 'too easy chair' to take a long walk: and just as natural was the wish to stir, under my circumstances, as it would be under his.

I lingered at the gates; I lingered on the lawn; I paced backwards and forwards on the pavement; the shutters of the glass door were closed; I could not see into the interior; and both my eyes and spirit seemed drawn from the gloomy house – from the grey hollow filled with rayless cells, as it appeared to me – to that sky expanded before me, a blue sea absolved from taint of cloud; the moon ascending it in solemn march; her orb seeming to look up as she left the hilltops, from behind which she had come, far and farther below her, and aspired to the zenith, midnight dark in its fathomless depth and measureless distance; and for those trembling stars that followed her course; they made my heart tremble, my veins glow when I viewed them. Little things recall us to earth; the clock struck in the hall; that sufficed; I turned from moon and stars, opened a side-door, and went in.

The hall was not dark, nor yet was it lit, only by the high-hung bronze lamp; a warm glow suffused both it and the lower steps of the oak staircase. This ruddy shine issued from the great dining-room, whose two-leaved door stood open, and showed a genial fire in the grate, glancing on marble hearth and brass fire-irons, and revealing purple draperies and polished furniture, in the most pleasant radiance. It revealed, too, a group near the mantelpiece: I had scarcely caught it, and scarcely become aware of a cheerful mingling of voices, amongst which I seemed to distinguish the tones of Adèle, when the door closed.

I hastened to Mrs Fairfax's room; there was a fire there too, but no candle, and no Mrs Fairfax. Instead, all alone, sitting upright on the rug, and gazing with gravity at the blaze, I beheld a great black and white long-haired dog, just like the Gytrash of the lane. It was so like it that I went forward and said – 'Pilot,' and the thing got up and came to me and snuffed me. I caressed him, and he wagged his great tail; but he looked an eerie creature to be alone with, and I could not tell whence he had come. I rang the bell, for I wanted a candle; and I wanted, too, to get an account of this visitant. Leah entered.

'What dog is this?'

'He came with master.'

'With whom?'

'With master – Mr Rochester – he is just arrived.'

'Indeed! and is Mrs Fairfax with him?'

'Yes, and Miss Adèle; they are in the dining-room, and John is gone for a surgeon; for master has had an accident; his horse fell and his ankle is sprained.'

'Did the horse fall in Hay Lane?'

'Yes, coming downhill; it slipped on some ice.'

'Ah! Bring me a candle, will you, Leah?'

Leah brought it; she entered, followed by Mrs Fairfax, who repeated the news; adding that Mr Carter the surgeon was come, and was now with Mr Rochester: then she hurried out to give orders about tea, and I went upstairs to take off my things.

# *Chapter 13*

Mr Rochester, it seems, by the surgeon's orders, went to bed early that night; nor did he rise soon next morning. When he did come down, it was to attend to business: his agent and some of his tenants were arrived, and waiting to speak with him.

Adèle and I had now to vacate the library: it would be in daily requisition as a reception-room for callers. A fire was lit in an apartment upstairs, and there I carried our books, and arranged it for the future schoolroom. I discerned in the course of the morning that Thornfield Hall was a changed place: no longer silent as a church, it echoed every hour or two to a knock at the door, or a clang of the bell: steps, too, often traversed the hall, and new voices spoke in different keys below; a rill from the outer world was flowing through it; it had a master: for my part, I liked it better.

Adèle was not easy to teach that day; she could not apply: she kept running to the door and looking over the banisters to see if she could get a glimpse of Mr Rochester; then she coined pretexts to go downstairs, in order, as I shrewdly suspected, to visit the library, where I knew she was not wanted; then, when I got a little angry, and made her sit still, she continued to talk incessantly of her 'ami, M. Edouard Fairfax *de* Rochester', as she dubbed him (I had not before heard his prenomens), and to conjecture what presents he had brought her: for it appears he had intimated the night before, that when his luggage came from Millcote, there would be found amongst it a little box in whose contents she had an interest.

'Et cela doit signifier,' said she, 'qu'il y aura là dedans un cadeau pour moi, et peut-être pour vous aussi, mademoiselle. Monsieur a parlé de vous: il m'a demandé le nom de ma gouvernante, et si elle n'était pas une petite personne, assez mince et un peu pâle. J'ai dit qu'oui: car c'est vrai, n'est-ce pas, mademoiselle?'

I and my pupil dined as usual in Mrs Fairfax's parlour; the afternoon was wild and snowy, and we passed it in the schoolroom. At dark I allowed Adèle to put away books and work, and to run downstairs; for, from the comparative silence below, and from the cessation of appeals to the doorbell, I conjectured that Mr Rochester was now at liberty. Left alone, I walked to the window; but nothing was to be seen thence: twilight and snowflakes together thickened the air, and hid the very shrubs on the lawn. I let down the curtain and went back to the fireside.

In the clear embers I was tracing a view, not unlike a picture I remembered to have seen of the castle of Heidelberg, on the Rhine, when Mrs Fairfax came in, breaking up by her entrance the fiery mosaic I had been piecing together, and scattering too some heavy unwelcome thoughts that were beginning to throng on my solitude.

'Mr Rochester would be glad if you and your pupil would take tea with him in the drawing-room this evening,' said she: 'he has been so much engaged all day that he could not ask to see you before.'

'When is his tea-time?' I enquired.

'Oh, at six o'clock: he keeps early hours in the country. You had better change your frock now; I will go with you and fasten it. Here is a candle.'

'Is it necessary to change my frock?'

'Yes, you had better: I always dress for the evening when Mr Rochester is here.'

This additional ceremony seemed somewhat stately; however, I repaired to my room, and, with Mrs Fairfax's aid, replaced my black stuff dress by one of black silk; the best and the only additional one I had, except one of light grey, which, in my Lowood notions of the toilette, I thought too fine to be worn, except on first-rate occasions.

'You want a brooch,' said Mrs Fairfax. I had a single little pearl ornament which Miss Temple gave me as a parting keepsake: I put it on, and then we went downstairs. Unused as I was to strangers, it was rather a trial to appear thus formally summoned in Mr Rochester's presence. I let Mrs Fairfax precede me into the dining-room, and kept in her shade as we crossed that apartment; and, passing the arch, whose curtain was now dropped, entered the elegant recess beyond.

Two wax candles stood lighted on the table, and two on the mantelpiece; basking in the light and heat of a superb fire, lay Pilot – Adèle knelt near him. Half reclined on a couch appeared Mr Rochester, his foot supported by the cushion; he was looking at Adèle and the dog: the fire shone full on his face. I knew my traveller with his broad and jetty eyebrows; his square forehead, made squarer by the horizontal sweep of his black hair. I recognised his decisive nose, more remarkable for character than beauty; his full nostrils, denoting, I thought, choler; his grim mouth, chin, and jaw – yes, all three were very grim, and no mistake. His shape, now divested of cloak, I perceived harmonised in squareness with his physiognomy: I suppose it was a good figure in the athletic sense of the term – broad chested and thin flanked, though neither tall nor graceful.

Mr Rochester must have been aware of the entrance of Mrs Fairfax and myself; but it appeared he was not in the mood to notice us, for he never lifted his head as we approached.

'Here is Miss Eyre, sir,' said Mrs Fairfax, in her quiet way. He bowed, still not taking his eyes from the group of the dog and child.

'Let Miss Eyre be seated,' said he: and there was something in the forced stiff bow, in the impatient yet formal tone, which seemed further to express, 'What the deuce is it to me whether Miss Eyre be there or not? At this moment I am not disposed to accost her.'

I sat down quite disembarrassed. A reception of finished politeness would probably have confused me: I could not have returned or repaid it by answering grace and elegance on my part; but harsh caprice laid me under no obligation; on the contrary, a decent quiescence, under the freak of manner, gave me the advantage. Besides, the eccentricity of the proceeding was piquant: I felt interested to see how he would go on.

He went on as a statue would, that is, he neither spoke nor moved. Mrs Fairfax seemed to think it necessary that someone should be amiable, and she began to talk. Kindly, as usual – and, as usual, rather trite – she condoled with him on the pressure of business he had had all day; on the annoyance it must have been to him with that painful sprain: then she commended his patience and perseverance in going through with it.

'Madam, I should like some tea,' was the sole rejoinder she got. She hastened to ring the bell; and when the tray came, she proceeded to arrange the cups, spoons, etc., with assiduous celerity. I and Adèle went to the table; but the master did not leave his couch.

'Will you hand Mr Rochester's cup?' said Mrs Fairfax to me; 'Adèle might perhaps spill it.'

I did as requested. As he took the cup from my hand, Adèle, thinking the moment propitious for making a request in my favour, cried out – 'N'est-ce pas, monsieur, qu'il y a un cadeau pour Mlle Eyre dans votre petit coffre?'

'Who talks of cadeaux?' said he gruffly. 'Did you expect a present, Miss Eyre? Are you fond of presents?' and he searched my face with eyes that I saw were dark, irate, and piercing.

'I hardly know, sir; I have little experience of them: they are generally thought pleasant things.'

'Generally thought? But what do *you* think?'

'I should be obliged to take time, sir, before I could give you an answer worthy of your acceptance: a present has many faces to it, has it not? and one should consider all, before pronouncing an opinion as to its nature.'

'Miss Eyre, you are not so unsophisticated as Adèle: she demands a "cadeau", clamorously, the moment she sees me: you beat about the bush.'

'Because I have less confidence in my deserts than Adèle has: she can prefer the claim of old acquaintance, and the right too of custom; for she says you have always been in the habit of giving her playthings; but if I had to make out a case I should be puzzled, since I am a stranger, and have done nothing to entitle me to an acknowledgement.'

'Oh, don't fall back on over-modesty! I have examined Adèle, and find you have taken great pains with her: she is not bright, she has no talents; yet in a short time she has made much improvement.'

'Sir, you have now given me my "cadeau"; I am obliged to you: it is the meed teachers most covet – praise of their pupils' progress.'

'Humph!' said Mr Rochester, and he took his tea in silence.

'Come to the fire,' said the master, when the tray was taken away, and Mrs Fairfax had settled into a corner with her knitting; while Adèle was leading me by the hand round the room, showing me the beautiful books and ornaments on the consoles and chiffonnières. We obeyed, as in duty bound; Adèle wanted to take a seat on my knee, but she was ordered to amuse herself with Pilot.

'You have been resident in my house three months?'

'Yes, sir.'

'And you came from?'

'From Lowood School, in —shire.'

'Ah! a charitable concern. How long were you there?'

'Eight years.'

'Eight years! you must be tenacious of life. I thought half the time in such a place would have done up any constitution! No wonder you have rather the look of another world. I marvelled where you had got that sort of face. When you came on me in Hay Lane last night, I thought unaccountably of fairy tales, and had half a mind to demand whether you had bewitched my horse: I am not sure yet. Who are your parents?'

'I have none.'

'Nor ever had, I suppose: do you remember them?'

'No.'

'I thought not. And so you were waiting for your people when you sat on that stile?'

'For whom, sir?'

'For the men in green: it was a proper moonlight evening for them. Did I break through one of your rings, that you spread that damned ice on the causeway?'

I shook my head. 'The men in green all forsook England a hundred years ago,' said I, speaking as seriously as he had done. 'And not even in Hay Lane, or the fields about it, could you find a trace of them. I don't think either summer or harvest, or winter moon, will ever shine on their revels more.'

Mrs Fairfax had dropped her knitting, and, with raised eyebrows, seemed wondering what sort of talk this was.

'Well,' resumed Mr Rochester, 'if you disown parents, you must have some sort of kinsfolk: uncles and aunts?'

'No; none that I ever saw.'

'And your home?'

'I have none.'

'Where do your brothers and sisters live?'

'I have no brothers or sisters.'

'Who recommended you to come here?'

'I advertised, and Mrs Fairfax answered my advertisement.'

'Yes,' said the good lady, who now knew what ground we were upon, 'and I am daily thankful for the choice Providence led me to make. Miss Eyre has been an invaluable companion to me, and a kind and careful teacher to Adèle.'

'Don't trouble yourself to give her a character,' returned Mr Rochester: 'eulogiums will not bias me; I shall judge for myself. She began by felling my horse.'

'Sir?' said Mrs Fairfax.

'I have to thank her for this sprain.'

The widow looked bewildered.

'Miss Eyre, have you ever lived in a town?'

'No, sir.'

'Have you seen much society?'

'None but the pupils and teachers of Lowood, and now the inmates of Thornfield.'

'Have you read much?'

'Only such books as came in my way; and they have not been numerous or very learned.'

'You have lived the life of a nun: no doubt you are well drilled in religious forms; Brocklehurst, who I understand directs Lowood, is a parson, is he not?'

'Yes, sir.'

'And you girls probably worshipped him, as a convent full of *religieuses* would worship their director.'

'Oh, no.'

'You are very cool! No! What! a novice not worship her priest! That sounds blasphemous.'

'I disliked Mr Brocklehurst; and I was not alone in the feeling. He is a harsh man; at once pompous and meddling; he cut off our hair; and for economy's sake bought us bad needles and thread, with which we could hardly sew.'

'That was very false economy,' remarked Mrs Fairfax, who now again caught the drift of the dialogue.

'And was that the head and front of his offending?' demanded Mr Rochester.

'He starved us when he had the sole superintendence of the provision department, before the committee was appointed; and he bored us with long lectures once a week, and with evening readings from books of his own inditing, about sudden deaths and judgements, which made us afraid to go to bed.'

'What age were you when you went to Lowood?'

'About ten.'

'And you stayed there eight years: you are now, then, eighteen?'

I assented.

'Arithmetic, you see, is useful; without its aid, I should hardly have been able to guess your age. It is a point difficult to fix where the features and countenance are so much at variance as in your case. And now what did you learn at Lowood? Can you play?'

'A little.'

'Of course: that is the established answer. Go into the library – I mean, if you please. (Excuse my tone of command; I am used to say, "Do this," and it is done: I cannot alter my customary habits for one new inmate.) – Go, then, into the library; take a candle with you; leave the door open; sit down to the piano, and play a tune.'

I departed, obeying his directions.

'Enough!' he called out in a few minutes. 'You play *a little*, I see; like any other English schoolgirl; perhaps rather better than some, but not well.'

I closed the piano and returned. Mr Rochester continued – 'Adèle showed me some sketches this morning, which she said were yours. I don't know whether they were entirely of your doing; probably a master aided you?'

'No, indeed!' I interjected.

'Ah! that pricks pride. Well, fetch me your portfolio, if you can vouch for its contents being original; but don't pass your word unless you are certain: I can recognise patchwork.'

'Then I will say nothing, and you shall judge for yourself, sir.'

I brought the portfolio from the library.

'Approach the table,' said he; and I wheeled it to his couch. Adèle and Mrs Fairfax drew near to see the pictures.

'No crowding,' said Mr Rochester: 'take the drawings from my hand as I finish with them; but don't push your faces up to mine.'

He deliberately scrutinised each sketch and painting. Three he laid aside; the others, when he had examined them, he swept from him.

'Take them off to the other table, Mrs Fairfax,' said he, 'and look at them with Adèle; you' (glancing at me) 'resume your seat, and answer my questions. I perceive those pictures were done by one hand: was that hand yours?'

'Yes.'

'And when did you find time to do them? They have taken much time, and some thought.'

'I did them in the last two vacations I spent at Lowood, when I had no other occupation.'

'Where did you get your copies?'

'Out of my head.'

'That head I see now on your shoulders?'

'Yes, sir.'

'Has it other furniture of the same kind within?'

'I should think it may have: I should hope – better.'

He spread the pictures before him, and again surveyed them alternately.

While he is so occupied, I will tell you, reader, what they are: and first, I must premise that they are nothing wonderful. The subjects had, indeed, risen vividly on my mind. As I saw them with the spiritual eye, before I attempted to embody them, they were striking; but my hand would not second my fancy, and in each case it had wrought out but a pale portrait of the thing I had conceived.

These pictures were in watercolours. The first represented clouds low and livid, rolling over a swollen sea: all the distance was in eclipse; so, too, was the foreground; or rather, the nearest billows, for there was no land. One gleam of light lifted into relief a half-submerged mast, on which sat a cormorant, dark and large, with wings flecked with foam; its beak held a gold bracelet set with gems, that I had touched with as brilliant tints as my palette could yield, and as glittering distinctness as my pencil could impart. Sinking below the bird and mast, a drowned corpse glanced through the green water; a fair arm was the only limb clearly visible, whence the bracelet had been washed or torn.

The second picture contained for foreground only the dim peak of a hill, with grass and some leaves slanting as if by a breeze. Beyond and above spread an expanse of sky, dark blue as at twilight: rising into the sky was a woman's shape to the bust, portrayed in tints as dusk and soft as I could combine. The dim forehead was crowned with a star; the lineaments below were seen as through the suffusion of vapour; the eyes shone dark and wild; the hair streamed shadowy, like a beamless cloud torn by storm or by electric travail. On the neck lay a pale reflection like moonlight; the same faint lustre touched the train of thin clouds from which rose and bowed this vision of the Evening Star.

The third showed the pinnacle of an iceberg piercing a polar winter sky: a muster of northern lights reared their dim lances, close serried, along the horizon. Throwing these into distance, rose, in the foreground, a head, a colossal head, inclined towards the iceberg, and resting against it. Two thin hands, joined under the forehead, and supporting it, drew up before the lower features a sable veil; a brow quite bloodless, white as bone, and an eye hollow and fixed, blank of meaning but for the glassiness of despair, alone were visible. Above the temples, amidst wreathed turban folds of black drapery, vague in its character and consistency as cloud, gleamed a ring of white flame, gemmed with sparkles of a more lurid tinge. This pale crescent was 'the likeness of a kingly crown'; what it diademed was 'the shape which shape had none.'

'Were you happy when you painted these pictures?' asked Mr Rochester presently.

'I was absorbed, sir: yes, and I was happy. To paint them, in short, was to enjoy one of the keenest pleasures I have ever known.'

'That is not saying much. Your pleasures, by your own account, have been few; but I dare say you did exist in a kind of artist's dreamland while you blent and arranged these strange tints. Did you sit at them long each day?'

'I had nothing else to do, because it was the vacation, and I sat at them from morning till noon, and from noon till night: the length of the midsummer days favoured my inclination to apply.'

'And you felt self-satisfied with the result of your ardent labours?'

'Far from it. I was tormented by the contrast between my idea and my handiwork: in each case I had imagined something which I was quite powerless to realise.'

'Not quite: you have secured the shadow of your thought; but no more, probably. You had not enough of the artist's skill and science to give it full being: yet the drawings are, for a schoolgirl, peculiar. As to the thoughts, they are elfish. These eyes in the Evening Star you must have seen in a dream. How could you make them look so clear, and yet not at all brilliant? for the planet above quells their rays. And what meaning is that in their solemn depth? And who taught you to paint wind. There is a high gale in that sky, and on this hilltop. Where did you see Latmos? For that is Latmos. There! put the drawings away!'

I had scarce tied the strings of the portfolio, when, looking at his watch, he said abruptly – 'It is nine o'clock: what are you about, Miss Eyre, to let Adèle sit up so long? Take her to bed.'

Adèle went to kiss him before quitting the room: he endured the caress, but scarcely seemed to relish it more than Pilot would have done, nor so much.

'I wish you all good-night, now,' said he, making a movement of the hand towards the door, in token that he was tired of our company, and wished to dismiss us. Mrs Fairfax folded up her knitting: I took my portfolio: we curtseyed to him, received a frigid bow in return, and so withdrew.

'You said Mr Rochester was not strikingly peculiar, Mrs Fairfax,' I observed, when I rejoined her in her room, after putting Adèle to bed.

'Well, is he?'

'I think so: he is very changeful and abrupt.'

'True: no doubt he may appear so to a stranger, but I am so accustomed to his manner, I never think of it; and then, if he has peculiarities of temper, allowance should be made.'

'Why?'

'Partly because it is his nature – and we can none of us help our nature; and partly because he has painful thoughts, no doubt, to harass him, and make his spirits unequal.'

'What about?'

'Family troubles, for one thing.'

'But he has no family.'

'Not now, but he has had – or, at least, relatives. He lost his elder brother a few years since.'

'His *elder* brother?'

'Yes. The present Mr Rochester has not been very long in possession of the property; only about nine years.'

'Nine years is a tolerable time. Was he so very fond of his brother as to be still inconsolable for his loss?'

'Why, no – perhaps not. I believe there were some misunderstandings between them. Mr Rowland Rochester was not quite just to Mr Edward; and perhaps he prejudiced his father against him. The old gentleman was fond of money, and anxious to keep the family estate together. He did not like to diminish the property by division, and yet he was anxious that Mr Edward should have wealth, too, to keep up the consequence of the name; and, soon after he was of age, some steps were taken that were not quite fair, and made a great deal of mischief. Old Mr Rochester and Mr Rowland combined to bring Mr Edward into what he considered a painful position, for the sake of making his fortune: what the precise nature of that position was I never clearly knew, but his spirit could not brook what he had to suffer in it. He is not very forgiving: he broke with his family, and now for many years he has led an unsettled kind of life. I don't think he has ever been resident at Thornfield for a fortnight together, since the death of his brother without a will left him master of the estate; and, indeed, no wonder he shuns the old place.'

'Why should he shun it?'

'Perhaps he thinks it gloomy.'

The answer was evasive. I should have liked something clearer; but Mrs Fairfax either could not, or would not, give me more explicit information of the origin and nature of Mr Rochester's trials. She averred they were a mystery to herself, and that what she knew was chiefly from conjecture. It was evident, indeed, that she wished me to drop the subject, which I did accordingly.

## *Chapter 14*

For several subsequent days I saw little of Mr Rochester. In the mornings he seemed much engaged with business, and, in the afternoon, gentlemen from Millcote or the neighbourhood called, and sometimes stayed to dine with him. When his sprain was well enough to admit of horse exercise, he rode out a good deal; probably to return these visits, as he generally did not come back till late at night.

During this interval, even Adèle was seldom sent for to his presence, and all my acquaintance with him was confined to an occasional *rencontre* in the hall, on the stairs, or in the gallery, when he would sometimes pass me haughtily and coldly, just acknowledging my presence by a distant nod or a cool glance, and sometimes bow and smile with gentlemanlike affability. His changes of mood did not offend me, because I saw that I had nothing to do with their alternation; the ebb and flow depended on causes quite disconnected with me.

One day he had had company to dinner, and had sent for my portfolio; in order, doubtless, to exhibit its contents: the gentlemen went away early, to attend a public meeting at Millcote, as Mrs Fairfax informed me; but the night being wet and inclement, Mr Rochester did not accompany them. Soon after they were gone he rang the bell: a message came that I and Adèle were to go downstairs. I brushed Adèle's hair and made her neat, and having ascertained that I was myself in my usual Quaker trim, where there was nothing to retouch – all being too close and plain, braided locks included, to admit of disarrangement – we descended, Adèle wondering whether the *petit coffre* was at length come; for, owing to some mistake, its arrival had hitherto been delayed. She was gratified: there it stood, a little carton, on the table when we entered the dining-room. She appeared to know it by instinct.

'Ma boîte! ma boîte!' exclaimed she, running towards it.

'Yes, there is your "boîte" at last: take it into a corner, you genuine daughter of Paris, and amuse yourself with disembowelling it,' said the deep and rather sarcastic voice of Mr Rochester, proceeding from the depths of an immense easy-chair at the fireside. 'And mind,' he continued, 'don't bother me with any details of the anatomical process, or any notice of the condition of the entrails: let your operation be conducted in silence: tiens-toi tranquille, enfant; comprends-tu?'

Adèle seemed scarcely to need the warning; she had already retired to a sofa with her treasure, and was busy untying the cord which secured the lid. Having removed this impediment, and lifted certain silvery envelopes of tissue paper, she merely exclaimed – 'Oh ciel! Que c'est beau!' and then remained absorbed in ecstatic contemplation.

'Is Miss Eyre there?' now demanded the master, half rising from his seat to look round to the door, near which I still stood.

'Ah! well, come forward; be seated here.' He drew a chair near his own. 'I am not fond of the prattle of children,' he continued; 'for, old bachelor as I am, I have no pleasant associations connected with their lisp. It would be intolerable to me to pass a whole evening tête-à-tête with a brat. Don't draw that chair farther off, Miss Eyre; sit down exactly where I placed it – if you please, that is. Confound these civilities! I continually forget them. Nor do I particularly affect simple-minded old ladies. By the by, I must have mine in mind; it won't do to neglect her; she is a Fairfax, or wed to one; and blood is said to be thicker than water.'

He rang, and despatched an invitation to Mrs Fairfax, who soon arrived, knitting-basket in hand.

'Good-evening, madam; I sent to you for a charitable purpose. I have forbidden Adèle to talk to me about her presents, and she is bursting with repletion; have the goodness to serve her as auditress and interlocutrice; it will be one of the most benevolent acts you ever performed.'

Adèle, indeed, no sooner saw Mrs Fairfax, than she summoned her to her sofa, and there quickly filled her lap with the porcelain, the ivory, the waxen contents of her 'boîte'; pouring out, meantime, explanations and raptures in such broken English as she was mistress of.

'Now I have performed the part of a good host,' pursued Mr Rochester, 'put my guests into the way of amusing each other, I ought to be at liberty to attend to my own pleasure. Miss Eyre, draw your chair still a little farther forward: you are yet too far back; I cannot see you without disturbing my position in this comfortable chair, which I have no mind to do.'

I did as I was bid, though I would much rather have remained somewhat in the shade; but Mr Rochester had such a direct way of giving orders, it seemed a matter of course to obey him promptly.

We were, as I have said, in the dining-room: the lustre, which had been lit for dinner, filled the room with a festal breadth of light; the large fire was all red and clear; the purple curtains hung rich and ample before the lofty window and loftier arch; everything was still, save the subdued chat of Adèle (she dared not speak loud), and, filling up each pause, the beating of winter rain against the panes.

Mr Rochester, as he sat in his damask-covered chair, looked different to what I had seen him look before; not quite so stern – much less gloomy. There was a smile on his lips, and his eyes sparkled, whether with wine or not, I am not sure; but I think it very probable. He was, in short, in his after-dinner mood; more expanded and genial, and also more self-indulgent than the frigid and rigid temper of the morning; still he looked preciously grim, cushioning his massive head against the swelling back of his chair, and receiving the light of the fire on his granite-hewn features, and in his great, dark eyes; for he had great, dark eyes, and very fine eyes, too – not without a certain change in their depths sometimes, which, if it was not softness, reminded you, at least, of that feeling.

He had been looking two minutes at the fire, and I had been looking the same length of time at him, when, turning suddenly, he caught my gaze fastened on his physiognomy.

'You examine me, Miss Eyre,' said he: 'do you think me handsome?'

I should, if I had deliberated, have replied to this question by something conventionally vague and polite; but the answer somehow slipped from my tongue before I was aware – 'No, sir.'

'Ah! By my word! there is something singular about you,' said he: 'you have the air of a little *nonnette*; quaint, quiet, grave, and simple, as you sit with your hands before you, and your eyes generally bent on the carpet (except, by the by, when they are directed piercingly to my face; as just now, for instance); and when one asks you a question, or makes a remark to which you are obliged to reply, you rap out a round rejoinder, which, if not blunt, is at least brusque. What do you mean by it?'

'Sir, I was too plain; I beg your pardon. I ought to have replied that it was not easy to give an impromptu answer to a question about appearances; that tastes mostly differ; and that beauty is of little consequence, or something of that sort.'

'You ought to have replied no such thing. Beauty of little consequence, indeed! And so, under pretence of softening the previous outrage, of stroking and soothing me into placidity, you stick a sly penknife under my ear! Go on: what fault do you find with me, pray? I suppose I have all my limbs and all my features like any other man?'

'Mr Rochester, allow me to disown my first answer: I intended no pointed repartee: it was only a blunder.'

'Just so: I think so: and you shall be answerable for it. Criticise me: does my forehead not please you?'

He lifted up the sable waves of hair which lay horizontally over his brow, and showed a solid enough mass of intellectual organs, but an abrupt deficiency where the suave sign of benevolence should have risen.

'Now, ma'am, am I a fool?'

'Far from it, sir. You would, perhaps, think me rude if I enquired in return whether you are a philanthropist?'

'There again! Another stick of the penknife, when she pretended to pat my head: and that is because I said I did not like the society of children and old women (low be it spoken!). No, young lady, I am not a general philanthropist; but I bear a conscience'; and he pointed to the prominences which are said to indicate that faculty, and which, fortunately for him, were sufficiently conspicuous; giving, indeed, a marked breadth to the upper part of his head: 'and, besides, I once had a kind of rude tenderness of heart. When I was as old as you, I was a feeling fellow enough; partial to the unfledged, unfostered, and unlucky; but Fortune has knocked me about since: she has even kneaded me with her knuckles, and now I flatter myself I am hard and tough as an India-rubber ball; pervious, though, through a chink or two still, and with one sentient point in the middle of the lump. Yes: does that leave hope for me?'

'Hope of what, sir?'

'Of my final re-transformation from India-rubber back to flesh?'

'Decidedly he has had too much wine,' I thought; and I did not know what answer to make to his queer question: how could I tell whether he was capable of being re-transformed?

'You looked very much puzzled, Miss Eyre; and though you are not pretty any more than I am handsome, yet a puzzled air becomes you; besides, it is convenient, for it keeps those searching eyes of yours away from my physiognomy, and busies them with the worsted flowers of the rug; so puzzle on. Young lady, I am disposed to be gregarious and communicative tonight.'

With this announcement he rose from his chair, and stood, leaning his arm on the marble mantelpiece: in that attitude his shape was seen plainly as well as his face; his unusual breadth of chest, disproportionate almost to his length of limb. I am sure most people would have thought him an ugly man; yet there was so much unconscious pride in his port; so much ease in his demeanour; such a look of complete indifference to his own external appearance; so haughty a reliance on the power of other qualities, intrinsic or adventitious, to atone for the lack of mere personal attractiveness, that, in looking at him, one inevitably shared the indifference, and, even in a blind, imperfect sense, put faith in the confidence.

'I am disposed to be gregarious and communicative tonight,' he repeated, 'and that is why I sent for you: the fire and the chandelier were not sufficient company for me; nor would Pilot have been, for none of these can talk. Adèle is a degree better, but still far below the mark; Mrs Fairfax ditto; you, I am persuaded, can suit me if you will: you puzzled me the first evening I invited you down here. I have almost forgotten you since: other ideas have driven yours from my head; but tonight I am resolved to be at ease; to dismiss what importunes, and recall what pleases. It would please me now to draw you out – to learn more of you – therefore speak.'

Instead of speaking, I smiled; and not a very complacent or submissive smile either.

'Speak,' he urged.

'What about, sir?'

'Whatever you like. I leave both the choice of subject and the manner of treating it entirely to yourself.'

Accordingly I sat and said nothing: 'If he expects me to talk for the mere sake of talking and showing off, he will find he has addressed himself to the wrong person,' I thought.

'You are dumb, Miss Eyre.'

I was dumb still. He bent his head a little towards me, and with a single hasty glance seemed to dive into my eyes.

'Stubborn?' he said, 'and annoyed. Ah! it is consistent. I put my request in an absurd, almost insolent form. Miss Eyre, I beg your pardon. The fact is, once for all, I don't wish to treat you like an inferior: that is' (correcting himself), 'I claim only such superiority as must result from twenty years' difference in age and a century's advance in experience. This is legitimate, *et j'y tiens*, as Adèle would say; and it is by virtue of this superiority, and this alone, that I desire you to have the goodness to talk to me a little now, and divert my thoughts, which are galled with dwelling on one point – cankering as a rusty nail.'

He had deigned an explanation, almost an apology, and I did not feel insensible to his condescension, and would not seem so.

'I am willing to amuse you, if I can, sir – quite willing; but I cannot introduce a topic, because how do I know what will interest you? Ask me questions, and I will do my best to answer them.'

'Then, in the first place, do you agree with me that I have a right to be a little masterful, abrupt, perhaps exacting, sometimes, on the grounds I stated, namely, that I am old enough to be your father, and that I have battled through a varied experience with many men of many nations, and roamed over half the globe, while you have lived quietly with one set of people in one house?'

'Do as you please, sir.'

'That is no answer; or rather it is a very irritating, because a very evasive one. Reply clearly.'

'I don't think, sir, you have a right to command me, merely because you are older than I, or because you have seen more of the world than I have; your claim to superiority depends on the use you have made of your time and experience.'

'Humph! Promptly spoken. But I won't allow that, seeing that it would never suit my case, as I have made an indifferent, not to say a bad, use of both advantages. Leaving superiority out of the question, then, you must still agree to receive my orders now and then, without being piqued or hurt by the tone of command. Will you?'

I smiled: I thought to myself Mr Rochester is peculiar – he seems to forget that he pays me £30 per annum for receiving his orders.

'The smile is very well,' said he, catching instantly the passing expression; 'but speak too.'

'I was thinking, sir, that very few masters would trouble themselves to enquire whether or not their paid subordinates were piqued and hurt by their orders.'

'Paid subordinates! What! you are my paid subordinate, are you? Oh yes, I had forgotten the salary! Well then, on that mercenary ground, will you agree to let me hector a little?'

'No, sir, not on that ground; but, on the ground that you did forget it, and that you care whether or not a dependant is comfortable in his dependency, I agree heartily.'

'And will you consent to dispense with a great many conventional forms and phrases, without thinking that the omission arises from insolence?'

'I am sure, sir, I should never mistake informality for insolence: one I rather like, the other nothing free-born would submit to, even for a salary.'

'Humbug! Most things free-born will submit to anything for a salary; therefore, keep to yourself, and don't venture on generalities of which you are intensely ignorant. However, I mentally shake hands with you for your answer, despite its inaccuracy; and as much for the manner in which it was said, as for the substance of the speech; the manner was frank and sincere; one does not often see such a manner: no, on the contrary, affectation, or coldness, or stupid, coarse-minded misapprehension of one's meaning are the usual rewards of candour. Not three in three thousand raw school-girl-governesses would have answered me as you have just done. But I don't mean to flatter you: if you are cast in a different mould to the majority, it is no merit of yours: Nature did it. And then, after all, I go too fast in my conclusions: for what I yet know, you may be no better than the rest; you may have intolerable defects to counterbalance your few good points.'

'And so may you,' I thought. My eye met his as the idea crossed my mind: he seemed to read the glance, answering as if its import had been spoken as well as imagined – 'Yes, yes, you are right,' said he; 'I have plenty of faults of my own: I know it, and I don't wish to palliate them, I assure you. God wot I need not be too severe about others; I have a past existence, a series of deeds, a colour of life to contemplate within my own breast, which might well call my sneers and censures from my neighbours to myself. I started, or rather (for like other defaulters, I like to lay half the blame on ill fortune and adverse circumstances) was thrust on to a wrong tack at the age of one-and-twenty, and have never recovered the right course since: but I might have been very different; I might have been as good as you – wiser – almost as stainless. I envy you your peace of mind, your clean conscience, your unpolluted memory. Little girl, a memory without blot or contamination must be an exquisite treasure – an inexhaustible source of pure refreshment: is it not?'

'How was your memory when you were eighteen, sir?'

'All right then; limpid, salubrious: no gush of bilge water had turned it to fetid puddle. I was your equal at eighteen – quite your equal. Nature meant me to be, on the whole, a good man, Miss Eyre; one of the better kind, and you see I am not so. You would say you don't see it; at least I flatter myself I read as much in your eye (beware, by the by, what you express with that organ; I am quick at interpreting its language). Then take my word for it, I am not a villain: you are not to suppose that – not to attribute to me any such bad eminence; but, owing, I verily believe, rather to circumstances than to my natural bent, I am a trite commonplace sinner, hackneyed in all the poor petty dissipations with which the rich and worthless try to put on life. Do you wonder that I avow this to you? Know, that in the course of your future life you will often find yourself elected the involuntary confidant of your acquaintances' secrets: people will instinctively find out, as I have done, that it is not your forte to tell of yourself, but to listen while others talk of themselves; they will feel, too, that you listen with no malevolent scorn of their indiscretion, but with a kind of innate sympathy; not the less comforting and encouraging because it is very unobtrusive in its manifestations.'

'How do you know? – how can you guess all this, sir?'

'I know it well; therefore I proceed almost as freely as if I were writing my thoughts in a diary. You would say, I should have been superior to circumstances; so I should – so I should; but you see I was not. When fate wronged me, I had not the wisdom to remain cool: I turned desperate; then I degenerated. Now, when any vicious simpleton excites my disgust by his paltry ribaldry, I cannot flatter myself that I am better than he: I am forced to confess that he and I are on a level. I wish I had stood firm – God knows I do! Dread remorse when you are tempted to err, Miss Eyre; remorse is the poison of life.'

'Repentance is said to be its cure, sir.'

'It is not its cure. Reformation may be its cure; and I could reform – I have strength yet for that – if – but where is the use of thinking of it, hampered, burdened, cursed as I am? Besides, since happiness is irrevocably denied me, I have a right to get pleasure out of life: and I *will* get it, cost what it may.'

'Then you will degenerate still more, sir.'

'Possibly: yet why should I, if I can get sweet, fresh pleasure? And I may get it as sweet and fresh as the wild honey the bee gathers on the moor.'

'It will sting – it will taste bitter, sir.'

'How do you know? – you never tried it. How very serious – how very solemn you look: and you are as ignorant of the matter as this cameo head' (taking one from the mantelpiece). 'You have no right to preach to me, you neophyte, that have not passed the porch of life, and are absolutely unacquainted with its mysteries.'

'I only remind you of your own words, sir: you said error brought remorse, and you pronounced remorse the poison of existence.'

'And who talks of error now? I scarcely think the notion that flittered across my brain was an error. I believe it was an inspiration rather than a temptation: it was very genial, very soothing – I know that. Here it comes again! It is no devil, I assure you; or if it be, it has put on the robes of an angel of light. I think I must admit so fair a guest when it asks entrance to my heart.'

'Distrust it, sir; it is not a true angel.'

'Once more, how do you know? By what instinct do you pretend to distinguish between a fallen seraph of the abyss and a messenger from the eternal throne – between a guide and a seducer?'

'I judged by your countenance, sir, which was troubled when you said the suggestion had returned upon you. I feel sure it will work you more misery if you listen to it.'

'Not at all – it bears the most gracious message in the world: for the rest, you are not my conscience-keeper, so don't make yourself uneasy. Here, come in, bonny wanderer!'

He said this as if he spoke to a vision, viewless to any eye but his own; then, folding his arms, which he had half extended, on his chest, he seemed to enclose in their embrace the invisible being.

'Now,' he continued, again addressing me, 'I have received the pilgrim – a disguised deity, as I verily believe. Already it has done me good: my heart was a sort of charnel; it will now be a shrine.'

'To speak truth, sir, I don't understand you at all: I cannot keep up the conversation, because it has got out of my depth. Only one thing, I know: you said you were not as good as you should like to be, and that you regretted your own imperfection; one thing I can comprehend: you intimated that to have a sullied memory was a perpetual bane. It seems to me, that if you tried hard, you would in time find it possible to become what you yourself would approve; and that if from this day you began with resolution to correct your thoughts and actions, you would in a few years have laid up a new and stainless store of recollections, to which you might revert with pleasure.'

'Justly thought; rightly said, Miss Eyre; and, at this moment, I am paving hell with energy.'

'Sir?'

'I am laying down good intentions, which I believe durable as flint. Certainly, my associates and pursuits shall be other than they have been.'

'And better?'

'And better – so much better as pure ore is than foul dross. You seem to doubt me; I don't doubt myself: I know what my aim is, what my motives are; and at this moment I pass a law, unalterable as that of the Medes and Persians, that both are right.'

'They cannot be, sir, if they require a new statute to legalise them.'

'They are, Miss Eyre, though they absolutely require a new statute: unheard-of combinations or circumstances demand unheard-of rules.'

'That sounds a dangerous maxim, sir; because one can see at once that it is liable to abuse.'

'Sententious sage! so it is: but I swear by my household gods not to abuse it.'

'You are human and fallible.'

'I am: so are you – what then?'

'The human and fallible should not arrogate a power with which the divine and perfect alone can be safely entrusted.'

'What power?'

'That of saying of any strange, unsanctioned line of action, "Let it be right." '

' "Let it be right" – the very words: you have pronounced them.'

'*May* it be right then,' I said, as I rose, deeming it useless to continue a discourse which was all darkness to me; and, besides, sensible that the character of my interlocutor was beyond my penetration; at least, beyond its present reach; and feeling the uncertainty, the vague sense of insecurity, which accompanies a conviction of ignorance.

'Where are you going?'

'To put Adèle to bed: it is past her bedtime.'

'You are afraid of me, because I talk like a Sphynx.'

'Your language is enigmatical, sir: but though I am bewildered, I am certainly not afraid.'

'You *are* afraid – your self-love dreads a blunder.'

'In that sense I do feel apprehensive – I have no wish to talk nonsense.'

'If you did, it would be in such a grave, quiet manner, I should mistake it for sense. Do you never laugh, Miss Eyre? Don't trouble yourself to answer – I see you laugh rarely; but you can laugh very merrily: believe me, you are not naturally austere, any more than I am naturally vicious. The Lowood constraint still clings to you somewhat; controlling your features, muffling your voice, and restricting your limbs; and you fear in the presence of a man and a brother – or father, or master, or what you will – to smile too gaily, speak too freely, or move too quickly: but, in time, I think you will learn to be natural with me, as I find it impossible to be conventional with you; and then your looks and movements will have more vivacity and variety than they dare offer now. I see at intervals the glance of a curious sort of bird through the close-set bars of a cage: a vivid, restless, resolute captive is there; were it but free, it would soar cloud-high. You are still bent on going?'

'It has struck nine, sir.'

'Never mind, wait a minute: Adèle is not ready to go to bed yet. My position, Miss Eyre, with my back to the fire, and my face to the room, favours observation. While talking to you, I have also occasionally watched Adèle (I have my own reasons for thinking her a curious study, reasons that I may, nay, that I shall, impart to you someday). She pulled out of her box, about ten minutes ago, a little pink silk frock; rapture lit her face as she unfolded it; coquetry runs in her blood, blends with her brains, and seasons the marrow of her bones. "Il faut que je l'essaie!" cried she, "et à l'instant même!" and she rushed out of the room. She is now with Sophie, undergoing a robing process: in a few minutes she will re-enter; and I know what I shall see, a miniature of Céline Varens, as she used to appear on the boards at the rising of – . But never mind that. However, my tenderest feelings are about to receive a shock: such is my presentiment; stay now, to see whether it will be realised.'

Ere long, Adèle's little foot was heard tripping across the hall. She entered, transformed as her guardian had predicted. A dress of rose-coloured satin, very short, and as full in the skirt as it could be gathered, replaced the brown frock she had previously worn; a wreath of rosebuds circled her forehead; her feet were dressed in silk stockings and small white satin sandals.

'Est-ce que ma robe va bien?' cried she, bounding forwards; 'et mes souliers? et mes bas? Tenez, je crois que je vais danser!'

And spreading out her dress, she chasséed across the room; till, having reached Mr Rochester, she wheeled lightly round before him on tiptoe, then dropped on one knee at his feet, exclaiming – 'Monsieur, je vous remercie mille fois de votre bonté'; then rising, she added, 'C'est comme cela que maman faisait, n'est-ce pas, monsieur?'

'Pre-cise-ly!' was the answer; 'and, "comme cela," she charmed my English gold out of my British breeches' pocket. I have been green, too, Miss Eyre, ay, grass green: not a more vernal tint freshens you now than once freshened me. My Spring is gone, however, but it has left me that French floweret on my hands, which, in some moods, I would fain be rid of. Not valuing now the root whence it sprang; having found that it was of a sort which nothing but gold dust could manure, I have but half a liking to the blossom, especially when it looks so artificial as just now. I keep it and rear it rather on the Roman Catholic principle of expiating numerous sins, great or small, by one good work. I'll explain all this someday. Good-night.'

## *Chapter 15*

Mr Rochester did, on a future occasion, explain it. It was one afternoon, when he chanced to meet me and Adèle in the grounds: and while she played with Pilot and her shuttlecock, he asked me to walk up and down a long beech avenue within sight of her.

He then said that she was the daughter of a French opera-dancer, Céline Varens, towards whom he had once cherished what he called a '*grande passion*'. This passion Céline had professed to return with even superior ardour. He thought himself her idol, ugly as he was: he believed, as he said, that she preferred his '*taille d'athlète*' to the elegance of the Apollo Belvidere.

'And, Miss Eyre, so much was I flattered by this preference of the Gallic sylph for her British gnome, that I installed her in an hotel; gave her a complete establishment of servants, a carriage, cashmeres, diamonds, dentelles, etc. In short, I began the process of ruining myself in the received style, like any other spoony. I had not, it seems, the originality to chalk out a new road to shame and destruction, but trod the old track with stupid exactness not to deviate an inch from the beaten centre. I had – as I deserved to have – the fate of all other spoonies. Happening to call one evening when Céline did not expect me, I found her out; but it was a warm night, and I was tired with strolling through Paris, so I sat down in her boudoir; happy to breathe the air consecrated so lately by her presence. No, I exaggerate; I never thought there was any consecrating virtue about her: it was rather a sort of pastille perfume she had left; a scent of musk and amber, than an odour of sanctity. I was just beginning to stifle with the fumes of conservatory flowers and sprinkled essences, when I bethought myself to open the window and step out on to the balcony. It was moonlight and gaslight besides, and very still and serene. The balcony was furnished with a chair or two; I sat down, and took out a cigar, I will take one now, if you will excuse me.'

Here ensued a pause, filled up by the producing and lighting of a cigar; having placed it to his lips and breathed a trail of Havannah incense on the freezing and sunless air, he went on – 'I liked bonbons too in those days, Miss Eyre, and I was *croquant* – (overlook the barbarism) – *croquant* chocolate comfits, and smoking alternately, watching meantime the equipages that rolled along the fashionable streets towards the neighbouring opera-house, when in an elegant close carriage drawn by a beautiful pair of English horses, and distinctly seen in the brilliant city-night, I recognised the "voiture" I had given Céline. She was returning: of course my heart thumped with impatience against the iron rails I leant upon. The carriage stopped, as I had expected, at the hotel door; my flame (that is the very word for an opera inamorata) alighted: though muffled in a cloak – an unnecessary encumbrance, by the by, on so warm a June evening – I knew her instantly by her little foot, seen peeping from the skirt of her dress, as she skipped from the carriage step. Bending over the balcony, I was about to murmur "Mon ange" – in a tone, of course, which should be audible to the ear of love alone – when a figure jumped from the carriage after her; cloaked also; but that was a spurred heel which had rung on the pavement, and that was a hatted head which now passed under the arched *porte cochère* of the hotel.

'You never felt jealousy, did you, Miss Eyre? Of course not: I need not ask you; because you never felt love. You have both sentiments yet to experience: your soul sleeps; the shock is yet to be given which shall waken it. You think all existence lapses in as quiet a flow as that in which your youth has hitherto slid away. Floating on with closed eyes and muffled ears, you neither see the rocks bristling not far off in the bed of the flood, nor hear the breakers boil at their base. But I tell you – and you may mark my words – you will come someday to a craggy pass in the channel, where the whole of life's stream will be broken up into whirl and tumult, foam and noise: either you will be dashed to atoms on crag points, or lifted up and borne on by some master-wave into a calmer current – as I am now.

'I like this day; I like that sky of steel; I like the sternness and stillness of the world under this frost. I like Thornfield, its antiquity, its retirement, its old crow trees and thorn trees, its grey facade, and lines of dark windows reflecting that metal welkin: and yet how long have I abhorred the very thought of it, shunned it like a great plague-house? How I do still abhor – '

He ground his teeth and was silent: he arrested his step and struck his boot against the hard ground. Some hated thought seemed to have him in its grip, and to hold him so tightly that he could not advance.

We were ascending the avenue when he thus paused; the hall was before us. Lifting his eye to its battlements, he cast over them a glare such as I never saw before or since. Pain, shame, ire, impatience, disgust, detestation, seemed momentarily to hold a quivering conflict in the large pupil dilating under his ebon eyebrow. Wild was the wrestle which should be paramount; but another feeling rose and triumphed: something hard and cynical: self-willed and resolute: it settled his passion and petrified his countenance: he went on – 'During the moment I was silent, Miss Eyre, I was arranging a point with my destiny. She stood there, by that beech-trunk – a hag like one of those who appeared to Macbeth on the heath of Forres. "You like Thornfield?" she said, lifting her finger; and then she wrote in the air a memento, which ran in lurid hieroglyphics all along the house-front, between the upper and lower row of windows, "Like it if you can! Like it if you dare!"

' "I will like it," said I; "I dare like it;" and' (he subjoined moodily) 'I will keep my word; I will break obstacles to happiness, to goodness – yes, goodness. I wish to be a better man than I have been, than I am; as Job's leviathan broke the spear, the dart, and the habergeon, hindrances which others count as iron and brass, I will esteem but straw and rotten wood.'

Adèle here ran before him with her shuttlecock. 'Away!' he cried harshly; 'keep at a distance, child; or go in to Sophie!' Continuing then to pursue his walk in silence, I ventured to recall him to the point whence he had abruptly diverged – 'Did you leave the balcony, sir,' I asked, 'when Mlle Varens entered?'

I almost expected a rebuff for this hardly well-timed question, but, on the contrary, waking out of his scowling abstraction, he turned his eyes towards me, and the shade seemed to clear off his brow. 'Oh, I had forgotten Céline! Well, to resume. When I saw my charmer thus come in accompanied by a cavalier, I seemed to hear a hiss, and the green snake of jealousy, rising on undulating coils from the moonlit balcony, glided within my waistcoat, and ate its way in two minutes to my heart's core. Strange!' he exclaimed, suddenly starting again from the point. 'Strange that I should choose you for the confidant of all this, young lady; passing strange that you should listen to me quietly, as if it were the most usual thing in the world for a man like me to tell stories of his opera-mistresses to a quaint, inexperienced girl like you! But the last singularity explains the first, as I intimated once before: you, with your gravity, considerateness, and caution were made to be the recipient of secrets. Besides, I know what sort of a mind I have placed in communication with my own: I know it is one not liable to take infection: it is a peculiar mind: it is a unique one. Happily I do not mean to harm it: but, if I did, it would not take harm from me. The more you and I converse, the better; for while I cannot blight you, you may refresh me.' After this digression he proceeded – 'I remained in the balcony. "They will come to her boudoir, no doubt," thought I: "let me prepare an ambush." So putting my hand in through the open window, I drew the curtain over it, leaving only an opening through which I could take observations; then I closed the casement, all but a chink just wide enough to furnish an outlet to lovers' whispered vows: then I stole back to my chair; and as I resumed it the pair came in. My eye was quickly at the aperture. Céline's chambermaid entered, lit a lamp, left it on the table, and withdrew. The couple were thus revealed to me clearly: both removed their cloaks, and there was "the Varens", shining in satin and jewels, my gifts of course, and there was her companion in an officer's uniform; and I knew him for a young roué of a vicomte – a brainless and vicious youth whom I had sometimes met in society, and had never thought of hating because I despised him so absolutely. On recognising him, the fang of the snake Jealousy was instantly broken; because at the same moment my love for Céline sank under an extinguisher. A woman who could betray me for such a rival was not worth contending for; she deserved only scorn; less, however, than I, who had been her dupe.

'They began to talk; their conversation eased me completely: frivolous, mercenary, heartless, and senseless, it was rather calculated to weary than enrage a listener. A card of mine lay on the table; this being perceived, brought my name under discussion. Neither of them possessed energy or wit to belabour me soundly, but they insulted me as coarsely as they could in their little way: especially Céline, who even waxed rather brilliant on my personal defects – deformities she termed them. Now it had been her custom to launch out into fervent admiration of what she called my "*beauté mâle*": wherein she differed diametrically from you, who told me point-blank, at the second interview, that you did not think me handsome. The contrast struck me at the time and – '

Adèle here came running up again.

'Monsieur, John has just been to say that your agent has called and wishes to see you.'

'Ah! in that case I must abridge. Opening the window, I walked in upon them; liberated Céline from my protection; gave her notice to vacate her hotel; offered her a purse for immediate exigencies; disregarded screams, hysterics, prayers, protestations, convulsions; made an appointment with the vicomte for a meeting at the Bois de Boulogne. Next morning I had the pleasure of encountering him; left a bullet in one of his poor etiolated arms, feeble as the wing of a chicken in the pip, and then thought I had done with the whole crew. But unluckily the Varens, six months before, had given me this filette Adèle, who, she affirmed, was my daughter; and perhaps she may be, though I see no proofs of such grim paternity written in her countenance: Pilot is more like me than she. Some years after I had broken with the mother, she abandoned her child, and ran away to Italy with a musician or singer. I acknowledged no natural claim on Adèle's part to be supported by me, nor do I now acknowledge any, for I am not her father; but hearing that she was quite destitute, I e'en took the poor thing out of the slime and mud of Paris, and transplanted it here, to grow up clean in the wholesome soil of an English country garden. Mrs Fairfax found you to train it; but now you know that it is the illegitimate offspring of a French opera-girl, you will perhaps think differently of your post and protégée: you will be coming to me someday with notice that you have found another place – that you beg me to look out for a new governess, etc. – Eh?'

'No: Adèle is not answerable for either her mother's faults or yours: I have a regard for her; and now that I know she is, in a sense, parentless – forsaken by her mother and disowned by you, sir – I shall cling closer to her than before. How could I possibly prefer the spoilt pet of a wealthy family, who would hate her governess as a nuisance, to a lonely little orphan, who leans towards her as a friend?'

'Oh, that is the light in which you view it! Well, I must go in now; and you too: it darkens.'

But I stayed out a few minutes longer with Adèle and Pilot – ran a race with her, and played a game of battledore and shuttlecock. When we went in, and I had removed her bonnet and coat, I took her on my knee; kept her there an hour, allowing her to prattle as she liked: not rebuking even some little freedoms and trivialities into which she was apt to stray when much noticed, and which betrayed in her a superficiality of character, inherited probably from her mother, hardly congenial to an English mind. Still she had her merits; and I was disposed to appreciate all that was good in her to the utmost. I sought in her countenance and features a likeness to Mr Rochester, but found none: no trait, no turn of expression announced relationship. It was a pity: if she could but have been proved to resemble him, he would have thought more of her.

It was not till after I had withdrawn to my own chamber for the night, that I steadily reviewed the tale Mr Rochester had told me. As he had said, there was probably nothing at all extraordinary in the substance of the narrative itself: a wealthy Englishman's passion for a French dancer, and her treachery to him, were everyday matters enough, no doubt, in society; but there was something decidedly strange in the paroxysm of emotion which had suddenly seized him when he was in the act of expressing the present contentment of his mood, and his newly revived pleasure in the old hall and its environs. I meditated wonderingly on this incident; but gradually quitting it, as I found it for the present inexplicable, I turned to the consideration of my master's manner to myself. The confidence he had thought fit to repose in me seemed a tribute to my discretion: I regarded and accepted it as such. His deportment had now for some weeks been more uniform towards me than at the first. I never seemed in his way; he did not take fits of chilling hauteur: when he met me unexpectedly, the encounter seemed welcome; he had always a word and sometimes a smile for me: when summoned by formal invitation to his presence, I was honoured by a cordiality of reception that made me feel I really possessed the power to amuse him, and that these evening conferences were sought as much for his pleasure as for my benefit.

I, indeed, talked comparatively little, but I heard him talk with relish. It was his nature to be communicative; he liked to open to a mind unacquainted with the world glimpses of its scenes and ways (I do not mean its corrupt scenes and wicked ways, but such as derived their interest from the great scale on which they were acted, the strange novelty by which they were characterised); and I had a keen delight in receiving the new ideas he offered, in imagining the new pictures he portrayed, and following him in thought through the new regions he disclosed, never startled or troubled by one noxious allusion.

The ease of his manner freed me from painful restraint: the friendly frankness, as correct as cordial, with which he treated me, drew me to him. I felt at times as if he were my relation rather than my master: yet he was imperious sometimes still; but I did not mind that; I saw it was his way. So happy, so gratified did I become with this new interest added to life, that I ceased to pine after kindred: my thin crescent-destiny seemed to enlarge; the blanks of existence were filled up; my bodily health improved; I gathered flesh and strength.

And was Mr Rochester now ugly in my eyes? No, reader: gratitude, and many associations, all pleasurable and genial, made his face the object I best liked to see; his presence in a room was more cheering than the brightest fire. Yet I had not forgotten his faults; indeed, I could not, for he brought them frequently before me. He was proud, sardonic, harsh to inferiority of every description: in my secret soul I knew that his great kindness to me was balanced by unjust severity to many others. He was moody, too; unaccountably so; I more than once, when sent for to read to him, found him sitting in his library alone, with his head bent on his folded arms; and, when he looked up, a morose, almost a malignant, scowl blackened his features. But I believed that his moodiness, his harshness, and his former faults of morality (I say *former*, for now he seemed corrected of them) had their source in some cruel cross of fate. I believed he was naturally a man of better tendencies, higher principles, and purer tastes than such as circumstances had developed, education instilled, or destiny encouraged. I thought there were excellent materials in him; though for the present they hung together somewhat spoiled and tangled. I cannot deny that I grieved for his grief, whatever that was, and would have given much to assuage it.

Though I had now extinguished my candle and was laid down in bed, I could not sleep for thinking of his look when he paused in the avenue, and told how his destiny had risen up before him, and dared him to be happy at Thornfield.

'Why not?' I asked myself. 'What alienates him from the house? Will he leave it again soon? Mrs Fairfax said he seldom stayed here longer than a fortnight at a time; and he has now been resident eight weeks. If he does go, the change will be doleful. Suppose he should be absent spring, summer, and autumn: how joyless sunshine and fine days will seem!'

I hardly know whether I had slept or not after this musing; at any rate, I started wide awake on hearing a vague murmur, peculiar and lugubrious, which sounded, I thought, just above me. I wished I had kept my candle burning: the night was drearily dark; my spirits were depressed. I rose and sat up in bed, listening. The sound was hushed.

I tried again to sleep; but my heart beat anxiously: my inward tranquillity was broken. The clock, far down in the hall, struck two. Just then it seemed my chamber-door was touched; as if fingers had swept the panels in groping a way along the dark gallery outside. I said, 'Who is there?' Nothing answered. I was chilled with fear.

All at once I remembered that it might be Pilot, who, when the kitchen-door chanced to be left open, not unfrequently found his way up to the threshold of Mr Rochester's chamber: I had seen him lying there myself in the mornings. The idea calmed me somewhat: I lay down. Silence composes the nerves; and as an unbroken hush now reigned again through the whole house, I began to feel the return of slumber. But it was not fated that I should sleep that night. A dream had scarcely approached my ear, when it fled affrighted, scared by a marrow-freezing incident enough.

This was a demoniac laugh – low, suppressed, and deep – uttered, as it seemed, at the very keyhole of my chamber door. The head of my bed was near the door, and I thought at first the goblin-laugher stood at my bedside – or rather, crouched by my pillow: but I rose, looked round, and could see nothing; while, as I still gazed, the unnatural sound was reiterated: and I knew it came from behind the panels. My first impulse was to rise and fasten the bolt; my next, again to cry out, 'Who is there?'

Something gurgled and moaned. Ere long, steps retreated up the gallery towards the third-storey staircase: a door had lately been made to shut in that staircase; I heard it open and close, and all was still.

'Was that Grace Poole? and is she possessed with a devil?' thought I. Impossible now to remain longer by myself: I must go to Mrs Fairfax. I hurried on my frock and a shawl; I withdrew the bolt and opened the door with a trembling hand. There was a candle burning just outside, and on the matting in the gallery. I was surprised at this circumstance: but still more was I amazed to perceive the air quite dim, as if filled with smoke; and, while looking to the right hand and left, to find whence these blue wreaths issued, I became further aware of a strong smell of burning.

Something creaked: it was a door ajar; and that door was Mr Rochester's, and the smoke rushed in a cloud from thence. I thought no more of Mrs Fairfax; I thought no more of Grace Poole, or the laugh: in an instant, I was within the chamber. Tongues of flame darted round the bed: the curtains were on fire. In the midst of blaze and vapour, Mr Rochester lay stretched motionless, in deep sleep.

'Wake! wake!' I cried. I shook him, but he only murmured and turned: the smoke had stupefied him. Not a moment could be lost: the very sheets were kindling, I rushed to his basin and ewer; fortunately, one was wide and the other deep, and both were filled with water. I heaved them up, deluged the bed and its occupant, flew back to my own room, brought my own water-jug, baptised the couch afresh, and, by God's aid, succeeded in extinguishing the flames which were devouring it.

The hiss of the quenched element, the breakage of a pitcher which I flung from my hand when I had emptied it, and, above all, the splash of the shower-bath I had liberally bestowed, roused Mr Rochester at last. Though it was now dark, I knew he was awake; because I heard him fulminating strange anathemas at finding himself lying in a pool of water.

'Is there a flood?' he cried.

'No, sir,' I answered; 'but there has been a fire: get up, do; you are quenched now; I will fetch you a candle.'

'In the name of all the elves in Christendom, is that Jane Eyre?' he demanded. 'What have you done with me, witch, sorceress? Who is in the room besides you? Have you plotted to drown me?'

'I will fetch you a candle, sir; and, in Heaven's name, get up. Somebody has plotted something: you cannot too soon find out who and what it is.'

'There! I am up now; but at your peril you fetch a candle yet: wait two minutes till I get into some dry garments, if any dry there be – yes, here is my dressing-gown. Now run!'

I did run; I brought the candle which still remained in the gallery. He took it from my hand, held it up, and surveyed the bed, all blackened and scorched, the sheets drenched, the carpet round swimming in water.

'What is it? and who did it?' he asked.

I briefly related to him what had transpired: the strange laugh I had heard in the gallery; the step ascending to the third storey; the smoke, the smell of fire which had conducted me to his room; in what state I had found matters there, and how I had deluged him with all the water I could lay hands on.

He listened very gravely; his face, as I went on, expressed more concern than astonishment; he did not immediately speak when I had concluded.

'Shall I call Mrs Fairfax?' I asked.

'Mrs Fairfax? No; what the deuce would you call her for? What can she do? Let her sleep unmolested.'

'Then I will fetch Leah, and wake John and his wife.'

'Not at all: just be still. You have a shawl on. If you are not warm enough, you may take my cloak yonder; wrap it about you, and sit down in the armchair:

there, I will put it on. Now place your feet on the stool, to keep them out of the wet. I am going to leave you a few minutes. I shall take the candle. Remain where you are till I return; be as still as a mouse. I must pay a visit to the second storey. Don't move, remember, or call anyone.'

He went: I watched the light withdraw. He passed up the gallery very softly, unclosed the staircase door with as little noise as possible, shut it after him, and the last ray vanished. I was left in total darkness. I listened for some noise, but heard nothing. A very long time elapsed. I grew weary: it was cold, in spite of the cloak; and then I did not see the use of staying, as I was not to rouse the house. I was on the point of risking Mr Rochester's displeasure by disobeying his orders, when the light once more gleamed dimly on the gallery wall, and I heard his unshod feet tread the matting. 'I hope it is he,' thought I, 'and not something worse.'

He re-entered, pale and very gloomy. 'I have found it all out,' said he, setting his candle down on the washstand; 'it is as I thought.'

'How, sir?'

He made no reply, but stood with his arms folded, looking on the ground. At the end of a few minutes he enquired in rather a peculiar tone – 'I forget whether you said you saw anything when you opened your chamber door.'

'No, sir, only the candlestick on the ground.'

'But you heard an odd laugh? You have heard that laugh before, I should think, or something like it?'

'Yes, sir: there is a woman who sews here, called Grace Poole, she laughs in that way. She is a singular person.'

'Just so. Grace Poole – you have guessed it. She is, as you say, singular – very. Well, I shall reflect on the subject. Meantime, I am glad that you are the only person, besides myself, acquainted with the precise details of tonight's incident. You are no talking fool: say nothing about it. I will account for this state of affairs' (pointing to the bed): 'and now return to your own room. I shall do very well on the sofa in the library for the rest of the night. It is near four: in two hours the servants will be up.'

'Good-night, then, sir,' said I, departing.

He seemed surprised – very inconsistently so, as he had just told me to go.

'What!' he exclaimed, 'are you quitting me already, and in that way?'

'You said I might go, sir.'

'But not without taking leave; not without a word or two of acknowledgement and goodwill: not, in short, in that brief, dry fashion. Why, you have saved my life! – snatched me from a horrible and excruciating death! and you walk past me as if we were mutual strangers! At least shake hands.'

He held out his hand; I gave him mine: he took it first in one, then in both his own.

'You have saved my life: I have a pleasure in owing you so immense a debt. I cannot say more. Nothing else that has being would have been tolerable to me in the character of creditor for such an obligation: but you: it is different; I feel your benefits no burden, Jane.'

He paused; gazed at me: words almost visible trembled on his lips, but his voice was checked.

'Good-night again, sir. There is no debt, benefit, burden, obligation, in the case.'

'I knew,' he continued, 'you would do me good in some way, at some time; I saw it in your eyes when I first beheld you: their expression and smile did not' – (again he stopped) – 'did not' (he proceeded hastily) 'strike delight to my very inmost heart so for nothing. People talk of natural sympathies; I have heard of good genii: there are grains of truth in the wildest fable. My cherished preserver, good-night!'

Strange energy was in his voice, strange fire in his look.

'I am glad I happened to be awake,' I said: and then I was going.

'What! you *will* go?'

'I am cold, sir.'

'Cold? Yes, and standing in a pool! Go, then, Jane; go!' But he still retained my hand, and I could not free it. I bethought myself of an expedient.

'I think I hear Mrs Fairfax move, sir,' said I.

'Well, leave me': he relaxed his fingers, and I was gone.

I regained my couch, but never thought of sleep. Till morning dawned I was tossed on a buoyant but unquiet sea, where billows of trouble rolled under surges of joy. I thought sometimes I saw beyond its wild waters a shore, sweet as the hills of Beulah; and now and then a freshening gale, wakened by hope, bore my spirit triumphantly towards the bourne: but I could not reach it, even in fancy – a counteracting breeze blew off land, and continually drove me back. Sense would resist delirium: judgement would warn passion. Too feverish to rest, I rose as soon as day dawned.

## *Chapter 16*

I both wished and feared to see Mr Rochester on the day which followed this sleepless night: I wanted to hear his voice again, yet feared to meet his eye. During the early part of the morning, I momentarily expected his coming; he was not in the frequent habit of entering the schoolroom, but he did step in for a few minutes sometimes, and I had the impression that he was sure to visit it that day.

But the morning passed just as usual: nothing happened to interrupt the quiet course of Adèle's studies; only soon after breakfast, I heard some bustle in the neighbourhood of Mr Rochester's chamber, Mrs Fairfax's voice, and Leah's, and the cook's – that is, John's wife – and even John's own gruff tones. There were exclamations of 'What a mercy master was not burnt in his bed!' 'It is always dangerous to keep a candle lit at night.' 'How providential that he had presence of mind to think of the water-jug!' 'I wonder he waked nobody!' 'It is to be hoped he will not take cold with sleeping on the library sofa,' etc.

To much confabulation succeeded a sound of scrubbing and setting to rights; and when I passed the room, in going downstairs to dinner, I saw through the open door that all was again restored to complete order; only the bed was stripped of its hangings. Leah stood up in the window-seat, rubbing the panes of glass dimmed with smoke. I was about to address her, for I wished to know what account had been given of the affair: but, on advancing, I saw a second person in the chamber – a woman sitting on a chair by the bedside, and sewing rings to new curtains. That woman was no other than Grace Poole.

There she sat, staid and taciturn-looking, as usual, in her brown stuff gown, her check apron, white handkerchief, and cap. She was intent on her work, in which her whole thoughts seemed absorbed: on her hard forehead, and in her commonplace features, was nothing either of the paleness or desperation one would have expected to see marking the countenance of a woman who had attempted murder, and whose intended victim had followed her last night to her lair, and (as I believed), charged her with the crime she wished to perpetrate. I was amazed – confounded. She looked up, while I still gazed at her: no start, no increase or failure of colour betrayed emotion, consciousness of guilt, or fear of detection. She said 'Good-morning, Miss,' in her usual phlegmatic and brief manner; and taking up another ring and more tape, went on with her sewing.

'I will put her to some test,' thought I: 'such absolute impenetrability is past comprehension.'

'Good-morning, Grace,' I said. 'Has anything happened here? I thought I heard the servants all talking together a while ago.'

'Only master had been reading in his bed last night; he fell asleep with his candle lit, and the curtains got on fire; but, fortunately, he awoke before the bedclothes or the woodwork caught, and contrived to quench the flames with the water in the ewer.'

'A strange affair!' I said, in a low voice: then looking at her fixedly – 'Did Mr Rochester wake nobody? Did no one hear him move?'

She again raised her eyes to me, and this time there was something of consciousness in their expression. She seemed to examine me warily; then she answered – 'The servants sleep so far off, you know, Miss, they would not be likely to hear. Mrs Fairfax's room and yours are the nearest to master's; but Mrs Fairfax said she heard nothing: when people get elderly, they often sleep heavy.' She paused, and then added, with a sort of assumed indifference, but still in a marked and significant tone – 'But you are young, Miss, and I should say a light sleeper: perhaps you may have heard a noise?'

'I did,' said I, dropping my voice, so that Leah, who was still polishing the panes, could not hear me, 'and at first I thought it was Pilot: but Pilot cannot laugh; and I am certain I heard a laugh, and a strange one.'

She took a new needleful of thread, waxed it carefully, threaded her needle with a steady hand, and then observed, with perfect composure – 'It is hardly likely master would laugh, I should think, Miss, when he was in such danger: you must have been dreaming.'

'I was not dreaming,' I said, with some warmth, for her brazen coolness provoked me. Again she looked at me; and with the same scrutinising and conscious eye.

'Have you told master that you heard a laugh?' she enquired.

'I have not had the opportunity of speaking to him this morning.'

'You did not think of opening your door and looking out into the gallery?' she further asked.

She appeared to be cross-questioning me, attempting to draw from me information unawares. The idea struck me that if she discovered I knew or suspected her guilt, she would be playing off some of her malignant pranks on me; I thought it advisable to be on my guard.

'On the contrary,' said I, 'I bolted my door.'

'Then you are not in the habit of bolting your door every night before you get into bed?'

'Fiend! she wants to know my habits, that she may lay her plans accordingly!' Indignation again prevailed over prudence: I replied sharply, 'Hitherto I have often omitted to fasten the bolt: I did not think it necessary. I was not aware any danger or annoyance was to be dreaded at Thornfield Hall: but in future' (and I laid marked stress on the words) 'I shall take good care to make all secure before I venture to lie down.'

'It will be wise so to do,' was her answer: 'this neighbourhood is as quiet as any I know, and I never heard of the hall being attempted by robbers since it was a house; though there are hundreds of pounds' worth of plate in the plate-closet, as is well known. And you see, for such a large house, there are very few servants, because master has never lived here much; and when he does come, being a bachelor, he needs little waiting on: but I always think it best to err on the safe side; a door is soon fastened, and it is as well to have a drawn bolt between one and any mischief that may be about. A deal of people, Miss, are for trusting all to Providence; but I say Providence will not dispense with the means, though He often blesses them when they are used discreetly.' And here she closed her harangue: a long one for her, and uttered with the demureness of a Quakeress.

I still stood absolutely dumfoundered at what appeared to me her miraculous self-possession, and most inscrutable hypocrisy, when the cook entered.

'Mrs Poole,' said she, addressing Grace, 'the servants' dinner will soon be ready: will you come down?'

'No; just put my pint of porter and bit of pudding on a tray, and I'll carry it upstairs.'

'You'll have some meat?'

'Just a morsel, and a taste of cheese, that's all.'

'And the sago?'

'Never mind it at present: I shall be coming down before tea-time: I'll make it myself.'

The cook here turned to me, saying that Mrs Fairfax was waiting for me: so I departed.

I hardly heard Mrs Fairfax's account of the curtain conflagration during dinner, so much was I occupied in puzzling my brains over the enigmatical character of Grace Poole, and still more in pondering the problem of her position at Thornfield and questioning why she had not been given into custody that morning, or, at the very least, dismissed from her master's service. He had almost as much as declared his conviction of her criminality last night: what mysterious cause withheld him from accusing her? Why had he enjoined me, too, to secrecy? It was strange: a bold, vindictive, and haughty gentleman seemed somehow in the power of one of the meanest of his dependants; so much in her power, that even when she lifted her hand against his life, he dared not openly charge her with the attempt, much less punish her for it.

Had Grace been young and handsome, I should have been tempted to think that tenderer feelings than prudence or fear influenced Mr Rochester in her behalf; but, hard-favoured and matronly as she was, the idea could not be admitted. 'Yet,' I reflected, 'she has been young once; her youth would be contemporary with her master's: Mrs Fairfax told me once, she had lived here many years. I don't think she can ever have been pretty; but, for aught I know, she may possess originality and strength of character to compensate for the want of personal advantages. Mr Rochester is an amateur of the decided and eccentric: Grace is eccentric at least. What if a former caprice (a freak very possible to a nature so sudden and headstrong as his) has delivered him into her power, and she now exercises over his actions a secret influence, the result of his own indiscretion, which he cannot shake off, and dare not disregard?' But, having reached this point of conjecture, Mrs Poole's square, flat figure, and uncomely, dry, even coarse face, recurred so distinctly to my mind's eye, that I thought, 'No; impossible! my supposition cannot be correct. Yet,' suggested the secret voice which talks to us in our own hearts, '*you* are not beautiful either, and perhaps Mr Rochester approves you: at any rate, you have often felt as if he did; and last night – remember his words; remember his look; remember his voice!'

I well remembered all; language, glance, and tone seemed at the moment vividly renewed. I was now in the schoolroom; Adèle was drawing; I bent over her and directed her pencil. She looked up with a sort of start.

'Qu'avez-vous, mademoiselle?' said she. 'Vos doigts tremblent comme la feuille, et vos joues sont rouges: mais, rouges comme des cerises!'

'I am hot, Adèle, with stooping!' She went on sketching; I went on thinking.

I hastened to drive from my mind the hateful notion I had been conceiving respecting Grace Poole; it disgusted me. I compared myself with her, and found we were different. Bessie Leaven had said I was quite a lady; and she spoke truth – I was a lady. And now I looked much better than I did when Bessie saw me; I had more colour and more flesh, more life, more vivacity, because I had brighter hopes and keener enjoyments.

'Evening approaches,' said I, as I looked towards the window. 'I have never heard Mr Rochester's voice or step in the house today; but surely I shall see him before night: I feared the meeting in the morning; now I desire it, because expectation has been so long baffled that it is grown impatient.'

When dusk actually closed, and when Adèle left me to go and play in the nursery with Sophie, I did most keenly desire it. I listened for the bell to ring below; I listened for Leah coming up with a message; I fancied sometimes I heard Mr Rochester's own tread, and I turned to the door, expecting it to open and admit him. The door remained shut; darkness only came in through the window. Still it was not late; he often sent for me at seven and eight o'clock, and it was yet but six. Surely I should not be wholly disappointed tonight, when I had so many things to say to him! I wanted again to introduce the subject of Grace Poole, and to hear what he would answer; I wanted to ask him plainly if he really believed it was she who had made last night's hideous attempt; and if so, why he kept her wickedness a secret. It little mattered whether my curiosity irritated him; I knew the pleasure of vexing and soothing him by turns; it was one I chiefly delighted in, and a sure instinct always prevented me from going too far; beyond the verge of provocation I never ventured; on the extreme brink I liked well to try my skill. Retaining every minute form of respect, every propriety of my station, I could still meet him in argument without fear or uneasy restraint; this suited both him and me.

A tread creaked on the stairs at last. Leah made her appearance; but it was only to intimate that tea was ready in Mrs Fairfax's room. Thither I repaired, glad at least to go downstairs; for that brought me, I imagined, nearer to Mr Rochester's presence.

'You must want your tea,' said the good lady, as I joined her; 'you ate so little at dinner. I am afraid,' she continued, 'you are not well today: you look flushed and feverish.'

'Oh, quite well! I never felt better.'

'Then you must prove it by evincing a good appetite; will you fill the teapot while I knit off this needle?' Having completed her task, she rose to draw down the blind, which she had hitherto kept up, by way, I suppose, of making the most of daylight, though dusk was now fast deepening into total obscurity.

'It is fair tonight,' said she, as she looked through the panes, 'though not starlight; Mr Rochester has, on the whole, had a favourable day for his journey.'

'Journey! – Is Mr Rochester gone anywhere? I did not know he was out.'

'Oh, he set off the moment he had breakfasted! He is gone to the Leas, Mr Eshton's place, ten miles on the other side Millcote. I believe there is quite a party assembled there; Lord Ingram, Sir George Lynn, Colonel Dent, and others.'

'Do you expect him back tonight?'

'No – nor tomorrow either; I should think he is very likely to stay a week or more: when these fine, fashionable people get together, they are so surrounded by elegance and gaiety, so well provided with all that can please and entertain, they are in no hurry to separate. Gentlemen especially are often in request on such occasions; and Mr Rochester is so talented and so lively in society, that I believe he is a general favourite: the ladies are very fond of him; though you would not think his appearance calculated to recommend him particularly in their eyes: but I suppose his acquirements and abilities, perhaps his wealth and good blood, make amends for any little fault of look.'

'Are there ladies at the Leas?'

'There are Mrs Eshton and her three daughters – very elegant young ladies indeed; and there are the Honourable Blanche and Mary Ingram, most beautiful women, I suppose: indeed I have seen Blanche, six or seven years since, when she was a girl of eighteen. She came here to a Christmas ball and party Mr Rochester gave. You should have seen the dining-room that day – how richly it was decorated, how brilliantly lit up! I should think there were fifty ladies and gentlemen present – all of the first county families; and Miss Ingram was considered the belle of the evening.'

'You saw her, you say, Mrs Fairfax: what was she like?'

'Yes, I saw her. The dining-room doors were thrown open; and, as it was Christmas-time, the servants were allowed to assemble in the hall, to hear some of the ladies sing and play. Mr Rochester would have me to come in, and I sat down in a quiet corner and watched them. I never saw a more splendid scene: the ladies were magnificently dressed; most of them – at least most of the younger ones – looked handsome; but Miss Ingram was certainly the queen.'

'And what was she like?'

'Tall, fine bust, sloping shoulders; long, graceful neck: olive complexion, dark and clear; noble features; eyes rather like Mr Rochester's: large and black, and as brilliant as her jewels. And then she had such a fine head of hair; raven-black and so becomingly arranged: a crown of thick plaits behind, and in front the longest, the glossiest curls I ever saw. She was dressed in pure white; an amber-coloured scarf was passed over her shoulder and across her breast tied at the side, and descending in long, fringed ends below her knee. She wore an amber-coloured flower, too, in her hair: it contrasted well with the jetty mass of her curls.'

'She was greatly admired, of course?'

'Yes, indeed: and not only for her beauty, but for her accomplishments. She was one of the ladies who sang: a gentleman accompanied her on the piano. She and Mr Rochester sang a duet.'

'Mr Rochester? I was not aware he could sing.'

'Oh! he has a fine bass voice, and an excellent taste for music.'

'And Miss Ingram: what sort of a voice had she?'

'A very rich and powerful one: she sang delightfully; it was a treat to listen to her; and she played afterwards. I am no judge of music, but Mr Rochester is; and I heard him say her execution was remarkably good.'

'And this beautiful and accomplished lady, she is not yet married.'

'It appears not: I fancy neither she nor her sister have very large fortunes. Old Lord Ingram's estates were chiefly entailed, and the eldest son came in for everything almost.'

'But I wonder no wealthy nobleman or gentleman has taken a fancy to her: Mr Rochester, for instance. He is rich, is he not?'

'Oh! yes. But you see there is a considerable difference in age: Mr Rochester is nearly forty; she is but twenty-five.'

'What of that? More unequal matches are made every day.'

'True: yet I should scarcely fancy Mr Rochester would entertain an idea of the sort. But you eat nothing: you have scarcely tasted since you began tea.'

'No: I am too thirsty to eat. Will you let me have another cup?'

I was about again to revert to the probability of a union between Mr Rochester and the beautiful Blanche; but Adèle came in, and the conversation was turned into another channel.

When once more alone, I reviewed the information I had got; looked into my heart, examined its thoughts and feelings, and endeavoured to bring back with a strict hand such as had been straying through imagination's boundless and trackless waste, into the safe fold of common sense.

Arraigned at my own bar, Memory having given her evidence of the hopes, wishes, sentiments I had been cherishing since last night – of the general state of mind in which I had indulged for nearly a fortnight past; Reason having come forward and told, in her own quiet way, a plain, unvarnished tale, showing how I had rejected the real, and rabidly devoured the ideal – I pronounced judgement to this effect: That a greater fool than Jane Eyre had never breathed the breath of life; that a more fantastic idiot had never surfeited herself on sweet lies, and swallowed poison as if it were nectar.

'*You*,' I said, 'a favourite with Mr Rochester? *You* gifted with the power of pleasing him? *You* of importance to him in any way? Go! your folly sickens me. And you have derived pleasure from occasional tokens of preference – equivocal tokens shown by a gentleman of family and a man of the world to a dependant and a novice. How dared you? Poor stupid dupe! – Could not even self-interest make you wiser? You repeated to yourself this morning the brief scene of last night? – Cover your face and be ashamed! He said something in praise of your eyes, did he? Blind puppy! Open their bleared lids and look on your own accursed senselessness! It does good to no woman to be flattered by her superior, who cannot possibly intend to marry her; and it is madness in all women to let a secret love kindle within them, which, if unreturned and unknown, must devour the life that feeds it; and, if discovered and responded to, must lead, *ignis-fatuus*-like, into miry wilds whence there is no extrication.

'Listen, then, Jane Eyre, to your sentence: tomorrow, place the glass before you, and draw in chalk your own picture, faithfully, without softening one defect; omit no harsh line, smooth away no displeasing irregularity; write under it, "Portrait of a Governess, disconnected, poor, and plain".

'Afterwards, take a piece of smooth ivory – you have one prepared in your drawing-box: take your palette, mix your freshest, finest, clearest tints; choose your most delicate camel-hair pencils; delineate carefully the loveliest face you can imagine; paint it in your softest shades and sweetest hues, according to the description given by Mrs Fairfax of Blanche Ingram; remember the raven ringlets, the oriental eye; What! you revert to Mr Rochester as a model! Order! No snivel! – no sentiment! – no regret! I will endure only sense and resolution. Recall the august yet harmonious lineaments, the Grecian neck and bust; let the round and dazzling arm be visible, and the delicate hand; omit neither diamond ring nor gold bracelet; portray faithfully the attire, aerial lace and glistening satin, graceful scarf and golden rose; call it "Blanche, an accomplished lady of rank".

'Whenever, in future, you should chance to fancy Mr Rochester thinks well of you, take out these two pictures and compare them: say, "Mr Rochester might probably win that noble lady's love, if he chose to strive for it; is it likely he would waste a serious thought on this indigent and insignificant plebeian?" '

'I'll do it,' I resolved: and having framed this determination, I grew calm, and fell asleep.

I kept my word. An hour or two sufficed to sketch my own portrait in crayons; and in less than a fortnight I had completed an ivory miniature of an imaginary Blanche Ingram. It looked a lovely face enough, and when compared with the real head in chalk, the contrast was as great as self-control could desire. I derived benefit from the task: it had kept my head and hands employed, and had given force and fixedness to the new impressions I wished to stamp indelibly on my heart.

Ere long, I had reason to congratulate myself on the course of wholesome discipline to which I had thus forced my feelings to submit. Thanks to it, I was able to meet subsequent occurrences with a decent calm, which, had they found me unprepared, I should probably have been unequal to maintain, even externally.

## *Chapter 17*

A week passed, and no news arrived of Mr Rochester: ten days, and still he did not come. Mrs Fairfax said she should not be surprised if he were to go straight from the Leas to London, and thence to the Continent, and not show his face again at Thornfield for a year to come; he had not unfrequently quitted it in a manner quite as abrupt and unexpected. When I heard this, I was beginning to feel a strange chill and failing at the heart. I was actually permitting myself to experience a sickening sense of disappointment; but rallying my wits, and recollecting my principles, I at once called my sensations to order; and it was wonderful how I got over the temporary blunder – how I cleared up the mistake of supposing Mr Rochester's movements a matter in which I had any cause to take a vital interest. Not that I humbled myself by a slavish notion of inferiority: on the contrary, I just said – 'You have nothing to do with the master of Thornfield, further than to receive the salary he gives you for teaching his protégée, and to be grateful for such respectful and kind treatment as, if you do your duty, you have a right to expect at his hands. Be sure that is the only tie he seriously acknowledges between you and him; so don't make him the object of your fine feelings, your raptures, agonies, and so forth. He is not of your order: keep to your caste, and be too self-respecting to lavish the love of the whole heart, soul, and strength, where such a gift is not wanted and would be despised.'

I went on with my day's business tranquilly; but ever and anon vague suggestions kept wandering across my brain of reasons why I should quit Thornfield; and I kept involuntarily framing advertisements and pondering conjectures about new situations: these thoughts I did not think it necessary to check; they might germinate and bear fruit if they could.

Mr Rochester had been absent upwards of a fortnight, when the post brought Mrs Fairfax a letter.

'It is from the master,' said she, as she looked at the direction. 'Now I suppose we shall know whether we are to expect his return or not.'

And while she broke the seal and perused the document, I went on taking my coffee (we were at breakfast): it was hot, and I attributed to that circumstance a fiery glow which suddenly rose to my face. Why my hand shook, and why I involuntarily spilt half the contents of my cup into my saucer, I did not choose to consider.

'Well, I sometimes think we are too quiet; but we run a chance of being busy enough now: for a little while at least,' said Mrs Fairfax, still holding the note before her spectacles.

Ere I permitted myself to request an explanation, I tied the string of Adèle's pinafore, which happened to be loose: having helped her also to another bun and refilled her mug with milk, I said, nonchalantly – 'Mr Rochester is not likely to return soon, I suppose?'

'Indeed he is – in three days, he says: that will be next Thursday; and not alone either. I don't know how many of the fine people at the Leas are coming with him: he sends directions for all the best bedrooms to be prepared; and the library and drawing-rooms are to be cleaned out; and I am to get more kitchen hands from the George Inn, at Millcote, and from wherever else I can; and the ladies will bring their maids and the gentlemen their valets: so we shall have a full house of it.' And Mrs Fairfax swallowed her breakfast and hastened away to commence operations.

The three days were, as she had foretold, busy enough. I had thought all the rooms at Thornfield beautifully clean and well arranged; but it appears I was mistaken. Three women were got to help; and such scrubbing, such brushing, such washing of paint and beating of carpets, such taking down and putting up of pictures, such polishing of mirrors and lustres, such lighting of fires in bedrooms, such airing of sheets and feather-beds on hearths, I never beheld, either before or since. Adèle ran quite wild in the midst of it: the preparations for company and the prospect of their arrival, seemed to throw her into ecstasies. She would have Sophie to look over all her 'toilettes', as she called frocks; to furbish up any that were '*passées*', and to air and arrange the new. For herself, she did nothing but caper about in the front chambers, jump on and off the bedsteads, and lie on the mattresses and piled-up bolsters and pillows before the enormous fires roaring in the chimneys. From school duties she was exonerated: Mrs Fairfax had pressed me into her service, and I was all day in the storeroom, helping (or hindering) her and the cook; learning to make custards and cheese-cakes and French pastry, to truss game and garnish dessert-dishes.

The party were expected to arrive on Thursday afternoon, in time for dinner at six. During the intervening period I had no time to nurse chimeras; and I believe I was as active and gay as anybody – Adèle excepted. Still, now and then, I received a damping check to my cheerfulness; and was, in spite of myself, thrown back on the region of doubts and portents, and dark conjectures. This was when I chanced to see the third-storey staircase door (which of late had always been kept locked) open slowly, and give passage to the form of Grace Poole, in prim cap, white apron, and handkerchief; when I watched her glide along the gallery, her quiet tread muffled in a list slipper; when I saw her look into the bustling, topsy-turvy bedrooms, just say a word, perhaps, to the charwoman about the proper way to polish a grate, or clean a marble mantelpiece, or take stains from papered walls, and then pass on. She would thus descend to the kitchen once a day, eat her dinner, smoke a moderate pipe on the hearth, and go back, carrying her pot of porter with her, for her private solace, in her own gloomy, upper haunt. Only one hour in the twenty-four did she pass with her fellow-servants below; all the rest of her time was spent in some low-ceiled, oaken chamber of the second storey: there she sat and sewed – and probably laughed drearily to herself, as companionless as a prisoner in his dungeon.

The strangest thing of all was, that not a soul in the house, except me, noticed her habits, or seemed to marvel at them: no one discussed her position or employment; no one pitied her solitude or isolation. I once, indeed, overheard part of a dialogue between Leah and one of the charwomen, of which Grace formed the subject. Leah had been saying something I had not caught, and the charwoman remarked – 'She gets good wages, I guess?'

'Yes,' said Leah; 'I wish I had as good; not that mine are to complain of, there's no stinginess at Thornfield; but they're not one fifth of the sum Mrs Poole receives. And she is laying by: she goes every quarter to the bank at Millcote. I should not wonder but she has saved enough to keep her independent if she liked to leave; but I suppose she's got used to the place; and then she's not forty yet, and strong and able for anything. It is too soon for her to give up business.'

'She is a good hand, I dare say,' said the charwoman.

'Ah! – she understands what she has to do, nobody better,' rejoined Leah significantly; 'and it is not everyone could fill her shoes – not for all the money she gets.'

'That it is not!' was the reply. 'I wonder whether the master – '

The charwoman was going on; but here Leah turned and perceived me, and she instantly gave her companion a nudge.

'Doesn't she know?' I heard the woman whisper.

Leah shook her head, and the conversation was of course dropped. All I had gathered from it amounted to this, that there was a mystery at Thornfield; and that from participation in that mystery I was purposely excluded.

Thursday came: all work had been completed the previous evening; carpets were laid down, bed-hangings festooned, radiant white counterpanes spread, toilet tables arranged, furniture rubbed, flowers piled in vases: both chambers and saloons looked as fresh and bright as hands could make them. The hall, too, was scoured; and the great carved clock, as well as the steps and banisters of the staircase, were polished to the brightness of glass; in the dining-room, the sideboard flashed resplendent with plate; in the drawing-room and boudoir, vases of exotics bloomed on all sides. Afternoon arrived: Mrs Fairfax assumed her best black satin gown, her gloves, and her gold watch; for it was her part to receive the company, to conduct the ladies to their rooms, etc. Adèle, too, would be dressed: though I thought she had little chance of being introduced to the party that day at least. However, to please her, I allowed Sophie to apparel her in one of her short, full muslin frocks. For myself, I had no need to make any change; I should not be called upon to quit my sanctum of the schoolroom; for a sanctum it was now become to me, 'a very pleasant refuge in time of trouble.'

It had been a mild, serene spring day – one of those days which, towards the end of March or the beginning of April, rise shining over the earth as heralds of summer. It was drawing to an end now; but the evening was even warm, and I sat at work in the schoolroom with the window open.

'It gets late,' said Mrs Fairfax, entering in rustling state. 'I am glad I ordered dinner an hour after the time Mr Rochester mentioned; for it is past six now. I have sent John down to the gates to see if there is anything on the road: one can see a long way from thence in the direction of Millcote.' She went to the window. 'Here he is!' said she. 'Well, John' (leaning out), 'any news?'

'They're coming, ma'am,' was the answer. 'They'll be here in ten minutes.'

Adèle flew to the window. I followed, taking care to stand on one side, so that, screened by the curtain, I could see without being seen.

The ten minutes John had given seemed very long, but at last wheels were heard; four equestrians galloped up the drive, and after them came two open carriages. Fluttering veils and waving plumes filled the vehicles; two of the cavaliers were young, dashing-looking gentlemen; the third was Mr Rochester, on his black horse, Mesrour, Pilot bounding before him; at his side rode a lady, and he and she were the first of the party. Her purple riding-habit almost swept the ground, her veil streamed long on the breeze; mingling with its transparent folds, and gleaming through them, shone rich raven ringlets.

'Miss Ingram!' exclaimed Mrs Fairfax, and away she hurried to her post below.

The cavalcade, following the sweep of the drive, quickly turned the angle of the house, and I lost sight of it. Adèle now petitioned to go down; but I took her on my knee, and gave her to understand that she must not on any account think of venturing in sight of the ladies, either now or at any other time, unless expressly sent for: that Mr Rochester would be very angry, etc. Some natural tears she shed on being told this; but as I began to look very grave, she consented at last to wipe them.

A joyous stir was now audible in the hall: gentlemen's deep tones and ladies' silvery accents blent harmoniously together, and distinguishable above all, though not loud, was the sonorous voice of the master of Thornfield Hall, welcoming his fair and gallant guests under its roof. Then light steps ascended the stairs; and there was a tripping through the gallery, and soft cheerful laughs, and opening and closing doors, and, for a time, a hush.

'Elles changent de toilettes,' said Adèle; who, listening attentively, had followed every movement; and she sighed.

'Chez maman,' said she, 'quand il y avait du monde, je le suivais partout, au salon et à leurs chambres; souvent je regardais les femmes de chambre coiffer et habiller les dames, et c'était si amusant: comme cela on apprend.'

'Don't you feel hungry, Adèle?'

'Mais oui, mademoiselle: voilà cinq ou six heures que nous n'avons pas mangé.'

'Well now, while the ladies are in their rooms, I will venture down and get you something to eat.'

And issuing from my asylum with precaution, I sought a back-stairs which conducted directly to the kitchen. All in that region was fire and commotion; the soup and fish were in the last stage of projection, and the cook hung over her crucibles in a frame of mind and body threatening spontaneous combustion. In the servants' hall two coachmen and three gentlemen's gentlemen stood or sat round the fire; the abigails, I suppose, were upstairs with their mistresses; the new servants, that had been hired from Millcote, were bustling about everywhere. Threading this chaos, I at last reached the larder; there I took possession of a cold chicken, a roll of bread, some tarts, a plate or two and a knife and fork: with this booty I made a hasty retreat. I had regained the gallery, and was just shutting the back-door behind me, when an accelerated hum warned me that the ladies were about to issue from their chambers. I could not proceed to the schoolroom without passing some of their doors, and running the risk of being surprised with my cargo of victualage; so I stood still at this end, which, being windowless, was dark: quite dark now, for the sun was set and twilight gathering.

Presently the chambers gave up their fair tenants one after another: each came out gaily and airily, with dress that gleamed lustrous through the dusk. For a moment they stood grouped together at the other extremity of the gallery, conversing in a key of sweet subdued vivacity: they then descended the staircase almost as noiselessly as a bright mist rolls down a hill. Their collective appearance had left on me an impression of high-born elegance, such as I had never before received.

I found Adèle peeping through the schoolroom door, which she held ajar. 'What beautiful ladies!' cried she in English. 'Oh, I wish I might go to them! Do you think Mr Rochester will send for us by and by, after dinner?'

'No, indeed, I don't; Mr Rochester has something else to think about. Never mind the ladies tonight; perhaps you will see them tomorrow: here is your dinner.'

She was really hungry, so the chicken and tarts served to divert her attention for a time. It was well I secured this forage, or both she, I, and Sophie, to whom I conveyed a share of our repast, would have run a chance of getting no dinner at all: everyone downstairs was too much engaged to think of us. The dessert was not carried out till after nine, and at ten footmen were still running to and fro with trays and coffee-cups. I allowed Adèle to sit up much later than usual; for she declared she could not possibly go to sleep while the doors kept opening and shutting below and people bustling about. Besides, she added, a message might possibly come from Mr Rochester when she was undressed; 'et alors quel dommage!'

the fancy miniature I had painted of her; and thirdly – it will out! – whether it were such as I should fancy likely to suit Mr Rochester's taste.

As far as person went, she answered point for point, both to my picture and Mrs Fairfax's description. The noble bust, the sloping shoulders, the graceful neck, the dark eyes and black ringlets were all there; but her face? Her face was like her mother's; a youthful unfurrowed likeness: the same low brow, the same high features, the same pride. It was not, however, so saturnine a pride! she laughed continually; her laugh was satirical, and so was the habitual expression of her arched and haughty lip.

Genius is said to be self-conscious. I cannot tell whether Miss Ingram was a genius, but she was self-conscious – remarkably self-conscious indeed. She entered into a discourse on botany with the gentle Mrs Dent. It seemed Mrs Dent had not studied that science: though, as she said, she liked flowers, 'especially wild ones'; Miss Ingram had, and she ran over its vocabulary with an air. I presently perceived she was (what is vernacularly termed) *trailing* Mrs Dent; that is, playing on her ignorance: her *trail* might be clever, but it was decidedly not good-natured. She played: her execution was brilliant; she sang, her voice was fine; she talked French apart to her mama; and she talked it well, with fluency and with a good accent.

Mary had a milder and more open countenance than Blanche; softer features too, and a skin some shades fairer (Miss Ingram was dark as a Spaniard) – but Mary was deficient in life: her face lacked expression, her eye lustre; she had nothing to say, and having once taken her seat, remained fixed like a statue in its niche. The sisters were both attired in spotless white.

And did I now think Miss Ingram such a choice as Mr Rochester would be likely to make? I could not tell – I did not know his taste in female beauty. If he liked the majestic, she was the very type of majesty: then she was accomplished, sprightly. Most gentlemen would admire her, I thought; and that he *did* admire her, I already seemed to have obtained proof: to remove the last shade of doubt, it remained but to see them together.

You are not to suppose, reader, that Adèle has all this time been sitting motionless on the stool at my feet: no; when the ladies entered, she rose, advanced to meet them, made a stately reverence, and said with gravity – 'Bon jour, mesdames.'

And Miss Ingram had looked down at her with a mocking air, and exclaimed, 'Oh, what a little puppet!'

Lady Lynn had remarked, 'It is Mr Rochester's ward, I suppose – the little French girl he was speaking of.'

Mrs Dent had kindly taken her hand, and given her a kiss. Amy and Louisa Eshton had cried out simultaneously – 'What a love of a child!'

And then they had called her to a sofa, where she now sat, ensconced between them, chattering alternately in French and broken English; absorbing not only the young ladies' attention, but that of Mrs Eshton and Lady Lynn, and getting spoilt to her heart's content.

At last coffee is brought in, and the gentlemen are summoned. I sit in the



I told her stories as long as she would listen to them; and then for a change I took her out into the gallery. The hall lamp was now lit, and it amused her to look over the balustrade and watch the servants passing backwards and forwards. When the evening was far advanced, a sound of music issued from the drawing-room, whither the piano had been removed; Adèle and I sat down on the top step of the stairs to listen. Presently a voice blent with the rich tones of the instrument; it was a lady who sang, and very sweet her notes were. The solo over, a duet followed, and then a glee: a joyous conversational murmur filled up the intervals. I listened long: suddenly I discovered that my ear was wholly intent on analysing the mingled sounds, and trying to discriminate amidst the confusion of accents those of Mr Rochester; and when it caught them, which it soon did, it found a further task in framing the tones, rendered by distance inarticulate, into words.

The clock struck eleven. I looked at Adèle, whose head leant against my shoulder; her eyes were waxing heavy, so I took her up in my arms and carried her off to bed. It was near one before the gentlemen and ladies sought their chambers.

The next day was as fine as its predecessor: it was devoted by the party to an excursion to some site in the neighbourhood. They set out early in the forenoon, some on horseback, the rest in carriages; I witnessed both the departure and the return. Miss Ingram, as before, was the only lady equestrian; and, as before, Mr Rochester galloped at her side; the two rode a little apart from the rest. I pointed out this circumstance to Mrs Fairfax, who was standing at the window with me – 'You said it was not likely they should think of being married,' said I, 'but you see Mr Rochester evidently prefers her to any of the other ladies.'

'Yes, I dare say: no doubt he admires her.'

'And she him,' I added; 'look how she leans her head towards him as if she were conversing confidentially; I wish I could see her face; I have never had a glimpse of it yet.'

'You will see her this evening,' answered Mrs Fairfax. 'I happened to remark to Mr Rochester how much Adèle wished to be introduced to the ladies, and he said: "Oh! let her come into the drawing-room after dinner; and request Miss Eyre to accompany her." '

'Yes; he said that from mere politeness: I need not go, I am sure,' I answered.

'Well, I observed to him that as you were unused to company, I did not think you would like appearing before so gay a party – all strangers; and he replied, in his quick way – "Nonsense! If she objects, tell her it is my particular wish; and if she resists, say I shall come and fetch her in case of contumacy." '

'I will not give him that trouble,' I answered. 'I will go, if no better may be; but I don't like it. Shall you be there, Mrs Fairfax?'

'No; I pleaded off, and he admitted my plea. I'll tell you how to manage so as to avoid the embarrassment of making a formal entrance, which is the most disagreeable part of the business. You must go into the drawing-room while it is empty, before the ladies leave the dinner-table; choose your seat in any quiet nook you like; you need not stay long after the gentlemen come in, unless you please: just let Mr Rochester see you are there and then slip away – nobody will notice you.'

'Will these people remain long, do you think?'

'Perhaps two or three weeks, certainly not more. After the Easter recess, Sir George Lynn, who was lately elected member for Millcote, will have to go up to town and take his seat; I dare say Mr Rochester will accompany him: it surprises me that he has already made so protracted a stay at Thornfield.'

It was with some trepidation that I perceived the hour approach when I was to repair with my charge to the drawing-room. Adèle had been in a state of ecstasy all day, after hearing she was to be presented to the ladies in the evening; and it was not till Sophie commenced the operation of dressing her that she sobered down. Then the importance of the process quickly steadied her, and by the time she had her curls arranged in well-smoothed, drooping clusters, her pink satin frock put on, her long sash tied, and her lace mittens adjusted, she looked as grave as any judge. No need to warn her not to disarrange her attire: when she was dressed, she sat demurely down in her little chair, taking care previously to lift up the satin skirt for fear she should crease it, and assured me she would not stir thence till I was ready. This I quickly was: my best dress (the silver-grey one, purchased for Miss Temple's wedding, and never worn since) was soon put on; my hair was soon smoothed; my sole ornament, the pearl brooch, soon assumed. We descended.

Fortunately there was another entrance to the drawing-room than that through the saloon where they were all seated at dinner. We found the apartment vacant; a large fire burning silently on the marble hearth, and wax candles shining in bright solitude, amid the exquisite flowers with which the tables were adorned. The crimson curtain hung before the arch: slight as was the separation this drapery formed from the party in the adjoining saloon, they spoke in so low a key that nothing of their conversation could be distinguished beyond a soothing murmur.

Adèle, who appeared to be still under the influence of a most solemnising impression, sat down, without a word, on the footstool I pointed out to her. I retired to a window-seat, and taking a book from a table near, endeavoured to read. Adèle brought her stool to my feet; ere long she touched my knee.

'What is it, Adèle?'

'Est-ce que je ne puis pas prendre une seule de ces fleurs magnifiques, mademoiselle? Seulement pour completer ma toilette.'

'You think too much of your "toilette", Adèle: but you may have a flower.' And I took a rose from a vase and fastened it in her sash. She sighed a sigh of ineffable satisfaction, as if her cup of happiness were now full. I turned my face away to conceal a smile I could not suppress: there was something ludicrous as well as painful in the little Parisienne's earnest and innate devotion to matters of dress.

A soft sound of rising now became audible; the curtain was swept back from the arch; through it appeared the dining-room, with its lit lustre pouring down light on the silver and glass of a magnificent dessert-service covering a long table; a band of ladies stood in the opening; they entered, and the curtain fell behind them.



There were but eight; yet, somehow, as they flocked in, impression of a much larger number. Some of them were very ta dressed in white; and all had a sweeping amplitude of array th magnify their persons as a mist magnifies the moon. I rose and them: one or two bent their heads in return, the others only stare

They dispersed about the room, reminding me, by the lightness a of their movements, of a flock of white plumy birds. Some of them t selves in half-reclining positions on the sofas and ottomans: some be tables and examined the flowers and books: the rest gathered in a gr the fire: all talked in a low but clear tone which seemed habitual to the their names afterwards, and may as well mention them now.

First, there was Mrs Eshton and two of her daughters. She had evide a handsome woman, and was well preserved still. Of her daughters, t Amy, was rather little: naïve, and childlike in face and manner, and p form; her white muslin dress and blue sash became her well. The second was taller and more elegant in figure; with a very pretty face, of that o French term *minois chiffoné*: both sisters were fair as lilies.

Lady Lynn was a large and stout personage of about forty, very ere haughty-looking, richly dressed in a satin robe of changeful sheen: her da shone glossily under the shade of an azure plume, and within the circlet of of gems.

Mrs Colonel Dent was less showy; but, I thought, more lady-like. She slight figure, a pale, gentle face, and fair hair. Her black satin dress, her sc rich foreign lace, and her pearl ornaments, pleased me better than the rai radiance of the titled dame.

But the three most distinguished – partly, perhaps, because the tallest fig of the band – were the Dowager Lady Ingram and her daughters, Blanche Mary. They were all three of the loftiest stature of women. The Dowager mi be between forty and fifty: her shape was still fine; her hair (by candleligh least) still black; her teeth, too, were still apparently perfect. Most people wo have termed her a splendid woman of her age: and so she was, no dou physically speaking; but then there was an expression of almost insupportab haughtiness in her bearing and countenance. She had Roman features a a double chin, disappearing into a throat like a pillar: these features appeare to me not only inflated and darkened, but even furrowed with pride; and th chin was sustained by the same principle, in a position of almost preternatura erectness. She had, likewise, a fierce and a hard eye: it reminded me of Mr Reed's; she mouthed her words in speaking; her voice was deep, its inflections very pompous, very dogmatical, very intolerable, in short. A crimson velvet robe, and a shawl turban of some gold-wrought Indian fabric, invested her (I suppose she thought) with a truly imperial dignity.

Blanche and Mary were of equal stature, straight and tall as poplars. Mary was too slim for her height, but Blanche was moulded like a Dian. I regarded her, of course, with special interest. First, I wished to see whether her appearance accorded with Mrs Fairfax's description; secondly, whether it at all resembled

shade – if any shade there be in this brilliantly-lit apartment; the window-curtain half hides me. Again the arch yawns; they come. The collective appearance of the gentlemen, like that of the ladies, is very imposing: they are all costumed in black; most of them are tall, some young. Henry and Frederick Lynn are very dashing sparks indeed; and Colonel Dent is a fine soldierly man. Mr Eshton, the magistrate of the district, is gentlemanlike: his hair is quite white, his eyebrows and whiskers still dark, which gives him something of the appearance of a 'père noble de théâtre'. Lord Ingram, like his sisters, is very tall; like them, also, he is handsome; but he shares Mary's apathetic and listless look: he seems to have more length of limb than vivacity of blood or vigour of brain.

And where is Mr Rochester?

He comes in last: I am not looking at the arch, yet I see him enter. I try to concentrate my attention on those netting-needles, on the meshes of the purse I am forming – I wish to think only of the work I have in my hands, to see only the silver beads and silk threads that lie in my lap; whereas, I distinctly behold his figure, and I inevitably recall the moment when I last saw it; just after I had rendered him, what he deemed, an essential service, and he, holding my hand, and looking down on my face, surveyed me with eyes that revealed a heart full and eager to overflow; in whose emotions I had a part. How near had I approached him at that moment! What had occurred since, calculated to change his and my relative positions? Yet now, how distant, how far estranged we were! So far estranged, that I did not expect him to come and speak to me. I did not wonder, when, without looking at me, he took a seat at the other side of the room, and began conversing with some of the ladies.

No sooner did I see that his attention was riveted on them, and that I might gaze without being observed, than my eyes were drawn involuntarily to his face; I could not keep their lids under control: they would rise, and the irids would fix on him. I looked, and had an acute pleasure in looking, a precious yet poignant pleasure; pure gold, with a steely point of agony: a pleasure like what the thirst-perishing man might feel who knows the well to which he has crept is poisoned, yet stoops and drinks divine draughts nevertheless.

Most true is it that 'beauty is in the eye of the gazer'. My master's colourless, olive face, square, massive brow, broad and jetty eyebrows, deep eyes, strong features, firm, grim mouth, all energy, decision, will, were not beautiful, according to rule; but they were more than beautiful to me; they were full of an interest, an influence that quite mastered me, that took my feelings from my own power and fettered them in his. I had not intended to love him; the reader knows I had wrought hard to extirpate from my soul the germs of love there detected; and now, at the first renewed view of him, they spontaneously arrived, green and strong! He made me love him without looking at me.

I compared him with his guests. What was the gallant grace of the Lynns, the languid elegance of Lord Ingram, even the military distinction of Colonel Dent, contrasted with his look of native pith and genuine power? I had no sympathy in their appearance, their expression: yet I could imagine that most observers would call them attractive, handsome, imposing; while they would pronounce Mr Rochester at once harsh-featured and melancholy-looking. I saw them smile, laugh – it was nothing; the light of the candles had as much soul in it as their smile; the tinkle of the bell as much significance as their laugh. I saw Mr Rochester smile: his stern features softened; his eye grew both brilliant and gentle, its ray both searching and sweet. He was talking, at the moment, to Louisa and Amy Eshton. I wondered to see them receive with calm that look which seemed to me so penetrating: I expected their eyes to fall, their colour to rise under it; yet I was glad when I found they were in no sense moved. 'He is not to them what he is to me,' I thought: 'he is not of their kind. I believe he is of mine; I am sure he is – I feel akin to him – I understand the language of his countenance and movements: though rank and wealth sever us widely, I have something in my brain and heart, in my blood and nerves, that assimilates me mentally to him. Did I say, a few days since, that I had nothing to do with him but to receive my salary at his hands? Did I forbid myself to think of him in any other light than as a paymaster? Blasphemy against nature! Every good, true, vigorous feeling I have gathers impulsively round him. I know I must conceal my sentiments: I must smother hope; I must remember that he cannot care much for me. For when I say that I am of his kind, I do not mean that I have his force to influence, and his spell to attract; I mean only that I have certain tastes and feelings in common with him. I must, then, repeat continually that we are for ever sundered: and yet, while I breathe and think, I must love him.'

Coffee is handed. The ladies, since the gentlemen entered, have become lively as larks; conversation waxes brisk and merry. Colonel Dent and Mr Eshton argue on politics; their wives listen. The two proud dowagers, Lady Lynn and Lady Ingram, confabulate together. Sir George – whom, by the by, I have forgotten to describe, a very big, and very fresh-looking country gentleman, stands before their sofa, coffee-cup in hand, and occasionally puts in a word. Mr Frederick Lynn has taken a seat beside Mary Ingram, and is showing her the engravings of a splendid volume: she looks, smiles now and then, but apparently says little. The tall and phlegmatic Lord Ingram leans with folded arms on the chair-back of the little and lively Amy Eshton; she glances up at him, and chatters like a wren: she likes him better than she does Mr Rochester. Henry Lynn has taken possession of an ottoman at the feet of Louisa: Adèle shares it with him: he is trying to talk French with her, and Louisa laughs at his blunders. With whom will Blanche Ingram pair? She is standing alone at the table, bending gracefully over an album. She seems waiting to be sought; but she will not wait too long: she herself selects a mate.

Mr Rochester, having quitted the Eshtons, stands on the hearth as solitary as she stands by the table: she confronts him, taking her station on the opposite side of the mantelpiece.

'Mr Rochester, I thought you were not fond of children?'

'Nor am I.'

'Then, what induced you to take charge of such a little doll as that?' (pointing to Adèle). 'Where did you pick her up?'

'I did not pick her up; she was left on my hands.'

'You should have sent her to school.'

'I could not afford it: schools are so dear.'

'Why, I suppose you have a governess for her: I saw a person with her just now – is she gone? Oh, no! there she is still, behind the window-curtain. You pay her, of course; I should think it quite as expensive, more so; for you have them both to keep in addition.'

I feared – or should I say, hoped? – the allusion to me would make Mr Rochester glance my way; and I involuntarily shrank farther into the shade: but he never turned his eyes.

'I have not considered the subject,' said he indifferently, looking straight before him.

'No, you men never do consider economy and common sense. You should hear mama on the chapter of governesses: Mary and I have had, I should think, a dozen at least in our day; half of them detestable and the rest ridiculous, and all incubi – were they not, mama?'

'Did you speak, my own?'

The young lady thus claimed as the dowager's special property, reiterated her question with an explanation.

'My dearest, don't mention governesses; the word makes me nervous. I have suffered a martyrdom from their incompetency and caprice. I thank Heaven I have now done with them!'

Mrs Dent here bent over to the pious lady, and whispered something in her ear; I suppose, from the answer elicited, it was a reminder that one of the anathematised race was present.

'Tant pis!' said her ladyship, 'I hope it may do her good!' Then, in a lower tone, but still loud enough for me to hear, 'I noticed her; I am a judge of physiognomy, and in hers I see all the faults of her class.'

'What are they, madam?' enquired Mr Rochester aloud.

'I will tell you in your private ear,' replied she, wagging her turban three times with portentous significancy.

'But my curiosity will be past its appetite; it craves food now.'

'Ask Blanche; she is nearer you than I.'

'Oh, don't refer him to me, mama! I have just one word to say of the whole tribe; they are a nuisance. Not that I ever suffered much from them; I took care to turn the tables. What tricks Theodore and I used to play on our Miss Wilsons, and Mrs Greys, and Mme Jouberts! Mary was always too sleepy to join in a plot with spirit. The best fun was with Mme Joubert: Miss Wilson was a poor sickly thing, lachrymose and low-spirited, not worth the trouble of vanquishing, in short; and Mrs Grey was coarse and insensible; no blow took effect on her. But poor Mme Joubert! I see her yet in her raging passions, when we had driven her to extremities – spilt our tea, crumbled our bread and butter, tossed our books up to the ceiling, and played a charivari with the ruler and desk, the fender and fire-irons. Theodore, do you remember those merry days?'

'Yaas, to be sure I do,' drawled Lord Ingram; 'and the poor old stick used to cry out "Oh you villains childs!" – and then we sermonised her on the presumption of attempting to teach such clever blades as we were, when she was herself so ignorant.'

'We did; and, Tedo, you know, I helped you in prosecuting (or persecuting) your tutor, whey-faced Mr Vining – the parson in the pip, as we used to call him. He and Miss Wilson took the liberty of falling in love with each other – at least Tedo and I thought so; we surprised sundry tender glances and sighs which we interpreted as tokens of "la belle passion", and I promise you the public soon had the benefit of our discovery; we employed it as a sort of lever to hoist our dead-weights from the house. Dear mama, there, as soon as she got an inkling of the business, found out that it was of an immoral tendency. Did you not, my lady-mother?'

'Certainly, my best. And I was quite right: depend on that: there are a thousand reasons why liaisons between governesses and tutors should never be tolerated a moment in any well-regulated house; firstly – '

'Oh, gracious, mama! Spare us the enumeration! *Au reste*, we all know them: danger of bad example to innocence of childhood; distractions and consequent neglect of duty on the part of the attached – mutual alliance and reliance; confidence thence resulting – insolence accompanying – mutiny and general blow-up. Am I right, Baroness Ingram, of Ingram Park?'

'My lily-flower, you are right now, as always.'

'Then no more need be said: change the subject.'

Amy Eshton, not hearing or not heeding this dictum, joined in with her soft, infantine tone: 'Louisa and I used to quiz our governess too; but she was such a good creature, she would bear anything: nothing put her out. She was never cross with us; was she, Louisa?'

'No, never: we might do what we pleased; ransack her desk and her work-box, and turn her drawers inside out; and she was so good-natured, she would give us anything we asked for.'

'I suppose, now,' said Miss Ingram, curling her lip sarcastically, 'we shall have an abstract of the memoirs of all the governesses extant: in order to avert such a visitation, I again move the introduction of a new topic. Mr Rochester, do you second my motion?'

'Madam, I support you on this point, as on every other.'

'Then on me be the onus of bringing it forward. Signior Eduardo, are you in voice tonight?'

'Donna Bianca, if you command it, I will be.'

'Then, signior, I lay on you my sovereign behest to furbish up your lungs and other vocal organs, as they will be wanted on my royal service.'

'Who would not be the Rizzio of so divine a Mary?'

'A fig for Rizzio!' cried she, tossing her head with all its curls, as she moved to the piano. 'It is my opinion the fiddler David must have been an insipid sort of fellow; I like black Bothwell better: to my mind a man is nothing without a spice of the devil in him; and history may say what it will of James Hepburn, but I have a notion, he was just the sort of wild, fierce, bandit hero whom I could have consented to gift with my hand.'

'Gentlemen, you hear! Now which of you most resembles Bothwell?' cried Mr Rochester.

'I should say the preference lies with you,' responded Colonel Dent.

'On my honour, I am much obliged to you,' was the reply.

Miss Ingram, who had now seated herself with proud grace at the piano, spreading out her snowy robes in queenly amplitude, commenced a brilliant prelude; talking meantime. She appeared to be on her high horse tonight; both her words and her air seemed intended to excite not only the admiration, but the amazement of her auditors: she was evidently bent on striking them as something very dashing and daring indeed.

'Oh, I am so sick of the young men of the present day!' exclaimed she, rattling away at the instrument. 'Poor, puny things, not fit to stir a step beyond papa's park gates: nor to go even so far without mama's permission and guardianship! Creatures so absorbed in care about their pretty faces, and their white hands, and their small feet; as if a man had anything to do with beauty! As if loveliness were not the special prerogative of woman – her legitimate appanage and heritage! I grant an ugly *woman* is a blot on the fair face of creation; but as to the *gentlemen*, let them be solicitous to possess only strength and valour: let their motto be: Hunt, shoot, and fight: the rest is not worth a fillip. Such should be my device, were I a man.'

'Whenever I marry,' she continued after a pause which none interrupted, 'I am resolved my husband shall not be a rival, but a foil to me. I will suffer no competitor near the throne; I shall exact an undivided homage: his devotions shall not be shared between me and the shape he sees in his mirror. Mr Rochester, now sing, and I will play for you.'

'I am all obedience,' was the response.

'Here then is a Corsair-song. Know that I dote on Corsairs; and for that reason, sing it *con spirito*.'

'Commands from Miss Ingram's lips would put spirit into a mug of milk and water.'

'Take care, then: if you don't please me, I will shame you by showing how such things *should* be done.'

'That is offering a premium on incapacity: I shall now endeavour to fail.'

'Gardez-vous en bien! If you err wilfully, I shall devise a proportionate punishment.'

'Miss Ingram ought to be clement, for she has it in her power to inflict a chastisement beyond mortal endurance.'

'Ha! explain!' commanded the lady.

'Pardon me, madam: no need of explanation; your own fine sense must inform you that one of your frowns would be a sufficient substitute for capital punishment.'

'Sing!' said she, and again touching the piano, she commenced an accompaniment in spirited style.

'Now is my time to slip away,' thought I: but the tones that then severed the air arrested me. Mrs Fairfax had said Mr Rochester possessed a fine voice: he did – a mellow, powerful bass, into which he threw his own feeling, his own force: finding a way through the ear to the heart, and there waking sensation strangely. I waited till the last deep and full vibration had expired – till the tide of talk, checked an instant, had resumed its flow; I then quitted my sheltered corner and made my exit by the side-door, which was fortunately near. Thence a narrow passage led into the hall: in crossing it, I perceived my sandal was loose; I stopped to tie it, kneeling down for that purpose on the mat at the foot of the staircase. I heard the dining-room door unclose; a gentleman came out; rising hastily, I stood face to face with him: it was Mr Rochester.

'How do you do?' he asked.

'I am very well, sir.'

'Why did you not come and speak to me in the room?'

I thought I might have retorted the question on him who put it: but I would not take that freedom. I answered – 'I did not wish to disturb you, as you seemed engaged, sir.'

'What have you been doing during my absence?'

'Nothing particular; teaching Adèle as usual.'

'And getting a good deal paler than you were – as I saw at first sight. What is the matter?'

'Nothing at all, sir.'

'Did you take any cold that night you half drowned me?'

'Not the least.'

'Return to the drawing-room: you are deserting too early.'

'I am tired, sir.'

He looked at me for a minute.

'And a little depressed,' he said. 'What about? Tell me.'

'Nothing – nothing, sir. I am not depressed.'

'But I affirm that you are: so much depressed that a few more words would bring tears to your eyes – indeed, they are there now, shining and swimming; and a bead has slipped from the lash and fallen on to the flag. If I had time, and was not in mortal dread of some prating prig of a servant passing, I would know what all this means. Well, tonight I excuse you; but understand that so long as my visitors stay, I expect you to appear in the drawing-room every evening; it is my wish; don't neglect it. Now go, and send Sophie for Adèle. Good-night, my – ' He stopped, bit his lip, and abruptly left me.

## *Chapter 18*

Merry days were these at Thornfield Hall; and busy days too: how different from the first three months of stillness, monotony, and solitude I had passed beneath its roof! All sad feelings seemed now driven from the house, all gloomy associations forgotten: there was life everywhere, movement all day long. You could not now traverse the gallery, once so hushed, nor enter the front chambers, once so tenantless, without encountering a smart lady's-maid or a dandy valet.

The kitchen, the butler's pantry, the servants' hall, the entrance hall, were equally alive; and the saloons were only left void and still when the blue sky and halcyon sunshine of the genial spring weather called their occupants out into the grounds. Even when that weather was broken, and continuous rain set in for some days, no damp seemed cast over enjoyment: indoor amusements only became more lively and varied, in consequence of the stop put to outdoor gaiety.

I wondered what they were going to do the first evening a change of entertainment was proposed: they spoke of 'playing charades,' but in my ignorance I did not understand the term. The servants were called in, the dining-room tables wheeled away, the lights otherwise disposed, the chairs placed in a semicircle opposite the arch. While Mr Rochester and the other gentlemen directed these alterations, the ladies were running up and down stairs ringing for their maids. Mrs Fairfax was summoned to give information respecting the resources of the house in shawls, dresses, draperies of any kind; and certain wardrobes of the third storey were ransacked, and their contents, in the shape of brocaded and hooped petticoats, satin sacques, black modes, lace lappets, etc., were brought down in armfuls by the abigails; then a selection was made, and such things as were chosen were carried to the boudoir within the drawing-room.

Meantime, Mr Rochester had again summoned the ladies round him, and was selecting certain of their number to be of his party. 'Miss Ingram is mine, of course,' said he: afterwards he named the two Misses Eshton, and Mrs Dent. He looked at me: I happened to be near him, as I had been fastening the clasp of Mrs Dent's bracelet, which had got loose.

'Will you play?' he asked. I shook my head. He did not insist, which I rather feared he would have done; he allowed me to return quietly to my usual seat.

He and his aids now withdrew behind the curtain: the other party, which was headed by Colonel Dent, sat down on the crescent of chairs. One of the gentlemen, Mr Eshton, observing me, seemed to propose that I should be asked to join them; but Lady Ingram instantly negatived the notion.

'No,' I heard her say: 'she looks too stupid for any game of the sort.'

Ere long a bell tinkled, and the curtain drew up. Within the arch, the bulky figure of Sir George Lynn, whom Mr Rochester had likewise chosen, was seen enveloped in a white sheet: before him, on a table, lay open a large book; and at his side stood Amy Eshton, draped in Mr Rochester's cloak, and holding a book in her hand. Somebody, unseen, rang the bell merrily; then Adèle (who had insisted on being one of her guardian's party), bounded forward, scattering round her the contents of a basket of flowers she carried on her arm. Then appeared the magnificent figure of Miss Ingram, clad in white, a long veil on her head, and a wreath of roses round her brow; by her side walked Mr Rochester, and together they drew near the table. They knelt; while Mrs Dent and Louisa Eshton, dressed also in white, took up their stations behind them. A ceremony followed, in dumb show, in which it was easy to recognise the pantomime of a marriage. At its termination, Colonel Dent, and his party consulted in whispers for two minutes, then the Colonel called out – 'Bride!' Mr Rochester bowed, and the curtain fell.

A considerable interval elapsed before it again rose. Its second rising displayed a more elaborately prepared scene than the last. The drawing-room, as I have before observed, was raised two steps above the dining-room, and on the top of the upper step, placed a yard or two back within the room, appeared a large marble basin, which I recognised as an ornament of the conservatory – where it usually stood, surrounded by exotics, and tenanted by gold fish – and whence it must have been transported with some trouble, on account of its size and weight.

Seated on the carpet, by the side of this basin, was seen Mr Rochester, costumed in shawls, with a turban on his head. His dark eyes and swarthy skin and Paynim features suited the costume exactly: he looked the very model of an Eastern emir, an agent or a victim of the bowstring. Presently advanced into view Miss Ingram. She, too, was attired in oriental fashion: a crimson scarf tied sash-like round the waist; an embroidered handkerchief knotted about her temples; her beautifully moulded arms bare, one of them upraised in the act of supporting a pitcher, poised gracefully on her head. Both her cast of form and feature, her complexion and her general air, suggested the idea of some Israelitish princess of the patriarchal days; and such was doubtless the character she intended to represent.

She approached the basin, and bent over it as if to fill her pitcher; she again lifted it to her head. The personage on the well-brink now seemed to accost her; to make some request: 'She hasted, let down her pitcher on her hand, and gave him to drink.' From the bosom of his robe he then produced a casket, opened it and showed magnificent bracelets and earrings; she acted astonishment and admiration; kneeling, he laid the treasure at her feet; incredulity and delight were expressed by her looks and gestures; the stranger fastened the bracelets on her arms and the rings in her ears. It was Eliezer and Rebecca: the camels only were wanting.

The divining party again laid their heads together: apparently they could not agree about the word or syllable the scene illustrated. Colonel Dent, their spokesman, demanded 'the tableau of the whole'; whereupon the curtain again descended.

On its third rising only a portion of the drawing-room was disclosed; the rest being concealed by a screen, hung with some sort of dark and coarse drapery. The marble basin was removed; in its place stood a deal table and a kitchen chair: these objects were visible by a very dim light proceeding from a horn lantern, the wax candles being all extinguished.

Amidst this sordid scene, sat a man with his clenched hands resting on his knees, and his eyes bent on the ground. I knew Mr Rochester; though the begrimed face, the disordered dress (his coat hanging loose from one arm, as if it had been almost torn from his back in a scuffle), the desperate and scowling countenance, the rough, bristling hair might well have disguised him. As he moved, a chain clanked; to his wrists were attached fetters.

'Bridewell!' exclaimed Colonel Dent, and the charade was solved.

A sufficient interval having elapsed for the performers to resume their ordinary costume, they re-entered the dining-room. Mr Rochester led in Miss Ingram; she was complimenting him on his acting.

'Do you know,' said she, 'that, of the three characters, I liked you in the last best? Oh, had you but lived a few years earlier, what a gallant gentleman-highwayman you would have made!'

'Is all the soot washed from my face?' he asked, turning it towards her.

'Alas! yes: the more's the pity! Nothing could be more becoming to your complexion than that ruffian's rouge.'

'You would like a hero of the road then?'

'An English hero of the road would be the next best thing to an Italian bandit; and that could only be surpassed by a Levantine pirate.'

'Well, whatever I am, remember you are my wife; we were married an hour since, in the presence of all these witnesses.' She giggled, and her colour rose.

'Now, Dent,' continued Mr Rochester, 'it is your turn.' And as the other party withdrew, he and his band took the vacated seats. Miss Ingram placed herself at her leader's right hand; the other diviners filled the chairs on each side of him and her. I did not now watch the actors; I no longer waited with interest for the curtain to rise; my attention was absorbed by the spectators; my eyes, erewhile fixed on the arch, were now irresistibly attracted to the semicircle of chairs. What charade Colonel Dent and his party played, what word they chose, how they acquitted themselves, I no longer remember; but I still see the consultation which followed each scene: I see Mr Rochester turn to Miss Ingram, and Miss Ingram to him; I see her incline her head towards him, till the jetty curls almost touch his shoulder and wave against his cheek; I hear their mutual whisperings; I recall their interchanged glances; and something even of the feeling roused by the spectacle returns in memory at this moment.

I have told you, reader, that I had learnt to love Mr Rochester: I could not unlove him now, merely because I found that he had ceased to notice me – because I might pass hours in his presence, and he would never once turn his eyes in my direction – because I saw all his attentions appropriated by a great lady, who scorned to touch me with the hem of her robes as she passed; who, if ever her dark and imperious eye fell on me by chance, would withdraw it instantly as from an object too mean to merit observation. I could not unlove him, because I felt sure he would soon marry this very lady – because I read daily in her a proud security in his intentions respecting her – because I witnessed hourly in him a style of courtship which, if careless and choosing rather to be sought than to seek, was yet, in its very carelessness, captivating, and in its very pride, irresistible.

There was nothing to cool or banish love in these circumstances, though much to create despair. Much too, you will think, reader, to engender jealousy: if a woman, in my position, could presume to be jealous of a woman in Miss Ingram's. But I was not jealous: or very rarely; the nature of the pain I suffered could not be explained by that word. Miss Ingram was a mark beneath jealousy: she was too inferior to excite the feeling. Pardon the seeming paradox; I mean what I say. She was very showy, but she was not genuine: she had a fine person, many brilliant attainments; but her mind was poor, her heart barren by nature: nothing bloomed spontaneously on that soil; no unforced natural fruit delighted by its freshness. She was not good; she was not original: she used to repeat sounding phrases from books: she never offered, nor had, an opinion of her own. She advocated a high tone of sentiment; but she did not know the sensations of sympathy and pity; tenderness and truth were not in her. Too often she betrayed this, by the undue vent she gave to a spiteful antipathy she had conceived against little Adèle: pushing her away with some contumelious epithet if she happened to approach her; sometimes ordering her from the room, and always treating her with coldness and acrimony. Other eyes besides mine watched these manifestations of character – watched them closely, keenly, shrewdly. Yes; the future bridegroom, Mr Rochester himself, exercised over his intended a ceaseless surveillance; and it was from this sagacity – this guardedness of his – this perfect, clear consciousness of his fair one's defects – this obvious absence of passion in his sentiments towards her, that my ever-torturing pain arose.

I saw he was going to marry her, for family, perhaps political reasons, because her rank and connections suited him; I felt he had not given her his love, and that her qualifications were ill adapted to win from him that treasure. This was the point – this was where the nerve was touched and teased – this was where the fever was sustained and fed: *she could not charm him.*

If she had managed the victory at once, and he had yielded and sincerely laid his heart at her feet, I should have covered my face, turned to the wall, and (figuratively) have died to them. If Miss Ingram had been a good and noble woman, endowed with force, fervour, kindness, sense, I should have had one vital struggle with two tigers – jealousy and despair: then, my heart torn out and devoured, I should have admired her – acknowledged her excellence, and been quiet for the rest of my days: and the more absolute her superiority, the deeper would have been my admiration – the more truly tranquil my quiescence. But as matters really stood, to watch Miss Ingram's efforts at fascinating Mr Rochester, to witness their repeated failure – herself unconscious that they did fail; vainly fancying that each shaft launched hit the mark, and infatuatedly pluming herself on success, when her pride and self-complacency repelled further and further what she wished to allure – to witness *this*, was to be at once under ceaseless excitation and ruthless restraint.

Because, when she failed, I saw how she might have succeeded. Arrows that continually glanced off from Mr Rochester's breast and fell harmless at his feet, might, I knew, if shot by a surer hand, have quivered keen in his proud heart – have called love into his stern eye, and softness into his sardonic face; or, better still, without weapons a silent conquest might have been won.

'Why can she not influence him more, when she is privileged to draw so near to him?' I asked myself. 'Surely she cannot truly like him, or not like him with true affection! If she did, she need not coin her smiles so lavishly, flash her glances so unremittingly, manufacture airs so elaborate, graces so multitudinous. It seems to me that she might, by merely sitting quietly at his side, saying little and looking less, get nigher his heart. I have seen in his face a far different expression from that which hardens it now while she is so vivaciously accosting him; but then it came of itself: it was not elicited by meretricious arts and calculated manoeuvres; and one had but to accept it – to answer what he asked without pretension, to address him when needful without grimace – and it increased and grew kinder and more genial, and warmed one like a fostering sunbeam. How will she manage to please him when they are married? I do not think she will manage it; and yet it might be managed; and his wife might, I verily believe, be the very happiest woman the sun shines on.'

I have not yet said anything condemnatory of Mr Rochester's project of marrying for interest and connections. It surprised me when I first discovered that such was his intention: I had thought him a man unlikely to be influenced by motives so commonplace in his choice of a wife; but the longer I considered the position, education, etc., of the parties, the less I felt justified in judging and blaming either him or Miss Ingram for acting in conformity to ideas and principles instilled into them, doubtless, from their childhood. All their class held these principles: I supposed, then, they had reasons for holding them such as I could not fathom. It seemed to me that, were I a gentleman like him, I would take to my bosom only such a wife as I could love; but the very obviousness of the advantages to the husband's own happiness offered by this plan convinced me that there must be arguments against its general adoption of which I was quite ignorant: otherwise I felt sure all the world would act as I wished to act.

But in other points, as well as this, I was growing very lenient to my master: I was forgetting all his faults, for which I had once kept a sharp look-out. It had formerly been my endeavour to study all sides of his character: to take the bad with the good; and from the just weighing of both, to form an equitable judgement. Now I saw no bad. The sarcasm that had repelled, the harshness that had startled me once, were only like keen condiments in a choice dish: their presence was pungent, but their absence would be felt as comparatively insipid. And as for the vague something – was it a sinister or a sorrowful, a designing or a desponding expression? – that opened upon a careful observer, now and then, in his eye, and closed again before one could fathom the strange depth partially disclosed; that something which used to make me fear and shrink, as if I had been wandering amongst volcanic-looking hills, and had suddenly felt the ground quiver and seen it gape: that something, I, at intervals, beheld still; and with throbbing heart, but not with palsied nerves. Instead of wishing to shun, I longed only to dare – to divine it; and I thought Miss Ingram happy, because one day she might look into the abyss at her leisure, explore its secrets and analyse their nature.

Meantime, while I thought only of my master and his future bride – saw only them, heard only their discourse, and considered only their movements of importance – the rest of the party were occupied with their own separate interests and pleasures. The Ladies Lynn and Ingram continued to consort in solemn conferences, where they nodded their two turbans at each other, and held up their four hands in confronting gestures of surprise, or mystery, or horror, according to the theme on which their gossip ran, like a pair of magnified puppets. Mild Mrs Dent talked with good-natured Mrs Eshton; and the two sometimes bestowed a courteous word or smile on me. Sir George Lynn, Colonel Dent, and Mr Eshton discussed politics, or county affairs, or justice business. Lord Ingram flirted with Amy Eshton; Louisa played and sang to and with one of the Messrs Lynn; and Mary Ingram listened languidly to the gallant speeches of the other. Sometimes all, as with one consent, suspended their by-play to observe and listen to the principal actors: for, after all, Mr Rochester and – because closely connected with him – Miss Ingram were the life and soul of the party. If he was absent from the room an hour, a perceptible dullness seemed to steal over the spirits of his guests; and his re-entrance was sure to give a fresh impulse to the vivacity of conversation.

The want of his animating influence appeared to be peculiarly felt one day that he had been summoned to Millcote on business, and was not likely to return till late. The afternoon was wet: a walk the party had proposed to take to see a gypsy camp, lately pitched on a common beyond Hay, was consequently deferred. Some of the gentlemen were gone to the stables: the younger ones, together with the younger ladies, were playing billiards in the billiard-room. The dowagers Ingram and Lynn sought solace in a quiet game at cards. Blanche Ingram, after having repelled, by supercilious taciturnity, some efforts of Mrs Dent and Mrs Eshton to draw her into conversation, had first murmured over some sentimental tunes and airs on the piano, and then, having fetched a novel from the library, had flung herself in haughty listlessness on a sofa, and prepared to beguile, by the spell of fiction the tedious hours of absence. The room and the house were silent: only now and then the merriment of the billiard-players was heard from above.

It was verging on dusk, and the clock had already given warning of the hour to dress for dinner, when little Adèle, who knelt by me in the drawing-room window-seat, suddenly exclaimed – 'Voilà M. Rochester, qui revient!'

I turned, and Miss Ingram darted forwards from her sofa: the others, too, looked up from their several occupations; for at the same time a crunching of wheels and a splashing tramp of horse-hoofs became audible on the wet gravel. A post-chaise was approaching.

'What can possess him to come home in that style?' said Miss Ingram. 'He rode Mesrour (the black horse), did he not, when he went out? and Pilot was with him: what has he done with the animals?'

As she said this, she approached her tall person and ample garments so near the window, that I was obliged to bend back almost to the breaking of my spine: in her eagerness she did not observe me at first, but when she did, she curled her lip and moved to another casement. The post-chaise stopped; the driver rang the doorbell, and a gentleman alighted attired in travelling garb; but it was not Mr Rochester; it was a tall, fashionable-looking man, a stranger.

'How provoking!' exclaimed Miss Ingram: 'you tiresome monkey!' (apostrophising Adèle), 'who perched you up in the window to give false intelligence?' and she cast on me an angry glance, as if I were in fault.

Some parleying was audible in the hall, and soon the newcomer entered. He bowed to Lady Ingram, as deeming her the eldest lady present.

'It appears I come at an inopportune time, madam,' said he, 'when my friend, Mr Rochester, is from home; but I arrive from a very long journey, and I think I may presume so far on old and intimate acquaintance as to instal myself here till he returns.'

His manner was polite; his accent, in speaking, struck me as being somewhat unusual, not precisely foreign, but still not altogether English: his age might be about Mr Rochester's, between thirty and forty; his complexion was singularly sallow: otherwise he was a fine-looking man, at first sight especially. On closer examination, you detected something in his face that displeased, or rather that failed to please. His features were regular, but too relaxed: his eye was large and well cut, but the life looking out of it was a tame, vacant life – at least so I thought.

The sound of the dressing-bell dispersed the party. It was not till after dinner that I saw him again: he then seemed quite at his ease. But I liked his physiognomy even less than before: it struck me as being at the same time unsettled and inanimate. His eye wandered, and had no meaning in its wandering: this gave him an odd look, such as I never remembered to have seen. For a handsome and not an unamiable-looking man, he repelled me exceedingly: there was no power in that smooth-skinned face of a full oval shape: no firmness in that aquiline nose and small cherry mouth; there was no thought on the low, even forehead; no command in that blank, brown eye.

As I sat in my usual nook, and looked at him with the light of the girandoles on the mantelpiece beaming full over him – for he occupied an armchair drawn close to the fire, and kept shrinking still nearer, as if he were cold – I compared him with Mr Rochester. I think (with deference be it spoken) the contrast could not be much greater between a sleek gander and a fierce falcon: between a meek sheep and the rough-coated keen-eyed dog, its guardian.

He had spoken of Mr Rochester as an old friend. A curious friendship theirs must have been: a pointed illustration, indeed, of the old adage that 'extremes meet.'

Two or three of the gentlemen sat near him, and I caught at times scraps of their conversation across the room. At first I could not make much sense of what I heard; for the discourse of Louisa Eshton and Mary Ingram, who sat nearer to me, confused the fragmentary sentences that reached me at intervals. These last were discussing the stranger; they both called him 'a beautiful man'. Louisa said he was 'a love of a creature', and she 'adored him'; and Mary instanced his 'pretty little mouth, and nice nose', as her ideal of the charming.

'And what a sweet-tempered forehead he has!' cried Louisa, 'so smooth – none of those frowning irregularities I dislike so much; and such a placid eye and smile!'

And then, to my great relief, Mr Henry Lynn summoned them to the other side of the room, to settle some point about the deferred excursion to Hay Common.

I was now able to concentrate my attention on the group by the fire, and I presently gathered that the newcomer was called Mr Mason; then I learned that he was but just arrived in England, and that he came from some hot country: which was the reason, doubtless, his face was so sallow, and that he sat so near the hearth, and wore a surtout in the house. Presently the words Jamaica, Kingston, Spanish Town, indicated the West Indies as his residence; and it was with no little surprise I gathered, ere long, that he had there first seen and become acquainted with Mr Rochester. He spoke of his friend's dislike of the burning heats, the hurricanes, and rainy seasons of that region. I knew Mr Rochester had been a traveller: Mrs Fairfax had said so; but I thought the continent of Europe had bounded his wanderings; till now I had never heard a hint given of visits to more distant shores.

I was pondering these things, when an incident, and a somewhat unexpected one, broke the thread of my musings. Mr Mason, shivering as someone chanced to open the door, asked for more coal to be put on the fire, which had burnt out its flame, though its mass of cinder still shone hot and red. The footman who brought the coal, in going out, stopped near Mr Eshton's chair, and said something to him in a low voice, of which I heard only the words, 'old woman' – 'quite troublesome.'

'Tell her she shall be put in the stocks if she does not take herself off,' replied the magistrate.

'No – stop!' interrupted Colonel Dent. 'Don't send her away, Eshton; we might turn the thing to account; better consult the ladies.' And speaking aloud, he continued – 'Ladies, you talked of going to Hay Common to visit the gypsy camp; Sam here says that one of the old Mother Bunches is in the servants' hall at this moment, and insists upon being brought in before "the quality", to tell them their fortunes. Would you like to see her?'

'Surely, colonel,' cried Lady Ingram, 'you would not encourage such a low impostor? Dismiss her, by all means, at once!'

'But I cannot persuade her to go away, my lady,' said the footman; 'nor can any of the servants: Mrs Fairfax is with her just now, entreating her to be gone; but she has taken a chair in the chimney-corner, and says nothing shall stir her from it till she gets leave to come in here.'

'What does she want?' asked Mrs Eshton.

' "To tell the gentry their fortunes," she says, ma'am; and she swears she must and will do it.'

'What is she like?' enquired the Misses Eshton, in a breath.

'A shockingly ugly old creature, miss; almost as black as a crock.'

'Why, she's a real sorceress!' cried Frederick Lynn. 'Let us have her in, of course.'

'To be sure,' rejoined his brother; 'it would be a thousand pities to throw away such a chance of fun.'

'My dear boys, what are you thinking about?' exclaimed Mrs Lynn.

'I cannot possibly countenance any such inconsistent proceeding,' chimed in the Dowager Ingram.

'Indeed, mama, but you can – and will,' pronounced the haughty voice of Blanche, as she turned round on the piano-stool; where till now she had sat silent, apparently examining sundry sheets of music. 'I have a curiosity to hear my fortune told: therefore, Sam, order the beldame forward.'

'My darling Blanche! recollect – '

'I do – I recollect all you can suggest; and I must have my will – quick, Sam!'

'Yes – yes – yes!' cried all the juveniles, both ladies and gentlemen. 'Let her come – it will be excellent sport!'

The footman still lingered. 'She looks such a rough one,' said he.

'Go!' ejaculated Miss Ingram, and the man went.

Excitement instantly seized the whole party: a running fire of raillery and jests was proceeding when Sam returned.

'She won't come now,' said he. 'She says it's not her mission to appear before the "vulgar herd" (them's her words). I must show her into a room by herself, and then those who wish to consult her must go to her one by one.'

'You see now, my queenly Blanche,' began Lady Ingram, 'she encroaches. Be advised, my angel girl – and – '

'Show her into the library, of course,' cut in the 'angel girl.' 'It is not my mission to listen to her before the vulgar herd either: I mean to have her all to myself. Is there a fire in the library?'

'Yes, ma'am – but she looks such a tinker.'

'Cease that chatter, blockhead! and do my bidding.'

Again Sam vanished; and mystery, animation, expectation rose to full flow once more.

'She's ready now,' said the footman, as he reappeared. 'She wishes to know who will be her first visitor.'

'I think I had better just look in upon her before any of the ladies go,' said Colonel Dent.

'Tell her, Sam, a gentleman is coming.'

Sam went and returned.

'She says, sir, that she'll have no gentlemen; they need not trouble themselves to come near her; nor,' he added, with difficulty suppressing a titter, 'any ladies either, except the young and single.'

'By Jove, she has taste!' exclaimed Henry Lynn.

Miss Ingram rose solemnly: 'I go first,' she said, in a tone which might have befitted the leader of a forlorn hope, mounting a breach in the van of his men.

'Oh, my best! oh, my dearest! pause – reflect!' was her mama's cry; but she swept past her in stately silence, passed through the door which Colonel Dent held open, and we heard her enter the library.

A comparative silence ensued. Lady Ingram thought it 'le cas' to wring her hands: which she did accordingly. Miss Mary declared she felt, for her part, she never dared venture. Amy and Louisa Eshton tittered under their breath, and looked a little frightened.

The minutes passed very slowly: fifteen were counted before the library-door again opened. Miss Ingram returned to us through the arch.

Would she laugh? Would she take it as a joke? All eyes met her with a glance of eager curiosity, and she met all eyes with one of rebuff and coldness; she looked neither flurried nor merry: she walked stiffly to her seat, and took it in silence.

'Well, Blanche?' said Lord Ingram.

'What did she say, sister?' asked Mary.

'What did you think? How do you feel? Is she a real fortune-teller?' demanded the Misses Eshton.

'Now, now, good people,' returned Miss Ingram, 'don't press upon me. Really your organs of wonder and credulity are easily excited: you seem, by the importance you all – my good mama included – ascribe to this matter, absolutely to believe we have a genuine witch in the house, who is in close alliance with the old gentleman. I have seen a gypsy vagabond; she has practised in hackneyed fashion the science of palmistry and told me what such people usually tell. My whim is gratified; and now I think Mr Eshton will do well to put the hag in the stocks tomorrow morning, as he threatened.'

Miss Ingram took a book, leant back in her chair, and so declined further conversation. I watched her for nearly half an hour: during all that time she never turned a page, and her face grew momently darker, more dissatisfied, and more sourly expressive of disappointment. She had obviously not heard anything to her advantage: and it seemed to me, from her prolonged fit of gloom and taciturnity, that she herself, notwithstanding her professed indifference, attached undue importance to whatever revelations had been made her.

Meantime, Mary Ingram, Amy and Louisa Eshton, declared they dared not go alone; and yet they all wished to go. A negotiation was opened through the medium of the ambassador, Sam; and after much pacing to and fro, till, I think, the said Sam's calves must have ached with the exercise, permission was at last, with great difficulty, extorted from the rigorous Sibyl, for the three to wait upon her in a body.

Their visit was not so still as Miss Ingram's had been: we heard hysterical giggling and little shrieks proceeding from the library; and at the end of about twenty minutes they burst the door open, and came running across the hall, as if they were half-scared out of their wits.

'I am sure she is something not right!' they cried, one and all. 'She told us such things! She knows all about us!' and they sank breathless into the various seats the gentlemen hastened to bring them.

Pressed for further explanation, they declared she had told them of things they had said and done when they were mere children; described books and ornaments they had in their boudoirs at home: keepsakes that different relations had presented to them. They affirmed that she had even divined their thoughts, and had whispered in the ear of each the name of the person she liked best in the world, and informed them of what they most wished for.

Here the gentlemen interposed with earnest petitions to be further enlightened on these two last-named points; but they got only blushes, ejaculations, tremors, and titters, in return for their importunity. The matrons, meantime, offered vinaigrettes and wielded fans; and again and again reiterated the expression of their concern that their warning had not been taken in time; and the elder gentlemen laughed, and the younger urged their services on the agitated fair ones.

In the midst of the tumult, and while my eyes and ears were fully engaged in the scene before me, I heard a hem close at my elbow: I turned, and saw Sam.

'If you please, miss, the gypsy declares that there is another young single lady in the room who has not been to her yet, and she swears she will not go till she has seen all. I thought it must be you: there is no one else for it. What shall I tell her?'

'Oh, I will go by all means,' I answered: and I was glad of the unexpected opportunity to gratify my much-excited curiosity. I slipped out of the room, unobserved by any eye – for the company were gathered in one mass about the trembling trio just returned – and I closed the door quietly behind me.

'If you like, miss,' said Sam, 'I'll wait in the hall for you; and if she frightens you, just call and I'll come in.'

'No, Sam, return to the kitchen: I am not in the least afraid.' Nor was I; but I was a good deal interested and excited.

## *Chapter 19*

The library looked tranquil enough as I entered it, and the Sibyl – if Sibyl she were – was seated snugly enough in an easy-chair at the chimney-corner. She had on a red cloak and a black bonnet: or rather, a broad-brimmed gypsy hat, tied down with a striped handkerchief under her chin. An extinguished candle stood on the table; she was bending over the fire, and seemed reading in a little black book, like a prayer-book, by the light of the blaze: she muttered the words to herself, as most old women do, while she read; she did not desist immediately on my entrance: it appeared she wished to finish a paragraph.

I stood on the rug and warmed my hands, which were rather cold with sitting at a distance from the drawing-room fire. I felt now as composed as ever I did in my life: there was nothing indeed in the gypsy's appearance to trouble one's calm. She shut her book and slowly looked up; her hat-brim partially shaded her face, yet I could see, as she raised it, that it was a strange one. It looked all brown and black: elf-locks bristled out from beneath a white band which passed under her chin, and came half over her cheeks, or rather jaws: her eye confronted me at once, with a bold and direct gaze.

'Well, and you want your fortune told?' she said, in a voice as decided as her glance, as harsh as her features.

'I don't care about it, mother; you may please yourself: but I ought to warn you, I have no faith.'

'It's like your impudence to say so: I expected it of you; I heard it in your step as you crossed the threshold.'

'Did you? You've a quick ear.'

'I have; and a quick eye and a quick brain.'

'You need them all in your trade.'

'I do; especially when I've customers like you to deal with. Why don't you tremble?'

'I'm not cold.'

'Why don't you turn pale?'

'I am not sick.'

'Why don't you consult my art?'

'I'm not silly.'

The old crone 'nichered' a laugh under her bonnet and bandage; she then drew out a short black pipe, and lighting it began to smoke. Having indulged a while in this sedative, she raised her bent body, took the pipe from her lips, and while gazing steadily at the fire, said very deliberately – 'You are cold; you are sick; and you are silly.'

'Prove it,' I rejoined.

'I will, in few words. You are cold, because you are alone: no contact strikes the fire from you that is in you. You are sick; because the best of feelings, the highest and the sweetest given to man, keeps far away from you. You are silly, because, suffer as you may, you will not beckon it to approach, nor will you stir one step to meet it where it waits you.'

She again put her short black pipe to her lips, and renewed her smoking with vigour.

'You might say all that to almost anyone who you knew lived as a solitary dependent in a great house.'

'I might say it to almost anyone: but would it be true of almost anyone?'

'In my circumstances.'

'Yes; just so, in *your* circumstances: but find me another precisely placed as you are.'

'It would be easy to find you thousands.'

'You could scarcely find me one. If you knew it, you are peculiarly situated: very near happiness; yes, within reach of it. The materials are all prepared; there only wants a movement to combine them. Chance laid them somewhat apart; let them be once approached and bliss results.'

'I don't understand enigmas. I never could guess a riddle in my life.'

'If you wish me to speak more plainly, show me your palm.'

'And I must cross it with silver, I suppose?'

'To be sure.'

I gave her a shilling: she put it into an old stocking-foot which she took out of her pocket, and having tied it round and returned it, she told me to hold out my hand. I did. She approached her face to the palm, and pored over it without touching it.

'It is too fine,' said she. 'I can make nothing of such a hand as that; almost without lines: besides, what is in a palm? Destiny is not written there.'

'I believe you,' said I.

'No,' she continued, 'it is in the face: on the forehead, about the eyes, in the eyes themselves, in the lines of the mouth. Kneel, and lift up your head.'

'Ah! now you are coming to reality,' I said, as I obeyed her. 'I shall begin to put some faith in you presently.'

I knelt within half a yard of her. She stirred the fire, so that a ripple of light broke from the disturbed coal: the glare, however, as she sat, only threw her face into deeper shadow: mine, it illumined.

'I wonder with what feelings you came to me tonight,' she said, when she had examined me a while. 'I wonder what thoughts are busy in your heart during all the hours you sit in yonder room with the fine people flitting before you like shapes in a magic-lantern: just as little sympathetic communion passing between you and them as if they were really mere shadows of human forms, and not the actual substance.'

'I feel tired often, sleepy sometimes, but seldom sad.'

'Then you have some secret hope to buoy you up and please you with whispers of the future?'

'Not I. The utmost I hope is, to save money enough out of my earnings to set up a school someday in a little house rented by myself.'

'A mean nutriment for the spirit to exist on: and sitting in that window-seat (you see I know your habits) – '

'You have learned them from the servants.'

'Ah! you think yourself sharp. Well, perhaps I have: to speak truth, I have an acquaintance with one of them, Mrs Poole – '

I started to my feet when I heard the name.

'You have – have you?' thought I; 'there is diablerie in the business after all, then!'

'Don't be alarmed,' continued the strange being; 'she's a safe hand is Mrs Poole: close and quiet; anyone may repose confidence in her. But, as I was saying: sitting in that window-seat, do you think of nothing but your future school? Have you no present interest in any of the company who occupy the sofas and chairs before you? Is there not one face you study? One figure whose movements you follow with at least curiosity?'

'I like to observe all the faces and all the figures.'

'But do you never single one from the rest – or it may be, two?'

'I do frequently; when the gestures or looks of a pair seem telling a tale: it amuses me to watch them.'

'What tale do you like best to hear?'

'Oh, I have not much choice! They generally run on the same theme – courtship; and promise to end in the same catastrophe – marriage.'

'And do you like that monotonous theme?'

'Positively, I don't care about it: it is nothing to me.'

'Nothing to you? When a lady, young and full of life and health, charming with beauty and endowed with the gifts of rank and fortune, sits and smiles in the eyes of a gentleman you – '

'I what?'

'You know – and perhaps think well of.'

'I don't know the gentlemen here. I have scarcely interchanged a syllable with one of them; and as to thinking well of them, I consider some respectable, and stately, and middle-aged, and others young, dashing, handsome, and lively: but certainly they are all at liberty to be the recipients of whose smiles they please, without my feeling disposed to consider the transaction of any moment to me.'

'You don't know the gentlemen here? You have not exchanged a syllable with one of them? Will you say that of the master of the house!'

'He is not at home.'

'A profound remark! A most ingenious quibble! He went to Millcote this morning, and will be back here tonight or tomorrow: does that circumstance exclude him from the list of your acquaintance – blot him, as it were, out of existence?'

'No; but I can scarcely see what Mr Rochester has to do with the theme you had introduced.

'I was talking of ladies smiling in the eyes of gentlemen; and of late so many smiles have been shed into Mr Rochester's eyes that they overflow like two cups filled above the brim: have you never remarked that?'

'Mr Rochester has a right to enjoy the society of his guests.'

'No question about his right: but have you never observed that, of all the tales told here about matrimony, Mr Rochester has been favoured with the most lively and the most continuous?'

'The eagerness of a listener quickens the tongue of a narrator.' I said this rather to myself than to the gypsy, whose strange talk, voice, manner, had by this time wrapped me in a kind of dream. One unexpected sentence came from her lips after another, till I got involved in a web of mystification; and wondered what unseen spirit had been sitting for weeks by my heart watching its workings and taking record of every pulse.

'Eagerness of a listener!' repeated she: 'yes; Mr Rochester has sat by the hour, his ear inclined to the fascinating lips that took such delight in their task of communicating; and Mr Rochester was so willing to receive and looked so grateful for the pastime given him; you have noticed this?'

'Grateful! I cannot remember detecting gratitude in his face.'

'Detecting! You have analysed, then. And what did you detect, if not gratitude?'

I said nothing.

'You have seen love: have you not? – and, looking forward, you have seen him married, and beheld his bride happy?'

'Humph! Not exactly. Your witch's skill is rather at fault sometimes.'

'What the devil have you seen, then?'

'Never mind: I came here to enquire, not to confess. Is it known that Mr Rochester is to be married?'

'Yes; and to the beautiful Miss Ingram.'

'Shortly?'

'Appearances would warrant that conclusion: and, no doubt (though, with an audacity that wants chastising out of you, you seem to question it), they will be a superlatively happy pair. He must love such a handsome, noble, witty, accomplished lady; and probably she loves him, or, if not his person, at least his purse. I know she considers the Rochester estate eligible to the last degree; though (God pardon me!) I told her something on that point about an hour ago which made her look wondrous grave: the corners of her mouth fell half an inch. I would advise her black-aviced suitor to look out: if another comes, with a longer or clearer rent-roll, he's dished – '

'But, mother, I did not come to hear Mr Rochester's fortune: I came to hear my own; and you have told me nothing of it.'

'Your fortune is yet doubtful: when I examined your face, one trait contradicted another. Chance has meted you a measure of happiness: that I know. I knew it before I came here this evening. She has laid it carefully on one side for you. I saw her do it. It depends on yourself to stretch out your hand, and take it up: but whether you will do so, is the problem I study. Kneel again on the rug.'

'Don't keep me long; the fire scorches me.'

I knelt. She did not stoop towards me, but only gazed, leaning back in her chair. She began muttering, 'The flame flickers in the eye; the eye shines like dew; it looks soft and full of feeling; it smiles at my jargon: it is susceptible; impression follows impression through its clear sphere; where it ceases to smile, it is sad; an unconscious lassitude weighs on the lid: that signifies melancholy resulting from loneliness. It turns from me; it will not suffer further scrutiny; it seems to deny, by a mocking glance, the truth of the discoveries I have already made, to disown the charge both of sensibility and chagrin: its pride and reserve only confirm me in my opinion. The eye is favourable.

'As to the mouth, it delights at times in laughter; it is disposed to impart all that the brain conceives; though I dare say it would be silent on much the heart experiences. Mobile and flexible, it was never intended to be compressed in the eternal silence of solitude; it is a mouth which should speak much and smile often, and have human affection for its interlocutor. That feature too is propitious.

'I see no enemy to a fortunate issue but in the brow; and that brow professes to say, "I can live alone, if self-respect and circumstances require me so to do. I need not sell my soul to buy bliss. I have an inward treasure born with me, which can keep me alive if all extraneous delights should be withheld, or offered only at a price I cannot afford to give." The forehead declares, "Reason sits firm and holds the reins, and she will not let the feelings burst away and hurry her to wild chasms. The passions may rage furiously, like true heathens, as they are; and the desires may imagine all sorts of vain things: but judgement shall still have the last word in every argument, and the casting vote in every decision. Strong wind, earthquake-shock, and fire may pass by: but I shall follow the guiding of that still small voice which interprets the dictates of conscience."

'Well said, forehead; your declaration shall be respected. I have formed my plans – right plans I deem them – and in them I have attended to the claims of conscience, the counsels of reason. I know how soon youth would fade and bloom perish, if, in the cup of bliss offered, but one dreg of shame, or one flavour of remorse were detected; and I do not want sacrifice, sorrow, dissolution – such is not my taste. I wish to foster, not to blight – to earn gratitude, not to wring tears of blood – no, nor of brine: my harvest must be in smiles, in endearments, in sweet – That will do. I think I rave in a kind of exquisite delirium. I should wish now to protract this moment *ad infinitum*; but I dare not. So far I have governed myself thoroughly. I have acted as I inwardly swore I would act; but further might try me beyond my strength. Rise, Miss Eyre: leave me; "the play is played out." '

Where was I? Did I wake or sleep? Had I been dreaming? Did I dream still? The old woman's voice had changed: her accent, her gesture, and all were familiar to me as my own face in a glass – as the speech of my own tongue. I got up, but did not go. I looked; I stirred the fire, and I looked again: but she drew her bonnet and her bandage closer about her face, and again beckoned me to depart. The flame illuminated her hand stretched out: roused now, and on the alert for discoveries, I at once noticed that hand. It was no more the withered limb of eld than my own; it was a rounded supple member, with smooth fingers, symmetrically turned; a broad ring flashed on the little finger, and stooping forward, I looked at it, and saw a gem I had seen a hundred times before. Again I looked at the face; which was no longer turned from me – on the contrary, the bonnet was doffed, the bandage displaced, the head advanced.

'Well, Jane, do you know me?' asked the familiar voice.

'Only take off the red cloak, sir, and then – '

'But the string is in a knot – help me.'

'Break it, sir.'

'There, then – "Off, ye lendings!" ' And Mr Rochester stepped out of his disguise.

'Now, sir, what a strange idea!'

'But well carried out, eh? Don't you think so?'

'With the ladies you must have managed well.'

'But not with you?'

'You did not act the character of a gypsy with me.'

'What character did I act? My own?'

'No; some unaccountable one. In short, I believe you have been trying to draw me out – or in; you have been talking nonsense to make me talk nonsense. It is scarcely fair, sir.'

'Do you forgive me, Jane?'

'I cannot tell till I have thought it all over. If, on reflection, I find I have fallen into no great absurdity, I shall try to forgive you; but it was not right.'

'Oh, you have been very correct – very careful, very sensible.'

I reflected, and thought, on the whole, I had. It was a comfort; but, indeed, I had been on my guard almost from the beginning of the interview. Something of masquerade I suspected. I knew gypsies and fortune-tellers did not express themselves as this seeming old woman had expressed herself; besides I had noted her feigned voice, her anxiety to conceal her features. But my mind had been running on Grace Poole – that living enigma, that mystery of mysteries, as I considered her. I had never thought of Mr Rochester.

'Well,' said he, 'what are you musing about? What does that grave smile signify?'

'Wonder and self-congratulation, sir. I have your permission to retire now, I suppose?'

'No; stay a moment; and tell me what the people in the drawing-room yonder are doing.'

'Discussing the gypsy, I dare say.'

'Sit down! – Let me hear what they said about me.'

'I had better not stay long, sir; it must be near eleven o'clock. Oh, are you aware, Mr Rochester that a stranger has arrived here since you left this morning?'

'A stranger! – no; who can it be? I expected no one; is he gone?'

'No; he said he had known you long, and that he could take the liberty of installing himself here till you returned.'

'The devil he did! Did he give his name?'

'His name is Mason, sir; and he comes from the West Indies; from Spanish Town, in Jamaica, I think.'

Mr Rochester was standing near me; he had taken my hand, as if to lead me to a chair. As I spoke he gave my wrist a convulsive grip; the smile on his lips froze: apparently a spasm caught his breath.

'Mason! – the West Indies!' he said, in the tone one might fancy a speaking automaton to enounce its single words; 'Mason! – the West Indies!' he reiterated; and he went over the syllables three times, growing in the intervals of speaking, whiter than ashes: he hardly seemed to know what he was doing.

'Do you feel ill, sir?' I enquired.

'Jane, I've got a blow; I've got a blow, Jane!' He staggered.

'Oh, lean on me, sir.'

'Jane, you offered me your shoulder once before; let me have it now.'

'Yes, sir, yes; and my arm.'

He sat down, and made me sit beside him. Holding my hand in both his own, he chafed it; gazing on me, at the same time, with the most troubled and dreary look.

'My little friend!' said he, 'I wish I were in a quiet island with only you; and trouble, and danger, and hideous recollections removed from me.'

'Can I help you, sir? – I'd give my life to serve you.'

'Jane, if aid is wanted, I'll seek it at your hands; I promise you that.'

'Thank you, sir. Tell me what to do, I'll try, at least, to do it.'

'Fetch me now, Jane, a glass of wine from the dining-room: they will be at supper there; and tell me if Mason is with them, and what he is doing.'

I went. I found all the party in the dining-room at supper, as Mr Rochester had said; they were not seated at table, the supper was arranged on the sideboard; each had taken what he chose, and they stood about here and there in groups, their plates and glasses in their hands. Everyone seemed in high glee; laughter and conversation were general and animated. Mr Mason stood near the fire, talking to Colonel and Mrs Dent, and appeared as merry as any of them. I filled a wineglass (I saw Miss Ingram watch me frowningly as I did so: she thought I was taking a liberty, I dare say), and I returned to the library.

Mr Rochester's extreme pallor had disappeared, and he looked once more firm and stern. He took the glass from my hand.

'Here is to your health, ministrant spirit!' he said. He swallowed the contents and returned it to me. 'What are they doing, Jane?'

'Laughing and talking, sir.'

'They don't look grave and mysterious, as if they had heard something strange?'

'Not at all: they are full of jests and gaiety.'

'And Mason?'

'He was laughing too.'

'If all these people came in a body and spat at me, what would you do, Jane?'

'Turn them out of the room, sir, if I could.'

He half smiled. 'But if I were to go to them, and they only looked at me coldly, and whispered sneeringly amongst each other, and then dropped off and left me one by one, what then? Would you go with them?'

'I rather think not, sir: I should have more pleasure in staying with you.'

'To comfort me?'

'Yes, sir, to comfort you, as well as I could.'

'And if they laid you under a ban for adhering to me?'

'I, probably, should know nothing about their ban; and if I did, I should care nothing about it.'

'Then, you could dare censure for my sake?'

'I could dare it for the sake of any friend who deserved my adherence; as you, I am sure, do.'

'Go back now into the room; step quietly up to Mason, and whisper in his ear that Mr Rochester is come and wishes to see him: show him in here and then leave me.'

'Yes, sir.'

I did his behest. The company all stared at me as I passed straight among them. I sought Mr Mason, delivered the message, and preceded him from the room: I ushered him into the library, and then I went upstairs.

At a late hour, after I had been in bed some time, I heard the visitors repair to their chambers: I distinguished Mr Rochester's voice, and heard him say, 'This way, Mason; this is your room.'

He spoke cheerfully: the gay tones set my heart at ease. I was soon asleep.

## *Chapter 20*

I had forgotten to draw my curtain, which I usually did, and also to let down my window-blind. The consequence was, that when the moon, which was full and bright (for the night was fine), came in her course to that space in the sky opposite my casement, and looked in at me through the unveiled panes, her glorious gaze roused me. Awaking in the dead of night, I opened my eyes on her disk – silver-white and crystal clear. It was beautiful, but too solemn: I half rose, and stretched my arm to draw the curtain.

Good God! What a cry!

The night – its silence – its rest, was rent in twain by a savage, a sharp, a shrilly sound that ran from end to end of Thornfield Hall.

My pulse stopped: my heart stood still; my stretched arm was paralysed. The cry died, and was not renewed. Indeed, whatever being uttered that fearful shriek could not soon repeat it: not the widest-winged condor on the Andes could, twice in succession, send out such a yell from the cloud shrouding his eyrie. The thing delivering such utterance must rest ere it could repeat the effort.

It came out of the third storey; for it passed overhead. And overhead – yes, in the room just above my chamber-ceiling – I now heard a struggle: a deadly one it seemed from the noise; and a half-smothered voice shouted – 'Help! help! help!' three times rapidly.

'Will no one come?' it cried; and then, while the staggering and stamping went on wildly, I distinguished through plank and plaster: 'Rochester! Rochester! for God's sake, come!'

A chamber-door opened: someone ran, or rushed, along the gallery. Another step stamped on the flooring above and something fell; and there was silence.

I had put on some clothes, though horror shook all my limbs; I issued from my apartment. The sleepers were all aroused: ejaculations, terrified murmurs sounded in every room; door after door unclosed; one looked out and another looked out; the gallery filled. Gentlemen and ladies alike had quitted their beds; and 'Oh! what is it?' – 'Who is hurt?' – 'What has happened?' – 'Fetch a light!' – 'Is it fire?' – 'Are there robbers?' – 'Where shall we run?' was demanded confusedly on all hands. But for the moonlight they would have been in complete darkness. They ran to and fro; they crowded together: some sobbed, some stumbled: the confusion was inextricable.

'Where the devil is Rochester?' cried Colonel Dent. 'I cannot find him in his bed.'

'Here! here!' was shouted in return. 'Be composed, all of you: I'm coming.'

And the door at the end of the gallery opened, and Mr Rochester advanced with a candle: he had just descended from the upper storey. One of the ladies ran to him directly; she seized his arm: it was Miss Ingram.

'What awful event has taken place?' said she. 'Speak! let us know the worst at once!'

'But don't pull me down or strangle me,' he replied: for the Misses Eshton were clinging about him now; and the two dowagers, in vast white wrappers, were bearing down on him like ships in full sail.

'All's right! – all's right!' he cried. 'It's a mere rehearsal of *Much Ado about Nothing*. Ladies, keep off, or I shall wax dangerous.'

And dangerous he looked: his black eyes darted sparks. Calming himself by an effort, he added – 'A servant has had the nightmare; that is all. She's an excitable, nervous person: she construed her dream into an apparition, or something of that sort, no doubt; and has taken a fit with fright. Now, then, I must see you all back into your rooms; for, till the house is settled, she cannot be looked after. Gentlemen, have the goodness to set the ladies the example. Miss Ingram, I am sure you will not fail in evincing superiority to idle terrors. Amy and Louisa, return to your nests like a pair of doves, as you are. Mesdames' (to the dowagers), 'you will take cold to a dead certainty, if you stay in this chill gallery any longer.'

And so, by dint of alternate coaxing and commanding, he contrived to get them all once more enclosed in their separate dormitories. I did not wait to be ordered back to mine, but retreated unnoticed, as unnoticed I had left it.

Not, however, to go to bed: on the contrary, I began and dressed myself carefully. The sounds I had heard after the scream, and the words that had been uttered, had probably been heard only by me; for they had proceeded from the room above mine: but they assured me that it was not a servant's dream which had thus struck horror through the house; and that the explanation Mr Rochester had given was merely an invention framed to pacify his guests. I dressed, then, to be ready for emergencies. When dressed, I sat a long time by the window looking out over the silent grounds and silvered fields and waiting for I knew not what. It seemed to me that some event must follow the strange cry, struggle, and call.

No: stillness returned: each murmur and movement ceased gradually, and in about an hour Thornfield Hall was again as hushed as a desert. It seemed that sleep and night had resumed their empire. Meantime the moon declined: she was about to set. Not liking to sit in the cold and darkness, I thought I would lie down on my bed, dressed as I was. I left the window, and moved with little noise across the carpet; as I stooped to take off my shoes, a cautious hand tapped low at the door.

'Am I wanted?' I asked.

'Are you up?' asked the voice I expected to hear viz., my master's.

'Yes, sir.'

'And dressed?'

'Yes.'

'Come out, then, quietly.'

I obeyed. Mr Rochester stood in the gallery holding a light.

'I want you,' he said: 'come this way: take your time, and make no noise.'

My slippers were thin: I could walk the matted floor as softly as a cat. He glided up the gallery and up the stairs, and stopped in the dark, low corridor of the fateful third storey: I had followed and stood at his side.

'Have you a sponge in your room?' he asked in a whisper.

'Yes, sir.'

'Have you any salts – volatile salts?'

'Yes.'

'Go back and fetch both.'

I returned, sought the sponge on the washstand, the salts in my drawer, and once more retraced my steps. He still waited; he held a key in his hand:

approaching one of the small, black doors, he put it in the lock; he paused, and addressed me again.

'You don't turn sick at the sight of blood?'

'I think I shall not: I have never been tried yet.'

I felt a thrill while I answered him; but no coldness, and no faintness.

'Just give me your hand,' he said: 'it will not do to risk a fainting fit.'

I put my fingers into his. 'Warm and steady,' was his remark: he turned the key and opened the door.

I saw a room I remembered to have seen before, the day Mrs Fairfax showed me over the house: it was hung with tapestry; but the tapestry was now looped up in one part, and there was a door apparent, which had then been concealed. This door was open; a light shone out of the room within: I heard thence a snarling, snatching sound, almost like a dog quarrelling. Mr Rochester, putting down his candle, said to me, 'Wait a minute,' and he went forward to the inner apartment. A shout of laughter greeted his entrance; noisy at first, and terminating in Grace Poole's own goblin ha! ha! *She* then was there. He made some sort of arrangement without speaking, though I heard a low voice address him: he came out and closed the door behind him.

'Here, Jane!' he said; and I walked round to the other side of a large bed, which with its drawn curtains concealed a considerable portion of the chamber. An easy-chair was near the bed-head: a man sat in it, dressed with the exception of his coat; he was still; his head leant back; his eyes were closed. Mr Rochester held the candle over him; I recognised in his pale and seemingly lifeless face – the stranger, Mason: I saw too that his linen on one side and one arm was almost soaked in blood.

'Hold the candle,' said Mr Rochester, and I took it: he fetched a basin of water from the washstand: 'Hold that,' said he. I obeyed. He took the sponge; dipped it in, and moistened the corpse-like face; he asked for my smelling-bottle, and applied it to the nostrils. Mr Mason shortly unclosed his eyes; he groaned. Mr Rochester opened the shirt of the wounded man, whose arm and shoulder were bandaged: he sponged away blood, trickling fast down.

'Is there immediate danger?' murmured Mr Mason.

'Pooh! No – a mere scratch. Don't be so overcome, man: bear up! I'll fetch a surgeon for you now, myself: you'll be able to be removed by morning, I hope. Jane,' he continued.

'Sir?'

'I shall have to leave you in this room with this gentleman, for an hour, or perhaps two hours: you will sponge the blood as I do when it returns: if he feels faint, you will put the glass of water on that stand to his lips, and your salts to his nose. You will not speak to him on any pretext – and – Richard, it will be at the peril of your life if you speak to her: open your lips – agitate yourself – and I'll not answer for the consequences.'

Again the poor man groaned; he looked as if he dared not move; fear, either of death or of something else, appeared almost to paralyse him. Mr Rochester put the now bloody sponge into my hand, and I proceeded to use it as he had done.

He watched me a second, then saying, 'Remember! – No conversation,' he left the room. I experienced a strange feeling as the key grated in the lock, and the sound of his retreating step ceased to be heard.

Here then I was in the third storey, fastened into one of its mystic cells; night around me; a pale and bloody spectacle under my eyes and hands; a murderess hardly separated from me by a single door: yes – that was appalling – the rest I could bear; but I shuddered at the thought of Grace Poole bursting out upon me.

I must keep to my post, however. I must watch this ghastly countenance – these blue, still lips forbidden to unclose – these eyes now shut, now opening, now wandering through the room, now fixing on me, and ever glazed with the dullness of horror. I must dip my hand again and again in the basin of blood and water, and wipe away the trickling gore. I must see the light of the unsnuffed candle wane on my employment; the shadows darken on the wrought, antique tapestry round me, and grow black under the hangings of the vast old bed, and quiver strangely over the doors of a great cabinet opposite – whose front, divided into twelve panels, bore, in grim design, the heads of the twelve apostles, each enclosed in its separate panel as in a frame; while above them at the top rose an ebon crucifix and a dying Christ.

According as the shifting obscurity and flickering gleam hovered here or glanced there, it was now the bearded physician, Luke, that bent his brow; now St John's long hair that waved; and anon the devilish face of Judas, that grew out of the panel, and seemed gathering life and threatening a revelation of the arch-traitor – of Satan himself – in his subordinate's form.

Amidst all this, I had to listen as well as watch: to listen for the movements of the wild beast or the fiend in yonder side den. But since Mr Rochester's visit it seemed spellbound: all the night I heard but three sounds at three long intervals, a step creak, a momentary renewal of the snarling, canine noise, and a deep human groan.

Then my own thoughts worried me. What crime was this, that lived incarnate in this sequestered mansion, and could neither be expelled nor subdued by the owner? – what mystery, that broke out now in fire and now in blood, at the deadest hours of night? What creature was it, that, masked in an ordinary woman's face and shape, uttered the voice, now of a mocking demon, and anon of a carrion-seeking bird of prey?

And this man I bent over – this commonplace, quiet stranger – how had he become involved in the web of horror? and why had the Fury flown at him? What made him seek this quarter of the house at an untimely season, when he should have been asleep in bed? I had heard Mr Rochester assign him an apartment below – what brought him here? And why, now, was he so tame under the violence or treachery done him? Why did he so quietly submit to the concealment Mr Rochester enforced? Why *did* Mr Rochester enforce this concealment? His guest had been outraged, his own life on a former occasion had been hideously plotted against; and both attempts he smothered in secrecy and sank in oblivion! Lastly, I saw Mr Mason was submissive to Mr Rochester;

that the impetuous will of the latter held complete sway over the inertness of the former: the few words which had passed between them assured me of this. It was evident that in their former intercourse, the passive disposition of the one had been habitually influenced by the active energy of the other: whence then had arisen Mr Rochester's dismay when he heard of Mr Mason's arrival? Why had the mere name of this unresisting individual – whom his word now sufficed to control like a child – fallen on him, a few hours since, as a thunderbolt might fall on an oak?

Oh! I could not forget his look and his paleness when he whispered: 'Jane, I have got a blow – I have got a blow, Jane.' I could not forget how the arm had trembled which he rested on my shoulder: and it was no light matter which could thus bow the resolute spirit and thrill the vigorous frame of Fairfax Rochester.

'When will he come? When will he come?' I cried inwardly, as the night lingered and lingered – as my bleeding patient drooped, moaned, sickened: and neither day nor aid arrived. I had, again and again, held the water to Mason's white lips; again and again offered him the stimulating salts: my efforts seemed ineffectual: either bodily or mental suffering, or loss of blood, or all three combined, were fast prostrating his strength. He moaned so, and looked so weak, wild, and lost, I feared he was dying; and I might not even speak to him.

The candle, wasted at last, went out; as it expired, I perceived streaks of grey light edging the window curtains: dawn was then approaching. Presently I heard Pilot bark far below, out of his distant kennel in the courtyard: hope revived. Nor was it unwarranted: in five minutes more the grating key, the yielding lock, warned me my watch was relieved. It could not have lasted more than two hours: many a week has seemed shorter.

Mr Rochester entered, and with him the surgeon he had been to fetch.

'Now, Carter, be on the alert,' he said to this last: 'I give you but half an hour for dressing the wound, fastening the bandages, getting the patient downstairs and all.'

'But is he fit to move, sir?'

'No doubt of it; it is nothing serious; he is nervous, his spirits must be kept up. Come, set to work.'

Mr Rochester drew back the thick curtain, drew up the holland blind, let in all the daylight he could; and I was surprised and cheered to see how far dawn was advanced: what rosy streaks were beginning to brighten the east. Then he approached Mason, whom the surgeon was already handling.

'Now, my good fellow, how are you?' he asked.

'She's done for me, I fear,' was the faint reply.

'Not a whit! – courage! This day fortnight you'll hardly be a pin the worse of it: you've lost a little blood; that's all. Carter, assure him there's no danger.'

'I can do that conscientiously,' said Carter, who had now undone the bandages; 'only I wish I could have got here sooner: he would not have bled so much – but how is this? The flesh on the shoulder is torn as well as cut. This wound was not done with a knife: there have been teeth here!'

'She bit me,' he murmured. 'She worried me like a tigress, when Rochester got the knife from her.'

'You should not have yielded: you should have grappled with her at once,' said Mr Rochester.

'But under such circumstances, what could one do?' returned Mason. 'Oh, it was frightful!' he added, shuddering. 'And I did not expect it: she looked so quiet at first.'

'I warned you,' was his friend's answer; 'I said – be on your guard when you go near her. Besides, you might have waited till tomorrow, and had me with you: it was mere folly to attempt the interview tonight, and alone.'

'I thought I could have done some good.'

'You thought! you thought! Yes, it makes me impatient to hear you: but, however, you have suffered, and are likely to suffer enough for not taking my advice; so I'll say no more. Carter – hurry! – hurry! The sun will soon rise, and I must have him off.'

'Directly, sir; the shoulder is just bandaged. I must look to this other wound in the arm: she has had her teeth here too, I think.'

'She sucked the blood: she said she'd drain my heart,' said Mason.

I saw Mr Rochester shudder: a singularly marked expression of disgust, horror, hatred, warped his countenance almost to distortion, but he only said – 'Come, be silent, Richard, and never mind her gibberish: don't repeat it.'

'I wish I could forget it,' was the answer.

'You will when you are out of the country: when you get back to Spanish Town, you may think of her as dead and buried – or rather, you need not think of her at all.'

'Impossible to forget this night!'

'It is not impossible: have some energy, man. You thought you were as dead as a herring two hours since, and you are all alive and talking now. There! – Carter has done with you or nearly so; I'll make you decent in a trice. Jane' (he turned to me for the first time since his re-entrance), 'take this key: go down into my bedroom, and walk straight forward into my dressing-room: open the top drawer of the wardrobe and take out a clean shirt and neck-handkerchief: bring them here; and be nimble.'

I went; sought the repository he had mentioned, found the articles named, and returned with them.

'Now,' said he, 'go to the other side of the bed while I order his toilet; but don't leave the room: you may be wanted again.'

I retired as directed.

'Was anybody stirring below when you went down, Jane?' enquired Mr Rochester presently.

'No, sir; all was very still.'

'We shall get you off cannily, Dick: and it will be better, both for your sake, and for that of the poor creature in yonder. I have striven long to avoid exposure, and I should not like it to come at last. Here, Carter, help him on with his waistcoat. Where did you leave your furred cloak? You can't travel a mile without that, I know, in this damned cold climate. In your room? – Jane, run down to Mr Mason's room, the one next mine, and fetch a cloak you will see there.'

Again I ran, and again returned, bearing an immense mantle lined and edged with fur.

'Now, I've another errand for you,' said my untiring master; 'you must away to my room again. What a mercy you are shod with velvet, Jane! – a clod-hopping messenger would never do at this juncture. You must open the middle drawer of my toilet-table and take out a little phial and a little glass you will find there, quick!'

I flew thither and back, bringing the desired vessels.

'That's well! Now, doctor, I shall take the liberty of administering a dose myself, on my own responsibility. I got thus cordial at Rome, of an Italian charlatan – a fellow you would have kicked, Carter. It is no a thing to be used indiscriminately, but it is good upon occasion: as now, for instance. Jane, a little water.'

He held out the tiny glass, and I half-filled it from the water-bottle on the washstand.

'That will do; now wet the lip of the phial.'

I did so; he measured twelve drops of a crimson liquid, and presented it to Mason.

'Drink, Richard: it will give you the heart you lack for an hour or so.'

'But will it hurt me? – is it inflammatory?'

'Drink! drink! drink!'

Mr Mason obeyed, because it was evidently useless to resist. He was dressed now: he still looked pale, but he was no longer gory and sullied. Mr Rochester let him sit three minutes after he had swallowed the liquid; he then took his arm – 'Now I am sure you can get on your feet,' he said – 'try.'

The patient rose.

'Carter, take him under the other shoulder. Be of good cheer, Richard; step out – that's it!'

'I do feel better,' remarked Mr Mason.

'I am sure you do. Now, Jane, trip on before us away to the backstairs; unbolt the side-passage door, and tell the driver of the post-chaise you will see in the yard – or just outside, for I told him not to drive his rattling wheels over the pavement – to be ready; we are coming: and, Jane, if anyone is about, come to the foot of the stairs and hem.'

It was by this time half-past five, and the sun was on the point of rising; but I found the kitchen still dark and silent. The side-passage door was fastened; I opened it with as little noise as possible: all the yard was quiet; but the gates stood wide open, and there was a post-chaise, with horses ready harnessed, and driver seated on the box, stationed outside. I approached him, and said the gentlemen were coming; he nodded: then I looked carefully round and listened. The stillness of early morning slumbered everywhere; the curtains were yet drawn over the servants' chamber windows; little birds were just twittering in the blossom-blanched orchard trees, whose boughs drooped like white garlands over the wall enclosing one side of the yard; the carriage horses stamped from time to time in their closed stables: all else was still.

The gentlemen now appeared. Mason, supported by Mr Rochester and the surgeon, seemed to walk with tolerable ease: they assisted him into the chaise; Carter followed.

'Take care of him,' said Mr Rochester to the latter, 'and keep him at your house till he is quite well: I shall ride over in a day or two to see how he gets on. Richard, how is it with you?'

'The fresh air revives me, Fairfax.'

'Leave the window open on his side, Carter; there is no wind – goodbye, Dick.'

'Fairfax – '

'Well, what is it?'

'Let her be taken care of; let her be treated as tenderly as may be: let her – ' he stopped and burst into tears.

'I do my best; and have done it, and will do it,' was the answer: he shut up the chaise door, and the vehicle drove away.

'Yet would to God there was an end of all this!' added Mr Rochester, as he closed and barred the heavy yard-gates.

This done, he moved with slow step and abstracted air towards a door in the wall bordering the orchard. I, supposing he had done with me, prepared to return to the house; again, however, I heard him call 'Jane!' He had opened the portal and stood at it, waiting for me.

'Come where there is some freshness, for a few moments,' he said; 'that house is a mere dungeon: don't you feel it so?'

'It seems to me a splendid mansion, sir.'

'The glamour of inexperience is over your eyes,' he answered; 'and you see it through a charmed medium: you cannot discern that the gilding is slime and the silk draperies cobwebs; that the marble is sordid slate, and the polished woods mere refuse chips and scaly bark. Now *here*' (he pointed to the leafy enclosure we had entered) 'all is real, sweet, and pure.'

He strayed down a walk edged with box, with apple trees, pear trees, and cherry trees on one side, and a border on the other full of all sorts of old-fashioned flowers, stocks, sweet-williams, primroses, pansies, mingled with southernwood, sweet-briar, and various fragrant herbs. They were fresh now as a succession of April showers and gleams, followed by a lovely spring morning, could make them: the sun was just entering the dappled east, and his light illumined the wreathed and dewy orchard trees and shone down the quiet walks under them.

'Jane, will you have a flower?'

He gathered a half-blown rose, the first on the bush, and offered it to me.

'Thank you, sir.'

'Do you like this sunrise, Jane? That sky with its high and light clouds which are sure to melt away as the day waxes warm – this placid and balmy atmosphere?'

'I do, very much.'

'You have passed a strange night, Jane.'

'Yes, sir.'

'And it has made you look pale – were you afraid when I left you alone with Mason?'

'I was afraid of someone coming out of the inner room.'

'But I had fastened the door – I had the key in my pocket: I should have been a careless shepherd if I had left a lamb – my pet lamb – so near a wolf's den, unguarded: you were safe.'

'Will Grace Poole live here still, sir?'

'Oh yes! don't trouble your head about her – put the thing out of your thoughts.'

'Yet it seems to me your life is hardly secure while she stays.'

'Never fear – I will take care of myself.'

'Is the danger you apprehended last night gone by now, sir?'

'I cannot vouch for that till Mason is out of England: nor even then. To live, for me, Jane, is to stand on a crater-crust which may crack and spew fire any day.'

'But Mr Mason seems a man easily led. Your influence, sir, is evidently potent with him: he will never set you at defiance or wilfully injure you.'

'Oh no! Mason will not defy me; nor, knowing it, will he hurt me – but, unintentionally, he might in a moment, by one careless word, deprive me, if not of life, yet for ever of happiness.'

'Tell him to be cautious, sir: let him know what you fear, and show him how to avert the danger.'

He laughed sardonically, hastily took my hand, and as hastily threw it from him.

'If I could do that, simpleton, where would the danger be? Annihilated in a moment. Ever since I have known Mason, I have only had to say to him "Do that," and the thing has been done. But I cannot give him orders in this case: I cannot say "Beware of harming me, Richard"; for it is imperative that I should keep him ignorant that harm to me is possible. Now you look puzzled; and I will puzzle you further. You are my little friend, are you not?'

'I like to serve you, sir, and to obey you in all that is right.'

'Precisely: I see you do. I see genuine contentment in your gait and mien, your eye and face, when you are helping me and pleasing me – working for me, and with me, in, as you characteristically say, "*all that is right*": for if I bid you do what you thought wrong, there would be no light-footed running, no neat-handed alacrity, no lively glance and animated complexion. My friend would then turn to me, quiet and pale, and would say, "No, sir; that is impossible: I cannot do it, because it is wrong"; and would become immutable as a fixed star. Well, you too have power over me, and may injure me: yet I dare not show you where I am vulnerable, lest, faithful and friendly as you are, you should transfix me at once.'

'If you have no more to fear from Mr Mason than you have from me, sir, you are very safe.'

'God grant it may be so! Here, Jane, is an arbour; sit down.'

The arbour was an arch in the wall, lined with ivy; it contained a rustic seat. Mr Rochester took it, leaving room, however, for me: but I stood before him.

'Sit,' he said; 'the bench is long enough for two. You don't hesitate to take a place at my side, do you? Is that wrong, Jane?'

I answered him by assuming it: to refuse would, I felt, have been unwise.

'Now, my little friend, while the sun drinks the dew – while all the flowers in this old garden awake and expand, and the birds fetch their young ones' breakfast out of the Thornfield, and the early bees do their first spell of work – I'll put a case to you, which you must endeavour to suppose your own: but first, look at me, and tell me you are at ease, and not fearing that I err in detaining you, or that you err in staying.'

'No, sir; I am content.'

'Well then, Jane, call to aid your fancy: suppose you were no longer a girl well reared and disciplined, but a wild boy indulged from childhood upwards; imagine yourself in a remote foreign land; conceive that you there commit a capital error, no matter of what nature or from what motives, but one whose consequences must follow you through life and taint all your existence. Mind, I don't say a *crime*; I am not speaking of shedding of blood or any other guilty act, which might make the perpetrator amenable to the law: my word is *error*. The results of what you have done become in time to you utterly insupportable; you take measures to obtain relief: unusual measures, but neither unlawful nor culpable. Still you are miserable; for hope has quitted you on the very confines of life: your sun at noon darkens in an eclipse, which you feel will not leave it till the time of setting. Bitter and base associations have become the sole food of your memory: you wander here and there, seeking rest in exile: happiness in pleasure – I mean in heartless, sensual pleasure such as dulls intellect and blights feeling. Heart-weary and soul-withered, you come home after years of voluntary banishment: you make a new acquaintance – how or where no matter: you find in this stranger much of the good and bright qualities which you have sought for twenty years, and never before encountered; and they are all fresh, healthy, without soil and without taint. Such society revives, regenerates: you feel better days come back – higher wishes, purer feelings; you desire to recommence your life, and to spend what remains to you of days in a way more worthy of an immortal being. To attain this end, are you justified in overleaping an obstacle of custom – a mere conventional impediment which neither your conscience sanctifies nor your judgement approves?'

He paused for an answer: and what was I to say? Oh, for some good spirit to suggest a judicious and satisfactory response! Vain aspiration! The west wind whispered in the ivy round me; but no gentle Ariel borrowed its breath as a medium of speech: the birds sang in the tree-tops; but their song, however sweet, was inarticulate.

Again Mr Rochester propounded his query: 'Is the wandering and sinful, but now rest-seeking and repentant, man justified in daring the world's opinion, in order to attach to him for ever this gentle, gracious, genial stranger, thereby securing his own peace of mind and regeneration of life?'

'Sir,' I answered, 'a wanderer's repose or a sinner's reformation should never depend on a fellow-creature. Men and women die; philosophers falter in wisdom, and Christians in goodness: if anyone you know has suffered and erred, let him look higher than his equals for strength to amend and solace to heal.'

'But the instrument – the instrument! God, who does the work, ordains the instrument. I have myself – I tell it you without parable – been a worldly, dissipated, restless man; and I believe I have found the instrument for my cure in – '

He paused: the birds went on carolling, the leaves lightly rustling. I almost wondered they did not check their songs and whispers to catch the suspended revelation; but they would have had to wait many minutes – so long was the silence protracted. At last I looked up at the tardy speaker: he was looking eagerly at me.

'Little friend,' said he, in quite a changed tone – while his face changed too, losing all its softness and gravity, and becoming harsh and sarcastic – 'you have noticed my tender penchant for Miss Ingram: don't you think if I married her she would regenerate me with a vengeance?'

He got up instantly, went quite to the other end of the walk, and when he came back he was humming a tune.

'Jane, Jane,' said he, stopping before me, 'you are quite pale with your vigils: don't you curse me for disturbing your rest?'

'Curse you? No, sir.'

'Shake hands in confirmation of the word. What cold fingers! They were warmer last night when I touched them at the door of the mysterious chamber. Jane, when will you watch with me again?'

'Whenever I can be useful, sir.'

'For instance, the night before I am married! I am sure I shall not be able to sleep. Will you promise to sit up with me to bear me company? To you I can talk of my lovely one: for now you have seen her and know her.'

'Yes, sir.'

'She's a rare one, is she not, Jane?'

'Yes, sir.'

'A strapper – a real strapper, Jane: big, brown, and buxom; with hair just such as the ladies of Carthage must have had. Bless me! there's Dent and Lynn in the stables! Go in by the shrubbery, through that wicket.'

As I went one way, he went another, and I heard him in the yard, saying cheerfully – 'Mason got the start of you all this morning; he was gone before sunrise: I rose at four to see him off.'

## *Chapter 21*

Presentiments are strange things! and so are sympathies; and so are signs; and the three combined make one mystery to which humanity has not yet found the key. I never laughed at presentiments in my life, because I have had strange ones of my own. Sympathies, I believe, exist (for instance, between far-distant, long-absent, wholly estranged relatives asserting, notwithstanding their alienation, the unity of the source to which each traces his origin) whose workings baffle mortal comprehension. And signs, for aught we know, may be but the sympathies of Nature with man.

When I was a little girl, only six years old, I one night heard Bessie Leaven say to Martha Abbot that she had been dreaming about a little child; and that to dream of children was a sure sign of trouble, either to oneself or one's kin. The saying might have worn out of my memory, had not a circumstance immediately followed which served indelibly to fix it there. The next day Bessie was sent for home to the deathbed of her little sister.

Of late I had often recalled this saying and this incident; for during the past week scarcely a night had gone over my couch that had not brought with it a dream of an infant, which I sometimes hushed in my arms, sometimes dandled on my knee, sometimes watched playing with daisies on a lawn, or again, dabbling its hands in running water. It was a wailing child this night, and a laughing one the next: now it nestled close to me, and now it ran from me; but whatever mood the apparition evinced, whatever aspect it wore, it failed not for seven successive nights to meet me the moment I entered the land of slumber.

I did not like this iteration of one idea – this strange recurrence of one image, and I grew nervous as bedtime approached and the hour of the vision drew near. It was from companionship with this baby-phantom I had been roused on that moonlight night when I heard the cry; and it was on the afternoon of the day following I was summoned downstairs by a message that someone wanted me in Mrs Fairfax's room. On repairing thither, I found a man waiting for me, having the appearance of a gentleman's servant: he was dressed in deep mourning, and the hat he held in his hand was surrounded with a crape band.

'I dare say you hardly remember me, Miss,' he said, rising as I entered; 'but my name is Leaven: I lived coachman with Mrs Reed when you were at Gateshead, eight or nine years since, and I live there still.'

'Oh, Robert! how do you do? I remember you very well: you used to give me a ride sometimes on Miss Georgiana's bay pony. And how is Bessie? You are married to Bessie?'

'Yes, Miss: my wife is very hearty, thank you; she brought me another little one about two months since – we have three now – and both mother and child are thriving.'

'And are the family well at the house, Robert?'

'I am sorry I can't give you better news of them, Miss: they are very badly at present – in great trouble.'

'I hope no one is dead,' I said, glancing at his black dress. He too looked down at the crape round his hat and replied – 'Mr John died yesterday was a week, at his chambers in London.'

'Mr John?'

'Yes.'

'And how does his mother bear it?'

'Why, you see, Miss Eyre, it is not a common mishap: his life has been very wild: these last three years he gave himself up to strange ways, and his death was shocking.'

'I heard from Bessie he was not doing well.'

'Doing well! He could not do worse: he ruined his health and his estate amongst the worst men and the worst women. He got into debt and into jail: his mother helped him out twice, but as soon as he was free he returned to his old companions and habits. His head was not strong: the knaves he lived amongst fooled him beyond anything I ever heard. He came down to Gateshead about three weeks ago and wanted missis to give up all to him. Missis refused: her means have long been much reduced by his extravagance; so he went back again, and the next news was that he was dead. How he died, God knows! – they say he killed himself.'

I was silent: the tidings were frightful. Robert Leaven resumed – 'Missis had been out of health herself for some time: she had got very stout, but was not strong with it; and the loss of money and fear of poverty were quite breaking her down. The information about Mr John's death and the manner of it came too suddenly: it brought on a stroke. She was three days without speaking; but last Tuesday she seemed rather better: she appeared as if she wanted to say something, and kept making signs to my wife and mumbling. It was only yesterday morning, however, that Bessie understood she was pronouncing your name; and at last she made out the words, "Bring Jane – fetch Jane Eyre: I want to speak to her." Bessie is not sure whether she is in her right mind, or means anything by the words; but she told Miss Reed and Miss Georgiana, and advised them to send for you. The young ladies put it off at first; but their mother grew so restless, and said, "Jane, Jane," so many times, that at last they consented. I left Gateshead yesterday: and if you can get ready, Miss, I should like to take you back with me early tomorrow morning.'

'Yes, Robert, I shall be ready: it seems to me that I ought to go.'

'I think so too, Miss. Bessie said she was sure you would not refuse: but I suppose you will have to ask leave before you can get off?'

'Yes; and I will do it now'; and having directed him to the servants' hall, and recommended him to the care of John's wife, and the attentions of John himself, I went in search of Mr Rochester.

He was not in any of the lower rooms; he was not in the yard, the stables, or the grounds. I asked Mrs Fairfax if she had seen him; yes: she believed he was playing billiards with Miss Ingram. To the billiard-room I hastened: the click of balls and the hum of voices resounded thence; Mr Rochester, Miss Ingram, the two Misses Eshton, and their admirers, were all busied in the game. It required some courage to disturb so interesting a party; my errand, however, was one I could not defer, so I approached the master where he stood at Miss Ingram's side. She turned as I drew near, and looked at me haughtily: her eyes seemed to demand, 'What can the creeping creature want now?' and when I said, in a low voice, 'Mr Rochester,' she made a movement as if tempted to order me away. I remember her appearance at the moment – it was very graceful and very striking: she wore a morning robe of sky-blue crape; a gauzy azure scarf was twisted in her hair. She had been all animation with the game, and irritated pride did not lower the expression of her haughty lineaments.

'Does that person want you?' she enquired of Mr Rochester; and Mr Rochester turned to see who the 'person' was. He made a curious grimace – one of his strange and equivocal demonstrations – threw down his cue and followed me from the room.

'Well, Jane?' he said, as he rested his back against the schoolroom door, which he had shut.

'If you please, sir, I want leave of absence for a week or two.'

'What to do? – where to go?'

'To see a sick lady who has sent for me.'

'What sick lady? – where does she live?'

'At Gateshead, in —shire.'

'—shire? That is a hundred miles off! Who may she be that sends for people to see her that distance?'

'Her name is Reed, sir – Mrs Reed.'

'Reed of Gateshead? There was a Reed of Gateshead, a magistrate.'

'It is his widow, sir.'

'And what have you to do with her? How do you know her?'

'Mr Reed was my uncle – my mother's brother.'

'The deuce he was! You never told me that before: you always said you had no relations.'

'None that would own me, sir. Mr Reed is dead, and his wife cast me off.'

'Why?'

'Because I was poor, and burdensome, and she disliked me.'

'But Reed left children? – you must have cousins? Sir George Lynn was talking of a Reed of Gateshead yesterday, who, he said, was one of the veriest rascals on town; and Ingram was mentioning a Georgiana Reed of the same place, who was much admired for her beauty a season or two ago in London.'

'John Reed is dead, too, sir: he ruined himself and half-ruined his family, and is supposed to have committed suicide. The news so shocked his mother that it brought on an apoplectic attack.'

'And what good can you do her? Nonsense, Jane! I would never think of running a hundred miles to see an old lady who will, perhaps, be dead before you reach her: besides, you say she cast you off.'

'Yes, sir, but that is long ago; and when her circumstances were very different: I could not be easy to neglect her wishes now.'

'How long will you stay?'

'As short a time as possible, sir.'

'Promise me only to stay a week – '

'I had better not pass my word: I might be obliged to break it.'

'At all events you *will* come back: you will not be induced under any pretext to take up a permanent residence with her?'

'Oh, no! I shall certainly return if all be well.'

'And who goes with you? You don't travel a hundred miles alone.'

'No, sir, she has sent her coachman.'

'A person to be trusted?'

'Yes, sir, he has lived ten years in the family.'

Mr Rochester meditated. 'When do you wish to go?'

'Early tomorrow morning, sir.'

'Well, you must have some money; you can't travel without money, and I dare say you have not much: I have given you no salary yet. How much have you in the world, Jane?' he asked, smiling.

I drew out my purse; a meagre thing it was. 'Five shillings, sir.' He took the purse, poured the hoard into his palm, and chuckled over it as if its scantiness amused him. Soon he produced his pocket-book: 'Here,' said he, offering me a note; it was fifty pounds, and he owed me but fifteen. I told him I had no change.

'I don't want change; you know that. Take your wages.'

I declined accepting more than was my due. He scowled at first; then, as if recollecting something, he said – 'Right, right! Better not give you all now: you would, perhaps, stay away three months if you had fifty pounds. There are ten; is it not plenty?'

'Yes, sir, but now you owe me five.'

'Come back for it, then; I am your banker for forty pounds.'

'Mr Rochester, I may as well mention another matter of business to you while I have the opportunity.'

'Matter of business? I am curious to hear it.'

'You have as good as informed me, sir, that you are going shortly to be married?'

'Yes; what then?'

'In that case, sir, Adèle ought to go to school: I am sure you will perceive the necessity of it.'

'To get her out of my bride's way, who might otherwise walk over her rather too emphatically? There's sense in the suggestion; not a doubt of it. Adèle, as you say, must go to school; and you, of course, must march straight to – the devil?'

'I hope not, sir; but I must seek another situation somewhere.'

'In course!' he exclaimed, with a twang of voice and a distortion of features equally fantastic and ludicrous. He looked at me some minutes.

'And old Madam Reed, or the Misses, her daughters, will be solicited by you to seek a place, I suppose?'

'No, sir; I am not on such terms with my relatives as would justify me in asking favours of them – but I shall advertise.'

'You shall walk up the pyramids of Egypt!' he growled. 'At your peril you advertise! I wish I had only offered you a sovereign instead of ten pounds. Give me back nine pounds, Jane; I've a use for it.'

'And so have I, sir,' I returned, putting my hands and my purse behind me. 'I could not spare the money on any account.'

'Little niggard!' said he, 'refusing me a pecuniary request! Give me five pounds, Jane.'

'Not five shillings, sir; nor five pence.'

'Just let me look at the cash.'

'No, sir; you are not to be trusted.'

'Jane!'

'Sir?'

'Promise me one thing.'

'I'll promise you anything, sir, that I think I am likely to perform.'

'Not to advertise: and to trust this quest of a situation to me. I'll find you one in time.'

'I shall be glad so to do, sir, if you, in your turn, will promise that I and Adèle shall be both safe out of the house before your bride enters it.'

'Very well! very well! I'll pledge my word on it. You go tomorrow, then?'

'Yes, sir; early.'

'Shall you come down to the drawing-room after dinner?'

'No, sir, I must prepare for the journey.'

'Then you and I must bid goodbye for a little while?'

'I suppose so, sir.'

'And how do people perform that ceremony of parting, Jane? Teach me; I'm not quite up to it.'

'They say, Farewell, or any other form they prefer.'

'Then say it.'

'Farewell, Mr Rochester, for the present.'

'What must I say?'

'The same, if you like, sir.'

'Farewell, Miss Eyre, for the present; is that all?'

'Yes?'

'It seems stingy, to my notions, and dry, and unfriendly. I should like something else: a little addition to the rite. If one shook hands, for instance; but no – that would not content me either. So you'll do no more than say Farewell, Jane?'

'It is enough, sir: as much goodwill may be conveyed in one hearty word as in many.'

'Very likely; but it is blank and cool – "Farewell." '

'How long is he going to stand with his back against that door?' I asked myself; 'I want to commence my packing.' The dinner-bell rang, and suddenly away he bolted, without another syllable: I saw him no more during the day, and was off before he had risen in the morning.

I reached the lodge at Gateshead about five o'clock in the afternoon of the first of May: I stepped in there before going up to the hall. It was very clean and neat: the ornamental windows were hung with little white curtains; the floor was spotless; the grate and fire-irons were burnished bright, and the fire burnt clear. Bessie sat on the hearth, nursing her last-born, and Robert and his sister played quietly in a corner.

'Bless you! – I knew you would come!' exclaimed Mrs Leaven, as I entered.

'Yes, Bessie,' said I, after I had kissed her; 'and I trust I am not too late. How is Mrs Reed? – Alive still, I hope.'

'Yes, she is alive; and more sensible and collected than she was. The doctor says she may linger a week or two yet; but he hardly thinks she will finally recover.'

'Has she mentioned me lately?'

'She was talking of you only this morning, and wishing you would come: but she is sleeping now, or was ten minutes ago, when I was up at the house. She generally lies in a kind of lethargy all the afternoon, and wakes up about six or seven. Will you rest yourself here an hour, Miss, and then I will go up with you?'

Robert here entered, and Bessie laid her sleeping child in the cradle and went to welcome him: afterwards she insisted on my taking off my bonnet and having some tea; for she said I looked pale and tired. I was glad to accept her hospitality; and I submitted to be relieved of my travelling garb just as passively as I used to let her undress me when a child.

Old times crowded fast back on me as I watched her bustling about – setting out the tea-tray with her best china, cutting bread and butter, toasting a teacake, and, between whiles, giving little Robert or Jane an occasional tap or push, just as she used to give me in former days. Bessie had retained her quick temper as well as her light foot and good looks.

Tea ready, I was going to approach the table; but she desired me to sit still, quite in her old peremptory tones. I must be served at the fireside, she said; and she placed before me a little round stand with my cup and a plate of toast, absolutely as she used to accommodate me with some privately purloined dainty on a nursery chair: and I smiled and obeyed her as in bygone days.

She wanted to know if I was happy at Thornfield Hall, and what sort of a person the mistress was; and when I told her there was only a master, whether he was a nice gentleman, and if I liked him. I told her he was rather an ugly man, but quite a gentleman; and that he treated me kindly, and I was content. Then I went on to describe to her the gay company that had lately been staying at the house; and to these details Bessie listened with interest: they were precisely of the kind she relished.

In such conversation an hour was soon gone: Bessie restored to me my bonnet, etc., and, accompanied by her, I quitted the lodge for the hall. It was also accompanied by her that I had, nearly nine years ago, walked down the path I was now ascending. On a dark, misty, raw morning in January, I had left a hostile roof with a desperate and embittered heart – a sense of outlawry and almost of reprobation – to seek the chilly harbourage of Lowood: that bourne so far away and unexplored. The same hostile roof now again rose before me: my prospects were doubtful yet; and I had yet an aching heart. I still felt as a wanderer on the face of the earth; but I experienced firmer trust in myself and my own powers, and less withering dread of oppression. The gaping wound of my wrongs, too, was now quite healed; and the flame of resentment extinguished.

'You shall go into the breakfast-room first,' said Bessie, as she preceded me through the hall; 'the young ladies will be there.'

In another moment I was within that apartment. There was every article of furniture looking just as it did on the morning I was first introduced to Mr Brocklehurst: the very rug he had stood upon still covered the hearth. Glancing at the bookcases, I thought I could distinguish the two volumes of Bewick's *British Birds* occupying their old place on the third shelf, and *Gulliver's Travels* and the *Arabian Nights* ranged just above. The inanimate objects were not changed; but the living things had altered past recognition.

Two young ladies appeared before me; one very tall, almost as tall as Miss Ingram – very thin too, with a sallow face and severe mien. There was something ascetic in her look, which was augmented by the extreme plainness of a straight-skirted, black, stuff dress, a starched linen collar, hair combed away from the temples, and the nun-like ornament of a string of ebony beads and a crucifix. This I felt sure was Eliza, though I could trace little resemblance to her former self in that elongated and colourless visage.

The other was as certainly Georgiana: but not the Georgiana I remembered – the slim and fairy-like girl of eleven. This was a full-blown, very plump damsel, fair as waxwork, with handsome and regular features, languishing blue eyes, and ringleted yellow hair. The hue of her dress was black too; but its fashion was so different from her sister's – so much more flowing and becoming – it looked as stylish as the other's looked puritanical.

In each of the sisters there was one trait of the mother – and only one; the thin and pallid elder daughter had her parent's Cairngorm eye: the blooming and luxuriant younger girl had her contour of jaw and chin – perhaps a little softened, but still imparting an indescribable hardness to the countenance, otherwise so voluptuous and buxom.

Both ladies, as I advanced, rose to welcome me, and both addressed me by the name of 'Miss Eyre'. Eliza's greeting was delivered in a short, abrupt voice, without a smile; and then she sat down again, fixed her eyes on the fire, and seemed to forget me. Georgiana added to her 'How d'ye do?' several commonplaces about my journey, the weather, and so on, uttered in rather a drawling tone: and accompanied by sundry side-glances that measured me from head to foot – now traversing the folds of my drab merino pelisse, and now lingering on the plain trimming of my cottage bonnet. Young ladies have a remarkable way of letting you know that they think you a 'quiz' without actually saying the words. A certain superciliousness of look, coolness of manner, nonchalance of tone, express fully their sentiments on the point, without committing them by any positive rudeness in word or deed.

A sneer, however, whether covert or open, had now no longer that power over me it once possessed: as I sat between my cousins, I was surprised to find how easy I felt under the total neglect of the one and the semi-sarcastic attentions of the other – Eliza did not mortify, nor Georgiana ruffle me. The fact was, I had other things to think about; within the last few months feelings had been stirred in me so much more potent than any they could raise – pains and pleasures so much more acute and exquisite had been excited than any it was in their power to inflict or bestow – that their airs gave me no concern either for good or bad.

'How is Mrs Reed?' I asked soon, looking calmly at Georgiana, who thought fit to bridle at the direct address, as if it were an unexpected liberty.

'Mrs Reed? Ah! mama, you mean; she is extremely poorly: I doubt if you can see her tonight.'

'If,' said I, 'you would just step upstairs and tell her I am come, I should be much obliged to you.'

Georgiana almost started, and she opened her blue eyes wild and wide. 'I know she had a particular wish to see me,' I added, 'and I would not defer attending to her desire longer than is absolutely necessary.'

'Mama dislikes being disturbed in an evening,' remarked Eliza. I soon rose, quietly took off my bonnet and gloves, uninvited, and said I would just step out to Bessie – who was, I dared say, in the kitchen – and ask her to ascertain whether Mrs Reed was disposed to receive me or not tonight. I went, and having found Bessie and despatched her on my errand, I proceeded to take further measures. It had heretofore been my habit always to shrink from arrogance: received as I had been today, I should, a year ago, have resolved to quit Gateshead the very next morning; now, it was disclosed to me all at once that that would be a foolish plan. I had taken a journey of a hundred miles to see my aunt, and I must stay with her till she was better – or dead: as to her daughters' pride or folly, I must put it on one side, make myself independent of it. So I addressed the housekeeper; asked her to show me a room, told her I should probably be a visitor here for a week or two, had my trunk conveyed to my chamber, and followed it thither my self: I met Bessie on the landing.

'Missis is awake,' said she; 'I have told her you are here: come and let us see if she will know you.'

I did not need to be guided to the well-known room, to which I had so often been summoned for chastisement or reprimand in former days. I hastened before Bessie; I softly opened the door: a shaded light stood on the table, for it was now getting dark. There was the great four-post bed with amber hangings as of old; there the toilet-table, the armchair, and the footstool, at which I had a hundred times been sentenced to kneel, to ask pardon for offences by me uncommitted. I looked into a certain corner near, half expecting to see the slim outline of a once dreaded switch which used to lurk there, waiting to leap out imp-like and lace my quivering palm or shrinking neck. I approached the bed; I opened the curtains and leant over the high-piled pillows.

Well did I remember Mrs Reed's face, and I eagerly sought the familiar image. It is a happy thing that time quells the longings of vengeance and hushes the promptings of rage and aversion. I had left this woman in bitterness and hate, and I came back to her now with no other emotion than a sort of ruth for her great sufferings, and a strong yearning to forget and forgive all injuries – to be reconciled and clasp hands in amity.

The well-known face was there: stern, relentless as ever – there was that peculiar eye which nothing could melt, and the somewhat raised, imperious, despotic eyebrow. How often had it lowered on me menace and hate! and how the recollection of childhood's terrors and sorrows revived as I traced its harsh line now! And yet I stooped down and kissed her: she looked at me.

'Is this Jane Eyre?' she said.

'Yes, Aunt Reed. How are you, dear aunt?'

I had once vowed that I would never call her aunt again: I thought it no sin to forget and break that vow now. My fingers had fastened on her hand which lay outside the sheet: had she pressed mine kindly, I should at that moment have experienced true pleasure. But unimpressionable natures are not so soon softened, nor are natural antipathies so readily eradicated. Mrs Reed took her hand away, and, turning her face rather from me, she remarked that the night was warm. Again she regarded me so icily, I felt at once that her opinion of me – her feeling towards me – was unchanged and unchangeable. I knew by her stony eye – opaque to tenderness, indissoluble to tears – that she was resolved to consider me bad to the last; because to believe me good would give her no generous pleasure: only a sense of mortification.

I felt pain, and then I felt ire; and then I felt a determination to subdue her – to be her mistress in spite both of her nature and her will. My tears had risen, just as in childhood: I ordered them back to their source. I brought a chair to the bed-head: I sat down and leaned over the pillow.

'You sent for me,' I said, 'and I am here; and it is my intention to stay till I see how you get on.'

'Oh, of course! You have seen my daughters?'

'Yes.'

'Well, you may tell them I wish you to stay till I can talk some things over with you I have on my mind: tonight it is too late, and I have a difficulty in recalling them. But there was something I wished to say – let me see – '

The wandering look and changed utterance told what wreck had taken place in her once vigorous frame. Turning restlessly, she drew the bedclothes round her; my elbow, resting on a corner of the quilt, fixed it down: she was at once irritated.

'Sit up!' said she; 'don't annoy me with holding the clothes fast. Are you Jane Eyre?'

'I am Jane Eyre.'

'I have had more trouble with that child than anyone would believe. Such a burden to be left on my hands – and so much annoyance as she caused me, daily and hourly, with her incomprehensible disposition, and her sudden starts of temper, and her continual, unnatural watchings of one's movements! I declare she talked to me once like something mad, or like a fiend – no child ever spoke or looked as she did; I was glad to get her away from the house. What did they do with her at Lowood? The fever broke out there, and many of the pupils died. She, however, did not die: but I said she did – I wish she had died!'

'A strange wish, Mrs Reed; why do you hate her so?'

'I had a dislike to her mother always; for she was my husband's only sister, and a great favourite with him: he opposed the family's disowning her when she made her low marriage; and when news came of her death, he wept like a simpleton. He would send for the baby; though I entreated him rather to put it out to nurse and pay for its maintenance. I hated it the first time I set my eyes on it – a sickly, whining pining thing! It would wail in its cradle all night long – not screaming heartily like any other child, but whimpering and moaning. Reed pitied it; and he used to nurse it and notice it as if it had been his own: more, indeed, than he ever noticed his own at that age. He would try to make my children friendly to the little beggar: the darlings could not bear it, and he was angry with them when they showed their dislike. In his last illness, he had it brought continually to his bedside; and but an hour before he died, he bound me by vow to keep the creature. I would as soon have been charged with a pauper brat out of a workhouse: but he was weak, naturally weak. John does not at all resemble his father, and I am glad of it: John is like me and like my brothers – he is quite a Gibson. Oh, I wish he would cease tormenting me with letters for money? I have no more money to give him: we are getting poor. I must send away half the servants and shut up part of the house; or let it off. I can never submit to do that – yet how are we to get on? Two-thirds of my income goes in paying the interest of mortgages. John gambles dreadfully, and always loses – poor boy! He is beset by sharpers: John is sunk and degraded – his look is frightful – I feel ashamed for him when I see him.'

She was getting much excited. 'I think I had better leave her now,' said I to Bessie, who stood on the other side of the bed.

'Perhaps you had, Miss: but she often talks in this way towards night – in the morning she is calmer.'

I rose. 'Stop!' exclaimed Mrs Reed, 'there is another thing I wished to say. He threatens me – he continually threatens me with his own death, or mine: and I dream sometimes that I see him laid out with a great wound in his throat, or with a swollen and blackened face. I am come to a strange pass: I have heavy troubles. What is to be done? How is the money to be had?'

Bessie now endeavoured to persuade her to take a sedative draught: she succeeded with difficulty. Soon after, Mrs Reed grew more composed, and sank into a dozing state. I then left her.

More than ten days elapsed before I had again any conversation with her. She continued either delirious or lethargic; and the doctor forbade everything which could painfully excite her. Meantime, I got on as well as I could with Georgiana and Eliza. They were very cold, indeed, at first. Eliza would sit half the day sewing, reading, or writing, and scarcely utter a word either to me or her sister. Georgiana would chatter nonsense to her canary bird by the hour, and take no notice of me. But I was determined not to seem at a loss for occupation or amusement: I had brought my drawing materials with me, and they served me for both.

Provided with a case of pencils, and some sheets of paper, I used to take a seat apart from them, near the window, and busy myself in sketching fancy vignettes, representing any scene that happened momentarily to shape itself in the ever-shifting kaleidoscope of imagination: a glimpse of sea between two rocks; the rising moon, and a ship crossing its disk; a group of reeds and water-flags, and a naiad's head, crowned with lotus-flowers, rising out of them; an elf sitting in a hedge-sparrow's nest, under a wreath of hawthorn-bloom.

One morning I fell to sketching a face: what sort of a face it was to be, I did not care or know. I took a soft black pencil, gave it a broad point, and worked away. Soon I had traced on the paper a broad and prominent forehead and a square lower outline of visage: that contour gave me pleasure; my fingers proceeded actively to fill it with features. Strongly-marked horizontal eyebrows must be traced under that brow; then followed, naturally, a well-defined nose, with a straight ridge and full nostrils; then a flexible-looking mouth, by no means narrow; then a firm chin, with a decided cleft down the middle of it: of course, some black whiskers were wanted, and some jetty hair, tufted on the temples, and waved above the forehead. Now for the eyes: I had left them to the last, because they required the most careful working. I drew them large; I shaped them well: the eyelashes I traced long and sombre; the irids lustrous and large. 'Good! but not quite the thing,' I thought, as I surveyed the effect: 'they want more force and spirit'; and I wrought the shades blacker, that the lights might flash more brilliantly – a happy touch or two secured success. There, I had a friend's face under my gaze; and what did it signify that those young ladies turned their backs on me? I looked at it; I smiled at the speaking likeness: I was absorbed and content.

'Is that a portrait of someone you know?' asked Eliza, who had approached me unnoticed. I responded that it was merely a fancy head, and hurried it beneath the other sheets. Of course, I lied: it was, in fact, a very faithful representation of Mr Rochester. But what was that to her, or to anyone but myself? Georgiana also advanced to look. The other drawings pleased her much, but she called that 'an ugly man.' They both seemed surprised at my skill. I offered to sketch their portraits; and each, in turn, sat for a pencil outline. Then Georgiana produced her album. I promised to contribute a watercolour drawing: this put her at once into good humour. She proposed a walk in the grounds. Before we had been out two hours, we were deep in a confidential conversation: she had favoured me with a description of the brilliant winter she had spent in London two seasons ago – of the admiration she had there excited – the attention she had received; and I even got hints of the titled conquest she had made. In the course of the afternoon and evening these hints were enlarged on: various soft conversations were reported, and sentimental scenes represented; and, in short, a volume of a novel of fashionable life was that day improvised by her for my benefit. The communications were renewed from day to day: they always ran on the same theme – herself, her loves, and woes. It was strange she never once adverted either to her mother's illness, or her brother's death, or the present gloomy state of the family prospects. Her mind seemed wholly taken up with reminiscences of past gaiety, and aspirations after dissipations to come. She passed about five minutes each day in her mother's sickroom, and no more.

Eliza still spoke little: she had evidently no time to talk. I never saw a busier person than she seemed to be; yet it was difficult to say what she did: or rather, to discover any result of her diligence. She had an alarm to call her up early. I know not how she occupied herself before breakfast, but after that meal she divided her time into regular portions, and each hour had its allotted task. Three times a day she studied a little book, which I found, on inspection, was a Common Prayer Book. I asked her once what was the great attraction of that volume, and she said, 'The Rubric.' Three hours she gave to stitching, with gold thread, the border of a square crimson cloth, almost large enough for a carpet. In answer to my enquiries after the use of this article, she informed me it was a covering for the altar of a new church lately erected near Gateshead. Two hours she devoted to her diary; two to working by herself in the kitchen-garden; and one to the regulation of her accounts. She seemed to want no company; no conversation. I believe she was happy in her way: this routine sufficed for her; and nothing annoyed her so much as the occurrence of any incident which forced her to vary its clockwork regularity.

She told me one evening, when more disposed to be communicative than usual, that John's conduct, and the threatened ruin of the family, had been a source of profound affliction to her: but she had now, she said, settled her mind, and formed her resolution. Her own fortune she had taken care to secure; and when her mother died – and it was wholly improbable, she tranquilly remarked, that she should either recover or linger long – she would execute a long-cherished project: seek a retirement where punctual habits would be permanently secured from disturbance, and place safe barriers between herself and a frivolous world. I asked if Georgiana would accompany her.

'Of course not. Georgiana and she had nothing in common: they never had had. She would not be burdened with her society for any consideration. Georgiana should take her own course; and she, Eliza, would take hers.'

Georgiana, when not unburdening her heart to me, spent most of her time in lying on the sofa, fretting about the dullness of the house, and wishing over and over again that her aunt Gibson would send her an invitation up to town. 'It would be so much better,' she said, 'if she could only get out of the way for a month or two, till all was over.' I did not ask what she meant by 'all being over', but I suppose she referred to the expected decease of her mother and the gloomy sequel of funeral rites. Eliza generally took no more notice of her sister's indolence and complaints than if no such murmuring, lounging object had been before her. One day, however, as she put away her account-book and unfolded her embroidery, she suddenly took her up thus – 'Georgiana, a more vain and absurd animal than you was certainly never allowed to cumber the earth. You had no right to be born, for you make no use of life. Instead of living for, in, and with yourself, as a reasonable being ought, you seek only to fasten your feebleness on some other person's strength: if no one can be found willing to burden her or himself with such a fat, weak, puffy, useless thing, you cry out that you are ill-treated, neglected, miserable. Then, too, existence for you must be a scene of continual change and excitement, or else the world is a dungeon: you must be admired, you must be courted, you must be flattered – you must have music, dancing, and society – or you languish, you die away. Have you no sense to devise a system which will make you independent of all efforts, and all wills, but your own? Take one day; share it into sections; to each section apportion its task: leave no stray unemployed quarters of an hour, ten minutes, five minutes – include all; do each piece of business in its turn with method, with rigid regularity. The day will close almost before you are aware it has begun; and you are indebted to no one for helping you to get rid of one vacant moment: you have had to seek no one's company, conversation, sympathy, forbearance; you have lived, in short, as an independent being ought to do. Take this advice: the first and last I shall offer you; then you will not want me or anyone else, happen what may. Neglect it – go on as heretofore, craving, whining, and idling – and suffer the results of your idiocy, however bad and insufferable they may be. I tell you this plainly; and listen: for though I shall no more repeat what I am now about to say, I shall steadily act on it. After my mother's death, I wash my hands of you: from the day her coffin is carried to the vault in Gateshead Church, you and I will be as separate as if we had never known each other. You need not think that because we chanced to be born of the same parents, I shall suffer you to fasten me down by even the feeblest claim: I can tell you this – if the whole human race, ourselves excepted, were swept away, and we two stood alone on the earth, I would leave you in the old world, and betake myself to the new.'

She closed her lips.

'You might have spared yourself the trouble of delivering that tirade,' answered Georgiana. 'Everybody knows you are the most selfish, heartless creature in existence: and *I* know your spiteful hatred towards me: I have had a specimen of it before in the trick you played me about Lord Edwin Vere: you could not bear me to be raised above you, to have a title, to be received into circles where you dare not show your face, and so you acted the spy and informer, and ruined my prospects for ever.' Georgiana took out her handkerchief and blew her nose for an hour afterwards; Eliza sat cold, impassible, and assiduously industrious.

True, generous feeling is made small account of by some, but here were two natures rendered, the one intolerably acrid, the other despicably savourless for the want of it. Feeling without judgement is a washy draught indeed; but judgement untempered by feeling is too bitter and husky a morsel for human deglutition.

It was a wet and windy afternoon: Georgiana had fallen asleep on the sofa over the perusal of a novel; Eliza was gone to attend a saint's-day service at the new church – for in matters of religion she was a rigid formalist: no weather ever prevented the punctual discharge of what she considered her devotional duties; fair or foul, she went to church thrice every Sunday, and as often on weekdays as there were prayers.

I bethought myself to go upstairs and see how the dying woman sped, who lay there almost unheeded: the very servants paid her but a remittent attention: the hired nurse, being little looked after, would slip out of the room whenever she could. Bessie was faithful; but she had her own family to mind, and could only come occasionally to the hall. I found the sickroom unwatched, as I had expected: no nurse was there; the patient lay still, and seemingly lethargic; her livid face sunk in the pillows: the fire was dying in the grate. I renewed the fuel, rearranged the bedclothes, gazed awhile on her who could not now gaze on me, and then I moved away to the window.

The rain beat strongly against the panes, the wind blew tempestuously: 'One lies there,' I thought, 'who will soon be beyond the war of earthly elements. Whither will that spirit – now struggling to quit its material tenement – flit when at length released?'

In pondering the great mystery, I thought of Helen Burns, recalled her dying words – her faith – her doctrine of the equality of disembodied souls. I was still listening in thought to her well-remembered tones – still picturing her pale and spiritual aspect, her wasted face and sublime gaze, as she lay on her placid deathbed, and whispered her longing to be restored to her divine Father's bosom – when a feeble voice murmured from the couch behind: 'Who is that?'

I knew Mrs Reed had not spoken for days: was she reviving? I went up to her.

'It is I, Aunt Reed.'

'Who – I?' was her answer. 'Who are you?' looking at me with surprise and a sort of alarm, but still not wildly. 'You are quite a stranger to me – where is Bessie?'

'She is at the lodge, aunt.'

'Aunt,' she repeated. 'Who calls me aunt? You are not one of the Gibsons; and yet I know you – that face, and the eyes and forehead, are quite familiar to me: you are like – why, you are like Jane Eyre!'

I said nothing: I was afraid of occasioning some shock by declaring my identity.

'Yet,' said she, 'I am afraid it is a mistake: my thoughts deceive me. I wished to see Jane Eyre, and I fancy a likeness where none exists: besides, in eight years she must be so changed.' I now gently assured her that I was the person she supposed and desired me to be: and seeing that I was understood, and that her senses were quite collected, I explained how Bessie had sent her husband to fetch me from Thornfield.

'I am very ill, I know,' she said ere long. 'I was trying to turn myself a few minutes since, and find I cannot move a limb. It is as well I should ease my mind before I die: what we think little of in health, burdens us at such an hour as the present is to me. Is the nurse here? or is there no one in the room but you?'

I assured her we were alone.

'Well, I have twice done you a wrong which I regret now. One was in breaking the promise which I gave my husband to bring you up as my own child; the other – ' she stopped. 'After all, it is of no great importance, perhaps,' she murmured to herself: 'and then I may get better; and to humble myself so to her is painful.'

She made an effort to alter her position, but failed: her face changed; she seemed to experience some inward sensation – the precursor, perhaps, of the last pang.

'Well, I must get it over. Eternity is before me: I had better tell her. Go to my dressing-case, open it, and take out a letter you will see there.'

I obeyed her directions. 'Read the letter,' she said.

It was short, and thus conceived:

MADAM – Will you have the goodness to send me the address of my niece, Jane Eyre, and to tell me how she is? It is my intention to write shortly and desire her to come to me at Madeira. Providence has blessed my endeavours to secure a competency; and as I am unmarried and childless, I wish to adopt her during my life, and bequeath her at my death whatever I may have to leave.

I am, Madam, etc., etc.,

JOHN EYRE
*Madeira*

It was dated three years back.

'Why did I never hear of this?' I asked.

'Because I disliked you too fixedly and thoroughly ever to lend a hand in lifting you to prosperity. I could not forget your conduct to me, Jane – the fury with which you once turned on me; the tone in which you declared you abhorred me the worst of anybody in the world; the unchildlike look and voice with which you affirmed that the very thought of me made you sick, and asserted that I had treated you with miserable cruelty. I could not forget my own sensations when you thus started up and poured out the venom of your mind: I felt fear as if an animal that I had struck or pushed had looked up at me with human eyes and cursed me in a man's voice. Bring me some water! Oh, make haste!'

'Dear Mrs Reed,' said I, as I offered her the draught she required, 'think no more of all this, let it pass away from your mind. Forgive me for my passionate language: I was a child then; eight, nine years have passed since that day.'

She heeded nothing of what I said; but when she had tasted the water and drawn breath, she went on thus – 'I tell you I could not forget it; and I took my revenge: for you to be adopted by your uncle, and placed in a state of ease and comfort, was what I could not endure. I wrote to him; I said I was sorry for his disappointment, but Jane Eyre was dead: she had died of typhus fever at Lowood. Now act as you please: write and contradict my assertion – expose my falsehood as soon as you like. You were born, I think, to be my torment: my last hour is racked by the recollection of a deed which, but for you, I should never have been tempted to commit.'

'If you could but be persuaded to think no more of it, aunt, and to regard me with kindness and forgiveness – '

'You have a very bad disposition,' said she, 'and one to this day I feel it impossible to understand: how for nine years you could be patient and quiescent under any treatment, and in the tenth break out all fire and violence, I can never comprehend.'

'My disposition is not so bad as you think: I am passionate, but not vindictive. Many a time, as a little child, I should have been glad to love you if you would have let me; and I long earnestly to be reconciled to you now: kiss me, aunt.'

I approached my cheek to her lips: she would not touch it. She said I oppressed her by leaning over the bed, and again demanded water. As I laid her down – for I raised her and supported her on my arm while she drank – I covered her ice-cold and clammy hand with mine: the feeble fingers shrank from my touch – the glazing eyes shunned my gaze.

'Love me, then, or hate me, as you will,' I said at last, 'you have my full and free forgiveness: ask now for God's, and be at peace.'

Poor, suffering woman! it was too late for her to make now the effort to change her habitual frame of mind: living, she had ever hated me – dying, she must hate me still.

The nurse now entered, and Bessie followed. I yet lingered half an hour longer, hoping to see some sign of amity: but she gave none. She was fast relapsing into stupor; nor did her mind again rally: at twelve o'clock that night she died. I was not present to close her eyes, nor were either of her daughters. They came to tell us the next morning that all was over. She was by that time laid out. Eliza and I went to look at her: Georgiana, who had burst out into loud weeping, said she dared not go. There was stretched Sarah Reed's once robust and active frame, rigid and still: her eye of flint was covered with its cold lid; her brow and strong traits wore yet the impress of her inexorable soul. A strange and solemn object was that corpse to me. I gazed on it with gloom and pain: nothing soft, nothing sweet, nothing pitying, or hopeful, or subduing did it inspire; only a grating anguish for *her* woes – not *my* loss – and a sombre tearless dismay at the fearfulness of death in such a form.

Eliza surveyed her parent calmly. After a silence of some minutes she observed – 'With her constitution she should have lived to a good old age: her life was shortened by trouble.' And then a spasm constricted her mouth for an instant: as it passed away she turned and left the room, and so did I. Neither of us had dropped a tear.

## *Chapter 22*

Mr Rochester had given me but one week's leave of absence: yet a month elapsed before I quitted Gateshead. I wished to leave immediately after the funeral, but Georgiana entreated me to stay till she could get off to London, whither she was now at last invited by her uncle, Mr Gibson, who had come down to direct his sister's interment and settle the family affairs. Georgiana said she dreaded being left alone with Eliza; from her she got neither sympathy in her dejection, support in her fears, nor aid in her preparations; so I bore with her feeble-minded wailings and selfish lamentations as well as I could, and did my best in sewing for her and packing her dresses. It is true, that while I worked, she would idle; and I thought to myself, 'If you and I were destined to live always together, cousin, we would commence matters on a different footing. I should not settle tamely down into being the forbearing party; I should assign you your share of labour, and compel you to accomplish it, or else it should be left undone: I should insist, also, on your keeping some of those drawling, half-insincere complaints hushed in your own breast. It is only because our connection happens to be very transitory, and comes at a peculiarly mournful season, that I consent thus to render it so patient and compliant on my part.'

At last I saw Georgiana off; but now it was Eliza's turn to request me to stay another week. Her plans required all her time and attention, she said; she was about to depart for some unknown bourne; and all day long she stayed in her own room, her door bolted within, filling trunks, emptying drawers, burning papers, and holding no communication with anyone. She wished me to look after the house, to see callers, and answer notes of condolence.

One morning she told me I was at liberty. 'And,' she added, 'I am obliged to you for your valuable services and discreet conduct! There is some difference between living with such an one as you and with Georgiana: you perform your own part in life and burden no one. Tomorrow,' she continued, 'I set out for the Continent. I shall take up my abode in a religious house near Lisle – a nunnery you would call it; there I shall be quiet and unmolested. I shall devote myself for a time to the examination of the Roman Catholic dogmas, and to a careful study of the workings of their system: if I find it to be, as I half suspect it is, the one best calculated to ensure the doing of all things decently and in order, I shall embrace the tenets of Rome and probably take the veil.'

I neither expressed surprise at this resolution nor attempted to dissuade her from it. 'The vocation will fit you to a hair,' I thought: 'much good may it do you!'

When we parted, she said: 'Goodbye, cousin Jane Eyre; I wish you well: you have some sense.'

I then returned: 'You are not without sense, cousin Eliza; but what you have, I suppose, in another year will be walled up alive in a French convent. However, it is not my business, and so it suits you, I don't much care.'

'You are in the right,' said she; and with these words we each went our separate way. As I shall not have occasion to refer either to her or her sister again, I may as well mention here, that Georgiana made an advantageous match with a wealthy worn-out man of fashion, and that Eliza actually took the veil, and is at this day superior of the convent where she passed the period of her novitiate, and which she endowed with her fortune.

How people feel when they are returning home from an absence, long or short, I did not know: I had never experienced the sensation. I had known what it was to come back to Gateshead when a child after a long walk, to be scolded for looking cold or gloomy; and later, what it was to come back from church to Lowood, to long for a plenteous meal and a good fire, and to be unable to get either. Neither of these returnings was very pleasant or desirable: no magnet drew me to a given point, increasing in its strength of attraction the nearer I came. The return to Thornfield was yet to be tried.

My journey seemed tedious – very tedious: fifty miles one day, a night spent at an inn; fifty miles the next day. During the first twelve hours I thought of Mrs Reed in her last moments; I saw her disfigured and discoloured face, and heard her strangely altered voice. I mused on the funeral day, the coffin, the hearse, the black train of tenants and servants – few was the number of relatives – the gaping vault, the silent church, the solemn service. Then I thought of Eliza and Georgiana; I beheld one the cynosure of a ballroom, the other the inmate of a convent cell; and I dwelt on and analysed their separate peculiarities of person and character. The evening arrival at the great town of — scattered these thoughts; night gave them quite another turn: laid down on my traveller's bed, I left reminiscence for anticipation.

I was going back to Thornfield: but how long was I to stay there? Not long; of that I was sure. I had heard from Mrs Fairfax in the interim of my absence: the party at the hall was dispersed; Mr Rochester had left for London three weeks ago, but he was then expected to return in a fortnight. Mrs Fairfax surmised that he was gone to make arrangements for his wedding, as he had talked of purchasing a new carriage: she said the idea of his marrying Miss Ingram still seemed strange to her; but from what everybody said, and from what she had herself seen, she could no longer doubt that the event would shortly take place. 'You would be strangely incredulous if you did doubt it,' was my mental comment. 'I don't doubt it.'

The question followed, 'Where was I to go?' I dreamt of Miss Ingram all the night: in a vivid morning dream I saw her closing the gates of Thornfield against me and pointing me out another road; and Mr Rochester looked on with his arms folded – smiling sardonically, as it seemed, at both her and me.

I had not notified to Mrs Fairfax the exact day of my return; for I did not wish either car or carriage to meet me at Millcote. I proposed to walk the distance quietly by myself; and very quietly, after leaving my box in the ostler's care, did I slip away from the George Inn, about six o'clock of a June evening, and take the old road to Thornfield: a road which lay chiefly through fields, and was now little frequented.

It was not a bright or splendid summer evening, though fair and soft: the haymakers were at work all along the road; and the sky, though far from cloudless, was such as promised well for the future: its blue – where blue was visible – was mild and settled, and its cloud strata high and thin. The west, too, was warm: no watery gleam chilled it – it seemed as if there was a fire lit, an altar burning behind its screen of marbled vapour, and out of apertures shone a golden redness.

I felt glad as the road shortened before me: so glad that I stopped once to ask myself what that joy meant: and to remind reason that it was not to my home I was going, or to a permanent resting-place, or to a place where fond friends looked out for me and waited my arrival. 'Mrs Fairfax will smile you a calm welcome, to be sure,' said I; 'and little Adèle will clap her hands and jump to see you: but you know very well you are thinking of another than they, and that he is not thinking of you.'

But what is so headstrong as youth? What so blind as inexperience? These affirmed that it was pleasure enough to have the privilege of again looking on Mr Rochester, whether he looked on me or not; and they added – 'Hasten! hasten!

be with him while you may: but a few more days or weeks, at most, and you are parted from him for ever!' And then I strangled a new-born agony – a deformed thing which I could not persuade myself to own and rear – and ran on.

They are making hay, too, in Thornfield meadows: or rather, the labourers are just quitting their work, and returning home with their rakes on their shoulders, now, at the hour I arrive. I have but a field or two to traverse, and then I shall cross the road and reach the gates. How full the hedges are of roses! But I have no time to gather any; I want to be at the house. I passed a tall briar, shooting leafy and flowery branches across the path; I see the narrow stile with stone steps; and I see – Mr Rochester sitting there, a book and a pencil in his hand; he is writing.

Well, he is not a ghost; yet every nerve I have is unstrung: for a moment I am beyond my own mastery. What does it mean? I did not think I should tremble in this way when I saw him, or lose my voice or the power of motion in his presence. I will go back as soon as I can stir: I need not make an absolute fool of myself. I know another way to the house. It does not signify if I knew twenty ways; for he has seen me.

'Hillo!' he cries; and he puts up his book and his pencil. 'There you are! Come on, if you please.'

I suppose I do come on; though in what fashion I know not; being scarcely cognisant of my movements, and solicitous only to appear calm; and, above all, to control the working muscles of my face – which I feel rebel insolently against my will, and struggle to express what I had resolved to conceal. But I have a veil – it is down: I may make shift yet to behave with decent composure.

'And this is Jane Eyre? Are you coming from Millcote, and on foot? Yes – just one of your tricks: not to send for a carriage, and come clattering over street and road like a common mortal, but to steal into the vicinage of your home along with twilight, just as if you were a dream or a shade. What the deuce have you done with yourself this last month?'

'I have been with my aunt, sir, who is dead.'

'A true Janian reply! Good angels be my guard. She comes from the other world – from the abode of people who are dead; and tells me so when she meets me alone here in the gloaming! If I dared, I'd touch you, to see if you are substance or shadow, you elf! – but I'd as soon offer to take hold of a blue *ignis fatuus* light in a marsh. Truant! truant!' he added, when he had paused an instant. 'Absent from me a whole month, and forgetting me quite, I'll be sworn!'

I knew there would be pleasure in meeting my master again, even though broken by the fear that he was so soon to cease to be my master, and by the knowledge that I was nothing to him: but there was ever in Mr Rochester (so at least I thought) such a wealth of the power of communicating happiness, that to taste but of the crumbs he scattered to stray and stranger birds like me, was to feast genially. His last words were balm: they seemed to imply that it imported something to him whether I forgot him or not. And he had spoken of Thornfield as my home – would that it were my home!

He did not leave the stile, and I hardly liked to ask to go by. I enquired soon if he had not been to London.

'Yes; I suppose you found that out by second-sight.'

'Mrs Fairfax told me in a letter.'

'And did she inform you what I went to do?'

'Oh, yes, sir! Everybody knew your errand.'

'You must see the carriage, Jane, and tell me if you don't think it will suit Mrs Rochester exactly; and whether she won't look like Queen Boadicea, leaning back against those purple cushions. I wish, Jane, I were a trifle better adapted to match with her externally. Tell me now, fairy as you are – can't you give me a charm, or a philtre, or something of that sort, to make me a handsome man?'

'It would be past the power of magic, sir'; and, in thought, I added, 'A loving eye is all the charm needed: to such you are handsome enough; or rather your sternness has a power beyond beauty.'

Mr Rochester had sometimes read my unspoken thoughts with an acumen to me incomprehensible: in the present instance he took no notice of my abrupt vocal response; but he smiled at me with a certain smile he had of his own, and which he used but on rare occasions. He seemed to think it too good for common purposes: it was the real sunshine of feeling – he shed it over me now.

'Pass, Janet,' said he, making room for me to cross the stile: 'go up home, and stay your weary little wandering feet at a friend's threshold.'

All I had now to do was to obey him in silence: no need for me to colloquise further. I got over the stile without a word, and meant to leave him calmly. An impulse held me fast – a force turned me round. I said – or something in me said for me, and in spite of me – 'Thank you, Mr Rochester, for your great kindness. I am strangely glad to get back again to you: and wherever you are is my home – my only home.'

I walked on so fast that even he could hardly have overtaken me had he tried. Little Adèle was half wild with delight when she saw me. Mrs Fairfax received me with her usual plain friendliness. Leah smiled, and even Sophie bid me 'bon soir' with glee. This was very pleasant; there is no happiness like that of being loved by your fellow-creatures, and feeling that your presence is an addition to their comfort.

I that evening shut my eyes resolutely against the future: I stopped my ears against the voice that kept warning me of near separation and coming grief. When tea was over and Mrs Fairfax had taken her knitting, and I had assumed a low seat near her, and Adèle, kneeling on the carpet, had nestled close up to me, and a sense of mutual affection seemed to surround us with a ring of golden peace, I uttered a silent prayer that we might not be parted far or soon; but when, as we thus sat, Mr Rochester entered, unannounced, and looking at us, seemed to take pleasure in the spectacle of a group so amicable – when he said he supposed the old lady was all right now that she had got her adopted daughter back again, and added that he saw Adèle was 'prête à croquer sa petite maman Anglaise' – I half ventured to hope that he would, even after his marriage, keep us together somewhere under the shelter of his protection, and not quite exiled from the sunshine of his presence.

A fortnight of dubious calm succeeded my return to Thornfield Hall. Nothing was said of the master's marriage, and I saw no preparation going on for such an event. Almost every day I asked Mrs Fairfax if she had yet heard anything decided: her answer was always in the negative. Once she said she had actually put the question to Mr Rochester as to when he was going to bring his bride home; but he had answered her only by a joke and one of his queer looks, and she could not tell what to make of him.

One thing specially surprised me, and that was, there were no journeyings backward and forward, no visits to Ingram Park: to be sure it was twenty miles off, on the borders of another county; but what was that distance to an ardent lover? To so practised and indefatigable a horseman as Mr Rochester, it would be but a morning's ride. I began to cherish hopes I had no right to conceive: that the match was broken off; that rumour had been mistaken; that one or both parties had changed their minds. I used to look at my master's face to see if it were sad or fierce; but I could not remember the time when it had been so uniformly clear of clouds or evil feelings. If, in the moments I and my pupil spent with him, I lacked spirits and sank into inevitable dejection, he became even gay. Never had he called me more frequently to his presence; never been kinder to me when there – and, alas! never had I loved him so well.

## *Chapter 23*

A splendid Midsummer shone over England: skies so pure, suns so radiant as were then seen in long succession, seldom favour even singly, our wave-girt land. It was as if a band of Italian days had come from the South, like a flock of glorious passenger birds, and lighted to rest them on the cliffs of Albion. The hay was all got in; the fields round Thornfield were green and shorn; the roads white and baked; the trees were in their dark prime; hedge and wood, full-leaved and deeply tinted, contrasted well with the sunny hue of the cleared meadows between.

On Midsummer-eve, Adèle, weary with gathering wild strawberries in Hay Lane half the day, had gone to bed with the sun. I watched her drop asleep, and when I left her, I sought the garden.

It was now the sweetest hour of the twenty-four: 'Day its fervid fires had wasted,' and dew fell cool on panting plain and scorched summit. Where the sun had gone down in simple state – pure of the pomp of clouds – spread a solemn purple, burning with the light of red jewel and furnace flame at one point, on one hill-peak, and extending high and wide, soft and still softer, over half heaven. The east had its own charm of fine deep blue, and its own modest gem, a rising and solitary star: soon it would boast the moon; but she was yet beneath the horizon.

I walked a while on the pavement; but a subtle, well-known scent – that of a cigar – stole from some window; I saw the library casement open a hand-breadth; I knew I might be watched thence; so I went apart into the orchard. No nook in the grounds more sheltered and more Eden-like; it was full of trees, it bloomed with flowers: a very high wall shut it out from the court, on one side; on the other, a beech avenue screened it from the lawn. At the bottom was a sunk fence; its sole separation from lonely fields: a winding walk, bordered with laurels and terminating in a giant horse-chestnut, circled at the base by a seat, led down to the fence. Here one could wander unseen. While such honeydew fell, such silence reigned, such gloaming gathered, I felt as if I could haunt such shade for ever; but in threading the flower and fruit parterres at the upper part of the enclosure, enticed there by the light the now rising moon cast on this more open quarter, my step is stayed – not by sound, not by sight, but once more by a warning fragrance.

Sweet-briar and southernwood, jasmine, pink, and rose have long been yielding their evening sacrifice of incense: this new scent is neither of shrub nor flower; it is – I know it well – it is Mr Rochester's cigar. I look round and I listen. I see trees laden with ripening fruit. I hear a nightingale warbling in a wood half a mile off; no moving form is visible, no coming step audible; but that perfume increases: I must flee. I make for the wicket leading to the shrubbery, and I see Mr Rochester entering. I step aside into the ivy recess; he will not stay long: he will soon return whence he came, and if I sit still he will never see me.

But no – eventide is as pleasant to him as to me, and this antique garden as attractive; and he strolls on, now lifting the gooseberry-tree branches to look at the fruit, large as plums, with which they are laden; now taking a ripe cherry from the wall; now stooping towards a knot of flowers, either to inhale their fragrance or to admire the dew-beads on their petals. A great moth goes humming by me; it alights on a plant at Mr Rochester's foot: he sees it, and bends to examine it.

'Now, he has his back towards me,' thought I, 'and he is occupied too; perhaps, if I walk softly, I can slip away unnoticed.'

I trod on an edging of turf that the crackle of the pebbly gravel might not betray me: he was standing among the beds at a yard or two distant from where I had to pass; the moth apparently engaged him. 'I shall get by very well,' I meditated. As I crossed his shadow, thrown long over the garden by the moon, not yet risen high, he said quietly, without turning – 'Jane, come and look at this fellow.'

I had made no noise: he had not eyes behind – could his shadow feel? I started at first, and then I approached him.

'Look at his wings,' said he, 'he reminds me rather of a West Indian insect; one does not often see so large and gay a night-rover in England; there! he is flown.'

The moth roamed away. I was sheepishly retreating also; but Mr Rochester followed me, and when we reached the wicket, he said – 'Turn back: on so lovely a night it is a shame to sit in the house; and surely no one can wish to go to bed while sunset is thus at meeting with moonrise.'

It is one of my faults, that though my tongue is sometimes prompt enough at an answer, there are times when it sadly fails me in framing an excuse; and always the lapse occurs at some crisis, when a facile word or plausible pretext is specially wanted to get me out of painful embarrassment. I did not like to walk at this hour alone with Mr Rochester in the shadowy orchard; but I could not find a reason to allege for leaving him. I followed with lagging step, and thoughts busily bent on discovering a means of extrication; but he himself looked so composed and so grave also, I became ashamed of feeling any confusion: the evil – if evil existent or prospective there was – seemed to lie with me only; his mind was unconscious and quiet.

'Jane,' he recommenced, as we entered the laurel walk, and slowly strayed down in the direction of the sunk fence and the horse-chestnut, 'Thornfield is a pleasant place in summer, is it not?'

'Yes, sir.'

'You must have become in some degree attached to the house, you, who have an eye for natural beauties, and a good deal of the organ of Adhesiveness?'

'I am attached to it, indeed.'

'And though I don't comprehend how it is, I perceive you have acquired a degree of regard for that foolish little child Adèle, too; and even for simple dame Fairfax?'

'Yes, sir; in different ways, I have an affection for both.'

'And would be sorry to part with them?'

'Yes.'

'Pity!' he said, and sighed and paused. 'It is always the way of events in this life,' he continued presently: 'no sooner have you got settled in a pleasant resting-place, than a voice calls out to you to rise and move on, for the hour of repose is expired.'

'Must I move on, sir?' I asked. 'Must I leave Thornfield?'

'I believe you must, Jane. I am sorry, Janet, but I believe indeed you must.'

This was a blow: but I did not let it prostrate me.

'Well, sir, I shall be ready when the order to march comes.'

'It is come now – I must give it tonight.'

'Then you *are* going to be married, sir?'

'Ex–act–ly – pre–cise–ly: with your usual acuteness, you have hit the nail straight on the head.'

'Soon, sir?'

'Very soon, my – that is, Miss Eyre: and you'll remember, Jane, the first time I, or Rumour, plainly intimated to you that it was my intention to put my old bachelor's neck into the sacred noose, to enter into the holy estate of matrimony – to take Miss Ingram to my bosom, in short (she's an extensive armful: but that's not to the point – one can't have too much of such a very excellent thing as my beautiful Blanche): well, as I was saying – listen to me, Jane! You're not turning your head to look after more moths, are you? That was only a lady-clock, child, "flying away home". I wish to remind you that it was you who first said to me, with that discretion I respect in you – with that foresight, prudence, and humility which befit your responsible and dependent position – that in case I married Miss Ingram, both you and little Adèle had better trot forthwith. I pass over the sort of slur conveyed in this suggestion on the character of my beloved; indeed, when you are far away, Janet, I'll try to forget it: I shall notice only its wisdom; which is such that I have made it my law of action. Adèle must go to school; and you, Miss Eyre, must get a new situation.'

'Yes, sir, I will advertise immediately: and meantime, I suppose – ' I was going to say, 'I suppose I may stay here, till I find another shelter to betake myself to': but I stopped, feeling it would not do to risk a long sentence, for my voice was not quite under command.

'In about a month I hope to be a bridegroom,' continued Mr Rochester; 'and in the interim, I shall myself look out for employment and an asylum for you.'

'Thank you, sir; I am sorry to give – '

'Oh, no need to apologise! I consider that when a dependent does her duty as well as you have done yours, she has a sort of claim upon her employer for any little assistance he can conveniently render her; indeed I have already, through my future mother-in-law, heard of a place that I think will suit: it is to undertake the education of the five daughters of Mrs Dionysius O'Gall of Bitternutt Lodge, Connaught, Ireland. You'll like Ireland, I think: they're such warm-hearted people there, they say.'

'It is a long way off, sir.'

'No matter – a girl of your sense will not object to the voyage or the distance.'

'Not the voyage, but the distance: and then the sea is a barrier – '

'From what, Jane?'

'From England and from Thornfield: and – '

'Well?'

'From *you*, sir.'

I said this almost involuntarily, and, with as little sanction of free will, my tears gushed out. I did not cry so as to be heard, however; I avoided sobbing. The thought of Mrs O'Gall and Bitternutt Lodge struck cold to my heart; and colder the thought of all the brine and foam, destined, as it seemed, to rush between me and the master at whose side I now walked, and coldest the remembrance of the wider ocean – wealth, caste, custom intervened between me and what I naturally and inevitably loved.

'It is a long way,' I again said.

'It is, to be sure; and when you get to Bitternutt Lodge, Connaught, Ireland, I shall never see you again, Jane: that's morally certain. I never go over to Ireland, not having myself much of a fancy for the country. We have been good friends, Jane; have we not?'

'Yes, sir.'

'And when friends are on the eve of separation, they like to spend the little time that remains to them close to each other. Come! we'll talk over the voyage and the parting quietly half an hour or so, while the stars enter into their shining life up in heaven yonder: here is the chestnut tree: here is the bench at its old roots. Come, we will sit there in peace tonight, though we should never more be destined to sit there together.' He seated me and himself.

'It is a long way to Ireland, Janet; and I am sorry to send my little friend on such weary travels: but if I can't do better, how is it to be helped? Are you anything akin to me, do you think, Jane?'

I could risk no sort of answer by this time: my heart was still.

'Because,' he said, 'I sometimes have a queer feeling with regard to you – especially when you are near me, as now: it is as if I had a string somewhere under my left ribs, tightly and inextricably knotted to a similar string situated in the corresponding quarter of your little frame. And if that boisterous Channel, and two hundred miles or so of land come broad between us, I am afraid that cord of communion will be snapped; and then I've a nervous notion I should take to bleeding inwardly. As for you, you'd forget me.'

'That I *never* should, sir: you know – ' Impossible to proceed.

'Jane, do you hear that nightingale singing in the wood? Listen!'

In listening, I sobbed convulsively; for I could repress what I endured no longer; I was obliged to yield, and I was shaken from head to foot with acute distress. When I did speak, it was only to express an impetuous wish that I had never been born, or never come to Thornfield.

'Because you are sorry to leave it?'

The vehemence of emotion, stirred by grief and love within me, was claiming mastery, and struggling for full sway, and asserting a right to predominate, to overcome, to live, rise, and reign at last: yes, and to speak.

'I grieve to leave Thornfield: I love Thornfield: I love it, because I have lived in it a full and delightful life, momentarily at least. I have not been trampled on. I have not been petrified. I have not been buried with inferior minds, and excluded from every glimpse of communion with what is bright and energetic and high. I have talked, face to face, with what I reverence, with what I delight in, with an original, a vigorous, an expanded mind. I have known you, Mr Rochester; and it strikes me with terror and anguish to feel I absolutely must be torn from you for ever. I see the necessity of departure; and it is like looking on the necessity of death.'

'Where do you see the necessity?' he asked suddenly.

'Where? You, sir, have placed it before me.'

'In what shape?'

'In the shape of Miss Ingram; a noble and beautiful woman, your bride.'

'My bride! What bride? I have no bride!'

'But you will have.'

'Yes; I will! – I will!' He set his teeth.

'Then I must go: you have said it yourself.'

'No: you must stay! I swear it – and the oath shall be kept.'

'I tell you I must go!' I retorted, roused to something like passion. 'Do you think I can stay to become nothing to you? Do you think I am an automaton? – a machine without feelings? and can bear to have my morsel of bread snatched from my lips, and my drop of living water dashed from my cup? Do you think, re was hope in its aspect and life in its colour; and my eyes y had beheld the fount of fruition, and borrowed beams from the I had often been unwilling to look at my master, because I feared e pleased at my look; but I was sure I might lift my face to his now, his affection by its expression. I took a plain but clean and light ss from my drawer and put it on: it seemed no attire had ever so well e, because none had I ever worn in so blissful a mood.

ot surprised, when I ran down into the hall, to see that a brilliant June , had succeeded to the tempest of the night; and to feel, through the ass door, the breathing of a fresh and fragrant breeze. Nature must be me when I was so happy. A beggar-woman and her little boy – pale, d objects both – were coming up the walk, and I ran down and gave them he money I happened to have in my purse – some three or four shillings: od or bad, they must partake of my jubilee. The rooks cawed, and blither birds ng; but nothing was so merry or so musical as my own rejoicing heart.

Mrs Fairfax surprised me by looking out of the window with a sad countenance, and saying gravely – 'Miss Eyre, will you come to breakfast?' During the meal she was quiet and cool: but I could not undeceive her then. I must wait for my master to give explanations; and so must she. I ate what I could, and then I hastened upstairs. I met Adèle leaving the schoolroom.

'Where are you going? It is time for lessons.'

'Mr Rochester has sent me away to the nursery.'

'Where is he?'

'In there,' pointing to the apartment she had left; and I went in, and there he stood.

'Come and bid me good-morning,' said he. I gladly advanced; and it was not merely a cold word now, or even a shake of the hand that I received, but an embrace and a kiss. It seemed natural: it seemed genial to be so well loved, so caressed by him.

'Jane, you look blooming, and smiling, and pretty,' said he: 'truly pretty this morning. Is this my pale, little elf? Is this my mustard-seed? This little sunny-faced girl with the dimpled cheek and rosy lips; the satin-smooth hazel hair, and the radiant hazel eyes?' (I had green eyes, reader; but you must excuse the mistake: for him they were new-dyed, I suppose.)

'It is Jane Eyre, sir.'

'Soon to be Jane Rochester,' he added: 'in four weeks, Janet; not a day more. Do you hear that?'

I did, and I could not quite comprehend it: it made me giddy. The feeling, the announcement sent through me, was something stronger than was consistent with joy – something that smote and stunned: it was, I think almost fear.

'You blushed, and now you are white, Jane: what is that for?'

'Because you gave me a new name – Jane Rochester; and it seems so strange.'

'Yes, Mrs Rochester,' said he; 'young Mrs Rochester – Fairfax Rochester's girl-bride.'

'It can never be, sir; it does not sound likely. Human beings never enjoy



because I am poor, obscure, plain, and little, I am soulless and heartless? You think wrong! – I have as much soul as you, and full as much heart! And if God had gifted me with some beauty and much wealth, I should have made it as hard for you to leave me, as it is now for me to leave you. I am not talking to you now through the medium of custom, conventionalities, nor even of mortal flesh; it is my spirit that addresses your spirit; just as if both had passed through the grave, and we stood at God's feet, equal, as we are!'

'As we are!' repeated Mr Rochester – 'so,' he added, enclosing me in his arms, gathering me to his breast, pressing his lips on my lips: 'so, Jane!'

'Yes, so, sir,' I rejoined: 'and yet not so; for you are a married man – or as good as a married man, and wed to one inferior to you – to one with whom you have no sympathy – whom I do not believe you truly love; for I have seen and heard you sneer at her. I would scorn such a union: therefore I am better than you – let me go!'

'Where, Jane? To Ireland?'

'Yes – to Ireland. I have spoken my mind, and can go anywhere now.'

'Jane, be still; don't struggle so, like a wild frantic bird that is rending its own plumage in its desperation.'

'I am no bird; and no net ensnares me; I am a free human being with an independent will, which I now exert to leave you.'

Another effort set me at liberty, and I stood erect before him.

'And your will shall decide your destiny,' he said: 'I offer you my hand, my heart, and a share of all my possessions.'

'You play a farce, which I merely laugh at.'

'I ask you to pass through life at my side – to be my second self, and best earthly companion.'

'For that fate you have already made your choice, and must abide by it.'

'Jane, be still a few moments: you are over-excited: I will be still too.'

A waft of wind came sweeping down the laurel-walk and trembled through the boughs of the chestnut: it wandered away – away – to an indefinite distance – it died. The nightingale's song was then the only voice of the hour: in listening to it, I again wept. Mr Rochester sat quiet, looking at me gently and seriously. Some time passed before he spoke; he at last said – 'Come to my side, Jane, and let us explain and understand one another.'

'I will never again come to your side: I am torn away now, and cannot return.'

'But, Jane, I summon you as my wife: it is you only I intend to marry.'

I was silent: I thought he mocked me.

'Come, Jane – come hither.'

'Your bride stands between us.'

He rose, and with a stride reached me.

'My bride is here,' he said, again drawing me to him, 'because my equal is here, and my likeness. Jane, will you marry me?'

Still I did not answer, and still I writhed myself from grasp: for I was still incredulous.

'Do you doubt me, Jane?'

'Entirely.'

'You have no faith in me?'

'Not a whit.'

'Am I a liar in your eyes?' he asked passionately. 'Little sceptic, you *shall* be convinced. What love have I for Miss Ingram? None: and that you know. What love has she for me? None: as I have taken pains to prove: I caused a rumour to reach her that my fortune was not a third of what was supposed, and after that I presented myself to see the result; it was coldness both from her and her mother. I would not – I could not – marry Miss Ingram. You – you strange, you almost unearthly thing! – I love as my own flesh. You – poor and obscure, and small and plain as you are – I entreat to accept me as a husband.'

'What, me!' I ejaculated, beginning in his earnestness – and especially in his incivility – to credit his sincerity: 'me who have not a friend in the world but you – if you are my friend: not a shilling but what you have given me?'

'You, Jane, I must have you for my own – entirely my own. Will you be mine? Say yes, quickly.'

'Mr Rochester, let me look at your face: turn to the moonlight.'

'Why?'

'Because I want to read your countenance – turn!'

'There! you will find it scarcely more legible than a crumpled, scratched page. Read on: only make haste, for I suffer.'

His face was very much agitated and very much flushed, and there were strong workings in the features, and strange gleams in the eyes.

'Oh, Jane, you torture me!' he exclaimed. 'With that searching and yet faithful and generous look, you torture me!'

'How can I do that? If you are true, and your offer real, my only feelings to you must be gratitude and devotion – they cannot torture.'

'Gratitude!' he ejaculated; and added wildly – 'Jane, accept me quickly. Say, Edward – give me my name – Edward – I will marry you.'

'Are you in earnest? Do you truly love me? Do you sincerely wish me to be your wife?'

'I do; and if an oath is necessary to satisfy you, I swear it.'

'Then, sir, I will marry you.'

'Edward – my little wife!'

'Dear Edward!'

'Come to me – come to me entirely now,' said he; and added, in his deepest tone, speaking in my ear as his cheek was laid on mine, 'Make my happiness – I will make yours.'

'God pardon me!' he subjoined ere long; 'and man meddle not with me: I have her, and will hold her.'

'There is no one to meddle, sir. I have no kindred to interfere.'

'No – that is the best of it,' he said. And if I had loved him less I should have thought his accent and look of exultation savage; but, sitting by him, roused from the nightmare of parting – called to the paradise of union – I thought only of the bliss given me to drink in so abundant a flow. Again and again he said, 'Are you



happy, Jane?' And again and again I
'It will atone – it will atone. H
comfortless? Will I not guar
my heart, and constancy in my
my Maker sanctions what I do.
thereof. For man's opinion – I defy

But what had befallen the night? T
shadow: I could scarcely see my master's
chestnut tree? it writhed and groaned; whi
came sweeping over us.

'We must go in,' said Mr Rochester: 'the w
with thee till morning, Jane.'

'And so,' thought I, 'could I with you.' I should
livid, vivid spark leapt out of a cloud at which I was
crack, a crash, and a close rattling peal; and I thought only
eyes against Mr Rochester's shoulder.

The rain rushed down. He hurried me up the walk, through
into the house; but we were quite wet before we could pass the
was taking off my shawl in the hall, and shaking the water out of
hair, when Mrs Fairfax emerged from her room. I did not observe
nor did Mr Rochester. The lamp was lit. The clock was on the stroke o

'Hasten to take off your wet things,' said he; 'and before you go, good-n
good-night, my darling!'

He kissed me repeatedly. When I looked up, on leaving his arms, there stood the widow, pale, grave, and amazed. I only smiled at her, and ran upstairs. 'Explanation will do for another time,' thought I. Still, when I reached my chamber, I felt a pang at the idea she should even temporarily misconstrue what she had seen. But joy soon effaced every other feeling, and loud as the wind blew, near and deep as the thunder crashed, fierce and frequent as the lightning gleamed, cataract-like as the rain fell during a storm of two hours' duration, I experienced no fear and little awe. Mr Rochester came thrice to my door in the course of it, to ask if I was safe and tranquil: and that was comfort, that was strength for anything.

Before I left my bed in the morning, little Adèle came running in to tell me that the great horse-chestnut at the bottom of the orchard had been struck by lightning in the night, and half of it split away.

## *Chapter 24*

As I rose and dressed, I thought over what had happened, and wondered if it were a dream. I could not be certain of the reality till I had seen Mr Rochester again, and heard him renew his words of love and promise.

While arranging my hair, I looked at my face in the glass, and felt it was no



longer plain: the
seemed as if the
lustrous ripple
he could not b
and not coo
summer dr
become m
I was n
morning
open g
gladso
ragg
all t
go
sa

complete happiness in this world. I was not born for a different destiny to the rest of my species: to imagine such a lot befalling me is a fairy tale – a day-dream.'

'Which I can and will realise. I shall begin today. This morning I wrote to my banker in London to send me certain jewels he has in his keeping, heirlooms for the ladies of Thornfield. In a day or two I hope to pour them into your lap: for every privilege, every attention shall be yours that I would accord a peer's daughter, if about to marry her.'

'Oh, sir! – never mind jewels! I don't like to hear them spoken of. Jewels for Jane Eyre sounds unnatural and strange: I would rather not have them.'

'I will myself put the diamond chain round your neck, and the circlet on your forehead, which it will become: for nature, at least, has stamped her patent of nobility on this brow, Jane; and I will clasp the bracelets on these fine wrists, and load these fairy-like fingers with rings.'

'No, no, sir! think of other subjects, and speak of other things, and in another strain. Don't address me as if I were a beauty; I am your plain, Quakerish governess.'

'You are a beauty in my eyes, and a beauty just after the desire of my heart, delicate and aërial.'

'Puny and insignificant, you mean. You are dreaming, sir, or you are sneering. For God's sake, don't be ironical!'

'I will make the world acknowledge you a beauty, too,' he went on, while I really became uneasy at the strain he had adopted, because I felt he was either deluding himself or trying to delude me. 'I will attire my Jane in satin and lace, and she shall have roses in her hair; and I will cover the head I love best with a priceless veil.'

'And then you won't know me, sir; and I shall not be your Jane Eyre any longer, but an ape in a harlequin's jacket – a jay in borrowed plumes. I would as soon see you, Mr Rochester, tricked out in stage-trappings, as myself clad in a court-lady's robe; and I don't call you handsome, sir, though I love you most dearly: far too dearly to flatter you. Don't flatter me.'

He pursued his theme, however, without noticing my deprecation. 'This very day I shall take you in the carriage to Millcote, and you must choose some dresses for yourself. I told you we shall be married in four weeks. The wedding is to take place quietly, in the church down below yonder; and then I shall waft you away at once to town. After a brief stay there, I shall bear my treasure to regions nearer the sun: to French vineyards and Italian plains; and she shall see whatever is famous in old story and in modern record: she shall taste, too, of the life of cities; and she shall learn to value herself by just comparison with others.'

'Shall I travel? – and with you, sir?'

'You shall sojourn at Paris, Rome, and Naples: at Florence, Venice, and Vienna: all the ground I have wandered over shall be re-trodden by you: wherever I stamped my hoof, your sylph's foot shall step also. Ten years since, I flew through Europe half mad; with disgust, hate, and rage as my companions: now I shall revisit it healed and cleansed, with a very angel as my comforter.'

I laughed at him as he said this. 'I am not an angel,' I asserted; 'and I will not be one till I die: I will be myself. Mr Rochester, you must neither expect nor exact anything celestial of me – for you will not get it, any more than I shall get it of you: which I do not at all anticipate.'

'What do you anticipate of me?'

'For a little while you will perhaps be as you are now, a very little while; and then you will turn cool; and then you will be capricious; and then you will be stern, and I shall have much ado to please you: but when you get well used to me, you will perhaps like me again, *like* me, I say, not *love* me. I suppose your love will effervesce in six months, or less. I have observed in books written by men, that period assigned as the farthest to which a husband's ardour extends. Yet, after all, as a friend and companion, I hope never to become quite distasteful to my dear master.'

'Distasteful! and like you again! I think I shall like you again, and yet again: and I will make you confess I do not only *like*, but *love* you – with truth, fervour, constancy.'

'Yet are you not capricious, sir?'

'To women who please me only by their faces, I am the very devil when I find out they have neither souls nor hearts – when they open to me a perspective of flatness, triviality, and perhaps imbecility, coarseness, and ill-temper: but to the clear eye and eloquent tongue, to the soul made of fire, and the character that bends but does not break – at once supple and stable, tractable and consistent – I am ever tender and true.'

'Had you ever experience of such a character, sir? Did you ever love such an one?'

'I love it now.'

'But before me: if I, indeed, in any respect come up to your difficult standard?'

'I never met your likeness. Jane, you please me, and you master me – you seem to submit, and I like the sense of pliancy you impart; and while I am twining the soft, silken skein round my finger, it sends a thrill up my arm to my heart. I am influenced – conquered; and the influence is sweeter than I can express; and the conquest I undergo has a witchery beyond any triumph I can win. Why do you smile, Jane? What does that inexplicable, that uncanny turn of countenance mean?'

'I was thinking, sir (you will excuse the idea; it was involuntary), I was thinking of Hercules and Samson with their charmers – '

'You were, you little elfish – '

'Hush, sir! You don't talk very wisely just now; any more than those gentlemen acted very wisely. However, had they been married, they would no doubt by their severity as husbands have made up for their softness as suitors; and so will you, I fear. I wonder how you will answer me a year hence, should I ask a favour it does not suit your convenience or pleasure to grant.'

'Ask me something now, Janet – the least thing; I desire to be entreated – '

'Indeed I will, sir; I have my petition all ready.'

'Speak! But if you look up and smile with that countenance, I shall swear concession before I know to what, and that will make a fool of me.'

'Not at all, sir; I ask only this: don't send for the jewels, and don't crown me with roses: you might as well put a border of gold lace round that plain pocket-handkerchief you have there.'

'I might as well "gild refined gold." I know it: your request is granted then – for the time. I will remand the order I despatched to my banker. But you have not yet asked for anything; you have prayed a gift to be withdrawn: try again.'

'Well then, sir, have the goodness to gratify my curiosity, which is much piqued on one point.'

He looked disturbed. 'What? what?' he said hastily. 'Curiosity is a dangerous petition: it is well I have not taken a vow to accord every request – '

'But there can be no danger in complying with this, sir.'

'Utter it, Jane: but I wish that instead of a mere enquiry into, perhaps, a secret, it was a wish for half my estate.'

'Now, King Ahasuerus! What do I want with half your estate? Do you think I am a Jew-usurer, seeking good investment in land? I would much rather have all your confidence. You will not exclude me from your confidence if you admit me to your heart?'

'You are welcome to all my confidence that is worth having, Jane; but for God's sake, don't desire a useless burden! Don't long for poison – don't turn out a downright Eve on my hands!'

'Why not, sir? You have just been telling me how much you liked to be conquered, and how pleasant over-persuasion is to you. Don't you think I had better take advantage of the confession, and begin and coax and entreat – even cry and be sulky if necessary – for the sake of a mere essay of my power?'

'I dare you to any such experiment. Encroach, presume, and the game is up.'

'Is it, sir? You soon give in. How stern you look now! Your eyebrows have become as thick as my finger, and your forehead resembles what, in some very astonishing poetry, I once saw styled, "a blue-piled thunderloft." That will be your married look, sir, I suppose?'

'If that will be *your* married look, I, as a Christian, will soon give up the notion of consorting with a mere sprite or salamander. But what had you to ask, thing, out with it?'

'There, you are less than civil now; and I like rudeness a great deal better than flattery. I had rather be a *thing* than an angel. This is what I have to ask, Why did you take such pains to make me believe you wished to marry Miss Ingram?'

'Is that all? Thank God it is no worse!' And now he unknit his black brows; looked down, smiling at me, and stroked my hair, as if well pleased at seeing a danger averted. 'I think I may confess,' he continued, 'even although I should make you a little indignant, Jane – and I have seen what a fire-spirit you can be when you are indignant. You glowed in the cool moonlight last night, when you mutinied against fate, and claimed your rank as my equal. Janet, by the by, it was you who made me the offer.'

'Of course I did. But to the point if you please, sir – Miss Ingram?'

'Well, I feigned courtship of Miss Ingram, because I wished to render you as madly in love with me as I was with you; and I knew jealousy would be the best ally I could call in for the furtherance of that end.'

'Excellent! Now you are small – not one whit bigger than the end of my little finger. It was a burning shame and a scandalous disgrace to act in that way. Did you think nothing of Miss Ingram's feelings, sir?'

'Her feelings are concentrated in one – pride; and that needs humbling. Were you jealous, Jane?'

'Never mind, Mr Rochester: it is in no way interesting to you to know that. Answer me truly once more. Do you think Miss Ingram will not suffer from your dishonest coquetry? Won't she feel forsaken and deserted?'

'Impossible! – when I told you how she, on the contrary, deserted me: the idea of my insolvency cooled, or rather extinguished, her flame in a moment.'

'You have a curious, designing mind, Mr Rochester. I am afraid your principles on some points are eccentric.'

'My principles were never trained, Jane: they may have grown a little awry for want of attention.'

'Once again, seriously; may I enjoy the great good that has been vouchsafed to me, without fearing that anyone else is suffering the bitter pain I myself felt a while ago?'

'That you may, my good little girl: there is not another being in the world has the same pure love for me as yourself – for I lay that pleasant unction to my soul, Jane, a belief in your affection.'

I turned my lips to the hand that lay on my shoulder. I loved him very much – more than I could trust myself to say – more than words had power to express. 'Ask something more,' he said presently; 'it is my delight to be entreated, and to yield.'

I was again ready with my request. 'Communicate your intentions to Mrs Fairfax, sir: she saw me with you last night in the hall, and she was shocked. Give her some explanation before I see her again. It pains me to be misjudged by so good a woman.'

'Go to your room, and put on your bonnet,' he replied. 'I mean you to accompany me to Millcote this morning; and while you prepare for the drive, I will enlighten the old lady's understanding. Did she think, Janet, you had given the world for love, and considered it well lost?'

'I believe she thought I had forgotten my station, and yours, sir.'

'Station! station! – your station is in my heart, and on the necks of those who would insult you, now or hereafter. Go.'

I was soon dressed; and when I heard Mr Rochester quit Mrs Fairfax's parlour, I hurried down to it. The old lady had been reading her morning portion of Scripture – the Lesson for the day; her Bible lay open before her, and her spectacles were upon it. Her occupation, suspended by Mr Rochester's announcement, seemed now forgotten: her eyes, fixed on the blank wall opposite, expressed the surprise of a quiet mind stirred by unwonted tidings. Seeing me, she roused herself: she made a sort of effort to smile, and framed a few words of congratulation; but the smile expired, and the sentence was abandoned unfinished. She put up her spectacles, shut the Bible, and pushed her chair back from the table.

'I feel so astonished,' she began, 'I hardly know what to say to you, Miss Eyre. I have surely not been dreaming, have I? Sometimes I half fall asleep when I am sitting alone and fancy things that have never happened. It has seemed to me more than once when I have been in a doze, that my dear husband, who died fifteen years since, has come in and sat down beside me; and that I have even heard him call me by my name, Alice, as he used to do. Now, can you tell me whether it is actually true that Mr Rochester has asked you to marry him? Don't laugh at me. But I really thought he came in here five minutes ago, and said that in a month you would be his wife.'

'He has said the same thing to me,' I replied.

'He has! Do you believe him? Have you accepted him?'

'Yes.'

She looked at me bewildered.

'I could never have thought it. He is a proud man: all the Rochesters were proud: and his father, at least, liked money. He, too, has always been called careful. He means to marry you?'

'He tells me so.'

She surveyed my whole person: in her eyes I read that they had there found no charm powerful enough to solve the enigma.

'It passes me!' she continued; 'but no doubt it is true since you say so. How it will answer, I cannot tell: I really don't know. Equality of position and fortune is often advisable in such cases; and there are twenty years of difference in your ages. He might almost be your father.'

'No, indeed, Mrs Fairfax!' exclaimed I, nettled; 'he is nothing like my father! No one, who saw us together, would suppose it for an instant. Mr Rochester looks as young, and is as young, as some men at five-and-twenty.'

'Is it really for love he is going to marry you?' she asked.

I was so hurt by her coldness and scepticism, that the tears rose to my eyes.

'I am sorry to grieve you,' pursued the widow; 'but you are so young, and so little acquainted with men, I wished to put you on your guard. It is an old saying that "all is not gold that glitters"; and in this case I do fear there will be something found to be different to what either you or I expect.'

'Why? – am I a monster?' I said: 'is it impossible that Mr Rochester should have a sincere affection for me?'

'No: you are very well; and much improved of late; and Mr Rochester, I dare say, is fond of you. I have always noticed that you were a sort of pet of his. There are times when, for your sake, I have been a little uneasy at his marked preference, and have wished to put you on your guard: but I did not like to suggest even the possibility of wrong. I knew such an idea would shock, perhaps offend you; and you were so discreet, and so thoroughly modest and sensible, I hoped you might be trusted to protect yourself. Last night I cannot tell you what I suffered when I sought all over the house, and could find you nowhere, nor the master either; and then, at twelve o'clock, saw you come in with him.'

'Well, never mind that now,' I interrupted impatiently; 'it is enough that all was right.'

'I hope all will be right in the end,' she said: 'but believe me, you cannot be too careful. Try and keep Mr Rochester at a distance: distrust yourself as well as him. Gentlemen in his station are not accustomed to marry their governesses.'

I was growing truly irritated: happily, Adèle ran in.

'Let me go, let me go to Millcote too!' she cried. 'Mr Rochester won't: though there is so much room in the new carriage. Beg him to let me go, mademoiselle.'

'That I will, Adèle'; and I hastened away with her, glad to quit my gloomy monitress. The carriage was ready: they were bringing it round to the front, and my master was pacing the pavement, Pilot following him backwards and forwards.

'Adèle may accompany us, may she not, sir?'

'I told her no. I'll have no brats! – I'll have only you.'

'Do let her go, Mr Rochester, if you please: it would be better.'

'Not it: she will be a restraint.'

He was quite peremptory, both in look and voice. The chill of Mrs Fairfax's warnings, and the damp of her doubts were upon me: something of unsubstantiality and uncertainty had beset my hopes. I half lost the sense of power over him. I was about mechanically to obey him, without further remonstrance; but as he helped me into the carriage, he looked at my face.

'What is the matter?' he asked; 'all the sunshine is gone. Do you really wish the bairn to go? Will it annoy you if she is left behind?'

'I would far rather she went, sir.'

'Then off for your bonnet, and back like a flash of lightning!' cried he to Adèle.

She obeyed him with what speed she might.

'After all, a single morning's interruption will not matter much,' said he, 'when I mean shortly to claim you – your thoughts, conversation, and company – for life.'

Adèle, when lifted in, commenced kissing me, by way of expressing her gratitude for my intercession: she was instantly stowed away into a corner on the other side of him. She then peeped round to where I sat; so stern a neighbour was too restrictive; to him, in his present fractious mood, she dared whisper no observations, nor ask of him any information.

'Let her come to me,' I entreated: 'she will, perhaps, trouble you, sir: there is plenty of room on this side.' He handed her over as if she had been a lapdog. 'I'll send her to school yet,' he said, but now he was smiling.

Adèle heard him, and asked if she was to go to school 'sans mademoiselle?'

'Yes,' he replied, 'absolutely sans mademoiselle; for I am to take mademoiselle to the moon, and there I shall seek a cave in one of the white valleys among the volcano-tops, and mademoiselle shall live with me there, and only me.'

'She will have nothing to eat: you will starve her,' observed Adèle.

'I shall gather manna for her morning and night: the plains and hillsides in the moon are bleached with manna, Adèle.'

'She will want to warm herself: what will she do for a fire?'

'Fire rises out of the lunar mountains: when she is cold, I'll carry her up to a peak, and lay her down on the edge of a crater.'

'Oh, qu'elle y sera mal – peu comfortable! And her clothes, they will wear out: how can she get new ones?'

Mr Rochester professed to be puzzled. 'Hem!' said he. 'What would you do, Adèle? Cudgel your brains for an expedient. How would a white or a pink cloud answer for a gown, do you think? And one could cut a pretty enough scarf out of a rainbow.'

'She is far better as she is,' concluded Adèle, after musing some time: 'besides, she would get tired of living with only you in the moon. If I were mademoiselle, I would never consent to go with you.'

'She has consented: she has pledged her word.'

'But you can't get her there; there is no road to the moon: it is all air; and neither you nor she can fly.'

'Adèle, look at that field.' We were now outside Thornfield gates, and bowling lightly along the smooth road to Millcote, where the dust was well laid by the thunderstorm, and where the low hedges and lofty timber trees on each side glistened green and rain-refreshed.

'In that field, Adèle, I was walking late one evening about a fortnight since – the evening of the day you helped me to make hay in the orchard meadows; and as I was tired with raking swaths, I sat down to rest me on a stile; and there I took out a little book and a pencil, and began to write about a misfortune that befell me long ago, and a wish I had for happy days to come: I was writing away very fast, though daylight was fading from the leaf, when something came up the path and stopped two yards off me. I looked at it. It was a little thing with a veil of gossamer on its head. I beckoned it to come near me; it stood soon at my knee. I never spoke to it, and it never spoke to me, in words; but I read its eyes, and it read mine; and our speechless colloquy was to this effect – 'It was a fairy, and come from Elf-land, it said; and its errand was to make me happy: I must go with it out of the common world to a lonely place – such as the moon, for instance – and it nodded its head towards her horn, rising over Hayhill: it told me of the alabaster cave and silver vale where we might live. I said I should like to go; but reminded it, as you did me, that I had no wings to fly.

' "Oh," returned the fairy, "that does not signify! Here is a talisman will remove all difficulties"; and she held out a pretty gold ring. "Put it," she said, "on the fourth finger of my left hand, and I am yours, and you are mine; and we shall leave earth, and make our own heaven yonder." She nodded again at the moon. The ring, Adèle, is in my breeches-pocket, under the disguise of a sovereign: but I mean soon to change it to a ring again.'

'But what has mademoiselle to do with it? I don't care for the fairy: you said it was mademoiselle you would take to the moon?'

'Mademoiselle is a fairy,' he said, whispering mysteriously. Whereupon I told her not to mind his badinage; and she, on her part, evinced a fund of genuine French scepticism: denominating Mr Rochester 'un vrai menteur', and assuring him that she made no account whatever of his 'contes de fée', and that 'du reste, il n'y avait pas de fées, et quand même il y en avait': she was sure they would never appear to him, nor ever give him rings, or offer to live with him in the moon.

The hour spent at Millcote was a somewhat harassing one to me. Mr Rochester obliged me to go to a certain silk warehouse: there I was ordered to choose half a dozen dresses. I hated the business, I begged leave to defer it: no – it should be gone through with now. By dint of entreaties expressed- in energetic whispers, I reduced the half-dozen to two: these, however, he vowed he would select himself. With anxiety I watched his eye rove over the gay stores: he fixed on a rich silk of the most brilliant amethyst dye, and a superb pink satin. I told him in a new series of whispers, that he might as well buy me a gold gown and a silver bonnet at once: I should certainly never venture to wear his choice. With infinite difficulty, for he was stubborn as a stone, I persuaded him to make an exchange in favour of a sober black satin and pearl-grey silk. 'It might pass for the present,' he said; 'but he would yet see me glittering like a parterre.'

Glad was I to get him out of the silk warehouse, and then out of a jeweller's shop: the more he bought me, the more my cheek burned with a sense of annoyance and degradation. As we re-entered the carriage, and I sat back feverish and fagged, I remembered what, in the hurry of events, dark and bright, I had wholly forgotten – the letter of my uncle, John Eyre, to Mrs Reed: his intention to adopt me and make me his legatee. 'It would, indeed, be a relief,' I thought, 'if I had ever so small an independency; I never can bear being dressed like a doll by Mr Rochester, or sitting like a second Danae with the golden shower falling daily round me. I will write to Madeira the moment I get home, and tell my uncle John I am going to be married, and to whom: if I had but a prospect of one day bringing Mr Rochester an accession of fortune, I could better endure to be kept by him now.' And somewhat relieved by this idea (which I failed not to execute that day), I ventured once more to meet my master's and lover's eye, which most pertinaciously sought mine, though I averted both face and gaze. He smiled; and I thought his smile was such as a sultan might, in a blissful and fond moment, bestow on a slave his gold and gems had enriched: I crushed his hand, which was ever hunting mine, vigorously, and thrust it back to him red with the passionate pressure.

'You need not look in that way,' I said; 'if you do, I'll wear nothing but my old Lowood frocks to the end of the chapter. I'll be married in this lilac gingham: you may make a dressing-gown for yourself out of the pearl-grey silk, and an infinite series of waistcoats out of the black satin.'

He chuckled; he rubbed his hands. 'Oh, it is rich to see and hear her?' he exclaimed. 'Is she original? Is she piquant? I would not exchange this one little English girl for the Grand Turk's whole seraglio, gazelle-eyes, houri forms, and all!'

The Eastern allusion bit me again. 'I'll not stand you an inch in the stead of a seraglio,' I said; 'so don't consider me an equivalent for one. If you have a fancy for anything in that line, away with you, sir, to the bazaars of Stamboul without delay, and lay out in extensive slave-purchases some of that spare cash you seem at a loss to spend satisfactorily here.'

'And what will you do, Janet, while I am bargaining for so many tons of flesh and such an assortment of black eyes?'

'I'll be preparing myself to go out as a missionary to preach liberty to them that are enslaved – your harem inmates amongst the rest. I'll get admitted there, and I'll stir up mutiny; and you, three-tailed bashaw as you are, sir, shall in a trice find yourself fettered amongst our hands: nor will I, for one, consent to cut your bonds till you have signed a charter, the most liberal that despot ever yet conferred.'

'I would consent to be at your mercy, Jane.'

'I would have no mercy, Mr Rochester, if you supplicated for it with an eye like that. While you looked so, I should be certain that whatever charter you might grant under coercion, your first act, when released, would be to violate its conditions.'

'Why, Jane, what would you have? I fear you will compel me to go through a private marriage ceremony, besides that performed at the altar. You will stipulate, I see, for peculiar terms – what will they be?'

'I only want an easy mind, sir; not crushed by crowded obligations. Do you remember what you said of Céline Varens? – of the diamonds, the cashmeres you gave her? I will not be your English Céline Varens. I shall continue to act as Adèle's governess; by that I shall earn my board and lodging, and thirty pounds a year besides. I'll furnish my own wardrobe out of that money, and you shall give me nothing but – '

'Well, but what?'

'Your regard; and if I give you mine in return, that debt will be quit.'

'Well, for cool native impudence and pure innate pride, you haven't your equal,' said he. We were now approaching Thornfield. 'Will it please you to dine with me today?' he asked, as we re-entered the gates.

'No, thank you, sir.'

'And what for, "no, thank you?" if one may enquire.'

'I never have dined with you, sir: and I see no reason why I should now: till – '

'Till what? You delight in half-phrases.'

'Till I can't help it.'

'Do you suppose I eat like an ogre or a ghoul, that you dread being the companion of my repast?'

'I have formed no supposition on the subject, sir; but I want to go on as usual for another month.'

'You will give up your governessing slavery at once.'

'Indeed, begging your pardon, sir, I shall not. I shall just go on with it as usual. I shall keep out of your way all day, as I have been accustomed to do: you may send for me in the evening, when you feel disposed to see me, and I'll come then; but at no other time.'

'I want a smoke, Jane, or a pinch of snuff, to comfort me under all this, "pour me donner une contenance," as Adèle would say; and unfortunately I have neither my cigar-case nor my snuff-box. But listen – whisper. It is your time now, little tyrant, but it will be mine presently; and when once I have fairly seized you, to have and to hold, I'll just – figuratively speaking – attach you to a chain like this' (touching his watch-guard). 'Yes, bonny wee thing, I'll wear you in my bosom, lest my jewel I should tyne.'

He said this as he helped me to alight from the carriage, and while he afterwards lifted out Adèle, I entered the house, and made good my retreat upstairs.

He duly summoned me to his presence in the evening. I had prepared an occupation for him; for I was determined not to spend the whole time in a tête-à-tête conversation. I remembered his fine voice; I knew he liked to sing – good singers generally do. I was no vocalist myself, and, in his fastidious judgement, no musician, either; but I delighted in listening when the performance was good. No sooner had twilight, that hour of romance, began to lower her blue and starry banner over the lattice, than I rose, opened the piano, and entreated him, for the love of heaven, to give me a song. He said I was a capricious witch, and that he would rather sing another time; but I averred that no time was like the present.

'Did I like his voice?' he asked.

'Very much.' I was not fond of pampering that susceptible vanity of his; but for once, and from motives of expediency, I would e'en soothe and stimulate it.

'Then, Jane, you must play the accompaniment.'

'Very well, sir, I will try.'

I did try, but was presently swept off the stool and denominated 'a little bungler.' Being pushed unceremoniously to one side – which was precisely what I wished – he usurped my place, and proceeded to accompany himself: for he could play as well as sing. I hied me to the window-recess. And while I sat there and looked out on the still trees and dim lawn, to a sweet air was sung in mellow tones the following strain:

The truest love that ever heart
  Felt at its kindled core,
Did through each vein, in quickened start,
  The tide of being pour.

Her coming was my hope each day,
  Her parting was my pain;
The chance that did her steps delay
  Was ice in every vein.

I dreamed it would be nameless bliss,
  As I loved, loved to be;
And to this object did I press
  As blind as eagerly.

But wide as pathless was the space
  That lay our lives between,
And dangerous as the foamy race
  Of ocean-surges green.

And haunted as a robber-path
  Through wilderness or wood;
For Might and Right, and Woe and Wrath,
  Between our spirits stood.

I dangers dared; I hindrance scorned;
  I omens did defy:
Whatever menaced, harassed, warned,
  I passed impetuous by.

On sped my rainbow, fast as light;
  I flew as in a dream;
For glorious rose upon my sight
  That child of Shower and Gleam.

Still bright on clouds of suffering dim
  Shines that soft, solemn joy;
Nor care I now, how dense and grim
  Disasters gather nigh.

I care not in this moment sweet,
  Though all I have rushed o'er
Should come on pinion, strong and fleet,
  Proclaiming vengeance sore:

Though haughty Hate should strike me down,
  Right, bar approach to me,
And grinding Might, with furious frown,
  Swear endless enmity.

My love has placed her little hand
  With noble faith in mine,
And vowed that wedlock's sacred band
  Our nature shall entwine.

My love has sworn, with sealing kiss,
  With me to live – to die;
I have at last my nameless bliss:
  As I love – loved am I!

He rose and came towards me, and I saw his face all kindled, and his full falcon-eye flashing, and tenderness and passion in every lineament. I quailed momentarily – then I rallied. Soft scene, daring demonstration, I would not have; and I stood in peril of both: a weapon of defence must be prepared – I whetted my tongue: as he reached me, I asked with asperity, 'whom he was going to marry now?'

'That was a strange question to be put by his darling Jane.'

'Indeed! I considered it a very natural and necessary one: he had talked of his future wife dying with him. What did he mean by such a pagan idea? *I* had no intention of dying with him – he might depend on that.'

'Oh, all he longed, all he prayed for, was that I might live with him! Death was not for such as I.'

'Indeed it was: I had as good a right to die when my time came as he had: but I should bide that time, and not be hurried away in a suttee.'

'Would I forgive him for the selfish idea, and prove my pardon by a reconciling kiss?'

'No: I would rather be excused.'

Here I heard myself apostrophised as a 'hard little thing'; and it was added, 'any other woman would have been melted to marrow at hearing such stanzas crooned in her praise.'

I assured him I was naturally hard – very flinty, and that he would often find me so; and that, moreover, I was determined to show him divers rugged points in my character before the ensuing four weeks elapsed: he should know fully what sort of a bargain he had made, while there was yet time to rescind it.

'Would I be quiet and talk rationally?'

'I would be quiet if he liked, and as to talking rationally, I flattered myself I was doing that now.'

He fretted, pished, and pshawed. 'Very good,' I thought; 'you may fume and fidget as you please: but this is the best plan to pursue with you, I am certain. I like you more than I can say; but I'll not sink into a bathos of sentiment: and with this needle of repartee I'll keep you from the edge of the gulf too; and, moreover, maintain by its pungent aid that distance between you and myself most conducive to our real mutual advantage.'

From less to more, I worked him up to considerable irritation; then, after he had retired, in dudgeon, quite to the other end of the room, I got up, and saying, 'I wish you good-night, sir,' in my natural and wonted respectful manner, I slipped out by the side-door and got away.

The system thus entered on, I pursued during the whole season of probation; and with the best success. He was kept, to be sure, rather cross and crusty; but on the whole I could see he was excellently entertained, and that a lamb-like submission and turtle-dove sensibility, while fostering his despotism more, would have pleased his judgement, satisfied his common-sense, and even suited his taste less.

In other people's presence I was, as formerly, deferential and quiet; any other line of conduct being uncalled for: it was only in the evening conferences I thus thwarted and afflicted him. He continued to send for me punctually the moment the clock struck seven; though when I appeared before him now, he had no such honeyed terms as 'love' and 'darling' on his lips: the best words at my service were 'provoking puppet', 'malicious elf', 'sprite', 'changeling', etc. For caresses, too, I now got grimaces; for a pressure of the hand, a pinch on the arm; for a kiss on the cheek, a severe tweak of the ear. It was all right: at present I decidedly preferred these fierce favours to anything more tender. Mrs Fairfax, I saw, approved me: her anxiety on my account vanished; therefore I was certain I did well. Meantime, Mr Rochester affirmed I was wearing him to skin and bone, and threatened awful vengeance for my present conduct at some period fast coming. I laughed in my sleeve at his menaces. 'I can keep you in reasonable check now,' I reflected; 'and I don't doubt to be able to do it hereafter: if one expedient loses its virtue, another must be devised.'

Yet after all my task was not an easy one; often I would rather have pleased than teased him. My future husband was becoming to me my whole world; and more than the world: almost my hope of heaven. He stood between me and every thought of religion, as an eclipse intervenes between man and the broad sun. I could not, in those days, see God for His creature: of whom I had made an idol.

## *Chapter 25*

The month of courtship had wasted: its very last hours were being numbered. There was no putting off the day that advanced – the bridal day; and all preparations for its arrival were complete. *I*, at least, had nothing more to do: there were my trunks, packed, locked, corded, ranged in a row along the wall of my little chamber; tomorrow, at this time, they would be far on their road to London: and so should I (d.v.), or rather, not I, but one Jane Rochester, a person whom as yet I knew not. The cards of address alone remained to nail on: they lay, four little squares, in the drawer. Mr Rochester had himself written the direction, 'Mrs Rochester, — Hotel, London', on each: I could not persuade myself to affix them, or to have them affixed. Mrs Rochester! She did not exist: she would not be born till tomorrow, sometime after eight o'clock a.m.; and I would wait to be assured she had come into the world alive before I assigned to her all that property. It was enough that in yonder closet, opposite my dressing-table, garments said to be hers had already displaced my black stuff Lowood frock and straw bonnet: for not to me appertained that suit of wedding raiment; the pearl-coloured robe, the vapoury veil pendent from the usurped portmanteau. I shut the closet to conceal the strange, wraith-like apparel it contained; which, at this evening hour – nine o'clock – gave out certainly a most ghostly shimmer through the shadow of my apartment. 'I will leave you by yourself, white dream,' I said. 'I am feverish: I hear the wind blowing: I will go out of doors and feel it.'

It was not only the hurry of preparation that made me feverish; not only the anticipation of the great change – the new life which was to commence tomorrow: both these circumstances had their share, doubtless, in producing that restless, excited mood which hurried me forth at this late hour into the darkening grounds: but a third cause influenced my mind more than they.

I had at heart a strange and anxious thought. Something had happened which I could not comprehend; no one knew of or had seen the event but myself: it had taken place the preceding night. Mr Rochester that night was absent from home;

nor was he yet returned: business had called him to a small estate of two or three farms he possessed thirty miles off – business it was requisite he should settle in person, previous to his meditated departure from England. I waited now his return; eager to disburden my mind, and to seek of him the solution of the enigma that perplexed me. Stay till he comes, reader: and, when I disclose my secret to him, you shall share the confidence.

I sought the orchard, driven to its shelter by the wind, which all day had blown strong and full from the south, without, however, bringing a speck of rain. Instead of subsiding as night drew on, it seemed to augment its rush and deepen its roar: the trees blew steadfastly one way, never writhing round, and scarcely tossing back their boughs once in an hour; so continuous was the strain bending their branchy heads northward – the clouds drifted from pole to pole, fast following, mass on mass: no glimpse of blue sky had been visible that July day.

It was not without a certain wild pleasure I ran before the wind, delivering my trouble of mind to the measureless air-torrent thundering through space. Descending the laurel walk, I faced the wreck of the chestnut tree; it stood up black and riven: the trunk, split down the centre, gaped ghastly. The cloven halves were not broken from each other, for the firm base and strong roots kept them unsundered below; though community of vitality was destroyed – the sap could flow no more: their great boughs on each side were dead, and next winter's tempests would be sure to fell one or both to earth: as yet, however, they might be said to form one tree – a ruin, but an entire ruin.

'You did right to hold fast to each other,' I said: as if the monster-splinters were living things, and could hear me. 'I think, scathed as you look, and charred and scorched, there must be a little sense of life in you yet, rising out of that adhesion at the faithful, honest roots: you will never have green leaves more – never more see birds making nests and singing idylls in your boughs; the time of pleasure and love is over with you: but you are not desolate: each of you has a comrade to sympathise with him in his decay.' As I looked up at them, the moon appeared momentarily in that part of the sky which filled their fissure; her disk was blood-red and half overcast; she seemed to throw on me one bewildered, dreary glance, and buried herself again instantly in the deep drift of cloud. The wind fell, for a second, round Thornfield; but far away over wood and water, poured a wild, melancholy wail: it was sad to listen to, and I ran off again.

Here and there I strayed through the orchard, gathered up the apples with which the grass round the tree roots was thickly strewn; then I employed myself in dividing the ripe from the unripe; I carried them into the house and put them away in the storeroom. Then I repaired to the library to ascertain whether the fire was lit, for, though summer, I knew on such a gloomy evening Mr Rochester would like to see a cheerful hearth when he came in: yes, the fire had been kindled sometime, and burnt well. I placed his armchair by the chimney-corner: I wheeled the table near it: I let down the curtain, and had the candles brought in ready for lighting. More restless than ever, when I had completed these arrangements I could not sit still, nor even remain in the house: a little timepiece in the room and the old clock in the hall simultaneously struck ten.

'How late it grows!' I said. 'I will run down to the gates: it is moonlight at intervals; I can see a good way on the road. He may be coming now, and to meet him will save some minutes of suspense.'

The wind roared high in the great trees which embowered the gates; but the road as far as I could see, to the right hand and the left, was all still and solitary: save for the shadows of clouds crossing it at intervals as the moon looked out, it was but a long pale line, unvaried by one moving speck.

A puerile tear dimmed my eye while I looked – a tear of disappointment and impatience; ashamed of it, I wiped it away. I lingered; the moon shut herself wholly within her chamber, and drew close her curtain of dense cloud: the night grew dark; rain came driving fast on the gale.

'I wish he would come! I wish he would come!' I exclaimed, seized with hypochondriac foreboding. I had expected his arrival before tea; now it was dark: what could keep him? Had an accident happened? The event of last night again recurred to me. I interpreted it as a warning of disaster. I feared my hopes were too bright to be realised; and I had enjoyed so much bliss lately that I imagined my fortune had passed its meridian, and must now decline.

'Well, I cannot return to the house,' I thought; 'I cannot sit by the fireside, while he is abroad in inclement weather: better tire my limbs than strain my heart; I will go forward and meet him.'

I set out; I walked fast, but not far: ere I had measured a quarter of a mile, I heard the tramp of hoofs; a horseman came on, full gallop; a dog ran by his side. Away with evil presentiment! It was he: here he was, mounted on Mesrour, followed by Pilot. He saw me; for the moon had opened a blue field in the sky, and rode in it watery bright: he took his hat off, and waved it round his head. I now ran to meet him.

'There!' he exclaimed, as he stretched out his hand and bent from the saddle: 'you can't do without me, that is evident. Step on my boot-toe; give me both hands: mount!'

I obeyed: joy made me agile: I sprang up before him. A hearty kissing I got for a welcome, and some boastful triumph, which I swallowed as well as I could. He checked himself in his exultation to demand, 'But is there anything the matter, Janet, that you come to meet me at such an hour? Is there anything wrong?'

'No, but I thought you would never come. I could not bear to wait in the house for you, especially with this rain and wind.'

'Rain and wind, indeed! Yes, you are dripping like a mermaid; pull my cloak round you: but I think you are feverish, Jane: both your cheek and hand are burning hot. I ask again, is there anything the matter?'

'Nothing now; I am neither afraid nor unhappy.'

'Then you have been both?'

'Rather: but I'll tell you all about it by and by, sir, and I dare say you will only laugh at me for my pains.'

'I'll laugh at you heartily when tomorrow is past; till then I dare not: my prize is not certain. This is you, who have been as slippery as an eel this last month, and as thorny as a briar-rose? I could not lay a finger anywhere but I was pricked;

and now I seem to have gathered up a stray lamb in my arms. You wandered out of the fold to seek your shepherd, did you, Jane?'

'I wanted you: but don't boast. Here we are at Thornfield: now let me get down.'

He landed me on the pavement. As John took his horse, and he followed me into the hall, he told me to make haste and put something dry on, and then return to him in the library; and he stopped me, as I made for the staircase, to extort a promise that I would not be long: nor was I long; in five minutes I rejoined him. I found him at supper.

'Take a seat and bear me company, Jane: please God, it is the last meal but one you will eat at Thornfield Hall for a long time.'

I sat down near him, but told him I could not eat.

'Is it because you have the prospect of a journey before you, Jane? Is it the thoughts of going to London that takes away your appetite?'

'I cannot see my prospects clearly tonight, sir; and I hardly know what thoughts I have in my head. Everything in life seems unreal.'

'Except me: I am substantial enough – touch me.'

'You, sir, are the most phantom-like of all: you are a mere dream.'

He held out his hand, laughing. 'Is that a dream?' said he, placing it close to my eyes. He had a rounded, muscular, and vigorous hand, as well as a long, strong arm.

'Yes; though I touch it, it is a dream,' said I, as I put it down from before my face. 'Sir, have you finished supper?'

'Yes, Jane.'

I rang the bell and ordered away the tray. When we were again alone, I stirred the fire, and then took a low seat at my master's knee.

'It is near midnight,' I said.

'Yes: but remember, Jane, you promised to wake with me the night before my wedding.'

'I did; and I will keep my promise, for an hour or two at least: I have no wish to go to bed.'

'Are all your arrangements complete?'

'All, sir.'

'And on my part likewise,' he returned, 'I have settled everything; and we shall leave Thornfield tomorrow, within half an hour after our return from church.'

'Very well, sir.'

'With what an extraordinary smile you uttered that word – "very well", Jane! What a bright spot of colour you have on each cheek! and how strangely your eyes glitter! Are you well?'

'I believe I am.'

'Believe! What is the matter? Tell me what you feel.'

'I could not, sir: no words could tell you what I feel. I wish this present hour would never end: who knows with what fate the next may come charged?'

'This is hypochondria, Jane. You have been overexcited, or over-fatigued.'

'Do you, sir, feel calm and happy?'

'Calm? – no: but happy – to the heart's core.'

I looked up at him to read the signs of bliss in his face: it was ardent and flushed.

'Give me your confidence, Jane,' he said: 'relieve your mind of any weight that oppresses it, by imparting it to me. What do you fear? – that I shall not prove a good husband?'

'It is the idea farthest from my thoughts.'

'Are you apprehensive of the new sphere you are about to enter? – of the new life into which you are passing?'

'No.'

'You puzzle me, Jane: your look and tone of sorrowful audacity perplex and pain me. I want an explanation.'

'Then, sir, listen. You were from home last night?'

'I was: I know that; and you hinted a while ago at something which had happened in my absence: nothing, probably, of consequence; but, in short, it has disturbed you. Let me hear it. Mrs Fairfax has said something, perhaps? or you have overheard the servants talk? – your sensitive self-respect has been wounded?'

'No, sir.' It struck twelve – I waited till the timepiece had concluded its silver chime, and the clock its hoarse, vibrating stroke, and then I proceeded.

'All day yesterday I was very busy, and very happy in my ceaseless bustle; for I am not, as you seem to think, troubled by any haunting fears about the new sphere, et cetera: I think it a glorious thing to have the hope of living with you, because I love you. No, sir, don't caress me now – let me talk undisturbed. Yesterday I trusted well in Providence, and believed that events were working together for your good and mine: it was a fine day, if you recollect – the calmness of the air and sky forbade apprehensions respecting your safety or comfort on your journey. I walked a little while on the pavement after tea, thinking of you; and I beheld you in imagination so near me, I scarcely missed your actual presence. I thought of the life that lay before me – *your* life, sir – an existence more expansive and stirring than my own: as much more so as the depths of the sea to which the brook runs are than the shallows of its own strait channel. I wondered why moralists call this world a dreary wilderness: for me it blossomed like a rose. Just at sunset, the air turned cold and the sky cloudy: I went in, Sophie called me upstairs to look at my wedding-dress, which they had just brought; and under it in the box I found your present – the veil which, in your princely extravagance, you sent for from London: resolved, I suppose, since I would not have jewels, to cheat me into accepting something as costly. I smiled as I unfolded it, and devised how I would tease you about your aristocratic tastes, and your efforts to masque your plebeian bride in the attributes of a peeress. I thought how I would carry down to you the square of unembroidered blond I had myself prepared as a covering for my low-born head, and ask if that was not good enough for a woman who could bring her husband neither fortune, beauty, nor connections. I saw plainly how you would look; and heard your impetuous republican answers, and your haughty disavowal of any necessity on your part to augment your wealth, or elevate your standing, by marrying either a purse or a coronet.'

'How well you read me, you witch!' interposed Mr Rochester: 'but what did you find in the veil besides its embroidery? Did you find poison, or a dagger, that you look so mournful now?'

'No, no, sir; besides the delicacy and richness of the fabric, I found nothing save Fairfax Rochester's pride; and that did not scare me, because I am used to the sight of the demon. But, sir, as it grew dark, the wind rose: it blew yesterday evening, not as it blows now – wild and high – but "with a sullen, moaning sound" far more eerie. I wished you were at home. I came into this room, and the sight of the empty chair and fireless hearth chilled me. For some time after I went to bed, I could not sleep – a sense of anxious excitement distressed me. The gale still rising, seemed to my ear to muffle a mournful under-sound; whether in the house or abroad I could not at first tell, but it recurred, doubtful yet doleful at every lull; at last I made out it must be some dog howling at a distance. I was glad when it ceased. On sleeping, I continued in dreams the idea of a dark and gusty night. I continued also the wish to be with you, and experienced a strange, regretful consciousness of some barrier dividing us. During all my first sleep, I was following the windings of an unknown road; total obscurity environed me; rain pelted me; I was burdened with the charge of a little child: a very small creature, too young and feeble to walk, and which shivered in my cold arms, and wailed piteously in my ear. I thought, sir, that you were on the road a long way before me; and I strained every nerve to overtake you, and made effort on effort to utter your name and entreat you to stop – but my movements were fettered, and my voice still died away inarticulate; while you, I felt, withdrew farther and farther every moment.'

'And these dreams weigh on your spirits now, Jane, when I am close to you? Little nervous subject! Forget visionary woe, and think only of real happiness! You say you love me, Janet: yes – I will not forget that; and you cannot deny it. *Those* words did not die inarticulate on your lips. I heard them clear and soft: a thought too solemn perhaps, but sweet as music – "I think it is a glorious thing to have the hope of living with you, Edward, because I love you." Do you love me, Jane? – repeat it.'

'I do, sir – I do, with my whole heart.'

'Well,' he said, after some minutes' silence, 'it is strange; but that sentence has penetrated my breast painfully. Why? I think because you said it with such an earnest, religious energy, and because your upward gaze at me now is the very sublime of faith, truth, and devotion: it is too much as if some spirit were near me. Look wicked, Jane: as you know well how to look: coin one of your wild, shy, provoking smiles, tell me you hate me – tease me, vex me; do anything but move me: I would rather be incensed than saddened.'

'I will tease you and vex you to your heart's content, when I have finished my tale: but hear me to the end.'

'I thought, Jane, you had told me all. I thought I had found the source of your melancholy in a dream.'

I shook my head. 'What! is there more? But I will not believe it to be anything important. I warn you of incredulity beforehand. Go on.'

The disquietude of his air, the somewhat apprehensive impatience of his manner, surprised me: but I proceeded.

'I dreamt another dream, sir: that Thornfield Hall was a dreary ruin, the retreat of bats and owls. I thought that of all the stately front nothing remained but a shell-like wall, very high and very fragile-looking. I wandered, on a moonlight night, through the grass-grown enclosure within: here I stumbled over a marble hearth, and there over a fallen fragment of cornice. Wrapped up in a shawl, I still carried the unknown little child: I might not lay it down anywhere, however tired were my arms – however much its weight impeded my progress, I must retain it. I heard the gallop of a horse at a distance on the road; I was sure it was you; and you were departing for many years and for a distant country. I climbed the thin wall with frantic perilous haste, eager to catch one glimpse of you from the top: the stones rolled from under my feet, the ivy branches I grasped gave way, the child clung round my neck in terror, and almost strangled me; at last I gained the summit. I saw you like a speck on a white track, lessening every moment. The blast blew so strong I could not stand. I sat down on the narrow ledge; I hushed the scared infant in my lap: you turned an angle of the road: I bent forward to take a last look; the wall crumbled; I was shaken; the child rolled from my knee, I lost my balance, fell, and woke.'

'Now, Jane, that is all.'

'All the preface, sir; the tale is yet to come. On waking, a gleam dazzled my eyes; I thought – Oh, it is daylight! But I was mistaken; it was only candlelight. Sophie, I supposed, had come in. There was a light in the dressing-table, and the door of the closet, where, before going to bed, I had hung my wedding-dress and veil, stood open; I heard a rustling there. I asked, "Sophie, what are you doing?" No one answered; but a form emerged from the closet; it took the light, held it aloft, and surveyed the garments pendent from the portmanteau. "Sophie! Sophie!" I again cried: and still it was silent. I had risen up in bed, I bent forward: first surprise, then bewilderment, came over me; and then my blood crept cold through my veins. Mr Rochester, this was not Sophie, it was not Leah, it was not Mrs Fairfax: it was not – no, I was sure of it, and am still – it was not even that strange woman, Grace Poole.'

'It must have been one of them,' interrupted my master.

'No, sir, I solemnly assure you to the contrary. The shape standing before me had never crossed my eyes within the precincts of Thornfield Hall before; the height, the contour were new to me.'

'Describe it, Jane.'

'It seemed, sir, a woman, tall and large, with thick and dark hair hanging long down her back. I know not what dress she had on: it was white and straight; but whether gown, sheet, or shroud, I cannot tell.'

'Did you see her face?'

'Not at first. But presently she took my veil from its place; she held it up, gazed at it long, and then she threw it over her own head, and turned to the mirror. At that moment I saw the reflection of the visage and features quite distinctly in the dark oblong glass.'

'And how were they?'

'Fearful and ghastly to me – oh, sir, I never saw a face like it! It was a discoloured face – it was a savage face. I wish I could forget the roll of the red eyes and the fearful blackened inflation of the lineaments!'

'Ghosts are usually pale, Jane.'

'This, sir, was purple: the lips were swelled and dark; the brow furrowed: the black eyebrows widely raised over the bloodshot eyes. Shall I tell you of what it reminded me?'

'You may.'

'Of the foul German spectre – the Vampyre.'

'Ah! – what did it do?'

'Sir, it removed my veil from its gaunt head, rent it in two parts, and flinging both on the floor, trampled on them.'

'Afterwards?'

'It drew aside the window-curtain and looked out; perhaps it saw dawn approaching, for, taking the candle, it retreated to the door. Just at my bedside, the figure stopped: the fiery eyes glared upon me – she thrust up her candle close to my face, and extinguished it under my eyes. I was aware her lurid visage flamed over mine, and I lost consciousness: for the second time in my life – only the second time – I became insensible from terror.'

'Who was with you when you revived?'

'No one, sir, but the broad day. I rose, bathed my head and face in water, drank a long draught; felt that though enfeebled I was not ill, and determined that to none but you would I impart this vision. Now sir, tell me who and what that woman was?'

'The creature of an over-stimulated brain; that is certain. I must be careful of you, my treasure: nerves like yours were not made for rough handling.'

'Sir, depend on it, my nerves were not in fault; the thing was real: the transaction actually took place.'

'And your previous dreams, were they real too? Is Thornfield Hall a ruin? Am I severed from you by insuperable obstacles? Am I leaving you without a tear – without a kiss – without a word?'

'Not yet.'

'Am I about to do it? Why, the day is already commenced which is to bind us indissolubly; and when we are once united, there shall be no recurrence of these mental terrors: I guarantee that.'

'Mental terrors, sir! I wish I could believe them to be only such: I wish it more now than ever; since even you cannot explain to me the mystery of that awful visitant.'

'And since I cannot do it, Jane, it must have been unreal.'

'But, sir, when I said so to myself on rising this morning, and when I looked round the room to gather courage and comfort from the cheerful aspect of each familiar object in full daylight, there – on the carpet – I saw what gave the distinct lie to my hypothesis, the veil, torn from top to bottom in two halves!'

I felt Mr Rochester start and shudder; he hastily flung his arms round me. 'Thank God!' he exclaimed, 'that if anything malignant did come near you last night, it was only the veil that was harmed. Oh, to think what might have happened!'

He drew his breath short, and strained me so close to him, I could scarcely pant. After some minutes' silence, he continued, cheerily – 'Now, Janet, I'll explain to you all about it. It was half dream, half reality. A woman did, I doubt not, enter your room: and that woman was – must have been – Grace Poole. You call her a strange being yourself: from all you know, you have reason so to call her – what did she do to me? what to Mason? In a state between sleeping and waking, you noticed her entrance and her actions; but feverish, almost delirious as you were, you ascribed to her a goblin appearance different from her own: the long dishevelled hair, the swelled black face, the exaggerated stature, were figments of imagination; results of nightmare: the spiteful tearing of the veil was real: and it is like her. I see you would ask why I keep such a woman in my house: when we have been married a year and a day, I will tell you; but not now. Are you satisfied, Jane? Do you accept my solution of the mystery?'

I reflected, and in truth it appeared to me the only possible one: satisfied I was not, but to please him I endeavoured to appear so – relieved, I certainly did feel; so I answered him with a contented smile. And now, as it was long past one, I prepared to leave him.

'Does not Sophie sleep with Adèle in the nursery?' he asked, as I lit my candle.

'Yes, sir.'

'And there is room enough in Adèle's little bed for you. You must share it with her tonight, Jane: it is no wonder that the incident you have related should make you nervous, and I would rather you did not sleep alone: promise me to go to the nursery.'

'I shall be very glad to do so, sir.'

'And fasten the door securely on the inside. Wake Sophie when you go upstairs, under pretence of requesting her to rouse you in good time tomorrow; for you must be dressed and have finished breakfast before eight. And now, no more sombre thoughts: chase dull care away, Janet. Don't you hear to what soft whispers the wind has fallen? and there is no more beating of rain against the window-panes: look here' (he lifted up the curtain) – 'it is a lovely night!'

It was. Half heaven was pure and stainless: the clouds, now trooping before the wind, which had shifted to the west, were filing off eastward in long, silvered columns. The moon shone peacefully.

'Well,' said Mr Rochester, gazing enquiringly into my eyes, 'how is my Janet now?'

'The night is serene, sir; and so am I.'

'And you will not dream of separation and sorrow tonight; but of happy love and blissful union.'

This prediction was but half fulfilled: I did not indeed dream of sorrow, but as little did I dream of Joy; for I never slept at all. With little Adèle in my arms, I watched the slumber of childhood – so tranquil so passionless, so innocent – and waited for the coming day: all my life was awake and astir in my frame: and as soon as the sun rose I rose too. I remember Adèle clung to me as I left her: I remember I kissed her as I loosened her little hands from my neck; and I cried over her with strange emotion, and quitted her because I feared my sobs would break her still sound repose. She seemed the emblem of my past life; and he I was now to array myself to meet, the dread, but adored, type of my unknown future day.

## *Chapter 26*

Sophie came at seven to dress me: she was very long indeed in accomplishing her task; so long that Mr Rochester, grown, I suppose, impatient of my delay, sent up to ask why I did not come. She was just fastening my veil (the plain square of blond after all) to my hair with a brooch; I hurried from under her hands as soon as I could.

'Stop!' she cried in French. 'Look at yourself in the mirror: you have not taken one peep.'

So I turned at the door: I saw a robed and veiled figure, so unlike my usual self that it seemed almost the image of a stranger. 'Jane!' called a voice, and I hastened down. I was received at the foot of the stairs by Mr Rochester.

'Lingerer!' he said, 'my brain is on fire with impatience, and you tarry so long!'

He took me into the dining-room, surveyed me keenly all over, pronounced me 'fair as a lily, and not only the pride of his life, but the desire of his eyes,' and then telling me he would give me but ten minutes to eat some breakfast, he rang the bell. One of his lately hired servants, a footman, answered it.

'Is John getting the carriage ready?'

'Yes, sir.'

'Is the luggage brought down?'

'They are bringing it down, sir.'

'Go you to the church: see if Mr Wood (the clergyman) and the clerk are there: return and tell me.'

The church, as the reader knows, was but just beyond the gates; the footman soon returned.

'Mr Wood is in the vestry, sir, putting on his surplice.'

'And the carriage?'

'The horses are harnessing.'

'We shall not want it to go to church; but it must be ready the moment we return: all the boxes and luggage arranged and strapped on, and the coachman in his seat.'

'Yes, sir.'

'Jane, are you ready?'

I rose. There were no groomsmen, no bridesmaids, no relatives to wait for or marshal: none but Mr Rochester and I. Mrs Fairfax stood in the hall as we passed. I would fain have spoken to her, but my hand was held by a grasp of iron: I was hurried along by a stride I could hardly follow; and to look at Mr Rochester's face was to feel that not a second of delay would be tolerated for any purpose. I wonder what other bridegroom ever looked as he did – so bent up to a purpose, so grimly resolute: or who, under such steadfast brows, ever revealed such flaming and flashing eyes.

I know not whether the day was fair or foul; in descending the drive, I gazed neither on sky nor earth: my heart was with my eyes; and both seemed migrated into Mr Rochester's frame. I wanted to see the invisible thing on which, as we went along, he appeared to fasten a glance fierce and fell. I wanted to feel the thoughts whose force he seemed breasting and resisting.

At the churchyard wicket he stopped: he discovered I was quite out of breath. 'Am I cruel in my love?' he said. 'Delay an instant: lean on me, Jane.'

And now I can recall the picture of the grey old house of God rising calm before me, of a rook wheeling round the steeple, of a ruddy morning sky beyond. I remember something, too, of the green grave-mounds; and I have not forgotten, either, two figures of strangers straying amongst the low hillocks and reading the mementoes graven on the few mossy headstones. I noticed them, because, as they saw us, they passed round to the back of the church; and I doubted not they were going to enter by the side-aisle door and witness the ceremony. By Mr Rochester they were not observed; he was earnestly looking at my face, from which the blood had, I dare say, momentarily fled: for I felt my forehead dewy, and my cheeks and lips cold. When I rallied, which I soon did, he walked gently with me up the path to the porch.

We entered the quiet and humble temple; the priest waited in his white surplice at the lowly altar, the clerk beside him. All was still: two shadows only moved in a remote corner. My conjecture had been correct: the strangers had slipped in before us, and they now stood by the vault of the Rochesters, their backs towards us, viewing through the rails the old time-stained marble tomb, where a kneeling angel guarded the remains of Damer de Rochester, slain at Marston Moor in the time of the civil wars, and of Elizabeth, his wife.

Our place was taken at the communion rails. Hearing a cautious step behind me, I glanced over my shoulder: one of the strangers – a gentleman, evidently – was advancing up the chancel. The service began. The explanation of the intent of matrimony was gone through; and then the clergyman came a step farther forward, and, bending slightly towards Mr Rochester, went on.

'I require and charge you both (as ye will answer at the dreadful day of judgement, when the secrets of all hearts shall be disclosed), that if either of you know any impediment why ye may not lawfully be joined together in matrimony, ye do now confess it; for be ye well assured that so many as are coupled together otherwise than God's Word doth allow, are not joined together by God, neither is their matrimony lawful.'

He paused, as the custom is. When is the pause after that sentence ever broken by reply? Not, perhaps, once in a hundred years. And the clergyman, who had not lifted his eyes from his book, and had held his breath but for a moment, was proceeding: his hand was already stretched towards Mr Rochester, as his lips unclosed to ask, 'Wilt thou have this woman for thy wedded wife? – ' when a distinct and near voice said – 'The marriage cannot go on: I declare the existence of an impediment.'

The clergyman looked up at the speaker and stood mute; the clerk did the same; Mr Rochester moved slightly, as if an earthquake had rolled under his feet: taking a firmer footing, and not turning his head or eyes, he said, 'Proceed.'

Profound silence fell when he had uttered that word, with deep but low intonation. Presently Mr Wood said – 'I cannot proceed without some investigation into what has been asserted, and evidence of its truth or falsehood.'

'The ceremony is quite broken off,' subjoined the voice behind us. 'I am in a condition to prove my allegation: an insuperable impediment to this marriage exists.'

Mr Rochester heard, but heeded not: he stood stubborn and rigid, making no movement but to possess himself of my hand. What a hot and strong grasp he had! and how like quarried marble was his pale, firm, massive front at this moment! How his eye shone, still watchful, and yet wild beneath!

Mr Wood seemed at a loss. 'What is the nature of the impediment?' he asked. 'Perhaps it may be got over – explained away?'

'Hardly,' was the answer. 'I have called it insuperable, and I speak advisedly.'

The speaker came forward and leaned on the rails. He continued, uttering each word distinctly, calmly, steadily, but not loudly – 'It simply consists in the existence of a previous marriage. Mr Rochester has a wife now living.'

My nerves vibrated to those low-spoken words as they had never vibrated to thunder – my blood felt their subtle violence as it had never felt frost or fire; but I was collected, and in no danger of swooning. I looked at Mr Rochester: I made him look at me. His whole face was colourless rock: his eye was both spark and flint. He disavowed nothing: he seemed as if he would defy all things. Without speaking, without smiling, without seeming to recognise in me a human being, he only twined my waist with his arm and riveted me to his side.

'Who are you?' he asked of the intruder.

'My name is Briggs, a solicitor of — Street, London.'

'And you would thrust on me a wife?'

'I would remind you of your lady's existence, sir, which the law recognises, if you do not.'

'Favour me with an account of her – with her name, her parentage, her place of abode.'

'Certainly.' Mr Briggs calmly took a paper from his pocket, and read out in a sort of official, nasal voice: ' "I affirm and can prove that on the 20th of October AD (a date of fifteen years back), Edward Fairfax Rochester, of Thornfield Hall, in the county of —, and of Ferndean Manor, in —shire, England, was married to my sister, Bertha Antoinetta Mason, daughter of Jonas Mason, merchant, and of Antoinetta his wife, a Creole, at — church, Spanish Town, Jamaica. The record of the marriage will be found in the register of that church – a copy of it is now in my possession. Signed, Richard Mason." '

'That – if a genuine document – may prove I have been married, but it does not prove that the woman mentioned therein as my wife is still living.'

'She was living three months ago,' returned the lawyer.

'How do you know?'

'I have a witness to the fact, whose testimony even you, sir, will scarcely controvert.'

'Produce him – or go to hell.'

'I will produce him first – he is on the spot. Mr Mason, have the goodness to step forward.'

Mr Rochester, on hearing the name, set his teeth; he experienced, too, a sort of strong convulsive quiver; near to him as I was, I felt the spasmodic movement of fury or despair run through his frame. The second stranger, who had hitherto lingered in the background, now drew near; a pale face looked over the solicitor's shoulder – yes, it was Mason himself. Mr Rochester turned and glared at him. His eye, as I have often said, was a black eye: it had now a tawny, nay, a bloody light in its gloom; and his face flushed – olive cheek and hueless forehead received a glow as from spreading, ascending heart-fire: and he stirred, lifted his strong arm – he could have struck Mason, dashed him on the church-floor, shocked by ruthless blow the breath from his body – but Mason shrank away, and cried faintly, 'Good God!' Contempt fell cool on Mr Rochester – his passion died as if a blight had shrivelled it up: he only asked – 'What have *you* to say?'

An inaudible reply escaped Mason's white lips.

'The devil is in it if you cannot answer distinctly. I again demand, what have *you* to say?'

'Sir – sir,' interrupted the clergyman, 'do not forget you are in a sacred place.' Then addressing Mason, he enquired gently, 'Are you aware, sir, whether or not this gentleman's wife is still living?'

'Courage,' urged the lawyer, 'speak out.'

'She is now living at Thornfield Hall,' said Mason, in more articulate tones: 'I saw her there last April. I am her brother.'

'At Thornfield Hall!' ejaculated the clergyman. 'Impossible! I am an old resident in this neighbourhood, sir, and I never heard of a Mrs Rochester at Thornfield Hall.'

I saw a grim smile contort Mr Rochester's lips, and he muttered – 'No, by God! I took care that none should hear of it – or of her under that name.' He mused – for ten minutes he held counsel with himself: he formed his resolve, and announced it – 'Enough! all shall bolt out at once, like the bullet from the barrel. Wood, close your book and take off your surplice; John Green (to the clerk), leave the church: there will be no wedding today.' The man obeyed.

Mr Rochester continued, hardily and recklessly: 'Bigamy is an ugly word! – I meant, however, to be a bigamist; but fate has out-manoeuvred me, or Providence has checked me, perhaps the last. I am little better than a devil at this moment; and, as my pastor there would tell me, deserve no doubt the sternest judgements of God, even to the quenchless fire and deathless worm. Gentlemen, my plan is broken up: what this lawyer and his client say is true: I have been married, and the woman to whom I was married lives! You say you never heard of a Mrs Rochester at the house up yonder, Wood; but I dare say you have many a time inclined your ear to gossip about the mysterious lunatic kept there under watch and ward. Some have whispered to you that she is my bastard half-sister: some, my cast-off mistress. I now inform you that she is my wife, whom I married fifteen years ago, Bertha Mason by name; sister of this resolute personage, who is now, with his quivering limbs and white cheeks, showing you what a stout heart men may bear. Cheer up, Dick! – never fear me! – I'd almost as soon strike a woman as you. Bertha Mason is mad; and she came of a mad family; idiots and maniacs through three generations! Her mother, the Creole, was both a madwoman and a drunkard! – as I found out after I had wed the daughter: for they were silent on family secrets before. Bertha, like a dutiful child, copied her parent in both points. I had a charming partner – pure, wise, modest: you can fancy I was a happy man. I went through rich scenes! Oh! my experience has been heavenly, if you only knew it! But I owe you no further explanation. Briggs, Wood, Mason, I invite you all to come up to the house and visit Mrs Poole's patient, and *my wife*! You shall see what sort of a being I was cheated into espousing, and judge whether or not I had a right to break the compact, and seek sympathy with something at least human. This girl,' he continued, looking at me, 'knew no more than you, Wood, of the disgusting secret: she thought all was fair and legal, and never dreamt she was going to be entrapped into a feigned union with a defrauded wretch, already bound to a bad, mad, and embruted partner! Come all of you – follow!'

Still holding me fast, he left the church: the three gentlemen came after. At the front door of the hall we found the carriage.

'Take it back to the coach-house, John,' said Mr Rochester coolly: 'it will not be wanted today.'

At our entrance, Mrs Fairfax, Adèle, Sophie, Leah, advanced to meet and greet us.

'To the right-about – every soul!' cried the master; 'away with your congratulations! Who wants them? Not I! – they are fifteen years too late!'

He passed on and ascended the stairs, still holding my hand, and still beckoning the gentlemen to follow him, which they did. We mounted the first staircase, passed up the gallery, proceeded to the third storey: the low, black door, opened by Mr Rochester's master-key, admitted us to the tapestried room, with its great bed and its pictorial cabinet.

'You know this place, Mason,' said our guide; 'she bit and stabbed you here.'

He lifted the hangings from the wall, uncovering the second door: this, too, he opened. In a room without a window, there burnt a fire guarded by a high and strong fender, and a lamp suspended from the ceiling by a chain. Grace Poole bent over the fire, apparently cooking something in a saucepan. In the deep shade, at the farther end of the room, a figure ran backwards and forwards. What it was, whether beast or human being, one could not, at first sight, tell: it grovelled, seemingly, on all fours; it snatched and growled like some strange wild animal: but it was covered with clothing, and a quantity of dark, grizzled hair, wild as a mane, hid its head and face.

'Good-morrow, Mrs Poole!' said Mr Rochester. 'How are you? and how is your charge today?'

'We're tolerable, sir, I thank you,' replied Grace, lifting the boiling mess carefully on to the hob: 'rather snappish, but not 'rageous.'

A fierce cry seemed to give the lie to her favourable report: the clothed hyena rose up, and stood tall on its hind-feet.

'Ah! sir, she sees you!' exclaimed Grace: 'you'd better not stay.'

'Only a few moments, Grace: you must allow me a few moments.'

'Take care then, sir! – for God's sake, take care!'

The maniac bellowed: she parted her shaggy locks from her visage, and gazed wildly at her visitors. I recognised well that purple face, those bloated features. Mrs Poole advanced.

'Keep out of the way,' said Mr Rochester, thrusting her aside: 'she has no knife now, I suppose, and I'm on my guard.'

'One never knows what she has, sir: she is so cunning: it is not in mortal discretion to fathom her craft.'

'We had better leave her,' whispered Mason.

'Go to the devil!' was his brother-in-law's recommendation.

' 'Ware!' cried Grace. The three gentlemen retreated simultaneously. Mr Rochester flung me behind him; the lunatic sprang and grappled his throat viciously, and laid her teeth to his cheek: they struggled. She was a big woman, in stature almost equalling her husband, and corpulent besides: she showed virile force in the contest – more than once she almost throttled him, athletic as he was. He could have settled her with a well-planted blow: but he would not strike: he would only wrestle. At last he mastered her arms; Grace Poole gave him a cord, and he pinioned them behind her: with more rope, which was at hand, he bound her to a chair. The operation was performed amidst the fiercest yells and the most convulsive plunges. Mr Rochester then turned to the spectators: he looked at them with a smile both acrid and desolate.

'That is *my wife*,' said he. 'Such is the sole conjugal embrace I am ever to know – such are the endearments which are to solace my leisure hours! And *this* is what I wished to have' (laying his hand on my shoulder): 'this young girl, who stands so grave and quiet at the mouth of hell, looking collectedly at the gambols of a demon. I wanted her just as a change after that fierce ragout. Wood and Briggs, look at the difference! Compare these clear eyes with the red balls yonder – this face with that mask – this form with that bulk; then judge me, priest of the gospel and man of the law, and remember with what judgement ye judge ye shall be judged! Off with you now. I must shut up my prize.'

We all withdrew. Mr Rochester stayed a moment behind us, to give some further order to Grace Poole. The solicitor addressed me as he descended the stair.

'You, madam,' said he, 'are cleared from all blame: your uncle will be glad to hear it – if, indeed, he should be still living – when Mr Mason returns to Madeira.'

'My uncle! What of him? Do you know him?'

'Mr Mason does. Mr Eyre has been the Funchal correspondent of his house for some years. When your uncle received your letter intimating the contemplated union between yourself and Mr Rochester, Mr Mason, who was staying at Madeira to recruit his health, on his way back to Jamaica, happened to be with him. Mr Eyre mentioned the intelligence; for he knew that my client here was acquainted with a gentleman of the name of Rochester. Mr Mason, astonished and distressed as you may suppose, revealed the real state of matters. Your uncle, I am sorry to say, is now on a sick-bed; from which, considering the nature of his disease – decline – and the stage it has reached, it is unlikely he will ever rise. He could not then hasten to England himself, to extricate you from the snare into which you had fallen, but he implored Mr Mason to lose no time in taking steps to prevent the false marriage. He referred him to me for assistance. I used all despatch, and am thankful I was not too late: as you, doubtless, must be also. Were I not morally certain that your uncle will be dead ere you reach Madeira, I would advise you to accompany Mr Mason back; but as it is, I think you had better remain in England till you can hear further, either from or of Mr Eyre. Have we anything else to stay for?' he enquired of Mr Mason.

'No, no – let us be gone,' was the anxious reply; and without waiting to take leave of Mr Rochester, they made their exit at the hall door. The clergyman stayed to exchange a few sentences, either of admonition or reproof, with his haughty parishioner; this duty done, he too departed.

I heard him go as I stood at the half-open door of my own room, to which I had now withdrawn. The house cleared, I shut myself in, fastened the bolt that none might intrude, and proceeded – not to weep, not to mourn, I was yet too calm for that, but – mechanically to take off the wedding-dress, and replace it by the stuff gown I had worn yesterday, as I thought, for the last time. I then sat down: I felt weak and tired. I leaned my arms on a table, and my head dropped on them. And now I thought: till now I had only heard, seen, moved – followed up and down where I was led or dragged – watched event rush on event, disclosure open beyond disclosure: but *now, I thought*.

The morning had been a quiet morning enough – all except the brief scene with the lunatic: the transaction in the church had not been noisy; there was no explosion of passion, no loud altercation, no dispute, no defiance or challenge, no tears, no sobs: a few words had been spoken, a calmly pronounced objection to the marriage made; some stern, short questions put by Mr Rochester; answers, explanations given, evidence adduced; an open admission of the truth had been uttered by my master; then the living proof had been seen; the intruders were gone, and all was over. I was in my own room as usual – just myself, without obvious change: nothing had smitten me, or scathed me, or maimed me. And yet where was the Jane Eyre of yesterday? – where was her life? – where were her prospects?

Jane Eyre, who had been an ardent, expectant woman – almost a bride, was a cold, solitary girl again: her life was pale; her prospects were desolate. A Christmas frost had come at midsummer; a white December storm had whirled over June; ice glazed the ripe apples, drifts crushed the blowing roses; on hayfield and cornfield lay a frozen shroud: lanes which last night blushed full of flowers, today were pathless with untrodden snow; and the woods, which twelve hours since waved leafy and fragrant as groves between the tropics, now spread, waste, wild, and white as pine-forests in wintry Norway. My hopes were all dead – struck with a subtle doom, such as, in one night, fell on all the first-born in the land of Egypt. I looked on my cherished wishes, yesterday so blooming and glowing; they lay stark, chill, livid corpses that could never revive. I looked at my love: that feeling which was my master's – which he had created; it shivered in my heart, like a suffering child in a cold cradle; sickness and anguish had seized it; it could not seek Mr Rochester's arms – it could not derive warmth from his breast. Oh, never more could it turn to him; for faith was blighted – confidence destroyed! Mr Rochester was not to me what he had been; for he was not what I had thought him. I would not ascribe vice to him; I would not say he had betrayed me; but the attribute of stainless truth was gone from his idea, and from his presence I must go: that I perceived well. When – how – whither, I could not yet discern; but he himself, I doubted not, would hurry me from Thornfield. Real affection, it seemed, he could not have for me; it had been only fitful passion: that was balked; he would want me no more. I should fear even to cross his path now: my view must be hateful to him. Oh, how blind had been my eyes! How weak my conduct!

My eyes were covered and closed: eddying darkness seemed to swim round me, and reflection came in as black and confused a flow. Self-abandoned, relaxed, and effortless, I seemed to have laid me down in the dried-up bed of a great river; I heard a flood loosened in remote mountains, and felt the torrent come: to rise I had no will, to flee I had no strength. I lay faint, longing to be dead. One idea only still throbbed lifelike within me – a remembrance of God: it begot an unuttered prayer: these words went wandering up and down in my rayless mind, as something that should be whispered, but no energy was found to express them – 'Be not far from me, for trouble is near: there is none to help.'

It was near: and as I had lifted no petition to Heaven to avert it – as I had neither joined my hands, nor bent my knees, nor moved my lips – it came: in full heavy swing the torrent poured over me. The whole consciousness of my life lorn, my love lost, my hope quenched, my faith death-struck, swayed full and mighty above me in one sullen mass. That bitter hour cannot be described: in truth, 'the waters came into my soul; I sank in deep mire: I felt no standing; I came into deep waters; the floods overflowed me.'

## *Chapter 27*

Sometime in the afternoon I raised my head, and looking round and seeing the western sun gilding the sign of its decline on the wall, I asked, 'What am I to do?'

But the answer my mind gave – 'Leave Thornfield at once' – was so prompt, so dread, that I stopped my ears. I said I could not bear such words now. 'That I am not Edward Rochester's bride is the least part of my woe,' I alleged: 'that I have wakened out of most glorious dreams, and found them all void and vain, as a horror I could bear and master; but that I must leave him decidedly, instantly, entirely, is intolerable. I cannot do it.'

But, then, a voice within me averred that I could do it and foretold that I should do it. I wrestled with my own resolution: I wanted to be weak that I might avoid the awful passage of further suffering I saw laid out for me; and Conscience, turned tyrant, held Passion by the throat, told her tauntingly, she had yet but dipped her dainty foot in the slough, and swore that with that arm of iron he would thrust her down to unsounded depths of agony.

'Let me be torn away, then!' I cried. 'Let another help me!'

'No; you shall tear yourself away, none shall help you: you shall yourself pluck out your right eye; yourself cut off your right hand: your heart shall be the victim, and you the priest to transfix it.'

I rose up suddenly, terror-struck at the solitude which so ruthless a judge haunted, at the silence which so awful a voice filled. My head swam as I stood erect. I perceived that I was sickening from excitement and inanition; neither meat nor drink had passed my lips that day, for I had taken no breakfast. And, with a strange pang, I now reflected that, long as I had been shut up here, no message had been sent to ask how I was, or to invite me to come down: not even little Adèle had tapped at the door; not even Mrs Fairfax had sought me. 'Friends always forget those whom fortune forsakes,' I murmured, as I undrew the bolt and passed out. I stumbled over an obstacle: my head was still dizzy, my sight was dim, and my limbs were feeble. I could not soon recover myself. I fell, but not on to the ground; an outstretched arm caught me. I looked up – I was supported by Mr Rochester, who sat in a chair across my chamber threshold.

'You come out at last,' he said. 'Well, I have been waiting for you long, and listening: yet not one movement have I heard, nor one sob: five minutes more of that death-like hush, and I should have forced the lock like a burglar. So you shun me? – you shut yourself up and grieve alone! I would rather you had come and upbraided me with vehemence. You are passionate: I expected a scene of some kind. I was prepared for the hot rain of tears; only I wanted them to be shed on my breast: now a senseless floor has received them, or your drenched handkerchief. But I err: you have not wept at all! I see a white cheek and a faded eye, but no trace of tears. I suppose, then, your heart has been weeping blood?

'Well, Jane! not a word of reproach? Nothing bitter – nothing poignant?

Nothing to cut a feeling or sting a passion? You sit quietly where I have placed you, and regard me with a weary, passive look.

'Jane, I never meant to wound you thus. If the man who had but one little ewe lamb that was dear to him as a daughter, that ate of his bread and drank of his cup, and lay in his bosom, had by some mistake slaughtered it at the shambles, he would not have rued his bloody blunder more than I now rue mine. Will you ever forgive me?'

Reader, I forgave him at the moment and on the spot. There was such deep remorse in his eye, such true pity in his tone, such manly energy in his manner; and besides, there was such unchanged love in his whole look and mien – I forgave him all: yet not in words, not outwardly; only at my heart's core.

'You know I am a scoundrel, Jane?' ere long he enquired wistfully – wondering, I suppose, at my continued silence and tameness, the result rather of weakness than of will.

'Yes, sir.'

'Then tell me so roundly and sharply – don't spare me.'

'I cannot: I am tired and sick. I want some water.' He heaved a sort of shuddering sigh, and taking me in his arms, carried me downstairs. At first I did not know to what room he had borne me- all was cloudy to my glazed sight: presently I felt the reviving warmth of a fire; for, summer as it was, I had become icy cold in my chamber. He put wine to my lips; I tasted it and revived; then I ate something he offered me, and was soon myself. I was in the library – sitting in his chair – he was quite near. 'If I could go out of life now, without too sharp a pang, it would be well for me,' I thought; 'then I should not have to make the effort of cracking my heart-strings in rending them from among Mr Rochester's. I must leave him, it appears. I do not want to leave him – I cannot leave him.'

'How are you now, Jane?'

'Much better, sir; I shall be well soon.'

'Taste the wine again, Jane.'

I obeyed him; then he put the glass on the table, stood before me, and looked at me attentively. Suddenly he turned away, with an inarticulate exclamation, full of passionate emotion of some kind; he walked fast through the room and came back; he stooped towards me as if to kiss me; but I remembered caresses were now forbidden. I turned my face away and put his aside.

'What! – How is this?' he exclaimed hastily. 'Oh, I know! you won't kiss the husband of Bertha Mason? You consider my arms filled and my embraces appropriated?'

'At any rate, there is neither room nor claim for me, sir.'

'Why, Jane? I will spare you the trouble of much talking; I will answer for you – Because I have a wife already, you would reply. I guess rightly?'

'Yes.'

'If you think so, you must have a strange opinion of me; you must regard me as a plotting profligate – a base and low rake who has been simulating disinterested love in order to draw you into a snare deliberately laid, and strip you of honour and rob you of self-respect. What do you say to that? I see you can say nothing: in the first place, you are faint still, and have enough to do to draw your breath; in the second place, you cannot yet accustom yourself to accuse and revile me, and besides, the floodgates of tears are opened, and they would rush out if you spoke much; and you have no desire to expostulate, to upbraid, to make a scene: you are thinking how *to act* – *talking* you consider is of no use. I know you – I am on my guard.'

'Sir, I do not wish to act against you,' I said; and my unsteady voice warned me to curtail my sentence.

'Not in *your* sense of the word, but in *mine* you are scheming to destroy me. You have as good as said that I am a married man – as a married man you will shun me, keep out of my way: just now you have refused to kiss me. You intend to make yourself a complete stranger to me: to live under this roof only as Adèle's governess; if ever I say a friendly word to you, if ever a friendly feeling inclines you again to me, you will say, "That man had nearly made me his mistress: I must be ice and rock to him"; and ice and rock you will accordingly become.'

I cleared and steadied my voice to reply: 'All is changed about me, sir; I must change too – there is no doubt of that; and to avoid fluctuations of feeling, and continual combats with recollections and associations, there is only one way – Adèle must have a new governess, sir.'

'Oh, Adèle will go to school – I have settled that already; nor do I mean to torment you with the hideous associations and recollections of Thornfield Hall – this accursed place – this tent of Achan – this insolent vault, offering the ghastliness of living death to the light of the open sky – this narrow stone hell, with its one real fiend, worse than a legion of such as we imagine. Jane, you shall not stay here, nor will I. I was wrong ever to bring you to Thornfield Hall, knowing as I did how it was haunted. I charged them to conceal from you, before I ever saw you, all knowledge of the curse of the place; merely because I feared Adèle never would have a governess to stay if she knew with what inmate she was housed, and my plans would not permit me to remove the maniac elsewhere – though I possess an old house, Ferndean Manor, even more retired and hidden than this, where I could have lodged her safely enough, had not a scruple about the unhealthiness of the situation, in the heart of a wood, made my conscience recoil from the arrangement. Probably those damp walls would soon have eased me of her charge: but to each villain his own vice; and mine is not a tendency to indirect assassination, even of what I most hate.

'Concealing the madwoman's neighbourhood from you, however, was something like covering a child with a cloak and laying it down near an upas tree: that demon's vicinage is poisoned, and always was. But I'll shut up Thornfield Hall: I'll nail up the front door and board the lower windows: I'll give Mrs Poole two hundred a year to live here with *my wife*, as you term that fearful hag: Grace will do much for money, and she shall have her son, the keeper at Grimsby Retreat, to bear her company and be at hand to give her aid in the paroxysms, when *my wife* is prompted by her familiar to burn people in their beds at night, to stab them, to bite their flesh from their bones, and so on – '

'Sir,' I interrupted him, 'you are inexorable for that unfortunate lady: you speak of her with hate – with vindictive antipathy. It is cruel – she cannot help being mad.'

'Jane, my little darling (so I will call you, for so you are), you don't know what you are talking about; you misjudge me again: it is not because she is mad I hate her. If you were mad, do you think I should hate you?'

'I do indeed, sir.'

'Then you are mistaken, and you know nothing about me, and nothing about the sort of love of which I am capable. Every atom of your flesh is as dear to me as my own: in pain and sickness it would still be dear. Your mind is my treasure, and if it were broken, it would be my treasure still: if you raved, my arms should confine you, and not a strait waistcoat – your grasp, even in fury, would have a charm for me: if you flew at me as wildly as that woman did this morning, I should receive you in an embrace, at least as fond as it would be restrictive. I should not shrink from you with disgust as I did from her: in your quiet moments you should have no watcher and no nurse but me; and I could hang over you with untiring tenderness, though you gave me no smile in return; and never weary of gazing into your eyes, though they had no longer a ray of recognition for me. But why do I follow that train of ideas? I was talking of removing you from Thornfield. All, you know, is prepared for prompt departure: tomorrow you shall go. I only ask you to endure one more night under this roof, Jane; and then, farewell to its miseries and terrors for ever! I have a place to repair to, which will be a secure sanctuary from hateful reminiscences, from unwelcome intrusion – even from falsehood and slander.'

'And take Adèle with you, sir,' I interrupted; 'she will be a companion for you.'

'What do you mean, Jane? I told you I would send Adèle to school; and what do I want with a child for a companion, and not my own child, a French dancer's bastard? Why do you importune me about her! I say, why do you assign Adèle to me for a companion?'

'You spoke of a retirement, sir; and retirement and solitude are dull: too dull for you.'

'Solitude! solitude!' he reiterated with irritation. 'I see I must come to an explanation. I don't know what sphynx-like expression is forming in your countenance. *You* are to share my solitude. Do you understand?'

I shook my head: it required a degree of courage, excited as he was becoming, even to risk that mute sign of dissent. He had been walking fast about the room, and he stopped, as if suddenly rooted to one spot. He looked at me long and hard: I turned my eyes from him, fixed them on the fire, and tried to assume and maintain a quiet, collected aspect.

'Now for the hitch in Jane's character,' he said at last, speaking more calmly than from his look I had expected him to speak. 'The reel of silk has run smoothly enough so far; but I always knew there would come a knot and a puzzle: here it is. Now for vexation, and exasperation, and endless trouble! By God! I long to exert a fraction of Samson's strength, and break the entanglement like tow!'

He recommenced his walk, but soon again stopped, and this time just before me.

'Jane! will you hear reason?' (he stooped and approached his lips to my ear); 'because, if you won't, I'll try violence.' His voice was hoarse; his look that of a man who is just about to burst an insufferable bond and plunge headlong into wild license. I saw that in another moment, and with one impetus of frenzy more, I should be able to do nothing with him. The present – the passing second of time – was all I had in which to control and restrain him: a movement of repulsion, flight, fear would have sealed my doom, and his. But I was not afraid: not in the least. I felt an inward power; a sense of influence, which supported me. The crisis was perilous; but not without its charm: such as the Indian, perhaps, feels when he slips over the rapid in his canoe. I took hold of his clenched hand, loosened the contorted fingers, and said to him, soothingly – 'Sit down; I'll talk to you as long as you like, and hear all you have to say, whether reasonable or unreasonable.'

He sat down: but he did not get leave to speak directly. I had been struggling with tears for some time: I had taken great pains to repress them, because I knew he would not like to see me weep. Now, however, I considered it well to let them flow as freely and as long as they liked. If the flood annoyed him, so much the better. So I gave way and cried heartily.

Soon I heard him earnestly entreating me to be composed. I said I could not while he was in such a passion.

'But I am not angry, Jane: I only love you too well; and you had steeled your little pale face with such a resolute, frozen look, I could not endure it. Hush, now, and wipe your eyes.'

His softened voice announced that he was subdued; so I, in my turn, became calm. Now he made an effort to rest his head on my shoulder, but I would not permit it. Then he would draw me to him: no.

'Jane! Jane!' he said, in such an accent of bitter sadness it thrilled along every nerve I had; 'you don't love me, then? It was only my station, and the rank of my wife, that you valued? Now that you think me disqualified to become your husband, you recoil from my touch as if I were some toad or ape.'

These words cut me: yet what could I do or say? I ought probably to have done or said nothing; but I was so tortured by a sense of remorse at thus hurting his feelings, I could not control the wish to drop balm where I had wounded.

'I *do* love you,' I said, 'more than ever: but I must not show or indulge the feeling: and this is the last time I must express it.'

'The last time, Jane! What! do you think you can live with me, and see me daily, and yet, if you still love me, be always cold and distant?'

'No, sir; that I am certain I could not; and therefore I see there is but one way: but you will be furious if I mention it.'

'Oh, mention it! If I storm, you have the art of weeping.'

'Mr Rochester, I must leave you.'

'For how long, Jane? For a few minutes, while you smooth your hair – which is somewhat dishevelled; and bathe your face – which looks feverish?'

'I must leave Adèle and Thornfield. I must part with you for my whole life: I must begin a new existence among strange faces and strange scenes.'

'Of course: I told you you should. I pass over the madness about parting from me. You mean you must become a part of me. As to the new existence, it is all right: you shall yet be my wife: I am not married. You shall be Mrs Rochester – both virtually and nominally. I shall keep only to you so long as you and I live. You shall go to a place I have in the south of France: a whitewashed villa on the shores of the Mediterranean. There you shall live a happy, and guarded, and most innocent life. Never fear that I wish to lure you into error – to make you my mistress. Why did you shake your head? Jane, you must be reasonable, or in truth I shall again become frantic.'

His voice and hand quivered: his large nostrils dilated; his eye blazed: still I dared to speak.

'Sir, your wife is living: that is a fact acknowledged this morning by yourself. If I lived with you as you desire, I should then be your mistress: to say otherwise is sophistical – is false.'

'Jane, I am not a gentle-tempered man – you forget that: I am not long-enduring; I am not cool and dispassionate. Out of pity to me and yourself, put your finger on my pulse, feel how it throbs, and – beware!'

He bared his wrist, and offered it to me: the blood was forsaking his cheek and lips, they were growing livid; I was distressed on all hands. To agitate him thus deeply, by a resistance he so abhorred, was cruel: to yield was out of the question. I did what human beings do instinctively when they are driven to utter extremity – looked for aid to one higher than man: the words 'God help me!' burst involuntarily from my lips.

'I am a fool!' cried Mr Rochester suddenly. 'I keep telling her I am not married, and do not explain to her why. I forget she knows nothing of the character of that woman, or of the circumstances attending my infernal union with her. Oh, I am certain Jane will agree with me in opinion, when she knows all that I know! Just put your hand in mine, Janet – that I may have the evidence of touch as well as sight, to prove you are near me – and I will in a few words show you the real state of the case. Can you listen to me?'

'Yes, sir; for hours if you will.'

'I ask only minutes. Jane, did you ever hear or know that I was not the eldest son of my house: that I had once a brother older than I?'

'I remember Mrs Fairfax told me so once.'

'And did you ever hear that my father was an avaricious, grasping man?'

'I have understood something to that effect.'

'Well, Jane, being so, it was his resolution to keep the property together; he could not bear the idea of dividing his estate and leaving me a fair portion: all, he resolved, should go to my brother, Rowland. Yet as little could he endure that a son of his should be a poor man. I must be provided for by a wealthy marriage. He sought me a partner betimes. Mr Mason, a West India planter and merchant, was his old acquaintance. He was certain his possessions were real and vast: he made enquiries. Mr Mason, he found, had a son and daughter; and he learned from him that he could and would give the latter a fortune of thirty thousand pounds: that sufficed. When I left college, I was sent out to Jamaica, to espouse a bride already courted for me. My father said nothing about her money; but he told me Miss Mason was the boast of Spanish Town for her beauty: and this was no lie. I found her a fine woman, in the style of Blanche Ingram: tall, dark, and majestic. Her family wished to secure me because I was of a good race; and so did she. They showed her to me in parties, splendidly dressed. I seldom saw her alone, and had very little private conversation with her. She flattered me, and lavishly displayed for my pleasure her charms and accomplishments. All the men in her circle seemed to admire her and envy me. I was dazzled, stimulated: my senses were excited; and being ignorant, raw, and inexperienced, I thought I loved her. There is no folly so besotted that the idiotic rivalries of society, the prurience, the rashness, the blindness of youth, will not hurry a man to its commission. Her relatives encouraged me; competitors piqued me; she allured me: a marriage was achieved almost before I knew where I was. Oh, I have no respect for myself when I think of that act! – an agony of inward contempt masters me. I never loved, I never esteemed, I did not even know her. I was not sure of the existence of one virtue in her nature: I had marked neither modesty, nor benevolence, nor candour, nor refinement in her mind or manners – and, I married her: gross, grovelling, mole-eyed blockhead that I was! With less sin I might have – But let me remember to whom I am speaking.

'My bride's mother I had never seen: I understood she was dead. The honey-moon over, I learned my mistake; she was only mad, and shut up in a lunatic asylum. There was a younger brother, too – a complete dumb idiot. The elder one, whom you have seen (and whom I cannot hate, whilst I abhor all his kindred, because he has some grains of affection in his feeble mind, shown in the continued interest he takes in his wretched sister, and also in a dog-like attachment he once bore me), will probably be in the same state one day. My father and my brother Rowland knew all this; but they thought only of the thirty thousand pounds, and joined in the plot against me.

'These were vile discoveries; but except for the treachery of concealment, I should have made them no subject of reproach to my wife, even when I found her nature wholly alien to mine, her tastes obnoxious to me, her cast of mind common, low, narrow, and singularly incapable of being led to anything higher, expanded to anything larger – when I found that I could not pass a single evening, nor even a single hour of the day with her in comfort; that kindly conversation could not be sustained between us, because whatever topic I started, immediately received from her a turn at once coarse and trite, perverse and imbecile – when I perceived that I should never have a quiet or settled household, because no servant would bear the continued outbreaks of her violent and unreasonable temper, or the vexations of her absurd, contradictory, exacting orders – even then I restrained myself: I eschewed upbraiding, I curtailed remonstrance; I tried to devour my repentance and disgust in secret; I repressed the deep antipathy I felt.

'Jane, I will not trouble you with abominable details: some strong words shall express what I have to say. I lived with that woman upstairs four years, and before that time she had tried me indeed: her character ripened and developed with frightful rapidity; her vices sprang up fast and rank: they were so strong, only cruelty could check them, and I would not use cruelty. What a pigmy intellect she had, and what giant propensities! How fearful were the curses those propensities entailed on me! Bertha Mason, the true daughter of an infamous mother, dragged me through all the hideous and degrading agonies which must attend a man bound to a wife at once intemperate and unchaste.

'My brother in the interval was dead, and at the end of the four years my father died too. I was rich enough now – yet poor to hideous indigence: a nature the most gross, impure, depraved I ever saw, was associated with mine, and called by the law and by society a part of me. And I could not rid myself of it by any legal proceedings: for the doctors now discovered that *my wife* was mad – her excesses had prematurely developed the germs of insanity. Jane, you don't like my narrative; you look almost sick – shall I defer the rest to another day?'

'No, sir, finish it now; I pity you – I do earnestly pity you.'

'Pity, Jane, from some people is a noxious and insulting sort of tribute, which one is justified in hurling back in the teeth of those who offer it; but that is the sort of pity native to callous, selfish hearts; it is a hybrid, egotistical pain at hearing of woes, crossed with ignorant contempt for those who have endured them. But that is not your pity, Jane; it is not the feeling of which your whole face is full at this moment – with which your eyes are now almost overflowing – with which your heart is heaving – with which your hand is trembling in mine. Your pity, my darling, is the suffering mother of love: its anguish is the very natal pang of the divine passion. I accept it, Jane; let the daughter have free advent – my arms wait to receive her.'

'Now, sir, proceed; what did you do when you found she was mad?'

'Jane, I approached the verge of despair; a remnant of self-respect was all that intervened between me and the gulf. In the eyes of the world, I was doubtless covered with grimy dishonour; but I resolved to be clean in my own sight – and to the last I repudiated the contamination of her crimes, and wrenched myself from connection with her mental defects. Still, society associated my name and person with hers; I yet saw her and heard her daily: something of her breath (faugh!) mixed with the air I breathed; and besides, I remembered I had once been her husband – that recollection was then, and is now, inexpressibly odious to me; moreover, I knew that while she lived I could never be the husband of another and better wife; and, though five years my senior (her family and her father had lied to me even in the particular of her age), she was likely to live as long as I, being as robust in frame as she was infirm in mind. Thus, at the age of twenty-six, I was hopeless.

'One night I had been awakened by her yells – (since the medical men had pronounced her mad, she had, of course, been shut up) – it was a fiery West Indian night; one of the description that frequently precede the hurricanes of those climates. Being unable to sleep in bed, I got up and opened the window. The air was like sulphur-steams – I could find no refreshment anywhere. Mosquitoes came buzzing in and hummed sullenly round the room; the sea, which I could hear from thence, rumbled dull like an earthquake – black clouds were casting up over it; the moon was setting in the waves, broad and red, like a hot cannon ball – she threw her last bloody glance over a world quivering with the ferment of tempest. I was physically influenced by the atmosphere and scene, and my ears were filled with the curses the maniac still shrieked out; wherein she momentarily mingled my name with such a tone of demon-hate, with such language! – no professed harlot ever had a fouler vocabulary than she: though two rooms off, I heard every word – the thin partitions of the West India house opposing but slight obstruction to her wolfish cries.

' "This life," said I at last, "is hell: this is the air – those are the sounds of the bottomless pit! I have a right to deliver myself from it if I can. The sufferings of this mortal state will leave me with the heavy flesh that now cumbers my soul. Of the fanatic's burning eternity I have no fear: there is not a future state worse than this present one – let me break away, and go home to God!"

'I said this whilst I knelt down at, and unlocked a trunk which contained a brace of loaded pistols: I meant to shoot myself. I only entertained the intention for a moment; for, not being insane, the crisis of exquisite and unalloyed despair, which had originated the wish and design of self-destruction, was past in a second.

'A wind fresh from Europe blew over the ocean and rushed through the open casement: the storm broke, streamed, thundered, blazed, and the air grew pure. I then framed and fixed a resolution. While I walked under the dripping orange trees of my wet garden, and amongst its drenched pomegranates and pineapples, and while the refulgent dawn of the tropics kindled round me – I reasoned thus, Jane – and now listen; for it was true Wisdom that consoled me in that hour, and showed me the right path to follow.

'The sweet wind from Europe was still whispering in the refreshed leaves, and the Atlantic was thundering in glorious liberty; my heart, dried up and scorched for a long time, swelled to the tone, and filled with living blood – my being longed for renewal – my soul thirsted for a pure draught. I saw hope revive – and felt regeneration possible. From a flowery arch at the bottom of my garden I gazed over the sea – bluer than the sky: the old world was beyond; clear prospects opened thus: ' "Go," said Hope, "and live again in Europe: there it is not known what a sullied name you bear, nor what a filthy burden is bound to you. You may take the maniac with you to England; confine her with due attendance and precautions at Thornfield: then travel yourself to what clime you will, and form what new tie you like. That woman, who has so abused your long-suffering, so sullied your name, so outraged your honour, so blighted your youth, is not your wife, nor are you her husband. See that she is cared for as her condition demands, and you have done all that God and humanity require of you. Let her identity, her connection with yourself, be buried in oblivion: you are bound to impart them to no living being. Place her in safety and comfort: shelter her degradation with secrecy, and leave her."

'I acted precisely on this suggestion. My father and brother had not made my marriage known to their acquaintance; because, in the very first letter I wrote to apprise them of the union – having already begun to experience extreme disgust of its consequences, and, from the family character and constitution, seeing a hideous future opening to me – I added an urgent charge to keep it secret: and very soon the infamous conduct of the wife my father had selected for me was such as to make him blush to own her as his daughter-in-law. Far from desiring to publish the connection, he became as anxious to conceal it as myself.

'To England, then, I conveyed her; a fearful voyage I had with such a monster in the vessel. Glad was I when I at last got her to Thornfield, and saw her safely lodged in that third-storey room, of whose secret inner cabinet she has now for ten years made a wild beast's den – a goblin's cell. I had some trouble in finding an attendant for her, as it was necessary to select one on whose fidelity dependence could be placed; for her ravings would inevitably betray my secret: besides, she had lucid intervals of days – sometimes weeks – which she filled up with abuse of me. At last I hired Grace Poole from the Grimsby Retreat. She and the surgeon, Carter (who dressed Mason's wounds that night he was stabbed and worried), are the only two I have ever admitted to my confidence. Mrs Fairfax may indeed have suspected something, but she could have gained no precise knowledge as to facts. Grace has, on the whole, proved a good keeper; though, owing partly to a fault of her own, of which it appears nothing can cure her, and which is incident to her harassing profession, her vigilance has been more than once lulled and baffled. The lunatic is both cunning and malignant; she has never failed to take advantage of her guardian's temporary lapses; once to secrete the knife with which she stabbed her brother, and twice to possess herself of the key of her cell, and issue therefrom in the night-time. On the first of these occasions, she perpetrated the attempt to burn me in my bed; on the second, she paid that ghastly visit to you. I thank Providence, who watched over you, that she then spent her fury on your wedding apparel, which perhaps brought back vague reminiscences of her own bridal days: but on what might have happened, I cannot endure to reflect. When I think of the thing which flew at my throat this morning, hanging its black and scarlet visage over the nest of my dove, my blood curdles – '

'And what, sir,' I asked, while he paused, 'did you do when you had settled her here? Where did you go?'

'What did I do, Jane? I transformed myself into a will-o'-the-wisp. Where did I go? I pursued wanderings as wild as those of the March-spirit. I sought the Continent, and went devious through all its lands. My fixed desire was to seek and find a good and intelligent woman, whom I could love: a contrast to the fury I left at Thornfield – '

'But you could not marry, sir.'

'I had determined and was convinced that I could and ought. It was not my original intention to deceive, as I have deceived you. I meant to tell my tale plainly, and make my proposals openly: and it appeared to me so absolutely rational that I should be considered free to love and be loved, I never doubted some woman might be found willing and able to understand my case and accept me, in spite of the curse with which I was burdened.'

'Well, sir?'

'When you are inquisitive, Jane, you always make me smile. You open your eyes like an eager bird, and make every now and then a restless movement, as if answers in speech did not flow fast enough for you, and you wanted to read the tablet of one's heart. But before I go on, tell me what you mean by your "Well, sir?" It is a small phrase very frequent with you; and which many a time has drawn me on and on through interminable talk: I don't very well know why.'

'I mean, What next? How did you proceed? What came of such an event?'

'Precisely! and what do you wish to know now?'

'Whether you found anyone you liked: whether you asked her to marry you; and what she said.'

'I can tell you whether I found anyone I liked, and whether I asked her to marry me: but what she said is yet to be recorded in the book of Fate. For ten long years I roved about, living first in one capital, then another: sometimes in St Petersburg; oftener in Paris; occasionally in Rome, Naples, and Florence. Provided with plenty of money and the passport of an old name, I could choose my own society: no circles were closed against me. I sought my ideal of a woman amongst English ladies, French countesses, Italian signoras, and German gräfinnen. I could not find her. Sometimes, for a fleeting moment, I thought I caught a glance, heard a tone, beheld a form, which announced the realisation of my dream: but I was presently undeceived. You are not to suppose that I desired perfection, either of mind or person. I longed only for what suited me – for the antipodes of the Creole: and I longed vainly. Amongst them all I found not one whom, had I been ever so free, I – warned as I was of the risks, the horrors, the loathings of incongruous unions – would have asked to marry me. Disappointment made me reckless. I tried dissipation – never debauchery: that I hated, and hate. That was my Indian Messalina's attribute: rooted disgust at it and her restrained me much, even in pleasure. Any enjoyment that bordered on riot seemed to approach me to her and her vices, and I eschewed it.

'Yet I could not live alone; so I tried the companionship of mistresses. The first I chose was Céline Varens – another of those steps which make a man spurn himself when he recalls them. You already know what she was, and how my liaison with her terminated. She had two successors: an Italian, Giacinta, and a German, Clara; both considered singularly handsome. What was their beauty to me in a few weeks? Giacinta was unprincipled and violent: I tired of her in three months. Clara was honest and quiet; but heavy, mindless, and unimpressible: not one whit to my taste. I was glad to give her a sufficient sum to set her up in a good line of business, and so get decently rid of her. But, Jane, I see by your face you are not forming a very favourable opinion of me just now. You think me an unfeeling, loose-principled rake: don't you?'

'I don't like you so well as I have done sometimes, indeed, sir. Did it not seem to you in the least wrong to live in that way, first with one mistress and then another? You talk of it as a mere matter of course.'

'It was with me; and I did not like it. It was a grovelling fashion of existence: I should never like to return to it. Hiring a mistress is the next worse thing to buying a slave: both are often by nature, and always by position, inferior: and to live familiarly with inferiors is degrading. I now hate the recollection of the time I passed with Céline, Giacinta, and Clara.'

I felt the truth of these words; and I drew from them the certain inference, that if I were so far to forget myself and all the teaching that had ever been instilled into me, as – under any pretext – with any justification – through any temptation – to become the successor of these poor girls, he would one day regard me with the same feeling which now in his mind desecrated their memory. I did not give utterance to this conviction: it was enough to feel it. I impressed it on my heart, that it might remain there to serve me as aid in the time of trial.

'Now, Jane, why don't you say "Well, sir?" I have not done. You are looking grave. You disapprove of me still, I see. But let me come to the point. Last January, rid of all mistresses – in a harsh, bitter frame of mind, the result of a useless, roving, lonely life – corroded with disappointment, sourly disposed against all men, and especially against all *woman*kind (for I began to regard the notion of an intellectual, faithful, loving woman as a mere dream), recalled by business, I came back to England.

'On a frosty winter afternoon, I rode in sight of Thornfield Hall. Abhorred spot! I expected no peace – no pleasure there. On a stile in Hay Lane I saw a quiet little figure sitting by itself. I passed it as negligently as I did the pollard willow opposite to it: I had no presentiment of what it would be to me; no inward warning that the arbitress of my life – my genius for good or evil – waited there in humble guise. I did not know it, even when, on the occasion of Mesrour's accident, it came up and gravely offered me help. Childish and slender creature! It seemed as if a linnet had hopped to my foot and proposed to bear me on its tiny wing. I was surly; but the thing would not go: it stood by me with strange perseverance, and looked and spoke with a sort of authority. I must be aided, and by that hand: and aided I was.

'When once I had pressed the frail shoulder, something new – a fresh sap and sense – stole into my frame. It was well I had learnt that this elf must return to me – that it belonged to my house down below – or I could not have felt it pass away from under my hand, and seen it vanish behind the dim hedge, without singular regret. I heard you come home that night, Jane, though probably you were not aware that I thought of you or watched for you. The next day I observed you – myself unseen – for half an hour, while you played with Adèle in the gallery. It was a snowy day, I recollect, and you could not go out of doors. I was in my room; the door was ajar: I could both listen and watch. Adèle claimed your outward attention for a while; yet I fancied your thoughts were elsewhere: but you were very patient with her, my little Jane; you talked to her and amused her a long time. When at last she left you, you lapsed at once into deep reverie: you betook yourself slowly to pace the gallery. Now and then, in passing a casement, you glanced out at the thick-falling snow; you listened to the sobbing wind, and again you paced gently on and dreamed. I think those day visions were not dark: there was a pleasurable illumination in your eye occasionally, a soft excitement in your aspect, which told of no bitter, bilious, hypochondriac brooding: your look revealed rather the sweet musings of youth when its spirit follows on willing wings the flight of Hope up and on to an ideal heaven. The voice of Mrs Fairfax, speaking to a servant in the hall, wakened you: and how curiously you smiled to and at yourself, Janet! There was much sense in your smile: it was very shrewd, and seemed to make light of your own abstraction. It seemed to say – "My fine visions are all very well, but I must not forget they are absolutely unreal. I have a rosy sky and a green flowery Eden in my brain; but without, I am perfectly aware, lies at my feet a rough tract to travel, and around me gather black tempests to encounter." You ran downstairs and demanded of Mrs Fairfax some occupation: the weekly house accounts to make up, or something of that sort, I think it was. I was vexed with you for getting out of my sight.

'Impatiently I waited for evening, when I might summon you to my presence. An unusual – to me – a perfectly new character I suspected was yours: I desired to search it deeper and know it better. You entered the room with a look and air at once shy and independent: you were quaintly dressed – much as you are now. I made you talk: ere long I found you full of strange contrasts. Your garb and manner were restricted by rule; your air was often diffident, and altogether that of one refined by nature, but absolutely unused to society, and a good deal afraid of making herself disadvantageously conspicuous by some solecism or blunder; yet when addressed, you lifted a keen, a daring, and a glowing eye to your interlocutor's face: there was penetration and power in each glance you gave; when plied by close questions, you found ready and round answers. Very soon you seemed to get used to me: I believe you felt the existence of sympathy between you and your grim and cross master, Jane; for it was astonishing to see how quickly a certain pleasant ease tranquillised your manner: snarl as I would, you showed no surprise, fear, annoyance, or displeasure at my moroseness; you watched me, and now and then smiled at me with a simple yet sagacious grace I cannot describe. I was at once content and stimulated with what I saw: I liked what I had seen, and wished to see more. Yet, for a long time, I treated you distantly, and sought your company rarely. I was an intellectual epicure, and wished to prolong the gratification of making this novel and piquant acquaintance: besides, I was for a while troubled with a haunting fear that if I handled the flower freely its bloom would fade – the sweet charm of freshness would leave it. I did not then know that it was no transitory blossom, but rather the radiant resemblance of one, cut in an indestructible gem. Moreover, I wished to see whether you would seek me if I shunned you – but you did not; you kept in the schoolroom as still as your own desk and easel; if by chance I met you, you passed me as soon, and with as little token of recognition, as was consistent with respect. Your habitual expression in those days, Jane, was a thoughtful look; not despondent, for you were not sickly; but not buoyant, for you had little hope, and no actual pleasure. I wondered what you thought of me, or if you ever thought of me, and resolved to find this out.

'I resumed my notice of you. There was something glad in your glance, and genial in your manner, when you conversed: I saw you had a social heart; it was the silent schoolroom – it was the tedium of your life – that made you mournful. I permitted myself the delight of being kind to you; kindness stirred emotion soon: your face became soft in expression, your tones gentle; I liked my name pronounced by your lips in a grateful happy accent. I used to enjoy a chance meeting with you, Jane, at this time: there was a curious hesitation in your manner: you glanced at me with a slight trouble – a hovering doubt: you did not know what my caprice might be – whether I was going to play the master and be stern, or the friend and be benignant. I was now too fond of you often to simulate the first whim; and, when I stretched my hand out cordially, such bloom and light and bliss rose to your young, wistful features, I had much ado often to avoid straining you then and there to my heart.'

'Don't talk any more of those days, sir,' I interrupted, furtively dashing away some tears from my eyes; his language was torture to me; for I knew what I must do – and do soon – and all these reminiscences, and these revelations of his feelings, only made my work more difficult.

'No, Jane,' he returned: 'what necessity is there to dwell on the Past, when the Present is so much surer – the Future so much brighter?'

I shuddered to hear the infatuated assertion.

'You see now how the case stands – do you not?' he continued. 'After a youth and manhood passed half in unutterable misery and half in dreary solitude, I have for the first time found what I can truly love – I have found *you*. You are my sympathy – my better self – my good angel. I am bound to you with a strong attachment. I think you good, gifted, lovely: a fervent, a solemn passion is conceived in my heart; it leans to you, draws you to my centre and spring of life, wraps my existence about you, and, kindling in pure, powerful flame, fuses you and me in one.

'It was because I felt and knew this, that I resolved to marry you. To tell me that I had already a wife is empty mockery: you know now that I had but a hideous demon. I was wrong to attempt to deceive you; but I feared a stubbornness that exists in your character. I feared early instilled prejudice: I wanted to have you safe before hazarding confidences. This was cowardly: I should have appealed to your nobleness and magnanimity at first, as I do now – opened to you plainly my life of agony – described to you my hunger and thirst after a higher and worthier existence – shown to you, not my *resolution* (that word is weak), but my resistless *bent* to love faithfully and well, where I am faithfully and well loved in return. Then I should have asked you to accept my pledge of fidelity and to give me yours. Jane – give it me now.'

A pause.

'Why are you silent, Jane?'

I was experiencing an ordeal: a hand of fiery iron grasped my vitals. Terrible moment: full of struggle, blackness, burning! Not a human being that ever lived could wish to be loved better than I was loved; and him who thus loved me I absolutely worshipped: and I must renounce love and idol. One drear word comprised my intolerable duty – 'Depart!'

'Jane, you understand what I want of you? Just this promise – "I will be yours, Mr Rochester." '

'Mr Rochester, I will *not* be yours.'

Another long silence.

'Jane!' recommenced he, with a gentleness that broke me down with grief, and turned me stone-cold with ominous terror – for this still voice was the pant of a lion rising – 'Jane, do you mean to go one way in the world, and to let me go another?'

'I do.'

'Jane' (bending towards and embracing me), 'do you mean it now?'

'I do.'

'And now?' softly kissing my forehead and cheek.

'I do,' extricating myself from restraint rapidly and completely.

'Oh, Jane, this is bitter! This – this is wicked. It would not be wicked to love me.'

'It would to obey you.'

A wild look raised his brows – crossed his features: he rose; but he forbore yet. I laid my hand on the back of a chair for support: I shook, I feared – but I resolved.

'One instant, Jane. Give one glance to my horrible life when you are gone. All happiness will be torn away with you. What then is left? For a wife I have but the maniac upstairs: as well might you refer me to some corpse in yonder churchyard. What shall I do, Jane? Where turn for a companion and for some hope?'

'Do as I do: trust in God and yourself. Believe in heaven. Hope to meet again there.'

'Then you will not yield?'

'No.'

'Then you condemn me to live wretched and to die accursed?' His voice rose.

'I advise you to live sinless, and I wish you to die tranquil.'

'Then you snatch love and innocence from me? You fling me back on lust for a passion – vice for an occupation?'

'Mr Rochester, I no more assign this fate to you than I grasp at it for myself. We were born to strive and endure – you as well as I: do so. You will forget me before I forget you.'

'You make me a liar by such language: you sully my honour. I declared I could not change: you tell me to my face I shall change soon. And what a distortion in your judgement, what a perversity in your ideas, is proved by your conduct! Is it better to drive a fellow-creature to despair than to transgress a mere human law, no man being injured by the breach? for you have neither relatives nor acquaintances whom you need fear to offend by living with me?'

This was true: and while he spoke my very conscience and reason turned traitors against me, and charged me with crime in resisting him. They spoke almost as loud as Feeling: and that clamoured wildly. 'Oh, comply!' it said. 'Think of his misery; think of his danger – look at his state when left alone; remember his headlong nature; consider the recklessness following on despair – soothe him; save him; love him; tell him you love him and will be his. Who in the world cares for *you*? or who will be injured by what you do?'

Still indomitable was the reply – '*I* care for myself. The more solitary, the more friendless, the more unsustained I am, the more I will respect myself. I will keep the law given by God; sanctioned by man. I will hold to the principles received by me when I was sane, and not mad – as I am now. Laws and principles are not for the times when there is no temptation: they are for such moments as this, when body and soul rise in mutiny against their rigour; stringent are they; inviolate they shall be. If at my individual convenience I might break them, what would be their worth? They have a worth – so I have always believed; and if I cannot believe it now, it is because I am insane – quite insane: with my veins running fire, and my heart beating faster than I can count its throbs. Preconceived opinions, foregone determinations, are all I have at this hour to stand by: there I plant my foot.'

I did. Mr Rochester, reading my countenance, saw I had done so. His fury was wrought to the highest: he must yield to it for a moment, whatever followed; he crossed the floor and seized my arm and grasped my waist. He seemed to devour me with his flaming glance: physically, I felt, at the moment, powerless as stubble exposed to the draught and glow of a furnace: mentally, I still possessed my soul, and with it the certainty of ultimate safety. The soul, fortunately, has an Interpreter – often an unconscious, but still truthful interpreter – in the eye. My eye rose to his; and while I looked in his fierce face I gave an involuntary sigh; his grip was painful, and my overtaxed strength almost exhausted.

'Never,' said he, as he ground his teeth, 'never was anything at once so frail and so indomitable. A mere reed she feels in my hand!' (And he shook me with the force of his hold.) 'I could bend her with my finger and thumb: and what good would it do if I bent, if I uptore, if I crushed her? Consider that eye: consider the resolute, wild, free thing looking out of it, defying me, with more than courage – with a stern triumph. Whatever I do with its cage, I cannot get at it – the savage, beautiful creature! If I tear, if I rend the slight prison, my outrage will only let the captive loose. Conqueror I might be of the house; but the inmate would escape to heaven before I could call myself possessor of its clay dwelling-place. And it is you, spirit – with will and energy, and virtue and purity – that I want: not alone your brittle frame. Of yourself you could come with soft flight and nestle against my heart, if you would: seized against your will, you will elude the grasp like an essence – you will vanish ere I inhale your fragrance. Oh! come, Jane, come!'

As he said this, he released me from his clutch, and only looked at me. The look was far worse to resist than the frantic strain: only an idiot, however, would have succumbed now. I had dared and baffled his fury; I must elude his sorrow: I retired to the door.

'You are going, Jane?'

'I am going, sir.'

'You are leaving me?'

'Yes.'

'You will not come? You will not be my comforter, my rescuer? My deep love, my wild woe, my frantic prayer, are all nothing to you?'

What unutterable pathos was in his voice! How hard it was to reiterate firmly, 'I am going.'

'Jane!'

'Mr Rochester!'

'Withdraw, then, I consent; but remember, you leave me here in anguish. Go up to your own room; think over all I have said, and, Jane, cast a glance on my sufferings – think of me.'

He turned away; he threw himself on his face on the sofa. 'Oh, Jane! my hope – my love – my life!' broke in anguish from his lips. Then came a deep, strong sob.

I had already gained the door; but, reader, I walked back – walked back as determinedly as I had retreated. I knelt down by him; I turned his face from the cushion to me; I kissed his cheek; I smoothed his hair with my hand.

'God bless you, my dear master!' I said. 'God keep you from harm and wrong – direct you, solace you – reward you well for your past kindness to me.'

'Little Jane's love would have been my best reward,' he answered; 'without it, my heart is broken. But Jane will give me her love: yes – nobly, generously.'

Up the blood rushed to his face; forth flashed the fire from his eyes; erect he sprang; he held his arms out; but I evaded the embrace, and at once quitted the room.

'Farewell!' was the cry of my heart as I left him. Despair added, 'Farewell for ever!'

That night I never thought to sleep; but a slumber fell on me as soon as I lay down in bed. I was transported in thought to the scenes of childhood: I dreamt I lay in the red-room at Gateshead; that the night was dark, and my mind impressed with strange fears. The light that long ago had struck me into syncope, recalled in this vision, seemed glidingly to mount the wall, and tremblingly to pause in the centre of the obscured ceiling. I lifted up my head to look: the roof resolved to clouds, high and dim; the gleam was such as the moon imparts to vapours she is about to sever. I watched her come – watched with the strangest anticipation; as though some word of doom were to be written on her disk. She broke forth as never moon yet burst from cloud: a hand first penetrated the sable folds and waved them away; then, not a moon, but a white human form shone in the azure, inclining a glorious brow earthward. It gazed and gazed on me. It spoke to my spirit: immeasurably distant was the tone, yet so near, it whispered in my heart – 'My daughter, flee temptation.'

'Mother, I will.'

So I answered after I had waked from the trance-like dream. It was yet night, but July nights are short: soon after midnight, dawn comes. 'It cannot be too early to commence the task I have to fulfil,' thought I. I rose: I was dressed; for I had taken off nothing but my shoes. I knew where to find in my drawers some linen, a locket, a ring. In seeking these articles, I encountered the beads of a pearl necklace Mr Rochester had forced me to accept a few days ago. I left that; it was not mine: it was the visionary bride's who had melted in air. The other articles I made up in a parcel; my purse, containing twenty shillings (it was all I had), I put in my pocket: I tied on my straw bonnet, pinned my shawl, took the parcel and my slippers, which I would not put on yet, and stole from my room.

'Farewell, kind Mrs Fairfax!' I whispered, as glided past her door. 'Farewell, my darling Adèle!' I said, as I glanced towards the nursery. No thought could be admitted of entering to embrace her. I had to deceive a fine ear: for aught I knew it might now be listening.

I would have got past Mr Rochester's chamber without a pause; but my heart momentarily stopping its beat at that threshold, my foot was forced to stop also. No sleep was there: the inmate was walking restlessly from wall to wall; and again and again he sighed while I listened. There was a heaven – a temporary heaven – in this room for me, if I chose: I had but to go in and to say – 'Mr Rochester, I will love you and live with you through life till death,' and a fount of rapture would spring to my lips. I thought of this.

That kind master, who could not sleep now, was waiting with impatience for day. He would send for me in the morning; I should be gone. He would have me sought for: vainly. He would feel himself forsaken; his love rejected: he would suffer; perhaps grow desperate. I thought of this too. My hand moved towards the lock: I caught it back, and glided on.

Drearily I wound my way downstairs: I knew what I had to do, and I did it mechanically. I sought the key of the side-door in the kitchen; I sought, too, a phial of oil and a feather; I oiled the key and the lock. I got some water, I got some bread: for perhaps I should have to walk far; and my strength, sorely shaken of late, must not break down. All this I did without one sound. I opened the door, passed out, shut it softly. Dim dawn glimmered in the yard. The great gates were closed and locked; but a wicket in one of them was only latched. Through that I departed, it, too, I shut; and now I was out of Thornfield.

A mile off, beyond the fields, lay a road which stretched in the contrary direction to Millcote; a road I had never travelled, but often noticed, and wondered where it led: thither I bent my steps. No reflection was to be allowed now: not one glance was to be cast back; not even one forward. Not one thought was to be given either to the past or the future. The first was a page so heavenly sweet – so deadly sad – that to read one line of it would dissolve my courage and break down my energy. The last was an awful blank: something like the world when the deluge was gone by.

I skirted fields, and hedges, and lanes till after sunrise. I believe it was a lovely summer morning: I know my shoes, which I had put on when I left the house, were soon wet with dew. But I looked neither to rising sun, nor smiling sky, nor wakening nature. He who is taken out to pass through a fair scene to the scaffold, thinks not of the flowers that smile on his road, but of the block and axe-edge; of the disseverment of bone and vein; of the grave gaping at the end: and I thought of drear flight and homeless wandering – and oh! with agony I thought of what I left. I could not help it. I thought of him now – in his room – watching the sunrise; hoping I should soon come to say I would stay with him and be his. I longed to be his; I panted to return: it was not too late; I could yet spare him the bitter pang of bereavement. As yet my flight, I was sure, was undiscovered. I could go back and be his comforter – his pride; his redeemer from misery, perhaps from ruin. Oh, that fear of his self-abandonment – far worse than my abandonment – how it goaded me! It was a barbed arrowhead in my breast; it tore me when I tried to extract it; it sickened me when remembrance thrust it farther in. Birds began singing in brake and copse: birds were faithful to their mates; birds were emblems of love What was I? In the midst of my pain of heart and frantic effort of principle, I abhorred myself. I had no solace from self-approbation: none even from self-respect. I had injured – wounded – left my master. I was hateful in my own eyes. Still I could not turn, nor retrace one step. God must have led me on. As to my own will or conscience, impassioned grief had trampled one and stifled the other. I was weeping wildly as I walked along my solitary way: fast, fast I went like one delirious. A weakness, beginning inwardly, extending to the limbs, seized me, and I fell: I lay on the ground some minutes, pressing my face to the wet turf. I had some fear – or hope – that here I should die: but I was soon up; crawling forwards on my hands and knees, and then again raised to my feet – as eager and as determined as ever to reach the road.

When I got there, I was forced to sit to rest me under the hedge; and while I sat, I heard wheels, and saw a coach come on. I stood up and lifted my hand; it stopped. I asked where it was going: the driver named a place a long way off, and where I was sure Mr Rochester had no connections. I asked for what sum he would take me there; he said thirty shillings; I answered I had but twenty; well, he would try to make it do. He further gave me leave to get into the inside, as the vehicle was empty: I entered, was shut in, and it rolled on its way.

Gentle reader, may you never feel what I then felt! May your eyes never shed such stormy, scalding, heart-wrung tears as poured from mine. May you never appeal to Heaven in prayers so hopeless and so agonised as in that hour left my lips; for never may you, like me, dread to be the instrument of evil to what you wholly love.

## *Chapter 28*

Two days are passed. It is a summer evening; the coachman has set me down at a place called Whitcross; he could take me no farther for the sum I had given, and I was not possessed of another shilling in the world. The coach is a mile off by this time; I am alone. At this moment I discover that I forgot to take my parcel out of the pocket of the coach, where I had placed it for safety; there it remains, there it must remain; and now, I am absolutely destitute.

Whitcross is no town, nor even a hamlet; it is but a stone pillar set up where four roads meet: whitewashed, I suppose, to be more obvious at a distance and in darkness. Four arms spring from its summit: the nearest town to which these point is, according to the inscription, distant ten miles; the farthest, above twenty. From the well-known names of these towns I learn in what county I have lighted; a north-midland shire, dusk with moorland, ridged with mountain: this I see. There are great moors behind and on each hand of me; there are waves of mountains far beyond that deep valley at my feet. The population here must be thin, and I see no passengers on these roads: they stretch out east, west, north, and south – white, broad, lonely; they are all cut in the moor, and the heather grows deep and wild to their very verge. Yet a chance traveller might pass by; and I wish no eye to see me now: strangers would wonder what I am doing, lingering here at the signpost, evidently objectless and lost. I might be questioned: I could give no answer but what would sound incredible and excite suspicion. Not a tie holds me to human society at this moment – not a charm or hope calls me where my fellow-creatures are – none that saw me would have a kind thought or a good wish for me. I have no relative but the universal mother, Nature: I will seek her breast and ask repose.

I struck straight into the heath; I held on to a hollow I saw deeply furrowing the brown moorside; I waded knee-deep in its dark growth; I turned with its turnings, and finding a moss-blackened granite crag in a hidden angle, I sat down under it. High banks of moor were about me; the crag protected my head: the sky was over that.

Some time passed before I felt tranquil even here: I had a vague dread that wild cattle might be near, or that some sportsman or poacher might discover me. If a gust of wind swept the waste, I looked up, fearing it was the rush of a bull; if a plover whistled, I imagined it a man. Finding my apprehensions unfounded, however, and calmed by the deep silence that reigned as evening declined at nightfall, I took confidence. As yet I had not thought; I had only listened, watched, dreaded; now I regained the faculty of reflection.

What was I to do? Where to go? Oh, intolerable questions, when I could do nothing and go nowhere! – when a long way must yet be measured by my weary, trembling limbs before I could reach human habitation – when cold charity must be entreated before I could get a lodging: reluctant sympathy importuned, almost certain repulse incurred, before my tale could be listened to, or one of my wants relieved!

I touched the heath: it was dry, and yet warm with the heat of the summer day. I looked at the sky; it was pure: a kindly star twinkled just above the chasm ridge. The day fell, but with propitious softness; no breeze whispered. Nature seemed to me benign and good; I thought she loved me, outcast as I was; and I, who from man could anticipate only mistrust, rejection, insult, clung to her with filial fondness. Tonight, at least, I would be her guest, as I was her child: my mother would lodge me without money and without price. I had one morsel of bread yet: the remnant of a roll I had bought in a town we passed through at noon with a stray penny – my last coin. I saw ripe bilberries gleaming here and there, like jet beads in the heath: I gathered a handful and ate them with the bread. My hunger, sharp before, was, if not satisfied, appeased by this hermit's meal. I said my evening prayers at its conclusion, and then chose my couch.

Beside the crag the heath was very deep: when I lay down my feet were buried in it; rising high on each side, it left only a narrow space for the night-air to invade. I folded my shawl double, and spread it over me for a coverlet; a low, mossy swell was my pillow. Thus lodged, I was not, at least at the commencement of the night, cold.

My rest might have been blissful enough, only a sad heart broke it. It plained of its gaping wounds, its inward bleeding, its riven chords. It trembled for Mr Rochester and his doom; it bemoaned him with bitter pity; it demanded him with ceaseless longing; and, impotent as a bird with both wings broken, it still quivered its shattered pinions in vain attempts to seek him.

Worn out with this torture of thought, I rose to my knees. Night was come, and her planets were risen: a safe, still night: too serene for the companionship of fear. We know that God is everywhere; but certainly we feel His presence most when His works are on the grandest scale spread before us; and it is in the unclouded night-sky, where His worlds wheel their silent course, that we read clearest His infinitude, His omnipotence, His omnipresence. I had risen to my knees to pray for Mr Rochester. Looking up, I, with tear-dimmed eyes, saw the mighty Milky Way. Remembering what it was – what countless systems there swept space like a soft trace of light – I felt the might and strength of God. Sure was I of His efficiency to save what He had made: convinced I grew that neither earth should perish, nor one of the souls it treasured. I turned my prayer to thanksgiving: the Source of Life was also the Saviour of spirits. Mr Rochester was safe: he was God's, and by God would he be guarded. I again nestled to the breast of the hill and ere long in sleep forgot sorrow.

But next day, Want came to me pale and bare. Long after the little birds had left their nests; long after bees had come in the sweet prime of day to gather the heath honey before the dew was dried – when the long morning shadows were curtailed, and the sun filled earth and sky – I got up, and I looked round me.

What a still, hot, perfect day! What a golden desert this spreading moor! Everywhere sunshine. I wished I could live in it and on it. I saw a lizard run over the crag; I saw a bee busy among the sweet bilberries. I would fain at the moment have become bee or lizard, that I might have found fitting nutriment, permanent shelter here. But I was a human being, and had a human being's wants: I must not linger where there was nothing to supply them. I rose; I looked back at the bed I had left. Hopeless of the future, I wished but this – that my Maker had that night thought good to require my soul of me while I slept; and that this weary frame, absolved by death from further conflict with fate, had now but to decay quietly, and mingle in peace with the soil of this wilderness. Life, however, was yet in my possession, with all its requirements, and pains, and responsibilities. The burden must be carried; the want provided for; the suffering endured; the responsibility fulfilled. I set out.

Whitcross regained, I followed a road which led from the sun, now fervent and high. By no other circumstance had I will to decide my choice. I walked a long time, and when I thought I had nearly done enough, and might conscientiously yield to the fatigue that almost overpowered me – might relax this forced action, and, sitting down on a stone I saw near, submit resistlessly to the apathy that clogged heart and limb – I heard a bell chime – a church bell.

I turned in the direction of the sound, and there, amongst the romantic hills, whose changes and aspect I had ceased to note an hour ago, I saw a hamlet and a spire. All the valley at my right hand was full of pasture-fields, and cornfields, and wood; and a glittering stream ran zigzag through the varied shades of green, the mellowing grain, the sombre woodland, the clear and sunny lea. Recalled by the rumbling of wheels to the road before me, I saw a heavily-laden waggon labouring up the hill, and not far beyond were two cows and their drover. Human life and human labour were near. I must struggle on: strive to live and bend to toil like the rest.

About two o'clock p.m. I entered the village. At the bottom of its one street there was a little shop with some cakes of bread in the window. I coveted a cake of bread. With that refreshment I could perhaps regain a degree of energy: without it, it would be difficult to proceed. The wish to have some strength and some vigour returned to me as soon as I was amongst my fellow-beings. I felt it would be degrading to faint with hunger on the causeway of a hamlet. Had I nothing about me I could offer in exchange for one of these rolls? I considered. I had a small silk handkerchief tied round my throat; I had my gloves. I could hardly tell how men and women in extremities of destitution proceeded. I did not know whether either of these articles would be accepted: probably they would not; but I must try.

I entered the shop: a woman was there. Seeing a respectably-dressed person, a lady as she supposed, she came forward with civility. How could she serve me? I was seized with shame: my tongue would not utter the request I had prepared. I dared not offer her the half-worn gloves, the creased handkerchief: besides, I felt it would be absurd. I only begged permission to sit down a moment, as I was tired. Disappointed in the expectation of a customer, she coolly acceded to my request. She pointed to a seat; I sank into it. I felt sorely urged to weep; but conscious how unseasonable such a manifestation would be, I restrained it. Soon I asked her 'if there were any dressmaker or plain-workwoman in the village?'

'Yes; two or three. Quite as many as there was employment for.'

I reflected. I was driven to the point now. I was brought face to face with Necessity. I stood in the position of one without a resource, without a friend, without a coin. I must do something. What? I must apply somewhere. Where?

'Did she know of any place in the neighbourhood where a servant was wanted?'

'Nay; she couldn't say.'

'What was the chief trade in this place? What did most of the people do?'

'Some were farm labourers; a good deal worked at Mr Oliver's needle-factory, and at the foundry.'

'Did Mr Oliver employ women?'

'Nay; it was men's work.'

'And what do the women do?'

'I knawn't,' was the answer. 'Some does one thing, and some another. Poor folk mun get on as they can.'

She seemed to be tired of my questions: and, indeed, what claim had I to importune her? A neighbour or two came in; my chair was evidently wanted. I took leave.

I passed up the street, looking as I went at all the houses to the right hand and to the left; but I could discover no pretext, nor see an inducement to enter any. I rambled round the hamlet, going sometimes to a little distance and returning again, for an hour or more. Much exhausted, and suffering greatly now for want of food, I turned aside into a lane and sat down under the hedge. Ere many minutes had elapsed, I was again on my feet, however, and again searching something – a resource, or at least an informant. A pretty little house stood at the top of the lane, with a garden before it, exquisitely neat and brilliantly blooming. I stopped at it. What business had I to approach the white door or touch the glittering knocker? In what way could it possibly be the interest of the inhabitants of that dwelling to serve me? Yet I drew near and knocked. A mild-looking, cleanly-attired young woman opened the door. In such a voice as might be expected from a hopeless heart and fainting frame – a voice wretchedly low and faltering – I asked if a servant was wanted here?

'No,' said she; 'we do not keep a servant.'

'Can you tell me where I could get employment of any kind?' I continued. 'I am a stranger, without acquaintance in this place. I want some work: no matter what.'

But it was not her business to think for me, or to seek a place for me: besides, in her eyes, how doubtful must have appeared my character, position, tale. She shook her head, she 'was sorry she could give me no information,' and the white door closed, quite gently and civilly: but it shut me out. If she had held it open a little longer, I believe I should have begged a piece of bread; for I was now brought low.

I could not bear to return to the sordid village, where, besides, no prospect of aid was visible. I should have longed rather to deviate to a wood I saw not far off, which appeared in its thick shade to offer inviting shelter; but I was so sick, so weak, so gnawed with nature's cravings, instinct kept me roaming round abodes where there was a chance of food. Solitude would be no solitude – rest no rest – while the vulture, hunger, thus sank beak and talons in my side.

I drew near houses; I left them, and came back again, and again I wandered away: always repelled by the consciousness of having no claim to ask – no right to expect interest in my isolated lot. Meantime, the afternoon advanced, while I thus wandered about like a lost and starving dog. In crossing a field, I saw the church spire before me: I hastened towards it. Near the churchyard, and in the middle of a garden, stood a well-built though small house, which I had no doubt was the parsonage. I remembered that strangers who arrive at a place where they have no friends, and who want employment, sometimes apply to the clergyman for introduction and aid. It is the clergyman's function to help – at least with advice – those who wished to help themselves. I seemed to have something like a right to seek counsel here. Renewing then my courage, and gathering my feeble remains of strength, I pushed on. I reached the house, and knocked at the kitchen-door. An old woman opened: I asked was this the parsonage?

'Yes.'

'Was the clergyman in?'

'No.'

'Would he be in soon?'

'No, he was gone from home.'

'To a distance?'

'Not so far – happen three mile. He had been called away by the sudden death of his father: he was at Marsh End now, and would very likely stay there a fortnight longer.'

'Was there any lady of the house?'

'Nay, there was naught but her, and she was housekeeper'; and of her, reader, I could not bear to ask the relief for want of which I was sinking; I could not yet beg; and again I crawled away.

Once more I took off my handkerchief – once more I thought of the cakes of bread in the little shop. Oh, for but a crust! for but one mouthful to allay the pang of famine! Instinctively I turned my face again to the village; I found the shop again, and I went in; and though others were there besides the woman I ventured the request – 'Would she give me a roll for this handkerchief?'

She looked at me with evident suspicion: 'Nay, she never sold stuff i' that way.'

Almost desperate, I asked for half a cake; she again refused. 'How could she tell where I had got the handkerchief?' she said.

'Would she take my gloves?'

'No! what could she do with them?'

Reader, it is not pleasant to dwell on these details. Some say there is enjoyment in looking back to painful experience past; but at this day I can scarcely bear to review the times to which I allude: the moral degradation, blent with the physical suffering, form too distressing a recollection ever to be willingly dwelt on. I blamed none of those who repulsed me. I felt it was what was to be expected, and what could not be helped: an ordinary beggar is frequently an object of suspicion; a well-dressed beggar inevitably so. To be sure, what I begged was employment; but whose business was it to provide me with employment? Not, certainly, that of persons who saw me then for the first time, and who knew nothing about my character. And as to the woman who would not take my handkerchief in exchange for her bread, why, she was right, if the offer appeared to her sinister or the exchange unprofitable. Let me condense now. I am sick of the subject.

A little before dark I passed a farmhouse, at the open door of which the farmer was sitting, eating his supper of bread and cheese. I stopped and said – 'Will you give me a piece of bread? for I am very hungry.' He cast on me a glance of surprise; but without answering, he cut a thick slice from his loaf, and gave it to me. I imagine he did not think I was a beggar, but only an eccentric sort of lady, who had taken a fancy to his brown loaf. As soon as I was out of sight of his house, I sat down and ate it.

I could not hope to get a lodging under a roof, and sought it in the wood I have before alluded to. But my night was wretched, my rest broken: the ground was damp, the air cold: besides, intruders passed near me more than once, and I had again and again to change my quarters: no sense of safety or tranquillity befriended me. Towards morning it rained; the whole of the following day was wet. Do not ask me, reader, to give a minute account of that day; as before, I sought work; as before, I was repulsed; as before, I starved; but once did food pass my lips. At the door of a cottage I saw a little girl about to throw a mess of cold porridge into a pig trough. 'Will you give me that?' I asked.

She stared at me. 'Mother!' she exclaimed, 'there is a woman wants me to give her this porridge.'

'Well, lass,' replied a voice within, 'give it her if she's a beggar. T' pig doesn't want it.'

The girl emptied the stiffened mould into my hands and I devoured it ravenously.

As the wet twilight deepened, I stopped in a solitary bridle-path, which I had been pursuing an hour or more.

'My strength is quite failing me,' I said in a soliloquy. 'I feel I cannot go much farther. Shall I be an outcast again this night? While the rain descends so, must I lay my head on the cold, drenched ground? I fear I cannot do otherwise: for who will receive me? But it will be very dreadful, with this feeling of hunger, faintness, chill, and this sense of desolation – this total prostration of hope. In all likelihood, though, I should die before morning. And why cannot I reconcile myself to the prospect of death? Why do I struggle to retain a valueless life? Because I know, or believe, Mr Rochester is living: and then, to die of want and cold is a fate to which nature cannot submit passively. Oh, Providence! sustain me a little longer! Aid! – direct me!'

My glazed eye wandered over the dim and misty landscape. I saw I had strayed far from the village: it was quite out of sight. The very cultivation surrounding it had disappeared. I had, by cross-ways and by-paths, once more drawn near the tract of moorland; and now, only a few fields, almost as wild and unproductive as the heath from which they were scarcely reclaimed, lay between me and the dusky hill.

'Well, I would rather die yonder than in a street or on a frequented road,' I reflected. 'And far better that crows and ravens – if any ravens there be in these regions – should pick my flesh from my bones, than that they should be prisoned in a workhouse coffin and moulder in a pauper's grave.'

To the hill, then, I turned. I reached it. It remained now only to find a hollow where I could lie down, and feel at least hidden, if not secure. But all the surface of the waste looked level. It showed no variation but of tint: green, where rush and moss overgrew the marshes; black, where the dry soil bore only heath. Dark as it was getting, I could still see these changes, though but as mere alternations of light and shade; for colour had faded with the daylight.

My eye still roved over the sullen swell and along the moor-edge, vanishing amidst the wildest scenery, when at one dim point, far in among the marshes and the ridges, a light sprang up. 'That is an *ignis fatuus*,' was my first thought; and I expected it would soon vanish. It burnt on, however, quite steadily, neither receding nor advancing. 'Is it, then, a bonfire just kindled?' I questioned. I watched to see whether it would spread: but no; as it did not diminish, so it did not enlarge. 'It may be a candle in a house,' I then conjectured; 'but if so, I can never reach it. It is much too far away: and were it within a yard of me, what would it avail? I should but knock at the door to have it shut in my face.'

And I sank down where I stood, and hid my face against the ground. I lay still a while: the night-wind swept over the hill and over me, and died moaning in the distance; the rain fell fast, wetting me afresh to the skin. Could I but have stiffened to the still frost – the friendly numbness of death – it might have pelted on; I should not have felt it; but my yet living flesh shuddered at its chilling influence. I rose ere long.

The light was yet there, shining dim but constant through the rain. I tried to walk again: I dragged my exhausted limbs slowly towards it. It led me aslant over the hill, through a wide bog, which would have been impassable in winter, and was splashy and shaking even now, in the height of summer. Here I fell twice; but as often I rose and rallied my faculties. This light was my forlorn hope: I must gain it.

Having crossed the marsh, I saw a trace of white over the moor. I approached it; it was a road or a track: it led straight up to the light, which now beamed from a sort of knoll, amidst a clump of trees – firs, apparently, from what I could distinguish of the character of their forms and foliage through the gloom. My star vanished as I drew near: some obstacle had intervened between me and it. I put out my hand to feel the dark mass before me: I discriminated the rough stones of a low wall – above it, something like palisades, and within, a high and prickly hedge. I groped on. Again a whitish object gleamed before me: it was a gate – a wicket; it moved on its hinges as I touched it. On each side stood a sable bush – holly or yew.

Entering the gate and passing the shrubs, the silhouette of a house rose to view, black, low, and rather long; but the guiding light shone nowhere. All was obscurity. Were the inmates retired to rest? I feared it must be so. In seeking the door, I turned an angle: there shot out the friendly gleam again, from the lozenged panes of a very small latticed window, within a foot of the ground, made still smaller by the growth of ivy or some other creeping plant, whose leaves clustered thick over the portion of the house wall in which it was set. The aperture was so screened and narrow, that curtain or shutter had been deemed unnecessary; and when I stooped down and put aside the spray of foliage shooting over it, I could see all within. I could see clearly a room with a sanded floor, clean scoured; a dresser of walnut, with pewter plates ranged in rows, reflecting the redness and radiance of a glowing peat-fire. I could see a clock, a white deal table, some chairs. The candle, whose ray had been my beacon, burnt on the table; and by its light an elderly woman, somewhat rough-looking, but scrupulously clean, like all about her, was knitting a stocking.

I noticed these objects cursorily only – in them there was nothing extraordinary. A group of more interest appeared near the hearth, sitting still amidst the rosy peace and warmth suffusing it. Two young, graceful women – ladies in every point – sat, one in a low rocking-chair, the other on a lower stool; both wore deep mourning of crape and bombazeen, which sombre garb singularly set off very fair necks and faces: a large old pointer dog rested its massive head on the knee of one girl – in the lap of the other was cushioned a black cat.

A strange place was this humble kitchen for such occupants! Who were they? They could not be the daughters of the elderly person at the table; for she looked like a rustic, and they were all delicacy and cultivation. I had nowhere seen such faces as theirs: and yet, as I gazed on them, I seemed intimate with every lineament. I cannot call them handsome – they were too pale and grave for the word: as they each bent over a book, they looked thoughtful almost to severity. A stand between them supported a second candle and two great volumes, to which they frequently referred, comparing them, seemingly, with the smaller books they held in their hands, like people consulting a dictionary to aid them in the task of translation. This scene was as silent as if all the figures had been shadows and the firelit apartment a picture: so hushed was it, I could hear the cinders fall from the grate, the clock tick in its obscure corner; and I even fancied I could distinguish the click-click of the woman's knitting-needles. When, therefore, a voice broke the strange stillness at last, it was audible enough to me.

'Listen, Diana,' said one of the absorbed students; 'Franz and old Daniel are together in the night-time, and Franz is telling a dream from which he has awakened in terror – listen!' And in a low voice she read something, of which not one word was intelligible to me; for it was in an unknown tongue – neither French nor Latin. Whether it were Greek or German I could not tell.

'That is strong,' she said, when she had finished: 'I relish it.' The other girl, who had lifted her head to listen to her sister, repeated, while she gazed at the fire, a line of what had been read. At a later day, I knew the language and the book; therefore, I will here quote the line: though, when I first heard it, it was only like a stroke on sounding brass to me – conveying no meaning: ' "Da trat hervor Einer, anzusehen wie die Sternen Nacht." Good! good!' she exclaimed, while her dark and deep eye sparkled. 'There you have a dim and mighty archangel fitly set before you! The line is worth a hundred pages of fustian. "Ich wäge die Gedanken in der Schale meines Zornes und die Werke mit dem Gewichte meines Grimms." I like it!'

Both were again silent.

'Is there ony country where they talk i' that way?' asked the old woman, looking up from her knitting.

'Yes, Hannah – a far larger country than England, where they talk in no other way.'

'Well, for sure case, I knawn't how they can understand t'one t'other: and if either o' ye went there, ye could tell what they said, I guess?'

'We could probably tell something of what they said, but not all – for we are not as clever as you think us, Hannah. We don't speak German, and we cannot read it without a dictionary to help us.'

'And what good does it do you?'

'We mean to teach it sometime – or at least the elements, as they say; and then we shall get more money than we do now.'

'Varry like: but give ower studying; ye've done enough for tonight.'

'I think we have: at least I'm tired. Mary, are you?'

'Mortally: after all, it's tough work fagging away at a language with no master but a lexicon.'

'It is, especially such a language as this crabbed but glorious Deutsch. I wonder when St John will come home.'

'Surely he will not be long now: it is just ten' (looking at a little gold watch she drew from her girdle). 'It rains fast, Hannah: will you have the goodness to look at the fire in the parlour?'

The woman rose: she opened a door, through which I dimly saw a passage: soon I heard her stir a fire in an inner room; she presently came back.

'Ah, childer!' said she, 'it fair troubles me to go into yond' room now: it looks so lonesome wi' the chair empty and set back in a corner.'

She wiped her eyes with her apron: the two girls, grave before, looked sad now.

'But he is in a better place,' continued Hannah: 'we shouldn't wish him here again. And then, nobody need to have a quieter death nor he had.'

'You say he never mentioned us?' enquired one of the ladies.

'He hadn't time, bairn: he was gone in a minute, was your father. He had been a bit ailing like the day before, but naught to signify; and when Mr St John asked if he would like either o' ye to be sent for, he fair laughed at him. He began again with a bit of a heaviness in his head the next day – that is, a fortnight sin' – and he went to sleep and niver wakened: he wor a'most stark when your brother went into t' chamber and fand him. Ah, childer! that's t' last o' t' old stock – for ye and Mr St John is like of different soart to them 'at's gone; for all your mother wor mich i' your way, and a'most as book-learned. She wor the pictur' o' ye, Mary: Diana is more like your father.'

I thought them so similar I could not tell where the old servant (for such I now concluded her to be) saw the difference. Both were fair complexioned and slenderly made; both possessed faces full of distinction and intelligence. One, to be sure, had hair a shade darker than the other, and there was a difference in their style of wearing it; Mary's pale brown locks were parted and braided smooth: Diana's duskier tresses covered her neck with thick curls. The clock struck ten.

'Ye'll want your supper, I am sure,' observed Hannah; 'and so will Mr St John when he comes in.'

And she proceeded to prepare the meal. The ladies rose; they seemed about to withdraw to the parlour.

Till this moment, I had been so intent on watching them, their appearance and conversation had excited in me so keen an interest, I had half-forgotten my own wretched position: now it recurred to me. More desolate, more desperate than ever, it seemed from contrast. And how impossible did it appear to touch the inmates of this house with concern on my behalf; to make them believe in the truth of my wants and woes – to induce them to vouchsafe a rest for my wanderings! As I groped out the door, and knocked at it hesitatingly, I felt that last idea to be a mere chimera. Hannah opened.

'What do you want?' she enquired, in a voice of surprise, as she surveyed me by the light of the candle she held.

'May I speak to your mistresses?' I said.

'You had better tell me what you have to say to them. Where do you come from?'

'I am a stranger.'

'What is your business here at this hour?'

'I want a night's shelter in an out-house or anywhere, and a morsel of bread to eat.'

Distrust, the very feeling I dreaded, appeared in Hannah's face. 'I'll give you a piece of bread,' she said, after a pause; 'but we can't take in a vagrant to lodge. It isn't likely.'

'Do let me speak to your mistresses.'

'No, not I. What can they do for you? You should not be roving about now; it looks very ill.'

'But where shall I go if you drive me away? What shall I do?'

'Oh, I'll warrant you know where to go and what to do. Mind you don't do wrong, that's all. Here is a penny; now go – '

'A penny cannot feed me, and I have no strength to go farther. Don't shut the door: oh, don't, for God's sake!'

'I must; the rain is driving in – '

'Tell the young ladies. Let me see them – '

'Indeed, I will not. You are not what you ought to be, or you wouldn't make such a noise. Move off.'

'But I must die if I am turned away.'

'Not you. I'm fear'd you have some ill plans agate that bring you about folk's houses at this time o' night. If you've any followers – housebreakers or suchlike – anywhere near, you may tell them we are not by ourselves in the house; we have a gentleman, and dogs, and guns.' Here the honest but inflexible servant clapped the door to and bolted it within.

This was the climax. A pang of exquisite suffering – a throe of true despair – rent and heaved my heart. Worn out, indeed, I was; not another step could I stir. I sank on the wet doorstep: I groaned – I wrung my hands – I wept in utter anguish. Oh, this spectre of death! Oh, this last hour, approaching in such horror! Alas, this isolation – this banishment from my kind! Not only the anchor of hope, but the footing of fortitude was gone – at least for a moment; but the last I soon endeavoured to regain.

'I can but die,' I said, 'and I believe in God. Let me try to wait His will in silence.'

These words I not only thought, but uttered; and thrusting back all my misery into my heart, I made an effort to compel it to remain there dumb and still.

'All men must die,' said a voice quite close at hand; 'but all are not condemned to meet a lingering and premature doom, such as yours would be if you perished here of want.'

'Who or what speaks?' I asked, terrified at the unexpected sound, and incapable now of deriving from any occurrence a hope of aid. A form was near – what form, the pitch-dark night and my enfeebled vision prevented me from distinguishing. With a loud long knock, the newcomer appealed to the door.

'Is it you, Mr St John?' cried Hannah.

'Yes – yes; open quickly.'

'Well, how wet and cold you must be, such a wild night as it is! Come in – your sisters are quite uneasy about you, and I believe there are bad folks about. There has been a beggar-woman – I declare she is not gone yet! – laid down there. Get up! for shame! Move off, I say!'

'Hush, Hannah! I have a word to say to the woman. You have done your duty in excluding, now let me do mine in admitting her. I was near, and listened to both you and her. I think this is a peculiar case – I must at least examine into it. Young woman, rise, and pass before me into the house.'

With difficulty I obeyed him. Presently I stood within that clean, bright kitchen – on the very hearth – trembling, sickening; conscious of an aspect in the last degree ghastly, wild, and weather-beaten. The two ladies, their brother, Mr St John, the old servant, were all gazing at me.

'St John, who is it?' I heard one ask.

'I cannot tell: I found her at the door,' was the reply.

'She does look white,' said Hannah.

'As white as clay or death,' was responded. 'She will fall: let her sit.'

And indeed my head swam: I dropped, but a chair received me. I still possessed my senses, though just now I could not speak.

'Perhaps a little water would restore her. Hannah, fetch some. But she is worn to nothing. How very thin, and how very bloodless!'

'A mere spectre!'

'Is she ill, or only famished?'

'Famished, I think. Hannah, is that milk? Give it me, and a piece of bread.'

Diana (I knew her by the long curls which I saw drooping between me and the fire as she bent over me) broke some bread, dipped it in milk, and put it to my lips. Her face was near mine: I saw there was pity in it, and I felt sympathy in her hurried breathing. In her simple words, too, the same balm-like emotion spoke: 'Try to eat.'

'Yes – try,' repeated Mary gently; and Mary's hand removed my sodden bonnet and lifted my head. I tasted what they offered me: feebly at first, eagerly soon.

'Not too much at first – restrain her,' said the brother; 'she has had enough.' And he withdrew the cup of milk and the plate of bread.

'A little more, St John – look at the avidity in her eyes.'

'No more at present, sister. Try if she can speak now – ask her her name.'

I felt I could speak, and I answered – 'My name is Jane Elliott.' Anxious as ever to avoid discovery, I had before resolved to assume an *alias*.

'And where do you live? Where are your friends?'

I was silent.

'Can we send for anyone you know?'

I shook my head.

'What account can you give of yourself?'

Somehow, now that I had once crossed the threshold of this house, and once was brought face to face with its owners, I felt no longer outcast, vagrant, and disowned by the wide world. I dared to put off the mendicant – to resume my natural manner and character. I began once more to know myself; and when Mr St John demanded an account – which at present I was far too weak to render – I said after a brief pause – 'Sir, I can give you no details tonight.'

'But what, then,' said he, 'do you expect me to do for you?'

'Nothing,' I replied. My strength sufficed for but short answers. Diana took the word – 'Do you mean,' she asked, 'that we have now given you what aid you require? and that we may dismiss you to the moor and the rainy night?'

I looked at her. She had, I thought, a remarkable countenance, instinct both with power and goodness. I took sudden courage. Answering her compassionate gaze with a smile, I said – 'I will trust you. If I were a masterless and stray dog, I know that you would not turn me from your hearth tonight: as it is, I really have no fear. Do with me and for me as you like; but excuse me from much discourse – my breath is short – I feel a spasm when I speak.' All three surveyed me, and all three were silent.

'Hannah,' said Mr St John, at last, 'let her sit there at present, and ask her no questions; in ten minutes more, give her the remainder of that milk and bread. Mary and Diana, let us go into the parlour and talk the matter over.'

They withdrew. Very soon one of the ladies returned – I could not tell which. A kind of pleasant stupor was stealing over me as I sat by the genial fire. In an undertone she gave some directions to Hannah. Ere long, with the servant's aid, I contrived to mount a staircase; my dripping clothes were removed; soon a warm, dry bed received me. I thanked God – experienced amidst unutterable exhaustion a glow of grateful joy – and slept.

## *Chapter 29*

The recollection of about three days and nights succeeding this is very dim in my mind. I can recall some sensations felt in that interval; but few thoughts framed, and no actions performed. I knew I was in a small room and in a narrow bed. To that bed I seemed to have grown; I lay on it motionless as a stone; and to have torn me from it would have been almost to kill me. I took no note of the lapse of time – of the change from morning to noon, from noon to evening. I observed when anyone entered or left the apartment: I could even tell who they were; I could understand what was said when the speaker stood near to me; but I could not answer; to open my lips or move my limbs was equally impossible. Hannah, the servant, was my most frequent visitor. Her coming disturbed me. I had a feeling that she wished me away: that she did not understand me or my circumstances; that she was prejudiced against me. Diana and Mary appeared in the chamber once or twice a day. They would whisper sentences of this sort at my bedside – 'It is very well we took her in.'

'Yes; she would certainly have been found dead at the door in the morning had she been left out all night. I wonder what she has gone through?'

'Strange hardships, I imagine – poor, emaciated, pallid wanderer!'

'She is not an uneducated person, I should think, by her manner of speaking; her accent was quite pure; and the clothes she took off, though splashed and wet, were little worn and fine.'

'She has a peculiar face; fleshless and haggard as it is, I rather like it; and when in good health and animated, I can fancy her physiognomy would be agreeable.'

Never once in their dialogues did I hear a syllable of regret at the hospitality they had extended to me, or of suspicion of, or aversion to, myself. I was comforted.

Mr St John came but once: he looked at me, and said my state of lethargy was the result of reaction from excessive and protracted fatigue. He pronounced it needless to send for a doctor: nature, he was sure, would manage best, left to herself. He said every nerve had been overstrained in some way, and the whole system must sleep torpid a while. There was no disease. He imagined my recovery would be rapid enough when once commenced. These opinions he delivered in a few words, in a quiet, low voice; and added, after a pause, in the tone of a man little accustomed to expansive comment, 'Rather an unusual physiognomy; certainly, not indicative of vulgarity or degradation.'

'Far otherwise,' responded Diana. 'To speak truth, St John, my heart rather warms to the poor little soul. I wish we may be able to benefit her permanently.'

'That is hardly likely,' was the reply. 'You will find she is some young lady who has had a misunderstanding with her friends, and has probably injudiciously left them. We may, perhaps, succeed in restoring her to them, if she is not obstinate: but I trace lines of force in her face which make me sceptical of her tractability.' He stood considering me some minutes; then added, 'She looks sensible, but not at all handsome.'

'She is so ill, St John.'

'Ill or well, she would always be plain. The grace and harmony of beauty are quite wanting in those features.'

On the third day I was better; on the fourth, I could speak, move, rise in bed, and turn. Hannah had brought me some gruel and dry toast, about, as I supposed, the dinner-hour. I had eaten with relish: the food was good – void of the feverish flavour which had hitherto poisoned what I had swallowed. When she left me, I felt comparatively strong and revived: ere long satiety of repose and desire for action stirred me. I wished to rise; but what could I put on? Only my damp and bemired apparel; in which I had slept on the ground and fallen in the marsh. I felt ashamed to appear before my benefactors so clad. I was spared the humiliation.

On a chair by the bedside were all my own things, clean and dry. My black silk frock hung against the wall. The traces of the bog were removed from it; the creases left by the wet smoothed out: it was quite decent. My very shoes and stockings were purified and rendered presentable. There were the means of washing in the room, and a comb and brush to smooth my hair. After a weary process, and resting every five minutes, I succeeded in dressing myself. My clothes hung loose on me; for I was much wasted, but I covered deficiencies with a shawl, and once more, clean and respectable looking – no speck of the dirt, no trace of the disorder I so hated, and which seemed so to degrade me, left – I crept down a stone staircase with the aid of the banisters, to a narrow low passage, and found my way presently to the kitchen.

It was full of the fragrance of new bread and the warmth of a generous fire. Hannah was baking. Prejudices, it is well known, are most difficult to eradicate from the heart whose soil has never been loosened or fertilised by education: they grow there, firm as weeds among stones. Hannah had been cold and stiff, indeed, at the first: latterly she had begun to relent a little; and when she saw me come in tidy and well-dressed, she even smiled.

'What, you have got up!' she said. 'You are better, then. You may sit you down in my chair on the hearthstone, if you will.'

She pointed to the rocking-chair: I took it. She bustled about, examining me every now and then with the corner of her eye. Turning to me, as she took some loaves from the oven, she asked bluntly – 'Did you ever go a-begging afore you came here?'

I was indignant for a moment; but remembering that anger was out of the question, and that I had indeed appeared as a beggar to her, I answered quietly, but still not without a certain marked firmness – 'You are mistaken in supposing me a beggar. I am no beggar; any more than yourself or your young ladies.'

After a pause she said, 'I dunnut understand that: you've like no house, nor no brass, I guess?'

'The want of house or brass (by which I suppose you mean money) does not make a beggar in your sense of the word.'

'Are you book-learned?' she enquired presently.

'Yes, very.'

'But you've never been to a boarding-school?'

'I was at a boarding-school eight years.'

She opened her eyes wide. 'Whatever cannot ye keep yourself for, then?'

'I have kept myself; and, I trust, shall keep myself again. What are you going to do with these gooseberries?' I enquired, as she brought out a basket of the fruit.

'Mak' 'em into pies.'

'Give them to me and I'll pick them.'

'Nay; I dunnut want ye to do nought.'

'But I must do something. Let me have them.'

She consented; and she even brought me a clean towel to spread over my dress, 'lest,' as she said, 'I should mucky it.'

'Ye've not been used to sarvant's wark, I see by your hands,' she remarked. 'Happen ye've been a dressmaker?'

'No, you are wrong. And now, never mind what I have been: don't trouble your head further about me; but tell me the name of the house where we are.'

'Some calls it Marsh End, and some calls it Moor House.'

'And the gentleman who lives here is called Mr St John?'

'Nay; he doesn't live here: he is only staying a while. When he is at home, he is in his own parish at Morton.'

'That village a few miles off?'

'Aye.'

'And what is he?'

'He is a parson.'

I remembered the answer of the old housekeeper at the parsonage, when I had asked to see the clergyman. 'This, then, was his father's residence?'

'Aye; old Mr Rivers lived here, and his father, and grandfather, and gurt [great] grandfather afore him.'

'The name, then, of that gentleman, is Mr St John Rivers?'

'Aye; St John is like his kirstened name.'

'And his sisters are called Diana and Mary Rivers?'

'Yes.'

'Their father is dead?'

'Dead three weeks sin' of a stroke.'

'They have no mother?'

'The mistress has been dead this mony a year.'

'Have you lived with the family long?'

'I've lived here thirty year. I nursed them all three.'

'That proves you must have been an honest and faithful servant. I will say so much for you, though you have had the incivility to call me a beggar.'

She again regarded me with a surprised stare. 'I believe,' she said, 'I was quite mista'en in my thoughts of you: but there is so mony cheats goes about, you mun forgie me.'

'And though,' I continued, rather severely, 'you wished to turn me from the door, on a night when you should not have shut out a dog.'

'Well, it was hard: but what can a body do? I thought more o' th' childer nor of mysel: poor things! They've like nobody to tak' care on 'em but me. I'm like to look sharpish.'

I maintained a grave silence for some minutes.

'You munnut think too hardly of me,' she again remarked.

'But I do think hardly of you,' I said; 'and I'll tell you why – not so much because you refused to give me shelter, or regarded me as an impostor, as because you just now made it a species of reproach that I had no "brass" and no house. Some of the best people that ever lived have been as destitute as I am; and if you are a Christian, you ought not to consider poverty a crime.'

'No more I ought,' said she: 'Mr St John tells me so too; and I see I wor wrang – but I've clear a different notion on you now to what I had. You look a raight down dacent little crater.'

'That will do – I forgive you now. Shake hands.'

She put her floury and horny hand into mine; another and heartier smile illumined her rough face, and from that moment we were friends.

Hannah was evidently fond of talking. While I picked the fruit, and she made the paste for the pies, she proceeded to give me sundry details about her deceased master and mistress, and 'the childer', as she called the young people.

Old Mr Rivers, she said, was a plain man enough, but a gentleman, and of as ancient a family as could be found. Marsh End had belonged to the Rivers ever since it was a house: and it was, she affirmed, 'aboon two hundred year old – for all it looked but a small, humble place, naught to compare wi' Mr Oliver's grand hall down i' Morton Vale. But she could remember Bill Oliver's father a journeyman needlemaker; and th' Rivers wor gentry i' th' owd days o' th' Henrys, as onybody might see by looking into th' registers i' Morton Church vestry.' Still, she allowed, 'the owd maister was like other folk – naught mich out o' th' common way: stark mad o' shooting, and farming, and sichlike'. The mistress was different. She was a great reader, and studied a deal; and the 'bairns' had taken after her. There was nothing like them in these parts, nor ever had been; they had liked learning, all three, almost from the time they could speak; and they had always been 'of a mak' of their own'. Mr St John, when he grew up, would go to college and be a parson; and the girls, as soon as they left school, would seek places as governesses: for they had told her their father had some years ago lost a great deal of money by a man he had trusted turning bankrupt; and as he was now not rich enough to give them fortunes, they must provide for themselves. They had lived very little at home for a long while, and were only come now to stay a few weeks on account of their father's death; but they did so like Marsh End and Morton, and all these moors and hills about. They had been in London, and many other grand towns; but they always said there was no place like home; and then they were so agreeable with each other – never fell out nor 'threaped'. She did not know where there was such a family for being united.

Having finished my task of gooseberry picking, I asked where the two ladies and their brother were now.

'Gone over to Morton for a walk; but they would be back in half an hour to tea.'

They returned within the time Hannah had allotted them: they entered by the kitchen door. Mr St John, when he saw me, merely bowed and passed through; the two ladies stopped: Mary, in a few words, kindly and calmly expressed the pleasure she felt in seeing me well enough to be able to come down; Diana took my hand: she shook her head at me.

'You should have waited for my leave to descend,' she said. 'You still look very pale – and so thin! Poor child! – poor girl!'

Diana had a voice toned, to my ear, like the cooing of a dove. She possessed eyes whose gaze I delighted to encounter. Her whole face seemed to me full of charm. Mary's countenance was equally intelligent – her features equally pretty; but her expression was more reserved, and her manners, though gentle, more distant. Diana looked and spoke with a certain authority: she had a will, evidently. It was my nature to feel pleasure in yielding to an authority supported like hers, and to bend, where my conscience and self-respect permitted, to an active will.

'And what business have you here?' she continued. 'It is not your place. Mary and I sit in the kitchen sometimes, because at home we like to be free, even to license – but you are a visitor, and must go into the parlour.'

'I am very well here.'

'Not at all, with Hannah bustling about and covering you with flour.'

'Besides, the fire is too hot for you,' interposed Mary.

'To be sure,' added her sister. 'Come, you must be obedient.' And still holding my hand she made me rise, and led me into the inner room.

'Sit there,' she said, placing me on the sofa, 'while we take our things off and get the tea ready; it is another privilege we exercise in our little moorland home – to prepare our own meals when we are so inclined, or when Hannah is baking, brewing, washing, or ironing.'

She closed the door, leaving me solus with Mr St John, who sat opposite, a book or newspaper in his hand. I examined first, the parlour, and then its occupant.

The parlour was rather a small room, very plainly furnished, yet comfortable, because clean and neat. The old-fashioned chairs were very bright, and the walnut-wood table was like a looking-glass. A few strange, antique portraits of the men and women of other days decorated the stained walls; a cupboard with glass doors contained some books and an ancient set of china. There was no superfluous ornament in the room – not one modern piece of furniture, save a brace of work-boxes and a lady's desk in rosewood, which stood on a side-table: everything – including the carpet and curtains – looked at once well worn and well saved.

Mr St John – sitting as still as one of the dusty pictures on the walls, keeping his eyes fixed on the page he perused, and his lips mutely sealed – was easy enough to examine. Had he been a statue instead of a man, he could not have been easier. He was young – perhaps from twenty-eight to thirty – tall, slender; his face riveted the eye; it was like a Greek face, very pure in outline: quite a straight, classic nose; quite an Athenian mouth and chin. It is seldom, indeed, an English face comes so near the antique models as did his. He might well be a little shocked at the irregularity of my lineaments, his own being so harmonious. His eyes were large and blue, with brown lashes; his high forehead, colourless as ivory, was partially streaked over by careless locks of fair hair.

This is a gentle delineation, is it not, reader? Yet he whom it describes scarcely impressed one with the idea of a gentle, a yielding, an impressible, or even of a placid nature. Quiescent as he now sat, there was something about his nostril, his mouth, his brow, which, to my perceptions, indicated elements within either restless, or hard, or eager. He did not speak to me one word, nor even direct to me one glance, till his sisters returned. Diana, as she passed in and out, in the course of preparing tea, brought me a little cake, baked on the top of the oven.

'Eat that now,' she said: 'you must be hungry. Hannah says you have had nothing but some gruel since breakfast.'

I did not refuse it, for my appetite was awakened and keen. Mr Rivers now closed his book, approached the table, and, as he took a seat, fixed his blue pictorial-looking eyes full on me. There was an unceremonious directness, a searching, decided steadfastness in his gaze now, which told that intention, and not diffidence, had hitherto kept it averted from the stranger. 'You are very hungry,' he said.

'I am, sir.' It is my way – it always was my way, by instinct – ever to meet the brief with brevity, the direct with plainness.

'It is well for you that a low fever has forced you to abstain for the last three days: there would have been danger in yielding to the cravings of your appetite at first. Now you may eat, though still not immoderately.'

'I trust I shall not eat long at your expense, sir,' was my very clumsily-contrived, unpolished answer.

'No,' he said coolly: 'when you have indicated to us the residence of your friends, we can write to them, and you may be restored to home.'

'That, I must plainly tell you, is out of my power to do; being absolutely without home and friends.'

The three looked at me, but not distrustfully; I felt there was no suspicion in their glances: there was more of curiosity. I speak particularly of the young ladies. St John's eyes, though clear enough in a literal sense, in a figurative one were difficult to fathom. He seemed to use them rather as instruments to search other people's thoughts, than as agents to reveal his own: the which combination of keenness and reserve was considerably more calculated to embarrass than to encourage.

'Do you mean to say,' he asked, 'that you are completely isolated from every connection?'

'I do. Not a tie links me to any living thing: not a claim do I possess to admittance under any roof in England.'

'A most singular position at your age!'

Here I saw his glance directed to my hands, which were folded on the table before me. I wondered what he sought there: his words soon explained the quest.

'You have never been married? You are a spinster?'

Diana laughed. 'Why, she can't be above seventeen or eighteen years old, St John,' said she.

'I am near nineteen: but I am not married. No.'

I felt a burning glow mount to my face; for bitter and agitating recollections were awakened by the allusion to marriage. They all saw the embarrassment and the emotion. Diana and Mary relieved me by turning their eyes elsewhere than to my crimsoned visage; but the colder and sterner brother continued to gaze, till the trouble he had excited forced out tears as well as colour.

'Where did you last reside?' he now asked.

'You are too inquisitive, St John,' murmured Mary in a low voice; but he leaned over the table and required an answer by a second firm and piercing look.

'The name of the place where, and of the person with whom I lived, is my secret,' I replied concisely.

'Which, if you like, you have, in my opinion, a right to keep, both from St John and every other questioner,' remarked Diana.

'Yet if I know nothing about you or your history, I cannot help you,' he said. 'And you need help, do you not?'

'I need it, and I seek it so far, sir, that some true philanthropist will put me in the way of getting work which I can do, and the remuneration for which will keep me, if but in the barest necessaries of life.'

'I know not whether I am a true philanthropist; yet I am willing to aid you to the utmost of my power in a purpose so honest. First, then, tell me what you have been accustomed to do, and what you *can* do.'

I had now swallowed my tea. I was mightily refreshed by the beverage; as much so as a giant with wine: it gave new tone to my unstrung nerves, and enabled me to address this penetrating young judge steadily.

'Mr Rivers,' I said, turning to him, and looking at him, as he looked at me, openly and without diffidence, 'you and your sisters have done me a great service – the greatest man can do his fellow-being; you have rescued me, by your noble hospitality, from death. This benefit conferred gives you an unlimited claim on my gratitude, and a claim, to a certain extent, on my confidence. I will tell you as much of the history of the wanderer you have harboured, as I can tell without compromising my own peace of mind – my own security, moral and physical, and that of others.

'I am an orphan, the daughter of a clergyman. My parents died before I could know them. I was brought up a dependant; educated in a charitable institution. I will even tell you the name of the establishment, where I passed six years as a pupil, and two as a teacher – Lowood Orphan Asylum, —shire: you will have heard of it, Mr Rivers? – the Revd Robert Brocklehurst is the treasurer.'

'I have heard of Mr Brocklehurst, and I have seen the school.'

'I left Lowood nearly a year since to become a private governess. I obtained a good situation, and was happy. This place I was obliged to leave four days before I came here. The reason of my departure I cannot and ought not to explain: it would be useless, dangerous, and would sound incredible. No blame attached to me: I am as free from culpability as any one of you three. Miserable I am, and must be for a time; for the catastrophe which drove me from a house I had found a paradise was of a strange and direful nature. I observed but two points in planning my departure – speed, secrecy: to secure these, I had to leave behind me everything I possessed except a small parcel; which, in my hurry and trouble of mind, I forgot to take out of the coach that brought me to Whitcross. To this neighbourhood, then, I came, quite destitute. I slept two nights in the open air, and wandered about two days without crossing a threshold: but twice in that space of time did I taste food; and it was when brought by hunger, exhaustion, and despair almost to the last gasp, that you, Mr Rivers, forbade me to perish of want at your door, and took me under the shelter of your roof. I know all your sisters have done for me since – for I have not been insensible during my seeming torpor – and I owe to their spontaneous, genuine, genial compassion as large a debt as to your evangelical charity.'

'Don't make her talk any more now, St John,' said Diana, as I paused; 'she is evidently not yet fit for excitement. Come to the sofa and sit down now, Miss Elliott.'

I gave an involuntary half start at hearing the *alias:* I had forgotten my new name. Mr Rivers, whom nothing seemed to escape, noticed it at once.

'You said your name was Jane Elliott?' he observed.

'I did say so; and it is the name by which I think it expedient to be called at present, but it is not my real name, and when I hear it, it sounds strange to me.'

'Your real name you will not give?'

'No: I fear discovery above all things; and whatever disclosure would lead to it, I avoid.'

'You are quite right, I am sure,' said Diana. 'Now do, brother, let her be at peace a while.'

But when St John had mused a few moments he recommenced as imperturbably and with as much acumen as ever.

'You would not like to be long dependent on our hospitality – you would wish, I see, to dispense as soon as may be with my sisters' compassion, and, above all with my *charity* (I am quite sensible of the distinction drawn, nor do I resent it – it is just): you desire to be independent of us?'

'I do: I have already said so. Show me how to work, or how to seek work: that is all I now ask; then let me go, if it be but to the meanest cottage; but till then, allow me to stay here: I dread another essay of the horrors of homeless destitution.'

'Indeed you *shall* stay here,' said Diana, putting her white hand on my head. 'You *shall*,' repeated Mary, in the tone of undemonstrative sincerity which seemed natural to her.

'My sisters, you see, have a pleasure in keeping you,' said Mr St John, 'as they would have a pleasure in keeping and cherishing a half-frozen bird, some wintry wind might have driven through their casement. I feel more inclination to put you in the way of keeping yourself, and shall endeavour to do so; but observe, my sphere is narrow. I am but the incumbent of a poor country parish: my aid must be of the humblest sort. And if you are inclined to despise the day of small things, seek some more efficient succour than such as I can offer.'

'She has already said that she is willing to do anything honest she *can* do,' answered Diana for me; 'and you know, St John, she has no choice of helpers: she is forced to put up with such crusty people as you.'

'I will be a dressmaker; I will be a plain-workwoman; I will be a servant, a nurse-girl, if I can be no better,' I answered.

'Right,' said Mr St John, quite coolly. 'If such is your spirit, I promise to aid you, in my own time and way.'

He now resumed the book with which he had been occupied before tea. I soon withdrew, for I had talked as much, and sat up as long, as my present strength would permit.

## *Chapter 30*

The more I knew of the inmates of Moor House, the better I liked them. In a few days I had so far recovered my health that I could sit up all day, and walk out sometimes. I could join with Diana and Mary in all their occupations; converse with them as much as they wished, and aid them when and where they would allow me. There was a reviving pleasure in this intercourse, of a kind now tasted by me for the first time – the pleasure arising from perfect congeniality of tastes, sentiments, and principles.

I liked to read what they liked to read: what they enjoyed, delighted me; what they approved, I reverenced. They loved their sequestered home. I, too, in the grey, small, antique structure, with its low roof, its latticed casements, its mouldering walls, its avenue of aged firs – all grown aslant under the stress of mountain winds; its garden, dark with yew and holly – and where no flowers but of the hardiest species would bloom – found a charm both potent and permanent. They clung to the purple moors behind and around their dwelling – to the hollow vale into which the pebbly bridle-path leading from their gate descended, and which wound between fern-banks first, and then amongst a few of the wildest little pasture-fields that ever bordered a wilderness of heath, or gave sustenance to a flock of grey moorland sheep, with their little mossy-faced lambs: they clung to this scene, I say, with a perfect enthusiasm of attachment. I could comprehend the feeling, and share both its strength and truth. I saw the fascination of the locality. I felt the consecration of its loneliness: my eye feasted on the outline of swell and sweep – on the wild colouring communicated to ridge and dell by moss, by heath-bell, by flower-sprinkled turf, by brilliant bracken, and mellow granite crag. These details were just to me what they were to them – so many pure and sweet sources of pleasure. The strong blast and the soft breeze; the rough and the halcyon day; the hours of sunrise and sunset; the moonlight and the clouded night, developed for me, in these regions, the same attraction as for them – wound round my faculties the same spell that entranced theirs.

Indoors we agreed equally well. They were both more accomplished and better read than I was; but with eagerness I followed in the path of knowledge they had trodden before me. I devoured the books they lent me: then it was full satisfaction to discuss with them in the evening what I had perused during the day. Thought fitted thought; opinion met opinion: we coincided, in short, perfectly.

If in our trio there was a superior and a leader, it was Diana. Physically, she far excelled me: she was handsome; she was vigorous. In her animal spirits there was an affluence of life and certainty of flow, such as excited my wonder, while it baffled my comprehension. I could talk a while when the evening commenced, but the first gush of vivacity and fluency gone, I was fain to sit on a stool at Diana's feet, to rest my head on her knee, and listen alternately to her and Mary, while they sounded thoroughly the topic on which I had but touched. Diana offered to teach me German. I liked to learn of her: I saw the part of instructress pleased and suited her; that of scholar pleased and suited me no less. Our natures dovetailed: mutual affection – of the strongest kind – was the result. They discovered I could draw: their pencils and colour-boxes were immediately at my service. My skill, greater in this one point than theirs, surprised and charmed them. Mary would sit and watch me by the hour together: then she would take lessons; and a docile, intelligent, assiduous pupil she made. Thus occupied, and mutually entertained, days passed like hours, and weeks like days.

As to Mr St John, the intimacy which had arisen so naturally and rapidly between me and his sisters did not extend to him. One reason of the distance yet observed between us was, that he was comparatively seldom at home: a large proportion of his time appeared devoted to visiting the sick and poor among the scattered population of his parish.

No weather seemed to hinder him in these pastoral excursions: rain or fair, he would, when his hours of morning study were over, take his hat, and, followed by his father's old pointer, Carlo, go out on his mission of love or duty – I scarcely know in which light he regarded it. Sometimes, when the day was very unfavourable, his sisters would expostulate. He would then say, with a peculiar smile, more solemn than cheerful – 'And if I let a gust of wind or a sprinkling of rain turn me aside from these easy tasks, what preparation would such sloth be for the future I propose to myself?'

Diana and Mary's general answer to this question was a sigh, and some minutes of apparently mournful meditation.

But besides his frequent absences, there was another barrier to friendship with him: he seemed of a reserved, an abstracted, and even of a brooding nature. Zealous in his ministerial labours, blameless in his life and habits, he yet did not appear to enjoy that mental serenity, that inward content, which should be the reward of every sincere Christian and practical philanthropist. Often, of an evening, when he sat at the window, his desk and papers before him, he would cease reading or writing, rest his chin on his hand, and deliver himself up to I know not what course of thought; but that it was perturbed and exciting might be seen in the frequent flash and changeful dilation of his eye.

I think, moreover, that Nature was not to him that treasury of delight it was to his sisters. He expressed once, and but once in my hearing, a strong sense of the rugged charm of the hills, and an inborn affection for the dark roof and hoary walls he called his home; but there was more of gloom than pleasure in the tone and words in which the sentiment was manifested; and never did he seem to roam the moors for the sake of their soothing silence – never seek out or dwell upon the thousand peaceful delights they could yield.

Incommunicative as he was, some time elapsed before I had an opportunity of gauging his mind. I first got an idea of its calibre when I heard him preach in his own church at Morton. I wish I could describe that sermon: but it is past my power. I cannot even render faithfully the effect it produced on me.

It began calm – and indeed, as far as delivery and pitch of voice went, it was calm to the end: an earnestly felt, yet strictly restrained zeal breathed soon in the distinct accents, and prompted the nervous language. This grew to force – compressed, condensed, controlled. The heart was thrilled, the mind astonished, by the power of the preacher: neither were softened. Throughout there was a strange bitterness; an absence of consolatory gentleness; stern allusions to Calvinistic doctrines – election, predestination, reprobation – were frequent; and each reference to these points sounded like a sentence pronounced for doom. When he had done, instead of feeling better, calmer, more enlightened by his discourse, I experienced an expressible sadness; for it seemed to me – I know not whether equally so to others – that the eloquence to which I had been listening had sprung from a depth where lay turbid dregs of disappointment – where moved troubling impulses of insatiate yearnings and disquieting aspirations. I was sure St John Rivers – pure-lived, conscientious, zealous as he was – had not yet found that peace of God which passeth all understanding: he had no more found it, I thought, than had I with my concealed and racking regrets for my broken idol and lost elysium – regrets to which I have latterly avoided referring, but which possessed me and tyrannised over me ruthlessly.

Meantime a month was gone. Diana and Mary were soon to leave Moor House, and return to the far different life and scene which awaited them, as governesses in a large, fashionable, south-of-England city, where each held a situation in families by whose wealthy and haughty members they were regarded only as humble dependants, and who neither knew nor sought out their innate excellences, and appreciated only their acquired accomplishments as they appreciated the skill of their cook or the taste of their waiting-woman. Mr St John had said nothing to me yet about the employment he had promised to obtain for me; yet it became urgent that I should have a vocation of some kind. One morning, being left alone with him a few minutes in the parlour, I ventured to approach the window-recess – which his table, chair, and desk consecrated as a kind of study – and I was going to speak, though not very well knowing in what words to frame my enquiry – for it is at all times difficult to break the ice of reserve glassing over such natures as his – when he saved me the trouble by being the first to commence a dialogue.

Looking up as I drew near – 'You have a question to ask of me?' he said.

'Yes; I wish to know whether you have heard of any service I can offer myself to undertake?'

'I found or devised something for you three weeks ago; but as you seemed both useful and happy here – as my sisters had evidently become attached to you, and your society gave them unusual pleasure – I deemed it inexpedient to break in on your mutual comfort till their approaching departure from Marsh End should render yours necessary.'

'And they will go in three days now?' I said.

'Yes; and when they go, I shall return to the parsonage at Morton: Hannah will accompany me; and this old house will be shut up.'

I waited a few moments, expecting he would go on with the subject first broached: but he seemed to have entered another train of reflection: his look denoted abstraction from me and my business. I was obliged to recall him to a theme which was of necessity one of close and anxious interest to me.

'What is the employment you had in view, Mr Rivers? I hope this delay will not have increased the difficulty of securing it.'

'Oh, no; since it is an employment which depends only on me to give, and you to accept.'

He again paused: there seemed a reluctance to continue. I grew impatient: a restless movement or two, and an eager and exacting glance fastened on his face, conveyed the feeling to him as effectually as words could have done, and with less trouble.

'You need be in no hurry to hear,' he said: 'let me frankly tell you, I have nothing eligible or profitable to suggest. Before I explain, recall, if you please, my notice, clearly given, that if I helped you, it must be as the blind man would help the lame. I am poor; for I find that, when I have paid my father's debts, all the patrimony remaining to me will be this crumbling grange, the row of scathed firs behind, and the patch of moorish soil, with the yew trees and holly bushes in front. I am obscure: Rivers is an old name; but of the three sole descendants of the race, two earn the dependant's crust among strangers, and the third considers himself an alien from his native country – not only for life, but in death. Yes, and deems, and is bound to deem, himself honoured by the lot, and aspires but after the day when the cross of separation from fleshly ties shall be laid on his shoulders, and when the Head of that church-militant of whose humblest members he is one, shall give the word, "Rise, follow Me!" '

St John said these words as he pronounced his sermons, with a quiet, deep voice; with an unflushed cheek, and a coruscating radiance of glance. He resumed – 'And since I am myself poor and obscure, I can offer you but a service of poverty and obscurity. *You* may even think it degrading – for I see now your habits have been what the world calls refined: your tastes lean to the ideal, and your society has at least been amongst the educated; but *I* consider that no service degrades which can better our race. I hold that the more arid and unreclaimed the soil where the Christian labourer's task of tillage is appointed him – the scantier the meed his toil brings – the higher the honour. His, under such circumstances, is the destiny of the pioneer; and the first pioneers of the Gospel were the Apostles – their captain was Jesus, the Redeemer, Himself.'

'Well?' I said, as he again paused – 'proceed.'

He looked at me before he proceeded: indeed, he seemed leisurely to read my face, as if its features and lines were characters on a page. The conclusions drawn from this scrutiny he partially expressed in his succeeding observations.

'I believe you will accept the post I offer you,' said he, 'and hold it for a while: not permanently, though: any more than I could permanently keep the narrow and narrowing – the tranquil, hidden office of English country incumbent; for in your nature is an alloy as detrimental to repose as that in mine, though of a different kind.'

'Do explain,' I urged, when he halted once more.

'I will; and you shall hear how poor the proposal is, how trivial – how cramping. I shall not stay long at Morton, now that my father is dead, and that I am my own master. I shall leave the place probably in the course of a twelve-month; but while I do stay, I will exert myself to the utmost for its improvement. Morton, when I came to it two years ago, had no school: the children of the poor were excluded from every hope of progress. I established one for boys: I mean now to open a second school for girls. I have hired a building for the purpose, with a cottage of two rooms attached to it for the mistress's house. Her salary will be thirty pounds a year: her house is already furnished, very simply, but sufficiently, by the kindness of a lady, Miss Oliver; the only daughter of the sole rich man in my parish – Mr Oliver, the proprietor of a needle-factory and iron-foundry in the valley. The same lady pays for the education and clothing of an orphan from the workhouse, on condition that she shall aid the mistress in such menial offices connected with her own house and the school as her occupation of teaching will prevent her having time to discharge in person. Will you be this mistress?'

He put the question rather hurriedly; he seemed half to expect an indignant, or at least a disdainful rejection of the offer: not knowing all my thoughts and feelings, though guessing some, he could not tell in what light the lot would appear to me. In truth it was humble – but then it was sheltered, and I wanted a safe asylum: it was plodding – but then, compared with that of a governess in a rich house, it was independent; and the fear of servitude with strangers entered my soul like iron: it was not ignoble – not unworthy – not mentally degrading. I made my decision.

'I thank you for the proposal, Mr Rivers, and I accept it with all my heart.'

'But you comprehend me?' he said. 'It is a village school: your scholars will be only poor girls – cottagers' children – at the best, farmers' daughters. Knitting, sewing, reading, writing, ciphering, will be all you will have to teach. What will you do with your accomplishments? What, with the largest portion of your mind – sentiments – tastes?'

'Save them till they are wanted. They will keep.'

'You know what you undertake, then?'

'I do.'

He now smiled: and not a bitter or a sad smile, but one well pleased and deeply gratified.

'And when will you commence the exercise of your function?'

'I will go to my house tomorrow, and open the school, if you like, next week.'

'Very well: so be it.'

He rose and walked through the room. Standing still, he again looked at me. He shook his head.

'What do you disapprove of, Mr Rivers?' I asked.

'You will not stay at Morton long: no, no!'

'Why? What is your reason for saying so?'

'I read it in your eye; it is not of that description which promises the maintenance of an even tenor in life.'

'I am not ambitious.'

He started at the word 'ambitious.' He repeated, 'No. What made you think of ambition? Who is ambitious? I know I am: but how did you find it out?'

'I was speaking of myself.'

'Well, if you are not ambitious, you are – ' He paused.

'What?'

'I was going to say, impassioned: but perhaps you would have misunderstood the word, and been displeased. I mean, that human affections and sympathies have a most powerful hold on you. I am sure you cannot long be content to pass your leisure in solitude, and to devote your working hours to a monotonous labour wholly void of stimulus: any more than I can be content,' he added, with emphasis, 'to live here buried in morass, pent in with mountains – my nature, that God gave me, contravened; my faculties, heaven-bestowed, paralysed – made useless. You hear now how I contradict myself. I, who preached contentment with a humble lot, and justified the vocation even of hewers of wood and drawers of water in God's service – I, His ordained minister, almost rave in my restlessness. Well, propensities and principles must be reconciled by some means.'

He left the room. In this brief hour I had learnt more of him than in the whole previous month: yet still he puzzled me.

Diana and Mary Rivers became more sad and silent as the day approached for leaving their brother and their home. They both tried to appear as usual; but the sorrow they had to struggle against was one that could not be entirely conquered or concealed. Diana intimated that this would be a different parting from any they had ever yet known. It would probably, as far as St John was concerned, be a parting for years: it might be a parting for life.

'He will sacrifice all to his long-framed resolves,' she said: 'natural affection and feelings more potent still. St John looks quiet, Jane; but he hides a fever in his vitals. You would think him gentle, yet in some things he is inexorable as death; and the worst of it is, my conscience will hardly permit me to dissuade him from his severe decision: certainly, I cannot for a moment blame him for it. It is right, noble, Christian: yet it breaks my heart!' And the tears gushed to her fine eyes. Mary bent her head low over her work.

'We are now without father: we shall soon be without home and brother,' she murmured.

At that moment a little accident supervened, which seemed decreed by fate purposely to prove the truth of the adage, that 'misfortunes never come singly,' and to add to their distresses the vexing one of the slip between the cup and the lip. St John passed the window reading a letter. He entered.

'Our uncle John is dead,' said he.

Both the sisters seemed struck: not shocked or appalled; the tidings appeared in their eyes rather momentous than afflicting.

'Dead?' repeated Diana.

'Yes.'

She riveted a searching gaze on her brother's face. 'And what then?' she demanded, in a low voice.

'What then, Die?' he replied, maintaining a marble immobility of feature. 'What then? Why – nothing. Read.'

He threw the letter into her lap. She glanced over it, and handed it to Mary. Mary perused it in silence, and returned it to her brother. All three looked at each other, and all three smiled – a dreary, pensive smile enough.

'Amen! We can yet live,' said Diana at last.

'At any rate, it makes us no worse off than we were before,' remarked Mary.

'Only it forces rather strongly on the mind the picture of what *might have been*,' said Mr Rivers, 'and contrasts it somewhat too vividly with what *is*.'

He folded the letter, locked it in his desk, and again went out.

For some minutes no one spoke. Diana then turned to me.

'Jane, you will wonder at us and our mysteries,' she said, 'and think us hard-hearted beings not to be more moved at the death of so near a relation as an uncle; but we have never seen him or known him. He was my mother's brother. My father and he quarrelled long ago. It was by his advice that my father risked most of his property in the speculation that ruined him. Mutual recrimination passed between them: they parted in anger, and were never reconciled. My uncle engaged afterwards in more prosperous undertakings: it appears he realised a fortune of twenty thousand pounds. He was never married, and had no near kindred but ourselves and one other person, not more closely related than we. My father always cherished the idea that he would atone for his error by leaving his possessions to us; that letter informs us that he has bequeathed every penny to the other relation, with the exception of thirty guineas, to be divided between St John, Diana, and Mary Rivers, for the purchase of three mourning rings. He had a right, of course, to do as he pleased: and yet a momentary damp is cast on the spirits by the receipt of such news. Mary and I would have esteemed ourselves rich with a thousand pounds each; and to St John such a sum would have been valuable, for the good it would have enabled him to do.'

This explanation given, the subject was dropped, and no further reference made to it by either Mr Rivers or his sisters. The next day I left Marsh End for Morton. The day after, Diana and Mary quitted it for distant B—. In a week, Mr Rivers and Hannah repaired to the parsonage: and so the old grange was abandoned.

## *Chapter 31*

My home, then, when I at last find a home, is a cottage; a little room with whitewashed walls and a sanded floor, containing four painted chairs and a table, a clock, a cupboard, with two or three plates and dishes, and a set of tea-things in delf. Above, a chamber of the same dimensions as the kitchen, with a deal bedstead and chest of drawers; small, yet too large to be filled with my scanty wardrobe: though the kindness of my gentle and generous friends has increased that, by a modest stock of such things as are necessary.

It is evening. I have dismissed, with the fee of an orange, the little orphan who serves me as a hand-maid. I am sitting alone on the hearth. This morning, the village school opened. I had twenty scholars. But three of the number can read: none write or cipher. Several knit, and a few sew a little. They speak with the broadest accent of the district. At present, they and I have a difficulty in understanding each other's language. Some of them are unmannered, rough, intractable, as well as ignorant; but others are docile, have a wish to learn, and evince a disposition that pleases me. I must not forget that these coarsely-clad little peasants are of flesh and blood as good as the scions of gentlest genealogy; and that the germs of native excellence, refinement, intelligence, kind feeling, are as likely to exist in their hearts as in those of the best-born. My duty will be to develop these germs: surely I shall find some happiness in discharging that office. Much enjoyment I do not expect in the life opening before me: yet it will, doubtless, if I regulate my mind, and exert my powers as I ought, yield me enough to live on from day to day.

Was I very gleeful, settled, content, during the hours I passed in yonder bare, humble schoolroom this morning and afternoon? Not to deceive myself, I must reply – No: I felt desolate to a degree. I felt – yes, idiot that I am – I felt degraded. I doubted I had taken a step which sank instead of raising me in the scale of social existence. I was weakly dismayed at the ignorance, the poverty, the coarseness of all I heard and saw round me. But let me not hate and despise myself too much for these feelings; I know them to be wrong – that is a great step gained; I shall strive to overcome them. Tomorrow, I trust, I shall get the better of them partially; and in a few weeks, perhaps, they will be quite subdued. In a few months, it is possible, the happiness of seeing progress, and a change for the better in my scholars may substitute gratification for disgust.

Meantime, let me ask myself one question – Which is better? – To have surrendered to temptation; listened to passion; made no painful effort – no struggle; but to have sunk down in the silken snare; fallen asleep on the flowers covering it; wakened in a southern clime, amongst the luxuries of a pleasure villa: to have been now living in France, Mr Rochester's mistress; delirious with his love half my time – for he would – oh, yes, he would have loved me well for a while. He *did* love me – no one will ever love me so again. I shall never more know the sweet homage given to beauty, youth, and grace – for never to anyone else shall I seem to possess these charms. He was fond and proud of me – it is what no man besides will ever be. But where am I wandering, and what am I saying, and above all, feeling? Whether is it better, I ask, to be a slave in a fool's paradise at Marseilles – fevered with delusive bliss one hour – suffocating with the bitterest tears of remorse and shame the next – or to be a village-schoolmistress, free and honest, in a breezy mountain nook in the healthy heart of England?

Yes; I feel now that I was right when I adhered to principle and law, and scorned and crushed the insane promptings of a frenzied moment. God directed me to a correct choice: I thank His providence for the guidance!

Having brought my eventide musings to this point, I rose, went to my door, and looked at the sunset of the harvest-day, and at the quiet fields before my cottage, which, with the school, was distant half a mile from the village. The birds were singing their last strains – 'The air was mild, the dew was balm'.

While I looked, I thought myself happy, and was surprised to find myself ere long weeping – and why? For the doom which had reft me from adhesion to my master: for him I was no more to see; for the desperate grief and fatal fury – consequences of my departure – which might now, perhaps, be dragging him from the path of right, too far to leave hope of ultimate restoration thither. At this thought, I turned my face aside from the lovely sky of eve and lonely vale of Morton – I say *lonely*, for in that bend of it visible to me there was no building apparent save the church and the parsonage, half-hid in trees, and, quite at the extremity, the roof of Vale Hall, where the rich Mr Oliver and his daughter lived. I hid my eyes, and leant my head against the stone frame of my door; but soon a slight noise near the wicket which shut in my tiny garden from the meadow beyond it made me look up. A dog – old Carlo, Mr Rivers' pointer, as I saw in a moment – was pushing the gate with his nose, and St John himself leant upon it with folded arms; his brow knit, his gaze, grave almost to displeasure, fixed on me. I asked him to come in.

'No, I cannot stay; I have only brought you a little parcel my sisters left for you. I think it contains a colour-box, pencils, and paper.'

I approached to take it: a welcome gift it was. He examined my face, I thought, with austerity, as I came near: the traces of tears were doubtless very visible upon it.

'Have you found your first day's work harder than you expected?' he asked.

'Oh, no! On the contrary, I think in time I shall get on with my scholars very well.'

'But perhaps your accommodations – your cottage – your furniture – have disappointed your expectations? They are, in truth, scanty enough; but – ' I interrupted – 'My cottage is clean and weather-proof; my furniture sufficient and commodious. All I see has made me thankful, not despondent. I am not absolutely such a fool and sensualist as to regret the absence of a carpet, a sofa, and silver plate; besides, five weeks ago I had nothing – I was an outcast, a beggar, a vagrant; now I have acquaintance, a home, a business. I wonder at the goodness of God; the generosity of my friends; the bounty of my lot. I do not repine.'

'But you feel solitude an oppression? The little house there behind you is dark and empty.'

'I have hardly had time yet to enjoy a sense of tranquillity, much less to grow impatient under one of loneliness.'

'Very well; I hope you feel the content you express: at any rate, your good sense will tell you that it is too soon yet to yield to the vacillating fears of Lot's wife. What you had left before I saw you, of course I do not know; but I counsel you to resist firmly every temptation which would incline you to look back: pursue your present career steadily, for some months at least.'

'It is what I mean to do,' I answered. St John continued – 'It is hard work to control the workings of inclination and turn the bent of nature; but that it may be done, I know from experience. God has given us, in a measure, the power to make our own fate; and when our energies seem to demand a sustenance they cannot get – when our will strains after a path we may not follow – we need neither starve from inanition, nor stand still in despair: we have but to seek another nourishment for the mind, as strong as the forbidden food it longed to taste – and perhaps purer; and to hew out for the adventurous foot a road as direct and broad as the one Fortune has blocked up against us, if rougher than it.

'A year ago I was myself intensely miserable, because I thought I had made a mistake in entering the ministry: its uniform duties wearied me to death. I burnt for the more active life of the world – for the more exciting toils of a literary career – for the destiny of an artist, author, orator; anything rather than that of a priest: yes, the heart of a politician, of a soldier, of a votary of glory, a lover of renown, a luster after power, beat under my curate's surplice. I considered; my life was so wretched, it must be changed, or I must die. After a season of darkness and struggling, light broke and relief fell: my cramped existence all at once spread out to a plain without bounds – my powers heard a call from heaven to rise, gather their full strength, spread their wings, and mount beyond ken. God had an errand for me; to bear which afar, to deliver it well, skill and strength, courage and eloquence, the best qualifications of soldier, statesman, and orator, were all needed: for these all centre in the good missionary.

'A missionary I resolved to be. From that moment my state of mind changed; the fetters dissolved and dropped from every faculty, leaving nothing of bondage but its galling soreness – which time only can heal. My father, indeed, opposed the determination, but since his death, I have not a legitimate obstacle to contend with; some affairs settled, a successor for Morton provided, an entanglement or two of the feelings broken through or cut asunder – a last conflict with human weakness, in which I know I shall overcome, because I have vowed that I *will* overcome – and I leave Europe for the East.'

He said this, in his peculiar, subdued, yet emphatic voice; looking, when he had ceased speaking, not at me, but at the setting sun, at which I looked too. Both he and I had our backs towards the path leading up the field to the wicket. We had heard no step on that grass-grown track; the water running in the vale was the one lulling sound of the hour and scene; we might well then start when a gay voice, sweet as a silver bell, exclaimed – 'Good-evening, Mr Rivers. And good-evening, old Carlo. Your dog is quicker to recognise his friends than you are, sir; he pricked his ears and wagged his tail when I was at the bottom of the field, and you have your back towards me now.'

It was true. Though Mr Rivers had started at the first of those musical accents, as if a thunderbolt had split a cloud over his head, he stood yet, at the close of the sentence, in the same attitude in which the speaker had surprised him – his arm resting on the gate, his face directed towards the west. He turned at last, with measured deliberation. A vision, as it seemed to me, had risen at his side. There appeared, within three feet of him, a form clad in pure white – a youthful, graceful form: full, yet fine in contour; and when, after bending to caress Carlo, it lifted up its head, and threw back a long veil, there bloomed under his glance a face of perfect beauty. Perfect beauty is a strong expression; but I do not retrace or qualify it: as sweet features as ever the temperate clime of Albion moulded; as pure hues of rose and lily as ever her humid gales and vapoury skies generated and screened, justified, in this instance, the term. No charm was wanting, no defect was perceptible; the young girl had regular and delicate lineaments; eyes shaped and coloured as we see them in lovely pictures, large, and dark, and full; the long and shadowy eyelash which encircles a fine eye with so soft a fascination; the pencilled brow which gives such clearness; the white smooth forehead, which adds such repose to the livelier beauties of tint and ray; the cheek oval, fresh, and smooth; the lips, fresh too, ruddy, healthy, sweetly formed; the even and gleaming teeth without flaw; the small dimpled chin; the ornament of rich, plenteous tresses – all advantages, in short, which, combined, realise the ideal of beauty, were fully hers. I wondered, as I looked at this fair creature: I admired her with my whole heart. Nature had surely formed her in a partial mood; and, forgetting her usual stinted stepmother dole of gifts, had endowed this, her darling, with a grand-dame's bounty.

What did St John Rivers think of this earthly angel? I naturally asked myself that question as I saw him turn to her and look at her; and, as naturally, I sought the answer to the enquiry in his countenance. He had already withdrawn his eye from the Peri, and was looking at a humble tuft of daisies which grew by the wicket.

'A lovely evening, but late for you to be out alone,' he said, as he crushed the snowy heads of the closed flowers with his foot.

'Oh, I only came home from S—' (she mentioned the name of a large town some twenty miles distant) 'this afternoon. Papa told me you had opened your school, and that the new mistress was come; and so I put on my bonnet after tea, and ran up the valley to see her: this is she?' pointing to me.

'It is,' said St John.

'Do you think you shall like Morton?' she asked of me, with a direct and naïve simplicity of tone and manner, pleasing, if childlike.

'I hope I shall. I have many inducements to do so.'

'Did you find your scholars as attentive as you expected?'

'Quite.'

'Do you like your house?'

'Very much.'

'Have I furnished it nicely?'

'Very nicely, indeed.'

'And made a good choice of an attendant for you in Alice Wood?'

'You have indeed. She is teachable and handy.' (This then, I thought, is Miss Oliver, the heiress; favoured, it seems, in the gifts of fortune, as well as in those of nature! What happy combination of the planets presided over her birth, I wonder?)

'I shall come up and help you to teach sometimes,' she added. 'It will be a change for me to visit you now and then; and I like a change. Mr Rivers, I have been *so* gay during my stay at S—. Last night, or rather this morning, I was dancing till two o'clock. The —th regiment are stationed there since the riots; and the officers are the most agreeable men in the world: they put all our young knife-grinders and scissor merchants to shame.'

It seemed to me that Mr St John's under lip protruded, and his upper lip curled a moment. His mouth certainly looked a good deal compressed, and the lower part of his face unusually stern and square, as the laughing girl gave him this information. He lifted his gaze, too, from the daisies, and turned it on her. An unsmiling, a searching, a meaning gaze it was. She answered it with a second laugh, and laughter well became her youth, her roses, her dimples, her bright eyes.

As he stood, mute and grave, she again fell to caressing Carlo. 'Poor Carlo loves me,' said she. '*He* is not stern and distant to his friends; and if he could speak, he would not be silent.'

As she patted the dog's head, bending with native grace before his young and austere master, I saw a glow rise to that master's face. I saw his solemn eye melt with sudden fire, and flicker with resistless emotion. Flushed and kindled thus, he looked nearly as beautiful for a man as she for a woman. His chest heaved once, as if his large heart, weary of despotic constriction, had expanded, despite the will, and made a vigorous bound for the attainment of liberty. But he curbed it, I think, as a resolute rider would curb a rearing steed. He responded neither by word nor movement to the gentle advances made him.

'Papa says you never come to see us now,' continued Miss Oliver, looking up. 'You are quite a stranger at Vale Hall. He is alone this evening, and not very well: will you return with me and visit him?'

'It is not a seasonable hour to intrude on Mr Oliver,' answered St John.

'Not a seasonable hour! But I declare it is. It is just the hour when papa most wants company: when the works are closed and he has no business to occupy him. Now, Mr Rivers, *do* come. Why are you so very shy, and so very sombre?' She filled up the hiatus his silence left by a reply of her own.

'I forgot!' she exclaimed, shaking her beautiful curled head, as if shocked at herself. 'I am so giddy and thoughtless! *Do* excuse me. It had slipped my memory that you have good reasons to be indisposed for joining in my chatter. Diana and Mary have left you, and Moor House is shut up, and you are so lonely. I am sure I pity you. Do come and see papa.'

'Not tonight, Miss Rosamond, not tonight.'

Mr St John spoke almost like an automaton: himself only knew the effort it cost him thus to refuse.

'Well, if you are so obstinate, I will leave you; for I dare not stay any longer: the dew begins to fall. Good-evening!'

She held out her hand. He just touched it. 'Good-evening!' he repeated, in a voice low and hollow as an echo. She turned, but in a moment returned.

'Are you well?' she asked. Well might she put the question: his face was blanched as her gown.

'Quite well,' he enunciated; and, with a bow, he left the gate. She went one way; he another. She turned twice to gaze after him as she tripped fairy-like down the field; he, as he strode firmly across, never turned at all.

This spectacle of another's suffering and sacrifice rapt my thoughts from exclusive meditation on my own. Diana Rivers had designated her brother 'inexorable as death'. She had not exaggerated.

## *Chapter 32*

I continued the labours of the village-school as actively and faithfully as I could. It was truly hard work at first. Some time elapsed before, with all my efforts, I could comprehend my scholars and their nature. Wholly untaught, with faculties quite torpid, they seemed to me hopelessly dull; and, at first sight, all dull alike: but I soon found I was mistaken. There was a difference amongst them as amongst the educated; and when I got to know them, and they me, this difference rapidly developed itself. Their amazement at me, my language, my rules, and ways, once subsided, I found some of these heavy-looking, gaping rustics wake up into sharp-witted girls enough. Many showed themselves obliging, and amiable too; and I discovered amongst them not a few examples of natural politeness, and innate self-respect, as well as of excellent capacity, that won both my goodwill and my admiration. These soon took a pleasure in doing their work well, in keeping their persons neat, in learning their tasks regularly, in acquiring quiet and orderly manners. The rapidity of their progress, in some instances, was even surprising; and an honest and happy pride I took in it: besides, I began personally to like some of the best girls; and they liked me. I had amongst my scholars several farmers' daughters: young women grown, almost. These could already read, write, and sew; and to them I taught the elements of grammar, geography, history, and the finer kinds of needlework. I found estimable characters amongst them – characters desirous of information and disposed for improvement – with whom I passed many a pleasant evening hour in their own homes. Their parents then (the farmer and his wife) loaded me with attentions. There was an enjoyment in accepting their simple kindness, and in repaying it by a consideration – a scrupulous regard to their feelings – to which they were not, perhaps, at all times accustomed, and which both charmed and benefited them; because, while it elevated them in their own eyes, it made them emulous to merit the deferential treatment they received.

I felt I became a favourite in the neighbourhood. Whenever I went out, I heard on all sides cordial salutations, and was welcomed with friendly smiles. To live amidst general regard, though it be but the regard of working people, is like 'sitting in sunshine, calm and sweet'; serene inward feelings bud and bloom under the ray. At this period of my life, my heart far oftener swelled with thankfulness than sank with dejection: and yet, reader, to tell you all, in the midst of this calm, this useful existence – after a day passed in honourable exertion amongst my scholars, an evening spent in drawing or reading contentedly alone – I used to rush into strange dreams at night: dreams many-coloured, agitated, full of the ideal, the stirring, the stormy – dreams where, amidst unusual scenes, charged with adventure, with agitating risk and romantic chance, I still again and again met Mr Rochester, always at some exciting crisis; and then the sense of being in his arms, hearing his voice, meeting his eye, touching his hand and cheek, loving him, being loved by him – the hope of passing a lifetime at his side, would be renewed, with all its first force and fire. Then I awoke. Then I recalled where I was, and how situated. Then I rose up on my curtainless bed, trembling and quivering; and then the still, dark night witnessed the convulsion of despair, and heard the burst of passion. By nine o'clock the next morning I was punctually opening the school; tranquil, settled, prepared for the steady duties of the day.

Rosamond Oliver kept her word in coming to visit me. Her call at the school was generally made in the course of her morning ride. She would canter up to the door on her pony, followed by a mounted livery servant. Anything more exquisite than her appearance, in her purple habit, with her Amazon's cap of black velvet placed gracefully above the long curls that kissed her cheek and floated to her shoulders, can scarcely be imagined: and it was thus she would enter the rustic building, and glide through the dazzled ranks of the village children. She generally came at the hour when Mr Rivers was engaged in giving his daily catechising lesson. Keenly, I fear, did the eye of the visitress pierce the young pastor's heart. A sort of instinct seemed to warn him of her entrance, even when he did not see it; and when he was looking quite away from the door, if she appeared at it, his cheek would glow, and his marble-seeming features, though they refused to relax, changed indescribably, and in their very quiescence became expressive of a repressed fervour, stronger than working muscle or darting glance could indicate.

Of course, she knew her power: indeed, he did not, because he could not, conceal it from her. In spite of his Christian stoicism, when she went up and addressed him, and smiled gaily, encouragingly, even fondly in his face, his hand would tremble and his eye burn. He seemed to say, with his sad and resolute look, if he did not say it with his lips, 'I love you, and I know you prefer me. It is not despair of success that keeps me dumb. If I offered my heart, I believe you would accept it. But that heart is already laid on a sacred altar: the fire is arranged round it. It will soon be no more than a sacrifice consumed.'

And then she would pout like a disappointed child; a pensive cloud would soften her radiant vivacity; she would withdraw her hand hastily from his, and turn in transient petulance from his aspect, at once so heroic and so martyr-like. St John, no doubt, would have given the world to follow, recall, retain her, when she thus left him; but he would not give one chance of heaven, nor relinquish, for the elysium of her love, one hope of the true, eternal Paradise. Besides, he could not bind all that he had in his nature – the rover, the aspirant, the poet, the priest – in the limits of a single passion. He could not – he would not – renounce his wild field of mission warfare for the parlours and the peace of Vale Hall. I learnt so much from himself in an inroad I once, despite his reserve, had the daring to make on his confidence.

Miss Oliver already honoured me with frequent visits to my cottage. I had learnt her whole character, which was without mystery or disguise: she was coquettish, but not heartless; exacting, but not worthlessly selfish. She had been indulged from her birth, but was not absolutely spoilt. She was hasty, but good-humoured; vain (she could not help it, when every glance in the glass showed her such a flush of loveliness), but not affected; liberal-handed; innocent of the pride of wealth; ingenuous; sufficiently intelligent; gay, lively, and unthinking: she was very charming, in short, even to a cool observer of her own sex like me; but she was not profoundly interesting or thoroughly impressive. A very different sort of mind was hers from that, for instance, of the sisters of St John. Still, I liked her almost as I liked my pupil Adèle; except that, for a child whom we have watched over and taught, a closer affection is engendered than we can give an equally attractive adult acquaintance.

She had taken an amiable caprice to me. She said I was like Mr Rivers, only, certainly, she allowed, 'not one-tenth so handsome, though I was a nice neat little soul enough, but he was an angel'. I was, however, good, clever, composed, and firm, like him. I was a *lusus naturae*, she affirmed, as a village schoolmistress: she was sure my previous history, if known, would make a delightful romance.

One evening, while, with her usual childlike activity, and thoughtless yet not offensive inquisitiveness, she was rummaging the cupboard and the table-drawer of my little kitchen, she discovered first two French books, a volume of Schiller, a German grammar and dictionary, and then my drawing-materials and some sketches, including a pencil-head of a pretty little cherub-like girl, one of my scholars, and sundry views from nature, taken in the Vale of Morton and on the surrounding moors. She was first transfixed with surprise, and then electrified with delight.

'Had I done these pictures? Did I know French and German? What a love – what a miracle I was! I drew better than her master in the first school in S—. Would I sketch a portrait of her, to show to papa?'

'With pleasure,' I replied; and I felt a thrill of artist-delight at the idea of copying from so perfect and radiant a model. She had then on a dark-blue silk dress; her arms and her neck were bare; her only ornament was her chestnut tresses, which waved over her shoulders with all the wild grace of natural curls. I took a sheet of fine cardboard, and drew a careful outline. I promised myself the pleasure of colouring it; and, as it was getting late then, I told her she must come and sit another day.

She made such a report of me to her father, that Mr Oliver himself accompanied her next evening – a tall, massive-featured, middle-aged, and grey-headed man, at whose side his lovely daughter looked like a bright flower near a hoary turret. He appeared a taciturn, and perhaps a proud personage; but he was very kind to me. The sketch of Rosamond's portrait pleased him highly: he said I must make a finished picture of it. He insisted, too, on my coming the next day to spend the evening at Vale Hall.

I went. I found it a large, handsome residence, showing abundant evidences of wealth in the proprietor. Rosamond was full of glee and pleasure all the time I stayed. Her father was affable; and when he entered into conversation with me after tea, he expressed in strong terms his approbation of what I had done in Morton school, and said he only feared, from what he saw and heard, I was too good for the place, and would soon quit it for one more suitable.

'Indeed,' cried Rosamond, 'she is clever enough to be a governess in a high family, papa.'

I thought I would far rather be where I am than in any high family in the land. Mr Oliver spoke of Mr Rivers – of the Rivers family – with great respect. He said it was a very old name in that neighbourhood; that the ancestors of the house were wealthy; that all Morton had once belonged to them; that even now he considered the representative of that house might, if he liked, make an alliance with the best. He accounted it a pity that so fine and talented a young man should have formed the design of going out as a missionary; it was quite throwing a valuable life away. It appeared, then, that her father would throw no obstacle in the way of Rosamond's union with St John. Mr Oliver evidently regarded the young clergyman's good birth, old name, and sacred profession as sufficient compensation for the want of fortune.

It was the 5th of November, and a holiday. My little servant, after helping me to clean my house, was gone, well satisfied with the fee of a penny for her aid. All about me was spotless and bright – scoured floor, polished grate, and well-rubbed chairs. I had also made myself neat, and had now the afternoon before me to spend as I would.

The translation of a few pages of German occupied an hour; then I got my palette and pencils, and fell to the more soothing, because easier occupation, of completing Rosamond Oliver's miniature. The head was finished already: there was but the background to tint and the drapery to shade off; a touch of carmine, too, to add to the ripe lips – a soft curl here and there to the tresses – a deeper tinge to the shadow of the lash under the azured eyelid. I was absorbed in the execution of these nice details, when, after one rapid tap, my door unclosed, admitting St John Rivers.

'I am come to see how you are spending your holiday,' he said. 'Not, I hope, in thought? No, that is well: while you draw you will not feel lonely. You see, I mistrust you still, though you have borne up wonderfully so far. I have brought you a book for evening solace,' and he laid on the table a new publication – a poem: one of those genuine productions so often vouchsafed to the fortunate public of those days – the golden age of modern literature. Alas! the readers of our era are less favoured. But courage! I will not pause either to accuse or repine. I know poetry is not dead, nor genius lost; nor has Mammon gained power over either, to bind or slay: they will both assert their existence, their presence, their liberty and strength again one day. Powerful angels, safe in heaven! they smile when sordid souls triumph, and feeble ones weep over their destruction. Poetry destroyed? Genius banished? No! Mediocrity, no: do not let envy prompt you to the thought. No; they not only live, but reign and redeem: and without their divine influence spread everywhere, you would be in hell – the hell of your own meanness.

While I was eagerly glancing at the bright pages of *Marmion* (for *Marmion* it was), St John stooped to examine my drawing. His tall figure sprang erect again with a start: he said nothing. I looked up at him: he shunned my eye. I knew his thoughts well, and could read his heart plainly; at the moment I felt calmer and cooler than he: I had then temporarily the advantage of him, and I conceived an inclination to do him some good, if I could.

'With all his firmness and self-control,' thought I, 'he tasks himself too far: locks every feeling and pang within – expresses, confesses, imparts nothing. I am sure it would benefit him to talk a little about this sweet Rosamond, whom he thinks he ought not to marry: I will make him talk.'

I said first, 'Take a chair, Mr Rivers.' But he answered, as he always did, that he could not stay. 'Very well,' I responded, mentally, 'stand if you like; but you shall not go just yet, I am determined: solitude is at least as bad for you as it is for me. I'll try if I cannot discover the secret spring of your confidence, and find an aperture in that marble breast through which I can shed one drop of the balm of sympathy.'

'Is this portrait like?' I asked bluntly.

'Like! Like whom? I did not observe it closely.'

'You did, Mr Rivers.'

He almost started at my sudden and strange abruptness: he looked at me astonished. 'Oh, that is nothing yet,' I muttered within. 'I don't mean to be baffled by a little stiffness on your part; I'm prepared to go to considerable lengths.' I continued, 'You observed it closely and distinctly; but I have no objection to your looking at it again,' and I rose and placed it in his hand.

'A well-executed picture,' he said; 'very soft, clear colouring; very graceful and correct drawing.'

'Yes, yes; I know all that. But what of the resemblance? Who is it like?'

Mastering some hesitation, he answered, 'Miss Oliver, I presume.'

'Of course. And now, sir, to reward you for the accurate guess, I will promise to paint you a careful and faithful duplicate of this very picture, provided you admit that the gift would be acceptable to you. I don't wish to throw away my time and trouble on an offering you would deem worthless.'

He continued to gaze at the picture: the longer he looked, the firmer he held it, the more he seemed to covet it. 'It is like!' he murmured; 'the eye is well managed: the colour, light, expression, are perfect. It smiles!'

'Would it comfort, or would it wound you to have a similar painting? Tell me that. When you are at Madagascar, or at the Cape, or in India, would it be a consolation to have that memento in your possession? or would the sight of it bring recollections calculated to enervate and distress?'

He now furtively raised his eyes: he glanced at me, irresolute, disturbed: he again surveyed the picture.

'That I should like to have it is certain: whether it would be judicious or wise is another question.'

Since I had ascertained that Rosamond really preferred him, and that her father was not likely to oppose the match, I – less exalted in my views than St John – had been strongly disposed in my own heart to advocate their union. It seemed to me that, should he become the possessor of Mr Oliver's large fortune, he might do as much good with it as if he went and laid his genius out to wither, and his strength to waste, under a tropical sun. With this persuasion I now answered – 'As far as I can see, it would be wiser and more judicious if you were to take to yourself the original at once.'

By this time he had sat down: he had laid the picture on the table before him, and with his brow supported on both hands, hung fondly over it. I discerned he was now neither angry nor shocked at my audacity. I saw even that to be thus frankly addressed on a subject he had deemed unapproachable – to hear it thus freely handled – was beginning to be felt by him as a new pleasure – an unhoped-for relief. Reserved people often really need the frank discussion of their sentiments and griefs more than the expansive. The sternest-seeming stoic is human after all; and to 'burst' with boldness and goodwill into 'the silent sea' of their souls is often to confer on them the first of obligations.

'She likes you, I am sure,' said I, as I stood behind his chair, 'and her father respects you. Moreover, she is a sweet girl – rather thoughtless; but you would have sufficient thought for both yourself and her. You ought to marry her.'

'*Does* she like me?' he asked.

'Certainly; better than she likes anyone else. She talks of you continually: there is no subject she enjoys so much or touches upon so often.'

'It is very pleasant to hear this,' he said – 'very: go on for another quarter of an hour.' And he actually took out his watch and laid it upon the table to measure the time.

'But where is the use of going on,' I asked, 'when you are probably preparing some iron blow of contradiction, or forging a fresh chain to fetter your heart?'

'Don't imagine such hard things. Fancy me yielding and melting, as I am doing: human love rising like a freshly opened fountain in my mind and overflowing with sweet inundation all the field I have so carefully and with such labour prepared – so assiduously sown with the seeds of good intentions, of self-denying plans. And now it is deluged with a nectarous flood – the young germs swamped – delicious poison cankering them: now I see myself stretched on an ottoman in the drawing-room at Vale Hall at my bride Rosamond Oliver's feet: she is talking to me with her sweet voice – gazing down on me with those eyes your skilful hand has copied so well – smiling at me with these coral lips. She is mine – I am hers – this present life and passing world suffice to me. Hush! say nothing – my heart is full of delight – my senses are entranced – let the time I marked pass in peace.'

I humoured him: the watch ticked on: he breathed fast and low: I stood silent. Amidst this hush the quarter sped; he replaced the watch, laid the picture down, rose, and stood on the hearth.

'Now,' said he, 'that little space was given to delirium and delusion. I rested my temples on the breast of temptation, and put my neck voluntarily under her yoke of flowers; I tasted her cup. The pillow was burning: there is an asp in the garland: the wine has a bitter taste: her promises are hollow – her offers false: I see and know all this.'

I gazed at him in wonder.

'It is strange,' pursued he, 'that while I love Rosamond Oliver so wildly – with all the intensity, indeed, of a first passion, the object of which is exquisitely beautiful, graceful, and fascinating – I experience at the same time a calm, unwarped consciousness that she would not make me a good wife; that she is not the partner suited to me; that I should discover this within a year after marriage; and that to twelve months' rapture would succeed a lifetime of regret. This I know.'

'Strange indeed!' I could not help ejaculating.

'While something in me,' he went on, 'is acutely sensible to her charms, something else is as deeply impressed with her defects: they are such that she could sympathise in nothing I aspired to – co-operate in nothing I undertook. Rosamond a sufferer, a labourer, a female apostle? Rosamond a missionary's wife? No!'

'But you need not be a missionary. You might relinquish that scheme.'

'Relinquish! What! my vocation? My great work? My foundation laid on earth for a mansion in heaven? My hopes of being numbered in the band who have merged all ambitions in the glorious one of bettering their race – of carrying knowledge into the realms of ignorance – of substituting peace for war – freedom for bondage – religion for superstition – the hope of heaven for the fear of hell? Must I relinquish that? It is dearer than the blood in my veins. It is what I have to look forward to, and to live for.'

After a considerable pause, I said – 'And Miss Oliver? Are her disappointment and sorrow of no interest to you?'

'Miss Oliver is ever surrounded by suitors and flatterers: in less than a month, my image will be effaced from her heart. She will forget me; and will marry, probably, someone who will make her far happier than I should do.'

'You speak coolly enough; but you suffer in the conflict. You are wasting away.'

'No. If I get a little thin, it is with anxiety about my prospects, yet unsettled – my departure, continually procrastinated. Only this morning, I received intelligence that the successor, whose arrival I have been so long expecting, cannot be ready to replace me for three months to come yet; and perhaps the three months may extend to six.'

'You tremble and become flushed whenever Miss Oliver enters the schoolroom.'

Again the surprised expression crossed his face. He had not imagined that a woman would dare to speak so to a man. For me, I felt at home in this sort of discourse. I could never rest in communication with strong, discreet, and refined minds, whether male or female, till I had passed the outworks of conventional reserve, and crossed the threshold of confidence, and won a place by their heart's very hearthstone.

'You *are* original,' said he, 'and not timid. There is something brave in your spirit, as well as penetrating in your eye; but allow me to assure you that you partially misinterpret my emotions. You think them more profound and potent than they are. You give me a larger allowance of sympathy than I have a just claim to. When I colour, and when I shake before Miss Oliver, I do not pity myself. I scorn the weakness. I know it is ignoble: a mere fever of the flesh: not, I declare, the convulsion of the soul. *That* is just as fixed as a rock, firm set in the depths of a restless sea. Know me to be what I am – a cold, hard man.'

I smiled incredulously.

'You have taken my confidence by storm,' he continued, 'and now it is much at your service. I am simply, in my original state – stripped of that blood-bleached robe with which Christianity covers human deformity – a cold, hard, ambitious man. Natural affection only, of all the sentiments, has permanent power over me. Reason, and not feeling, is my guide; my ambition is unlimited: my desire to rise higher, to do more than others, insatiable. I honour endurance, perseverance, industry, talent; because these are the means by which men achieve great ends and mount to lofty eminence. I watch your career with interest, because I consider you a specimen of a diligent, orderly, energetic woman: not because I deeply compassionate what you have gone through, or what you still suffer.'

'You would describe yourself as a mere pagan philosopher,' I said.

'No. There is this difference between me and deistic philosophers: I believe; and I believe the Gospel. You missed your epithet. I am not a pagan, but a Christian philosopher – a follower of the sect of Jesus. As His disciple I adopt His pure, His merciful, His benignant doctrines. I advocate them: I am sworn to spread them. Won in youth to religion, she has cultivated my original qualities thus: From the minute germ, natural affection, she has developed the overshadowing tree, philanthropy. From the wild stringy root of human uprightness, she has reared a due sense of the Divine justice. Of the ambition to win power and renown for my wretched self, she has formed the ambition to spread my Master's kingdom; to achieve victories for the standard of the cross. So much has religion done for me; turning the original materials to the best account; pruning and training nature. But she could not eradicate nature: nor will it be eradicated "till this mortal shall put on immortality".'

Having said this, he took his hat, which lay on the table beside my palette. Once more he looked at the portrait.

'She *is* lovely,' he murmured. 'She is well named the Rose of the World, indeed!'

'And may I not paint one like it for you?'

'*Cui bono?* No.'

He drew over the picture the sheet of thin paper on which I was accustomed to rest my hand in painting, to prevent the cardboard from being sullied. What he suddenly saw on this blank paper, it was impossible for me to tell; but something had caught his eye. He took it up with a snatch; he looked at the edge; then shot a glance at me, inexpressibly peculiar, and quite incomprehensible: a glance that seemed to take and make note of every point in my shape, face, and dress; for it traversed all, quick, keen as lightning. His lips parted, as if to speak: but he checked the coming sentence, whatever it was.

'What is the matter?' I asked.

'Nothing in the world,' was the reply; and, replacing the paper, I saw him dexterously tear a narrow slip from the margin. It disappeared in his glove; and, with one hasty nod and 'good-afternoon', he vanished.

'Well!' I exclaimed, using an expression of the district, 'that caps the globe, however!'

I, in my turn, scrutinised the paper; but saw nothing on it save a few dingy stains of paint where I had tried the tint in my pencil. I pondered the mystery a minute or two; but finding it insolvable, and being certain it could not be of much moment, I dismissed, and soon forgot it.

## *Chapter 33*

When Mr St John went, it was beginning to snow; the whirling storm continued all night. The next day a keen wind brought fresh and blinding falls; by twilight the valley was drifted up and almost impassable. I had closed my shutter, laid a mat to the door to prevent the snow from blowing in under it, trimmed my fire, and after sitting nearly an hour on the hearth listening to the muffled fury of the tempest, I lit a candle, took down *Marmion*, and beginning –

Day set on Norham's castled steep,
And Tweed's fair river broad and deep
And Cheviot's mountains lone;
The massive towers, the donjon keep
The flanking walls that round them sweep,
In yellow lustre shone –

I soon forgot storm in music.

I heard a noise: the wind, I thought, shook the door. No; it was St John Rivers, who, lifting the latch, came in out of the frozen hurricane – the howling darkness – and stood before me: the cloak that covered his tall figure all white as a glacier. I was almost in consternation, so little had I expected any guest from the blocked-up vale that night.

'Any ill news?' I demanded. 'Has anything happened?'

'No. How very easily alarmed you are?' he answered, removing his cloak and hanging it up against the door, towards which he again coolly pushed the mat which his entrance had deranged. He stamped the snow from his boots.

'I shall sully the purity of your floor,' said he, 'but you must excuse me for once.' Then he approached the fire. 'I have had hard work to get here, I assure you,' he observed, as he warmed his hands over the flame. 'One drift took me up to the waist; happily the snow is quite soft yet.'

'But why are you come?' I could not forbear saying.

'Rather an inhospitable question to put to a visitor; but since you ask it, I answer simply to have a little talk with you; I got tired of my mute books and empty rooms. Besides, since yesterday I have experienced the excitement of a person to whom a tale has been half-told, and who is impatient to hear the sequel.'

He sat down. I recalled his singular conduct of yesterday, and really I began to fear his wits were touched. If he were insane, however, his was a very cool and collected insanity: I had never seen that handsome-featured face of his look more like chiselled marble than it did just now, as he put aside his snow-wet hair from his forehead and let the firelight shine free on his pale brow and cheek as pale, where it grieved me to discover the hollow trace of care or sorrow now so plainly graved. I waited, expecting he would say something I could at least comprehend; but his hand was now at his chin, his finger on his lip: he was thinking. It struck me that his hand looked wasted like his face. A perhaps uncalled-for gush of pity came over my heart: I was moved to say – 'I wish Diana or Mary would come and live with you: it is too bad that you should be quite alone; and you are recklessly rash about your own health.'

'Not at all,' said he: 'I care for myself when necessary. I am well now. What do you see amiss in me?'

This was said with a careless, abstracted indifference which showed that my solicitude was, at least in his opinion, wholly superfluous. I was silenced.

He still slowly moved his finger over his upper lip, and still his eye dwelt dreamily on the glowing grate; thinking it urgent to say something, I asked him presently if he felt any cold draught from the door, which was behind him.

'No, no!' he responded shortly and somewhat testily.

'Well,' I reflected, 'if you won't talk, you may be still; I'll let you alone now, and return to my book.'

So I snuffed the candle and resumed the perusal of *Marmion*. He soon stirred; my eye was instantly drawn to his movements; he only took out a morocco pocketbook, thence produced a letter, which he read in silence, folded it, put it back, relapsed into meditation. It was vain to try to read with such an inscrutable fixture before me; nor could I, in my impatience, consent to be dumb; he might rebuff me if he liked, but talk I would.

'Have you heard from Diana and Mary lately?'

'Not since the letter I showed you a week ago.'

'There has not been any change made about your own arrangements? You will not be summoned to leave England sooner than you expected?'

'I fear not, indeed: such chance is too good to befall me.' Baffled so far, I changed my ground. I bethought myself to talk about the school and my scholars.

'Mary Garrett's mother is better, and Mary came back to the school this morning, and I shall have four new girls next week from the Foundry Close – they would have come today but for the snow.'

'Indeed!'

'Mr Oliver pays for two.'

'Does he?'

'He means to give the whole school a treat at Christmas.'

'I know.'

'Was it your suggestion?'

'No.'

'Whose, then?'

'His daughter's, I think.'

'It is like her: she is so good-natured.'

'Yes.'

Again came the blank of a pause: the clock struck eight strokes. It aroused him; he uncrossed his legs, sat erect, turned to me.

'Leave your book a moment, and come a little nearer the fire,' he said.

Wondering, and of my wonder finding no end, I complied.

'Half an hour ago,' he pursued, 'I spoke of my impatience to hear the sequel of a tale: on reflection, I find the matter will be better managed by my assuming the narrator's part, and converting you into a listener. Before commencing, it is but fair to warn you that the story will sound somewhat hackneyed in your ears; but stale details often regain a degree of freshness when they pass through new lips. For the rest, whether trite or novel, it is short.

'Mr Rivers!' I interrupted.

'I can guess your feelings,' he said, 'but restrain them for a while: I have nearly finished; hear me to the end. Of Mr Rochester's character I know nothing, but the one fact that he professed to offer honourable marriage to this young girl, and that at the very altar she discovered he had a wife yet alive, though a lunatic. What his subsequent conduct and proposals were is a matter of pure conjecture; but when an event transpired which rendered enquiry after the governess necessary, it was discovered she was gone – no one could tell when, where, or how. She had left Thornfield Hall in the night; every research after her course had been vain: the country had been scoured far and wide; no vestige of information could be gathered respecting her. Yet that she should be found is become a matter of serious urgency: advertisements have been put in all the papers; I myself have received a letter from one Mr Briggs, a solicitor, communicating the details I have just imparted. Is it not an odd tale?'

'Just tell me this,' said I, 'and since you know so much, you surely *can* tell it me – what of Mr Rochester? How and where is he? What is he doing? Is he well?'

'I am ignorant of all concerning Mr Rochester: the letter never mentions him but to narrate the fraudulent and illegal attempt I have adverted to. You should rather ask the name of the governess – the nature of the event which requires her appearance.'

'Did no one go to Thornfield Hall, then? Did no one see Mr Rochester?'

'I suppose not.'

'But they wrote to him?'

'Of course.'

'And what did he say? Who has his letters?'

'Mr Briggs intimates that the answer to his application was not from Mr Rochester, but from a lady: it is signed "Alice Fairfax".'

I felt cold and dismayed: my worst fears then were probably true: he had in all probability left England and rushed in reckless desperation to some former haunt on the Continent. And what opiate for his severe sufferings – what object for his strong passions – had he sought there? I dared not answer the question. Oh, my poor master – once almost my husband – whom I had often called 'my dear Edward!'

'He must have been a bad man,' observed Mr Rivers.

'You don't know him – don't pronounce an opinion upon him,' I said, with warmth.

'Very well,' he answered quietly: 'and indeed my head is otherwise occupied than with him: I have my tale to finish. Since you won't ask the governess's name, I must tell it of my own accord. Stay! I have it here – it is always more satisfactory to see important points written down, fairly committed to black and white.'

And the pocket-book was again deliberately produced, opened, sought through; from one of its compartments was extracted a shabby slip of paper, hastily torn off: I recognised in its texture and its stains of ultramarine, and lake, and vermilion, the ravished margin of the portrait-cover. He got up, held it close to my eyes: and I read, traced in Indian ink, in my own handwriting, the words 'Jane Eyre' – the work doubtless of some moment of abstraction.

'Briggs wrote to me of a Jane Eyre:' he said, 'the advertisements demanded a Jane Eyre: I knew a Jane Elliott. I confess I had my suspicions, but it was only yesterday afternoon they were at once resolved into certainty. You own the name and renounce the *alias*?'

'Yes – yes; but where is Mr Briggs? He perhaps knows more of Mr Rochester than you do.'

'Briggs is in London. I should doubt his knowing anything at all about Mr Rochester; it is not in Mr Rochester he is interested. Meantime, you forget essential points in pursuing trifles: you do not enquire why Mr Briggs sought after you – what he wanted with you.'

'Well, what did he want?'

'Merely to tell you that your uncle, Mr Eyre of Madeira, is dead; that he has left you all his property, and that you are now rich – merely that – nothing more.'

'I! – rich?'

'Yes, you, rich – quite an heiress.'

Silence succeeded.

'You must prove your identity of course,' resumed St John presently: 'a step which will offer no difficulties; you can then enter on immediate possession. Your fortune is vested in the English funds; Briggs has the will and the necessary documents.'

Here was a new card turned up! It is a fine thing, reader, to be lifted in a moment from indigence to wealth – a very fine thing; but not a matter one can comprehend or consequently enjoy, all at once. And then there are other chances in life far more thrilling and rapture-giving: *this* is solid, an affair of the actual world, nothing ideal about it: all its associations are solid and sober, and its manifestations are the same. One does not jump, and spring, and shout hurrah! at hearing one has got a fortune; one begins to consider responsibilities, and to ponder business; on a base of steady satisfaction rise certain grave cares, and we contain ourselves, and brood over our bliss with a solemn brow.

Besides, the words Legacy, Bequest, go side by side with the words, Death, Funeral. My uncle I had heard was dead – my only relative; ever since being made aware of his existence, I had cherished the hope of one day seeing him:

now, I never should. And then this money came only to me: not to me and a rejoicing family, but to my isolated self. It was a grand boon doubtless; and independence would be glorious – yes, I felt that – *that* thought swelled my heart.

'You unbend your forehead at last,' said Mr Rivers. 'I thought Medusa had looked at you, and that you were turning to stone. Perhaps now you will ask how much you are worth?'

'How much am I worth?'

'Oh, a trifle! Nothing of course to speak of – twenty thousand pounds, I think they say – but what is that?'

'Twenty thousand pounds?'

Here was a new stunner – I had been calculating on four or five thousand. This news actually took my breath for a moment: Mr St John, whom I had never heard laugh before, laughed now.

'Well,' said he, 'if you had committed a murder, and I had told you your crime was discovered, you could scarcely look more aghast.'

'It is a large sum – don't you think there is a mistake?'

'No mistake at all.'

'Perhaps you have read the figures wrong – it may be two thousand!'

'It is written in letters, not figures, twenty thousand.'

I again felt rather like an individual of but average gastronomical powers sitting down to feast alone at a table spread with provisions for a hundred. Mr Rivers rose now and put his cloak on.

'If it were not such a very wild night,' he said, 'I would send Hannah down to keep you company: you look too desperately miserable to be left alone. But Hannah, poor woman! could not stride the drifts so well as I: her legs are not quite so long: so I must e'en leave you to your sorrows. Good-night.'

He was lifting the latch: a sudden thought occurred to me.

'Stop one minute!' I cried.

'Well?'

'It puzzles me to know why Mr Briggs wrote to you about me; or how he knew you, or could fancy that you, living in such an out-of-the-way place, had the power to aid in my discovery.'

'Oh! I am a clergyman,' he said; 'and the clergy are often appealed to about odd matters.' Again the latch rattled.

'No; that does not satisfy me!' I exclaimed: and indeed there was something in the hasty and unexplanatory reply which, instead of allaying, piqued my curiosity more than ever.

'It is a very strange piece of business,' I added; 'I must know more about it.'

'Another time.'

'No; tonight! – tonight!' and as he turned from the door, I placed myself between it and him. He looked rather embarrassed.

'You certainly shall not go till you have told me all,' I said.

'I would rather not just now.'

'You shall! – you must!'

'I would rather Diana or Mary informed you.'

Of course these objections wrought my eagerness to a climax: gratified it must be, and that without delay; and I told him so.

'But I apprised you that I was a hard man,' said he, 'difficult to persuade.'

'And I am a hard woman, impossible to put off.'

'And then,' he pursued, 'I am cold: no fervour infects me.'

'Whereas I am hot, and fire dissolves ice. The blaze there has thawed all the snow from your cloak; by the same token, it has streamed on to my floor, and made it like a trampled street. As you hope ever to be forgiven, Mr Rivers, the high crime and misdemeanour of spoiling a sanded kitchen, tell me what I wish to know.'

'Well, then,' he said, 'I yield; if not to your earnestness, to your perseverance: as stone is worn by continual dropping. Besides, you must know someday, as well now as later. Your name is Jane Eyre?'

'Of course: that was all settled before.'

'You are not, perhaps, aware that I am your namesake? – that I was christened St John Eyre Rivers?'

'No, indeed! I remember now seeing the letter E comprised in your initials written in books you have at different times lent me; but I never asked for what name it stood. But what then? Surely – '

I stopped: I could not trust myself to entertain, much less to express, the thought that rushed upon me – that embodied itself, that, in a second, stood out a strong, solid probability. Circumstances knit themselves, fitted themselves, shot into order: the chain that had been lying hitherto a formless lump of links was drawn out straight, every ring was perfect, the connection complete. I knew, by instinct, how the matter stood, before St John had said another word; but I cannot expect the reader to have the same intuitive perception, so I must repeat his explanation.

'My mother's name was Eyre; she had two brothers; one a clergyman, who married Miss Jane Reed, of Gateshead; the other, John Eyre, Esq., merchant, late of Funchal, Madeira. Mr Briggs, being Mr Eyre's solicitor, wrote to us last August to inform us of our uncle's death, and to say that he had left his property to his brother the clergyman's orphan daughter, overlooking us, in consequence of a quarrel, never forgiven, between him and my father. He wrote again a few weeks since, to intimate that the heiress was lost, and asking if we knew anything of her. A name casually written on a slip of paper has enabled me to find her out. You know the rest.' Again he was going, but I set my back against the door.

'Do let me speak,' I said; 'let me have one moment to draw breath and reflect.' I paused – he stood before me, hat in hand, looking composed enough. I resumed – 'Your mother was my father's sister?'

'Yes.'

'My aunt, consequently?'

He bowed.

'My uncle John was your uncle John? You, Diana, and Mary are his sister's children, as I am his brother's child?'

'Undeniably.'

'You three, then, are my cousins; half our blood on each side flows from the same source?'

'We are cousins; yes.'

I surveyed him. It seemed I had found a brother: one I could be proud of, one I could love; and two sisters, whose qualities were such, that, when I knew them but as mere strangers, they had inspired me with genuine affection and admiration. The two girls, on whom, kneeling down on the wet ground, and looking through the low, latticed window of Moor House kitchen, I had gazed with so bitter a mixture of interest and despair, were my near kinswomen; and the young and stately gentleman who had found me almost dying at his threshold was my blood relation. Glorious discovery to a lonely wretch! This was wealth indeed! – wealth to the heart! – a mine of pure, genial affections. This was a blessing, bright, vivid, and exhilarating; not like the ponderous gift of gold: rich and welcome enough in its way, but sobering from its weight. I now clapped my hands in sudden joy – my pulse bounded, my veins thrilled.

'Oh, I am glad! – I am glad!' I exclaimed.

St John smiled. 'Did I not say you neglected essential points to pursue trifles?' he asked. 'You were serious when I told you you had got a fortune; and now, for a matter of no moment, you are excited.'

'What *can* you mean? It may be of no moment to you; you have sisters and don't care for a cousin; but I had nobody; and now three relations, or two, if you don't choose to be counted, are born into my world full-grown. I say again, I am glad!'

I walked fast through the room: I stopped, half suffocated with the thoughts that rose faster than I could receive, comprehend, settle them: thoughts of what might, could, would, and should be, and that ere long. I looked at the blank wall: it seemed a sky thick with ascending stars, every one lit me to a purpose or delight. Those who had saved my life, whom, till this hour, I had loved barrenly, I could now benefit. They were under a yoke, I could free them: they were scattered, I could reunite them: the independence the affluence which was mine, might be theirs too. Were we not four? Twenty thousand pounds shared equally, would be five thousand each, enough and to spare: justice would be done, mutual happiness secured. Now the wealth did not weigh on me: now it was not a mere bequest of coin, it was a legacy of life, hope, enjoyment.

How I looked while these ideas were taking my spirit by storm, I cannot tell; but I perceived soon that Mr Rivers had placed a chair behind me, and was gently attempting to make me sit down on it. He also advised me to be composed; I scorned the insinuation of helplessness and distraction, shook off his hand, and began to walk about again.

'Write to Diana and Mary tomorrow,' I said, 'and tell them to come home directly. Diana said they would both consider themselves rich with a thousand pounds, so with five thousand they will do very well.'

'Tell me where I can get you a glass of water,' said St John; 'you must really make an effort to tranquillise your feelings.'

'Nonsense! and what sort of an effect will the bequest have on you? Will it keep you in England, induce you to marry Miss Oliver, and settle down like an ordinary mortal?'

'You wander: your head becomes confused. I have been too abrupt in communicating the news; it has excited you beyond your strength.'

'Mr Rivers! you quite put me out of patience: I am rational enough; it is you who misunderstand, or rather who affect to misunderstand.'

'Perhaps, if you explained yourself a little more fully, I should comprehend better.'

'Explain! What is there to explain? You cannot fail to see that twenty thousand pounds, the sum in question, divided equally between the nephew and three nieces of our uncle, will give five thousand to each? What I want is, that you should write to your sisters and tell them of the fortune that has accrued to them.'

'To you, you mean.'

'I have intimated my view of the case: I am incapable of taking any other. I am not brutally selfish, blindly unjust, or fiendishly ungrateful. Besides, I am resolved I will have a home and connections. I like Moor House, and I will live at Moor House; I like Diana and Mary, and I will attach myself for life to Diana and Mary. It would please and benefit me to have five thousand pounds; it would torment and oppress me to have twenty thousand; which, moreover, could never be mine in justice, though it might in law. I abandon to you, then, what is absolutely superfluous to me. Let there be no opposition, and no discussion about it; let us agree amongst each other, and decide the point at once.'

'This is acting on first impulses; you must take days to consider such a matter, ere your word can be regarded as valid.'

'Oh! if all you doubt is my sincerity, I am easy: you see the justice of the case?'

'I *do* see a certain justice; but it is contrary to all custom. Besides, the entire fortune is your right: my uncle gained it by his own efforts; he was free to leave it to whom he would: he left it to you. After all, justice permits you to keep it: you may, with a clear conscience, consider it absolutely your own.'

'With me,' said I, 'it is fully as much a matter of feeling as of conscience: I must indulge my feelings; I so seldom have had an opportunity of doing so. Were you to argue, object, and annoy me for a year, I could not forego the delicious pleasure of which I have caught a glimpse – that of repaying, in part, a mighty obligation, and winning to myself lifelong friends.'

'You think so now,' rejoined St John, 'because you do not know what it is to possess, nor consequently to enjoy wealth: you cannot form a notion of the importance twenty thousand pounds would give you; of the place it would enable you to take in society; of the prospects it would open to you: you cannot – '

'And you,' I interrupted, 'cannot at all imagine the craving I have for fraternal and sisterly love. I never had a home, I never had brothers or sisters; I must and will have them now: you are not reluctant to admit me and own me, are you?'

'Jane, I will be your brother – my sisters will be your sisters – without stipulating for this sacrifice of your just rights.'

'Brother? Yes; at the distance of a thousand leagues! Sisters? Yes; slaving amongst strangers! I, wealthy – gorged with gold I never earned and do not merit! You, penniless! Famous equality and fraternisation! Close union! Intimate attachment!'

'But, Jane, your aspirations after family ties and domestic happiness may be realised otherwise than by the means you contemplate: you may marry.'

'Nonsense, again! Marry! I don't want to marry, and never shall marry.'

'That is saying too much: such hazardous affirmations are a proof of the excitement under which you labour.'

'It is not saying too much: I know what I feel, and how averse are my inclinations to the bare thought of marriage. No one would take me for love; and I will not be regarded in the light of a mere money speculation. And I do not want a stranger – unsympathising, alien, different from me; I want my kindred: those with whom I have full fellow-feeling. Say again you will be my brother: when you uttered the words I was satisfied, happy; repeat them, if you can, repeat them sincerely.'

'I think I can. I know I have always loved my own sisters; and I know on what my affection for them is grounded, respect for their worth and admiration of their talents. You too have principle and mind: your tastes and habits resemble Diana's and Mary's; your presence is always agreeable to me; in your conversation I have already for some time found a salutary solace. I feel I can easily and naturally make room in my heart for you, as my third and youngest sister.'

'Thank you: that contents me for tonight. Now you had better go; for if you stay longer, you will perhaps irritate me afresh by some mistrustful scruple.'

'And the school, Miss Eyre? It must now be shut up, I suppose?'

'No. I will retain my post of mistress till you get a substitute.'

He smiled approbation: we shook hands, and he took leave.

I need not narrate in detail the further struggles I had, and arguments I used, to get matters regarding the legacy settled as I wished. My task was a very hard one; but, as I was absolutely resolved – as my cousins saw at length that my mind was really and immutably fixed on making a just division of the property – as they must in their own hearts have felt the equity of the intention; and must, besides, have been innately conscious that in my place they would have done precisely what I wished to do – they yielded at length so far as to consent to put the affair to arbitration. The judges chosen were Mr Oliver and an able lawyer: both coincided in my opinion: I carried my point. The instruments of transfer were drawn out: St John, Diana, Mary, and I, each became possessed of a competency.

## *Chapter 34*

It was near Christmas by the time all was settled: the season of general holiday approached. I now closed Morton school, taking care that the parting should not be barren on my side. Good fortune opens the hand as well as the heart wonderfully; and to give somewhat when we have largely received, is but to afford a vent to the unusual ebullition of the sensations. I had long felt with pleasure that many of my rustic scholars liked me, and when we parted, that consciousness was confirmed: they manifested their affection plainly and strongly. Deep was my gratification to find I had really a place in their unsophisticated hearts: I promised them that never a week should pass in future that I did not visit them, and give them an hour's teaching in their school.

Mr Rivers came up as, having seen the classes, now numbering sixty girls, file out before me, and locked the door, I stood with the key in my hand, exchanging a few words of special farewell with some half-dozen of my best scholars: as decent, respectable, modest, and well-informed young women as could be found in the ranks of the British peasantry. And that is saying a great deal; for after all, the British peasantry are the best taught, best mannered, most self-respecting of any in Europe: since those days I have seen paysannes and Bäuerinnen; and the best of them seemed to me ignorant, coarse, and besotted, compared with my Morton girls.

'Do you consider you have got your reward for a season of exertion?' asked Mr Rivers, when they were gone. 'Does not the consciousness of having done some real good in your day and generation give pleasure?

'Doubtless.'

'And you have only toiled a few months! Would not a life devoted to the task of regenerating your race be well spent?'

'Yes,' I said; 'but I could not go on for ever so: I want to enjoy my own faculties as well as to cultivate those of other people. I must enjoy them now; don't recall either my mind or body to the school; I am out of it and disposed for full holiday.'

He looked grave. 'What now? What sudden eagerness is this you evince? What are you going to do?'

'To be active: as active as I can. And first I must beg you to set Hannah at liberty, and get somebody else to wait on you.'

'Do you want her?'

'Yes, to go with me to Moor House. Diana and Mary will be at home in a week, and I want to have everything in order against their arrival.'

'I understand. I thought you were for flying off on some excursion. It is better so: Hannah shall go with you.'

'Tell her to be ready by tomorrow then; and here is the schoolroom key: I will give you the key of my cottage in the morning.'

He took it. 'You give it up very gleefully,' said he; 'I don't quite understand your light-heartedness, because I cannot tell what employment you propose to yourself as a substitute for the one you are relinquishing. What aim, what purpose, what ambition in life have you now?'

'My first aim will be to *clean down* (do you comprehend the full force of the expression?) – to *clean down* Moor House from chamber to cellar; my next to rub it up with bees-wax, oil, and an indefinite number of cloths, till it glitters again; my third, to arrange every chair, table, bed, carpet, with mathematical precision; afterwards I shall go near to ruin you in coals and peat to keep up good fires in every room; and lastly, the two days preceding that on which your sisters are expected will be devoted by Hannah and me to such a beating of eggs, sorting of currants, grating of spices, compounding of Christmas cakes, chopping up of materials for mince-pies, and solemnising of other culinary rites, as words can convey but an inadequate notion of to the uninitiated like you. My purpose, in short, is to have all things in an absolutely perfect state of readiness for Diana and Mary before next Thursday; and my ambition is to give them a beau-ideal of a welcome when they come.'

St John smiled slightly: still he was dissatisfied.

'It is all very well for the present,' said he; 'but seriously, I trust that when the first flush of vivacity is over, you will look a little higher than domestic endearments and household joys.'

'The best things the world has!' I interrupted.

'No, Jane, no: this world is not the scene of fruition; do not attempt to make it so: nor of rest; do not turn slothful.'

'I mean, on the contrary, to be busy.'

'Jane, I excuse you for the present: two months' grace I allow you for the full enjoyment of your new position, and for pleasing yourself with this late-found charm of relationship; but *then*, I hope you will begin to look beyond Moor House and Morton, and sisterly society, and the selfish calm and sensual comfort of civilised affluence. I hope your energies will then once more trouble you with their strength.'

I looked at him with surprise. 'St John,' I said, 'I think you are almost wicked to talk so. I am disposed to be as content as a queen, and you try to stir me up to restlessness! To what end?'

'To the end of turning to profit the talents which God has committed to your keeping; and of which He will surely one day demand a strict account. Jane, I shall watch you closely and anxiously – I warn you of that. And try to restrain the disproportionate fervour with which you throw yourself into commonplace home pleasures. Don't cling so tenaciously to ties of the flesh; save your constancy and ardour for an adequate cause; forbear to waste them on trite transient objects. Do you hear, Jane?'

'Yes; just as if you were speaking Greek. I feel I have adequate cause to be happy, and I *will* be happy. Goodbye!'

Happy at Moor House I was, and hard I worked; and so did Hannah: she was charmed to see how jovial I could be amidst the bustle of a house turned topsy-turvy – how I could brush, and dust, and clean, and cook. And really, after a day or two of confusion worse confounded, it was delightful by degrees to invoke order from the chaos ourselves had made. I had previously taken a journey to S— to purchase some new furniture: my cousins having given me *carte blanche* to effect what alterations I pleased, and a sum having been set aside for that purpose. The ordinary sitting-room and bedrooms I left much as they were: for I knew Diana and Mary would derive more pleasure from seeing again the old homely tables, and chairs, and beds, than from the spectacle of the smartest innovations. Still some novelty was necessary, to give to their return the piquancy with which I wished it to be invested. Dark handsome new carpets and curtains, an arrangement of some carefully selected antique ornaments in porcelain and bronze, new coverings, and mirrors, and dressing-cases, for the toilet tables, answered the end: they looked fresh without being glaring. A spare parlour and bedroom I refurnished entirely, with old mahogany and crimson upholstery: I laid canvas on the passage, and carpets on the stairs. When all was finished, I thought Moor House as complete a model of bright modest snugness within, as it was, at this season, a specimen of wintry waste and desert dreariness without.

The eventful Thursday at length came. They were expected about dark, and ere dusk fires were lit upstairs and below; the kitchen was in perfect trim; Hannah and I were dressed, and all was in readiness.

St John arrived first. I had entreated him to keep quite clear of the house till everything was arranged: and, indeed, the bare idea of the commotion, at once sordid and trivial, going on within its walls sufficed to scare him to estrangement. He found me in the kitchen, watching the progress of certain cakes for tea, then baking. Approaching the hearth, he asked, 'If I was at last satisfied with housemaid's work?' I answered by inviting him to accompany me on a general inspection of the result of my labours. With some difficulty, I got him to make the tour of the house. He just looked in at the doors I opened; and when he had wandered upstairs and downstairs, he said I must have gone through a great deal of fatigue and trouble to have effected such considerable changes in so short a time: but not a syllable did he utter indicating pleasure in the improved aspect of his abode.

This silence damped me. I thought perhaps the alterations had disturbed some old associations he valued. I enquired whether this was the case: no doubt in a somewhat crestfallen tone.

'Not at all; he had, on the contrary, remarked that I had scrupulously respected every association: he feared, indeed, I must have bestowed more thought on the matter than it was worth. How many minutes, for instance, had I devoted to studying the arrangement of this very room? – By the by, could I tell him where such a book was?'

I showed him the volume on the shelf: he took it down, and withdrawing to his accustomed window recess, he began to read it.

Now, I did not like this, reader. St John was a good man; but I began to feel he had spoken truth of himself when he said he was hard and cold. The humanities and amenities of life had no attraction for him – its peaceful enjoyments no charm. Literally, he lived only to aspire – after what was good and great, certainly; but still he would never rest, nor approve of others resting round him. As I looked at his lofty forehead, still and pale as a white stone – at his fine lineaments fixed in study – I comprehended all at once that he would hardly make a good husband: that it would be a trying thing to be his wife. I understood, as by inspiration, the nature of his love for Miss Oliver; I agreed with him that it was but a love of the senses. I comprehended how he should despise himself for the feverish influence it exercised over him; how he should wish to stifle and destroy it; how he should mistrust its ever conducing permanently to his happiness or hers. I saw he was of the material from which nature hews her heroes – Christian and Pagan – her lawgivers, her statesmen, her conquerors: a steadfast bulwark for great interests to rest upon; but, at the fireside, too often a cold cumbrous column, gloomy and out of place.

'This parlour is not his sphere,' I reflected: 'the Himalayan ridge or Caffre bush, even the plague-cursed Guinea Coast swamp would suit him better. Well may he eschew the calm of domestic life; it is not his element: there his faculties stagnate – they cannot develop or appear to advantage. It is in scenes of strife and danger – where courage is proved, and energy exercised, and fortitude tasked – that he will speak and move, the leader and superior. A merry child would have the advantage of him on this hearth. He is right to choose a missionary's career – I see it now.'

'They are coming! they are coming!' cried Hannah, throwing open the parlour door. At the same moment old Carlo barked joyfully. Out I ran. It was now dark; but a rumbling of wheels was audible. Hannah soon had a lantern lit. The vehicle had stopped at the wicket; the driver opened the door: first one well-known form, then another, stepped out. In a minute I had my face under their bonnets, in contact first with Mary's soft cheek, then with Diana's flowing curls. They laughed – kissed me – then Hannah: patted Carlo, who was half wild with delight; asked eagerly if all was well; and being assured in the affirmative, hastened into the house.

They were stiff with their long and jolting drive from Whitcross, and chilled with the frosty night air; but their pleasant countenances expanded to the cheerful firelight. While the driver and Hannah brought in the boxes, they demanded St John. At this moment he advanced from the parlour. They both threw their arms round his neck at once. He gave each one quiet kiss, said in a low tone a few words of welcome, stood a while to be talked to, and then, intimating that he supposed they would soon rejoin him in the parlour, withdrew there as to a place of refuge.

I had lit their candles to go upstairs, but Diana had first to give hospitable orders respecting the driver; this done, both followed me. They were delighted with the renovation and decorations of their rooms; with the new drapery, and fresh carpets, and rich tinted china vases: they expressed their gratification ungrudgingly. I had the pleasure of feeling that my arrangements met their wishes exactly, and that what I had done added a vivid charm to their joyous return home.

Sweet was that evening. My cousins, full of exhilaration, were so eloquent in narrative and comment, that their fluency covered St John's taciturnity: he was sincerely glad to see his sisters; but in their glow of fervour and flow of joy he could not sympathise. The event of the day – that is, the return of Diana and Mary – pleased him; but the accompaniments of that event, the glad tumult, the garrulous glee of reception irked him: I saw he wished the calmer morrow was come. In the very meridian of the night's enjoyment, about an hour after tea, a rap was heard at the door. Hannah entered with the intimation that 'a poor lad was come, at that unlikely time, to fetch Mr Rivers to see his mother, who was drawing away.'

'Where does she live, Hannah?'

'Clear up at Whitcross Brow, almost four miles off, and moor and moss all the way.'

'Tell him I will go.'

'I'm sure, sir, you had better not. It's the worst road to travel after dark that can be: there's no track at all over the bog. And then it is such a bitter night – the keenest wind you ever felt. You had better send word, sir, that you will be there in the morning.'

But he was already in the passage, putting on his cloak; and without one objection, one murmur, he departed. It was then nine o'clock: he did not return till midnight. Starved and tired enough he was: but he looked happier than when he set out. He had performed an act of duty; made an exertion; felt his own strength to do and deny, and was on better terms with himself.

I am afraid the whole of the ensuing week tried his patience. It was Christmas week: we took to no settled employment, but spent it in a sort of merry domestic dissipation. The air of the moors, the freedom of home, the dawn of prosperity, acted on Diana and Mary's spirits like some life-giving elixir: they were gay from morning till noon, and from noon till night. They could always talk; and their discourse, witty, pithy, original, had such charms for me, that I preferred listening to, and sharing in it, to doing anything else. St John did not rebuke our vivacity; but he escaped from it: he was seldom in the house; his parish was large, the population scattered, and he found daily business in visiting the sick and poor in its different districts.

One morning at breakfast, Diana, after looking a little pensive for some minutes, asked him, 'If his plans were yet unchanged.'

'Unchanged and unchangeable,' was the reply. And he proceeded to inform us that his departure from England was now definitely fixed for the ensuing year.

'And Rosamond Oliver?' suggested Mary, the words seeming to escape her lips involuntarily: for no sooner had she uttered them, than she made a gesture as if wishing to recall them. St John had a book in his hand – it was his unsocial custom to read at meals – he closed it, and looked up.

'Rosamond Oliver,' said he, 'is about to be married to Mr Granby, one of the best connected and most estimable residents in S—, grandson and heir to Sir Frederic Granby: I had the intelligence from her father yesterday.'

His sisters looked at each other and at me; we all three looked at him: he was serene as glass.

'The match must have been got up hastily,' said Diana: 'they cannot have known each other long.'

'But two months: they met in October at the county ball at S—. But where there are no obstacles to a union, as in the present case, where the connection is in every point desirable, delays are unnecessary: they will be married as soon as S— Place, which Sir Frederic gives up to them, can be refitted for their reception.'

The first time I found St John alone after this communication, I felt tempted to enquire if the event distressed him: but he seemed so little to need sympathy, that, so far from venturing to offer him more, I experienced some shame at the recollection of what I had already hazarded. Besides, I was out of practice in talking to him: his reserve was again frozen over, and my frankness was congealed beneath it. He had not kept his promise of treating me like his sisters; he continually made little, chilling differences between us, which did not at all tend to the development of cordiality: in short, now that I was acknowledged his kinswoman, and lived under the same roof with him, I felt the distance between us to be far greater than when he had known me only as the village schoolmistress. When I remembered how far I had once been admitted to his confidence, I could hardly comprehend his present frigidity.

Such being the case, I felt not a little surprised when he raised his head suddenly from the desk over which he was stooping, and said – 'You see, Jane, the battle is fought and the victory won.'

Startled at being thus addressed, I did not immediately reply: after a moment's hesitation I answered – 'But are you sure you are not in the position of those conquerors whose triumphs have cost them too dear? Would not such another ruin you?'

'I think not; and if I were, it does not much signify; I shall never be called upon to contend for such another. The event of the conflict is decisive: my way is now clear; I thank God for it!' So saying, he returned to his papers and his silence.

As our mutual happiness (i.e., Diana's, Mary's, and mine) settled into a quieter character, and we resumed our usual habits and regular studies, St John stayed more at home: he sat with us in the same room, sometimes for hours together. While Mary drew, Diana pursued a course of encyclopaedic reading she had (to my awe and amazement) undertaken, and I fagged away at German, he pondered a mystic lore of his own: that of some Eastern tongue, the acquisition of which he thought necessary to his plans.

Thus engaged, he appeared, sitting in his own recess, quiet and absorbed enough; but that blue eye of his had a habit of leaving the outlandish-looking grammar, and wandering over, and sometimes fixing upon us, his fellow-students, with a curious intensity of observation: if caught, it would be instantly withdrawn; yet ever and anon, it returned searchingly to our table. I wondered what it meant: I wondered, too, at the punctual satisfaction he never failed to exhibit on an occasion that seemed to me of small moment, namely, my weekly visit to Morton school; and still more was I puzzled when, if the day was unfavourable, if there was snow, or rain, or high wind, and his sisters urged me not to go, he would invariably make light of their solicitude, and encourage me to accomplish the task without regard to the elements.

'Jane is not such a weakling as you would make her,' he would say: 'she can bear a mountain blast, or a shower, or a few flakes of snow, as well as any of us. Her constitution is both sound and elastic; better calculated to endure variations of climate than many more robust.'

And when I returned, sometimes a good deal tired, and not a little weather-beaten, I never dared complain, because I saw that to murmur would be to vex him: on all occasions fortitude pleased him; the reverse was a special annoyance.

One afternoon, however, I got leave to stay at home, because I really had a cold. His sisters were gone to Morton in my stead: I sat reading Schiller; he, deciphering his crabbed Oriental scrolls. As I exchanged a translation for an exercise, I happened to look his way: there I found myself under the influence of the ever-watchful blue eye. How long it had been searching me through and through, and over and over, I cannot tell: so keen was it, and yet so cold, I felt for the moment superstitious – as if I were sitting in the room with something uncanny.

'Jane, what are you doing?'

'Learning German.'

'I want you to give up German and learn Hindustani.'

'You are not in earnest?'

'In such earnest that I must have it so: and I will tell you why.'

He then went on to explain that Hindustani was the language he was himself at present studying; that, as he advanced, he was apt to forget the commencement; that it would assist him greatly to have a pupil with whom he might again and again go over the elements, and so fix them thoroughly in his mind; that his choice had hovered for some time between me and his sisters; but that he had fixed on me because he saw I could sit at a task the longest of the three. Would I do him this favour? I should not, perhaps, have to make the sacrifice long, as it wanted now barely three months to his departure.

St John was not a man to be lightly refused: you felt that every impression made on him, either for pain or pleasure, was deep-graved and permanent. I consented. When Diana and Mary returned, the former found her scholar transferred from her to her brother: she laughed, and both she and Mary agreed that St John should never have persuaded them to such a step. He answered quietly – 'I know it.'

I found him a very patient, very forbearing, and yet an exacting master: he expected me to do a great deal; and when I fulfilled his expectations, he, in his own way, fully testified his approbation. By degrees, he acquired a certain influence over me that took away my liberty of mind: his praise and notice were more restraining than his indifference. I could no longer talk or laugh freely when he was by, because a tiresomely importunate instinct reminded me that vivacity (at least in me) was distasteful to him. I was so fully aware that only serious moods and occupations were acceptable, that in his presence every effort to sustain or follow any other became vain: I fell under a freezing spell.

When he said 'go,' I went; 'come,' I came; 'do this,' I did it. But I did not love my servitude: I wished, many a time, he had continued to neglect me.

One evening when, at bedtime, his sisters and I stood round him, bidding him good-night, he kissed each of them, as was his custom; and, as was equally his custom, he gave me his hand. Diana, who chanced to be in a frolicsome humour (*she* was not painfully controlled by his will; for hers, in another way, was as strong), exclaimed – 'St John! you used to call Jane your third sister, but you don't treat her as such: you should kiss her too.'

She pushed me towards him. I thought Diana very provoking, and felt uncomfortably confused; and while I was thus thinking and feeling, St John bent his head; his Greek face was brought to a level with mine, his eyes questioned my eyes piercingly – he kissed me. There are no such things as marble kisses or ice kisses, or I should say my ecclesiastical cousin's salute belonged to one of these classes; but there may be experiment kisses, and his was an experiment kiss. When given, he viewed me to learn the result; it was not striking: I am sure I did not blush; perhaps I might have turned a little pale, for I felt as if this kiss were a seal affixed to my fetters. He never omitted the ceremony afterwards, and the gravity and quiescence with which I underwent it, seemed to invest it for him with a certain charm.

As for me, I daily wished more to please him; but to do so, I felt daily more and more that I must disown half my nature, stifle half my faculties, wrest my tastes from their original bent, force myself to the adoption of pursuits for which I had no natural vocation. He wanted to train me to an elevation I could never reach; it racked me hourly to aspire to the standard he uplifted. The thing was as impossible as to mould my irregular features to his correct and classic pattern, to give to my changeable green eyes the sea-blue tint and solemn lustre of his own.

Not his ascendancy alone, however, held me in thrall at present. Of late it had been easy enough for me to look sad: a cankering evil sat at my heart and drained my happiness at its source – the evil of suspense.

Perhaps you think I had forgotten Mr Rochester, reader, amidst these changes of place and fortune. Not for a moment. His idea was still with me, because it was not a vapour sunshine could disperse, nor a sand-traced effigy storms could wash away; it was a name graven on a tablet, fated to last as long as the marble it inscribed. The craving to know what had become of him followed me everywhere; when I was at Morton, I re-entered my cottage every evening to think of that; and now at Moor House, I sought my bedroom each night to brood over it.

In the course of my necessary correspondence with Mr Briggs about the will, I had enquired if he knew anything of Mr Rochester's present residence and state of health; but, as St John had conjectured, he was quite ignorant of all concerning him. I then wrote to Mrs Fairfax, entreating information on the subject. I had calculated with certainty on this step answering my end: I felt sure it would elicit an early answer. I was astonished when a fortnight passed without reply; but when two months wore away, and day after day the post arrived and brought nothing for me, I fell a prey to the keenest anxiety.

I wrote again: there was a chance of my first letter having missed. Renewed hope followed renewed effort: it shone like the former for some weeks, then, like it, it faded, flickered: not a line, not a word reached me. When half a year wasted in vain expectancy, my hope died out, and then I felt dark indeed.

A fine spring shone round me, which I could not enjoy. Summer approached; Diana tried to cheer me: she said I looked ill, and wished to accompany me to the seaside. This St John opposed; he said I did not want dissipation, I wanted employment; my present life was too purposeless, I required an aim; and, I suppose, by way of supplying deficiencies, he prolonged still further my lessons in Hindustani, and grew more urgent in requiring their accomplishment: and I, like a fool, never thought of resisting him – I could not resist him.

One day I had come to my studies in lower spirits than usual; the ebb was occasioned by a poignantly felt disappointment. Hannah had told me in the morning there was a letter for me, and when I went down to take it, almost certain that the long-looked-for tidings were vouchsafed me at last, I found only an unimportant note from Mr Briggs on business. The bitter check had wrung from me some tears; and now, as I sat poring over the crabbed characters and flourishing tropes of an Indian scribe, my eyes filled again.

St John called me to his side to read; in attempting to do this my voice failed me: words were lost in sobs. He and I were the only occupants of the parlour: Diana was practising her music in the drawing-room, Mary was gardening – it was a very fine May day, clear, sunny, and breezy. My companion expressed no surprise at this emotion, nor did he question me as to its cause; he only said – 'We will wait a few minutes, Jane, till you are more composed.' And while I smothered the paroxysm with all haste, he sat calm and patient, leaning on his desk, and looking like a physician watching with the eye of science an expected and fully understood crisis in a patient's malady. Having stifled my sobs, wiped my eyes, and muttered something about not being very well that morning, I resumed my task, and succeeded in completing it. St John put away my books and his, locked his desk, and said – 'Now, Jane, you shall take a walk; and with me.'

'I will call Diana and Mary.'

'No; I want only one companion this morning, and that must be you. Put on your things, go out by the kitchen-door: take the road towards the head of Marsh Glen: I will join you in a moment.'

I know no medium: I never in my life have known any medium in my dealings with positive, hard characters, antagonistic to my own, between absolute submission and determined revolt. I have always faithfully observed the one, up to the very moment of bursting, sometimes with volcanic vehemence, into the other; and as neither present circumstances warranted, nor my present mood inclined me to mutiny, I observed careful obedience to St John's directions; and in ten minutes I was treading the wild track of the glen, side by side with him.

The breeze was from the west: it came over the hills, sweet with scents of heath and rush; the sky was of stainless blue; the stream descending the ravine, swelled with past spring rains, poured along plentiful and clear, catching golden gleams from the sun, and sapphire tints from the firmament. As we advanced and left the track, we trod a soft turf, mossy fine and emerald green, minutely enamelled with a tiny white flower, and spangled with a star-like yellow blossom: the hills, meantime, shut us quite in; for the glen, towards its head, wound to their very core.

'Let us rest here,' said St John, as we reached the first stragglers of a battalion of rocks, guarding a sort of pass, beyond which the beck rushed down a waterfall; and where, still a little farther, the mountain shook off turf and flower, had only heath for raiment and crag for gem – where it exaggerated the wild to the savage, and exchanged the fresh for the frowning – where it guarded the forlorn hope of solitude, and a last refuge for silence.

I took a seat: St John stood near me. He looked up the pass and down the hollow; his glance wandered away with the stream, and returned to traverse the unclouded heaven which coloured it: he removed his hat, let the breeze stir his hair and kiss his brow. He seemed in communion with the genius of the haunt: with his eye he bade farewell to something.

'And I shall see it again,' he said aloud, 'in dreams when I sleep by the Ganges: and again in a more remote hour – when another slumber overcomes me – on the shore of a darker stream!'

Strange words of a strange love! An austere patriot's passion for his fatherland! He sat down; for half an hour we never spoke; neither he to me nor I to him: that interval past, he recommenced – 'Jane, I go in six weeks; I have taken my berth in an East Indiaman which sails on the 20th of June.'

'God will protect you; for you have undertaken His work,' I answered.

'Yes,' said he, 'there is my glory and joy. I am the servant of an infallible Master. I am not going out under human guidance, subject to the defective laws and erring control of my feeble fellow-worms: my king, my lawgiver, my captain, is the All-perfect. It seems strange to me that all round me do not burn to enlist under the same banner, to join in the same enterprise.'

'All have not your powers, and it would be folly for the feeble to wish to march with the strong.'

'I do not speak to the feeble, or think of them: I address only such as are worthy of the work, and competent to accomplish it.'

'Those are few in number, and difficult to discover.'

'You say truly; but when found, it is right to stir them up – to urge and exhort them to the effort – to show them what their gifts are, and why they were given – to speak Heaven's message in their ear, to offer them, direct from God, a place in the ranks of His chosen.'

'If they are really qualified for the task, will not their own hearts be the first to inform them of it?'

I felt as if an awful charm was framing round and gathering over me: I trembled to hear some fatal word spoken which would at once declare and rivet the spell.

'And what does *your* heart say?' demanded St John.

'My heart is mute – my heart is mute,' I answered struck and thrilled.

'Then I must speak for it,' continued the deep relentless voice. 'Jane, come with me to India: come as my helpmeet and fellow-labourer.'

The glen and sky spun round: the hills heaved! It was as if I had heard a summons from Heaven – as if a visionary messenger, like him of Macedonia, had enounced, 'Come over and help us!' But I was no apostle, I could not behold the herald, I could not receive his call.

'Oh, St John!' I cried, 'have some mercy!'

I appealed to one who, in the discharge of what he believed his duty, knew neither mercy nor remorse. He continued – 'God and nature intended you for a missionary's wife. It is not personal, but mental endowments they have given you: you are formed for labour, not for love. A missionary's wife you must – shall be. You shall be mine: I claim you – not for my pleasure, but for my Sovereign's service.'

'I am not fit for it: I have no vocation,' I said.

He had calculated on these first objections: he was not irritated by them. Indeed, as he leaned back against the crag behind him, folded his arms on his chest, and fixed his countenance, I saw he was prepared for a long and trying opposition, and had taken in a stock of patience to last him to its close – resolved, however, that that close should be conquest for him.

'Humility, Jane,' said he, 'is the groundwork of Christian virtues: you say right that you are not fit for the work. Who is fit for it? Or who, that ever was truly called, believed himself worthy of the summons? I, for instance, am but dust and ashes. With St Paul, I acknowledge myself the chiefest of sinners; but I do not suffer this sense of my personal vileness to daunt me. I know my Leader: that He is just as well as mighty; and while He has chosen a feeble instrument to perform a great task, He will, from the boundless stores of His providence, supply the inadequacy of the means to the end. Think like me, Jane – trust like me. It is the Rock of Ages I ask you to lean on: do not doubt but it will bear the weight of your human weakness.'

'I do not understand a missionary life: I have never studied missionary labours.'

'There I, humble as I am, can give you the aid you want: I can set you your task from hour to hour; stand by you always; help you from moment to moment. This I could do in the beginning: soon (for I know your powers) you would be as strong and apt as myself, and would not require my help.'

'But my powers – where are they for this undertaking? I do not feel them. Nothing speaks or stirs in me while you talk. I am sensible of no light kindling – no life quickening – no voice counselling or cheering. Oh, I wish I could make you see how much my mind is at this moment like a rayless dungeon, with one shrinking fear fettered in its depths – the fear of being persuaded by you to attempt what I cannot accomplish!'

'I have an answer for you – hear it. I have watched you ever since we first met: I have made you my study for ten months. I have proved you in that time by sundry tests: and what have I seen and elicited? In the village school I found you could perform well, punctually, uprightly, labour uncongenial to your habits and inclinations; I saw you could perform it with capacity and tact: you could win while you controlled. In the calm with which you learnt you had become suddenly rich, I read a mind clear of the vice of Demas: lucre had no undue power over you. In the resolute readiness with which you cut your wealth into four shares, keeping but one to yourself, and relinquishing the three others to the claim of abstract justice, I recognised a soul that revelled in the flame and excitement of sacrifice. In the tractability with which, at my wish, you forsook a study in which you were interested, and adopted another because it interested me; in the untiring assiduity with which you have since persevered in it – in the unflagging energy and unshaken temper with which you have met its difficulties – I acknowledge the complement of the qualities I seek. Jane, you are docile, diligent, disinterested, faithful, constant, and courageous; very gentle, and very heroic: cease to mistrust yourself – I can trust you unreservedly. As a conductress of Indian schools, and a helper amongst Indian women, your assistance will be to me invaluable.'

My iron shroud contracted round me; persuasion advanced with slow, sure step. Shut my eyes as I would, these last words of his succeeded in making the way, which had seemed blocked up, comparatively clear. My work, which had appeared so vague, so hopelessly diffuse, condensed itself as he proceeded, and assumed a definite form under his shaping hand. He waited for an answer. I demanded a quarter of an hour to think, before I again hazarded a reply.

'Very willingly,' he rejoined; and rising, he strode a little distance up the pass, threw himself down on a swell of heath, and there lay still.

'I *can* do what he wants me to do: I am forced to see and acknowledge that,' I meditated, 'that is, if life be spared me. But I feel mine is not the existence to be long protracted under an Indian sun. What then? He does not care for that: when my time came to die, he would resign me, in all serenity and sanctity, to the God who gave me. The case is very plain before me. In leaving England, I should leave a loved but empty land – Mr Rochester is not there; and if he were, what is, what can that ever be to me? My business is to live without him now: nothing so absurd, so weak as to drag on from day to day, as if I were waiting some impossible change in circumstances, which might reunite me to him. Of course (as St John once said) I must seek another interest in life to replace the one lost: is not the occupation he now offers me truly the most glorious man can adopt or God assign? Is it not, by its noble cares and sublime results, the one best calculated to fill the void left by uptorn affections and demolished hopes? I believe I must say, Yes – and yet I shudder. Alas! If I join St John, I abandon half myself: if I go to India, I go to premature death. And how will the interval between leaving England for India, and India for the grave, be filled? Oh, I know well! That, too, is very clear to my vision. By straining to satisfy St John till my sinews ache, I *shall* satisfy him – to the finest central point and farthest outward circle of his expectations. If I *do* go with him – if I *do* make the sacrifice he urges I will make it absolutely: I will throw all on the altar – heart, vitals, the entire victim. He will never love me; but he shall approve me; I will show him energies he has not yet seen, resources he has never suspected. Yes, I can work as hard as he can, and with as little grudging.

'Consent, then, to his demand is possible: but for one item – one dreadful item. It is – that he asks me to be his wife, and has no more of a husband's heart for me than that frowning giant of a rock, down which the stream is foaming in yonder gorge. He prizes me as a soldier would a good weapon, and that is all. Unmarried to him, this would never grieve me; but can I let him complete his calculations – coolly put into practice his plans – go through the wedding ceremony? Can I receive from him the bridal ring, endure all the forms of love (which I doubt not he would scrupulously observe) and know that the spirit was quite absent? Can I bear the consciousness that every endearment he bestows is a sacrifice made on principle? No: such a martyrdom would be monstrous. I will never undergo it. As his sister, I might accompany him – not as his wife: I will tell him so.'

I looked towards the knoll: there he lay, still as a prostrate column; his face turned to me: his eye beaming watchful and keen. He started to his feet and approached me.

'I am ready to go to India, if I may go free.'

'Your answer requires a commentary,' he said; 'it is not clear.'

'You have hitherto been my adopted brother – I, your adopted sister: let us continue as such: you and I had better not marry.'

He shook his head. 'Adopted fraternity will not do in this case. If you were my real sister it would be different: I should take you, and seek no wife. But as it is, either our union must be consecrated and sealed by marriage, or it cannot exist: practical obstacles oppose themselves to any other plan. Do you not see it, Jane? Consider a moment – your strong sense will guide you.'

I did consider; and still my sense, such as it was, directed me only to the fact that we did not love each other as man and wife should: and therefore it inferred we ought not to marry. I said so. 'St John,' I returned, 'I regard you as a brother – you, me as a sister: so let us continue.'

'We cannot – we cannot,' he answered, with short, sharp determination: 'it would not do. You have said you will go with me to India: remember – you have said that.'

'Conditionally.'

'Well – well. To the main point – the departure with me from England, the co-operation with me in my future labours – you do not object. You have already as good as put your hand to the plough: you are too consistent to withdraw it. You have but one end to keep in view – how the work you have undertaken can best be done. Simplify your complicated interests, feelings, thoughts, wishes, aims; merge all considerations in one purpose: that of fulfilling with effect – with power – the mission of your great Master. To do so, you must have a co-adjutor: not a brother – that is a loose tie – but a husband. I, too, do not want a sister: a sister might any day be taken from me. I want a wife: the sole helpmeet I can influence efficiently in life, and retain absolutely till death.'

I shuddered as he spoke: I felt his influence in my marrow – his hold on my limbs.

'Seek one elsewhere than in me, St John: seek one fitted to you.'

'One fitted to my purpose, you mean – fitted to my vocation. Again I tell you it is not the insignificant private individual – the mere man, with the man's selfish senses – I wish to mate: it is the missionary.'

'And I will give the missionary my energies – it is all he wants – but not myself: that would be only adding the husk and shell to the kernel. For them he has no use: I retain them.'

'You cannot – you ought not. Do you think God will be satisfied with half an oblation? Will He accept a mutilated sacrifice? It is the cause of God I advocate: it is under His standard I enlist you. I cannot accept on His behalf a divided allegiance: it must be entire.'

'Oh! I will give my heart to God,' I said. '*You* do not want it.'

I will not swear, reader, that there was not something of repressed sarcasm both in the tone in which I uttered this sentence, and in the feeling that accompanied it. I had silently feared St John till now, because I had not understood him. He had held me in awe, because he had held me in doubt. How much of him was saint, how much mortal, I could not heretofore tell: but revelations were being made in this conference: the analysis of his nature was proceeding before my eyes. I saw his fallibilities: I comprehended them. I understood that, sitting there where I did, on the bank of heath, and with that handsome form before me, I sat at the feet of a man, erring as I. The veil fell from his hardness and despotism. Having felt in him the presence of these qualities, I felt his imperfection and took courage. I was with an equal – one with whom I might argue – one whom, if I saw good, I might resist.

He was silent after I had uttered the last sentence, and I presently risked an upward glance at his countenance. His eye, bent on me, expressed at once stern surprise and keen enquiry. 'Is she sarcastic, and sarcastic to *me*!' it seemed to say. 'What does this signify?'

'Do not let us forget that this is a solemn matter,' he said ere long; 'one of which we may neither think nor talk lightly without sin. I trust, Jane, you are in earnest when you say you will give your heart to God: it is all I want. Once wrench your heart from man, and fix it on your Maker, the advancement of that Maker's spiritual kingdom on earth will be your chief delight and endeavour; you will be ready to do at once whatever furthers that end. You will see what impetus would be given to your efforts and mine by our physical and mental union in marriage: the only union that gives a character of permanent conformity to the destinies and designs of human beings; and, passing over all minor caprices – all trivial difficulties and delicacies of feeling – all scruple about the degree, kind, strength or tenderness of mere personal inclination – you will hasten to enter into that union at once.'

'Shall I?' I said briefly; and I looked at his features, beautiful in their harmony, but strangely formidable in their still severity; at his brow, commanding but not open; at his eyes, bright and deep and searching, but never soft; at his tall imposing figure; and fancied myself in idea *his wife*. Oh! it would never do! As his curate, his comrade, all would be right: I would cross oceans with him in that capacity; toil under Eastern suns, in Asian deserts with him in that office; admire and emulate his courage and devotion and vigour; accommodate quietly to his masterhood; smile undisturbed at his ineradicable ambition; discriminate the Christian from the man: profoundly esteem the one, and freely forgive the other. I should suffer often, no doubt, attached to him only in this capacity: my body would be under rather a stringent yoke, but my heart and mind would be free. I should still have my unblighted self to turn to: my natural unenslaved feelings with which to communicate in moments of loneliness. There would be recesses in my mind which would be only mine, to which he never came, and sentiments growing there fresh and sheltered which his austerity could never blight, nor his measured warrior-march trample down: but as his wife – at his side always, and always restrained, and always checked – forced to keep the fire of my nature continually low, to compel it to burn inwardly and never utter a cry, though the imprisoned flame consumed vital after vital – *this* would be unendurable.

'St John!' I exclaimed, when I had got so far in my meditation.

'Well?' he answered icily.

'I repeat I freely consent to go with you as your fellow-missionary, but not as your wife; I cannot marry you and become part of you.'

'A part of me you must become,' he answered steadily: 'otherwise the whole bargain is void. How can I, a man not yet thirty, take out with me to India a girl of nineteen, unless she be married to me? How can we be for ever together – sometimes in solitudes, sometimes amidst savage tribes – and unwed?'

'Very well,' I said shortly; 'under the circumstances, quite as well as if I were either your real sister, or a man and a clergyman like yourself.'

'It is known that you are not my sister; I cannot introduce you as such: to attempt it would be to fasten injurious suspicions on us both. And for the rest, though you have a man's vigorous brain, you have a woman's heart and – it would not do.'

'It would do,' I affirmed with some disdain, 'perfectly well. I have a woman's heart, but not where you are concerned; for you I have only a comrade's constancy; a fellow-soldier's frankness, fidelity, fraternity, if you like; a neophyte's respect and submission to his hierophant: nothing more – don't fear.'

'It is what I want,' he said, speaking to himself; 'it is just what I want. And there are obstacles in the way: they must be hewn down. Jane, you would not repent marrying me – be certain of that; we *must* be married. I repeat it: there is no other way; and undoubtedly enough of love would follow upon marriage to render the union right even in your eyes.'

'I scorn your idea of love,' I could not help saying, as I rose up and stood before him, leaning my back against the rock. 'I scorn the counterfeit sentiment you offer: yes, St John, and I scorn you when you offer it.'

He looked at me fixedly, compressing his well-cut lips while he did so. Whether he was incensed or surprised, or what, it was not easy to tell: he could command his countenance thoroughly.

'I scarcely expected to hear that expression from you,' he said: 'I think I have done and uttered nothing to deserve scorn.'

I was touched by his gentle tone, and overawed by his high, calm mien.

'Forgive me the words, St John; but it is your own fault that I have been roused to speak so unguardedly. You have introduced a topic on which our natures are at variance – a topic we should never discuss: the very name of love is an apple of discord between us. If the reality were required, what should we do? How should we feel? My dear cousin, abandon your scheme of marriage – forget it.'

'No,' said he; 'it is a long-cherished scheme, and the only one which can secure my great end: but I shall urge you no further at present. Tomorrow, I leave home for Cambridge: I have many friends there to whom I should wish to say farewell. I shall be absent a fortnight – take that space of time to consider my offer: and do not forget that if you reject it, it is not me you deny, but God. Through my means, He opens to you a noble career; as my wife only can you enter upon it. Refuse to be my wife, and you limit yourself for ever to a track of selfish ease and barren obscurity. Tremble lest in that case you should be numbered with those who have denied the faith, and are worse than infidels!'

He had done. Turning from me, he once more 'Looked to river, looked to hill'. But this time his feelings were all pent in his heart: I was not worthy to hear them uttered. As I walked by his side homeward, I read well in his iron silence all he felt towards me: the disappointment of an austere and despotic nature, which has met resistance where it expected submission – the disapprobation of a cool, inflexible judgement, which has detected in another feelings and views in which it has no power to sympathise: in short, as a man, he would have wished to coerce me into obedience: it was only as a sincere Christian he bore so patiently with my perversity, and allowed so long a space for reflection and repentance.

That night, after he had kissed his sisters, he thought proper to forget even to shake hands with me, but left the room in silence. I – who, though I had no love, had much friendship for him – was hurt by the marked omission: so much hurt that tears started to my eyes.

'I see you and St John have been quarrelling, Jane,' said Diana, 'during your walk on the moor. But go after him; he is now lingering in the passage expecting you – he will make it up.'

I have not much pride under such circumstances: I would always rather be happy than dignified; and I ran after him – he stood at the foot of the stairs.

'Good-night, St John,' said I.

'Good-night, Jane,' he replied calmly.

'Then shake hands,' I added.

What a cold, loose touch he impressed on my fingers! He was deeply displeased by what had occurred that day; cordiality would not warm, nor tears move him. No happy reconciliation was to be had with him – no cheering smile or generous word: but still the Christian was patient and placid; and when I asked him if he forgave me, he answered that he was not in the habit of cherishing the remembrance of vexation; that he had nothing to forgive, not having been offended.

And with that answer he left me. I would much rather he had knocked me down.

## *Chapter 35*

He did not leave for Cambridge the next day, as he had said he would. He deferred his departure a whole week, and during that time he made me feel what severe punishment a good yet stern, a conscientious yet implacable man can inflict on one who has offended him. Without one overt act of hostility, one upbraiding word he contrived to impress me momently with the conviction that I was put beyond the pale of his favour.

Not that St John harboured a spirit of unchristian vindictiveness – not that he would have injured a hair of my head, if it had been fully in his power to do so. Both by nature and principle, he was superior to the mean gratification of vengeance: he had forgiven me for saying I scorned him and his love, but he had not forgotten the words; and as long as he and I lived he never would forget them. I saw by his look, when he turned to me, that they were always written on the air between me and him; whenever I spoke, they sounded in my voice to his ear, and their echo toned every answer he gave me.

He did not abstain from conversing with me: he even called me as usual each morning to join him at his desk; and I fear the corrupt man within him had a pleasure unimparted to, and unshared by, the pure Christian, in evincing with what skill he could, while acting and speaking apparently just as usual, extract from every deed and every phrase the spirit of interest and approval which had formerly communicated a certain austere charm to his language and manner. To me, he was in reality become no longer flesh, but marble; his eye was a cold, bright, blue gem; his tongue a speaking instrument – nothing more.

All this was torture to me – refined, lingering torture. It kept up a slow fire of indignation and a trembling trouble of grief, which harassed and crushed me altogether. I felt how – if I were his wife, this good man, pure as the deep sunless source, could soon kill me, without drawing from my veins a single drop of blood, or receiving on his own crystal conscience the faintest stain of crime. Especially I felt this when I made any attempt to propitiate him. No ruth met my ruth. *He* experienced no suffering from estrangement – no yearning after reconciliation; and though, more than once, my fast falling tears blistered the page over which we both bent, they produced no more effect on him than if his heart had been really a matter of stone or metal. To his sisters, meantime, he was somewhat kinder than usual: as if afraid that mere coldness would not sufficiently convince me how completely I was banished and banned, he added the force of contrast; and this I am sure he did not by malice, but on principle.

The night before he left home, happening to see him walking in the garden about sunset, and remembering, as I looked at him, that this man, alienated as he now was, had once saved my life, and that we were near relations, I was moved to make a last attempt to regain his friendship. I went out and approached him as he stood leaning over the little gate; I spoke to the point at once.

'St John, I am unhappy because you are still angry with me. Let us be friends.'

'I hope we are friends,' was the unmoved reply; while he still watched the rising of the moon, which he had been contemplating as I approached.

'No, St John, we are not friends as we were. You know that.'

'Are we not? That is wrong. For my part, I wish you no ill and all good.'

'I believe you, St John; for I am sure you are incapable of wishing anyone ill; but, as I am your kinswoman, I should desire somewhat more of affection than that sort of general philanthropy you extend to mere strangers.'

'Of course,' he said. 'Your wish is reasonable, and I am far from regarding you as a stranger.'

This, spoken in a cool, tranquil tone, was mortifying and baffling enough. Had I attended to the suggestions of pride and ire, I should immediately have left him; but something worked within me more strongly than those feelings could. I deeply venerated my cousin's talent and principle. His friendship was of value to me: to lose it tried me severely. I would not so soon relinquish the attempt to reconquer it.

'Must we part in this way, St John? And when you go to India, will you leave me so, without a kinder word than you have yet spoken?'

He now turned quite from the moon and faced me. 'When I go to India, Jane, will I leave you! What! do you not go to India?'

'You said I could not unless I married you.'

'And you will not marry me! You adhere to that resolution?'

Reader, do you know, as I do, what terror those cold people can put into the ice of their questions? How much of the fall of the avalanche is in their anger? of the breaking up of the frozen sea in their displeasure?

'No, St John, I will not marry you. I adhere to my resolution.'

The avalanche had shaken and slid a little forward but it did not yet crash down.

'Once more, why this refusal?' he asked.

'Formerly,' I answered, 'because you did not love me; now, I reply, because you almost hate me. If I were to marry you, you would kill me. You are killing me now.'

His lips and cheeks turned white – quite white.

'*I should kill you – I am killing you?* Your words are such as ought not to be used: violent, unfeminine, and untrue. They betray an unfortunate state of mind: they merit severe reproof: they would seem inexcusable, but that it is the duty of man to forgive his fellow even until seventy-and-seven times.'

I had finished the business now. While earnestly wishing to erase from his mind the trace of my former offence, I had stamped on that tenacious surface another and far deeper impression: I had burnt it in.

'Now you will indeed hate me,' I said. 'It is useless to attempt to conciliate you: I see I have made an eternal enemy of you.'

A fresh wrong did these words inflict: the worse, because they touched on the truth. That bloodless lip quivered to a temporary spasm. I knew the steely ire I had whetted. I was heart-wrung.

'You utterly misinterpret my words,' I said, at once seizing his hand: 'I have no intention to grieve or pain you – indeed, I have not.'

Most bitterly he smiled – most decidedly he withdrew his hand from mine. 'And now you recall your promise, and will not go to India at all, I presume?' said he, after a considerable pause.

'Yes, I will, as your assistant,' I answered.

A very long silence succeeded. What struggle there was in him between Nature and Grace in this interval, I cannot tell: only singular gleams scintillated in his eyes, and strange shadows passed over his face. He spoke at last.

'I before proved to you the absurdity of a single woman of your age proposing to accompany abroad a single man of mine. I proved it to you in such terms as, I should have thought, would have prevented your ever again alluding to the plan. That you have done so, I regret – for your sake.'

I interrupted him. Anything like a tangible reproach gave me courage at once. 'Keep to common sense, St John: you are verging on nonsense. You pretend to be shocked by what I have said. You are not really shocked: for, with your superior mind, you cannot be either so dull or so conceited as to misunderstand my meaning. I say again, I will be your curate, if you like, but never your wife.'

Again he turned lividly pale; but, as before, controlled his passion perfectly. He answered emphatically but calmly – 'A female curate, who is not my wife, would never suit me. With me, then, it seems, you cannot go: but if you are sincere in your offer, I will, while in town, speak to a married missionary, whose wife needs a co-adjutor. Your own fortune will make you independent of the Society's aid; and thus you may still be spared the dishonour of breaking your promise and deserting the band you engaged to join.'

Now I never had, as the reader knows, either given any formal promise or entered into any engagement; and this language was all much too hard and much too despotic for the occasion. I replied – 'There is no dishonour, no breach of promise, no desertion in the case. I am not under the slightest obligation to go to India, especially with strangers. With you I would have ventured much, because I admire, confide in, and, as a sister, I love you; but I am convinced that, go when and with whom I would, I should not live long in that climate.'

'Ah! you are afraid of yourself,' he said, curling his lip.

'I am. God did not give me my life to throw away; and to do as you wish me would, I begin to think, be almost equivalent to committing suicide. Moreover, before I definitively resolve on quitting England, I will know for certain whether I cannot be of greater use by remaining in it than by leaving it.'

'What do you mean?'

'It would be fruitless to attempt to explain; but there is a point on which I have long endured painful doubt, and I can go nowhere till by some means that doubt is removed.'

'I know where your heart turns and to what it clings. The interest you cherish is lawless and unconsecrated. Long since you ought to have crushed it: now you should blush to allude to it. You think of Mr Rochester?'

It was true. I confessed it by silence.

'Are you going to seek Mr Rochester?'

'I must find out what is become of him.'

'It remains for me, then,' he said, 'to remember you in my prayers, and to entreat God for you, in all earnestness, that you may not indeed become a castaway. I had thought I recognised in you one of the chosen. But God sees not as man sees: *His* will be done.'

He opened the gate, passed through it, and strayed away down the glen. He was soon out of sight.

On re-entering the parlour, I found Diana standing at the window, looking very thoughtful. Diana was a great deal taller than I: she put her hand on my shoulder, and, stooping, examined my face.

'Jane,' she said, 'you are always agitated and pale now. I am sure there is something the matter. Tell me what business St John and you have on hands. I have watched you this half hour from the window; you must forgive my being such a spy, but for a long time I have fancied I hardly know what. St John is a strange being – '

She paused – I did not speak: soon she resumed – 'That brother of mine cherishes peculiar views of some sort respecting you, I am sure: he has long distinguished you by a notice and interest he never showed to anyone else – to what end? I wish he loved you – does he, Jane?'

I put her cool hand to my hot forehead; 'No, Die, not one whit.'

'Then why does he follow you so with his eyes, and get you so frequently alone with him, and keep you so continually at his side? Mary and I had both concluded he wished you to marry him.'

'He does – he has asked me to be his wife.'

Diana clapped her hands. 'That is just what we hoped and thought! And you will marry him, Jane, won't you? And then he will stay in England.'

'Far from that, Diana; his sole idea in proposing to me is to procure a fitting fellow-labourer in his Indian toils.'

'What! He wishes you to go to India?'

'Yes.'

'Madness!' she exclaimed. 'You would not live three months there, I am certain. You never shall go: you have not consented, have you, Jane?'

'I have refused to marry him – '

'And have consequently displeased him?' she suggested.

'Deeply: he will never forgive me, I fear: yet I offered to accompany him as his sister.'

'It was frantic folly to do so, Jane. Think of the task you undertook – one of incessant fatigue, where fatigue kills even the strong, and you are weak. St John – you know him – would urge you to impossibilities: with him there would be no permission to rest during the hot hours; and unfortunately, I have noticed, whatever he exacts, you force yourself to perform. I am astonished you found courage to refuse his hand. You do not love him then, Jane?'

'Not as a husband.'

'Yet he is a handsome fellow.'

'And I am so plain, you see, Die. We should never suit.'

'Plain! You? Not at all. You are much too pretty, as well as too good, to be grilled alive in Calcutta.' And again she earnestly conjured me to give up all thoughts of going out with her brother.

'I must indeed,' I said; 'for when just now I repeated the offer of serving him for a deacon, he expressed himself shocked at my want of decency. He seemed to think I had committed an impropriety in proposing to accompany him unmarried: as if I had not from the first hoped to find in him a brother, and habitually regarded him as such.'

'What makes you say he does not love you, Jane?'

'You should hear himself on the subject. He has again and again explained that it is not himself, but his office he wishes to mate. He has told me I am formed for labour – not for love: which is true, no doubt. But, in my opinion, if I am not formed for love, it follows that I am not formed for marriage. Would it not be strange, Die, to be chained for life to a man who regarded one but as a useful tool?'

'Insupportable – unnatural – out of the question!'

'And then,' I continued, 'though I have only sisterly affection for him now, yet, if forced to be his wife, I can imagine the possibility of conceiving an inevitable, strange, torturing kind of love for him, because he is so talented; and there is often a certain heroic grandeur in his look, manner, and conversation. In that case, my lot would become unspeakably wretched. He would not want me to love him; and if I showed the feeling, he would make me sensible that it was a superfluity, unrequired by him, unbecoming in me. I know he would.'

'And yet St John is a good man,' said Diana.

'He is a good and a great man; but he forgets, pitilessly, the feelings and claims of little people, in pursuing his own large views. It is better, therefore, for the insignificant to keep out of his way, lest, in his progress, he should trample them down. Here he comes! I will leave you, Diana.' And I hastened upstairs as I saw him entering the garden.

But I was forced to meet him again at supper. During that meal he appeared just as composed as usual. I had thought he would hardly speak to me, and I was certain he had given up the pursuit of his matrimonial scheme: the sequel showed I was mistaken on both points. He addressed me precisely in his ordinary manner, or what had, of late, been his ordinary manner – one scrupulously polite. No doubt he had invoked the help of the Holy Spirit to subdue the anger I had roused in him, and now believed he had forgiven me once more.

For the evening reading before prayers, he selected the twenty-first chapter of Revelation. It was at all times pleasant to listen while from his lips fell the words of the Bible: never did his fine voice sound at once so sweet and full – never did his manner become so impressive in its noble simplicity, as when he delivered the oracles of God: and tonight that voice took a more solemn tone – that manner a more thrilling meaning – as he sat in the midst of his household circle (the May moon shining in through the uncurtained window, and rendering almost unnecessary the light of the candle on the table): as he sat there, bending over the great old Bible, and described from its page the vision of the new heaven and the new earth – told how God would come to dwell with men, how He would wipe away all tears from their eyes, and promised that there should be no more death, neither sorrow nor crying, nor any more pain, because the former things were passed away.

The succeeding words thrilled me strangely as he spoke them: especially as I felt, by the slight, indescribable alteration in sound, that in uttering them, his eye had turned on me.

'He that overcometh shall inherit all things; and I will be his God, and he shall be my son. But,' was slowly, distinctly read, 'the fearful, the unbelieving, etc., shall have their part in the lake which burneth with fire and brimstone, which is the second death.'

Henceforward, I knew what fate St John feared for me.

A calm, subdued triumph, blent with a longing earnestness, marked his enunciation of the last glorious verses of that chapter. The reader believed his name was already written in the Lamb's book of life, and he yearned after the hour which should admit him to the city to which the kings of the earth bring their glory and honour; which has no need of sun or moon to shine in it, because the glory of God lightens it, and the Lamb is the light thereof.

In the prayer following the chapter, all his energy gathered – all his stern zeal woke: he was in deep earnest, wrestling with God, and resolved on a conquest. He supplicated strength for the weak-hearted; guidance for wanderers from the fold: a return, even at the eleventh hour, for those whom the temptations of the world and the flesh were luring from the narrow path. He asked, he urged, he claimed the boon of a brand snatched from the burning. Earnestness is ever deeply solemn: first, as I listened to that prayer, I wondered at his; then, when it continued and rose, I was touched by it, and at last awed. He felt the greatness and goodness of his purpose so sincerely: others who heard him plead for it, could not but feel it too.

The prayer over, we took leave of him: he was to go at a very early hour in the morning. Diana and Mary having kissed him, left the room – in compliance, I think, with a whispered hint from him: I tendered my hand, and wished him a pleasant journey.

'Thank you, Jane. As I said, I shall return from Cambridge in a fortnight: that space, then, is yet left you for reflection. If I listened to human pride, I should say no more to you of marriage with me; but I listen to my duty, and keep steadily in view my first aim – to do all things to the glory of God. My Master was long-suffering: so will I be. I cannot give you up to perdition as a vessel of wrath: repent – resolve, while there is yet time. Remember, we are bid to work while it is day – warned that "the night cometh when no man shall work." Remember the fate of Dives, who had his good things in this life. God give you strength to choose that better part which shall not be taken from you!'

He laid his hand on my head as he uttered the last words. He had spoken earnestly, mildly: his look was not, indeed, that of a lover beholding his mistress, but it was that of a pastor recalling his wandering sheep – or better, of a guardian angel watching the soul for which he is responsible. All men of talent, whether they be men of feeling or not; whether they be zealots, or aspirants, or despots – provided only they be sincere – have their sublime moments, when they subdue and rule. I felt veneration for St John – veneration so strong that its impetus thrust me at once to the point I had so long shunned. I was tempted to cease struggling with him – to rush down the torrent of his will into the gulf of his existence, and there lose my own. I was almost as hard beset by him now as I had been once before, in a different way, by another. I was a fool both times. To have yielded then would have been an error of principle; to have yielded now would have been an error of judgement. So I think at this hour, when I look back to the crisis through the quiet medium of time: I was unconscious of folly at the instant.

I stood motionless under my hierophant's touch. My refusals were forgotten – my fears overcome – my wrestlings paralysed. The Impossible – i.e., my marriage with St John – was fast becoming the Possible. All was changing utterly with a sudden sweep. Religion called – Angels beckoned – God commanded – life rolled together like a scroll – death's gates opening, showed eternity beyond: it seemed, that for safety and bliss there, all here might be sacrificed in a second. The dim room was full of visions.

'Could you decide now?' asked the missionary. The enquiry was put in gentle tones: he drew me to him as gently. Oh, that gentleness! how far more potent is it than force! I could resist St John's wrath: I grew pliant as a reed under his kindness. Yet I knew all the time, if I yielded now, I should not the less be made to repent, someday, of my former rebellion. His nature was not changed by one hour of solemn prayer: it was only elevated.

'I could decide if I were but certain,' I answered: 'were I but convinced that it is God's will I should marry you, I could vow to marry you here and now – come afterwards what would!'

'My prayers are heard!' ejaculated St John. He pressed his hand firmer on my head, as if he claimed me: he surrounded me with his arm, *almost* as if he loved me (I say *almost* – I knew the difference – for I had felt what it was to be loved; but, like him, I had now put love out of the question, and thought only of duty). I contended with my inward dimness of vision, before which clouds yet rolled. I sincerely, deeply, fervently longed to do what was right; and only that. 'Show me, show me the path!' I entreated of Heaven. I was excited more than I had ever been; and whether what followed was the effect of excitement the reader shall judge.

All the house was still; for I believe all, except St John and myself, were now retired to rest. The one candle was dying out: the room was full of moonlight. My heart beat fast and thick: I heard its throb. Suddenly it stood still to an inexpressible feeling that thrilled it through, and passed at once to my head and extremities. The feeling was not like - an electric shock, but it was quite as sharp, as strange, as startling: it acted on my senses as if their utmost activity hitherto had been but torpor, from which they were now summoned and forced to wake. They rose expectant: eye and ear waited while the flesh quivered on my bones.

'What have you heard? What do you see?' asked St John. I saw nothing, but I heard a voice somewhere cry – 'Jane! Jane! Jane!' – nothing more.

'O God! what is it?' I gasped.

I might have said, 'Where is it?' for it did not seem in the room – nor in the house – nor in the garden; it did not come out of the air – nor from under the earth – nor from overhead. I had heard it – where, or whence, for ever impossible to know! And it was the voice of a human being – a known, loved, well-remembered voice – that of Edward Fairfax Rochester; and it spoke in pain and woe, wildly, eerily, urgently.

'I am coming!' I cried. 'Wait for me! Oh, I will come!' I flew to the door and looked into the passage: it was dark. I ran out into the garden: it was void.

'Where are you?' I exclaimed.

The hills beyond Marsh Glen sent the answer faintly back – 'Where are you?' I listened. The wind sighed low in the firs: all was moorland loneliness and midnight hush.

'Down superstition!' I commented, as that spectre rose up black by the black yew at the gate. 'This is not thy deception, nor thy witchcraft: it is the work of nature. She was roused, and did – no miracle – but her best.'

I broke from St John, who had followed, and would have detained me. It was *my* time to assume ascendency. *My* powers were in-play and in force. I told him to forbear question or remark; I desired him to leave me: I must and would be alone. He obeyed at once. Where there is energy to command well enough, obedience never fails. I mounted to my chamber; locked myself in; fell on my knees; and prayed in my way – a different way to St John's, but effective in its own fashion. I seemed to penetrate very near a Mighty Spirit; and my soul rushed out in gratitude at His feet. I rose from the thanksgiving – took a resolve – and lay down, unscared, enlightened – eager but for the daylight.

## *Chapter 36*

The daylight came. I rose at dawn. I busied myself for an hour or two with arranging my things in my chamber, drawers, and wardrobe, in the order wherein I should wish to leave them during a brief absence. Meantime, I heard St John quit his room.

He stopped at my door: I feared he would knock – no, but a slip of paper was passed under the door. I took it up. It bore these words –

> You left me too suddenly last night. Had you stayed but a little longer, you would have laid your hand on the Christian's cross and the angel's crown. I shall expect your clear decision when I return this day fortnight. Meantime, watch and pray that you enter not into temptation: the spirit, I trust, is willing, but the flesh, I see, is weak. I shall pray for you hourly.
>
> Yours, ST JOHN

'My spirit,' I answered mentally, 'is willing to do what is right; and my flesh, I hope, is strong enough to accomplish the will of Heaven, when once that will is distinctly known to me. At any rate, it shall be strong enough to search – enquire – to grope an outlet from this cloud of doubt, and find the open day of certainty.'

It was the first of June; yet the morning was overcast and chilly: rain beat fast on my casement. I heard the front-door open, and St John pass out. Looking through the window, I saw him traverse the garden. He took the way over the misty moors in the direction of Whitcross – there he would meet the coach.

'In a few more hours I shall succeed you in that track, cousin,' thought I: 'I too have a coach to meet at Whitcross. I too have some to see and ask after in England, before I depart for ever.'

It wanted yet two hours of breakfast-time. I filled the interval in walking softly about my room, and pondering the visitation which had given my plans their present bent. I recalled that inward sensation I had experienced: for I could recall it, with all its unspeakable strangeness. I recalled the voice I had heard; again I questioned whence it came, as vainly as before: it seemed in *me* – not in the external world. I asked was it a mere nervous impression – a delusion? I could not conceive or believe: it was more like an inspiration. The wondrous shock of feeling had come like the earthquake which shook the foundations of Paul and Silas's prison; it had opened the doors of the soul's cell and loosed its bands – it had wakened it out of its sleep, whence it sprang trembling, listening, aghast; then vibrated thrice a cry on my startled ear, and in my quaking heart and through my spirit, which neither feared nor shook, but exulted as if in joy over the success of one effort it had been privileged to make, independent of the cumbrous body.

'Ere many days,' I said, as I terminated my musings, 'I will know something of him whose voice seemed last night to summon me. Letters have proved of no avail – personal enquiry shall replace them.'

At breakfast I announced to Diana and Mary that I was going a journey, and should be absent at least four days.

'Alone, Jane?' they asked.

'Yes; it was to see or hear news of a friend about whom I had for some time been uneasy.'

They might have said, as I have no doubt they thought, that they had believed me to be without any friends save them: for, indeed, I had often said so; but, with their true natural delicacy, they abstained from comment, except that Diana asked me if I was sure I was well enough to travel. I looked very pale, she observed. I replied, that nothing ailed me save anxiety of mind, which I hoped soon to alleviate.

It was easy to make my further arrangements; for I was troubled with no enquiries – no surmises. Having once explained to them that I could not now be explicit about my plans, they kindly and wisely acquiesced in the silence with which I pursued them, according to me the privilege of free action I should under similar circumstances have accorded them.

I left Moor House at three o'clock p.m., and soon after four I stood at the foot of the signpost of Whitcross, waiting the arrival of the coach which was to take me to distant Thornfield. Amidst the silence of those solitary roads and desert hills, I heard it approach from a great distance. It was the same vehicle whence, a year ago, I had alighted one summer evening on this very spot – how desolate, and hopeless, and objectless! It stopped as I beckoned. I entered – not now obliged to part with my whole fortune as the price of its accommodation. Once more on the road to Thornfield, I felt like the messenger-pigeon flying home.

It was a journey of six-and-thirty hours. I had set out from Whitcross on a Tuesday afternoon, and early on the succeeding Thursday morning the coach stopped to water the horses at a wayside inn, situated in the midst of scenery whose green hedges and large fields and low pastoral hills (how mild of feature and verdant of hue compared with the stern North-Midland moors of Morton!) met my eye like the lineaments of a once familiar face. Yes, I knew the character of this landscape: I was sure we were near my bourne.

'How far is Thornfield Hall from here?' I asked of the ostler.

'Just two miles, ma'am, across the fields.'

'My journey is closed,' I thought to myself. I got out of the coach, gave a box I had into the ostler's charge, to be kept till I called for it; paid my fare; satisfied the coachman, and was going: the brightening day gleamed on the sign of the inn, and I read in gilt letters, 'The Rochester Arms'. My heart leapt up: I was already on my master's very lands. It fell again: the thought struck it: 'Your master himself may be beyond the British Channel, for aught you know: and then, if he is at Thornfield Hall, towards which you hasten, who besides him is there? His lunatic wife: and you have nothing to do with him: you dare not speak to him or seek his presence. You have lost your labour – you had better go no farther,' urged the monitor. 'Ask information of the people at the inn; they can give you all you seek: they can solve your doubts at once. Go up to that man, and enquire if Mr Rochester be at home.'

The suggestion was sensible, and yet I could not force myself to act on it. I so dreaded a reply that would crush me with despair. To prolong doubt was to prolong hope. I might yet once more see the Hall under the ray of her star. There was the stile before me – the very fields through which I had hurried, blind, deaf, distracted with a revengeful fury tracking and scourging me, on the morning I fled from Thornfield: ere I well knew what course I had resolved to take, I was in the midst of them. How fast I walked! How I ran sometimes! How I looked forward to catch the first view of the well-known woods! With what feelings I welcomed single trees I knew, and familiar glimpses of meadow and hill between them!

At last the woods rose; the rookery clustered dark; a loud cawing broke the morning stillness. Strange delight inspired me: on I hastened. Another field crossed – a lane threaded – and there were the courtyard walls – the back offices: the house itself, the rookery still hid. 'My first view of it shall be in front,' I determined, 'where its bold battlements will strike the eye nobly at once, and where I can single out my master's very window: perhaps he will be standing at it – he rises early: perhaps he is now walking in the orchard, or on the pavement in front. Could I but see him! – but a moment! Surely, in that case, I should not be so mad as to run to him? I cannot tell – I am not certain. And if I did – what then?

God bless him! What then? Who would be hurt by my once more tasting the life his glance can give me? I rave: perhaps at this moment he is watching the sun rise over the Pyrenees, or on the tideless sea of the south.'

I had coasted along the lower wall of the orchard – turned its angle: there was a gate just there, opening into the meadow, between two stone pillars crowned by stone balls. From behind one pillar I could peep round quietly at the full front of the mansion. I advanced my head with precaution, desirous to ascertain if any bedroom window-blinds were yet drawn up: battlements, windows, long front – all from this sheltered station were at my command.

The crows sailing overhead perhaps watched me while I took this survey. I wonder what they thought. They must have considered I was very careful and timid at first, and that gradually I grew very bold and reckless. A peep, and then a long stare; and then a departure from my niche and a straying out into the meadow; and a sudden stop full in front of the great mansion, and a protracted, hardy gaze towards it. 'What affectation of diffidence was this at first?' they might have demanded; 'what stupid regardlessness now?'

Hear an illustration, reader.

A lover finds his mistress asleep on a mossy bank; he wishes to catch a glimpse of her fair face without waking her. He steals softly over the grass, careful to make no sound; he pauses – fancying she has stirred: he withdraws: not for worlds would he be seen. All is still: he again advances: he bends above her; a light veil rests on her features: he lifts it, bends lower; now his eyes anticipate the vision of beauty – warm, and blooming, and lovely, in rest. How hurried was their first glance! But how they fix! How he starts! How he suddenly and vehemently clasps in both arms the form he dared not, a moment since, touch with his finger! How he calls aloud a name, and drops his burden, and gazes on it wildly! He thus grasps and cries, and gazes, because he no longer fears to waken by any sound he can utter – by any movement he can make. He thought his love slept sweetly: he finds she is stone dead.

I looked with timorous joy towards a stately house: I saw a blackened ruin.

No need to cower behind a gatepost, indeed! – to peep up at chamber lattices, fearing life was astir behind them! No need to listen for doors opening – to fancy steps on the pavement or the gravel-walk! The lawn, the grounds were trodden and waste: the portal yawned void. The front was, as I had once seen it in a dream, but a shell-like wall, very high and very fragile-looking, perforated with paneless windows: no roof, no battlements, no chimneys – all had crashed in.

And there was the silence of death about it: the solitude of a lonesome wild. No wonder that letters addressed to people here had never received an answer: as well despatch epistles to a vault in a church aisle. The grim blackness of the stones told by what fate the Hall had fallen – by conflagration: but how kindled? What story belonged to this disaster? What loss, besides mortar and marble and woodwork had followed upon it? Had life been wrecked as well as property? If so, whose? Dreadful question: there was no one here to answer it – not even dumb sign, mute token.

In wandering round the shattered walls and through the devastated interior, I gathered evidence that the calamity was not of late occurrence. Winter snows, I thought, had drifted through that void arch, winter rains beaten in at those hollow casements; for, amidst the drenched piles of rubbish, spring had cherished vegetation: grass and weed grew here and there between the stones and fallen rafters. And oh! where meantime was the hapless owner of this wreck? In what land? Under what auspices? My eye involuntarily wandered to the grey church tower near the gates, and I asked, 'Is he with Damer de Rochester, sharing the shelter of his narrow marble house?'

Some answer must be had to these questions. I could find it nowhere but at the inn, and thither, ere long, I returned. The host himself brought my breakfast into the parlour. I requested him to shut the door and sit down: I had some questions to ask him. But when he complied, I scarcely knew how to begin, such horror had I of the possible answers. And yet the spectacle of desolation I had just left prepared me in a measure for a tale of misery. The host was a respectable-looking, middle-aged man.

'You know Thornfield Hall, of course?' I managed to say at last.

'Yes, ma'am; I lived there once.'

'Did you?' Not in my time, I thought: you are a stranger to me.

'I was the late Mr Rochester's butler,' he added.

The late! I seem to have received, with full force, the blow I had been trying to evade.

'The late!' I gasped. 'Is he dead?'

'I mean the present gentleman, Mr Edward's father,' he explained. I breathed again: my blood resumed its flow. Fully assured by these words that Mr Edward – *my* Mr Rochester (God bless him, wherever he was!) – was at least alive: was, in short, 'the present gentleman'. Gladdening words! It seemed I could hear all that was to come – whatever the disclosures might be – with comparative tranquillity. Since he was not in the grave, I could bear, I thought, to learn that he was at the Antipodes.

'Is Mr Rochester living at Thornfield Hall now?' I asked, knowing, of course, what the answer would be, but yet desirous of deferring the direct question as to where he really was.

'No, ma'am – oh, no! No one is living there. I suppose you are a stranger in these parts, or you would have heard what happened last autumn, Thornfield Hall is quite a ruin: it was burnt down just about harvest-time. A dreadful calamity! such an immense quantity of valuable property destroyed: hardly any of the furniture could be saved. The fire broke out at dead of night, and before the engines arrived from Millcote, the building was one mass of flame. It was a terrible spectacle: I witnessed it myself.'

'At dead of night!' I muttered. Yes, that was ever the hour of fatality at Thornfield. 'Was it known how it originated?' I demanded.

'They guessed, ma'am: they guessed. Indeed, I should say it was ascertained beyond a doubt. You are not perhaps aware,' he continued, edging his chair a little nearer the table, and speaking low, 'that there was a lady – a – a lunatic, kept in the house?'

'I have heard something of it.'

'She was kept in very close confinement, ma'am; people even for some years was not absolutely certain of her existence. No one saw her: they only knew by rumour that such a person was at the Hall; and who or what she was it was difficult to conjecture. They said Mr Edward had brought her from abroad, and some believed she had been his mistress. But a queer thing happened a year since – a very queer thing.'

I feared now to hear my own story. I endeavoured to recall him to the main fact.

'And this lady?'

'This lady, ma'am,' he answered, 'turned out to be Mr Rochester's wife! The discovery was brought about in the strangest way. There was a young lady, a governess at the Hall, that Mr Rochester fell in – '

'But the fire,' I suggested.

'I'm coming to that, ma'am – that Mr Edward fell in love with. The servants say they never saw anybody so much in love as he was: he was after her continually. They used to watch him – servants will, you know, ma'am – and he set store on her past everything: for all, nobody but him thought her so very handsome. She was a little small thing, they say, almost like a child. I never saw her myself; but I've heard Leah the housemaid, tell of her. Leah liked her well enough. Mr Rochester was about forty, and this governess not twenty; and you see, when gentlemen of his age fall in love with girls, they are often like as if they were bewitched. Well, he would marry her.'

'You shall tell me this part of the story another time,' I said; 'but now I have a particular reason for wishing to hear all about the fire. Was it suspected that this lunatic, Mrs Rochester, had any hand in it?'

'You've hit it, ma'am: it's quite certain that it was her, and nobody but her, that set it going. She had a woman to take care of her called Mrs Poole – an able woman in her line, and very trustworthy, but for one fault – a fault common to a deal of them nurses and matrons – *she kept a private bottle of gin by her*, and now and then took a drop over-much. It is excusable, for she had a hard life of it: but still it was dangerous; for when Mrs Poole was fast asleep after the gin and water, the mad lady, who was as cunning as a witch, would take the keys out of her pocket, let herself out of her chamber, and go roaming about the house, doing any wild mischief that came into her head. They say she had nearly burnt her husband in his bed once: but I don't know about that. However, on this night, she set fire first to the hangings of the room next her own, and then she got down to a lower storey, and made her way to the chamber that had been the governess's – (she was like as if she knew somehow how matters had gone on, and had a spite at her) – and she kindled the bed there; but there was nobody sleeping in it, fortunately. The governess had run away two months before; and for all Mr Rochester sought her as if she had been the most precious thing he had in the world, he never could hear a word of her; and he grew savage – quite savage on his disappointment: he never was a wild man, but he got dangerous after he lost her. He would be alone, too. He sent Mrs Fairfax, the housekeeper, away to her friends at a distance; but he did it handsomely, for he settled an annuity on her for life: and she deserved it – she was a very good woman. Miss Adèle, a ward he had, was put to school. He broke off acquaintance with all the gentry, and shut himself up like a hermit at the Hall.'

'What! did he not leave England?'

'Leave England? Bless you, no! He would not cross the door-stones of the house, except at night, when he walked just like a ghost about the grounds and in the orchard as if he had lost his senses – which it is my opinion he had; for a more spirited, bolder, keener gentleman than he was before that midge of a governess crossed him, you never saw, ma'am. He was not a man given to wine, or cards, or racing, as some are, and he was not so very handsome; but he had a courage and a will of his own, if ever man had. I knew him from a boy, you see: and for my part, I have often wished that Miss Eyre had been sunk in the sea before she came to Thornfield Hall.'

'Then Mr Rochester was at home when the fire broke out?'

'Yes, indeed was he; and he went up to the attics when all was burning above and below, and got the servants out of their beds and helped them down himself, and went back to get his mad wife out of her cell. And then they called out to him that she was on the roof, where she was standing, waving her arms, above the battlements, and shouting out till they could hear her a mile off: I saw her and heard her with my own eyes. She was a big woman, and had long black hair: we could see it streaming against the flames as she stood. I witnessed, and several more witnessed, Mr Rochester ascend through the skylight on to the roof; we heard him call "Bertha!" We saw him approach her; and then, ma'am, she yelled and gave a spring, and the next minute she lay smashed on the pavement.'

'Dead?'

'Dead! Ay, dead as the stones on which her brains and blood were scattered.'

'Good God!'

'You may well say so, ma'am: it was frightful!'

He shuddered.

'And afterwards?' I urged.

'Well, ma'am, afterwards the house was burnt to the ground: there are only some bits of walls standing now.'

'Were any other lives lost?'

'No – perhaps it would have been better if there had.'

'What do you mean?'

'Poor Mr Edward!' he ejaculated, 'I little thought ever to have seen it! Some say it was a just judgement on him for keeping his first marriage secret, and wanting to take another wife while he had one living: but I pity him, for my part.'

'You said he was alive?' I exclaimed.

'Yes, yes: he is alive; but many think he had better be dead.'

'Why? How?' My blood was again running cold. 'Where is he?' I demanded. 'Is he in England?'

'Ay – ay – he's in England; he can't get out of England, I fancy – he's a fixture now.'

What agony was this! And the man seemed resolved to protract it.

'He is stone-blind,' he said at last. 'Yes, he is stone-blind, is Mr Edward.'

I had dreaded worse. I had dreaded he was mad. I summoned strength to ask what had caused this calamity.

'It was all his own courage, and a body may say, his kindness, in a way, ma'am: he wouldn't leave the house till everyone else was out before him. As he came down the great staircase at last, after Mrs Rochester had flung herself from the battlements, there was a great crash – all fell. He was taken out from under the ruins, alive, but sadly hurt: a beam had fallen in such a way as to protect him partly; but one eye was knocked out, and one hand so crushed that Mr Carter, the surgeon, had to amputate it directly. The other eye inflamed: he lost the sight of that also. He is now helpless, indeed – blind and a cripple.'

'Where is he? Where does he now live?'

'At Ferndean, a manor-house on a farm he has, about thirty miles off: quite a desolate spot.'

'Who is with him?'

'Old John and his wife: he would have none else. He is quite broken down, they say.'

'Have you any sort of conveyance?'

'We have a chaise, ma'am, a very handsome chaise.'

'Let it be got ready instantly; and if your post-boy can drive me to Ferndean before dark this day, I'll pay both you and him twice the hire you usually demand.'

## *Chapter 37*

The manor-house of Ferndean was a building of considerable antiquity, moderate size, and no architectural pretensions, deep buried in a wood. I had heard of it before. Mr Rochester often spoke of it, and sometimes went there. His father had purchased the estate for the sake of the game covers. He would have let the house, but could find no tenant, in consequence of its ineligible and insalubrious site. Ferndean then remained uninhabited and unfurnished, with the exception of some two or three rooms fitted up for the accommodation of the squire when he went there in the season to shoot.

To this house I came just ere dark on an evening marked by the characteristics of sad sky, cold gale, and continued small penetrating rain. The last mile I performed on foot, having dismissed the chaise and driver with the double remuneration I had promised. Even when within a very short distance of the manor-house, you could see nothing of it, so thick and dark grew the timber of the gloomy wood about it. Iron gates between granite pillars showed me where to enter, and passing through them, I found myself at once in the twilight of close-ranked trees. There was a grass-grown track descending the forest aisle between hoar and knotty shafts and under branched arches. I followed it, expecting soon to reach the dwelling; but it stretched on and on, it wound far and farther: no sign of habitation or grounds was visible.

I thought I had taken a wrong direction and lost my way. The darkness of natural as well as of sylvan dusk gathered over me. I looked round in search of another road. There was none: all was interwoven stem, columnar trunk, dense summer foliage – no opening anywhere.

I proceeded: at last my way opened, the trees thinned a little; presently I beheld a railing, then the house scarce, by this dim light, distinguishable from the trees, so dank and green were its decaying walls. Entering a portal, fastened only by a latch, I stood amidst a space of enclosed ground, from which the wood swept away in a semicircle. There were no flowers, no garden-beds; only a broad gravel-walk girdling a grass-plat, and this set in the heavy frame of the forest. The house presented two pointed gables in its front; the windows were latticed and narrow: the front door was narrow too, one step led up to it. The whole looked, as the host of the Rochester Arms had said, 'quite a desolate spot.' It was as still as a church on a weekday: the pattering rain on the forest leaves was the only sound audible in its vicinage.

'Can there be life here?' I asked.

Yes, life of some kind there was; for I heard a movement – that narrow front-door was unclosing, and some shape was about to issue from the grange.

It opened slowly: a figure came out into the twilight and stood on the step; a man without a hat: he stretched forth his hand as if to feel whether it rained. Dusk as it was, I had recognised him – it was my master, Edward Fairfax Rochester, and no other.

I stayed my step, almost my breath, and stood to watch him – to examine him, myself unseen, and alas! to him invisible. It was a sudden meeting, and one in which rapture was kept well in check by pain. I had no difficulty in restraining my voice from exclamation, my step from hasty advance.

His form was of the same strong and stalwart contour as ever: his port was still erect, his hair was still raven black; nor were his features altered or sunk: not in one year's space, by any sorrow, could his athletic strength be quelled or his vigorous prime blighted. But in his countenance I saw a change: that looked desperate and brooding – that reminded me of some wronged and fettered wild beast or bird, dangerous to approach in his sullen woe. The caged eagle, whose gold-ringed eyes cruelty has extinguished, might look as looked that sightless Samson.

And, reader, do you think I feared him in his blind ferocity? – if you do, you little know me. A soft hope blent with my sorrow that soon I should dare to drop a kiss on that brow of rock, and on those lips so sternly sealed beneath it: but not yet. I would not accost him yet.

He descended the one step, and advanced slowly and gropingly towards the grass-plat. Where was his daring stride now? Then he paused, as if he knew not which way to turn. He lifted his hand and opened his eyelids; gazed blank, and with a straining effort, on the sky, and toward the amphitheatre of trees: one saw that all to him was void darkness. He stretched his right hand (the left arm, the mutilated one, he kept hidden in his bosom); he seemed to wish by touch to gain an idea of what lay around him: he met but vacancy still; for the trees were some yards off where he stood. He relinquished the endeavour, folded his arms, and stood quiet and mute in the rain, now falling fast on his uncovered head. At this moment John approached him from some quarter.

'Will you take my arm, sir?' he said; 'there is a heavy shower coming on: had you not better go in?'

'Let me alone,' was the answer.

John withdrew without having observed me. Mr Rochester now tried to walk about: vainly, all was too uncertain. He groped his way back to the house, and, re-entering it, closed the door.

I now drew near and knocked: John's wife opened for me. 'Mary,' I said, 'how are you?'

She started as if she had seen a ghost: I calmed her. To her hurried 'Is it really you, miss, come at this late hour to this lonely place?' I answered by taking her hand; and then I followed her into the kitchen, where John now sat by a good fire. I explained to them, in a few words, that I had heard all which had happened since I left Thornfield, and that I was come to see Mr Rochester. I asked John to go down to the turnpike-house, where I had dismissed the chaise, and bring my trunk, which I had left there: and then, while I removed my bonnet and shawl, I questioned Mary as to whether I could be accommodated at the Manor House for the night; and finding that arrangements to that effect, though difficult, would not be impossible, I informed her I should stay. Just at this moment the parlour-bell rang.

'When you go in,' said I, 'tell your master that a person wishes to speak to him, but do not give my name.'

'I don't think he will see you,' she answered; 'he refuses everybody.'

When she returned, I enquired what he had said.

'You are to send in your name and your business,' she replied. She then proceeded to fill a glass with water, and place it on a tray, together with candles.

'Is that what he rang for?' I asked.

'Yes: he always has candles brought in at dark, though he is blind.'

'Give the tray to me; I will carry it in.'

I took it from her hand: she pointed me out the parlour door. The tray shook as I held it; the water spilt from the glass; my heart struck my ribs loud and fast. Mary opened the door for me, and shut it behind me.

This parlour looked gloomy: a neglected handful of fire burnt low in the grate; and, leaning over it, with his head supported against the high, old-fashioned mantelpiece, appeared the blind tenant of the room. His old dog, Pilot, lay on one side, removed out of the way, and coiled up as if afraid of being inadvertently trodden upon. Pilot pricked up his ears when I came in: then he jumped up with a yelp and a whine, and bounded towards me: he almost knocked the tray from my hands. I set it on the table; then patted him, and said softly, 'Lie down!' Mr Rochester turned mechanically to *see* what the commotion was: but as he *saw* nothing, he returned and sighed.

'Give me the water, Mary,' he said.

I approached him with the now only half-filled glass; Pilot followed me, still excited.

'What is the matter?' he enquired.

'Down, Pilot!' I again said. He checked the water on its way to his lips, and seemed to listen: he drank, and put the glass down. 'This is you, Mary, is it not?'

'Mary is in the kitchen,' I answered.

He put out his hand with a quick gesture, but not seeing where I stood, he did not touch me. 'Who is this? Who is this?' he demanded, trying, as it seemed, to *see* with those sightless eyes – unavailing and distressing attempt! 'Answer me – speak again!' he ordered, imperiously and aloud.

'Will you have a little more water, sir? I spilt half of what was in the glass,' I said.

'*Who* is it? *What* is it? Who speaks?'

'Pilot knows me, and John and Mary know I am here. I came only this evening,' I answered.

'Great God! – what delusion has come over me? What sweet madness has seized me?'

'No delusion – no madness: your mind, sir, is too strong for delusion, your health too sound for frenzy.'

'And where is the speaker? Is it only a voice? Oh! I *cannot* see, but I must feel, or my heart will stop and my brain burst. Whatever – whoever you are – be perceptible to the touch or I cannot live!'

He groped; I arrested his wandering hand, and prisoned it in both mine.

'Her very fingers!' he cried; 'her small, slight fingers! If so there must be more of her.'

The muscular hand broke from my custody; my arm was seized, my shoulder – neck – waist – I was entwined and gathered to him.

'Is it Jane? *What* is it? This is her shape – this her size – '

'And this her voice,' I added. 'She is all here: her heart, too. God bless you, sir! I am glad to be so near you again.'

'Jane Eyre! – Jane Eyre,' was all he said.

'My dear master,' I answered, 'I am Jane Eyre: I have found you out – I am come back to you.'

'In truth? – in the flesh? My living Jane?'

'You touch me, sir, you hold me, and fast enough: I am not cold like a corpse, nor vacant like air, am I?'

'My living darling! These are certainly her limbs, and these her features; but I cannot be so blest, after all my misery. It is a dream; such dreams as I have had at night when I have clasped her once more to my heart, as I do now; and kissed her, as thus – and felt that she loved me, and trusted that she would not leave me.'

'Which I never will, sir, from this day.'

'Never will, says the vision? But I always woke and found it an empty mockery; and I was desolate and abandoned – my life dark, lonely, hopeless – my soul athirst and forbidden to drink – my heart famished and never to be fed. Gentle, soft dream, nestling in my arms now, you will fly, too, as your sisters have all fled before you: but kiss me before you go – embrace me, Jane.'

'There, sir – and there!'

I pressed my lips to his once brilliant and now rayless eyes – I swept his hair from his brow, and kissed that too. He suddenly seemed to arouse himself: the conviction of the reality of all this seized him.

'It is you – is it, Jane? You are come back to me then?'

'I am.'

'And you do not lie dead in some ditch under some stream? And you are not a pining outcast amongst strangers?'

'No, sir! I am an independent woman now.'

'Independent! What do you mean, Jane?'

'My uncle in Madeira is dead, and he left me five thousand pounds.'

'Ah! this is practical – this is real!' he cried: 'I should never dream that. Besides, there is that peculiar voice of hers, so animating and piquant, as well as soft: it cheers my withered heart; it puts life into it. What, Janet! Are you an independent woman? A rich woman?'

'Quite rich, sir. If you won't let me live with you, I can build a house of my own close up to your door, and you may come and sit in my parlour when you want company of an evening.'

'But as you are rich, Jane, you have now, no doubt, friends who will look after you, and not suffer you to devote yourself to a blind lameter like me?'

'I told you I am independent, sir, as well as rich: I am my own mistress.'

'And you will stay with me?'

'Certainly – unless you object. I will be your neighbour, your nurse, your housekeeper. I find you lonely: I will be your companion – to read to you, to walk with you, to sit with you, to wait on you, to be eyes and hands to you. Cease to look so melancholy, my dear master; you shall not be left desolate, so long as I live.'

He replied not: he seemed serious – abstracted; he sighed; he half-opened his lips as if to speak: he closed them again. I felt a little embarrassed. Perhaps I had too rashly overleaped conventionalities; and he, like St John, saw impropriety in my inconsiderateness. I had indeed made my proposal from the idea that he wished and would ask me to be his wife: an expectation, not the less certain because unexpressed, had buoyed me up, that he would claim me at once as his own. But no hint to that effect escaping him and his countenance becoming more overcast, I suddenly remembered that I might have been all wrong, and was perhaps playing the fool unwittingly; and I began gently to withdraw myself from his arms – but he eagerly snatched me closer.

'No – no – Jane; you must not go. No – I have touched you, heard you, felt the comfort of your presence – the sweetness of your consolation: I cannot give up these joys. I have little left in myself – I must have you. The world may laugh – may call me absurd, selfish – but it does not signify. My very soul demands you: it will be satisfied, or it will take deadly vengeance on its frame.'

'Well, sir, I will stay with you: I have said so.'

'Yes – but you understand one thing by staying with me; and I understand another. You, perhaps, could make up your mind to be about my hand and chair – to wait on me as a kind little nurse (for you have an affectionate heart and a generous spirit, which prompt you to make sacrifices for those you pity), and that ought to suffice for me no doubt. I suppose I should now entertain none but fatherly feelings for you: do you think so? Come – tell me.'

'I will think what you like, sir: I am content to be only your nurse, if you think it better.'

'But you cannot always be my nurse, Janet: you are young – you must marry one day.'

'I don't care about being married.'

'You should care, Janet: if I were what I once was, I would try to make you care – but – a sightless block!'

He relapsed again into gloom. I, on the contrary, became more cheerful, and took fresh courage: these last words gave me an insight as to where the difficulty lay; and as it was no difficulty with me, I felt quite relieved from my previous embarrassment. I resumed a livelier vein of conversation.

'It is time someone undertook to rehumanise you,' said I, parting his thick and long uncut locks; 'for I see you are being metamorphosed into a lion, or something of that sort. You have a "faux air" of Nebuchadnezzar in the fields about you, that is certain: your hair reminds me of eagles' feathers; whether your nails are grown like birds' claws or not, I have not yet noticed.'

'On this arm, I have neither hand nor nails,' he said, drawing the mutilated limb from his breast, and showing it to me. 'It is a mere stump – a ghastly sight! Don't you think so, Jane?'

'It is a pity to see it; and a pity to see your eyes – and the scar of fire on your forehead: and the worst of it is, one is in danger of loving you too well for all this; and making too much of you.'

'I thought you would be revolted, Jane, when you saw my arm, and my cicatrised visage.'

'Did you? Don't tell me so – lest I should say something disparaging to your judgement. Now, let me leave you an instant, to make a better fire, and have the hearth swept up. Can you tell when there is a good fire?'

'Yes; with the right eye I see a glow – a ruddy haze.'

'And you see the candles?'

'Very dimly – each is a luminous cloud.'

'Can you see me?'

'No, my fairy: but I am only too thankful to hear and feel you.'

'When do you take supper?'

'I never take supper.'

'But you shall have some tonight. I am hungry: so are you, I dare say, only you forget.'

Summoning Mary, I soon had the room in more cheerful order: I prepared him, likewise, a comfortable repast. My spirits were excited, and with pleasure and ease I talked to him during supper, and for a long time after. There was no harassing restraint, no repressing of glee and vivacity with him; for with him I was at perfect ease, because I knew I suited him; all I said or did seemed either to console or revive him. Delightful consciousness! It brought to life and light my whole nature: in his presence I thoroughly lived; and he lived in mine. Blind as he was, smiles played over his face, Joy dawned on his forehead: his lineaments softened and warmed.

After supper, he began to ask me many questions, of where I had been, what I had been doing, how I had found him out; but I gave him only very partial replies: it was too late to enter into particulars that night. Besides, I wished to touch no deep-thrilling chord – to open no fresh well of emotion in his heart: my sole present aim was to cheer him. Cheered, as I have said, he was: and yet but by fits. If a moment's silence broke the conversation, he would turn restless, touch me, then say, 'Jane.'

'You are altogether a human being, Jane? You are certain of that?'

'I conscientiously believe so, Mr Rochester.'

'Yet how, on this dark and doleful evening, could you so suddenly rise on my lone hearth? I stretched my hand to take a glass of water from a hireling, and it was given me by you: I asked a question, expecting John's wife to answer me, and your voice spoke at my ear.'

'Because I had come in, in Mary's stead, with the tray.'

'And there is enchantment in the very hour I am now spending with you. Who can tell what a dark, dreary, hopeless life I have dragged on for months past? Doing nothing, expecting nothing; merging night in day; feeling but the sensation of cold when I let the fire go out, of hunger when I forgot to eat: and then a ceaseless sorrow, and, at times, a very delirium of desire to behold my Jane again. Yes: for her restoration I longed, far more than for that of my lost sight. How can it be that Jane is with me, and says she loves me? Will she not depart as suddenly as she came? Tomorrow, I fear I shall find her no more.'

A commonplace, practical reply, out of the train of his own disturbed ideas, was, I was sure, the best and most reassuring for him in this frame of mind. I passed my finger over his eyebrows, and remarked that they were scorched, and that I would apply something which would make them grow as broad and black as ever.

'Where is the use of doing me good in any way, beneficent spirit, when, at some fatal moment, you will again desert me – passing like a shadow, whither and how to me unknown, and for me remaining afterwards undiscoverable?'

'Have you a pocket-comb about you, sir?'

'What for, Jane?'

'Just to comb out this shaggy black mane. I find you rather alarming, when I examine you close at hand: you talk of my being a fairy, but I am sure, you are more like a brownie.'

'Am I hideous, Jane?'

'Very, sir: you always were, you know.'

'Humph! The wickedness has not been taken out of you, wherever you have sojourned.'

'Yet I have been with good people; far better than you: a hundred times better people; possessed of ideas and views you never entertained in your life: quite more refined and exalted.'

'Who the deuce have you been with?'

'If you twist in that way you will make me pull the hair out of your head; and then I think you will cease to entertain doubts of my substantiality.'

'Who have you been with, Jane?'

'You shall not get it out of me tonight, sir; you must wait till tomorrow; to leave my tale half told, will, you know, be a sort of security that I shall appear at your breakfast table to finish it. By the by, I must mind not to rise on your hearth with only a glass of water then: I must bring an egg at the least, to say nothing of fried ham.'

'You mocking changeling – fairy-born and human-bred! You make me feel as I have not felt these twelve months. If Saul could have had you for his David, the evil spirit would have been exorcised without the aid of the harp.'

'There, sir, you are redd up and made decent. Now I'll leave you: I have been travelling these last three days, and I believe I am tired. Good-night.'

'Just one word, Jane: were there only ladies in the house where you have been?'

I laughed and made my escape, still laughing as I ran upstairs. 'A good idea!' I thought with glee. 'I see I have the means of fretting him out of his melancholy for some time to come.'

Very early the next morning I heard him up and astir, wandering from one room to another. As soon as Mary came down I heard the question: 'Is Miss Eyre here?' Then: 'Which room did you put her into? Was it dry? Is she up? Go and ask if she wants anything; and when she will come down.'

I came down as soon as I thought there was a prospect of breakfast. Entering the room very softly, I had a view of him before he discovered my presence. It was mournful, indeed, to witness the subjugation of that vigorous spirit to a corporeal infirmity. He sat in his chair – still, but not at rest: expectant evidently; the lines of now habitual sadness marking his strong features. His countenance reminded one of a lamp quenched, waiting to be re-lit – and alas! it was not himself that could now kindle the lustre of animated expression: he was dependent on another for that office! I had meant to be gay and careless, but the powerlessness of the strong man touched my heart to the quick: still I accosted him with what vivacity I could.

'It is a bright, sunny morning, sir,' I said. 'The rain is over and gone, and there is a tender shining after it: you shall have a walk soon.'

I had wakened the glow: his features beamed.

'Oh, you are indeed there, my skylark! Come to me. You are not gone: not vanished? I heard one of your kind an hour ago, singing high over the wood: but its song had no music for me, any more than the rising sun had rays. All the melody on earth is concentrated in my Jane's tongue to my ear (I am glad it is not naturally a silent one): all the sunshine I can feel is in her presence.'

The water stood in my eyes to hear this avowal of his dependence; just as if a royal eagle, chained to a perch, should be forced to entreat a sparrow to become its purveyor. But I would not be lachrymose: I dashed off the salt drops, and busied myself with preparing breakfast.

Most of the morning was spent in the open air. I led him out of the wet and wild wood into some cheerful fields: I described to him how brilliantly green they were; how the flowers and hedges looked refreshed; how sparklingly blue was the sky. I sought a seat for him in a hidden and lovely spot, a dry stump of a tree; nor did I refuse to let him, when seated, place me on his knee. Why should I, when both he and I were happier near than apart? Pilot lay beside us: all was quiet. He broke out suddenly while clasping me in his arms – 'Cruel, cruel deserter! Oh, Jane, what did I feel when I discovered you had fled from Thornfield, and when I could nowhere find you; and, after examining your apartment, ascertained that you had taken no money, nor anything which could serve as an equivalent! A pearl necklace I had given you lay untouched in its little casket; your trunks were left corded and locked as they had been prepared for the bridal tour. What could my darling do, I asked, left destitute and penniless? And what did she do? Let me hear now.' Thus urged, I began the narrative of my experience for the last year. I softened considerably what related to the three days of wandering and starvation, because to have told him all would have been to inflict unnecessary pain: the little I did say lacerated his faithful heart deeper than I wished.

I should not have left him thus, he said, without any means of making my way: I should have told him my intention. I should have confided in him: he would never have forced me to be his mistress. Violent as he had seemed in his despair, he, in truth, loved me far too well and too tenderly to constitute himself my tyrant: he would have given me half his fortune, without demanding so much as a kiss in return, rather that I should have flung myself friendless on the wide world. I had endured, he was certain, more than I had confessed to him.

'Well, whatever my sufferings had been, they were very short,' I answered: and then I proceeded to tell him how I had been received at Moor House; how I had obtained the office of schoolmistress, etc. The accession of fortune, the discovery of my relations, followed in due order. Of course, St John Rivers' name came in frequently in the progress of my tale. When I had done, that name was immediately taken up.

'This St John, then, is your cousin?'

'Yes.'

'You have spoken of him often: do you like him?'

'He was a very good man, sir; I could not help liking him.'

'A good man. Does that mean a respectable well-conducted man of fifty? Or what does it mean?'

'St John was only twenty-nine, sir.'

' "*Jeune encore*", as the French say. Is he a person of low stature, phlegmatic, and plain. A person whose goodness consists rather in his guiltlessness of vice, than in his prowess in virtue.'

'He is untiringly active. Great and exalted deeds are what he lives to perform.'

'But his brain? That is probably rather soft? He means well: but you shrug your shoulders to hear him talk?'

'He talks little, sir: what he does say is ever to the point. His brain is first-rate, I should think not impressible, but vigorous.'

'Is he an able man, then?'

'Truly able.'

'A thoroughly educated man?'

'St John is an accomplished and profound scholar.'

'His manners, I think, you said are not to your taste? – priggish and parsonic?'

'I never mentioned his manners; but, unless I had a very bad taste, they must suit it; they are polished, calm, and gentlemanlike.'

'His appearance, I forget what description you gave of his appearance; a sort of raw curate, half strangled with his white neckcloth, and stilted up on his thick-soled high-lows, eh?'

'St John dresses well. He is a handsome man: tall, fair, with blue eyes, and a Grecian profile.'

*(Aside.)* 'Damn him!' – (*To me.*) 'Did you like him, Jane?'

'Yes, Mr Rochester, I liked him: but you asked me that before.'

I perceived, of course, the drift of my interlocutor. Jealousy had got hold of him: she stung him; but the sting was salutary: it gave him respite from the gnawing fang of melancholy. I would not, therefore, immediately charm the snake.

'Perhaps you would rather not sit any longer on my knee, Miss Eyre?' was the next somewhat unexpected observation.

'Why not, Mr Rochester?'

'The picture you have just drawn is suggestive of a rather too overwhelming contrast. Your words have delineated very prettily a graceful Apollo: he is present to your imagination, tall, fair, blue-eyed, and with a Grecian profile. Your eyes dwell on a Vulcan, a real blacksmith, brown, broad-shouldered: and blind and lame into the bargain.'

'I never thought of it, before; but you certainly are rather like Vulcan, sir.'

'Well, you can leave me, ma'am: but before you go' (and he retained me by a firmer grasp than ever), 'you will be pleased just to answer me a question or two.' He paused.

'What questions, Mr Rochester?'

Then followed this cross examination.

'St John made you schoolmistress of Morton before he knew you were his cousin?'

'Yes.'

'You would often see him? He would visit the school sometimes?'

'Daily.'

'He would approve of your plans, Jane? I know they would be clever, for you are a talented creature!'

'He approved of them – yes.'

'He would discover many things in you he could not have expected to find? Some of your accomplishments are not ordinary.'

'I don't know about that.'

'You had a little cottage near the school, you say: did he ever come there to see you?'

'Now and then.'

'Of an evening?'

'Once or twice.'

A pause.

'How long did you reside with him and his sisters after the cousinship was discovered?'

'Five months.'

'Did Rivers spend much time with the ladies of his family?'

'Yes; the back parlour was both his study and ours: he sat near the window, and we by the table.'

'Did he study much?'

'A good deal.'

'What?'

'Hindustani.'

'And what did you do meantime?'

'I learnt German, at first.'

'Did he teach you?'

'He did not understand German.'

'Did he teach you nothing?'

'A little Hindustani.'

'Rivers taught you Hindustani?'

'Yes, sir.'

'And his sisters also?'

'No.'

'Only you?'

'Only me.'

'Did you ask to learn?'

'No.'

'He wished to teach you?'

'Yes.'

A second pause.

'Why did he wish it? Of what use could Hindustani be to you?'

'He intended me to go with him to India.'

'Ah! here I reach the root of the matter. He wanted you to marry him?'

'He asked me to marry him.'

'That is a fiction – an impudent invention to vex me.'

'I beg your pardon, it is the literal truth: he asked me more than once, and was as stiff about urging his point as ever you could be.'

'Miss Eyre, I repeat it, you can leave me. How often am I to say the same thing? Why do you remain pertinaciously perched on my knee, when I have given you notice to quit?'

'Because I am comfortable there.'

'No, Jane, you are not comfortable there, because your heart is not with me: it is with this cousin – this St John. Oh, till this moment, I thought my little

Jane was all mine! I had a belief she loved me even when she left me: that was an atom of sweet in much bitter. Long as we have been parted, hot tears as I have wept over our separation, I never thought that while I was mourning her, she was loving another! But it is useless grieving. Jane, leave me: go and marry Rivers.'

'Shake me off, then, sir, push me away, for I'll not leave you of my own accord.'

'Jane, I ever like your tone of voice: it still renews hope, it sounds so truthful. When I hear it, it carries me back a year. I forget that you have formed a new tie, But I am not a fool – go – '

'Where must I go, sir?'

'Your own way – with the husband you have chosen.'

'Who is that?'

'You know – this St John Rivers.'

'He is not my husband, nor ever will be. He does not love me: I do not love him. He loves (as he *can* love, and that is not as you love) a beautiful young lady called Rosamond. He wanted to marry me only because he thought I should make a suitable missionary's wife, which she would not have done. He is good and great, but severe; and, for me, cold as an iceberg. He is not like you, sir: I am not happy at his side, nor near him, nor with him. He has no indulgence for me – no fondness. He sees nothing attractive in me; not even youth only a few useful mental points – Then I must leave you, sir, to go to him?'

I shuddered involuntarily, and clung instinctively closer to my blind but beloved master. He smiled.

'What, Jane! Is this true? Is such really the state of matters between you and Rivers?'

'Absolutely, sir! Oh, you need not be jealous! I wanted to tease you a little to make you less sad: I thought anger would be better than grief. But if you wish me to love you, could you but see how much I *do* love you, you would be proud and content. All my heart is yours, sir: it belongs to you; and with you it would remain, were fate to exile the rest of me from your presence for ever.'

Again, as he kissed me, painful thoughts darkened his aspect.

'My seared vision! My crippled strength!' he murmured regretfully.

I caressed, in order to soothe him. I knew of what he was thinking, and wanted to speak for him, but dared not. As he turned aside his face a minute, I saw a tear slide from under the sealed eyelid, and trickle down the manly cheek. My heart swelled.

'I am no better than the old lightning-struck chestnut tree in Thornfield orchard,' he remarked ere long. 'And what right would that ruin have to bid a budding woodbine cover its decay with freshness?'

'You are no ruin, sir – no lightning-struck tree: you are green and vigorous. Plants will grow about your roots, whether you ask them or not, because they take delight in your bountiful shadow, and as they grow they will lean towards you, and wind round you, because your strength offers them so safe a prop.'

Again he smiled: I gave him comfort.

'You speak of friends, Jane?' he asked.

'Yes, of friends,' I answered rather hesitatingly: for I knew I meant more than friends, but could not tell what other word to employ. He helped me.

'Ah! Jane. But I want a wife.'

'Do you, sir?'

'Yes: is it news to you?'

'Of course: you said nothing about it before.'

'Is it unwelcome news?'

'That depends on circumstances, sir – on your choice.'

'Which you shall make for me, Jane. I will abide by your decision.'

'Choose then, sir – her *who loves you best*.'

'I will at least choose – *her I love best*. Jane, will you marry me?'

'Yes, sir.'

'A poor blind man, whom you will have to lead about by the hand?'

'Yes, sir.'

'A crippled man, twenty years older than you, whom you will have to wait on?'

'Yes, sir.'

'Truly, Jane?'

'Most truly, sir.'

'Oh! my darling! God bless you and reward you!'

'Mr Rochester, if ever I did a good deed in my life – if ever I thought a good thought – if ever I prayed a sincere and blameless prayer – if ever I wished a righteous wish, I am rewarded now. To be your wife is, for me, to be as happy as I can be on earth.'

'Because you delight in sacrifice.'

'Sacrifice! What do I sacrifice? Famine for food, expectation for content. To be privileged to put my arms round what I value – to press my lips to what I love – to repose on what I trust: is that to make a sacrifice? If so, then certainly I delight in sacrifice.'

'And to bear with my infirmities, Jane: to overlook my deficiencies.'

'Which are none, sir, to me. I love you better now, when I can really be useful, to you, than I did in your state of proud independence, when you disdained every part but that of the giver and protector.'

'Hitherto I have hated to be helped – to be led: henceforth, I feel I shall hate it no more. I did not like to put my hand into a hireling's, but it is pleasant to feel it circled by Jane's little fingers. I preferred utter loneliness to the constant attendance of servants; but Jane's soft ministry will be a perpetual joy. Jane suits me: do I suit her?'

'To the finest fibre of my nature, sir.'

'The case being so, we have nothing in the world to wait for: we must be married instantly.'

He looked and spoke with eagerness: his old impetuosity was rising.

'We must become one flesh without any delay, Jane: there is but the licence to get – then we marry.'

'Mr Rochester, I have just discovered the sun is far declined from its meridian, and Pilot is actually gone home to his dinner. Let me look at your watch.'

'Fasten it into your girdle, Janet, and keep it henceforward: I have no use for it.'

'It is nearly four o'clock in the afternoon, sir. Don't you feel hungry?'

'The third day from this must be our wedding-day, Jane. Never mind fine clothes and jewels, now: all that is not worth a fillip.'

'The sun has dried up all the raindrops, sir. The breeze is still: it is quite hot.'

'Do you know, Jane, I have your little pearl necklace at this moment fastened round my bronze scrag under my cravat? I have worn it since the day I lost my only treasure, as a memento of her.'

'We will go home through the wood: that will be the shadiest way.'

He pursued his own thoughts without heeding me.

'Jane! you think me, I dare say, an irreligious dog: but my heart swells with gratitude to the beneficent God of this earth just now. He sees not as man sees, but far clearer: judges not as man judges, but far more wisely. I did wrong: I would have sullied my innocent flower – breathed guilt on its purity: the Omnipotent snatched it from me. I, in my stiff-necked rebellion, almost cursed the dispensation: instead of bending to the decree, I defied it. Divine justice pursued its course; disasters came thick on me: I was forced to pass through the valley of the shadow of death. *His* chastisements are mighty; and one smote me which has humbled me for ever. You know I was proud of my strength: but what is it now, when I must give it over to foreign guidance, as a child does its weakness? Of late, Jane – only – only of late – I began to see and acknowledge the hand of God in my doom. I began to experience remorse, repentance; the wish for reconcilement to my Maker. I began sometimes to pray: very brief prayers they were, but very sincere.

'Some days since: nay, I can number them – four; it was last Monday night, a singular mood came over me: one in which grief replaced frenzy – sorrow, sullenness. I had long had the impression that since I could nowhere find you, you must be dead. Late that night – perhaps it might be between eleven and twelve o'clock – ere I retired to my dreary rest, I supplicated God, that, if it seemed good to Him, I might soon be taken from this life, and admitted to that world to come, where there was still hope of rejoining Jane.

'I was in my own room, and sitting by the window, which was open: it soothed me to feel the balmy night-air; though I could see no stars, and only by a vague, luminous haze, knew the presence of a moon. I longed for thee, Janet! Oh, I longed for thee both with soul and flesh! I asked of God, at once in anguish and humility, if I had not been long enough desolate, afflicted, tormented; and might not soon taste bliss and peace once more. That I merited all I endured, I acknowledged – that I could scarcely endure more, I pleaded; and the alpha and omega of my heart's wishes broke involuntarily from my lips in the words – "Jane! Jane! Jane!" '

'Did you speak these words aloud?'

'I did, Jane. If any listener had heard me, he would have thought me mad: I pronounced them with such frantic energy.'

'And it was last Monday night, somewhere near midnight?'

'Yes; but the time is of no consequence: what followed is the strange point. You will think me superstitious – some superstition I have in my blood, and always had: nevertheless, this is true – true at least it is that I heard what I now relate.

'As I exclaimed "Jane! Jane! Jane!" a voice – I cannot tell whence the voice came, but I know whose voice it was – replied, "I am coming: wait for me;" and a moment after, went whispering on the wind the words – "Where are you?"

'I'll tell you, if I can, the idea, the picture these words opened to my mind: yet it is difficult to express what I want to express. Ferndean is buried, as you see, in a heavy wood, where sound falls dull, and dies unreverberating. "Where are you?" seemed spoken amongst mountains; for I heard a hill-sent echo repeat the words. Cooler and fresher at the moment the gale seemed to visit my brow: I could have deemed that in some wild, lone scene, I and Jane were meeting. In spirit, I believe we must have met. You no doubt were, at that hour, in unconscious sleep, Jane: perhaps your soul wandered from its cell to comfort mine; for those were your accents – as certain as I live – they were yours!'

Reader, it was on Monday night – near midnight – that I too had received the mysterious summons: those were the very words by which I replied to it. I listened to Mr Rochester's narrative, but made no disclosure in return. The coincidence struck me as too awful and inexplicable to be communicated or discussed. If I told anything, my tale would be such as must necessarily make a profound impression on the mind of my hearer: and that mind, yet from its sufferings too prone to gloom, needed not the deeper shade of the supernatural. I kept these things then, and pondered them in my heart.

'You cannot now wonder,' continued my master, 'that when you rose upon me so unexpectedly last night, I had difficulty in believing you any other than a mere voice and vision, something that would melt to silence and annihilation, as the midnight whisper and mountain echo had melted before. Now, I thank God! I know it to be otherwise. Yes, I thank God!'

He put me off his knee, rose, and reverently lifting his hat from his brow, and bending his sightless eyes to the earth, he stood in mute devotion. Only the last words of the worship were audible.

'I thank my Maker, that, in the midst of judgement, he has remembered mercy. I humbly entreat my Redeemer to give me strength to lead henceforth a purer life than I have done hitherto!'

Then he stretched his hand out to be led. I took that dear hand, held it a moment to my lips, then let it pass round my shoulder: being so much lower of stature than he, I served both for his prop and guide. We entered the wood, and wended homeward.

# *Chapter 38*

## CONCLUSION

Reader, I married him. A quiet wedding we had: he and I, the parson and clerk, were alone present. When we got back from church, I went into the kitchen of the manor-house, where Mary was cooking the dinner and John cleaning the knives, and I said – 'Mary, I have been married to Mr Rochester this morning.' The housekeeper and her husband were both of that decent phlegmatic order of people to whom one may at any time safely communicate a remarkable piece of news without incurring the danger of having one's ears pierced by some shrill ejaculation, and subsequently stunned by a torrent of wordy wonderment. Mary did look up, and she did stare at me: the ladle with which she was basting a pair of chickens roasting at the fire, did for some three minutes hang suspended in air; and for the same space of time John's knives also had rest from the polishing process: but Mary, bending again over the roast, said only – 'Have you, Miss? Well, for sure!'

A short time after she pursued – 'I seed you go out with the master, but I didn't know you were gone to church to be wed;' and she basted away. John, when I turned to him, was grinning from ear to ear.

'I telled Mary how it would be,' he said: 'I knew what Mr Edward' (John was an old servant, and had known his master when he was the cadet of the house, therefore, he often gave him his Christian name) – 'I knew what Mr Edward would do; and I was certain he would not wait long neither: and he's done right, for aught I know. I wish you joy, Miss!' and he politely pulled his forelock.

'Thank you, John. Mr Rochester told me to give you and Mary this.' I put into his hand a five-pound note. Without waiting to hear more, I left the kitchen. In passing the door of that sanctum some time after, I caught the words – 'She'll happen do better for him nor ony o' t' grand ladies.' And again, 'If she ben't one o' th' handsomest, she's noan faâl and varry good-natured; and i' his een she's fair beautiful, onybody may see that.'

I wrote to Moor House and to Cambridge immediately, to say what I had done: fully explaining also why I had thus acted. Diana and Mary approved the step unreservedly. Diana announced that she would just give me time to get over the honeymoon, and then she would come and see me.

'She had better not wait till then, Jane,' said Mr Rochester, when I read her letter to him; 'if she does; she will be too late, for our honeymoon will shine our life long: its beams will only fade over your grave or mine.'

How St John received the news, I don't know: he never answered the letter in which I communicated it: yet six months after he wrote to me, without, however, mentioning Mr Rochester's name or alluding to my marriage. His letter was then calm, and, though very serious, kind. He has maintained a regular, though not frequent, correspondence ever since: he hopes I am happy, and trusts I am not of those who live without God in the world, and only mind earthly things.

You have not quite forgotten little Adèle, have you, reader? I had not; I soon asked and obtained leave of Mr Rochester, to go and see her at the school where he had placed her. Her frantic joy at beholding me again moved me much. She looked pale and thin: she said she was not happy. I found the rules of the establishment were too strict, its course of study too severe for a child of her age: I took her home with me. I meant to become her governess once more, but I soon found this impracticable; my time and cares were now required by another – my husband needed them all. So I sought out a school conducted on a more indulgent system, and near enough to permit of my visiting her often, and bringing her home sometimes. I took care she should never want for anything that could contribute to her comfort: she soon settled in her new abode, became very happy there, and made fair progress in her studies. As she grew up, a sound English education corrected in a great measure her French defects; and when she left school, I found in her a pleasing and obliging companion: docile, good-tempered, and well-principled. By her grateful attention to me and mine, she has long since well repaid any little kindness I ever had it in my power to offer her.

My tale draws to its close: one word respecting my experience of married life, and one brief glance at the fortunes of those whose names have most frequently recurred in this narrative, and I have done.

I have now been married ten years. I know what it is to live entirely for and with what I love best on earth. I hold myself supremely blest – blest beyond what language can express; because I am my husband's life as fully as he is mine. No woman was ever nearer to her mate than I am: ever more absolutely bone of his bone and flesh of his flesh. I know no weariness of my Edward's society: he knows none of mine, any more than we each do of the pulsation of the heart that beats in our separate bosoms; consequently, we are ever together. To be together is for us to be at once as free as in solitude, as gay as in company. We talk, I believe, all day long: to talk to each other is but a more animated and an audible thinking. All my confidence is bestowed on him, all his confidence is devoted to me; we are precisely suited in character – perfect concord is the result.

Mr Rochester continued blind the first two years of our union: perhaps it was that circumstance that drew us so very near – that knit us so very close: for I was then his vision, as I am still his right hand. Literally, I was (what he often called me) the apple of his eye. He saw nature – he saw books through me; and never did I weary of gazing for his behalf, and of putting into words the effect of field, tree, town, river, cloud, sunbeam – of the landscape before us; of the weather round us and impressing by sound on his ear what light could no longer stamp on his eye. Never did I weary of reading to him; never did I weary of conducting him where he wished to go: of doing for him what he wished to be done. And there was a pleasure in my services, most full, most exquisite, even though sad – because he claimed these services without painful shame or damping humiliation. He loved me so truly, that he knew no reluctance in profiting by my attendance: he felt I loved him so fondly, that to yield that attendance was to indulge my sweetest wishes.

One morning at the end of the two years, as I was writing a letter to his dictation, he came and bent over me, and said – 'Jane, have you a glittering ornament round your neck?'

I had a gold watch-chain: I answered 'Yes.'

'And have you a pale-blue dress on?'

I had. He informed me then, that for some time he had fancied the obscurity clouding one eye was becoming less dense; and that now he was sure of it.

He and I went up to London. He had the advice of an eminent oculist; and he eventually recovered the sight of that one eye. He cannot now see very distinctly: he cannot read or write much; but he can find his way without being led by the hand: the sky is no longer a blank to him – the earth no longer a void. When his first-born was put into his arms, he could see that the boy had inherited his own eyes, as they once were – large, brilliant, and black. On that occasion, he again, with a full heart, acknowledged that God had tempered judgement with mercy.

My Edward and I, then, are happy: and the more so, because those we most love are happy likewise. Diana and Mary Rivers are both married: alternately, once every year, they come to see us, and we go to see them. Diana's husband is a captain in the navy, a gallant officer and a good man. Mary's is a clergyman, a college friend of her brother's, and, from his attainments and principles, worthy of the connection. Both Captain Fitzjames and Mr Wharton love their wives, and are loved by them.

As to St John Rivers, he left England: he went to India. He entered on the path he had marked for himself; he pursues it still. A more resolute, indefatigable pioneer never wrought amidst rocks and dangers. Firm, faithful, and devoted, full of energy, and zeal, and truth, he labours for his race; he clears their painful way to improvement; he hews down like a giant the prejudices of creed and caste that encumber it. He may be stern; he may be exacting; he may be ambitious yet; but his is the sternness of the warrior Greatheart, who guards his pilgrim convoy from the onslaught of Apollyon. His is the exaction of the apostle, who speaks but for Christ, when he says – 'Whosoever will come after me, let him deny himself, and take up his cross and follow me.' His is the ambition of the high master-spirit, which aims to fill a place in the first rank of those who are redeemed from the earth – who stand without fault before the throne of God, who share the last mighty victories of the Lamb, who are called, and chosen, and faithful.

St John is unmarried: he never will marry now. Himself has hitherto sufficed to the toil, and the toil draws near its close: his glorious sun hastens to its setting. The last letter I received from him drew from my eyes human tears, and yet filled my heart with divine joy: he anticipated his sure reward, his incorruptible crown. I know that a stranger's hand will write to me next, to say that the good and faithful servant has been called at length into the joy of his Lord. And why weep for this? No fear of death will darken St John's last hour: his mind will be unclouded, his heart will be undaunted, his hope will be sure, his faith steadfast. His own words are a pledge of this – 'My Master,' he says, 'has forewarned me. Daily He announces more distinctly, "Surely I come quickly!" and hourly I more eagerly respond, "Amen; even so come, Lord Jesus!" '

# WUTHERING HEIGHTS

# Wuthering Heights

EMILY BRONTË

## *Chapter 1*

1801 – I have just returned from a visit to my landlord – the solitary neighbour that I shall be troubled with. This is certainly a beautiful country! In all England, I do not believe that I could have fixed on a situation so completely removed from the stir of society. A perfect misanthropist's Heaven: and Mr Heathcliff and I are such a suitable pair to divide the desolation between us. A capital fellow! He little imagined how my heart warmed towards him when I beheld his black eyes withdraw so suspiciously under their brows, as I rode up, and when his fingers sheltered themselves, with a jealous resolution, still further in his waistcoat, as I announced my name.

'Mr Heathcliff?' I said.

A nod was the answer.

'Mr Lockwood your new tenant, sir. I do myself the honour of calling as soon as possible after my arrival, to express the hope that I have not inconvenienced you by my perseverance in soliciting the occupation of Thrushcross Grange: I heard yesterday you had had some thoughts – '

'Thrushcross Grange is my own, sir,' he interrupted, wincing. 'I should not allow anyone to inconvenience me, if I could hinder it – walk in!'

The 'walk in' was uttered with closed teeth, and expressed the sentiment, 'Go to the Deuce': even the gate over which he leant manifested no sympathising movement to the words; and I think that circumstance determined me to accept the invitation: I felt interested in a man who seemed more exaggeratedly reserved than myself.

When he saw my horse's breast fairly pushing the barrier, he did pull out his hand to unchain it, and then sullenly preceded me up the causeway, calling, as we entered the court – 'Joseph, take Mr Lockwood's horse; and bring up some wine.'

'Here we have the whole establishment of domestics, I suppose,' was the reflection, suggested by this compound order. 'No wonder the grass grows up between the flags, and cattle are the only hedge-cutters.'

Joseph was an elderly, nay, an old man: very old, perhaps, though hale and sinewy. 'The Lord help us!' he soliloquised in an undertone of peevish displeasure, while relieving me of my horse: looking, meantime, in my face so sourly that I charitably conjectured he must have need of divine aid to digest his dinner, and his pious ejaculation had no reference to my unexpected advent.

Wuthering Heights is the name of Mr Heathcliff's dwelling. 'Wuthering' being a significant provincial adjective, descriptive of the atmospheric tumult to which its station is exposed in stormy weather. Pure, bracing ventilation they must have up there at all times, indeed: one may guess the power of the north wind blowing over the edge, by the excessive slant of a few stunted firs at the end of the house; and by a range of gaunt thorns all stretching their limbs one way, as if craving alms of the sun. Happily, the architect had foresight to build it strong: the narrow windows are deeply set in the wall, and the corners defended with large jutting stones.

Before passing the threshold, I paused to admire a quantity of grotesque carving lavished over the front, and especially about the principal door; above which, among a wilderness of crumbling griffins and shameless little boys, I detected the date '1500', and the name 'Hareton Earnshaw'. I would have made a few comments, and requested a short history of the place from the surly owner; but his attitude at the door appeared to demand my speedy entrance, or complete departure, and I had no desire to aggravate his impatience previous to inspecting the penetralium.

One step brought us into the family sitting-room, without any introductory lobby or passage: they call it here 'the house' pre-eminently. It includes kitchen and parlour, generally; but I believe at Wuthering Heights the kitchen is forced to retreat altogether into another quarter: at least I distinguished a chatter of tongues, and a clatter of culinary utensils, deep within; and I observed no signs of roasting, boiling, or baking, about the huge fireplace; nor any glitter of copper saucepans and tin colanders on the walls. One end, indeed, reflected splendidly both light and heat from ranks of immense pewter dishes, interspersed with silver jugs and tankards, towering row after row, on a vast oak dresser, to the very roof. The latter had never been underdrawn: its entire anatomy lay bare to an enquiring eye, except where a frame of wood laden with oatcakes and clusters of legs of beef, mutton, and ham, concealed it. Above the chimney were sundry villainous old guns, and a couple of horse-pistols: and, by way of ornament, three gaudily painted canisters disposed along its ledge. The floor was of smooth, white stone; the chairs, high-backed, primitive structures, painted green: one or two heavy black ones lurking in the shade. In an arch under the dresser, reposed a huge, liver-coloured bitch pointer, surrounded by a swarm of squealing puppies; and other dogs haunted other recesses.

The apartment and furniture would have been nothing extraordinary as belonging to a homely, northern farmer, with a stubborn countenance, and stalwart limbs set out to advantage in knee-breeches and gaiters. Such an individual seated in his armchair, his mug of ale frothing on the round table before him, is to be seen in any circuit of five or six miles among these hills, if you go at the right time after dinner. But Mr Heathcliff forms a singular contrast to his abode and style of living. He is a dark-skinned gypsy in aspect, in dress and manners a gentleman: that is, as much a gentleman as many a country squire: rather slovenly, perhaps, yet not looking amiss with his negligence, because he has an erect and handsome figure; and rather morose. Possibly, some people might suspect him of a degree of underbred pride; I have a sympathetic chord within that tells me it is nothing of the sort: I know, by instinct, his reserve springs from an aversion to showy displays of feeling – to manifestations of mutual kindliness. He'll love and hate equally under cover, and esteem it a species of impertinence to be loved or hated again. No, I'm running on too fast: I bestow my own attributes over liberally on him. Mr

Heathcliff may have entirely dissimilar reasons for keeping his hand out of the way when he meets a would-be acquaintance, to those which actuate me. Let me hope my constitution is almost peculiar: my dear mother used to say I should never have a comfortable home; and only last summer I proved myself perfectly unworthy of one.

While enjoying a month of fine weather at the seacoast, I was thrown into the company of a most fascinating creature: a real goddess in my eyes, as long as she took no notice of me. I 'never told my love' vocally; still, if looks have language, the merest idiot might have guessed I was over head and ears: she understood me at last, and looked a return – the sweetest of all imaginable looks. And what did I do? I confess it with shame – shrunk icily into myself, like a snail; at every glance retired colder and farther; till finally the poor innocent was led to doubt her own senses, and, overwhelmed with confusion at her supposed mistake, persuaded her mamma to decamp. By this curious turn of disposition I have gained the reputation of deliberate heartlessness; how undeserved, I alone can appreciate.

I took a seat at the end of the hearthstone opposite that towards which my landlord advanced, and filled up an interval of silence by attempting to caress the canine mother, who had left her nursery, and was sneaking wolfishly to the back of my legs, her lip curled up, and her white teeth watering for a snatch. My caress provoked a long, guttural gnarl.

'You'd better let the dog alone,' growled Mr Heathcliff in unison, checking fiercer demonstrations with a punch of his foot. 'She's not accustomed to be spoiled – not kept for a pet.' Then, striding to a side door, he shouted again, 'Joseph!'

Joseph mumbled indistinctly in the depths of the cellar, but gave no intimation of ascending; so his master dived down to him, leaving me *vis-à-vis* the ruffianly bitch and a pair of grim shaggy sheepdogs, who shared with her a jealous guardianship over all my movements. Not anxious to come in contact with their fangs, I sat still; but, imagining they would scarcely understand tacit insults, I unfortunately indulged in winking and making faces at the trio, and some turn of my physiognomy so irritated madam, that she suddenly broke into a fury, and leapt on my knees. I flung her back, and hastened to interpose the table between us. This proceeding roused the whole hive. Half a dozen four-footed fiends, of various sizes and ages, issued from hidden dens to the common centre. I felt my heels and coat-laps peculiar subjects of assault; and, parrying off the larger combatants as effectually as I could with the poker, I was constrained to demand, aloud, assistance from some of the household in re-establishing peace.

Mr Heathcliff and his man climbed the cellar steps with vexatious phlegm: I don't think they moved one second faster than usual, though the hearth was an absolute tempest of worrying and yelping. Happily, an inhabitant of the kitchen made more dispatch: a lusty dame, with tucked-up gown, bare arms, and fire-flushed cheeks, rushed into the midst of us flourishing a frying-pan: and used that weapon, and her tongue, to such purpose, that the storm subsided magically, and she only remained, heaving like a sea after a high wind, when her master entered on the scene.

'What the devil is the matter?' he asked, eyeing me in a manner I could ill endure after this inhospitable treatment.

'What the devil, indeed!' I muttered. 'The herd of possessed swine could have had no worse spirits in them than those animals of yours, sir. You might as well leave a stranger with a brood of tigers!'

'They won't meddle with persons who touch nothing,' he remarked, putting the bottle before me, and restoring the displaced table. 'The dogs do right to be vigilant. Take a glass of wine?'

'No thank you.'

'Not bitten, are you?'

'If I had been, I would have set my signet on the biter.'

Heathcliff's countenance relaxed into a grin.

'Come, come,' he said, 'you are flurried, Mr Lockwood. Here, take a little wine. Guests are so exceedingly rare in this house that I and my dogs, I am willing to own, hardly know how to receive them. Your health, sir!'

I bowed and returned the pledge; beginning to perceive that it would be foolish to sit sulking for the misbehaviour of a pack of curs: besides, I felt loath to yield the fellow further amusement at my expense; since his humour took that turn. He – probably swayed by prudential considerations of the folly of offending a good tenant – relaxed a little in the laconic style of chipping off his pronouns and auxiliary verbs, and introduced what he supposed would be a subject of interest to me – a discourse on the advantages and disadvantages of my present place of retirement. I found him very intelligent on the topics we touched; and before I went home, I was encouraged so far as to volunteer another visit tomorrow. He evidently wished no repetition of my intrusion. I shall go, notwithstanding. It is astonishing how sociable I feel myself compared with him.

## *Chapter 2*

Yesterday afternoon set in misty and cold. I had half a mind to spend it by my study fire, instead of wading through heath and mud to Wuthering Heights. On coming up from dinner, however (N.B. – I dine between twelve and one o'clock; the housekeeper, a matronly lady, taken as a fixture along with the house, could not, or would not, comprehend my request that I might be served at five), on mounting the stairs with this lazy intention, and stepping into the room, I saw a servant-girl on her knees, surrounded by brushes, and coal-scuttles; and raising an infernal dust as she extinguished the flames with heaps of cinders. This spectacle drove me back immediately; I took my hat, and, after a four miles' walk, arrived at Heathcliff's garden gate just in time to escape the first feathery flakes of a snow-shower.

On that bleak hilltop the earth was hard with a black frost, and the air made me shiver through every limb. Being unable to remove the chain, I jumped over, and, running up the flagged causeway bordered with straggling gooseberry bushes, knocked vainly for admittance, till my knuckles tingled, and the dogs howled.

'Wretched inmates!' I ejaculated, mentally, 'you deserve perpetual isolation from your species for your churlish inhospitality. At least, I would not keep my doors barred in the daytime. I don't care – I will get in!' So resolved, I grasped the latch and shook it vehemently. Vinegar-faced Joseph projected his head from a round window of the barn.

'Whet are ye for?' he shouted. 'T' maister's dahn i' t' fowld. Goa rahnd by th' end ut' laith, if yah went tuh spake tull him.'

'Is there nobody inside to open the door?' I hallooed, responsively.

'They's nobbut t' missis; and shoo'll nut oppen 't an ye mak yer flaysome dins till neeght.'

'Why? cannot you tell her who I am, eh, Joseph?'

'Nor-ne me! Aw'll hae noa hend wi't,' muttered the head vanishing.

The snow began to drive thickly. I seized the handle to essay another trial; when a young man without coat, and shouldering a pitchfork, appeared in the yard behind. He hailed me to follow him, and, after marching through a wash-house, and a paved area containing a coal-shed, pump, and pigeon-cote, we at length arrived in the huge, warm, cheerful apartment, where I was formerly received. It glowed delightfully in the radiance of an immense fire, compounded of coal, peat, and wood; and near the table, laid for a plentiful evening meal, I was pleased to observe the 'missis,' an individual whose existence I had never previously suspected. I bowed and waited, thinking she would bid me take a seat. She looked at me, leaning back in her chair, and remained motionless and mute.

'Rough weather!' I remarked. 'I'm afraid, Mrs Heathcliff, the door must bear the consequence of your servants' leisure attendance: I had hard work to make them hear me!'

She never opened her mouth. I stared – she stared also. At any rate, she kept her eyes on me in a cool, regardless manner, exceedingly embarrassing and disagreeable.

'Sit down,' said the young man, gruffly. 'He'll be in soon.'

I obeyed; and hemmed, and called the villain Juno, who deigned, at this second interview, to move the extreme tip of her tail, in token of owning my acquaintance.

'A beautiful animal!' I commenced again. 'Do you intend parting with the little ones, madam?'

'They are not mine,' said the amiable hostess, more repellingly than Heathcliff himself could have replied.

'Ah, your favourites are among these!' I continued, turning to an obscure cushion full of something like cats.

'A strange choice of favourites!' she observed scornfully.

Unluckily, it was a heap of dead rabbits. I hemmed once more, and drew closer to the hearth, repeating my comment on the wildness of the evening.

'You should not have come out,' she said, rising and reaching from the chimney-piece two of the painted canisters.

Her position before was sheltered from the light; now, I had a distinct view of her whole figure and countenance. She was slender, and apparently scarcely past girlhood: an admirable form, and the most exquisite little face that I have ever had the pleasure of beholding: small features, very fair; flaxen ringlets, or rather golden, hanging loose on her delicate neck; and eyes, had they been agreeable in expression, they would have been irresistible: fortunately for my susceptible heart, the only sentiment they evinced hovered between scorn and a kind of desperation, singularly unnatural to be detected there.

The canisters were almost out of her reach; I made a motion to aid her; she turned upon me as a miser might turn if anyone attempted to assist him in counting his gold.

'I don't want your help,' she snapped; 'I can get them for myself.'

'I beg your pardon,' I hastened to reply.

'Were you asked to tea?' she demanded, tying an apron over her neat black frock, and standing with a spoonful of the leaf poised over the pot.

'I shall be glad to have a cup,' I answered.

'Were you asked?' she repeated.

'No,' I said, half smiling. 'You are the proper person to ask me.'

She flung the tea back, spoon and all; and resumed her chair in a pet, her forehead corrugated, and her red under-lip pushed out, like a child's, ready to cry.

Meanwhile, the young man had slung on to his person a decidedly shabby upper garment, and, erecting himself before the blaze, looked down on me, from the corner of his eyes, for all the world as if there were some mortal feud unavenged between us. I began to doubt whether he were a servant or not: his dress and speech were both rude, entirely devoid of the superiority observable in Mr and Mrs Heathcliff; his thick, brown curls were rough and uncultivated, his whiskers encroached bearishly over his cheeks, and his hands were embrowned like those of the common labourer: still his bearing was free, almost haughty, and he showed none of a domestic's assiduity in attending on the lady of the house. In the absence of clear proofs of his condition, I deemed it best to abstain from noticing his curious conduct; and, five minutes afterwards, the entrance of Heathcliff relieved me, in some measure, from my uncomfortable state.

'You see, sir, I am come, according to promise!' I exclaimed, assuming the cheerful; 'and I fear I shall be weather-bound for half an hour, if you can afford me shelter during that space.'

'Half an hour?' he said, shaking the white flakes from his clothes; 'I wonder you should select the thick of a snowstorm to ramble about in. Do you know that you run a risk of being lost in the marshes? People familiar with these moors often miss their road on such evenings; and, I can tell you, there is no chance of a change at present.'

'Perhaps I can get a guide among your lads, and he might stay at the Grange till morning – could you spare me one?'

'No, I could not.'

'Oh, indeed! Well, then, I must trust to my own sagacity.'

'Umph!'

'Are you going to mak' th' tea?' demanded he of the shabby coat, shifting his ferocious gaze from me to the young lady.

'Is *he* to have any?' she asked, appealing to Heathcliff.

'Get it ready, will you?' was the answer uttered so savagely that I started. The tone in which the words were said, revealed a genuine bad nature. I no longer felt inclined to call Heathcliff a capital fellow. When the preparations were finished, he invited me with – 'Now, sir, bring forward your chair.' And we all, including the rustic youth, drew round the table: an austere silence prevailing while we discussed our meal.

I thought, if I had caused the cloud, it was my duty to make an effort to dispel it. They could not every day sit so grim and taciturn; and it was impossible, however ill-tempered they might be, that the universal scowl they wore was their everyday countenance.

'It is strange,' I began, in the interval of swallowing one cup of tea and receiving another – 'it is strange how custom can mould our tastes and ideas: many could not imagine the existence of happiness in a life of such complete exile from the world as you spend, Mr Heathcliff; yet, I'll venture to say, that, surrounded by your family, and with your amiable lady as the presiding genius over your home and heart – '

'My amiable lady!' he interrupted, with an almost diabolical sneer on his face. 'Where is she – my amiable lady?'

'Mrs Heathcliff, your wife, I mean.'

'Well, yes – Oh! you would intimate that her spirit has taken the post of ministering angel, and guards the fortunes of Wuthering Heights, even when her body is gone. Is that it?'

Perceiving myself in a blunder, I attempted to correct it. I might have seen that there was too great a disparity between the ages of the parties to make it likely that they were man and wife. One was about forty; a period of mental vigour at which men seldom cherish the delusion of being married for love, by girls: that dream is reserved for the solace of our declining years. The other did not look seventeen.

Then it flashed upon me – 'The clown at my elbow, who is drinking his tea out of a basin and eating his bread with unwashed hands, may be her husband. Heathcliff, junior, of course. Here is the consequence of being buried alive: she has thrown herself away upon that boor, from sheer ignorance that better individuals existed! A sad pity – I must beware how I cause her to regret her choice.' The last reflection may seem conceited; it was not. My neighbour struck me as bordering on repulsive; I knew, through experience, that I was tolerably attractive.

'Mrs Heathcliff is my daughter-in-law,' said Heathcliff, corroborating my surmise. He turned, as he spoke, a peculiar look in her direction, a look of hatred unless he has a most perverse set of facial muscles that will not, like those of other people, interpret the language of his soul.

'Ah, certainly – I see now: you are the favoured possessor of the beneficent fairy,' I remarked, turning to my neighbour.

This was worse than before: the youth grew crimson, and clenched his fist, with every appearance of a meditated assault. But he seemed to recollect himself, presently; and smothered the storm in a brutal curse, muttered on my behalf: which, however, I took care not to notice.

'Unhappy in your conjectures, sir!' observed my host: 'we neither of us have the privilege of owning your good fairy; her mate is dead. I said she was my daughter-in-law, therefore, she must have married my son.'

'And this young man is – '

'Not my son, assuredly!'

Heathcliff smiled again, as if it were rather too bold a jest to attribute the paternity of that bear to him.

'My name is Hareton Earnshaw,' growled the other; 'and I'd counsel you to respect it!'

'I've shown no disrespect,' was my reply, laughing internally at the dignity with which he announced himself.

He fixed his eye on me longer than I cared to return the stare, for fear I might be tempted either to box his ears, or render my hilarity audible. I began to feel unmistakably out of place in that pleasant family circle. The dismal spiritual atmosphere overcame, and more than neutralised the glowing physical comforts round me; and I resolved to be cautious how I ventured under those rafters a third time.

The business of eating being concluded, and no one uttering a word of sociable conversation, I approached a window to examine the weather. A sorrowful sight I saw: dark night coming down prematurely, and sky and hills mingled in one bitter whirl of wind and suffocating snow.

'I don't think it possible for me to get home now, without a guide,' I could not help exclaiming. 'The roads will be buried already; and, if they were bare, I could scarcely distinguish a foot in advance.'

'Hareton, drive those dozen sheep into the barn porch. They'll be covered if left in the fold all night: and put a plank before them,' said Heathcliff.

'How must I do?' I continued, with rising irritation.

There was no reply to my question; and on looking round I saw only Joseph bringing in a pail of porridge for the dogs, and Mrs Heathcliff leaning over the fire, diverting herself with burning a bundle of matches which had fallen from the chimney-piece as she restored the tea-canister to its place.

The former, when he had deposited his burden, took a critical survey of the room; and, in cracked tones, grated out – 'Aw woonder hagh yah can faishion tuh stand thear i' idleness un war, when all on 'em's goan aght! Bud yah 're a nowt, and it's noa use talking – yah'll niver mend uh yer ill ways; bud, goa raight tuh t' divil, like yer mother afore ye!'

I imagined, for a moment, that this piece of eloquence was addressed to me; and, sufficiently enraged, stepped towards the aged rascal with an intention of kicking him out of the door. Mrs Heathcliff, however, checked me by her answer.

'You scandalous old hypocrite!' she replied. 'Are you not afraid of being carried away bodily, whenever you mention the devil's name? I warn you to refrain from provoking me, or I'll ask your adbuction as a special favour. Stop, look here, Joseph,' she continued, taking a long, dark book from a shelf. 'I'll show you how far I've progressed in the Black Art: I shall soon be competent to make a clear house of it. The red cow didn't die by chance; and your rheumatism can hardly be reckoned among providential visitations!'

'Oh, wicked, wicked!' gasped the elder; 'may the Lord deliver us from evil!'

'No, reprobate! you are a castaway – be off, or I'll hurt you seriously! I'll have you all modelled in wax and clay; and the first who passes the limits I fix, shall – I'll not say what he shall be done to – but, you'll see! Go, I'm looking at you!'

The little witch put a mock malignity into her beautiful eyes, and Joseph, trembling with sincere horror, hurried out praying and ejaculating 'wicked' as he went. I thought her conduct must be prompted by a species of dreary fun; and, now that we were alone, I endeavoured to interest her in my distress.

'Mrs Heathcliff,' I said, earnestly, 'you must excuse me for troubling you – I presume, because, with that face, I'm sure you cannot help being good-hearted. Do point out some landmarks by which I may know my way home: I have no more idea how to get there than you would have how to get to London!'

'Take the road you came,' she answered, ensconcing herself in a chair, with a candle, and the long book open before her. 'It is brief advice, but as sound as I can give.'

'Then, if you hear of me being discovered dead in a bog or a pit full of snow, your conscience won't whisper that it is partly your fault?'

'How so? I cannot escort you. They wouldn't let me go to the end of the garden-wall.'

'*You!* I should be very sorry to ask you to cross the threshold, for my convenience, on such a night,' I cried. 'I want you to *tell* me my way, not to *show* it; or else to persuade Mr Heathcliff to give me a guide.'

'Who? There is himself, Earnshaw, Zillah, Joseph, and I. Which would you have?'

'Are there no boys at the farm?'

'No, those are all.'

'Then, it follows that I am compelled to stay.'

'That you may settle with your host. I have nothing to do with it.'

'I hope it will be a lesson to you, to make no more rash journeys on these hills,' cried Heathcliff's stern voice from the kitchen entrance. 'As to staying here, I don't keep accommodations for visitors: you must share a bed with Hareton, or Joseph, if you do.'

'I can sleep on a chair in this room,' I replied.

'No, no! A stranger is a stranger, be he rich or poor: it will not suit me to permit anyone the range of the place while I am off guard!' said the unmannerly wretch.

With this insult, my patience was at an end. I uttered an expression of disgust, and pushed past him into the yard, running against Earnshaw in my haste. It was so dark that I could not see the means of exit; and, as I wandered round, I heard another specimen of their civil behaviour amongst each other. At first, the young man appeared about to befriend me.

'I'll go with him as far as the park,' he said.

'You'll go with him to hell!' exclaimed his master, or whatever relation he bore. 'And who is to look after the horses, eh?'

'A man's life is of more consequence than one evening's neglect of the horses: somebody must go,' murmured Mrs Heathcliff, more kindly than I expected.

'Not at your command!' retorted Hareton. 'If you set store on him, you'd better be quiet.'

'Then I hope his ghost will haunt you; and I hope Mr Heathcliff will never get another tenant, till the Grange is a ruin!' she answered sharply.

'Hearken, hearken, shoo's cursing on em!' muttered Joseph, towards whom I had been steering.

He sat within earshot, milking the cows by the light of a lantern, which I seized unceremoniously, and, calling out that I would send it back on the morrow, rushed to the nearest postern.

'Maister, maister, he's staling t' lantern!' shouted the ancient, pursuing my retreat. 'Hey, Gnasher! Hey, dog! Hey, Wolf, holld him, holld him!'

On opening the little door, two hairy monsters flew at my throat, bearing me down and extinguishing the light; while a mingled guffaw, from Heathcliff and Hareton, put the copestone on my rage and humiliation. Fortunately, the beasts seemed more bent on stretching their paws, and yawning, and flourishing their tails, than devouring me alive; but they would suffer no resurrection, and I was forced to lie till their malignant masters pleased to deliver me: then hatless, and trembling with wrath, I ordered the miscreants to let me out – on their peril to keep me one minute longer – with several incoherent threats of retaliation that, in their indefinite depth of virulency, smacked of King Lear.

The vehemence of my agitation brought on a copious bleeding at the nose, and still Heathcliff laughed, and still I scolded. I don't know what would have concluded the scene, had there not been one person at hand rather more rational than myself, and more benevolent than my entertainer. This was Zillah, the stout housewife; who at length issued forth to enquire into the nature of the uproar. She thought that some of them had been laying violent hands on me; and, not daring to attack her master, she turned her vocal artillery against the younger scoundrel.

'Well, Mr Earnshaw,' she cried, 'I wonder what you'll have agait next! Are we going to murder folk on our very door-stones? I see this house will never do for me – look at t' poor lad, he's fair choking! Wisht, wisht! you mun'n't go on so. Come in, and I'll cure that. There now, hold ye still.'

With these words she suddenly splashed a pint of icy water down my neck, and pulled me into the kitchen. Mr Heathcliff followed, his accidental merriment expiring quickly in his habitual moroseness.

I was sick exceedingly, and dizzy and faint; and thus compelled, perforce, to accept lodgings under his roof. He told Zillah to give me a glass of brandy, and then passed on to the inner room; while she condoled with me on my sorry predicament, and having obeyed his orders, whereby I was somewhat revived, ushered me to bed.

## Chapter 3

While leading the way upstairs, she recommended that I should hide the candle, and not make a noise; for her master had an odd notion about the chamber she would put me in, and never let anybody lodge there willingly. I asked the reason. She did not know, she answered: she had only lived there a year or two; and they had so many queer goings on, she could not begin to be curious.

Too stupified to be curious myself, I fastened my door and glanced round for the bed. The whole furniture consisted of a chair, a clothes-press, and a large oak case, with squares cut out near the top, resembling coach windows. Having approached this structure, I looked inside, and perceived it to be a singular sort of old-fashioned couch, very conveniently designed to obviate the necessity for every member of the family having a room to himself. In fact, it formed a little closet, and the ledge of a window, which it enclosed, served as a table. I slid back the panelled sides, got in with my light, pulled them together again, and felt secure against the vigilance of Heathcliff, and everyone else.

The ledge, where I placed my candle, had a few mildewed books piled up in one corner; and it was covered with writing scratched on the paint. This writing, however, was nothing but a name repeated in all kinds of characters, large and small – *Catherine Earnshaw*, here and there varied to *Catherine Heathcliff*, and then again to *Catherine Linton*.

In vapid listlessness I leant my head against the window, and continued spelling over Catherine Earnshaw – Heathcliff – Linton, till my eyes closed; but they had not rested five minutes when a glare of white letters started from the dark, as vivid as spectres – the air swarmed with Catherines; and rousing myself to dispel the obtrusive name, I discovered my candle wick reclining on one of the antique volumes, and perfuming the place with an odour of roasted calfskin. I snuffed it off, and, very ill at ease under the influence of cold and lingering nausea, sat up and spread open the injured tome on my knee. It was a Testament, in lean type, and smelling dreadfully musty: a flyleaf bore the inscription – 'Catherine Earnshaw, her book,' and a date some quarter of a century back. I shut it, and took up another, and another, till I had examined all. Catherine's library was select, and its state of dilapidation proved it to have been well used; though not altogether for a legitimate purpose: scarcely one chapter had escaped a pen-and-ink commentary – at least, the appearance of one – covering every morsel of blank that the printer had left. Some were detached sentences; other parts took the form of a regular diary, scrawled in an unformed, childish hand. At the top of an extra page (quite a treasure, probably, when first lighted on) I was greatly amused to behold an excellent caricature of my friend Joseph – rudely yet powerfully sketched. An immediate interest kindled within me for the unknown Catherine, and I began, forthwith, to decipher her faded hieroglyphics.

'An awful Sunday!' commenced the paragraph beneath. 'I wish my father were back again. Hindley is a detestable substitute – his conduct to Heathcliff is atrocious – H. and I are going to rebel – we took our initiatory step this evening.

'All day had been flooding with rain; we could not go to church, so Joseph must needs get up a congregation in the garret; and, while Hindley and his wife basked downstairs before a comfortable fire – doing anything but reading their Bibles, I'll answer for it – Heathcliff, myself, and the unhappy ploughboy were commanded to take our prayer-books, and mount: we were ranged in a row, on a sack of corn, groaning and shivering, and hoping that Joseph would shiver too, so that he might give us a short homily for his own sake. A vain idea! The service lasted precisely three hours; and yet my brother had the face to exclaim, when he saw us descending, "What, done already?" On Sunday evenings we used to be permitted to play, if we did not make much noise; now a mere titter is sufficient to send us into corners!

' "You forget you have a master here," says the tyrant. "I'll demolish the first who puts me out of temper! I insist on perfect sobriety and silence. Oh, boy! was that you? Frances, darling, pull his hair as you go by: I heard him snap his fingers." Frances pulled his hair heartily, and then went and seated herself on her husband's knee; and there they were, like two babies, kissing and talking nonsense by the hour – foolish palaver that we should be ashamed of. We made ourselves as snug as our means allowed in the arch of the dresser. I had just fastened our pinafores together, and hung them up for a curtain, when in comes Joseph, on an errand from the stables.

'He tears down my handiwork, boxes my ears, and croaks – "T' maister nobbut just buried, and Sabbath nut oe'red, und t' sahnd uh't gospel still i' yer lugs, and yah darr be laiking! shame on ye! sit ye dahn, ill childer! they's good books eneugh if ye'll read 'em: sit ye dahn, and think uh yer sowls!"

'Saying this, he compelled us so to square our positions that we might receive from the far-off fire a dull ray to show us the text of the lumber he thrust upon us. I could not bear the employment. I took my dingy volume by the scroop, and hurled it into the dog-kennel, vowing I hated a good book. Heathcliff kicked his to the same place. Then there was a hubbub!

' "Maister Hindley!" shouted our chaplain. "Maister, coom hither! Miss Cathy's riven th' back off *Th' Helmet uh Salvation*, un' Heathcliff's pawsed his fit intuh t' first part uh *T' Brooad Way to Destruction*! It's fair flaysome ut yah let 'em goa on this gait. Ech! th' owd man ud uh laced 'em properly – bud he's goan!"

'Hindley hurried up from his paradise on the hearth, and seizing one of us by the collar, and the other by the arm, hurled both into the back-kitchen; where, Joseph asseverated, "owd Nick" would fetch us as sure as we were living: and, so comforted, we each sought a separate nook to await his advent. I reached this book, and a pot of ink from the shelf, and pushed the house-door ajar to give me light, and I have got the time on with writing for twenty minutes; but my companion is impatient, and proposes that we should appropriate the dairy woman's cloak, and have a scamper on the moors, under its shelter. A pleasant suggestion – and then, if the surly old man come in, he may believe his prophecy verified – we cannot be damper, or colder, in the rain than we are here.'

I suppose Catherine fulfilled her project, for the next sentence took up another subject: she waxed lachrymose.

'How little did I dream that Hindley would ever make me cry so!' she wrote. 'My head aches, till I cannot keep it on the pillow; and still I can't give over. Poor Heathcliff! Hindley calls him a vagabond, and won't let him sit with us, nor eat with us any more; and, he says, he and I must not play together, and threatens to turn him out of the house if we break his orders. He has been blaming our father (how dared he?) for treating H. too liberally; and swears he will reduce him to his right place – '

I began to nod drowsily over the dim page: my eye wandered from manuscript to print. I saw a red ornamented title – 'Seventy Times Seven, and the First of the Seventy-First. A Pious Discourse delivered by the Reverend Jabes Branderham, in the Chapel of Gimmerden Sough'. And while I was, half consciously, worrying my brain to guess what Jabes Branderham would make of his subject, I sank back in bed, and fell asleep. Alas, for the effects of bad tea and bad temper! What else could it be that made me pass such a terrible night? I don't remember another that I can at all compare with it since I was capable of suffering.

I began to dream, almost before I ceased to be sensible of my locality. I thought it was morning; and I had set out on my way home, with Joseph for a guide. The snow lay yards deep in our road; and, as we floundered on, my companion wearied me with constant reproaches that I had not brought a pilgrim's staff: telling me that I could never get into the house without one, and boastfully flourishing a heavy-headed cudgel, which I understood to be so denominated. For a moment I considered it absurd that I should need such a weapon to gain admittance into my own residence. Then a new idea flashed across me. I was not going there: we were journeying to hear the famous Jabes Branderham preach from the text – 'Seventy Times Seven'; and either Joseph, the preacher, or I had committed the 'First of the Seventy-First', and were to be publicly exposed and excommunicated.

We came to the chapel. I have passed it really in my walks, twice or thrice; it lies in a hollow, between two hills: an elevated hollow, near a swamp, whose peaty moisture is said to answer all the purposes of embalming on the few corpses deposited there. The roof has been kept whole hitherto; but as the clergyman's stipend is only twenty pounds per annum, and a house with two rooms, threatening speedily to determine into one, no clergyman will undertake the duties of pastor: especially as it is currently reported that his flock would rather let him starve than increase the living by one penny from their own pockets. However, in my dream, Jabes had a full and attentive congregation; and he preached – good God! what a sermon: divided into *four hundred and ninety* parts, each fully equal to an ordinary address from the pulpit, and each discussing a separate sin! Where he searched for them, I cannot tell. He had his private manner of interpreting the phrase, and it seemed necessary the brother should sin different sins on every occasion. They were of the most curious character: odd transgressions that I never imagined previously.

Oh, how weary I grew. How I writhed, and yawned, and nodded, and revived! How I pinched and pricked myself, and rubbed my eyes, and stood up, and sat down again, and nudged Joseph to inform me if he would *ever* have done. I was condemned to hear all out: finally, he reached the '*First of the Seventy-First*'. At that crisis, a sudden inspiration descended on me; I was moved to rise and denounce Jabes Branderham as the sinner of the sin that no Christian need pardon.

'Sir,' I exclaimed, 'sitting here within these four walls, at one stretch, I have endured and forgiven the four hundred and ninety heads of your discourse. Seventy times seven times have I plucked up my hat and been about to depart – Seventy times seven times have you preposterously forced me to resume my seat. The four hundred and ninety first is too much. Fellow-martyrs, have at him! Drag him down, and crush him to atoms, that the place which knows him may know him no more!'

'*Thou art the Man!*' cried Jabes, after a solemn pause, leaning over his cushion. 'Seventy times seven times didst thou gapingly contort thy visage – seventy times seven did I take counsel with my soul – Lo, this is human weakness: this also may be absolved! The First of the Seventy-First is come. Brethren, execute upon him the judgement written. Such honour have all His saints!'

With that concluding word the whole assembly, exalting their pilgrim's staves, rushed round me in a body; and I, having no weapon to raise in self-defence, commenced grappling with Joseph, my nearest and most ferocious assailant, for his. In the confluence of the multitude, several clubs crossed; blows, aimed at me, fell on other sconces. Presently the whole chapel resounded with rappings and counter-rappings: every man's hand was against his neighbour; and Branderham, unwilling to remain idle, poured forth his zeal in a shower of loud taps on the boards of the pulpit, which responded so smartly that, at last, to my unspeakable relief, they woke me. And what was it that had suggested the tremendous tumult? What had played Jabes's part in the row? Merely the branch of a fir tree that touched my lattice, as the blast wailed by, and rattled its dry cones against the panes! I listened doubtingly an instant; detected the disturber, then turned and dosed, and dreamt again: if possible, still more disagreeably than before.

This time, I remembered I was lying in the oak closet, and I heard distinctly the gusty wind, and the driving of the snow; I heard, also, the fir bough repeat its teasing sound, and ascribed it to the right cause: but it annoyed me so much, that I resolved to silence it, if possible; and, I thought, I rose and endeavoured to unhasp the casement. The hook was soldered into the staple: a circumstance observed by me when awake, but forgotten. 'I must stop it, nevertheless!' I muttered, knocking my knuckles through the glass, and stretching an arm out to seize the importunate branch; instead of which, my fingers closed on the fingers of a little, ice-cold hand! The intense horror of nightmare came over me: I tried to draw back my arm, but the hand clung to it, and a most melancholy voice sobbed, 'Let me in – let me in!' 'Who are you?' I asked, struggling, meanwhile, to disengage myself. 'Catherine Linton,' it replied shiveringly (why did I think of *Linton*? I had read *Earnshaw* twenty times for Linton). 'I'm come home: I'd lost my way on the moor!' As it spoke, I discerned, obscurely, a child's face looking through the window. Terror made me cruel; and, finding it useless to attempt shaking the creature off, I pulled its wrist on to the broken pane, and rubbed it to and fro till the blood ran down and soaked the bedclothes: still it wailed, 'Let me in!' and maintained its tenacious gripe, almost maddening me with fear. 'How can I!' I said at length. 'Let *me* go, if you want me to let you in!' The fingers relaxed, I snatched mine through the hole, hurriedly piled the books up in a pyramid against it, and stopped my ears to exclude the lamentable prayer. I seemed to keep them closed above a quarter of an hour; yet, the instant I listened again, there was the doleful cry moaning on! 'Begone!' I shouted, 'I'll never let you in, not if you beg for twenty years.' 'It is twenty years,' mourned the voice: 'twenty years. I've been a waif for twenty years!' Thereat began a feeble scratching outside, and the pile of books moved as if thrust forward. I tried to jump up; but could not stir a limb; and so yelled aloud, in a frenzy of fright. To my confusion, I discovered the yell was not ideal: hasty footsteps approached my chamber door; somebody pushed it open, with a vigorous hand, and a light glimmered through the squares at the top of the bed. I sat shuddering yet, and wiping the perspiration from my forehead: the intruder appeared to hesitate, and muttered to himself. At last, he said in a half-whisper, plainly not expecting an answer, 'Is anyone here?' I considered it best to confess my presence; for I knew Heathcliff's accents, and feared he might search further, if I kept quiet. With this intention, I turned and opened the panels. I shall not soon forget the effect my action produced.

Heathcliff stood near the entrance, in his shirt and trousers; with a candle dripping over his fingers, and his face as white as the wall behind him. The first creak of the oak startled him like an electric shock: the light leaped from his hold to a distance of some feet, and his agitation was so extreme, that he could hardly pick it up.

'It is only your guest, sir,' I called out, desirous to spare him the humiliation of exposing his cowardice further. 'I had the misfortune to scream in my sleep, owing to a frightful nightmare. I'm sorry I disturbed you.'

'Oh, God confound you, Mr Lockwood! I wish you were at the —' commenced my host, setting the candle on a chair, because he found it impossible to hold it steady. 'And who showed you up to this room?' he continued, crushing his nails into his palms, and grinding his teeth to subdue the maxillary convulsions. 'Who was it? I've a good mind to turn them out of the house this moment!'

'It was your servant, Zillah,' I replied, flinging myself on to the floor, and rapidly resuming my garments. 'I should not care if you did, Mr Heathcliff; she richly deserves it. I suppose that she wanted to get another proof that the place was haunted, at my expense. Well, it is – swarming with ghosts and goblins! You have reason in shutting it up, I assure you. No one will thank you for a dose in such a den!"

'What do you mean?' asked Heathcliff, 'and what are you doing? Lie down and finish out the night, since you *are* here; but, for Heaven's sake! Don't repeat that horrid noise: nothing could excuse it, unless you were having your throat cut!'

'If the little fiend had got in at the window, she probably would have strangled me!' I returned. 'I'm not going to endure the persecutions of your hospitable ancestors again. Was not the Reverend Jabes Branderham akin to you on the mother's side? And that minx, Catherine Linton, or Earnshaw, or however she was called – she must have been a changeling – wicked little soul! She told me she had been walking the earth these twenty years; a just punishment for her mortal transgressions, I've no doubt!'

Scarcely were these words uttered, when I recollected the association of Heathcliff's with Catherine's name in the book, which had completely slipped from my memory, till thus awakened. I blushed at my inconsideration; but, without showing further consciousness of the offence, I hastened to add – 'The truth is, sir, I passed the first part of the night in' – here I stopped afresh – I was about to say 'perusing those old volumes', then it would have revealed my knowledge of their written, as well as their printed, contents; so, correcting myself, I went on – 'in spelling over the name scratched on that window-ledge. A monotonous occupation, calculated to set me asleep, like counting, or – '

'What *can* you mean by talking in this way to *me*?' thundered Heathcliff with savage vehemence. 'How – how *dare* you, under my roof? – God! he's mad to speak so!' And he struck his forehead with rage.

I did not know whether to resent this language or pursue my explanation; but he seemed so powerfully affected that I took pity and proceeded with my dreams; affirming I had never heard the appellation of 'Catherine Linton' before, but reading it often over produced an impression which personified itself when I had no longer my imagination under control. Heathcliff gradually fell back into the shelter of the bed, as I spoke; finally sitting down almost concealed behind it. I guessed, however, by his irregular and intercepted breathing, that he struggled to vanquish an excess of violent emotion. Not liking to show him that I heard the conflict, I continued my toilette rather noisily, looked at my watch, and soliloquised on the length of the night: 'Not three o'clock yet! I could have taken oath it had been six. Time stagnates here: we must surely have retired to rest at eight!'

'Always at nine in winter, and always rise at four,' said my host, suppressing a groan: and, as I fancied, by the motion of his shadow's arm, dashing a tear from his eyes. 'Mr Lockwood,' he added, 'you may go into my room: you'll only be in the way, coming downstairs so early; and your childish outcry has sent sleep to the devil for me.'

'And for me, too,' I replied. 'I'll walk in the yard till daylight, and then I'll be off; and you need not dread a repetition of my intrusion. I am now quite cured of seeking pleasure in society, be it country or town. A sensible man ought to find sufficient company in himself.'

'Delightful company!' muttered Heathcliff. 'Take the candle, and go where you please. I shall join you directly. Keep out of the yard, though, the dogs are unchained; and the house – Juno mounts sentinel there, and – nay, you can only ramble about the steps and passages. But, away with you! I'll come in two minutes!'

I obeyed, so far as to quit the chamber; when, ignorant where the narrow lobbies led, I stood still, and was witness, involuntarily, to a piece of superstition on the part of my landlord, which belied, oddly, his apparent sense. He got on to the bed, and wrenched open the lattice, bursting, as he pulled at it, into an uncontrollable passion of tears. 'Come in! come in!' he sobbed. 'Cathy, do come. Oh do – *once* more! Oh! My heart's darling! hear me *this* time, Catherine, at last!' The spectre showed a spectre's ordinary caprice; it gave no sign of being; but the snow and wind whirled wildly through, even reaching my station, and blowing out the light.

There was such anguish in the gush of grief that accompanied this raving, that my compassion made me overlook its folly, and I drew off, half angry to have listened at all, and vexed at having related my ridiculous nightmare, since it produced that agony; though *why*, was beyond my comprehension. I descended cautiously to the lower regions, and landed in the back-kitchen, where a gleam of fire, raked compactly together, enabled me to rekindle my candle. Nothing was stirring except a brindled, grey cat, which crept from the ashes, and saluted me with a querulous mew.

Two benches, shaped in sections of a circle, nearly enclosed the hearth; on one of these I stretched myself, and Grimalkin mounted the other. We were both of us nodding, ere anyone invaded our retreat, and then it was Joseph, shuffling down a wooden ladder that vanished in the roof, through a trap: the ascent to his garret, I suppose. He cast a sinister look at the little flame which I had enticed to play between the ribs, swept the cat from its elevation, and bestowing himself in the vacancy, commenced the operation of stuffing a three-inch pipe with tobacco. My presence in his sanctum was evidently esteemed a piece of impudence too shameful for remark: he silently applied the tube to his lips, folded his arms, and puffed away. I let him enjoy the luxury unannoyed; and after sucking out the last wreath, and heaving a profound sigh, he got up, and departed as solemnly as he came.

A more elastic footstep entered next; and now I opened my mouth for a 'good-morning', but closed it again, the salutation unachieved; for Hareton Earnshaw was performing his orisons *sotto voce*, in a series of curses directed against every object he touched, while he rummaged a corner for a spade or shovel to dig through the drifts. He glanced over the back of the bench, dilating his nostrils, and thought as little of exchanging civilities with me as with my companion the cat. I guessed, by his preparations, that egress was allowed, and, leaving my hard couch, made a movement to follow him. He noticed this, and thrust at an inner door with the end of his spade, intimating by an inarticulate sound that there was the place where I must go, if I changed my locality.

It opened into the house, where the females were already astir. Zillah urging flakes of flame up the chimney with a colossal bellows; and Mrs Heathcliff, kneeling on the hearth, reading a book by the aid of the blaze. She held her hand interposed between the furnace-heat and her eyes, and seemed absorbed in her occupation; desisting from it only to chide the servant for covering her with sparks, or to push away a dog, now and then, that snoozled its nose over-forwardly into her face. I was surprised to see Heathcliff there also. He stood by the fire, his back towards me, just finishing a stormy scene to poor Zillah; who ever and anon interrupted her labour to pluck up the corner of her apron, and heave an indignant groan.

'And you, you worthless —,' he broke out as I entered, turning to his daughter-in-law, and employing an epithet as harmless as duck, or sheep, but generally represented by a dash. 'There you are, at your idle tricks again? The rest of them do earn their bread – you live on my charity! Put your trash away, and find something to do. You shall pay me for the plague of having you eternally in my sight – do you hear, damnable jade?'

'I'll put my trash away, because you can make me, if I refuse,' answered the young lady, closing her book, and throwing it on a chair. 'But I'll not do anything, though you should swear your tongue out, except what I please!'

Heathcliff lifted his hand, and the speaker sprang to a safer distance, obviously acquainted with its weight. Having no desire to be entertained by a cat-and-dog combat, I stepped forward briskly, as if eager to partake the warmth of the hearth, and innocent of any knowledge of the interrupted dispute. Each had enough decorum to suspend further hostilities: Heathcliff placed his fists, out of temptation, in his pockets; Mrs Heathcliff curled her lip, and walked to a seat far off, where she kept her word by playing the part of a statue during the remainder of my stay. That was not long. I declined joining their breakfast, and, at the first gleam of dawn, took an opportunity of escaping into the free air, now clear and still, and cold as impalpable ice.

My landlord hallooed for me to stop, ere I reached the bottom of the garden, and offered to accompany me across the moor. It was well he did, for the whole hill-back was one billowy, white ocean; the swells and falls not indicating corresponding rises and depressions in the ground: many pits, at least, were filled to a level; and entire ranges of mounds, the refuse of the quarries, blotted out from the chart which my yesterday's walk left pictured in my mind. I had remarked on one side of the road, at intervals of six or seven yards, a line of upright stones, continued through the whole length of the barren: these were erected, and daubed with lime on purpose to serve as guides in the dark; and also when a fall, like the present, confounded the deep swamps on either hand with the firmer path: but, excepting a dirty dot pointing up here and there, all traces of their existence had vanished: and my companion found it necessary to warn me frequently to steer to the right or left, when I imagined I was following, correctly, the windings of the road.

We exchanged little conversation, and he halted at the entrance of Thrushcross park, saying I could make no error there. Our adieux were limited to a hasty bow, and then I pushed forward, trusting to my own resources; for the porter's lodge is untenanted as yet. The distance from the gate to the Grange is two miles: I believe I managed to make it four; what with losing myself among the trees, and sinking up to the neck in snow: a predicament which only those who have experienced it can appreciate. At any rate, whatever were my wanderings, the clock chimed twelve as I entered the house; and that gave exactly an hour for every mile of the usual way from Wuthering Heights.

My human fixture and her satellites rushed to welcome me; exclaiming, tumultuously, they had completely given me up: everybody conjectured that I perished last night; and they were wondering how they must set about the search for my remains. I bid them be quiet, now that they saw me returned, and, benumbed to my very heart, I dragged upstairs; whence, after putting on dry clothes, and pacing to and fro thirty or forty minutes, to restore the animal heat, I am adjourned to my study, feeble as a kitten: almost too much so to enjoy the cheerful fire and smoking coffee which the servant has prepared for my refreshment.

## *Chapter 4*

What vain weathercocks we are! I, who had determined to hold myself independent of all social intercourse, and thanked my stars that, at length, I had lighted on a spot where it was next to impracticable – I, weak wretch, after maintaining till dusk a struggle with low spirits and solitude, was finally compelled to strike my colours: and, under pretence of gaining information concerning the necessities of my establishment, I desired Mrs Dean, when she brought in supper, to sit down while I ate it; hoping sincerely she would prove a regular gossip, and either rouse me to animation or lull me to sleep by her talk.

'You have lived here a considerable time,' I commenced; 'did you not say sixteen years?'

'Eighteen, sir: I came, when the mistress was married, to wait on her; after she died, the master retained me for his housekeeper.'

'Indeed.'

There ensued a pause. She was not a gossip, I feared; unless about her own affairs, and those could hardly interest me. However, having studied for an interval, with a fist on either knee, and a cloud of meditation over her ruddy countenance, she ejaculated – 'Ah, times are greatly changed since then!'

'Yes,' I remarked, 'you've seen a good many alterations, I suppose?'

'I have: and troubles too,' she said.

'Oh, I'll turn the talk on my landlord's family!' I thought to myself. 'A good subject to start – and that pretty girl-widow, I should like to know her history: whether she be a native of the country, or, as is more probable, an exotic that the surly *indigenae* will not recognise for kin.' With this intention I asked Mrs Dean why Heathcliff let Thrushcross Grange, and preferred living in a situation and residence so much inferior. 'Is he not rich enough to keep the estate in good order?' I enquired.

'Rich, sir!' she returned. 'He has nobody knows what money, and every year it increases. Yes, yes, he's rich enough to live in a finer house than this: but he's very near – close-handed; and, if he had meant to flit to Thrushcross Grange, as soon as he heard of a good tenant he could not have borne to miss the chance of getting a few hundreds more. It is strange people should be so greedy, when they are alone in the world!'

'He had a son, it seems?'

'Yes, he had one – he is dead.'

'And that young lady, Mrs Heathcliff, is his widow?'

'Yes.'

'Where did she come from originally?'

'Why, sir, she is my late master's daughter: Catherine Linton was her maiden name. I nursed her, poor thing! I did wish Mr Heathcliff would remove here, and then we might have been together again.'

'What! Catherine Linton?' I exclaimed, astonished. But a minute's reflection convinced me it was not my ghostly Catherine. 'Then,' I continued, 'my predecessor's name was Linton?'

'It was.'

'And who is that Earnshaw, Hareton Earnshaw, who lives with Mr Heathcliff? Are they relations?'

'No; he is the late Mrs Linton's nephew.

'The young lady's cousin, then?'

'Yes; and her husband was her cousin also: one on the mother's, the other on the father's side: Heathcliff married Mr Linton's sister.'

'I see the house at Wuthering Heights has "Earnshaw" carved over the front door. Are they an old family?'

'Very old, sir; and Hareton is the last of them, as our Miss Cathy is of us – I mean, of the Lintons. Have you been to Wuthering Heights? I beg pardon for asking; but I should like to hear how she is.'

'Mrs Heathcliff? she looked very well, and very handsome; yet, I think, not very happy.'

'Oh dear, I don't wonder! And how did you like the master?'

'A rough fellow, rather, Mrs Dean. Is not that his character?'

'Rough as a saw-edge, and hard as whinstone! The less you meddle with him the better.'

'He must have had some ups and downs in life to make him such a churl. Do you know anything of his history?'

'It's a cuckoo's, sir – I know all about it: except where he was born, and who were his parents, and how he got his money, at first. And Hareton has been cast out like an unfledged dunnock! The unfortunate lad is the only one in all this parish that does not guess how he has been cheated.'

'Well, Mrs Dean, it will be a charitable deed to tell me something of my neighbours: I feel I shall not rest, if I go to bed; so be good enough to sit and chat an hour.'

'Oh, certainly, sir! I'll just fetch a little sewing, and then I'll sit as long as you please. But you've caught cold: I saw you shivering, and you must have some gruel to drive it out.'

The worthy woman bustled off, and I crouched nearer the fire; my head felt hot, and the rest of me chill: moreover I was excited, almost to a pitch of foolishness, through my nerves and brain. This caused me to feel, not uncomfortable, but rather fearful (as I am still) of serious effects from the incidents of today and yesterday. She returned presently, bringing a smoking basin and a basket of work; and, having placed the former on the hob, drew in her seat, evidently pleased to find me so companionable.

Before I came to live here, she commenced – waiting no further invitation to her story – I was almost always at Wuthering Heights; because my mother had nursed Mr Hindley Earnshaw, that was Hareton's father, and I got used to playing with the children: I ran errands too, and helped to make hay, and hung about the farm ready for anything that anybody would set me to. One fine summer morning – it was the beginning of harvest, I remember – Mr Earnshaw, the old master, came downstairs, dressed for a journey; and after he had told Joseph what was to be done during the day, he turned to Hindley, and Cathy, and me – for I sat eating my porridge with them – and he said, speaking to his son, 'Now, my bonny man, I'm going to Liverpool today, what shall I bring you? You may choose what you like: only let it be little, for I shall walk there and back: sixty miles each way, that is a long spell!' Hindley named a fiddle, and then he asked Miss Cathy; she was hardly six years old, but she could ride any horse in the stable, and she chose a whip. He did not forget me; for he had a kind heart, though he was rather severe sometimes. He promised to bring me a pocketful of apples and pears, and then he kissed his children, goodbye, and set off.

It seemed a long while to us all – the three days of his absence – and often did little Cathy ask when he would be home. Mrs Earnshaw expected him by supper-time, on the third evening, and she put the meal off hour after hour; there were no signs of his coming, however, and at last the children got tired of running down to the gate to look. Then it grew dark; she would have had them to bed, but they begged sadly to be allowed to stay up; and, just about eleven o'clock, the door-latch was raised quietly, and in stepped the master. He threw himself into a chair, laughing and groaning, and bid them all stand off, for he was nearly killed – he would not have such another walk for the three kingdoms.

'And at the end of it, to be flighted to death!' he said, opening his greatcoat, which he held bundled up in his arms. 'See here, wife! I was never so beaten with anything in my life: but you must e'en take it as a gift of God; though it's as dark almost as if it came from the devil.'

We crowded round, and over Miss Cathy's head I had a peep at a dirty, ragged, black-haired child; big enough both to walk and talk: indeed, its face looked older than Catherine's; yet, when it was set on its feet, it only stared round, and repeated over and over again some gibberish, that nobody could understand. I was frightened, and Mrs Earnshaw was ready to fling it out of doors: she did fly up, asking how he could fashion to bring that gypsy brat into the house, when they had their own bairns to feed and fend for? What he meant to do with it, and whether he were mad? The master tried to explain the matter; but he was really half dead with fatigue, and all that I could make out, amongst her scolding, was a tale of his seeing it starving, and houseless, and as good as dumb, in the streets of Liverpool; where he picked it up and enquired for its owner. Not a soul knew to whom it belonged, he said; and his money and time being both limited, he thought it better to take it home with him at once, than run into vain expenses there: because he was determined he would not leave it as he found it. Well, the conclusion was that my mistress grumbled herself calm; and Mr Earnshaw told me to wash it, and give it clean things, and let it sleep with the children.

Hindley and Cathy contented themselves with looking and listening till peace was restored: then, both began searching their father's pockets for the presents he had promised them. The former was a boy of fourteen, but when he drew out what had been a fiddle, crushed to morsels in the greatcoat, he blubbered aloud; and Cathy, when she learnt the master had lost her whip in attending on the stranger, showed her humour by grinning and spitting at the stupid little thing; earning for her pains a sound blow from her father to teach her cleaner manners. They entirely refused to have it in bed with them, or even in their room; and I had no more sense, so I put it on the landing of the stairs, hoping it might be gone on the morrow. By chance, or else attracted by hearing his voice, it crept to Mr Earnshaw's door, and there he found it on quitting his chamber. Enquiries were made as to how it got there; I was obliged to confess, and in recompense for my cowardice and inhumanity was sent out of the house.

This was Heathcliff's first introduction to the family. On coming back a few days afterwards (for I did not consider my banishment perpetual) I found they had christened him 'Heathcliff': it was the name of a son who died in childhood, and it has served him ever since, both for Christian and surname. Miss Cathy and he were now very thick; but Hindley hated him: and to say the truth I did the same; and we plagued and went on with him shamefully: for I wasn't reasonable enough to feel my injustice, and the mistress never put in a word on his behalf when she saw him wronged.

He seemed a sullen, patient child; hardened, perhaps, to ill-treatment: he would stand Hindley's blows without winking or shedding a tear, and my pinches moved him only to draw in a breath and open his eyes, as if he had hurt himself by accident and nobody was to blame. This endurance made old Earnshaw furious, when he discovered his son persecuting the poor, fatherless child, as he called him. He took to Heathcliff strangely, believing all he said (for that matter, he said precious little, and generally the truth), and petting him up far above Cathy, who was too mischievous and wayward for a favourite.

So, from the very beginning, he bred bad feeling in the house; and at Mrs Earnshaw's death, which happened in less than two years after, the young master had learnt to regard his father as an oppressor rather than a friend, and Heathcliff as a usurper of his father's affections and his privileges, and he grew bitter with brooding over these injuries. I sympathised awhile; but when the children fell ill of the measles, and I had to tend them, and take on me the cares of a woman at once, I changed my ideas. Heathcliff was dangerously sick; and while he lay at the worst he would have me constantly by his pillow: I suppose he felt I did a good deal for him, and he hadn't the wit to guess that I was compelled to do it. However, I will say this, he was the quietest child that ever nurse watched over. The difference between him and the others forced me to be less partial.

Cathy and her brother harassed me terribly; *he* was as uncomplaining as a lamb; though hardness, not gentleness, made him give little trouble.

He got through, and the doctor affirmed it was in a great measure owing to me, and praised me for my care. I was vain of his commendations, and softened towards the being by whose means I earned them, and thus Hindley lost his last ally: still I couldn't dote on Heathcliff, and I wondered often what my master saw to admire so much in the sullen boy, who never, to my recollection, repaid his indulgence by any sign of gratitude. He was not insolent to his benefactor, he was simply insensible; though knowing perfectly the hold he had on his heart, and conscious he had only to speak and all the house would be obliged to bend to his wishes.

As an instance, I remember Mr Earnshaw once bought a couple of colts at the parish fair, and gave the lads each one. Heathcliff took the handsomest, but it soon fell lame, and when he discovered it, he said to Hindley – 'You must exchange horses with me: I don't like mine; and if you won't I shall tell your father of the three thrashings you've given me this week, and show him my arm, which is black to the shoulder.' Hindley put out his tongue, and cuffed him over the ears. 'You'd better do it at once,' he persisted, escaping to the porch (they were in the stable): 'you will have to; and if I speak of these blows, you'll get them again with interest.' 'Off, dog!' cried Hindley, threatening him with an iron weight used for weighing potatoes and hay. 'Throw it,' he replied, standing still, 'and then I'll tell how you boasted that you would turn me out of doors as soon as he died, and see whether he will not turn you out directly.' Hindley threw it, hitting him on the breast, and down he fell, but staggered up immediately, breathless and white; and, had not I prevented it, he would have gone just so to the master, and got full revenge by letting his condition plead for him, intimating who had caused it. 'Take my colt, gypsy, then!' said young Earnshaw. 'And I pray that he may break your neck: take him, and be damned, you beggarly interloper! and wheedle my father out of all he has: only afterwards show him what you are, imp of Satan – And take that, I hope he'll kick out your brains!'

Heathcliff had gone to loose the beast, and shift it to his own stall; he was passing behind it, when Hindley finished his speech by knocking him under its feet, and without stopping to examine whether his hopes were fulfilled, ran away as fast as he could. I was surprised to witness how coolly the child gathered himself up, and went on with his intention; exchanging saddles and all, and then sitting down on a bundle of hay to overcome the qualm which the violent blow occasioned, before he entered the house. I persuaded him easily to let me lay the blame of his bruises on the horse: he minded little what tale was told since he had what he wanted. He complained so seldom, indeed, of such stirs as these, that I really thought him not vindictive: I was deceived completely, as you will hear.

## *Chapter 5*

In the course of time, Mr Earnshaw began to fail. He had been active and healthy, yet his strength left him suddenly; and when he was confined to the chimney-corner he grew grievously irritable. A nothing vexed him; and suspected slights of his authority nearly threw him into fits. This was especially to be remarked if anyone attempted to impose upon, or domineer over, his favourite: he was painfully jealous lest a word should be spoken amiss to him; seeming to have got into his head the notion that, because he liked Heathcliff, all hated, and longed to do him an ill-turn. It was a disadvantage to the lad; for the kinder among us did not wish to fret the master, so we humoured his partiality; and that humouring was rich nourishment to the child's pride and black tempers. Still it became in a manner necessary; twice, or thrice, Hindley's manifestations of scorn, while his father was near, roused the old man to a fury: he seized his stick to strike him, and shook with rage that he could not do it.

At last, our curate, (we had a curate then who made the living answer by teaching the little Lintons and Earnshaws, and farming his bit of land himself), he advised that the young man should be sent to college; and Mr Earnshaw agreed, though with a heavy spirit, for he said – 'Hindley was naught, and would never thrive as where he wandered.'

I hoped heartily we should have peace now. It hurt me to think the master should be made uncomfortable by his own good deed. I fancied the discontent of age and disease arose from his family disagreements; as he would have it that it did: really, you know, sir, it was in his sinking frame. We might have got on tolerably, notwithstanding, but for two people, Miss Cathy and Joseph, the servant: you saw him, I dare say, up yonder. He was, and is yet, most likely, the wearisomest, self-righteous pharisee that ever ransacked a Bible to rake the promises to himself and fling the curses on his neighbours. By his knack of sermonising and pious discoursing, he contrived to make a great impression on Mr Earnshaw; and the more feeble the master became, the more influence he gained. He was relentless in worrying him about his soul's concerns, and about ruling his children rigidly. He encouraged him to regard Hindley as a reprobate; and, night after night, he regularly grumbled out a long string of tales against Heathcliff and Catherine: always minding to flatter Earnshaw's weakness by heaping the heaviest blame on the last.

Certainly, she had ways with her such as I never saw a child take up before; and she put all of us past our patience fifty times and oftener in a day: from the hour she came downstairs till the hour she went to bed, we had not a minute's security that she wouldn't be in mischief. Her spirits were always at high-water-mark, her tongue always going – singing, laughing, and plaguing everybody who would not do the same. A wild, wicked slip she was – but she had the bonniest eye, and sweetest smile, and lightest foot in the parish: and, after all, I believe she meant no harm; for when once she made you cry in good earnest, it seldom happened that she would not keep you company, and oblige you to be quiet that you might comfort her. She was much too fond of Heathcliff. The greatest punishment we could invent for her was to keep her separate from him; yet she got chided more than any of us on his account. In play, she liked exceedingly to act the little mistress; using her hands freely, and commanding her companions: she did so to me, but I would not bear slapping and ordering: and so I let her know.

Now, Mr Earnshaw did not understand jokes from his children: he had always been strict and grave with them; and Catherine, on her part, had no idea why her father should be crosser and less patient in his ailing condition, than he was in his prime. His peevish reproofs wakened in her a naughty delight to provoke him: she was never so happy as when we were all scolding her at once, and she defying us with her bold, saucy look, and her ready words; turning Joseph's religious curses into ridicule, baiting me, and doing just what her father hated most, showing how her pretended insolence, which he thought real, had more power over Heathcliff than his kindness: how the boy would do *her* bidding in anything, and *his* only when it suited his own inclination. After behaving as badly as possible all day, she sometimes came fondling to make it up at night. 'Nay, Cathy,' the old man would say, 'I cannot love thee; thou'rt worse than thy brother. Go, say thy prayers, child, and ask God's pardon. I doubt thy mother and I must rue that we ever reared thee!' That made her cry, at first; and then, being repulsed continually hardened her, and she laughed if I told her to say she was sorry for her faults, and beg to be forgiven.

But the hour came, at last, that ended Mr Earnshaw's troubles on earth. He died quietly in his chair one October evening, seated by the fireside. A high wind blustered round the house, and roared in the chimney: it sounded wild and stormy, yet it was not cold, and we were all together – I, a little removed from the hearth, busy at my knitting, and Joseph reading his Bible near the table (for the servants generally sat in the house then, after their work was done). Miss Cathy had been sick, and that made her still; she leant against her father's knee, and Heathcliff was lying on the floor with his head in her lap. I remember the master, before he fell into a doze, stroking her bonny hair – it pleased him rarely to see her gentle – and saying – 'Why canst thou not always be a good lass, Cathy?' And she turned her face up to his, and laughed, and answered, 'Why cannot you always be a good man, father?' But as soon as she saw him vexed again, she kissed his hand, and said she would sing him to sleep. She began singing very low, till his fingers dropped from hers, and his head sank on his breast. Then I told her to hush, and not stir, for fear she should wake him. We all kept as mute as mice a full half-hour, and should have done longer, only Joseph, having finished his chapter, got up and said that he must rouse the master for prayers and bed. He stepped forward, and called him by name, and touched his shoulder; but he would not move, so he took the candle and looked at him. I thought there was something wrong as he set down the light, and seizing the children each by an arm, whispered them to 'frame upstairs, and make little din – they might pray alone that evening – he had summut to do'.

'I shall bid father good-night first,' said Catherine, putting her arms round his neck before we could hinder her. The poor thing discovered her loss directly – she screamed out – 'Oh, he's dead, Heathcliff! he's dead!' And they both set up a heartbreaking cry.

I joined my wail to theirs, loud and bitter; but Joseph asked what we could be thinking of to roar in that way over a saint in heaven. He told me to put on my cloak and run to Gimmerton for the doctor and the parson. I could not guess the use that either would be of, then. However, I went, through wind and rain, and brought one, the doctor, back with me; the other said he would come in the morning. Leaving Joseph to explain matters, I ran to the children's room: their door was ajar, I saw they had never laid down, though it was past midnight; but they were calmer, and did not need me to console them. The little souls were comforting each other with better thoughts than I could have hit on: no parson in the world ever pictured heaven so beautifully as they did, in their innocent talk; and, while I sobbed, and listened, I could not help wishing we were all there safe together.

## *Chapter 6*

Mr Hindley came home to the funeral; and – a thing that amazed us, and set the neighbours gossiping right and left – he brought a wife with him. What she was, and where she was born, he never informed us: probably, she had neither money nor name to recommend her, or he would scarcely have kept the union from his father.

She was not one that would have disturbed the house much on her own account. Every object she saw, the moment she crossed the threshold, appeared to delight her; and every circumstance that took place about her: except the preparing for the burial, and the presence of the mourners. I thought she was half silly, from her behaviour while that went on: she ran into her chamber, and made me come with her, though I should have been dressing the children; and there she sat shivering and clasping her hands, and asking repeatedly – 'Are they gone yet?' Then she began describing with hysterical emotion the effect it produced on her to see black; and started, and trembled, and, at last, fell a-weeping – and when I asked what was the matter? answered, she didn't know; but she felt so afraid of dying! I imagined her as little likely to die as myself. She was rather thin, but young, and fresh complexioned, and her eyes sparkled as bright as diamonds. I did remark, to be sure, that mounting the stairs made her breathe very quick; that the least sudden noise set her all in a quiver, and that she coughed troublesomely sometimes: but I knew nothing of what these symptoms portended, and had no impulse to sympathise with her. We don't in general take to foreigners, here, Mr Lockwood, unless they take to us first.

Young Earnshaw was altered considerably in the three years of his absence. He had grown sparer, and lost his colour, and spoke and dressed quite differently; and, on the very day of his return, he told Joseph and me we must thenceforth quarter ourselves in the back-kitchen, and leave the house for him. Indeed, he would have carpeted and papered a small spare room for a parlour; but his wife expressed such pleasure at the white floor and huge glowing fireplace, at the pewter dishes and delf-case, and dog-kennel, and the wide space there was to move about in where they usually sat, that he thought it unnecessary to her comfort, and so dropped the intention.

She expressed pleasure, too, at finding a sister among her new acquaintance; and she prattled to Catherine, and kissed her, and ran about with her, and gave her quantities of presents, at the beginning. Her affection tired very soon, however, and when she grew peevish, Hindley became tyrannical. A few words from her, evincing a dislike to Heathcliff, were enough to rouse in him all his old hatred of the boy. He drove him from their company to the servants, deprived him of the instructions of the curate, and insisted that he should labour out of doors instead; compelling him to do so as hard as any other lad on the farm.

He bore his degradation pretty well at first, because Cathy taught him what she learnt, and worked or played with him in the fields. They both promised fair to grow up as rude as savages; the young master being entirely negligent how they behaved, and what they did, so they kept clear of him. He would not even have seen after their going to church on Sundays, only Joseph and the curate reprimanded his carelessness when they absented themselves; and that reminded him to order Heathcliff a flogging, and Catherine a fast from dinner or supper. But it was one of their chief amusements to run away to the moors in the morning and remain there all day, and the after punishment grew a mere thing to laugh at. The curate might set as many chapters as he pleased for Catherine to get by heart, and Joseph might thrash Heathcliff till his arm ached; they forgot everything the minute they were together again: at least the minute they had contrived some naughty plan of revenge; and many a time I've cried to myself to watch them growing more reckless daily, and I not daring to speak a syllable, for fear of losing the small power I still retained over the unfriended creatures. One Sunday evening, it chanced that they were banished from the sitting-room, for making a noise, or a light offence of the kind; and when I went to call them to supper, I could discover them nowhere. We searched the house, above and below, and the yard and stables; they were invisible: and, at last, Hindley in a passion told us to bolt the doors, and swore nobody should let them in that night. The household went to bed; and I, too anxious to lie down, opened my lattice and put my head out to hearken, though it rained: determined to admit them in spite of the prohibition, should they return. In a while, I distinguished steps coming up the road, and the light of a lantern glimmered through the gate. I threw a shawl over my head and ran to prevent them from waking Mr Earnshaw by knocking. There was Heathcliff, by himself: it gave me a start to see him alone.

'Where is Miss Catherine?' I cried hurriedly. 'No accident, I hope?' 'At Thrushcross Grange,' he answered; 'and I would have been there too, but they had not the manners to ask me to stay.' 'Well, you will catch it!' I said: 'you'll never be content till you're sent about your business. What in the world led you wandering to Thrushcross Grange?' 'Let me get off my wet clothes, and I'll tell you all about it, Nelly,' he replied. I bid him beware of rousing the master, and while he undressed and I waited to put out the candle, he continued – 'Cathy and I escaped from the wash-house to have a ramble at liberty, and getting a glimpse of the Grange lights, we thought we would just go and see whether the Lintons passed their Sunday evenings standing shivering in corners, while their father and mother sat eating and drinking, and singing and laughing, and burning their eyes out before the fire. Do you think they do? Or reading sermons, and being catechised by their manservant, and set to learn a column of Scripture names, if they don't answer properly?' 'Probably not,' I responded. 'They are good children, no doubt, and don't deserve the treatment you receive, for your bad conduct.' 'Don't you cant, Nelly,' he said: 'nonsense! We ran from the top of the Heights to the park, without stopping – Catherine completely beaten in the race, because she was barefoot. You'll have to seek for her shoes in the bog tomorrow. We crept through a broken hedge, groped our way up the path, and planted ourselves on a flower-plot under the drawing-room window. The light came from thence; they had not put up the shutters, and the curtains were only half closed. Both of us were able to look in by standing on the basement, and clinging to the ledge, and we saw – ah! it was beautiful – a splendid place carpeted with crimson, and crimson-covered chairs and tables, and a pure white ceiling bordered by gold, a shower of glass-drops hanging in silver chains from the centre, and shimmering with little soft tapers. Old Mr and Mrs Linton were not there; Edgar and his sister had it entirely to themselves. Shouldn't they have been happy? We should have thought ourselves in heaven! And now, guess what your good children were doing? Isabella – I believe she is eleven, a year younger than Cathy – lay screaming at the farther end of the room, shrieking as if witches were running red-hot needles into her. Edgar stood on the hearth weeping silently, and in the middle of the table sat a little dog, shaking its paw and yelping; which, from their mutual accusations, we understood they had nearly pulled in two between them. The idiots! That was their pleasure! to quarrel who should hold a heap of warm hair, and each begin to cry because both, after struggling to get it, refused to take it. We laughed outright at the petted things; we did despise them! When would you catch me wishing to have what Catherine wanted? Or find us by ourselves, seeking entertainment in yelling, and sobbing, and rolling on the ground, divided by the whole room? I'd not exchange, for a thousand lives, my condition here, for Edgar Linton's at Thrushcross Grange – not if I might have the privilege of flinging Joseph off the highest gable, and painting the house-front with Hindley's blood!'

'Hush, hush!' I interrupted. 'Still you have not told me, Heathcliff, how Catherine is left behind?'

'I told you we laughed,' he answered. 'The Lintons heard us, and with one accord, they shot like arrows to the door; there was silence, and then a cry, "Oh, mamma, mamma! Oh, papa! Oh, mamma, come here. Oh, papa, oh!" They really did howl out something in that way. We made frightful noises to terrify them still more, and then we dropped off the ledge, because somebody was drawing the bars, and we felt we had better flee. I had Cathy by the hand, and was urging her on, when all at once she fell down. "Run, Heathcliff, run!" she whispered. "They have let the bulldog loose, and he holds me!" The devil had seized her ankle, Nelly: I heard his abominable snorting. She did not yell out – no! She would have scorned to do it, if she had been spitted on the horns of a mad cow. I did, though: I vociferated curses enough to annihilate any fiend in Christendom; and I got a stone and thrust it between his jaws, and tried with all my might to cram it down his throat. A beast of a servant came up with a lantern, at last, shouting – "Keep fast, Skulker, keep fast!" He changed his note, however, when he saw Skulker's game. The dog was throttled off; his huge, purple tongue hanging half a foot out of his mouth, and his pendant lips streaming with bloody slaver. The man took Cathy up; she was sick, not from fear, I'm certain, but from pain. He carried her in; I followed, grumbling execrations and vengeance. "What prey, Robert?" hallooed Linton from the entrance. "Skulker has caught a little girl, sir," he replied; "and there's a lad here," he added, making a clutch at me, "who looks an out-and-outer! Very like, the robbers were for putting them through the window to open the doors to the gang after all were asleep, that they might murder us at their ease. Hold your tongue, you foul-mouthed thief, you! You shall go to the gallows for this. Mr Linton, sir, don't lay by your gun." "No, no, Robert," said the old fool. "The rascals knew that yesterday was my rent-day: they thought to have me cleverly. Come in; I'll furnish them a reception. There, John, fasten the chain. Give Skulker some water, Jenny. To beard a magistrate in his stronghold, and on the Sabbath, too! Where will their insolence stop? Oh, my dear Mary, look here! Don't be afraid, it is but a boy – yet the villain scowls so plainly in his face; would it not be a kindness to the country to hang him at once, before he shows his nature in acts as well as features?" He pulled me under the chandelier, and Mrs Linton placed her spectacles on her nose and raised her hands in horror. The cowardly children crept nearer, also, Isabella lisping – "Frightful thing! Put him in the cellar, papa. He's exactly like the son of the fortune-teller, that stole my tame pheasant. Isn't he, Edgar?"

'While they examined me, Cathy came round; she heard the last speech, and laughed. Edgar Linton, after an inquisitive stare, collected sufficient wit to recognise her. They see us at church, you know, though we seldom meet them elsewhere. "That's Miss Earnshaw!" he whispered to his mother, "and look how Skulker has bitten her – how her foot bleeds!"

' "Miss Earnshaw? Nonsense!" cried the dame; "Miss Earnshaw scouring the country with a gypsy! And yet, my dear, the child is in mourning – surely it is – and she may be lamed for life!"

' "What culpable carelessness in her brother!" exclaimed Mr Linton, turning from me to Catherine. "I've understood from Shielders" ' (that was the curate, sir) ' "that he lets her grow up in absolute heathenism. But who is this? Where did she pick up this companion? Oho! I declare he is that strange acquisition my late neighbour made, in his journey to Liverpool – a little Lascar, or an American or Spanish castaway."

' "A wicked boy, at all events," remarked the old lady, "and quite unfit for a decent house! Did you notice his language, Linton? I'm shocked that my children should have heard it."

'I recommenced cursing – don't be angry, Nelly – and so Robert was ordered to take me off. I refused to go without Cathy; he dragged me into the garden, pushed the lantern into my hand, assured me that Mr Earnshaw should be informed of my behaviour, and, bidding me march directly, secured the door again. The curtains were still looped up at one corner, and I resumed my station as spy; because, if Catherine had wished to return, I intended shattering their great glass panes to a million of fragments, unless they let her out. She sat on the sofa quietly. Mrs Linton took off the grey cloak of the dairy maid which we had borrowed for our excursion, shaking her head and expostulating with her, I suppose: she was a young lady, and they made a distinction between her treatment and mine. Then the woman-servant brought a basin of warm water, and washed her feet; and Mr Linton mixed a tumbler of negus, and Isabella emptied a plateful of cakes into her lap, and Edgar stood gaping at a distance. Afterwards, they dried and combed her beautiful hair, and gave her a pair of enormous slippers, and wheeled her to the fire; and I left her, as merry as she could be, dividing her food between the little dog and Skulker, whose nose she pinched as she ate; and kindling a spark of spirit in the vacant blue eyes of the Lintons – a dim reflection from her own enchanting face. I saw they were full of stupid admiration; she is so immeasurably superior to them – to everybody on earth, is she not, Nelly?'

'There will more come of this business than you reckon on,' I answered, covering him up and extinguishing the light. 'You are incurable, Heathcliff; and Mr Hindley will have to proceed to extremities, see if he won't.' My words came truer than I desired. The luckless adventure made Earnshaw furious. And then Mr Linton, to mend matters, paid us a visit himself on the morrow; and read the young master such a lecture on the road he guided his family, that he was stirred to look about him, in earnest. Heathcliff received no flogging, but he was told that the first word he spoke to Miss Catherine should ensure a dismissal; and Miss Earnshaw undertook to keep her sister-in-law in due restraint when she returned home; employing art, not force: with force she would have found it impossible.

## *Chapter 7*

Cathy stayed at Thrushcross Grange five weeks: till Christmas. By that time her ankle was thoroughly cured, and her manners much improved. The mistress visited her often in the interval, and commenced her plan of reform by trying to raise her self-respect with fine clothes and flattery, which she took readily; so that, instead of a wild, hatless little savage jumping into the house, and rushing to squeeze us all breathless, there lighted from a handsome black pony a very dignified person, with brown ringlets falling from the cover of a feathered beaver, and a long cloth habit, which she was obliged to hold up with both hands that she might sail in. Hindley lifted her from her horse, exclaiming delightedly, 'Why, Cathy, you are quite a beauty! I should scarcely have known you: you look like a lady now. Isabella Linton is not to be compared with her, is she, Frances?'

'Isabella has not her natural advantages,' replied his wife: 'but she must mind and not grow wild again here. Ellen, help Miss Catherine off with her things – Stay, dear, you will disarrange your curls – let me untie your hat.'

I removed the habit, and there shone forth, beneath a grand plaid silk frock, white trousers, and burnished shoes; and, while her eyes sparkled joyfully when the dogs came bounding up to welcome her, she dare hardly touch them lest they should fawn upon her splendid garments. She kissed me gently: I was all flour making the Christmas cake, and it would not have done to give me a hug; and, then, she looked round for Heathcliff. Mr and Mrs Earnshaw watched anxiously their meeting; thinking it would enable them to judge, in some measure, what grounds they had for hoping to succeed in separating the two friends.

Heathcliff was hard to discover, at first. If he were careless, and uncared for, before Catherine's absence, he had been ten times more so since. Nobody but I even did him the kindness to call him a dirty boy, and bid him wash himself, once a week; and children of his age seldom have a natural pleasure in soap and water. Therefore, not to mention his clothes, which had seen three months' service in mire and dust, and his thick uncombed hair, the surface of his face and hands was dismally beclouded. He might well skulk behind the settle, on beholding such a bright, graceful damsel enter the house, instead of a rough-headed counterpart of himself, as he expected. 'Is Heathcliff not here?' she demanded, pulling off her gloves, and displaying fingers wonderfully whitened with doing nothing and staying in doors.

'Heathcliff, you may come forward,' cried Mr Hindley, enjoying his discomfiture, and gratified to see what a forbidding young blackguard he would be compelled to present himself. 'You may come and wish Miss Catherine welcome, like the other servants.'

Cathy, catching a glimpse of her friend in his concealment, flew to embrace him; she bestowed seven or eight kisses on his cheek within the second, and then stopped, and drawing back, burst into a laugh, exclaiming, 'Why, how very black and cross you look! and how – how funny and grim! But that's because I'm used to Edgar and Isabella Linton. Well, Heathcliff, have you forgotten me?'

She had some reason to put the question, for shame and pride threw double gloom over his countenance, and kept him immoveable.

'Shake hands, Heathcliff,' said Mr Earnshaw, condescendingly; 'once in a way, that is permitted.'

'I shall not,' replied the boy, finding his tongue at last; 'I shall not stand to be laughed at. I shall not bear it!'

And he would have broken from the circle, but Miss Cathy seized him again.

'I did not mean to laugh at you,' she said; 'I could not hinder myself:

Heathcliff, shake hands, at least! What are you sulky for? It was only that you looked odd. If you wash your face, and brush your hair, it will be all right: but you are so dirty!'

She gazed concernedly at the dusky fingers she held in her own, and also at her dress; which she feared had gained no embellishment from its contact with his.

'You needn't have touched me!' he answered, following her eye and snatching away his hand. 'I shall be as dirty as I please: and I like to be dirty, and I will be dirty.'

With that he dashed head foremost out of the room, amid the merriment of the master and mistress, and to the serious disturbance of Catherine; who could not comprehend how her remarks should have produced such an exhibition of bad temper.

After playing lady's maid to the new comer, and putting my cakes in the oven, and making the house and kitchen cheerful with great fires, befitting Christmas Eve, I prepared to sit down and amuse myself by singing carols, all alone; regardless of Joseph's affirmations that he considered the merry tunes I chose as next door to songs. He had retired to private prayer in his chamber, and Mr and Mrs Earnshaw were engaging missy's attention by sundry gay trifles bought for her to present to the little Lintons, as an acknowledgment of their kindness. They had invited them to spend the morrow at Wuthering Heights, and the invitation had been accepted, on one condition: Mrs Linton begged that her darlings might be kept carefully apart from that 'naughty swearing boy'.

Under these circumstances I remained solitary. I smelt the rich scent of the heating spices: and admired the shining kitchen utensils, the polished clock, decked in holly, the silver mugs ranged on a tray ready to be filled with mulled ale for supper; and above all, the speckless purity of my particular care – the scoured and well-swept floor. I gave due inward applause to every object, and then I remembered how old Earnshaw used to come in when all was tidied, and call me a cant lass, and slip a shilling into my hand as a Christmas box; and from that I went on to think of his fondness for Heathcliff, and his dread lest he should suffer neglect after death had removed him; and that naturally led me to consider the poor lad's situation now, and from singing I changed my mind to crying. It struck me soon, however, there would be more sense in endeavouring to repair some of his wrongs than shedding tears over them: I got up and walked into the court to seek him. He was not far; I found him smoothing the glossy coat of the new pony in the stable, and feeding the other beasts, according to custom.

'Make haste, Heathcliff!' I said, 'the kitchen is so comfortable; and Joseph is upstairs: make haste, and let me dress you smart before Miss Cathy comes out, and then you can sit together, with the whole hearth to yourselves, and have a long chatter till bedtime.'

He proceeded with his task and never turned his head towards me.

'Come – are you coming?' I continued. 'There's a little cake for each of you, nearly enough; and you'll need half-an-hour's donning.'

I waited five minutes, but getting no answer left him . . . Catherine supped with her brother and sister-in-law: Joseph and I joined at an unsociable meal, seasoned with reproofs on one side and sauciness on the other. His cake and cheese remained on the table all night for the fairies. He managed to continue work till nine o'clock, and then marched dumb and dour to his chamber.

Cathy sat up late, having a world of things to order for the reception of her new friends: she came into the kitchen once to speak to her old one; but he was gone, and she only stayed to ask what was the matter with him, and then went back. In the morning he rose early; and as it was a holiday, carried his ill-humour on to the moors; not reappearing till the family were departed for church. Fasting and reflection seemed to have brought him to a better spirit.

He hung about me for a while, and having screwed up his courage, exclaimed abruptly – 'Nelly, make me decent, I'm going to be good.'

'High time, Heathcliff,' I said; 'you *have* grieved Catherine: she's sorry she ever came home, I dare say! It looks as if you envied her, because she is more thought of than you.'

The notion of *envying* Catherine was incomprehensible to him, but the notion of grieving her he understood clearly enough.

'Did she say she was grieved?' he enquired, looking very serious.

'She cried when I told her you were off again this morning.'

'Well, *I* cried last night,' he returned, 'and I had more reason to cry than she.'

'Yes; you had the reason of going to bed with a proud heart and an empty stomach,' said I. 'Proud people breed sad sorrows for themselves. But, if you be ashamed of your touchiness, you must ask pardon, mind, when she comes in. You must go up and offer to kiss her, and say – you know best what to say; only do it heartily, and not as if you thought her converted into a stranger by her grand dress. And now, though I have dinner to get ready, I'll steal time to arrange you so that Edgar Linton shall look quite a doll beside you: and that he does. You are younger, and yet, I'll be bound, you are taller and twice as broad across the shoulders: you could knock him down in a twinkling; don't you feel that you could?'

Heathcliff's face brightened a moment; then it was overcast afresh, and he sighed.

'But, Nelly, if I knocked him down twenty times, that wouldn't make him less handsome or me more so. I wish I had light hair and a fair skin, and was dressed and behaved as well, and had a chance of being as rich as he will be!'

'And cried for mama, at every turn,' I added, 'and trembled if a country lad heaved his fist against you, and sat at home all day for a shower of rain. Oh, Heathcliff, you are showing a poor spirit! Come to the glass, and I'll let you see what you should wish. Do you mark those two lines between your eyes; and those thick brows, that instead of rising arched, sink in the middle; and that couple of black fiends, so deeply buried, who never open their windows boldly, but lurk glinting under them, like devil's spies? Wish and learn to smooth away the surly wrinkles, to raise your lids frankly, and change the fiends to confident, innocent angels, suspecting and doubting nothing, and always seeing friends where they are not sure of foes. Don't get the expression of a vicious cur that appears to know the kicks it gets are its desert, and yet hates all the world, as well as the kicker, for what it suffers.'

'In other words, I must wish for Edgar Linton's great blue eyes and even forehead,' he replied. 'I do – and that won't help me to them.'

'A good heart will help you to a bonny face, my lad,' I continued, 'if you were a regular black; and a bad one will turn the bonniest into something worse than ugly. And now that we've done washing, and combing, and sulking – tell me whether you don't think yourself rather handsome? I'll tell you, I do. You're fit for a prince in disguise. Who knows but your father was Emperor of China, and your mother an Indian queen, each of them able to buy up, with one week's income, Wuthering Heights and Thrushcross Grange together? And you were kidnapped by wicked sailors and brought to England. Were I in your place, I would frame high notions of my birth; and the thoughts of what I was should give me courage and dignity to support the oppressions of a little farmer!'

So I chattered on; and Heathcliff gradually lost his frown and began to look quite pleasant, when all at once our conversation was interrupted by a rumbling sound moving up the road and entering the court. He ran to the window and I to the door, just in time to behold the two Lintons descend from the family carriage, smothered in cloaks and furs, and the Earnshaws dismount from their horses: they often rode to church in winter. Catherine took a hand of each of the children, and brought them into the house and set them before the fire, which quickly put colour into their white faces.

I urged my companion to hasten now and show his amiable humour, and he willingly obeyed; but ill-luck would have it that, as he opened the door leading from the kitchen on one side, Hindley opened it on the other. They met, and the master, irritated at seeing him clean and cheerful; or, perhaps, eager to keep his promise to Mrs Linton, shoved him back with a sudden thrust, and angrily bade Joseph 'keep the fellow out of the room – send him into the garret till dinner is over. He'll be cramming his fingers in the tarts and stealing the fruit, if left alone with them a minute.'

'Nay, sir,' I could not avoid answering, 'he'll touch nothing, not he: and I suppose he must have his share of the dainties as well as we.'

'He shall have his share of my hand, if I catch him downstairs again till dark,' cried Hindley. Begone, you vagabond! What! you are attempting the coxcomb, are you? Wait till I get hold of those elegant locks – see if I won't pull them a bit longer!'

'They are long enough already,' observed Master Linton, peeping from the doorway; 'I wonder they don't make his head ache. It's like a colt's mane over his eyes!'

He ventured this remark without any intention to insult; but Heathcliff's violent nature was not prepared to endure the appearance of impertinence from one whom he seemed to hate, even then, as a rival. He seized a tureen of hot apple sauce, the first thing that came under his gripe, and dashed it full against the speaker's face and neck; who instantly commenced a lament that brought Isabella and Catherine hurrying to the place. Mr Earnshaw snatched up the culprit directly and conveyed him to his chamber; where, doubtless, he administered a rough remedy to cool the fit of passion, for he reappeared red and breathless. I got the dishcloth, and, rather spitefully, scrubbed Edgar's nose and mouth, affirming it served him right for meddling. His sister began weeping to go home, and Cathy stood by, confounded, blushing for all.

'You should not have spoken to him!' she expostulated with Master Linton. 'He was in a bad temper, and now you've spoilt your visit; and he'll be flogged: I hate him to be flogged! I can't eat my dinner. Why did you speak to him, Edgar?'

'I didn't,' sobbed the youth, escaping from my hands, and finishing the remainder of the purification with his cambric pocket-handkerchief. 'I promised mamma that I wouldn't say one word to him, and I didn't.'

'Well, don't cry,' replied Catherine, contemptuously; 'you're not killed. Don't make more mischief; my brother is coming: be quiet! Give over, Isabella! Has anybody hurt *you*?'

'There, there, children – to your seats!' cried Hindley, bustling in. 'That brute of a lad has warmed me nicely. Next time, Master Edgar, take the law into your own fists – it will give you an appetite!'

The little party recovered its equanimity at sight of the fragrant feast. They were hungry after their ride, and easily consoled, since no real harm had befallen them. Mr Earnshaw carved bountiful platefuls, and the mistress made them merry with lively talk. I waited behind her chair, and was pained to behold Catherine, with dry eyes and an indifferent air, commence cutting up the wing of a goose before her. 'An unfeeling child,' I thought to myself; 'how lightly she dismisses her old playmate's troubles. I could not have imagined her to be so selfish.' She lifted a mouthful to her lips; then she set it down again: her cheeks flushed, and the tears gushed over them. She slipped her fork to the floor, and hastily dived under the cloth to conceal her emotion. I did not call her unfeeling long; for I perceived she was in purgatory throughout the day, and wearying to find an opportunity of getting by herself, or paying a visit to Heathcliff, who had been locked up by the master: as I discovered, on endeavouring to introduce to him a private mess of victuals.

In the evening we had a dance. Cathy begged that he might be liberated then, as Isabella Linton had no partner; her entreaties were vain, and I was appointed to supply the deficiency. We got rid of all gloom in the excitement of the exercise, and our pleasure was increased by the arrival of the Gimmerton band, mustering fifteen strong: a trumpet, a trombone, clarionets, bassoons, French horns, and a bass viol, besides singers. They go the rounds of all the respectable houses, and receive contributions every Christmas, and we esteemed it a first-rate treat to hear them. After the usual carols had been sung, we set them to songs and glees. Mrs Earnshaw loved the music, and so they gave us plenty.

Catherine loved it too; but she said it sounded sweetest at the top of the steps, and she went up in the dark: I followed. They shut the house door below, never noting our absence, it was so full of people. She made no stay at the stairs' head, but mounted farther, to the garret where Heathcliff was confined, and called him. He stubbornly declined answering for a while; she persevered, and finally persuaded him to hold communion with her through the boards. I let the poor things converse unmolested, till I supposed the songs were going to cease, and the singers to get some refreshment; then, I clambered up the ladder to warn her. Instead of finding her outside, I heard her voice within. The little monkey had crept by the skylight of one garret along the roof, into the skylight of the other, and it was with the utmost difficulty I could coax her out again. When she did come, Heathcliff came with her, and she insisted that I should take him into the kitchen, as my fellow-servant had gone to a neighbour's to be removed from the sound of our 'devil's psalmody', as it pleased him to call it. I told them I intended by no means to encourage their tricks; but as the prisoner had never broken his fast since yesterday's dinner, I would wink at his cheating Mr Hindley that once. He went down; I set him a stool by the fire, and offered him a quantity of good things; but he was sick and could eat little, and my attempts to entertain him were thrown away. He leant his two elbows on his knees, and his chin on his hands, and remained wrapped in dumb meditation.

On my enquiring the subject of his thoughts, he answered gravely – 'I'm trying to settle how I shall pay Hindley back. I don't care how long I wait, if I can only do it at last. I hope he will not die before I do!'

'For shame, Heathcliff!' said I. 'It is for God to punish wicked people; we should learn to forgive.'

'No, God won't have the satisfaction that I shall,' he returned. 'I only wish I knew the best way! Let me alone, and I'll plan it out: while I'm thinking of that I don't feel pain.'

But, Mr Lockwood, I forget these tales cannot divert you. I'm annoyed how I should dream of chattering on at such a rate: and your gruel cold, and you nodding for bed! I could have told Heathcliff's history, all that you need hear, in half a dozen words.

Thus interrupting herself, the housekeeper rose, and proceeded to lay aside her sewing; but I felt incapable of moving from the hearth, and I was very far from nodding. 'Sit still, Mrs Dean,' I cried, 'do sit still, another half-hour! You've done just right to tell the story leisurely. That is the method I like; and you must finish in the same style. I am interested in every character you have mentioned, more or less.'

'The clock is on the stroke of eleven, sir.'

'No matter – I'm not accustomed to go to bed in the long hours. One or two is early enough for a person who lies till ten.'

'You shouldn't lie till ten. There's the very prime of the morning gone long before that time. A person who has not done one half his day's work by ten o'clock, runs a chance of leaving the other half undone.'

'Nevertheless, Mrs Dean, resume your chair; because tomorrow I intend lengthening the night till afternoon. I prognosticate for myself an obstinate cold, at least.'

'I hope not, sir. Well, you must allow me to leap over some three years; during that space Mrs Earnshaw – '

'No, no, I'll allow nothing of the sort! Are you acquainted with the mood of mind in which, if you were seated alone, and the cat licking its kitten on the rug before you, you would watch the operation so intently that puss's neglect of one ear would put you seriously out of temper?'

'A terribly lazy mood, I should say.'

'On the contrary, a tiresomely active one. It is mine, at present: and, therefore, continue minutely. I perceive that people in these regions acquire over people in towns the value that a spider in a dungeon does over a spider in a cottage, to their various occupants; and yet the deepened attraction is not entirely owing to the situation of the looker-on. They *do* live more in earnest, more in themselves, and less in surface change, and frivolous external things. I could fancy a love for life here almost possible; and I was a fixed unbeliever in any love of a year's standing. One state resembles setting a hungry man down to a single dish, on which he may concentrate his entire appetite and do it justice; the other, introducing him to a table laid out by French cooks: he can perhaps extract as much enjoyment from the whole; but each part is a mere atom in his regard and remembrance.'

'Oh! here we are the same as anywhere else, when you get to know us,' observed Mrs Dean, somewhat puzzled at my speech.

'Excuse me,' I responded; 'you, my good friend, are a striking evidence against that assertion. Excepting a few provincialisms of slight consequence, you have no marks of the manners which I am habituated to consider peculiar to your class. I am sure you have thought a great deal more than the generality of servants think. You have been compelled to cultivate your reflective faculties for want of occasions for frittering your life away in silly trifles.'

Mrs Dean laughed.

'I certainly esteem myself a steady, reasonable kind of body,' she said; 'not exactly from living among the hills and seeing one set of faces, and one series of actions, from year's end to year's end; but I have undergone sharp discipline, which has taught me wisdom: and then, I have read more than you would fancy, Mr Lockwood. You could not open a book in this library that I have not looked into, and got something out of also: unless it be that range of Greek and Latin, and that of French; and those I know one from another: it is as much as you can expect of a poor man's daughter. However, if I am to follow my story in true gossip's fashion, I had better go on; and instead of leaping three years, I will be content to pass to the next summer – the summer of 1778, that is nearly twenty-three years ago.'

## *Chapter 8*

On the morning of a fine June day, my first bonny little nursling, and the last of the ancient Earnshaw stock, was born. We were busy with the hay in a far away field, when the girl that usually brought our breakfasts came running an hour too soon, across the meadow and up the lane, calling me as she ran.

'Oh, such a grand bairn!' she panted out. 'The finest lad that ever breathed! But the doctor says missis must go: he says she's been in a consumption these many months. I heard him tell Mr Hindley: and now she has nothing to keep her, and she'll be dead before winter. You must come home directly. You're to nurse it, Nelly: to feed it with sugar and milk, and take care of it day and night. I wish I were you, because it will be all yours when there is no missis!'

'But is she very ill?' I asked, flinging down my rake, and tying my bonnet.

'I guess she is; yet she looks bravely,' replied the girl, 'and she talks as if she thought of living to see it grow a man. She's out of her head for joy, it's such a beauty! If I were her, I'm certain I should not die: I should get better at the bare sight of it, in spite of Kenneth. I was fairly mad at him. Dame Archer brought the cherub down to master, in the house, and his face just began to light up, then the old croaker steps forward, and says he – "Earnshaw, it's a blessing your wife has been spared to leave you this son. When she came, I felt convinced we shouldn't keep her long; and now, I must tell you, the winter will probably finish her. Don't take on, and fret about it too much: it can't be helped. And besides, you should have known better than to choose such a rush of a lass!" '

'And what did the master answer?' I enquired.

'I think he swore: but I didn't mind him, I was straining to see the bairn,' and she began again to describe it rapturously. I, as zealous as herself, hurried eagerly home to admire, on my part; though I was very sad for Hindley's sake. He had room in his heart only for two idols – his wife and himself: he doted on both, and adored one, and I couldn't conceive how he would bear the loss.

When we got to Wuthering Heights, there he stood at the front door; and, as I passed in, I asked, 'how was the baby?'

'Nearly ready to run about, Nell!' he replied, putting on a cheerful smile.

'And the mistress?' I ventured to enquire; 'the doctor says she's – '

'Damn the doctor!' he interrupted, reddening. 'Frances is quite right: she'll be perfectly well by this time next week. Are you going upstairs? will you tell her that I'll come, if she'll promise not to talk. I left her because she would not hold her tongue; and she must – tell her Mr Kenneth says she must be quiet.'

I delivered this message to Mrs Earnshaw: she seemed in flighty spirits, and replied merrily – 'I hardly spoke a word, Ellen, and there he has gone out twice, crying. Well, say I promise I won't speak: but that does not bind me not to laugh at him!'

Poor soul! Till within a week of her death that gay heart never failed her; and her husband persisted doggedly, nay, furiously, in affirming her health improved every day.

When Kenneth warned him that his medicines were useless at that stage of the malady, and he needn't put him to further expense by attending her, he retorted – 'I know you need not – she 's well – she does not want any more attendance from you! She never was in a consumption. It was a fever; and it is gone: her pulse is as slow as mine now, and her cheek as cool.'

He told his wife the same story, and she seemed to believe him: but one night, while leaning on his shoulder in the act of saying she thought she should be able to get up tomorrow, a fit of coughing took her – a very slight one – he raised her in his arms; she put her two hands about his neck, her face changed, and she was dead.

As the girl had anticipated, the child Hareton fell wholly into my hands. Mr Earnshaw, provided he saw him healthy and never heard him cry, was contented, as far as regarded him. For himself, he grew desperate: his sorrow was of that kind that will not lament. He neither wept nor prayed; he cursed and defied: execrated God and man, and gave himself up to reckless dissipation. The servants could not bear his tyrannical and evil conduct long: Joseph and I were the only two that would stay. I had not the heart to leave my charge; and besides, you know, I had been his foster-sister, and excused his behaviour more readily than a stranger would. Joseph remained to hector over tenants and labourers; and because it was his vocation to be where he had plenty of wickedness to reprove.

The master's bad ways and bad companions formed a pretty example for Catherine and Heathcliff. His treatment of the latter was enough to make a fiend of a saint. And, truly, it appeared as if the lad *were* possessed of something diabolical at that period. He delighted to witness Hindley degrading himself past redemption; and became daily more notable for savage sullenness and ferocity. I could not half tell what an infernal house we had. The curate dropped calling, and nobody decent came near us, at last; unless Edgar Linton's visits to Miss Cathy might be an exception. At fifteen she was the queen of the countryside; she had no peer; and she did turn out a haughty, headstrong creature! I own I did not like her, after her infancy was past; and I vexed her frequently by trying to bring down her arrogance: she never took an aversion to me, though. She had a wondrous constancy to old attachments: even Heathcliff kept his hold on her affections unalterably; and young Linton, with all his superiority, found it difficult to make an equally deep impression. He was my late master: that is his portrait over the fireplace. It used to hang on one side, and his wife's on the other; but hers has been removed, or else you might see something of what she was. Can you make that out?

Mrs Dean raised the candle, and I discerned a soft-featured face, exceedingly resembling the young lady at the Heights, but more pensive and amiable in expression. It formed a sweet picture. The long light hair curled slightly on the temples; the eyes were large and serious; the figure almost too graceful. I did not marvel how Catherine Earnshaw could forget her first friend for such an individual. I marvelled much how he, with a mind to correspond with his person, could fancy my idea of Catherine Earnshaw.

'A very agreeable portrait, I observed to the housekeeper. 'Is it like?'

'Yes,' she answered; 'but he looked better when he was animated; that is his everyday countenance: he wanted spirit in general.'

Catherine had kept up her acquaintance with the Lintons since her five weeks' residence among them; and as she had no temptation to show her rough side in their company, and had the sense to be ashamed of being rude where she experienced such invariable courtesy, she imposed unwittingly on the old lady and gentleman, by her ingenious cordiality; gained the admiration of Isabella, and the heart and soul of her brother: acquisitions that flattered her from the first, for she was full of ambition, and led her to adopt a double character without exactly intending to deceive anyone. In the place where she had heard Heathcliff termed a 'vulgar young ruffian,' and 'worse than a brute,' she took care not to act like him; but at home she had small inclination to practise politeness that would only be laughed at, and restrain an unruly nature when it would bring her neither credit nor praise.

Mr Edgar seldom mustered courage to visit Wuthering Heights openly. He had a terror of Earnshaw's reputation, and shrunk from encountering him; and yet he was always received with our best attempts at civility: the master himself avoided offending him, knowing why he came; and if he could not be gracious, kept out of the way. I rather think his appearance there was distasteful to Catherine: she was not artful, never played the coquette, and had evidently an objection to her two friends meeting at all; for when Heathcliff expressed contempt of Linton in his presence, she could not half coincide, as she did in his absence; and when Linton evinced disgust and antipathy to Heathcliff, she dare not treat his sentiments with indifference, as if depreciation of her playmate were of scarcely any consequence to her. I've had many a laugh at her perplexities and untold troubles, which she vainly strove to hide from my mockery. That sounds ill-natured: but she was so proud, it became really impossible to pity her distresses, till she should be chastened into more humility. She did bring herself, finally, to confess, and confide in me: there was not a soul else that she might fashion into an adviser.

Mr Hindley had gone from home, one afternoon, and Heathcliff presumed to give himself a holiday on the strength of it. He had reached the age of sixteen then, I think, and without having bad features, or being deficient in intellect, he contrived to convey an impression of inward and outward repulsiveness that his present aspect retains no traces of. In the first place, he had by that time lost the benefit of his early education: continual hard work, begun soon and concluded late, had extinguished any curiosity he once possessed in pursuit of knowledge, and any love for books or learning. His childhood's sense of superiority, instilled into him by the favours of old Mr Earnshaw, was faded away. He struggled long to keep up an equality with Catherine in her studies, and yielded with poignant though silent regret: but he yielded completely; and there was no prevailing on him to take a step in the way of moving upward, when he found he must, necessarily, sink beneath his former level. Then personal appearance sympathised with mental deterioration: he acquired a slouching gait, and ignoble look; his naturally reserved disposition was exaggerated into an almost idiotic excess of unsociable moroseness; and he took a grim pleasure, apparently, in exciting the aversion rather than the esteem of his few acquaintance.

Catherine and he were constant companions still at his seasons of respite from labour; but he had ceased to express his fondness for her in words, and recoiled with angry suspicion from her girlish caresses, as if conscious there could be no gratification in lavishing such marks of affection on him. On the before-named occasion he came into the house to announce his intention of doing nothing, while I was assisting Miss Cathy to arrange her dress: she had not reckoned on his taking it into his head to be idle: and imagining she would have the whole place to herself, she managed, by some means, to inform Mr Edgar of her brother's absence, and was then preparing to receive him.

'Cathy, are you busy this afternoon?' asked Heathcliff. 'Are you going anywhere?'

'No, it is raining,' she answered.

'Why have you that silk frock on, then?' he said. 'Nobody coming here, I hope?'

'Not that I know of,' stammered miss: 'but you should be in the field now, Heathcliff. It is an hour past dinner time: I thought you were gone.'

'Hindley does not often free us from his accursed presence,' observed the boy. 'I'll not work any more today: I'll stay with you.'

'Oh, but Joseph will tell,' she suggested: 'you'd better go!'

'Joseph is loading lime on the farther side of Pennistow Crag; it will take him till dark, and he'll never know.'

So saying, he lounged to the fire, and sat down. Catherine reflected an instant, with knitted brows – she found it needful to smooth the way for an intrusion. 'Isabella and Edgar Linton talked of calling this afternoon,' she said, at the conclusion of a minute's silence. 'As it rains, I hardly expect them; but they may come, and if they do, you run the risk of being scolded for no good.'

'Order Ellen to say you are engaged, Cathy,' he persisted; 'don't turn me out for those pitiful, silly friends of yours! I'm on the point, sometimes, of complaining that they – but I'll not – '

'That they what?' cried Catherine, gazing at him with a troubled countenance. 'Oh, Nelly!' she added petulantly, jerking her head away from my hands, 'you've combed my hair quite out of curl! That's enough; let me alone. What are you on the point of complaining about, Heathcliff?'

'Nothing – only look at the almanac on that wall,' he pointed to a framed sheet hanging near the window, and continued – 'The crosses are for the evenings you have spent with the Lintons, the dots for those spent with me. Do you see? I've marked every day.'

'Yes – very foolish: as if I took notice!' replied Catherine in a peevish tone. 'And where is the sense of that?'

'To show that I *do* take notice,' said Heathcliff.

'And should I always be sitting with you?' she demanded, growing more irritated. 'What good do I get? What do you talk about? You might be dumb, or a baby, for anything you say to amuse me, or for anything you do, either!'

'You never told me before that I talked too little, or that you disliked my company, Cathy!' exclaimed Heathcliff in much agitation.

'It's no company at all, when people know nothing and say nothing,' she muttered.

Her companion rose up, but he hadn't time to express his feelings further, for a horse's feet were heard on the flags, and having knocked gently, young Linton entered, his face brilliant with delight at the unexpected summons he had received. Doubtless Catherine marked the difference between her friends, as one came in and the other went out. The contrast resembled what you see in exchanging a bleak, hilly, coal country for a beautiful fertile valley; and his voice and greeting were as opposite as his aspect. He had a sweet, low manner of speaking, and pronounced his words as you do: that's less gruff than we talk here, and softer.

'I'm not come too soon, am I?' he said, casting a look at me: I had begun to wipe the plate, and tidy some drawers at the far end in the dresser.

'No,' answered Catherine. 'What are you doing there, Nelly?'

'My work, miss,' I replied. (Mr Hindley had given me directions to make a third party in any private visits Linton chose to pay.)

She stepped behind me and whispered crossly, 'Take yourself and your dusters off; when company are in the house, servants don't commence scouring and cleaning in the room where they are!'

'It's a good opportunity, now that master is away,' I answered aloud: 'he hates me to be fidgeting over these things in his presence. I'm sure Mr Edgar will excuse me.'

'I hate you to be fidgeting in *my* presence,' exclaimed the young lady imperiously, not allowing her guest time to speak: she had failed to recover her equanimity since the little dispute with Heathcliff.

'I'm sorry for it, Miss Catherine,' was my response; and I proceeded assiduously with my occupation.

She, supposing Edgar could not see her, snatched the cloth from my hand, and pinched me, with a prolonged wrench, very spitefully on the arm. I've said I did not love her, and rather relished mortifying her vanity now and then: besides, she hurt me extremely; so I started up from my knees, and screamed out, 'Oh, miss, that's a nasty trick! You have no right to nip me, and I'm not going to bear it.'

'I didn't touch you, you lying creature!' cried she, her fingers tingling to repeat the act, and her ears red with rage. She never had power to conceal her passion, it always set her whole complexion in a blaze.

'What's that, then?' I retorted, showing a decided purple witness to refute her.

She stamped her foot, wavered a moment, and then, irresistibly impelled by the naughty spirit within her, slapped me on the cheek a stinging blow that filled both eyes with water.

'Catherine, love! Catherine!' interposed Linton, greatly shocked at the double fault of falsehood and violence which his idol had committed.

'Leave the room, Ellen!' she repeated, trembling all over.

Little Hareton, who followed me everywhere, and was sitting near me on the floor, at seeing my tears commenced crying himself, and sobbed out complaints against 'wicked aunt Cathy,' which drew her fury on to his unlucky head: she seized his shoulders, and shook him till the poor child waxed livid, and Edgar thoughtlessly laid hold of her hands to deliver him. In an instant one was wrung free, and the astonished young man felt it applied over his own ear in a way that could not be mistaken for jest. He drew back in consternation. I lifted Hareton in my arms, and walked off to the kitchen with him, leaving the door of communication open, for I was curious to watch how they would settle their disagreement. The insulted visitor moved to the spot where he had laid his hat, pale and with a quivering lip.

'That's right!' I said to myself. 'Take warning and begone! It's a kindness to let you have a glimpse of her genuine disposition.'

'Where are you going?' demanded Catherine, advancing to the door.

He swerved aside, and attempted to pass.

'You must not go!' she exclaimed energetically.

'I must and shall!' he replied in a subdued voice.

'No,' she persisted, grasping the handle; 'not yet, Edgar Linton: sit down; you shall not leave me in that temper. I should be miserable all night, and I won't be miserable for you!'

'Can I stay after you have struck me?' asked Linton.

Catherine was mute.

'You've made me afraid and ashamed of you,' he continued; 'I'll not come here again!'

Her eyes began to glisten, and her lids to twinkle.

'And you told a deliberate untruth!' he said.

'I didn't!' she cried, recovering her speech; 'I did nothing deliberately. Well, go, if you please – get away! And now I'll cry – I'll cry myself sick!'

She dropped down on her knees by a chair, and set to weeping in serious earnest. Edgar persevered in his resolution as far as the court; there he lingered. I resolved to encourage him.

'Miss is dreadfully wayward, sir,' I called out. 'As bad as any marred child: you'd better be riding home, or else she will be sick, only to grieve us.'

The soft thing looked askance through the window: he possessed the power to depart, as much as a cat possesses the power to leave a mouse half killed, or a bird half eaten. Ah, I thought, there will be no saving him – He's doomed, and flies to his fate! And so it was: he turned abruptly, hastened into the house again, shut the door behind him; and when I went in a while after to inform them that Earnshaw had come home rabid drunk, ready to pull the old place about our ears (his ordinary frame of mind in that condition), I saw the quarrel had merely effected a closer intimacy – had broken the outworks of youthful timidity, and enabled them to forsake the disguise of friendship, and confess themselves lovers.

Intelligence of Mr Hindley's arrival drove Linton speedily to his horse, and

Catherine to her chamber. I went to hide little Hareton, and to take the shot out of the master's fowling-piece, which he was fond of playing with in his insane excitement, to the hazard of the lives of any who provoked, or even attracted his notice too much; and I had hit upon the plan of removing it, that he might do less mischief if he did go the length of firing the gun.

## *Chapter 9*

He entered, vociferating oaths dreadful to hear; and caught me in the act of stowing his son away in the kitchen cupboard. Hareton was impressed with a wholesome terror of encountering either his wild-beast's fondness or his madman's rage; for in one he ran a chance of being squeezed and kissed to death, and in the other of being flung into the fire, or dashed against the wall; and the poor thing remained perfectly quiet wherever I chose to put him.

'There, I've found it out at last!' cried Hindley, pulling me back by the skin of my neck, like a dog. 'By heaven and hell, you've sworn between you to murder that child! I know how it is, now, that he is always out of my way. But, with the help of Satan, I shall make you swallow the carving-knife, Nelly! You needn't laugh; for I've just crammed Kenneth, head-downmost, in the Blackhorse marsh; and two is the same as one – and I want to kill some of you: I shall have no rest till I do!'

'But I don't like the carving-knife, Mr Hindley,' I answered; 'it has been cutting red herrings. I'd rather be shot, if you please.'

'You'd rather be damned!' he said; 'and so you shall. No law in England can hinder a man from keeping his house decent, and mine's abominable! open your mouth.'

He held the knife in his hand, and pushed its point between my teeth: but, for my part, I was never much afraid of his vagaries. I spat out, and affirmed it tasted detestably – I would not take it on any account.

'Oh!' said he, releasing me, 'I see that hideous little villain is not Hareton: I beg your pardon, Nell. If it be, he deserves flaying alive for not running to welcome me, and for screaming as if I were a goblin. Unnatural cub, come hither! I'll teach thee to impose on a good-hearted, deluded father. Now, don't you think the lad would be handsomer cropped? It makes a dog fiercer, and I love something fierce – get me a scissors – something fierce and trim! Besides, it's infernal affectation – devilish conceit it is, to cherish our ears – we're asses enough without them. Hush, child, hush! Well then, it is my darling! wisht, dry thy eyes – there's a joy; kiss me. What! it won't? Kiss me, Hareton! Damn thee, kiss me! By God, as if I would rear such a monster! As sure as I'm living, I'll break the brat's neck.'

Poor Hareton was squalling and kicking in his father's arms with all his might, and redoubled his yells when he carried him upstairs and lifted him over the bannister. I cried out that he would frighten the child into fits, and ran to rescue him. As I reached them, Hindley leant forward on the rails to listen to a noise below; almost forgetting what he had in his hands. 'Who is that?' he asked, hearing someone approaching the stair's foot. I leant forward also, for the purpose of signing to Heathcliff, whose step I recognised, not to come further; and, at the instant when my eye quitted Hareton, he gave a sudden spring, delivered himself from the careless grasp that held him, and fell.

There was scarcely time to experience a thrill of horror before we saw that the little wretch was safe. Heathcliff arrived underneath just at the critical moment; by a natural impulse, he arrested his descent, and setting him on his feet, looked up to discover the author of the accident. A miser who has parted with a lucky lottery ticket for five shillings, and finds next day he has lost in the bargain five thousand pounds, could not show a blanker countenance than he did on beholding the figure of Mr Earnshaw above. It expressed, plainer than words could do, the intensest anguish at having made himself the instrument of thwarting his own revenge. Had it been dark, I dare say, he would have tried to remedy the mistake by smashing Hareton's skull on the steps; but, we witnessed his salvation; and I was presently below with my precious charge pressed to my heart. Hindley descended more leisurely, sobered and abashed.

'It is your fault, Ellen,' he said; 'you should have kept him out of sight: you should have taken him from me! Is he injured anywhere?'

'Injured!' I cried angrily. 'If he's not killed, he'll be an idiot! Oh! I wonder his mother does not rise from her grave to see how you use him. You're worse than a heathen – treating your own flesh and blood in that manner!'

He attempted to touch the child, who, on finding himself with me, sobbed off his terror directly. At the first finger his father laid on him, however, he shrieked again louder than before, and struggled as if he would go into convulsions.

'You shall not meddle with him!' I continued. 'He hates you – they all hate you – that's the truth! A happy family you have; and a pretty state you're come to!'

'I shall come to a prettier, yet, Nelly,' laughed the misguided man, recovering his hardness. 'At present, convey yourself and him away. And, hark you, Heathcliff! clear you too, quite from my reach and hearing . . . I wouldn't murder you tonight, unless, perhaps, I set the house on fire: but that's as my fancy goes.'

While saying this he took a pint bottle of brandy from the dresser, and poured some into a tumbler.

'Nay, don't!' I entreated. 'Mr Hindley, do take warning. Have mercy on this unfortunate boy, if you care nothing for yourself!'

'Anyone will do better for him than I shall,' he answered.

'Have mercy on your own soul!' I said, endeavouring to snatch the glass from his hand.

'Not I! On the contrary, I shall have great pleasure in sending it to perdition to punish its Maker,' exclaimed the blasphemer. 'Here's to its hearty damnation!'

He drank the spirits and impatiently bade us go; terminating his command with a sequel of horrid imprecations, too bad to repeat or remember.

'It's a pity he cannot kill himself with drink,' observed Heathcliff, muttering an echo of curses back when the door was shut. 'He's doing his very utmost; but his constitution defies him. Mr Kenneth says he would wager his mare, that he'll outlive any man on this side Gimmerton, and go to the grave a hoary sinner; unless some happy chance out of the common course befall him.'

I went into the kitchen, and sat down to lull my little lamb to sleep. Heathcliff, as I thought, walked through to the barn. It turned out afterwards that he only got as far as the other side the settle, when he flung himself on a bench by the wall, removed from the fire, and remained silent.

I was rocking Hareton on my knee, and humming a song that began –

> 'It was far in the night, and the bairnies grat,
> The mither beneath the mools heard that,'

when Miss Cathy, who had listened to the hubbub from her room, put her head in and whispered – 'Are you alone, Nelly?'

'Yes, miss,' I replied.

She entered and approached the hearth. I, supposing she was going to say something, looked up. The expression of her face seemed disturbed and anxious. Her lips were half asunder, as if she meant to speak, and she drew a breath; but it escaped in a sigh instead of a sentence. I resumed my song; not having forgotten her recent behaviour.

'Where's Heathcliff?' she said, interrupting me.

'About his work in the stable,' was my answer.

He did not contradict me; perhaps he had fallen into a dose. There followed another long pause, during which I perceived a drop or two trickle from Catherine's cheek to the flags. Is she sorry for her shameful conduct? I asked myself. That will be a novelty: but she may come to the point as she will – I shan't help her! No, she felt small trouble regarding any subject, save her own concerns.

'Oh, dear!' she cried at last. 'I'm very unhappy!'

'A pity,' observed I. 'You're hard to please: so many friends and so few cares, and can't make yourself content!'

'Nelly, will you keep a secret for me?' she pursued, kneeling down by me, and lifting her winsome eyes to my face with that sort of look which turns off bad temper, even when one has all the right in the world to indulge it.

'Is it worth keeping?' I enquired, less sulkily.

'Yes, and it worries me, and I must let it out! I want to know what I should do. Today, Edgar Linton has asked me to marry him, and I've given him an answer. Now, before I tell you whether it was a consent or denial, you tell me which it ought to have been.'

'Really, Miss Catherine, how can I know?' I replied. 'To be sure, considering the exhibition you performed in his presence this afternoon, I might say it would be wise to refuse him: since he asked you after that, he must be either hopelessly stupid or a venturesome fool.'

'If you talk so, I won't tell you any more,' she returned, peevishly, rising to her feet. 'I accepted him, Nelly. Be quick, and say whether I was wrong!'

'You accepted him! then what good is it discussing the matter? You have pledged your word, and cannot retract.'

'But, say whether I should have done so – do!' she exclaimed in an irritated tone; chafing her hands together, and frowning.

'There are many things to be considered before that question can be answered properly,' I said sententiously. 'First and foremost, do you love Mr Edgar?'

'Who can help it? Of course I do,' she answered.

Then I put her through the following catechism: for a girl of twenty-two, it was not injudicious.

'Why do you love him, Miss Cathy?'

'Nonsense, I do – that's sufficient.'

'By no means; you must say why?'

'Well, because he is handsome, and pleasant to be with.'

'Bad!' was my commentary.

'And because he is young and cheerful.'

'Bad, still.'

'And because he loves me.'

'Indifferent, coming there.'

'And he will be rich, and I shall like to be the greatest woman of the neighbourhood, and I shall be proud of having such a husband.'

'Worst of all. And now say how you love him?'

'As everybody loves – You're silly, Nelly.'

'Not at all – Answer.'

'I love the ground under his feet, and the air over his head, and everything he touches, and every word he says. I love all his looks, and all his actions, and him entirely and altogether. There now!'

'And why?'

'Nay, you are making a jest of it: it is exceedingly ill-natured! It's no jest to me!' said the young lady, scowling, and turning her face to the fire.

'I'm very far from jesting, Miss Catherine,' I replied. 'You love Mr Edgar, because he is handsome, and young, and cheerful, and rich, and loves you. The last, however, goes for nothing: you would love him without that, probably; and with it you wouldn't, unless he possessed the four former attractions.'

'No, to be sure not: I should only pity him – hate him, perhaps, if he were ugly, and a clown.'

'But there are several other handsome, rich young men in the world: handsomer, possibly, and richer than he is. What should hinder you from loving them?'

'If there be any, they are out of my way: I've seen none like Edgar.'

'You may see some; and he won't always be handsome, and young, and may not always be rich.'

'He is now; and I have only to do with the present. I wish you would speak rationally.'

'Well, that settles it: if you have only to do with the present, marry Mr Linton.'

'I don't want your permission for that – I *shall* marry him: and yet you have not told me whether I'm right.'

'Perfectly right; if people be right to marry only for the present. And now, let us hear what you are unhappy about. Your brother will be pleased . . . The old lady and gentleman will not object, I think; you will escape from a disorderly comfortless home into a wealthy, respectable one; and you love Edgar, and Edgar loves you. All seems smooth and easy: where is the obstacle?'

'*Here!* and *here!*' replied Catherine, striking one hand on her forehead, and the other on her breast 'in whichever place the soul lives. In my soul and in my heart, I'm convinced I'm wrong!'

'That's very strange! I cannot make it out.'

'It's my secret. But if you will not mock at me, I'll explain it: I can't do it distinctly; but I'll give you a feeling of how I feel.'

She seated herself by me again: her countenance grew sadder and graver, and her clasped hands trembled.

'Nelly, do you never dream queer dreams?' she said, suddenly, after some minutes' reflection.

'Yes, now and then,' I answered.

'And so do I. I've dreamt in my life dreams that have stayed with me ever after, and changed my ideas: they've gone through and through me, like wine through water, and altered the colour of my mind. And this is one: I'm going to tell it – but take care not to smile at any part of it.'

'Oh! don't, Miss Catherine!' I cried. 'We're dismal enough without conjuring up ghosts and visions to perplex us. Come, come, be merry and like yourself! Look at little Hareton! *He's* dreaming nothing dreary. How sweetly he smiles in his sleep!'

'Yes; and how sweetly his father curses in his solitude! You remember him, I dare say, when he was just such another as that chubby thing: nearly as young and innocent. However, Nelly, I shall oblige you to listen: it's not long: and I've no power to be merry tonight.'

'I won't hear it, I won't hear it!' I repeated, hastily.

I was superstitious about dreams then, and am still; and Catherine had an unusual gloom in her aspect, that made me dread something from which I might shape a prophecy, and foresee a fearful catastrophe. She was vexed, but she did not proceed. Apparently taking up another subject, she recommenced in a short time.

'If I were in heaven, Nelly, I should be extremely miserable.'

'Because you are not fit to go there,' I answered. 'All sinners would be miserable in heaven.'

'But it is not for that. I dreamt once that I was there.'

'I tell you I won't harken to your dreams, Miss Catherine! I'll go to bed,' I interrupted again.

She laughed, and held me down; for I made a motion to leave my chair.

'This is nothing,' cried she: 'I was only going to say that heaven did not seem to be my home; and I broke my heart with weeping to come back to earth; and the angels were so angry that they flung me out into the middle of the heath on the top of Wuthering Heights; where I woke sobbing for joy. That will do to explain my secret, as well as the other. I've no more business to marry Edgar Linton than I have to be in heaven; and if the wicked man in there had not brought Heathcliff so low, I shouldn't have thought of it. It would degrade me to marry Heathcliff now; so he shall never know how I love him: and that, not because he's handsome, Nelly, but because he's more myself than I am. Whatever our souls are made of, his and mine are the same; and Linton's is as different as a moonbeam from lightning, or frost from fire.'

Ere this speech ended, I became sensible of Heathcliff's presence. Having noticed a slight movement, I turned my head, and saw him rise from the bench, and steal out noiselessly. He had listened till he heard Catherine say it would degrade her to marry him, and then he staid, to hear no farther. My companion, sitting on the ground, was prevented by the back of the settle from remarking his presence or departure; but I started, and bade her hush!

'Why?' she asked, gazing nervously round.

'Joseph is here,' I answered, catching opportunely the roll of his cartwheels up the road; 'and Heathcliff will come in with him. I'm not sure whether he were not at the door this moment.'

'Oh, he couldn't overhear me at the door!' said she. 'Give me Hareton, while you get the supper, and when it is ready ask me to sup with you. I want to cheat my uncomfortable conscience, and be convinced that Heathcliff has no notion of these things. He has not, has he? He does not know what being in love is?'

'I see no reason that he should not know, as well as you,' I returned; 'and if *you* are his choice, he'll be the most unfortunate creature that ever was born! As soon as you become Mrs Linton, he loses friend, and love, and all! Have you considered how you'll bear the separation, and how he'll bear to be quite deserted in the world? Because, Miss Catherine – '

'He quite deserted! We separated!' she exclaimed, with an accent of indignation. 'Who is to separate us, pray? They'll meet the fate of Milo! Not as long as I live, Ellen: for no mortal creature. Every Linton on the face of the earth might melt into nothing, before I could consent to forsake Heathcliff. Oh, that's not what I intend – that's not what I mean! I shouldn't be Mrs Linton were such a price demanded! He'll be as much to me as he has been all his lifetime. Edgar must shake off his antipathy, and tolerate him, at least. He will, when he learns my true feelings towards him. Nelly, I see now, you think me a selfish wretch; but did it never strike you that if Heathcliff and I married, we should be beggars? Whereas, if I marry Linton, I can aid Heathcliff to rise, and place him out of my brother's power.'

'With your husband's money, Miss Catherine?' I asked. 'You'll find him not so pliable as you calculate upon: and though I'm hardly a judge, I think that's the worst motive you've given yet for being the wife of young Linton.'

'It is not,' retorted she; 'it is the best! The others were the satisfaction of my whims: and for Edgar's sake, too, to satisfy him. This is for the sake of one who comprehends in his person my feelings to Edgar and myself. I cannot express it; but surely you and everybody have a notion that there is or should be an existence of yours beyond you. What were the use of my creation, if I were entirely contained here? My great miseries in this world have been Heathcliff's miseries, and I watched and felt each from the beginning: my great thought in living is himself. If all else perished, and *he* remained, I should still continue to be; and if all else remained, and he were annihilated, the universe would turn to a mighty stranger: I should not seem a part of it. My love for Linton is like the foliage in the woods: time will change it, I'm well aware, as winter changes the trees. My love for Heathcliff resembles the eternal rocks beneath: a source of little visible delight, but necessary. Nelly, I *am* Heathcliff! He's always, always in my mind: not as a pleasure, any more than I am always a pleasure to myself, but as my own being. So don't talk of our separation again: it is impracticable; and – '

She paused, and hid her face in the folds of my gown; but I jerked it forcibly away. I was out of patience with her folly!

'If I can make any sense of your nonsense, miss,' I said, 'it only goes to convince me that you are ignorant of the duties you undertake in marrying; or else that you are a wicked, unprincipled girl. But trouble me with no more secrets: I'll not promise to keep them.'

'You'll keep that?' she asked, eagerly.

'No, I'll not promise,' I repeated.

She was about to insist, when the entrance of Joseph finished our conversation; and Catherine removed her seat to a corner, and nursed Hareton, while I made the supper. After it was cooked, my fellow-servant and I began to quarrel who should carry some to Mr Hindley; and we didn't settle it till all was nearly cold. Then we came to the agreement that we would let him ask, if he wanted any; for we feared particularly to go into his presence when he had been some time alone.

'Und hah isn't that nowt comed in frough th' field, be this time? What is he abaht? girt eedle seeght!' demanded the old man, looking round for Heathcliff.

'I'll call him,' I replied. 'He's in the barn, I've no doubt.'

I went and called, but got no answer. On returning, I whispered to Catherine that he had heard a good part of what she said, I was sure; and told how I saw him quit the kitchen just as she complained of her brother's conduct regarding him. She jumped up in a fine fright, flung Hareton on to the settle, and ran to seek for her friend herself; not taking leisure to consider why she was so flurried, or how her talk would have affected him. She was absent such a while that Joseph proposed we should wait no longer. He cunningly conjectured they were staying away in order to avoid hearing his protracted blessing. They were 'ill eneugh for ony fahl manners,' he affirmed. And on their behalf he added that night a special prayer to the usual quarter of an hour's supplication before meat, and would have tacked another to the end of the grace, had not his young mistress broken in upon him with a hurried command that he must run down the road, and, wherever Heathcliff had rambled, find and make him re-enter directly!

'I want to speak to him, and I *must*, before I go upstairs,' she said. 'And the gate is open: he is somewhere out of hearing; for he would not reply, though I shouted at the top of the fold as loud as I could.'

Joseph objected at first; she was too much in earnest, however, to suffer contradiction; and at last he placed his hat on his head, and walked grumbling forth.

Meantime, Catherine paced up and down the floor, exclaiming – 'I wonder where he is – I wonder where he *can* be! What did I say, Nelly? I've forgotten. Was he vexed at my bad humour this afternoon?

Dear! tell me what I've said to grieve him? I do wish he'd come. I do wish he would!'

'What a noise for nothing!' I cried, though rather uneasy myself. 'What a trifle scares you! It's surely no great cause of alarm that Heathcliff should take a moonlight saunter on the moors, or even lie too sulky to speak to us in the hayloft. I'll engage he's lurking there. See if I don't ferret him out!'

I departed to renew my search; its result was disappointment, and Joseph's quest ended in the same.

'You lad gets war un war!' observed he on re-entering. 'He's left th' yate ut t'full swing, and miss's pony has trodden dahn two rigs uh corn, un plottered through, raight o'er intuh t'meadow! Hahsomdiver, t' maister 'ull play t' devil to morn, and he'll do weel. He's patience itsseln wi'sich careless, offald craters – patience itsseln he is! Bud he'll nut be soa allus – yah's see, all on ye! Yah mum'n't drive him aht uf his heead fur nowt!'

'Have you found Heathcliff, you ass?' interrupted Catherine. 'Have you been looking for him, as I ordered?'

'Aw sud more likker look for th' horse,' he replied. 'It 'ud be tuh more sense. Bud, aw can look for norther horse, nur man uf a neeght loike this – as black as t' chimbley! Und Hathecliff's noan t' chap tuh coom ut *maw* whistle – happen he'll be less hard uh hearing wi' *ye*!'

It *was* a very dark evening for summer: the clouds appeared inclined to thunder, and I said we had better all sit down: the approaching rain would be certain to bring him home without further trouble. However, Catherine would not be persuaded into tranquillity. She kept wandering to and fro, from the gate to the door, in a state of agitation which permitted no repose; and at length took up a permanent position on one side of the wall, near the road: where, heedless of my expostulations and the growling thunder, and the great drops that began to plash around her, she remained, calling at intervals, and then listening, and then crying outright. She beat Hareton, or any child, at a good passionate fit of crying.

About midnight, while we still sat up, the storm came rattling over the Heights in full fury. There was a violent wind, as well as thunder, and either one or the other split a tree off at the corner of the building: a huge bough fell across the roof, and knocked down a portion of the east chimney-stack, sending a clatter of stones and soot into the kitchen fire. We thought a bolt had fallen in the middle of us; and Joseph swung on to his knees, beseeching the Lord to remember the patriarchs Noah and Lot, and, as in former times, spare the righteous, though he smote the ungodly. I felt some sentiment that it must be a judgement on us also. The Jonah, in my mind, was Mr Earnshaw; and I shook the handle of his den that I might ascertain if he were yet living. He replied audibly enough, in a fashion which made my companion vociferate, more clamorously than before, that a wide distinction might be drawn between saints like himself and sinners like his master. But the uproar passed away in twenty minutes, leaving us all unharmed; excepting Cathy, who got thoroughly drenched for her obstinacy in refusing to take shelter, and standing bonnetless and shawlless to catch as much water as she could with her hair and clothes. She came in and lay down on the settle, all soaked as she was, turning her face to the back, and putting her hands before it.

'Well, miss!' I exclaimed, touching her shoulder; 'you are not bent on getting your death, are you? Do you know what o'clock it is? Half-past twelve. Come, come to bed! there's no use waiting longer on that foolish boy: he'll be gone to Gimmerton, and he'll stay there now. He guesses we shouldn't wake for him till this late hour: at least, he guesses that only Mr Hindley would be up; and he'd rather avoid having the door opened by the master.'

'Nay, nay, he's noan at Gimmerton!' said Joseph. 'Aw'sniver wonder, bud he's at t' bothom ufa bug-hoile. This visitation worn't for nowt, und aw wod hev ye tuh look aht, miss – yah muh be t' next. Thank Hivin for all! All warks togither for gooid tuh them as is chozzen, and piked aht froo' th' rubbidge! Yah knaw whet t' Scripture ses – ' And he began quoting several texts, referring us to the chapters and verses, where we might find them.

I, having vainly begged the wilful girl to rise and remove her wet things, left him preaching and her shivering, and betook myself to bed with little Hareton, who slept as fast as if everyone had been sleeping round him. I heard Joseph read on a while afterwards; then I distinguished his slow step on the ladder, and then I dropped asleep.

Coming down somewhat later than usual, I saw, by the sunbeams piercing the chinks of the shutters, Miss Catherine still seated near the fireplace. The house door was ajar, too; light entered from its unclosed windows; Hindley had come out, and stood on the kitchen hearth, haggard and drowsy.

'What ails you, Cathy?' he was saying when I entered: 'you look as dismal as a drowned whelp. Why are you so damp and pale, child?'

'I've been wet,' she answered reluctantly, 'and I'm cold, that's all.'

'Oh, she is naughty!' I cried, perceiving the master to be tolerably sober. 'She got steeped in the shower of yesterday evening, and there she has sat the night through, and I couldn't prevail on her to stir.'

Mr Earnshaw stared at us in surprise. 'The night through,' he repeated. 'What kept her up? Not fear of the thunder, surely? That was over hours since.'

Neither of us wished to mention Heathcliff's absence, as long as we could conceal it; so I replied, I didn't know how she took it into her head to sit up; and she said nothing. The morning was fresh and cool; I threw back the lattice, and presently the room filled with sweet scents from the garden; but Catherine called peevishly to me, 'Ellen, shut the window. I'm starving!' And her teeth chattered as she shrunk closer to the almost extinguished embers.

'She's ill,' said Hindley, taking her wrist; 'I suppose that's the reason she would not go to bed. Damn it! I don't want to be troubled with more sickness here. What took you into the rain?'

'Running after t' lads, as usuald!' croaked Joseph, catching an opportunity, from our hesitation, to thrust in his evil tongue. 'If Aw wur yah, maister, Aw'd just slam t' boards i' their faces all on 'em, gentle and simple! Never a day ut yah're off, but yon cat uh Linton comes sneaking hither; and Miss Nelly shoo's a fine lass! shoo sits watching for ye i' t' kitchen; and as yah're in at one door, he's aht at t' other; und, then, wer grand lady goes a coorting uf hor side! It's bonny behaviour, lurking amang t' fields, after twelve ut' night, wi' that fahl, flaysome divil uf a gipsy, Heathcliff! They think *Aw*'m blind; but Aw'm noan, nowt ut t'soart! Aw seed young Linton, boath coming and going, and Aw seed *yah*' (directing his discourse to me). 'Yah gooid fur nowt, slattenly witch! nip up und bolt intuh th' hahs, t' minute yah heard t' maister's horse fit clatter up t' road.'

'Silence, eavesdropper!' cried Catherine; 'None of your insolence, before me! Edgar Linton came yesterday, by chance, Hindley; and it was *I* who told him to be off: because, I knew you would not like to have met him as you were.'

'You lie, Cathy, no doubt,' answered her brother, 'and you are a confounded simpleton! But never mind Linton at present: tell me, were you not with Heathcliff last night? Speak the truth, now. You need not be afraid of harming him: though I hate him as much as ever, he did me a good turn a short time since, that will make my conscience tender of breaking his neck. To prevent it, I shall send him about his business, this very morning; and after he's gone, I'd advise you all to look sharp: I shall only have the more humour for you.'

'I never saw Heathcliff last night,' answered Catherine, beginning to sob bitterly: 'and if you do turn him out of doors, I'll go with him. But, perhaps, you'll never have an opportunity: perhaps he's gone.' Here she burst into uncontrollable grief, and the remainder of her words were inarticulate.

Hindley lavished on her a torrent of scornful abuse, and bade her get to her room immediately, or she shouldn't cry for nothing! I obliged her to obey; and I shall never forget what a scene she acted when we reached her chamber: it terrified me. I thought she was going mad, and I begged Joseph to run for the doctor. It proved the commencement of delirium: Mr Kenneth, as soon as he saw her, pronounced her dangerously ill; she had a fever. He bled her, and he told me to let her live on whey, and water gruel; and take care she did not throw herself downstairs or out of the window; and then he left: for he had enough to do in the parish, where two or three miles was the ordinary distance between cottage and cottage.

Though I cannot say I made a gentle nurse, and Joseph and the master were no better; and though our patient was as wearisome and headstrong as a patient could be, she weathered it through. Old Mrs Linton paid us several visits, to be sure, and set things to rights, and scolded and ordered us all; and when Catherine was convalescent, she insisted on conveying her to Thrushcross Grange: for which deliverance we were very grateful. But the poor dame had reason to repent of her kindness: she and her husband both took the fever, and died within a few days of each other.

Our young lady returned to us, saucier and more passionate, and haughtier than ever. Heathcliff had never been heard of since the evening of the thunderstorm; and, one day, I had the misfortune, when she provoked me exceedingly, to lay the blame of his disappearance on her: where indeed it belonged, as she well knew. From that period, for several months, she ceased to hold any communication with me, save in the relation of a mere servant. Joseph fell under a ban also: he *would* speak his mind, and lecture her all the same as if she were a little girl; and she esteemed herself a woman, and our mistress, and thought that her recent illness gave her a claim to be treated with consideration. Then the doctor had said that she would not bear crossing much; she ought to have her own way; and it was nothing less than murder in her eyes for anyone to presume to stand up and contradict her. From Mr Earnshaw and his companions she kept aloof; and tutored by Kenneth, and serious threats of a fit that often attended her rages, her brother allowed her whatever she pleased to demand, and generally avoided aggravating her fiery temper. He was rather *too* indulgent in humouring her caprices; not from affection, but from pride: he wished earnestly to see her bring honour to the family by an alliance with the Lintons, and as long as she let him alone she might trample us like slaves, for aught he cared! Edgar Linton, as multitudes have been before and will be after him, was infatuated; and believed himself the happiest man alive on the day he led her to Gimmerton chapel, three years subsequent to his father's death.

Much against my inclination, I was persuaded to leave Wuthering Heights and accompany her here. Little Hareton was nearly five years old, and I had just begun to teach him his letters. We made a sad parting; but Catherine's tears were more powerful than ours. When I refused to go, and when she found her entreaties did not move me, she went lamenting to her husband and brother. The former offered me munificent wages; the latter ordered me to pack up: he wanted no women in the house, he said, now that there was no mistress; and as to Hareton, the curate should take him in hand, by and by. And so I had but one choice left: to do as I was ordered. I told the master he got rid of all decent people only to run to ruin a little faster; I kissed Hareton goodbye; and since then he has been a stranger: and it's very queer to think it, but I've no doubt he has completely forgotten all about Ellen Dean, and that he was ever more than all the world to her, and she to him!

At this point of the housekeeper's story, she chanced to glance towards the timepiece over the chimney; and was in amazement on seeing the minute-hand measure half-past one. She would not hear of staying a second longer: in truth, I felt rather disposed to defer the sequel of her narrative myself. And now that she is vanished to her rest, and I have meditated for another hour or two, I shall summon courage to go, also, in spite of aching laziness of head and limbs.

## *Chapter 10*

A charming introduction to a hermit's life! Four weeks' torture, tossing and sickness! Oh, these bleak winds and bitter northern skies, and impassable roads, and dilatory country surgeons!

And, oh, this dearth of the human physiognomy! and, worse than all, the terrible intimation of Kenneth that I need not expect to be out of doors till spring!

Mr Heathcliff has just honoured me with a call. About seven days ago he sent me a brace of grouse – the last of the season. Scoundrel! He is not altogether guiltless in this illness of mine; and that I had a great mind to tell him. But, alas! how could I offend a man who was charitable enough to sit at my bedside a good hour, and talk on some other subject than pills, and draughts, blisters, and leeches? This is quite an easy interval. I am too weak to read; yet I feel as if I could enjoy something interesting. Why not have up Mrs Dean to finish her tale? I can recollect its chief incidents, as far as she had gone. Yes: I remember her hero had run off, and never been heard of for three years; and the heroine was married. I'll ring: she'll be delighted to find me capable of talking cheerfully. Mrs Dean came.

'It wants twenty minutes, sir, to taking the medicine,' she commenced.

'Away, away with it!' I replied; 'I desire to have —'

'The doctor says you must drop the powders.'

'With all my heart! Don't interrupt me. Come and take your seat here. Keep your fingers from that bitter phalanx of vials. Draw your knitting out of your pocket – that will do – now continue the history of Mr Heathcliff, from where you left off, to the present day. Did he finish his education on the Continent, and come back a gentleman? Or did he get a sizar's place at college, or escape to America, and earn honours by drawing blood from his foster country? Or make a fortune more promptly, on the English highways?'

'He may have done a little in all these vocations, Mr Lockwood; but I couldn't give my word for any. I stated before that I didn't know how he gained his money; neither am I aware of the means he took to raise his mind from the savage ignorance into which it was sunk: but, with your leave, I'll proceed in my own fashion, if you think it will amuse and not weary you. Are you feeling better this morning?'

'Much.'

'That's good news.'

I got Miss Catherine and myself to Thrushcross Grange; and, to my agreeable disappointment, she behaved infinitely better than I dared to expect. She seemed almost over fond of Mr Linton; and even to his sister, she showed plenty of affection. They were both very attentive to her comfort, certainly. It was not the thorn bending to the honeysuckles, but the honeysuckles embracing the thorn. There were no mutual concessions: one stood erect, and the others yielded: and who *can* be ill-natured and bad-tempered when they encounter neither opposition nor indifference? I observed that Mr Edgar had a deep-rooted fear of ruffling her humour. He concealed it from her; but if ever he heard me answer sharply, or saw any other servant grow cloudy at some imperious order of hers, he would show his trouble by a frown of displeasure that never darkened on his own account. He many a time spoke sternly to me about my pertness; and averred that the stab of a knife could not inflict a worse pang than he suffered at seeing his lady vexed. Not to grieve a kind master, I learned to be less touchy; and, for the space of half a year, the gunpowder lay as harmless as sand, because no fire came near to explode it. Catherine had seasons of gloom and silence, now and then: they were respected with sympathising silence by her husband, who ascribed them to an alteration in her constitution, produced by her perilous illness; as she was never subject to depression of spirits before. The return of sunshine was welcomed by answering sunshine from him. I believe I may assert that they were really in possession of deep and growing happiness.

It ended. Well, we *must* be for ourselves in the long run; the mild and generous are only more justly selfish than the domineering; and it ended when circumstances caused each to feel that the one's interest was not the chief consideration in the other's thoughts. On a mellow evening in September, I was coming from the garden with a heavy basket of apples which I had been gathering. It had got dusk, and the moon looked over the high wall of the court, causing undefined shadows to lurk in the corners of the numerous projecting portions of the building. I set my burden on the house steps by the kitchen door, and lingered to rest, and drew in a few more breaths of the soft, sweet air; my eyes were on the moon, and my back to the entrance, when I heard a voice behind me say – 'Nelly, is that you?'

It was a deep voice, and foreign in tone; yet there was something in the manner of pronouncing my name which made it sound familiar. I turned about to discover who spoke, fearfully; for the doors were shut, and I had seen nobody on approaching the steps. Something stirred in the porch; and, moving nearer, I distinguished a tall man dressed in dark clothes, with dark face and hair. He leant against the side, and held his fingers on the latch as if intending to open for himself. 'Who can it be?' I thought. 'Mr Earnshaw? Oh, no! The voice has no resemblance to his.'

'I have waited here an hour,' he resumed, while I continued staring; 'and the whole of that time all round has been as still as death. I dared not enter. You do not know me? Look, I'm not a stranger!'

A ray fell on his features; the cheeks were sallow, and half covered with black whiskers; the brows lowering, the eyes deep set and singular. I remembered the eyes.

'What!' I cried, uncertain whether to regard him as a worldly visitor, and I raised my hands in amazement. 'What! you come back? Is it really you? Is it?'

'Yes, Heathcliff,' he replied, glancing from me up to the windows, which reflected a score of glittering moons, but showed no lights from within. 'Are they at home? Where is she? Nelly, you are not glad! You needn't be so disturbed. Is she here? Speak! I want to have one word with her – your mistress. Go, and say some person from Gimmerton desires to see her.'

'How will she take it?' I exclaimed. 'What will she do? The surprise bewilders me – it will put her out of her head! And you *are* Heathcliff? But altered! Nay, there's no comprehending it. Have you been for a soldier?'

'Go and carry my message,' he interrupted impatiently. 'I'm in hell till you do!'

He lifted the latch, and I entered; but when I got to the parlour where Mr and Mrs Linton were, I could not persuade myself to proceed. At length, I resolved on making an excuse to ask if they would have the candles lighted, and I opened the door.

They sat together in a window whose lattice lay back against the wall, and displayed, beyond the garden trees and the wild green park, the valley of Gimmerton, with a long line of mist winding nearly to its top (for very soon after you pass the chapel, as you may have noticed, the sough that runs from the marshes joins a beck which follows the bend of the glen). Wuthering Heights rose above this silvery vapour; but our old house was invisible; it rather dips down on the other side. Both the room and its occupants, and the scene they gazed on, looked wondrously peaceful. I shrank reluctantly from performing my errand; and was actually going away leaving it unsaid, after having put my question about the candles, when a sense of my folly compelled me to return, and mutter, 'A person from Gimmerton wishes to see you, ma'am.'

'What does he want?' asked Mrs Linton.

'I did not question him,' I answered.

'Well, close the curtains, Nelly,' she said; 'and bring up tea. I'll be back again directly.'

She quitted the apartment; Mr Edgar enquired, carelessly, who it was.

'Someone mistress does not expect,' I replied. 'That Heathcliff – you recollect him, sir – who used to live at Mr Earnshaw's.'

'What, the gipsy – the plough-boy?' he cried. 'Why did you not say so to Catherine?'

'Hush! you must not call him by those names, master,' I said. 'She'd be sadly grieved to hear you. She was nearly heartbroken when he ran off. I guess his return will make a jubilee to her.'

Mr Linton walked to a window on the other side of the room that overlooked the court. He unfastened it, and leant out. I suppose they were below, for he exclaimed quickly, 'Don't stand there, love! Bring the person in, if it be anyone particular.' Ere long, I heard the click of the latch, and Catherine flew upstairs, breathless and wild; too excited to show gladness: indeed, by her face, you would rather have surmised an awful calamity.

'Oh, Edgar, Edgar!' she panted, flinging her arms round his neck. 'Oh, Edgar, darling! Heathcliff's come back – he is!' And she tightened her embrace to a squeeze.

'Well, well,' cried her husband, crossly, 'don't strangle me for that! He never struck me as such a marvellous treasure. There is no need to be frantic!'

'I know you didn't like him,' she answered, repressing a little the intensity of her delight. 'Yet, for my sake, you must be friends now. Shall I tell him to come up now?'

'Here?' he said, 'into the parlour?'

'Where else?' she asked.

He looked vexed, and suggested the kitchen as a more suitable place for him. Mrs Linton eyed him with a droll expression – half angry, half laughing at his fastidiousness.

'No,' she added, after a while; 'I cannot sit in the kitchen. Set two tables here, Ellen: one for your master and Miss Isabella, being gentry; the other for Heathcliff and myself, being of the lower orders. Will that please you, dear? Or must I have a fire lighted elsewhere? If so, give directions. I'll run down and secure my guest. I'm afraid the joy is too great to be real!'

She was about to dart off again; but Edgar arrested her.

'*You* bid him step up,' he said, addressing me; 'and, Catherine, try to be glad, without being absurd! The whole household need not witness the sight of your welcoming a runaway servant as a brother.'

I descended, and found Heathcliff waiting under the porch, evidently anticipating an invitation to enter. He followed my guidance with out waste of words, and I ushered him into the presence of the master and mistress, whose flushed cheeks betrayed signs of warm talking. But the lady's glowed with another feeling when her friend appeared at the door: she sprang forward, took both his hands, and led him to Linton; and then she *seized* Linton's reluctant fingers and crushed them into his. Now fully revealed by the fire and candlelight, I was amazed, more than ever, to behold the transformation of Heathcliff. He had grown a tall, athletic, well-formed man; beside whom, my master seemed quite slender and youth-like. His upright carriage suggested the idea of his having been in the army. His countenance was much older in expression and decision of feature than Mr Linton's; it looked intelligent, and retained no marks of former degradation. A half-civilised ferocity lurked yet in the depressed brows and eyes full of black fire, but it was subdued; and his manner was even dignified: quite divested of roughness, though too stern for grace. My master's surprise equalled or exceeded mine: he remained for a minute at a loss how to address the ploughboy, as he had called him. Heathcliff dropped his slight hand, and stood looking at him coolly till he chose to speak.

'Sit down, sir,' he said, at length. 'Mrs Linton, recalling old times, would have me give you a cordial reception; and, of course, I am gratified when anything occurs to please her.'

'And I also,' answered Heathcliff, 'especially if it be anything in which I have a part. I shall stay an hour or two willingly.'

He took a seat opposite Catherine, who kept her gaze fixed on him as if she feared he would vanish were she to remove it. He did not raise his to her often: a quick glance now and then sufficed; but it flashed back, each time more confidently, the undisguised delight he drank from hers. They were too much absorbed in their mutual joy to suffer embarrassment. Not so Mr Edgar: he grew pale with pure annoyance: a feeling that reached its climax when his lady rose, and stepping across the rug, seized Heathcliff's hands again, and laughed like one beside herself.

'I shall think it a dream tomorrow!' she cried. 'I shall not be able to believe that I have seen, and touched, and spoken to you once more. And yet, cruel Heathcliff! you don't deserve this welcome. To be absent and silent for three years, and never to think of me!'

'A little more than you have thought of me,' he murmured. 'I heard of your marriage, Cathy, not long since; and, while waiting in the yard below, I meditated this plan – just to have one glimpse of your face: a stare of surprise, perhaps, and pretended pleasure; afterwards settle my score with Hindley; and then prevent the law by doing execution on myself. Your welcome has put these ideas out of my mind; but beware of meeting me with another aspect next time! Nay, you'll not drive me off again. You were really sorry for me, were you? Well, there was cause. I've fought through a bitter life since I last heard your voice; and you must forgive me, for I struggled only for you!'

'Catherine, unless we are to have cold tea, please to come to the table,' interrupted Linton, striving to preserve his ordinary tone, and a due measure of politeness. 'Mr Heathcliff will have a long walk, wherever he may lodge tonight; and I'm thirsty.'

She took her post before the urn; and Miss Isabella came, summoned by the bell; then, having handed their chairs forward, I left the room. The meal hardly endured ten minutes. Catherine's cup was never filled: she could neither eat nor drink. Edgar had made a slop in his saucer, and scarcely swallowed a mouthful. Their guest did not protract his stay that evening above an hour longer. I asked, as he departed, if he went to Gimmerton?

'No, to Wuthering Heights,' he answered: 'Mr Earnshaw invited me, when I called this morning.'

Mr Earnshaw invited *him*! and *he* called on Mr Earnshaw! I pondered this sentence painfully after he was gone. Is he turning out a bit of a hypocrite and coming into the country to work mischief under a cloak? I mused: I had a presentiment, in the bottom of my heart, that he had better have remained away.

About the middle of the night, I was wakened from my first nap by Mrs Linton gliding into my chamber, taking a seat on my bedside, and pulling me by the hair to rouse me.

'I cannot rest, Ellen,' she said, by way of apology. 'And I want some living creature to keep me company in my happiness! Edgar is sulky, because I'm glad of a thing that does not interest him: he refuses to open his mouth, except to utter pettish, silly speeches; and he affirmed I was cruel and selfish for wishing to talk when he was so sick and sleepy. He always contrives to be sick at the least cross! I gave a few sentences of commendation to Heathcliff, and he, either for a headache or a pang of envy, began to cry: so I got up and left him.'

'What use is it praising Heathcliff to him?' I answered. 'As lads they had an aversion to each other, and Heathcliff would hate just as much to hear him praised: it's human nature. Let Mr Linton alone about him, unless you would like an open quarrel between them.'

'But does it not show great weakness?' pursued she. 'I'm not envious; I never feel hurt at the brightness of Isabella's yellow hair and the whiteness of her skin, at her dainty elegance, and the fondness all the family exhibit for her. Even you, Nelly, if we have a dispute sometimes, you back Isabella at once; and I yield like a foolish mother: I call her a darling, and flatter her into a good temper. It pleases her brother to see us cordial, and that pleases me. But they are very much alike: they are spoiled children, and fancy the world was made for their accommodation; and though I humour both, I think a smart chastisement might improve them, all the same.'

'You're mistaken, Mrs Linton,' said I. 'They humour you: I know what there would be to do if they did not. You can well afford to indulge their passing whims as long as their business is to anticipate all your desires. You may, however, fall out, at last, over something of equal consequence to both sides; and then those you term weak are very capable of being as obstinate as you.'

'And then we shall fight to the death, shan't we, Nelly?' she returned, laughing. 'No! I tell you, I have such faith in Linton's love, that I believe I might kill him, and he wouldn't wish to retaliate.'

I advised her to value him the more for his affection.

'I do,' she answered, 'but he needn't resort to whining for trifles. It is childish; and, instead of melting into tears because I said that Heathcliff was now worthy of anyone's regard, and it would honour the first gentleman in the country to be his friend, he ought to have said it for me, and been delighted from sympathy. He must get accustomed to him, and he may as well like him: considering how Heathcliff has reason to object to him, I'm sure he behaved excellently!'

'What do you think of his going to Wuthering Heights?' I enquired. 'He is reformed in every respect, apparently: quite a Christian: offering the right hand of fellowship to his enemies all around!'

'He explained it,' she replied. 'I wondered as much as you. He said he called to gather information concerning me from you, supposing you resided there still, and Joseph told Hindley, who came out and fell to questioning him of what he had been doing, and how he had been living; and finally, desired him to walk in. There were some persons sitting at cards; Heathcliff joined them; my brother lost some money to him, and, finding him plentifully supplied, he requested that he would come again in the evening: to which he consented. Hindley is too reckless to select his acquaintance prudently: he doesn't trouble himself to reflect on the causes he might have for mistrusting one whom he has basely injured. But, Heathcliff affirms his principal reason for resuming a connection with his ancient persecutor is a wish to install himself in quarters at walking distance from the Grange, and an attachment to the house where we lived together; and likewise a hope that I shall have more opportunities of seeing him there than I could have if he settled in Gimmerton. He means to offer liberal payment for permission to lodge at the Heights; and doubtless my brother's covetousness will prompt him to accept the terms: he was always greedy; though what he grasps with one hand he flings away with the other.'

'It's a nice place for a young man to fix his dwelling in!' said I. 'Have you no fear of the consequences, Mrs Linton?'

'None for my friend,' she replied: 'his strong head will keep him from danger; a little for Hindley: but he can't be made morally worse than he is; and I stand between him and bodily harm. The event of this evening has reconciled me to God and humanity! I had risen in angry rebellion against Providence. Oh, I've endured very, very bitter misery, Nelly! If that creature knew how bitter, he'd be ashamed to cloud its removal with idle petulance. It was kindness for him which induced me to bear it alone: had I expressed the agony I frequently felt, he would have been taught to long for its alleviation as ardently as I. However, it's over, and I'll take no revenge on his folly; I can afford to suffer anything hereafter! Should the meanest thing alive slap me on the cheek, I'd not only turn the other, but I'd ask pardon for provoking it; and, as a proof, I'll go make my peace with Edgar instantly. Good-night! I'm an angel!'

In this self-complacent conviction she departed; and the success of her fulfilled resolution was obvious on the morrow: Mr Linton had not only abjured his peevishness (though his spirits seemed still subdued by Catherine's exuberance of vivacity), but he ventured no objection to her taking Isabella with her to Wuthering Heights in the afternoon; and she rewarded him with such a summer of sweetness and affection in return, as made the house a paradise for several days; both master and servants profiting from the perpetual sunshine.

Heathcliff – Mr Heathcliff I should say in future – used the liberty of visiting at Thrushcross Grange cautiously, at first: he seemed estimating how far its owner would bear his intrusion. Catherine, also, deemed it judicious to moderate her expressions of pleasure in receiving him; and he gradually established his right to be expected. He retained a great deal of the reserve for which his boyhood was remarkable; and that served to repress all startling demonstrations of feeling. My master's uneasiness experienced a lull, and further circumstances diverted it into another channel for a space.

His new source of trouble sprang from the not anticipated misfortune of Isabella Linton evincing a sudden and irresistible attraction towards the tolerated guest. She was at that time a charming young lady of eighteen; infantile in manners, though possessed of keen wit, keen feelings, and a keen temper, too, if irritated. Her brother, who loved her tenderly, was appalled at this fantastic preference. Leaving aside the degradation of an alliance with a nameless man, and the possible fact that his property, in default of heirs male, might pass into such a one's power, he had sense to comprehend Heathcliff's disposition: to know that, though his exterior was altered, his mind was unchangeable, and unchanged. And he dreaded that mind: it revolted him: he shrank forebodingly from the idea of committing Isabella to its keeping. He would have recoiled still more had he been aware that her attachment rose unsolicited, and was bestowed where it awakened no reciprocation of sentiment; for the minute he discovered its existence, he laid the blame on Heathcliff's deliberate designing.

We had all remarked, during some time, that Miss Linton fretted and pined over something. She grew cross and wearisome; snapping at and teasing Catherine continually, at the imminent risk of exhausting her limited patience. We excused her to a certain extent, on the plea of ill-health: she was dwindling and fading before our eyes. But one day, when she had been particularly wayward, rejecting her breakfast, complaining that the servants did not do what she told them; that the mistress would allow her to be nothing in the house, and Edgar neglected her; that she had caught a cold with the doors being left open, and we let the parlour fire go out on purpose to vex her, with a hundred yet more frivolous accusations, Mrs Linton peremptorily insisted that she should get to bed; and, having scolded her heartily, threatened to send for the doctor. Mention of Kenneth caused her to exclaim, instantly, that her health was perfect, and it was only Catherine's harshness which made her unhappy.

'How can you say I am harsh, you naughty fondling?' cried the mistress, amazed at the unreasonable assertion. 'You are surely losing your reason. When have I been harsh, tell me?'

'Yesterday,' sobbed Isabella, 'and now!'

'Yesterday!' said her sister-in-law. 'On what occasion?'

'In our walk along the moor: you told me to ramble where I pleased, while you sauntered on with Mr Heathcliff!'

'And that's your notion of harshness?' said Catherine, laughing. 'It was no hint that your company was superfluous: we didn't care whether you kept with us or not; I merely thought Heathcliff's talk would have nothing entertaining for your ears.'

'Oh no,' wept the young lady; 'you wished me away, because you know I liked to be there!'

'Is she sane?' asked Mrs Linton, appealing to me. 'I'll repeat our conversation, word for word, Isabella; and you point out any charm it could have had for you.'

'I don't mind the conversation,' she answered. 'I wanted to be with – '

'Well!' said Catherine, perceiving her hesitate to complete the sentence.

'With him: and I won't be always sent off!' she continued, kindling up. 'You are a dog in the manger, Cathy, and desire no one to be loved but yourself!'

'You are an impertinent little monkey!' exclaimed Mrs Linton, in surprise. 'But I'll not believe this idiocy! It is impossible that you can covet the admiration of Heathcliff – that you can consider him an agreeable person! I hope I have misunderstood you, Isabella?

'No, you have not,' said the infatuated girl. 'I love him more than ever you loved Edgar; and he might love me, if you would let him!'

'I wouldn't be you for a kingdom, then!' Catherine declared, emphatically: and she seemed to speak sincerely. 'Nelly, help me to convince her of her madness. Tell her what Heathcliff is: an unreclaimed creature, without refinement, without cultivation: an arid wilderness of furze and whinstone. I'd as soon put that little canary into the park on a winter's day, as recommend you to bestow your heart on him! It is deplorable ignorance of his character, child, and nothing else, which makes that dream enter your head. Pray, don't imagine that he conceals depths of benevolence and affection beneath a stern exterior! He's not a rough diamond – a pearl-containing oyster of a rustic: he's a fierce, pitiless, wolfish man. I never say to him, "Let this or that enemy alone, because it would be ungenerous or cruel to harm them"; I say, "Let them alone, because *I* should hate them to be wronged": and he'd crush you like a sparrow's egg, Isabella, if he found you a troublesome charge. I know he couldn't love a Linton; and yet he'd be quite capable of marrying your fortune and expectations: avarice is growing with him a besetting sin. There's my picture: and I'm his friend – so much so, that had he thought seriously to catch you, I should, perhaps, have held my tongue, and let you fall into his trap.'

Miss Linton regarded her sister-in-law with indignation. 'For shame! for shame!' she repeated, angrily. 'You are worse than twenty foes, you poisonous friend!'

'Ah! you won't believe me, then?' said Catherine. 'You think I speak from wicked selfishness?'

'I'm certain you do,' retorted Isabella; 'and I shudder at you!'

'Good!' cried the other. 'Try for yourself, if that be your spirit: I have done, and yield the argument to your saucy insolence.'

'And I must suffer for her egotism!' she sobbed, as Mrs Linton left the room. 'All, all is against me: she has blighted my single consolation. But she uttered falsehoods, didn't she? Mr Heathcliff is not a fiend: he has an honourable soul, and a true one, or how could he remember her?'

'Banish him from your thoughts, miss,' I said. 'He's a bird of bad omen: no mate for you. Mrs Linton spoke strongly, and yet I can't contradict her. She is better acquainted with his heart than I, or anyone besides; and she never would represent him as worse than he is. Honest people don't hide their deeds. How has he been living? How has he got rich? Why is he staying at Wuthering Heights, the house of a man whom he abhors? They say Mr Earnshaw is worse and worse since he came. They sit up all night together continually, and Hindley has been borrowing money on his land, and does nothing but play and drink: I heard only a week ago – it was Joseph who told me – I met him at Gimmerton: "Nelly," he said, "we's hae a Crahnr's 'quest enah, at ahr folks. One on 'em's a'most getten his finger cut off wi' hauding t' other froo'sticking hisseln loike a cawlf. That's maister, yah knaw, ut's soa up uh going tuh t' grand 'sizes. He 's noan feard uh t' Bench uh judges, norther Paul, nur Peter, nur John, nor Mathew, nor noan on 'em, nut he! He fair like's he langs tuh set his brazened face agean 'em! And yon bonny lad Heathcliff, yah mind, he's a rare un! He can girn a laugh, as weel's onybody at a raight divil's jest. Does he niver say nowt of his fine living amang us, when he goas tuh t' Grange? This is t' way on 't – up at sun-dahn; dice, brandy, cloised shutters, und can'le lught till next day, at nooin: then, t'fooil gangs banning un raving tuh his cham'er, makking dacent fowks dig thur fingers i' thur lugs fur varry shaume; un' the knave, wah, he earn cahnt his brass, un' ate, un' sleep, un' off tuh his neighbour's tuh gossip wi' t' wife. I' course, he tells Dame Catherine hah hor father's goold runs intuh his pocket, and her fathur's son gallops dahn t' Broad road, while he flees afore tuh oppen t' pikes?" Now, Miss Linton, Joseph is an old rascal, but no liar; and, if his account of Heathcliff's conduct be true, you would never think of desiring such a husband, would you?'

'You are leagued with the rest, Ellen!' she replied. 'I'll not listen to your slanders. What malevolence you must have to wish to convince me that there is no happiness in the world!'

Whether she would have got over this fancy if left to herself, or persevered in nursing it perpetually, I cannot say: she had little time to reflect. The day after, there was a justice-meeting at the next town; my master was obliged to attend; and Mr Heathcliff, aware of his absence, called rather earlier than usual. Catherine and Isabella were sitting in the library, on hostile terms, but silent. The latter alarmed at her recent indiscretion, and the disclosure she had made of her secret feelings in a transient fit of passion; the former, on mature consideration, really offended with her companion; and, if she laughed again at her pertness, inclined to make it no laughing matter to *her*. She did laugh as she saw Heathcliff pass the window. I was sweeping the hearth, and I noticed a mischievous smile on her lips. Isabella, absorbed in her meditations, or a book, remained till the door opened; and it was too late to attempt an escape, which she would gladly have done had it been practicable.

'Come in, that's right!' exclaimed the mistress, gaily, pulling a chair to the fire. 'Here are two people sadly in need of a third to thaw the ice between them; and you are the very one we should both of us choose. Heathcliff, I'm proud to show you, at last, somebody that dotes on you more than myself. I expect you to feel flattered. Nay, it's not Nelly; don't look at her! My poor little sister-in-law is breaking her heart by mere contemplation of your physical and moral beauty. It lies in your own power to be Edgar's brother! No, no, Isabella, you sha'n't run off,' she continued, arresting, with feigned playfulness, the confounded girl, who had risen indignantly. 'We were quarrelling like cats about you, Heathcliff, and I was fairly beaten in protestations of devotion and admiration: and, moreover, I was informed that if I would but have the manners to stand aside, my rival, as she will have herself to be, would shoot a shaft into your soul that would fix you for ever, and send my image into eternal oblivion!'

'Catherine!' said Isabella, calling up her dignity, and disdaining to struggle from the tight grasp that held her. 'I'd thank you to adhere to the truth and not slander me, even in joke! Mr Heathcliff, be kind enough to bid this friend of yours release me: she forgets that you and I are not intimate acquaintances; and what amuses her is painful to me beyond expression.'

As the guest answered nothing, but took his seat, and looked thoroughly indifferent what sentiments she cherished concerning him, she turned and whispered an earnest appeal for liberty to her tormentor.

'By no means!' cried Mrs Linton in answer.

'I won't be named a dog in the manger again. You *shall* stay: now then! Heathcliff, why don't you evince satisfaction at my pleasant news? Isabella swears that the love Edgar has for me is nothing to that she entertains for you. I'm sure she made some speech of the kind; did she not, Ellen? And she has fasted ever since the day before yesterday's walk, from sorrow and rage that I despatched her out of your society under the idea of its being unacceptable.'

'I think you belie her,' said Heathcliff, twisting his chair to face them. 'She wishes to be out of my society now, at any rate!'

And he stared hard at the object of discourse, as one might do at a strange repulsive animal: a centipede from the Indies, for instance, which curiosity leads one to examine in spite of the aversion it raises. The poor thing couldn't bear that: she grew white and red in rapid succession, and, while tears beaded her lashes, bent the strength of her small fingers to loosen the firm clutch of Catherine; and perceiving that as fast as she raised one finger off her arm another closed down, and she could not remove the whole together, she began to make use of her nails; and their sharpness presently ornamented the detainer's with crescents of red.

'There's a tigress!' exclaimed Mrs Linton, setting her free, and shaking her hand with pain. 'Begone, for God's sake, and hide your vixen face! How foolish to reveal those talons to *him*. Can't you fancy the conclusions he'll draw? Look, Heathcliff! they are instruments that will do execution – you must beware of your eyes.'

'I'd wrench them off her fingers, if they ever menaced me,' he answered, brutally, when the door had closed after her. 'But what did you mean by teasing the creature in that manner, Cathy? You were not speaking the truth, were you?'

'I assure you I was,' she returned. 'She has been pining for your sake several weeks; and raving about you this morning, and pouring forth a deluge of abuse, because I represented your failings in a plain light, for the purpose of mitigating her adoration. But don't notice it further: I wished to punish her sauciness, that's all. I like her too well, my dear Heathcliff, to let you absolutely seize and devour her up.'

'And I like her too ill to attempt it,' said he, 'except in a very ghoulish fashion. You'd hear of odd things if I lived alone with that mawkish, waxen face: the most ordinary would be painting on its white the colours of the rainbow, and turning the blue eyes black, every day or two: they detestably resemble Linton's.'

'Delectably!' observed Catherine. 'They are dove's eyes – angel's!'

'She's her brother's heir, is she not?' he asked, after a brief silence.

'I should be sorry to think so,' returned his companion. 'Half a dozen nephews shall erase her title, please Heaven. Abstract your mind from the subject at present: you are too prone to covet your neighbour's goods; remember *this* neighbour's goods are mine.'

'If they were *mine*, they would be none the less that,' said Heathcliff; 'but though Isabella Linton may be silly, she is scarcely mad; and, in short, we'll dismiss the matter, as you advise.'

From their tongues, they did dismiss it; and Catherine, probably, from her thoughts. The other, I felt certain, recalled it often in the course of the evening. I saw him smile to himself – grin rather – and lapse into ominous musing whenever Mrs Linton had occasion to be absent from the apartment.

I determined to watch his movements. My heart invariably cleaved to the master's, in preference to Catherine's side: with reason I imagined, for he was kind, and trustful, and honourable; and she – she could not be called the *opposite*, yet she seemed to allow herself such wide latitude, that I had little faith in her principles, and still less sympathy for her feelings. I wanted something to happen which might have the effect of freeing both Wuthering Heights and the Grange of Mr Heathcliff, quietly; leaving us as we had been prior to his advent. His visits were a continual nightmare to me; and, I suspected, to my master also. His abode at the Heights was an oppression past explaining. I felt that God had forsaken the stray sheep there to its own wicked wanderings, and an evil beast prowled between it and the fold, waiting his time to spring and destroy.

## *Chapter 11*

Sometimes, while meditating on these things in solitude, I've got up in a sudden terror, and put on my bonnet to go and see how all was at the farm. I've persuaded my conscience that it was a duty to warn him how people talked regarding his ways; and then I've recollected his confirmed bad habits, and, hopeless of benefiting him, have flinched from re-entering the dismal house, doubting if I could bear to be taken at my word.

One time I passed the old gate, going out of my way, on a journey to Gimmerton. It was about the period that my narrative has reached: a bright frosty afternoon; the ground bare, and the road hard and dry. I came to a stone where the highway branches off on to the moor at your left hand; a rough sand-pillar, with the letters W. H. cut on its north side, on the east, G., and on the southwest, T. G. It serves as guidepost to the Grange, and Heights, and village. The sun shone yellow on its grey head, reminding me of summer; and I cannot say why, but all at once, a gush of child's sensations flowed into my heart. Hindley and I held it a favourite spot twenty years before I gazed long at the weather-worn block; and, stooping down, perceived a hole near the bottom still full of snail-shells and pebbles, which we were very fond of storing there with more perishable things; and, as fresh as reality, it appeared that I beheld my early playmate seated on the withered turf: his dark, square head bent forward, and his little hand scooping out the earth with a piece of slate. 'Poor Hindley!' I exclaimed, involuntarily. I started: my bodily eye was cheated into a momentary belief that the child lifted its face and stared straight into mine! It vanished in a twinkling; but immediately I felt an irresistible yearning to be at the Heights. Superstition urged me to comply with this impulse: supposing he should be dead! I thought – or should die soon! – supposing it were a sign of death! The nearer I got to the house the more agitated I grew; and on catching sight of it I trembled every limb. The apparition had outstripped me: it stood looking through the gate. That was my first idea on observing an elf-locked, brown-eyed boy setting his ruddy countenance against the bars. Further reflection suggested this must be Hareton, *my* Hareton, not altered greatly since I left him, ten months since.

'God bless thee, darling!' I cried, forgetting instantaneously my foolish fears. 'Hareton, it's Nelly! Nelly, thy nurse.'

He retreated out of arm's length, and picked up a large flint.

'I am come to see thy father, Hareton,' I added, guessing from the action that Nelly, if she lived in his memory at all, was not recognised as one with me.

He raised his missile to hurl it; I commenced a soothing speech, but could not stay his hand: the stone struck my bonnet; and then ensued, from the stammering lips of the little fellow, a string of curses, which, whether he comprehended them or not, were delivered with practised emphasis, and distorted his baby features into a shocking expression of malignity. You may be certain this grieved more than angered me. Fit to cry, I took an orange from my pocket, and offered it to propitiate him. He hesitated, and then snatched it from my hold; as if he fancied I only intended to tempt and disappoint him. I showed another, keeping it out of his reach.

'Who has taught you those fine words, my bairn?' I enquired. 'The curate?'

'Damn the curate, and thee! Gie me that,' he replied.

'Tell us where you got your lessons, and you shall have it,' said I. 'Who's your master?'

'Devil daddy,' was his answer.

'And what do you learn from daddy?' I continued.

He jumped at the fruit; I raised it higher. 'What does he teach you?' I asked.

'Naught,' said he, 'but to keep out of his gait. Daddy cannot bide me, because I swear at him.'

'Ah! and the devil teaches you to swear at daddy?' I observed.

'Ay – nay,' he drawled.

'Who, then?'

'Heathcliff.'

I asked if he liked Mr Heathcliff.

'Ay!' he answered again.

Desiring to have his reasons for liking him, I could only gather the sentences – 'I known't: he pays dad back what he gies to me – he curses daddy for cursing me. He says I mun do as I will.'

'And the curate does not teach you to read and write, then?' I pursued.

'No, I was told the curate should have his — teeth dashed down his — throat, if he stepped over the threshold – Heathcliff had promised that!'

I put the orange in his hand, and bade him tell his father that a woman called Nelly Dean was waiting to speak with him, by the garden gate. He went up the walk, and entered the house; but, instead of Hindley, Heathcliff appeared on the door stones; and I turned directly and ran down the road as hard as ever I could race, making no halt till I gained the guide post, and feeling as scared as if I had raised a goblin. This is not much connected with Miss Isabella's affair; except that it urged me to resolve further on mounting vigilant guard, and doing my utmost to check the spread of such bad influence at the Grange: even though I should wake a domestic storm, by thwarting Mrs Linton's pleasure.

The next time Heathcliff came, my young lady chanced to be feeding some pigeons in the court. She had never spoken a word to her sister-in-law for three days; but she had likewise dropped her fretful complaining, and we found it a great comfort. Heathcliff had not the habit of bestowing a single unnecessary civility on Miss Linton, I knew. Now, as soon as he beheld her, his first precaution was to take a sweeping survey of the house-front. I was standing by the kitchen window, but I drew out of sight. He then stepped across the pavement to her, and said something: she seemed embarrassed, and desirous of getting away; to prevent it, he laid his hand on her arm. She averted her face: he apparently put some question which she had no mind to answer. There was another rapid glance at the house, and supposing himself unseen, the scoundrel had the impudence to embrace her.

'Judas! Traitor!' I ejaculated. 'You are a hypocrite, too, are you? A deliberate deceiver.'

'Who is, Nelly?' said Catherine's voice at my elbow: I had been over-intent on watching the pair outside to mark her entrance.

'Your worthless friend!' I answered warmly: 'the sneaking rascal yonder. Ah, he has caught a glimpse of us – he is coming in! I wonder will he have the art to find a plausible excuse for making love to miss, when he told you he hated her?'

Mrs Linton saw Isabella tear herself free, and run into the garden; and a minute after, Heathcliff opened the door. I couldn't withhold giving some loose to my indignation; but Catherine angrily insisted on silence, and threatened to order me out of the kitchen, if I dared to be so presumptuous as to put in my insolent tongue.

'To hear you, people might think you were the mistress!' she cried. 'You want setting down in your right place! Heathcliff, what are you about, raising this stir? I said you must let Isabella alone! I beg you will, unless you are tired of being received here, and wish Linton to draw the bolts against you!'

'God forbid that he should try!' answered the black villain. I detested him just then. 'God keep him meek and patient! Every day I grow madder after sending him to heaven!'

'Hush!' said Catherine, shutting the inner door. 'Don't vex me. Why have you disregarded my request? Did she come across you on purpose?'

'What is it to you?' he growled. 'I have a right to kiss her, if she chooses; and you have no right to object. I'm not *your* husband: *you* needn't be jealous of me!'

'I'm not jealous of you,' replied the mistress; 'I'm jealous for you. Clear your face: you shan't scowl at me! If you like Isabella, you shall marry her. But do you like her? Tell the truth, Heathcliff! There, you won't answer. I'm certain you don't!'

'And would Mr Linton approve of his sister marrying that man?' I enquired.

'Mr Linton should approve,' returned my lady decisively.

'He might spare himself the trouble,' said Heathcliff: 'I could do as well without his approbation. And as to you, Catherine, I have a mind to speak a few words now, while we are at it. I want you to be aware that I *know* you have treated me infernally – infernally! Do you hear? And if you flatter yourself that I don't perceive it, you are a fool; and if you think I can be consoled by sweet words, you are an idiot; and if you fancy I'll suffer unrevenged, I'll convince you of the contrary, in a very little while! Meantime, thank you for telling me your sister-in-law's secret: I swear I'll make the most of it. And stand you aside!'

'What new phase of his character is this?' exclaimed Mrs Linton, in amazement. 'I've treated you infernally – and you'll take revenge! How will you take it, ungrateful brute? How have I treated you infernally?'

'I seek no revenge on you,' replied Heathcliff less vehemently. 'That's not the plan. The tyrant grinds down his slaves and they don't turn against him; they crush those beneath them. You are welcome to torture me to death for your amusement, only allow me to amuse myself a little in the same style, and refrain from insult as much as you are able. Having levelled my palace, don't erect a hovel and complacently admire your own charity in giving me that for a home. If I imagined you really wished me to marry Isabella, I'd cut my throat!'

'Oh, the evil is that I am *not* jealous, is it?' cried Catherine. 'Well, I won't repeat my offer of a wife: it is as bad as offering Satan a lost soul. Your bliss lies, like his, in inflicting misery. You prove it. Edgar is restored from the ill-temper he gave way to at your coming; I begin to be secure and tranquil; and you, restless to know us at peace, appear resolved on exciting a quarrel. Quarrel with Edgar, if you please, Heathcliff, and deceive his sister: you'll hit on exactly the most efficient method of revenging yourself on me.'

The conversation ceased. Mrs Linton sat down by the fire, flushed and gloomy. The spirit which served her was growing intractable: she could neither lay nor control it. He stood on the hearth with folded arms, brooding on his evil thoughts; and in this position I left them to seek the master, who was wondering what kept Catherine below so long.

'Ellen,' said he, when I entered, 'have you seen your mistress?'

'Yes; she's in the kitchen, sir,' I answered. 'She's sadly put out by Mr Heathcliff's behaviour: and, indeed, I do think it's time to arrange his visits on another footing. There's harm in being too soft, and now it's come to this – ' And I related the scene in the court, and, as near as I dared, the whole subsequent dispute. I fancied it could not be very prejudicial to Mrs Linton; unless she made it so afterwards, by assuming the defensive for her guest. Edgar Linton had difficulty in hearing me to the close. His first words revealed that he did not clear his wife of blame.

'This is insufferable!' he exclaimed. 'It is disgraceful that she should own him for a friend, and force his company on me! Call me two men out of the hall, Ellen. Catherine shall linger no longer to argue with the low ruffian – I have humoured her enough.'

He descended, and bidding the servants wait in the passage, went, followed by me, to the kitchen. Its occupants had recommenced their angry discussion: Mrs Linton, at least, was scolding with renewed vigour; Heathcliff had moved to the window, and hung his head, somewhat cowed by her violent rating apparently. He saw the master first, and made a hasty motion that she should be silent; which she obeyed, abruptly, on discovering the reason of his intimation. 'How is this?' said Linton, addressing her; 'what notion of propriety must you have to remain here, after the language which has been held to you by that blackguard? I suppose, because it is his ordinary talk, you think nothing of it: you are habituated to his baseness, and, perhaps, imagine I can get used to it too!'

'Have you been listening at the door, Edgar?' asked the mistress, in a tone particularly calculated to provoke her husband, implying both carelessness and contempt of his irritation. Heathcliff, who had raised his eyes at the former speech, gave a sneering laugh at the latter; on purpose, it seemed, to draw Mr Linton's attention to him. He succeeded; but Edgar did not mean to entertain him with any high flights of passion.

'I have been so far forbearing with you, sir,' he said, quietly; 'not that I was ignorant of your miserable, degraded character, but I felt you were only partly responsible for that; and Catherine wishing to keep up your acquaintance, I acquiesced – foolishly. Your presence is a moral poison that would contaminate the most virtuous: for that cause, and to prevent worse consequences, I shall deny you hereafter admission into this house, and give notice now that I require your instant departure. Three minutes' delay will render it involuntary and ignominious.'

Heathcliff measured the height and breadth of the speaker with an eye full of derision.

'Cathy, this lamb of yours threatens like a bull!' he said. 'It is in danger of splitting its skull against my knuckles. By God! Mr Linton, I'm mortally sorry that you are not worth knocking down!'

My master glanced towards the passage, and signed me to fetch the men: he had no intention of hazarding a personal encounter. I obeyed the hint; but Mrs Linton, suspecting something, followed; and when I attempted to call them, she pulled me back, slammed the door to, and locked it.

'Fair means!' she said, in answer to her husband's look of angry surprise. 'If you have not the courage to attack him, make an apology, or allow yourself to be beaten. It will correct you of feigning more valour than you possess. No, I'll swallow the key before you shall get it! I'm delightfully rewarded for my kindness to each! After constant indulgence of one's weak nature, and the other's bad one, I earn, for thanks, two samples of blind ingratitude, stupid to absurdity! Edgar, I was defending you and yours; and I wish Heathcliff may flog you sick, for daring to think an evil thought of me!'

It did not need the medium of a flogging to produce that effect on the master. He tried to wrest the key from Catherine's grasp, and for safety she flung it into the hottest part of the fire; whereupon Mr Edgar was taken with a nervous trembling, and his countenance grew deadly pale. For his life he could not avert that access of emotion: mingled anguish and humiliation overcame him completely. He leant on the back of a chair, and covered his face.

'Oh! Heavens! In old days this would win you knight- hood!' exclaimed Mrs Linton. 'We are vanquished! we are vanquished! Heathcliff would as soon lift a finger at you as the king would march his army against a colony of mice. Cheer up! you sha'n't be hurt! Your type is not a lamb, it's a sucking leveret.'

'I wish you joy of the milk-blooded coward, Cathy!' said her friend. 'I compliment you on your taste. And that is the slavering, shivering thing you preferred to me! I would not strike him with my fist, but I'd kick him with my foot, and experience considerable satisfaction. Is he weeping, or is he going to faint for fear?'

The fellow approached and gave the chair on which Linton rested a push. He'd better have kept his distance: my master quickly sprang erect, and struck him full on the throat a blow that would have levelled a slighter man. It took his breath for a minute; and, while he choked, Mr Linton walked out by the back door into the yard, and from thence, to the front entrance.

'There! you've done with coming here,' cried Catherine. 'Get away, now; he'll return with a brace of pistols, and half a dozen assistants. If he did overhear us, of course, he'd never forgive you. You've played me an ill turn, Heathcliff! But, go – make haste! I'd rather see Edgar at bay than you.'

'Do you suppose I'm going with that blow burning in my gullet?' he thundered. 'By hell, no! I'll crush his ribs in like a rotten hazelnut, before I cross the threshold! If I don't floor him now, I shall murder him some time; so, as you value his existence, let me get at him!'

'He is not coming,' I interposed, framing a bit of a lie. 'There's the coachman, and the two gardeners; you'll surely not wait to be thrust into the road by them! Each has a bludgeon; and master will, very likely, be watching from the parlour windows to see that they fulfil his orders.'

The gardeners and coachman *were* there; but Linton was with them. They had already entered the court. Heathcliff, on second thoughts, resolved to avoid a struggle against three underlings: he seized the poker, smashed the lock from the inner door, and made his escape as they tramped in.

Mrs Linton, who was very much excited, bade me accompany her upstairs. She did not know my share in contributing to the disturbance, and I was anxious to keep her in ignorance.

'I'm nearly distracted, Nelly!' she exclaimed, throwing herself on the sofa. 'A thousand smiths' hammers are beating in my head! Tell Isabella to shun me; this uproar is owing to her; and should she or anyone else aggravate my anger at present, I shall get wild. And, Nelly, say to Edgar, if you see him again tonight, that I'm in danger of being seriously ill. I wish it may prove true. He has startled and distressed me shockingly! I want to frighten him. Besides, he might come and begin a string of abuse or complainings; I'm certain I should recriminate, and God knows where we should end! Will you do so, my good Nelly? You are aware that I am no way blameable in this matter. What possessed him to turn listener? Heathcliff's talk was outrageous, after you left us; but I could soon have diverted him from Isabella, and the rest meant nothing. Now, all is dashed wrong by the fool's-craving to hear evil of self that haunts some people like a demon! Had Edgar never gathered our conversation, he would never have been the worse for it. Really, when he opened on me in that unreasonable tone of displeasure, after I had scolded Heathcliff till I was hoarse for *him*, I did not care, hardly, what they did to each other; especially as I felt that, however the scene closed, we should all be driven asunder for nobody knows how long! Well, if I cannot keep Heathcliff for my friend – if Edgar will be mean and jealous, I'll try to break their hearts by breaking my own. That will be a prompt way of finishing all, when I am pushed to extremity! But it's a deed to be reserved for a forlorn hope; I'd not take Linton by surprise with it. To this point he has been discreet in dreading to provoke me; you must represent the peril of quitting that policy, and remind him of my passionate temper, verging, when kindled, on frenzy. I wish you could dismiss that apathy out of your countenance, and look rather more anxious about me!'

The stolidity with which I received these instructions was, no doubt, rather exasperating: for they were delivered in perfect sincerity; but I believed a person who could plan the turning of her fits of passion to account, beforehand, might, by exerting her will, manage to control herself tolerably, even while under their influence; and I did not wish to 'frighten' her husband, as she said, and multiply his annoyances for the purpose of serving her selfishness. Therefore I said nothing when I met the master coming towards the parlour; but I took the liberty of turning back to listen whether they would resume their quarrel together. He began to speak first.

'Remain where you are, Catherine,' he said; without any anger in his voice, but with much sorrowful despondency. 'I shall not stay. I am neither come to wrangle nor be reconciled; but I wish just to learn whether, after this evening's events, you intend to continue your intimacy with – '

'Oh, for mercy's sake,' interrupted the mistress, stamping her foot, 'for mercy's sake, let us hear no more of it now! Your cold blood cannot be worked into a fever: your veins are full of ice-water; but mine are boiling, and the sight of such chillness makes them dance.'

'To get rid of me, answer my question,' persevered Mr Linton. 'You *must* answer it; and that violence does not alarm me. I have found that you can be as stoical as anyone, when you please. Will you give up Heathcliff hereafter, or will you give up me? It is impossible for you to be *my* friend and *his* at the same time; and I absolutely *require* to know which you choose.'

'I require to be let alone!' exclaimed Catherine, furiously. 'I demand it! Don't you see I can scarcely stand? Edgar, you – you leave me!'

She rung the bell till it broke with a twang; I entered leisurely. It was enough to try the temper of a saint, such senseless, wicked rages! There she lay dashing her head against the arm of the sofa, and grinding her teeth, so that you might fancy she would crash them to splinters! Mr Linton stood looking at her in sudden compunction and fear. He told me to fetch some water. She had no breath for speaking. I brought a glass full; and, as she would not drink, I sprinkled it on her face. In few seconds she stretched herself out stiff, and turned up her eyes, while her cheeks, at once blanched and livid, assumed the aspect of death. Linton looked terrified.

'There is nothing in the world the matter,' I whispered. I did not want him to yield, though I could not help being afraid in my heart.

'She has blood on her lips!' he said, shuddering.

'Never mind!' I answered, tartly. And I told him how she had resolved, previous to his coming, on exhibiting a fit of frenzy. I incautiously gave the account aloud, and she heard me; for she started up – her hair flying over her shoulders, her eyes flashing, the muscles of her neck and arms standing out preternaturally. I made up my mind for broken bones, at least; but she only glared about her for an instant, and then rushed from the room. The master directed me to follow; I did, to her chamber door: she hindered me from going farther by securing it against me.

As she never offered to descend to breakfast next morning, I went to ask whether she would have some carried up. 'No!' she replied, peremptorily. The same question was repeated at dinner and tea; and again on the morrow after, and received the same answer. Mr Linton, on his part, spent his time in the library, and did not enquire concerning his wife's occupations. Isabella and he had had an hour's interview, during which he tried to elicit from her some sentiment of proper horror for Heathcliff's advances: but he could make nothing of her evasive replies, and was obliged to close the examination unsatisfactorily; adding, however, a solemn warning, that if she were so insane as to encourage that worthless suitor, it would dissolve all bonds of relationship between herself and him.

## *Chapter 12*

While Miss Linton moped about the park and garden, always silent, and almost always in tears; and her brother shut himself up among books that he never opened – wearying, I guessed, with a continual vague expectation that Catherine, repenting her conduct, would come of her own accord to ask pardon, and seek a reconciliation – and *she* fasted pertinaciously, under the idea, probably, that at every meal, Edgar was ready to choke for her absence, and pride alone held him from running to cast himself at her feet; I went about my household duties, convinced that the Grange had but one sensible soul in its walls, and that lodged in my body. I wasted no condolences on miss, nor any expostulations on my mistress; nor did I pay attention to the sighs of my master, who yearned to hear his lady's name, since he might not hear her voice. I determined they should come about as they pleased for me; and though it was a tiresomely slow process, I began to rejoice at length in a faint dawn of its progress: as I thought at first.

Mrs Linton on the third day unbarred her door, and having finished the water in her pitcher and decanter, desired a renewed supply, and a basin of gruel, for she believed she was dying. That I set down as a speech meant for Edgar's ears; I believed no such thing, so I kept it to myself, and brought her some tea and dry toast. She eat and drank eagerly; and sank back on her pillow again, clenching her hands and groaning. 'Oh, I will die,' she exclaimed, 'since no one cares anything about me. I wish I had not taken that.' Then a good while after I heard her murmur, 'No, I'll not die – he'd be glad – he does not love me at all – he would never miss me!'

'Did you want anything, ma'am?' I enquired, still preserving my external composure, in spite of her ghastly countenance and strange exaggerated manner.

'What is that apathetic being doing?' she demanded, pushing the thick entangled locks from her wasted face. 'Has he fallen into a lethargy, or is he dead?'

'Neither,' replied I; 'if you mean Mr Linton. He's tolerably well, I think, though his studies occupy him rather more than they ought: he is continually among his books, since he has no other society.'

I should not have spoken so if I had known her true condition, but I could not get rid of the notion that she acted a part of her disorder.

'Among his books!' she cried, confounded. 'And I dying! I on the brink of the grave! My God! does he know how I'm altered?' continued she, staring at her reflection in a mirror hanging against the opposite wall. 'Is that Catherine Linton? He imagines me in a pet – in play, perhaps. Cannot you inform him that it is frightful earnest? Nelly, if it be not too late, as soon as I learn how he feels, I'll choose between these two; either to starve at once – that would be no punishment unless he had a heart – or to recover, and leave the country. Are you speaking the truth about him now? Take care. Is he actually so utterly indifferent for my life?

'Why, ma'am,' I answered, 'the master has no idea of your being deranged; and of course he does not fear that you will let yourself die of hunger.'

'You think not? Cannot you tell him I will?' she returned. 'Persuade him! speak of your own mind: say you are certain I will!'

'No, you forget, Mrs Linton,' I suggested, 'that you have eaten some food with a relish this evening, and tomorrow you will perceive its good effects.'

'If I were only sure it would kill him,' she interrupted, 'I'd kill myself directly! These three awful nights, I've never closed my lids – and oh, I've been tormented! I've been haunted, Nelly! But I begin to fancy you don't like me. How strange! I thought, though everybody hated and despised each other, they could not avoid loving me. And they have all turned to enemies in a few hours: *they* have, I'm positive; the people *here*. How dreary to meet death, surrounded by their cold faces! Isabella, terrified and repelled, afraid to enter the room, it would be so terrible to watch Catherine go. And Edgar standing solemnly by to see it over; then offering prayers of thanks to God for restoring peace to his house, and going back to his *books*! What in the name of all that feels has he to do with *books* when I am dying?'

She could not bear the notion which I had put into her head of Mr Linton's philosophical resignation. Tossing about, she increased her feverish bewilderment to madness, and tore the pillow with her teeth; then raising herself up all burning, desired that I would open the window. We were in the middle of winter, the wind blew strong from the north-east, and I objected. Both the expressions flitting over her face, and the changes of her moods, began to alarm me terribly; and brought to my recollection her former illness, and the doctor's injunction that she should not be crossed. A minute previously she was violent; now, supported on one arm, and not noticing my refusal to obey her, she seemed to find childish diversion in pulling the feathers from the rents she had just made, and ranging them on the sheet according to their different species: her mind had strayed to other associations.

'That's a turkey's,' she murmured to herself; 'and this is a wild duck's; and this is a pigeon's. Ah, they put pigeons' feathers in the pillows – no wonder I couldn't die! Let me take care to throw it on the floor when I lie down. And here is a moorcock's; and this – I should know it among a thousand – it's a lapwing's. Bonny bird; wheeling over our heads in the middle of the moor. It wanted to get to its nest, for the clouds had touched the swells, and it felt rain coming. This feather was picked up from the heath, the bird was not shot: we saw its nest in the winter, full of little skeletons. Heathcliff set a trap over it, and the old ones dare not come. I made him promise he'd never shoot a lapwing after that, and he didn't. Yes, here are more! Did he shoot my lapwings, Nelly? Are they red, any of them? Let me look.'

'Give over with that baby-work!' I interrupted, dragging the pillow away, and turning the holes towards the mattress, for she was removing its contents by handfuls. 'Lie down and shut your eyes: you're wandering. There's a mess! The down is flying about like snow.'

I went here and there collecting it.

'I see in you, Nelly,' she continued, dreamily, 'an aged woman: you have grey hair and bent shoulders. This bed is the fairy cave under Penistone Crag, and you are gathering elf-bolts to hurt our heifers; pretending, while I am near, that they are only locks of wool. That's what you'll come to fifty years hence: I know you are not so now. I'm not wandering: you're mistaken, or else I should believe you really *were* that withered hag, and I should think I *was* under Penistone Crag; and I'm conscious it's night, and there are two candles on the table making the black press shine like jet.'

'The black press? Where is that?' I asked. 'You are talking in your sleep!'

'It's against the wall, as it always is,' she replied. 'It *does* appear odd – I see a face in it!'

'There is no press in the room, and never was,' said I, resuming my seat, and looping up the curtain that I might watch her.

'Don't *you* see that face?' she enquired, gazing earnestly at the mirror.

And say what I could, I was incapable of making her comprehend it to be her own; so I rose and covered it with a shawl.

'It's behind there still!' she pursued, anxiously. 'And it stirred. Who is it? I hope it will not come out when you are gone! Oh! Nelly, the room is haunted! I'm afraid of being alone!'

I took her hand in mine, and bid her be composed; for a succession of shudders convulsed her frame, and she *would* keep straining her gaze towards the glass.

'There's nobody here!' I insisted. 'It was *yourself*, Mrs Linton: you knew it a while since.'

'Myself!' she gasped, 'and the clock is striking twelve! It's true, then! that's dreadful!'

Her fingers clutched the clothes, and gathered them over her eyes. I attempted to steal to the door with an intention of calling her husband; but I was summoned back by a piercing shriek – the shawl had dropped from the frame.

'Why, what *is* the matter?' cried I. 'Who is coward now? Wake up! That is the glass – the mirror, Mrs Linton; and you see yourself in it and there am I, too, by your side.'

Trembling and bewildered, she held me fast, but the horror gradually passed from her countenance; its paleness gave place to a glow of shame.

'Oh, dear! I thought I was at home,' she sighed. 'I thought I was lying in my chamber at Wuthering Heights. Because I'm weak, my brain got confused, and I screamed unconsciously. Don't say anything; but stay with me. I dread sleeping: my dreams appal me.'

'A sound sleep would do you good, ma'am,' I answered; 'and I hope this suffering will prevent your trying starving again.'

'Oh, if I were but in my own bed in the old house!' she went on bitterly, wringing her hands. 'And that wind sounding in the firs by the lattice. Do let me feel it – it comes straight down the moor – do let me have one breath!'

To pacify her, I held the casement ajar a few seconds. A cold blast rushed through; I closed it, and returned to my post. She lay still now, her face bathed in tears. Exhaustion of body had entirely subdued her spirit: our fiery Catherine was no better than a wailing child.

'How long is it since I shut myself in here?' she asked, suddenly reviving.

'It was Monday evening,' I replied, 'and this is Thurs-day night, or rather Friday morning, at present.'

'What! of the same week?' she exclaimed. 'Only that brief time?'

'Long enough to live on nothing but cold water and ill-temper,' observed I.

'Well, it seems a weary number of hours,' she muttered doubtfully: 'it must be more. I remember being in the parlour after they had quarrelled, and Edgar being cruelly provoking, and me running into this room desperate. As soon as ever I had barred the door, utter blackness overwhelmed me, and I fell on the floor. I couldn't explain to Edgar how certain I felt of having a fit, or going raging mad, if he persisted in teasing me! I had no command of tongue, or brain, and he did not guess my agony, perhaps: it barely left me sense to try to escape from him and his voice. Before I recovered sufficiently to see and hear, it began to be dawn, and, Nelly, I'll tell you what I thought, and what has kept recurring and recurring till I feared for my reason. I thought as I lay there, with my head against that table leg, and my eyes dimly discerning the grey square of the window, that I was enclosed in the oak-panelled bed at home; and my heart ached with some great grief which, just waking, I could not recollect. I pondered, and worried myself to discover what it could be, and, most strangely, the whole last seven years of my life grew a blank! I did not recall that they had been at all. I was a child; my father was just buried, and my misery arose from the separation that Hindley had ordered between me and Heathcliff. I was laid alone, for the first time; and, rousing from a dismal dose after a night of weeping, I lifted my hand to push the panels aside: it struck the table-top! I swept it along the carpet, and then memory burst in: my late anguish was swallowed in a paroxysm of despair. I cannot say why I felt so wildly wretched: it must have been temporary derangement, for there is scarcely cause – but, supposing at twelve years old, I had been wrenched from the Heights, and every early association, and my all in all, as Heathcliff was at that time, and been converted at a stroke into Mrs Linton, the lady of Thrushcross Grange, and the wife of a stranger: an exile, and outcast, thenceforth, from what had been my world – you may fancy a glimpse of the abyss where I grovelled! Shake your head as you will, Nelly, *you* have helped to unsettle me! You should have spoken to Edgar, indeed you should, and compelled him to leave me quiet! Oh, I'm burning!

'I wish I were out of doors! I wish I were a girl again, half savage and hardy, and free . . . and laughing at injuries, not maddening under them! Why am I so changed? why does my blood rush into a hell of tumult at a few words? I'm sure I should be myself were I once among the heather on those hills. Open the window again wide: fasten it open! Quick, why don't you move?'

'Because I won't give you your death of cold,' I answered.

'You won't give me a chance of life, you mean,' she said sullenly. 'However, I'm not helpless yet; I'll open it myself.'

And sliding from the bed before I could hinder her, she crossed the room, walking very uncertainly, threw it back, and bent out, careless of the frosty air that cut about her shoulders as keen as a knife. I entreated, and finally attempted to force her to retire. But I soon found her delirious strength much surpassed mine (she *was* delirious, I became convinced by her subsequent actions and ravings). There was no moon, and everything beneath lay in misty darkness: not a light gleamed from any house, far or near – all had been extinguished long ago; and those at Wuthering Heights were never visible – still she asserted she caught their shining.

'Look!' she cried eagerly, 'that's my room with the candle in it, and the trees swaying before it . . . and the other candle is in Joseph's garret . . . Joseph sits up late, doesn't he? He's waiting till I come home that he may lock the gate . . . Well, he'll wait a while yet. It's a rough journey, and a sad heart to travel it; and we must pass by Gimmerton kirk, to go that journey! We've braved its ghosts often together, and dared each other to stand among the graves and ask them to come . . . But Heathcliff, if I dare you now, will you venture? If you do, I'll keep you. I'll not lie there by myself: they may bury me twelve feet deep, and throw the church down over me, but I won't rest till you are with me. I never will!'

She paused, and resumed with a strange smile. 'He's considering – he'd rather I'd come to him! Find a way, then! not through that kirkyard . . . You are slow! Be content, you always followed me!'

Perceiving it vain to argue against her insanity, I was planning how I could reach something to wrap about her, without quitting my hold of herself, for I could not trust her alone by the gaping lattice; when, to my consternation, I heard the rattle of the door-handle, and Mr Linton entered. He had only then come from the library; and, in passing through the lobby, had noticed our talking and been attracted by curiosity, or fear, to examine what it signified, at that late hour.

'Oh, sir!' I cried, checking the exclamation risen to his lips at the sight which met him, and the bleak atmosphere of the chamber. 'My poor mistress is ill, and she quite masters me: I cannot manage her at all; pray, come and persuade her to go to bed. Forget your anger, for she's hard to guide any way but her own.'

'Catherine ill?' he said, hastening to us. 'Shut the window, Ellen! Catherine! why . . . '

He was silent; the haggardness of Mrs Linton's appearance smote him speechless, and he could only glance from her to me in horrified astonishment.

'She's been fretting here,' I continued, 'and eating scarcely anything, and never complaining: she would admit none of us till this evening, and so we couldn't inform you of her state, as we were not aware of it ourselves; but it is nothing.'

I felt I uttered my explanations awkwardly; the master frowned. 'It is nothing, is it, Ellen Dean?' he said sternly. 'You shall account more clearly for keeping me ignorant of this!' And he took his wife in his arms, and looked at her with anguish.

At first she gave him no glance of recognition: he was invisible to her abstracted gaze. The delirium was not fixed, however; having weaned her eyes from contemplating the outer darkness, by degrees she centred her attention on him, and discovered who it was that held her.

'Ah! You are come, are you, Edgar Linton?' she said with angry animation . . . 'You are one of those things that are ever found when least wanted, and when you are wanted, never! I suppose we shall have plenty of lamentations now . . . I see we shall . . . but they can't keep me from my narrow home out yonder: my resting-place, where I'm bound before spring is over! There it is: not among the Lintons, mind, under the chapel-roof, but in the open air, with a headstone; and you may please yourself, whether you go to them or come to me!'

'Catherine, what have you done?' commenced the master. 'Am I nothing to you any more? Do you love that wretch Heath – '

'Hush!' cried Mrs Linton. 'Hush, this moment! You mention that name and I end the matter instantly, by a spring from the window!

What you touch at present you may have; but my soul will be on that hilltop before you lay hands on me again. I don't want you, Edgar: I'm past wanting you. Return to your books. I'm glad you possess a consolation, for all you had in me is gone.'

'Her mind wanders, sir,' I interposed. 'She has been talking nonsense the whole evening; but, let her have quiet, and proper attendance, and she'll rally . . . Hereafter, we must be cautious how we vex her.'

'I desire no further advice from you,' answered Mr Linton. 'You knew your mistress's nature, and you encouraged me to harass her. And not to give me one hint of how she has been these three days! It was heartless! Months of sickness could not cause such a change!'

I began to defend myself, thinking it too bad to be blamed for another's wicked waywardness. 'I knew Mrs Linton's nature to be headstrong and domineering,' cried I; 'but I didn't know that you wished to foster her fierce temper! I didn't know that, to humour her, I should wink at Mr Heathcliff. I performed the duty of a faithful servant in telling you, and I have got a faithful servant's wages! Well, it will teach me to be careful next time. Next time you may gather intelligence for yourself!'

'The next time you bring a tale to me, you shall quit my service, Ellen Dean,' he replied.

'You'd rather hear nothing about it, I suppose, then, Mr Linton?' said I. 'Heathcliff has your permission to come a-courting to miss, and to drop in at every opportunity your absence offers, on purpose to poison the mistress against you?'

Confused as Catherine was, her wits were alert at applying our conversation.

'Ah! Nelly has played traitor,' she exclaimed, passionately. 'Nelly is my hidden enemy. You witch! So you do seek elf-bolts to hurt us! Let me go, and I'll make her rue! I'll make her howl a recantation!'

A maniac's fury kindled under her brows; she struggled desperately to disengage herself from Linton's arms. I felt no inclination to tarry the event; and, resolving to seek medical aid on my own responsibility, I quitted the chamber.

In passing the garden to reach the road, at a place where a bridle hook is driven into the wall, I saw something white moved irregularly, evidently by another agent than the wind. Notwithstanding my hurry, I staid to examine it, lest ever after I should have the conviction impressed on my imagination that it was a creature of the other world. My surprise and perplexity were great to discover, by touch more than vision, Miss Isabella's springer, Fanny, suspended to a handkerchief, and nearly at its last gasp. I quickly released the animal, and lifted it into the garden. I had seen it follow its mistress upstairs, when she went to bed; and wondered much how it could have got out there, and what mischievous person had treated it so. While untying the knot round the hook, it seemed to me that I repeatedly caught the beat of horses' feet galloping at some distance; but there were such a number of things to occupy my reflections that I hardly gave the circumstance a thought: though it was a strange sound, in that place, at two o'clock in the morning.

Mr Kenneth was fortunately just issuing from his house to see a patient in the village as I came up the street; and my account of Catherine Linton's malady induced him to accompany me back immediately. He was a plain rough man; and he made no scruple to speak his doubts of her surviving this second attack; unless she were more submissive to his directions than she had shown herself before.

'Nelly Dean,' said he, 'I can't help fancying there's an extra cause for this. What has there been to do at the Grange? We've odd reports up here. A stout, hearty lass like Catherine does not fall ill for a trifle; and that sort of people should not either. It's hard work bringing them through fevers, and such things. How did it begin?'

'The master will inform you,' I answered; 'but you are acquainted with the

Earnshaws' violent dispositions, and Mrs Linton caps them all. I may say this; it commenced in a quarrel. She was struck during a tempest of passion with a kind of fit. That's her account, at least; for she flew off in the height of it, and locked herself up. Afterwards, she refused to eat, and now she alternately raves and remains in a half-dream; knowing those about her, but having her mind filled with all sorts of strange ideas and illusions.'

'Mr Linton will be sorry?' observed Kenneth, interrogatively.

'Sorry? he'll break his heart should anything happen!' I replied. 'Don't alarm him more than necessary.'

'Well, I told him to beware,' said my companion; 'and he must bide the consequences of neglecting my warning! Hasn't he been thick with Mr Heathcliff lately?'

'Heathcliff frequently visits at the Grange,' answered I, 'though more on the strength of the mistress having known him when a boy, than because the master likes his company. At present, he's discharged from the trouble of calling; owing to some presumptuous aspirations after Miss Linton which he manifested. I hardly think he'll be taken in again.'

'And does Miss Linton turn a cold shoulder on him?' was the doctor's next question.

'I'm not in her confidence,' returned I, reluctant to continue the subject.

'No, she's a sly one,' he remarked, shaking his head. 'She keeps her own counsel! But she's a real little fool. I have it from good authority, that, last night (and a pretty night it was!) she and Heathcliff were walking in the plantation at the back of your house, above two hours; and he pressed her not to go in again, but just mount his horse and away with him! My informant said she could only put him off by pledging her word of honour to be prepared on their first meeting after that: when it was to be, he didn't hear; but you urge Mr Linton to look sharp!'

This news filled me with fresh fears; I outstripped Kenneth, and ran most of the way back. The little dog was yelping in the garden yet. I spared a minute to open the gate for it, but instead of going to the house door, it coursed up and down snuffing the grass, and would have escaped to the road, had I not seized and conveyed it in with me. On ascending to Isabella's room, my suspicions were confirmed: it was empty. Had I been a few hours sooner, Mrs Linton's illness might have arrested her rash step.

But what could be done now? There was a bare possibility of overtaking them if I pursued instantly. *I* could not pursue them, however; and I dare not rouse the family, and fill the place with confusion; still less unfold the business to my master, absorbed as he was in his present calamity, and having no heart to spare for a second grief! I saw nothing for it but to hold my tongue, and suffer matters to take their course; and Kenneth being arrived, I went with a badly composed countenance to announce him. Catherine lay in a troubled sleep: her husband had succeeded in soothing the access of frenzy; he now hung over her pillow, watching every shade, and every change of her painfully expressive features.

The doctor, on examining the case for himself, spoke hopefully to him of its having a favourable termination, if we could only preserve around her perfect and constant tranquillity. To me, he signified the threatening danger was not so much death, as permanent alienation of intellect.

I did not close my eyes that night, nor did Mr Linton: indeed, we never went to bed; and the servants were all up long before the usual hour, moving through the house with stealthy tread, and exchanging whispers as they encountered each other in their vocations. Everyone was active, but Miss Isabella; and they began to remark how sound she slept: her brother, too, asked if she had risen, and seemed impatient for her presence, and hurt that she showed so little anxiety for her sister-in-law. I trembled lest he should send me to call her; but I was spared the pain of being the first proclaimant of her flight. One of the maids, a thoughtless girl, who had been on an early errand to Gimmerton, came panting upstairs, open-mouthed, and dashed into the chamber, crying – 'Oh, dear, dear! What mun we have next? Master, master, our young lady – '

'Hold your noise!' cried I hastily, enraged at her clamorous manner.

'Speak lower, Mary – What is the matter?' said Mr Linton. 'What ails your young lady?'

'She's gone, she's gone! Yon' Heathcliff's run off wi' her!' gasped the girl.

'That is not true!' exclaimed Linton, rising in agitation. 'It cannot be: how has the idea entered your head? Ellen Dean, go and seek her. It is incredible: it cannot be.'

As he spoke he took the servant to the door, and then repeated his demand to know her reasons for such an assertion.

'Why, I met on the road a lad that fetches milk here,' she stammered, 'and he asked whether we wern't in trouble at the Grange. I thought he meant for missis's sickness, so I answered, yes. Then says he, "they's somebody gone after 'em, I guess?" I stared. He saw I knew naught about it, and he told how a gentleman and lady had stopped to have a horse's shoe fastened at a blacksmith's shop, two miles out of Gimmerton, not very long after midnight! and how the blacksmith's lass had got up to spy who they were: she knew them both directly. And she noticed the man – Heathcliff it was, she felt certain, nob'dy could mistake him, besides – put a sovereign in her father's hand for payment. The lady had a cloak about her face; but having desired a sup of water, while she drank, it fell back, and she saw her very plain. Heathcliff held both bridles as they rode on, and they set their faces from the village, and went as fast as the rough roads would let them. The lass said nothing to her father, but she told it all over Gimmerton this morning.'

I ran and peeped, for form's sake, into Isabella's room; confirming, when I returned, the servant's statement. Mr Linton had resumed his seat by the bed; on my re-entrance, he raised his eyes, read the meaning of my blank aspect, and dropped them without giving an order, or uttering a word.

'Are we to try any measures for overtaking and bringing her back,' I enquired. 'How should we do?'

'She went of her own accord,' answered the master; 'she had a right to go if she pleased. Trouble me no more about her. Hereafter she is only my sister in name: not because I disown her, but because she has disowned me.'

And that was all he said on the subject: he did not make a single enquiry further, nor mention her in any way, except directing me to send what property she had in the house to her fresh home, wherever it was, when I knew it.

## *Chapter 13*

For two months the fugitives remained absent; in those two months, Mrs Linton encountered and conquered the worst shock of what was denominated a brain fever. No mother could have nursed an only child more devotedly than Edgar tended her. Day and night he was watching, and patiently enduring all the annoyances that irritable nerves and a shaken reason could inflict; and, though Kenneth remarked that what he saved from the grave would only recompense his care by forming the source of constant future anxiety – in fact, that his health and strength were being sacrificed to preserve a mere ruin of humanity – he knew no limits in gratitude and joy when Catherine's life was declared out of danger; and hour after hour he would sit beside her, tracing the gradual return to bodily health, and flattering his too sanguine hopes with the illusion that her mind would settle back to its right balance also, and she would soon be entirely her former self.

The first time she left her chamber was at the commencement of the following March. Mr Linton had put on her pillow, in the morning, a handful of golden crocuses; her eye, long stranger to any gleam of pleasure, caught them in waking, and shone delighted as she gathered them eagerly together.

'These are the earliest flowers at the Heights,' she exclaimed. 'They remind me of soft thaw winds, and warm sunshine, and nearly melted snow. Edgar, is there not a south wind, and is not the snow almost gone?'

'The snow is quite gone down here, darling,' replied her husband; 'and I only see two white spots on the whole range of moors: the sky is blue, and the larks are singing, and the becks and brooks are all brim full. Catherine, last spring at this time, I was longing to have you under this roof: now, I wish you were a mile or two up those hills: the air blows so sweetly, I feel that it would cure you.'

'I shall never be there, but once more,' said the invalid; 'and then you'll leave me, and I shall remain for ever. Next spring you'll long again to have me under this roof, and you'll look back and think you were happy today.'

Linton lavished on her the kindest caresses, and tried to cheer her by the fondest words; but, vaguely regarding the flowers, she let the tears collect on her lashes and stream down her cheeks unheeding. We knew she was really better, and, therefore, decided that long confinement to a single place produced much of this despondency, and it might be partially removed by a change of scene. The master told me to light a fire in the many-weeks'-deserted parlour, and to set an easy-chair in the sunshine by the window; and then he brought her down, and she sat a long while enjoying the genial heat, and, as we expected, revived by the objects round her: which, though familiar, were free from the dreary associations investing her hated sick-chamber. By evening, she seemed greatly exhausted; yet no arguments could persuade her to return to that apartment, and I had to arrange the parlour sofa for her bed, till another room could be prepared. To obviate the fatigue of mounting and descending the stairs, we fitted up this, where you lie at present: on the same floor with the parlour; and she was soon strong enough to move from one to the other, leaning on Edgar's arm. Ah, I thought myself, she might recover, so waited on as she was. And there was double cause to desire it, for on her existence depended that of another: we cherished the hope that in a little while, Mr Linton's heart would be gladdened, and his lands secured from a stranger's gripe, by the birth of an heir.

I should mention that Isabella sent to her brother, some six weeks from her departure, a short note, announcing her marriage with Heathcliff. It appeared dry and cold; but at the bottom was dotted in with pencil an obscure apology, and an entreaty for kind remembrance and reconciliation, if her proceeding had offended him: asserting that she could not help it then, and being done, she had now no power to repeal it. Linton did not reply to this, I believe; and, in a fortnight more, I got a long letter which I considered odd, coming from the pen of a bride just out of the honeymoon. I'll read it: for I keep it yet. Any relic of the dead is precious, if they were valued living.

Dear Ellen, it begins.

I came last night to Wuthering Heights, and heard, for the first time, that Catherine has been, and is yet, very ill. I must not write to her, I suppose, and my brother is either too angry or too distressed to answer what I send him. Still, I must write to somebody, and the only choice left me is you.

Inform Edgar that I'd give the world to see his face again – that my heart returned to Thrushcross Grange in twenty-four hours after I left it, and is there at this moment, full of warm feelings for him, and Catherine! *I can't follow it though* – (those words are underlined) they need not expect me, and they may draw what conclusions they please; taking care, however, to lay nothing it the door of my weak will or deficient affection.

The remainder of the letter is for yourself alone. I want to ask you two questions; the first is – How did you contrive to preserve the common sympathies of human nature when you resided here? I cannot recognise any sentiment which those around share with me.

The second question, I have great interest in; it is this – Is Mr Heathcliff a man? If so, is he mad? And if not, is he a devil? I shan't tell my reasons for making this enquiry; but I beseech you to explain, if you can, what I have married: that is, when you call to see me; and you must call, Ellen, very soon. Don't write but come, and bring me something from Edgar.

Now, you shall hear how I have been received in my new home, as I am led to imagine the Heights will be. It is to amuse myself that I dwell on such subjects as the lack of external comforts: they never occupy my thoughts, except at the moment when I miss them. I should laugh and dance for joy, if I found their absence was the total of my miseries, and the rest was an unnatural dream!

The sun set behind the Grange, as we turned on to the moors; by that, I judged it to be six o'clock; and my companion halted half an hour, to inspect the park, and the gardens, and, probably, the place itself, as well as he could; so it was dark when we dismounted in the paved yard of the farmhouse, and your old fellow-servant, Joseph, issued out to receive us by the light of a dip candle. He did it with a courtesy that redounded to his credit. His first act was to elevate his torch to a level with my face, squint malignantly, project his under lip, and turn away.

Then he took the two horses, and led them into the stables; reappearing for the purpose of locking the outer gate, as if we lived in an ancient castle.

Heathcliff stayed to speak to him, and I entered the kitchen – a dingy, untidy hole; I dare say you would not know it, it is so changed since it was in your charge. By the fire stood a ruffianly child, strong in limb and dirty in garb, with a look of Catherine in his eyes and about his mouth.

'This is Edgar's legal nephew,' I reflected – 'mine in a manner; I must shake hands, and – yes – I must kiss him. It is right to establish a good understanding at the beginning.'

I approached, and, attempting to take his chubby fist, said – 'How do you do, my dear?'

He replied in a jargon I did not comprehend. 'Shall you and I be friends, Hareton?' was my next essay at conversation.

An oath, and a threat to set Throttler on me if I did not 'frame off', rewarded my perseverance.

'Hey, Throttler, lad!' whispered the little wretch, rousing a half-bred bulldog from its lair in a corner. 'Now, wilt tuh be ganging?' he asked authoritatively.

Love for my life urged a compliance; I stepped over the threshold to wait till the others should enter. Mr Heathcliff was nowhere visible; and Joseph, whom I followed to the stables, and requested to accompany me in, after staring and muttering to himself, screwed up his nose and replied – 'Mim! mim! mim! Did iver Christian body hear owt like it? Minching un' munching! Hah can Aw tell whet ye say?'

'I say, I wish you to come with me into the house!' I cried, thinking him deaf, yet highly disgusted at his rudeness.

'Nor nuh me! Aw getten summut else to do,' he answered, and continued his work; moving his lantern jaws meanwhile, and surveying my dress and countenance (the former a great deal too fine, but the latter, I'm sure, as sad as he could desire) with sovereign contempt.

I walked round the yard, and through a wicket, to another door, at which I took the liberty of knocking, in hopes some more civil servant might show himself. After a short suspense, it was opened by a tall, gaunt man, without neckerchief, and otherwise extremely slovenly; his features were lost in masses of shaggy hair that hung on his shoulders; and *his* eyes, too, were like a ghostly Catherine's, with all their beauty annihilated.

'What's your business here?' he demanded, grimly. 'Who are you?'

'My name *was* Isabella Linton,' I replied. 'You've seen me before, sir. I'm lately married to Mr Heathcliff, and he has brought me here – I suppose by your permission.'

'Is he come back, then?' asked the hermit, glaring like a hungry wolf.

'Yes – we came just now,' I said; 'but he left me by the kitchen door; and when I would have gone in, your little boy played sentinel over the place, and frightened me off by the help of a bulldog.'

'It's well the hellish villain has kept his word!' growled my future host, searching the darkness beyond me in expectation of discovering Heathcliff; and then he indulged in a soliloquy of execrations, and threats of what he would have done had the 'fiend' deceived him.

I repented having tried this second entrance, and was almost inclined to slip away before he finished cursing, but ere I could execute that intention, he ordered me in, and shut and re-fastened the door. There was a great fire, and that was all the light in the huge apartment, whose floor had grown a uniform grey; and the once brilliant pewter dishes, which used to attract my gaze when I was a girl, partook of a similar obscurity, created by tarnish and dust. I enquired whether I might call the maid, and be conducted to a bedroom? Mr Earnshaw vouchsafed no answer. He walked up and down, with his hands in his pockets, apparently quite forgetting my presence; and his abstraction was evidently so deep, and his whole aspect so misanthropical, that I shrank from disturbing him again.

You'll not be surprised, Ellen, at my feeling particularly cheerless, seated in worse than solitude on that inhospitable hearth, and remembering that four miles distant lay my delightful home, containing the only people I loved on earth; and there might as well be the Atlantic to part us, instead of those four miles: I could not overpass them! I questioned with myself – where must I turn for comfort? And – mind you don't tell Edgar, or Catherine – above every sorrow beside, this rose pre-eminent: despair at finding nobody who could or would be my ally against Heathcliff! I had sought shelter at Wuthering Heights, almost gladly, because I was secured by that arrangement from living alone with him; but he knew the people we were coming amongst, and he did not fear their intermeddling.

I sat and thought a doleful time; the clock struck eight, and nine, and still my companion paced to and fro, his head bent on his breast, and perfectly silent, unless a groan or a bitter ejaculation forced itself out at intervals. I listened to detect a woman's voice in the house, and filled the interim with wild regrets and dismal anticipations, which, at last, spoke audibly in irrepressible sighing and weeping. I was not aware how openly I grieved, till Earnshaw halted opposite, in his measured walk, and gave me a stare of newly-awakened surprise.

Taking advantage of his recovered attention, I exclaimed – 'I'm tired with my journey, and I want to go to bed! Where is the maidservant? Direct me to her, as she won't come to me!'

'We have none,' he answered; 'you must wait on yourself!'

'Where must I sleep, then?' I sobbed; I was beyond regarding self-respect, weighed down by fatigue and wretchedness.

'Joseph will show you Heathcliff's chamber,' said he; 'open that door – he's in there.'

I was going to obey, but he suddenly arrested me, and added in the strangest tone – 'Be so good as to turn your lock, and draw your bolt – don't omit it!'

'Well!' I said. 'But why, Mr Earnshaw?' I did not relish the notion of deliberately fastening myself in with Heathcliff.

'Look here!' he replied, pulling from his waistcoat a curiously constructed pistol, having a double-edged spring knife attached to the barrel. 'That's a great tempter to a desperate man, is it not? I cannot resist going up with this every night, and trying his door. If once I find it open, he's done for! I do it invariably, even though the minute before I have been recalling a hundred reasons that should make me refrain: it is some devil that urges me to thwart my own schemes by killing him – you fight against that devil for love as long as you may; when the time comes, not all the angels in heaven shall save him!'

I surveyed the weapon inquisitively; a hideous notion struck me: how powerful I should be possessing such an instrument! I took it from his hand, and touched the blade. He looked astonished at the expression my face assumed during a brief second: it was not horror, it was covetousness. He snatched the pistol back, jealously; shut the knife, and returned it to its concealment.

'I don't care if you tell him,' said he. 'Put him on his guard, and watch for him. You know the terms we are on, I see: his danger does not shock you.'

'What has Heathcliff done to you?' I asked. 'In what has he wronged you, to warrant this appalling hatred? Wouldn't it be wiser to bid him quit the house?'

'No!' thundered Earnshaw; 'should he offer to leave me, he's a dead man: persuade him to attempt it, and you are a murderess! Am I to lose *all*, without a chance of retrieval? Is Hareton to be a beggar? Oh, damnation! I *will* have it back: and I'll have *his* gold too: and then his blood; and hell shall have his soul! It will be ten times blacker with that guest than ever it was before!'

You've acquainted me, Ellen, with your old master's habits. He is clearly on the verge of madness: he was so last night at least. I shuddered to be near him, and thought on the servant's ill-bred moroseness as comparatively agreeable. He now recommenced his moody walk, and I raised the latch, and escaped into the kitchen. Joseph was bending over the fire, peering into a large pan that swung above it; and a wooden bowl of oatmeal stood on the settle close by. The contents of the pan began to boil, and he turned to plunge his hand into the bowl; I conjectured that this preparation was probably for our supper, and, being hungry, I resolved it should be eatable; so, crying out sharply, '*I*'ll make the porridge!' I removed the vessel out of his reach, and proceeded to take off my hat and riding habit. 'Mr Earnshaw,' I continued, 'directs me to wait on myself: I will. I'm not going to act the lady among you, for fear I should starve.'

'Gooid Lord!' he muttered, sitting down, and stroking his ribbed stockings from the knee to the ankle. 'If they's tuh be fresh ortherings – just when aw getten used tuh two maisters, if aw mun hev a *mistress* set o'er my heead, it's loike time tuh be flitting. Aw niver *did* think tuh say t' day ut aw mud lave th' owld place – but aw daht it's nigh at hend!'

This lamentation drew no notice from me: I went briskly to work, sighing to remember a period when it would have been all merry fun; but compelled speedily to drive off the remembrance. It racked me to recall past happiness, and the greater peril there was of conjuring up its apparition, the quicker the thible ran round, and the faster the handfuls of meal fell into the water. Joseph beheld my style of cookery with growing indignation.

'Thear!' he ejaculated. 'Hareton, thah willut sup thy porridge tuh neeght; they'll be nowt bud lumps as big as maw nave. Thear, agean! Aw'd fling in bowl un all, if aw wer yah! Thear, pale t' guilp off, un' then yah'll hae done wi't. Bang, bang. It's a marcy t' bothom isn't deaved aht!'

It *was* rather a rough mess, I own, when poured into the basins; four had been provided, and a gallon pitcher of new milk was brought from the dairy, which Hareton seized and commenced drinking and spilling from the expansive lip. I expostulated, and desired that he should have his in a mug; affirming that I could not taste the liquid treated so dirtily. The old cynic chose to be vastly offended at this nicety; assuring me, repeatedly, that 'the barn was every bit as gooid' as I, 'and every bit as wollsome,' and wondering how I could fashion to be so conceited. Meanwhile, the infant ruffian continued sucking; and glowered up at me defyingly, as he slavered into the jug.

'I shall have my supper in another room,' I said. 'Have you no place you call a parlour?'

'*Parlour!*' he echoed, sneeringly, '*parlour!* Nay, we've noa *parlours*. If yah dunnut loike wer company, they's maister's; un' if yah dunnut loike maister, they's us.'

'Then I shall go upstairs,' I answered; 'shew me a chamber.'

I put my basin on a tray, and went myself to fetch some more milk. With great grumblings, the fellow rose, and preceded me in my ascent: we mounted to the garrets; he opening a door, now and then, to look into the apartments we passed.

'Here's a rahm,' he said, at last, flinging back a cranky board on hinges. 'It's weel eneugh tuh ate a few porridge in. They's a pack uh corn i' t' corner, thear, meeterly clane; if yah're feared uh muckying yer grand silk cloes, spread yer hankerchir ut t' top on 't.'

The 'rahm' was a kind of lumber-hole smelling strong of malt and grain; various sacks of which articles were piled around, leaving a wide, bare space in the middle.

'Why, man!' I exclaimed, facing him angrily, 'this is not a place to sleep in. I wish to see my bedroom.'

'*Bed-rume!*' he repeated, in a tone of mockery. 'Yah's see all t' *bed-rumes* thear is – yon's mine.'

He pointed into the second garret, only differing from the first in being more naked about the walls, and having a large, low, curtainless bed, with an indigo-coloured quilt, at one end.

'What do I want with yours?' I retorted. 'I suppose Mr Heathcliff does not lodge at the top of the house, does he?'

'Oh, it's Maister *Hathecliff's* yah're wenting?' cried he, as if making a new discovery. 'Couldn't ye uh said soa, at onst? Un then, aw mud uh telled ye, baht all this wark, ut that's just one yah cannut sea – he allas keeps it locked, un' nob'dy iver mells on 't but hisseln.'

'You've a nice house, Joseph,' I could not refrain from observing, 'and pleasant inmates; and I think the concentrated essence of all the madness in the world took up its abode in my brain the day I linked my fate with theirs! However, that is not to the present purpose – there are other rooms. For Heaven's sake, be quick, and let me settle somewhere!'

He made no reply to this adjuration; only plodding doggedly down the wooden steps, and halting before an apartment which, from that halt and the superior quality of its furniture, I conjectured to be the best one. There was a carpet: a good one, but the pattern was obliterated by dust; a fireplace hung with cut paper, dropping to pieces; a handsome oak-bedstead with ample crimson curtains of rather expensive material and modern make; but they had evidently experienced rough usage; the valances hung in festoons, wrenched from their rings, and the iron rod supporting them was bent in an arc, on one side, causing the drapery to trail upon the floor. The chairs were also damaged, many of them severely; and deep indentations deformed the panels of the walls. I was endeavouring to gather resolution for entering, and taking possession, when my fool of a guide announced, 'This here is t' maister's.' My supper by this time was cold, my appetite gone, and my patience exhausted. I insisted on being provided instantly with a place of refuge, and means of repose.

'Whear the divil,' began the religious elder. 'The Lord bless us! The Lord forgie us! Whear the *hell*, wold ye gang? Ye marred, wearisome nowt! Yah seen all bud Hareton's bit uf a cham'er. They's nut another hoile tuh lig dahn in i' th' hahse!'

I was so vexed, I flung my tray and its contents on the ground; and then seated myself at the stair head, hid my face in my hands, and cried.

'Ech! ech!' exclaimed Joseph. 'Weel done, Miss Cathy! Weel done, Miss Cathy! Hahsiver, t' maister sall just tum'le o'er them brocken pots; un' then we's hear summut; we's hear hah it's tuh be. Gooid-for-nowt madling! yah desarve pining froo this tuh Churstmas, flinging t' precious gifts uh God under fooit i' yer flaysome rages! Bud, aw'm mista'en if yah shew yer sperrit lang. Will Hathecliff bide sich bonny ways, think ye? Aw nobbut wish he muh cotch ye i' that plisky. Aw nobbut wish he may.'

And so he went scolding to his den beneath, taking the candle with him; and I remained in the dark. The period of reflection succeeding this silly action, compelled me to admit the necessity of smothering my pride and choking my wrath, and bestirring myself to remove its effects. An unexpected aid presently appeared in the shape of Throttler, whom I now recognised as a son of our old Skulker: it had spent its whelphood at the Grange, and was given by my father to Mr Hindley. I fancy it knew me: it pushed its nose against mine by way of salute, and then hastened to devour the porridge; while I groped from step to step, collecting the shattered earthenware, and drying the spatters of milk from the bannister with my pocket-handkerchief. Our labours were scarcely over when I heard Earnshaw's tread in the passage; my assistant tucked in his tail, and pressed to the wall: I stole into the nearest doorway. The dog's endeavour to avoid him was unsuccessful; as I guessed by a scutter downstairs, and a prolonged, piteous yelping. I had better luck: he passed on, entered his chamber, and shut the door.

Directly after Joseph came up with Hareton, to put him to bed. I had found shelter in Hareton's room, and the old man, on seeing me, said – 'They's rahm fur boath yah, un yer pride, nah, aw sud think i' th' hahse. It's empty; yah muh hev it all tuh yerseln, un Him as allas maks a third, i' sich ill company!'

Gladly did I take advantage of this intimation; and the minute I flung myself into a chair, by the fire, I nodded, and slept. My slumber was deep and sweet, though over far too soon. Mr Heathcliff awoke me; he had just come in, and demanded, in his loving manner, what I was doing there? I told him the cause of my staying up so late – that he had the key of our room in his pocket. The adjective *our* gave mortal offence. He swore it was not, nor ever should be mine; and he'd – but I'll not repeat his language, nor describe his habitual conduct: he is ingenious and unresting in seeking to gain my abhorrence! I sometimes wonder at him with an intensity that deadens my fear: yet, I assure you, a tiger or a venomous serpent could not rouse terror in me equal to that which he wakens. He told me of Catherine's illness, and accused my brother of causing it; promising that I should be Edgar's proxy in suffering, till he could get hold of him.

I do hate him – I am wretched – I have been a fool! Beware of uttering one breath of this to anyone at the Grange. I shall expect you every day – don't disappoint me! Isabella.

## *Chapter 14*

As soon as I had perused this epistle, I went to the master, and informed him that his sister had arrived at the Heights, and sent me a letter expressing her sorrow for Mrs Linton's situation, and her ardent desire to see him; with a wish that he would transmit to her, as early as possible, some token of forgiveness by me.

'Forgiveness!' said Linton. 'I have nothing to forgive her, Ellen. You may call at Wuthering Heights this afternoon, if you like, and say that I am not *angry*, but I'm *sorry* to have lost her; especially as I can never think she'll be happy. It is out of the question my going to see her, however: we are eternally divided; and should she really wish to oblige me, let her persuade the villain she has married to leave the country.'

'And you won't write her a little note, sir?' I asked imploringly.

'No,' he answered. 'It is needless. My communication with Heathcliff's family shall be as sparing as his with mine. It shall not exist!'

Mr Edgar's coldness depressed me exceedingly; and all the way from the Grange I puzzled my brains how to put more heart into what he said, when I repeated it; and how to soften his refusal of even a few lines to console Isabella. I dare say she had been on the watch for me since morning: I saw her looking through the lattice, as I came up the garden causeway, and I nodded to her; but she drew back, as if afraid of being observed. I entered without knocking. There never was such a dreary, dismal scene as the formerly cheerful house presented! I must confess, that if I had been in the young lady's place, I would, at least, have swept the hearth, and wiped the tables with a duster. But she already partook of the pervading spirit of neglect which encompassed her. Her pretty face was wan and listless; her hair uncurled: some locks hanging lankly down, and some carelessly twisted round her head. Probably she had not touched her dress since yester-evening. Hindley was not there. Mr Heathcliff sat at a table, turning over some papers in his pocketbook; but he rose when I appeared, asked me how I did, quite friendly, and offered me a chair. He was the only thing there that seemed decent; and I thought he never looked better. So much had circumstances altered their positions, that he would certainly have struck a stranger as a born and bred gentleman, and his wife as a thorough little slattern! She came forward eagerly to greet me; and held out one hand to take the expected letter. I shook my head. She wouldn't understand the hint, but followed me to a sideboard, where I went to lay my bonnet, and importuned me in a whisper to give her directly what I had brought.

Heathcliff guessed the meaning of her manoeuvres, and said – 'If you have got anything for Isabella (as no doubt you have, Nelly), give it to her. You needn't make a secret of it: we have no secrets between us.'

'Oh, I have nothing,' I replied, thinking it best to speak the truth at once. 'My master bid me tell his sister that she must not expect either a letter or a visit from him at present. He sends his love, ma'am, and his wishes for your happiness, and his pardon for the grief you have occasioned; but he thinks that after this time, his household and the household here should drop intercommunication, as nothing good could come of keeping it up.'

Mrs Heathcliff's lip quivered slightly, and she returned to her seat in the window. Her husband took his stand on the hearthstone, near me, and began to put questions concerning Catherine. I told him as much as I thought proper of her illness, and he extorted from me, by cross-examination, most of the facts connected with its origin. I blamed her, as she deserved, for bringing it all on herself; and ended by hoping that he would follow Mr Linton's example, and avoid future interference with his family, for good or evil.

'Mrs Linton is now just recovering,' I said; 'she'll never be like she was, but her life is spared; and if you really have a regard for her, you'll shun crossing her way again: nay, you'll move out of this country entirely; and that you may not regret it, I'll inform you Catherine Linton is as different now from your old friend Catherine Earnshaw, as that young lady is different from me. Her appearance is changed greatly, her character much more so; and the person who is compelled, of necessity, to be her companion, will only sustain his affection hereafter by the remembrance of what she once was, by common humanity, and a sense of duty!'

'That is quite possible,' remarked Heathcliff, forcing himself to seem calm: 'quite possible that your master should have nothing but common humanity and a sense of duty to fall back upon. But do you imagine that I shall leave Catherine to his *duty* and *humanity*? and can you compare my feelings respecting Catherine to his? Before you leave this house, I must exact a promise from you, that you'll get me an interview with her: consent, or refuse, I *will* see her! What do you say?'

'I say, Mr Heathcliff,' I replied, 'you must not: you never shall, through my means. Another encounter between you and the master would kill her altogether.'

'With your aid, that may be avoided,' he continued; 'and should there be danger of such an event – should he be the cause of adding a single trouble more to her existence – why, I think, I shall be justified in going to extremes! I wish you had sincerity enough to tell me whether Catherine would suffer greatly from his loss: the fear that she would restrains me. And there you see the distinction between our feelings: had he been in my place and I in his, though I hated him with a hatred that turned my life to gall, I never would have raised a hand against him. You may look incredulous, if you please! I never would have banished him from her society as long as she desired his. The moment her regard ceased, I would have torn his heart out, and drank his blood! But, till then – if you don't believe me, you don't know me – till then, I would have died by inches before I touched a single hair of his head!'

'And yet,' I interrupted, 'you have no scruples in completely ruining all hopes of her perfect restoration, by thrusting yourself into her remembrance now, when she has nearly forgotten you, and involving her in a new tumult of discord and distress.'

'You suppose she has nearly forgotten me?' he said. 'Oh, Nelly! You know she has not! You know as well as I do, that for every thought she spends on Linton, she spends a thousand on me! At a most miserable period of my life, I had a notion of the kind: it haunted me on my return to the neighbourhood last summer; but only her own assurance could make me admit the horrible idea again. And then, Linton would be nothing, nor Hindley, nor all the dreams that ever I dreamt. Two words would comprehend my future – *death* and *hell*: existence, after losing her, would be hell. Yet I was a fool to fancy for a moment that she valued Edgar Linton's attachment more than mine. If he loved with all the powers of his puny being, he couldn't love as much in eighty years as I could in a day. And Catherine has a heart as deep as I have: the sea could be as readily contained in that horse-trough, as her whole affection be monopolised by him. Tush! He is scarcely a degree dearer to her than her dog, or her horse. It is not in him to be loved like me: how can she love in him what he has not?'

'Catherine and Edgar are as fond of each other as any two people can be,' cried Isabella, with sudden vivacity. 'No one has a right to talk in that manner, and I won't hear my brother depreciated in silence!'

'Your brother is wondrous fond of you too, isn't he?' observed Heathcliff scornfully. 'He turns you adrift on the world with surprising alacrity.'

'He is not aware of what I suffer,' she replied. 'I didn't tell him that.'

'You have been telling him something, then: you have written, have you?'

'To say that I was married, I did write – you saw the note.'

'And nothing since?'

'No.'

'My young lady is looking sadly the worse for her change of condition,' I remarked. 'Somebody's love comes short in her case, obviously: whose, I may guess; but, perhaps, I shouldn't say.'

'I should guess it was her own,' said Heathcliff. 'She degenerates into a mere slut! She is tired of trying to please me, uncommonly early. You'd hardly credit it, but the very morrow of our wedding, she was weeping to go home. However, she'll suit this house so much the better for not being over nice, and I'll take care she does not disgrace me by rambling abroad.'

'Well, sir,' returned I, 'I hope you'll consider that Mrs Heathcliff is accustomed to be looked after and waited on; and that she has been brought up like an only daughter, whom, everyone was ready to serve. You must let her have a maid to keep things tidy about her, and you must treat her kindly. Whatever be your notion of Mr Edgar, you cannot doubt that she has a capacity for strong attachments, or she wouldn't have abandoned the elegancies, and comforts, and friends of her former home, to fix contentedly, in such a wilderness as this, with you.'

'She abandoned them under a delusion,' he answered; 'picturing in me a hero of romance, and expecting unlimited indulgences from my chivalrous devotion. I can hardly regard her in the light of a rational creature, so obstinately has she persisted in forming a fabulous notion of my character, and acting on the false impressions she cherished. But, at last, I think she begins to know me: I don't perceive the silly smiles and grimaces that provoked me at first; and the senseless incapability of discerning that I was in earnest when I gave her my opinion of her infatuation and herself. It was a marvellous effort of perspicacity to discover that I did not love her. I believed, at one time, no lessons could teach her that! And yet it is poorly learnt; for this morning she announced, as a piece of appalling intelligence, that I had actually succeeded in making her hate me! A positive labour of Hercules, I assure you! If it be achieved, I have cause to return thanks. Can I trust your assertion, Isabella? Are you sure you hate me? If I let you alone for half a day, won't you come sighing and wheedling to me again? I dare say she would rather I had seemed all tenderness before you: it wounds her vanity to have the truth exposed. But I don't care who knows that the passion was wholly on one side; and I never told her a lie about it. She cannot accuse me of showing a bit of deceitful softness. The first thing she saw me do, on coming out of the Grange, was to hang up her little dog; and when she pleaded for it, the first words I uttered were a wish that I had the hanging of every being belonging to her, except one: possibly she took that exception for herself. But no brutality disgusted her: I suppose she has an innate admiration of it, if only her precious person were secure from injury! Now, was it not the depth of absurdity – of genuine idiocy, for that pitiful, slavish, mean-minded brach to dream that I could love her? Tell your master, Nelly, that I never, in all my life, met with such an abject thing as she is. She even disgraces the name of Linton; and I've sometimes relented, from pure lack of invention, in my experiments on what she could endure, and still creep shamefully cringing back! But tell him, also, to set his fraternal and magisterial heart at ease, that I keep strictly within the limits of the law. I have avoided, up to this period, giving her the slightest right to claim a separation; and, what's more, she'd thank nobody for dividing us. If she desired to go she might: the nuisance of her presence outweighs the gratification to be derived from tormenting her!'

'Mr Heathcliff,' said I, 'this is the talk of a madman, and your wife, most likely, is convinced you are mad; and, for that reason, she has borne with you hitherto: but now that you say she may go, she'll doubtless avail herself of the permission. You are not so bewitched, ma'am, are you, as to remain with him of your own accord?'

'Take care, Ellen!' answered Isabella, her eyes sparkling irefully; there was no misdoubting by their expression, the full success of her partner's endeavours to make himself detested. 'Don't put faith in a single word he speaks. He's a lying fiend! A monster, and not a human being! I've been told I might leave him before; and I've made the attempt, but I dare not repeat it! Only, Ellen, promise you'll not mention a syllable of his infamous conversation to my brother or Catherine. Whatever he may pretend, he wishes to provoke Edgar to desperation: he says he has married me on purpose to obtain power over him; and he shan't obtain it – I'll die first! I just hope, I pray, that he may forget his diabolical prudence, and kill me! The single pleasure I can imagine, is to die, or to see him dead!'

'There – that will do for the present!' said Heathcliff. 'If you are called upon in a court of law, you'll remember her language, Nelly! And take a good look at that countenance: she's near the point which would suit me. No; you're not fit to be your own guardian, Isabella, now; and I, being your legal protector, must retain you in my custody, however distasteful the obligation may be. Go upstairs; I have something to say to Ellen Dean in private. That's not the way: upstairs, I tell you! Why, this is the road upstairs, child!'

He seized, and thrust her from the room; and returned muttering – 'I have no pity! I have no pity! The more the worms writhe, the more I yearn to crush out their entrails! It is a moral teething; and I grind with greater energy, in proportion to the increase of pain.'

'Do you understand what the word pity means?' I said, hastening to resume my bonnet. 'Did you ever feel a touch of it in your life?'

'Put that down!' he interrupted, perceiving my intention to depart. 'You are not going yet. Come here now, Nelly: I must either persuade or compel you to aid me in fulfilling my determination to see Catherine, and that without delay. I swear that I meditate no harm: I don't desire to cause any disturbance, or to exasperate or insult Mr Linton; I only wish to hear from herself how she is, and why she has been ill; and to ask if anything that I could do would be of use to her. Last night, I was in the Grange garden six hours, and I'll return there tonight; and every night I'll haunt the place, and every day, till I find an opportunity of entering. If Edgar Linton meets me, I shall not hesitate to knock him down, and give him enough to ensure his quiescence while I stay. If his servants oppose me,

I shall threaten them off with these pistols. But wouldn't it be better to prevent my coming in contact with them, or their master? And you could do it so easily. I'd warn you when I came, and then you might let me in unobserved, as soon as she was alone, and watch till I departed, your conscience quite calm: you would be hindering mischief.'

I protested against playing that treacherous part in my employer's house: and besides, I urged the cruelty and selfishness of his destroying Mrs Linton's tranquillity for his satisfaction. 'The commonest occurrence startles her painfully,' I said. 'She's all nerves, and she couldn't bear the surprise, I'm positive. Don't persist, sir! Or else, I shall be obliged to inform my master of your designs; and he'll take measures to secure his house and its inmates from any such unwarrantable intrusions!'

'In that case, I'll take measures to secure you, woman!' exclaimed Heathcliff; 'you shall not leave Wuthering Heights till tomorrow morning. It is a foolish story to assert that Catherine could not bear to see me; and as to surprising her, I don't desire it: you must prepare her – ask her if I may come. You say she never mentions my name, and that I am never mentioned to her. To whom should she mention me if I am a forbidden topic in the house? She thinks you are all spies for her husband. Oh, I've no doubt she's in hell among you! I guess by her silence, as much as anything, what she feels. You say she is often restless, and anxious looking: is that a proof of tranquillity? You talk of her mind being unsettled. How the devil could it be otherwise in her frightful isolation? And that insipid, paltry creature attending her from *duty* and *humanity*! From *pity* and *charity*! He might as well plant an oak in a flowerpot, and expect it to thrive, as imagine he can restore her to vigour in the soil of his shallow cares! Let us settle it at once; will you stay here, and am I to fight my way to Catherine over Linton and his footmen? Or will you be my friend, as you have been hitherto, and do what I request? Decide! because there is no reason for my lingering another minute, if you persist in your stubborn ill-nature!'

Well, Mr Lockwood, I argued and complained, and flatly refused him fifty times; but in the long run he forced me to an agreement. I engaged to carry a letter from him to my mistress; and should she consent, I promised to let him have intelligence of Linton's next absence from home, when he might come, and get in as he was able: I wouldn't be there, and my fellow servants should be equally out of the way. Was it right or wrong? I fear it was wrong, though expedient. I thought I prevented another explosion by my compliance; and I thought, too, it might create a favourable crisis in Catherine's mental illness: and then I remembered Mr Edgar's stern rebuke of my carrying tales; and I tried to smooth away all disquietude on the subject, by affirming, with frequent iteration, that that betrayal of trust, if it merited so harsh an appellation, should be the last. Notwithstanding, my journey homeward was sadder than my journey thither; and many misgivings I had, ere I could prevail on myself to put the missive into Mrs Linton's hand.

But here is Kenneth; I'll go down, and tell him how much better you are. My history is *dree*, as we say, and will serve to wile away another morning.

Dree, and dreary! I reflected as the good woman descended to receive the doctor; and not exactly of a kind which I should have chosen to amuse me. But never mind! I'll extract wholesome medicines from Mrs Dean's bitter herbs; and firstly, let me beware of the fascination that lurks in Catherine Heathcliff's brilliant eyes. I should be in a curious taking if I surrendered my heart to that young person, and the daughter turned out a second edition of the mother!

## *Chapter 15*

Another week over – and I am so many days nearer health, and spring! I have now heard all my neighbour's history, at different sittings, as the housekeeper could spare time from more important occupations. I'll continue it in her own words, only a little condensed. She is, on the whole, a very fair narrator, and I don't think I could improve her style.

In the evening, she said, the evening of my visit to the Heights, I knew, as well as if I saw him, that Mr Heathcliff was about the place; and I shunned going out, because I still carried his letter in my pocket, and didn't want to be threatened, or teased any more. I had made up my mind not to give it till my master went somewhere, as I could not guess how its receipt would affect Catherine. The consequence was, that it did not reach her before the lapse of three days. The fourth was Sunday, and I brought it into her room after the family were gone to church. There was a man servant left to keep the house with me, and we generally made a practice of locking the doors during the hours of service; but on that occasion the weather was so warm and pleasant that I set them wide open, and, to fulfil my engagement, as I knew who would be coming, I told my companion that the mistress wished very much for some oranges, and he must run over to the village and get a few, to be paid for on the morrow. He departed, and I went upstairs.

Mrs Linton sat in a loose, white dress, with a light shawl over her shoulders, in the recess of the open window, as usual. Her thick, long hair had been partly removed at the beginning of her illness, and now she wore it simply combed in its natural tresses over her temples and neck. Her appearance was altered, as I had told Heathcliff; but when she was calm, there seemed unearthly beauty in the change. The flash of her eyes had been succeeded by a dreamy and melancholy softness; they no longer gave the impression of looking at the objects around her: they appeared always to gaze beyond, and far beyond – you would have said out of this world. Then, the paleness of her face – its haggard aspect having vanished as she recovered flesh – and the peculiar expression arising from her mental state, though painfully suggestive of their causes, added to the touching interest which she awakened; and – invariably to me, I know, and to any person who saw her, I should think – refuted more tangible proofs of convalescence, and stamped her as one doomed to decay.

A book lay spread on the sill before her, and the scarcely perceptible wind fluttered its leaves at intervals. I believe Linton had laid it there: for she never endeavoured to divert herself with reading, or occupation of any kind, and he would spend many an hour in trying to entice her attention to some subject which had formerly been her amusement. She was conscious of his aim, and in her better moods endured his efforts placidly, only showing their uselessness by now and then suppressing a wearied sigh, and checking him at last with the saddest of smiles and kisses. At other times, she would turn petulantly away, and hide her face in her hands, or even push him off angrily; and then he took care to let her alone, for he was certain of doing no good.

Gimmerton chapel bells were still ringing; and the full, mellow flow of the beck in the valley came soothingly on the ear. It was a sweet substitute for the yet absent murmur of the summer foliage, which drowned that music about the Grange when the trees were in leaf. At Wuthering Heights it always sounded on quiet days following a great thaw or a season of steady rain. And of Wuthering Heights Catherine was thinking as she listened: that is, if she thought or listened at all; but she had the vague, distant look I mentioned before, which expressed no recognition of material things either by ear or eye.

'There's a letter for you, Mrs Linton,' I said, gently inserting it in one hand that rested on her knee. 'You must read it immediately, because it wants an answer. Shall I break the seal?' 'Yes,' she answered, without altering the direction of her eyes. I opened it – it was very short. 'Now,' I continued, 'read it.'

She drew away her, hand, and let it fall. I replaced it in her lap, and stood waiting till it should please her to glance down; but that movement was so long delayed that at last I resumed – 'Must I read it, ma'am? It is from Mr Heathcliff.'

There was a start and a troubled gleam of recollection, and a struggle to arrange her ideas. She lifted the letter, and seemed to peruse it; and when she came to the signature she sighed: yet still I found she had not gathered its import, for, upon my desiring to hear her reply, she merely pointed to the name, and gazed at me with mournful and questioning eagerness.

'Well, he wishes to see you,' said I, guessing her need of an interpreter. 'He's in the garden by this time, and impatient to know what answer I shall bring.'

As I spoke, I observed a large dog lying on the sunny grass beneath, raise its ears as if about to bark, and then smoothing them back, announce, by a wag of the tail, that someone approached whom it did not consider a stranger. Mrs Linton bent forward, and listened breathlessly. The minute after a step traversed the hall; the open house was too tempting for Heathcliff to resist walking in: most likely he supposed that I was inclined to shirk my promise, and so resolved to trust to his own audacity. With straining eagerness Catherine gazed towards the entrance of her chamber. He did not hit the right room directly; she motioned me to admit him; but he found it out, ere I could reach the door, and in a stride or two was at her side, and had her grasped in his arms.

He neither spoke nor loosed his hold for some five minutes, during which period he bestowed more kisses than ever he gave in his life before, I dare say: but then my mistress had kissed him first, and I plainly saw that he could hardly bear, for downright agony, to look into her face! The same conviction had stricken him as me, from the instant he beheld her, that there was no prospect of ultimate recovery there – she was fated, sure to die.

'Oh, Cathy! Oh, my life! how can I bear it?' Was the first sentence he uttered, in a tone that did not seek to disguise his despair. And now he stared at her so earnestly that I thought the very intensity of his gaze would bring tears into his eyes; but they burned with anguish: they did not melt.

'What now?' said Catherine, leaning back, and returning his look with a suddenly clouded brow: her humour was a mere vane for constantly varying caprices. 'You and Edgar have broken my heart, Heathcliff! And you both come to bewail the deed to me, as if you were the people to be pitied! I shall not pity you, not I. You have killed me – and thriven on it, I think. How strong you are! How many years do you mean to live after I am gone?'

Heathcliff had knelt on one knee to embrace her; he attempted to rise, but she seized his hair, and kept him down.

'I wish I could hold you,' she continued, bitterly, 'till we were both dead! I shouldn't care what you suffered. I care nothing for your sufferings. Why shouldn't you suffer? I do! Will you forget me? Will you be happy when I am in the earth? Will you say twenty years hence, "That's the grave of Catherine Earnshaw. I loved her long ago, and was wretched to lose her; but it is past. I've loved many others since: my children are dearer to me than she was; and, at death, I shall not rejoice that I am going to her: I shall be sorry that I must leave them!" Will you say so, Heathcliff?'

'Don't torture me till I'm as mad as yourself,' cried he, wrenching his head free, and grinding his teeth.

The two, to a cool spectator, made a strange and fearful picture. Well might Catherine deem that heaven would be a land of exile to her, unless with her mortal body she cast away her mortal character also. Her present countenance had a wild vindictiveness in its white cheek, and a bloodless lip and scintillating eye; and she retained in her closed fingers a portion of the locks she had been grasping. As to her companion, while raising himself with one hand, he had taken her arm with the other; and so inadequate was his stock of gentleness to the requirements of her condition, that on his letting go I saw four distinct impressions left blue in the colourless skin.

'Are you possessed with a devil,' he pursued, savagely, 'to talk in that manner to me when you are dying? Do you reflect that all those words will be branded in my memory, and eating deeper eternally after you have left me? You know you lie to say I have killed you: and, Catherine, you know that I could as soon forget you as my existence! Is it not sufficient for your infernal selfishness, that while you are at peace I shall writhe in the torments of hell?'

'I shall not be at peace,' moaned Catherine, recalled to a sense of physical weakness by the violent, unequal throbbing of her heart, which beat visibly and audibly under this excess of agitation.

She said nothing further till the paroxysm was over; then she continued, more kindly – 'I'm not wishing you greater torment than I have, Heathcliff. I only wish us never to be parted: and should a word of mine distress you hereafter, think I feel the same distress underground, and for my own sake, forgive me! Come here and kneel down again! You never harmed me in your life. Nay, if you nurse anger, that will be worse to remember than my harsh words! Won't you come here again? Do!'

Heathcliff went to the back of her chair, and leant over, but not so far as to let her see his face, which was livid with emotion. She bent round to look at him; he would not permit it: turning abruptly, he walked to the fireplace, where he stood, silent, with his back towards us. Mrs Linton's glance followed him suspiciously: every movement woke a new sentiment in her.

After a pause, and a prolonged gaze, she resumed; addressing me in accents of indignant disappointment – 'Oh, you see, Nelly, he would not relent a moment to keep me out of the grave. *That* is how I'm loved! Well, never mind. That is not *my* Heathcliff. I shall love mine yet; and take him with me: he's in my soul. And,' added she musingly, 'the thing that irks me most is this shattered prison, after all. I'm tired, tired of being enclosed here. I'm wearying to escape into that glorious world, and to be always there: not seeing it dimly through tears, and yearning for it through the walls of an aching heart; but really with it, and in it. Nelly, you think you are better and more fortunate than I; in full health and strength: you are sorry for me – very soon that will be altered. I shall be sorry for *you*. I shall be incomparably beyond and above you all. I *wonder* he won't be near me!' She went on to herself. 'I thought he wished it. Heathcliff, dear! you should not be sullen now. Do come to me, Heathcliff.'

In her eagerness she rose and supported herself on the arm of the chair. At that earnest appeal he turned to her, looking absolutely desperate. His eyes wide, and wet at last, flashed fiercely on her; his breast heaved convulsively. An instant they held asunder, and then how they met I hardly saw, but Catherine made a spring, and he caught her, and they were locked in an embrace from which I thought my mistress would never be released alive: in fact, to my eyes, she seemed directly insensible. He flung himself into the nearest seat, and on my approaching hurriedly to ascertain if she had fainted, he gnashed at me, and foamed like a mad dog, and gathered her to him with greedy jealousy. I did not feel as if I were in the company of a creature of my own species: it appeared that he would not understand, though I spoke to him; so I stood off, and held my tongue, in great perplexity.

A movement of Catherine's relieved me a little presently: she put up her hand to clasp his neck, and bring her cheek to his as he held her; while he, in return, covering her with frantic caresses, said wildly – 'You teach me now how cruel you've been – cruel and false. *Why* did you despise me? *Why* did you betray your own heart, Cathy? I have not one word of comfort. You deserve this. You have killed yourself. Yes, you may kiss me, and cry; and wring out my kisses and tears: they'll blight you – they'll damn you. You loved me – then what *right* had you to leave me? What right – answer me – for the poor fancy you felt for Linton? Because misery, and degradation, and death, and nothing that God or satan could inflict would have parted us, *you*, of your own will, did it. I have not broken your heart – *you* have broken it; and in breaking it, you have broken mine. So much the worse for me, that I am strong. Do I want to live? What kind of living will it be when you – oh, God! Would *you* like to live with your soul in the grave?'

'Let me alone. Let me alone,' sobbed Catherine. 'If I've done wrong, I'm dying for it. It is enough! You left me too: but I won't upbraid you! I forgive you. Forgive me!'

'It is hard to forgive, and to look at those eyes, and feel those wasted hands,' he answered. 'Kiss me again; and don't let me see your eyes! I forgive what you have done to me. I love *my* murderer – but *yours*! How can I?

They were silent – their faces hid against each other, and washed by each other's tears. At least, I suppose the weeping was on both sides; as it seemed Heathcliff *could* weep on a great occasion like this.

I grew very uncomfortable, meanwhile; for the afternoon wore fast away, the man whom I had sent off returned from his errand, and I could distinguish, by the shine of the westering sun up the valley, a concourse thickening outside Gimmerton chapel porch.

'Service is over,' I announced. 'My master will be here in half an hour.'

Heathcliff groaned a curse, and strained Catherine closer: she never moved.

Ere long I perceived a group of the servants passing up the road towards the kitchen wing. Mr Linton was not far behind; he opened the gate himself and sauntered slowly up, probably enjoying the lovely afternoon that breathed as soft as summer.

'Now he is here,' I exclaimed. 'For Heaven's sake, hurry down! You'll not meet anyone on the front stairs. Do be quick; and stay among the trees till he is fairly in.'

'I must go, Cathy,' said Heathcliff, seeking to extricate himself from his companion's arms. 'But, if I live, I'll see you again before you are asleep. I won't stray five yards from your window.'

'You must not go!' she answered, holding him as firmly as her strength allowed. 'You shall not, I tell you.'

'For one hour,' he pleaded, earnestly.

'Not for one minute,' she replied.

'I *must* – Linton will be up immediately,' persisted the alarmed intruder.

He would have risen, and unfixed her fingers by the act – she clung fast, gasping: there was mad resolution in her face.

'No!' she shrieked. 'Oh, don't, don't go. It is the last time! Edgar will not hurt us. Heathcliff, I shall die! I shall die!'

'Damn the fool! There he is,' cried Heathcliff, sinking back into his seat. 'Hush, my darling! Hush, hush, Catherine! I'll stay. If he shot me so, I'd expire with a blessing on my lips.'

And there they were fast again. I heard my master mounting the stairs – the cold sweat ran from my forehead: I was horrified.

'Are you going to listen to her ravings?' I said, passionately. 'She does not know what she says. Will you ruin her, because she has not wit to help herself? Get up! You could be free instantly. That is the most diabolical deed that ever you did. We are all done for – master, mistress, and servant.'

I wrung my hands, and cried out; and Mr Linton hastened his step at the noise. In the midst of my agitation, I was sincerely glad to observe that Catherine's arms had fallen relaxed, and her head hung down.

'She's fainted, or dead,' I thought: 'so much the better. Far better that she should be dead, than lingering a burden and a misery-maker to all about her.'

Edgar sprang to his unbidden guest, blanched with astonishment and rage. What he meant to do, I cannot tell; however, the other stopped all demonstrations, at once, by placing the lifeless-looking form in his arms.

'Look there!' he said. 'Unless you be a fiend, help her first – then you shall speak to me!'

He walked into the parlour, and sat down. Mr Linton summoned me, and with great difficulty, and after resorting to many means, we managed to restore her to sensation; but she was all bewildered; she sighed, and moaned, and knew nobody. Edgar, in his anxiety for her, forgot her hated friend. I did not. I went, at the earliest opportunity, and besought him to depart; affirming that Catherine was better, and he should hear from me in the morning, how she passed the night.

'I shall not refuse to go out of doors,' he answered; 'but I shall stay in the garden: and, Nelly, mind you keep your word tomorrow. I shall be under those larch trees. Mind! Or I pay another visit, whether Linton be in or not.'

He sent a rapid glance through the half-open door of the chamber, and, ascertaining that what I stated was apparently true, delivered the house of his luckless presence.

## *Chapter 16*

About twelve o'clock, that night, was born the Catherine you saw at Wuthering Heights: a puny, seven months' child; and two hours after the mother died, having never recovered sufficient consciousness to miss Heathcliff, or know Edgar. The latter's distraction at his bereavement is a subject too painful to be dwelt on; its after effects showed how deep the sorrow sank. A great addition, in my eyes, was his being left without an heir. I bemoaned that, as I gazed on the feeble orphan; and I mentally abused old Linton for (what was only natural partiality) the securing his estate to his own daughter, instead of his son's. An unwelcomed infant it was, poor thing! It might have wailed out of life, and nobody cared a morsel, during those first hours of existence. We redeemed the neglect afterwards; but its beginning was as friendless as its end is likely to be.

Next morning – bright and cheerful out of doors – stole softened in through the blinds of the silent room, and suffused the couch and its occupant with a mellow, tender glow. Edgar Linton had his head laid on the pillow, and his eyes shut. His young and fair features were almost as deathlike as those of the form beside him, and almost as fixed: but *his* was the hush of exhausted anguish, and *hers* of perfect peace. Her brow smooth, her lids closed, her lips wearing the expression of a smile; no angel in heaven could be more beautiful than she appeared. And I partook of the infinite calm in which she lay: my mind was never in a holier frame than while I gazed on that untroubled image of Divine rest. I instinctively echoed the words she had uttered a few hours before: 'Incomparably beyond and above us all! Whether still on earth or now in heaven, her spirit is at home with God!'

I don't know if it be a peculiarity in me, but I am seldom otherwise than happy while watching in the chamber of death, should no frenzied or despairing mourner share the duty with me. I see a repose that neither earth nor hell can break, and I feel an assurance of the endless and shadowless hereafter – the Eternity they have entered – where life is boundless in its duration, and love in its sympathy, and joy in its fullness. I noticed on that occasion how much selfishness there is even in a love like Mr Linton's, when he so regretted Catherine's blessed release! To be sure, one might have doubted, after the wayward and impatient existence she had led, whether she merited a haven of peace at last. One might doubt in seasons of cold reflection; but not then, in the presence of her corpse. It asserted its own tranquillity, which seemed a pledge of equal quiet to its former inhabitant.

Do you believe such people *are* happy in the other world, sir? I'd give a great deal to know. I declined answering Mrs Dean's question, which struck me as something heterodox. She proceeded:

Retracing the course of Catherine Linton, I fear we have no right to think she is; but we'll leave her with her Maker.

The master looked asleep, and I ventured soon after sunrise to quit the room and steal out to the pure refreshing air. The servants thought me gone to shake off the drowsiness of my protracted watch; in reality, my chief motive was seeing Mr Heathcliff. If he had remained among the larches all night, he would have heard nothing of the stir at the Grange; unless, perhaps, he might catch the gallop of the messenger going to Gimmerton. If he had come nearer, he would probably be aware, from the lights flitting to and fro, and the opening and shutting of the outer doors, that all was not right within. I wished, yet feared, to find him. I felt the terrible news must be told, and I longed to get it over; but *how* to do it, I did not know. He was there – at least a few yards further in the park; leant against an old ash tree, his hat off, and his hair soaked with the dew that had gathered on the budded branches, and fell pattering round him. He had been standing a long time in that position, for I saw a pair of ouzels passing and repassing scarcely three feet from him, busy in building their nest, and regarding his proximity no more than that of a piece of timber. They flew off at my approach, and he raised his eyes and spoke: 'She's dead!' he said; 'I've not waited for you to learn that. Put your handkerchief away – don't snivel before me. Damn you all! she wants none of *your* tears!'

I was weeping as much for him as her: we do sometimes pity creatures that have none of the feeling either for themselves or others; and when I first looked into his face, I perceived that he had got intelligence of the catastrophe; and a foolish notion struck me that his heart was quelled and he prayed, because his lips moved and his gaze was bent on the ground.

'Yes, she's dead!' I answered, checking my sobs and drying my cheeks. 'Gone to heaven, I hope; where we may, everyone, join her, if we take due warning and leave our evil ways to follow good!'

'Did *she* take due warning, then?' asked Heathcliff, attempting a sneer. 'Did she die like a saint? Come, give me a true history of the event. How did – '

He endeavoured to pronounce the name, but could not manage it; and compressing his mouth he held a silent combat with his inward agony, defying, meanwhile, my sympathy with an unflinching, ferocious stare. 'How did she die?' he resumed, at last – fain, notwithstanding his hardihood, to have a support behind him; for, after the struggle, he trembled, in spite of himself, to his very finger-ends.

'Poor wretch!' I thought; 'you have a heart and nerves the same as your brother men! Why should you be anxious to conceal them? Your pride cannot blind God! You tempt him to wring them, till he forces a cry of humiliation.'

'Quietly as a lamb!' I answered, aloud. 'She drew a sigh, and stretched herself, like a child reviving, and sinking again to sleep; and five minutes after I felt one little pulse at her heart, and nothing more!'

'And – did she ever mention me?' he asked, hesitating, as if he dreaded the answer to his question would introduce details that he could not bear to hear.

'Her senses never returned: she recognised nobody from the time you left her,' I said. 'She lies with a sweet smile on her face; and her latest ideas wandered back to pleasant early days. Her life closed in a gentle dream – may she wake as kindly in the other world!'

'May she wake in torment!' he cried, with frightful vehemence, stamping his foot, and groaning in a sudden paroxysm of ungovernable passion. 'Why, she's a liar to the end! Where is she? Not *there* – not in heaven – not perished – where? Oh! you said you cared nothing for my sufferings! And I pray one prayer – I repeat it till my tongue stiffens – Catherine Earnshaw, may you not rest as long as I am living! You said I killed you – haunt me, then! The murdered *do* haunt their murderers. I believe – I know that ghosts *have* wandered on earth. Be with me always – take any form – drive me mad! Only *do* not leave me in this abyss, where I cannot find you! Oh, God! It is unutterable! I *cannot* live without my life! I *cannot* live without my soul!'

He dashed his head against the knotted trunk; and, lifting up his eyes, howled, not like a man, but like a savage beast getting goaded to death with knives and spears. I observed several splashes of blood about the bark of the tree, and his hand and forehead were both stained; probably the scene I witnessed was a repetition of others acted during the night. It hardly moved my compassion – it appalled me: still I felt reluctant to quit him so. But the moment he recollected himself enough to notice me watching, he thundered a command for me to go, and I obeyed. He was beyond my skill to quiet or console!

Mrs Linton's funeral was appointed to take place on the Friday following her decease; and till then her coffin remained uncovered, and strewn with flowers and scented leaves, in the great drawing-room. Linton spent his days and nights there, a sleepless guardian; and – a circumstance concealed from all but me –

Heathcliff spent his nights, at least, outside, equally a stranger to repose. I held no communication with him: still I was conscious of his design to enter, if he could; and on the Tuesday, a little after dark, when my master, from sheer fatigue, had been compelled to retire a couple of hours, I went and opened one of the windows, moved by his perseverance to give him a chance of bestowing on the fading image of his idol one final adieu. He did not omit to avail himself of the opportunity, cautiously and briefly: too cautiously to betray his presence by the slightest noise. Indeed, I shouldn't have discovered that he had been there, except for the disarrangement of the drapery about the corpse's face, and for observing on the floor a curl of light hair, fastened with a silver thread; which, on examination, I ascertained to have been taken from a locket hung round Catherine's neck. Heathcliff had opened the trinket and cast out its contents, replacing them by a black lock of his own. I twisted the two, and enclosed them together.

Mr Earnshaw was, of course, invited to attend the remains of his sister to the grave; and he sent no excuse, but he never came; so that, besides her husband, the mourners were wholly composed of tenants and servants. Isabella was not asked.

The place of Catherine's interment, to the surprise of the villagers, was neither in the chapel, under the carved monument of the Lintons, nor yet by the tombs of her own relations, outside. It was dug on a green slope in a corner of the kirkyard, where the wall is so low that heath and bilberry plants have climbed over it from the moor; and peat mould almost buries it. Her husband lies in the same spot now; and they have each a simple headstone above, and a plain grey block at their feet, to mark the graves.

## *Chapter 17*

That Friday made the last of our fine days, for a month. In the evening, the weather broke; the wind shifted from south to northeast, and brought rain first, and then sleet and snow. On the morrow one could hardly imagine that there had been three weeks of summer: the primroses and crocuses were hidden under wintry drifts; the larks were silent, the young leaves of the early trees smitten and blackened. And dreary, and chill, and dismal that morrow did creep over! My master kept his room; I took possession of the lonely parlour, converting it into a nursery: and there I was sitting, with the moaning doll of a child laid on my knee; rocking it to and fro, and watching, meanwhile, the still driving flakes build up the uncurtained window, when the door opened, and some person entered, out of breath and laughing! My anger was greater than my astonishment for a minute. I supposed it one of the maids, and I cried – 'Have done! How dare you show your giddiness here? What would Mr Linton say if he heard you?'

'Excuse me!' answered a familiar voice; 'but I know Edgar is in bed, and I cannot stop myself.'

With that the speaker came forward to the fire, panting and holding her hand to her side.

'I have run the whole way from Wuthering Heights!' she continued, after a pause; 'except where I've flown. I couldn't count the number of falls I've had. Oh, I'm aching all over! Don't be alarmed! There shall be an explanation as soon as I can give it; only just have the goodness to step out and order the carriage to take me on to Gimmerton, and tell a servant to seek up a few clothes in my wardrobe.'

The intruder was Mrs Heathcliff. She certainly seemed in no laughing predicament: her hair streamed on her shoulders, dripping with snow and water; she was dressed in the girlish dress she commonly wore, befitting her age more than her position: a low frock with short sleeves, and nothing on either head or neck. The frock was of light silk, and clung to her with wet, and her feet were protected merely by thin slippers; add to this a deep cut under one ear, which only the cold prevented from bleeding profusely, a white face scratched and bruised, and a frame hardly able to support itself, through fatigue; and you may fancy my first fright was not much allayed when I had leisure to examine her.

'My dear young lady,' I exclaimed, 'I'll stir nowhere, and hear nothing, till you have removed every article of your clothes, and put on dry things; and certainly you shall not go to Gimmerton tonight, so it is needless to order the carriage.'

'Certainly, I shall,' she said; 'walking or riding: yet I've no objection to dress myself decently. And – ah, see how it flows down my neck now! The fire does make it smart.'

She insisted on my fulfilling her directions, before she would let me touch her; and not till after the coachman had been instructed to get ready, and a maid set to pack up some necessary attire, did I obtain her consent for binding the wound and helping to change her garments.

'Now, Ellen,' she said, when my task was finished, and she was seated in an easy chair on the hearth, with a cup of tea before her, 'you sit down opposite me, and put poor Catherine's baby away: I don't like to see it! You mustn't think I care little for Catherine, because I behaved so foolishly on entering: I've cried too, bitterly – yes, more than anyone else has reason to cry. We parted unreconciled, you remember, and I shan't forgive myself. But, for all that, I was not going to sympathise with him – the brute beast! O, give me the poker! This is the last thing of his I have about me:' she slipped the gold ring from her third finger, and threw it on the floor. 'I'll smash it!' she continued, striking it with childish spite, 'and then I'll burn it!' And she took and dropped the misused article among the coals. 'There! he shall buy another, if he gets me back again. He'd be capable of coming to seek me, to tease Edgar – I dare not stay, lest that notion should possess his wicked head! And besides, Edgar has not been kind, has he? And I won't come suing for his assistance; nor will I bring him into more trouble. Necessity compelled me to seek shelter here; though, if I had not learnt he was out of the way, I'd have halted at the kitchen, washed my face, warmed myself, got you to bring what I wanted, and departed again to anywhere out of the reach of my accursed – of that incarnate goblin! Ah, he was in such a fury! If he had caught me! It's a pity Earnshaw is not his match in strength: I wouldn't have run till I'd seen him all but demolished, had Hindley been able to do it!'

'Well, don't talk so fast, miss!' I interrupted, 'you'll disorder the handkerchief I have tied round your face, and make the cut bleed again. Drink your tea, and take breath, and give over laughing: laughter is sadly out of place under this roof, and in your condition!'

'An undeniable truth,' she replied. 'Listen to that child! It maintains a constant wail – send it out of my hearing for an hour; I shan't stay any longer.'

I rang the bell, and committed it to a servant's care; and then I enquired what had urged her to escape from Wuthering Heights in such an unlikely plight, and where she meant to go, as she refused remaining with us.

'I ought, and I wish to remain,' answered she, 'to cheer Edgar and take care of the baby, for two things, and because the Grange is my right home. But I tell you he wouldn't let me! Do you think he could bear to see me grow fat and merry; and could bear to think that we were tranquil, and not resolve on poisoning our comfort? Now, I have the satisfaction of being sure that he detests me to the point of its annoying him seriously to have me within earshot, or eyesight: I notice, when I enter his presence, the muscles of his countenance are involuntarily distorted into an expression of hatred; partly arising from his knowledge of the good causes I have to feel that sentiment for him, and partly from original aversion. It is strong enough to make me feel pretty certain that he would not chase me over England, supposing I contrived a clear escape; and therefore I must get quite away. I've recovered from my first desire to be killed by him: I'd rather he'd kill himself! He has extinguished my love effectually, and so I'm at my ease. I can recollect yet how I loved him; and can dimly imagine that I could still be loving him, if – no, no! Even if he had doted on me, the devilish nature would have revealed its existence somehow. Catherine had an awfully perverted taste to esteem him so dearly, knowing him so well. Monster! would that he could be blotted out of creation, and out of my memory!'

'Hush, hush! He's a human being,' I said. 'Be more charitable: there are worse men than he is yet!'

'He's not a human being,' she retorted; 'and he has no claim on my charity. I gave him my heart, and he took and pinched it to death; and flung it back to me. People feel with their hearts, Ellen: and since he has destroyed mine, I have not power to feel for him: and I would not, though he groaned from this to his dying day, and wept tears of blood for Catherine! No, indeed, indeed, I wouldn't!' And here Isabella began to cry; but, immediately dashing the water from her lashes, she recommenced. 'You asked, what has driven me to flight at last? I was compelled to attempt it, because I had succeeded in rousing his rage a pitch above his malignity. Pulling out the nerves with red hot pincers requires more coolness than knocking on the head. He was worked up to forget the fiendish prudence he boasted of, and proceeded to murderous violence. I experienced pleasure in being able to exasperate him: the sense of pleasure woke my instinct of self-preservation, so I fairly broke free; and if ever I come into his hands again he is welcome to a signal revenge.

'Yesterday, you know, Mr Earnshaw should have been at the funeral. He kept himself sober for the purpose – tolerably sober: not going to bed mad at six o'clock and getting up drunk at twelve. Consequently, he rose, in suicidal low spirits, as fit for the church as for a dance; and instead, he sat down by the fire and swallowed gin or brandy by tumblerfuls.

'Heathcliff – I shudder to name him! has been a stranger in the house from last Sunday till today. Whether the angels have fed him, or his kin beneath, I cannot tell; but he has not eaten a meal with us for nearly a week. He has just come home at dawn, and gone upstairs to his chamber; locking himself in – as if anybody dreamt of coveting his company! There he has continued, praying like a methodist: only the deity he implored is senseless dust and ashes; and God, when addressed, was curiously confounded with his own black father! After concluding these precious orisons – and they lasted generally till he grew hoarse and his voice was strangled in his throat – he would be off again; always straight down to the Grange! I wonder Edgar did not send for a constable, and give him into custody! For me, grieved as I was about Catherine, it was impossible to avoid regarding this season of deliverance from degrading oppression as a holiday.

'I recovered spirits sufficient to hear Joseph's eternal lectures without weeping, and to move up and down the house less with the foot of a frightened thief than formerly. You wouldn't think that I should cry at anything Joseph could say; but he and Hareton are detestable companions. I'd rather sit with Hindley, and hear his awful talk, than with "t' little maister" and his staunch supporter, that odious old man! When Heathcliff is in, I'm often obliged to seek the kitchen and their society, or starve among the damp uninhabited chambers; when he is not, as was the case this week, I establish a table and chair at one corner of the house fire, and never mind how Mr Earnshaw may occupy himself; and he does not interfere with my arrangements. He is quieter now than he used to be, if no one provokes him: more sullen and depressed, and less furious. Joseph affirms he's sure he's an altered man: that the Lord has touched his heart, and he is saved "so as by fire". I'm puzzled to detect signs of the favourable change: but it is not my business.

'Yester-evening I sat in my nook reading some old books till late on towards twelve. It seemed so dismal to go upstairs, with the wild snow blowing outside, and my thoughts continually reverting to the kirkyard and the new-made grave! I dared hardly lift my eyes from the page before me, that melancholy scene so instantly usurped its place. Hindley sat opposite, his head leant on his hand; perhaps meditating on the same subject. He had ceased drinking at a point below irrationality, and had neither stirred nor spoken during two or three hours. There was no sound through the house but the moaning wind which shook the windows every now and then, the faint crackling of the coals, and the click of my snuffers as I removed at intervals the long wick of the candle. Hareton and Joseph were probably fast asleep in bed. It was very, very sad: and while I read I sighed, for it seemed as if all joy had vanished from the world, never to be restored.

'The doleful silence was broken at length by the sound of the kitchen latch:

Heathcliff had returned from his watch earlier than usual; owing, I suppose, to the sudden storm. That entrance was fastened, and we heard him coming round to get in by the other. I rose with an irrepressible expression of what I felt on my lips, which induced my companion, who had been staring towards the door, to turn and look at me.

' "I'll keep him out five minutes," he exclaimed. "You won't object?"

' "No, you may keep him out the whole night for me," I answered. "Do! put the key in the lock, and draw the bolts."

'Earnshaw accomplished this ere his guest reached the front; he then came and brought his chair to the other side of my table, leaning over it, and searching in my eyes, a sympathy with the burning hate that gleamed from his: as he both looked and felt like an assassin, he couldn't exactly find that; but he discovered enough to encourage him to speak.

' "You, and I," he said, "have each a great debt to settle with the man out yonder! If we were neither of us cowards, we might combine to discharge it. Are you as soft as your brother? Are you willing to endure to the last, and not once attempt a repayment?"

' "I'm weary of enduring now," I replied; "and I'd be glad of a retaliation that wouldn't recoil on myself; but treachery and violence are spears pointed at both ends: they wound those who resort to them, worse than their enemies."

' "Treachery and violence are a just return for treachery and violence!" cried Hindley. "Mrs Heathcliff, I'll ask you to do nothing, but sit still and be dumb. Tell me now, can you? I'm sure you would have as much pleasure as I in witnessing the conclusion of the fiend's existence; he'll be *your* death unless you overreach him; and he'll be *my* ruin. Damn the hellish villain! He knocks at the door as if he were master here already! Promise to hold your tongue, and before that clock strikes – it wants three minutes of one – you're a free woman!"

'He took the implements which I described to you in my letter from his breast, and would have turned down the candle. I snatched it away, however, and seized his arm.

' "I'll not hold my tongue!" I said; "you mustn't touch him. Let the door remain shut, and be quiet!"

' "No! I've formed my resolution, and by God, I'll execute it!" cried the desperate being. "I'll do you a kindness in spite of yourself, and Hareton justice! And you needn't trouble your head to screen me; Catherine is gone. Nobody alive would regret me, or be ashamed, though I cut my throat this minute – and it's time to make an end!"

'I might as well have struggled with a bear, or reasoned with a lunatic. The only resource left me was to run to a lattice and warn his intended victim of the fate which awaited him.

' "You'd better seek shelter somewhere else tonight!" I exclaimed in a rather triumphant tone. "Mr Earnshaw has a mind to shoot you, if you persist in endeavouring to enter."

' "You'd better open the door, you —," he answered, addressing me by some elegant term that I don't care to repeat.

' "I shall not meddle in the matter," I retorted again. "Come in and get shot, if you please! I've done my duty."

'With that I shut the window and returned to my place by the fire; having too small a stock of hypocrisy at my command to pretend any anxiety for the danger that menaced him. Earnshaw swore passionately at me: affirming that I loved the villain yet; and calling me all sorts of names for the base spirit I evinced. And I, in my secret heart, (and conscience never reproached me) thought what a blessing it would be for *him*, should Heathcliff put him out of misery; and what a blessing for *me*, should he send Heathcliff to his right abode! As I sat nursing these reflections, the casement behind me was banged on to the floor by a blow from the latter individual, and his black countenance looked blightingly through. The stanchions stood too close to suffer his shoulders to follow, and I smiled, exulting in my fancied security. His hair and clothes were whitened with snow, and his sharp cannibal teeth, revealed by cold and wrath, gleamed through the dark.

' "Isabella, let me in, or I'll make you repent!" he "girned", as Joseph calls it.

' "I cannot commit murder," I replied. "Mr Hindley stands sentinel with a knife and loaded pistol."

' "Let me in by the kitchen door," he said.

' "Hindley will be there before me," I answered: "and that's a poor love of yours that cannot bear a shower of snow! We were left at peace in our beds as long as the summer moon shone, but the moment a blast of winter returns, you must run for shelter! Heathcliff, if I were you, I'd go stretch myself over her grave and die like a faithful dog. The world is surely not worth living in now, is it? You had distinctly impressed on me the idea that Catherine was the whole joy of your life: I can't imagine how you think of surviving her loss."

' "He's there, is he?" exclaimed my companion, rushing to the gap. "If I can get my arm out I can hit him!"

'I'm afraid, Ellen, you'll set me down as really wicked; but you don't know all, so don't judge. I wouldn't have aided or abetted an attempt on even *his* life for anything. Wish that he were dead, I must; and therefore I was fearfully disappointed, and unnerved by terror for the consequences of my taunting speech, when he flung himself on Earnshaw's weapon and wrenched it from his grasp.

'The charge exploded, and the knife, in springing back, closed into its owner's wrist. Heathcliff pulled it away by main force, slitting up the flesh as it passed on, and thrust it dripping into his pocket. He then took a stone, struck down the division between two windows, and sprung in. His adversary had fallen senseless with excessive pain, and the flow of blood that gushed from an artery or a large vein. The ruffian kicked and trampled on him, and dashed his head repeatedly against the flags, holding me with one hand, meantime, to prevent me summoning Joseph. He exerted preter-human self-denial in abstaining from finishing him completely; but getting out of breath he finally desisted, and dragged the apparently inanimate body on to the settle. There he tore off the sleeve of Earnshaw's coat, and bound up the wound with brutal roughness; spitting and cursing during the operation as energetically as he had kicked before. Being at liberty, I lost no time in seeking the old servant; who, having gathered by degrees the purport of my hasty tale, hurried below, gasping, as he descended the steps two at once.

' "Whet is thur tuh do, nah? Whet is thur tuh do, nah?"

' "There's this to do," thundered Heathcliff, "that your master's mad; and should he last another month, I'll have him to an asylum. And how the devil did you come to fasten me out, you toothless hound? Don't stand muttering and mumbling there. Come, I'm not going to nurse him. Wash that stuff away; and mind the sparks of your candle – it is more than half brandy!"

' "Und soa, yah been murthering on him?" exclaimed Joseph, lifting his hands and eyes in horror. "If iver Aw seed a seeght loike this! May the Lord – "

'Heathcliff gave him a push on to his knees in the middle of the blood, and flung a towel to him; but instead of proceeding to dry it up, he joined his hands, and began a prayer which excited my laughter from its odd phraseology. I was in the condition of mind to be shocked at nothing: in fact, I was as reckless as some malefactors show themselves at the foot of the gallows.

' "Oh, I forgot you," said the tyrant. "You shall do that. Down with you. And you conspire with him against me, do you, viper? There, that is work fit for you!'

'He shook me till my teeth rattled, and pitched me beside Joseph, who steadily concluded his supplications and then rose, vowing he would set off for the Grange directly. Mr Linton was a magistrate, and though he had fifty wives dead, he should enquire into this. He was so obstinate in his resolution, that Heathcliff deemed it expedient to compel from my lips a recapitulation of what had taken place; standing over me, heaving with malevolence, as I reluctantly delivered the account in answer to his questions. It required a great deal of labour to satisfy the old man that he was not the aggressor; especially with my hardly wrung replies. However, Mr Earnshaw soon convinced him that he was alive still; he hastened to administer a dose of spirits, and by their succour his master presently regained motion and consciousness. Heathcliff, aware that he was ignorant of the treatment received while insensible, called him deliriously intoxicated; and said he should not notice his atrocious conduct further, but advised him to get to bed. To my joy, he left us, after giving this judicious counsel, and Hindley stretched himself on the hearthstone. I departed to my own room, marvelling that I had escaped so easily.

'This morning, when I came down, about half an hour before noon, Mr Earnshaw was sitting by the fire, deadly sick; his evil genius, almost as gaunt and ghastly, leant against the chimney. Neither appeared inclined to dine, and, having waited till all was cold on the table, I commenced alone. Nothing hindered me from eating heartily, and I experienced a certain sense of satisfaction and superiority, as, at intervals, I cast a look towards my silent companions, and felt the comfort of a quiet conscience within me. After I had done, I ventured on the unusual liberty of drawing near the fire, going round Earnshaw's seat, and kneeling in the corner beside him.

'Heathcliff did not glance my way, and I gazed up, and contemplated his features almost as confidently as if they had been turned to stone. His forehead, that I once thought so manly, and that I now think so diabolical, was shaded with a heavy cloud; his basilisk eyes were nearly quenched by sleeplessness – and weeping, perhaps, for the lashes were wet then; his lips devoid of their ferocious sneer, and sealed in an expression of unspeakable sadness. Had it been another, I would have covered my face, in the presence of such grief. In *his* case, I was gratified; and, ignoble as it seems to insult a fallen enemy, I couldn't miss this chance of sticking in a dart: his weakness was the only time when I could taste the delight of paying wrong for wrong.'

'Fie, fie, miss!' I interrupted. 'One might suppose you had never opened a Bible in your life. If God afflict your enemies, surely that ought to suffice you. It is both mean and presumptuous to add your torture to his!'

'In general, I'll allow that it would be, Ellen,' she continued; 'but what misery laid on Heathcliff could content me, unless I have a hand in it? I'd rather he suffered *less*, if I might cause his sufferings and he might *know* that I was the cause. Oh, I owe him so much. On only one condition can I hope to forgive him. It is, if I may take an eye for an eye, a tooth for a tooth; for every wrench of agony return a wrench: reduce him to my level. As he was the first to injure, make him the first to implore pardon; and then – why then, Ellen, I might show you some generosity. But it is utterly impossible I can ever be revenged, and therefore I cannot forgive him. Hindley wanted some water, and I handed him a glass, and asked him how he was.

' "Not as ill as I wish," he replied. "But leaving out my arm, every inch of me is as sore as if I had been fighting with a legion of imps!"

' "Yes, no wonder," was my next remark. "Catherine used to boast that she stood between you and bodily harm: she meant that certain persons would not hurt you for fear of offending her. It's well people don't *really* rise from their grave, or, last night, she might have witnessed a repulsive scene! Are not you bruised, and cut over your chest and shoulders?"

' "I can't say," he answered: "but what do you mean? Did he dare to strike me when I was down?"

' "He trampled on, and kicked you, and dashed you on the ground," I whispered. "And his mouth watered to tear you with his teeth; because, he's only half a man – not so much."

'Mr Earnshaw looked up, like me, to the countenance of our mutual foe; who, absorbed in his anguish, seemed insensible to anything around him: the longer he stood, the plainer his reflections revealed their blackness through his features.

' "Oh, if God would but give me strength to strangle him in my last agony, I'd go to hell with joy," groaned the impatient man, writhing to rise, and sinking back in despair, convinced of his inadequacy for the struggle.

' "Nay, it's enough that he has murdered one of you," I observed aloud. "At the Grange, everyone knows your sister would have been living now, had it not been for Mr Heathcliff. After all, it is preferable to be hated than loved by him. When I recollect how happy we were – how happy Catherine was before he came – I'm fit to curse the day."

'Most likely, Heathcliff noticed more the truth of what was said, than the spirit of the person who said it. His attention was roused, I saw, for his eyes rained down tears among the ashes, and he drew his breath in suffocating sighs. I stared full at him, and laughed scornfully. The clouded windows of hell flashed a moment towards me; the fiend which usually looked out, however, was so dimmed and drowned that I did not fear to hazard another sound of derision.

' "Get up, and begone out of my sight," said the mourner.

'I guessed he uttered those words, at least, though his voice was hardly intelligible.

' "I beg your pardon," I replied. "But I loved Catherine too; and her brother requires attendance which, for her sake, I shall supply. Now that she's dead, I see her in Hindley: Hindley has exactly her eyes, if you had not tried to gouge them out, and made them black and red; and her – "

' "Get up, wretched idiot, before I stamp you to death!" he cried, making a movement that caused me to make one also.

' "But then," I continued, holding myself ready to flee; "if poor Catherine had trusted you, and assumed the ridiculous, contemptible, degrading title of Mrs Heathcliff, she would soon have presented a similar picture! *She* wouldn't have borne your abominable behaviour quietly: her detestation and disgust must have found voice."

'The back of the settle and Earnshaw's person interposed between me and him; so instead of endeavouring to reach me, he snatched a dinner knife from the table and flung it at my head. It struck beneath my ear, and stopped the sentence I was uttering; but, pulling it out, I sprang to the door and delivered another which I hope went a little deeper than his missile. The last glimpse I caught of him was a furious rush on his part, checked by the embrace of his host; and both fell locked together on the hearth. In my flight through the kitchen I bid Joseph speed to his master; I knocked over Hareton, who was hanging a litter of puppies from a chair-back in the doorway; and, blest as a soul escaped from purgatory, I bounded, leaped, and flew down the steep road; then, quitting its windings, shot direct across the moor, rolling over banks, and wading through marshes: precipitating myself, in fact, towards the beacon light of the Grange. And far rather would I be condemned to a perpetual dwelling in the infernal regions, than, even for one night, abide beneath the roof of Wuthering Heights again.'

Isabella ceased speaking, and took a drink of tea; then she rose, and bidding me put on her bonnet, and a great shawl I had brought, and turning a deaf ear to my entreaties for her to remain another hour, she stepped on to a chair, kissed Edgar's and Catherine's portraits, bestowed a similar salute on me, and descended to the carriage, accompanied by Fanny, who yelped wild with joy at recovering her mistress. She was driven away, never to revisit this neighbourhood: but a regular correspondence was established between her and my master when things were more settled. I believe her new abode was in the south, near London; there she had a son born, a few months subsequent to her escape. He was christened Linton, and, from the first, she reported him to be an ailing, peevish creature.

Mr Heathcliff, meeting me one day in the village, enquired where she lived. I refused to tell. He remarked that it was not of any moment, only she must beware of coming to her brother: she should not be with him, if he had to keep her himself. Though I would give no information, he discovered, through some of the other servants, both her place of residence and the existence of the child. Still he didn't molest her: for which forbearance she might thank his aversion, I suppose.

He often asked about the infant, when he saw me; and on hearing its name, smiled grimly, and observed – 'They wish me to hate it too, do they?'

'I don't think they wish you to know anything about it,' I answered.

'But I'll have it,' he said, 'when I want it. They may reckon on that!'

Fortunately, its mother died before the time arrived, some thirteen years after the decease of Catherine, when Linton was twelve, or a little more.

On the day succeeding Isabella's unexpected visit, I had no opportunity of speaking to my master: he shunned conversation, and was fit for discussing nothing. When I could get him to listen, I saw it pleased him that his sister had left her husband; whom he abhorred with an intensity which the mildness of his nature would scarcely seem to allow. So deep and sensitive was his aversion, that he refrained from going anywhere where he was likely to see or hear of Heathcliff. Grief, and that together, transformed him into a complete hermit: he threw up his office of magistrate, ceased even to attend church, avoided the village on all occasions, and spent a life of entire seclusion within the limits of his park and grounds; only varied by solitary rambles on the moors, and visits to the grave of his wife, mostly at evening, or early morning before other wanderers were abroad. But he was too good to be thoroughly unhappy long. *He* didn't pray for Catherine's soul to haunt him: time brought resignation, and a melancholy sweeter than common joy. He recalled her memory with ardent, tender love, and hopeful aspiring to the better world, where, he doubted not, she was gone.

And he had earthly consolation and affections, also. For a few days, I said, he seemed regardless of the puny successor to the departed: that coldness melted as fast as snow in April, and ere the tiny thing could stammer a word or totter a step, it wielded a despot's sceptre in his heart. It was named Catherine; but he never called it the name in full, as he had never called the first Catherine short: probably because Heathcliff had a habit of doing so. The little one was always Cathy: it formed to him a distinction from the mother, and yet, a connection with her; and his attachment sprang from its relation to her, far more than from its being his own.

I used to draw a comparison between him and Hindley Earnshaw, and perplex myself to explain satisfactorily why their conduct was so opposite in similar circumstances. They had both been fond husbands, and were both attached to their children; and I could not see how they shouldn't both have taken the same road, for good or evil. But, I thought in my mind, Hindley, with apparently the stronger head, has shown himself sadly the worse and the weaker man. When his ship struck, the captain abandoned his post; and the crew, instead of trying to save her, rushed into riot and confusion, leaving no hope for their luckless vessel.

Linton, on the contrary, displayed the true courage of a loyal and faithful soul: he trusted God; and God comforted him. One hoped, and the other despaired: they chose their own lots, and were righteously doomed to endure them. But you'll not want to hear my moralising, Mr Lockwood; you'll judge as well as I can, all these things: at least, you'll think you will, and that's the same. The end of Earnshaw was what might have been expected; it followed fast on his sister's: there were scarcely six months between them. We, at the Grange, never got a very succinct account of his state preceding it; all that I did learn was on occasion of going to aid in the preparations for the funeral.

Mr Kenneth came to announce the event to my master.

'Well, Nelly,' said he, riding into the yard one morning, too early not to alarm me with an instant presentiment of bad news, 'It's yours and my turn to go into mourning at present. Who's given us the slip now, do you think?'

'Who?' I asked in a flurry.

'Why, guess!' he returned, dismounting, and slinging his bridle on a hook by the door. 'And nip up the corner of your apron: I'm certain you'll need it.'

'Not Mr Heathcliff, surely?' I exclaimed.

'What! would you have tears for him?' said the doctor. 'No, Heathcliff's a tough young fellow: he looks blooming today. I've just seen him. He's rapidly regaining flesh since he lost his better half.'

'Who is it, then, Mr Kenneth?' I repeated impatiently.

'Hindley Earnshaw! Your old friend Hindley,' he replied, 'and my wicked gossip: though he's been too wild for me this long while. There! I said we should draw water. But cheer up! He died true to his character: drunk as a lord. Poor lad; I'm sorry, too. One can't help missing an old companion: though he had the worst tricks with him that ever man imagined, and has done me many a rascally turn. He's barely twenty-seven, it seems; that's your own age: who would have thought you were born in one year?'

I confess this blow was greater to me than the shock of Mrs Linton's death: ancient associations lingered round my heart; I sat down in the porch and wept as for a blood relation, desiring Kenneth to get another servant to introduce him to the master. I could not hinder myself from pondering on the question – 'Had he had fair play?' Whatever I did, that idea would bother me: it was so tiresomely pertinacious that I resolved on requesting leave to go to Wuthering Heights, and assist in the last duties to the dead. Mr Linton was extremely reluctant to consent, but I pleaded eloquently for the friendless condition in which he lay; and I said my old master and foster-brother had a claim on my services as strong as his own. Besides, I reminded him that the child Hareton was his wife's nephew, and, in the absence of nearer kin, he ought to act as its guardian; and he ought to and must enquire how the property was left, and look over the concerns of his brother-in-law. He was unfit for attending to such matters then, but he bid me speak to his lawyer; and at length permitted me to go. His lawyer had been Earnshaw's also: I called at the village, and asked him to accompany me. He shook his head, and advised that Heathcliff should be let alone; affirming, if the truth were known, Hareton would be found little else than a beggar.

'His father died in debt,' he said; 'the whole property is mortgaged, and the sole chance for the natural heir is to allow him an opportunity of creating some interest in the creditor's heart, that he may be inclined to deal leniently towards him.'

When I reached the Heights, I explained that I had come to see everything carried on decently; and Joseph, who appeared in sufficient distress, expressed satisfaction at my presence. Mr Heathcliff said he did not perceive that I was wanted; but I might stay and order the arrangements for the funeral, if I chose.

'Correctly,' he remarked, 'that fool's body should be buried at the crossroads, without ceremony of any kind. I happened to leave him ten minutes yesterday afternoon, and in that interval he fastened the two doors of the house against me, and he has spent the night in drinking himself to death deliberately! We broke in this morning, for we heard him snorting like a horse; and there he was, laid over the settle: flaying and scalping would not have wakened him. I sent for Kenneth, and he came; but not till the beast had changed into carrion; he was both dead and cold, and stark; and so you'll allow, it was useless making more stir about him!'

The old servant confirmed this statement, but muttered – 'Aw'd rayther he'd goan hisseln fur t' doctor! Aw sud uh taen tent uh t' maister better nur him – un he warn't deead when Aw left, nowt uh t' soart!'

I insisted on the funeral being respectable. Mr Heathcliff said I might have my own way there too: only, he desired me to remember that the money for the whole affair came out of his pocket. He maintained a hard, careless deportment, indicative of neither joy nor sorrow: if anything, it expressed a flinty gratification at a piece of difficult work successfully executed. I observed once, indeed, something like exultation in his aspect: it was just when the people were bearing the coffin from the house. He had the hypocrisy to represent a mourner: and previous to following with Hareton, he lifted the unfortunate child on to the table and muttered, with peculiar gusto, 'Now, my bonny lad, you are *mine*! And we'll see if one tree won't grow as crooked as another, with the same wind to twist it!' The unsuspecting thing was pleased at this speech: he played with Heathcliff's whiskers, and stroked his cheek; but I divined its meaning, and observed tartly, 'That boy must go back with me to Thrushcross Grange, sir. There is nothing in the world less yours than he is!'

'Does Linton say so?' he demanded.

'Of course – he has ordered me to take him,' I replied.

'Well,' said the scoundrel, 'we'll not argue the subject now: but I have a fancy to try my hand at rearing a young one; so intimate to your master that I must supply the place of this with my own, if he attempt to remove it. I don't engage to let Hareton go, undisputed; but I'll be pretty sure to make the other come! Remember to tell him.'

This hint was enough to bind our hands. I repeated its substance on my return; and Edgar Linton, little interested at the commencement, spoke no more of interfering. I'm not aware that he could have done it to any purpose, had he been ever so willing.

The guest was now the master of Wuthering Heights: he held firm possession, and proved to the attorney – who, in his turn, proved it to Mr Linton – that

Earnshaw had mortgaged every yard of land he owned, for cash to supply his mania for gaming; and he, Heathcliff, was the mortgagee. In that manner Hareton, who should now be the first gentleman in the neighbourhood, was reduced to a state of complete dependence on his father's inveterate enemy; and lives in his own house as a servant, deprived of the advantage of wages, and quite unable to right himself, because of his friendlessness, and his ignorance that he has been wronged.

## *Chapter 18*

The twelve years, continued Mrs Dean, following that dismal period, were the happiest of my life: my greatest troubles in their passage rose from our little lady's trifling illnesses, which she had to experience in common with all children, rich and poor. For the rest, after the first six months, she grew like a larch, and could walk and talk too, in her own way, before the heath blossomed a second time over Mrs Linton's dust. She was the most winning thing that ever brought sunshine into a desolate house: a real beauty in face, with the Earnshaws' handsome dark eyes, but the Lintons' fair skin, and small features, and yellow curling hair. Her spirit was high, though not rough, and qualified by a heart sensitive and lively to excess in its affections. That capacity for intense attachments reminded me of her mother: still she did not resemble her; for she could be soft and mild as a dove, and she had a gentle voice and pensive expression: her anger was never furious; her love never fierce: it was deep and tender. However, it must be acknowledged, she had faults to foil her gifts. A propensity to be saucy was one; and a perverse will, that indulged children invariably acquire, whether they be good tempered or cross. If a servant chanced to vex her, it was always – 'I shall tell papa!' And if he reproved her, even by a look, you would have thought it a heartbreaking business: I don't believe he ever did speak a harsh word to her. He took her education entirely on himself, and made it an amusement. Fortunately, curiosity and a quick intellect urged her into an apt scholar: she learnt rapidly and eagerly, and did honour to his teaching.

Till she reached the age of thirteen, she had not once been beyond the range of the park by herself. Mr Linton would take her with him a mile or so outside, on rare occasions; but he trusted her to no one else. Gimmerton was an unsubstantial name in her ears; the chapel, the only building she had approached or entered, except her own home. Wuthering Heights and Mr Heathcliff did not exist for her: she was a perfect recluse; and, apparently, perfectly contented. Sometimes, indeed, while surveying the country from her nursery window, she would observe – 'Ellen, how long will it be before I can walk to the top of those hills? I wonder what lies on the other side – is it the sea?'

'No, Miss Cathy,' I would answer; 'it is hills again, just like these.'

'And what are those golden rocks like, when you stand under them?' she once asked.

The abrupt descent of Penistone Craggs particularly attracted her notice; especially when the setting sun shone on it and the topmost heights, and the whole extent of landscape besides lay in shadow. I explained that they were bare masses of stone, with hardly enough earth in their clefts to nourish a stunted tree.

'And why are they bright so long after it is evening here?' she pursued.

'Because they are a great deal higher up than we are,' replied I; 'you could not climb them, they are too high and steep. In winter the frost is always there before it comes to us; and deep into summer I have found snow under that black hollow on the northeast side!'

'Oh, you have been on them!' she cried, gleefully. 'Then I can go, too, when I am a woman. Has papa been, Ellen?'

'Papa would tell you, miss,' I answered, hastily, 'that they are not worth the trouble of visiting. The moors, where you ramble with him, are much nicer; and Thrushcross park is the finest place in the world.'

'But I know the park, and I don't know those,' she murmured to herself. 'And I should delight to look round me from the brow of that tallest point: my little pony Minny shall take me sometime.'

One of the maids mentioning the Fairy cave, quite turned her head with a desire to fulfil this project: she teased Mr Linton about it; and he promised she should have the journey when she got older. But Miss Catherine measured her age by months, and, 'Now, am I old enough to go to Penistone Craggs?' was the constant question in her mouth. The road thither wound close by Wuthering Heights. Edgar had not the heart to pass it; so she received as constantly the answer, 'Not yet, love: not yet.'

I said Mrs Heathcliff lived above a dozen years after quitting her husband. Her family were of a delicate constitution: she and Edgar both lacked the ruddy health that you will generally meet in these parts. What her last illness was, I am not certain: I conjecture, they died of the same thing, a kind of fever, slow at its commencement, but incurable, and rapidly consuming life towards the close. She wrote to inform her brother of the probable conclusion of a four months' indisposition under which she had suffered; and entreated him to come to her, if possible; for she had much to settle, and she wished to bid him adieu, and deliver Linton safely into his hands. Her hope was, that Linton might be left with him, as he had been with her: his father, she would fain convince herself, had no desire to assume the burden of his maintenance or education. My master hesitated not a moment in complying with her request: reluctant as he was to leave home at ordinary calls, he flew to answer this; commending Catherine to my peculiar vigilance, in his absence, with reiterated orders that she must not wander out of the park, even under my escort: he did not calculate on her going unaccompanied.

He was away three weeks: the first day or two, my charge sat in a corner of the library, too sad for either reading or playing: in that quiet state she caused me little trouble; but it was succeeded by an interval of impatient, fretful weariness; and being too busy, and too old then, to run up and down amusing her, I hit on a method by which she might entertain herself. I used to send her on travels round the grounds – now on foot, and now on a pony: indulging her with a patient audience of all her real and imaginary adventures, when she returned.

The summer shone in full prime; and she took such a taste for this solitary rambling that she often contrived to remain out from breakfast till tea; and then the evenings were spent in recounting her fanciful tales. I did not fear her breaking bounds; because the gates were generally locked, and I thought she would scarcely venture forth alone, if they had stood wide open. Unluckily, my confidence proved misplaced. Catherine came to me, one morning, at eight o'clock, and said she was that day an Arabian merchant, going to cross the desert with his caravan; and I must give her plenty of provision for herself and beasts: a horse, and three camels, personated by a large hound and a couple of pointers. I got together good store of dainties, and slung them in a basket on one side of the saddle; and she sprang up as gay as a fairy, sheltered by her wide-brimmed hat and gauze veil from the July sun, and trotted off with a merry laugh, mocking my cautious counsel to avoid galloping, and come back early. The naughty thing never made her appearance at tea. One traveller, the hound, being an old dog and fond of its ease, returned; but neither Cathy, nor the pony, nor the two pointers were visible in any direction; and I despatched emissaries down this path, and that path, and at last went wandering in search of her myself. There was a labourer working at a fence round a plantation, on the borders of the grounds. I enquired of him if he had seen our young lady.

'I saw her at morn,' he replied; 'she would have me to cut her a hazel switch, and then she leapt her galloway over the hedge yonder, where it is lowest, and galloped out of sight.'

You may guess how I felt at hearing this news. It struck me directly she must have started for Penistone Craggs. 'What will become of her?' I ejaculated, pushing through a gap which the man was repairing, and making straight to the highroad. I walked as if for a wager, mile after mile, till a turn brought me in view of the Heights; but no Catherine could I detect, far or near. The Craggs lie about a mile and a half beyond Mr Heathcliff's place, and that is four from the Grange, so I began to fear night would fall ere I could reach them. 'And what if she should have slipped in clambering among them,' I reflected, 'and been killed, or broken some of her bones?' My suspense was truly painful; and, at first, it gave me delightful relief to observe, in hurrying by the farmhouse, Charlie, the fiercest of the pointers, lying under a window, with swelled head and bleeding ear. I opened the wicket and ran to the door, knocking vehemently for admittance. A woman whom I knew, and who formerly lived at Gimmerton, answered: she had been servant there since the death of Mr Earnshaw.

'Ah,' said she, 'you are come a seeking your little mistress! Don't be frightened. She's here safe: but I'm glad it isn't the master.'

'He is not at home then, is he?' I panted, quite breathless with quick walking and alarm.

'No, no,' she replied: 'both he and Joseph are off, and I think they won't return this hour or more. Step in and rest you a bit.'

I entered, and beheld my stray lamb seated on the hearth, rocking herself in a little chair that had been her mother's when a child. Her hat was hung against the wall and she seemed perfectly at home, laughing and chattering, in the best spirits imaginable, to Hareton – now a great, strong lad of eighteen – who stared at her with considerable curiosity and astonishment: comprehending precious little of the fluent succession of remarks and questions which her tongue never ceased pouring forth.

'Very well, miss!' I exclaimed, concealing my joy under an angry countenance. 'This is your last ride, till papa comes back. I'll not trust you over the threshold again, you naughty, naughty girl!'

'Aha, Ellen!' she cried, gaily, jumping up, and running to my side. 'I shall have a pretty story to tell tonight: and so you've found me out. Have you ever been here in your life before?'

'Put that hat on, and home at once,' said I. 'I'm dreadfully grieved at you, Miss Cathy: you've done extremely wrong! It's no use pouting and crying: that won't repay the trouble I've had, scouring the country after you. To think how Mr Linton charged me to keep you in; and you stealing off so! It shows you are a cunning little fox, and nobody will put faith in you any more.'

'What have I done?' sobbed she, instantly checked. 'Papa charged me nothing: he'll not scold me, Ellen – he's never cross, like you!'

'Come, come!' I repeated. 'I'll tie the riband. Now, let us have no petulance. Oh, for shame. You thirteen years old, and such a baby!'

This exclamation was caused by her pushing the hat from her head, and retreating to the chimney out of my reach.

'Nay,' said the servant, 'don't be hard on the bonny lass, Mrs Dean. We made her stop: she'd fain have ridden forwards, afeard you should be uneasy. But Hareton offered to go with her, and I thought he should: it's a wild road over the hills.'

Hareton, during the discussion, stood with his hands in his pockets, too awkward to speak; though he looked as if he did not relish my intrusion.

'How long am I to wait?' I continued, disregarding the woman's interference. 'It will be dark in ten minutes. Where is the pony, Miss Cathy? And where is Phoenix? I shall leave you unless you be quick; so please yourself.'

'The pony is in the yard,' she replied, 'and Phoenix is shut in there. He's bitten – and so is Charlie. I was going to tell you all about it; but you are in a bad temper, and don't deserve to hear.'

I picked up her hat, and approached to reinstate it; but perceiving that the people of the house took her part, she commenced capering round the room; and on my giving chase, ran like a mouse over and under and behind the furniture, rendering it ridiculous for me to pursue. Hareton and the woman laughed, and she joined them, and waxed more impertinent still; till I cried, in great irritation – 'Well, Miss Cathy, if you were aware whose house this is, you'd be glad enough to get out.'

'It's *your* father's, isn't it?' said she, turning to Hareton.

'Nay,' he replied, looking down, and blushing bashfully.

He could not stand a steady gaze from her eyes, though they were just his own.

'Whose, then – your master's?' she asked.

He coloured deeper, with a different feeling, muttered an oath, and turned away.

'Who is his master?' continued the tiresome girl, appealing to me. 'He talked about "our house", and "our folk". I thought he had been the owner's son. And he never said, miss: he should have done, shouldn't he, if he's a servant?'

Hareton grew black as a thundercloud, at this childish speech. I silently shook my questioner, and at last succeeded in equipping her for departure.

'Now, get my horse,' she said, addressing her unknown kinsman as she would one of the stable-boys at the Grange. 'And you may come with me. I want to see where the goblin-hunter rises in the marsh, and to hear about the *fairishes*, as you call them: but make haste! What's the matter? Get my horse, I say.'

'I'll see thee damned before I be *thy* servant!' growled the lad.

'You'll see me *what*?' asked Catherine in surprise.

'Damned – thou saucy witch!' he replied.

'There, Miss Cathy! You see you have got into pretty company,' I interposed. 'Nice words to be used to a young lady! Pray don't begin to dispute with him. Come, let us seek for Minny ourselves, and begone.'

'But Ellen,' cried she, staring, fixed in astonishment. 'How dare he speak so to me? Mustn't he be made to do as I ask him? You wicked creature, I shall tell papa what you said – Now then!'

Hareton did not appear to feel this threat; so the tears sprung into her eyes with indignation.

'You bring the pony,' she exclaimed, turning to the woman, 'and let my dog free this moment!'

'Softly, miss,' answered the addressed: 'you'll lose nothing by being civil. Though Mr Hareton, there, be not the master's son, he's your cousin; and I was never hired to serve you.'

'*He* my cousin!' cried Cathy, with a scornful laugh.

'Yes, indeed,' responded her reprover.

'Oh, Ellen! Don't let them say such things,' she pursued in great trouble. 'Papa is gone to fetch my cousin from London: my cousin is a gentleman's son. That my – ' she stopped, and wept outright; upset at the bare notion of relationship with such a clown.

'Hush, hush!' I whispered, 'people can have many cousins and of all sorts, Miss Cathy, without being any the worse for it; only they needn't keep their company, if they be disagreeable and bad.'

'He's not – he's not my cousin, Ellen!' she went on, gathering fresh grief from reflection, and flinging herself into my arms for refuge from the idea.

I was much vexed at her and the servant for their mutual revelations; having no doubt of Linton's approaching arrival, communicated by the former, being reported to Mr Heathcliff; and feeling as confident that Catherine's first thought on her father's return would be to seek an explanation of the latter's assertion concerning her rude-bred kindred. Hareton, recovering from his disgust at being taken for a servant, seemed moved by her distress; and, having fetched the pony round to the door, he took, to propitiate her, a fine crooked-legged terrier whelp from the kennel, and putting it into her hand bid her wisht! For he meant naught. Pausing in her lamentations, she surveyed him with a glance of awe and horror, then burst forth anew.

I could scarcely refrain from smiling at this antipathy to the poor fellow; who was a well-made, athletic youth, good looking in features, and stout and healthy, but attired in garments befitting his daily occupations of working on the farm, and lounging among the moors after rabbits and game. Still, I thought I could detect in his physiognomy a mind owning better qualities than his father ever possessed. Good things lost amid a wilderness of weeds, to be sure, whose rankness far over-topped their neglected growth; yet, notwithstanding, evidence of a wealthy soil, that might yield luxuriant crops under other and favourable circumstances. Mr Heathcliff, I believe, had not treated him physically ill; thanks to his fearless nature, which offered no temptation to that course of oppression: it had none of the timid susceptibility that would have given zest to ill-treatment, in Heathcliff's judgement. He appeared to have bent his malevolence on making him a brute: he was never taught to read or write; never rebuked for any bad habit which did not annoy his keeper; never led a single step towards virtue, or guarded by a single precept against vice. And from what I heard, Joseph contributed much to his deterioration, by a narrow-minded partiality which prompted him to flatter and pet him, as a boy, because he was the head of the old family. And as he had been in the habit of accusing Catherine Earnshaw and Heathcliff, when children, of putting the master past his patience, and compelling him to seek solace in drink by what he termed their 'offalld ways', so at present he laid the whole burden of Hareton's faults on the shoulders of the usurper of his property. If the lad swore, he wouldn't correct him: nor however culpably he behaved. It gave Joseph satisfaction, apparently, to watch him go the worst lengths: he allowed that he was ruined: that his soul was abandoned to perdition; but then, he reflected that Heathcliff must answer for it. Hareton's blood would be required at his hands; and there lay immense consolation in that thought. Joseph had instilled into him a pride of name, and of his lineage; he would, had he dared, have fostered hate between him and the present owner of the Heights: but his dread of that owner amounted to superstition; and he confined his feelings regarding him to muttered innuendoes and private comminations. I don't pretend to be intimately acquainted with the mode of living customary in those days at Wuthering Heights: I only speak from hearsay; for I saw little. The villagers affirmed Mr Heathcliff was *near*, and a cruel hard landlord to his tenants; but the house, inside, had regained its ancient aspect of comfort under female management, and the scenes of riot common in Hindley's time were not now enacted within its walls. The master was too gloomy to seek companionship with any people, good or bad; and he is yet.

This, however, is not making progress with my story. Miss Cathy rejected the peace-offering of the terrier, and demanded her own dogs, Charlie and Phoenix. They came limping, and hanging their heads; and we set out for home, sadly out of sorts, every one of us. I could not wring from my little lady how she had spent the day; except that, as I supposed, the goal of her pilgrimage was Penistone Craggs; and she arrived without adventure to the gate of the farmhouse, when Hareton happened to issue forth, attended by some canine followers, who attacked her train. They had a smart battle, before their owners could separate them: that formed an introduction. Catherine told Hareton who she was, and where she was going; and asked him to show her the way; finally, beguiling him to accompany her. He opened the mysteries of the fairy cave, and twenty other queer places. But, being in disgrace, I was not favoured with a description of the interesting objects she saw. I could gather, however, that her guide had been a favourite till she hurt his feelings by addressing him as a servant; and Heathcliff's housekeeper hurt hers by calling him her cousin. Then the language he had held to her rankled in her heart; she who was always 'love', and 'darling', and 'queen', and 'angel', with everybody at the Grange, to be insulted so shockingly by a stranger! She did not comprehend it; and hard work I had to obtain a promise that she would not lay the grievance before her father. I explained how he objected to the whole household at the Heights, and how sorry he would be to find she had been there; but I insisted most on the fact, that if she revealed my negligence of his orders, he would perhaps be so angry, that I should have to leave; and Cathy couldn't bear that prospect: she pledged her word, and kept it, for my sake. After all, she was a sweet little girl.

## *Chapter 19*

A letter, edged with black, announced the day of my master's return. Isabella was dead; and he wrote to bid me get mourning for his daughter, and arrange a room, and other accommodations, for his youthful nephew. Catherine ran wild with joy at the idea of welcoming her father back; and indulged most sanguine anticipations of the innumerable excellences of her 'real' cousin. The evening of their expected arrival came. Since early morning, she had been busy ordering her own small affairs; and now, attired in her new black frock – poor thing! Her aunt's death impressed her with no definite sorrow – she obliged me, by constant worrying, to walk with her down through the grounds to meet them.

'Linton is just six months younger than I am,' she chattered, as we strolled leisurely over the swells and hollows of mossy turf, under shadow of the trees. 'How delightful it will be to have him for a playfellow! Aunt Isabella sent papa a beautiful lock of his hair; it was lighter than mine – more flaxen, and quite as fine. I have it carefully preserved in a little glass box; and I've often thought what pleasure it would be to see its owner. Oh! I am happy – and papa, dear, dear papa! Come, Ellen, let us run! Come run!'

She ran, and returned and ran again, many times before my sober footsteps reached the gate, and then she seated herself on the grassy bank beside the path, and tried to wait patiently, but that was impossible: she couldn't be still a minute.

'How long they are!' she exclaimed. 'Ah, I see some dust on the road – they are coming! No! When will they be here? May we not go a little way – half a mile, Ellen: only just half a mile? Do say yes, to that clump of birches at the turn!'

I refused staunchly: and, at length, her suspense was ended: the travelling carriage rolled in sight. Miss Cathy shrieked, and stretched out her arms, as soon as she caught her father's face looking from the window. He descended, nearly as eager as herself; and a considerable interval elapsed ere they had a thought to spare for any but themselves. While they exchanged caresses, I took a peep in to see after Linton. He was asleep in a corner, wrapped in a warm, fur-lined cloak, as if it had been winter. A pale, delicate, effeminate boy, who might have been taken for my master's younger brother, so strong was the resemblance: but there was a sickly peevishness in his aspect that Edgar Linton never had. The latter saw me looking; and having shaken hands, advised me to close the door, and leave him undisturbed; for the journey had fatigued him. Cathy would fain have taken one glance, but her father told her to come on, and they walked together up the park, while I hastened before to prepare the servants.

'Now, darling,' said Mr Linton, addressing his daughter, as they halted at the bottom of the front steps: 'your cousin is not so strong or so merry as you are, and he has lost his mother, remember, a very short time since; therefore, don't expect him to play and run about with you directly. And don't harass him much by talking: let him be quiet this evening, at least, will you?

'Yes, yes, papa,' answered Catherine: 'but I do want to see him; and he hasn't once looked out.'

The carriage stopped; and the sleeper, being roused, was lifted to the ground by his uncle.

'This is your cousin Cathy, Linton,' he said, putting their little hands together. 'She's fond of you already; and mind you don't grieve her by crying tonight. Try to be cheerful now; the travelling is at an end, and you have nothing to do but rest and amuse yourself as you please.'

'Let me go to bed, then,' answered the boy, shrinking from Catherine's salute; and he put his fingers to his eyes to remove incipient tears.

'Come, come, there's a good child,' I whispered, leading him in. 'You'll make her weep too – see how sorry she is for you!'

I do not know whether it were sorrow for him, but his cousin put on as sad a countenance as himself, and returned to her father. All three entered, and mounted to the library, where tea was laid ready. I proceeded to remove Linton's cap and mantle, and placed him on a chair by the table; but he was no sooner seated than he began to cry afresh. My master enquired what was the matter.

'I can't sit on a chair,' sobbed the boy.

'Go to the sofa, then, and Ellen shall bring you some tea,' answered his uncle, patiently.

He had been greatly tried during the journey, I felt convinced, by his fretful ailing charge. Linton slowly trailed himself off, and lay down. Cathy carried a footstool and her cup to his side. At first she sat silent; but that could not last: she had resolved to make a pet of her little cousin, as she would have him to be; and she commenced stroking his curls, and kissing his cheek, and offering him tea in her saucer, like a baby. This pleased him, for he was not much better: he dried his eyes, and lightened into a faint smile.

'Oh, he'll do very well,' said the master to me, after watching them a minute. 'Very well, if we can keep him, Ellen. The company of a child of his own age will instil new spirit into him soon, and by wishing for strength he'll gain it.'

'Ay, if we can keep him!' I mused to myself; and sore misgivings came over me that there was slight hope of that. And then, I thought, however will that weakling live at Wuthering Heights, between his father and Hareton? what playmates and instructors they'll be. Our doubts were presently decided – even earlier than I expected. I had just taken the children upstairs, after tea was finished, and seen Linton asleep – he would not suffer me to leave him till that was the case – I had come down, and was standing by the table in the hall, lighting a bedroom candle for Mr Edgar, when a maid stepped out of the kitchen and informed me that Mr Heathcliff's servant Joseph was at the door, and wished to speak with the master.

'I shall ask him what he wants first,' I said, in considerable trepidation. 'A very unlikely hour to be troubling people, and the instant they have returned from a long journey. I don't think the master can see him.'

Joseph had advanced through the kitchen as I uttered these words, and now presented himself in the hall. He was donned in his Sunday garments, with his most sanctimonious and sourest face, and, holding his hat in one hand and his stick in the other, he proceeded to clean his shoes on the mat.

'Good-evening, Joseph,' I said, coldly. 'What business brings you here tonight?'

'It's Maister Linton Aw mun spake tull,' he answered, waving me disdainfully aside.

'Mr Linton is going to bed; unless you have something particular to say, I'm sure he won't hear it now,' I continued. 'You had better sit down in there, and entrust your message to me.'

'Which is his rahm?' pursued the fellow, surveying the range of closed doors.

I perceived he was bent on refusing my mediation, so very reluctantly I went up to the library, and announced the unseasonable visitor, advising that he should be dismissed till next day. Mr Linton had no time to empower me to do so, for he mounted close at my heels, and, pushing into the apartment, planted himself at the far side of the table, with his two fists clapped on the head of his stick, and began in an elevated tone, as if anticipating opposition – 'Hathecliff has send me for his lad, un Aw munn't goa back 'baht him.'

Edgar Linton was silent a minute; an expression of exceeding sorrow overcast his features: he would have pitied the child on his own account; but, recalling Isabella's hopes and fears, and anxious wishes for her son, and her commendations of him to his care, he grieved bitterly at the prospect of yielding him up, and searched in his heart how it might be avoided. No plan offered itself: the very exhibition of any desire to keep him would have rendered the claimant more peremptory: there was nothing left but to resign him. However, he was not going to rouse him from his sleep.

'Tell Mr Heathcliff,' he answered, calmly, 'that his son shall come to Wuthering Heights tomorrow. He is in bed, and too tired to go the distance now. You may also tell him that the mother of Linton desired him to remain under my guardianship; and, at present, his health is very precarious.'

'Noa!' said Joseph, giving a thud with his prop on the floor, and assuming an authoritative air. 'Noa! that manes nowt – Hathecliff maks noa 'cahnt uh t' mother, nur yah norther; Bud he'll hev his lad; und Aw mun tak him – soa nah yah knaw!'

'You shall not tonight!' answered Linton, decisively. 'Walk downstairs at once, and repeat to your master what I have said. Ellen, show him down. Go –'

And, aiding the indignant elder with a lift by the arm, he rid the room of him, and closed the door.

'Varrah weel!' shouted Joseph, as he slowly drew off. 'Tuh morn, he's come hisseln, un'thrust *him* aht, if yah darr!'

## *Chapter 20*

To obviate the danger of this threat being fulfilled, Mr Linton commissioned me to take the boy home early, on Catherine's pony; and, said he – 'As we shall now have no influence over his destiny, good or bad, you must say nothing of where he is gone to my daughter: she cannot associate with him hereafter, and it is better for her to remain in ignorance of his proximity; lest she should be restless, and anxious to visit the Heights – merely tell her, his father sent for him suddenly, and he has been obliged to leave us.'

Linton was very reluctant to be roused from his bed at five o'clock, and astonished to be informed that he must prepare for further travelling; but I softened off the matter by stating that he was going to spend some time with his father, Mr Heathcliff, who wished to see him so much, he did not like to defer the pleasure till he should recover from his late journey.

'My father!' he cried, in strange perplexity. 'Mamma never told me I had a father. Where does he live? I'd rather stay with uncle.'

'He lives a little distance from the Grange,' I replied; 'just beyond those hills: not so far, but you may walk over here when you get hearty. And you should be glad to go home, and to see him. You must try to love him, as you did your mother, and then he will love you.'

'But why have I not heard of him before?' asked Linton. 'Why didn't mamma and he live together, as other people do?'

'He had business to keep him in the north,' I answered, 'and your mother's health required her to reside in the south.'

'And why didn't mamma speak to me about him?' persevered the child. 'She often talked of uncle, and I learnt to love him long ago. How am I to love papa? I don't know him.'

'Oh, all children love their parents,' I said. 'Your mother, perhaps, thought you would want to be with him if she mentioned him often to you. Let us make haste. An early ride on such a beautiful morning is much preferable to an hour's more sleep.'

'Is *she* to go with us,' he demanded: 'the little girl I saw yesterday?'

'Not now,' replied I.

'Is uncle?' he continued.

'No, I shall be your companion there,' I said.

Linton sank back on his pillow, and fell into a brown study.

'I won't go without uncle,' he cried at length; 'I can't tell where you mean to take me.'

I attempted to persuade him of the naughtiness of showing reluctance to meet his father; still he obstinately resisted any progress towards dressing, and I had to call for my master's assistance in coaxing him out of bed. The poor thing was finally got off with several delusive assurances that his absence should be short; that Mr Edgar and Cathy would visit him, and other promises, equally ill-founded, which I invented and reiterated at intervals throughout the way. The pure heather-scented air, and the bright sunshine, and the gentle canter of Minny, relieved his despondency, after a while. He began to put questions concerning his new home, and its inhabitants, with greater interest and liveliness.

'Is Wuthering Heights as pleasant a place as Thrushcross Grange?' he enquired, turning to take a last glance into the valley, whence a light mist mounted and formed a fleecy cloud on the skirts of the blue.

'It is not so buried in trees,' I replied, 'and it is not quite so large, but you can see the country beautifully, all round; and the air is healthier for you – fresher and dryer. You will, perhaps, think the building old and dark at first; though it is a respectable house: the next best in the neighbourhood. And you will have such nice rambles on the moors. Hareton Earnshaw – that is Miss Cathy's other cousin, and so yours in a manner – will show you all the sweetest spots; and you can bring a book in fine weather, and make a green hollow your study; and, now and then, your uncle may join you in a walk: he does, frequently, walk out on the hills.'

'And what is my father like?' he asked. 'Is he as young and handsome as uncle?'

'He's as young,' said I; 'but he has black hair and eyes, and looks sterner; and he is taller and bigger altogether. He'll not seem to you so gentle and kind at first, perhaps, because it is not his way – still, mind you be frank and cordial with him; and naturally he'll be fonder of you than any uncle, for you are his own.'

'Black hair and eyes!' mused Linton. 'I can't fancy him. Then I am not like him, am I?'

'Not much,' I answered . . . not a morsel, I thought, surveying with regret the white complexion and slim frame of my companion, and his large languid eyes . . . his mother's eyes, save that, unless a morbid touchiness kindled them a moment, they had not a vestige of her sparkling spirit.

'How strange that he should never come to see mama, and me!' he murmured. 'Has he ever seen me? If he have, I must have been a baby – I remember not a single thing about him!'

'Why, Master Linton,' said I, 'three hundred miles is a great distance; and ten years seem very different in length to a grown-up person compared with what they do to you. It is probable Mr Heathcliff proposed going, from summer to summer, but never found a convenient opportunity; and now it is too late. Don't trouble him with questions on the subject: it will disturb him for no good.'

The boy was fully occupied with his own cogitations for the remainder of the ride, till we halted before the farmhouse garden gate. I watched to catch his impressions in his countenance. He surveyed the carved front and low-browed lattices, the straggling gooseberry bushes and crooked firs, with solemn intentness, and then shook his head: his private feelings entirely disapproved of the exterior of his new abode. But he had sense to postpone complaining: there might be compensation within. Before he dismounted, I went and opened the door. It was half-past six; the family had just finished breakfast; the servant was clearing and wiping down the table: Joseph stood by his master's chair telling some tale concerning a lame horse; and Hareton was preparing for the hayfield.

'Hallo, Nelly!' cried Mr Heathcliff, when he saw me. 'I feared I should have to come down and fetch my property myself. You've brought it, have you? Let us see what we can make of it.'

He got up and strode to the door: Hareton and Joseph followed in gaping curiosity. Poor Linton ran a frightened eye over the faces of the three.

'Sure–ly,' said Joseph after a grave inspection, 'he's swopped wi' ye, maister, an' yon's his lass!'

Heathcliff, having stared his son into an ague of confusion, uttered a scornful laugh.

'God! What a beauty! What a lovely, charming thing!' he exclaimed. 'Haven't they reared it on snails and sour milk, Nelly? Oh, damn my soul! But that's worse than I expected – and the devil knows I was not sanguine!'

I bid the trembling and bewildered child get down, and enter. He did not thoroughly comprehend the meaning of his father's speech, or whether it were intended for him: indeed, he was not yet certain that the grim, sneering stranger was his father; but he clung to me with growing trepidation; and on Mr Heathcliff's taking a seat, and bidding him 'come hither', he hid his face on my shoulder, and wept.

'Tut, tut!' said Heathcliff, stretching out a hand and dragging him roughly between his knees, and then holding up his head by the chin. 'None of that nonsense! We're not going to hurt thee, Linton – isn't that thy name? Thou art thy mother's child, entirely! Where is *my* share in thee, puling chicken?'

He took off the boy's cap and pushed back his thick flaxen curls, felt his slender arms and his small fingers; during which examination Linton ceased crying, and lifted his great blue eyes to inspect the inspector.

'Do you know me?' asked Heathcliff, having satisfied himself that the limbs were all equally frail and feeble.

'No,' said Linton, with a gaze of vacant fear.

'You've heard of me, I dare say?'

'No,' he replied again.

'No? What a shame of your mother, never to waken your filial regard for me! You are my son, then, I'll tell you; and your mother was a wicked slut to leave you in ignorance of the sort of father you possessed. Now, don't wince, and colour up! Though it *is* something to see you have not white blood. Be a good lad; and I'll do for you. Nelly, if you be tired you may sit down; if not, get home again. I guess you'll report what you hear, and see, to the cipher at the Grange; and this thing won't be settled while you linger about it.'

'Well,' replied I, 'I hope you'll be kind to the boy, Mr Heathcliff, or you'll not keep him long; and he's all you have akin in the wide world, that you will ever know – remember.'

'I'll be *very* kind to him, you needn't fear,' he said, laughing. 'Only nobody else must be kind to him: I'm jealous of monopolising his affection. And, to begin my kindness, Joseph! Bring the lad some breakfast. Hareton, you infernal calf, begone to your work. Yes, Nell,' he added when they had departed, 'my son is prospective owner of your place, and I should not wish him to die till I was certain of being his successor. Besides, he's *mine*, and I want the triumph of seeing *my* descendant fairly lord of their estates: my child hiring their children to till their fathers' lands for wages. That is the sole consideration which can make me endure the whelp: I despise him for himself, and hate him for the memories he revives! But that consideration is sufficient: he's as safe with me, and shall be tended as carefully as your master tends his own. I have a room upstairs, furnished for him in handsome style; I've engaged a tutor, also, to come three times a week, from twenty miles distance, to teach him what he pleases to learn. I've ordered Hareton to obey him: and in fact I've arranged everything with a view to preserve the superior and the gentleman in him, above his associates. I do regret, however, that he so little deserves the trouble: if I wished any blessing in the world, it was to find him a worthy object of pride; and I'm bitterly disappointed with the wheyfaced whining wretch!'

While he was speaking, Joseph returned, bearing a basin of milk-porridge, and placed it before Linton. He stirred round the homely mess with a look of aversion, and affirmed he could not eat it. I saw the old manservant shared largely in his master's scorn of the child; though he was compelled to retain the sentiment in his heart, because Heathcliff plainly meant his underlings to hold him in honour.

'Cannot ate it?' repeated he, peering in Linton's face, and subduing his voice to a whisper, for fear of being overheard. 'But Maister Hareton nivir ate nowt else, when he wer a little un: und what wer gooid eneugh fur him's gooid eneugh fur yah, Aw's rayther think!'

'I *shan't* eat it!' answered Linton, snappishly. 'Take it away.'

Joseph snatched up the food indignantly, and brought it to us.

'Is there owt ails th' victuals?' he asked, thrusting the tray under Heathcliff's nose.

'What should ail them?' he said.

'Wah!' answered Joseph, 'yon dainty chap says he cannut ate 'em. Bud Aw guess it's raight! His mother wer just soa – we wer a'most too mucky tuh sow t' corn fur makking her breead.'

'Don't mention his mother to me,' said the master, angrily. 'Get him something that he can eat, that's all. What is his usual food, Nelly?'

I suggested boiled milk or tea; and the housekeeper received instructions to prepare some. Come, I reflected, his father's selfishness may contribute to his comfort. He perceives his delicate constitution, and the necessity of treating him tolerably. I'll console Mr Edgar by acquainting him with the turn Heathcliff's humour has taken. Having no excuse for lingering longer, I slipped out, while Linton was engaged in timidly rebuffing the advances of a friendly sheepdog. But he was too much on the alert to be cheated: as I closed the door, I heard a cry, and a frantic repetition of the words – 'Don't leave me! I'll not stay here! I'll not stay here!'

Then the latch was raised and fell: they did not suffer him to come forth. I mounted Minny, and urged her to a trot; and so my brief guardianship ended.

## *Chapter 21*

We had sad work with little Cathy that day: she rose in high glee, eager to join her cousin; and such passionate tears and lamentations followed the news of his departure, that Edgar himself was obliged to sooth her, by affirming he should come back soon: he added, however, 'if I can get him'; and there were no hopes of that. This promise poorly pacified her; but time was more potent; and though still at intervals she enquired of her father when Linton would return, before she did see him again his features had waxed so dim in her memory that she did not recognise him.

When I chanced to encounter the housekeeper of Wuthering Heights, in paying business-visits to Gimmerton, I used to ask how the young master got on; for he lived almost as secluded as Catherine herself, and was never to be seen. I could gather from her that he continued in weak health, and was a tiresome inmate. She said Mr Heathcliff seemed to dislike him ever longer and worse, though he took some trouble to conceal it. He had an antipathy to the sound of his voice, and could not do at all with his sitting in the same room with him many minutes together. There seldom passed much talk between them: Linton learnt his lessons and spent his evenings in a small apartment they called the parlour: or else lay in bed all day: for he was constantly getting coughs, and colds, and aches, and pains of some sort.

'And I never knew such a fainthearted creature,' added the woman; 'nor one so careful of hisseln. He *will* go on, if I leave the window open a bit late in the evening. Oh! it's killing, a breath of night air! And he must have a fire in the middle of summer; and Joseph's bacca pipe is poison; and he must always have sweets and dainties, and always milk, milk for ever – heeding naught how the rest of us are pinched in winter; and there he'll sit, wrapped in his furred cloak in his chair by the fire, and some toast and water or other slop on the hob to sip at; and if Hareton, for pity, comes to amuse him – Hareton is not bad-natured, though he's rough – they're sure to part, one swearing and the other crying. I believe the master would relish Earnshaw's thrashing him to a mummy, if he were not his son; and I'm certain he would be fit to turn him out of doors, if he knew half the nursing he gives hisseln. But then, he won't go into danger of temptation: he never enters the parlour, and should Linton show those ways in the house where he is, he sends him upstairs directly.'

I divined, from this account, that utter lack of sympathy had rendered young Heathcliff selfish and disagreeable, if he were not so originally; and my interest in him, consequently, decayed: though still I was moved with a sense of grief at his lot, and a wish that he had been left with us.

Mr Edgar encouraged me to gain information: he thought a great deal about him, I fancy, and would have run some risk to see him; and he told me once to ask the housekeeper whether he ever came into the village? She said he had only been twice, on horseback, accompanying his father; and both times he pretended to be quite knocked up for three or four days afterwards. That housekeeper left, if I recollect rightly, two years after he came; and another, whom I did not know, was her successor: she lives there still.

Time wore on at the Grange in its former pleasant way, till Miss Cathy reached sixteen. On the anniversary of her birth we never manifested any signs of rejoicing, because it was also the anniversary of my late mistress's death. Her father invariably spent that day alone in the library; and walked, at dusk, as far as Gimmerton kirkyard, where he would frequently prolong his stay beyond midnight. Therefore Catherine was thrown on her own resources for amusement.

This twentieth of March was a beautiful spring day, and when her father had retired, my young lady came down dressed for going out, and said she had asked to have a ramble on the edge of the moors with me; and Mr Linton had given her leave, if we went only a short distance and were back within the hour.

'So make haste, Ellen!' she cried. 'I know where I wish to go; where a colony of moor-game are settled: I want to see whether they have made their nests yet.'

'That must be a good distance up,' I answered; 'they don't breed on the edge of the moor.'

'No, it's not,' she said. 'I've gone very near with papa.'

I put on my bonnet and sallied out, thinking nothing more of the matter. She bounded before me, and returned to my side, and was off again like a young greyhound; and, at first, I found plenty of entertainment in listening to the larks singing far and near, and enjoying the sweet, warm sunshine; and watching her, my pet, and my delight, with her golden ringlets flying loose behind, and her bright cheek, as soft and pure in its bloom as a wild rose, and her eyes radiant with cloudless pleasure. She was a happy creature, and an angel, in those days. It's a pity she could not be content.

'Well,' said I, 'where are your moor-game, Miss Cathy? We should be at them: the Grange park-fence is a great way off now.'

'Oh, a little farther – only a little farther, Ellen,' was her answer, continually. 'Climb to that hillock, pass that bank, and by the time you reach the other side I shall have raised the birds.'

But there were so many hillocks and banks to climb and pass, that, at length, I began to be weary, and told her we must halt, and retrace our steps. I shouted to her, as she had outstripped me, a long way; she either did not hear or did not regard, for she still sprang on, and I was compelled to follow. Finally, she dived into a hollow; and before I came in sight of her again, she was two miles nearer Wuthering Heights than her own home; and I beheld a couple of persons arrest her, one of whom I felt convinced was Mr Heathcliff himself.

Cathy had been caught in the fact of plundering, or, at least, hunting out the nests of the grouse. The Heights were Heathcliff's land, and he was reproving the poacher.

'I've neither taken any nor found any,' she said, as I toiled to them, expanding her hands in corroboration of the statement. 'I didn't mean to take them; but papa told me there were quantities up here, and I wished to see the eggs.'

Heathcliff glanced at me with an ill-meaning smile, expressing his acquaintance with the party, and, consequently, his malevolence towards it, and demanded who 'papa' was?

'Mr Linton of Thrushcross Grange,' she replied. 'I thought you did not know me, or you wouldn't have spoken in that way.'

'You suppose papa is highly esteemed and respected, then?' he said, sarcastically.

'And what are you?' enquired Catherine, gazing curiously on the speaker. 'That man I've seen before. Is he your son?'

She pointed to Hareton, the other individual, who had gained nothing but increased bulk and strength by the addition of two years to his age: he seemed as awkward and rough as ever.

'Miss Cathy,' I interrupted, 'it will be three hours instead of one that we are out, presently. We really must go back.'

'No, that man is not my son,' answered Heathcliff, pushing me aside. 'But I have one, and you have seen him before, too; and, though your nurse is in a hurry, I think both you and she would be the better for a little rest. Will you just turn this nab of heath, and walk into my house ? You'll get home earlier for the ease; and you shall receive a kind welcome.'

I whispered Catherine that she mustn't, on any account, accede to the proposal: it was entirely out of the question.

'Why?' she asked, aloud. 'I'm tired of running, and the ground is dewy: I can't sit here. Let us go, Ellen. Besides, he says I have seen his son. He's mistaken, I think; but I guess where he lives: at the farmhouse I visited in coming from Penistone Craggs. Don't you?'

'I do. Come, Nelly, hold your tongue – it will be a treat for her to look in on us. Hareton, get forwards with the lass. You shall walk with me, Nelly.'

'No, she's not going to any such place,' I cried, struggling to release my arm, which he had seized: but she was almost at the door-stones already, scampering round the brow at full speed. Her appointed companion did not pretend to escort her: he shied off by the roadside, and vanished.

'Mr Heathcliff, it's very wrong,' I continued: 'you know you mean no good.

And there she'll see Linton, and all will be told, as soon as ever we return; and I shall have the blame.'

'I want her to see Linton,' he answered; 'he's looking better these few days: it's not often he's fit to be seen. And we'll soon persuade her to keep the visit secret: where is the harm of it?'

'The harm of it is, that her father would hate me if he found I suffered her to enter your house; and I am convinced you have a bad design in encouraging her to do so,' I replied.

'My design is as honest as possible. I'll inform you of its whole scope,' he said. 'That the two cousins may fall in love, and get married. I'm acting generously to your master: his young chit has no expectations, and should she second my wishes, she'll be provided for at once as joint successor with Linton.'

'If Linton died,' I answered, 'and his life is quite uncertain, Catherine would be the heir.'

'No, she would not,' he said. 'There is no clause in the will to secure it so: his property would go to me; but, to prevent disputes, I desire their union, and am resolved to bring it about.'

'And I'm resolved she shall never approach your house with me again,' I returned, as we reached the gate, where Miss Cathy waited our coming.

Heathcliff bid me be quiet; and, preceding us up the path, hastened to open the door. My young lady gave him several looks, as if she could not exactly make up her mind what to think of him; but now he smiled when he met her eye, and softened his voice in addressing her; and I was foolish enough to imagine the memory of her mother might disarm him from desiring her injury. Linton stood on the hearth. He had been out, walking in the fields, for his cap was on, and he was calling to Joseph to bring him dry shoes. He had grown tall of his age, still wanting some months of sixteen. His features were pretty yet, and his eye and complexion brighter than I remembered them, though with merely temporary lustre borrowed from the salubrious air and genial sun.

'Now, who is that?' asked Mr Heathcliff, turning to Cathy. 'Can you tell?'

'Your son?' she said, having doubtfully surveyed, first one and then the other.

'Yes, yes,' answered he: 'but is this the only time you have beheld him? Think! Ah! you have a short memory. Linton, don't you recall your cousin, that you used to tease us so with wishing to see?'

'What, Linton!' cried Cathy, kindling into joyful surprise at the name. 'Is that little Linton? He's taller than I am! Are you, Linton?'

The youth stepped forward, and acknowledged himself: she kissed him fervently, and they gazed with wonder at the change time had wrought in the appearance of each. Catherine had reached her full height; her figure was both plump and slender, elastic as steel, and her whole aspect sparkling with health and spirits. Linton's looks and movements were very languid, and his form extremely slight; but there was a grace in his manner that mitigated these defects, and rendered him not unpleasing. After exchanging numerous marks of fondness with him, his cousin went to Mr Heathcliff, who lingered by the door, dividing his attention between the objects inside and those that lay without: pretending, that is, to observe the latter, and really noting the former alone.

'And you are my uncle, then!' she cried, reaching up to salute him. 'I thought I liked you, though you were cross, at first. Why don't you visit at the Grange with Linton? To live all these years such close neighbours, and never see us, is odd: what have you done so for?'

'I visited it once or twice too often before you were born,' he answered. 'There – damn it! If you have any kisses to spare, give them to Linton: they are thrown away on me.'

'Naughty Ellen!' exclaimed Catherine, flying to attack me next with her lavish caresses. 'Wicked Ellen! to try to hinder me from entering. But I'll take this walk every morning in future: may I, uncle? And sometimes bring papa. Won't you be glad to see us?'

'Of course!' replied the uncle, with a hardly suppressed grimace, resulting from his deep aversion to both the proposed visitors. 'But stay,' he continued, turning towards the young lady. 'Now I think of it, I'd better tell you. Mr Linton has a prejudice against me: we quarrelled at one time of our lives, with unchristian ferocity; and, if you mention coming here to him, he'll put a veto on your visits altogether. Therefore, you must not mention it, unless you be careless of seeing your cousin hereafter: you may come, if you will, but you must not mention it.'

'Why did you quarrel?' asked Catherine, considerably crestfallen.

'He thought me too poor to wed his sister,' answered Heathcliff, 'and was grieved that I got her: his pride was hurt, and he'll never forgive it.'

'That's wrong!' said the young lady: 'some time, I'll tell him so. But Linton and I have no share in your quarrel. I'll not come here, then; he shall come to the Grange.'

'It will be too far for me,' murmured her cousin: 'to walk four miles would kill me. No, come here, Miss Catherine, now and then: not every morning, but once or twice a week.'

The father launched towards his son a glance of bitter contempt.

'I am afraid, Nelly, I shall lose my labour,' he muttered to me. 'Miss Catherine, as the ninny calls her, will discover his value, and send him to the devil. Now, if it had been Hareton! – Do you know that, twenty times a day, I covet Hareton, with all his degradation? I'd have loved the lad had he been someone else. But I think he's safe from *her* love. I'll pit him against that paltry creature, unless it bestir itself briskly. We calculate it will scarcely last till it is eighteen. Oh, confound the vapid thing! He's absorbed in drying his feet, and never looks at her – Linton!'

'Yes, father,' answered the boy.

'Have you nothing to show your cousin, anywhere about; not even a rabbit, or a weasel's nest? Take her into the garden, before you change your shoes; and into the stable to see your horse.'

'Wouldn't you rather sit here?' asked Linton, addressing Cathy in a tone which expressed reluctance to move again.

'I don't know,' she replied, casting a longing look to the door, and evidently eager to be active.

He kept his seat, and shrank closer to the fire. Heathcliff rose, and went into the kitchen, and from thence to the yard, calling out for Hareton. Hareton responded, and presently the two re-entered. The young man had been washing himself, as was visible by the glow on his cheeks, and his wetted hair.

'Oh, I'll ask *you*, uncle,' cried Miss Cathy, recollecting the housekeeper's assertion. 'That is not my cousin, is he?'

'Yes,' he replied, 'your mother's nephew. Don't you like him?'

Catherine looked queer.

'Is he not a handsome lad?' he continued.

The uncivil little thing stood on tiptoe, and whispered a sentence in Heathcliff's ear. He laughed; Hareton darkened: I perceived he was very sensitive to suspected slights, and had obviously a dim notion of his inferiority. But his master or guardian chased the frown by exclaiming – 'You'll be the favourite among us, Hareton! She says you are a – what was it? Well, something very flattering. Here! you go with her round the farm. And behave like a gentleman, mind! Don't use any bad words; and don't stare, when the young lady is not looking at you, and be ready to hide your face when she is; and, when you speak, say your words slowly, and keep your hands out of your pockets. Be off, and entertain her as nicely as you can.'

He watched the couple walking past the window. Earnshaw had his countenance completely averted from his companion. He seemed studying the familiar landscape with a stranger's and an artist's interest. Catherine took a sly look at him, expressing small admiration. She then turned her attention to seeking out objects of amusement for herself, and tripped merrily on, lilting a tune to supply the lack of conversation.

'I've tied his tongue,' observed Heathcliff. 'He'll not venture a single syllable, all the time! Nelly, you recollect me at his age – nay, some years younger. Did I ever look so stupid: so "gaumless", as Joseph calls it?'

'Worse,' I replied, 'because more sullen with it.'

'I've a pleasure in him,' he continued reflecting aloud. 'He has satisfied my expectations. If he were a born fool I should not enjoy it half so much. But he's no fool; and I can sympathise with all his feelings, having felt them myself. I know what he suffers now, for instance, exactly: it is merely a beginning of what he shall suffer, though. And he'll never be able to emerge from his bathos of coarseness and ignorance. I've got him faster than his scoundrel of a father secured me, and lower; for he takes a pride in his brutishness. I've taught him to scorn everything extra animal as silly and weak. Don't you think Hindley would be proud of his son, if he could see him? almost as proud as I am of mine. But there's this difference; one is gold put to the use of paving-stones, and the other is tin polished to ape a service of silver. *Mine* has nothing valuable about it; yet I shall have the merit of making it go as far as such poor stuff can go. *His* had first rate qualities, and they are lost: rendered worse than unavailing. I have nothing to regret; he would have more than any, but I, are aware of. And the best of it is, Hareton is damnably fond of me! You'll own that I've out-matched Hindley there. If the dead villain could rise from his grave to abuse me for his offspring's wrongs, I should have the fun of seeing the said offspring fight him back again, indignant that he should dare to rail at the one friend he has in the world!'

Heathcliff chuckled a fiendish laugh at the idea. I made no reply, because I saw that he expected none. Meantime, our young companion, who sat too removed from us to hear what was said, began to evince symptoms of uneasiness, probably repenting that he had denied himself the treat of Catherine's society for fear of a little fatigue. His father remarked the restless glances wandering to the window, and the hand irresolutely extended towards his cap.

'Get up, you idle boy!' he exclaimed with assumed heartiness. 'Away after them! they are just at the corner, by the stand of hives.'

Linton gathered his energies, and left the hearth. The lattice was open, and, as he stepped out, I heard Cathy enquiring of her unsociable attendant, what was that inscription over the door? Hareton stared up, and scratched his head like a true clown.

'It's some damnable writing,' he answered. 'I cannot read it.'

'Can't read it?' cried Catherine; 'I can read it: it's English. But I want to know why it is there.'

Linton giggled – the first appearance of mirth he had exhibited.

'He does not know his letters,' he said to his cousin. 'Could you believe in the existence of such a colossal dunce?'

'Is he all as he should be?' asked Miss Cathy seriously; 'or is he simple: not right? I've questioned him twice now, and each time he looked so stupid I think he does not understand me. I can hardly understand *him*, I'm sure!'

Linton repeated his laugh, and glanced at Hareton tauntingly; who certainly did not seem quite clear of comprehension at that moment.

'There's nothing the matter, but laziness, is there, Earnshaw?' he said. 'My cousin fancies you are an idiot. There you experience the consequence of scorning "book-larning", as you would say. Have you noticed, Catherine, his frightful Yorkshire pronunciation?'

'Why, where the devil is the use on 't?' growled Hareton, more ready in answering his daily companion. He was about to enlarge further, but the two youngsters broke into a noisy fit of merriment; my giddy miss being delighted to discover that she might turn his strange talk to matter of amusement.

'Where is the use of the devil in that sentence?' tittered Linton. 'Papa told you not to say any bad words, and you can't open your mouth without one. Do try to behave like a gentleman, now do!'

'If thou wern't more a lass than a lad, I'd fell thee this minute, I would; pitiful lath of a crater!' retorted the angry boor, retreating, while his face burnt with mingled rage and mortification; for he was conscious of being insulted, and embarrassed how to resent it.

Mr Heathcliff having overheard the conversation, as well as I, smiled when he saw him go; but immediately afterwards cast a look of singular aversion on the flippant pair, who remained chattering in the doorway: the boy finding animation enough while discussing Hareton's faults and deficiencies, and relating anecdotes of his goings on; and the girl relishing his pert and spiteful sayings, without considering the ill-nature they evinced: but I began to dislike, more than to compassionate, Linton, and to excuse his father, in some measure, for holding him cheap.

We stayed till afternoon: I could not tear Miss Cathy away, before; but happily my master had not quitted his apartment, and remained ignorant of our prolonged absence. As we walked home, I would fain have enlightened my charge on the characters of the people we had quitted; but she got it into her head that I was prejudiced against them.

'Aha!' she cried, 'you take papa's side, Ellen: you are partial, I know; or else you wouldn't have cheated me so many years into the notion that Linton lived a long way from here. I'm really extremely angry, only, I'm so pleased, I can't show it! But you must hold your tongue about my uncle: he's *my* uncle, remember; and I'll scold papa for quarrelling with him.'

And so she ran on, till I dropped endeavouring to convince her of her mistake. She did not mention the visit that night, because she did not see Mr Linton. Next day it all came out, sadly to my chagrin; and still I was not altogether sorry: I thought the burden of directing and warning would be more efficiently borne by him than me, but he was too timid in giving satisfactory reasons for his wish that she would shun connection with the household of the Heights, and Catherine liked good reasons for every restraint that harassed her petted will.

'Papa!' she exclaimed, after the morning's salutations, 'guess whom I saw yesterday, in my walk on the moors. Ah, papa, you started! You've not done right, have you, now? I saw – But listen, and you shall hear how I found you out, and Ellen, who is in league with you, and yet pretended to pity me so, when I kept hoping, and was always disappointed about Linton's coming back!'

She gave a faithful account of her excursion and its consequences; and my master, though he cast more than one reproachful look at me, said nothing till she had concluded. Then he drew her to him, and asked if she knew why he had concealed Linton's near neighbourhood from her? Could she think it was to deny her a pleasure that she might harmlessly enjoy?

'It was because you disliked Mr Heathcliff,' she answered.

'Then you believe I care more for my own feelings than yours, Cathy?' he said. 'No, it was not because I disliked Mr Heathcliff, but because Mr Heathcliff dislikes me; and is a most diabolical man, delighting to wrong and ruin those he hates, if they give him the slightest opportunity. I knew that you could not keep up an acquaintance with your cousin, without being brought into contact with him; and I knew he would detest you, on my account; so for your own good, and nothing else, I took precautions that you should not see Linton again. I meant to explain this some time as you grew older, and I'm sorry I delayed it.'

'But Mr Heathcliff was quite cordial, papa,' observed Catherine, not at all convinced; 'and *he* didn't object to our seeing each other: he said I might come to his house when I pleased; only I must not tell you, because you had quarrelled with him, and would not forgive him for marrying Aunt Isabella. And you won't. *You* are the one to be blamed: he is willing to let *us* be friends, at least; Linton and I; and you are not.'

My master, perceiving that she would not take his word for her uncle-in-law's evil disposition, gave a hasty sketch of his conduct to Isabella, and the manner in which Wuthering Heights became his property. He could not bear to discourse long upon the topic; for though he spoke little of it, he still felt the same horror and detestation of his ancient enemy that had occupied his heart ever since Mrs Linton's death. 'She might have been living yet, if it had not been for him!' was his constant bitter reflection; and, in his eyes, Heathcliff seemed a murderer. Miss Cathy – conversant with no bad deeds except her own slight acts of disobedience, injustice, and passion, rising from hot temper and thoughtlessness, and repented of on the day they were committed – was amazed at the blackness of spirit that could brood on and cover revenge for years, and deliberately prosecute its plans without a visitation of remorse. She appeared so deeply impressed and shocked at this new view of human nature – excluded from all her studies and all her ideas till now – that Mr Edgar deemed it unnecessary to pursue the subject. He merely added – 'You will know hereafter, darling, why I wish you to avoid his house and family; now, return to your old employments and amusements, and think no more about them!'

Catherine kissed her father, and sat down quietly to her lessons for a couple of hours, according to custom; then she accompanied him into the grounds, and the whole day passed as usual: but in the evening, when she had retired to her room, and I went to help her to undress, I found her crying, on her knees by the bedside.

'Oh, fie, silly child!' I exclaimed. 'If you had any real griefs, you'd be ashamed to waste a tear on this little contrariety. You never had one shadow of substantial sorrow, Miss Catherine. Suppose, for a minute, that master and I were dead, and you were by yourself in the world: how would you feel then? Compare the present occasion with such an affliction as that, and be thankful for the friends you have, instead of coveting more.'

'I'm not crying for myself, Ellen,' she answered, 'it's for him. He expected to see me again tomorrow, and there, he'll be so disappointed: and he'll wait for me, and I shan't come!'

'Nonsense!' said I, 'do you imagine he has thought as much of you as you have of him? Hasn't he Hareton for a companion? Not one in a hundred would weep at losing a relation they had just seen twice, for two afternoons. Linton will conjecture how it is, and trouble himself no further about you.'

'But may I not write a note to tell him why I cannot come?' she asked, rising to her feet. 'And just send those books I promised to lend him? His books are not as nice as mine, and he wanted to have them extremely, when I told him how interesting they were. May I not, Ellen?'

'No, indeed! no, indeed!' replied I with decision. 'Then he would write to you, and there'd never be an end of it. No, Miss Catherine, the acquaintance must be dropped entirely: so papa expects, and I shall see that it is done.'

'But how can one little note – ' she recommenced, putting on an imploring countenance.

'Silence!' I interrupted. 'We'll not begin with your little notes. Get into bed.'

She threw at me a very naughty look, so naughty that I would not kiss her good-night at first: I covered her up, and shut her door, in great displeasure; but, repenting halfway, I returned softly, and lo! there was miss, standing at the table with a bit of blank paper before her and a pencil in her hand, which she guiltily slipped out of sight, on my re-entrance.

'You'll get nobody to take that, Catherine,' I said, 'if you write it; and at present I shall put out your candle.'

I set the extinguisher on the flame, receiving as I did so a slap on my hand, and a petulant 'cross thing!' I then quitted her again, and she drew the bolt in one of her worst, most peevish humours. The letter was finished and forwarded to its destination by a milk-fetcher who came from the village: but that I didn't learn till some time afterwards. Weeks passed on, and Cathy recovered her temper; though she grew wondrous fond of stealing off to corners by herself; and often, if I came near her suddenly while reading, she would start and bend over the book, evidently desirous to hide it; and I detected edges of loose paper sticking out beyond the leaves. She also got a trick of coming down early in the morning, and lingering about the kitchen, as if she were expecting the arrival of something: and she had a small drawer in a cabinet in the library, which she would trifle over for hours, and whose key she took special care to remove when she left it.

One day, as she inspected this drawer, I observed that the playthings and trinkets, which recently formed its contents, were transmuted into bits of folded paper. My curiosity and suspicions were roused; I determined to take a peep at her mysterious treasures; so, at night, as soon as she and my master were safe upstairs, I searched and readily found among my house keys one that would fit the lock. Having opened, I emptied the whole contents into my apron, and took them with me to examine at leisure in my own chamber. Though I could not but suspect, I was still surprised to discover that they were a mass of correspondence – daily, almost, it must have been – from Linton Heathcliff: answers to documents forwarded by her. The earlier dated were embarrassed and short; gradually, however, they expanded into copious love letters, foolish as the age of the writer rendered natural, yet with touches, here and there, which I thought were borrowed from a more experienced source. Some of them struck me as singularly odd compounds of ardour and flatness; commencing in strong feeling, and concluding in the affected, wordy way that a schoolboy might use to a fancied, incorporeal sweetheart. Whether they satisfied Cathy, I don't know; but they appeared very worthless trash to me. After turning over as many as I thought proper, I tied them in a handkerchief and set them aside, re-locking the vacant drawer.

Following her habit, my young lady descended early, and visited the kitchen: I watched her go to the door, on the arrival of a certain little boy; and, while the dairy maid filled his can, she tucked something into his jacket pocket, and plucked something out. I went round by the garden, and laid wait for the messenger; who fought valorously to defend his trust, and we spilt the milk between us; but I succeeding in abstracting the epistle; and, threatening serious consequences if he did not look sharp home, I remained under the wall and perused Miss Cathy's affectionate composition. It was more simple and more eloquent than her cousin's: very pretty and very silly. I shook my head, and went meditating into the house. The day being wet, she could not divert herself with rambling about the park; so, at the conclusion of her morning studies, she resorted to the solace of the drawer. Her father sat reading at the table; and I, on purpose, had sought a bit of work in some unripped fringes of the window curtain, keeping my eye steadily fixed on her proceedings. Never did any bird flying back to a plundered nest which it had left brimfull of chirping young ones, express more complete despair in its anguished cries and flutterings, than she by her single 'Oh!' and the change that transfigured her late happy countenance. Mr Linton looked up.

'What is the matter, love? Have you hurt yourself?' he said.

His tone and look assured her *he* had not been the discoverer of the hoard.

'No, papa – ' she gasped. 'Ellen! Ellen! Come upstairs – I'm sick!'

I obeyed her summons, and accompanied her out.

'Oh, Ellen! You have got them,' she commenced immediately, dropping on her knees, when we were enclosed alone. 'O, give them to me, and I'll never never do so again! Don't tell papa. You have not told papa, Ellen, say you have not! I've been exceedingly naughty, but I won't do it any more!'

With a grave severity in my manner, I bid her stand up.

'So,' I exclaimed, 'Miss Catherine, you are tolerably far on, it seems: you may well be ashamed of them! A fine bundle of trash you study in your leisure hours, to be sure: why it's good enough to be printed! And what do you suppose the master will think, when I display it before him? I haven't shown it yet, but you needn't imagine I shall keep your ridiculous secrets. For shame! And you must have led the way in writing such absurdities: he would not have thought of beginning, I'm certain.'

'I didn't! I didn't!' sobbed Cathy, fit to break her heart. 'I didn't once think of loving him till – '

'*Loving!*' cried I, as scornfully as I could utter the word. '*Loving!* Did anybody ever hear the like! I might just as well talk of loving the miller who comes once a year to buy our corn. Pretty loving, indeed! and both times together you have seen Linton hardly four hours in your life! Now here is the babyish trash. I'm going with it to the library; and we'll see what your father says to such *loving*.'

She sprang at her precious epistles, but I held them above my head; and then she poured out further frantic entreaties that I would burn them – do anything rather than show them. And being really fully as inclined to laugh as scold – for I esteemed it all girlish vanity – I at length relented in a measure, and asked – 'If I consent to burn them, will you promise faithfully, neither to send nor receive a letter again, nor a book (for I perceive you have sent him books), nor locks of hair, nor rings, nor playthings?'

'We don't send playthings!' cried Catherine, her pride overcoming her shame.

'Nor anything at all, then, my lady!' I said. 'Unless you will, here I go.'

'I promise, Ellen!' she cried, catching my dress. 'Oh, put them in the fire, do, do!'

But when I proceeded to open a place with the poker, the sacrifice was too painful to be borne. She earnestly supplicated that I would spare her one or two.

'One or two, Ellen, to keep for Linton's sake!'

I unknotted the handkerchief, and commenced dropping them in from an angle, and the flame curled up the chimney.

'I will have one, you cruel wretch!' she screamed, darting her hand into the fire, and drawing forth some half consumed fragments, at the expense of her fingers.

'Very well – and I will have some to exhibit to papa!' I answered, shaking back the rest into the bundle, and turning anew to the door.

She emptied her blackened pieces into the flames, and motioned me to finish the immolation. It was done; I stirred up the ashes, and interred them under a shovel full of coals; and she mutely, and with a sense of intense injury, retired to her private apartment. I descended to tell my master that the young lady's qualm of sickness was almost gone, but I judged it best for her to lie down a while. She wouldn't dine; but she reappeared at tea, pale, and red about the eyes, and marvellously subdued in outward aspect.

Next morning, I answered the letter by a slip of paper, inscribed, 'Master Heathcliff is requested to send no more notes to Miss Linton, as she will not receive them.' And, thenceforth, the little boy came with vacant pockets.

## *Chapter* 22

Summer drew to an end, and early autumn: it was past Michaelmas, but the harvest was late that year, and a few of our fields were still uncleared. Mr Linton and his daughter would frequently walk out among the reapers; at the carrying of the last sheaves, they stayed till dusk, and the evening happening to be chill and damp, my master caught a bad cold, that settling obstinately on his lungs, confined him indoors throughout the whole of the winter, nearly without intermission.

Poor Cathy, frightened from her little romance, had been considerably sadder and duller since its abandonment; and her father insisted on her reading less, and taking more exercise. She had his companionship no longer; I esteemed it a duty to supply its lack, as much as possible, with mine: an inefficient substitute, for I could only spare two or three hours, from my numerous diurnal occupations, to follow her footsteps, and then my society was obviously less desirable than his.

On an afternoon in October, or the beginning of November – a fresh watery afternoon, when the turf and paths were rustling with moist, withered leaves, and the cold, blue sky was half hidden by clouds – dark grey streamers, rapidly mounting from the west, and boding abundant rain – I requested my young lady to forego her ramble because I was certain of showers. She refused; and I unwillingly donned a cloak, and took my umbrella to accompany her on a stroll to the bottom of the park: a formal walk which she generally affected if low-spirited – and that she invariably was when Mr Edgar had been worse than ordinary; a thing never known from his confession, but guessed both by her and me from his increased silence, and the melancholy of his countenance. She went sadly on: there was no running or bounding now, though the chill wind might well have tempted her to a race. And often, from the side of my eye, I could detect her raising a hand, and brushing something off her cheek. I gazed round for a means of diverting her thoughts. On one side of the road rose a high, rough bank, where hazels and stunted oaks, with their roots half exposed, held uncertain tenure: the soil was too loose for the latter; and strong winds had blown some nearly horizontal. In summer, Miss Catherine delighted to climb along these trunks, and sit in the branches, swinging twenty feet above the ground; and I, pleased with her agility and her light, childish heart, still considered it proper to scold every time I caught her at such an elevation, but so that she knew there was no necessity for descending. From dinner to tea she would lie in her breeze-rocked cradle, doing nothing except singing old songs – my nursery lore – to herself, or watching the birds, joint tenants, feed and entice their young ones to fly: or nestling with closed lids, half thinking, half dreaming, happier than words can express.

'Look, miss!' I exclaimed, pointing to a nook under the roots of one twisted tree. 'Winter is not here yet. There's a little flower, up yonder, the last bud from the multitude of bluebells that clouded those turf steps in July with a lilac mist. Will you clamber up, and pluck it to show to papa?'

Cathy stared a long time at the lonely blossom trembling in its earthy shelter, and replied, at length – 'No, I'll not touch it: but it looks melancholy, does it not, Ellen?'

'Yes,' I observed, 'about as starved and sackless as you: your cheeks are bloodless; let us take hold of hands and run. You're so low, I dare say I shall keep up with you.'

'No,' she repeated, and continued sauntering on, pausing, at intervals, to muse over a bit of moss, or a tuft of blanched grass, or a fungus spreading its bright orange among the heaps of brown foliage; and, ever and anon, her hand was lifted to her averted face.

'Catherine, why are you crying, love?' I asked, approaching and putting my arm over her shoulder. 'You mustn't cry because papa has a cold; be thankful it is nothing worse.'

She now put no further restraint on her tears; her breath was stifled by sobs.

'Oh, it *will* be something worse,' she said. 'And what shall I do when papa and you leave me, and I am by myself? I can't forget your words, Ellen; they are always in my ear. How life will be changed, how dreary the world will be, when papa and you are dead.'

'None can tell, whether you won't die before us,' I replied. 'It's wrong to anticipate evil. We'll hope there are years and years to come before any of us go: master is young, and I am strong, and hardly forty-five. My mother lived till eighty, a canty dame to the last. And suppose Mr Linton were spared till he saw sixty, that would be more years than you have counted, miss. And would it not be foolish to mourn a calamity above twenty years beforehand?'

'But Aunt Isabella was younger than papa,' she remarked, gazing up with timid hope to seek further consolation.

'Aunt Isabella had not you and me to nurse her,' I replied. 'She wasn't as happy as master: she hadn't as much to live for. All you need do, is to wait well on your father, and cheer him by letting him see you cheerful; and avoid giving him anxiety on any subject: mind that, Cathy! I'll not disguise but you might kill him, if you were wild and reckless, and cherished a foolish, fanciful affection for the son of a person who would be glad to have him in his grave; and allowed him to discover that you fretted over the separation he has judged it expedient to make.'

'I fret about nothing on earth except papa's illness,' answered my companion. 'I care for nothing in comparison with papa. And I'll never – never – oh, never, while I have my senses, do an act or say a word to vex him. I love him better than myself, Ellen; and I know it by this: I pray every night that I may live after him; because I would rather be miserable than that he should be: that proves I love him better than myself.'

'Good words,' I replied. 'But deeds must prove it also; and after he is well, remember you don't forget resolutions formed in the hour of fear.'

As we talked, we neared a door that opened on the road; and my young lady, lightening into sunshine again, climbed up, and seated herself on the top of the wall, reaching over to gather some hips that bloomed scarlet on the summit branches of the wild rose trees, shadowing the highway side: the lower fruit had disappeared, but only birds could touch the upper, except from Cathy's present station. In stretching to pull them, her hat fell off; and as the door was locked, she proposed scrambling down to recover it. I bid her be cautious lest she got a fall, and she nimbly disappeared. But the return was no such easy matter: the stones were smooth and neatly cemented, and the rosebushes and blackberry stragglers could yield no assistance in re-ascending. I, like a fool, didn't recollect that, till I heard her laughing and exclaiming – 'Ellen, you'll have to fetch the key, or else I must run round to the porter's lodge. I can't scale the ramparts on this side!'

'Stay where you are,' I answered, 'I have my bundle of keys in my pocket: perhaps I may manage to open it; if not, I'll go.'

Catherine amused herself with dancing to and fro before the door, while I tried all the large keys in succession. I had applied the last, and found that none would do; so, repeating my desire that she would remain there, I was about to hurry home as fast as I could, when an approaching sound arrested me. It was the trot of a horse; Cathy's dance stopped; and in a minute the horse stopped also.

'Who is that?' I whispered.

'Ellen, I wish you could open the door,' whispered back my companion, anxiously.

'Ho, Miss Linton!' cried a deep voice (the rider's). 'I'm glad to meet you. Don't be in haste to enter, for I have an explanation to ask and obtain.'

'I shan't speak to you, Mr Heathcliff,' answered Catherine. 'Papa says you are a wicked man, and you hate both him and me; and Ellen says the same.'

'That is nothing to the purpose,' said Heathcliff. (He it was.) 'I don't hate my son, I suppose; and it is concerning him that I demand your attention. Yes! You have cause to blush. Two or three months since, were you not in the habit of writing to Linton? Making love in play, eh? You deserved, both of you, flogging for that!

You especially, the elder, and less sensitive, as it turns out. I've got your letters, and if you give me any pertness I'll send them to your father. I presume you grew weary of the amusement and dropped it, didn't you? Well, you dropped Linton with it, into a Slough of Despond. He was in earnest: in love, really. As true as I live, he's dying for you; breaking his heart at your fickleness: not figuratively, but actually. Though Hareton has made him a standing jest for six weeks, and I have used more serious measures, and attempted to frighten him out of his idiocy, he gets worse daily; and he'll be under the sod before summer, unless you restore him!'

'How can you lie so glaringly to the poor child!' I called from the inside. 'Pray ride on! How can you deliberately get up such paltry falsehoods? Miss Cathy, I'll knock the lock off with a stone: you won't believe that vile nonsense. You can feel in yourself, it is impossible that a person should die for the love of a stranger.'

'I was not aware there were eavesdroppers,' muttered the detected villain. 'Worthy Mrs Dean, I like you, but I don't like your double dealing,' he added, aloud. 'How could *you* lie so glaringly, as to affirm I hated the "poor child"? and invent bugbear stories to terrify her from my door-stones? Catherine Linton (the very name warms me), my bonny lass, I shall be from home all this week; go and see if I have not spoken truth: do, there's a darling! Just imagine your father in my place, and Linton in yours; then think how you would value your careless lover if he refused to stir a step to comfort you, when your father, himself, entreated him; and don't, from pure stupidity, fall into the same error. I swear, on my salvation, he's going to his grave, and none but you can save him!'

The lock gave way, and I issued out.

'I swear Linton is dying,' repeated Heathcliff, looking hard at me. 'And grief and disappointment are hastening his death. Nelly, if you won't let her go, you can walk over yourself. But I shall not return till this time next week; and I think your master himself would scarcely object to her visiting her cousin!'

'Come in,' said I, taking Cathy by the arm and half forcing her to re-enter; for she lingered, viewing with troubled eyes the features of the speaker, too stern to express his inward deceit.

He pushed his horse close, and, bending down, observed – 'Miss Catherine, I'll own to you that I have little patience with Linton; and Hareton and Joseph have less. I'll own that he's with a harsh set. He pines for kindness, as well as love; and a kind word from you would be his best medicine. Don't mind Mrs Dean's cruel cautions; but be generous, and contrive to see him. He dreams of you day and night, and cannot be persuaded that you don't hate him, since you neither write nor call.'

I closed the door, and rolled a stone to assist the loosened lock in holding it; and spreading my umbrella, I drew my charge underneath: for the rain began to drive through the moaning branches of the trees, and warned us to avoid delay.

Our hurry prevented any comment on the encounter with Heathcliff, as we stretched towards home; but I divined instinctively that Catherine's heart was clouded now in double darkness. Her features were so sad, they did not seem hers: she evidently regarded what she had heard as every syllable true.

The master had retired to rest before we came in. Cathy stole to his room to enquire how he was; he had fallen asleep. She returned, and asked me to sit with her in the library. We took our tea together; and afterwards she lay down on the rug, and told me not to talk for she was weary. I got a book, and pretended to read. As soon as she supposed me absorbed in my occupation, she recommenced her silent weeping: it appeared, at present, her favourite diversion. I suffered her to enjoy it a while; then I expostulated: deriding and ridiculing all Mr Heathcliff's assertions about his son, as if I were certain she would coincide. Alas! I hadn't the skill to counteract the effect his account had produced: it was just what he intended.

'You may be right, Ellen,' she answered; 'but I shall never feel at ease till I know. And I must tell Linton it is not my fault that I don't write; and convince him that I shall not change.'

What use were anger and protestations against her silly credulity? We parted that night – hostile; but next day beheld me on the road to Wuthering Heights, by the side of my wilful young mistress's pony. I couldn't bear to witness her sorrow: to see her pale, dejected countenance, and heavy eyes; and I yielded, in the faint hope that Linton himself might prove, by his reception of us, how little of the tale was founded on fact.

## *Chapter 23*

The rainy night had ushered in a misty morning – half frost, half drizzle – and temporary brooks crossed our path, gurgling from the uplands. My feet were thoroughly wetted; I was cross and low: exactly the humour suited for making the most of these disagreeable things. We entered the farmhouse by the kitchen way, to ascertain whether Mr Heathcliff were really absent; because I put slight faith in his own affirmation.

Joseph seemed sitting in a sort of elysium alone, beside a roaring fire; a quart of ale on the table near him, bristling with large pieces of toasted oat cake; and his black, short pipe in his mouth. Catherine ran to the hearth to warm herself. I asked if the master was in? My question remained so long unanswered, that I thought the old man had grown deaf, and repeated it louder.

'Na–ay!' he snarled, or rather screamed through his nose. 'Na–ay! yah muh goa back whear yah coom frough.'

'Joseph!' cried a peevish voice, simultaneously with me, from the inner room. 'How often am I to call you? There are only a few red ashes now. Joseph! Come this moment.'

Vigorous puffs, and a resolute stare into the grate, declared he had no ear for this appeal. The housekeeper and Hareton were invisible; one gone on an errand, and the other at his work, probably. We knew Linton's tones and entered.

'Oh, I hope you'll die in a garret! Starved to death,' said the boy, mistaking our approach for that of his negligent attendant.

He stopped, on observing his error; his cousin flew to him.

'Is that you, Miss Linton?' he said, raising his head from the arm of the great chair, in which he reclined. 'No – don't kiss me. It takes my breath – dear me! Papa said you would call,' continued he, after recovering a little from Catherine's embrace; while she stood by looking very contrite. 'Will you shut the door, if you please? you left it open; and those – those *detestable* creatures won't bring coals to the fire. It's so cold!'

I stirred up the cinders, and fetched a scuttle full myself. The invalid complained of being covered with ashes; but he had a tiresome cough, and looked feverish and ill, so I did not rebuke his temper.

'Well, Linton,' murmured Catherine, when his corrugated brow relaxed. 'Are you glad to see me? Can I do you any good?'

'Why didn't you come before?' he said. 'You should have come, instead of writing. It tired me dreadfully, writing those long letters. I'd far rather have talked to you. Now, I can neither bear to talk, nor anything else. I wonder where Zillah is! Will you,' looking at me, 'step into the kitchen and see?'

I had received no thanks for my other service; and being unwilling to run to and fro at his behest, I replied – 'Nobody is out there but Joseph.'

'I want to drink,' he exclaimed, fretfully, turning away. 'Zillah is constantly gadding off to Gimmerton since papa went. It's miserable! And I'm obliged to come down here – they resolved never to hear me upstairs.'

'Is your father attentive to you, Master Heathcliff?' I asked, perceiving Catherine to be checked in her friendly advances.

'Attentive? He makes *them* a little more attentive, at least,' he cried. 'The wretches! Do you know, Miss Linton, that brute Hareton laughs at me! I hate him! indeed, I hate them all: they are odious beings.'

Cathy began searching for some water; she lighted on a pitcher in the dresser, filled a tumbler, and brought it. He bid her add a spoonful of wine from a bottle on the table; and having swallowed a small portion, appeared more tranquil, and said she was very kind.

'And are you glad to see me?' asked she, reiterating her former question, and pleased to detect the faint dawn of a smile.

'Yes, I am. It's something new to hear a voice like yours!' he replied. 'But I *have* been vexed, because you wouldn't come. And papa swore it was owing to me: he called me a pitiful, shuffling, worthless thing; and said you despised me; and if he had been in my place, he would be more the master of the Grange than your father, by this time. But you don't despise me, do you miss – '

'I wish you would say Catherine, or Cathy,' interrupted my young lady. 'Despise you? No! Next to papa, and Ellen, I love you better than anybody living. I don't love Mr Heathcliff, though; and I dare not come when he returns: will he stay away many days?'

'Not many,' answered Linton; 'but he goes on to the moors frequently, since the shooting season commenced; and you might spend an hour or two with me, in his absence. Do! Say you will! I think I should not be peevish with you: you'd not provoke me, and you'd be always ready to help me, wouldn't you?'

'Yes,' said Catherine, stroking his long soft hair; 'if I could only get papa's consent, I'd spend half my time with you. Pretty Linton! I wish you were my brother.'

'And then you would like me as well as your father?' observed he, more cheerfully. 'But papa says you would love me better than him and all the world, if you were my wife; so I'd rather you were that.'

'No! I should never love anybody better than papa,' she returned gravely. 'And people hate their wives, sometimes; but not their sisters and brothers: and if you were the latter, you would live with us, and papa would be as fond of you as he is of me.'

Linton denied that people ever hated their wives; but Cathy affirmed they did, and, in her wisdom, instanced his own father's aversion to her aunt. I endeavoured to stop her thoughtless tongue. I couldn't succeed till everything she knew was out. Master Heathcliff, much irritated, asserted her relation was false.

'Papa told me; and papa does not tell falsehoods!' she answered pertly.

'*My* papa scorns yours!' cried Linton. 'He calls him a sneaking fool!'

'Yours is a wicked man,' retorted Catherine; 'and you are very naughty to dare to repeat what he says. He must be wicked, to have made Aunt Isabella leave him as she did!'

'She didn't leave him,' said the boy: 'you shan't contradict me!'

'She did!' cried my young lady.

'Well, I'll tell *you* something!' said Linton. 'Your mother hated your father: now then.'

'Oh!' exclaimed Catherine, too enraged to continue.

'And she loved mine!' added he.

'You little liar! I hate you now,' she panted, and her face grew red with passion.

'She did! She did!' sang Linton, sinking into the recess of his chair, and leaning back his head to enjoy the agitation of the other disputant, who stood behind.

'Hush, Master Heathcliff!' I said; 'that's your father's tale too, I suppose.'

'It isn't: you hold your tongue!' he answered. 'She did, she did, Catherine! She did, she did!'

Cathy, beside herself, gave the chair a violent push, and caused him to fall against one arm. He was immediately seized by a suffocating cough that soon ended his triumph. It lasted so long that it frightened even me. As to his cousin, she wept with all her might; aghast at the mischief she had done: though she said nothing. I held him till the fit exhausted itself. Then he thrust me away, and leant his head down silently. Catherine quelled her lamentations also, took a seat opposite, and looked solemnly into the fire.

'How do you feel now, Master Heathcliff?' I enquired after waiting ten minutes.

'I wish *she* felt as I do,' he replied: 'spiteful, cruel thing! Hareton never touches me: he never struck me in his life. And I was better today: and there – ' his voice died in a whimper.

'*I* didn't strike you!' muttered Cathy, chewing her lip to prevent another burst of emotion.

He sighed and moaned like one under great suffering, and kept it up for a quarter of an hour; on purpose to distress his cousin, apparently, for whenever he caught a stifled sob from her he put renewed pain and pathos into the inflections of his voice.

'I'm sorry I hurt you, Linton,' she said at length, racked beyond endurance. 'But *I* couldn't have been hurt by that little push, and I had no idea that you could, either: you're not much, are you, Linton? Don't let me go home thinking I've done you harm. Answer! Speak to me.'

'I can't speak to you,' he murmured; 'you've hurt me so, that I shall lie awake all night, choking with this cough! If you had it you'd know what it was: but *you*'ll be comfortably asleep, while I'm in agony – and nobody near me! I wonder how you would like to pass those fearful nights!' And he began to wail aloud, for very pity of himself.

'Since you are in the habit of passing dreadful nights,' I said, 'it won't be miss who spoils your ease: you'd be the same had she never come. However, she shall not disturb you again; and perhaps you'll get quieter when we leave you.'

'Must I go?' asked Catherine dolefully, bending over him. 'Do you want me to go, Linton?'

'You can't alter what you've done,' he replied pettishly, shrinking from her, 'unless you alter it for the worse, by teasing me into a fever.'

'Well, then I must go?' she repeated.

'Let me alone, at least,' said he; 'I can't bear your talking!'

She lingered, and resisted my persuasions to departure, a tiresome while; but as he neither looked up nor spoke, she finally made a movement to the door and I followed. We were recalled by a scream. Linton had slid from his seat on to the hearthstone, and lay writhing in the mere perverseness of an indulged plague of a child, determined to be as grievous and harassing as it can. I thoroughly gauged his disposition from his behaviour, and saw at once it would be folly to attempt humouring him. Not so my companion: she ran back in terror, knelt down, and cried, and soothed, and entreated, till he grew quiet from lack of breath: by no means from compunction at distressing her.

'I shall lift him on the settle,' I said, 'and he may roll about as he pleases: we can't stop to watch him. I hope you are satisfied, Miss Cathy, that *you* are not the person to benefit him, and that his condition of health is not occasioned by attachment to you. Now then, there he is! Come away: as soon as he knows there is nobody by to care for his nonsense, he'll be glad to lie still!'

She placed a cushion under his head, and offered him some water; he rejected the latter, and tossed uneasily on the former, as if it were a stone or a block of wood. She tried to put it more comfortably.

'I can't do with that,' he said; 'it's not high enough!'

Catherine brought another to lay above it.

'That's *too* high!' murmured the provoking thing.

'How must I arrange it, then?' she asked despairingly.

He twined himself up to her, as she half knelt by the settle, and converted her shoulder into a support.

'No, that won't do,' I said. 'You'll be content with the cushion, Master Heathcliff. Miss has wasted too much time on you already: we cannot remain five minutes longer.'

'Yes, yes, we can!' replied Cathy. 'He's good and patient now. He's beginning to think I shall have far greater misery than he will tonight, if I believe he is the worse for my visit; and then, I dare not come again. Tell the truth about it, Linton; for I mustn't come, if I have hurt you.'

'You must come, to cure me,' he answered. 'You ought to come because you have hurt me: you know you have, extremely! I was not as ill when you entered as I am at present – was I?'

'But you've made yourself ill by crying, and being in a passion.'

'I didn't do it all,' said his cousin. 'However, we'll be friends now. And you want me: you would wish to see me sometimes, really?'

'I told you I did,' he replied impatiently. 'Sit on the settle and let me lean on your knee. That's as mama used to do, whole afternoons together. Sit quite still, and don't talk: but you may sing a song if you can sing; or you may say a nice long interesting ballad – one of those you promised to teach me; or a story. I'd rather have a ballad, though: begin.'

Catherine repeated the longest she could remember. The employment pleased both mightily. Linton would have another, and after that another, notwithstanding my strenuous objections; and so they went on until the clock struck twelve, and we heard Hareton in the court, returning for his dinner.

'And tomorrow, Catherine, will you be here tomorrow?' asked young Heathcliff, holding her frock as she rose reluctantly.

'No!' I answered, 'nor next day neither.' She, however, gave a different response, evidently, for his forehead cleared as she stooped and whispered in his ear.

'You won't go tomorrow, recollect, miss!' I commenced, when we were out of the house. 'You are not dreaming of it, are you?'

She smiled.

'Oh, I'll take good care,' I continued: 'I'll have that lock mended, and you can escape by no way else.'

'I can get over the wall,' she said, laughing. 'The Grange is not a prison, Ellen, and you are not my jailer. And besides, I'm almost seventeen: I'm a woman. And I'm certain Linton would recover quickly if he had me to look after him. I'm older than he is, you know, and wiser: less childish, am I not? And he'll soon do as I direct him, with some slight coaxing. He's a pretty little darling when he's good. I'd make such a pet of him, if he were mine. We should never quarrel, should we, after we were used to each other? Don't you like him, Ellen?'

'Like him?' I exclaimed. 'The worst-tempered bit of a sickly slip that ever struggled into its teens! Happily, as Mr Heathcliff conjectured, he'll not win twenty! I doubt whether he'll see spring, indeed. And small loss to his family whenever he drops off. And lucky it is for us that his father took him: the kinder he was treated, the more tedious and selfish he'd be! I'm glad you have no chance of having him for a husband, Miss Catherine!'

My companion waxed serious at hearing this speech. To speak of his death so regardlessly wounded her feelings.

'He's younger than I,' she answered, after a protracted pause of meditation, 'and he ought to live the longest: he will – he must live as long as I do. He's as strong now as when he first came into the North; I'm positive of that! It's only a cold that ails him, the same as papa has. You say papa will get better, and why shouldn't he?'

'Well, well,' I cried, 'after all, we needn't trouble ourselves; for listen, miss – and mind, I'll keep my word – if you attempt going to Wuthering Heights again, with or without me, I shall inform Mr Linton, and, unless he allow it, the intimacy with your cousin must not be revived.'

'It has been revived!' muttered Cathy sulkily.

'Must not be continued, then!' I said.

'We'll see!' was her reply, and she set off at a gallop, leaving me to toil in the rear.

We both reached home before our dinner-time; my master supposed we had been wandering through the park, and therefore he demanded no explanation of our absence. As soon as I entered, I hastened to change my soaked shoes and stockings; but sitting such a while at the Heights had done the mischief. On the succeeding morning I was laid up, and during three weeks I remained incapacitated for attending to my duties: a calamity never experienced prior to that period, and never, I am thankful to say, since.

My little mistress behaved like an angel in coming to wait on me, and cheer my solitude: the confinement brought me exceedingly low. It is wearisome, to a stirring active body: but few have slighter reasons for complaint than I had. The moment Catherine left Mr Linton's room, she appeared at my bedside. Her day was divided between us; no amusement usurped a minute: she neglected her meals, her studies, and her play; and she was the fondest nurse that ever watched. She must have had a warm heart, when she loved her father so, to give so much to me!

I said her days were divided between us; but the master retired early, and I generally needed nothing after six o'clock, thus the evening was her own. Poor thing! I never considered what she did with herself after tea. And though frequently, when she looked in to bid me good-night, I remarked a fresh colour in her cheeks and a pinkness over her slender fingers; instead of fancying the hue borrowed from a cold ride across the moors, I laid it to the charge of a hot fire in the library.

## *Chapter 24*

At the close of three weeks, I was able to quit my chamber, and move about the house. And on the first occasion of my sitting up in the evening, I asked Catherine to read to me, because my eyes were weak. We were in the library, the master having gone to bed: she consented, rather unwillingly, I fancied; and imagining my sort of books did not suit her, I bid her please herself in the choice of what she perused. She selected one of her own favourites, and got forward steadily about an hour; then came frequent questions.

'Ellen, are not you tired? Hadn't you better lie down now? You'll be sick, keeping up so long, Ellen.'

'No, no, dear, I'm not tired,' I returned, continually.

Perceiving me immovable, she essayed another method of showing her dis-relish for her occupation. It changed to yawning, and stretching, and – 'Ellen, I'm tired.'

'Give over then and talk,' I answered.

That was worse: she fretted and sighed, and looked at her watch till eight, and finally went to her room, completely overdone with sleep; judging by her peevish, heavy look, and the constant rubbing she inflicted on her eyes. The following night she seemed more impatient still; and on the third from recovering my company, she complained of a headache, and left me. I thought her conduct odd; and having remained alone a long while, I resolved on going, and enquiring whether she were better, and asking her to come and lie on the sofa, instead of upstairs in the dark. No Catherine could I discover upstairs, and none below. The servants affirmed they had not seen her. I listened at Mr Edgar's door; all was silence. I returned to her apartment, extinguished my candle, and seated myself in the window.

The moon shone bright; a sprinkling of snow covered the ground, and I reflected that she might, possibly, have taken it into her head to walk about the garden, for refreshment. I did detect a figure creeping along the inner fence of the park; but it was not my young mistress: on its emerging into the light, I recognised one of the grooms. He stood a considerable period, viewing the carriage-road through the grounds; then started off at a brisk pace, as if he had detected something, and reappeared presently, leading miss's pony; and there she was, just dismounted, and walking by its side. The man took his charge stealthily across the grass towards the stable. Cathy entered by the casement-window of the drawing-room, and glided noiselessly up to where I awaited her. She put the door gently to, slipped off her snowy shoes, untied her hat, and was proceeding, unconscious of my espionage, to lay aside her mantle, when I suddenly rose and revealed myself. The surprise petrified her an instant: she uttered an inarticulate exclamation, and stood fixed.

'My dear Miss Catherine,' I began, too vividly impressed by her recent kindness to break into a scold, 'where have you been riding out at this hour? And why should you try to deceive me, by telling a tale? Where have you been? Speak!'

'To the bottom of the park,' she stammered. 'I didn't tell a tale.'

'And nowhere else?' I demanded.

'No,' was the muttered reply.

'Oh, Catherine!' I cried, sorrowfully. 'You know you have been doing wrong, or you wouldn't be driven to uttering an untruth to me. That does grieve me. I'd rather be three months ill, than hear you frame a deliberate lie.'

She sprang forward, and bursting into tears, threw her arms round my neck.

'Well Ellen, I'm so afraid of you being angry,' she said. 'Promise not to be angry, and you shall know the very truth. I hate to hide it.'

We sat down in the window-seat; I assured her I would not scold, whatever her secret might be, and I guessed it, of course; so she commenced – 'I've been to Wuthering Heights, Ellen, and I've never missed going a day since you fell ill; except thrice before, and twice after you left your room. I gave Michael books and pictures to prepare Minny every evening, and to put her back in the stable: you mustn't scold *him* either, mind. I was at the Heights by half-past six, and generally stayed till half-past eight, and then galloped home. It was not to amuse myself that I went: I was often wretched all the time. Now and then, I was happy: once in a week perhaps. At first, I expected there would be sad work persuading you to let me keep my word to Linton: for I had engaged to call again next day, when we quitted him; but, as you stayed upstairs on the morrow, I escaped that trouble; and while Michael was refastening the lock of the park door in the afternoon, I got possession of the key, and told him how my cousin wished me to visit him, because he was sick, and couldn't come to the Grange; and how papa would object to my going; and then I negotiated with him about the pony.

'He is fond of reading, and he thinks of leaving soon to get married; so he offered, if I would lend him books out of the library, to do what I wished: but I preferred giving him my own, and that satisfied him better.

'On my second visit, Linton seemed in lively spirits; and Zillah (that is their housekeeper) made us a clean room and a good fire, and told us that, as Joseph was out at a prayer-meeting and Hareton Earnshaw was off with his dogs – robbing our woods of pheasants, as I heard afterwards – we might do what we liked. She brought me some warm wine and gingerbread, and appeared exceedingly good-natured; and Linton sat in the armchair, and I in the little rocking chair on the hearthstone, and we laughed and talked so merrily, and found so much to say: we planned where we would go, and what we would do in summer. I needn't repeat that, because you would call it silly.

'One time, however, we were near quarrelling. He said the pleasantest manner of spending a hot July day was lying from morning till evening on a bank of heath in the middle of the moors, with the bees humming dreamily about among the bloom, and the larks singing high up over head, and the blue sky and bright sun shining steadily and cloudlessly. That was his most perfect idea of heaven's happiness: mine was rocking in a rustling green tree, with a west wind blowing, and bright white clouds flitting rapidly above; and not only larks, but throstles, and blackbirds, and linnets, and cuckoos pouring out music on every side, and the moors seen at a distance, broken into cool dusky dells; but close by great swells of long grass undulating in waves to the breeze; and woods and sounding water, and the whole world awake and wild with joy. He wanted all to lie in an ecstacy of peace; I wanted all to sparkle, and dance in a glorious jubilee. I said his heaven would be only half alive; and he said mine would be drunk: I said I should fall asleep in his; and he said he could not breathe in mine, and began to grow very snappish. At last, we agreed to try both, as soon as the right weather came; and then we kissed each other and were friends.

'After sitting still an hour, I looked at the great room with its smooth uncarpeted floor, and thought how nice it would be to play in, if we removed the table; and I asked Linton to call Zillah in to help us, and we'd have a game at blind-man's buff; she should try to catch us; you used to, you know, Ellen. He wouldn't: there was no pleasure in it, he said; but he consented to play at ball with me. We found two in a cupboard, among a heap of old toys: tops, and hoops, battledores, and shuttlecocks. One was marked C., and the other H.; I wished to have the C., because that stood for Catherine, and the H. might be for Heathcliff, his name; but the bran came out of H., and Linton didn't like it. I beat him constantly: and he got cross again, and coughed, and returned to his chair. That night, though, he easily recovered his good humour: he was charmed with two or three pretty songs – *your* songs, Ellen; and when I was obliged to go, he begged and entreated me to come the following evening; and I promised. Minny and I went flying home as light as air; and I dreamt of Wuthering Heights and my sweet, darling cousin, till morning.

'On the morrow, I was sad; partly because you were poorly, and partly that I wished my father knew, and approved of my excursions: but it was beautiful moonlight after tea; and, as I rode on, the gloom cleared. I shall have another happy evening, I thought to myself; and what delights me more, my pretty Linton will. I trotted up their garden, and was turning round to the back, when that fellow Earnshaw met me, took my bridle, and bid me go in by the front entrance. He patted Minny's neck, and said she was a bonny beast, and appeared as if he wanted me to speak to him. I only told him to leave my horse alone, or else it would kick him. He answered in his vulgar accent, "It wouldn't do mitch hurt if it did"; and surveyed its legs with a smile. I was half inclined to make it try; however, he moved off to open the door, and, as he raised the latch, he looked up to the inscription above, and said, with a stupid mixture of awkwardness and elation – ' "Miss Catherine! I can read yon, nah."

' "Wonderful," I exclaimed. "Pray let us hear you – you *are* grown clever!"

'He spelt, and drawled over by syllables, the name – "Hareton Earnshaw."

' "And the figures?" I cried, encouragingly, perceiving that he came to a dead halt.

' "I cannot tell them yet," he answered.

' "Oh, you dunce!" I said, laughing heartily at his failure.

'The fool stared, with a grin hovering about his lips, and a scowl gathering over his eyes, as if uncertain whether he might not join in my mirth: whether it were not pleasant familiarity, or what it really was, contempt. I settled his doubts, by suddenly retrieving my gravity and desiring him to walk away, for I came to see Linton not him. He reddened – I saw that by the moonlight – dropped his hand from the latch, and skulked off, a picture of mortified vanity. He imagined himself to be as accomplished as Linton, I suppose, because he could spell his own name; and was marvellously discomfited that I didn't think the same.'

'Stop, Miss Catherine, dear!' I interrupted. 'I shall not scold, but I don't like your conduct there. If you had remembered that Hareton was your cousin as much as Master Heathcliff, you would have felt how improper it was to behave in that way. At least, it was praiseworthy ambition for him to desire to be as accomplished as Linton; and probably he did not learn merely to show off: you had made him ashamed of his ignorance before, I have no doubt; and he wished to remedy it and please you. To sneer at his imperfect attempt was very bad breeding. Had *you* been brought up in his circumstances, would you be less rude? He was as quick and as intelligent a child as ever you were; and I'm hurt that he should be despised now, because that base Heathcliff has treated him so unjustly.'

'Well, Ellen, you won't cry about it, will you?' she exclaimed, surprised at my earnestness. 'But wait, and you shall hear if he conned his A B C to please me; and if it were worth while being civil to the brute. I entered; Linton was lying on the settle, and half got up to welcome me.

' "I'm ill tonight, Catherine, love," he said; "and you must have all the talk, and let me listen. Come, and sit by me. I was sure you wouldn't break your word, and I'll make you promise again, before you go."

'I knew now that I mustn't tease him, as he was ill; and I spoke softly and put no questions, and avoided irritating him in any way. I had brought some of my nicest books for him; he asked me to read a little of one, and I was about to comply, when Earnshaw burst the door open: having gathered venom with reflection. He advanced direct to us, seized Linton by the arm, and swung him off the seat.

' "Get to thy own room!" he said in a voice almost inarticulate with passion; and his face looked swelled and furious. "Take her there if she comes to see thee: thou shalln't keep me out of this. Begone, wi' ye both!"

'He swore at us, and left Linton no time to answer, nearly throwing him into the kitchen; and he clenched his fist as I followed, seemingly longing to knock me down. I was afraid for a moment, and I let one volume fall; he kicked it after me, and shut us out. I heard a malignant, crackly laugh by the fire, and turning, beheld that odious Joseph standing rubbing his bony hands, and quivering.

' "Aw wer sure he'd sarve ye eht! He's a grand lad! He's getten t' raight sperrit in him! *He* knaws – aye, he knaws, as weel as Aw do, who sud be t' maister yonder – ech, ech, ech! He mad ye skift properly! Ech, ech, ech!"

' "Where must we go?" I said to my cousin, disregarding the old wretch's mockery.

'Linton was white and trembling. He was not pretty then, Ellen: Oh no! He looked frightful! For his thin face and large eyes were wrought into an expression of frantic, powerless fury. He grasped the handle of the door, and shook it: it was fastened inside.

' "If you don't let me in I'll kill you! – if you don't let me in I'll kill you!" he rather shrieked than said. "Devil! devil! – I'll kill you – I'll kill you!"

'Joseph uttered his croaking laugh again.

' "Thear that's t' father!" he cried. "That's father! We've allas summut uh orther side in us. Niver heed Hareton, lad – dunnut be 'feard – he cannot get at thee!"

'I took hold of Linton's hands, and tried to pull him away; but he shrieked so shockingly that I dared not proceed. At last, his cries were choked by a dreadful fit of coughing; blood gushed from his mouth, and he fell on the ground. I ran into the yard, sick with terror; and called for Zillah, as loud as I could. She soon heard me: she was milking the cows in a shed behind the barn, and hurrying from her work, she enquired what there was to do? I hadn't breath to explain; dragging her in, I looked about for Linton. Earnshaw had come out to examine the mischief he had caused, and he was then conveying the poor thing upstairs. Zillah and I ascended after him; but he stopped me at the top of the steps, and said I shouldn't go in: I must go home. I exclaimed that he had killed Linton, and I *would* enter. Joseph locked the door, and declared I should do "no sich stuff", and asked me whether I were "bahn to be as mad as him". I stood crying, till the housekeeper reappeared. She affirmed that he would be better in a bit, but he couldn't do with that shrieking and din; and she took me, and nearly carried me into the house.

'Ellen, I was ready to tear my hair off my head! I sobbed and wept so that my eyes were almost blind; and the ruffian you have such sympathy with stood opposite: presuming every now and then to bid me "wisht", and denying that it was his fault; and finally, frightened by my assertions that I would tell papa, and that he should be put in prison and hanged, he commenced blubbering himself, and hurried out to hide his cowardly agitation. Still, I was not rid of him: when at length they compelled me to depart, and I had got some hundred yards off the premises, he suddenly issued from the shadow of the roadside, and checked Minny and took hold of me.

' "Miss Catherine, I'm ill grieved," he began, "but it's raything too bad – "

'I gave him a cut with my whip, thinking perhaps he would murder me. He let go, thundering one of his horrid curses, and I galloped home more than half out of my senses.

'I didn't bid you good-night, that evening, and I didn't go to Wuthering Heights, the next: I wished to, exceedingly; but I was strangely excited, and dreaded to hear that Linton was dead, sometimes; and sometimes shuddered at the thought of encountering Hareton. On the third day I took courage: at least, I couldn't bear longer suspense, and stole off once more. I went at five o'clock, and walked; fancying I might manage to creep into the house, and up to Linton's room, unobserved. However, the dogs gave notice of my approach.

Zillah received me, and saying "the lad was mending nicely", showed me into a small, tidy, carpeted apartment, where, to my inexpressible joy, I beheld Linton laid on a little sofa, reading one of my books. But he would neither speak to me nor look at me, through a whole hour, Ellen: he has such an unhappy temper. And what quite confounded me, when he did open his mouth it was to utter the falsehood that I had occasioned the uproar, and Hareton was not to blame! Unable to reply, except passionately, I got up and walked from the room. He sent after me a faint "Catherine!" He did not reckon on being answered so: but I wouldn't turn back; and the morrow was the second day on which I stayed at home, nearly determined to visit him no more. But it was so miserable going to bed, and getting up, and never hearing anything about him, that my resolution melted into air before it was properly formed. It *had* appeared wrong to take the journey once; now it seemed wrong to refrain. Michael came to ask if he must saddle Minny; I said "Yes," and considered myself doing a duty as she bore me over the hills. I was forced to pass the front windows to get to the court: it was no use trying to conceal my presence.

' "Young master is in the house," said Zillah, as she saw me making for the parlour. I went in; Earnshaw was there also, but he quitted the room directly. Linton sat in the great arm chair half asleep; walking up to the fire, I began in a serious tone, partly meaning it to be true – ' "As you don't like me, Linton, and as you think I come on purpose to hurt you, and pretend that I do so every time, this is our last meeting: let us say goodbye; and tell Mr Heathcliff that you have no wish to see me, and that he mustn't invent any more falsehoods on the subject.'

' "Sit down and take your hat off, Catherine," he answered. "You are so much happier than I am, you ought to be better. Papa talks enough of my defects, and shows enough scorn of me, to make it natural I should doubt myself. I doubt whether I am not altogether as worthless as he calls me, frequently; and then I feel so cross and bitter, I hate everybody! I *am* worthless, and bad in temper, and bad in spirit, almost always; and if you choose, you *may* say goodbye: you'll get rid of an annoyance. Only, Catherine, do me this justice: believe that if I might be as sweet, and as kind, and as good as you are, I would be; as willingly, and more so, than as happy and as healthy. And believe that your kindness has made me love you deeper than if I deserved your love: and though I couldn't, and cannot help showing my nature to you, I regret it and repent it; and shall regret and repent it till I die!"

'I felt he spoke the truth; and I felt I must forgive him: and, though he should quarrel the next moment, I must forgive him again. We were reconciled; but we cried, both of us, the whole time I stayed: not entirely for sorrow; yet I *was* sorry Linton had that distorted nature. He'll never let his friends be at ease, and he'll never be at ease himself! I have always gone to his little parlour, since that night; because his father returned the day after.

'About three times, I think, we have been merry and hopeful, as we were the first evening; the rest of my visits were dreary and troubled: now with his selfishness and spite, and now with his sufferings: but I've learnt to endure the former with nearly as little resentment as the latter. Mr Heathcliff purposely avoids me; I have hardly seen him at all. Last Sunday, indeed, coming earlier than usual, I heard him abusing poor Linton, cruelly, for his conduct of the night before. I can't tell how he knew of it, unless he listened. Linton had certainly behaved provokingly: however, it was the business of nobody but me, and I interrupted Mr Heathcliff's lecture by entering and telling him so. He burst into a laugh, and went away, saying he was glad I took that view of the matter. Since then, I've told Linton he must whisper his bitter things. Now, Ellen, you have heard all; and I can't be prevented from going to Wuthering Heights, except by inflicting misery on two people; whereas, if you'll only not tell papa, my going need disturb the tranquillity of none. You'll not tell, will you? It will be very heartless if you do.'

'I'll make up my mind on that point by tomorrow, Miss Catherine,' I replied. 'It requires some study; and so I'll leave you to your rest, and go think it over.'

I thought it over aloud, in my master's presence; walking straight from her room to his, and relating the whole story: with the exception of her conversations with her cousin, and any mention of Hareton. Mr Linton was alarmed and distressed more than he would acknowledge to me. In the morning, Catherine learnt my betrayal of her confidence, and she learnt also that her secret visits were to end. In vain she wept and writhed against the interdict, and implored her father to have pity on Linton: all she got to comfort her was a promise that he would write, and give him leave to come to the Grange when he pleased; but explaining that he must no longer expect to see Catherine at Wuthering Heights. Perhaps, had he been aware of his nephew's disposition and state of health, he would have seen fit to withhold even that slight consolation.

## *Chapter 25*

'These things happened last winter, sir,' said Mrs Dean; 'hardly more than a year ago. Last winter, I did not think, at another twelve months' end, I should be amusing a stranger to the family with relating them! Yet, who knows how long you'll be a stranger? You're too young to rest always contented, living by yourself; and I some way fancy, no one could see Catherine Linton, and not love her. You smile; but why do you look so lively and interested, when I talk about her? And why have you asked me to hang her picture over your fireplace? and why – '

'Stop, my good friend!' I cried. 'It may be very possible that *I* should love her; but would she love me? I doubt it too much to venture my tranquillity by running into temptation: and then my home is not here. I'm of the busy world, and to its arms I must return. Go on. Was Catherine obedient to her father's commands?'

'She was,' continued the housekeeper. 'Her affection for him was still the chief sentiment in her heart; and he spoke without anger: he spoke in the deep tenderness of one about to leave his treasure amid perils and foes, where his remembered words would be the only aid that he could bequeath to guide her. He said to me, a few days afterwards,

'"I wish my nephew would write, Ellen, or call. Tell me, sincerely, what you think of him: is he changed for the better, or is there a prospect of improvement, as he grows a man?"

'"He's very delicate, sir," I replied; "and scarcely likely to reach manhood: but this I can say, he does not resemble his father; and if Miss Catherine had the misfortune to marry him, he would not be beyond her control: unless she were extremely and foolishly indulgent. However, master, you'll have plenty of time to get acquainted with him, and see whether he would suit her: it wants four years and more to his being of age."

Edgar sighed; and, walking to the window, looked out towards Gimmerton kirk. It was a misty afternoon, but the February sun shone dimly, and we could just distinguish the two fir trees in the yard, and the sparely scattered gravestones.

'I've prayed often,' he half soliloquised, 'for the approach of what is coming; and now I begin to shrink, and fear it. I thought the memory of the hour I came down that glen a bridegroom would be less sweet than the anticipation that I was soon, in a few months, or, possibly, weeks, to be carried up, and laid in its lonely hollow! Ellen, I've been very happy with my little Cathy. Through winter nights and summer days she was a living hope at my side. But I've been as happy musing by myself among those stones, under that old church: lying, through the long June evenings, on the green mound of her mother's grave, and wishing, yearning for the time when I might lie beneath it. What can I do for Cathy? How must I quit her? I'd not care one moment for Linton being Heathcliff's son; nor for his taking her from me, if he could console her for my loss. I'd not care that Heathcliff gained his ends, and triumphed in robbing me of my last blessing! But should Linton be unworthy – only a feeble tool to his father – I cannot abandon her to him! And, hard though it be to crush her buoyant spirit, I must persevere in making her sad while I live, and leaving her solitary when I die. Darling! I'd rather resign her to God, and lay her in the earth before me.'

'Resign her to God, as it is, sir,' I answered, 'and if we should lose you – which may He forbid – under His providence, I'll stand her friend and counsellor to the last. Miss Catherine is a good girl: I don't fear that she will go wilfully wrong; and people who do their duty are always finally rewarded.'

Spring advanced; yet my master gathered no real strength, though he resumed his walks in the grounds with his daughter. To her inexperienced notions, this itself was a sign of convalescence; and then his cheek was often flushed, and his eyes were bright: she felt sure of his recovering.

On her seventeenth birthday, he did not visit the churchyard: it was raining, and I observed – 'You'll surely not go out tonight, sir?'

He answered – 'No, I'll defer it, this year, a little longer.'

He wrote again to Linton, expressing his great desire to see him; and, had the invalid been presentable, I've no doubt his father would have permitted him to come. As it was, being instructed, he returned an answer, intimating that Mr Heathcliff objected to his calling at the Grange; but his uncle's kind remembrance delighted him, and he hoped to meet him, sometimes, in his rambles, and personally to petition that his cousin and he might not remain long so utterly divided.

That part of his letter was simple, and probably his own. Heathcliff knew he could plead eloquently enough for Catherine's company, then – 'I do not ask,' he said, 'that she may visit here; but, am I never to see her, because my father forbids me to go to her home, and you forbid her to come to mine? Do, now and then, ride with her towards the Heights; and let us exchange a few words, in your presence! We have done nothing to deserve this separation; and you are not angry with me: you have no reason to dislike me, you allow, yourself. Dear uncle! Send me a kind note tomorrow, and leave to join you anywhere you please, except at Thrushcross Grange. I believe an interview would convince you that my father's character is not mine: he affirms I am more your nephew than his son; and though I have faults which render me unworthy of Catherine, she has excused them, and, for her sake, you should also. You enquire after my health – it is better; but while I remain cut off from all hope, and doomed to solitude, or the society of those who never did and never will like me, how can I be cheerful and well?'

Edgar, though he felt for the boy, could not consent to grant his request; because he could not accompany Catherine. He said, in summer, perhaps, they might meet: meantime, he wished him to continue writing at intervals, and engaged to give him what advice and comfort he was able by letter; being well aware of his hard position in his family. Linton complied; and had he been unrestrained, would probably have spoiled all by filling his epistles with complaints and lamentations: but his father kept a sharp watch over him; and, of course, insisted on every line that my master sent being shown; so, instead of penning his peculiar personal sufferings and distresses, the themes constantly uppermost in his thoughts, he harped on the cruel obligation of being held asunder from his friend and love; and gently intimated that Mr Linton must allow an interview soon, or he should fear he was purposely deceiving him with empty promises.

Cathy was a powerful ally at home; and, between them, they at length persuaded my master to acquiesce in their having a ride or a walk together, about once a week, under my guardianship, and on the moors nearest the Grange: for June found him still declining; and though he had set aside, yearly, a portion of his income for my young lady's fortune, he had a natural desire that she might retain – or at least return in a short time to – the house of her ancestors; and he considered her only prospect of doing that was by a union with his heir; he had no idea that the latter was failing almost as fast as himself; nor had anyone, I believe: no doctor visited the Heights, and no one saw Master Heathcliff to make report of his condition, among us. I, for my part, began to fancy my forebodings were false, and that he must be actually rallying, when he mentioned riding and walking on the moors, and seemed so earnest in pursuing his object. I could not picture a father treating a dying child as tyrannically and wickedly as I afterwards learnt Heathcliff had treated him, to compel this apparent eagerness: his efforts redoubling the more imminently his avaricious and unfeeling plans were threatened with defeat by death.

## *Chapter 26*

Summer was already past its prime, when Edgar reluctantly yielded his assent to their entreaties, and Catherine and I set out on our first ride to join her cousin. It was a close, sultry day: devoid of sunshine, but with a sky too dappled and hazy to threaten rain; and our place of meeting had been fixed at the guide-stone, by the crossroads.

On arriving there, however, a little herd-boy, despatched as a messenger, told us that – 'Maister Linton wer just ut this side th' Heights: and he'd be mitch obleeged to us to gang on a bit further.'

'Then Master Linton has forgot the first injunction of his uncle,' I observed: 'he bid us keep on the Grange land, and here we are, off at once.'

'Well, we'll turn our horses' heads round, when we reach him,' answered my companion, 'our excursion shall lie towards home.'

But when we reached him, and that was scarcely a quarter of a mile from his own door, we found he had no horse; and we were forced to dismount, and leave ours to graze.

He lay on the heath, awaiting our approach, and did not rise till we came within a few yards. Then he walked so feebly, and looked so pale, that I immediately exclaimed – 'Why, Master Heathcliff, you are not fit for enjoying a ramble, this morning. How ill you do look!'

Catherine surveyed him with grief and astonishment; and changed the ejaculation of joy on her lips, to one of alarm; and the congratulation on their long postponed meeting to an anxious enquiry, whether he were worse than usual?

'No – better – better!' he panted, trembling, and retaining her hand as if he needed its support, while his large blue eyes wandered timidly over her; the hollowness round them transforming to haggard wildness the languid expression they once possessed.

'But you have been worse,' persisted his cousin; 'worse than when I saw you last – you are thinner, and – '

'I'm tired,' he interrupted, hurriedly. 'It is too hot for walking, let us rest here. And, in the morning, I often feel sick – papa says I grow so fast.'

Badly satisfied, Cathy sat down, and he reclined beside her.

'This is something like your paradise,' said she, making an effort at cheerfulness. 'You recollect the two days we agreed to spend in the place and way each thought pleasantest? This is nearly yours, only there are clouds; but then they are so soft and mellow, it is nicer than sunshine. Next week, if you can, we'll ride down to the Grange Park, and try mine.'

Linton did not appear to remember what she talked of; and he had evidently great difficulty in sustaining any kind of conversation. His lack of interest in the subjects she started, and his equal incapacity to contribute to her entertainment, were so obvious, that she could not conceal her disappointment. An indefinite alteration had come over his whole person and manner. The pettishness that might be caressed into fondness, had yielded to a listless apathy; there was less of the peevish temper of a child which frets and teases on purpose to be soothed, and more of the self-absorbed moroseness of a confirmed invalid, repelling consolation, and ready to regard the good-humoured mirth of others, as an insult. Catherine perceived, as well as I did, that he held it rather a punishment, than a gratification, to endure our company; and she made no scruple of proposing, presently, to depart. That proposal, unexpectedly, roused Linton from his lethargy, and threw him into a strange state of agitation. He glanced fearfully towards the Heights, begging she would remain another half-hour, at least.

'But, I think,' said Cathy, 'you'd be more comfortable at home than sitting here; and I cannot amuse you today, I see, by my tales, and songs, and chatter: you have grown wiser than I, in these six months; you have little taste for my diversions now; or else, if I could amuse you, I'd willingly stay.'

'Stay to rest yourself,' he replied. 'And, Catherine, don't think, or say that I'm *very* unwell: it is the heavy weather and heat that make me dull; and I walked about, before you came, a great deal, for me. Tell uncle, I'm in tolerable health, will you?'

'I'll tell him that *you* say so, Linton. I couldn't affirm that you are,' observed my young lady, wondering at his pertinacious assertion of what was evidently an untruth.

'And be here again next Thursday,' continued he, shunning her puzzled gaze. 'And give him my thanks for permitting you to come – my best thanks, Catherine. And – and, if you *did* meet my father, and he asked you about me, don't lead him to suppose that I've been extremely silent and stupid: don't look sad and downcast, as you *are* doing – he'll be angry.'

'I care nothing for his anger,' exclaimed Cathy, imagining she would be its object.

'But I do,' said her cousin, shuddering. '*Don't* provoke him against me, Catherine, for he is very hard.'

'Is he severe to you, Master Heathcliff?' I enquired. 'Has he grown weary of indulgence, and passed from passive, to active hatred?'

Linton looked at me, but did not answer; and, after keeping her seat by his side another ten minutes, during which his head fell drowsily on his breast, and he uttered nothing except suppressed moans of exhaustion or pain, Cathy began to seek solace in looking for bilberries, and sharing the produce of her researches with me: she did not offer them to him, for she saw further notice would only weary and annoy.

'Is it half an hour now, Ellen!' she whispered in my ear, at last. 'I can't tell why we should stay. He's asleep, and papa will be wanting us back.'

'Well, we must not leave him asleep,' I answered; 'wait till he wakes, and be patient. You were mighty eager to set off, but your longing to see poor Linton has soon evaporated!'

'Why did *he* wish to see me?' returned Catherine. 'In his crassest humours, formerly, I liked him better than I do in his present curious mood. It's just as if it were a task he was compelled to perform – this interview – for fear his father should scold him. But I'm hardly going to come to give Mr Heathcliff pleasure; whatever reason he may have for ordering Linton to undergo this penance. And, though I'm glad he's better in health, I'm sorry he's so much less pleasant, and so much less affectionate to me.'

'You think he *is* better in health, then?' I said.

'Yes,' she answered; 'because he always made such a great deal of his sufferings, you know. He is not tolerably well, as he told me to tell papa; but he's better, very likely.'

'There you differ with me, Miss Cathy,' I remarked; 'I should conjecture him to be far worse.'

Linton here started from his slumber in bewildered terror, and asked if anyone had called his name.

'No,' said Catherine; 'unless in dreams. I cannot conceive how you manage to close, out of doors, in the morning.'

'I thought I heard my father,' he gasped, glancing up to the frowning nab above us. 'You are sure nobody spoke?'

'Quite sure,' replied his cousin. 'Only Ellen and I were disputing concerning your health. Are you truly stronger, Linton, than when we separated in winter? If you be, I'm certain one thing is not stronger – your regard for me – speak, are you?'

The tears gushed from Linton's eyes as he answered, 'Yes, yes, I am!' And, still under the spell of the imaginary voice, his gaze wandered up and down to detect its owner. Cathy rose. 'For today we must part,' she said. 'And I won't conceal that I have been sadly disappointed with our meeting, though I'll mention it to nobody but you: not that I stand in awe of Mr Heathcliff!'

'Hush,' murmured Linton; 'for God's sake, hush! He's coming.' And he clung to Catherine's arm, striving to detain her; but at that announcement she hastily disengaged herself, and whistled to Minny, who obeyed like a dog.

'I'll be here next Thursday,' she cried, springing to the saddle. 'Goodbye. Quick, Ellen!'

And so we left him, scarcely conscious of our departure, so absorbed was he in anticipating his father's approach.

Before we reached home, Catherine's displeasure softened into a perplexed sensation of pity and regret, largely blended with vague, uneasy doubts about Linton's actual circumstances, physical and social: in which I partook, though I counselled her not to say much; for a second journey would make us better judges. My master requested an account of our on-goings: His nephew's offering of thanks was duly delivered, Miss Cathy gently touching on the rest: I also, threw little light on his enquiries, for I hardly knew what to hide, and what to reveal.

## *Chapter 27*

Seven days glided away, every one marking its course by the henceforth rapid alteration of Edgar Linton's state. The havoc that months had previously wrought was now emulated by the inroads of hours. Catherine, we would fain have deluded yet; but her own quick spirit refused to delude her: it divined in secret, and brooded on the dreadful probability, gradually ripening into certainty. She had not the heart to mention her ride, when Thursday came round; I mentioned it for her, and obtained permission to order her out of doors: for the library, where her father stopped a short time daily – the brief period he could bear to sit up – and his chamber, had become her whole world. She grudged each moment that did not find her bending over his pillow, or seated by his side. Her countenance grew wan with watching and sorrow, and my master gladly dismissed her to what he flattered himself would be a happy change of scene and society; drawing comfort from the hope that she would not now be left entirely alone after his death.

He had a fixed idea, I guessed by several observations he let fall, that as his nephew resembled him in person, he would resemble him in mind; for Linton's letters bore few or no indications of his defective character. And I, through pardonable weakness, refrained from correcting the error; asking myself what good there would be in disturbing his last moments with information that he had neither power nor opportunity to turn to account.

We deferred our excursion till the afternoon; a golden afternoon of August: every breath from the hills so full of life, that it seemed whoever respired it, though dying, might revive. Catherine's face was just like the landscape – shadows and sunshine flitting over it in rapid succession; but the shadows rested longer, and the sunshine was more transient; and her poor little heart reproached itself for even that passing forgetfulness of its cares.

We discerned Linton watching at the same spot he had selected before. My young mistress alighted, and told me that as she was resolved to stay a very little while, I had better hold the pony and remain on horseback; but I dissented: I wouldn't risk losing sight of the charge committed to me a minute; so we climbed the slope of heath together. Master Heathcliff received us with greater animation on this occasion: not the animation of high spirits though, nor yet of joy; it looked more like fear.

'It is late!' he said, speaking short and with difficulty. 'Is not your father very ill? I thought you wouldn't come.'

'*Why* won't you be candid?' cried Catherine, swallowing her greeting. 'Why cannot you say at once, you don't want me? It is strange Linton, that for the second time, you have brought me here on purpose, apparently, to distress us both, and for no reason besides!'

Linton shivered, and glanced at her, half supplicating, half ashamed; but his cousin's patience was not sufficient to endure this enigmatical behaviour.

'My father *is* very ill,' she said; 'and why am I called from his bedside – why didn't you send to absolve me from my promise, when you wished I wouldn't keep it? Come! I desire an explanation: playing and trifling are completely banished out of my mind; and I can't dance attendance on your affectations, now!'

'My affectations!' he murmured; 'what are they? For Heaven's sake Catherine, don't look so angry! Despise me as much as you please; I am a worthless, cowardly wretch: I can't be scorned enough! but I'm too mean for your anger – hate my father, and spare me, for contempt.'

'Nonsense!' cried Catherine, in a passion. 'Foolish, silly boy! And there! He trembles, as if I were really going to touch him! You needn't bespeak contempt, Linton: anybody will have it spontaneously, at your service. Get off! I shall return home: it is folly dragging you from the hearthstone, and pretending – what do we pretend? Let go my frock! If I pitied you for crying and looking so very frightened, you should spurn such pity. Ellen, tell him how disgraceful this conduct is. Rise, and don't degrade yourself into an abject reptile – *don't*.'

With streaming face and an expression of agony, Linton had thrown his nerveless frame along the ground: he seemed convulsed with exquisite terror.

'Oh!' he sobbed, 'I cannot bear it! Catherine, Catherine, I'm a traitor too, and I dare not tell you! But leave me and I shall be killed! *Dear* Catherine, my life is in your hands: and you have said you loved me – and if you did, it wouldn't harm you. You'll not go, then? kind, sweet, good Catherine! And perhaps you *will* consent – and he'll let me die with you!'

My young lady, on witnessing his intense anguish, stooped to raise him. The old feeling of indulgent tenderness overcame her vexation, and she grew thoroughly moved and alarmed.

'Consent to what?' she asked. 'To stay? Tell me the meaning of this strange talk, and I will. You contradict your own words, and distract me! Be calm and frank, and confess at once all that weighs on your heart. You wouldn't injure me, Linton, would you? You wouldn't let any enemy hurt me, if you could prevent it? I'll believe you are a coward, for yourself, but not a cowardly betrayer of your best friend.'

'But my father threatened me,' gasped the boy, clasping his attenuated fingers, 'and I dread him – I dread him! I *dare* not tell!'

'Oh well!' said Catherine, with scornful compassion, 'keep your secret, *I'm* no coward – save yourself: I'm not afraid!'

Her magnanimity provoked his tears: he wept wildly, kissing her supporting hands, and yet could not summon courage to speak out. I was cogitating what the mystery might be, and determined Catherine should never suffer to benefit him or anyone else, by my good will; when hearing a rustle among the ling, I looked up, and saw Mr Heathcliff almost close upon us, descending the Heights. He didn't cast a glance towards my companions, though they were sufficiently near for Linton's sobs to be audible; but hailing me in the almost hearty tone he assumed to none besides, and the sincerity of which, I couldn't avoid doubting, he said – 'It is something to see you so near to my house, Nelly! How are you at the Grange? Let us hear! The rumour goes,' he added in a lower tone, 'that Edgar Linton is on his deathbed: perhaps they exaggerate his illness?'

'No; my master is dying,' I replied: 'it is true enough. A sad thing it will be for us all, but a blessing for him!'

'How long will he last, do you think?' he asked.

'I don't know,' I said.

'Because,' he continued, looking at the two young people, who were fixed under his eye – Linton appeared as if he could not venture to stir, or raise his head, and Catherine could not move, on his account – 'Because that lad yonder, seems determined to beat me; and I'd thank his uncle to be quick, and go before him – Hallo! Has the whelp been playing that game long? I *did* give him some lessons about snivelling. Is he pretty lively with Miss Linton generally?'

'Lively? no – he has shown the greatest distress,' I answered. 'To see him, I should say, that instead of rambling with his sweetheart on the hills, he ought to be in bed, under the hands of a doctor.'

'He shall be, in a day or two,' muttered Heathcliff. 'But first – get up, Linton! Get up!' he shouted. 'Don't grovel on the ground, there – up this moment!'

Linton had sunk prostrate again in another paroxysm of helpless fear, caused by his father's glance towards him, I suppose: there was nothing else to produce such humiliation. He made several efforts to obey, but his little strength was annihilated for the time, and he fell back again with a moan. Mr Heathcliff advanced, and lifted him to lean against a ridge of turf.

'Now,' said he, with curbed ferocity, 'I'm getting angry; and if you don't command that paltry spirit of yours – *Damn* you! Get up, directly!'

'I will, father!' he panted. 'Only, let me alone, or I shall faint! I've done as you wished, I'm sure. Catherine will tell you that I – that I – have been cheerful. Ah! keep by me Catherine; give me your hand.'

'Take mine,' said his father; 'stand on your feet. There now – she'll lend you her arm: that's right, look at *her*. You would imagine I was the devil himself; Miss Linton, to excite such horror. Be so kind as to walk home with him, will you? He shudders, if I touch him.'

'Linton, dear!' whispered Catherine, 'I can't go to Wuthering Heights . . . papa has forbidden me . . . He'll not harm you: why are you so afraid?'

'I can never re-enter that house,' he answered. 'I'm *not* to re-enter it without you!'

'Stop . . . ' cried his father. 'We'll respect Catherine's filial scruples. Nelly, take him in, and I'll follow your advice concerning the doctor, without delay.'

'You'll do well,' replied I, 'but I must remain with my mistress. To mind your son is not my business.'

'You are very stiff,' said Heathcliff, 'I know that: but you'll force me to pinch the baby, and make it scream, before it moves your charity. Come then, my hero. Are you willing to return, escorted by me?'

He approached once more, and made as if he would seize the fragile being; but shrinking back, Linton clung to his cousin, and implored her to accompany him, with a frantic importunity that admitted no denial. However I disapproved,

I couldn't hinder her: indeed how could she have refused him herself? What was filling him with dread we had no means of discerning; but there he was, powerless under its gripe, and any addition seemed capable of shocking him into idiocy.

We reached the threshold; Catherine walked in; and I stood waiting till she had conducted the invalid to a chair, expecting her out immediately; when Mr Heathcliff, pushing me forward, exclaimed – 'My house is not stricken with the plague, Nelly; and I have a mind to be hospitable today: sit down, and allow me to shut the door.'

He shut and locked it also. I started.

'You shall have tea, before you go home,' he added. 'I am by myself. Hareton is gone with some cattle to the lees – and Zillah and Joseph are off on a journey of pleasure. And, though I'm used to being alone, I'd rather have some interesting company, if I can get it. Miss Linton, take your seat by *him*. I give you what I have: the present is hardly worth accepting; but, I have nothing else to offer. It is Linton, I mean. How she does stare! It's odd what a savage feeling I have to anything that seems afraid of me! Had I been born where laws are less strict, and tastes less dainty, I should treat myself to a slow vivisection of those two, as an evening's amusement.'

He drew in his breath, struck the table, and swore to himself, 'By hell! I hate them.'

'I'm not afraid of you!' exclaimed Catherine, who could not hear the latter part of his speech. She stepped close up; her black eyes flashing with passion and resolution. 'Give me that key: I will have it!' she said. 'I wouldn't eat or drink here, if I were starving.'

Heathcliff had the key in his hand that remained on the table. He looked up, seized with a sort of surprise at her boldness; or, possibly, reminded by her voice and glance, of the person from whom she inherited it. She snatched at the instrument, and half succeeded in getting it out of his loosened fingers: but her action recalled him to the present; he recovered it speedily.

'Now, Catherine Linton,' he said, 'stand off, or I shall knock you down; and that will make Mrs Dean mad.'

Regardless of this warning, she captured his closed hand and its contents again. 'We *will* go!' she repeated, exerting her utmost efforts to cause the iron muscles to relax; and finding that her nails made no impression, she applied her teeth pretty sharply. Heathcliff glanced at me a glance that kept me from interfering a moment. Catherine was too intent on his fingers to notice his face. He opened them suddenly, and resigned the object of dispute; but, ere she had well secured it, he seized her with the liberated hand, and, pulling her on his knee, administered with the other a shower of terrific slaps on both sides of the head, each sufficient to have fulfilled his threat, had she been able to fall.

At this diabolical violence, I rushed on him furiously. 'You villain!' I began to cry, 'you villain!' A touch on the chest silenced me: I am stout, and soon put out of breath; and, what with that and the rage, I staggered dizzily back, and felt ready to suffocate, or to burst a blood-vessel.

The scene was over in two minutes; Catherine, released, put her two hands to her temples, and looked just as if she were not sure whether her ears were off or on. She trembled like a reed, poor thing, and leant against the table perfectly bewildered.

'I know how to chastise children, you see,' said the scoundrel, grimly, as he stooped to repossess himself of the key, which had dropped to the floor. 'Go to Linton now, as I told you; and cry at your ease! I shall be your father, tomorrow – all the father you'll have in a few days – and you shall have plenty of that – you can bear plenty – you're no weakling – you shall have a daily taste, if I catch such a devil of a temper in your eyes again!'

Cathy ran to me instead of Linton, and knelt down, and put her burning cheek on my lap, weeping aloud. Her cousin had shrunk into a corner of the settle, as quiet as a mouse, congratulating himself, I dare say, that the correction had lighted on another than him. Mr Heathcliff, perceiving us all confounded, rose, and expeditiously made the tea himself. The cups and saucers were laid ready. He poured it out, and handed me a cup.

'Wash away your spleen,' he said. 'And help your own naughty pet and mine. It is not poisoned, though I prepared it. I'm going out to seek your horses.'

Our first thought, on his departure, was to force an exit somewhere. We tried the kitchen door, but that was fastened outside: we looked at the windows – they were too narrow for even Cathy's little figure.

'Master Linton,' I cried, seeing we were regularly imprisoned; 'you know what your diabolical father is after, and you shall tell us, or I'll box your ears, as he has done your cousin's.'

'Yes, Linton; you must tell,' said Catherine. 'It was for your sake I came; and it will be wickedly ungrateful if you refuse.'

'Give me some tea, I'm thirsty, and then I'll tell you,' he answered. 'Mrs Dean, go away. I don't like you standing over me. Now, Catherine, you are letting your tears fall into my cup! I won't drink that. Give me another.'

Catherine pushed another to him, and wiped her face. I felt disgusted at the little wretch's composure, since he was no longer in terror for himself. The anguish he had exhibited on the moor subsided as soon as ever he entered Wuthering Heights; so I guessed he had been menaced with an awful visitation of wrath if he failed in decoying us there; and, that accomplished, he had no further immediate fears.

'Papa wants us to be married,' he continued, after sipping some of the liquid. 'And he knows your papa wouldn't let us marry now; and he's afraid of my dying, if we wait; so we are to be married in the morning, and you are to stay here all night; and, if you do as he wishes, you shall return home next day, and take me with you.'

'Take you with her, pitiful changeling?' I exclaimed. '*You* marry? Why, the man is mad! Or he thinks us fools, everyone. And do you imagine that beautiful young lady, that healthy, hearty girl, will tie herself to a little perishing monkey like you? Are you cherishing the notion that *anybody*, let alone Miss Catherine Linton, would have you for a husband? You want whipping for bringing us in here at all, with your dastardly, puling tricks; and – don't look so silly now! I've a very good mind to shake you severely, for your contemptible treachery, and your imbecile conceit.'

I did give him a slight shaking; but it brought on the cough, and he took to his ordinary resource of moaning and weeping, and Catherine rebuked me.

'Stay all night? No!' she said, looking slowly round. 'Ellen, I'll burn that door down, but I'll get out.'

And she would have commenced the execution of her threat directly, but Linton was up in alarm, for his dear self, again.

He clasped her in his two feeble arms, sobbing – 'Won't you have me, and save me – not let me come to the Grange? Oh! darling Catherine! you mustn't go, and leave me, after all. You *must* obey my father, you *must*!'

'I must obey my own,' she replied, 'and relieve him from this cruel suspense. The whole night! What would he think? he'll be distressed already. I'll either break or burn a way out of the house. Be quiet! You're in no danger – but, if you hinder me – Linton, I love papa better than you!'

The mortal terror he felt of Mr Heathcliff's anger, restored to the boy his coward's eloquence. Catherine was near distraught: still, she persisted that she must go home, and tried entreaty, in her turn, persuading him to subdue his selfish agony.

While they were thus occupied, our jailer re-entered.

'Your beasts have trotted off;' he said, 'and – Now, Linton! Snivelling again? What has she been doing to you? Come, come – have done, and get to bed. In a month or two, my lad, you'll be able to pay her back her present tyrannies, with a vigorous hand. You're pining for pure love, are you not? Nothing else in the world: and she shall have you! There, to bed! Zillah won't be here tonight; you must undress yourself. Hush! Hold your noise! Once in your own room, I'll not come near you, you needn't fear. By chance, you've managed tolerably. I'll look to the rest.'

He spoke these words, holding the door open for his son to pass; and the latter achieved his exit exactly as a spaniel might, which suspected the person who attended on it of designing a spiteful squeeze. The lock was re-secured. Heathcliff approached the fire, where my mistress and I stood silent.

Catherine looked up, and instinctively raised her hand to her cheek: his neighbourhood revived a painful sensation. Anybody else would have been incapable of regarding the childish act with sternness, but he scowled on her, and muttered – 'Oh, you are not afraid of me? Your courage is well disguised: you *seem* damnably afraid!'

'I *am* afraid now,' she replied; 'because if I stay, papa will be miserable; and how can I endure making him miserable – when he – when he – Mr Heathcliff, *let* me go home! I promise to marry Linton: papa would like me to, and I love him – and why should you wish to force me to do what I'll willingly do of myself?'

'Let him dare to force you!' I cried. 'There's law in the land, thank God, there is! Though we *be* in an out-of-the-way place. I'd inform, if he were my own son, and it's felony without benefit of clergy!'

'Silence!' said the ruffian. 'To the devil with your clamour! I don't want *you* to speak. Miss Linton, I shall enjoy myself remarkably in thinking your father will be miserable: I shall not sleep for satisfaction. You could have hit on no surer way of fixing your residence under my roof, for the next twenty-four hours, than informing me that such an event would follow. As to your promise to marry Linton, I'll take care you shall keep it; for you shall not quit this place till it is fulfilled.'

'Send Ellen then, to let papa know I'm safe!' exclaimed Catherine, weeping bitterly. 'Or marry me now. Poor papa! Ellen, he'll think we're lost. What shall we do?'

'Not he! He'll think you are tired of waiting on him, and run off, for a little amusement,' answered Heathcliff. 'You cannot deny that you entered my house of your own accord, in contempt of his injunctions to the contrary. And it is quite natural that you should desire amusement at your age; and that you should weary of nursing a sick man, and that man *only* your father. Catherine, his happiest days were over when your days began. He cursed you, I dare say, for coming into the world (I did, at least). And it would just do if he cursed you as *he* went out of it. I'd join him. I don't love you! How should I? Weep away. As far as I can see, it will be your chief diversion hereafter; unless Linton make amends for other losses: and your provident parent appears to fancy he may. His letters of advice and consolation entertained me vastly. In his last, he recommended my jewel to be careful of his; and kind to her when he got her. Careful and kind – that's paternal. But Linton requires his whole stock of care and kindness for himself. Linton can play the little tyrant well. He'll undertake to torture any number of cats if their teeth be drawn, and their claws pared. You'll be able to tell his uncle fine tales of his *kindness*, when you get home again, I assure you.'

'You're right there!' I said; 'explain your son's character. Show his resemblance to yourself; and then, I hope, Miss Cathy will think twice before she takes the cockatrice!'

'I don't much mind speaking of his amiable qualities now,' he answered; 'because she must either accept him or remain a prisoner, and you along with her, till your master dies. I can detain you both, quite concealed, here. If you doubt, encourage her to retract her word, and you'll have an opportunity of judging!'

'I'll not retract my word,' said Catherine. 'I'll marry him, within this hour, if I may go to Thrushcross Grange afterwards. Mr Heathcliff, you're a cruel man, but you're not a fiend; and you won't, from *mere* malice, destroy, irrevocably, all my happiness. If papa thought I had left him, on purpose, and if he died before I returned, could I bear to live? I've given over crying: but I'm going to kneel here, at your knee; and I'll not get up, and I'll not take my eyes from your face, till you look back at me! No, don't turn away! *Do* look! You'll see nothing to provoke you. I don't hate you. I'm not angry that you struck me. Have you never loved *anybody*, in all your life, uncle? *Never?* Ah! you must look once – I'm so wretched – you can't help being sorry and pitying me.'

'Keep your eft's fingers off; and move, or I'll kick you!' cried Heathcliff, brutally repulsing her. 'I'd rather be hugged by a snake. How the devil can you dream of fawning on me? I *detest* you!'

He shrugged his shoulders: shook himself, indeed, as if his flesh crept with aversion; and thrust back his chair; while I got up, and opened my mouth, to commence a downright torrent of abuse; but I was rendered dumb in the middle of the first sentence, by a threat that I should be shown into a room by myself, the very next syllable I uttered. It was growing dark – we heard a sound of voices at the garden gate. Our host hurried out instantly: *he* had his wits about him; *we* had not. There was a talk of two or three minutes, and he returned alone.

'I thought it had been your cousin Hareton,' I observed to Catherine. 'I wish he would arrive! Who knows but he might take our part?'

'It was three servants sent to seek you from the Grange,' said Heathcliff, overhearing me. 'You should have opened a lattice and called out: but I could swear that chit is glad you didn't. She's glad to be obliged to stay, I'm certain.'

At learning the chance we had missed, we both gave vent to our grief without control; and he allowed us to wail on till nine o'clock. Then he bade us go upstairs, through the kitchen, to Zillah's chamber; and I whispered my companion to obey: perhaps we might contrive to get through the window there, or into a garret, and out by its skylight. The window, however, was narrow, like those below, and the garret trap was safe from our attempts; for we were fastened in as before. We neither of us lay down: Catherine took her station by the lattice, and watched anxiously for morning; a deep sigh being the only answer I could obtain to my frequent entreaties that she would try to rest. I seated myself in a chair, and rocked, to and fro, passing harsh judgement on my many derelictions of duty; from which, it struck me then, all the misfortunes of all my employers sprang. It was not the case, in reality, I am aware; but it was, in my imagination, that dismal night; and I thought Heathcliff himself less guilty than I.

At seven o'clock he came, and enquired if Miss Linton had risen. She ran to the door immediately, and answered, 'Yes.'

'Here, then,' he said, opening it, and pulling her out. I rose to follow, but he turned the lock again. I demanded my release.

'Be patient,' he replied; 'I'll send up your breakfast in a while.'

I thumped on the panels, and rattled the latch angrily; and Catherine asked why I was still shut up? He answered, I must try to endure it another hour, and they went away. I endured it two or three hours; at length, I heard a footstep, not Heathcliff's.

'I've brought you something to eat,' said a voice; 'oppen t' door!'

Complying eagerly, I beheld Hareton, laden with food enough to last me all day.

'Tak it,' he added, thrusting the tray into my hand.

'Stay one minute,' I began.

'Nay!' cried he, and retired, regardless of any prayers I could pour forth to detain him.

And there I remained enclosed, the whole day, and the whole of the next night; and another, and another. Five nights and four days I remained, altogether, seeing nobody but Hareton, once every morning; and he was a model of a jailer: surly, and dumb, and deaf to every attempt at moving his sense of justice or compassion.

## *Chapter 28*

On the fifth morning, or rather afternoon, a different step approached – lighter and shorter; and, this time, the person entered the room. It was Zillah; donned in her scarlet shawl, with a black silk bonnet on her head, and a willow basket swung to her arm.

'Eh, dear! Mrs Dean,' she exclaimed. 'Well! There is a talk about you at Gimmerton. I never thought but you were sunk in the Blackhorse marsh, and missy with you, till master told me you'd been found, and he'd lodged you here! What, and you must have got on an island, sure? And how long were you in the hole? Did master save you, Mrs Dean? But you're not so thin – you've not been so poorly, have you?'

'Your master is a true scoundrel!' I replied. 'But he shall answer for it. He needn't have raised that tale: it shall all be laid bare!'

'What do you mean?' asked Zillah. 'It's not his tale: they tell that in the village – about your being lost in the marsh; and I calls to Earnshaw, when I come in – "Eh, they's queer things, Mr Hareton, happened since I went off. It's a sad pity of that likely young lass, and cant Nelly Dean." He stared. I thought he had not heard aught, so I told him the rumour. The master listened, and he just smiled to himself, and said, "If they have been in the marsh, they are out now, Zillah. Nelly Dean is lodged, at this minute, in your room. You can tell her to flit, when you go up; here is the key. The bog-water got into her head, and she would have run home, quite flighty, but I fixed her, till she came round to her senses. You can bid her go to the Grange, at once, if she be able, and carry a message from me, that her young lady will follow in time to attend the squire's funeral." '

'Mr Edgar is not dead?' I gasped. 'Oh! Zillah, Zillah!'

'No, no; sit you down, my good mistress,' she replied; 'your right sickly yet. He's not dead; Doctor Kenneth thinks he may last another day. I met him on the road and asked.'

Instead of sitting down, I snatched my outdoor things, and hastened below, for the way was free. On entering the house, I looked about for someone to give information of Catherine. The place was filled with sunshine, and the door stood wide open; but nobody seemed at hand. As I hesitated whether to go off at once, or return and seek my mistress, a slight cough drew my attention to the hearth. Linton lay on the settle, sole tenant, sucking a stick of sugar-candy, and pursuing my movements with apathetic eyes. 'Where is Miss Catherine?' I demanded, sternly, supposing I could frighten him into giving intelligence, by catching him thus, alone. He sucked on like an innocent.

'Is she gone?' I said.

'No,' he replied; she's upstairs: she's not to go; we won't let her.'

'You won't let her, little idiot!' I exclaimed. 'Direct me to her room immediately, or I'll make you sing out sharply.'

'Papa would make you sing out, if you attempted to get there,' he answered. 'He says I'm not to be soft with Catherine: she's my wife, and it's shameful that she should wish to leave me! He says, she hates me, and wants me to die, that she may have my money; but she shan't have it: and she shan't go home! She never shall! – She may cry, and be sick as much as she pleases!'

He resumed his former occupation, closing his lids, as if he meant to drop asleep.

'Master Heathcliff,' I resumed, 'have you forgotten all Catherine's kindness to you, last winter, when you affirmed you loved her, and when she brought you books, and sung you songs, and came many a time through wind and snow to see you? She wept to miss one evening, because you would be disappointed; and you felt then, that she was a hundred times too good to you: and now you believe the lies your father tells, though you know he detests you both! And you join him against her. That's fine gratitude, is it not?'

The corner of Linton's mouth fell, and he took the sugar-candy from his lips.

'Did she come to Wuthering Heights, because she hated you?' I continued. 'Think for yourself!

As to your money, she does not even know that you will have any. And you say she's sick; and yet, you leave her alone, up there in a strange house! *You*, who have felt what it is to be so neglected! You could pity your own sufferings, and she pitied them, too, but you won't pity hers! I shed tears Master Heathcliff, you see – an elderly woman, and a servant merely – and you, after pretending such affection, and having reason to worship her, almost, store up every tear you have for yourself, and lie there quite at ease. Ah! You're a heartless, selfish boy!'

'I can't stay with her,' he answered crossly. 'I can't stay, by myself. She cries so I can't bear it. And she won't give over, though I say I'll call my father. I did call him once; and he threatened to strangle her, if she was not quiet; but she began again, the instant he left the room; moaning and grieving all night long, though I screamed for vexation that I couldn't sleep.'

'Is Mr Heathcliff out?' I enquired, perceiving that the wretched creature had no power to sympathise with his cousin's mental tortures.

'He's in the court,' he replied, 'talking to Doctor Kenneth who says uncle is dying, truly, at last. I'm glad, for I shall be master of the Grange after him – and Catherine always spoke of it as her house. It isn't hers! It's mine: papa says everything she has is mine. All her nice books are mine; she offered to give me them, and her pretty birds, and her pony Minny, if I would get the key of our room, and let her but; but I told her she had nothing to give, they were all, all mine. And then she cried, and took a little picture from her neck, and said I should have that two pictures in a gold case – on one side her mother, and on the other, uncle, when they were young. That was yesterday – I said *they* were mine, too; and tried to get them from her. The spiteful thing wouldn't let me: she pushed me off, and hurt me. I shrieked out – that frightens her – she heard papa coming, and she broke the hinges, and divided the case and gave me her mother's portrait; the other she attempted to hide: but papa asked what was the matter and I explained it. He took the one I had away; and ordered her to resign hers to me; she refused, and he – he struck her down, and wrenched it off the chain, and crushed it with his foot.'

'And were you pleased to see her struck?' I asked: having my designs in encouraging his talk.

'I winked,' he answered. 'I wink to see my father strike a dog, or a horse, he does it so hard. Yet I was glad at first – she deserved punishing for pushing me: but when papa was gone, she made me come to the window and showed me her cheek cut on the inside, against her teeth, and her mouth filling with blood; and then she gathered up the bits of the picture, and went and sat down with her face to the wall, and she has never spoken to me since: and I sometimes think she can't speak for pain. I don't like to think so! But she's a naughty thing for crying continually; and she looks so pale and wild, I'm afraid of her!'

'And you can get the key if you choose?' I said.

'Yes, when I am upstairs,' he answered; 'but I can't walk upstairs now.'

'In what apartment is it?' I asked.

'Oh,' he cried, 'I shan't tell *you* where it is! It is our secret. Nobody, neither Hareton, nor Zillah are to know. There! You've tired me – go away, go away!' And he turned his face on to his arm, and shut his eyes, again.

I considered it best to depart without seeing Mr Heathcliff; and bring a rescue for my young lady, from the Grange. On reaching it, the astonishment of my fellow servants to see me, and their joy also, was intense; and when they heard that their little mistress was safe, two or three were about to hurry up, and shout the news at Mr Edgar's door: but I bespoke the announcement of it, myself. How changed I found him, even in those few days! He lay an image of sadness, and resignation, waiting his death. Very young he looked: though his actual age was thirty-nine; one would have called him ten years younger, at least. He thought of Catherine for he murmured her name. I touched his hand, and spoke.

'Catherine is coming, dear master!' I whispered; 'she is alive, and well; and will be here I hope tonight.'

I trembled at the first effects of this intelligence: he half rose up, looked eagerly round the apartment, and then sunk back in a swoon. As soon as he recovered, I related our compulsory visit, and detention at the Heights. I said Heathcliff forced me to go in: which was not quite true. I uttered as little as possible against Linton; nor did I describe all his father's brutal conduct – my intentions being to add no bitterness, if I could help it, to his already overflowing cup.

He divined that one of his enemy's purposes was to secure the personal property, as well as the estate, to his son, or rather himself; yet why he did not wait till his decease, was a puzzle to my master, because ignorant how nearly he and his nephew would quit the world together. However, he felt that his will had better be altered: instead of leaving Catherine's fortune at her own disposal, he determined to put it in the hands of trustees, for her use during life; and for her children, if she had any, after her. By that means, it could not fall to Mr Heathcliff should Linton die.

Having received his orders, I despatched a man to fetch the attorney, and four more, provided with serviceable weapons, to demand my young lady of her jailer. Both parties were delayed very late. The single servant returned first. He said Mr Green, the lawyer, was out when he arrived at his house, and he had to wait two hours for his re-entrance; and then Mr Green told him he had a little business in the village that must be done; but he would be at Thrushcross Grange before morning. The four men came back unaccompanied, also. They brought word that Catherine was ill: too ill to quit her room; and Heathcliff would not suffer them to see her. I scolded the stupid fellows well, for listening to that tale, which I would not carry to my master; resolving to take a whole bevy up to the Heights, at daylight, and storm it, literally, unless the prisoner were quietly surrendered to us. Her father *shall* see her, I vowed, and vowed again, if that devil be killed on his own door-stones in trying to prevent it!

Happily, I was spared the journey, and the trouble. I had gone downstairs at three o'clock to fetch a jug of water; and was passing through the hall with it in my hand, when a sharp knock at the front door made me jump. 'Oh! It is Green,' I said, recollecting myself – 'only Green,' and I went on, intending to send somebody else to open it; but the knock was repeated: not loud, and still importunately. I put the jug on the bannister, and hastened to admit him myself. The harvest moon shone clear outside. It was not the attorney. My own sweet little mistress sprung on my neck, sobbing – 'Ellen! Ellen! Is papa alive?'

'Yes!' I cried: 'yes, my angel, he is. God be thanked, you are safe with us again!'

She wanted to run, breathless as she was, upstairs to Mr Linton's room; but I compelled her to sit down on a chair, and made her drink, and washed her pale face, chafing it into a faint colour with my apron. Then I said I must go first and tell of her arrival, imploring her to say she should be happy with young Heathcliff. She stared, but soon comprehending why I counselled her to utter the falsehood, she assured me she would not complain.

I couldn't abide to be present at their meeting. I stood outside the chamber-door a quarter of an hour, and hardly ventured near the bed, then. All was composed, however: Catherine's despair was as silent as her father's joy. She supported him calmly, in appearance; and he fixed on her features his raised eyes, that seemed dilating with ecstacy.

He died blissfully, Mr Lockwood: he died so. Kissing her cheek, he murmured, 'I am going to her; and you darling child shall come to us;' and never stirred or spoke again; but continued that rapt, radiant gaze, till his pulse imperceptibly stopped, and his soul departed. None could have noticed the exact minute of his death, it was so entirely without a struggle.

Whether Catherine had spent her tears, or whether the grief were too weighty to let them flow, she sat there dry-eyed till the sun rose: she sat till noon, and would still have remained, brooding over that deathbed, but I insisted on her coming away, and taking some repose. It was well I succeeded in removing her, for at dinner-time appeared the lawyer, having called at Wuthering Heights to get his instructions how to behave. He had sold himself to Mr Heathcliff, and that was the cause of his delay in obeying my master's summons. Fortunately, no thought of worldly affairs crossed the latter's mind, to disturb him, after his daughter's arrival.

Mr Green took upon himself to order everything and everybody about the place. He gave all the servants but me, notice to quit. He would have carried his delegated authority to the point of insisting that Edgar Linton should not be buried beside his wife, but in the chapel, with his family. There was the will however, to hinder that, and my loud protestations against any infringement of its directions. The funeral was hurried over; Catherine, Mrs Linton Heathcliff now, was suffered to stay at the Grange till her father's corpse had quitted it.

She told me that her anguish had at last spurred Linton to incur the risk of liberating her. She heard the men I sent, disputing at the door, and she gathered the sense of Heathcliff's answer. It drove her desperate. Linton, who had been conveyed up to the little parlour soon after I left, was terrified into fetching the key before his father re-ascended. He had the cunning to unlock, and re-lock the door, without shutting it; and when he should have gone to bed, he begged to sleep with Hareton, and his petition was granted, for once. Catherine stole out before break of day. She dare not try the doors, lest the dogs should raise an alarm; she visited the empty chambers, and examined their windows; and, luckily, lighting on her mother's, she got easily out of its lattice, and on to the ground, by means of the fir tree, close by. Her accomplice suffered for his share in the escape, notwithstanding his timid contrivances.

## *Chapter 29*

The evening after the funeral, my young lady and I were seated in the library; now musing mournfully – one of us despairingly – on our loss, now venturing conjectures as to the gloomy future.

We had just agreed the best destiny which could await Catherine, would be a permission to continue resident at the Grange; at least during Linton's life: he being allowed to join her there, and I to remain as housekeeper. That seemed rather too favourable an arrangement to be hoped for; and yet I did hope, and began to cheer up under the prospect of retaining my home, and my employment, and, above all, my beloved young mistress, when a servant – one of the discarded ones, not yet departed – rushed hastily in, and said, 'that devil Heathcliff' was coming through the court: should he fasten the door in his face?

If we had been mad enough to order that proceeding, we had not time. He made no ceremony of knocking, or announcing his name: he was master, and availed himself of the master's privilege to walk straight in, without saying a word. The sound of our informant's voice directed him to the library; he entered, and motioning him out, shut the door.

It was the same room into which he had been ushered, as a guest, eighteen years before: the same moon shone through the window; and the same autumn landscape lay outside. We had not yet lighted a candle, but all the apartment was visible, even to the portraits on the wall – the splendid head of Mrs Linton, and the graceful one of her husband. Heathcliff advanced to the hearth. Time had little altered his person either. There was the same man: his dark face rather sallower, and more composed, his frame a stone or two heavier, perhaps, and no other difference. Catherine had risen, with an impulse to dash out, when she saw him.

'Stop!' he said, arresting her by the arm. 'No more runnings away! Where would you go? I'm come to fetch you home; and I hope you'll be a dutiful daughter, and not encourage my son to further disobedience. I was embarrassed how to punish him, when I discovered his part in the business: he's such a cobweb, a pinch would annihilate him; but you'll see by his look that he has received his due! I brought him down one evening, the day before yesterday, and just set him in a chair, and never touched him afterwards. I sent Hareton out, and we had the room to ourselves. In two hours, I called Joseph to carry him up again; and, since then, my presence is as potent on his nerves as a ghost; and I fancy he sees me often, though I am not near. Hareton says he wakes and shrieks in the night by the hour together; and calls you to protect him from me; and, whether you like your precious mate or not, you must come: he's your concern now; I yield all my interest in him to you.'

'Why not let Catherine continue here?' I pleaded, 'and send Master Linton to her. As you hate them both, you'd not miss them: they *can* only be a daily plague to your unnatural heart.'

'I'm seeking a tenant for the Grange,' he answered; 'and I want my children about me, to be sure – besides, that lass owes me her services for her bread; I'm not going to nurture her in luxury and idleness after Linton is gone. Make haste and get ready now. And don't oblige me to compel you.'

'I shall,' said Catherine. 'Linton is all I have to love in the world, and, though you have done what you could to make him hateful to me, and me to him, you *cannot* make us hate each other! And I defy you to hurt him when I am by, and I defy you to frighten me.'

'You are a boastful champion,' replied Heathcliff; 'but I don't like you well enough to hurt him: you shall get the full benefit of the torment, as long as it lasts. It is not I who will make him hateful to you – it is his own sweet spirit. He's as bitter as gall at your desertion, and its consequences; don't expect thanks for this noble devotion. I heard him draw a pleasant picture to Zillah of what he would do, if he were as strong as I: the inclination is there, and his very weakness will sharpen his wits to find a substitute for strength.'

'I know he has a bad nature,' said Catherine: 'he's your son. But I'm glad I've a better, to forgive it; and I know he loves me, and for that reason I love him. Mr Heathcliff, *you* have *nobody* to love you; and, however miserable you make us, we shall still have the revenge of thinking that your cruelty arises from your greater misery! You *are* miserable, are you not? Lonely, like the devil, and envious like him? *Nobody* loves you – *nobody* will cry for you when you die! I wouldn't be you!'

Catherine spoke with a kind of dreary triumph: she seemed to have made up her mind to enter into the spirit of her future family, and draw pleasure from the griefs of her enemies.

'You shall be sorry to be yourself presently,' said her father-in-law, 'if you stand there another minute. Begone, witch, and get your things.'

She scornfully withdrew. In her absence, I began to beg for Zillah's place at the Heights, offering to resign mine to her; but he would suffer it on no account.

He bid me be silent; and then, for the first time, allowed himself a glance round the room, and a look at the pictures. Having studied Mrs Linton, he said – 'I shall have that home. Not because I need it, but – ' He turned abruptly to the fire, and continued, with what, for lack of a better word, I must call a smile – 'I'll tell you what I did yesterday! I got the sexton, who was digging Linton's grave, to remove the earth off her coffin-lid, and I opened it. I thought, once, I would have stayed there, when I saw her face again – it is hers yet – he had hard work to stir me; but he said it would change, if the air blew on it, and so I struck one side of the coffin loose, and covered it up: not Linton's side, damn him! I wish he'd been soldered in lead – and I bribed the sexton to pull it away, when I'm laid there, and slide mine out too. I'll have it made so, and then, by the time Linton gets to us, he'll not know which is which!'

'You were very wicked, Mr Heathcliff!' I exclaimed; 'were you not ashamed to disturb the dead?'

'I disturbed nobody, Nelly,' he replied; 'and I gave some ease to myself. I shall be a great deal more comfortable now; and you'll have a better chance of keeping me underground, when I get there. Disturbed her? No! She has disturbed me, night and day, through eighteen years – incessantly – remorselessly – till yesternight; and yesternight I was tranquil. I dreamt I was sleeping the last sleep by that sleeper, with my heart stopped and my cheek frozen against hers.'

'And if she had been dissolved into earth, or worse, what would you have dreamt of then?' I said.

'Of dissolving with her, and being more happy still!' he answered. 'Do you suppose I dread any change of that sort? I expected such a transformation on raising the lid, but I'm better pleased that it should not commence till I share it. Besides, unless I had received a distinct impression of her passionless features, that strange feeling would hardly have been removed. It began oddly. You know, I was wild after she died; and eternally, from dawn to dawn, praying her to return to me – her spirit – I have a strong faith in ghosts: I have a conviction that they can, and do exist, among us! The day she was buried, there came a fall of snow. In the evening I went to the churchyard. It blew bleak as winter – all round was solitary: I didn't fear that her fool of a husband would wander up the den so late; and no one else had business to bring them there. Being alone, and conscious two yards of loose earth was the sole barrier between us, I said to myself – "I'll have her in my arms again! If she be cold, I'll think it is this north wind that chills *me*; and if she be motionless, it is sleep." I got a spade from the toolhouse, and began to delve with all my might – it scraped the coffin; I fell to work with my hands; the wood commenced cracking about the screws, I was on the point of attaining my object, when it seemed that I heard a sigh from someone above, close at the edge of the grave, and bending down. "If I can only get this off," I muttered, "I wish they may shovel in the earth over us both!" and I wrenched more desperately still. There was another sigh, close at my ear. I appeared to feel the warm breath of it displacing the sleet-laden wind. I knew no living thing in flesh and blood was by; but as certainly as you perceive the approach to some substantial body in the dark, though it cannot be discerned, so certainly I felt that Cathy was there: not under me, but on the earth. A sudden sense of relief flowed, from my heart, through every limb. I relinquished my labour of agony, and turned consoled at once: unspeakably consoled. Her presence was with me: it remained while I refilled the grave, and led me home. You may laugh, if you will; but I was sure I should see her there. I was sure she was with me, and I could not help talking to her. Having reached the Heights, I rushed eagerly to the door. It was fastened; and, I remember, that accursed Earnshaw and my wife opposed my entrance. I remember stopping to kick the breath out of him, and then hurrying upstairs, to my room, and hers. I looked round impatiently – I felt her by me – I could *almost* see her, and yet I *could not*! I ought to have sweat blood then, from the anguish of my yearning – from the fervour of my supplications to have but one glimpse! I had not one. She showed herself, as she often was in life, a devil to me! And, since then, sometimes more and sometimes less, I've been the sport of that intolerable torture! Infernal – keeping my nerves at such a stretch, that, if they had not resembled catgut, they would, long ago, have relaxed to the feebleness of Linton's. When I sat in the house with Hareton, it seemed that on going out, I should meet her; when I walked on the moors I should meet her coming in. When I went from home, I hastened to return: she *must* be somewhere at the Heights, I was certain! And when I slept in her chamber – I was beaten out of that – I couldn't lie there; for the moment I closed my eyes, she was either outside the window, or sliding back the panels, or entering the room, or even resting her darling head on the same pillow as she did when a child. And I must open my lids to see. And so I opened and closed them a hundred times a night – to be always disappointed! It racked me! I've often groaned aloud, till that old rascal Joseph no doubt believed that my conscience was playing the fiend inside of me. Now, since I've seen her, I'm pacified – a little. It was a strange way of killing, not by inches, but by fractions of hairbreadths, to beguile me with the spectre of a hope, through eighteen years!'

Mr Heathcliff paused and wiped his forehead; his hair clung to it, wet with perspiration; his eyes were fixed on the red embers of the fire; the brows not contracted, but raised next the temples; diminishing the grim aspect of his countenance, but imparting a peculiar look of trouble, and a painful appearance of mental tension towards one absorbing subject. He only half addressed me, and I maintained silence – I didn't like to hear him talk! After a short period, he resumed his meditation on the picture, took it down and leant it against the sofa to contemplate it at better advantage; and while so occupied Catherine entered, announcing that she was ready, when her pony should be saddled.

'Send that over tomorrow,' said Heathcliff to me, then turning to her he added, 'You may do without your pony: it is a fine evening, and you'll need no ponies at Wuthering Heights; for what journeys you take, your own feet will serve you – come along.'

'Goodbye, Ellen!' whispered my dear little mistress. As she kissed me, her lips felt like ice. 'Come and see me Ellen, don't forget.'

'Take care you do no such thing, Mrs Dean!' said her new father. 'When I wish to speak to you I'll come here. I want none of your prying at my house!'

He signed her to precede him; and casting back a look that cut my heart, she obeyed. I watched them from the window, walk down the garden. Heathcliff fixed Catherine's arm under his: though she disputed the act, at first, evidently; and with rapid strides, he hurried her into the alley, whose trees concealed them.

## *Chapter 30*

I have paid a visit to the Heights, but I have not seen her since she left: Joseph held the door in his hand, when I called to ask after her, and wouldn't let me pass. He said Mrs Linton was 'thrang', and the master was not in. Zillah has told me something of the way they go on, otherwise I should hardly know who was dead and who living. She thinks Catherine haughty, and does not like her, I can guess by her talk. My young lady asked some aid of her when she first came; but Mr Heathcliff told her to follow her own business, and let his daughter-in-law look after herself; and Zillah willingly acquiesced, being a narrow-minded selfish woman. Catherine evinced a child's annoyance at this neglect; repaid it with contempt, and thus enlisted my informant among her enemies, as securely as if she had done her some great wrong. I had a long talk with Zillah, about six weeks ago, a little before you came, one day, when we foregathered on the moor; and this is what she told me.

'The first thing Mrs Linton did,' she said, 'on her arrival at the Heights, was to run upstairs without even wishing good-evening to me and Joseph; she shut herself into Linton's room, and remained till morning. Then, while the master and Earnshaw were at breakfast, she entered the house, and asked all in a quiver if the doctor might be sent for? Her cousin was very ill.

' "We know that!" answered Heathcliff; "but his life is not worth a farthing, and I won't spend a farthing on him."

' "But I cannot tell how to do," she said; "and if nobody will help me, he'll die!"

' "Walk out of the room," cried the master, "and let me never hear a word more about him! None here care what becomes of him; if you do, act the nurse; if you do not, lock him up and leave him."

'Then she began to bother me, and I said I'd had enough plague with the tiresome thing; we each had our tasks, and hers was to wait on Linton, Mr Heathcliff bid me leave that labour to her.

'How they managed together, I can't tell. I fancy he fretted a great deal, and moaned hisseln, night and day; and she had precious little rest, one could guess by her white face, and heavy eyes – she sometimes came into the kitchen all wildered like, and looked as if she would fain beg assistance; but I was not going to disobey the master: I never dare disobey him, Mrs Dean, and though I thought it wrong that Kenneth should not be sent for, it was no concern of mine, either to advise or complain; and I always refused to meddle. Once or twice, after we had gone to bed, I've happened to open my door again, and seen her sitting crying, on the stairs' top; and then I've shut myself in, quick, for fear of being moved to interfere. I did pity her then, I'm sure: still I didn't want to lose my place, you know!

'At last, one night she came boldly into my chamber, and frightened me out of my wits, by saying – ' "Tell Mr Heathcliff that his son is dying – I'm sure he is, this time. Get up, instantly, and tell him!"

'Having uttered this speech, she vanished again. I lay a quarter of an hour listening and trembling. Nothing stirred – the house was quiet.

' "She's mistaken," I said to myself. "He's got over it. I needn't disturb them." And I began to dose. But my sleep was marred a second time, by a sharp ringing of the bell – the only bell we have, put up on purpose for Linton; and the master called to me to see what was the matter, and inform them that he wouldn't have that noise repeated.

'I delivered Catherine's message. He cursed to himself, and in a few minutes came out with a lighted candle, and proceeded to their room. I followed. Mrs Heathcliff was seated by the bedside, with her hands folded on her knees. Her father-in-law went up, held the light to Linton's face, looked at him, and touched him; afterwards he turned to her.

' "Now – Catherine," he said, "how do you feel?"

'She was dumb.

' "How do you feel, Catherine?" he repeated.

' "He's safe, and I'm free," she answered: "I should feel well – but," she continued with a bitterness she couldn't conceal, "you have left me so long to struggle against death, alone, that I feel and see only death! I feel like death!"

'And she looked like it, too! I gave her a little wine. Hareton and Joseph, who had been wakened by the ringing, and the sound of feet, and heard our talk from outside, now entered. Joseph was fain, I believe, of the lad's removal; Hareton seemed a thought bothered: though he was more taken up with staring at Catherine than thinking of Linton. But the master bid him get off to bed again: we didn't want his help. He afterwards made Joseph remove the body to his chamber, and told me to return to mine, and Mrs Heathcliff remained by herself.

'In the morning, he sent me to tell her she must come down to breakfast: she had undressed, and appeared going to sleep; and said she was ill; at which I hardly wondered. I informed Mr Heathcliff, and he replied – "Well, let her be till after the funeral; and go up now and then to get her what is needful; and as soon as she seems better, tell me." '

Cathy stayed upstairs a fortnight, according to Zillah, who visited her twice a day, and would have been rather more friendly, but her attempts at increasing kindness were proudly and promptly repelled.

Heathcliff went up at once, to show her Linton's will. He had bequeathed the whole of his, and what had been her moveable property to his father. The poor creature was threatened, or coaxed, into that act during her week's absence, when his uncle died. The lands, being a minor, he could not meddle with. However, Mr Heathcliff has claimed and kept them in his wife's right, and his also: I suppose legally, at any rate Catherine, destitute of cash and friends, cannot disturb his possession.

'Nobody,' said Zillah, 'ever approached her door, except that once, but I . . . and nobody asked anything about her. The first occasion of her coming down into the house, was on a Sunday afternoon. She had cried out, when I carried up her dinner, that she couldn't bear any longer being in the cold; and I told her the master was going to Thrushcross Grange; and Earnshaw and I needn't hinder her from descending; so, as soon as she heard Heathcliff's horse trot off, she made her appearance, donned in black, and her yellow curls combed back behind her ears, as plain as a quaker: she couldn't comb them out.

'Joseph and I generally go to chapel on Sundays. (The kirk, you know, has no minister now,' explained Mrs Dean; 'and they call the Methodists' or Baptists' place, I can't say which it is, at Gimmerton, a chapel.) Joseph had gone,' she continued, 'but I thought proper to bide at home. Young folks are always the better for an elder's overlooking; and Hareton, with all his bashfulness, isn't a model of nice behaviour. I let him know that his cousin would very likely sit with us, and she had been always used to see the Sabbath respected; so he had as good leave his guns, and bits of indoor work alone, while she stayed. He coloured up at the news, and cast his eyes over his hands and clothes. The train-oil and gunpowder were shoved out of sight in a minute. I saw he meant to give her his company; and I guessed, by his way, he wanted to be presentable; so, laughing, as I durst not laugh when the master is by, I offered to help him, if he would, and joked at his confusion. He grew sullen, and began to swear.

'Now, Mrs Dean,' she went on, seeing me not pleased by her manner, 'you happen think your young lady too fine for Mr Hareton; and happen you're right: but, I own, I should love well to bring her pride a peg lower. And what will all her learning and her daintiness do for her, now? She's as poor as you or I: poorer, I'll be bound: you're saving, and I'm doing my little all, that road.'

Hareton allowed Zillah to give him her aid; and she flattered him into a good humour; so, when Catherine came, half forgetting her former insults, he tried to make himself agreeable, by the housekeeper's account.

'Missis walked in,' she said, 'as chill as an icicle, and as high as a princess. I got up and offered her my seat in the armchair. No, she turned up her nose at my civility. Earnshaw rose too, and bid her come to the settle, and sit close by the fire: he was sure she was starved.

' "I've been starved a month and more," she answered, resting on the word, as scornful as she could.

'And she got a chair for herself, and placed it at a distance from both of us.

Having sat till she was warm, she began to look round, and discovered a number of books in the dresser; she was instantly upon her feet again, stretching to reach them: but they were too high up. Her cousin, after watching her endeavours a while, at last summoned courage to help her; she held her frock, and he filled it with the first that came to hand.

'That was a great advance for the lad. She didn't thank him: still, he felt gratified that she had accepted his assistance, and ventured to stand behind as she examined them, and even to stoop and point out what struck his fancy in certain old pictures which they contained; nor was he daunted by the saucy style in which she jerked the page from his finger: he contented himself with going a bit farther back, and looking at her instead of the book. She continued reading, or seeking for something to read. His attention became, by degrees, quite centred in the study of her thick, silky curls: her face he couldn't see, and she couldn't see him. And, perhaps, not quite awake to what he did, but attracted like a child to a candle, at last he proceeded from staring to touching; he put out his hand and stroked one curl, as gently as if it were a bird. He might have stuck a knife into her neck, she started round in such a taking.

' "Get away, this moment! How dare you touch me? Why are you stopping there?" she cried, in a tone of disgust. "I can't endure you! I'll go upstairs again, if you come near me."

'Mr Hareton recoiled, looking as foolish as he could do: he sat down in the settle, very quiet, and she continued turning over her volumes, another half-hour; finally, Earnshaw crossed over, and whispered to me.

' "Will you ask her to read to us, Zillah? I'm stalled of doing naught; and I do like – I could like to hear her! Dunnot say I wanted it, but ask of yourseln."

' "Mr Hareton wishes you would read to us, ma'am," I said, immediately. "He'd take it very kind – he'd be much obliged."

'She frowned; and, looking up, answered – "Mr Hareton, and the whole set of you, will be good enough to understand that I reject any pretence at kindness you have the hypocrisy to offer! I despise you, and will have nothing to say to any of you! When I would have given my life for one kind word, even to see one of your faces, you all kept off. But I won't complain to you! I'm driven down here by the cold, not either to amuse you, or enjoy your society."

' "What could I ha' done?" began Earnshaw. "How was I to blame?"

' "Oh! you are an exception," answered Mrs Heathcliff. "I never missed such a concern as you."

' "But, I offered more than once, and asked," he said, kindling up at her pertness, "I asked Mr Heathcliff to let me wake for you – "

' "Be silent! I'll go out of doors, or anywhere, rather than have your disagreeable voice in my ear!" said my lady.

'Hareton muttered, she might go to hell, for him! and unslinging his gun, restrained himself from his Sunday occupations no longer. He talked now, freely enough; and she presently saw fit to retreat to her solitude: but the frost had set in, and, in spite of her pride, she was forced to condescend to our company, more and more. However, I took care there should be no further scorning at my good nature: ever since, I've been as stiff as herself; and she has no lover or liker among us: and she does not deserve one; for, let them say the least word to her, and she'll curl back without respect of anyone! She'll snap at the master himself, and as good as dares him to thrash her; and the more hurt she gets, the more venomous she grows.'

At first, on hearing this account from Zillah, I determined to leave my situation, take a cottage, and get Catherine to come and live with me: but Mr Heathcliff would as soon permit that, as he would set up Hareton in an independent house; and I can see no remedy, at present, unless she could marry again: and that scheme it does not come within my province to arrange.

Thus ended Mrs Dean's story. Notwithstanding the doctor's prophecy, I am rapidly recovering strength; and, though it be only the second week in January, I propose getting out on horseback in a day or two, and riding over to Wuthering Heights, to inform my landlord that I shall spend the next six months in London; and, if he likes, he may look out for another tenant to take the place, after October – I would not pass another winter here for much.

## *Chapter 31*

Yesterday was bright, calm, and frosty. I went to the Heights as I proposed: my housekeeper entreated me to bear a little note from her to her young lady, and I did not refuse, for the worthy woman was not conscious of anything odd in her request. The front door stood open, but the jealous gate was fastened, as at my last visit; I knocked, and invoked Earnshaw from among the garden beds; he unchained it, and I entered. The fellow is as handsome a rustic as need be seen. I took particular notice of him this time; but then he does his best, apparently, to make the least of his advantages.

I asked if Mr Heathcliff were at home? He answered, no; but he would be in at dinner time. It was eleven o'clock, and I announced my intention of going in, and waiting for him, at which he immediately flung down his tools and accompanied me, in the office of watchdog, not as a substitute for the host.

We entered together; Catherine was there, making herself useful in preparing some vegetables for the approaching meal; she looked more sulky, and less spirited than when I had seen her first. She hardly raised her eyes to notice me, and continued her employment with the same disregard to common forms of politeness, as before; never returning my bow and good-morning by the slightest acknowledgment.

'She does not seem so amiable,' I thought, 'as Mrs Dean would persuade me to believe. She's a beauty, it is true; but not an angel.'

Earnshaw surlily bid her remove her things to the kitchen. 'Remove them yourself,' she said, pushing them from her as soon as she had done; and retiring to a stool by the window, where she began to carve figures of birds and beasts out of the turnip parings in her lap. I approached her, pretending to desire a view of the garden; and, as I fancied, adroitly dropped Mrs Dean's note on to her knee, unnoticed by Hareton – but she asked aloud, 'What is that?' and chucked it off.

'A letter from your old acquaintance, the housekeeper at the Grange,' I answered, annoyed at her exposing my kind deed, and fearful lest it should be imagined a missive of my own. She would gladly have gathered it up at this information, but Hareton beat her; he seized, and put it in his waistcoat, saying Mr Heathcliff should look at it first. Thereat, Catherine silently turned her face from us, and, very stealthily, drew out her pocket-handkerchief and applied it to her eyes; and her cousin, after struggling a while to keep down his softer feelings, pulled out the letter and flung it on the floor beside her, as ungraciously as he could.

Catherine caught and perused it eagerly; then she put a few questions to me concerning the inmates, rational and irrational, of her former home; and gazing towards the hills, murmured in soliloquy – 'I should like to be riding Minny down there! I should like to be climbing up there – Oh! I'm tired – I'm *stalled*, Hareton!' And she leant her pretty head back against the sill, with half a yawn and half a sigh, and lapsed into an aspect of abstracted sadness: neither caring nor knowing whether we remarked her.

'Mrs Heathcliff,' I said, after sitting some time mute, 'are you not aware that I am an acquaintance of yours? So intimate, that I think it strange you won't come and speak to me. My housekeeper never wearies of talking about and praising you; and she'll be greatly disappointed if I return with no news of, or from you, except that you received her letter and said nothing!'

She appeared to wonder at this speech and asked – 'Does Ellen like you?'

'Yes, very well,' I replied unhesitatingly.

'You must tell her,' she continued, 'that I would answer her letter, but I have no materials for writing: not even a book from which I might tear a leaf.'

'No books!' I exclaimed. 'How do you contrive to live here without them? If I may take the liberty to enquire. Though provided with a large library, I'm frequently very dull at the Grange; take my books away, and I should be desperate!'

'I was always reading, when I had them,' said Catherine: 'and Mr Heathcliff never reads; so he took it into his head to destroy my books. I have not had a glimpse of one, for weeks. Only once, I searched through Joseph's store of theology, to his great irritation; and once, Hareton, I came upon a secret stock in your room . . . some Latin and Greek, and some tales and poetry: all old friends – I brought the last here – and you gathered them, as a magpie gathers silver spoons, for the mere love of stealing! They are of no use to you; or else you concealed them in the bad spirit, that as you cannot enjoy them, nobody else shall. Perhaps *your* envy counselled Mr Heathcliff to rob me of my treasures? But I've most of them written on my brain and printed in my heart, and you cannot deprive me of those!'

Earnshaw blushed crimson when his cousin made this revelation of his private literary accumulations, and stammered an indignant denial of her accusations.

'Mr Hareton is desirous of increasing his amount of knowledge,' I said, coming to his rescue. 'He is not *envious* but *emulous* of your attainments – He'll be a clever scholar in a few years!'

'And he wants *me* to sink into a dunce, meantime,' answered Catherine. 'Yes, I hear him trying to spell and read to himself, and pretty blunders he makes! I wish you would repeat Chevy Chase as you did yesterday: it was extremely funny! I heard you . . . and I heard you turning over the dictionary, to seek out the hard words, and then cursing, because you couldn't read their explanations!'

The young man evidently thought it too bad that he should be laughed at for his ignorance, and then laughed at for trying to remove it. I had a similar notion, and, remembering Mrs Dean's anecdote of his first attempt at enlightening the darkness in which he had been reared, I observed – 'But, Mrs Heathcliff, we have each had a commencement, and each stumbled and tottered on the threshold, and had our teachers scorned, instead of aiding us, we should stumble and totter yet.'

'Oh!' she replied, 'I don't wish to limit his acquirements . . . still, he has no right to appropriate what is mine, and make it ridiculous to me with his vile mistakes and mispronunciations! Those books, both prose and verse, were consecrated to me by other associations, and I hate to have them debased and profaned in his mouth! Besides, of all, he has selected my favourite pieces that I love the most to repeat, as if out of deliberate malice!'

Hareton's chest heaved in silence a minute: he laboured under a severe sense of mortification and wrath, which it was no easy task to suppress.

I rose and, from a gentlemanly idea of relieving his embarrassment, took up my station in the doorway, surveying the external prospect as I stood. He followed my example, and left the room; but presently reappeared, bearing half a dozen volumes in his hands, which he threw into Catherine's lap, exclaiming – 'Take them! I never want to hear, or read, or think of them again!'

'I won't have them, now,' she answered. 'I shall connect them with you, and hate them.'

She opened one that had obviously been often turned over, and read a portion in the drawling tone of a beginner; then laughed, and threw it from her. 'And listen,' she continued provokingly, commencing a verse of an old ballad in the same fashion.

But his self-love would endure no further torment: I heard, and not altogether disapprovingly, a manual check given to her saucy tongue – The little wretch had done her utmost to hurt her cousin's sensitive though uncultivated feelings, and a physical argument was the only mode he had of balancing the account and repaying its effects on the inflicter. He afterwards gathered the books and hurled them on the fire. I read in his countenance what anguish it was to offer that sacrifice to spleen – I fancied that as they consumed, he recalled the pleasure they had already imparted, and the triumph and ever-increasing pleasure he had anticipated from them; and I fancied, I guessed the incitement to his secret studies, also. He had been content with daily labour and rough animal enjoyments, till Catherine crossed his path. Shame at her scorn, and hope of her approval, were his first prompters to higher pursuits; and instead of guarding him from one, and winning him the other, his endeavours to raise himself had produced just the contrary result.

'Yes; that's all the good that such a brute as you can get from them!' cried Catherine, sucking her damaged lip, and watching the conflagration with indignant eyes.

'You'd *better* hold your tongue, now!' he answered fiercely.

And his agitation precluding further speech, he advanced hastily to the entrance, where I made way for him to pass. But, ere he had crossed the door-stones, Mr Heathcliff, coming up the causeway, encountered him, and laying hold of his shoulder, asked – 'What's to do now, my lad?'

'Naught, naught!' he said, and broke away, to enjoy his grief and anger in solitude.

Heathcliff gazed after him, and sighed.

'It will be odd, if I thwart myself!' he muttered, unconscious that I was behind him. 'But, when I look for his father in his face, I find *her* every day more! How the devil is he so like? I can hardly bear to see him.'

He bent his eyes to the ground, and walked moodily in. There was a restless, anxious expression in his countenance I had never remarked there before; and he looked sparer in person. His daughter-in-law, on perceiving him through the window, immediately escaped to the kitchen, so that I remained alone.

'I'm glad to see you out of doors again, Mr Lockwood.' he said in reply to my greeting, 'from selfish motives partly: I don't think I could readily supply your loss in this desolation. I've wondered, more than once, what brought you here.'

'An idle whim, I fear, sir,' was my answer; 'or else an idle whim is going to spirit me away. I shall set out for London, next week; and I must give you warning, that I feel no disposition to retain Thrushcross Grange beyond the twelve-months I agreed to rent it. I believe I shall not live there any more.'

'Oh, indeed! You're tired of being banished from the world, are you?' he said. 'But, if you be coming to plead off paying for a place you won't occupy, your journey is useless: I never relent in exacting my due, from anyone.'

'I'm coming to plead off nothing about it!' I exclaimed, considerably irritated. 'Should you wish it, I'll settle with you now,' and I drew my notebook from my pocket.

'No, no,' he replied coolly; 'you'll leave sufficient behind to cover your debts, if you fail to return: I'm not in such a hurry – sit down and take your dinner with us; a guest that is safe from repeating his visit can generally be made welcome. Catherine! Bring the things in: where are you?'

Catherine reappeared, bearing a tray of knives and forks.

'You may get your dinner with Joseph,' muttered Heathcliff aside, 'and remain in the kitchen till he is gone.'

She obeyed his directions very punctually: perhaps she had no temptation to transgress. Living among clowns and misanthropists, she probably cannot appreciate a better class of people, when she meets them.

With Mr Heathcliff, grim and saturnine, on one hand, and Hareton, absolutely dumb, on the other, I made a somewhat cheerless meal, and bid adieu early. I would have departed by the back way, to get a last glimpse of Catherine, and annoy old Joseph; but Hareton received orders to lead up my horse, and my host himself escorted me to the door, so I could not fulfil my wish.

'How dreary life gets over in that house!' I reflected, while riding down the road. 'What a realisation of something more romantic than a fairy tale it would have been for Mrs Linton Heathcliff, had she and I struck up an attachment, as her good nurse desired, and migrated together into the stirring atmosphere of the town!'

## *Chapter 32*

1802 – This September, I was invited to devastate the moors of a friend, in the North; and, on my journey to his abode, I unexpectedly came within fifteen miles of Gimmerton.

The ostler at a roadside public-house was holding a pail of water to refresh my horses, when a cart of very green oats, newly reaped, passed by, and he remarked – 'Yon's frough Gimmerton, nah! They're alias three wick' after other folk wi' ther harvest.'

'Gimmerton?' I repeated – my residence in that locality had already grown dim and dreamy. 'Ah! I know! How far is it from this?'

'Happen fourteen mile' o'er th' hills, and a rough road,' he answered.

A sudden impulse seized me to visit Thrushcross Grange. It was scarcely noon, and I conceived that I might as well pass the night under my own roof, as in an inn. Besides, I could spare a day easily, to arrange matters with my landlord, and thus save myself the trouble of invading the neighbourhood again. Having rested a while, I directed my servant to enquire the way to the village; and, with great fatigue to our beasts, we managed the distance in some three hours.

I left him there, and proceeded down the valley alone. The grey church looked greyer, and the lonely churchyard lonelier. I distinguished a moor sheep cropping the short turf on the graves. It was sweet, warm weather – too warm for travelling; but the heat did not hinder me from enjoying the delightful scenery above and below: had I seen it nearer August, I'm sure it would have tempted me to waste a month among its solitudes. In winter nothing more dreary, in summer nothing more divine, than those glens shut in by hills, and those bluff, bold swells of heath.

I reached the Grange before sunset, and knocked for admittance; but the family had retreated into the back premises, I judged by one thin, blue wreath curling from the kitchen chimney, and they did not hear. I rode into the court. Under the porch, a girl of nine or ten sat knitting, and an old woman reclined on the horse-steps, smoking a meditative pipe.

'Is Mrs Dean within?' I demanded of the dame.

'Mistress Dean? Nay!' she answered, 'shoo doesn't bide here; shoo's up at th' Heights.'

'Are you the housekeeper, then?' I continued.

'Eea, Aw keep th' hause,' she replied.

'Well, I'm Mr Lockwood, the master. Are there any rooms to lodge me in, I wonder? I wish to stay here all night.'

'T' maister!' she cried in astonishment. 'Whet, whoiver knew yah wur coming? Yah sud ha' send word! They's nowt norther dry – nor mensful abaht t' place: nowt there is n't!'

She threw down her pipe and bustled in, the girl followed, and I entered too; soon perceiving that her report was true, and, moreover, that I had almost upset her wits by my unwelcome apparition. I bid her be composed – I would go out for a walk; and, meantime, she must try to prepare a corner of a sitting-room for me to sup in, and a bedroom to sleep in. No sweeping and dusting, only good fires and dry sheets were necessary. She seemed willing to do her best; though she thrust the hearth-brush into the grates in mistake for the poker, and malappropriated several other articles of her craft: but I retired, confiding in her energy for a resting-place against my return. Wuthering Heights was the goal of my proposed excursion. An afterthought brought me back, when I had quitted the court.

'All well at the Heights?' I enquired of the woman.

'Eea, f'r owt Ee knaw!' she answered, skurrying away with a pan of hot cinders.

I would have asked why Mrs Dean had deserted the Grange, but it was impossible to delay her at such a crisis, so I turned away and made my exit, rambling leisurely along, with the glow of a sinking sun behind, and the mild glory of a rising moon in front – one fading, and the other brightening, as I quitted the park, and climbed the stony by-road branching off to Mr Heathcliff's dwelling. Before I arrived in sight of it, all that remained of day was a beamless, amber light along the west: but I could see every pebble on the path, and every blade of grass, by that splendid moon. I had neither to climb the gate, nor to knock – it yielded to my hand. That is an improvement! I thought. And I noticed another, by the aid of my nostrils; a fragrance of stocks and wall flowers, wafted on the air, from amongst the homely fruit trees.

Both doors and lattices were open; and yet, as is usually the case in a coal district, a fine, red fire illumined the chimney: the comfort which the eye derives from it, renders the extra heat endurable. But the house of Wuthering Heights is so large, that the inmates have plenty of space for withdrawing out of its influence; and, accordingly, what inmates there were had stationed themselves not far from one of the windows. I could both see them and hear them talk before I entered, and looked and listened in consequence; being moved thereto by a mingled sense of curiosity, and envy that grew as I lingered.

'Con-*trary*!' said a voice, as sweet as a silver bell – 'That for the third time, you dunce! I'm not going to tell you, again – Recollect, or I pull your hair!'

'Contrary, then,' answered another, in deep but softened tones. 'And now, kiss me, for minding so well.'

'No, read it over first correctly, without a single mistake.'

The male speaker began to read: he was a young man, respectably dressed, and seated at a table, having a book before him. His handsome features glowed with pleasure, and his eyes kept impatiently wandering from the page to a small white hand over his shoulder, which recalled him by a smart slap on the cheek, whenever its owner detected such signs of inattention. Its owner stood behind; her light shining ringlets blending, at intervals, with his brown locks, as she bent to superintend his studies; and her face – it was lucky he could not see her face, or he would never have been so steady – I could, and I bit my lip, in spite, at having thrown away the chance I might have had, of doing something besides staring at its smiting beauty.

The task was done, not free from further blunders; but the pupil claimed a reward, and received at least five kisses: which, however, he generously returned. Then, they came to the door, and from their conversation, I judged they were about to issue out and have a walk on the moors. I supposed I should be condemned in Hareton Earnshaw's heart, if not by his mouth, to the lowest pit in the infernal regions, if I showed my unfortunate person in his neighbourhood then; and feeling very mean and malignant, I skulked round to seek refuge in the kitchen.

There was unobstructed admittance on that side also; and, at the door, sat my old friend, Nelly Dean, sewing and singing a song, which was often interrupted from within, by harsh words of scorn and intolerance, uttered in far from musical accents.

'Aw'd rayther, by th' haulf, hev 'em swearing i' my lugs frough morn tuh neeght, nur hearken yah, hahsiver!' said the tenant of the kitchen, in answer to an unheard speech of Nelly's. 'It's a blazing shaime, ut Aw cannut oppen t' Blessed Book, bud yah set up them glories tuh sattan, un' all t' flay-some wickednesses ut iver wer born intuh t' warld! Oh! yah're a raight nowt; un' shoo's another; un' that poor lad 'ull be lost, atween ye. Poor lad!' he added, with a groan; 'he's witched, Aw'm sartin on 't! O, Lord, judge 'em, fur they's norther law nur justice amang wer rullers!'

'No! or we should be sitting in flaming faggots, I suppose,' retorted the singer. 'But wisht, old man, and read your Bible, like a Christian, and never mind me. This is "Fairy Annie's Wedding" – a bonny tune – it goes to a dance.'

Mrs Dean was about to recommence, when I advanced; and recognising me directly, she jumped to her feet, crying – 'Why, bless you, Mr Lockwood! How could you think of returning in this way? All's shut up at Thrushcross Grange. You should have given us notice!'

'I've arranged to be accommodated there, for as long as I shall stay,' I answered. 'I depart again tomorrow. And how are you transplanted here, Mrs Dean? tell me that.'

'Zillah left, and Mr Heathcliff wished me to come, soon after you went to London, and stay till you returned. But, step in, pray! Have you walked from Gimmerton this evening?'

'From the Grange,' I replied; 'and, while they make me lodging room there, I want to finish my business with your master; because I don't think of having another opportunity in a hurry.'

'What business, sir?' said Nelly, conducting me into the house. He's gone out at present, and won't return soon.'

'About the rent,' I answered.

'Oh! Then it is with Mrs Heathcliff you must settle,' she observed; 'or rather with me. She has not learnt to manage her affairs yet, and I act for her: there's nobody else.'

I looked surprised.

'Ah! You have not heard of Heathcliff's death, I see!' she continued.

'Heathcliff dead?' I exclaimed, astonished. 'How long ago?'

'Three months since: but, sit down, and let me take your hat, and I'll tell you all about it. Stop, you have had nothing to eat, have you?'

'I want nothing. I have ordered supper at home. You sit down too. I never dreamt of his dying! Let me hear how it came to pass. You say you don't expect them back for some time – the young people?'

'No – I have to scold them every evening, for their late rambles: but they don't care for me. At least, have a drink of our old ale; it will do you good: you seem weary.'

She hastened to fetch it, before I could refuse, and I heard Joseph asking whether 'it warn't a crying scandal that she should have fellies at her time of life? And then, to get them jocks out uh' t' Maister's cellar! He fair shaamed to 'bide still and see it.'

She did not stay to retaliate, but re-entered, in a minute, bearing a reaming silver pint, whose contents I lauded with becoming earnestness. And afterwards she furnished me with the sequel of Heathcliff's history. He had a 'queer' end, as she expressed it.

I was summoned to Wuthering Heights, within a fortnight of your leaving us, she said; and I obeyed joyfully, for Catherine's sake. My first interview with her grieved and shocked me! She had altered so much since our separation. Mr Heathcliff did not explain his reasons for taking a new mind about my coming here; he only told me he wanted me, and he was tired of seeing Catherine: I must make the little parlour my sitting-room, and keep her with me. It was enough if he were obliged to see her once or twice a day. She seemed pleased at this arrangement; and, by degrees, I smuggled over a great number of books, and other articles, that had formed her amusement at the Grange; and flattered myself we should get on in tolerable comfort. The delusion did not last long. Catherine, contented at first, in a brief space grew irritable and restless. For one thing, she was forbidden to move out of the garden, and it fretted her sadly to be confined to its narrow bounds, as Spring drew on; for another, in following the house, I was forced to quit her frequently, and she complained of loneliness: she preferred quarrelling with Joseph in the kitchen, to sitting at peace in her solitude. I did not mind their skirmishes: but Hareton was often obliged to seek the kitchen also, when the master wanted to have the house to himself; and though, in the beginning, she either left it at his approach, or quietly joined in my occupations, and shunned remarking or addressing him – and though he was always as sullen and silent as possible – after a while, she changed her behaviour, and became incapable of letting him alone: talking at him; commenting on his stupidity and idleness; expressing her wonder how he could endure the life he lived – how he could sit a whole evening staring into the fire, and dozing.

'He's just like a dog, is he not, Ellen?' she once observed, 'or a carthorse? He does his work, eats his food, and sleeps, eternally! What a blank, dreary mind he must have! Do you ever dream, Hareton? And, if you do, what is it about? But you can't speak to me!'

Then she looked at him; but he would neither open his mouth nor look again.

'He's perhaps dreaming now,' she continued. 'He twitched his shoulder as Juno twitches hers. Ask him, Ellen.'

'Mr Hareton will ask the master to send you upstairs, if you don't behave!' I said. He had not only twitched his shoulder but clenched his fist, as if tempted to use it.

'I know why Hareton never speaks, when I am in the kitchen,' she exclaimed, on another occasion. 'He is afraid I shall laugh at him. Ellen, what do you think? He began to teach himself to read once; and, because I laughed, he burned his books, and dropped it: was he not a fool?'

'Were not you naughty?' I said; 'answer me that.'

'Perhaps I was,' she went on; 'but I did not expect him to be so silly. Hareton, if I gave you a book, would you take it now? I'll try!'

She placed one she had been perusing on his hand; he flung it off, and muttered, if she did not give over, he would break her neck.

'Well, I shall put it here,' she said, 'in the table drawer; and I'm going to bed.'

Then she whispered me to watch whether he touched it, and departed. But he would not come near it; and so I informed her in the morning, to her great disappointment. I saw she was sorry for his persevering sulkiness and indolence: her conscience reproved her for frightening him off improving himself: she had done it effectually.

But her ingenuity was at work to remedy the injury: while I ironed, or pursued other stationary employments I could not well do in the parlour, she would bring some pleasant volume and read it aloud to me. When Hareton was there, she generally paused in an interesting part, and left the book lying about: that she did repeatedly; but he was as obstinate as a mule, and, instead of snatching at her bait, in wet weather he took to smoking with Joseph, and they sat like automatons, one on each side of the fire, the elder happily too deaf to understand her wicked nonsense, as he would have called it, the younger doing his best to seem to disregard it. On fine evenings the latter followed his shooting expeditions, and Catherine yawned and sighed, and teased me to talk to her, and ran off into the court or garden, the moment I began; and, as a last resource, cried and said, she was tired of living: her life was useless.

Mr Heathcliff, who grew more and more disinclined to society, had almost banished Earnshaw out of his apartment. Owing to an accident, at the commencement of March, he became for some days a fixture in the kitchen. His gun burst while out on the hills by himself; a splinter cut his arm, and he lost a good deal of blood before he could reach home. The consequence was, that, perforce, he was condemned to the fireside and tranquillity, till he made it up again. It suited Catherine to have him there: at any rate, it made her hate her room upstairs more than ever: and she would compel me to find out business below, that she might accompany me.

On Easter Monday, Joseph went to Gimmerton fair with some cattle; and, in the afternoon, I was busy getting up linen in the kitchen. Earnshaw sat, morose as usual, at the chimney corner, and my little mistress was beguiling an idle hour with drawing pictures on the window panes, varying her amusement by smothered bursts of songs, and whispered ejaculations, and quick glances of annoyance and impatience in the direction of her cousin, who steadfastly smoked, and looked into the grate.

At a notice that I could do with her no longer, intercepting my light, she removed to the hearthstone. I bestowed little attention on her proceedings, but, presently, I heard her begin – 'I've found out, Hareton, that I want – that I'm glad – that I should like you to be my cousin, now, if you had not grown so cross to me, and so rough.'

Hareton returned no answer.

'Hareton, Hareton, Hareton! do you hear?' she continued.

'Get off wi' ye!' he growled, with uncompromising gruffness.

'Let me take that pipe,' she said, cautiously advancing her hand, and abstracting it from his mouth.

Before he could attempt to recover it, it was broken, and behind the fire. He swore at her and seized another.

'Stop,' she cried, 'you must listen to me, first; and I can't speak while those clouds are floating in my face.'

'Will you go to the devil!' he exclaimed, ferociously, 'and let me be!'

'No,' she persisted, 'I won't: I can't tell what to do to make you talk to me; and you are determined not to understand. When I call you stupid, I don't mean anything: I don't mean that I despise you. Come, you shall take notice of me, Hareton: you are my cousin, and you shall own me.'

'I shall have naught to do wi' you, and your mucky pride, and your damned, mocking tricks!' he answered. 'I'll go to hell, body and soul, before I look sideways after you again! Side out of t' gait, now; this minute!'

Catherine frowned, and retreated to the window-seat, chewing her lip, and endeavouring, by humming an eccentric tune, to conceal a growing tendency to sob.

'You should be friends with your cousin, Mr Hareton,' I interrupted, 'since she repents of her sauciness! It would do you a great deal of good: it would make you another man, to have her for a companion.'

'A companion?' he cried; 'when she hates me, and does not think me fit to wipe her shoon! Nay, if it made me a king, I'd not be scorned for seeking her good will any more.'

'It is not I who hate you, it is you who hate me!' wept Cathy, no longer disguising her trouble. 'You hate me as much as Mr Heathcliff does, and more.'

'You're a damned liar,' began Earnshaw: 'why have I made him angry, by taking your part then, a hundred times? And that, when you sneered at, and despised me, and – Go on plaguing me, and I'll step in yonder, and say you worried me out of the kitchen!'

'I didn't know you took my part,' she answered, drying her eyes; 'and I was miserable and bitter at everybody; but, now I thank you, and beg you to forgive me, what can I do besides?'

She returned to the hearth, and frankly extended her hand. He blackened, and scowled like a thundercloud, and kept his fists resolutely clenched, and his gaze fixed on the ground.

Catherine, by instinct, must have divined it was obdurate perversity, and not dislike, that prompted this dogged conduct; for, after remaining an instant undecided, she stooped, and impressed on his cheek a gentle kiss. The little rogue thought I had not seen her, and, drawing back, she took her former station by the window, quite demurely. I shook my head reprovingly; and then she blushed, and whispered – 'Well! what should I have done, Ellen? He wouldn't shake hands, and he wouldn't look: I must show him some way that I like him – that I want to be friends.'

Whether the kiss convinced Hareton, I cannot tell: he was very careful, for some minutes, that his face should not be seen; and when he did raise it, he was sadly puzzled where to turn his eyes.

Catherine employed herself in wrapping a handsome book neatly in white paper; and having tied it with a bit of ribband, and addressed it to 'Mr Hareton Earnshaw,' she desired me to be her ambassadress, and convey the present to its destined recipient.

'And tell him, if he'll take it, I'll come and teach him to read it right,' she said; 'and, if he refuse it, I'll go upstairs, and never tease him again.'

I carried it, and repeated the message, anxiously watched by my employer. Hareton would not open his fingers, so I laid it on his knee. He did not strike it off, either. I returned to my work: Catherine leaned her head and arms on the table, till she heard the slight rustle of the covering being removed; then she stole away, and quietly seated herself beside her cousin. He trembled, and his face glowed: all his rudeness and all his surly harshness had deserted him: he could not summon courage, at first, to utter a syllable, in reply to her questioning look, and her murmured petition.

'Say you forgive me, Hareton, do! You can make me so happy, by speaking that little word.'

He muttered something inaudible.

'And you'll be my friend?' added Catherine, interrogatively.

'Nay! you'll be ashamed of me every day of your life,' he answered. 'And the more, the more you know me, and I cannot bide it.'

'So, you won't be my friend?' she said, smiling as sweet as honey, and creeping close up.

I overheard no further distinguishable talk, but on looking round again, I perceived two such radiant countenances bent over the page of the accepted book, that I did not doubt the treaty had been ratified, on both sides, and the enemies were, thenceforth, sworn allies.

The work they studied was full of costly pictures; and those, and their position, had charm enough to keep them unmoved, till Joseph came home. He, poor man, was perfectly aghast at the spectacle of Catherine seated on the same bench with Hareton Earnshaw, leaning her hand on his shoulder; and confounded at his favourite's endurance of her proximity. It affected him too deeply to allow an observation on the subject that night. His emotion was only revealed by the immense sighs he drew, as he solemnly spread his large Bible on the table, and overlaid it with dirty banknotes from his pocketbook, the produce of the day's transactions. At length, he summoned Hareton from his seat.

'Tak' these in tuh t' maister, lad,' he said, 'un' bide theare; Aw's gang up tuh my awn rahm. This hoile's norther mensful, nor seemly fur us – we mun side aht, and seearch another!'

'Come, Catherine,' I said, 'we must "side out" too: I've done my ironing, are you ready to go?'

'It is not eight o'clock!' she answered, rising unwillingly. 'Hareton, I'll leave this book upon the chimney-piece, and I'll bring some more tomorrow.'

'Ony books ut yah leave, Aw suall tak' intuh th' hahse,' said Joseph, 'un' it'ull be mitch if yah find 'em agean; soa, yah muh plase yourseln!'

Cathy threatened that his library should pay for hers; and, smiling as she passed Hareton, went singing upstairs: lighter of heart, I venture to say, than ever she had been under that roof before; except, perhaps, during her earliest visits to Linton.

The intimacy thus commenced, grew rapidly: though it encountered temporary interruptions. Earnshaw was not to be civilised with a wish; and my young lady was no philosopher, and no paragon of patience; but both their minds tending to the same point – one loving and desiring to esteem, and the other loving and desiring to be esteemed – they contrived in the end to reach it.

You see, Mr Lockwood, it was easy enough to win Mrs Heathcliff's heart. But now, I'm glad you did not try. The crown of all my wishes will be the union of those two. I shall envy no one on their wedding-day: there won't be a happier woman than myself in England!

## *Chapter 33*

On the morrow of that Monday, Earnshaw being still unable to follow his ordinary employments, and therefore remaining about the house, I speedily found it would be impracticable to retain my charge beside me, as heretofore. She got downstairs before me, and out into the garden, where she had seen her cousin performing some easy work; and when I went to bid them come to breakfast, I saw she had persuaded him to clear a large space of ground from currant and gooseberry bushes, and they were busy planning together an importation of plants from the Grange.

I was terrified at the devastation which had been accomplished in a brief half-hour; the black currant trees were the apple of Joseph's eye, and she had just fixed her choice of a flower bed in the midst of them!

'There! That will be all shewn to the master,' I exclaimed, 'the minute it is discovered. And what excuse have you to offer for taking such liberties with the garden? We shall have a fine explosion on the head of it: see if we don't! Mr Hareton, I wonder you should have no more wit, than to go and make that mess at her bidding!'

'I'd forgotten they were Joseph's,' answered Earnshaw, rather puzzled; 'but I'll tell him I did it.'

We always ate our meals with Mr Heathcliff. I held the mistress's post in making tea and carving; so I was indispensable at table. Catherine usually sat by me; but today, she stole nearer to Hareton, and I presently saw she would have no more discretion in her friendship, than she had in her hostility.

'Now, mind you don't talk with and notice your cousin too much,' were my whispered instructions as we entered the room. 'It will certainly annoy Mr Heathcliff, and he'll be mad at you both.'

'I'm not going to,' she answered.

The minute after, she had sidled to him, and was sticking primroses in his plate of porridge.

He dared not speak to her, there: he dared hardly look; and yet she went on teasing, till he was twice on the point of being provoked to laugh; and I frowned, and then, she glanced towards the master, whose mind was occupied on other subjects than his company, as his countenance evinced, and she grew serious for an instant, scrutinising him with deep gravity. Afterwards she turned, and recommenced her nonsense; at last, Hareton uttered a smothered laugh. Mr Heathcliff started; his eye rapidly surveyed our faces. Catherine met it with her accustomed look of nervousness, and yet defiance, which he abhorred.

'It is well you are out of my reach,' he exclaimed. 'What fiend possesses you to stare back at me, continually, with those infernal eyes? Down with them! And don't remind me of your existence again. I thought I had cured you of laughing!'

'It was me,' muttered Hareton.

'What do you say?' demanded the master.

Hareton looked at his plate, and did not repeat the confession. Mr Heathcliff looked at him a bit, and then silently resumed his breakfast, and his interrupted musing. We had nearly finished, and the two young people prudently shifted wider asunder, so I anticipated no further disturbance during that sitting; when Joseph appeared at the door, revealing by his quivering lip and furious eyes, that the outrage committed on his precious shrubs was detected.

He must have seen Cathy and her cousin about the spot before he examined it, for while his jaws worked like those of a cow chewing its cud, and rendered his speech difficult to understand, he began – 'Aw mun hev my wage, and Aw mun goa! Aw *hed* aimed tuh dee, wheare Aw'd sarved fur sixty year; un' Aw thowt

Aw'd lug my books up intuht' garret, 'un all my bits uh stuff, un' they sud hev t' kitchen tuh theirseln; fur t' sake uh quietness. It wur hard tuh gie up my awn hearthstun, bud Aw thowt Aw *could* do that! Bud, nah, shoo's taan my garden frough me, un' by th' heart! Maister, Aw cannot stand it! Yah muh bend tuh th' yoak, an ye will – *Aw'* noan used to 't and an ow'd man doesn't sooin get used tuh new barthens – Aw'd raythe arn my bite, an' my sup, wi' a hammer in th' road!'

'Now, now, idiot!' interrupted Heathcliff, 'cut it short! What's your grievance? I'll interfere in no quarrels between you and Nelly – She may thrust you into the coal-hole for anything I care.'

'It's noan Nelly!' answered Joseph. 'Aw sudn't shift fur Nelly – Nasty, ill nowt as shoo is, Thank God! *Shoo* cannot stale t' sowl uh nob'dy! Shoo wer niver soa handsome, bud whet a body mud look at her 'baht winking. It's yon flaysome, graceless quean, ut's witched ahr lad, wi' her bold een, un' her forrard ways – till – Nay! It fair brusts my heart! He's forgetten all E done for him, un made on him, un' goan un' riven up a whole row ut t' grandest currant trees, i' t' garden!' and here he lamented outright, unmanned by a sense of his bitter injuries, and Earnshaw's ingratitude and dangerous condition.

'Is the fool drunk?' asked Mr Heathcliff. 'Hareton, is it you he's finding fault with?'

'I've pulled up two or three bushes,' replied the young man; 'but I'm going to set 'em again.'

'And why have you pulled them up?' said the master.

Catherine wisely put in her tongue.

'We wanted to plant some flowers there,' she cried. 'I'm the only person to blame, for I wished him to do it.'

'And who the devil gave *you* leave to touch a stick about the place?' demanded her father-in-law, much surprised. 'And who ordered *you* to obey her?' he added, turning to Hareton.

The latter was speechless; his cousin replied – 'You shouldn't grudge a few yards of earth, for me to ornament, when you have taken all my land!'

'Your land, insolent slut? You never had any!' said Heathcliff.

'And my money,' she continued, returning his angry glare, and meantime, biting a piece of crust, the remnant of her breakfast.

'Silence!' he exclaimed. 'Get done, and begone!'

'And Hareton's land, and his money,' pursued the reckless thing. 'Hareton and I are friends now; and I shall tell him all about you!'

The master seemed confounded a moment: he grew pale, and rose up, eyeing her all the while, with an expression of mortal hate.

'If you strike me, Hareton will strike you!' she said; 'so you may as well sit down.'

'If Hareton does not turn you out of the room, I'll strike him to Hell,' thundered Heathcliff. 'Damnable witch! Dare you pretend to rouse him against me? Off with her! Do you hear? Fling her into the kitchen! I'll kill her, Ellen Dean, if you let her come into my sight again!'

Hareton tried under his breath to persuade her to go.

'Drag her away!' he cried savagely. 'Are you staying to talk?' And he approached to execute his own command.

'He'll not obey you, wicked man, any more!' said Catherine; 'and he'll soon detest you, as much as I do!'

'Wisht! wisht!' muttered the young man reproachfully. 'I will not hear you speak so to him – Have done.'

'But you won't let him strike me?' she cried.

'Come then!' he whispered earnestly.

It was too late: Heathcliff had caught hold of her.

'Now *you* go!' he said to Earnshaw. 'Accursed witch! this time she has provoked me, when I could not bear it; and I'll make her repent it for ever!'

He had his hand in her hair; Hareton attempted to release the locks, entreating him not to hurt her that once. His black eyes flashed; he seemed ready to tear Catherine in pieces, and I was just worked up to risk coming to the rescue, when of a sudden, his fingers relaxed, he shifted his grasp from her head, to her arm, and gazed intently in her face – Then, he drew his hand over his eyes, stood a moment to collect himself apparently, and turning anew to Catherine, said with assumed calmness, 'You must learn to avoid putting me in a passion, or I shall really murder you, some time! Go with Mrs Dean, and keep with her, and confine your insolence to her ears. As to Hareton Earnshaw, if I see him listen to you, I'll send him seeking his bread where he can get it! Your love will make him an outcast, and a beggar. Nelly, take her, and leave me, all of you! Leave me!'

I led my young lady out: she was too glad of her escape, to resist; the other followed, and Mr Heathcliff had the room to himself, till dinner. I had counselled Catherine to get hers upstairs; but, as soon as he perceived her vacant seat, he sent me to call her. He spoke to none of us, eat very little, and went out directly afterwards, intimating that he should not return before evening.

'The two new friends established themselves in the house, during his absence, where I heard Hareton sternly check his cousin, on her offering a revelation of her father-in-law's conduct to his father. He said he wouldn't suffer a word to be uttered to him, in his disparagement: if he were the devil, it didn't signify; he would stand by him; and he'd rather she would abuse himself, as she used to, than begin on Mr Heathcliff. Catherine was waxing cross at this; but he found means to make her hold her tongue, by asking, how she would like *him* to speak ill of her father? And then she comprehended that Earnshaw took the master's reputation home to himself; and was attached by ties stronger than reason could break – chains, forged by habit, which it would be cruel to attempt to loosen. She showed a good heart, thenceforth, in avoiding both complaints and expressions of antipathy concerning Heathcliff; and confessed to me her sorrow that she had endeavoured to raise a bad spirit between him and Hareton: indeed, I don't believe she has ever breathed a syllable, in the latter's hearing, against her oppressor, since.

When this slight disagreement was over, they were thick again, and as busy as possible, in their several occupations, of pupil, and teacher. I came in to sit with them, after I had done my work; and I felt so soothed and comforted to watch them, that I did not notice how time got on. You know, they both appeared in a measure my children: I had long been proud of one; and now, I was sure, the other would be a source of equal satisfaction. His honest, warm, and intelligent nature shook off rapidly the clouds of ignorance and degradation in which it had been bred; and Catherine's sincere commendations acted as a spur to his industry. His brightening mind brightened his features, and added spirit and nobility to their aspect: I could hardly fancy it the same individual I had beheld on the day I discovered my little lady at Wuthering Heights, after her expedition to the crags. While I admired, and they laboured, dusk drew on, and with it returned the master. He came upon us quite unexpectedly, entering by the front way, and had a full view of the whole three, ere we could raise our heads to glance at him. Well, I reflected, there was never a pleasanter, or more harmless sight; and it will be a burning shame to scold them. The red firelight glowed on their two bonny heads, and revealed their faces, animated with the eager interest of children; for, though he was twenty-three, and she eighteen, each had so much of novelty to feel and learn, that neither experienced nor evinced the sentiments of sober disenchanted maturity.

They lifted their eyes together, to encounter Mr Heathcliff: perhaps you have never remarked that their eyes are precisely similar, and they are those of Catherine Earnshaw. The present Catherine has no other likeness to her, except a breadth of forehead, and a certain arch of the nostril that makes her appear rather haughty, whether she will or not. With Hareton the resemblance is carried farther: it is singular, at all times – then it was particularly striking: because his senses were alert, and his mental faculties wakened to unwonted activity. I suppose this resemblance disarmed Mr Heathcliff: he walked to the hearth in evident agitation; but it quickly subsided, as he looked at the young man: or, I should say, altered its character; for it was there yet. He took the book from his hand, and glanced at the open page, then returned it without any observation; merely signing Catherine away: her companion lingered very little behind her, and I was about to depart also, but he bid me sit still.

'It is a poor conclusion, is it not,' he observed, having brooded a while on the scene he had just witnessed. 'An absurd termination to my violent exertions? I get levers and mattocks to demolish the two houses, and train myself to be capable of working like Hercules, and when everything is ready, and in my power, I find the will to lift a slate off either roof has vanished! My old enemies have not beaten me; now would be the precise time to revenge myself on their representatives: I could do it; and none could hinder me. But where is the use? I don't care for striking: I can't take the trouble to raise my hand! That sounds as if I had been labouring the whole time, only to exhibit a fine trait of magnanimity. It is far from being the case – I have lost the faculty of enjoying their destruction, and I am too idle to destroy for nothing.

'Nelly, there is a strange change approaching: I'm in its shadow at present. I take so little interest in my daily life, that I hardly remember to eat and drink. Those two, who have left the room are the only objects which retain a distinct material appearance to me; and, that appearance causes me pain, amounting to agony. About *her* I won't speak; and I don't desire to think; but I earnestly wish she were invisible: her presence invokes only maddening sensations. *He* moves me differently: and yet if I could do it without seeming insane, I'd never see him again! You'll perhaps think me rather inclined to become so,' he added, making an effort to smile, 'if I try to describe the thousand forms of past associations, and ideas he awakens, or embodies – But you'll not talk of what I tell you; and my mind is so eternally secluded in itself, it is tempting, at last, to turn it out to another.

'Five minutes ago, Hareton seemed a personification of my youth, not a human being: I felt to him in such a variety of ways, that it would have been impossible to have accosted him rationally.

'In the first place, his startling likeness to Catherine connected him fearfully with her. That however which you may suppose the most potent to arrest my imagination, is actually the least: for what is not connected with her to me? And what does not recall her? I cannot look down to this floor, but her features are shaped on the flags! In every cloud, in every tree – filling the air at night, and caught by glimpses in every object, by day I am surrounded with her image! The most ordinary faces of men, and women – my own features mock me with a resemblance. The entire world is a dreadful collection of memoranda that she did exist, and that I have lost her!

'Well, Hareton's aspect was the ghost of my immortal love, of my wild endeavours to hold my right, my degradation, my pride, my happiness, and my anguish –

'But it is frenzy to repeat these thoughts to you: only it will let you know, why, with a reluctance to be always alone, his society is no benefit, rather an aggravation of the constant torment I suffer: and it partly contributes to render me regardless how he and his cousin go on together. I can give them no attention, any more.'

'But what do you mean by a *change*, Mr Heathcliff?' I said, alarmed at his manner, though he was neither in danger of losing his senses, nor dying; according to my judgement he was quite strong and healthy; and, as to his reason, from childhood he had a delight in dwelling on dark things, and entertaining odd fancies. He might have had a monomania on the subject of his departed idol; but on every other point his wits were as sound as mine.

'I shall not know that, till it comes,' he said; 'I'm only half conscious of it now.'

'You have no feeling of illness, have you?' I asked.

'No, Nelly, I have not,' he answered.

'Then, you are not afraid of death?' I pursued.

'Afraid? No!' he replied. 'I have neither a fear, nor a presentiment, nor a hope of death. Why should I? With my hard constitution and temperate mode of living, and unperilous occupations, I ought to, and probably *shall* remain above ground, till there is scarcely a black hair on my head – And yet I cannot continue in this condition! I have to remind myself to breathe – almost to remind my heart to beat! And it is like bending back a stiff spring: it is by compulsion that I do the slightest act not prompted by one thought, and by compulsion, that I notice anything alive or dead, which is not associated with one universal idea. I have a single wish, and my whole being and faculties are yearning to attain it. They have yearned towards it so long, and so unwaveringly, that I'm convinced it *will* be reached – and *soon* – because it has devoured my existence: I am swallowed in the anticipation of its fulfilment. My confessions have not relieved me; but they may account for some otherwise unaccountable phases of humour which I show. O, God! It is a long fight, I wish it were over!'

He began to pace the room, muttering terrible things to himself, till I was inclined to believe, as he said Joseph did, that conscience had turned his heart to an earthly hell. I wondered greatly how it would end. Though he seldom before had revealed this state of mind, even by looks, it was his habitual mood, I had no doubt: he asserted it himself; but not a soul, from his general bearing, would have conjectured the fact. You did not, when you saw him, Mr Lockwood: and at the period of which I speak, he was just the same as then, only fonder of continued solitude, and perhaps still more laconic in company.

## Chapter 34

For some days after that evening, Mr Heathcliff shunned meeting us at meals; yet he would not consent, formally, to exclude Hareton and Cathy. He had an aversion to yielding so completely to his feelings, choosing rather to absent himself; and eating once in twenty-four hours seemed sufficient sustenance for him.

One night, after the family were in bed, I heard him go downstairs, and out at the front door. I did not hear him re-enter, and in the morning I found he was still away. We were in April then: the weather was sweet and warm, the grass as green as showers and sun could make it, and the two dwarf apple trees, near the southern wall, in full bloom. After breakfast, Catherine insisted on my bringing a chair, and sitting with my work under the fir trees at the end of the house; and she beguiled Hareton, who had perfectly recovered from his accident, to dig and arrange her little garden, which was shifted to that corner by the influence of Joseph's complaints. I was comfortably revelling in the spring fragrance around, and the beautiful soft blue overhead, when my young lady, who had run down near the gate to procure some primrose roots for a border, returned only half laden, and informed us that Mr Heathcliff was coming in. 'And he spoke to me,' she added, with a perplexed countenance.

'What did he say?' asked Hareton.

'He told me to begone as fast as I could,' she answered. 'But he looked so different from his usual look that I stopped a moment to stare at him.'

'How?' he enquired.

'Why, almost bright and cheerful – No, almost nothing – *very much* excited, and wild and glad!' she replied.

'Night-walking amuses him, then,' I remarked, affecting a careless manner: in reality, as surprised as she was; and, anxious to ascertain the truth of her statement, for to see the master looking glad would not be an everyday spectacle, I framed an excuse to go in. Heathcliff stood at the open door; he was pale, and he trembled: yet, certainly, he had a strange joyful glitter in his eyes that altered the aspect of his whole face.

'Will you have some breakfast?' I said. 'You must be hungry, rambling about all night!' I wanted to discover where he had been, but I did not like to ask directly.

'No, I'm not hungry,' he answered, averting his head, and speaking rather contemptuously, as if he guessed I was trying to divine the occasion of his good humour.

I felt perplexed: I didn't know whether it were not a proper opportunity to offer a bit of admonition.

'I don't think it right to wander out of doors,' I observed, 'instead of being in bed: it is not wise, at any rate, this moist season. I dare say you'll catch a bad cold, or a fever: you have something the matter with you now!'

'Nothing but what I can bear,' he replied; 'and with the greatest pleasure, provided you'll leave me alone: get in, and don't annoy me.'

I obeyed; and, in passing, I noticed he breathed as fast as a cat.

'Yes!' I reflected to myself, 'we shall have a fit of illness. I cannot conceive what he has been doing!'

That noon, he sat down to dinner with us, and received a heaped-up plate from my hands, as if he intended to make amends for previous fasting.

'I've neither cold nor fever, Nelly,' he remarked, in allusion to my morning's speech; 'and I'm ready to do justice to the food you give me.'

He took his knife and fork, and was going to commence eating, when the inclination appeared to become suddenly extinct. He laid them on the table, looked eagerly towards the window, then rose and went out. We saw him walking to and fro in the garden while we concluded our meal, and Earnshaw said he'd go and ask why he would not dine: he thought we had grieved him some way.

'Well, is he coming?' cried Catherine, when her cousin returned.

'Nay,' he answered; 'but he's not angry: he seemed rare and pleased indeed; only, I made him impatient by speaking to him twice; and then he bid me be off to you: he wondered how I could want the company of anybody else.'

I set his plate to keep warm on the fender: and after an hour or two he re-entered, when the room was clear, in no degree calmer: the same unnatural – it was unnatural – appearance of joy under his black brows; the same bloodless hue, and his teeth visible, now and then, in a kind of smile; his frame shivering, not as one shivers with chill or weakness, but as a tight-stretched cord vibrates – a strong thrilling, rather than trembling.

I will ask what is the matter, I thought, or who should? And I exclaimed – 'Have you heard any good news, Mr Heathcliff? You look uncommonly animated.'

'Where should good news come from, to me?' he said. 'I'm animated with hunger; and, seemingly, I must not eat.'

'Your dinner is here', I returned; 'why won't you get it?'

'I don't want it now,' he muttered, hastily: 'I'll wait till supper. And, Nelly, once for all, let me beg you to warn Hareton and the other away from me. I wish to be troubled by nobody: I wish to have this place to myself.'

'Is there some new reason for this banishment?' I enquired. 'Tell me why you are so queer, Mr Heathcliff? Where were you last night? I'm not putting the question through idle curiosity, but – '

'You are putting the question through very idle curiosity,' he interrupted, with a laugh. 'Yet, I'll answer it. Last night, I was on the threshold of hell. Today, I am within sight of my heaven. I have my eyes on it: hardly three feet to sever me! And now you'd better go – You'll neither see nor hear anything to frighten you, if you refrain from prying.'

Having swept the hearth and wiped the table, I departed more perplexed than ever.

He did not quit the house again that afternoon, and no one intruded on his solitude, till, at eight o'clock, I deemed it proper, though unsummoned, to carry a candle and his supper to him.

He was leaning against the ledge of an open lattice, but not looking out: his face was turned to the interior gloom. The fire had smouldered to ashes; the room was filled with the damp, mild air of the cloudy evening; and so still, that not only the murmur of the beck down Gimmerton was distinguishable, but its ripples and its gurgling over the pebbles, or through the large stones which it could not cover. I uttered an ejaculation of discontent at seeing the dismal grate, and commenced shutting the casements, one after another, till I came to his.

'Must I close this?' I asked, in order to rouse him; for he would not stir.

The light flashed on his features as I spoke. Oh, Mr Lockwood, I cannot express what a terrible start I got, by the momentary view! Those deep black eyes! That smile, and ghastly paleness! It appeared to me, not Mr Heathcliff, but a goblin; and, in my terror, I let the candle bend towards the wall, and it left me in darkness.

'Yes, close it,' he replied, in his familiar voice. 'There, that is pure awkwardness! Why did you hold the candle horizontally? Be quick, and bring another.'

I hurried out in a foolish state of dread, and said to Joseph – 'The master wishes you to take him a light and rekindle the fire.' For I dare not go in myself again just then.

Joseph rattled some fire into the shovel, and went: but he brought it back immediately, with the supper tray in his other hand, explaining that Mr Heathcliff was going to bed, and he wanted nothing to eat till morning. We heard him mount the stairs directly; he did not proceed to his ordinary chamber, but turned into that with the panelled bed: its window, as I mentioned before, is wide enough for anybody to get through; and it struck me that he plotted another midnight excursion, which he had rather we had no suspicion of.

'Is he a ghoul, or a vampire?' I mused. I had read of such hideous, incarnate demons. And then I set myself to reflect how I had tended him in infancy; and watched him grow to youth; and followed him almost through his whole course; and what absurd nonsense it was to yield to that sense of horror. 'But where did he come from, the little dark thing, harboured by a good man to his bane?' muttered superstition, as I dozed into unconsciousness. And I began, half dreaming, to weary myself with imaging some fit parentage for him; and repeating my waking meditations, I tracked his existence over again, with grim variations; at last, picturing his death and funeral: of which, all I can remember is, being exceedingly vexed at having the task of dictating an inscription for his monument, and consulting the sexton about it; and, as he had no surname, and we could not tell his age, we were obliged to content ourselves with the single word, 'Heathcliff'. That came true: we were. If you enter the kirkyard, you'll read on his headstone, only that, and the date of his death.

Dawn restored me to common sense. I rose, and went into the garden, as soon as I could see, to ascertain if there were any footmarks under his window. There were none. 'He has stayed at home,' I thought, 'and he'll be all right today!'

I prepared breakfast for the household, as was my usual custom, but told Hareton and Catherine to get theirs ere the master came down, for he lay late. They preferred taking it out of doors, under the trees, and I set a little table to accommodate them.

On my re-entrance, I found Mr Heathcliff below. He and Joseph were conversing about some farming business; he gave clear, minute directions concerning the matter discussed, but he spoke rapidly, and turned his head continually aside, and had the same excited expression, even more exaggerated. When Joseph quitted the room, he took his seat in the place he generally chose, and I put a basin of coffee before him. He drew it nearer, and then rested his arms on the table, and looked at the opposite wall, as I supposed, surveying one particular portion, up and down, with glittering, restless eyes, and with such eager interest that he stopped breathing, during half a minute together.

'Come now,' I exclaimed, pushing some bread against his hand. 'Eat and drink that, while it is hot: it has been waiting near an hour.'

He didn't notice me, and yet he smiled. I'd rather have seen him gnash his teeth than smile so.

'Mr Heathcliff! Master!' I cried. 'Don't for God's sake, stare as if you saw an unearthly vision.'

'Don't, for God's sake, shout so loud,' he replied. 'Turn round, and tell me, are we by ourselves?'

'Of course,' was my answer; 'of course we are!'

Still. I involuntarily obeyed him, as if I were not quite sure. With a sweep of his hand he cleared a vacant space in front among the breakfast things, and leant forward to gaze more at his ease.

Now, I perceived he was not looking at the wall; for when I regarded him alone, it seemed exactly that he gazed at something within two yards distance. And whatever it was, it communicated, apparently, both pleasure and pain, in exquisite extremes: at least, the anguished, yet raptured expression of his countenance suggested that idea. The fancied object was not fixed, either; his eyes pursued it with unwearied vigilance, and, even in speaking to me, were never weaned away. I vainly reminded him of his protracted abstinence from food: if he stirred to touch anything in compliance with my entreaties, if he stretched his hand out to get a piece of bread, his fingers clenched before they reached it, and remained on the table, forgetful of their aim.

I sat, a model of patience, trying to attract his absorbed attention from its engrossing speculation; till he grew irritable, and got up, asking why I would not allow him to have his own time in taking his meals? and saying that, on the next occasion, I needn't wait: I might set the things down and go. Having uttered these words he left the house, slowly sauntered down the garden path, and disappeared through the gate.

The hours crept anxiously by: another evening came. I did not retire to rest till late, and when I did, I could not sleep. He returned after midnight, and, instead of going to bed, shut himself into the room beneath. I listened, and tossed about; and, finally, dressed, and descended. It was too irksome to lie up there, harassing my brain with a hundred idle misgivings.

I distinguished Mr Heathcliff's step, restlessly measuring the floor; and he frequently broke the silence by a deep inspiration, resembling a groan. He muttered detached words also; the only one I could catch was the name of Catherine, coupled with some wild term of endearment or suffering; and spoken as one would speak to a person present: low and earnest, and wrung from the depth of his soul. I had not courage to walk straight into the apartment; but I desired to divert him from his reverie, and therefore fell foul of the kitchen fire, stirred it, and began to scrape the cinders. It drew him forth sooner than I expected. He opened the door immediately, and said – 'Nelly, come here – is it morning? Come in with your light.'

'It is striking four,' I answered. 'You want a candle to take upstairs: you might have lit one at this fire.'

'No, I don't wish to go upstairs,' he said. 'Come in, and kindle *me* a fire, and do anything there is to do about the room.'

'I must blow the coals red first, before I can carry any,' I replied, getting a chair and the bellows.

He roamed to and fro, meantime, in a state approaching distraction; his heavy sighs succeeding each other so thick as to leave no space for common breathing between.

'When day breaks I'll send for Green,' he said; 'I wish to make some legal enquiries of him while I can bestow a thought on those matters, and while I can act calmly. I have not written my will yet; and how to leave my property I cannot determine! I wish I could annihilate it from the face of the earth.'

'I would not talk so, Mr Heathcliff,' I interposed. 'Let your will be, a while: you'll be spared to repent of your many injustices, yet! I never expected that your nerves would be disordered: they are, at present, marvellously so, however; and almost entirely through your own fault. The way you've passed these three last days might knock up a Titan. Do take some food, and some repose. You need only look at yourself in a glass to see how you require both. Your cheeks are hollow, and your eyes bloodshot, like a person starving with hunger, and going blind with loss of sleep.'

'It is not my fault that I cannot eat or rest,' he replied. 'I assure you it is through no settled designs. I'll do both, as soon as I possibly can. But you might as well bid a man struggling in the water, rest within arm's length of the shore! I must reach it first, and then I'll rest. Well, never mind Mr Green: as to repenting of my injustices, I've done no injustice, and I repent of nothing – I'm too happy, and yet I'm not happy enough. My soul's bliss kills my body, but does not satisfy itself.'

'Happy, master?' I cried. 'Strange happiness! If you would hear me without being angry, I might offer some advice that would make you happier.'

'What is that?' he asked. 'Give it.'

'You are aware, Mr Heathcliff,' I said, 'that from the time you were thirteen years old, you have lived a selfish, unchristian life; and probably hardly had a Bible in your hands during all that period. You must have forgotten the contents of the book, and you may not have space to search it now. Could it be hurtful to send for someone – some minister of any denomination, it does not matter which, to explain it, and show you how very far you have erred from its precepts, and how unfit you will be for its heaven, unless a change takes place before you die?'

'I'm rather obliged than angry, Nelly,' he said, 'for you remind me of the manner that I desire to be buried in – It is to be carried to the churchyard, in the evening. You and Hareton may, if you please, accompany me: and mind, particularly, to notice that the sexton obeys my directions concerning the two coffins! No minister need come; nor need anything be said over me – I tell you, I have nearly attained *my* heaven; and that of others is altogether unvalued and uncoveted by me!'

'And supposing you persevered in your obstinate fast, and died by that means, and they refused to bury you in the precincts of the kirk?' I said, shocked at his godless indifference. 'How would you like it?'

'They won't do that,' he replied: 'if they did, you must have me removed secretly; and if you neglect it, you shall prove, practically, that the dead are not annihilated!'

As soon as he heard the other members of the family stirring he retired to his den, and I breathed freer. But in the afternoon, while Joseph and Hareton were at their work, he came into the kitchen again, and with a wild look, bid me come, and sit in the house: he wanted somebody with him. I declined; telling him plainly that his strange talk and manner frightened me, and I had neither the nerve nor the will to be his companion, alone.

'I believe you think me a fiend!' he said, with his dismal laugh: 'something too horrible to live under a decent roof!' Then turning to Catherine, who was there, and who drew behind me at his approach, he added, half sneeringly – 'Will *you* come, chuck? I'll not hurt you. No! To you, I've made myself worse than the devil. Well, there is *one* who won't shrink from my company! By God! She's relentless. Oh, damn it! It's unutterably too much for flesh and blood to bear – even mine.'

He solicited the society of no one more. At dusk, he went into his chamber.

Through the whole night, and far into the morning, we heard him groaning, and murmuring to himself. Hareton was anxious to enter; but I bid him fetch Mr Kenneth, and he should go in and see him.

When he came, and I requested admittance and tried to open the door, I found it locked; and Heathcliff bid us be damned. He was better, and would be left alone; so the doctor went away.

The following evening was very wet: indeed it poured down, till day-dawn; and, as I took my morning walk round the house, I observed the master's window swinging open, and the rain driving straight in. He cannot be in bed, I thought: those showers would drench him through! He must either be up or out. But I'll make no more ado, I'll go boldly and look!

Having succeeded in obtaining entrance with another key, I ran to unclose the panels, for the chamber was vacant; quickly pushing them aside, I peeped in. Mr Heathcliff was there – laid on his back. His eyes met mine so keen and fierce, I started; and then he seemed to smile.

I could not think him dead: but his face and throat were washed with rain; the bedclothes dripped, and he was perfectly still. The lattice, flapping to and fro, had grazed one hand that rested on the sill; no blood trickled from the broken skin, and when I put my fingers to it, I could doubt no more: he was dead and stark!

I hasped the window; I combed his black long hair from his forehead; I tried to close his eyes: to extinguish, if possible, that frightful, lifelike gaze of exultation, before anyone else beheld it. They would not shut: they seemed to sneer at my attempts; and his parted lips and sharp white teeth sneered too! Taken with another fit of cowardice, I cried out for Joseph. Joseph shuffled up and made a noise, but resolutely refused to meddle with him.

'Th' divil's harried off his soul,' he cried, 'and he muh hev his carcass intuh t' bargin, for ow't Aw care! Ech! what a wicked un he looks girnning at death!' and the old sinner grinned in mockery.

I thought he intended to cut a caper round the bed; but suddenly composing himself, he fell on his knees, and raised his hands, and returned thanks that the lawful master and the ancient stock were restored to their rights.

I felt stunned by the awful event; and my memory unavoidably recurred to former times with a sort of oppressive sadness. But poor Hareton, the most wronged, was the only one that really suffered much. He sat by the corpse all night, weeping in bitter earnest. He pressed its hand, and kissed the sarcastic, savage face that everyone else shrank from contemplating; and bemoaned him with that strong grief which springs naturally from a generous heart, though it be tough as tempered steel.

Kenneth was perplexed to pronounce of what disorder the master died. I concealed the fact of his having swallowed nothing for four days, fearing it might lead to trouble, and then, I am persuaded he did not abstain on purpose: it was the consequence of his strange illness, not the cause.

We buried him, to the scandal of the whole neighbourhood, as he had wished. Earnshaw, and I, the sexton and six men to carry the coffin, comprehended the whole attendance. The six men departed when they had let it down into the grave: we stayed to see it covered. Hareton, with a streaming face, dug green sods, and laid them over the brown mould himself: at present it is as smooth and verdant as its companion mounds – and I hope its tenant sleeps as soundly. But the country folks, if you asked them, would swear on their Bible that he *walks*. There are those who speak to having met him near the church, and on the moor, and even within this house. Idle tales, you'll say, and so say I. Yet that old man by the kitchen fire affirms he has seen two on 'em looking out of his chamber window, on every rainy night since his death – and an odd thing happened to me about a month ago. I was going to the Grange one evening – a dark evening threatening thunder – and, just at the turn of the Heights, I encountered a little boy with a sheep and two lambs before him; he was crying terribly, and I supposed the lambs were skittish, and would not be guided.

'What is the matter, my little man?' I asked.

'They's Heathcliff, and a woman, yonder, under t' Nab,' he blubbered, 'un' Aw darnut pass 'em.'

I saw nothing; but neither the sheep nor he would go on; so I bid him take the road lower down. He probably raised the phantoms from thinking, as he traversed the moors alone, on the nonsense he had heard his parents and companions repeat – yet still, I don't like being out in the dark, now; and I don't like being left by myself in this grim house: I cannot help it; I shall be glad when they leave it, and shift to the Grange!

'They are going to the Grange then?' I said.

'Yes,' answered Mrs Dean, 'as soon as they are married; and that will be on New Year's Day.'

'And who will live here then?'

'Why, Joseph will take care of the house, and, perhaps, a lad to keep him company. They will live in the kitchen, and the rest will be shut up.'

'For the use of such ghosts as choose to inhabit it,' I observed.

'No, Mr Lockwood,' said Nelly, shaking her head. 'I believe the dead are at peace, but it is not right to speak of them with levity.'

At that moment the garden gate swung to; the ramblers were returning.

'*They* are afraid of nothing,' I grumbled, watching their approach through the window.

'Together, they would brave satan and all his legions.'

As they stepped on to the door-stones, and halted to take a last look at the moon – or, more correctly, at each other, by her light – I felt irresistibly impelled to escape them again; and, pressing a remembrance into the hand of Mrs Dean, and disregarding her expostulations at my rudeness, I vanished through the kitchen as they opened the house door: and so should have confirmed Joseph in his opinion of his fellow-servant's gay indiscretions, had he not fortunately recognised me for a respectable character by the sweet ring of a sovereign at his feet.

My walk home was lengthened by a diversion in the direction of the kirk. When beneath its walls, I perceived decay had made progress, even in seven months: many a window showed black gaps deprived of glass; and slates jutted off, here and there, beyond the right line of the roof, to be gradually worked off in coming autumn storms.

I sought, and soon discovered, the three headstones on the slope next the moor: the middle one grey, and half buried in heath; Edgar Linton's only harmonised by the turf, and moss creeping up its foot; Heathcliff's still bare.

I lingered round them, under that benign sky: watched the moths fluttering among the heath and harebells; listened to the soft wind breathing through the grass; and wondered how anyone could ever imagine unquiet slumbers for the sleepers in that quiet earth.

# TESS OF THE D'URBEVILLES

# Tess of the d'Urbevilles

THOMAS HARDY

## AUTHOR'S EXPLANATORY NOTE TO THE FIRST EDITION

The main portion of the following story appeared – with slight modifications – in *The Graphic* newspaper; other chapters, more especially addressed to adult readers, in the *Fortnightly Review* and the *National Observer*, as episodic sketches. My thanks are tendered to the editors and proprietors of those periodicals for enabling me now to piece the trunk and limbs of the novel together, and print it complete, as originally written two years ago.

I will just add that the story is sent out in all sincerity of purpose, as an attempt to give artistic form to a true sequence of things; and in respect of the book's opinions and sentiments, I would ask any too genteel reader, who cannot endure to have said what everybody nowadays thinks and feels, to remember a well-worn sentence of St Jerome's: If an offence come out of the truth, better is it that the offence come than that the truth be concealed.

*November 1891*

## AUTHOR'S PREFACES TO THE FIFTH AND LATER EDITIONS

This novel being one wherein the great campaign of the heroine begins after an event in her experience which has usually been treated as fatal to her part of protagonist, or at least as the virtual ending of her enterprises and hopes, it was quite contrary to avowed conventions that the public should welcome the book, and agree with me in holding that there was something more to be said in fiction than had been said about the shaded side of a well-known catastrophe. But the responsive spirit in which *Tess of the d'Urbervilles* has been received by the readers of England and America would seem to prove that the plan of laying down a story on the lines of tacit opinion, instead of making it to square with the merely vocal formulae of society, is not altogether a wrong one, even when exemplified in so unequal and partial an achievement as the present. For this responsiveness I cannot refrain from expressing my thanks; and my regret is that, in a world where one so often hungers in vain for friendship, where even not to be wilfully misunderstood is felt as a kindness, I shall never meet in person these appreciative readers, male and female, and shake them by the hand.

I include amongst them the reviewers – by far the majority – who have so generously welcomed the tale. Their words show that they, like the others, have only too largely repaired my defects of narration by their own imaginative intuition.

Nevertheless, though the novel was intended to be neither didactic nor aggressive, but in the scenic parts to be representative simply, and in the contemplative to be oftener charged with impressions than with convictions, there have been objectors both to the matter and to the rendering.

The more austere of these maintain a conscientious difference of opinion concerning, among other things, subjects fit for art, and reveal an inability to associate the idea of the subtitle adjective with any but the artificial and derivative meaning which has resulted to it from the ordinances of civilisation. They ignore the meaning of the word in Nature, together with all aesthetic claims upon it, not to mention the spiritual interpretation afforded by the finest side of their own Christianity. Others dissent on grounds which are intrinsically no more than an assertion that the novel embodies the views of life prevalent at the end of the nineteenth century, and not those of an earlier and simpler generation – an assertion which I can only hope may be well founded. Let me repeat that a novel is an impression, not an argument; and there the matter must rest; as one is reminded by a passage which occurs in the letters of Schiller to Goethe on judges of this class: 'They are those who seek only their own ideas in a representation, and prize that which should be as higher than what is. The cause of the dispute, therefore, lies in the very first principles, and it would be utterly impossible to come to an understanding with them.' And again: 'As soon as I observe that anyone, when judging of poetical representations, considers anything more important than the inner Necessity and Truth, I have done with him.'

In the introductory words to the first edition I suggested the possible advent of the genteel person who would not be able to endure something or other in these pages. That person duly appeared among the aforesaid objectors. In one case he felt upset that it was not possible for him to read the book through three times, owing to my not having made that critical effort which 'alone can prove the salvation of such an one'. In another, he objected to such vulgar articles as the Devil's pitchfork, a lodging-house carving-knife and a shame-bought parasol appearing in a respectable story. In another place he was a gentleman who turned Christian for half an hour the better to express his grief that a disrespectful phrase about the Immortals should have been used; though the same innate gentility compelled him to excuse the author in words of pity that one cannot be too thankful for: 'He does but give us of his best.' I can assure this great critic that to exclaim illogically against the gods, singular or plural, is not such an original sin of mine as he seems to imagine. True, it may have some local originality; though if Shakespeare were an authority on history, which perhaps he is not, I could show that the sin was introduced into Wessex as early as the Heptarchy itself. Says Glo'ster in *Lear*, otherwise Ina, king of that country:

> 'As flies to wanton boys are we to the gods;
> They kill us for their sport.'

The remaining two or three manipulators of *Tess* were of the predetermined sort whom most writers and readers would gladly forget; professed literary boxers, who put on their convictions for the occasion; modern 'Hammers of Heretics'; sworn Discouragers, ever on the watch to prevent the tentative half-success from becoming the whole success later on; who pervert plain meanings, and grow personal under the name of practising the great historical method. However, they may have causes to advance, privileges to guard, traditions to keep going; some of which a mere tale-teller, who writes down how the things of the world strike him, without any ulterior intentions whatever, has overlooked, and may by pure inadvertence have run foul of when in the least aggressive mood. Perhaps some passing perception, the outcome of a dream hour, would, if generally acted on, cause such an assailant considerable inconvenience with respect to position, interests, family, servant, ox, ass, neighbour, or neighbour's wife. He therefore valiantly hides his personality behind a publisher's shutters, and cries 'Shame!' So densely is the world thronged that any shifting of positions, even the best warranted advance, galls somebody's kibe. Such shiftings often begin in sentiment, and such sentiment sometimes begins in a novel.

*July 1892*

The foregoing remarks were written during the early career of this story, when a spirited public and private criticism of its points was still fresh to the feelings. The pages are allowed to stand for what they are worth, as something once said; but probably they would not have been written now. Even in the short time which has elapsed since the book was first published, some of the critics who provoked the reply have 'gone down into silence', as if to remind one of the infinite unimportance of both their say and mine.

In the present edition it may be well to state, in response to inquiries from readers interested in landscape, prehistoric antiquities, and especially old English architecture, that the description of these backgrounds in this and its companion novels has been done from the real. Many features of the first two kinds have been given under their existing names: for instance, the Vale of Blackmoor, or Blakemore, Hambledon Hill, Bulbarrow, Nettlecombe Tout, Dogbury Hill, High-Stoy, Bubb-Down Hill, The Devil's Kitchen, Cross-in-Hand, Long-Ash Lane, Benvill Lane, Giant's Hill, Crimmercrock Lane, and Stonehenge. The rivers Froom or Frome, and Stour, are, of course, well known as such. And in planning the stories the idea was that large towns and points tending to mark the outline of Wessex – such as Bath, Plymouth, The Start, Portland Bill, Southampton, &c. – should be named outright. The scheme was not greatly elaborated, but, whatever its value, the names remain still.

In respect of places described under fictitious or ancient names – for reasons that seemed good at the time of writing – discerning persons have affirmed in print that they clearly recognise the originals: such as Shaftesbury in 'Shaston', Sturminster Newton in 'Stourcastle', Dorchester in 'Casterbridge', Salisbury in 'Melchester', Salisbury Plain in 'The Great Plain', Cranborne in 'Chase-borough', Cranborne Chase in 'The Chase', Beaminster in 'Emminster',

Bere Regis in 'Kingsbere', Woodbury Hill in 'Greenhill', Wool Bridge in 'Wellbridge', Hartfoot or Harput Lane in 'Stagfoot Lane', Hazelbury in 'Nuzzlebury', Bridport in 'Port-Bredy', Maiden Newton in 'Chalk Newton', a farm near Nettlecombe Tout in 'Flintcomb Ash', Sherborne in 'Sherton Abbas', Milton Abbey in 'Middleton Abbey', Cerne Abbas in 'Abbot's Cernel', Evershot in 'Evershead', Taunton in 'Toneborough', Bournemouth in 'Sandbourne', Winchester in 'Wintoncester', and so on. I shall not be the one to contradict them; I accept their statements as at least an indication of their real and kindly interest in the scenes.

*January 1895*

The present edition of this novel contains a few pages that have never appeared in any previous edition. When the detached episodes were collected as stated in the Preface of 1891, these pages were overlooked, though they were in the original manuscript. They occur in Chapter x.

Respecting the subtitle, to which allusion was made above, I may add that it was appended at the last moment, after reading the final proofs, as being the estimate left in a candid mind of the heroine's character – an estimate that nobody would be likely to dispute. It was disputed more than anything else in the book. *Melius fuerat non scribere*. But there it stands.

The novel was first published complete, in three volumes, in November 1891.

*March 1912*

*Contents*

# PHASE THE FIRST

## *The Maiden*

## *Chapter 1*

On an evening in the latter part of May a middle-aged man was walking homeward from Shaston to the village of Marlott, in the adjoining Vale of Blakemore or Blackmoor. The pair of legs that carried him were rickety, and there was a bias in his gait which inclined him somewhat to the left of a straight line. He occasionally gave a smart nod, as if in confirmation of some opinion, though he was not thinking of anything in particular. An empty egg-basket was slung upon his arm, the nap of his hat was ruffled, a patch being quite worn away at its brim where his thumb came in taking it off. Presently he was met by an elderly parson astride on a grey mare, who, as he rode, hummed a wandering tune.

'Good-night t'ee,' said the man with the basket.

'Good-night, Sir John,' said the parson.

The pedestrian, after another pace or two, halted, and turned round.

'Now, sir, begging your pardon; we met last market-day on this road about this time, and I said, "Good-night," and you made reply, "*Good-night, Sir John*," as now.'

'I did,' said the parson.

'And once before that – near a month ago.'

'I may have.'

'Then what might your meaning be in calling me "Sir John" these different times, when I be plain Jack Durbeyfield, the haggler?'

The parson rode a step or two nearer.

'It was only my whim,' he said; and, after a moment's hesitation: 'It was on account of a discovery I made some little time ago, whilst I was hunting up pedigrees for the new county history. I am Parson Tringham, the antiquary, of Stagfoot Lane. Don't you really know, Durbeyfield, that you are the lineal representative of the ancient and knightly family of the d'Urbervilles, who derive their descent from Sir Pagan d'Urberville, that renowned knight who came from Normandy with William the Conqueror, as appears by Battle Abbey Roll?'

'Never heard it before, sir!'

'Well it's true. Throw up your chin a moment, so that I may catch the profile of your face better. Yes, that's the d'Urberville nose and chin – a little debased. Your ancestor was one of the twelve knights who assisted the Lord of Estremavilla in Normandy in his conquest of Glamorganshire. Branches of your family held manors over all this part of England; their names appear in the Pipe Rolls in the time of King Stephen. In the reign of King John one of them was rich enough to give a manor to the Knights Hospitallers; and in Edward the II's time your forefather Brian was summoned to Westminster to attend the great Council there. You declined a little in Oliver Cromwell's time, but to no serious extent, and in Charles the Second's reign you were made Knights of the Royal Oak for your loyalty. Aye, there have been generations of Sir Johns among you, and if knighthood were hereditary, like a baronetcy, as it practically was in old times, when men were knighted from father to son, you would be Sir John now.'

'Ye don't say so!'

'In short,' concluded the parson, decisively smacking his leg with his switch, 'there's hardly such another family in England.'

'Daze my eyes, and isn't there?' said Durbeyfield. 'And here have I been knocking about, year after year, from pillar to post, as if I was no more than the commonest feller in the parish . . . And how long hev this news about me been knowed, Pa'son Tringham?'

The clergyman explained that, as far as he was aware, it had quite died out of knowledge, and could hardly be said to be known at all. His own investigations had begun on a day in the preceding spring when, having been engaged in tracing the vicissitudes of the d'Urberville family, he had observed Durbeyfield's name on his waggon, and had thereupon been led to make enquiries about his father and grandfather till he had no doubt on the subject.

'At first I resolved not to disturb you with such a useless piece of information,' said he. 'However, our impulses are too strong for our judgment sometimes. I thought you might perhaps know something of it all the while.'

'Well, I have heard once or twice, 'tis true, that my family had seen better days afore they came to Blackmoor. But I took no notice o't, thinking it to mean that we had once kept two horses where we now keep only one. I've got a wold silver spoon, and a wold graven seal at home, too; but, Lord, what's a spoon and seal?. . . And to think that I and these noble d'Urbervilles were one flesh all the time. 'Twas said that my gr't-grandfer had secrets, and didn't care to talk of where he came from . . . And where do we raise our smoke, now, parson, if I may make so bold; I mean, where do we d'Urbervilles live?'

'You don't live anywhere. You are extinct – as a county family.'

'That's bad.'

'Yes – what the mendacious family chronicles call extinct in the male line – that is, gone down – gone under.'

'Then where do we lie?'

'At Kingsbere-sub-Greenhill: rows and rows of you in your vaults, with your effigies under Purbeck-marble canopies.'

'And where be our family mansions and estates?'

'You haven't any.'

'Oh? No lands neither?'

'None; though you once had 'em in abundance, as I said, for your family consisted of numerous branches. In this county there was a seat of yours at Kingbere, and another at Sherton, and another at Millpond, and another at Lullstead, and another at Wellbridge.'

'And shall we ever come into our own again?'

'Ah – that I can't tell!'

'And what had I better do about it, sir?' asked Durbeyfield, after a pause.

'Oh – nothing, nothing; except chasten yourself with the thought of "how are the mighty fallen". It is a fact of some interest to the local historian and genealogist, nothing more. There are several families among the cottagers of this county of almost equal lustre. Good-night.'

'But you'll turn back and have a quart of beer wi' me on the strength o't, Pa'son Tringham? There's a very pretty brew in tap at the Pure Drop – though, to be sure, not so good as at Rolliver's.'

'No, thank you – not this evening, Durbeyfield. You've had enough already.' Concluding thus the parson rode on his way, with doubts as to his discretion in retailing this curious bit of lore.

When he was gone Durbeyfield walked a few steps in a profound reverie, and then sat down upon the grassy bank by the roadside, depositing his basket before him. In a few minutes a youth appeared in the distance, walking in the same direction as that which had been pursued by Durbeyfield. The latter, on seeing him, held up his hand, and the lad quickened his pace and came near.

'Boy, take up that basket! I want 'ee to go on an errand for me.'

The lath-like stripling frowned. 'Who be you, then, John Durbeyfield, to order me about and call me "boy"? You know my name as well as I know yours!'

'Do you, do you? That's the secret – that's the secret! Now obey my orders, and take the message I'm going to charge 'ee wi' . . . Well, Fred, I don't mind telling you that the secret is that I'm one of a noble race – it has been just found out by me this present afternoon, p.m.' And as he made the announcement, Durbeyfield, declining from his sitting position, luxuriously stretched himself out upon the bank among the daisies.

The lad stood before Durbeyfield, and contemplated his length from crown to toe.

'Sir John d'Urberville – that's who I am,' continued the prostrate man. 'That is if knights were baronets – which they be. 'Tis recorded in history all about me. Dost know of such a place, lad, as Kingsbere-sub-Greenhill?'

'Ees. I've been there to Greenhill Fair.'

'Well, under the church of that city there lie – '

' 'Tisn't a city, the place I mean; leastwise 'twaddn' when I was there – 'twas a little one-eyed, blinking sort o' place.'

'Never you mind the place, boy, that's not the question before us. Under the church of that there parish lie my ancestors – hundreds of 'em – in coats of mail and jewels, in gr't lead coffins weighing tons and tons. There's not a man in the county o' South-Wessex that's got grander and nobler skillentons in his family than I.'

'Oh?'

'Now take up that basket, and goo on to Marlott, and when you've come to the Pure Drop Inn, tell 'em to send a horse and carriage to me immed'ately, to carry me home. And in the bottom o' the carriage they be to put a noggin o' rum in a small bottle, and chalk it up to my account. And when you've done that go on to my house with the basket, and tell my wife to put away that washing, because she needn't finish it, and wait till I come home, as I've news to tell her.'

As the lad stood in a dubious attitude, Durbeyfield put his hand in his pocket, and produced a shilling, one of the chronically few that he possessed.

'Here's for your labour, lad.'

This made a difference in the young man's estimate of the position.

'Yes, Sir John. Thank 'ee. Anything else I can do for 'ee, Sir John?'

'Tell 'em at hwome that I should like for supper, – well, lamb's fry if they can get it; and if they can't, black-pot; and if they can't get that, well, chitterlings will do.'

'Yes, Sir John.'

The boy took up the basket, and as he set out the notes of a brass band were heard from the direction of the village.

'What's that?' said Durbeyfield. 'Not on account o' I?'

' 'Tis the women's club-walking, Sir John. Why, your da'ter is one o' the members.'

'To be sure – I'd quite forgot it in my thoughts of greater things! Well, vamp on to Marlott, will ye, and order that carriage, and maybe I'll drive round and inspect the club.'

The lad departed, and Durbeyfield lay waiting on the grass and daisies in the evening sun. Not a soul passed that way for a long while, and the faint notes of the band were the only human sounds audible within the rim of blue hills.

## *Chapter 2*

The village of Marlott lay amid the north-eastern undulations of the beautiful Vale of Blackmore or Blackmoor aforesaid, an engirdled and secluded region, for the most part untrodden as yet by tourist or landscape-painter, though within a four hours' journey from London.

It is a vale whose acquaintance is best made by viewing it from the summits of the hills that surround it – except perhaps during the droughts of summer. An unguided ramble into its recesses in bad weather is apt to engender dissatisfaction with its narrow, tortuous, and miry ways.

This fertile and sheltered tract of country, in which the fields are never brown and the springs never dry, is bounded on the south by the bold chalk ridge that embraces the prominences of Hambledon Hill, Bulbarrow, Nettlecombe-Tout, Dogbury, High Stoy, and Bubb Down. The traveller from the coast, who, after plodding northward for a score of miles over calcareous downs and corn-lands, suddenly reaches the verge of one of these escarpments, is surprised and delighted to behold, extended like a map beneath him, a country differing absolutely from that which he has passed through. Behind him the hills are open, the sun blazes down upon fields so large as to give an unenclosed character to the landscape, the lanes are white, the hedges low and plashed, the atmosphere colourless. Here, in the valley, the world seems to be constructed upon a smaller and more delicate scale; the fields are mere paddocks, so reduced that from this height their hedgerows appear a network of dark green threads overspreading the paler green of the grass. The atmosphere beneath is languorous, and is so tinged with azure that what artists call the middle distance partakes also of that hue, while the horizon beyond is of the deepest ultramarine. Arable lands are few and limited; with but slight exceptions the prospect is a broad rich mass of grass and trees, mantling minor hills and dales within the major. Such is the Vale of Blackmoor.

The district is of historic, no less than of topographical interest. The Vale was known in former times as the Forest of White Hart, from a curious legend of King Henry III's reign, in which the killing by a certain Thomas de la Lynd of a beautiful white hart which the king had run down and spared, was made the occasion of a heavy fine. In those days, and till comparatively recent times, the country was densely wooded. Even now, traces of its earlier condition are to be found in the old oak copses and irregular belts of timber that yet survive upon its slopes, and the hollow-trunked trees that shade so many of its pastures.

The forests have departed, but some old customs of their shades remain. Many, however, linger only in a metamorphosed or disguised form. The May-Day dance, for instance, was to be discerned on the afternoon under notice, in the guise of the club revel, or 'club-walking,' as it was there called.

It was an interesting event to the younger inhabitants of Marlott, though its real interest was not observed by the participators in the ceremony. Its singularity lay less in the retention of a custom of walking in procession and dancing on each anniversary than in the members being solely women. In men's clubs such celebrations were, though expiring, less uncommon; but either the natural shyness of the softer sex, or a sarcastic attitude on the part of male relatives, had denuded such women's clubs as remained (if any other did) of this their glory and consummation. The club of Marlott alone lived to uphold the local Cerealia. It had walked for hundreds of years, if not as benefit-club, as votive sisterhood of some sort; and it walked still.

The banded ones were all dressed in white gowns – a gay survival from Old Style days, when cheerfulness and Maytime were synonyms – days before the habit of taking long views had reduced emotions to a monotonous average. Their first exhibition of themselves was in a processional march of two and two round the parish. Ideal and real clashed slightly as the sun lit up their figures against the green hedges and creeper-laced house-fronts; for, though the whole troop wore white garments, no two whites were alike among them. Some approached pure blanching; some had a bluish pallor; some worn by the older characters (which had possibly lain by folded for many a year) inclined to a cadaverous tint, and to a Georgian style.

In addition to the distinction of a white frock, every woman and girl carried in her right hand a peeled willow wand, and in her left a bunch of white flowers. The peeling of the former, and the selection of the latter, had been an operation of personal care.

There were a few middle-aged and even elderly women in the train, their silver-wiry hair and wrinkled faces, scourged by time and trouble, having almost a grotesque, certainly a pathetic, appearance in such a jaunty situation. In a true view, perhaps, there was more to be gathered and told of each anxious and experienced one, to whom the years were drawing nigh when she should say, 'I have no pleasure in them,' than of her juvenile comrades. But let the elder be passed over here for those under whose bodices the life throbbed quick and warm.

The young girls formed, indeed, the majority of the band, and their heads of luxuriant hair reflected in the sunshine every tone of gold, and black, and brown. Some had beautiful eyes, others a beautiful nose, others a beautiful mouth and figure: few, if any, had all. A difficulty of arranging their lips in this crude exposure to public scrutiny, an inability to balance their heads, and to dissociate self-consciousness from their features, was apparent in them, and showed that they were genuine country girls, unaccustomed to many eyes.

And as each and all of them were warmed without by the sun, so each had a private little sun for her soul to bask in; some dream, some affection, some hobby, at least some remote and distant hope which, though perhaps starving to nothing, still lived on, as hopes will. Thus they were all cheerful, and many of them merry.

They came round by the Pure Drop Inn, and were turning out of the high road to pass through a wicket-gate into the meadows, when one of the women said – 'The Lord-a-Lord! Why, Tess Durbeyfield, if there isn't thy father riding hwome in a carriage!'

A young member of the band turned her head at the exclamation. She was a fine and handsome girl – not handsomer than some others, possibly – but her mobile peony mouth and large innocent eyes added eloquence to colour and shape. She wore a red ribbon in her hair, and was the only one of the white company who could boast of such a pronounced adornment. As she looked round Durbeyfield was seen moving along the road in a chaise belonging to the Pure Drop, driven by a frizzle-headed brawny damsel with her gown-sleeves rolled above her elbows. This was the cheerful servant of that establishment, who, in her part of factotum, turned groom and ostler at times. Durbeyfield, leaning back, and with his eyes closed luxuriously, was waving his hand above his head, and singing in a slow recitative – 'I've-got-a-gr't-family-vault-at-Kingsbere – and knighted fore-fathers-in-lead-coffins-there!'

The clubbists tittered, except the girl called Tess – in whom a slow heat seemed to rise at the sense that her father was making himself foolish in their eyes.

'He's tired, that's all,' she said hastily, 'and he has got a lift home, because our own horse has to rest today.'

'Bless thy simplicity, Tess,' said her companions. 'He's got his market-nitch. Haw-haw!'

'Look here; I won't walk another inch with you, if you say any jokes about him!' Tess cried, and the colour upon her cheeks spread over her face and neck. In a moment her eyes grew moist, and her glance drooped to the ground. Perceiving that they had really pained her they said no more, and order again prevailed. Tess's pride would not allow her to turn her head again, to learn what her father's meaning was, if he had any; and thus she moved on with the whole body to the enclosure where there was to be dancing on the green. By the time the spot was reached she had recovered her equanimity, and tapped her neighbour with her wand and talked as usual.

Tess Durbeyfield at this time of her life was a mere vessel of emotion untinctured by experience. The dialect was on her tongue to some extent, despite the village school: the characteristic intonation of that dialect for this district being the voicing approximately rendered by the syllable ur, probably as rich an utterance as any to be found in human speech. The pouted-up deep red mouth to which this syllable was native had hardly as yet settled into its definite shape, and her lower lip had a way of thrusting the middle of her top one upward, when they closed together after a word.

Phases of her childhood lurked in her aspect still. As she walked along today, for all her bouncing handsome womanliness, you could sometimes see her twelfth year in her cheeks, or her ninth sparkling from her eyes; and even her fifth would flit over the curves of her mouth now and then.

Yet few knew, and still fewer considered this. A small minority, mainly strangers, would look long at her in casually passing by, and grow momentarily fascinated by her freshness, and wonder if they would ever see her again: but to almost everybody she was a fine and picturesque country girl, and no more.

Nothing was seen or heard further of Durbeyfield in his triumphal chariot under the conduct of the ostleress, and the club having entered the allotted space, dancing began. As there were no men in the company the girls danced at first with each other, but when the hour for the close of labour drew on, the masculine inhabitants of the village, together with other idlers and pedestrians, gathered round the spot, and appeared inclined to negotiate for a partner.

Among these on-lookers were three young men of a superior class, carrying small knapsacks strapped to their shoulders, and stout sticks in their hands. Their general likeness to each other, and their consecutive ages, would almost have suggested that they might be, what in fact they were, brothers. The eldest wore the white tie, high waistcoat, and thin-brimmed hat of the regulation curate; the second was the normal undergraduate; the appearance of the third and youngest would hardly have been sufficient to characterise him; there was an uncribbed, uncabined aspect in his eyes and attire, implying that he had hardly as yet found the entrance to his professional groove. That he was a desultory tentative student of something and everything might only have been predicted of him.

These three brethren told casual acquaintance that they were spending their Whitsun holidays in a walking tour through the Vale of Blackmoor, their course being south-westerly from the town of Shaston on the north-east.

They leant over the gate by the highway, and enquired as to the meaning of the dance and the white-frocked maids. The two elder of the brothers were plainly not intending to linger more than a moment, but the spectacle of a bevy of girls dancing without male partners seemed to amuse the third, and make him in no hurry to move on. He unstrapped his knapsack, put it, with his stick, on the hedge-bank, and opened the gate.

'What are you going to do, Angel?' asked the eldest.

'I am inclined to go and have a fling with them. Why not all of us – just for a minute or two – it will not detain us long?'

'No – no; nonsense!' said the first. 'Dancing in public with a troop of country hoydens – suppose we should be seen! Come along, or it will be dark before we get to Stourcastle, and there's no place we can sleep at nearer than that; besides, we must get through another chapter of *A Counterblast to Agnosticism* before we turn in, now I have taken the trouble to bring the book.'

'All right – I'll overtake you and Cuthbert in five minutes; don't stop; I give my word that I will, Felix.'

The two elder reluctantly left him and walked on, taking their brother's knapsack to relieve him in following, and the youngest entered the field.

'This is a thousand pities,' he said gallantly, to two or three of the girls nearest him, as soon as there was a pause in the dance. 'Where are your partners, my dears?'

'They've not left off work yet,' answered one of the boldest. 'They'll be here by and by. Till then, will you be one, sir?'

'Certainly. But what's one among so many!'

'Better than none. 'Tis melancholy work facing and footing it to one of your own sort, and no clipsing and colling at all. Now, pick and choose.'

' 'Ssh – don't be so for'ard!' said a shyer girl.

The young man, thus invited, glanced them over, and attempted some discrimination; but, as the group were all so new to him, he could not very well exercise it. He took almost the first that came to hand, which was not the speaker, as she had expected; nor did it happen to be Tess Durbeyfield. Pedigree, ancestral skeletons, monumental record, the d'Urberville lineaments, did not help Tess in her life's battle as yet, even to the extent of attracting to her a dancing-partner over the heads of the commonest peasantry. So much for Norman blood unaided by Victorian lucre.

The name of the eclipsing girl, whatever it was, has not been handed down; but she was envied by all as the first who enjoyed the luxury of a masculine partner that evening. Yet such was the force of example that the village young men, who had not hastened to enter the gate while no intruder was in the way, now dropped in quickly, and soon the couples became leavened with rustic youth to a marked extent, till at length the plainest woman in the club was no longer compelled to foot it on the masculine side of the figure.

The church clock struck, when suddenly the student said that he must leave – he had been forgetting himself – he had to join his companions. As he fell out of the dance his eyes lighted on Tess Durbeyfield, whose own large orbs wore, to tell the truth, the faintest aspect of reproach that he had not chosen her. He, too, was sorry then that, owing to her backwardness, he had not observed her; and with that in his mind he left the pasture.

On account of his long delay he started in a flying-run down the lane westward, and had soon passed the hollow and mounted the next rise. He had not yet overtaken his brothers but he paused to get breath, and looked back. He could see the white figures of the girls in the green enclosure whirling about as they had whirled when he was among them. They seemed to have quite forgotten him already.

All of them, except, perhaps, one. This white shape stood apart by the hedge alone. From her position he knew it to be the pretty maiden with whom he had not danced. Trifling as the matter was, he yet instinctively felt that she was hurt by his oversight. He wished that he had asked her; he wished that he had enquired her name. She was so modest, so expressive, she had looked so soft in her thin white gown that he felt he had acted stupidly.

However, it could not be helped, and turning, and bending himself to a rapid walk, he dismissed the subject from his mind.

## *Chapter 3*

As for Tess Durbeyfield, she did not so easily dislodge the incident from her consideration. She had no spirit to dance again for a long time, though she might have had plenty of partners; but, ah! they did not speak so nicely as the strange young man had done. It was not till the rays of the sun had absorbed the young stranger's retreating figure on the hill that she shook off her temporary sadness and answered her would-be partner in the affirmative.

She remained with her comrades till dusk, and participated with a certain zest in the dancing; though, being heart-whole as yet, she enjoyed treading a measure purely for its own sake; little divining when she saw 'the soft torments, the bitter sweets, the pleasing pains, and the agreeable distresses' of those girls who had been wooed and won, what she herself was capable of in that kind. The struggles and wrangles of the lads for her hand in a jig were an amusement to her – no more; and when they became fierce she rebuked them.

She might have stayed even later, but the incident of her father's odd appearance and manner returned upon the girl's mind to make her anxious, and wondering what had become of him she dropped away from the dancers and bent her steps towards the end of the village at which the parental cottage lay.

While yet many score yards off, other rhythmic sounds than those she had quitted became audible to her; sounds that she knew well – so well. They were a regular series of thumpings from the interior of the house, occasioned by the violent rocking of a cradle upon a stone floor, to which movement a feminine voice kept time by singing, in a vigorous gallopade, the favourite ditty of 'The Spotted Cow' –

> I saw her lie do´–own in yon´– der green gro´–ove;
> Come, love!´ and I'll tell´ you where!´

The cradle-rocking and the song would cease simultaneously for a moment, and an exclamation at highest vocal pitch would take the place of the melody.

'God bless thy diment eyes! And thy waxen cheeks! And thy cherry mouth!

And thy Cubit's thighs! And every bit o' thy blessed body!'

After this invocation the rocking and the singing would recommence, and 'The Spotted Cow' proceed as before. So matters stood when Tess opened the door, and paused upon the mat within it surveying the scene.

The interior, in spite of the melody, struck upon the girl's senses with an unspeakable dreariness. From the holiday gaieties of the field – the white gowns, the nosegays, the willow-wands, the whirling movements on the green, the flash of gentle sentiment towards the stranger – to the yellow melancholy of this one-candled spectacle, what a step! Besides the jar of contrast there came to her a chill self-reproach that she had not returned sooner, to help her mother in these domesticities, instead of indulging herself out-of-doors.

There stood her mother amid the group of children, as Tess had left her, hanging over the Monday washing-tub, which had now, as always, lingered on to the end of the week. Out of that tub had come the day before – Tess felt it with a dreadful sting of remorse – the very white frock upon her back which she had so carelessly greened about the skirt on the damping grass – which had been wrung up and ironed by her mother's own hands.

As usual, Mrs Durbeyfield was balanced on one foot beside the tub, the other being engaged in the aforesaid business of rocking her youngest child. The cradle-rockers had done hard duty for so many years, under the weight of so many children, on that flagstone floor, that they were worn nearly flat, in consequence of which a huge jerk accompanied each swing of the cot, flinging the baby from side to side like a weaver's shuttle, as Mrs Durbeyfield, excited by her song, trod the rocker with all the spring that was left in her after a long day's seething in the suds.

Nick-knock, nick-knock, went the cradle; the candle-flame stretched itself tall, and began jigging up and down; the water dribbled from the matron's elbows, and the song galloped on to the end of the verse, Mrs Durbeyfield regarding her daughter the while. Even now, when burdened with a young family, Joan Durbeyfield was a passionate lover of tune. No ditty floated into Blackmoor Vale from the outer world but Tess's mother caught up its notation in a week.

There still faintly beamed from the woman's features something of the freshness, and even the prettiness, of her youth; rendering it probable that the personal charms which Tess could boast of were in main part her mother's gift, and therefore unknightly, unhistorical.

'I'll rock the cradle for 'ee, mother,' said the daughter gently. 'Or I'll take off my best frock and help you wring up? I thought you had finished long ago.'

Her mother bore Tess no ill-will for leaving the housework to her single-handed efforts for so long; indeed, Joan seldom upbraided her thereon at any time, feeling but slightly the lack of Tess's assistance whilst her instinctive plan for relieving herself of her labours lay in postponing them. Tonight, however, she was even in a blither mood than usual. There was a dreaminess, a preoccupation, an exaltation, in the maternal look which the girl could not understand.

'Well, I'm glad you've come,' her mother said, as soon as the last note had passed out of her. 'I want to go and fetch your father; but what's more'n that, I want to tell 'ee what have happened. Y'll be fess enough, my poppet, when th'st know!' (Mrs Durbeyfield habitually spoke the dialect; her daughter, who had passed the Sixth Standard in the National School under a London-trained mistress, spoke two languages: the dialect at home, more or less; ordinary English abroad and to persons of quality.)

'Since I've been away?' Tess asked.

'Ay!'

'Had it anything to do with father's making such a mommet of himself in thik carriage this afternoon? Why did 'er? I felt inclined to sink into the ground with shame!'

'That wer all a part of the larry! We've been found to be the greatest gentlefolk in the whole county – reaching all back long before Oliver Grumble's time – to the days of the Pagan Turks – with monuments, and vaults, and crests, and 'scutcheons, and the Lord knows what all. In Saint Charles's days we was made Knights o' the Royal Oak, our real name being d'Urberville! . . . Don't that make your bosom plim? 'Twas on this account that your father rode home in the vlee; not because he'd been drinking, as people supposed.'

'I'm glad of that. Will it do us any good, mother?'

'O yes! 'Tis thoughted that great things may come o't. No doubt a mampus of volk of our own rank will be down here in their carriages as soon as 'tis known. Your father learnt it on his way home from Shaston, and he has been telling me the whole pedigree of the matter.'

'Where is father now?' asked Tess suddenly.

Her mother gave irrelevant information by way of answer: 'He called to see the doctor today in Shaston. It is not consumption at all, it seems. It is fat round his heart, 'a says. There, it is like this.' Joan Durbeyfield, as she spoke, curved a sodden thumb and forefinger to the shape of the letter C, and used the other forefinger as a pointer. ' "At the present moment," he says to your father, "your heart is enclosed all round there, and all round there; this space is still open," 'a says. "As soon as it do meet, so," ' – Mrs Durbeyfield closed her fingers into a circle complete – ' "off you will go like a shadder, Mr Durbeyfield," 'a says. "You mid last ten years; you mid go off in ten months, or ten days." '

Tess looked alarmed. Her father possibly to go behind the eternal cloud so soon, notwithstanding this sudden greatness!

'But where *is* father?' she asked again.

Her mother put on a deprecating look. 'Now don't you be bursting out angry! The poor man – he felt so rafted after his uplifting by the pa'son's news – that he went up to Rolliver's half an hour ago. He do want to get up his strength for his journey tomorrow with that load of beehives, which must be delivered, family or no. He'll have to start shortly after twelve tonight, as the distance is so long.'

'Get up his strength!' said Tess impetuously, the tears welling to her eyes. 'O my God! Go to a public-house to get up his strength! And you as well agreed as he, mother!'

Her rebuke and her mood seemed to fill the whole room, and to impart a cowed look to the furniture, and candle, and children playing about, and to her mother's face.

'No,' said the latter touchily, 'I be not agreed. I have been waiting for 'ee to bide and keep house while I go fetch him.'

'I'll go.'

'O no, Tess. You see, it would be no use.'

Tess did not expostulate. She knew what her mother's objection meant. Mrs Durbeyfield's jacket and bonnet were already hanging slily upon a chair by her side, in readiness for this contemplated jaunt, the reason for which the matron deplored more than its necessity.

'And take the *Compleat Fortune-Teller* to the outhouse,' Joan continued, rapidly wiping her hands, and donning the garments.

The *Compleat Fortune-Teller* was an old thick volume, which lay on a table at her elbow, so worn by pocketing that the margins had reached the edge of the type. Tess took it up, and her mother started.

This going to hunt up her shiftless husband at the inn was one of Mrs Durbeyfield's still extant enjoyments in the muck and muddle of rearing children. To discover him at Rolliver's, to sit there for an hour or two by his side and dismiss all thought and care of the children during the interval, made her happy. A sort of halo, an occidental glow, came over life then. Troubles and other realities took on themselves a metaphysical impalpability, sinking to mere mental phenomena for serene contemplation, and no longer stood as pressing concretions which chafed body and soul. The youngsters, not immediately within sight, seemed rather bright and desirable appurtenances than otherwise; the incidents of daily life were not without humorousness and jollity in their aspect there. She felt a little as she had used to feel when she sat by her now wedded husband in the same spot during his wooing, shutting her eyes to his defects of character, and regarding him only in his ideal presentation as lover.

Tess, being left alone with the younger children, went first to the outhouse with the fortune-telling book, and stuffed it into the thatch. A curious fetishistic fear of this grimy volume on the part of her mother prevented her ever allowing it to stay in the house all night, and hither it was brought back whenever it had been consulted. Between the mother, with her fast-perishing lumber of superstitions, folklore, dialect and orally transmitted ballads, and the daughter, with her trained National teachings and Standard knowledge under an infinitely Revised Code, there was a gap of two hundred years as ordinarily understood. When they were together the Jacobean and the Victorian ages were juxtaposed.

Returning along the garden path Tess mused on what the mother could have wished to ascertain from the book on this particular day. She guessed the recent ancestral discovery to bear upon it, but did not divine that it solely concerned herself. Dismissing this, however, she busied herself with sprinkling the linen dried during the daytime, in company with her nine-year-old brother Abraham, and her sister Eliza-Louisa of twelve and a half, called ' 'Liza-Lu', the youngest ones being put to bed. There was an interval of four years and more between

Tess and the next of the family, the two who had filled the gap having died in their infancy, and this lent her a deputy-maternal attitude when she was alone with her juniors. Next in juvenility to Abraham came two more girls, Hope and Modesty; then a boy of three, and then the baby, who had just completed his first year.

All these young souls were passengers in the Durbeyfield ship – entirely dependent on the judgment of the two Durbeyfield adults for their pleasures, their necessities, their health, even their existence. If the heads of the Durbeyfield household chose to sail into difficulty, disaster, starvation, disease, degradation, death, thither were these half-dozen little captives under hatches compelled to sail with them – six helpless creatures, who had never been asked if they wished for life on any terms, much less if they wished for it on such hard conditions as were involved in being of the shiftless house of Durbeyfield. Some people would like to know whence the poet whose philosophy is in these days deemed as profound and trustworthy as his song is breezy and pure, gets his authority for speaking of 'Nature's holy plan.'

It grew later, and neither father nor mother reappeared. Tess looked out of the door, and took a mental journey through Marlott. The village was shutting its eyes. Candles and lamps were being put out everywhere: she could inwardly behold the extinguisher and the extended hand.

Her mother's fetching simply meant one more to fetch. Tess began to perceive that a man in indifferent health, who proposed to start on a journey before one in the morning, ought not to be at an inn at this late hour celebrating his ancient blood.

'Abraham,' she said to her little brother, 'do you put on your hat – you bain't afraid? – and go up to Rolliver's, and see what has gone wi' father and mother.'

The boy jumped promptly from his seat, and opened the door, and the night swallowed him up. Half an hour passed yet again; neither man, woman, nor child returned. Abraham, like his parents, seemed to have been limed and caught by the ensnaring inn.

'I must go myself,' she said.

'Liza-Lu then went to bed, and Tess, locking them all in, started on her way up the dark and crooked lane or street not made for hasty progress; a street laid out before inches of land had value, and when one-handed clocks sufficiently subdivided the day.

# *Chapter 4*

Rolliver's inn, the single alehouse at this end of the long and broken village, could only boast of an off-licence; hence, as nobody could legally drink on the premises, the amount of overt accommodation for consumers was strictly limited to a little board about six inches wide and two yards long, fixed to the garden palings by pieces of wire, so as to form a ledge. On this board thirsty strangers deposited their cups as they stood in the road and drank, and threw the dregs on the dusty ground to the pattern of Polynesia, and wished they could have a restful seat inside.

Thus the strangers. But there were also local customers who felt the same wish; and where there's a will there's a way.

In a large bedroom upstairs, the window of which was thickly curtained with a great woollen shawl lately discarded by the landlady Mrs Rolliver, were gathered on this evening nearly a dozen persons, all seeking beatitude; all old inhabitants of the nearer end of Marlott, and frequenters of this retreat. Not only did the distance to the Pure Drop, the fully-licensed tavern at the further part of the dispersed village, render its accommodation practically unavailable for dwellers at this end; but the far more serious question, the quality of the liquor, confirmed the prevalent opinion that it was better to drink with Rolliver in a corner of the housetop than with the other landlord in a wide house.

A gaunt four-post bedstead which stood in the room afforded sitting-space for several persons gathered round three of its sides; a couple more men had elevated themselves on a chest of drawers; another rested on the oak-carved 'cwoffer'; two on the washstand; another on the stool; and thus all were, somehow, seated at their ease. The stage of mental comfort to which they had arrived at this hour was one wherein their souls expanded beyond their skins, and spread their personalities warmly through the room. In this process the chamber and its furniture grew more and more dignified and luxurious; the shawl hanging at the window took upon itself the richness of tapestry; the brass handles of the chest of drawers were as golden knockers; and the carved bed-posts seemed to have some kinship with the magnificent pillars of Solomon's temple.

Mrs Durbeyfield, having quickly walked hitherward after parting from Tess, opened the front door, crossed the downstairs room, which was in deep gloom, and then unfastened the stair-door like one whose fingers knew the tricks of the latches well. Her ascent of the crooked staircase was a slower process, and her face, as it rose into the light above the last stair, encountered the gaze of all the party assembled in the bedroom.

' – Being a few private friends I've asked in to keep up club-walking at my own expense,' the landlady exclaimed at the sound of footsteps, as glibly as a child repeating the Catechism, while she peered over the stairs. 'Oh, 'tis you, Mrs Durbeyfield – Lard – how you frightened me! – I thought it might be some gaffer sent by Gover'ment.'

Mrs Durbeyfield was welcomed with glances and nods by the remainder of the conclave, and turned to where her husband sat. He was humming absently to himself, in a low tone: 'I be as good as some folks here and there! I've got a great family vault at Kingsbere-sub-Greenhill, and finer skillentons than any man in Wessex!'

'I've something to tell 'ee that's come into my head about that – a grand projick!' whispered his cheerful wife. 'Here, John, don't 'ee see me?' She nudged him, while he, looking through her as through a window-pane, went on with his recitative.

'Hush! Don't 'ee sing so loud, my good man,' said the landlady; 'in case any member of the Gover'ment should be passing, and take away my licends.'

'He's told 'ee what's happened to us, I suppose?' asked Mrs Durbeyfield.

'Yes – in a way. D'ye think there's any money hanging by it?'

'Ah, that's the secret,' said Joan Durbeyfield sagely. 'However, 'tis well to be kin to a coach, even if you don't ride in 'en.' She dropped her public voice, and continued in a low tone to her husband: 'I've been thinking since you brought the news that there's a great rich lady out by Trantridge, on the edge o' The Chase, of the name of d'Urberville.'

'Hey – what's that?' said Sir John.

She repeated the information. 'That lady must be our relation,' she said. 'And my projick is to send Tess to claim kin.'

'There *is* a lady of the name, now you mention it,' said Durbeyfield. 'Pa'son Tringham didn't think of that. But she's nothing beside we – a junior branch of us, no doubt, hailing long since King Norman's day.'

While this question was being discussed neither of the pair noticed, in their preoccupation, that little Abraham had crept into the room, and was awaiting an opportunity of asking them to return.

'She is rich, and she'd be sure to take notice o' the maid,' continued Mrs Durbeyfield; 'and 'twill be a very good thing. I don't see why two branches o' one family should not be on visiting terms.'

'Yes; and we'll all claim kin!' said Abraham brightly from under the bedstead. 'And we'll all go and see her when Tess has gone to live with her; and we'll ride in her coach and wear black clothes!'

'How do you come here, child? What nonsense be ye talking! Go away, and play on the stairs till father and mother be ready! . . . Well, Tess ought to go to this other member of our family. She'd be sure to win the lady – Tess would; and likely enough 'twould lead to some noble gentleman marrying her. In short, I know it.'

'How?'

'I tried her fate in the *Fortune-Teller*, and it brought out that very thing! . . . You should ha' seen how pretty she looked today; her skin is as sumple as a duchess's.'

'What says the maid herself to going?'

'I've not asked her. She don't know there is any such lady-relation yet. But it would certainly put her in the way of a grand marriage, and she won't say nay to going.'

'Tess is queer.'

'But she's tractable at bottom. Leave her to me.'

Though this conversation had been private, sufficient of its import reached the understandings of those around to suggest to them that the Durbeyfields had weightier concerns to talk of now than common folks had, and that Tess, their pretty eldest daughter, had fine prospects in store.

'Tess is a fine figure o' fun, as I said to myself today when I zeed her vamping round parish with the rest,' observed one of the elderly boozers in an undertone. 'But Joan Durbeyfield must mind that she don't get green malt in floor.' It was a local phrase which had a peculiar meaning, and there was no reply.

The conversation became inclusive, and presently other footsteps were heard crossing the room below.

' – Being a few private friends asked in tonight to keep up club-walking at my own expense.' The landlady had rapidly re-used the formula she kept on hand for intruders before she recognised that the newcomer was Tess.

Even to her mother's gaze the girl's young features looked sadly out of place amid the alcoholic vapours which floated here as no unsuitable medium for wrinkled middle-age; and hardly was a reproachful flash from Tess's dark eyes needed to make her father and mother rise from their seats, hastily finish their ale, and descend the stairs behind her, Mrs Rolliver's caution following their footsteps.

'No noise, please, if ye'll be so good, my dears; or I mid lose my licends, and be summons'd, and I don't know what all! 'Night t'ye!'

They went home together, Tess holding one arm of her father, and Mrs Durbeyfield the other. He had, in truth, drunk very little – not a fourth of the quantity which a systematic tippler could carry to church on a Sunday afternoon without a hitch in his eastings or genuflections; but the weakness of Sir John's constitution made mountains of his petty sins in this kind. On reaching the fresh air he was sufficiently unsteady to incline the row of three at one moment as if they were marching to London, and at another as if they were marching to Bath – which produced a comical effect, frequent enough in families on nocturnal home-goings; and, like most comical effects, not quite so comic after all. The two women valiantly disguised these forced excursions and countermarches as well as they could from Durbeyfield their cause, and from Abraham, and from themselves; and so they approached by degrees their own door, the head of the family bursting suddenly into his former refrain as he drew near, as if to fortify his soul at sight of the smallness of his present residence – 'I've got a fam–ily vault at Kingsbere!'

'Hush – don't be so silly, Jacky,' said his wife. 'Yours is not the only family that was of 'count in wold days. Look at the Anktells, and Horseys, and the Tringhams themselves – gone to seed a'most as much as you – though you was bigger folks than they, that's true. Thank God, I was never of no family, and have nothing to be ashamed of in that way!'

'Don't you be so sure o' that. From your nater 'tis my belief you've disgraced yourselves more than any o' us, and was kings and queens outright at one time.'

Tess turned the subject by saying what was far more prominent in her own mind at the moment than thoughts of her ancestry – 'I am afraid father won't be able to take the journey with the beehives tomorrow so early.'

'I? I shall be all right in an hour or two,' said Durbeyfield.

It was eleven o'clock before the family were all in bed, and two o'clock next morning was the latest hour for starting with the beehives if they were to be delivered to the retailers in Casterbridge before the Saturday market began, the way thither lying by bad roads over a distance of between twenty and thirty miles, and the horse and waggon being of the slowest. At half-past one Mrs Durbeyfield came into the large bedroom where Tess and all her little brothers and sisters slept.

'The poor man can't go,' she said to her eldest daughter, whose great eyes had opened the moment her mother's hand touched the door.

Tess sat up in bed, lost in a vague interspace between a dream and this information.

'But somebody must go,' she replied. 'It is late for the hives already. Swarming will soon be over for the year; and if we put off taking 'em till next week's market the call for 'em will be past, and they'll be thrown on our hands.'

Mrs Durbeyfield looked unequal to the emergency. 'Some young feller, perhaps, would go? One of them who were so much after dancing with 'ee yesterday,' she presently suggested.

'O no – I wouldn't have it for the world!' declared Tess proudly. 'And letting everybody know the reason – such a thing to be ashamed of! I think *I* could go if Abraham could go with me to kip me company.'

Her mother at length agreed to this arrangement. Little Abraham was aroused from his deep sleep in a corner of the same apartment, and made to put on his clothes while still mentally in the other world. Meanwhile Tess had hastily dressed herself; and the twain, lighting a lantern, went out to the stable. The rickety little waggon was already laden, and the girl led out the horse Prince, only a degree less rickety than the vehicle.

The poor creature looked wonderingly round at the night, at the lantern, at their two figures, as if he could not believe that at that hour, when every living thing was intended to be in shelter and at rest, he was called upon to go out and labour. They put a stock of candle-ends into the lantern, hung the latter to the off-side of the load, and directed the horse onward, walking at his shoulder at first during the uphill parts of the way, in order not to overload an animal of so little vigour. To cheer themselves as well as they could, they made an artificial morning with the lantern, some bread and butter, and their own conversation, the real morning being far from come. Abraham, as he more fully awoke (for he had moved in a sort of trance so far), began to talk of the strange shapes assumed by the various dark objects against the sky; of this tree that looked like a raging tiger springing from a lair; of that which resembled a giant's head.

When they had passed the little town of Stourcastle, dumbly somnolent under its thick brown thatch, they reached higher ground. Still higher, on their left, the elevation called Bulbarrow or Bealbarrow, well-nigh the highest in South Wessex, swelled into the sky, engirdled by its earthen trenches. From hereabout the long road was fairly level for some distance onward. They mounted in front of the waggon, and Abraham grew reflective.

'Tess!' he said in a preparatory tone, after a silence.

'Yes, Abraham.'

'Bain't you glad that we've become gentlefolk?'

'Not particular glad.'

'But you be glad that you 'm going to marry a gentleman?'

'What?' said Tess, lifting her face.

'That our great relation will help 'ee to marry a gentleman.'

'I? Our great relation? We have no such relation. What has put that into your head?'

'I heard 'em talking about it up at Rolliver's when I went to find father. There's a rich lady of our family out at Trantridge, and mother said that if you claimed kin with the lady, she'd put 'ee in the way of marrying a gentleman.'

His sister became abruptly still, and lapsed into a pondering silence. Abraham talked on, rather for the pleasure of utterance than for audition, so that his sister's abstraction was of no account. He leant back against the hives, and with upturned face made observations on the stars, whose cold pulses were beating amid the black hollows above, in serene dissociation from these two wisps of human life. He asked how far away those twinklers were, and whether God was on the other side of them. But ever and anon his childish prattle recurred to what impressed his imagination even more deeply than the wonders of creation. If Tess were made rich by marrying a gentleman, would she have money enough to buy a spyglass so large that it would draw the stars as near to her as Nettlecombe-Tout?

The renewed subject, which seemed to have impregnated the whole family, filled Tess with impatience.

'Never mind that now!' she exclaimed.

'Did you say the stars were worlds, Tess?'

'Yes.'

'All like ours?'

'I don't know; but I think so. They sometimes seem to be like the apples on our stubbard tree. Most of them splendid and sound – a few blighted.'

'Which do we live on – a splendid one or a blighted one?'

'A blighted one.'

' 'Tis very unlucky that we didn't pitch on a sound one, when there were so many more of 'em!'

'Yes.'

'Is it like that *really*, Tess?' said Abraham, turning to her much impressed, on reconsideration of this rare information. 'How would it have been if we had pitched on a sound one?'

'Well, father wouldn't have coughed and creeped about as he does, and wouldn't have got too tipsy to go this journey; and mother wouldn't have been always washing, and never getting finished.'

'And you would have been a rich lady ready-made, and not have had to be made rich by marrying a gentleman?'

'O Aby, don't – don't talk of that any more!'

Left to his reflections Abraham soon grew drowsy. Tess was not skilful in the management of a horse, but she thought that she could take upon herself the entire conduct of the load for the present, and allow Abraham to go to sleep if he wished to do so. She made him a sort of nest in front of the hives, in such a manner that he could not fall, and, taking the reins into her own hands, jogged on as before.

Prince required but slight attention, lacking energy for superfluous movements of any sort. With no longer a companion to distract her, Tess fell more deeply into reverie than ever, her back leaning against the hives. The mute procession past her shoulders of trees and hedges became attached to fantastic scenes outside reality, and the occasional heave of the wind became the sigh of some immense sad soul, conterminous with the universe in space, and with history in time.

Then, examining the mesh of events in her own life, she seemed to see the vanity of her father's pride; the gentlemanly suitor awaiting herself in her mother's fancy; to see him as a grimacing personage, laughing at her poverty, and her shrouded knightly ancestry. Everything grew more and more extravagant, and she no longer knew how time passed. A sudden jerk shook her in her seat, and Tess awoke from the sleep into which she, too, had fallen.

They were a long way further on than when she had lost consciousness, and the waggon had stopped. A hollow groan, unlike anything she had ever heard in her life, came from the front, followed by a shout of 'Hoi there!'

The lantern hanging at her waggon had gone out, but another was shining in her face – much brighter than her own had been. Something terrible had happened. The harness was entangled with an object which blocked the way.

In consternation Tess jumped down, and discovered the dreadful truth. The groan had proceeded from her father's poor horse Prince. The morning mail-cart, with its two noiseless wheels, speeding along these lanes like an arrow, as it always did, had driven into her slow and unlighted equipage. The pointed shaft of the cart had entered the breast of the unhappy Prince like a sword, and from the wound his life's blood was spouting in a stream, and falling with a hiss into the road.

In her despair Tess sprang forward and put her hand upon the hole, with the only result that she became splashed from face to skirt with the crimson drops. Then she stood helplessly looking on. Prince also stood firm and motionless as long as he could; till he suddenly sank down in a heap.

By this time the mail-cart man had joined her, and began dragging and unharnessing the hot form of Prince. But he was already dead, and, seeing that nothing more could be done immediately, the mail-cart man returned to his own animal, which was uninjured.

'You was on the wrong side,' he said. 'I am bound to go on with the mail-bags, so that the best thing for you to do is to bide here with your load. I'll send somebody to help you as soon as I can. It is getting daylight, and you have nothing to fear.'

He mounted and sped on his way; while Tess stood and waited. The atmosphere turned pale, the birds shook themselves in the hedges, arose, and twittered; the lane showed all its white features, and Tess showed hers, still whiter. The huge pool of blood in front of her was already assuming the iridescence of coagulation; and when the sun rose a hundred prismatic hues were reflected from it. Prince lay alongside still and stark; his eyes half open, the hole in his chest looking scarcely large enough to have let out all that had animated him.

' 'Tis all my doing – all mine!' the girl cried, gazing at the spectacle. 'No excuse for me – none. What will mother and father live on now? Aby, Aby!' She shook the child, who had slept soundly through the whole disaster. 'We can't go on with our load – Prince is killed!'

When Abraham realised all, the furrows of fifty years were extemporised on his young face.

'Why, I danced and laughed only yesterday!' she went on to herself. 'To think that I was such a fool!'

' 'Tis because we be on a blighted star, and not a sound one, isn't it, Tess?' murmured Abraham through his tears.

In silence they waited through an interval which seemed endless. At length a sound, and an approaching object, proved to them that the driver of the mail-cart had been as good as his word. A farmer's man from near Stourcastle came up, leading a strong cob. He was harnessed to the waggon of beehives in the place of Prince, and the load taken on towards Casterbridge.

The evening of the same day saw the empty waggon reach again the spot of the accident. Prince had lain there in the ditch since the morning; but the place of the blood-pool was still visible in the middle of the road, though scratched and scraped over by passing vehicles. All that was left of Prince was now hoisted into the waggon he had formerly hauled, and with his hoofs in the air, and his shoes shining in the setting sunlight, he retraced the eight or nine miles to Marlott.

Tess had gone back earlier. How to break the news was more than she could think. It was a relief to her tongue to find from the faces of her parents that they already knew of their loss, though this did not lessen the self-reproach which she continued to heap upon herself for her negligence.

But the very shiftlessness of the household rendered the misfortune a less terrifying one to them than it would have been to a thriving family, though in the present case it meant ruin, and in the other it would only have meant inconvenience. In the Durbeyfield countenances there was nothing of the red wrath that would have burnt upon the girl from parents more ambitious for her welfare. Nobody blamed Tess as she blamed herself.

When it was discovered that the knacker and tanner would give only a very few shillings for Prince's carcase because of his decrepitude, Durbeyfield rose to the occasion.

'No,' said he stoically, 'I won't sell his old body. When we d'Urbervilles was knights in the land, we didn't sell our chargers for cat's meat. Let 'em keep their shillings. He've served me well in his lifetime, and I won't part from him now.'

He worked harder the next day in digging a grave for Prince in the garden than he had worked for months to grow a crop for his family. When the hole was ready, Durbeyfield and his wife tied a rope round the horse and dragged him up the path towards it, the children following in funeral train. Abraham and 'Liza-Lu sobbed, Hope and Modesty discharged their griefs in loud blares which echoed from the walls; and when Prince was tumbled in they gathered round the grave. The bread-winner had been taken away from them; what would they do?

'Is he gone to heaven?' asked Abraham, between the sobs.

Then Durbeyfield began to shovel in the earth, and the children cried anew. All except Tess. Her face was dry and pale, as though she regarded herself in the light of a murderess.

## *Chapter 5*

The haggling business, which had mainly depended on the horse, became disorganised forthwith. Distress, if not penury, loomed in the distance. Durbeyfield was what was locally called a slack-twisted fellow; he had good strength to work at times; but the times could not be relied on to coincide with the hours of requirement; and, having been unaccustomed to the regular toil of the day-labourer, he was not particularly persistent when they did so coincide.

Tess, meanwhile, as the one who had dragged her parents into this quagmire, was silently wondering what she could do to help them out of it; and then her mother broached her scheme.

'We must take the ups wi' the downs, Tess,' said she; 'and never could your high blood have been found out at a more called-for moment. You must try your friends. Do ye know that there is a very rich Mrs d'Urberville living on the outskirts o' The Chase, who must be our relation? You must go to her and claim kin, and ask for some help in our trouble.'

'I shouldn't care to do that,' says Tess. 'If there is such a lady, 'twould be enough for us if she were friendly – not to expect her to give us help.'

'You could win her round to do anything, my dear. Besides, perhaps there's more in it than you know of. I've heard what I've heard, good-now.'

The oppressive sense of the harm she had done led Tess to be more deferential than she might otherwise have been to the maternal wish; but she could not understand why her mother should find such satisfaction in contemplating an enterprise of, to her, such doubtful profit. Her mother might have made enquiries, and have discovered that this Mrs d'Urberville was a lady of unequalled virtues and charity. But Tess's pride made the part of poor relation one of particular distaste to her.

'I'd rather try to get work,' she murmured.

'Durbeyfield, you can settle it,' said his wife, turning to where he sat in the background. 'If you say she ought to go, she will go.'

'I don't like my children going and making themselves beholden to strange kin,' murmured he. 'I'm the head of the noblest branch o' the family, and I ought to live up to it.'

His reasons for staying away were worse to Tess than her own objection to going. 'Well, as I killed the horse, mother,' she said mournfully, 'I suppose I ought to do something. I don't mind going and seeing her, but you must leave it to me about asking for help. And don't go thinking about her making a match for me – it is silly.'

'Very well said, Tess!' observed her father sententiously.

'Who said I had such a thought?' asked Joan.

'I fancy it is in your mind, mother. But I'll go.'

Rising early next day she walked to the hill-town called Shaston, and there took advantage of a van which twice in the week ran from Shaston eastward to Chaseborough, passing near Trantridge, the parish in which the vague and mysterious Mrs d'Urberville had her residence.

Tess Durbeyfield's route on this memorable morning lay amid the north-eastern undulations of the Vale in which she had been born, and in which her life had unfolded. The Vale of Blackmoor was to her the world, and its inhabitants the races thereof. From the gates and stiles of Marlott she had looked down its length in the wondering days of infancy, and what had been mystery to her then was not much less than mystery to her now. She had seen daily from her chamber-window towers, villages, faint white mansions; above all the town of Shaston standing majestically on its height; its windows shining like lamps in the evening sun. She had hardly ever visited the place, only a small tract even of the Vale and its environs being known to her by close inspection. Much less had she been far outside the valley. Every contour of the surrounding hills was as personal to her as that of her relatives' faces; but for what lay beyond her judgment was dependent on the teaching of the village school, where she had held a leading place at the time of her leaving, a year or two before this date.

In those early days she had been much loved by others of her own sex and age, and had used to be seen about the village as one of three – all nearly of the same year – walking home from school side by side; Tess the middle one – in a pink print pinafore, of a finely reticulated pattern, worn over a stuff frock that had lost its original colour for a nondescript tertiary – marching on upon long stalky legs, in tight stockings which had little ladder-like holes at the knees, torn by kneeling in the roads and banks in search of vegetable and mineral treasures; her then earth-coloured hair hanging like pot-hooks; the arms of the two outside girls resting round the waist of Tess; her arms on the shoulders of the two supporters.

As Tess grew older, and began to see how matters stood, she felt quite a Malthusian towards her mother for thoughtlessly giving her so many little sisters and brothers, when it was such a trouble to nurse and provide for them. Her mother's intelligence was that of a happy child: Joan Durbeyfield was simply an additional one, and that not the eldest, to her own long family of waiters on Providence.

However, Tess became humanely beneficent towards the small ones, and to help them as much as possible she used, as soon as she left school, to lend a hand at haymaking or harvesting on neighbouring farms; or, by preference, at milking or butter-making processes, which she had learnt when her father had owned cows; and being deft-fingered it was a kind of work in which she excelled.

Every day seemed to throw upon her young shoulders more of the family burdens, and that Tess should be the representative of the Durbeyfields at the d'Urberville mansion came as a thing of course. In this instance it must be admitted that the Durbeyfields were putting their fairest side outward.

She alighted from the van at Trantridge Cross, and ascended on foot a hill in the direction of the district known as The Chase, on the borders of which, as she had been informed, Mrs d'Urberville's seat, The Slopes, would be found. It was not a manorial home in the ordinary sense, with fields, and pastures, and a grumbling farmer, out of whom the owner had to squeeze an income for himself and his family by hook or by crook. It was more, far more; a country-house built for enjoyment pure and simple, with not an acre of troublesome land attached to it beyond what was required for residential purposes, and for a little fancy farm kept in hand by the owner, and tended by a bailiff.

The crimson brick lodge came first in sight, up to its eaves in dense evergreens. Tess thought this was the mansion itself till, passing through the side wicket with some trepidation, and onward to a point at which the drive took a turn, the house proper stood in full view. It was of recent erection – indeed almost new – and of the same rich red colour that formed such a contrast with the evergreens of the lodge. Far behind the corner of the house – which rose like a geranium bloom against the subdued colours around – stretched the soft azure landscape of The Chase – a truly venerable tract of forest land, one of the few remaining woodlands in England of undoubted primaeval date, wherein Druidical mistletoe was still found on aged oaks, and where enormous yew trees, not planted by the hand of man, grew as they had grown when they were pollarded for bows. All this sylvan antiquity, however, though visible from The Slopes, was outside the immediate boundaries of the estate.

Everything on this snug property was bright, thriving, and well kept; acres of glasshouses stretched down the inclines to the copses at their feet. Everything looked like money – like the last coin issued from the Mint. The stables, partly screened by Austrian pines and evergreen oaks, and fitted with every late appliance, were as dignified as Chapels-of-Ease. On the extensive lawn stood an ornamental tent, its door being towards her.

Simple Tess Durbeyfield stood at gaze, in a half-alarmed attitude, on the edge of the gravel sweep. Her feet had brought her onward to this point before she had quite realised where she was; and now all was contrary to her expectation.

'I thought we were an old family; but this is all new!' she said, in her artlessness. She wished that she had not fallen in so readily with her mother's plans for 'claiming kin', and had endeavoured to gain assistance nearer home.

The d'Urbervilles – or Stoke-d'Urbervilles, as they at first called themselves – who owned all this, were a somewhat unusual family to find in such an old-fashioned part of the country. Parson Tringham had spoken truly when he said that our shambling John Durbeyfield was the only really lineal representative of the old d'Urberville family existing in the county, or near it; he might have added, what he knew very well, that the Stoke-d'Urbervilles were no more d'Urbervilles of the true tree than he was himself. Yet it must be admitted that this family formed a very good stock whereon to regraft a name which sadly wanted such renovation.

When old Mr Simon Stoke, latterly deceased, had made his fortune as an honest merchant (some said money lender) in the North, he decided to settle as a county man in the South of England, out of hail of his business district; and in doing this he felt the necessity of recommencing with a name that would not too readily identify him with the smart tradesman of the past, and that would be less commonplace than the original bald stark words. Conning for an hour in the British Museum the pages of works devoted to extinct, half-extinct, obscured, and ruined families appertaining to the quarter of England in which he proposed to settle, he considered that *d'Urberville* looked and sounded as well as any of them: and d'Urberville accordingly was annexed to his own name for himself and his heirs eternally. Yet he was not an extravagant-minded man in this, and in constructing his family tree on the new basis was duly reasonable in framing his inter-marriages and aristocratic links, never inserting a single title above a rank of strict moderation.

Of this work of imagination poor Tess and her parents were naturally in ignorance – much to their discomfiture; indeed the very possibility of such annexations was unknown to them; who supposed that, though to be well-favoured might be the gift of fortune, a family name came by nature.

Tess still stood hesitating like a bather about to make his plunge, hardly knowing whether to retreat or to persevere, when a figure came forth from the dark triangular door of the tent. It was that of a tall young man, smoking.

He had an almost swarthy complexion, with full lips, badly moulded, though red and smooth, above which was a well-groomed black moustache with curled points, though his age could not be more than three-or four-and-twenty. Despite the touches of barbarism in his contours, there was a singular force in the gentleman's face, and in his bold rolling eye.

'Well, my Beauty, what can I do for you?' said he, coming forward. And perceiving that she stood quite confounded: 'Never mind me. I am Mr d'Urberville. Have you come to see me or my mother?'

This embodiment of a d'Urberville and a namesake differed even more from what Tess had expected than the house and grounds had differed. She had dreamed of an aged and dignified face, the sublimation of all the d'Urberville lineaments, furrowed with incarnate memories representing in hieroglyphic the centuries of her family's and England's history. But she screwed herself up to the work in hand, since she could not get out of it, and answered – 'I came to see your mother, sir.'

'I am afraid you cannot see her – she is an invalid,' replied the present representative of the spurious house; for this was Mr Alec, the only son of the lately deceased gentleman. 'Cannot I answer your purpose? What is the business you wish to see her about?'

'It isn't business – it is – I can hardly say what!'

'Pleasure?'

'Oh no. Why, sir, if I tell you, it will seem – '

Tess's sense of a certain ludicrousness in her errand was now so strong that, notwithstanding her awe of him, and her general discomfort at being here, her rosy lips curved towards a smile, much to the attraction of the swarthy Alexander.

'It is so very foolish,' she stammered; 'I fear I can't tell you!'

'Never mind; I like foolish things. Try again, my dear,' said he kindly.

'Mother asked me to come,' Tess continued; 'and, indeed, I was in the mind to do so myself likewise. But I did not think it would be like this. I came, sir, to tell you that we are of the same family as you.'

'Ho! Poor relations?'

'Yes.'

'Stokes?'

'No; d'Urbervilles.'

'Ay, ay; I mean d'Urbervilles.'

'Our names are worn away to Durbeyfield; but we have several proofs that we are d'Urbervilles. Antiquarians hold we are, – and – and we have an old seal, marked with a ramping lion on a shield, and a castle over him. And we have a very old silver spoon, round in the bowl like a little ladle, and marked with the same castle. But it is so worn that mother uses it to stir the pea-soup.'

'A castle argent is certainly my crest,' said he blandly. 'And my arms a lion rampant.'

'And so mother said we ought to make ourselves beknown to you – as we've lost our horse by a bad accident, and are the oldest branch o' the family.'

'Very kind of your mother, I'm sure. And I, for one, don't regret her step.' Alec looked at Tess as he spoke, in a way that made her blush a little. 'And so, my pretty girl, you've come on a friendly visit to us, as relations?'

'I suppose I have,' faltered Tess, looking uncomfortable again.

'Well – there's no harm in it. Where do you live? What are you?'

She gave him brief particulars; and responding to further enquiries told him that she was intending to go back by the same carrier who had brought her.

'It is a long while before he returns past Trantridge Cross. Supposing we walk round the grounds to pass the time, my pretty coz?'

Tess wished to abridge her visit as much as possible; but the young man was pressing, and she consented to accompany him. He conducted her about the lawns, and flower-beds, and conservatories; and thence to the fruit-garden and greenhouses, where he asked her if she liked strawberries.

'Yes,' said Tess, 'when they come.'

'They are already here.' D'Urberville began gathering specimens of the fruit for her, handing them back to her as he stooped; and, presently, selecting a specially fine product of the 'British Queen' variety, he stood up and held it by the stem to her mouth.

'No – no!' she said quickly, putting her fingers between his hand and her lips. 'I would rather take it in my own hand.'

'Nonsense!' he insisted; and in a slight distress she parted her lips and took it in.

They had spent some time wandering desultorily thus, Tess eating in a half-pleased, half-reluctant state whatever d'Urberville offered her. When she could consume no more of the strawberries he filled her little basket with them; and then the two passed round to the rose trees, whence he gathered blossoms and gave her to put in her bosom. She obeyed like one in a dream, and when she could affix no more he himself tucked a bud or two into her hat, and heaped her basket with others in the prodigality of his bounty. At last, looking at his watch, he said, 'Now, by the time you have had something to eat, it will be time for you to leave, if you want to catch the carrier to Shaston. Come here, and I'll see what grub I can find.'

Stoke-d'Urberville took her back to the lawn and into the tent, where he left her, soon reappearing with a basket of light luncheon, which he put before her himself. It was evidently the gentleman's wish not to be disturbed in this pleasant tête-à-tête by the servantry.

'Do you mind my smoking?' he asked.

'Oh, not at all, sir.'

He watched her pretty and unconscious munching through the skeins of smoke that pervaded the tent, and Tess Durbeyfield did not divine, as she innocently looked down at the roses in her bosom, that there behind the blue narcotic haze was potentially the 'tragic mischief' of her drama – one who stood fair to be the blood-red ray in the spectrum of her young life. She had an attribute which amounted to a disadvantage just now; and it was this that caused Alec d'Urberville's eyes to rivet themselves upon her. It was a luxuriance of aspect, a fullness of growth, which made her appear more of a woman than she really was. She had inherited the feature from her mother without the quality it denoted. It had troubled her mind occasionally, till her companions had said that it was a fault which time would cure.

She soon had finished her lunch. 'Now I am going home, sir,' she said, rising.

'And what do they call you?' he asked, as he accompanied her along the drive till they were out of sight of the house.

'Tess Durbeyfield, down at Marlott.'

'And you say your people have lost their horse?'

'I – killed him!' she answered, her eyes filling with tears as she gave particulars of Prince's death. 'And I don't know what to do for father on account of it!'

'I must think if I cannot do something. My mother must find a berth for you. But, Tess, no nonsense about "d'Urberville"; – "Durbeyfield" only, you know – quite another name.'

'I wish for no better, sir,' said she with something of dignity.

For a moment – only for a moment – when they were in the turning of the drive, between the tall rhododendrons and conifers, before the lodge became visible, he inclined his face towards her as if – but, no: he thought better of it, and let her go.

Thus the thing began. Had she perceived this meeting's import she might have asked why she was doomed to be seen and coveted that day by the wrong man, and not by some other man, the right and desired one in all respects – as nearly as humanity can supply the right and desired; yet to him who amongst her acquaintance might have approximated to this kind, she was but a transient impression, half forgotten.

In the ill-judged execution of the well-judged plan of things the call seldom produces the comer, the man to love rarely coincides with the hour for loving. Nature does not often say 'See!' to her poor creature at a time when seeing can lead to happy doing; or reply 'Here!' to a body's cry of 'Where?' till the hide-and-seek has become an irksome, outworn game. We may wonder whether at the acme and summit of the human progress these anachronisms will be corrected by a finer intuition, a closer interaction of the social machinery than that which now jolts us round and along; but such completeness is not to be prophesied, or even conceived as possible. Enough that in the present case, as in millions, it was not the two halves of a perfect whole that confronted each other at the perfect moment; a missing counterpart wandered independently about the earth waiting in crass obtuseness till the late time came. Out of which maladroit delay sprang anxieties, disappointments, shocks, catastrophes, and passing-strange destinies.

When d'Urberville got back to the tent he sat down astride on a chair reflecting, with a pleased gleam in his face. Then he broke into a loud laugh.

'Well, I'm damned! What a funny thing! Ha-ha-ha! And what a crumby girl!'

## *Chapter 6*

Tess went down the hill to Trantridge Cross, and inattentively waited to take her seat in the van returning from Chaseborough to Shaston. She did not know what the other occupants said to her as she entered, though she answered them; and when they had started anew she rode along with an inward and not an outward eye.

One among her fellow-travellers addressed her more pointedly than any had spoken before: 'Why, you be quite a posy! And such roses in early June!'

Then she became aware of the spectacle she presented to their surprised vision: roses at her breast; roses in her hat; roses and strawberries in her basket to the brim. She blushed, and said confusedly that the flowers had been given to her. When the passengers were not looking she stealthily removed the more prominent blooms from her hat and placed them in the basket, where she covered them with her handkerchief. Then she fell to reflecting again, and in looking downwards a thorn of the rose remaining in her breast accidentally pricked her chin. Like all the cottagers in Blackmoor Vale, Tess was steeped in fancies and prefigurative superstitions; she thought this an ill omen – the first she had noticed that day.

The van travelled only so far as Shaston, and there were several miles of pedestrian descent from that mountain-town into the vale of Marlott. Her mother had advised her to stay here for the night, at the house of a cottage-woman they knew, if she should feel too tired to come on; and this Tess did, not descending to her home till the following afternoon.

When she entered the house she perceived in a moment from her mother's triumphant manner that something had occurred in the interim.

'Oh yes; I know all about it! I told 'ee it would be all right, and now 'tis proved!'

'Since I've been away? What has?' said Tess rather wearily.

Her mother surveyed the girl up and down with arch approval, and went on banteringly: 'So you've brought 'em round!'

'How do you know, mother?'

'I've had a letter.'

Tess then remembered that there would have been time for this.

'They say – Mrs d'Urberville says – that she wants you to look after a little fowl-farm which is her hobby. But this is only her artful way of getting 'ee there without raising your hopes. She's going to own 'ee as kin – that's the meaning o't.'

'But I didn't see her.'

'You zid somebody, I suppose?'

'I saw her son.'

'And did he own 'ee?'

'Well – he called me Coz.'

'An' I knew it! Jacky – he called her Coz!' cried Joan to her husband. 'Well, he spoke to his mother, of course, and she do want 'ee there.'

'But I don't know that I am apt at tending fowls,' said the dubious Tess.

'Then I don't know who is apt. You've be'n born in the business, and brought up in it. They that be born in a business always know more about it than any 'prentice. Besides, that's only just a show of something for you to do, that you midn't feel beholden.'

'I don't altogether think I ought to go,' said Tess thoughtfully. 'Who wrote the letter? Will you let me look at it?'

'Mrs d'Urberville wrote it. Here it is.'

The letter was in the third person, and briefly informed Mrs Durbeyfield that her daughter's services would be useful to that lady in the management of her poultry-farm, that a comfortable room would be provided for her if she could come, and that the wages would be on a liberal scale if they liked her.

'Oh – that's all!' said Tess.

'You couldn't expect her to throw her arms round 'ee, an' to kiss and to coll 'ee all at once.'

Tess looked out of the window.

'I would rather stay here with father and you,' she said.

'But why?'

'I'd rather not tell you why, mother; indeed, I don't quite know why.'

A week afterwards she came in one evening from an unavailing search for some light occupation in the immediate neighbourhood. Her idea had been to get together sufficient money during the summer to purchase another horse. Hardly had she crossed the threshold before one of the children danced across the room, saying, 'The gentleman's been here!'

Her mother hastened to explain, smiles breaking from every inch of her person. Mrs d'Urberville's son had called on horseback, having been riding by chance in the direction of Marlott. He had wished to know, finally, in the name of his mother, if Tess could really come to manage the old lady's fowl-farm or not; the lad who had hitherto superintended the birds having proved untrustworthy. 'Mr d'Urberville says you must be a good girl if you are at all as you appear; he knows you must be worth your weight in gold. He is very much interested in 'ee – truth to tell.'

Tess seemed for the moment really pleased to hear that she had won such high opinion from a stranger when, in her own esteem, she had sunk so low.

'It is very good of him to think that,' she murmured; 'and if I was quite sure how it would be living there, I would go any-when.'

'He is a mighty handsome man!'

'I don't think so,' said Tess coldly.

'Well, there's your chance, whether or no; and I'm sure he wears a beautiful diamond ring!'

'Yes,' said little Abraham, brightly, from the window-bench; 'and I seed it! and it did twinkle when he put his hand up to his mistarshers. Mother, why did our grand relation keep on putting his hand up to his mistarshers?'

'Hark at that child!' cried Mrs Durbeyfield, with parenthetic admiration.

'Perhaps to show his diamond ring,' murmured Sir John, dreamily, from his chair.

'I'll think it over,' said Tess, leaving the room.

'Well, she's made a conquest o' the younger branch of us, straight off,' continued the matron to her husband, 'and she's a fool if she don't follow it up.'

'I don't quite like my children going away from home,' said the haggler. 'As the head of the family, the rest ought to come to me.'

'But do let her go, Jacky,' coaxed his poor witless wife. 'He's struck wi' her – you can see that. He called her Coz! He'll marry her, most likely, and make a lady of her; and then she'll be what her forefathers was.'

John Durbeyfield had more conceit than energy or health, and this supposition was pleasant to him.

'Well, perhaps, that's what young Mr d'Urberville means,' he admitted; 'and sure enough he mid have serious thoughts about improving his blood by linking on to the old line. Tess, the little rogue! And have she really paid 'em a visit to such an end as this?'

Meanwhile Tess was walking thoughtfully among the gooseberry-bushes in the garden, and over Prince's grave. When she came in her mother pursued her advantage.

'Well, what be you going to do?' she asked.

'I wish I had seen Mrs d'Urberville,' said Tess.

'I think you mid as well settle it. Then you'll see her soon enough.'

Her father coughed in his chair.

'I don't know what to say!' answered the girl restlessly. 'It is for you to decide. I killed the old horse, and I suppose I ought to do something to get ye a new one. But – but – I don't quite like Mr d'Urberville being there!'

The children, who had made use of this idea of Tess being taken up by their wealthy kinsfolk (which they imagined the other family to be) as a species of dolorifuge after the death of the horse, began to cry at Tess's reluctance, and teased and reproached her for hesitating.

'Tess won't go–o–o and be made a la–a–dy of! – no, she says she wo–o–on't!' they wailed, with square mouths. 'And we shan't have a nice new horse, and lots o' golden money to buy fairlings! And Tess won't look pretty in her best cloze no mo–o–ore!'

Her mother chimed in to the same tune: a certain way she had of making her labours in the house seem heavier than they were by prolonging them indefinitely, also weighed in the argument. Her father alone preserved an attitude of neutrality.

'I will go,' said Tess at last.

Her mother could not repress her consciousness of the nuptial vision conjured up by the girl's consent.

'That's right! For such a pretty maid as 'tis, this is a fine chance!'

Tess smiled crossly.

'I hope it is a chance for earning money. It is no other kind of chance. You had better say nothing of that silly sort about parish.'

Mrs Durbeyfield did not promise. She was not quite sure that she did not feel proud enough, after the visitor's remarks, to say a good deal.

Thus it was arranged; and the young girl wrote, agreeing to be ready to set out on any day on which she might be required. She was duly informed that Mrs d'Urberville was glad of her decision, and that a spring-cart should be sent to meet her and her luggage at the top of the Vale on the day after the morrow, when she must hold herself prepared to start. Mrs d'Urberville's handwriting seemed rather masculine.

'A cart?' murmured Joan Durbeyfield doubtingly. 'It might have been a carriage for her own kin!'

Having at last taken her course Tess was less restless and abstracted, going about her business with some self-assurance in the thought of acquiring another horse for her father by an occupation which would not be onerous. She had hoped to be a teacher at the school, but the fates seemed to decide otherwise. Being mentally older than her mother she did not regard Mrs Durbeyfield's matrimonial hopes for her in a serious aspect for a moment. The light-minded woman had been discovering good matches for her daughter almost from the year of her birth.

## *Chapter 7*

On the morning appointed for her departure Tess was awake before dawn – at the marginal minute of the dark when the grove is still mute, save for one prophetic bird who sings with a clear-voiced conviction that he at least knows the correct time of day, the rest preserving silence as if equally convinced that he is mistaken. She remained upstairs packing till breakfast-time, and then came down in her ordinary weekday clothes, her Sunday apparel being carefully folded in her box.

Her mother expostulated. 'You will never set out to see your folks without dressing up more the dand than that?'

'But I am going to work!' said Tess.

'Well, yes,' said Mrs Durbeyfield; and in a private tone, 'at first there mid be a little pretence o't . . . But I think it will be wiser of 'ee to put your best side outward,' she added.

'Very well; I suppose you know best,' replied Tess with calm abandonment.

And to please her parent the girl put herself quite in Joan's hands, saying serenely – 'Do what you like with me, mother.'

Mrs Durbeyfield was only too delighted at this tractability. First she fetched a great basin, and washed Tess's hair with such thoroughness that when dried and brushed it looked twice as much as at other times. She tied it with a broader pink ribbon than usual. Then she put upon her the white frock that Tess had worn at the club-walking, the airy fullness of which, supplementing her enlarged *coiffure*, imparted to her developing figure an amplitude which belied her age, and might cause her to be estimated as a woman when she was not much more than a child.

'I declare there's a hole in my stocking-heel!' said Tess.

'Never mind holes in your stockings – they don't speak! When I was a maid, so long as I had a pretty bonnet the devil might ha' found me in heels.'

Her mother's pride in the girl's appearance led her to step back, like a painter from his easel, and survey her work as a whole.

'You must zee yourself!' she cried. 'It is much better than you was t'other day.'

As the looking-glass was only large enough to reflect a very small portion of Tess's person at one time, Mrs Durbeyfield hung a black cloak outside the casement, and so made a large reflector of the panes, as it is the wont of bedecking cottagers to do. After this she went downstairs to her husband, who was sitting in the lower room.

'I'll tell 'ee what 'tis, Durbeyfield,' said she exultingly; 'he'll never have the heart not to love her. But whatever you do, don't zay too much to Tess of his fancy for her, and this chance she has got. She is such an odd maid that it mid zet her against him, or against going there, even now. If all goes well, I shall certainly be for making some return to pa'son at Stagfoot Lane for telling us – dear, good man!'

However, as the moment for the girl's setting out drew nigh, when the first excitement of the dressing had passed off, a slight misgiving found place in Joan Durbeyfield's mind. It prompted the matron to say that she would walk a little way – as far as to the point where the acclivity from the valley began its first steep ascent to the outer world. At the top Tess was going to be met with the spring-cart sent by the Stoke-d'Urbervilles, and her box had already been wheeled ahead towards this summit by a lad with trucks, to be in readiness.

Seeing their mother put on her bonnet the younger children clamoured to go with her.

'I do want to walk a little-ways wi' Sissy, now she's going to marry our gentleman-cousin, and wear fine cloze!'

'Now,' said Tess, flushing and turning quickly, 'I'll hear no more o' that! Mother, how could you ever put such stuff into their heads?'

'Going to work, my dears, for our rich relation, and help get enough money for a new horse,' said Mrs Durbeyfield pacifically.

'Goodbye, father,' said Tess, with a lumpy throat.

'Goodbye, my maid,' said Sir John, raising his head from his breast as he suspended his nap, induced by a slight excess this morning in honour of the occasion. 'Well, I hope my young friend will like such a comely sample of his own blood. And tell'n, Tess, that being sunk, quite, from our former grandeur, I'll sell him the title – yes, sell it – and at no unreasonable figure.'

'Not for less than a thousand pound!' cried Lady Durbeyfield.

'Tell'n – I'll take a thousand pound. Well, I'll take less, when I come to think o't. He'll adorn it better than a poor lammicken feller like myself can. Tell'n he shall hae it for a hundred. But I won't stand upon trifles – tell'n he shall hae it for fifty – for twenty pound! Yes, twenty pound – that's the lowest. Dammy, family honour is family honour, and I won't take a penny less!'

Tess's eyes were too full and her voice too choked to utter the sentiments that were in her. She turned quickly, and went out.

So the girls and their mother all walked together, a child on each side of Tess, holding her hand, and looking at her meditatively from time to time, as at one who was about to do great things; her mother just behind with the smallest; the group forming a picture of honest beauty flanked by innocence, and backed by simple-souled vanity. They followed the way till they reached the beginning of the ascent, on the crest of which the vehicle from Trantridge was to receive her, this limit having been fixed to save the horse the labour of the last slope. Far away behind the first hills the cliff-like dwellings of Shaston broke the line of the ridge. Nobody was visible in the elevated road which skirted the ascent save the lad whom they had sent on before them, sitting on the handle of the barrow that contained all Tess's worldly possessions.

'Bide here a bit, and the cart will soon come, no doubt,' said Mrs Durbeyfield. 'Yes, I see it yonder!'

It had come – appearing suddenly from behind the forehead of the nearest upland, and stopping beside the boy with the barrow. Her mother and the children thereupon decided to go no farther, and bidding them a hasty goodbye Tess bent her steps up the hill.

They saw her white shape draw near to the spring-cart, on which her box was already placed. But before she had quite reached it another vehicle shot out from a clump of trees on the summit, came round the bend of the road there, passed the luggage-cart, and halted beside Tess, who looked up as if in great surprise.

Her mother perceived, for the first time, that the second vehicle was not a humble conveyance like the first, but a spick-and-span gig or dog-cart, highly varnished and equipped. The driver was a young man of three-or four-and-twenty, with a cigar between his teeth; wearing a dandy cap, drab jacket, breeches of the same hue, white neckcloth, stick-up collar, and brown driving-gloves – in short, he was the handsome horsey young buck who had visited Joan a week or two before to get her answer about Tess.

Mrs Durbeyfield clapped her hands like a child. Then she looked down, then stared again. Could she be deceived as to the meaning of this?

'Is dat the gentleman-kinsman who'll make Sissy a lady?' asked the youngest child.

Meanwhile the muslined form of Tess could be seen standing still, undecided, beside this turn-out, whose owner was talking to her. Her seeming indecision was, in fact, more than indecision: it was misgiving. She would have preferred the humble cart. The young man dismounted, and appeared to urge her to ascend. She turned her face down the hill to her relatives, and regarded the little group. Something seemed to quicken her to a determination; possibly the thought that she had killed Prince. She suddenly stepped up; he mounted beside her, and immediately whipped on the horse. In a moment they had passed the slow cart with the box, and disappeared behind the shoulder of the hill.

Directly Tess was out of sight, and the interest of the matter as a drama was at an end, the little ones' eyes filled with tears. The youngest child said, 'I wish poor, poor Tess wasn't gone away to be a lady!' and, lowering the corners of his lips, burst out crying. The new point of view was infectious, and the next child did likewise, and then the next, till the whole three of them wailed loud.

There were tears also in Joan Durbeyfield's eyes as she turned to go home. But by the time she had got back to the village she was passively trusting to the favour of accident. However, in bed that night she sighed, and her husband asked her what was the matter.

'Oh, I don't know exactly,' she said. 'I was thinking that perhaps it would ha' been better if Tess had not gone.'

'Oughtn't ye to have thought of that before?'

'Well, 'tis a chance for the maid – Still, if 'twere the doing again, I wouldn't let her go till I had found out whether the gentleman is really a good-hearted young man and choice over her as his kinswoman.'

'Yes, you ought, perhaps, to ha' done that,' snored Sir John.

Joan Durbeyfield always managed to find consolation somewhere: 'Well, as one of the genuine stock, she ought to make her way with 'en, if she plays her trump card aright. And if he don't marry her afore he will after. For that he's all afire wi' love for her any eye can see.'

'What's her trump card? Her d'Urberville blood, you mean?'

'No, stupid; her face – as 'twas mine.'

## *Chapter 8*

Having mounted beside her, Alec d'Urberville drove rapidly along the crest of the first hill, chatting compliments to Tess as they went, the cart with her box being left far behind. Rising still, an immense landscape stretched around them on every side; behind, the green valley of her birth, before, a grey country of which she knew nothing except from her first brief visit to Trantridge. Thus they reached the verge of an incline down which the road stretched in a long straight descent of nearly a mile.

Ever since the accident with her father's horse Tess Durbeyfield, courageous as she naturally was, had been exceedingly timid on wheels; the least irregularity of motion startled her. She began to get uneasy at a certain recklessness in her conductor's driving.

'You will go down slow, sir, I suppose?' she said with attempted unconcern.

D'Urberville looked round upon her, nipped his cigar with the tips of his large white centre-teeth, and allowed his lips to smile slowly of themselves.

'Why, Tess,' he answered, after another whiff or two, 'it isn't a brave bouncing girl like you who asks that? Why, I always go down at full gallop. There's nothing like it for raising your spirits.'

'But perhaps you need not now?'

'Ah,' he said, shaking his head, 'there are two to be reckoned with. It is not me alone. Tib has to be considered, and she has a very queer temper.'

'Who?'

'Why, this mare. I fancy she looked round at me in a very grim way just then. Didn't you notice it?'

'Don't try to frighten me, sir,' said Tess stiffly.

'Well, I don't. If any living man can manage this horse I can: – I won't say any living man can do it – but if such has the power, I am he.'

'Why do you have such a horse?'

'Ah, well may you ask it! It was my fate, I suppose. Tib has killed one chap; and just after I bought her she nearly killed me. And then, take my word for it, I nearly killed her. But she's touchy still, very touchy; and one's life is hardly safe behind her sometimes.'

They were just beginning to descend; and it was evident that the horse, whether of her own will or of his (the latter being the more likely), knew so well the reckless performance expected of her that she hardly required a hint from behind.

Down, down, they sped, the wheels humming like a top, the dog-cart rocking right and left, its axis acquiring a slightly oblique set in relation to the line of progress; the figure of the horse rising and falling in undulations before them. Sometimes a wheel was off the ground, it seemed, for many yards; sometimes a stone was sent spinning over the hedge, and flinty sparks from the horse's hoofs outshone the daylight. The aspect of the straight road enlarged with their advance, the two banks dividing like a splitting stick; one rushing past at each shoulder.

The wind blew through Tess's white muslin to her very skin, and her washed hair flew out behind. She was determined to show no open fear, but she clutched d'Urberville's rein-arm.

'Don't touch my arm! We shall be thrown out if you do! Hold on round my waist!'

She grasped his waist, and so they reached the bottom.

'Safe, thank God, in spite of your fooling!' said she, her face on fire.

'Tess – fie! that's temper!' said d'Urberville.

' 'Tis truth.'

'Well, you need not let go your hold of me so thanklessly the moment you feel yourself out of danger.'

She had not considered what she had been doing; whether he were man or woman, stick or stone, in her involuntary hold on him. Recovering her reserve she sat without replying, and thus they reached the summit of another declivity.

'Now then, again!' said d'Urberville.

'No, no!' said Tess. 'Show more sense, do, please.'

'But when people find themselves on one of the highest points in the county, they must get down again,' he retorted.

He loosened rein, and away they went a second time. D'Urberville turned his face to her as they rocked, and said, in playful raillery: 'Now then, put your arms round my waist again, as you did before, my Beauty.'

'Never!' said Tess independently, holding on as well as she could without touching him.

'Let me put one little kiss on those holmberry lips, Tess, or even on that warmed cheek, and I'll stop – on my honour, I will!'

Tess, surprised beyond measure, slid farther back still on her seat, at which he urged the horse anew, and rocked her the more.

'Will nothing else do?' she cried at length, in desperation, her large eyes staring at him like those of a wild animal. This dressing her up so prettily by her mother had apparently been to lamentable purpose.

'Nothing, dear Tess,' he replied.

'Oh, I don't know – very well; I don't mind!' she panted miserably.

He drew rein, and as they slowed he was on the point of imprinting the desired salute, when, as if hardly yet aware of her own modesty, she dodged aside. His arms being occupied with the reins there was left him no power to prevent her manoeuvre.

'Now, damn it – I'll break both our necks!' swore her capriciously passionate companion. 'So you can go from your word like that, you young witch, can you?'

'Very well,' said Tess, 'I'll not move since you be so determined! But I – thought you would be kind to me, and protect me, as my kinsman!'

'Kinsman be hanged! Now!'

'But I don't want anybody to kiss me, sir!' she implored, a big tear beginning to roll down her face, and the corners of her mouth trembling in her attempts not to cry. 'And I wouldn't ha' come if I had known!'

He was inexorable, and she sat still, and d'Urberville gave her the kiss of mastery. No sooner had he done so than she flushed with shame, took out her handkerchief, and wiped the spot on her cheek that had been touched by his lips. His ardour was nettled at the sight, for the act on her part had been unconsciously done.

'You are mighty sensitive for a cottage girl!' said the young man.

Tess made no reply to this remark, of which, indeed, she did not quite comprehend the drift, unheeding the snub she had administered by her instinctive rub upon her cheek. She had, in fact, undone the kiss, as far as such a thing was physically possible. With a dim sense that he was vexed she looked steadily ahead as they trotted on near Melbury Down and Wingreen, till she saw, to her consternation, that there was yet another descent to be undergone.

'You shall be made sorry for that!' he resumed, his injured tone still remaining, as he flourished the whip anew. 'Unless, that is, you agree willingly to let me do it again, and no handkerchief.'

She sighed. 'Very well, sir!' she said. 'Oh – let me get my hat!'

At the moment of speaking her hat had blown off into the road, their present speed on the upland being by no means slow. D'Urberville pulled up, and said he would get it for her, but Tess was down on the other side.

She turned back and picked up the article.

'You look prettier with it off, upon my soul, if that's possible,' he said, contemplating her over the back of the vehicle. 'Now then, up again! What's the matter?'

The hat was in place and tied, but Tess had not stepped forward.

'No, sir,' she said, revealing the red and ivory of her mouth as her eye lit in defiant triumph; 'not again, if I know it!'

'What – you won't get up beside me?'

'No; I shall walk.'

' 'Tis five or six miles yet to Trantridge.'

'I don't care if 'tis dozens. Besides, the cart is behind.'

'You artful hussy! Now, tell me – didn't you make that hat blow off on purpose? I'll swear you did!'

Her strategic silence confirmed his suspicion.

Then d'Urberville cursed and swore at her, and called her everything he could think of for the trick. Turning the horse suddenly he tried to drive back upon her, and so hem her in between the gig and the hedge. But he could not do this short of injuring her.

'You ought to be ashamed of yourself for using such wicked words!' cried Tess with spirit, from the top of the hedge into which she had scrambled. 'I don't like 'ee at all! I hate and detest you! I'll go back to mother, I will!'

D'Urberville's bad temper cleared up at sight of hers; and he laughed heartily.

'Well, I like you all the better,' he said. 'Come, let there be peace. I'll never do it any more against your will. My life upon it now!'

Still Tess could not be induced to remount. She did not, however, object to his keeping his gig alongside her; and in this manner, at a slow pace, they advanced towards the village of Trantridge. From time to time d'Urberville exhibited a sort of fierce distress at the sight of the tramping he had driven her to undertake by his misdemeanour. She might in truth have safely trusted him now; but he had forfeited her confidence for the time, and she kept on the ground, progressing thoughtfully, as if wondering whether it would be wiser to return home. Her resolve, however, had been taken, and it seemed vacillating even to childishness to abandon it now, unless for graver reasons. How could she face her parents, get back her box, and disconcert the whole scheme for the rehabilitation of her family on such sentimental grounds?

A few minutes later the chimneys of The Slopes appeared in view, and in a snug nook to the right the poultry-farm and cottage of Tess's destination.

## *Chapter 9*

The community of fowls to which Tess had been appointed as supervisor, purveyor, nurse, surgeon, and friend, made its headquarters in an old thatched cottage standing in an enclosure that had once been a garden, but was now a trampled and sanded square. The house was overrun with ivy, its chimney being enlarged by the boughs of the parasite to the aspect of a ruined tower. The lower rooms were entirely given over to the birds, who walked about them with a proprietary air, as though the place had been built by themselves, and not by certain dusty copyholders who now lay east and west in the churchyard. The descendants of these bygone owners felt it almost as a slight to their family when the house which had so much of their affection, had cost so much of their forefathers' money, and had been in their possession for several generations before the d'Urbervilles came and built here, was indifferently turned into a fowl-house by Mrs Stoke-d'Urberville as soon as the property fell into hand according to law. ' 'Twas good enough for Christians in grandfather's time,' they said.

The rooms wherein dozens of infants had wailed at their nursing now resounded with the tapping of nascent chicks. Distracted hens in coops occupied spots where formerly stood chairs supporting sedate agriculturists. The chimney-corner and once blazing hearth was now filled with inverted beehives, in which the hens laid their eggs; while out of doors the plots that each succeeding householder had carefully shaped with his spade were torn by the cocks in wildest fashion.

The garden in which the cottage stood was surrounded by a wall, and could only be entered through a door.

When Tess had occupied herself about an hour the next morning in altering and improving the arrangements, according to her skilled ideas as the daughter of a professed poulterer, the door in the wall opened and a servant in white cap and apron entered. She had come from the manor-house.

'Mrs d'Urberville wants the fowls as usual,' she said; but perceiving that Tess did not quite understand, she explained, 'Mis'ess is a old lady, and blind.'

'Blind!' said Tess.

Almost before her misgiving at the news could find time to shape itself she took, under her companion's direction, two of the most beautiful of the Hamburghs in her arms, and followed the maidservant, who had likewise taken two, to the adjacent mansion, which, though ornate and imposing, showed traces everywhere on this side that some occupant of its chambers could bend to the love of dumb creatures – feathers floating within view of the front, and hen-coops standing on the grass.

In a sitting-room on the ground-floor, ensconced in an armchair with her back to the light, was the owner and mistress of the estate, a white-haired woman of not more than sixty, or even less, wearing a large cap. She had the mobile face frequent in those whose sight has decayed by stages, has been laboriously striven after, and reluctantly let go, rather than the stagnant mien apparent in persons long sightless or born blind. Tess walked up to this lady with her feathered charges – one sitting on each arm.

'Ah, you are the young woman come to look after my birds?' said Mrs d'Urberville, recognising a new footstep. 'I hope you will be kind to them. My bailiff tells me you are quite the proper person. Well, where are they? Ah, this is Strut! But he is hardly so lively today, is he? He is alarmed at being handled by a stranger, I suppose. And Phena too – yes, they are a little frightened – aren't you, dears? But they will soon get used to you.'

While the old lady had been speaking Tess and the other maid, in obedience to her gestures, had placed the fowls severally in her lap, and she had felt them over from head to tail, examining their beaks, their combs, the manes of the cocks, their wings, and their claws. Her touch enabled her to recognise them in a moment, and to discover if a single feather were crippled or draggled. She handled their crops, and knew what they had eaten, and if too little or too much; her face enacting a vivid pantomime of the criticisms passing in her mind.

The birds that the two girls had brought in were duly returned to the yard; and the process was repeated till all the pet cocks and hens had been submitted to the old woman – Hamburghs, Bantams, Cochins, Brahmas, Dorkings, and such other sorts as were in fashion just then – her perception of each visitor being seldom at fault as she received the bird upon her knees.

It reminded Tess of a Confirmation, in which Mrs d'Urberville was the bishop, the fowls the young people presented, and herself and the maidservant the parson and curate of the parish bringing them up. At the end of the ceremony Mrs d'Urberville abruptly asked Tess, wrinkling and twitching her face into undulations, 'Can you whistle?'

'Whistle, ma'am?'

'Yes, whistle tunes.'

Tess could whistle like most other country girls, though the accomplishment was one which she did not care to profess in genteel company. However, she blandly admitted that such was the fact.

'Then you will have to practise it every day. I had a lad who did it very well, but he has left. I want you to whistle to my bullfinches; as I cannot see them I like to hear them, and we teach 'em airs that way. Tell her where the cages are, Elizabeth. You must begin tomorrow, or they will go back in their piping. They have been neglected these several days.'

'Mr d'Urberville whistled to 'em this morning, ma'am,' said Elizabeth.

'He! Pooh!'

The old lady's face creased into furrows of repugnance, and she made no further reply.

Thus the reception of Tess by her fancied kinswoman terminated, and the birds were taken back to their quarters. The girl's surprise at Mrs d'Urberville's manner was not great; for since seeing the size of the house she had expected no more. But she was far from being aware that the old lady had never heard a word of the so-called kinship. She gathered that no great affection flowed between the blind woman and her son. But in that, too, she was mistaken. Mrs d'Urberville was not the first mother compelled to love her offspring resentfully, and to be bitterly fond.

In spite of the unpleasant initiation of the day before, Tess inclined to the freedom and novelty of her new position in the morning when the sun shone, now that she was once installed there; and she was curious to test her powers in the unexpected direction asked of her, so as to ascertain her chance of retaining her post. As soon as she was alone within the walled garden she sat herself down on a coop, and seriously screwed up her mouth for the long-neglected practice. She found her former ability to have degenerated to the production of a hollow rush of wind through the lips, and no clear note at all.

She remained fruitlessly blowing and blowing, wondering how she could have so grown out of the art which had come by nature, till she became aware of a movement among the ivy-boughs which cloaked the garden-wall no less than the cottage. Looking that way she beheld a form springing from the coping to the plot. It was Alec d'Urberville, whom she had not set eyes on since he had conducted her the day before to the door of the gardener's cottage where she had lodgings.

'Upon my honour!' cried he, 'there was never before such a beautiful thing in Nature or Art as you look, "Cousin" Tess ["Cousin" had a faint ring of mockery]. I have been watching you from over the wall – sitting like *Im*-patience on a monument, and pouting up that pretty red mouth to whistling shape, and whooing and whooing, and privately swearing, and never being able to produce a note. Why, you are quite cross because you can't do it.'

'I may be cross, but I didn't swear.'

'Ah! I understand why you are trying – those bullies! My mother wants you to carry on their musical education. How selfish of her! As if attending to these curst cocks and hens here were not enough work for any girl. I would flatly refuse, if I were you.'

'But she wants me particularly to do it, and to be ready by tomorrow morning.'

'Does she? Well then – I'll give you a lesson or two.'

'Oh no, you won't!' said Tess, withdrawing towards the door.

'Nonsense; I don't want to touch you. See – I'll stand on this side of the wire-netting, and you can keep on the other; so you may feel quite safe. Now, look here; you screw up your lips too harshly. There 'tis – so.'

He suited the action to the word, and whistled a line of 'Take, O take those lips away.' But the allusion was lost upon Tess.

'Now try,' said d'Urberville.

She attempted to look reserved; her face put on a sculptural severity. But he persisted in his demand, and at last, to get rid of him, she did put up her lips as directed for producing a clear note; laughing distressfully, however, and then blushing with vexation that she had laughed.

He encouraged her with 'Try again!'

Tess was quite serious, painfully serious by this time; and she tried – ultimately and unexpectedly emitting a real round sound. The momentary pleasure of success got the better of her; her eyes enlarged, and she involuntarily smiled in his face.

'That's it! Now I have started you – you'll go on beautifully. There – I said I would not come near you; and, in spite of such temptation as never before fell to mortal man, I'll keep my word . . . Tess, do you think my mother a queer old soul?'

'I don't know much of her yet, sir.'

'You'll find her so; she must be, to make you learn to whistle to her bullfinches. I am rather out of her books just now, but you will be quite in favour if you treat her livestock well. Good-morning. If you meet with any difficulties and want help here, don't go to the bailiff, come to me.'

It was in the economy of this *régime* that Tess Durbeyfield had undertaken to fill a place. Her first day's experiences were fairly typical of those which followed through many succeeding days. A familiarity with Alec d'Urberville's presence – which that young man carefully cultivated in her by playful dialogue, and by jestingly calling her his cousin when they were alone – removed much of her original shyness of him, without, however, implanting any feeling which could engender shyness of a new and tenderer kind. But she was more pliable under his hands than a mere companionship would have made her, owing to her unavoidable dependence upon his mother, and, through that lady's comparative helplessness, upon him.

She soon found that whistling to the bullfinches in Mrs d'Urberville's room was no such onerous business when she had regained the art, for she had caught from her musical mother numerous airs that suited those songsters admirably. A far more satisfactory time than when she practised in the garden was this whistling by the cages each morning. Unrestrained by the young man's presence she threw up her mouth, put her lips near the bars, and piped away in easeful grace to the attentive listeners.

Mrs d'Urberville slept in a large four-post bedstead hung with heavy damask curtains, and the bullfinches occupied the same apartment, where they flitted about freely at certain hours, and made little white spots on the furniture and upholstery. Once while Tess was at the window where the cages were ranged, giving her lesson as usual, she thought she heard a rustling behind the bed. The old lady was not present, and turning round the girl had an impression that the toes of a pair of boots were visible below the fringe of the curtains. Thereupon her whistling became so disjointed that the listener, if such there were, must have discovered her suspicion of his presence. She searched the curtains every morning after that, but never found anybody within them. Alec d'Urberville had evidently thought better of his freak to terrify her by an ambush of that kind.

## *Chapter 10*

Every village has its idiosyncrasy, its constitution, often its own code of morality. The levity of some of the younger women in and about Trantridge was marked, and was perhaps symptomatic of the choice spirit who ruled The Slopes in that vicinity. The place had also a more abiding defect; it drank hard. The staple conversation on the farms around was on the uselessness of saving money; and smockfrocked arithmeticians, leaning on their ploughs or hoes, would enter into calculations of great nicety to prove that parish relief was a fuller provision for a man in his old age than any which could result from savings out of their wages during a whole lifetime.

The chief pleasure of these philosophers lay in going every Saturday night, when work was done, to Chaseborough, a decayed market-town two or three miles distant; and, returning in the small hours of the next morning, to spend Sunday in sleeping off the dyspeptic effects of the curious compounds sold to them as beer by the monopolisers of the once independent inns.

For a long time Tess did not join in the weekly pilgrimages. But under pressure from matrons not much older than herself – for a field-man's wages being as high at twenty-one as at forty, marriage was early here – Tess at length consented to go. Her first experience of the journey afforded her more enjoyment than she had expected, the hilariousness of the others being quite contagious after her monotonous attention to the poultry-farm all the week. She went again and again. Being graceful and interesting, standing moreover on the momentary threshold of womanhood, her appearance drew down upon her some sly regards from loungers in the streets of Chaseborough; hence, though sometimes her journey to the town was made independently, she always searched for her fellows at nightfall, to have the protection of their companionship homeward.

This had gone on for a month or two when there came a Saturday in September, on which a fair and a market coincided; and the pilgrims from Trantridge sought double delights at the inns on that account. Tess's occupations made her late in setting out, so that her comrades reached the town long before her. It was a fine September evening, just before sunset, when yellow lights struggle with blue shades in hairlike lines, and the atmosphere itself forms a prospect without aid from more solid objects, except the innumerable winged insects that dance in it. Through this low-lit mistiness Tess walked leisurely along.

She did not discover the coincidence of the market with the fair till she had reached the place, by which time it was close upon dusk. Her limited marketing was soon completed; and then as usual she began to look about for some of the Trantridge cottagers.

At first she could not find them, and she was informed that most of them had gone to what they called a private little jig at the house of a hay-trusser and peat-dealer who had transactions with their farm. He lived in an out-of-the-way nook of the townlet, and in trying to find her course thither her eyes fell upon Mr d'Urberville standing at a street corner.

'What – my Beauty? You here so late?' he said.

She told him that she was simply waiting for company homeward.

'I'll see you again,' said he over her shoulder as she went on down the back lane.

Approaching the hay-trussers she could hear the fiddled notes of a reel proceeding from some building in the rear; but no sound of dancing was audible – an exceptional state of things for these parts, where as a rule the stamping drowned the music. The front door being open she could see straight through the house into the garden at the back as far as the shades of night would allow; and nobody appearing to her knock she traversed the dwelling and went up the path to the outhouse whence the sound had attracted her.

It was a windowless erection used for storage, and from the open door there floated into the obscurity a mist of yellow radiance, which at first Tess thought to be illuminated smoke. But on drawing nearer she perceived that it was a cloud of dust lit by candles within the outhouse, whose beams upon the haze carried forward the outline of the doorway into the wide night of the garden.

When she came close and looked in she beheld indistinct forms racing up and down to the figure of the dance, the silence of their footfalls arising from their being overshoe in 'scroff' – that is to say, the powdery residuum from the storage of peat and other products, the stirring of which by their turbulent feet created the nebulosity that involved the scene. Through this floating, fusty debris of peat and hay, mixed with the perspirations and warmth of the dancers, and forming together a sort of vegeto-human pollen, the muted fiddles feebly pushed their notes, in marked contrast to the spirit with which the measure was trodden out. They coughed as they danced, and laughed as they coughed. Of the rushing couples there could barely be discerned more than the high lights – the indistinctness shaping them to satyrs clasping nymphs – a multiplicity of Pans whirling a multiplicity of Syrinxes; Lotis attempting to elude Priapus, and always failing.

At intervals a couple would approach the doorway for ai longer veiling their features, the demigods resolved themselve personalities of her own next-door neighbours. Could Trant three short hours have metamorphosed itself thus madly!

Some Sileni of the throng sat on benches and hay-trusses by the of them recognised her.

'The maids don't think it respectable to dance at the Flower-d explained. 'They don't like to let everybody see which be their fa Besides, the house sometimes shuts up just when their jints begin to get So we come here and send out for liquor.'

'But when be any of you going home?' asked Tess with some anxiety.

'Now – a'most directly. This is all but the last jig.'

She waited. The reel drew to a close, and some of the party were in the n of starting. But others would not, and another dance was formed. This su would end it, thought Tess. But it merged in yet another. She became restle and uneasy; yet, having waited so long, it was necessary to wait longer; o account of the fair the roads were dotted with roving characters of possibly ill intent; and, though not fearful of measurable dangers, she feared the unknown. Had she been near Marlott she would have had less dread.

'Don't ye be nervous, my dear good soul,' expostulated, between his coughs, a young man with a wet face, and his straw hat so far back upon his head that the brim encircled it like the nimbus of a saint. 'What's yer hurry? Tomorrow is Sunday, thank God, and we can sleep it off in church-time. Now, have a turn with me?'

She did not abhor dancing, but she was not going to dance here. The movement grew more passionate: the fiddlers behind the luminous pillar of cloud now and then varied the air by playing on the wrong side of the bridge or with the back of the bow. But it did not matter; the panting shapes spun onwards.

They did not vary their partners if their inclination were to stick to previous ones. Changing partners simply meant that a satisfactory choice had not as yet been arrived at by one or other of the pair, and by this time every couple had been suitably matched. It was then that the ecstasy and the dream began, in which emotion was the matter of the universe, and matter but an adventitious intrusion likely to hinder you from spinning where you wanted to spin.

Suddenly there was a dull thump on the ground: a couple had fallen, and lay in a mixed heap. The next couple, unable to check its progress, came toppling over the obstacle. An inner cloud of dust rose around the prostrate figures amid the general one of the room, in which a twitching entanglement of arms and legs was discernible.

'You shall catch it for this, my gentleman, when you get home!' burst in female accents from the human heap – those of the unhappy partner of the man whose clumsiness had caused the mishap; she happened also to be his recently married wife, in which assortment there was nothing unusual at Trantridge as long as any affection remained between wedded couples; and, indeed, it was not ıcustomary in their later lives, to avoid making odd lots of the single people etween whom there might be a warm understanding.

A loud laugh from behind Tess's back, in the shade of the garden, united with he titter within the room. She looked round, and saw the red coal of a cigar: Alec d'Urberville was standing there alone. He beckoned to her, and she reluctantly retreated towards him.

'Well, my Beauty, what are you doing here?'

She was so tired after her long day and her walk that she confided her trouble to him – that she had been waiting ever since he saw her to have their company home, because the road at night was strange to her. 'But it seems they will never leave off, and I really think I will wait no longer.'

'Certainly do not. I have only a saddle-horse here today; but come to The Flower-de-Luce, and I'll hire a trap, and drive you home with me.'

Tess, though flattered, had never quite got over her original mistrust of him, and, despite their tardiness, she preferred to walk home with the work-folk. So she answered that she was much obliged to him, but would not trouble him. 'I have said that I will wait for 'em, and they will expect me to now.'

'Very well, Miss Independence. Please yourself . . . Then I shall not hurry . . . My good Lord, what a kick-up they are having there!'

He had not put himself forward into the light, but some of them had perceived him, and his presence led to a slight pause and a consideration of how the time was flying. As soon as he had re-lit a cigar and walked away the Trantridge people began to collect themselves from amid those who had come in from other farms, and prepared to leave in a body. Their bundles and baskets were gathered up, and half an hour later, when the clock-chime sounded a quarter past eleven, they were straggling along the lane which led up the hill towards their homes.

It was a three-mile walk, along a dry white road, made whiter tonight by the light of the moon.

Tess soon perceived as she walked in the flock, sometimes with this one, sometimes with that, that the fresh night air was producing staggerings and serpentine courses among the men who had partaken too freely; some of the more careless women also were wandering in their gait – to wit, a dark virago, Car Darch, dubbed Queen of Spades, till lately a favourite of d'Urberville's; Nancy, her sister, nicknamed the Queen of Diamonds; and the young married woman who had already tumbled down. Yet however terrestrial and lumpy their appearance just now to the mean unglamoured eye, to themselves the case was different. They followed the road with a sensation that they were soaring along in a supporting medium, possessed of original and profound thoughts, themselves and surrounding nature forming an organism of which all the parts harmoniously and joyously interpenetrated each other. They were as sublime as the moon and stars above them, and the moon and stars were as ardent as they.

Tess, however, had undergone such painful experiences of this kind in her father's house, that the discovery of their condition spoilt the pleasure she was beginning to feel in the moonlight journey. Yet she stuck to the party, for reasons above given.

In the open highway they had progressed in scattered order; but now their route was through a field-gate, and the foremost finding a difficulty in opening it they closed up together.

This leading pedestrian was Car the Queen of Spades, who carried a wicker-basket containing her mother's groceries, her own draperies, and other purchases for the week. The basket being large and heavy, Car had placed it for convenience of porterage on the top of her head, where it rode on in jeopardised balance as she walked with arms akimbo.

'Well – whatever is that a-creeping down thy back, Car Darch?' said one of the group suddenly.

All looked at Car. Her gown was a light cotton print, and from the back of her head a kind of rope could be seen descending to some distance below her waist, like a Chinaman's queue.

' 'Tis her hair falling down,' said another.

No; it was not her hair: it was a black stream of something oozing from her basket, and it glistened like a slimy snake in the cold still rays of the moon.

' 'Tis treacle,' said an observant matron.

Treacle it was. Car's poor old grandmother had a weakness for the sweet stuff. Honey she had in plenty out of her own hives, but treacle was what her soul desired, and Car had been about to give her a treat of surprise. Hastily lowering the basket the dark girl found that the vessel containing the syrup had been smashed within.

By this time there had arisen a shout of laughter at the extraordinary appearance of Car's back, which irritated the dark queen into getting rid of the disfigurement by the first sudden means available, and independently of the help of the scoffers. She rushed excitedly into the field they were about to cross, and flinging herself flat on her back upon the grass, began to wipe her gown as well as she could by spinning horizontally on the herbage and dragging herself over it upon her elbows.

The laughter rang louder; they clung to the gate, to the posts, rested on their staves, in the weakness engendered by their convulsions at the spectacle of Car. Our heroine, who had hitherto held her peace, at this wild moment could not help joining in with the rest.

It was a misfortune – in more ways than one. No sooner did the dark queen hear the soberer richer note of Tess among those of the other work-people than a long smouldering sense of rivalry inflamed her to madness. She sprang to her feet and closely faced the object of her dislike.

'How darest th' laugh at me, hussy!' she cried.

'I couldn't really help it when t'others did,' apologised Tess, still tittering.

'Ah, th'st think th' beest everybody, dostn't, because th' beest first favourite with He just now! But stop a bit, my lady, stop a bit! I'm as good as two of such! Look here – here's at 'ee!'

To Tess's horror the dark queen began stripping off the bodice of her gown –

which for the added reason of its ridiculed condition she was only too glad to be free of – till she had bared her plump neck, shoulders, and arms to the moonshine, under which they looked as luminous and beautiful as some Praxitelean creation, in their possession of the faultless rotundities of a lusty country girl. She closed her fists and squared up at Tess.

'Indeed, then, I shall not fight!' said the latter majestically; 'and if I had known you was of that sort, I wouldn't have so let myself down as to come with such a whorage as this is!'

The rather too inclusive speech brought down a torrent of vituperation from other quarters upon fair Tess's unlucky head, particularly from the Queen of Diamonds, who having stood in the relations to d'Urberville that Car had also been suspected of, united with the latter against the common enemy. Several other women also chimed in, with an animus which none of them would have been so fatuous as to show but for the rollicking evening they had passed. Thereupon, finding Tess unfairly browbeaten, the husbands and lovers tried to make peace by defending her; but the result of that attempt was directly to increase the war.

Tess was indignant and ashamed. She no longer minded the loneliness of the way and the lateness of the hour; her one object was to get away from the whole crew as soon as possible. She knew well enough that the better among them would repent of their passion next day. They were all now inside the field, and she was edging back to rush off alone when a horseman emerged almost silently from the corner of the hedge that screened the road, and Alec d'Urberville looked round upon them.

'What the devil is all this row about, work-folk?' he asked.

The explanation was not readily forthcoming; and, in truth, he did not require any. Having heard their voices while yet some way off he had ridden creepingly forward, and learnt enough to satisfy himself.

Tess was standing apart from the rest, near the gate. He bent over towards her. 'Jump up behind me,' he whispered, 'and we'll get shot of the screaming cats in a jiffy!'

She felt almost ready to faint, so vivid was her sense of the crisis. At almost any other moment of her life she would have refused such proffered aid and company, as she had refused them several times before; and now the loneliness would not of itself have forced her to do otherwise. But coming as the invitation did at the particular juncture when fear and indignation at these adversaries could be transformed by a spring of the foot into a triumph over them, she abandoned herself to her impulse, climbed the gate, put her toe upon his instep, and scrambled into the saddle behind him. The pair were speeding away into the distant grey by the time that the contentious revellers became aware of what had happened.

The Queen of Spades forgot the stain on her bodice, and stood beside the Queen of Diamonds and the new-married, staggering young woman – all with a gaze of fixity in the direction in which the horse's tramp was diminishing into silence on the road.

'What be ye looking at?' asked a man who had not observed the incident.

'Ho–ho–ho!' laughed dark Car.

'Hee–hee–hee!' laughed the tippling bride, as she steadied herself on the arm of her fond husband.

'Heu–heu–heu!' laughed dark Car's mother, stroking her moustache as she explained laconically: 'Out of the frying-pan into the fire!'

Then these children of the open air, whom even excess of alcohol could scarce injure permanently, betook themselves to the field-path; and as they went there moved onward with them, around the shadow of each one's head, a circle of opalised light, formed by the moon's rays upon the glistening sheet of dew. Each pedestrian could see no halo but his or her own, which never deserted the head-shadow, whatever its vulgar unsteadiness might be; but adhered to it, and persistently beautified it; till the erratic motions seemed an inherent part of the irradiation, and the fumes of their breathing a component of the night's mist; and the spirit of the scene, and of the moonlight, and of Nature, seemed harmoniously to mingle with the spirit of wine.

## *Chapter 11*

The twain cantered along for some time without speech, Tess as she clung to him still panting in her triumph, yet in other respects dubious. She had perceived that the horse was not the spirited one he sometimes rode, and felt no alarm on that score, though her seat was precarious enough despite her tight hold of him. She begged him to slow the animal to a walk, which Alec accordingly did.

'Neatly done, was it not, dear Tess?' he said by and by.

'Yes!' said she. 'I am sure I ought to be much obliged to you.

'And are you?'

She did not reply.

'Tess, why do you always dislike my kissing you?'

'I suppose – because I don't love you.'

'You are quite sure?'

'I am angry with you sometimes!'

'Ah, I half feared as much.' Nevertheless, Alec did not object to that confession. He knew that anything was better than frigidity. 'Why haven't you told me when I have made you angry?'

'You know very well why. Because I cannot help myself here.'

'I haven't offended you often by love-making?'

'You have sometimes.'

'How many times?'

'You know as well as I – too many times.'

'Every time I have tried?'

She was silent, and the horse ambled along for a considerable distance, till a faint luminous fog, which had hung in the hollows all the evening, became general and enveloped them. It seemed to hold the moonlight in suspension, rendering it more pervasive than in clear air. Whether on this account, or from absent-mindedness, or from sleepiness, she did not perceive that they had long ago passed the point at which the lane to Trantridge branched from the highway, and that her conductor had not taken the Trantridge track.

She was inexpressibly weary. She had risen at five o'clock every morning of that week, had been on foot the whole of each day, and on this evening had in addition walked the three miles to Chaseborough, waited three hours for her neighbours without eating or drinking, her impatience to start them preventing either; she had then walked a mile of the way home, and had undergone the excitement of the quarrel, till, with the slow progress of their steed, it was now nearly one o'clock. Only once, however, was she overcome by actual drowsiness. In that moment of oblivion her head sank gently against him.

D'Urberville stopped the horse, withdrew his feet from the stirrups, turned sideways on the saddle, and enclosed her waist with his arm to support her.

This immediately put her on the defensive, and with one of those sudden impulses of reprisal to which she was liable she gave him a little push from her. In his ticklish position he nearly lost his balance and only just avoided rolling over into the road, the horse, though a powerful one, being fortunately the quietest he rode.

'That is devilish unkind!' he said. 'I mean no harm – only to keep you from falling.'

She pondered suspiciously; till, thinking that this might after all be true, she relented, and said quite humbly, 'I beg your pardon, sir.'

'I won't pardon you unless you show some confidence in me. Good God!' he burst out, 'what am I, to be repulsed so by a mere chit like you? For near three mortal months have you trifled with my feelings, eluded me, and snubbed me; and I won't stand it!'

'I'll leave you tomorrow, sir.'

'No, you will not leave me tomorrow! Will you, I ask once more, show your belief in me by letting me clasp you with my arm? Come, between us two and nobody else, now. We know each other well; and you know that I love you, and think you the prettiest girl in the world, which you are. Mayn't I treat you as a lover?'

She drew a quick pettish breath of objection, writhing uneasily on her seat, looked far ahead, and murmured, 'I don't know – I wish – how can I say yes or no when – '

He settled the matter by clasping his arm round her as he desired, and Tess expressed no further negative. Thus they sidled slowly onward till it struck her they had been advancing for an unconscionable time – far longer than was usually occupied by the short journey from Chaseborough, even at this walking pace, and that they were no longer on hard road, but in a mere trackway.

'Why, where be we?' she exclaimed.

'Passing by a wood.'

'A wood – what wood? Surely we are quite out of the road?'

'A bit of The Chase – the oldest wood in England. It is a lovely night, and why should we not prolong our ride a little?'

'How could you be so treacherous!' said Tess, between archness and real dismay, and getting rid of his arm by pulling open his fingers one by one, though at the risk of slipping off herself. 'Just when I've been putting such trust in you, and obliging you to please you, because I thought I had wronged you by that push! Please set me down, and let me walk home.'

'You cannot walk home, darling, even if the air were clear. We are miles away from Trantridge, if I must tell you, and in this growing fog you might wander for hours among these trees.'

'Never mind that,' she coaxed. 'Put me down, I beg you. I don't mind where it is; only let me get down, sir, please!'

'Very well, then, I will – on one condition. Having brought you here to this out-of-the-way place, I feel myself responsible for your safe-conduct home, whatever you may yourself feel about it. As to your getting to Trantridge without assistance, it is quite impossible; for, to tell the truth, dear, owing to this fog, which so disguises everything, I don't quite know where we are myself. Now, if you will promise to wait beside the horse while I walk through the bushes till I come to some road or house, and ascertain exactly our whereabouts, I'll deposit you here willingly. When I come back I'll give you full directions, and if you insist upon walking you may; or you may ride – at your pleasure.'

She accepted these terms, and slid off on the near side, though not till he had stolen a cursory kiss. He sprang down on the other side.

'I suppose I must hold the horse?' said she.

'Oh no; it's not necessary,' replied Alec, patting the panting creature. 'He's had enough of it for tonight.'

He turned the horse's head into the bushes, hitched him on to a bough, and made a sort of couch or nest for her in the deep mass of dead leaves.

'Now, you sit there,' he said. 'The leaves have not got damp as yet. Just give an eye to the horse – it will be quite sufficient.'

He took a few steps away from her, but, returning, said, 'By the by, Tess, your father has a new cob today. Somebody gave it to him.'

'Somebody? You!'

D'Urberville nodded.

'O how very good of you that is!' she exclaimed, with a painful sense of the awkwardness of having to thank him just then.

'And the children have some toys.'

'I didn't know – you ever sent them anything!' she murmured, much moved. 'I almost wish you had not – yes, I almost wish it!'

'Why, dear?'

'It – hampers me so.'

'Tessy – don't you love me ever so little now?'

'I'm grateful,' she reluctantly admitted. 'But I fear I do not – ' The sudden vision of his passion for herself as a factor in this result so distressed her that, beginning with one slow tear, and then following with another, she wept outright.

'Don't cry, dear, dear one! Now sit down here, and wait till I come.' She passively sat down amid the leaves he had heaped, and shivered slightly. 'Are you cold?' he asked.

'Not very – a little.'

He touched her with his fingers, which sank into her as into down. 'You have only that puffy muslin dress on – how's that?'

'It's my best summer one. 'Twas very warm when I started, and I didn't know I was going to ride, and that it would be night.'

'Nights grow chilly in September. Let me see.' He pulled off a light overcoat that he had worn, and put it round her tenderly. 'That's it – now you'll feel warmer,' he continued. 'Now, my pretty, rest there; I shall soon be back again.'

Having buttoned the overcoat round her shoulders he plunged into the webs of vapour which by this time formed veils between the trees. She could hear the rustling of the branches as he ascended the adjoining slope, till his movements were no louder than the hopping of a bird, and finally died away. With the setting of the moon the pale light lessened, and Tess became invisible as she fell into reverie upon the leaves where he had left her.

In the meantime Alec d'Urberville had pushed on up the slope to clear his genuine doubt as to the quarter of The Chase they were in. He had, in fact, ridden quite at random for over an hour, taking any turning that came to hand in order to prolong companionship with her, and giving far more attention to Tess's moonlit person than to any wayside object. A little rest for the jaded animal being desirable, he did not hasten his search for landmarks. A clamber over the hill into the adjoining vale brought him to the fence of a highway whose contours he recognised, which settled the question of their whereabouts. D'Urberville thereupon turned back; but by this time the moon had quite gone down, and partly on account of the fog The Chase was wrapped in thick darkness, although morning was not far off. He was obliged to advance with outstretched hands to avoid contact with the boughs, and discovered that to hit the exact spot from which he had started was at first entirely beyond him. Roaming up and down, round and round, he at length heard a slight movement of the horse close at hand; and the sleeve of his overcoat unexpectedly caught his foot.

'Tess!' said d'Urberville.

There was no answer. The obscurity was now so great that he could see absolutely nothing but a pale nebulousness at his feet, which represented the white muslin figure he had left upon the dead leaves. Everything else was blackness alike. D'Urberville stooped; and heard a gentle regular breathing. He knelt and bent lower, till her breath warmed his face, and in a moment his cheek was in contact with hers. She was sleeping soundly, and upon her eyelashes there lingered tears.

Darkness and silence ruled everywhere around. Above them rose the primeval yews and oaks of The Chase, in which there poised gentle roosting birds in their last nap; and about them stole the hopping rabbits and hares. But, might some say, where was Tess's guardian angel? where was the providence of her simple faith? Perhaps, like that other god of whom the ironical Tishbite spoke, he was talking, or he was pursuing, or he was in a journey, or he was sleeping and not to be awaked.

Why it was that upon this beautiful feminine tissue, sensitive as gossamer, and practically blank as snow as yet, there should have been traced such a coarse pattern as it was doomed to receive; why so often the coarse appropriates the finer thus, the wrong man the woman, the wrong woman the man, many thousand years of analytical philosophy have failed to explain to our sense of order. One may, indeed, admit the possibility of a retribution lurking in the present catastrophe. Doubtless some of Tess d'Urberville's mailed ancestors rollicking home from a fray had dealt the same measure even more ruthlessly towards peasant girls of their time. But though to visit the sins of the fathers upon the children may be a morality good enough for divinities, it is scorned by average human nature; and it therefore does not mend the matter.

As Tess's own people down in those retreats are never tired of saying among each other in their fatalistic way: 'It was to be.' There lay the pity of it. An immeasurable social chasm was to divide our heroine's personality thereafter from that previous self of hers who stepped from her mother's door to try her fortune at Trantridge poultry-farm.

END OF PHASE THE FIRST

# PHASE THE SECOND

## *Maiden No More*

## *Chapter 12*

The basket was heavy and the bundle was large, but she lugged them along like a person who did not find her especial burden in material things. Occasionally she stopped to rest in a mechanical way by some gate or post; and then, giving the baggage another hitch upon her full round arm, went steadily on again.

It was a Sunday morning in late October, about four months after Tess Durbeyfield's arrival at Trantridge, and some few weeks subsequent to the night ride in The Chase. The time was not long past daybreak, and the yellow luminosity upon the horizon behind her back lighted the ridge towards which her face was set – the barrier of the vale wherein she had of late been a stranger – which she would have to climb over to reach her birthplace. The ascent was gradual on this side, and the soil and scenery differed much from those within Blackmore Vale. Even the character and accent of the two peoples had shades of difference, despite the amalgamating effects of a roundabout railway; so that, though less than twenty miles from the place of her sojourn at Trantridge, her native village had seemed a faraway spot. The field-folk shut in there traded northward and westward, travelled, courted, and married northward and westward, thought northward and westward; those on this side mainly directed their energies and attention to the east and south.

The incline was the same down which d'Urberville had driven her so wildly on that day in June. Tess went up the remainder of its length without stopping, and on reaching the edge of the escarpment gazed over the familiar green world beyond, now half veiled in mist. It was always beautiful from here; it was terribly beautiful to Tess today, for since her eyes last fell upon it she had learnt that the serpent hisses where the sweet birds sing, and her views of life had been totally changed for her by the lesson. Verily another girl than the simple one she had been at home was she who, bowed by thought, stood still here, and turned to look behind her. She could not bear to look forward into the Vale.

Ascending by the long white road that Tess herself had just laboured up, she saw a two-wheeled vehicle, beside which walked a man, who held up his hand to attract her attention.

She obeyed the signal to wait for him with unspeculative repose, and in a few minutes man and horse stopped beside her.

'Why did you slip away by stealth like this?' said d'Urberville, with upbraiding breathlessness; 'on a Sunday morning, too, when people were all in bed! I only discovered it by accident, and I have been driving like the deuce to overtake you. Just look at the mare. Why go off like this? You know that nobody wished to hinder your going. And how unnecessary it has been for you to toil along on foot, and encumber yourself with this heavy load! I have followed like a madman, simply to drive you the rest of the distance, if you won't come back.'

'I shan't come back,' said she.

'I thought you wouldn't – I said so! Well, then, put up your baskets, and let me help you on.'

She listlessly placed her basket and bundle within the dog-cart, and stepped up, and they sat side by side. She had no fear of him now, and in the cause of her confidence her sorrow lay.

D'Urberville mechanically lit a cigar, and the journey was continued with broken unemotional conversation on the commonplace objects by the wayside. He had quite forgotten his struggle to kiss her when, in the early summer, they had driven in the opposite direction along the same road. But she had not, and she sat now, like a puppet, replying to his remarks in monosyllables. After some miles they came in view of the clump of trees beyond which the village of Marlott stood. It was only then that her still face showed the least emotion, a tear or two beginning to trickle down.

'What are you crying for?' he coldly asked.

'I was only thinking that I was born over there,' murmured Tess.

'Well – we must all be born somewhere.'

'I wish I had never been born – there or anywhere else!'

'Pooh! Well, if you didn't wish to come to Trantridge why did you come?'

She did not reply.

'You didn't come for love of me, that I'll swear.'

' 'Tis quite true. If I had gone for love o' you, if I had ever sincerely loved you, if I loved you still, I should not so loathe and hate myself for my weakness as I do now! . . . My eyes were dazed by you for a little, and that was all.'

He shrugged his shoulders. She resumed – 'I didn't understand your meaning till it was too late.'

'That's what every woman says.'

'How can you dare to use such words!' she cried, turning impetuously upon him, her eyes flashing as the latent spirit (of which he was to see more someday) awoke in her. 'My God! I could knock you out of the gig! Did it never strike your mind that what every woman says some women may feel?'

'Very well,' he said, laughing; 'I am sorry to wound you. I did wrong – I admit it.' He dropped into some little bitterness as he continued: 'Only you needn't be so everlastingly flinging it in my face. I am ready to pay to the uttermost farthing. You know you need not work in the fields or the dairies again. You know you may clothe yourself with the best, instead of in the bald plain way you have lately affected, as if you couldn't get a ribbon more than you earn.'

Her lip lifted slightly, though there was little scorn, as a rule, in her large and impulsive nature.

'I have said I will not take anything more from you, and I will not – I cannot! I *should* be your creature to go on doing that, and I won't!'

'One would think you were a princess from your manner, in addition to a true and original d'Urberville – ha! ha! Well, Tess, dear, I can say no more. I suppose I am a bad fellow – a damn bad fellow. I was born bad, and I have lived bad, and I shall die bad in all probability. But, upon my lost soul, I won't be bad towards you again, Tess. And if certain circumstances should arise – you understand – in which you are in the least need, the least difficulty, send me one line, and you shall have by return whatever you require. I may not be at Trantridge – I am going to London for a time – I can't stand the old woman. But all letters will be forwarded.

She said that she did not wish him to drive her further, and they stopped just under the clump of trees. D'Urberville alighted, and lifted her down bodily in his arms, afterwards placing her articles on the ground beside her. She bowed to him slightly, her eye just lingering in his; and then she turned to take the parcels for departure.

Alec d'Urberville removed his cigar, bent towards her, and said – 'You are not going to turn away like that, dear? Come!'

'If you wish,' she answered indifferently. 'See how you've mastered me!'

She thereupon turned round and lifted her face to his, and remained like a marble term while he imprinted a kiss upon her cheek – half perfunctorily, half as if zest had not yet quite died out. Her eyes vaguely rested upon the remotest trees in the lane while the kiss was given, as though she were nearly unconscious of what he did.

'Now the other side, for old acquaintance' sake.'

She turned her head in the same passive way, as one might turn at the request of a sketcher or hairdresser, and he kissed the other side, his lips touching cheeks that were damp and smoothly chill as the skin of the mushrooms in the fields around.

'You don't give me your mouth and kiss me back. You never willingly do that – you'll never love me, I fear.'

'I have said so, often. It is true. I have never really and truly loved you, and I think I never can.' She added mournfully, 'Perhaps, of all things, a lie on this thing would do the most good to me now; but I have honour enough left, little as 'tis, not to tell that lie. If I did love you I may have the best o' causes for letting you know it. But I don't.'

He emitted a laboured breath, as if the scene were getting rather oppressive to his heart, or to his conscience, or to his gentility.

'Well, you are absurdly melancholy, Tess. I have no reason for flattering you now, and I can say plainly that you need not be so sad. You can hold your own for beauty against any woman of these parts, gentle or simple; I say it to you as a practical man and well-wisher. If you are wise you will show it to the world more than you do before it fades . . . And yet, Tess, will you come back to me? Upon my soul I don't like to let you go like this!'

'Never, never! I made up my mind as soon as I saw – what I ought to have seen sooner; and I won't come.'

'Then good-morning, my four months' cousin – goodbye!'

He leapt up lightly, arranged the reins, and was gone between the tall red-berried hedges.

Tess did not look after him, but slowly wound along the crooked lane. It was still early, and though the sun's lower limb was just free of the hill, his rays, ungenial and peering, addressed the eye rather than the touch as yet. There was not a human soul near. Sad October and her sadder self seemed the only two existences haunting that lane.

As she walked, however, some footsteps approached behind her, the footsteps of a man; and owing to the briskness of his advance he was close at her heels and had said 'Good-morning' before she had been long aware of his propinquity. He appeared to be an artisan of some sort, and carried a tin pot of red paint in his hand. He asked in a businesslike manner if he should take her basket, which she permitted him to do, walking beside him.

'It is early to be astir this Sabbath morn!' he said cheerfully.

'Yes,' said Tess.

'When most people are at rest from their week's work.'

She also assented to this.

'Though I do more real work today than all the week besides.'

'Do you?'

'All the week I work for the glory of man, and on Sunday for the glory of God. That's more real than the other – hey? I have a little to do here at this stile.' The man turned as he spoke to an opening at the roadside leading into a pasture. 'If you'll wait a moment,' he added, 'I shall not be long.'

As he had her basket she could not well do otherwise; and she waited, observing him. He set down her basket and the tin pot, and stirring the paint with the brush that was in it began painting large square letters on the middle board of the three composing the stile, placing a comma after each word, as if to give pause while that word was driven well home to the reader's heart; 'Thy, damnation, slumbereth, not.' 2 Peter 2: 3

Against the peaceful landscape, the pale, decaying tints of the copses, the blue air of the horizon and the lichened stile-boards, these staring vermilion words shone forth. They seemed to shout themselves out and make the atmosphere ring. Some people might have cried 'Alas, poor Theology!' at the hideous defacement – the last grotesque phase of a creed which had served mankind well in its time. But the words entered Tess with accusatory horror. It was as if this man had known her recent history; yet he was a total stranger.

Having finished his text he picked up her basket, and she mechanically resumed her walk beside him.

'Do you believe what you paint?' she asked in low tones.

'Believe that text? Do I believe in my own existence!'

'But,' said she tremulously, 'suppose your sin was not of your own seeking?'

He shook his head.

'I cannot split hairs on that burning query,' he said. 'I have walked hundreds of miles this past summer, painting these textes on every wall, gate, and stile in the length and breadth of this district. I leave their application to the hearts of the people who read 'em.'

'I think they are horrible,' said Tess. 'Crushing! killing!'

'That's what they are meant to be!' he replied in a trade voice. 'But you should read my hottest ones – them I kips for slums and seaports. They'd make ye wriggle! Not but what this is a very good text for rural districts . . . Ah –

there's a nice bit of blank wall up by that barn standing to waste. I must put one there – one that it will be good for dangerous young females like yerself to heed. Will ye wait, missy?'

'No,' said she; and taking her basket Tess trudged on. A little way forward she turned her head. The old grey wall began to advertise a similar fiery lettering to the first, with a strange and unwonted mien, as if distressed at duties it had never before been called upon to perform. It was with a sudden flush that she read and realised what was to be the inscription he was now halfway through; 'Thou, shalt, not, commit, —'

Her cheerful friend saw her looking, stopped his brush, and shouted – 'If you want to ask for edification on these things of moment, there's a very earnest good man going to preach a charity-sermon today in the parish you are going to – Mr Clare of Emminster. I'm not of his persuasion now, but he's a good man, and he'll expound as well as any parson I know. 'Twas he began the work in me.'

But Tess did not answer; she throbbingly resumed her walk, her eyes fixed on the ground. 'Pooh – I don't believe God said such things!' she murmured contemptuously when her flush had died away.

A plume of smoke soared up suddenly from her father's chimney, the sight of which made her heart ache. The aspect of the interior, when she reached it, made her heart ache more. Her mother, who had just come down stairs, turned to greet her from the fireplace, where she was kindling barked-oak twigs under the breakfast kettle. The young children were still above, as was also her father, it being Sunday morning, when he felt justified in lying an additional half-hour.

'Well! – my dear Tess!' exclaimed her surprised mother, jumping up and kissing the girl. 'How be ye? I didn't see you till you was in upon me! Have you come home to be married?'

'No, I have not come for that, mother.'

'Then for a holiday?'

'Yes – for a holiday; for a long holiday,' said Tess.

'What, isn't your cousin going to do the handsome thing?'

'He's not my cousin, and he's not going to marry me.'

Her mother eyed her narrowly.

'Come, you have not told me all,' she said.

Then Tess went up to her mother, put her face upon Joan's neck, and told.

'And yet th'st not got him to marry 'ee!' reiterated her mother. 'Any woman would have done it but you, after that!'

'Perhaps any woman would except me.'

'It would have been something like a story to come back with, if you had!' continued Mrs Durbeyfield, ready to burst into tears of vexation. 'After all the talk about you and him which has reached us here, who would have expected it to end like this! Why didn't ye think of doing some good for your family instead o' thinking only of yourself? See how I've got to teave and slave, and your poor weak father with his heart clogged like a dripping-pan. I did hope for something to come out o' this! To see what a pretty pair you and he made that day when you drove away together four months ago! See what he has given us – all, as we thought, because we were his kin. But if he's not, it must have been done because of his love for 'ee. And yet you've not got him to marry!'

Get Alec d'Urberville in the mind to marry her! He marry *her!* On matrimony he had never once said a word. And what if he had? How a convulsive snatching at social salvation might have impelled her to answer him she could not say. But her poor foolish mother little knew her present feeling towards this man. Perhaps it was unusual in the circumstances, unlucky, unaccountable; but there it was; and this, as she had said, was what made her detest herself. She had never wholly cared for him, she did not at all care for him now. She had dreaded him, winced before him, succumbed to adroit advantages he took of her helplessness; then, temporarily blinded by his ardent manners, had been stirred to confused surrender awhile: had suddenly despised and disliked him, and had run away. That was all. Hate him she did not quite; but he was dust and ashes to her, and even for her name's sake she scarcely wished to marry him.

'You ought to have been more careful if you didn't mean to get him to make you his wife!'

'O mother, my mother!' cried the agonised girl, turning passionately upon her parent as if her poor heart would break. 'How could I be expected to know? I was a child when I left this house four months ago. Why didn't you tell me there was danger in menfolk? Why didn't you warn me? Ladies know what to fend hands against, because they read novels that tell them of these tricks; but I never had the chance o' learning in that way, and you did not help me!'

Her mother was subdued.

'I thought if I spoke of his fond feelings and what they might lead to, you would be hontish wi' him and lose your chance,' she murmured, wiping her eyes with her apron. 'Well, we must make the best of it, I suppose. 'Tis nater, after all, and what do please God!'

## *Chapter 13*

The event of Tess Durbeyfield's return from the manor of her bogus kinsfolk was rumoured abroad, if rumour be not too large a word for a space of a square mile. In the afternoon several young girls of Marlott, former schoolfellows and acquaintances of Tess, called to see her, arriving dressed in their best starched and ironed, as became visitors to a person who had made a transcendent conquest (as they supposed), and sat round the room looking at her with great curiosity. For the fact that it was this said thirty-first cousin, Mr d'Urberville, who had fallen in love with her, a gentleman not altogether local, whose reputation as a reckless gallant and heart-breaker was beginning to spread beyond the immediate boundaries of Trantridge, lent Tess's supposed position, by its fearsomeness, a far higher fascination than it would have exercised if unhazardous.

Their interest was so deep that the younger ones whispered when her back was turned – 'How pretty she is; and how that best frock do set her off! I believe it cost an immense deal, and that it was a gift from him.'

Tess, who was reaching up to get the tea-things from the corner-cupboard, did not hear these commentaries. If she had heard them, she might soon have set her friends right on the matter. But her mother heard, and Joan's simple vanity having been denied the hope of a dashing marriage, fed itself as well as it could upon the sensation of a dashing flirtation. Upon the whole she felt gratified, even though such a limited and evanescent triumph should involve her daughter's reputation; it might end in marriage yet, and in the warmth of her responsiveness to their admiration she invited her visitors to stay to tea.

Their chatter, their laughter, their good-humoured innuendoes, above all, their flashes and flickerings of envy, revived Tess's spirits also; and, as the evening wore on, she caught the infection of their excitement, and grew almost gay. The marble hardness left her face, she moved with something of her old bounding step, and flushed in all her young beauty.

At moments, in spite of thought, she would reply to their enquiries with a manner of superiority, as if recognising that her experiences in the field of courtship had, indeed, been slightly enviable. But so far was she from being, in the words of Robert South, 'in love with her own ruin,' that the illusion was transient as lightning; cold reason came back to mock her spasmodic weakness; the ghastliness of her momentary pride would convict her, and recall her to reserved listlessness again.

And the despondency of the next morning's dawn, when it was no longer Sunday, but Monday; and no best clothes; and the laughing visitors were gone, and she awoke alone in her old bed, the innocent younger children breathing softly around her. In place of the excitement of her return, and the interest it had inspired, she saw before her a long and stony highway which she had to tread, without aid, and with little sympathy. Her depression was then terrible, and she could have hidden herself in a tomb.

In the course of a few weeks Tess revived sufficiently to show herself so far as was necessary to get to church one Sunday morning. She liked to hear the chanting – such as it was – and the old Psalms, and to join in the Morning Hymn. That innate love of melody, which she had inherited from her ballad-singing mother, gave the simplest music a power over her which could well-nigh drag her heart out of her bosom at times.

To be as much out of observation as possible for reasons of her own, and to escape the gallantries of the young men, she set out before the chiming began, and took a back seat under the gallery, close to the lumber, where only old men and women came, and where the bier stood on end among the churchyard tools.

Parishioners dropped in by twos and threes, deposited themselves in rows before her, rested three-quarters of a minute on their foreheads as if they were praying, though they were not; then sat up, and looked around. When the chants came on one of her favourites happened to be chosen among the rest – the old double chant 'Langdon' – but she did not know what it was called, though she would much have liked to know. She thought, without exactly wording the thought, how strange and godlike was a composer's power, who from the grave could lead through sequences of emotion, which he alone had felt at first, a girl like her who had never heard of his name, and never would have a clue to his personality.

The people who had turned their heads turned them again as the service proceeded; and at last observing her they whispered to each other. She knew what their whispers were about, grew sick at heart, and felt that she could come to church no more.

The bedroom which she shared with some of the children formed her retreat more continually than ever. Here, under her few square yards of thatch, she watched winds, and snows, and rains, gorgeous sunsets, and successive moons at their full. So close kept she that at length almost everybody thought she had gone away.

The only exercise that Tess took at this time was after dark; and it was then, when out in the woods, that she seemed least solitary. She knew how to hit to a hair's-breadth that moment of evening when the light and the darkness are so evenly balanced that the constraint of day and the suspense of night neutralise each other, leaving absolute mental liberty. It is then that the plight of being alive becomes attenuated to its least possible dimensions. She had no fear of the shadows; her sole idea seemed to be to shun mankind – or rather that cold accretion called the world, which, so terrible in the mass, is so unformidable, even pitiable, in its units.

On these lonely hills and dales her quiescent glide was of a piece with the element she moved in. Her flexuous and stealthy figure became an integral part of the scene. At times her whimsical fancy would intensify natural processes around her till they seemed a part of her own story. Rather they became a part of it; for the world is only a psychological phenomenon, and what they seemed they were. The midnight airs and gusts, moaning amongst the tightly-wrapped buds and bark of the winter twigs, were formulae of bitter reproach. A wet day was the expression of irremediable grief at her weakness in the mind of some vague ethical being whom she could not class definitely as the God of her childhood, and could not comprehend as any other.

But this encompassment of her own characterisation, based on shreds of convention, peopled by phantoms and voices antipathetic to her, was a sorry and mistaken creation of Tess's fancy – a cloud of moral hobgoblins by which she was terrified without reason. It was they that were out of harmony with the actual world, not she. Walking among the sleeping birds in the hedges, watching the skipping rabbits on a moonlit warren, or standing under a pheasant-laden bough, she looked upon herself as a figure of Guilt intruding into the haunts of Innocence. But all the while she was making a distinction where there was no difference. Feeling herself in antagonism she was quite in accord. She had been made to break an accepted social law, but no law known to the environment in which she fancied herself such an anomaly.

## *Chapter 14*

It was a hazy sunrise in August. The denser nocturnal vapours, attacked by the warm beams, were dividing and shrinking into isolated fleeces within hollows and coverts, where they waited till they should be dried away to nothing.

The sun, on account of the mist, had a curious sentient, personal look, demanding the masculine pronoun for its adequate expression. His present aspect, coupled with the lack of all human forms in the scene, explained the old-time heliolatries in a moment. One could feel that a saner religion had never prevailed under the sky. The luminary was a golden-haired, beaming, mild-eyed, Godlike creature, gazing down in the vigour and intentness of youth upon an earth that was brimming with interest for him.

His light, a little later, broke through chinks of cottage shutters, throwing stripes like red-hot pokers upon cupboards, chests of drawers, and other furniture within; and awakening harvesters who were not already astir.

But of all ruddy things that morning the brightest were two broad arms of painted wood, which rose from the margin of a yellow cornfield hard by Marlott village. They, with two others below, formed the revolving Maltese cross of the reaping-machine, which had been brought to the field on the previous evening to be ready for operations this day. The paint with which they were smeared, intensified in hue by the sunlight, imparted to them a look of having been dipped in liquid fire.

The field had already been 'opened'; that is to say, a lane a few feet wide had been hand-cut through the wheat along the whole circumference of the field, for the first passage of the horses and machine.

Two groups, one of men and lads, the other of women, had come down the lane just at the hour when the shadows of the eastern hedge-top struck the west hedge midway, so that the heads of the groups were enjoying sunrise while their feet were still in the dawn. They disappeared from the lane between the two stone posts which flanked the nearest field-gate.

Presently there arose from within a ticking like the lovemaking of the grasshopper. The machine had begun, and a moving concatenation of three horses and the aforesaid long rickety machine was visible over the gate, a driver sitting upon one of the hauling horses, and an attendant on the seat of the implement. Along one side of the field the whole wain went, the arms of the mechanical reaper revolving slowly, till it passed down the hill quite out of sight. In a minute it came up on the other side of the field at the same equable pace; the glistening brass star in the forehead of the fore horse first catching the eye as it rose into view over the stubble, then the bright arms, and then the whole machine.

The narrow lane of stubble encompassing the field grew wider with each circuit, and the standing corn was reduced to smaller area as the morning wore on. Rabbits, hares, snakes, rats, mice, retreated inwards as into a fastness, unaware of the ephemeral nature of their refuge, and of the doom that awaited them later in the day when, their covert shrinking to a more and more horrible narrowness, they were huddled together, friends and foes, till the last few yards of upright wheat fell also under the teeth of the unerring reaper, and they were every one put to death by the sticks and stones of the harvesters.

The reaping-machine left the fallen corn behind it in little heaps, each heap being of the quantity for a sheaf; and upon these the active binders in the rear laid their hands – mainly women, but some of them men in print shirts, and trousers supported round their waists by leather straps, rendering useless the two buttons behind, which twinkled and bristled with sunbeams at every movement of each wearer, as if they were a pair of eyes in the small of his back.

But those of the other sex were the most interesting of this company of binders, by reason of the charm which is acquired by woman when she becomes part and parcel of outdoor nature, and is not merely an object set down therein as at ordinary times. A field-man is a personality afield; a field-woman is a portion of the field; she has somehow lost her own margin, imbibed the essence of her surrounding, and assimilated herself with it.

The women – or rather girls, for they were mostly young – wore drawn cotton bonnets with great flapping curtains to keep off the sun, and gloves to prevent their hands being wounded by the stubble. There was one wearing a pale pink jacket, another in a cream-coloured tight-sleeved gown, another in a petticoat as red as the arms of the reaping-machine; and others, older, in the brown-rough 'wropper' or overall – the old-established and most appropriate dress of the field-woman, which the young ones were abandoning. This morning the eye returns involuntarily to the girl in the pink cotton jacket, she being the most flexuous and finely-drawn figure of them all. But her bonnet is pulled so far over her brow that none of her face is disclosed while she binds, though her complexion may be guessed from a stray twine or two of dark brown hair which extends below the curtain of her bonnet. Perhaps one reason why she seduces casual attention is that she never courts it, though the other women often gaze around them.

Her binding proceeds with clock-like monotony. From the sheaf last finished she draws a handful of ears, patting their tips with her left palm to bring them even. Then stooping low she moves forward, gathering the corn with both hands against her knees, and pushing her left gloved hand under the bundle to meet the right on the other side, holding the corn in an embrace like that of a lover. She brings the ends of the bond together, and kneels on the sheaf while she ties it, beating back her skirts now and then when lifted by the breeze. A bit of her naked arm is visible between the buff leather of the gauntlet and the sleeve of her gown; and as the day wears on its feminine smoothness becomes scarified by the stubble, and bleeds.

At intervals she stands up to rest, and to retie her disarranged apron, or to pull her bonnet straight. Then one can see the oval face of a handsome young woman with deep dark eyes and long heavy clinging tresses, which seem to clasp in a beseeching way anything they fall against. The cheeks are paler, the teeth more regular, the red lips thinner than is usual in a country-bred girl.

It is Tess Durbeyfield, otherwise d'Urberville, somewhat changed – the same, but not the same; at the present stage of her existence living as a stranger and an alien here, though it was no strange land that she was in. After a long seclusion she had come to a resolve to undertake outdoor work in her native village, the busiest season of the year in the agricultural world having arrived, and nothing that she could do within the house being so remunerative for the time as harvesting in the fields.

The movements of the other women were more or less similar to Tess's, the whole bevy of them drawing together like dancers in a quadrille at the completion of a sheaf by each, every one placing her sheaf on end against those of the rest, till a shock, or 'stitch' as it was here called, of ten or a dozen was formed.

They went to breakfast, and came again, and the work proceeded as before. As the hour of eleven drew near a person watching her might have noticed that every now and then Tess's glance flitted wistfully to the brow of the hill, though she did not pause in her sheafing. On the verge of the hour the heads of a group of children, of ages ranging from six to fourteen, rose over the stubbly convexity of the hill.

The face of Tess flushed slightly, but still she did not pause.

The eldest of the comers, a girl who wore a triangular shawl, its corners dragging on the stubble, carried in her arms what at first sight seemed to be a doll, but proved to be an infant in long clothes. Another brought some lunch. The harvesters ceased working, took their provisions, and sat down against one of the shocks. Here they fell to, the men plying a stone jar freely, and passing round a cup.

Tess Durbeyfield had been one of the last to suspend her labours. She sat down at the end of the shock, her face turned somewhat away from her companions. When she had deposited herself a man in a rabbit-skin cap and with a red handkerchief tucked into his belt, held the cup of ale over the top of the shock for her to drink. But she did not accept his offer. As soon as her lunch was spread she called up the big girl her sister, and took the baby off her, who, glad to be relieved of the burden, went away to the next shock and joined the other children playing there. Tess, with a curiously stealthy yet courageous movement, and with a still rising colour, unfastened her frock and began suckling the child.

The men who sat nearest considerately turned their faces towards the other end of the field, some of them beginning to smoke; one, with absent-minded fondness, regretfully stroking the jar that would no longer yield a stream. All the women but Tess fell into animated talk, and adjusted the disarranged knots of their hair.

When the infant had taken its fill the young mother sat it upright in her lap, and looking into the far distance dandled it with a gloomy indifference that was almost dislike; then all of a sudden she fell to violently kissing it some dozens of times as if she could never leave off, the child crying at the vehemence of an onset which strangely combined passionateness with contempt.

'She's fond of that there child, though she mid pretend to hate en, and say she wishes the baby and her too were in the churchyard,' observed the woman in the red petticoat.

'She'll soon leave off saying that,' replied the one in buff. 'Lord, 'tis wonderful what a body can get used to o' that sort in time!'

'A little more than persuading had to do wi' the coming o't, I reckon. There were they that heard a sobbing one night last year in The Chase; and it mid ha' gone hard wi' a certain party if folks had come along.'

'Well, a little more, or a little less, 'twas a thousand pities that it should have happened to she, of all others. But 'tis always the comeliest! The plain ones be as safe as churches – hey, Jenny?' The speaker turned to one of the group who certainly was not ill-defined as plain.

It was a thousand pities, indeed; it was impossible for even an enemy to feel otherwise on looking at Tess as she sat there, with her flower-like mouth and large tender eyes, neither black nor blue nor grey nor violet; rather all those shades together, and a hundred others, which could be seen if one looked into their irises – shade behind shade – tint beyond tint – around pupils that had no bottom; an almost standard woman, but for the slight incautiousness of character inherited from her race.

A resolution which had surprised herself had brought her into the fields this week for the first time during many months. After wearing and wasting her palpitating heart with every engine of regret that lonely inexperience could devise, common-sense had illumined her. She felt that she would do well to be useful again – to taste anew sweet independence at any price. The past was past; whatever it had been it was no more at hand. Whatever its consequences, time would close over them; they would all in a few years be as if they had never been, and she herself grassed down and forgotten. Meanwhile the trees were just as green as before; the birds sang and the sun shone as clearly now as ever. The familiar surroundings had not darkened because of her grief, nor sickened because of her pain.

She might have seen that what had bowed her head so profoundly – the thought of the world's concern at her situation – was founded on an illusion. She was not an existence, an experience, a passion, a structure of sensations, to anybody but herself. To all humankind besides Tess was only a passing thought. Even to friends she was no more than a frequently passing thought. If she made herself miserable the livelong night and day it was only this much to them – 'Ah, she makes herself unhappy.' If she tried to be cheerful, to dismiss all care, to take pleasure in the daylight, the flowers, the baby, she could only be this idea to them – 'Ah, she bears it very well.' Moreover, alone in a desert island would she have been wretched at what had happened to her? Not greatly. If she could have been but just created, to discover herself as a spouseless mother, with no experience of life except as the parent of a nameless child, would the position have caused her to despair? No, she would have taken it calmly, and found pleasures therein. Most of the misery had been generated by her conventional aspect, and not by her innate sensations.

Whatever Tess's reasoning, some spirit had induced her to dress herself up neatly as she had formerly done, and come out into the fields, harvest-hands being greatly in demand just then. This was why she had borne herself with dignity, and had looked people calmly in the face at times, even when holding the baby in her arms.

The harvest-men rose from the shock of corn, and stretched their limbs, and extinguished their pipes. The horses, which had been unharnessed and fed, were again attached to the scarlet machine. Tess, having quickly eaten her own meal, beckoned to her eldest sister to come and take away the baby, fastened her dress, put on the buff gloves again, and stooped anew to draw a bond from the last completed sheaf for the tying of the next.

In the afternoon and evening the proceedings of the morning were continued, Tess staying on till dusk with the body of harvesters. Then they all rode home in one of the largest wagons, in the company of a broad tarnished moon that had risen from the ground to the eastwards, its face resembling the outworn gold-leaf halo of some worm-eaten Tuscan saint. Tess's female companions sang songs, and showed themselves very sympathetic and glad at her reappearance out of doors, though they could not refrain from mischievously throwing in a few verses of the ballad about the maid who went to the merry green wood and came back a changed state. There are counterpoises and compensations in life; and the event which had made of her a social warning had also for the moment made her the most interesting personage in the village to many. Their friendliness won her still farther away from herself, their lively spirits were contagious, and she became almost gay.

But now that her moral sorrows were passing away a fresh one arose on the natural side of her which knew no social law. When she reached home it was to learn to her grief that the baby had been suddenly taken ill since the afternoon. Some such collapse had been probable, so tender and puny was its frame; but the event came as a shock nevertheless.

The baby's offence against society in coming into the world was forgotten by the girl-mother; her soul's desire was to continue that offence by preserving the life of the child. However, it soon grew clear that the hour of emancipation for that little prisoner of the flesh was to arrive earlier than her worst misgivings had conjectured. And when she had discovered this she was plunged into a misery which transcended that of the child's simple loss. Her baby had not been baptised.

Tess had drifted into a frame of mind which accepted passively the consideration that if she should have to burn for what she had done, burn she must, and there was an end of it. Like all village girls she was well grounded in the Holy Scriptures, and had dutifully studied the histories of Aholah and Aholibah, and knew the inferences to be drawn therefrom. But when the same question arose with regard to the baby, it had a very different colour. Her darling was about to die, and no salvation.

It was nearly bedtime, but she rushed downstairs and asked if she might send for the parson. The moment happened to be one at which her father's sense of the antique nobility of his family was highest, and his sensitiveness to the smudge which Tess had set upon that nobility most pronounced, for he had just returned from his weekly booze at Rolliver's Inn. No parson should come inside his door, he declared, prying into his affairs, just then, when, by her shame, it had become more necessary than ever to hide them. He locked the door and put the key in his pocket.

The household went to bed, and, distressed beyond measure, Tess retired also. She was continually waking as she lay, and in the middle of the night found that the baby was still worse. It was obviously dying – quietly and painlessly, but none the less surely.

In her misery she rocked herself upon the bed. The clock struck the solemn hour of one, that hour when fancy stalks outside reason, and malignant possibilities stand rock-firm as facts. She thought of the child consigned to the nethermost corner of hell, as its double doom for lack of baptism and lack of legitimacy; saw the archfiend tossing it with his three-pronged fork, like the one they used for heating the oven on baking days; to which picture she added many other quaint and curious details of torment sometimes taught the young in this Christian country. The lurid presentment so powerfully affected her imagination in the silence of the sleeping house that her nightgown became damp with perspiration, and the bedstead shook with each throb of her heart.

The infant's breathing grew more difficult, and the mother's mental tension increased. It was useless to devour the little thing with kisses; she could stay in bed no longer, and walked feverishly about the room.

'O merciful God, have pity; have pity upon my poor baby!' she cried. 'Heap as much anger as you want to upon me, and welcome; but pity the child!'

She leant against the chest of drawers, and murmured incoherent supplications for a long while, till she suddenly started up.

'Ah! perhaps baby can be saved! Perhaps it will be just the same!'

She spoke so brightly that it seemed as though her face might have shone in the gloom surrounding her.

She lit a candle, and went to a second and a third bed under the wall, where she awoke her young sisters and brothers, all of whom occupied the same room. Pulling out the washing-stand so that she could get behind it, she poured some water from a jug, and made them kneel around, putting their hands together with fingers exactly vertical. While the children, scarcely awake, awe-stricken at her manner, their eyes growing larger and larger, remained in this position, she took the baby from her bed – a child's child – so immature as scarce to seem a sufficient personality to endow its producer with the maternal title. Tess then stood erect with the infant on her arm beside the basin, the next sister held the Prayer-Book open before her, as the clerk at church held it before the parson; and thus the girl set about baptising her child.

Her figure looked singularly tall and imposing as she stood in her long white nightgown, a thick cable of twisted dark hair hanging straight down her back to her waist. The kindly dimness of the weak candle abstracted from her form and features the little blemishes which sunlight might have revealed – the stubble scratches upon her wrists, and the weariness of her eyes – her high enthusiasm having a transfiguring effect upon the face which had been her undoing, showing it as a thing of immaculate beauty, with a touch of dignity which was almost regal. The little ones kneeling round, their sleepy eyes blinking and red, awaited her preparations full of a suspended wonder which their physical heaviness at that hour would not allow to become active.

The most impressed of them said:

'Be you really going to christen him, Tess?'

The girl-mother replied in a grave affirmative.

'What's his name going to be?'

She had not thought of that, but a name suggested by a phrase in the book of Genesis came into her head as she proceeded with the baptismal service, and now she pronounced it:

'Sorrow, I baptise thee in the name of the Father, and of the Son, and of the Holy Ghost.'

She sprinkled the water, and there was silence.

'Say "Amen", children.'

The tiny voices piped in obedient response 'Amen!'

Tess went on:

'We receive this child' – and so forth – 'and do sign him with the sign of the Cross.'

Here she dipped her hand into the basin, and fervently drew an immense cross upon the baby with her forefinger, continuing with the customary sentences as to his manfully fighting against sin, the world, and the devil, and being a faithful soldier and servant unto his life's end. She duly went on with the Lord's Prayer, the children lisping it after her in a thin gnat-like wail, till, at the conclusion, raising their voices to clerk's pitch, they again piped into the silence, 'Amen!'

Then their sister, with much augmented confidence in the efficacy of this sacrament, poured forth from the bottom of her heart the thanksgiving that follows, uttering it boldly and triumphantly in the stopped-diapason note which her voice acquired when her heart was in her speech, and which will never be forgotten by those who knew her. The ecstasy of faith almost apotheosised her; it set upon her face a glowing irradiation, and brought a red spot into the middle of each cheek; while the miniature candle-flame inverted in her eye-pupils shone like a diamond. The children gazed up at her with more and more reverence, and no longer had a will for questioning. She did not look like Sissy to them now, but as a being large, towering, and awful – a divine personage with whom they had nothing in common.

Poor Sorrow's campaign against sin, the world, and the devil was doomed to be of limited brilliancy – luckily perhaps for himself, considering his beginnings. In the blue of the morning that fragile soldier and servant breathed his last, and when the other children awoke they cried bitterly, and begged Sissy to have another pretty baby.

The calmness which had possessed Tess since the christening remained with her in the infant's loss. In the daylight, indeed, she felt her terrors about his soul to have been somewhat exaggerated; whether well founded or not she had no uneasiness now, reasoning that if Providence would not ratify such an act of approximation she, for one, did not value the kind of heaven lost by the irregularity – either for herself or for her child.

So passed away Sorrow the Undesired – that intrusive creature, that bastard gift of shameless Nature who respects not the social law; a waif to whom eternal Time had been a matter of days merely, who knew not that such things as years and centuries ever were; to whom the cottage interior was the universe, the week's weather climate, newborn babyhood human existence, and the instinct to suck human knowledge.

Tess, who mused on the christening a good deal, wondered if it were doctrinally sufficient to secure a Christian burial for the child. Nobody could tell this but the parson of the parish, and he was a newcomer, and did not know her. She went to his house after dusk, and stood by the gate, but could not summon courage to go in. The enterprise would have been abandoned if she had not by accident met him coming homeward as she turned away. In the gloom she did not mind speaking freely.

'I should like to ask you something, sir.'

He expressed his willingness to listen, and she told the story of the baby's illness and the extemporised ordinance.

'And now, sir,' she added earnestly, 'can you tell me this – will it be just the same for him as if you had baptised him?'

Having the natural feelings of a tradesman at finding that a job he should have been called in for had been unskilfully botched by his customers among themselves, he was disposed to say no. Yet the dignity of the girl, the strange tenderness in her voice, combined to affect his nobler impulses – or rather those that he had left in him after ten years of endeavour to graft technical belief on actual scepticism. The man and the ecclesiastic fought within him, and the victory fell to the man.

'My dear girl,' he said, 'it will be just the same.'

'Then will you give him a Christian burial?' she asked quickly.

The vicar felt himself cornered. Hearing of the baby's illness, he had conscientiously gone to the house after nightfall to perform the rite, and, unaware that the refusal to admit him had come from Tess's father and not from Tess, he could not allow the plea of necessity for its irregular administration.

'Ah – that's another matter,' he said.

'Another matter – why?' asked Tess, rather warmly.

'Well – I would willingly do so if only we two were concerned. But I must not – for certain reasons.'

'Just for once, sir!'

'Really I must not.'

'O sir!' She seized his hand as she spoke.

He withdrew it, shaking his head.

'Then I don't like you!' she burst out, 'and I'll never come to your church no more!'

'Don't talk so rashly.'

'Perhaps it will be just the same to him if you don't? . . . Will it be just the same? Don't for God's sake speak as saint to sinner, but as you yourself to me myself – poor me!'

How the vicar reconciled his answer with the strict notions he supposed himself to hold on these subjects it is beyond a layman's power to tell, though not to excuse. Somewhat moved, he said in this case also – 'It will be just the same.'

So the baby was carried in a small deal box, under an ancient woman's shawl, to the churchyard that night, and buried by lantern-light, at the cost of a shilling and a pint of beer to the sexton, in that shabby corner of God's allotment where He lets the nettles grow, and where all unbaptised infants, notorious drunkards, suicides, and others of the conjecturally damned are laid. In spite of the untoward surroundings, however, Tess bravely made a little cross of two laths and a piece of string, and having bound it with flowers, she stuck it up at the head of the grave one evening when she could enter the churchyard without being seen, putting at the foot also a bunch of the same flowers in a little jar of water to keep them alive. What matter was it that on the outside of the jar the eye of mere observation noted the words 'Keelwell's Marmalade'? The eye of maternal affection did not see them in its vision of higher things.

## *Chapter 15*

'By experience,' says Roger Ascham, 'we find out a short way by a long wandering.' Not seldom that long wandering unfits us for further travel, and of what use is our experience to us then? Tess Durbeyfield's experience was of this incapacitating kind. At last she had learned what to do; but who would now accept her doing?

If before going to the d'Urbervilles' she had vigorously moved under the guidance of sundry gnomic texts and phrases known to her and to the world in general, no doubt she would never have been imposed on. But it had not been in Tess's power – nor is it in anybody's power – to feel the whole truth of golden opinions while it is possible to profit by them. She – and how many more – might have ironically said to God with Saint Augustine: 'Thou hast counselled a better course than Thou hast permitted.'

She remained at her father's house during the winter months, plucking fowls, or cramming turkeys and geese, or making clothes for her sisters and brothers out of some finery which d'Urberville had given her, and she had put by with contempt. Apply to him she would not. But she would often clasp her hands behind her head and muse when she was supposed to be working hard.

She philosophically noted dates as they came past in the revolution of the year; the disastrous night of her undoing at Trantridge with its dark background of The Chase; also the dates of the baby's birth and death; also her own birthday; and every other day individualised by incidents in which she had taken some share. She suddenly thought one afternoon, when looking in the glass at her fairness, that there was yet another date, of greater importance to her than those; that of her own death, when all these charms would have disappeared; a day which lay sly and unseen among all the other days of the year, giving no sign or sound when she annually passed over it; but not the less surely there. When was it? Why did she not feel the chill of each yearly encounter with such a cold relation? She had Jeremy Taylor's thought that some time in the future those who had known her would say: 'It is the —th, the day that poor Tess Durbeyfield died'; and there would be nothing singular to their minds in the statement. Of that day, doomed to be her terminus in time through all the ages, she did not know the place in month, week, season, or year.

Almost at a leap Tess thus changed from simple girl to complex woman. Symbols of reflectiveness passed into her face, and a note of tragedy at times into her voice. Her eyes grew larger and more eloquent. She became what would have been called a fine creature; her aspect was fair and arresting; her soul that of a woman whom the turbulent experiences of the last year or two had quite failed to demoralise. But for the world's opinion those experiences would have been simply a liberal education.

She had held so aloof of late that her trouble, never generally known, was nearly forgotten in Marlott. But it became evident to her that she could never be really comfortable again in a place which had seen the collapse of her family's attempt to 'claim kin' – and, through her, even closer union – with the rich d'Urbervilles. At least she could not be comfortable there till long years should have obliterated her keen consciousness of it. Yet even now Tess felt the pulse of hopeful life still warm within her; she might be happy in some nook which had no memories. To escape the past and all that appertained thereto was to annihilate it, and to do that she would have to get away.

Was once lost always lost really true of chastity? she would ask herself. She might prove it false if she could veil bygones. The recuperative power which pervaded organic nature was surely not denied to maidenhood alone.

She waited a long time without finding opportunity for a new departure. A particularly fine spring came round, and the stir of germination was almost audible in the buds; it moved her, as it moved the wild animals, and made her passionate to go. At last, one day in early May, a letter reached her from a former friend of her mother's, to whom she had addressed enquiries long before – a person whom she had never seen – that a skilful milkmaid was required at a dairy-house many miles to the southward, and that the dairyman would be glad to have her for the summer months.

It was not quite so far off as could have been wished; but it was probably far enough, her radius of movement and repute having been so small. To persons of limited spheres, miles are as geographical degrees, parishes as counties, counties as provinces and kingdoms.

On one point she was resolved: there should be no more d'Urberville air-castles in the dreams and deeds of her new life. She would be the dairymaid

Tess, and nothing more. Her mother knew Tess's feeling on this point so well, though no words had passed between them on the subject, that she never alluded to the knightly ancestry now.

Yet such is human inconsistency that one of the interests of the new place to her was the accidental virtue of its lying near her forefathers' country (for they were not Blakemore men, though her mother was Blakemore to the bone). The dairy called Talbothays, for which she was bound, stood not remotely from some of the former estates of the d'Urbervilles, near the great family vaults of her granddames and their powerful husbands. She would be able to look at them, and think not only that d'Urberville, like Babylon, had fallen, but that the individual innocence of a humble descendant could lapse as silently. All the while she wondered if any strange good thing might come of her being in her ancestral land; and some spirit within her rose automatically as the sap in the twigs. It was unexpended youth, surging up anew after its temporary check, and bringing with it hope, and the invincible instinct towards self-delight.

END OF PHASE THE SECOND

# PHASE THE THIRD

## *The Rally*

## *Chapter 16*

On a thyme-scented, bird-hatching morning in May, between two and three years after the return from Trantridge – silent reconstructive years for Tess Durbeyfield – she left her home for the second time.

Having packed up her luggage so that it could be sent to her later, she started in a hired trap for the little town of Stourcastle, through which it was necessary to pass on her journey, now in a direction almost opposite to that of her first adventuring. On the curve of the nearest hill she looked back regretfully at Marlott and her father's house, although she had been so anxious to get away.

Her kindred dwelling there would probably continue their daily lives as heretofore, with no great diminution of pleasure in their consciousness, although she would be far off, and they deprived of her smile. In a few days the children would engage in their games as merrily as ever, without the sense of any gap left by her departure. This leaving of the younger children she had decided to be for the best; were she to remain they would probably gain less good by her precepts than harm by her example.

She went through Stourcastle without pausing, and onward to a junction of highways, where she could await a carrier's van that ran to the south-west; for the railways which engirdled this interior tract of country had never yet struck across it. While waiting, however, there came along a farmer in his spring cart, driving approximately in the direction that she wished to pursue. Though he was a stranger to her she accepted his offer of a seat beside him, ignoring that its motive was a mere tribute to her countenance. He was going to Weatherbury, and by accompanying him thither she could walk the remainder of the distance instead of travelling in the van by way of Casterbridge.

Tess did not stop at Weatherbury, after this long drive, further than to make a slight nondescript meal at noon at a cottage to which the farmer recommended her. Thence she started on foot, basket in hand, to reach the wide upland of heath dividing this district from the low-lying meads of a further valley in which the dairy stood that was the aim and end of her day's pilgrimage.

Tess had never before visited this part of the country, and yet she felt akin to the landscape. Not so very far to the left of her she could discern a dark patch in the scenery, which enquiry confirmed her in supposing to be trees marking the environs of Kingsbere – in the church of which parish the bones of her ancestors – her useless ancestors – lay entombed.

She had no admiration for them now; she almost hated them for the dance they had led her; not a thing of all that had been theirs did she retain but the old seal and spoon. 'Pooh – I have as much of mother as father in me!' she said. 'All my prettiness comes from her, and she was only a dairymaid.'

The journey over the intervening uplands and lowlands of Egdon, when she reached them, was a more troublesome walk than she had anticipated, the distance being actually but a few miles. It was two hours, owing to sundry wrong turnings, ere she found herself on a summit commanding the long-sought-for vale, the Valley of the Great Dairies, the valley in which milk and butter grew to rankness, and were produced more profusely, if less delicately, than at her home – the verdant plain so well watered by the river Var or Froom.

It was intrinsically different from the Vale of Little Dairies, Blackmoor Vale, which, save during her disastrous sojourn at Trantridge, she had exclusively known till now. The world was drawn to a larger pattern here. The enclosures numbered fifty acres instead of ten, the farmsteads were more extended, the groups of cattle formed tribes hereabout; there only families. These myriads of cows stretching under her eyes from the far east to the far west outnumbered any she had ever seen at one glance before. The green lea was speckled as thickly with them as a canvas by Van Alsloot or Sallaert with burghers. The ripe hue of the red and dun kine absorbed the evening sunlight, which the white-coated animals returned to the eye in rays almost dazzling, even at the distant elevation on which she stood.

The bird's-eye perspective before her was not so luxuriantly beautiful, perhaps, as that other one which she knew so well; yet it was more cheering. It lacked the intensely blue atmosphere of the rival vale, and its heavy soils and scents; the new air was clear, bracing, ethereal. The river itself, which nourished the grass and cows of these renowned dairies, flowed not like the streams in Blackmoor. Those were slow, silent, often turbid; flowing over beds of mud into which the incautious wader might sink and vanish unawares. The Froom waters were clear as the pure River of Life shown to the Evangelist, rapid as the shadow of a cloud, with pebbly shallows that prattled to the sky all day long. There the water-flower was the lily; the crowfoot here.

Either the change in the quality of the air from heavy to light, or the sense of being amid new scenes where there were no invidious eyes upon her, sent up her spirits wonderfully. Her hopes mingled with the sunshine in an ideal photosphere which surrounded her as she bounded along against the soft south wind. She heard a pleasant voice in every breeze, and in every bird's note seemed to lurk a joy.

Her face had latterly changed with changing states of mind, continually fluctuating between beauty and ordinariness, according as the thoughts were gay or grave. One day she was pink and flawless; another pale and tragical. When she was pink she was feeling less than when pale; her more perfect beauty accorded with her less elevated mood; her more intense mood with her less perfect beauty. It was her best face physically that was now set against the south wind.

The irresistible, universal, automatic tendency to find sweet pleasure somewhere, which pervades all life, from the meanest to the highest, had at length mastered Tess. Being even now only a young woman of twenty, one who mentally and sentimentally had not finished growing, it was impossible that any event should have left upon her an impression that was not in time capable of transmutation.

And thus her spirits, and her thankfulness, and her hopes, rose higher and higher. She tried several ballads, but found them inadequate; till, recollecting the psalter that her eyes had so often wandered over of a Sunday morning before she had eaten of the tree of knowledge, she chanted: 'O ye Sun and Moon . . . O ye Stars . . . ye Green Things upon the Earth . . . ye Fowls of the Air . . . Beasts and Cattle . . . Children of Men . . . bless ye the Lord, praise Him and magnify Him for ever!'

She suddenly stopped and murmured: 'But perhaps I don't quite know the Lord as yet.'

And probably the half-unconscious rhapsody was a Fetishistic utterance in a Monotheistic setting; women whose chief companions are the forms and forces of outdoor Nature retain in their souls far more of the Pagan fantasy of their remote forefathers than of the systematised religion taught their race at later date. However, Tess found at least approximate expression for her feelings in the old *Benedicite* that she had lisped from infancy; and it was enough. Such high contentment with such a slight initial performance as that of having started towards a means of independent living was a part of the Durbeyfield temperament. Tess really wished to walk uprightly, while her father did nothing of the kind; but she resembled him in being content with immediate and small achievements, and in having no mind for laborious effort towards such petty social advancement as could alone be effected by a family so heavily handicapped as the once powerful d'Urbervilles were now.

There was, it might be said, the energy of her mother's unexpended family, as well as the natural energy of Tess's years, rekindled after the experience which had so overwhelmed her for the time. Let the truth be told – women do as a rule live through such humiliations, and regain their spirits, and again look about them with an interested eye. While there's life there's hope is a conviction not so entirely unknown to the 'betrayed' as some amiable theorists would have us believe.

Tess Durbeyfield, then, in good heart, and full of zest for life, descended the Egdon slopes lower and lower towards the dairy of her pilgrimage.

The marked difference, in the final particular, between the rival vales now showed itself. The secret of Blackmoor was best discovered from the heights around; to read aright the valley before her it was necessary to descend into its midst. When Tess had accomplished this feat she found herself to be standing on a carpeted level, which stretched to the east and west as far as the eye could reach.

The river had stolen from the higher tracts and brought in particles to the vale all this horizontal land; and now, exhausted, aged, and attenuated, lay serpentining along through the midst of its former spoils.

Not quite sure of her direction Tess stood still upon the hemmed expanse of verdant flatness, like a fly on a billiard-table of indefinite length, and of no more consequence to the surroundings than that fly. The sole effect of her presence upon the placid valley so far had been to excite the mind of a solitary heron, which, after descending to the ground not far from her path, stood with neck erect, looking at her.

Suddenly there arose from all parts of the lowland a prolonged and repeated call – 'Waow! waow! waow!'

From the furthest east to the furthest west the cries spread as if by contagion, accompanied in some cases by the barking of a dog. It was not the expression of the valley's consciousness that beautiful Tess had arrived, but the ordinary announcement of milking-time – half-past four o'clock, when the dairymen set about getting in the cows.

The red and white herd nearest at hand, which had been phlegmatically waiting for the call, now trooped towards the steading in the background, their great bags of milk swinging under them as they walked. Tess followed slowly in their rear, and entered the barton by the open gate through which they had entered before her. Long thatched sheds stretched round the enclosure, their slopes encrusted with vivid green moss, and their eaves supported by wooden posts rubbed to a glossy smoothness by the flanks of infinite cows and calves of bygone years, now passed to an oblivion almost inconceivable in its profundity. Between the posts were ranged the milchers, each exhibiting herself at the present moment to a whimsical eye in the rear as a circle on two stalks, down the centre of which a switch moved pendulum-wise; while the sun, lowering itself behind this patient row, threw their shadows accurately inwards upon the wall. Thus it threw shadows of these obscure and homely figures every evening with as much care over each contour as if it had been the profile of a Court beauty on a palace wall; copied them as diligently as it had copied Olympian shapes on marble façades long ago, or the outline of Alexander, Caesar, and the Pharaohs.

They were the less restful cows that were stalled. Those that would stand still of their own will were milked in the middle of the yard, where many of such better behaved ones stood waiting now – all prime milchers, such as were seldom seen out of this valley, and not always within it; nourished by the succulent feed which the water-meads supplied at this prime season of the year. Those of them that were spotted with white reflected the sunshine in dazzling brilliancy, and the polished brass knobs on their horns glittered with something of military display. Their large-veined udders hung ponderous as sandbags, the teats sticking out like the legs of a gypsy's crock; and as each animal lingered for her turn to arrive the milk oozed forth and fell in drops to the ground.

## *Chapter 17*

The dairymaids and men had flocked down from their cottages and out of the dairy-house with the arrival of the cows from the meads; the maids walking in pattens, not on account of the weather, but to keep their shoes above the mulch of the barton. Each girl sat down on her three-legged stool, her face sideways, her right cheek resting against the cow; and looked musingly along the animal's flank at Tess as she approached. The male milkers, with hat-brims turned down, resting flat on their foreheads and gazing on the ground, did not observe her.

One of these was a sturdy middle-aged man – whose long white 'pinner' was somewhat finer and cleaner than the wraps of the others, and whose jacket underneath had a presentable marketing aspect – the master-dairyman, of whom she was in quest, his double character as a working milker and buttermaker here during six days, and on the seventh as a man in shining broad-cloth in his family pew at church, being so marked as to have inspired a rhyme –

> Dairyman Dick
> All the week –
> On Sundays Mister Richard Crick.

Seeing Tess standing at gaze he went across to her.

The majority of dairymen have a cross manner at milking-time, but it happened that Mr Crick was glad to get a new hand – for the days were busy ones now – and he received her warmly; enquiring for her mother and the rest of the family – (though this as a matter of form merely, for in reality he had not been aware of Mrs Durbeyfield's existence till apprised of the fact by a brief business-letter about Tess).

'Oh – ay, as a lad I knowed your part o' the country very well,' he said terminatively. 'Though I've never been there since. And a aged woman of ninety that used to live nigh here, but is dead and gone long ago, told me that a family of some such name as yours in Blackmoor Vale came originally from these parts, and that 'twere a old ancient race that had all but perished off the earth – though the new generations didn't know it. But, Lord, I took no notice of the old woman's ramblings, not I.'

'Oh no – it is nothing,' said Tess.

Then the talk was of business only.

'You can milk 'em clean, my maidy? I don't want my cows going azew at this time o' year.'

She reassured him on that point, and he surveyed her up and down. She had been staying indoors a good deal, and her complexion had grown delicate.

'Quite sure you can stand it? 'Tis comfortable enough here for rough folk; but we don't live in a cowcumber frame.'

She declared that she could stand it, and her zest and willingness seemed to win him over.

'Well, I suppose you'll want a dish o' tay, or victuals of some sort, hey? Not yet? Well, do as ye like about it. But faith, if 'twas I, I should be as dry as a kex wi' travelling so far.'

'I'll begin milking now, to get my hand in,' said Tess.

She drank a little milk as temporary refreshment – to the surprise – indeed, slight contempt – of Dairyman Crick, to whose mind it had apparently never occurred that milk was good as a beverage.

'Oh, if ye can swaller that, be it so,' he said indifferently, while holding up the pail that she sipped from. ' 'Tis what I hain't touched for years – not I. Rot the stuff; it would lie in my innards like lead. You can try your hand upon she,' he pursued, nodding to the nearest cow. 'Not but what she do milk rather hard.

We've hard ones and we've easy ones, like other folks. However, you'll find out that soon enough.'

When Tess had changed her bonnet for a hood, and was really on her stool under the cow, and the milk was squirting from her fists into the pail, she appeared to feel that she really had laid a new foundation for her future. The conviction bred serenity, her pulse slowed, and she was able to look about her.

The milkers formed quite a little battalion of men and maids, the men operating on the hard-teated animals, the maids on the kindlier natures. It was a large dairy. There were nearly a hundred milchers under Crick's management, all told; and of the herd the master-dairyman milked six or eight with his own hands, unless away from home. These were the cows that milked hardest of all; for his journey-milkmen being more or less casually hired, he would not entrust this half-dozen to their treatment, lest, from indifference, they should not milk them fully; nor to the maids, lest they should fail in the same way for lack of finger-grip; with the result that in course of time the cows would 'go azew' – that is, dry up. It was not the loss for the moment that made slack milking so serious, but that with the decline of demand there came decline, and ultimately cessation, of supply.

After Tess had settled down to her cow there was for a time no talk in the barton, and not a sound interfered with the purr of the milk-jets into the numerous pails, except a momentary exclamation to one or other of the beasts requesting her to turn round or stand still. The only movements were those of the milkers' hands up and down, and the swing of the cows' tails. Thus they all worked on, encompassed by the vast flat mead which extended to either slope of the valley – a level landscape compounded of old landscapes long forgotten, and, no doubt, differing in character very greatly from the landscape they composed now.

'To my thinking,' said the dairyman, rising suddenly from a cow he had just finished off, snatching up his three-legged stool in one hand and the pail in the other, and moving on to the next hard-yielder in his vicinity; 'to my thinking, the cows don't gie down their milk today as usual. Upon my life, if Winker do begin keeping back like this, she'll not be worth going under by midsummer.'

' 'Tis because there's a new hand come among us,' said Jonathan Kail. 'I've noticed such things afore.'

'To be sure. It may be so. I didn't think o't.'

'I've been told that it goes up into their horns at such times,' said a dairymaid.

'Well, as to going up into their horns,' replied Dairyman Crick dubiously, as though even witchcraft might be limited by anatomical possibilities, 'I couldn't say; I certainly could not. But as nott cows will keep it back as well as the horned ones, I don't quite agree to it. Do ye know that riddle about the nott cows, Jonathan? Why do nott cows give less milk in a year than horned?'

'I don't!' interposed the milkmaid. 'Why do they?'

'Because there bain't so many of 'em,' said the dairyman. 'Howsomever, these gam'sters do certainly keep back their milk today. Folks, we must lift up a stave or two – that's the only cure for't.'

Songs were often resorted to in dairies hereabout as an enticement to the cows when they showed signs of withholding their usual yield; and the band of milkers at this request burst into melody – in purely businesslike tones, it is true, and with no great spontaneity; the result, according to their own belief, being a decided improvement during the song's continuance. When they had gone through fourteen or fifteen verses of a cheerful ballad about a murderer who was afraid to go to bed in the dark because he saw certain brimstone flames around him, one of the male milkers said – 'I wish singing on the stoop didn't use up so much of a man's wind! You should get your harp, sir; not but what a fiddle is best.'

Tess, who had given ear to this, thought the words were addressed to the dairyman, but she was wrong. A reply, in the shape of 'Why?' came as it were out of the belly of a dun cow in the stalls; it had been spoken by a milker behind the animal, whom she had not hitherto perceived.

'Oh yes; there's nothing like a fiddle,' said the dairyman. 'Though I do think that bulls are more moved by a tune than cows – at least that's my experience. Once there was an old aged man over at Mellstock – William Dewy by name – one of the family that used to do a good deal of business as tranters over there, Jonathan, do ye mind? – I knowed the man by sight as well as I know my own brother, in a manner of speaking. Well, this man was a coming home-along from a wedding where he had been playing his fiddle, one fine moonlight night, and for shortness' sake he took a cut across Forty-acres, a field lying that way, where a bull was out to grass. The bull seed William, and took after him, horns aground, begad; and though William runned his best, and hadn't *much* drink in him (considering 'twas a wedding, and the folks well off), he found he'd never reach the fence and get over in time to save himself. Well, as a last thought, he pulled out his fiddle as he runned, and struck up a jig, turning to the bull, and backing towards the corner. The bull softened down, and stood still, looking hard at William Dewy, who fiddled on and on; till a sort of a smile stole over the bull's face. But no sooner did William stop his playing and turn to get over hedge than the bull would stop his smiling and lower his horns towards the seat of William's breeches. Well, William had to turn about and play on, willy-nilly; and 'twas only three o'clock in the world, and 'a knowed that nobody would come that way for hours, and he so leery and tired that 'a didn't know what to do. When he had scraped till about four o'clock he felt that he verily would have to give over soon, and he said to himself, "There's only this last tune between me and eternal welfare! Heaven save me, or I'm a done man." Well, then he called to mind how he'd seen the cattle kneel o' Christmas Eves in the dead o' night. It was not Christmas Eve then, but it came into his head to play a trick upon the bull. So he broke into the 'Tivity Hymn, just as at Christmas carol-singing; when, lo and behold, down went the bull on his bended knees, in his ignorance just as if 'twere the true 'Tivity night and hour. As soon as his horned friend were down, William turned, clinked off like a long-dog, and jumped safe over hedge, before the praying bull had got on his feet again to take after him. William used to say that he'd seen a man look a fool a good many times, but never such a fool as that bull looked when he found his pious feelings had been played upon, and 'twas not Christmas Eve . . . Yes, William Dewy, that was the man's name; and I can tell you to a foot where's he a-lying in Mellstock Churchyard at this very moment – just between the second yew tree and the north aisle.'

'It's a curious story; it carries us back to mediaeval times, when faith was a living thing!'

The remark, singular for a dairy-yard, was murmured by the voice behind the dun cow; but as nobody understood the reference no notice was taken, except that the narrator seemed to think it might imply scepticism as to his tale.

'Well, 'tis quite true, sir, whether or no. I knowed the man well.'

'Oh yes; I have no doubt of it,' said the person behind the dun cow.

Tess's attention was thus attracted to the dairyman's interlocutor, of whom she could see but the merest patch, owing to his burying his head so persistently in the flank of the milcher. She could not understand why he should be addressed as 'sir' even by the dairyman himself. But no explanation was discernible; he remained under the cow long enough to have milked three, uttering a private ejaculation now and then, as if he could not get on.

'Take it gentle, sir; take it gentle,' said the dairyman. ' 'Tis knack, not strength that does it.'

'So I find,' said the other, standing up at last and stretching his arms. 'I think I have finished her, however, though she made my fingers ache.'

Tess could then see him at full length. He wore the ordinary white pinner and leather leggings of a dairy-farmer when milking, and his boots were clogged with the mulch of the yard; but this was all his local livery. Beneath it was something educated, reserved, subtle, sad, differing.

But the details of his aspect were temporarily thrust aside by the discovery that he was one whom she had seen before. Such vicissitudes had Tess passed through since that time that for a moment she could not remember where she had met him; and then it flashed upon her that he was the pedestrian who had joined in the club-dance at Marlott – the passing stranger who had come she knew not whence, had danced with others but not with her, had slightingly left her, and gone on his way with his friends.

The flood of memories brought back by this revival of an incident anterior to her troubles produced a momentary dismay lest, recognising her also, he should by some means discover her story. But it passed away when she found no sign of remembrance in him. She saw by degrees that since their first and only encounter his mobile face had grown more thoughtful, and had acquired a young man's shapely moustache and beard – the latter of the palest straw colour where it began upon his cheeks, and deepening to a warm brown farther from its root. Under his linen milking-pinner he wore a dark velveteen jacket, cord breeches and gaiters, and a starched white shirt. Without the milking-gear nobody could have guessed what he was. He might with equal probability have been an eccentric landowner or a gentlemanly ploughman. That he was but a novice at dairy-work she had realised in a moment from the time he had spent upon the milking of one cow.

Meanwhile many of the milkmaids had said to one another of the newcomer, 'How pretty she is!' with something of real generosity and admiration, though with a half hope that the auditors would qualify the assertion – which, strictly speaking they might have done, prettiness being an inexact definition of what struck the eye in Tess. When the milking was finished for the evening they straggled indoors, where Mrs Crick, the dairyman's wife – who was too respectable to go out milking herself, and wore a hot stuff gown in warm weather because the dairymaids wore prints – was giving an eye to the leads and things.

Only two or three of the maids, Tess learnt, slept in the dairy-house besides herself; most of the helpers going to their homes. She saw nothing at supper-time of the superior milker who had commented on the story, and asked no questions about him, the remainder of the evening being occupied in arranging her place in the bedchamber. It was a large room over the milkhouse, some thirty feet long; the sleeping-cots of the other three indoor milkmaids being in the same apartment. They were blooming young women, and, except one, rather older then herself. By bedtime Tess was thoroughly tired, and fell asleep immediately.

But one of the girls who occupied an adjoining bed was more wakeful than Tess, and would insist upon relating to the latter various particulars of the homestead into which she had just entered. The girl's whispered words mingled with the shades, and, to Tess's drowsy mind, they seemed to be generated by the darkness in which they floated.

'Mr Angel Clare – he that is learning milking, and that plays the harp – never says much to us. He is a pa'son's son, and is too much taken up wi' his own thoughts to notice girls. He is the dairyman's pupil – learning farming in all its branches. He has learnt sheep-farming at another place, and he's now mastering dairy-work . . . Yes, he is quite the gentleman-born. His father is the Reverent Mr Clare at Emminster – a good many miles from here.'

'Oh – I have heard of him,' said her companion, now awake. 'A very earnest clergyman, is he not?'

'Yes – that he is – the earnestest man in all Wessex, they say – the last of the old Low Church sort, they tell me – for all about here be what they call High. All his sons, except our Mr Clare, be made pa'sons too.'

Tess had not at this hour the curiosity to ask why the present Mr Clare was not made a parson like his brethren and gradually fell asleep again, the words of her informant coming to her along with the smell of the cheeses in the adjoining cheese-loft, and the measured dripping of the whey from the wrings downstairs.

## *Chapter 18*

Angel Clare rises out of the past not altogether as a distinct figure, but as an appreciative voice, a long regard of fixed abstracted eyes, and a mobility of mouth somewhat too small and delicately lined for a man's, though with an unexpectedly firm close of the lower lip now and then; enough to do away with any inference of indecision. Nevertheless, something nebulous, pre-occupied, vague, in his bearing and regard, marked him as one who probably had no very definite aim or concern about his material future. Yet as a lad people had said of him that he was one who might do anything if he tried.

He was the youngest son of his father, a poor parson at the other end of the county, and had arrived at Talbothays Dairy as a six months' pupil, after going the round of some other farms, his object being to acquire a practical skill in the various processes of farming, with a view either to the Colonies, or the tenure of a home-farm, as circumstances might decide.

His entry into the ranks of the agriculturists and breeders was a step in the young man's career which had been anticipated neither by himself nor by others.

Mr Clare the elder, whose first wife had died and left him a daughter, married a second late in life. This lady had somewhat unexpectedly brought him three sons, so that between Angel, the youngest, and his father the vicar there seemed to be almost a missing generation. Of these boys the aforesaid Angel, the child of his old age, was the only son who had not taken a University degree, though he was the single one of them whose early promise might have done full justice to an academical training.

Some two or three years before Angel's appearance at the Marlott dance, on a day when he had left school and was pursuing his studies at home, a parcel came to the vicarage from the local bookseller's, directed to the Reverend James Clare. The vicar having opened it and found it to contain a book, read a few pages; whereupon he jumped up from his seat and went straight to the shop with the book under his arm.

'Why has this been sent to my house?' he asked peremptorily, holding up the volume.

'It was ordered, sir.'

'Not by me, or anyone belonging to me, I am happy to say.'

The shopkeeper looked into his order-book.

'Oh, it has been misdirected, sir,' he said. 'It was ordered by Mr Angel Clare, and should have been sent to him.'

Mr Clare winced as if he had been struck. He went home pale and dejected, and called Angel into his study.

'Look into this book, my boy,' he said. 'What do you know about it?'

'I ordered it,' said Angel simply.

'What for?'

'To read.'

'How can you think of reading it?'

'How can I? Why – it is a system of philosophy. There is no more moral, or even religious, work published.'

'Yes – moral enough; I don't deny that. But religious! – and for *you*, who intend to be a minister of the Gospel!'

'Since you have alluded to the matter, father,' said the son, with anxious thought upon his face, 'I should like to say, once for all, that I should prefer not to take orders. I fear I could not conscientiously do so. I love the Church as one loves a parent. I shall always have the warmest affection for her. There is no institution for whose history I have a deeper admiration; but I cannot honestly be ordained her minister, as my brothers are, while she refuses to liberate her mind from an untenable redemptive theolatry.'

It had never occurred to the straightforward and simple-minded vicar that one of his own flesh and blood could come to this! He was stultified, shocked, paralysed. And if Angel were not going to enter the Church, what was the use of sending him to Cambridge? The University as a step to anything but ordination seemed, to this man of fixed ideas, a preface without a volume. He was a man not merely religious, but devout; a firm believer – not as the phrase is now elusively construed by theological thimble-riggers in the Church and out of it, but in the old and ardent sense of the Evangelical school: one who could

> Indeed opine
> That the Eternal and Divine
> Did, eighteen centuries ago
> In very truth . . .

Angel's father tried argument, persuasion, entreaty.

'No, father; I cannot underwrite Article Four (leave alone the rest), taking it "in the literal and grammatical sense" as required by the Declaration; and, therefore, I can't be a parson in the present state of affairs,' said Angel. 'My whole instinct in matters of religion is towards reconstruction; to quote your favourite Epistle to the Hebrews, "*the removing of those things that are shaken, as of things that are made, that those things which cannot be shaken may remain*".'

His father grieved so deeply that it made Angel quite ill to see him.

'What is the good of your mother and me economising and stinting ourselves to give you a University education, if it is not to be used for the honour and glory of God?' his father repeated.

'Why, that it may be used for the honour and glory of man, father.'

Perhaps if Angel had persevered he might have gone to Cambridge like his brothers. But the Vicar's view of that seat of learning as a stepping-stone to orders alone was quite a family tradition; and so rooted was the idea in his mind that perseverance began to appear to the sensitive son akin to an intent to misappropriate a trust, and wrong the pious heads of the household, who had been and were, as his father had hinted, compelled to exercise much thrift to carry out this uniform plan of education for the three young men.

'I will do without Cambridge,' said Angel at last. 'I feel that I have no right to go there in the circumstances.'

The effects of this decisive debate were not long in showing themselves. He spent years and years in desultory studies, undertakings, and meditations; he began to evince considerable indifference to social forms and observances. The material distinctions of rank and wealth he increasingly despised. Even the 'good old family' (to use a favourite phrase of a late local worthy) had no aroma for him unless there were good new resolutions in its representatives. As a balance to these austerities, when he went to live in London to see what the world was like, and with a view to practising a profession or business there, he was carried off his head, and nearly entrapped by a woman much older than himself, though luckily he escaped not greatly the worse for the experience.

Early association with country solitudes had bred in him an unconquerable, and almost unreasonable, aversion to modern town life, and shut him out from such success as he might have aspired to by following a mundane calling in the impracticability of the spiritual one. But something had to be done; he had wasted many valuable years; and having an acquaintance who was starting on a thriving life as a Colonial farmer, it occurred to Angel that this might be a lead in the right direction. Farming, either in the Colonies, America, or at home – farming, at any rate, after becoming well qualified for the business by a careful apprenticeship – that was a vocation which would probably afford an independence without the sacrifice of what he valued even more than a competency – intellectual liberty.

So we find Angel Clare at six-and-twenty here at Talbothays as a student of kine, and, as there were no houses near at hand in which he could get a comfortable lodging, a boarder at the dairyman's.

His room was an immense attic which ran the whole length of the dairy-house. It could only be reached by a ladder from the cheese-loft, and had been closed up for a long time till he arrived and selected it as his retreat. Here Clare had plenty of space, and could often be heard by the dairy-folk pacing up and down when the household had gone to rest. A portion was divided off at one end by a curtain, behind which was his bed, the outer part being furnished as a homely sitting-room.

At first he lived up above entirely, reading a good deal, and strumming upon an old harp which he had bought at a sale, saying when in a bitter humour that he might have to get his living by it in the streets some day. But he soon preferred to read human nature by taking his meals downstairs in the general dining-kitchen, with the dairyman and his wife, and the maids and men, who all together formed a lively assembly; for though but few milking hands slept in the house, several joined the family at meals. The longer Clare resided here the less objection had he to his company, and the more did he like to share quarters with them in common.

Much to his surprise he took, indeed, a real delight in their companionship. The conventional farm-folk of his imagination – personified in the newspaper-press by the pitiable dummy known as Hodge – were obliterated after a few days' residence. At close quarters no Hodge was to be seen. At first, it is true, when Clare's intelligence was fresh from a contrasting society, these friends with whom he now hobnobbed seemed a little strange. Sitting down as a level member of the dairyman's household seemed at the outset an undignified proceeding. The ideas, the modes, the surroundings, appeared retrogressive and unmeaning. But with living on there, day after day, the acute sojourner became conscious of a new aspect in the spectacle. Without any objective change whatever, variety had taken the place of monotonousness. His host and his host's household, his men and his maids, as they became intimately known to Clare, began to differentiate themselves as in a chemical process. The thought of Pascal's was brought home to him: 'A mesure qu'on a plus d'esprit, on trouve qu'il y a plus d'hommes originaux. Les gens du commun ne trouvent pas de différence entre les hommes.' The typical and unvarying Hodge ceased to exist. He had been disintegrated into a number of varied fellow-creatures – beings of many minds, beings infinite in difference; some happy, many serene, a few depressed, one here and there bright even to genius, some stupid, others wanton, others austere; some mutely Miltonic, some potentially Cromwellian; into men who had private views of each other, as he had of his friends; who could applaud or condemn each other, amuse or sadden themselves by the contemplation of each other's foibles or vices; men every one of whom walked in his own individual way the road to dusty death.

Unexpectedly he began to like the outdoor life for its own sake, and for what it brought, apart from its bearing on his own proposed career. Considering his position he became wonderfully free from the chronic melancholy which is taking hold of the civilised races with the decline of belief in a beneficent Power. For the first time of late years he could read as his musings inclined him, without any eye to cramming for a profession, since the few farming handbooks which he deemed it desirable to master occupied him but little time.

He grew away from old associations, and saw something new in life and humanity. Secondarily, he made close acquaintance with phenomena which he had before known but darkly – the seasons in their moods, morning and evening, night and noon, winds in their different tempers, trees, waters and mists, shades and silences, and the voices of inanimate things.

The early mornings were still sufficiently cool to render a fire acceptable in the large room wherein they breakfasted; and, by Mrs Crick's orders, who held that he was too genteel to mess at their table, it was Angel Clare's custom to sit in the yawning chimney-corner during the meal, his cup and saucer and plate being placed on a hinged flap at his elbow. The light from the long, wide, mullioned window opposite shone in upon his nook, and, assisted by a secondary light of cold blue quality which shone down the chimney, enabled him to read there easily whenever disposed to do so. Between Clare and the window was the table at which his companions sat, their munching profiles rising sharp against the panes; while to the side was the milk-house door, through which were visible the rectangular leads in rows, full to the brim with the morning's milk. At the further end the great churn could be seen revolving, and its slip-slopping heard – the moving power being discernible through the window in the form of a spiritless horse walking in a circle and driven by a boy.

For several days after Tess's arrival Clare, sitting abstractedly reading from some book, periodical, or piece of music just come by post, hardly noticed that she was present at table. She talked so little, and the other maids talked so much, that the babble did not strike him as possessing a new note, and he was ever in the habit of neglecting the particulars of an outward scene for the general impression. One day, however, when he had been conning one of his music-scores, and by force of imagination was hearing the tune in his head, he lapsed into listlessness, and the music-sheet rolled to the hearth. He looked at the fire of logs, with its one flame pirouetting on the top in a dying dance after the breakfast-cooking and boiling, and it seemed to jig to his inward tune; also at the two chimney crooks dangling down from the cotterel or cross-bar, plumed with soot which quivered to the same melody; also at the half-empty kettle whining an accompaniment. The conversation at the table mixed in with his phantasmal orchestra till he thought: 'What a fluty voice one of those milkmaids has! I suppose it is the new one.'

Clare looked round upon her, seated with the others.

She was not looking towards him. Indeed, owing to his long silence, his presence in the room was almost forgotten.

'I don't know about ghosts,' she was saying; 'but I do know that our souls can be made to go outside our bodies when we are alive.'

The dairyman turned to her with his mouth full, his eyes charged with serious enquiry, and his great knife and fork (breakfasts were breakfasts here) planted erect on the table, like the beginning of a gallows.

'What – really now? And is it so, maidy?' he said.

'A very easy way to feel 'em go,' continued Tess, 'is to lie on the grass at night and look straight up at some big bright star; and, by fixing your mind upon it, you will soon find that you are hundreds and hundreds o' miles away from your body, which you don't seem to want at all.'

The dairyman removed his hard gaze from Tess, and fixed it on his wife.

'Now that's a rum thing, Christianner – hey? To think o' the miles I've vamped o' starlight nights these last thirty year, courting, or trading, or for doctor, or for nurse, and yet never had the least notion o' that till now, or feeled my soul rise so much as an inch above my shirt-collar.'

The general attention being drawn to her, including that of the dairyman's pupil, Tess flushed, and remarking evasively that it was only a fancy, resumed her breakfast.

Clare continued to observe her. She soon finished her eating, and having a consciousness that Clare was regarding her, began to trace imaginary patterns on the tablecloth with her forefinger with the constraint of a domestic animal that perceives itself to be watched.

'What a fresh and virginal daughter of Nature that milkmaid is!' he said to himself.

And then he seemed to discern in her something that was familiar, something which carried him back into a joyous and unforeseeing past, before the necessity of taking thought had made the heavens grey. He concluded that he had beheld her before; where he could not tell. A casual encounter during some country ramble it certainly had been, and he was not greatly curious about it. But the circumstance was sufficient to lead him to select Tess in preference to the other pretty milkmaids when he wished to contemplate contiguous womankind.

## *Chapter 19*

In general the cows were milked as they presented themselves, without fancy or choice. But certain cows will show a fondness for a particular pair of hands, sometimes carrying this predilection so far as to refuse to stand at all except to their favourite, the pail of a stranger being unceremoniously kicked over.

It was Dairyman Crick's rule to insist on breaking down these partialities and aversions by constant interchange, since otherwise, in the event of a milkman or maid going away from the dairy, he was placed in a difficulty. The maids' private aims, however, were the reverse of the dairyman's rule, the daily selection by each damsel of the eight or ten cows to which she had grown accustomed rendering the operation on their willing udders surprisingly easy and effortless.

Tess, like her compeers, soon discovered which of the cows had a preference for her style of manipulation, and her fingers having become delicate from the long domiciliary imprisonments to which she had subjected herself at intervals during the last two or three years, she would have been glad to meet the milchers' views in this respect. Out of the whole ninety-five there were eight in particular – Dumpling, Fancy, Lofty, Mist, Old Pretty, Young Pretty, Tidy, and Loud – who, though the teats of one or two were as hard as carrots, gave down to her with a readiness that made her work on them a mere touch of the fingers. Knowing, however, the dairyman's wish, she endeavoured conscientiously to take the animals just as they came, excepting the very hard yielders which she could not yet manage.

But she soon found a curious correspondence between the ostensibly chance position of the cows and her wishes in this matter, till she felt that their order could not be the result of accident. The dairyman's pupil had lent a hand in getting the cows together of late, and at the fifth or sixth time she turned her eyes, as she rested against the cow, full of sly enquiry upon him.

'Mr Clare, you have ranged the cows!' she said, blushing; and in making the accusation symptoms of a smile gently lifted her upper lip in spite of her, so as to show the tips of her teeth, the lower lip remaining severely still.

'Well, it makes no difference,' said he. 'You will always be here to milk them.'

'Do you think so? I *hope* I shall! But I don't *know*.'

She was angry with herself afterwards, thinking that he, unaware of her grave reasons for liking this seclusion, might have mistaken her meaning. She had spoken so earnestly to him, as if his presence were somehow a factor in her wish. Her misgiving was such that at dusk, when the milking was over, she walked in the garden alone, to continue her regrets that she had disclosed to him her discovery of his considerateness.

It was a typical summer evening in June, the atmosphere being in such delicate equilibrium and so transmissive that inanimate objects seemed endowed with two or three senses, if not five. There was no distinction between the near and the far, and an auditor felt close to everything within the horizon. The soundlessness impressed her as a positive entity rather than as the mere negation of noise. It was broken by the strumming of strings.

Tess had heard those notes in the attic above her head. Dim, flattened, constrained by their confinement, they had never appealed to her as now, when they wandered in the still air with a stark quality like that of nudity. To speak absolutely, both instrument and execution were poor; but the relative is all, and as she listened Tess, like a fascinated bird, could not leave the spot. Far from leaving she drew up towards the performer, keeping behind the hedge that he might not guess her presence.

The outskirt of the garden in which Tess found herself had been left uncultivated for some years, and was now damp and rank with juicy grass which sent up mists of pollen at a touch; and with tall blooming weeds emitting offensive smells – weeds whose red and yellow and purple hues formed a polychrome as dazzling as that of cultivated flowers. She went stealthily as a cat through this profusion of growth, gathering cuckoo-spittle on her skirts, cracking snails that were underfoot, staining her hands with thistle-milk and slug-slime, and rubbing off upon her naked arms sticky blights which, though snow-white on the apple-tree trunks, made madder stains on her skin; thus she drew quite near to Clare, still unobserved of him.

Tess was conscious of neither time nor space. The exaltation which she had described as being producible at will by gazing at a star, came now without any determination of hers; she undulated upon the thin notes of the second-hand harp, and their harmonies passed like breezes through her, bringing tears into her eyes. The floating pollen seemed to be his notes made visible, and the dampness of the garden the weeping of the garden's sensibility. Though near nightfall, the rank-smelling weed-flowers glowed as if they would not close for intentness, and the waves of colour mixed with the waves of sound.

The light which still shone was derived mainly from a large hole in the western bank of cloud; it was like a piece of day left behind by accident, dusk having closed in elsewhere. He concluded his plaintive melody, a very simple performance, demanding no great skill; and she waited, thinking another might be begun. But, tired of playing, he had desultorily come round the fence, and was rambling up behind her. Tess, her cheeks on fire, moved away furtively, as if hardly moving at all.

Angel, however, saw her light summer gown, and he spoke; his low tones reaching her, though he was some distance off.

'What makes you draw off in that way, Tess?' said he. 'Are you afraid?'

'Oh no, sir . . . not of outdoor things; especially just now when the apple-blooth is falling, and everything so green.'

'But you have your indoor fears – eh?'

'Well – yes, sir.'

'What of?'

'I couldn't quite say.'

'The milk turning sour?'

'No.'

'Life in general?'

'Yes, sir.'

'Ah – so have I, very often. This hobble of being alive is rather serious, don't you think so?'

'It is – now you put it that way.'

'All the same, I shouldn't have expected a young girl like you to see it so just yet. How is it you do?'

She maintained a hesitating silence.

'Come, Tess, tell me in confidence.'

She thought that he meant what were the aspects of things to her, and replied shyly – 'The trees have inquisitive eyes, haven't they? – that is, seem as if they had. And the river says, – "Why do ye trouble me with your looks?" And you seem to see numbers of tomorrows just all in a line, the first of them the biggest and clearest, the others getting smaller and smaller as they stand farther away; but they all seem very fierce and cruel and as if they said, "I'm coming! Beware of me! Beware of me! . . . But *you*, sir, can raise up dreams with your music, and drive all such horrid fancies away!'

He was surprised to find this young woman – who though but a milkmaid had just that touch of rarity about her which might make her the envied of her housemates – shaping such sad imaginings. She was expressing in her own native phrases – assisted a little by her Sixth Standard training – feelings which might almost have been called those of the age – the ache of modernism. The perception arrested him less when he reflected that what are called advanced ideas are really in great part but the latest fashion in definition – a more accurate expression, by words in *logy* and *ism*, of sensations which men and women have vaguely grasped for centuries.

Still, it was strange that they should have come to her while yet so young; more than strange; it was impressive, interesting, pathetic. Not guessing the cause, there was nothing to remind him that experience is as to intensity, and not as to duration. Tess's passing corporeal blight had been her mental harvest.

Tess, on her part, could not understand why a man of clerical family and good education, and above physical want, should look upon it as a mishap to be alive. For the unhappy pilgrim herself there was very good reason. But how could this admirable and poetic man ever have descended into the Valley of Humiliation, have felt with the man of Uz – as she herself had felt two or three years ago – 'My soul chooseth strangling and death rather than my life. I loathe it; I would not live alway.'

It was true that he was at present out of his class. But she knew that was only because, like Peter the Great in a shipwright's yard, he was studying what he wanted to know. He did not milk cows because he was obliged to milk cows, but because he was learning how to be a rich and prosperous dairyman, landowner, agriculturist, and breeder of cattle. He would become an American or Australian Abraham, commanding like a monarch his flocks and his herds, his spotted and his ring-straked, his menservants and his maids. At times, nevertheless, it did seem unaccountable to her that a decidedly bookish, musical, thinking young man should have chosen deliberately to be a farmer, and not a clergyman, like his father and brothers.

Thus, neither having the clue to the other's secret, they were respectively puzzled at what each revealed, and awaited new knowledge of each other's character and moods without attempting to pry into each other's history.

Every day, every hour, brought to him one more little stroke of her nature, and to her one more of his. Tess was trying to lead a repressed life, but she little divined the strength of her own vitality.

At first Tess seemed to regard Angel Clare as an intelligence rather than as a man. As such she compared him with herself; and at every discovery of the abundance of his illuminations, of the distance between her own modest mental standpoint and the unmeasurable, Andean altitude of his, she became quite dejected, disheartened from all further effort on her own part whatever.

He observed her dejection one day, when he had casually mentioned something to her about pastoral life in ancient Greece. She was gathering the buds called 'lords and ladies' from the bank while he spoke.

'Why do you look so woebegone all of a sudden?' he asked.

'Oh, 'tis only – about my own self,' she said, with a frail laugh of sadness, fitfully beginning to peel 'a lady' meanwhile. 'Just a sense of what might have been with me! My life looks as if it had been wasted for want of chances! When I see what you know, what you have read, and seen, and thought, I feel what a nothing I am! I'm like the poor Queen of Sheba who lived in the Bible. There is no more spirit in me.'

'Bless my soul, don't go troubling about that! Why,' he said with some enthusiasm, 'I should be only too glad, my dear Tess, to help you to anything in the way of history, or any line of reading you would like to take up – '

'It is a lady again,' interrupted she, holding out the bud she had peeled.

'What?'

'I meant that there are always more ladies than lords when you come to peel them.'

'Never mind about the lords and ladies. Would you like to take up any course of study – history, for example?'

'Sometimes I feel I don't want to know anything more about it than I know already.'

'Why not?'

'Because what's the use of learning that I am one of a long row only – finding out that there is set down in some old book somebody just like me, and to know that I shall only act her part; making me sad, that's all. The best is not to remember that your nature and your past doings have been just like thousands' and thousands', and that your coming life and doings'll be like thousands' and thousands'.'

'What, really, then, you don't want to learn anything?'

'I shouldn't mind learning why – why the sun do shine on the just and the unjust alike,' she answered, with a slight quaver in her voice. 'But that's what books will not tell me.'

'Tess, fie for such bitterness!' Of course he spoke with a conventional sense of duty only, for that sort of wondering had not been unknown to himself in bygone days. And as he looked at the unpractised mouth and lips, he thought that such a daughter of the soil could only have caught up the sentiment by rote. She went on peeling the lords and ladies till Clare, regarding for a moment the wave-like curl of her lashes as they drooped with her bent gaze on her soft cheek, lingeringly went away. When he was gone she stood awhile, thoughtfully peeling the last bud; and then, awakening from her reverie, flung it and all the crowd of floral nobility impatiently on the ground, in an ebullition of displeasure with herself for her *niaiseries*, and with a quickening warmth in her heart of hearts.

How stupid he must think her! In an access of hunger for his good opinion she bethought herself of what she had latterly endeavoured to forget, so unpleasant had been its issues – the identity of her family with that of the knightly d'Urbervilles. Barren attribute as it was, disastrous as its discovery had been in many ways to her, perhaps Mr Clare, as a gentleman and a student of history, would respect her sufficiently to forget her childish conduct with the lords and ladies if he knew that those Purbeck-marble and alabaster people in Kingsbere Church really represented her own lineal forefathers; that she was no spurious d'Urberville, compounded of money and ambition like those at Trantridge, but true d'Urberville to the bone.

But, before venturing to make the revelation, dubious Tess indirectly sounded the dairyman as to its possible effect upon Mr Clare, by asking the former if Mr Clare had any great respect for old county families when they had lost all their money and land.

'Mr Clare,' said the dairyman emphatically, 'is one of the most rebellest rozums you ever knowed – not a bit like the rest of his family; and if there's one thing that he do hate more than another 'tis the notion of what's called a' old family. He says that it stands to reason that old families have done their spurt of work in past days, and can't have anything left in 'em now. There's the Billetts and the Drenkhards and the Greys and the St Quintins and the Hardys and the Goulds, who used to own the lands for miles down this valley; you could buy 'em all up now for an old song a'most. Why, our little Retty Priddle here, you know, is one of the Paridelles – the old family that used to own lots o' the lands out by King's-Hintock now owned by the Earl o' Wessex, afore even he or his was heard of. Well, Mr Clare found this out, and spoke quite scornful to the poor girl for days. "Ah!" he says to her, "you'll never make a good dairymaid! All your skill was used up ages ago in Palestine, and you must lie fallow for a thousand years to git strength for more deeds!" A boy came here t'other day asking for a job, and said his name was Matt, and when we asked him his surname he said he'd never heard that 'a had any surname, and when we asked why, he said he supposed his folks hadn't been 'stablished long enough. "Ah! you're the very boy I want!" says Mr Clare, jumping up and shaking hands wi'en; "I've great hopes of you;" and gave him half a crown. O no! he can't stomach old families!'

After hearing this caricature of Clare's opinions poor Tess was glad that she had not said a word in a weak moment about her family – even though it was so unusually old as almost to have gone round the circle and become a new one. Besides, another dairy-girl was as good as she, it seemed, in that respect. She held her tongue about the d'Urberville vault, and the Knight of the Conqueror whose name she bore. The insight afforded into Clare's character suggested to her that it was largely owing to her supposed untraditional newness that she had won interest in his eyes.

## *Chapter 20*

The season developed and matured. Another year's instalment of flowers, leaves, nightingales, thrushes, finches, and such ephemeral creatures, took up their positions where only a year ago others had stood in their place when these were nothing more than germs and inorganic particles. Rays from the sunrise drew forth the buds and stretched them into long stalks, lifted up sap in noiseless streams, opened petals, and sucked out scents in invisible jets and breathings.

Dairyman Crick's household of maids and men lived on comfortably, placidly, even merrily. Their position was perhaps the happiest of all positions in the social scale, being above the line at which neediness ends, and below the line at which the *convenances* begin to cramp natural feelings, and the stress of threadbare modishness makes too little of enough.

Thus passed the leafy time when arborescence seems to be the one thing aimed at out of doors. Tess and Clare unconsciously studied each other, ever balanced on the edge of a passion, yet apparently keeping out of it. All the while they were converging, under an irresistible law, as surely as two streams in one vale.

Tess had never in her recent life been so happy as she was now, possibly never would be so happy again. She was, for one thing, physically and mentally suited among these new surroundings. The sapling which had rooted down to a poisonous stratum on the spot of its sowing had been transplanted to a deeper soil. Moreover she, and Clare also, stood as yet on the debatable land between predilection and love; where no profundities have been reached; no reflections have set in, awkwardly enquiring, 'Whither does this new current tend to carry me? What does it mean to my future? How does it stand towards my past?'

Tess was the merest stray phenomenon to Angel Clare as yet – a rosy warming apparition which had only just acquired the attribute of persistence in his consciousness. So he allowed his mind to be occupied with her, deeming his preoccupation to be no more than a philosopher's regard of an exceedingly novel, fresh, and interesting specimen of womankind.

They met continually; they could not help it. They met daily in that strange and solemn interval, the twilight of the morning, in the violet or pink dawn; for it was necessary to rise early, so very early, here. Milking was done betimes; and before the milking came the skimming, which began at a little past three. It usually fell to the lot of someone or other of them to wake the rest, the first being aroused by an alarm-clock; and, as Tess was the latest arrival, and they soon discovered that she could be depended upon not to sleep through the alarm as the others did, this task was thrust most frequently upon her. No sooner had the hour of three struck and whizzed, than she left her room and ran to the dairyman's door; then up the ladder to Angel's, calling him in a loud whisper; then woke her fellow-milkmaids. By the time that Tess was dressed Clare was downstairs and out in the humid air. The remaining maids and the dairyman usually gave themselves another turn on the pillow, and did not appear till a quarter of an hour later.

The grey half-tones of daybreak are not the grey half-tones of the day's close, though the degree of their shade may be the same. In the twilight of the morning light seems active, darkness passive; in the twilight of evening it is the darkness which is active and crescent, and the light which is the drowsy reverse.

Being so often – possibly not always by chance – the first two persons to get up at the dairy-house, they seemed to themselves the first persons up of all the world. In these early days of her residence here Tess did not skim, but went out of doors at once after rising, where he was generally awaiting her. The spectral, half-compounded, aqueous light which pervaded the open mead, impressed them with a feeling of isolation, as if they were Adam and Eve. At this dim inceptive stage of the day Tess seemed to Clare to exhibit a dignified largeness both of disposition and physique, an almost regnant power, possibly because he knew that at that preternatural time hardly any woman so well endowed in person as she was likely to be walking in the open air within the boundaries of his horizon; very few in all England. Fair women are usually asleep at midsummer dawns. She was close at hand, and the rest were nowhere.

The mixed, singular, luminous gloom in which they walked along together to the spot where the cows lay, often made him think of the Resurrection hour. He little thought that the Magdalen might be at his side. Whilst all the landscape was in neutral shade his companion's face, which was the focus of his eyes, rising above the mist stratum, seemed to have a sort of phosphorescence upon it. She looked ghostly, as if she were merely a soul at large. In reality her face, without appearing to do so, had caught the cold gleam of day from the north-east; his own face, though he did not think of it, wore the same aspect to her.

It was then, as has been said, that she impressed him most deeply. She was no longer the milkmaid, but a visionary essence of woman – a whole sex condensed into one typical form. He called her Artemis, Demeter, and other fanciful names half teasingly, which she did not like because she did not understand them.

'Call me Tess,' she would say askance; and he did.

Then it would grow lighter, and her features would become simply feminine; they had changed from those of a divinity who could confer bliss to those of a being who craved it.

At these non-human hours they could get quite close to the waterfowl. Herons came, with a great bold noise as of opening doors and shutters, out of the boughs of a plantation which they frequented at the side of the mead; or, if already on the spot, hardily maintained their standing in the water as the pair walked by, watching them by moving their heads round in a slow, horizontal, passionless wheel, like the turn of puppets by clockwork.

They could then see the faint summer fogs in layers, woolly, level, and apparently no thicker than counterpanes, spread about the meadows in detached remnants of small extent. On the grey moisture of the grass were marks where the cows had lain through the night – dark-green islands of dry herbage the size of their carcases, in the general sea of dew. From each island proceeded a serpentine trail, by which the cow had rambled away to feed after getting up, at the end of which trail they found her; the snoring puff from her nostrils, when she recognised them, making an intenser little fog of her own amid the prevailing one. Then they drove the animals back to the barton, or sat down to milk them on the spot, as the case might require.

Or perhaps the summer fog was more general, and the meadows lay like a white sea, out of which the scattered trees rose like dangerous rocks. Birds would soar through it into the upper radiance, and hang on the wing sunning themselves, or alight on the wet rails subdividing the mead, which now shone like glass rods. Minute diamonds of moisture from the mist hung, too, upon Tess's eyelashes, and drops upon her hair, like seed pearls. When the day grew quite strong and commonplace these dried off her; moreover, Tess then lost her strange and ethereal beauty; her teeth, lips, and eyes scintillated in the sunbeams, and she was again the dazzlingly fair dairymaid only, who had to hold her own against the other women of the world.

About this time they would hear Dairyman Crick's voice, lecturing the non-resident milkers for arriving late, and speaking sharply to old Deborah Fyander for not washing her hands.

'For Heaven's sake, pop thy hands under the pump, Deb! Upon my soul, if the London folk only knowed of thee and thy slovenly ways, they'd swaller their milk and butter more mincing than they do a'ready; and that's saying a good deal.'

The milking progressed, till towards the end Tess and Clare, in common with the rest, could hear the heavy breakfast table dragged out from the wall in the kitchen by Mrs Crick, this being the invariable preliminary to each meal; the same horrible scrape accompanying its return journey when the table had been cleared.

## *Chapter 21*

There was a great stir in the milk-house just after breakfast. The churn revolved as usual, but the butter would not come. Whenever this happened the dairy was paralysed. Squish, squash, echoed the milk in the great cylinder, but never arose the sound they waited for.

Dairyman Crick and his wife, the milkmaids Tess, Marian Retty Priddle, Izz Huett, and the married ones from the cottages; also Mr Clare, Jonathan Kail, old Deborah, and the rest, stood gazing hopelessly at the churn; and the boy who kept the horse going outside put on moon-like eyes to show his sense of the situation. Even the melancholy horse himself seemed to look in at the window in enquiring despair at each walk round.

' 'Tis years since I went to Conjuror Trendle's son in Egdon – years!' said the dairyman bitterly. 'And he was nothing to what his father had been. I have said fifty times, if I have said once, that I don't believe in en; though he do cast folks' waters very true. But I shall have to go to 'n if he's alive. O yes, I shall have to go to 'n, if this sort of thing continnys!'

Even Mr Clare began to feel tragical at the dairyman's desperation.

'Conjuror Fall, t'other side of Casterbridge, that they used to call "Wide-O," was a very good man when I was a boy,' said Jonathan Kail. 'But he's rotten as touchwood by now.'

'My grandfather used to go to Conjuror Mynterne, out at Owlscombe, and a clever man a' were, so I've heard grandf'er say,' continued Mr Crick. 'But there's no such genuine folk about nowadays!'

Mrs Crick's mind kept nearer to the matter in hand.

'Perhaps somebody in the house is in love,' she said tentatively. 'I've heard tell in my younger days that that will cause it. Why, Crick – that maid we had years ago, do ye mind, and how the butter didn't come then – '

'Ah yes, yes! – but that isn't the rights o't. It had nothing to do with the love-making. I can mind all about it – 'twas the damage to the churn.'

He turned to Clare.

'Jack Dollop, a 'hore's-bird of a fellow we had here as milker at one time, sir, courted a young woman over at Mellstock, and deceived her as he had deceived many afore. But he had another sort o' woman to reckon wi' this time, and it was not the girl herself. One Holy Thursday of all days in the almanac, we was here as we mid be now, only there was no churning in hand, when we zid the girl's mother coming up to the door, wi' a great brass-mounted umbrella in her hand that would ha' felled an ox, and saying "Do Jack Dollop work here? – because I want him! I have a big bone to pick with he, I can assure 'n!" And some way behind her mother walked Jack's young woman, crying bitterly into her handkercher. "O Lard, here's a time!" said Jack, looking out o' winder at 'em. "She'll murder me! Where shall I get – where shall I – ? Don't tell her where I be!" And with that he scrambled into the churn through the trap-door, and shut himself inside, just as the young woman's mother busted into the milk-house. "The villain – where is he?" says she "I'll claw his face for'n, let me only catch him!" Well, she hunted about everywhere, ballyragging Jack by side and by seam, Jack lying a'most stifled inside the churn, and the poor maid – or young woman rather – standing at the door crying her eyes out. I shall never forget it, never! 'Twould have melted a marble stone! But she couldn't find him nowhere at all.'

The dairyman paused, and one or two words of comment came from the listeners.

Dairyman Crick's stories often seemed to be ended when they were not really so, and strangers were betrayed into premature interjections of finality; though old friends knew better. The narrator went on – 'Well, how the old woman should have had the wit to guess it I could never tell, but she found out that he was inside that there churn. Without saying a word she took hold of the winch (it was turned by handpower then), and round she swung him, and Jack began to flop about inside. "O Lard" stop the churn! let me out!" says he, popping out his head, "I shall be churned into a pummy!" (he was a cowardly chap in his heart, as such men mostly be). "Not till ye make amends for ravaging her virgin innocence!" says the old woman. "Stop the churn, you old witch!" screams he. "You call me old witch, do ye, you deceiver!" says she, "when ye ought to ha' been calling me mother-law these last five months!" And on went the churn, and Jack's bones rattled round again. Well, none of us ventured to interfere; and at last 'a promised to make it right wi' her. "Yes – I'll be as good as my word!" he said. And so it ended that day.'

While the listeners were smiling their comments there was a quick movement behind their backs, and they looked round. Tess, pale-faced, had gone to the door.

'How warm 'tis today!' she said, almost inaudibly.

It was warm, and none of them connected her withdrawal with the reminiscences of the dairyman. He went forward, and opened the door for her, saying with tender raillery – 'Why, maidy' (he frequently, with unconscious irony, gave her this pet name), 'the prettiest milker I've got in my dairy; you mustn't get so fagged as this at the first breath of summer weather, or we shall be finely put to for want of 'ee by dog-days, shan't we, Mr Clare?'

'I was faint – and – I think I am better out o' doors,' she said mechanically; and disappeared outside.

Fortunately for her the milk in the revolving churn at that moment changed its squashing for a decided flick-flack.

' 'Tis coming!' cried Mrs Crick, and the attention of all was called off from Tess.

That fair sufferer soon recovered herself externally; but she remained much depressed all the afternoon. When the evening milking was done she did not care to be with the rest of them, and went out of doors wandering along she knew not whither. She was wretched – O so wretched – at the perception that to her companions the dairyman's story had been rather a humorous narration than otherwise; none of them but herself seemed to see the sorrow of it; to a certainty, not one knew how cruelly it touched the tender place in her experience. The evening sun was now ugly to her, like a great inflamed wound in the sky. Only a solitary cracked-voiced reed-sparrow greeted her from the bushes by the river, in a sad, machine-made tone, resembling that of a past friend whose friendship she had outworn.

In these long June days the milkmaids, and, indeed, most of the household, went to bed at sunset or sooner, the morning work before milking being so early and heavy at a time of full pails. Tess usually accompanied her fellows upstairs. Tonight, however, she was the first to go to their common chamber; and she had dozed when the other girls came in. She saw them undressing in the orange light of the vanished sun, which flushed their forms with its colour; she dozed again, but she was reawakened by their voices, and quietly turned her eyes towards them.

Neither of her three chamber-companions had got into bed. They were standing in a group, in their nightgowns, barefooted, at the window, the last red rays of the west still warming their faces and necks, and the walls around them. All were watching somebody in the garden with deep interest, their three faces close together: a jovial and round one, a pale one with dark hair, and a fair one whose tresses were auburn.

'Don't push! You can see as well as I,' said Retty, the auburn-haired and youngest girl, without removing her eyes from the window.

' 'Tis no use for you to be in love with him any more than me, Retty Priddle,' said jolly-faced Marian, the eldest, slily. 'His thoughts be of other cheeks than thine!'

Retty Priddle still looked, and the others looked again.

'There he is again!' cried Izz Huett, the pale girl with dark damp hair and keenly cut lips.

'You needn't say anything, Izz,' answered Retty. 'For I zid you kissing his shade.'

'*What* did you see her doing?' asked Marian.

'Why – he was standing over the whey-tub to let off the whey, and the shade of his face came upon the wall behind, close to Izz, who was standing there filling a vat. She put her mouth against the wall and kissed the shade of his mouth; I zid her, though he didn't.'

'O Izz Huett!' said Marian.

A rosy spot came into the middle of Izz Huett's cheek.

'Well, there was no harm in it,' she declared, with attempted coolness. 'And if I be in love wi'en, so is Retty, too; and so be you, Marian, come to that.'

Marian's full face could not blush past its chronic pinkness.

'I!' she said. 'What a tale! Ah, there he is again! Dear eyes – dear face – dear Mr Clare!'

'There – you've owned it!'

'So have you – so have we all,' said Marian, with the dry frankness of complete indifference to opinion. 'It is silly to pretend otherwise amongst ourselves, though we need not own it to other folks. I would just marry 'n tomorrow!'

'So would I – and more,' murmured Izz Huett.

'And I too,' whispered the more timid Retty.

The listener grew warm.

'We can't all marry him,' said Izz.

'We shan't, either of us; which is worse still,' said the eldest. 'There he is again!'

They all three blew him a silent kiss.

'Why?' asked Retty quickly.

'Because he likes Tess Durbeyfield best,' said Marian, lowering her voice. 'I have watched him every day, and have found it out.'

There was a reflective silence.

'But she don't care anything for 'n?' at length breathed Retty.

'Well – I sometimes think that too.'

'But how silly all this is!' said Izz Huett impatiently. 'Of course he won't marry any one of us, or Tess either – a gentleman's son, who's going to be a great landowner and farmer abroad! More likely to ask us to come wi'en as farm-hands at so much a year!'

One sighed, and another sighed, and Marian's plump figure sighed biggest of all. Somebody in bed hard by sighed too. Tears came into the eyes of Retty Priddle, the pretty red-haired youngest – the last bud of the Paridelles, so important in the county annals. They watched silently a little longer, their three faces still close together as before, and the triple hues of their hair mingling. But the unconscious Mr Clare had gone indoors, and they saw him no more; and, the shades beginning to deepen, they crept into their beds. In a few minutes they heard him ascend the ladder to his own room. Marian was soon snoring, but Izz did not drop into forgetfulness for a long time. Retty Priddle cried herself to sleep.

The deeper-passioned Tess was very far from sleeping even then. This conversation was another of the bitter pills she had been obliged to swallow that day. Scarce the least feeling of jealousy arose in her breast. For that matter she knew herself to have the preference. Being more finely formed, better educated, and, though the youngest except Retty, more woman than either, she perceived that only the slightest ordinary care was necessary for holding her own in Angel Clare's heart against these her candid friends. But the grave question was, ought she to do this? There was, to be sure, hardly a ghost of a chance for either of them, in a serious sense; but there was, or had been, a chance of one or the other inspiring him with a passing fancy for her, and enjoying the pleasure of his attentions while he stayed here. Such unequal attachments had led to marriage; and she had heard from Mrs Crick that Mr Clare had one day asked, in a laughing way, what would be the use of his marrying a fine lady, and all the while ten thousand acres of Colonial pasture to feed, and cattle to rear, and corn to reap. A farm-woman would be the only sensible kind of wife for him. But whether Mr Clare had spoken seriously or not, why should she, who could never conscientiously allow any man to marry her now, and who had religiously determined that she never would be tempted to do so, draw off Mr Clare's attention from other women, for the brief happiness of sunning herself in his eyes while he remained at Talbothays?

## *Chapter 22*

They came downstairs yawning next morning; but skimming and milking were proceeded with as usual, and they went indoors to breakfast. Dairyman Crick was discovered stamping about the house. He had received a letter, in which a customer had complained that the butter had a twang.

'And begad, so 't have!' said the dairyman, who held in his left hand a wooden slice on which a lump of butter was stuck 'Yes – taste for yourself!'

Several of them gathered round him; and Mr Clare tasted, Tess tasted, also the other indoor milkmaids, one or two of the milking-men, and last of all Mrs Crick, who came out from the waiting breakfast-table. There certainly was a twang.

The dairyman, who had thrown himself into abstraction to better realise the taste, and so divine the particular species of noxious weed to which it appertained, suddenly exclaimed – ' 'Tis garlic! and I thought there wasn't a blade left in that mead!'

Then all the old hands remembered that a certain dry mead, into which a few of the cows had been admitted of late, had, in years gone by, spoilt the butter in the same way. The dairyman had not recognised the taste at that time, and thought the butter bewitched.

'We must overhaul that mead,' he resumed; 'this mustn't continny!'

All having armed themselves with old pointed knives they went out together. As the inimical plant could only be present in very microscopic dimensions to have escaped ordinary observation, to find it seemed rather a hopeless attempt in the stretch of rich grass before them. However, they formed themselves into line, all assisting, owing to the importance of the search; the dairyman at the upper end with Mr Clare, who had volunteered to help; then Tess, Marian, Izz Huett, and Retty; then Bill Lewell, Jonathan, and the married dairy-women – Beck Knibbs, with her woolly black hair and rolling eyes; and flaxen Frances, consumptive from the winter damps of the water-meads – who lived in their respective cottages.

With eyes fixed upon the ground they crept slowly across a strip of the field, returning a little further down in such a manner that, when they should have finished, not a single inch of the pasture but would have fallen under the eye of some one of them. It was a most tedious business, not more than half a dozen shoots of garlic being discoverable in the whole field; yet such was the herb's pungency that probably one bite of it by one cow had been sufficient to season the whole dairy's produce for the day.

Differing one from another in natures and moods so greatly as they did, they yet formed, bending, a curiously uniform row – automatic, noiseless; and an alien observer passing down the neighbouring lane might well have been excused for massing them as 'Hodge.' As they crept along, stooping low to discern the plant, a soft yellow gleam was reflected from the buttercups into their shaded faces, giving them an elfish, moonlit aspect, though the sun was pouring upon their backs in all the strength of noon.

Angel Clare, who communistically stuck to his rule of taking part with the rest in everything, glanced up now and then. It was not, of course, by accident that he walked next to Tess.

'Well, how are you?' he murmured.

'Very well, thank you, sir,' she replied demurely.

As they had been discussing a score of personal matters only half an hour before, the introductory style seemed a little superfluous. But they got no further in speech just then. They crept and crept, the hem of her petticoat just touching his gaiter, and his elbow sometimes brushing hers. At last the dairyman, who came next, could stand it no longer.

'Upon my soul and body, this here stooping do fairly make my back open and shut!' he exclaimed, straightening himself slowly with an excruciated look till quite upright. 'And you, maidy Tess, you wasn't well a day or two ago – this will make your head ache finely! Don't do any more, if you feel fainty; leave the rest to finish it.'

Dairyman Crick withdrew, and Tess dropped behind. Mr Clare also stepped out of line, and began privateering about for the weed. When she found him near her, her very tension at what she had heard the night before made her the first to speak.

'Don't they look pretty?' she said.

'Who?'

'Izzy Huett and Retty.'

Tess had moodily decided that either of these maidens would make a good farmer's wife, and that she ought to recommend them, and obscure her own wretched charms.

'Pretty? Well, yes – they are pretty girls – fresh looking. I have often thought so.'

'Though, poor dears, prettiness won't last long!'

'O no, unfortunately.'

'They are excellent dairy-women.'

'Yes: though not better than you.'

'They skim better than I.'

'Do they?'

Clare remained observing them – not without their observing him.

'She is colouring up,' continued Tess heroically.

'Who?'

'Retty Priddle.'

'Oh! Why is that?'

'Because you are looking at her.'

Self-sacrificing as her mood might be Tess could not well go further and cry, 'Marry one of them, if you really do want a dairywoman and not a lady; and don't think of marrying me!' She followed Dairyman Crick, and had the mournful satisfaction of seeing that Clare remained behind.

From this day she forced herself to take pains to avoid him – never allowing herself, as formerly, to remain long in his company, even if their juxtaposition were purely accidental. She gave the other three every chance.

Tess was woman enough to realise from their avowals to herself that Angel Clare had the honour of all the dairymaids in his keeping, and her perception of his care to avoid compromising the happiness of either in the least degree bred a tender respect in Tess for what she deemed, rightly or wrongly, the self-controlling sense of duty shown by him, a quality which she had never expected to find in one of the opposite sex, and in the absence of which more than one of the simple hearts who were his house-mates might have gone weeping on her pilgrimage.

## *Chapter 23*

The hot weather of July had crept upon them unawares, and the atmosphere of the flat vale hung heavy as an opiate over the dairy-folk, the cows, and the trees. Hot steaming rains fell frequently, making the grass where the cows fed yet more rank, and hindering the late haymaking in the other meads.

It was Sunday morning; the milking was done; the outdoor milkers had gone home. Tess and the other three were dressing themselves rapidly, the whole bevy having agreed to go together to Mellstock Church, which lay some three or four miles distant from the dairy-house. She had now been two months at Talbothays, and this was her first excursion.

All the preceding afternoon and night heavy thunderstorms had hissed down upon the meads, and washed some of the hay into the river; but this morning the sun shone out all the more brilliantly for the deluge, and the air was balmy and clear.

The crooked lane leading from their own parish to Mellstock ran along the lowest levels in a portion of its length, and when the girls reached the most depressed spot they found that the result of the rain had been to flood the lane over-shoe to a distance of some fifty yards. This would have been no serious hindrance on a weekday; they would have clicked through it in their high pattens and boots quite unconcerned; but on this day of vanity, this Sun's-day, when flesh went forth to coquet with flesh while hypocritically affecting business with spiritual things; on this occasion for wearing their white stockings and thin shoes, and their pink, white, and lilac gowns, on which every mud spot would be visible, the pool was an awkward impediment. They could hear the church-bell calling – as yet nearly a mile off.

'Who would have expected such a rise in the river in summertime!' said Marian, from the top of the roadside bank on which they had climbed, and were maintaining a precarious footing in the hope of creeping along its slope till they were past the pool.

'We can't get there anyhow, without walking right through it, or else going round the Turnpike way; and that would make us so very late!' said Retty, pausing hopelessly.

'And I do colour up so hot, walking into church late, and all the people staring round,' said Marian, 'that I hardly cool down again till we get into the That-it-may-please-Thees.'

While they stood clinging to the bank they heard a splashing round the bend of the road, and presently appeared Angel Clare, advancing along the lane towards them through the water.

Four hearts gave a big throb simultaneously.

His aspect was probably as un-Sabbatarian a one as a dogmatic parson's son often presented; his attire being his dairy clothes, long wading boots, a cabbage-leaf inside his hat to keep his head cool, with a thistle-spud to finish him off.

'He's not going to church,' said Marian.

'No – I wish he was!' murmured Tess.

Angel, in fact, rightly or wrongly (to adopt the safe phrase of evasive controversialists), preferred sermons in stones to sermons in churches and chapels on fine summer days. This morning, moreover, he had gone out to see if the damage to the hay by the flood was considerable or not. On his walk he observed the girls from a long distance, though they had been so occupied with their difficulties of passage as not to notice him. He knew that the water had risen at that spot, and that it would quite check their progress. So he had hastened on, with a dim idea of how he could help them – one of them in particular.

The rosy-cheeked, bright-eyed quartet looked so charming in their light summer attire, clinging to the roadside bank like pigeons on a roof-slope, that he stopped a moment to regard them before coming close. Their gauzy skirts had brushed up from the grass innumerable flies and butterflies which, unable to escape, remained caged in the transparent tissue as in an aviary. Angel's eye at last fell upon Tess, the hindmost of the four; she, being full of suppressed laughter at their dilemma, could not help meeting his glance radiantly.

He came beneath them in the water, which did not rise over his long boots; and stood looking at the entrapped flies and butterflies.

'Are you trying to get to church?' he said to Marian, who was in front, including the next two in his remark, but avoiding Tess.

'Yes, sir; and 'tis getting late; and my colour do come up so – '

'I'll carry you through the pool – every Jill of you.'

The whole four flushed as if one heart beat through them.

'I think you can't, sir,' said Marian.

'It is the only way for you to get past. Stand still. Nonsense – you are not too heavy! I'd carry you all four together. Now, Marian, attend,' he continued, 'and put your arms round my shoulders, so. Now! Hold on. That's well done.'

Marian had lowered herself upon his arm and shoulder as directed, and Angel strode off with her, his slim figure, as viewed from behind, looking like the mere stem to the great nosegay suggested by hers. They disappeared round the curve of the road, and only his sousing footsteps and the top ribbon of Marian's bonnet told where they were. In a few minutes he reappeared. Izz Huett was the next in order upon the bank.

'Here he comes,' she murmured, and they could hear that her lips were dry with emotion. 'And I have to put my arms round his neck and look into his face as Marian did.'

'There's nothing in that,' said Tess quickly.

'There's a time for everything,' continued Izz, unheeding. 'A time to embrace, and a time to refrain from embracing; the first is now going to be mine.'

'Fie – it is Scripture, Izz!'

'Yes,' said Izz, 'I've always a' ear at church for pretty verses.'

Angel Clare, to whom three-quarters of this performance was a commonplace act of kindness, now approached Izz. She quietly and dreamily lowered herself into his arms, and Angel methodically marched off with her. When he was heard returning for the third time Retty's throbbing heart could be almost seen to shake her. He went up to the red-haired girl, and while he was seizing her he glanced at Tess. His lips could not have pronounced more plainly, 'It will soon be you and I.' Her comprehension appeared in her face; she could not help it. There was an understanding between them.

Poor little Retty, though by far the lightest weight, was the most troublesome of Clare's burdens. Marian had been like a sack of meal, a dead weight of plumpness under which he had literally staggered. Izz had ridden sensibly and calmly. Retty was a bunch of hysterics.

However, he got through with the disquieted creature, deposited her, and returned. Tess could see over the hedge the distant three in a group, standing as he had placed them on the next rising ground. It was now her turn. She was embarrassed to discover that excitement at the proximity of Mr Clare's breath and eyes, which she had contemned in her companions, was intensified in herself; and as if fearful of betraying her secret she paltered with him at the last moment.

'I may be able to clim' along the bank perhaps – I can clim' better than they. You must be so tired, Mr Clare!'

'No, no, Tess,' said he quickly. And almost before she was aware she was seated in his arms and resting against his shoulder.

'Three Leahs to get one Rachel,' he whispered.

'They are better women than I,' she replied, magnanimously sticking to her resolve.

'Not to me,' said Angel.

He saw her grow warm at this; and they went some steps in silence.

'I hope I am not too heavy?' she said timidly.

'O no. You should lift Marian! Such a lump. You are like an undulating billow warmed by the sun. And all this fluff of muslin about you is the froth.'

'It is very pretty – if I seem like that to you.'

'Do you know that I have undergone three-quarters of this labour entirely for the sake of the fourth quarter?'

'No.'

'I did not expect such an event today.'

'Nor I . . . The water came up so sudden.'

That the rise in the water was what she understood him to refer to, the state of her breathing belied. Clare stood still and inclined his face towards hers.

'O Tessy!' he exclaimed.

The girl's cheeks burned to the breeze, and she could not look into his eyes for her emotion. It reminded Angel that he was somewhat unfairly taking advantage of an accidental position; and he went no further with it. No definite words of love had crossed their lips as yet, and suspension at this point was desirable now. However, he walked slowly, to make the remainder of the distance as long as possible; but at last they came to the bend, and the rest of their progress was in full view of the other three. The dry land was reached, and he set her down.

Her friends were looking with round thoughtful eyes at her and him, and she could see that they had been talking of her. He hastily bade them farewell, and splashed back along the stretch of submerged road.

The four moved on together as before, till Marian broke the silence by saying – 'No – in all truth; we have no chance against her!' She looked joylessly at Tess.

'What do you mean?' asked the latter.

'He likes 'ee best – the very best! We could see it as he brought 'ee. He would have kissed 'ee, if you had encouraged him to do it, ever so little.'

'No, no,' said she.

The gaiety with which they had set out had somehow vanished; and yet there was no enmity or malice between them. They were generous young souls; they had been reared in the lonely country nooks where fatalism is a strong sentiment, and they did not blame her. Such supplanting was to be.

Tess's heart ached. There was no concealing from herself the fact that she loved Angel Clare, perhaps all the more passionately from knowing that the others had also lost their hearts to him. There is contagion in this sentiment, especially among women. And yet that same hungry heart of hers compassionated her friends. Tess's honest nature had fought against this, but too feebly, and the natural result had followed.

'I will never stand in your way, nor in the way of either of you!' she declared to Retty that night in the bedroom (her tears running down). 'I can't help this, my dear! I don't think marrying is in his mind at all; but if he were ever to ask me I should refuse him, as I should refuse any man.'

'Oh! would you? Why?' said wondering Retty.

'It cannot be! But I will be plain. Putting myself quite on one side, I don't think he will choose either of you.'

'I have never expected it – thought of it!' moaned Retty. 'But O! I wish I was dead!'

The poor child, torn by a feeling which she hardly understood, turned to the other two girls who came upstairs just then.

'We be friends with her again,' she said to them. 'She thinks no more of his choosing her than we do.'

So the reserve went off, and they were confiding and warm.

'I don't seem to care what I do now,' said Marian, whose mood was tuned to its lowest bass. 'I was going to marry a dairyman at Stickleford, who's asked me twice; but – my soul – I would put an end to myself rather'n be his wife now! Why don't ye speak, Izz?'

'To confess, then,' murmured Izz, 'I made sure today that he was going to kiss me as he held me; and I lay still against his breast, hoping and hoping, and never moved at all. But he did not. I don't like biding here at Talbothays any longer! I shall go hwome.'

The air of the sleeping-chamber seemed to palpitate with the hopeless passion of the girls. They writhed feverishly under the oppressiveness of an emotion thrust on them by cruel Nature's law – an emotion which they had neither expected nor desired. The incident of the day had fanned the flame that was burning the inside of their hearts out, and the torture was almost more than they could endure. The differences which distinguished them as individuals were abstracted by this passion, and each was but portion of one organism called sex. There was so much frankness and so little jealousy because there was no hope. Each one was a girl of fair common sense, and she did not delude herself with any vain conceits, or deny her love, or give herself airs, in the idea of outshining the others. The full recognition of the futility of their infatuation, from a social point of view; its purposeless beginning; its self-bounded outlook; its lack of everything to justify its existence in the eye of civilisation (while lacking nothing in the eye of Nature); the one fact that it did exist, ecstasising them to a killing joy; all this imparted to them a resignation, a dignity, which a practical and sordid expectation of winning him as a husband would have destroyed.

They tossed and turned on their little beds, and the cheese-wring dripped monotonously downstairs.

'B' you awake, Tess?' whispered one, half an hour later.

It was Izz Huett's voice.

Tess replied in the affirmative, whereupon also Retty and Marian suddenly flung the bedclothes off them, and sighed – 'So be we!'

'I wonder what she is like – the lady they say his family have looked out for him!'

'I wonder,' said Izz.

'Some lady looked out for him?' gasped Tess, starting. 'I have never heard o' that!'

'O yes – 'tis whispered; a young lady of his own rank, chosen by his family; a Doctor of Divinity's daughter near his father's parish of Emminster; he don't much care for her, they say. But he is sure to marry her.'

They had heard so very little of this; yet it was enough to build up wretched dolorous dreams upon, there in the shade of the night. They pictured all the details of his being won round to consent, of the wedding preparations, of the bride's happiness, of her dress and veil, of her blissful home with him, when oblivion would have fallen upon themselves as far as he and their love were concerned. Thus they talked, and ached, and wept till sleep charmed their sorrow away.

After this disclosure Tess nourished no further foolish thought that there lurked any grave and deliberate import in Clare's attentions to her. It was a passing summer love of her face, for love's own temporary sake – nothing more. And the thorny crown of this sad conception was that she whom he really did prefer in a cursory way to the rest, she who knew herself to be more impassioned in nature, cleverer, more beautiful than they, was in the eyes of propriety far less worthy of him than the homelier ones whom he ignored.

## *Chapter 24*

Amid the oozing fatness and warm ferments of the Froom Vale, at a season when the rush of juices could almost be heard below the hiss of fertilisation, it was impossible that the most fanciful love should not grow passionate. The ready bosoms existing there were impregnated by their surroundings.

July passed over their heads, and the Thermidorean weather which came in its wake seemed an effort on the part of Nature to match the state of hearts at Talbothays Dairy. The air of the place, so fresh in the spring and early summer, was stagnant and enervating now. Its heavy scents weighed upon them, and at midday the landscape seemed lying in a swoon. Ethiopic scorchings browned the upper slopes of the pastures, but there was still bright green herbage here where the watercourses purled. And as Clare was oppressed by the outward heats, so was he burdened inwardly by waxing fervour of passion for the soft and silent Tess.

The rains having passed the uplands were dry. The wheels of the dairyman's spring cart, as he sped home from market, licked up the pulverised surface of the highway, and were followed by white ribands of dust, as if they had set a thin powder-train on fire. The cows jumped wildly over the five-barred barton-gate, maddened by the gadfly; Dairyman Crick kept his shirt-sleeves permanently rolled up from Monday to Saturday; open windows had no effect in ventilation without open doors, and in the dairy-garden the blackbirds and thrushes crept about under the currant-bushes, rather in the manner of quadrupeds than of winged creatures. The flies in the kitchen were lazy, teasing, and familiar, crawling about in unwonted places, on the floors, into drawers, and over the backs of the milkmaids' hands. Conversations were concerning sunstroke; while butter-making, and still more butter-keeping, was a despair.

They milked entirely in the meads for coolness and convenience, without driving in the cows. During the day the animals obsequiously followed the shadow of the smallest tree as it moved round the stem with the diurnal roll; and when the milkers came they could hardly stand still for the flies.

On one of these afternoons four or five unmilked cows chanced to stand apart from the general herd, behind the corner of a hedge, among them being Dumpling and Old Pretty, who loved Tess's hands above those of any other maid. When she rose from her stool under a finished cow Angel Clare, who had been observing her for some time, asked her if she would take the aforesaid creatures next. She silently assented, and with her stool at arm's length, and the pail against her knee, went round to where they stood. Soon the sound of Old Pretty's milk fizzing into the pail came through the hedge, and then Angel felt inclined to go round the corner also, to finish off a hard-yielding milcher who had strayed there, he being now as capable of this as the dairyman himself.

All the men, and some of the women, when milking, dug their foreheads into the cows and gazed into the pail. But a few – mainly the younger ones – rested their heads sideways. This was Tess Durbeyfield's habit, her temple pressing the milcher's flank, her eyes fixed on the far end of the meadow with the quiet of one lost in meditation. She was milking Old Pretty thus, and the sun chancing to be on the milking-side it shone flat upon her pink-gowned form and her white curtain-bonnet, and upon her profile, rendering it keen as a cameo cut from the dun background of the cow.

She did not know that Clare had followed her round, and that he sat under his cow watching her. The stillness of her head and features was remarkable: she might have been in a trance, her eyes open, yet unseeing. Nothing in the picture moved but Old Pretty's tail and Tess's pink hands, the latter so gently as to be a rhythmic pulsation only, as if they were obeying a reflex stimulus, like a beating heart.

How very lovable her face was to him. Yet there was nothing ethereal about it; all was real vitality, real warmth, real incarnation. And it was in her mouth that this culminated. Eyes almost as deep and speaking he had seen before, and cheeks perhaps as fair; brows as arched, a chin and throat almost as shapely; her mouth he had seen nothing to equal on the face of the earth. To a young man with the least fire in him that little upward lift in the middle of her red top lip was distracting, infatuating, maddening. He had never before seen a woman's lips and teeth which forced upon his mind with such persistent iteration the old Elizabethan simile of roses filled with snow. Perfect, he, as a lover, might have called them off-hand. But no – they were not perfect. And it was the touch of the imperfect upon the would-be perfect that gave the sweetness, because it was that which gave the humanity.

Clare had studied the curves of those lips so many times that he could reproduce them mentally with ease: and now, as they again confronted him, clothed with colour and life, they sent an *aura* over his flesh, a breeze through his nerves, which wellnigh produced a qualm; and actually produced, by some mysterious physiological process, a prosaic sneeze.

She then became conscious that he was observing her; but she would not show it by any change of position, though the curious dream-like fixity disappeared, and a close eye might easily have discerned that the rosiness of her face deepened, and then faded till only a tinge of it was left.

The influence that had passed into Clare like an excitation from the sky did not die down. Resolutions, reticences, prudences, fears, fell back like a defeated battalion. He jumped up from his seat, and, leaving his pail to be kicked over if the milcher had such a mind, went quickly towards the desire of his eyes, and, kneeling down beside her, clasped her in his arms.

Tess was taken completely by surprise, and she yielded to his embrace with unreflecting inevitableness. Having seen that it was really her lover who had advanced, and no one else, her lips parted, and she sank upon him in her momentary joy, with something very like an ecstatic cry.

He had been on the point of kissing that too tempting mouth, but he checked himself, for tender conscience' sake.

'Forgive me, Tess dear!' he whispered. 'I ought to have asked. I – did not know what I was doing. I do not mean it as a liberty. I am devoted to you, Tessy, dearest, in all sincerity!'

Old Pretty by this time had looked round, puzzled; and seeing two people crouching under her where, by immemorial custom, there should have been only one, lifted her hind leg crossly.

'She is angry – she doesn't know what we mean – she'll kick over the milk!' exclaimed Tess, gently striving to free herself, her eyes concerned with the quadruped's actions, her heart more deeply concerned with herself and Clare.

She slipped up from her seat, and they stood together, his arm still encircling her. Tess's eyes, fixed on distance, began to fill.

'Why do you cry, my darling?' he said.

'O – I don't know!' she murmured.

As she saw and felt more clearly the position she was in she became agitated and tried to withdraw.

'Well, I have betrayed my feeling, Tess, at last,' said he, with a curious sigh of desperation, signifying unconsciously that his heart had outrun his judgment. 'That I – love you dearly and truly I need not say. But I – it shall go no further now – it distresses you – I am as surprised as you are. You will not think I have presumed upon your defencelessness – been too quick and unreflecting, will you?'

'N' – I can't tell.'

He had allowed her to free herself; and in a minute or two the milking of each was resumed. Nobody had beheld the gravitation of the two into one; and when the dairyman came round by that screened nook a few minutes later there was not a sign to reveal that the markedly sundered pair were more to each other than mere acquaintance. Yet in the interval since Crick's last view of them something had occurred which changed the pivot of the universe for their two natures; something which, had he known its quality, the dairyman would have despised, as a practical man; yet which was based upon a more stubborn and resistless tendency than a whole heap of so-called practicalities. A veil had been whisked aside; the tract of each one's outlook was to have a new horizon thenceforward – for a short time or for a long.

END OF PHASE THE THIRD

# PHASE THE FOURTH

## *The Consequence*

## *Chapter 25*

Clare, restless, went out into the dusk when evening drew on, she who had won him having retired to her chamber.

The night was as sultry as the day. There was no coolness after dark unless on the grass. Roads, garden-paths, the house-fronts, the barton-walls were warm as hearths, and reflected the noontide temperature into the noctambulist's face.

He sat on the east gate of the dairy-yard, and knew not what to think of himself. Feeling had indeed smothered judgment that day.

Since the sudden embrace, three hours before, the twain had kept apart. She seemed stilled, almost alarmed, at what had occurred, while the novelty, unpremeditation, mastery of circumstance disquieted him – palpitating, contemplative being that he was. He could hardly realise their true relations to each other as yet, and what their mutual bearing should be before third parties thenceforward.

Angel had come as pupil to this dairy in the idea that his temporary existence here was to be the merest episode in his life, soon passed through and early forgotten; he had come as to a place from which as from a screened alcove he could calmly view the absorbing world without, and, apostrophising it with Walt Whitman:

> Crowds of men and women attired in the usual costumes,
> How curious you are to me!

resolve upon a plan for plunging into that world anew. But behold, the absorbing scene had been imported hither. What had been the engrossing world had dissolved into an uninteresting outer dumb-show; while here, in this apparently dim and unimpassioned place, novelty had volcanically started up, as it had never, for him, started up elsewhere.

Every window of the house being open Clare could hear across the yard each trivial sound of the retiring household. That dairy-house, so humble, so insignificant, so purely to him a place of constrained sojourn that he had never hitherto deemed it of sufficient importance to be reconnoitred as an object of any quality whatever in the landscape; what was it now? The aged and lichened brick gables breathed forth 'Stay!' The windows smiled, the door coaxed and beckoned, the creeper blushed confederacy. A personality within it was so far-reaching in her influence as to spread into and make the bricks, mortar, and whole overhanging sky throb with a burning sensibility. Whose was this mighty personality? A milkmaid's.

It was amazing, indeed, to find how great a matter the life of the obscure dairy had become to him. And though new love was to be held partly responsible for this it was not solely so. Many besides Angel have learnt that the magnitude of lives is not as to their external displacements, but as to their subjective experiences. The impressionable peasant leads a larger, fuller, more dramatic life than the pachydermatous king. Looking at it thus he found that life was to be seen of the same magnitude here as elsewhere.

Despite his heterodoxy, faults, and weaknesses, Clare was a man with a conscience. Tess was no insignificant creature to toy with and dismiss; but a woman living her precious life – a life which, to herself who endured or enjoyed it, possessed as great a dimension as the life of the mightiest to himself. Upon her sensations the whole world depended to Tess; through her existence all her fellow-creatures existed, to her. The universe itself only came into being for Tess on the particular day in the particular year in which she was born.

This consciousness upon which he had intruded was the single opportunity of existence ever vouchsafed to Tess by an unsympathetic First Cause – her all; her every and only chance. How then should he look upon her as of less consequence than himself; as a pretty trifle to caress and grow weary of; and not deal in the greatest seriousness with the affection which he knew that he had awakened in her – so fervid and so impressionable as she was under her reserve; in order that it might not agonise and wreck her?

To encounter her daily in the accustomed manner would be to develop what had begun. Living in such close relations, to meet meant to fall into endearment; flesh and blood could not resist it; and, having arrived at no conclusion as to the issue of such a tendency, he decided to hold aloof for the present from occupations in which they would be mutually engaged. As yet the harm done was small.

But it was not easy to carry out the resolution never to approach her. He was driven towards her by every heave of his pulse.

He thought he would go and see his friends. It might be possible to sound them upon this. In less than five months his term here would have ended, and after a few additional months spent upon other farms he would be fully equipped in agricultural knowledge, and in a position to start on his own account. Would not a farmer want a wife, and should a farmer's wife be a drawing-room wax-figure, or a woman who understood farming? Notwithstanding the pleasing answer returned to him by the silence he resolved to go his journey.

One morning when they sat down to breakfast at Talbothays Dairy some maid observed that she had not seen anything of Mr Clare that day.

'O no,' said Dairyman Crick. 'Mr Clare has gone hwome to Emminster to spend a few days wi' his kinsfolk.'

For four impassioned ones around that table the sunshine of the morning went out at a stroke, and the birds muffled their song. But neither girl by word or gesture revealed her blankness.

'He's getting on towards the end of his time wi' me,' added the dairyman, with a phlegm which unconsciously was brutal; 'and so I suppose he is beginning to see about his plans elsewhere.'

'How much longer is he to bide here?' asked Izz Huett, the only one of the gloom-stricken bevy who could trust her voice with the question.

The others waited for the dairyman's answer as if their lives hung upon it; Retty, with parted lips, gazing on the tablecloth, Marian with heat added to her redness, Tess throbbing and looking out at the meads.

'Well, I can't mind the exact day without looking at my memorandum-book,' replied Crick, with the same intolerable unconcern. 'And even that may be altered a bit. He'll bide to get a little practice in the calving out at the straw-yard, for certain. He'll hang on till the end of the year I should say.'

Four months or so of torturing ecstasy in his society – of 'pleasure girdled about with pain.' After that the blackness of unutterable night.

At this moment of the morning Angel Clare was riding along a narrow lane ten miles distant from the breakfasters, in the direction of his father's vicarage at Emminster, carrying, as well as he could, a little basket which contained some black-puddings and a bottle of mead, sent by Mrs Crick, with her kind respects, to his parents. The white lane stretched before him, and his eyes were upon it; but they were staring into next year, and not at the lane. He loved her; ought he to marry her? Dared he to marry her? What would his mother and his brothers say? What would he himself say a couple of years after the event? That would depend upon whether the germs of staunch comradeship underlay the temporary emotion, or whether it were a sensuous joy in her form only, with no substratum of everlastingness.

His father's hill-surrounded little town, the Tudor church-tower of red stone, the clump of trees near the vicarage, came at last into view beneath him, and he rode down towards the well-known gate. Casting a glance in the direction of the church before entering his home, he beheld standing by the vestry-door a group of girls, of ages between twelve and sixteen, apparently awaiting the arrival of some other one, who in a moment became visible; a figure somewhat older than the schoolgirls, wearing a broad-brimmed hat and highly-starched cambric morning-gown, with a couple of books in her hand.

Clare knew her well. He could not be sure that she observed him; he hoped she did not, so as to render it unnecessary that he should go and speak to her, blameless creature that she was. An overpowering reluctance to greet her made him decide that she had not seen him. The young lady was Miss Mercy Chant, the only daughter of his father's neighbour and friend, whom it was his parents' quiet hope that he might wed someday. She was great at Antinomianism and Bible-classes, and was plainly going to hold a class now. Clare's mind flew to the impassioned, summer-steeped heathens in the Var Vale, their rosy faces court-patched with cow-droppings; and to one the most impassioned of them all.

It was on the impulse of the moment that he had resolved to trot over to Emminster, and hence had not written to apprise his mother and father, aiming, however, to arrive about the breakfast hour, before they should have gone out to their parish duties. He was a little late, and they had already sat down to the morning meal. The group at the table jumped up to welcome him as soon as he entered. They were his father and mother, his brother the Reverend Felix – curate at a town in the adjoining county, home for the inside of a fortnight – and his other brother, the Reverend Cuthbert, the classical scholar, and Fellow and Dean of his College, down from Cambridge for the long vacation. His mother appeared in a cap and silver spectacles, and his father looked what in fact he was – an earnest, God-fearing man, somewhat gaunt, in years about sixty-five, his pale face lined with thought and purpose. Over their heads hung the picture of Angel's sister, the eldest of the family, sixteen years his senior, who had married a missionary and gone out to Africa.

Old Mr Clare was a clergyman of a type which, within the last twenty years, has wellnigh dropped out of contemporary life. A spiritual descendant in the direct line from Wycliff, Huss, Luther, Calvin; an Evangelical of the Evangelicals, a Conversionist, a man of Apostolic simplicity in life and thought, he had in his raw youth made up his mind once for all on the deeper questions of existence, and admitted no further reasoning on them thenceforward. He was regarded even by those of his own date and school of thinking as extreme; while, on the other hand, those totally opposed to him were unwillingly won to admiration for his thoroughness, and for the remarkable power he showed in dismissing all question as to principles in his energy for applying them. He loved Paul of Tarsus, liked St John, hated St James as much as he dared, and regarded with mixed feelings Timothy, Titus, and Philemon. The New Testament was less a Christiad than a Pauliad to his intelligence – less an argument than an intoxication. His creed of determinism was such that it almost amounted to a vice, and quite amounted, on its negative side, to a renunciative philosophy which had cousinship with that of Schopenhauer and Leopardi. He despised the Canons and Rubric, swore by the Articles, and deemed himself consistent through the whole category – which in a way he might have been. One thing he certainly was – sincere.

To the aesthetic, sensuous, pagan pleasure in natural life and lush womanhood which his son Angel had lately been experiencing in Var Vale, his temper would have been antipathetic in a high degree, had he either by enquiry or imagination been able to apprehend it. Once upon a time Angel had been so unlucky as to say to his father, in a moment of irritation, that it might have resulted far better for mankind if Greece had been the source of the religion of modern civilisation, and not Palestine; and his father's grief was of that blank description which could not realise that there might lurk a thousandth part of a truth, much less a half truth or a whole truth, in such a proposition. He had simply preached austerely at Angel for some time after. But the kindness of his heart was such that he never resented anything for long, and welcomed his son today with a smile which was as candidly sweet as a child's.

Angel sat down, and the place felt like home; yet he did not so much as formerly feel himself one of the family gathered there. Every time that he returned hither he was conscious of this divergence, and since he had last shared in the vicarage life it had grown even more distinctly foreign to his own than usual. Its transcendental aspirations – still unconsciously based on the geocentric view of things, a zenithal paradise, a nadiral hell – were as foreign to his own as if they had been the dreams of people on another planet. Latterly he had seen only Life, felt only the great passionate pulse of existence, unwarped, uncontorted, untrammelled by those creeds which futilely attempt to check what wisdom would be content to regulate.

On their part they saw a great difference in him, a growing divergence from the Angel Clare of former times. It was chiefly a difference in his manner that they noticed just now, particularly his brothers. He was getting to behave like a farmer; he flung his legs about; the muscles of his face had grown more expressive; his eyes looked as much information as his tongue spoke, and more. The manner of the scholar had nearly disappeared; still more the manner of the drawing-room young man. A prig would have said that he had lost culture, and a prude that he had become coarse. Such was the contagion of domiciliary fellowship with the Talbothays nymphs and swains.

After breakfast he walked with his two brothers, non-evangelical, well-educated, hallmarked young men, correct to their remotest fibre, such unimpeachable models as are turned out yearly by the lathe of a systematic tuition. They were both somewhat short-sighted, and when it was the custom to wear a single eyeglass and string they wore a single eyeglass and string; when it was the custom to wear a double glass they wore a double glass; when it was the custom to wear spectacles they wore spectacles straightway, all without reference to the particular variety of defect in their own vision. When Wordsworth was enthroned they carried pocket copies; and when Shelley was belittled they allowed him to grow dusty on their shelves. When Correggio's Holy Families were admired, they admired Correggio's Holy Families; when he was decried in favour of Velasquez, they sedulously followed suit without any personal objection.

If these two noticed Angel's growing social ineptness, he noticed their growing mental limitations. Felix seemed to him all Church; Cuthbert all College. His Diocesan Synod and Visitations were the mainsprings of the world to the one; Cambridge to the other. Each brother candidly recognised that there were a few unimportant scores of millions of outsiders in civilised society, persons who were neither University men nor churchmen; but they were to be tolerated rather than reckoned with and respected.

They were both dutiful and attentive sons, and were regular in their visits to their parents. Felix, though an offshoot from a far more recent point in the devolution of theology than his father, was less self-sacrificing and disinterested. More tolerant than his father of a contradictory opinion, in its aspect as a danger to its holder, he was less ready than his father to pardon it as a slight to his own teaching. Cuthbert was, upon the whole, the more liberal-minded, though, with greater subtlety, he had not so much heart.

As they walked along the hillside Angel's former feeling revived in him – that whatever their advantages by comparison with himself, neither saw or set forth life as it really was lived. Perhaps, as with many men, their opportunities of observation were not so good as their opportunities of expression. Neither had an adequate conception of the complicated forces at work outside the smooth and gentle current in which they and their associates floated. Neither saw the difference between local truth and universal truth; that what the inner world said in their clerical and academic hearing was quite a different thing from what the outer world was thinking.

'I suppose it is farming or nothing for you now, my dear fellow,' Felix was saying, among other things, to his youngest brother, as he looked through his spectacles at the distant fields with sad austerity. 'And, therefore, we must make the best of it. But I do entreat you to endeavour to keep as much as possible in touch with moral ideals. Farming, of course, means roughing it externally; but high thinking may go with plain living, nevertheless.'

'Of course it may,' said Angel. 'Was it not proved nineteen hundred years ago – if I may trespass upon your domain a little? Why should you think, Felix, that I am likely to drop my high thinking and my moral ideals?'

'Well, I fancied, from the tone of your letters and our conversation – it may be fancy only – that you were somehow losing intellectual grasp. Hasn't it struck you, Cuthbert?'

'Now, Felix,' said Angel drily, 'we are very good friends, you know; each of us treading our allotted circles; but if it comes to intellectual grasp, I think you, as a contented dogmatist, had better leave mine alone, and enquire what has become of yours.'

They returned down the hill to dinner, which was fixed at any time at which their father's and mother's morning work in the parish usually concluded. Convenience as regarded afternoon callers was the last thing to enter into the consideration of unselfish Mr and Mrs Clare; though the three sons were sufficiently in unison on this matter to wish that their parents would conform a little to modern notions.

The walk had made them hungry, Angel in particular, who was now an outdoor man, accustomed to the profuse *dapes inemptoe* of the dairyman's somewhat coarsely-laden table. But neither of the old people had arrived, and it was not till the sons were almost tired of waiting that their parents entered. The self-denying pair had been occupied in coaxing the appetites of some of their sick parishioners, whom they, somewhat inconsistently, tried to keep imprisoned in the flesh, their own appetites being quite forgotten.

The family sat down to table, and a frugal meal of cold viands was deposited before them. Angel looked round for Mrs Crick's black-puddings, which he had directed to be nicely grilled, as they did them at the dairy, and of which he wished his father and mother to appreciate the marvellous herbal savours as highly as he did himself.

'Ah! you are looking for the black-puddings, my dear boy,' observed Clare's mother. 'But I am sure you will not mind doing without them, as I am sure your father and I shall not, when you know the reason. I suggested to him that we should take Mrs Crick's kind present to the children of the man who can earn nothing just now because of his attacks of delirium tremens; and he agreed that it would be a great pleasure to them; so we did.'

'Of course,' said Angel cheerfully, looking round for the mead.

'I found the mead so extremely alcoholic,' continued his mother, 'that it was quite unfit for use as a beverage, but as valuable as rum or brandy in an emergency; so I have put it in my medicine-closet.'

'We never drink spirits at this table, on principle,' added his father.

'But what shall I tell the dairyman's wife?' said Angel.

'The truth, of course,' said his father.

'I rather wanted to say we enjoyed the mead and the black-puddings very much. She is a kind, jolly sort of body, and is sure to ask me directly I return.'

'You cannot, if we did not,' Mr Clare answered lucidly.

'Ah – no; though that mead was a drop of pretty tipple.'

'A what?' said Cuthbert and Felix both.

'Oh – 'tis an expression they use down at Talbothays,' replied Angel, blushing. He felt that his parents were right in their practice if wrong in their want of sentiment, and said no more.

## *Chapter 26*

It was not till the evening, after family prayers, that Angel found opportunity of broaching to his father one or two subjects near his heart. He had strung himself up to the purpose while kneeling behind his brothers on the carpet, studying the little nails in the heels of their walking boots. When the service was over they went out of the room with their mother, and Mr Clare and himself were left alone

The young man first discussed with the elder his plans for the attainment of his position as a farmer on an extensive scale – either in England or in the Colonies. His father then told him that, as he had not been put to the expense of sending Angel up to Cambridge, he had felt it his duty to set by a sum of money every year towards the purchase or lease of land for him someday, that he might not feel himself unduly slighted

'As far as worldly wealth goes,' continued his father, 'you will no doubt stand far superior to your brothers in a few years.'

This considerateness on old Mr Clare's part led Angel onward to the other and dearer subject. He observed to his father that he was then six-and-twenty, and that when he should start in the farming business he would require eyes in the back of his head to see to all matters – someone would be necessary to superintend the domestic labours of his establishment whilst he was afield. Would it not be well, therefore, for him to marry?

His father seemed to think this idea not unreasonable; and then Angel put the question – 'What kind of wife do you think would be best for me as a thrifty hard-working farmer?'

'A truly Christian woman, who will be a help and a comfort to you in your goings-out and your comings-in. Beyond that, it really matters little. Such an one can be found; indeed my earnest-minded friend and neighbour, Dr Chant – '

'But ought she not primarily to be able to milk cows, churn good butter, make immense cheeses; know how to sit hens and turkeys and rear chickens, to direct a field of labourers in an emergency, and estimate the value of sheep and calves?'

'Yes; a farmer's wife; yes, certainly. It would be desirable.' Mr Clare, the elder, had plainly never thought of these points before. 'I was going to add,' he said, 'that for a pure and saintly woman you will not find one more to your true advantage, and certainly not more to your mother's mind and my own, than your friend Mercy, whom you used to show a certain interest in. It is true that my neighbour Chant's daughter has lately caught up the fashion of the younger clergy round about us for decorating the Communion-table – altar, as I was shocked to hear her call it one day – with flowers and other stuff on festival occasions. But her father, who is quite as opposed to such flummery as I, says that can be cured. It is a mere girlish outbreak which, I am sure, will not be permanent.'

'Yes, yes; Mercy is good and devout, I know. But, father, don't you think that a young woman equally pure and virtuous as Miss Chant, but one who, in place of that lady's ecclesiastical accomplishments, understands the duties of farm life as well as a farmer himself, would suit me infinitely better?'

His father persisted in his conviction that a knowledge of a farmer's wife's duties came second to a Pauline view of humanity; and the impulsive Angel, wishing to honour his father's feelings and to advance the cause of his heart at the same time, grew specious. He said that fate or Providence had thrown in his way a woman who possessed every qualification to be the helpmate of an agriculturist, and was decidedly of a serious turn of mind. He would not say whether or not she had attached herself to the sound Low Church School of his father; but she would probably be open to conviction on that point; she was a regular church-goer of simple faith; honest-hearted, receptive, intelligent, graceful to a degree, chaste as a vestal, and, in personal appearance, exceptionally beautiful.

'Is she of a family such as you would care to marry into – a lady, in short?' asked his startled mother, who had come softly into the study during the conversation.

'She is not what in common parlance is called a lady,' said Angel, unflinchingly, 'for she is a cottager's daughter, as I am proud to say. But she is a lady, nevertheless – in feeling and nature.'

'Mercy Chant is of a very good family.'

'Pooh! – what's the advantage of that, mother?' said Angel quickly. 'How is family to avail the wife of a man who has to rough it as I have, and shall have to do?'

'Mercy is accomplished. And accomplishments have their charm,' returned his mother, looking at him through her silver spectacles.

'As to external accomplishments, what will be the use of them in the life I am going to lead? – while as to her reading, I can take that in hand. She'll be apt pupil enough, as you would say if you knew her. She's brim full of poetry – actualised poetry, if I may use the expression. She *lives* what paper-poets only write . . . And she is an unimpeachable Christian, I am sure; perhaps of the very tribe, genus, and species you desire to propagate.'

'O Angel, you are mocking!'

'Mother, I beg pardon. But as she really does attend Church almost every Sunday morning, and is a good Christian girl, I am sure you will tolerate any social shortcomings for the sake of that quality, and feel that I may do worse than choose her.' Angel waxed quite earnest on that rather automatic orthodoxy in his beloved Tess which (never dreaming that it might stand him in such good stead) he had been prone to slight when observing it practised by her and the other milkmaids, because of its obvious unreality amid beliefs essentially naturalistic.

In their sad doubts as to whether their son had himself any right whatever to the title he claimed for the unknown young woman, Mr and Mrs Clare began to feel it as an advantage not to be overlooked that she at least was sound in her views; especially as the conjunction of the pair must have arisen by an act of Providence; for Angel never would have made orthodoxy a condition of his choice. They said finally that it was better not to act in a hurry, but that they would not object to see her.

Angel therefore refrained from declaring more particulars now. He felt that, single-minded and self-sacrificing as his parents were, there yet existed certain latent prejudices of theirs, as middle-class people, which it would require some tact to overcome. For though legally at liberty to do as he chose, and though their daughter-in-law's qualifications could make no practical difference to their lives, in the probability of her living far away from them, he wished for affection's sake not to wound their sentiment in the most important decision of his life.

He observed his own inconsistencies in dwelling upon accidents in Tess's life as if they were vital features. It was for herself that he loved Tess; her soul, her heart, her substance – not for her skill in the dairy, her aptness as his scholar, and certainly not for her simple formal faith-professions. Her unsophisticated open-air existence required no varnish of conventionality to make it palatable to him. He held that education had as yet but little affected the beats of emotion and impulse on which domestic happiness depends. It was probable that, in the lapse of ages, improved systems of moral and intellectual training would appreciably, perhaps considerably, elevate the involuntary and even the unconscious instincts of human nature; but up to the present day culture, as far as he could see, might be said to have affected only the mental epiderm of those lives which had been brought under its influence. This belief was confirmed by his experience of women, which, having latterly been extended from the cultivated middle-class into the rural community, had taught him how much less was the intrinsic difference between the good and wise woman of one social stratum and the good and wise woman of another social stratum, than between the good and bad, the wise and the foolish, of the same stratum or class.

It was the morning of his departure. His brothers had already left the vicarage to proceed on a walking tour in the north, whence one was to return to his college, and the other to his curacy. Angel might have accompanied them, but preferred to rejoin his sweetheart at Talbothays. He would have been an awkward member of the party; for, though the most appreciative humanist, the most ideal religionist, even the best-versed Christologist of the three, there was alienation in the standing consciousness that his squareness would not fit the round hole that had been prepared for him. To neither Felix nor Cuthbert had he ventured to mention Tess.

His mother made him sandwiches, and his father accompanied him, on his own mare, a little way along the road. Having fairly well advanced his own affairs Angel listened in a willing silence, as they jogged on together through the shady lanes, to his father's account of his parish difficulties, and the coldness of brother clergymen whom he loved, because of his strict interpretations of the New Testament by the light of what they deemed a pernicious Calvinistic doctrine.

'Pernicious!' said Mr Clare, with genial scorn; and he proceeded to recount experiences which would show the absurdity of that idea. He told of wondrous conversions of evil livers of which he had been the instrument, not only amongst the poor, but amongst the rich and well-to-do; and he also candidly admitted many failures.

As an instance of the latter, he mentioned the case of a young upstart squire named d'Urberville, living some forty miles off, in the neighbourhood of Trantridge.

'Not one of the ancient d'Urbervilles of Kingsbere and other places?' asked his son. 'That curiously historic worn-out family with its ghostly legend of the coach-and-four?'

'O no. The original d'Urbervilles decayed and disappeared sixty or eighty years ago – at least, I believe so. This seems to be a new family which has taken the name; for the credit of the former knightly line I hope they are spurious, I'm sure. But it is odd to hear you express interest in old families. I thought you set less store by them even than I.'

'You misapprehend me, father; you often do,' said Angel with a little impatience. 'Politically I am sceptical as to the virtue of their being old. Some of the wise even among themselves "exclaim against their own succession," as Hamlet puts it; but lyrically, dramatically, and even historically, I am tenderly attached to them.'

This distinction, though by no means a subtle one, was yet too subtle for Mr Clare the elder, and he went on with the story he had been about to relate; which was that after the death of the senior so-called d'Urberville the young man developed the most culpable passions, though he had a blind mother, whose condition should have made him know better. A knowledge of his career having come to the ears of Mr Clare, when he was in that part of the country preaching missionary sermons, he boldly took occasion to speak to the delinquent on his spiritual state. Though he was a stranger, occupying another's pulpit, he had felt this to be his duty, and took for his text the words from St Luke: 'Thou fool, this night thy soul shall be required of thee!' The young man much resented this directness of attack, and in the war of words which followed when they met he did not scruple publicly to insult Mr Clare, without respect for his grey hairs.

Angel flushed with distress.

'Dear father,' he said sadly, 'I wish you would not expose yourself to such gratuitous pain from scoundrels!'

'Pain?' said his father, his rugged face shining in the ardour of self-abnegation. 'The only pain to me was pain on his account, poor, foolish young man. Do you suppose his incensed words could give me any pain, or even his blows? "Being reviled we bless; being persecuted we suffer it; being defamed we entreat; we are made as the filth of the world, and as the offscouring of all things unto this day." Those ancient and noble words to the Corinthians are strictly true at this present hour.'

'Not blows, father? He did not proceed to blows?'

'No, he did not. Though I have borne blows from men in a mad state of intoxication.'

'No!'

'A dozen times, my boy. What then? I have saved them from the guilt of murdering their own flesh and blood thereby; and they have lived to thank me, and praise God.'

'May this young man do the same!' said Angel fervently. 'But I fear otherwise, from what you say.'

'We'll hope, nevertheless,' said Mr Clare. 'And I continue to pray for him, though on this side of the grave we shall probably never meet again. But, after all, one of those poor words of mine may spring up in his heart as a good seed someday.'

Now, as always, Clare's father was sanguine as a child; and though the younger could not accept his parent's narrow dogma he revered his practice, and recognised the hero under the pietist. Perhaps he revered his father's practice even more now than ever, seeing that, in the question of making Tessy his wife, his father had not once thought of enquiring whether she were well provided or penniless. The same unworldliness was what had necessitated Angel's getting a living as a farmer, and would probably keep his brothers in the position of poor parsons for the term of their activities; yet Angel admired it none the less. Indeed, despite his own heterodoxy, Angel often felt that he was nearer to his father on the human side than was either of his brethren.

## *Chapter 27*

An uphill and downhill ride of twenty-odd miles through a garish midday atmosphere brought him in the afternoon to a detached knoll a mile or two west of Talbothays, whence he again looked into that green trough of sappiness and humidity, the valley of the Var or Froom. Immediately he began to descend from the upland to the fat alluvial soil below, the atmosphere grew heavier; the languid perfume of the summer fruits, the mists, the hay, the flowers, formed therein a vast pool of odour which at this hour seemed to make the animals, the very bees and butterflies, drowsy. Clare was now so familiar with the spot that he knew the individual cows by their names when, a long distance off, he saw them dotted about the meads. It was with a sense of luxury that he recognised his power of viewing life here from its inner side, in a way that had been quite foreign to him in his student-days; and, much as he loved his parents, he could not help being aware that to come here, as now, after an experience of home-life, affected him like throwing off splints and bandages; even the one customary curb on the humours of English rural societies being absent in this place, Talbothays having no resident landlord.

Not a human being was out of doors at the dairy. The denizens were all enjoying the usual afternoon nap of an hour or so which the exceedingly early hours kept in summertime rendered a necessity. At the door the wood-hooped pails, sodden and bleached by infinite scrubbings, hung like hats on a stand upon the forked and peeled limb of an oak fixed there for that purpose; all of them ready and dry for the evening milking. Angel entered, and went through the silent passages of the house to the back quarters, where he listened for a moment. Sustained snores came from the cart-house, where some of the men were lying down; the grunt and squeal of sweltering pigs arose from the still further distance. The large-leaved rhubarb and cabbage plants slept too, their broad limp surfaces hanging in the sun like half-closed umbrellas.

He unbridled and fed his horse, and as he re-entered the house the clock struck three. Three was the afternoon skimming-hour; and, with the stroke, Clare heard the creaking of the floorboards above, and then the touch of a descending foot on the stairs. It was Tess's, who in another moment came down before his eyes.

She had not heard him enter, and hardly realised his presence there. She was yawning, and he saw the red interior of her mouth as if it had been a snake's. She had stretched one arm so high above her coiled-up cable of hair that he could see its satin delicacy above the sunburn; her face was flushed with sleep, and her eyelids hung heavy over their pupils. The brim-fulness of her nature breathed from her. It was a moment when a woman's soul is more incarnate than at any other time; when the most spiritual beauty bespeaks itself flesh; and sex takes the outside place in the presentation.

Then those eyes flashed brightly through their filmy heaviness, before the remainder of her face was well awake. With an oddly compounded look of gladness, shyness, and surprise, she exclaimed – 'O Mr Clare! How you frightened me – I – '

There had not at first been time for her to think of the changed relations which his declaration had introduced; but the full sense of the matter rose up in her face when she encountered Clare's tender look as he stepped forward to the bottom stair.

'Dear, darling Tessy!' he whispered, putting his arm round her, and his face to her flushed cheek. 'Don't, for Heaven's sake, Mister me any more. I have hastened back so soon because of you!'

Tess's excitable heart beat against his by way of reply; and there they stood upon the red-brick floor of the entry, the sun slanting in by the window upon his back, as he held her tightly to his breast; upon her inclining face, upon the blue veins of her temple, upon her naked arm, and her neck, and into the depths of her hair. Having been lying down in her clothes she was warm as a sunned cat. At first she would not look straight up at him, but her eyes soon lifted and his plumbed the deepness of the ever-varying pupils, with their radiating fibrils of blue, and black, and grey, and violet, while she regarded him as Eve at her second waking might have regarded Adam.

'I've got to go a-skimming,' she pleaded, 'and I have on'y old Deb to help me today. Mrs Crick is gone to market with Mr Crick, and Retty is not well, and the others are gone out somewhere, and won't be home till milking.'

As they retreated to the milk-house Deborah Fyander appeared on the stairs.

'I have come back, Deborah,' said Mr Clare, upwards. 'So I can help Tess with the skimming; and, as you are very tired, I am sure, you needn't come down till milking-time.'

Possibly the Talbothays milk was not very thoroughly skimmed that afternoon. Tess was in a dream wherein familiar objects appeared as having light and shade and position, but no particular outline. Every time she held the skimmer under the pump to cool it for the work her hand trembled, the ardour of his affection being so palpable that she seemed to flinch under it like a plant in too burning a sun.

Then he pressed her again to his side, and when she had done running her forefinger round the leads to cut off the cream-edge, he cleaned it in nature's way; for the unconstrained manners of Talbothays dairy came convenient now.

'I may as well say it now as later, dearest,' he resumed gently. 'I wish to ask you something of a very practical nature, which I have been thinking of ever since that day last week in the meads. I shall soon want to marry, and, being a farmer, you see I shall require for my wife a woman who knows all about the management of farms. Will you be that woman, Tessy?'

He put it in that way that she might not think he had yielded to an impulse of which his head would disapprove.

She turned quite careworn. She had bowed to the inevitable result of proximity, the necessity of loving him; but she had not calculated upon this sudden corollary, which, indeed, Clare had put before her without quite meaning himself to do it so soon. With pain that was like the bitterness of dissolution she murmured the words of her indispensable and sworn answer as an honourable woman.

'O Mr Clare – I cannot be your wife – I cannot be!'

The sound of her own decision seemed to break Tess's very heart, and she bowed her face in her grief.

'But, Tess!' he said, amazed at her reply, and holding her still more greedily close. 'Do you say no? Surely you love me?'

'O yes, yes! And I would rather be yours than anybody's in the world,' returned the sweet and honest voice of the distressed girl. 'But I *cannot* marry you!'

'Tess,' he said, holding her at arm's length, 'you are engaged to marry someone else!'

'No, no!'

'Then why do you refuse me?'

'I don't want to marry! I have not thought of doing it. I cannot! I only want to love you.'

'But why?'

Driven to subterfuge, she stammered – 'Your father is a parson, and your mother wouldn' like you to marry such as me. She will want you to marry a lady.'

'Nonsense – I have spoken to them both. That was partly why I went home.'

'I feel I cannot – never, never!' she echoed.

'Is it too sudden to be asked thus, my Pretty?'

'Yes – I did not expect it.'

'If you will let it pass, please, Tessy, I will give you time,' he said. 'It was very abrupt to come home and speak to you all at once. I'll not allude to it again for a while.'

She again took up the shining skimmer, held it beneath the pump, and began anew. But she could not, as at other times hit the exact under-surface of the cream with the delicate dexterity required, try as she might; sometimes she was cutting down into the milk, sometimes in the air. She could hardly see, her eyes having filled with two blurring tears drawn forth by a grief which, to this her best friend and dear advocate, she could never explain.

'I can't skim – I can't!' she said, turning away from him.

Not to agitate and hinder her longer the considerate Clare began talking in a more general way:

'You quite misapprehend my parents. They are the most simple-mannered people alive, and quite unambitious. They are two of the few remaining Evangelical school. Tessy, are you an Evangelical?'

'I don't know.'

'You go to church very regularly, and our parson here is not very High, they tell me.'

Tess's ideas on the views of the parish clergyman, whom she heard every week, seemed to be rather more vague than Clare's, who had never heard him at all.

'I wish I could fix my mind on what I hear there more firmly than I do,' she remarked as a safe generality. 'It is often a great sorrow to me.'

She spoke so unaffectedly that Angel was sure in his heart that his father could not object to her on religious grounds, even though she did not know whether her principles were High, Low or Broad. He himself knew that, in reality, the confused beliefs which she held, apparently imbibed in childhood, were, if anything, Tractarian as to phraseology and Pantheistic as to essence. Confused or otherwise, to disturb them was his last desire:

> Leave thou thy sister, when she prays,
> Her early Heaven, her happy views;
> Nor thou with shadow'd hint confuse
> A life that leads melodious days.

He had occasionally thought the counsel less honest than musical; but he gladly conformed to it now.

He spoke further of the incidents of his visit, of his father's mode of life, of his zeal for his principles; she grew serener, and the undulations disappeared from her skimming; as she finished one lead after another he followed her, and drew the plugs for letting down the milk.

'I fancied you looked a little downcast when you came in,' she ventured to observe, anxious to keep away from the subject of herself.

'Yes – well, my father has been talking a good deal to me of his troubles and difficulties, and the subject always tends to depress me. He is so zealous that he gets many snubs and buffetings from people of a different way of thinking from himself, and I don't like to hear of such humiliations to a man of his age, the more particularly as I don't think earnestness does any good when carried so far. He has been telling me of a very unpleasant scene in which he took part quite recently. He went as the deputy of some missionary society to preach in the neighbourhood of Trantridge, a place forty miles from here, and made it his business to expostulate with a lax young cynic he met with somewhere about there – son of some landowner up that way – and who has a mother afflicted with blindness. My father addressed himself to the gentleman point-blank, and there was quite a disturbance. It was very foolish of my father, I must say, to intrude his conversation upon a stranger when the probabilities were so obvious that it would be useless. But whatever he thinks to be his duty, that he'll do, in season or out of season; and, of course, he makes many enemies, not only among the absolutely vicious, but among the easy-going, who hate being bothered. He says he glories in what happened, and that good may be done indirectly; but I wish he would not wear himself out now he is getting old, and would leave such pigs to their wallowing.'

Tess's look had grown hard and worn, and her ripe mouth tragical; but she no longer showed any tremulousness. Clare's revived thoughts of his father prevented his noticing her particularly; and so they went on down the white row of liquid rectangles till they had finished and drained them off, when the other maids returned, and took their pails, and Deb came to scald out the leads for the new milk. As Tess withdrew to go afield to the cows he said to her softly – 'And my question, Tessy?'

'O no – no!' replied she with grave hopelessness, as one who had heard anew the turmoil of her own past in the allusion to Alec d'Urberville. 'It *can't* be!'

She went out towards the mead, joining the other milkmaids with a bound, as if trying to make the open air drive away her sad constraint. All the girls drew onward to the spot where the cows were grazing in the farther mead, the bevy advancing with the bold grace of wild animals – the reckless unchastened motion of women accustomed to unlimited space – in which they abandoned themselves to the air as a swimmer to the wave. It seemed natural enough to him now that Tess was again in sight to choose a mate from unconstrained Nature, and not from the abodes of Art.

## *Chapter 28*

Her refusal, though unexpected, did not permanently daunt Clare. His experience of women was great enough for him to be aware that the negative often meant nothing more than the preface to the affirmative; and it was little enough for him not to know that in the manner of the present negative there lay a great exception to the dallyings of coyness. That she had already permitted him to make love to her he read as an additional assurance, not fully trowing that in the fields and pastures to 'sigh gratis' is by no means deemed waste; love-making being here more often accepted inconsiderately and for its own sweet sake than in the carking anxious homes of the ambitious, where a girl's craving for an establishment paralyses her healthy thought of a passion as an end.

'Tess, why did you say "no" in such a positive way?' he asked her in the course of a few days.

She started.

'Don't ask me. I told you why – partly. I am not good enough – not worthy enough.'

'How? Not fine lady enough?'

'Yes – something like that,' murmured she. 'Your friends would scorn me.'

'Indeed, you mistake them – my father and mother. As for my brothers, I don't care – ' He clasped his fingers behind her back to keep her from slipping away. 'Now – you did not mean it, sweet? – I am sure you did not! You have made me so restless that I cannot read, or play, or do anything. I am in no hurry, Tess, but I want to know – to hear from your own warm lips – that you will someday be mine – any time you may choose; but someday?'

She could only shake her head and look away from him.

Clare regarded her attentively, conned the characters of her face as if they had been hieroglyphics. The denial seemed real.

'Then I ought not to hold you in this way – ought I? I have no right to you – no right to seek out where you are, or walk with you! Honestly, Tess, do you love any other man?'

'How can you ask?' she said, with continued self-suppression.

'I almost know that you do not. But then, why do you repulse me?'

'I don't repulse you. I like you to – tell me you love me; and you may always tell me so as you go about with me – and never offend me.'

'But you will not accept me as a husband?'

'Ah – that's different – it is for your good, indeed, my dearest! O, believe me, it is only for your sake! I don't like to give myself the great happiness o' promising to be yours in that way – because – because I am *sure* I ought not to do it.'

'But you will make me happy!'

'Ah – you think so, but you don't know!'

At such times as this, apprehending the grounds of her refusal to be her modest sense of incompetence in matters social and polite, he would say that she was wonderfully well-informed and versatile – which was certainly true, her natural quickness, and her admiration for him, having led her to pick up his vocabulary, his accent, and fragments of his knowledge, to a surprising extent. After these tender contests and her victory she would go away by herself under the remotest cow, if at milking-time, or into the sedge, or into her room, if at a leisure interval, and mourn silently, not a minute after an apparently phlegmatic negative.

The struggle was so fearful; her own heart was so strongly on the side of his – two ardent hearts against one poor little conscience – that she tried to fortify her resolution by every means in her power. She had come to Talbothays with a made-up mind. On no account could she agree to a step which might afterwards cause bitter rueing to her husband for his blindness in wedding her. And she held that what her conscience had decided for her when her mind was unbiassed ought not to be overruled now.

'Why don't somebody tell him all about me?' she said. 'It was only forty miles off – why hasn't it reached here? Somebody must know!'

Yet nobody seemed to know; nobody told him.

For two or three days no more was said. She guessed from the sad countenances of her chamber companions that they regarded her not only as the favourite, but as the chosen; but they could see for themselves that she did not put herself in his way.

Tess had never before known a time in which the thread of her life was so distinctly twisted of two strands, positive pleasure and positive pain. At the next cheese-making the pair were again left alone together. The dairyman himself had been lending a hand; but Mr Crick, as well as his wife, seemed latterly to have acquired a suspicion of mutual interest between these two; though they walked so circumspectly that suspicion was but of the faintest. Anyhow, the dairyman left them to themselves.

They were breaking up the masses of curd before putting them into the vats. The operation resembled the act of crumbling bread on a large scale; and amid the immaculate whiteness of the curds Tess Durbeyfield's hands showed themselves of the pinkness of the rose. Angel, who was filling the vats with his handfuls, suddenly ceased, and laid his hands flat upon hers. Her sleeves were rolled far above the elbow, and bending lower he kissed the inside vein of her soft arm.

Although the early September weather was sultry, her arm, from her dabbling in the curds, was as cold and damp to his mouth as a new-gathered mushroom, and tasted of the whey. But she was such a sheaf of susceptibilities that her pulse was accelerated by the touch, her blood driven to her finger-ends, and the cool arms flushed hot. Then, as though her heart had said, 'Is coyness longer necessary? Truth is truth between man and woman, as between man and man,' she lifted her eyes, and they beamed devotedly into his, as her lip rose in a tender half-smile.

'Do you know why I did that, Tess?' he said.

'Because you love me very much!'

'Yes, and as a preliminary to a new entreaty.'

'Not *again*!'

She looked a sudden fear that her resistance might break down under her own desire.

'O, Tessy!' he went on, 'I *cannot* think why you are so tantalising. Why do you disappoint me so? You seem almost like a coquette, upon my life you do – a coquette of the first urban water! They blow hot and blow cold, just as you do; and it is the very last sort of thing to expect to find in a retreat like Talbothays . . . And yet, dearest,' he quickly added, observing how the remark had cut her, 'I know you to be the most honest, spotless creature that ever lived. So how can I suppose you a flirt? Tess, why don't you like the idea of being my wife, if you love me as you seem to do?'

'I have never said I don't like the idea, and I never could say it; because – it isn't true!'

The stress now getting beyond endurance her lip quivered, and she was obliged to go away. Clare was so pained and perplexed that he ran after and caught her in the passage.

'Tell me, tell me!' he said, passionately clasping her, in forgetfulness of his curdy hands: 'do tell me that you won't belong to anybody but me!'

'I will, I will tell you!' she exclaimed. 'And I will give you a complete answer, if you will let me go now. I will tell you my experiences – all about myself – all!'

'Your experiences, dear; yes, certainly; any number.' He expressed assent in loving satire, looking into her face. 'My Tess has, no doubt, almost as many experiences as that wild convolvulus out there on the garden hedge, that opened itself this morning for the first time. Tell me anything, but don't use that wretched expression any more about not being worthy of me.'

'I will try – not! And I'll give you my reasons tomorrow – next week.'

'Say on Sunday?'

'Yes, on Sunday.'

At last she got away, and did not stop in her retreat till she was in the thicket of pollard willows at the lower side of the barton, where she could be quite unseen. Here Tess flung herself down upon the rustling undergrowth of spear-grass, as upon a bed, and remained crouching in palpitating misery broken by momentary shoots of joy, which her fears about the ending could not altogether suppress.

In reality, she was drifting into acquiescence. Every seesaw of her breath, every wave of her blood, every pulse singing in her ears, was a voice that joined with nature in revolt against her scrupulousness. Reckless, inconsiderate acceptance of him; to close with him at the altar, revealing nothing, and chancing discovery; to snatch ripe pleasure before the iron teeth of pain could have time to shut upon her: that was what love counselled; and in almost a terror of ecstasy Tess divined that, despite her many months of lonely self-chastisement, wrestlings, communings, schemes to lead a future of austere isolation, love's counsel would prevail.

The afternoon advanced, and still she remained among the willows. She heard the rattle of taking down the pails from the forked stands; the 'waow-waow!' which accompanied the getting together of the cows. But she did not go to the milking. They would see her agitation; and the dairyman, thinking the cause to be love alone, would good-naturedly tease her; and that harassment could not be borne.

Her lover must have guessed her overwrought state, and invented some excuse for her non-appearance, for no enquiries were made or calls given. At half-past six the sun settled down upon the levels, with the aspect of a great forge in the heavens, and presently a monstrous pumpkin-like moon arose on the other hand. The pollard willows, tortured out of their natural shape by incessant choppings, became spiny-haired monsters as they stood up against it. She went in, and upstairs without a light.

It was now Wednesday. Thursday came, and Angel looked thoughtfully at her from a distance, but intruded in no way upon her. The indoor milkmaids, Marian and the rest, seemed to guess that something definite was afoot, for they did not force any remarks upon her in the bedchamber. Friday passed; Saturday. Tomorrow was the day.

'I shall give way – I shall say yes – I shall let myself marry him – I cannot help it!' she jealously panted, with her hot face to the pillow that night, on hearing one of the other girls sigh his name in her sleep. 'I can't bear to let anybody have him but me! Yet it is a wrong to him, and may kill him when he knows! O my heart – O – O – O!'

## *Chapter 29*

'Now, who mid ye think I've heard news o' this morning?' said Dairyman Crick, as he sat down to breakfast next day with a riddling gaze round upon the munching men and maids. 'Now, just who mid ye think?'

One guessed, and another guessed. Mrs Crick did not guess, because she knew already.

'Well,' said the dairyman, ' 'tis that slack-twisted 'hore's-bird of a feller, Jack Dollop. He's lately got married to a widow-woman.'

'Not Jack Dollop? A villain – to think o' that!' said a milker.

The name entered quickly into Tess Durbeyfield's consciousness, for it was the name of the lover who had wronged his sweetheart, and had afterwards been so roughly used by the young woman's mother in the butter-churn.

'And has he married the valiant matron's daughter, as he promised?' asked Angel Clare absently, as he turned over the newspaper he was reading at the little table to which he was always banished by Mrs Crick, in her sense of his gentility.

'Not he, sir. Never meant to,' replied the dairyman. 'As I say, 'tis a widow-woman, and she had money, it seems – fifty poun' a year or so; and that was all he was after. They were married in a great hurry; and then she told him that by marrying she had lost her fifty poun' a year. Just fancy the state o' my gentleman's mind at that news! Never such a cat-and-dog life as they've been leading ever since! Serves him well beright. But unluckily the poor woman gets the worst o't.'

'Well, the silly body should have told en sooner that the ghost of her first man would trouble him,' said Mrs Crick.

'Ay; ay,' responded the dairyman indecisively. 'Still, you can see exactly how 'twas. She wanted a home, and didn't like to run the risk of losing him. Don't ye think that was something like it, maidens?'

He glanced towards the row of girls.

'She ought to ha' told him just before they went to church, when he could hardly have backed out,' exclaimed Marian.

'Yes, she ought,' agreed Izz.

'She must have seen what he was after, and should ha' refused him,' cried Retty spasmodically.

'And what do you say, my dear?' asked the dairyman of Tess.

'I think she ought – to have told him the true state of things – or else refused him – I don't know,' replied Tess, the bread and butter choking her.

'Be cust if I'd have done either o't,' said Beck Knibbs, a married helper from one of the cottages. 'All's fair in love and war. I'd ha' married en just as she did, and if he'd said two words to me about not telling him beforehand anything whatsomdever about my first chap that I hadn't chose to tell, I'd ha' knocked him down wi' the rolling-pin – a scram little feller like he! Any woman could do it.'

The laughter which followed this sally was supplemented only by a sorry smile, for form's sake, from Tess. What was comedy to them was tragedy to her; and she could hardly bear their mirth. She soon rose from table, and, with an impression that Clare would soon follow her, went along a little wriggling path, now stepping to one side of the irrigating channels, and now to the other, till she stood by the main stream of the Var. Men had been cutting the water-weeds higher up the river, and masses of them were floating past her – moving islands of green crowfoot, whereon she might almost have ridden; long locks of which weed had lodged against the piles driven to keep the cows from crossing.

Yes, there was the pain of it. This question of a woman telling her story – the heaviest of crosses to herself – seemed but amusement to others. It was as if people should laugh at martyrdom.

'Tessy!' came from behind her, and Clare sprang across the gully, alighting beside her feet. 'My wife – soon!'

'No, no; I cannot. For your sake, O Mr Clare; for your sake, I say no!'

'Tess!'

'Still I say no!' she repeated.

Not expecting this he had put his arm lightly round her waist the moment after speaking, beneath her hanging tail of hair. (The younger dairymaids, including Tess, breakfasted with their hair loose on Sunday mornings before building it up extra high for attending church, a style they could not adopt when milking with their heads against the cows.) If she had said 'Yes' instead of 'No' he would have kissed her; it had evidently been his intention; but her determined negative deterred his scrupulous heart. Their condition of domiciliary comradeship put her, as the woman, to such disadvantage by its enforced intercourse, that he felt it unfair to her to exercise any pressure of blandishment which he might have honestly employed had she been better able to avoid him. He released her momentarily-imprisoned waist, and withheld the kiss.

It all turned on that release. What had given her strength to refuse him this time was solely the tale of the widow told by the dairyman; and that would have been overcome in another moment. But Angel said no more; his face was perplexed; he went away.

Day after day they met – somewhat less constantly than before; and thus two or three weeks went by. The end of September drew near, and she could see in his eye that he might ask her again.

His plan of procedure was different now – as though he had made up his mind that her negatives were, after all, only coyness and youth startled by the novelty of the proposal. The fitful evasiveness of her manner when the subject was under discussion countenanced the idea. So he played a more coaxing game; and while never going beyond words, or attempting the renewal of caresses, he did his utmost orally.

In this way Clare persistently wooed her in undertones like that of the purling milk – at the cow's side, at skimmings, at butter-makings, at cheese-makings, among broody poultry, and among farrowing pigs – as no milkmaid was ever wooed before by such a man.

Tess knew that she must break down. Neither a religious sense of a certain moral validity in the previous union nor a conscientious wish for candour could hold out against it much longer. She loved him so passionately, and he was so godlike in her eyes; and being, though untrained, instinctively refined, her nature cried for his tutelary guidance. And thus, though Tess kept repeating to herself, 'I can never be his wife,' the words were vain. A proof of her weakness lay in the very utterance of what calm strength would not have taken the trouble to formulate. Every sound of his voice beginning on the old subject stirred her with a terrifying bliss, and she coveted the recantation she feared.

His manner was – what man's is not? – so much that of one who would love and cherish and defend her under any conditions, changes, charges, or revelations, that her gloom lessened as she basked in it. The season meanwhile was drawing onward to the equinox, and though it was still fine, the days were much shorter. The dairy had again worked by morning candlelight for a long time; and a fresh renewal of Clare's pleading occurred one morning between three and four.

She had run up in her bedgown to his door to call him as usual; then had gone back to dress and call the others; and in ten minutes was walking to the head of the stairs with the candle in her hand. At the same moment he came down his steps from above in his shirt-sleeves and put his arm across the stairway.

'Now, Miss Flirt, before you go down,' he said peremptorily. 'It is a fortnight since I spoke, and this won't do any longer. You must tell me what you mean, or I shall have to leave this house. My door was ajar just now, and I saw you. For your own safety I must go. You don't know. Well? Is it to be yes at last?'

'I am only just up, Mr Clare, and it is too early to take me to task!' she pouted. 'You need not call me Flirt. 'Tis cruel and untrue. Wait till by and by. Please wait till by and by! I will really think seriously about it between now and then. Let me go downstairs!'

She looked a little like what he said she was as, holding the candle sideways, she tried to smile away the seriousness of her words.

'Call me Angel, then, and not Mr Clare.'

'Angel.'

'Angel dearest – why not?'

' 'Twould mean that I agree, wouldn't it?'

'It would only mean that you love me, even if you cannot marry me; and you were so good as to own that long ago.'

'Very well, then, "Angel dearest," if I *must*,' she murmured, looking at her candle, a roguish curl coming upon her mouth, notwithstanding her suspense.

Clare had resolved never to kiss her until he had obtained her promise; but somehow, as Tess stood there in her prettily tucked-up milking gown, her hair carelessly heaped upon her head till there should be leisure to arrange it when skimming and milking were done, he broke his resolve, and brought his lips to her cheek for one moment. She passed downstairs very quickly, never looking back at him or saying another word. The other maids were already down, and the subject was not pursued. Except Marian, they all looked wistfully and suspiciously at the pair, in the sad yellow rays which the morning candles emitted in contrast with the first cold signals of the dawn without.

When skimming was done – which, as the milk diminished with the approach of autumn, was a lessening process day by day – Retty and the rest went out. The lovers followed them.

'Our tremulous lives are so different from theirs, are they not?' he musingly observed to her, as he regarded the three figures tripping before him through the frigid pallor of opening day.

'Not so very different, I think,' she said.

'Why do you think that?'

'There are very few women's lives that are not – tremulous,' Tess replied, pausing over the new word as if it impressed her. 'There's more in those three than you think.'

'What is in them?'

'Almost either of 'em,' she began, 'would make – perhaps would make – a properer wife than I. And perhaps they love you as well as I – almost.'

'O, Tessy!'

There were signs that it was an exquisite relief to her to hear the impatient exclamation, though she had resolved so intrepidly to let generosity make one bid against herself. That was now done, and she had not the power to attempt self-immolation a second time then. They were joined by a milker from one of the cottages, and no more was said on that which concerned them so deeply. But Tess knew that this day would decide it.

In the afternoon several of the dairyman's household and assistants went down to the meads as usual, a long way from the dairy, where many of the cows were milked without being driven home. The supply was getting less as the animals advanced in calf, and the supernumerary milkers of the lush green season had been dismissed.

The work progressed leisurely. Each pailful was poured into tall cans that stood in a large spring-waggon which had been brought upon the scene; and when they were milked the cows trailed away.

Dairyman Crick, who was there with the rest, his wrapper gleaming miraculously white against a leaden evening sky, suddenly looked at his heavy watch.

'Why, 'tis later than I thought,' he said. 'Begad! We shan't be soon enough with this milk at the station, if we don't mind. There's no time today to take it home and mix it with the bulk afore sending off. It must go to station straight from here. Who'll drive it across?'

Mr Clare volunteered to do so, though it was none of his business, asking Tess to accompany him. The evening, though sunless, had been warm and muggy for the season, and Tess had come out with her milking-hood only, naked-armed and jacketless; certainly not dressed for a drive. She therefore replied by glancing over her scant habiliments; but Clare gently urged her. She assented by relinquishing her pail and stool to the dairyman to take home; and mounted the spring-waggon beside Clare.

## *Chapter 30*

In the diminishing daylight they went along the level roadway through the meads, which stretched away into grey miles, and were backed in the extreme edge of distance by the swarthy and abrupt slopes of Egdon Heath. On its summit stood clumps and stretches of fir trees, whose notched tips appeared like battlemented towers crowning black-fronted castles of enchantment.

They were so absorbed in the sense of being close to each other that they did not begin talking for a long while, the silence being broken only by the clucking of the milk in the tall cans behind them. The lane they followed was so solitary that the hazel nuts had remained on the boughs till they slipped from their shells, and the blackberries hung in heavy clusters. Every now and then Angel would fling the lash of his whip round one of these, pluck it off, and give it to his companion.

The dull sky soon began to tell its meaning by sending down herald-drops of rain, and the stagnant air of the day changed into a fitful breeze which played about their faces. The quick-silvery glaze on the rivers and pools vanished; from broad mirrors of light they changed to lustreless sheets of lead, with a surface like a rasp. But that spectacle did not affect her preoccupation. Her countenance, a natural carnation slightly embrowned by the season, had deepened its tinge with the beating of the raindrops; and her hair, which the pressure of the cows' flanks had, as usual, caused to tumble down from its fastenings and stray beyond the curtain of her calico bonnet, was made clammy by the moisture, till it hardly was better than seaweed.

'I ought not to have come, I suppose,' she murmured, looking at the sky.

'I am sorry for the rain,' said he. 'But how glad I am to have you here!'

Remote Egdon disappeared by degrees behind the liquid gauze. The evening grew darker, and the roads being crossed by gates it was not safe to drive faster than at a walking pace. The air was rather chill.

'I am so afraid you will get cold, with nothing upon your arms and shoulders,' he said. 'Creep close to me, and perhaps the drizzle won't hurt you much. I should be sorrier still if I did not think that the rain might be helping me.'

She imperceptibly crept closer, and he wrapped round them both a large piece of sail-cloth, which was sometimes used to keep the sun off the milk-cans. Tess held it from slipping off him as well as herself, Clare's hands being occupied.

'Now we are all right again. Ah – no we are not! It runs down into my neck a little, and it must still more into yours. That's better. Your arms are like wet marble, Tess. Wipe them in the cloth. Now, if you stay quiet, you will not get another drop. Well, dear – about that question of mine – that long-standing question?'

The only reply that he could hear for a little while was the smack of the horse's hoofs on the moistening road, and the cluck of the milk in the cans behind them.

'Do you remember what you said?'

'I do,' she replied.

'Before we get home, mind.'

'I'll try.'

He said no more then. As they drove on the fragment of an old manor house of Caroline date rose against the sky, and was in due course passed and left behind.

'That,' he observed, to entertain her, 'is an interesting old place – one of the several seats which belonged to an ancient Norman family formerly of great influence in this county, the d'Urbervilles. I never pass one of their residences without thinking of them. There is something very sad in the extinction of a family of renown, even if it was fierce, domineering, feudal renown.'

'Yes,' said Tess.

They crept along towards a point in the expanse of shade just at hand at which a feeble light was beginning to assert its presence, a spot where, by day, a fitful white streak of steam at intervals upon the dark green background denoted intermittent moments of contact between their secluded world and modern life. Modern life stretched out its steam feeler to this point three or four times a day, touched the native existences, and quickly withdrew its feeler again, as if what it touched had been uncongenial.

They reached the feeble light, which came from the smoky lamp of a little railway station; a poor enough terrestrial star, yet in one sense of more importance to Talbothays Dairy and mankind than the celestial ones to which it stood in such humiliating contrast. The cans of new milk were unladen in the rain, Tess getting a little shelter from a neighbouring holly tree.

Then there was the hissing of a train, which drew up almost silently upon the wet rails, and the milk was rapidly swung can by can into the truck. The light of the engine flashed for a second upon Tess Durbeyfield's figure, motionless under the great holly tree. No object could have looked more foreign to the gleaming cranks and wheels than this unsophisticated girl, with the round bare arms, the rainy face and hair, the suspended attitude of a friendly leopard at pause, the print gown of no date or fashion, and the cotton bonnet drooping on her brow.

She mounted again beside her lover, with a mute obedience characteristic of impassioned natures at times, and when they had wrapped themselves up over head and ears in the sailcloth again, they plunged back into the now thick night. Tess was so receptive that the few minutes of contact with the whirl of material progress lingered in her thought.

'Londoners will drink it at their breakfasts tomorrow, won't they?' she asked. 'Strange people that we have never seen.'

'Yes – I suppose they will. Though not as we send it. When its strength has been lowered, so that it may not get up into their heads.'

'Noble men and noble women, ambassadors and centurions, ladies and tradeswomen, and babies who have never seen a cow.'

'Well, yes; perhaps; particularly centurions.'

'Who don't know anything of us, and where it comes from; or think how we two drove miles across the moor tonight in the rain that it might reach 'em in time?'

'We did not drive entirely on account of these precious Londoners; we drove a little on our own – on account of that anxious matter which you will, I am sure, set at rest, dear Tess. Now, permit me to put it in this way. You belong to me already, you know; your heart, I mean. Does it not?'

'You know as well as I. O yes – yes!'

'Then, if your heart does, why not your hand?'

'My only reason was on account of you – on account of a question. I have something to tell you – '

'But suppose it to be entirely for my happiness, and my worldly convenience also?'

'O yes; if it is for your happiness and worldly convenience. But my life before I came here – I want – '

'Well, it is for my convenience as well as my happiness. If I have a very large farm, either English or colonial, you will be invaluable as a wife to me; better than a woman out of the largest mansion in the country. So please – please, dear Tessy, disabuse your mind of the feeling that you will stand in my way.'

'But my history. I want you to know it – you must let me tell you – you will not like me so well!'

'Tell it if you wish to, dearest. This precious history then. Yes, I was born at so and so, Anno Domini – '

'I was born at Marlott,' she said, catching at his words as a help, lightly as they were spoken. 'And I grew up there. And I was in the Sixth Standard when I left school, and they said I had great aptness, and should make a good teacher, so it was settled that I should be one. But there was trouble in my family; father was not very industrious, and he drank a little.'

'Yes, yes. Poor child! Nothing new.' He pressed her more closely to his side.

'And then – there is something very unusual about it – about me. I – I was – '

Tess's breath quickened.

'Yes, dearest. Never mind.'

'I – I – am not a Durbeyfield, but a d'Urberville – a descendant of the same family as those that owned the old house we passed. And – we are all gone to nothing!'

'A d'Urberville! – Indeed! And is that all the trouble, dear Tess?'

'Yes,' she answered faintly.

'Well – why should I love you less after knowing this?'

'I was told by the dairyman that you hated old families.'

He laughed.

'Well, it is true, in one sense. I do hate the aristocratic principle of blood before everything, and do think that as reasoners the only pedigrees we ought to respect are those spiritual ones of the wise and virtuous, without regard to corporeal paternity. But I am extremely interested in this news – you can have no idea how interested I am! Are you not interested yourself in being one of that well-known line?'

'No. I have thought it sad – especially since coming here, and knowing that many of the hills and fields I see once belonged to my father's people. But other hills and fields belonged to Retty's people, and perhaps others to Marian's, so that I don't value it particularly.'

'Yes – it is surprising how many of the present tillers of the soil were once owners of it, and I sometimes wonder that a certain school of politicians don't make capital of the circumstance; but they don't seem to know it . . . I wonder that I did not see the resemblance of your name to d'Urberville, and trace the manifest corruption. And this was the carking secret!'

She had not told. At the last moment her courage had failed her, she feared his blame for not telling him sooner; and her instinct of self-preservation was stronger than her candour.

'Of course,' continued the unwitting Clare, 'I should have been glad to know you to be descended exclusively from the long-suffering, dumb, unrecorded rank and file of the English nation, and not from the self-seeking few who made themselves powerful at the expense of the rest. But I am corrupted away from that by my affection for you, Tess [he laughed as he spoke], and made selfish likewise. For your own sake I rejoice in your descent. Society is hopelessly snobbish, and this fact of your extraction may make an appreciable difference to its acceptance of you as my wife, after I have made you the well-read woman that I mean to make you. My mother too, poor soul, will think so much better of you on account of it. Tess, you must spell your name correctly – d'Urberville – from this very day.'

'I like the other way rather best.'

'But you *must*, dearest! Good heavens, why dozens of mushroom millionaires would jump at such a possession! By the by, there's one of that kidney who has taken the name – where have I heard of him? – Up in the neighbourhood of The Chase, I think. Why, he is the very man who had that rumpus with my father I told you of. What an odd coincidence!'

'Angel, I think I would rather not take the name! It is unlucky, perhaps!'

She was agitated.

'Now then, Mistress Teresa d'Urberville, I have you. Take my name, and so you will escape yours! The secret is out, so why should you any longer refuse me?'

'If it is *sure* to make you happy to have me as your wife, and you feel that you do wish to marry me, *very, very* much – '

'I do, dearest, of course!'

'I mean, that it is only your wanting me very much, and being hardly able to keep alive without me, whatever my offences, that would make me feel I ought to say I will.'

'You will – you do say it, I know! You will be mine for ever and ever.'

He clasped her close and kissed her.

'Yes!'

She had no sooner said it than she burst into a dry hard sobbing, so violent that it seemed to rend her. Tess was not a hysterical girl by any means, and he was surprised.

'Why do you cry, dearest?'

'I can't tell – quite! – I arn so glad to think – of being yours, and making you happy!'

'But this does not seem very much like gladness, my Tessy!'

'I mean – I cry because I have broken down in my vow! I said I would die unmarried!'

'But, if you love me you would like me to be your husband?'

'Yes, yes, yes! But O, I sometimes wish I had never been born!'

'Now, my dear Tess, if I did not know that you are very much excited, and very inexperienced, I should say that remark was not very complimentary. How came you to wish that if you care for me? Do you care for me? I wish you would prove it in some way.'

'How can I prove it more than I have done?' she cried, in a distraction of tenderness. 'Will this prove it more?'

She clasped his neck, and for the first time Clare learnt what an impassioned woman's kisses were like upon the lips of one whom she loved with all her heart and soul, as Tess loved him.

'There – now do you believe?' she asked, flushed, and wiping her eyes.

'Yes. I never really doubted – never, never!'

So they drove on through the gloom, forming one bundle inside the sail-cloth, the horse going as he would, and the rain driving against them. She had consented. She might as well have agreed at first. The 'appetite for joy' which pervades all creation, that tremendous force which sways humanity to its purpose, as the tide sways the helpless weed, was not to be controlled by vague lucubrations over the social rubric.

'I must write to my mother,' she said. 'You don't mind my doing that?'

'Of course not, dear child. You are a child to me, Tess, not to know how very proper it is to write to your mother at such a time, and how wrong it would be in me to object. Where does she live?'

'At the same place – Marlott. On the further side of Blackmoor Vale.'

'Ah, then I *have* seen you before this summer – '

'Yes; at that dance on the green; but you would not dance with me. O, I hope that is of no ill-omen for us now!'

## *Chapter 31*

Tess wrote a most touching and urgent letter to her mother the very next day, and by the end of the week a response to her communication arrived in Joan Durbeyfield's wandering last-century hand.

> DEAR TESS – J write these few lines Hoping they will find you well, as they leave me at Present, thank God for it. Dear Tess, we are all glad to Hear that you are going really to be married soon. But with respect to your question, Tess, J say between ourselves, quite private but very strong, that on no account do you say a word of your Bygone Trouble to him. J did not tell everything to your Father, he being so Proud on account of his Respectability, which, perhaps, your Intended is the same. Many a woman – some of the Highest in the Land – have had a Trouble in their time; and why should you Trumpet yours when others don't Trumpet theirs? No girl would be such a Fool, specially as it is so long ago, and not your Fault at all. J shall answer the same if you ask me fifty times. Besides, you must bear in mind that, knowing it to be your Childish Nature to tell all that's in your heart – so simple! – J made you promise me never to let it out by Word or Deed, having your Welfare in my Mind; and you most solemnly did promise it going from this Door. J have not named either that Question or your coming marriage to your Father, as he would blab it everywhere, poor Simple Man.
>
> Dear Tess, keep up your Spirits, and we mean to send you a Hogshead of Cyder for your Wedding, knowing there is not much in your parts, and thin Sour Stuff what there is. So no more at present, and with kind love to your Young Man. – From your affectte. Mother,
>
> J. DURBEYFIELD

'O mother, mother!' murmured Tess.

She was recognising how light was the touch of events the most oppressive upon Mrs Durbeyfield's elastic spirit. Her mother did not see life as Tess saw it. That haunting episode of bygone days was to her mother but a passing accident. But perhaps her mother was right as to the course to be followed, whatever she might be in her reasons. Silence seemed, on the face of it, best for her adored one's happiness: silence it should be.

Thus steadied by a command from the only person in the world who had any shadow of right to control her action, Tess grew calmer. The responsibility was shifted, and her heart was lighter than it had been for weeks. The days of declining autumn which followed her assent, beginning with the month of October, formed a season through which she lived in spiritual altitudes more nearly approaching ecstasy than any other period of her life.

There was hardly a touch of earth in her love for Clare. To her sublime trustfulness he was all that goodness could be – knew all that a guide, philosopher, and friend should know. She thought every line in the contour of his person the perfection of masculine beauty, his soul the soul of a saint, his intellect that of a seer. The wisdom of her love for him, as love, sustained her dignity; she seemed to be wearing a crown. The compassion of his love for her, as she saw it, made her lift up her heart to him in devotion. He would sometimes catch her large, worshipful eyes, that had no bottom to them, looking at him from their depths, as if she saw something immortal before her.

She dismissed the past – trod upon it and put it out, as one treads on a coal that is smouldering and dangerous.

She had not known that men could be so disinterested, chivalrous, protective, in their love for women as he. Angel Clare was far from all that she thought him in this respect; absurdly far, indeed; but he was, in truth, more spiritual than animal; he had himself well in hand, and was singularly free from grossness. Though not cold-natured, he was rather bright than hot – less Byronic than Shelleyan; could love desperately, but with a love more especially inclined to the imaginative and ethereal; it was a fastidious emotion which could jealously guard the loved one against his very self. This amazed and enraptured Tess, whose slight experiences had been so infelicitous till now; and in her reaction from indignation against the male sex she swerved to excess of honour for Clare.

They unaffectedly sought each other's company; in her honest faith she did not disguise her desire to be with him. The sum of her instincts on this matter, if clearly stated, would have been that the elusive quality in her sex which attracts men in general might be distasteful to so perfect a man after an avowal of love, since it must in its very nature carry with it a suspicion of art.

The country custom of unreserved comradeship out of doors during betrothal was the only custom she knew, and to her it had no strangeness; though it seemed oddly anticipative to Clare till he saw how normal a thing she, in common with all the other dairy-folk, regarded it. Thus, during this October month of wonderful afternoons they roved along the meads by creeping paths which followed the brinks of trickling tributary brooks, hopping across by little wooden bridges to the other side, and back again. They were never out of the sound of some purling weir, whose buzz accompanied their own murmuring, while the beams of the sun, almost as horizontal as the mead itself, formed a pollen of radiance over the landscape. They saw tiny blue fogs in the shadows of trees and hedges, all the time that there was bright sunshine elsewhere. The sun was so near the ground, and the sward so flat, that the shadows of Clare and Tess would stretch a quarter of a mile ahead of them, like two long fingers pointing afar to where the green alluvial reaches abutted against the sloping sides of the vale.

Men were at work here and there – for it was the season for 'taking up' the meadows, or digging the little waterways clear for the winter irrigation, and mending their banks where trodden down by the cows. The shovelfuls of loam, black as jet, brought there by the river when it was as wide as the whole valley, were an essence of soils, pounded champaigns of the past, steeped, refined, and subtilised to extraordinary richness, out of which came all the fertility of the mead, and of the cattle grazing there.

Clare hardily kept his arm round her waist in sight of these watermen, with the air of a man who was accustomed to public dalliance, though actually as shy as she who, with lips parted and eyes askance on the labourers, wore the look of a wary animal the while.

'You are not ashamed of owning me as yours before them!' she said gladly.

'O no!'

'But if it should reach the ears of your friends at Emminster that you are walking about like this with me, a milkmaid – '

'The most bewitching milkmaid ever seen.'

'They might feel it a hurt to their dignity.'

'My dear girl – a d'Urberville hurt the dignity of a Clare! It is a grand card to play – that of your belonging to such a family, and I am reserving it for a grand effect when we are married, and have the proofs of your descent from Parson Tringham. Apart from that, my future is to be totally foreign to my family – it will not affect even the surface of their lives. We shall leave this part of England – perhaps England itself – and what does it matter how people regard us here? You will like going, will you not?'

She could answer no more than a bare affirmative, so great was the emotion aroused in her at the thought of going through the world with him as his own familiar friend. Her feelings almost filled her ears like a babble of waves, and surged up to her eyes. She put her hand in his, and thus they went on, to a place where the reflected sun glared up from the river, under a bridge, with a molten-metallic glow that dazzled their eyes, though the sun itself was hidden by the bridge. They stood still, whereupon little furred and feathered heads popped up from the smooth surface of the water; but, finding that the disturbing presences had paused, and not passed by, they disappeared again. Upon this river-brink they lingered till the fog began to close round them – which was very early in the evening at this time of the year – settling on the lashes of her eyes, where it rested like crystals, and on his brows and hair.

They walked later on Sundays, when it was quite dark. Some of the dairy-people, who were also out of doors on the first Sunday evening after their engagement, heard her impulsive speeches, ecstasised to fragments, though they were too far off to hear the words discoursed; noted the spasmodic catch in her remarks, broken into syllables by the leapings of her heart, as she walked leaning on his arm; her contented pauses, the occasional little laugh upon which her soul seemed to ride – the laugh of a woman in company with the man she loves and has won from all other women – unlike anything else in nature. They marked the buoyancy of her tread, like the skim of a bird which has not quite alighted.

Her affection for him was now the breath and life of Tess's being; it enveloped her as a photosphere, irradiated her into forgetfulness of her past sorrows, keeping back the gloomy spectres that would persist in their attempts to touch her – doubt, fear, moodiness, care, shame. She knew that they were waiting like wolves just outside the circumscribing light, but she had long spells of power to keep them in hungry subjection there.

A spiritual forgetfulness co-existed with an intellectual remembrance. She walked in brightness, but she knew that in the background those shapes of darkness were always spread. They might be receding, or they might be approaching, one or the other, a little every day.

One evening Tess and Clare were obliged to sit indoors keeping house, all the other occupants of the domicile being away. As they talked she looked thoughtfully up at him, and met his two appreciative eyes.

'I am not worthy of you – no, I am not!' she burst out, jumping up from her low stool as though appalled at his homage, and the fulness of her own joy thereat.

Clare, deeming the whole basis of her excitement to be that which was only the smaller part of it, said – 'I won't have you speak like it, dear Tess! Distinction does not consist in the facile use of a contemptible set of conventions, but in being numbered among those who are true, and honest, and just, and pure, and lovely, and of good report – as you are, my Tess.'

She struggled with the sob in her throat. How often had that string of excellences made her young heart ache in church of late years, and how strange that he should have cited them now.

'Why didn't you stay and love me when I – was sixteen; living with my little sisters and brothers, and you danced on the green? O, why didn't you, why didn't you!' she said, impetuously clasping her hands.

Angel began to comfort and reassure her, thinking to himself, truly enough, what a creature of moods she was, and how careful he would have to be of her when she depended for her happiness entirely on him.

'Ah – why didn't I stay!' he said. 'That is just what I feel. If I had only known! But you must not be so bitter in your regret – why should you be?'

With the woman's instinct to hide she diverged hastily – 'I should have had four years more of your heart than I can ever have now. Then I should not have wasted my time as I have done – I should have had so much longer happiness!'

It was no mature woman with a long dark vista of intrigue behind her who was tormented thus; but a girl of simple life, not yet one-and-twenty, who had been caught during her days of immaturity like a bird in a springe. To calm herself the more completely she rose from her little stool and left the room, overturning the stool with her skirts as she went.

He sat on by the cheerful firelight thrown from a bundle of green ash-sticks laid across the dogs; the sticks snapped pleasantly, and hissed out bubbles of sap from their ends. When she came back she was herself again.

'Do you not think you are just a wee bit capricious, fitful, Tess?' he said, good-humouredly, as he spread a cushion for her on the stool, and seated himself in the settle beside her. 'I wanted to ask you something, and just then you ran away.'

'Yes, perhaps I am capricious,' she murmured. She suddenly approached him, and put a hand upon each of his arms. 'No, Angel, I am not really so – by nature, I mean!' The more particularly to assure him that she was not, she placed herself close to him in the settle, and allowed her head to find a resting-place against Clare's shoulder. 'What did you want to ask me – I am sure I will answer it,' she continued humbly.

'Well, you love me, and have agreed to marry me, and hence there follows a thirdly, "When shall the day be?" '

'I like living like this.'

'But I must think of starting in business on my own hook with the new year, or a little later. And before I get involved in the multifarious details of my new position, I should like to have secured my partner.'

'But,' she timidly answered, 'to talk quite practically, wouldn't it be best not to marry till after all that? – Though I can't bear the thought o' your going away and leaving me here!'

'Of course you cannot – and it is not best in this case. I want you to help me in many ways in making my start. When shall it be? Why not a fortnight from now?'

'No,' she said, becoming grave: 'I have so many things to think of first.'

'But – '

He drew her gently nearer to him.

The reality of marriage was startling when it loomed so near. Before discussion of the question had proceeded further there walked round the corner of the settle into the full firelight of the apartment Mr Dairyman Crick, Mrs Crick, and two of the milkmaids.

Tess sprang like an elastic ball from his side to her feet, while her face flushed and her eyes shone in the firelight.

'I knew how it would be if I sat so close to him!' she cried with vexation. 'I said to myself, they are sure to come and catch us! But I wasn't really sitting on his knee, though it might ha' seemed as if I was almost!'

'Well – if so be you hadn't told us, I am sure we shouldn't ha' noticed that ye had been sitting anywhere at all in this light,' replied the dairyman. He continued to his wife, with the stolid mien of a man who understood nothing of the emotions relating to matrimony – 'Now, Christianer, that shows that folks should never fancy other folks be supposing things when they bain't. O no, I should never ha' thought a word of where she was a sitting to, if she hadn't told me – not I.'

'We are going to be married soon,' said Clare, with improvised phlegm.

'Ah – and be ye! Well, I am truly glad to hear it, sir. I've thought you mid do such a thing for some time. She's too good for a dairymaid – I said so the very first day I zid her – and a prize for any man; and what's more, a wonderful woman for a gentleman-farmer's wife; he won't be at the mercy of his baily wi' her at his side.'

Somehow Tess disappeared. She had been even more struck with the look of the girls who followed Crick than abashed by Crick's blunt praise.

After supper, when she reached her bedroom, they were all present. A light was burning, and each damsel was sitting up whitely in her bed, awaiting Tess, the whole like a row of avenging ghosts.

But she saw in a few moments that there was no malice in their mood. They could scarcely feel as a loss what they had never expected to have. Their condition was objective, contemplative.

'He's going to marry her!' murmured Retty, never taking eyes off Tess. 'How her face do show it!'

'You *be* going to marry him?' asked Marian.

'Yes,' said Tess.

'When?'

'Someday.'

They thought that this was evasiveness only.

'*Yes* – going to *marry* him – a gentleman!' repeated Izz Huett.

And by a sort of fascination the three girls, one after another, crept out of their beds, and came and stood barefooted round Tess. Retty put her hands upon Tess's shoulders, as if to realise her friend's corporeality after such a miracle, and the other two laid their arms round her waist, all looking into her face.

'How it do seem! Almost more than I can think of!' said Izz Huett.

Marian kissed Tess. 'Yes,' she murmured as she withdrew her lips.

'Was that because of love for her, or because other lips have touched there by now?' continued Izz drily to Marian.

'I wasn't thinking o' that,' said Marian simply. 'I was on'y feeling all the strangeness o't – that she is to be his wife, and nobody else. I don't say nay to it, nor either of us, because we did not think of it – only loved him. Still, nobody else is to marry'n in the world – no fine lady, nobody in silks and satins; but she who do live like we.'

'Are you sure you don't dislike me for it?' said Tess in a low voice.

They hung about her in their white nightgowns before replying, as if they considered their answer might lie in her look.

'I don't know – I don't know,' murmured Retty Priddle. 'I want to hate 'ee; but I cannot!'

'That's how I feel,' echoed Izz and Marian. 'I can't hate her. Somehow she hinders me!'

'He ought to marry one of you,' murmured Tess.

'Why?'

'You are all better than I.'

'We better than you?' said the girls in a low, slow whisper. 'No, no, dear Tess!'

'You are!' she contradicted impetuously. And suddenly tearing away from their clinging arms she burst into a hysterical fit of tears, bowing herself on the chest of drawers and repeating incessantly, 'O yes, yes, yes!'

Having once given way she could not stop her weeping.

'He ought to have had one of you!' she cried. 'I think I ought to make him even now! You would be better for him than – I don't know what I'm saying! O! O!'

They went up to her and clasped her round, but still her sobs tore her.

'Get some water,' said Marian. 'She's upset by us, poor thing, poor thing!'

They gently led her back to the side of her bed, where they kissed her warmly.

'You are best for'n,' said Marian. 'More ladylike, and a better scholar than we, especially since he has taught 'ee so much. But even you ought to be proud. You *be* proud, I'm sure!'

'Yes, I am,' she said; 'and I am ashamed at so breaking down.'

When they were all in bed, and the light was out, Marian whispered across to her – 'You will think of us when you be his wife, Tess, and of how we told 'ee that we loved him, and how we tried not to hate you, and did not hate you, and could not hate you, because you were his choice, and we never hoped to be chose by him.'

They were not aware that, at these words, salt, stinging tears trickled down upon Tess's pillow anew, and how she resolved, with a bursting heart, to tell all her history to Angel Clare, despite her mother's command – to let him for whom she lived and breathed despise her if he would and her mother regard her as a fool, rather than preserve a silence which might be deemed a treachery to him, and which somehow seemed a wrong to these.

## *Chapter 32*

This penitential mood kept her from naming the wedding-day. The beginning of November found its date still in abeyance, though he asked her at the most tempting times. But Tess's desire seemed to be for a perpetual betrothal in which everything should remain as it was then.

The meads were changing now; but it was still warm enough in early afternoons before milking to idle there awhile, and the state of dairy-work at this time of year allowed a spare hour for idling. Looking over the damp sod in the direction of the sun, a glistening ripple of gossamer webs was visible to their eyes under the luminary, like the track of moonlight on the sea. Gnats, knowing nothing of their brief glorification, wandered across the shimmer of this pathway, irradiated as if they bore fire within them, then passed out of its line, and were quite extinct. In the presence of these things he would remind her that the date was still the question.

Or he would ask her at night, when he accompanied her on some mission invented by Mrs Crick to give him the opportunity. This was mostly a journey to the farmhouse on the slopes above the vale, to enquire how the advanced cows were getting on in the straw-barton to which they were relegated. For it was a time of the year that brought great changes to the world of kine. Batches of the animals were sent away daily to this lying-in hospital, where they lived on straw till their calves were born, after which event, and as soon as the calf could walk, mother and offspring were driven back to the dairy. In the interval which elapsed before the calves were sold there was, of course, little milking to be done, but as soon as the calf had been taken away the milkmaids would have to set to work as usual.

Returning from one of these dark walks they reached a great gravel-cliff immediately over the levels, where they stood still and listened. The water was now high in the streams, squirting through the weirs, and tinkling under culverts; the smallest gullies were all full; there was no taking short cuts anywhere, and foot-passengers were compelled to follow the permanent ways. From the whole extent of the invisible vale came a multitudinous intonation; it forced upon their fancy that a great city lay below them, and that the murmur was the vociferation of its populace.

'It seems like tens of thousands of them,' said Tess; 'holding public-meetings in their market-places, arguing, preaching, quarrelling, sobbing, groaning, praying, and cursing.'

Clare was not particularly heeding.

'Did Crick speak to you today, dear, about his not wanting much assistance during the winter months?'

'No.'

'The cows are going dry rapidly.'

'Yes. Six or seven went to the straw-barton yesterday, and three the day before, making nearly twenty in the straw already. Ah – is it that the farmer don't want my help for the calving? O, I am not wanted here any more! And I have tried so hard to – '

'Crick didn't exactly say that he would no longer require you. But, knowing what our relations were, he said in the most good-natured and respectful manner possible that he supposed on my leaving at Christmas I should take you with me, and on my asking what he would do without you he merely observed that, as a matter of fact, it was a time of year when he could do with a very little female help. I am afraid I was sinner enough to feel rather glad that he was in this way forcing your hand.'

'I don't think you ought to have felt glad, Angel. Because 'tis always mournful not to be wanted, even if at the same time 'tis convenient.'

'Well, it is convenient – you have admitted that.' He put his finger upon her cheek. 'Ah!' he said.

'What?'

'I feel the red rising up at her having been caught! But why should I trifle so! We will not trifle – life is too serious.'

'It is. Perhaps I saw that before you did.'

She was seeing it then. To decline to marry him after all – in obedience to her emotion of last night – and leave the dairy, meant to go to some strange place, not a dairy; for milkmaids were not in request now calving-time was coming on; to go to some arable farm where no divine being like Angel Clare was. She hated the thought, and she hated more the thought of going home.

'So that, seriously, dearest Tess,' he continued, 'since you will probably have to leave at Christmas, it is in every way desirable and convenient that I should carry you off then as my property. Besides, if you were not the most uncalculating girl in the world you would know that we could not go on like this for ever.'

'I wish we could. That it would always be summer and autumn, and you always courting me, and always thinking as much of me as you have done through the past summertime!'

'I always shall.'

'O, I know you will!' she cried, with a sudden fervour of faith in him. 'Angel, I will fix the day when I will become yours for always!'

Thus at last it was arranged between them, during that dark walk home, amid the myriads of liquid voices on the right and left.

When they reached the dairy Mr and Mrs Crick were promptly told – with injunctions to secrecy; for each of the lovers was desirous that the marriage should be kept as private as possible. The dairyman, though he had thought of dismissing her soon, now made a great concern about losing her. What should he do about his skimming? Who would make the ornamental butter-pats for the Anglebury and Sandbourne ladies? Mrs Crick congratulated Tess on the shilly-shallying having at last come to an end, and said that directly she set eyes on Tess she divined that she was to be the chosen one of somebody who was no common outdoor man; Tess had looked so superior as she walked across the barton on that afternoon of her arrival; that she was of a good family she could have sworn. In point of fact Mrs Crick did remember thinking that Tess was graceful and good-looking as she approached; but the superiority might have been a growth of the imagination aided by subsequent knowledge.

Tess was now carried along upon the wings of the hours, without the sense of a will. The word had been given; the number of the day written down. Her naturally bright intelligence had begun to admit the fatalistic convictions common to field-folk and those who associate more extensively with natural phenomena than with their fellow-creatures; and she accordingly drifted into that passive responsiveness to all things her lover suggested, characteristic of the frame of mind.

But she wrote anew to her mother, ostensibly to notify the wedding-day; really to again implore her advice. It was a gentleman who had chosen her, which perhaps her mother had not sufficiently considered. A post-nuptial explanation, which might be accepted with a light heart by a rougher man, might not be received with the same feeling by him. But this communication brought no reply from Mrs Durbeyfield.

Despite Angel Clare's plausible representations to himself and to Tess of the practical need for their immediate marriage, there was in truth an element of precipitancy in the step, as became apparent at a later date. He loved her dearly, though perhaps rather ideally and fancifully than with the impassioned thoroughness of her feeling for him. He had entertained no notion, when doomed as he had thought to an unintellectual bucolic life, that such charms as he beheld in this idyllic creature would be found behind the scenes. Unsophistication was a thing to talk of; but he had not known how it really struck one until he came here. Yet he was very far from seeing his future track clearly, and it might be a year or two before he would be able to consider himself fairly started in life. The secret lay in the tinge of recklessness imparted to his career and character by the sense that he had been made to miss his true destiny through the prejudices of his family.

'Don't you think 'twould have been better for us to wait till you were quite settled in your midland farm?' she once asked timidly. (A midland farm was the idea just then.)

'To tell the truth, my Tess, I don't like you to be left anywhere away from my protection and sympathy.'

The reason was a good one, so far as it went. His influence over her had been so marked that she had caught his manner and habits, his speech and phrases, his likings and his aversions. And to leave her in farmland would be to let her slip back again out of accord with him. He wished to have her under his charge for another reason. His parents had naturally desired to see her once at least before he carried her off to a distant settlement, English or colonial; and as no opinion of theirs was to be allowed to change his intention, he judged that a couple of months' life with him in lodgings whilst seeking for an advantageous opening would be of some social assistance to her at what she might feel to be a trying ordeal – her presentation to his mother at the vicarage.

Next, he wished to see a little of the working of a flour-mill, having an idea that he might combine the use of one with corn-growing. The proprietor of a large old water-mill at Wellbridge – once the mill of an Abbey – had offered him the inspection of his time-honoured mode of procedure, and a hand in the operations for a few days, whenever he should choose to come. Clare paid a visit to the place, some few miles distant, one day at this time, to enquire particulars, and returned to Talbothays in the evening. She found him determined to spend a short time at the Wellbridge flour-mills. And what had determined him? Less the opportunity of an insight into grinding and bolting than the casual fact that lodgings were to be obtained in that very farmhouse which, before its mutilation, had been the mansion of a branch of the d'Urberville family. This was always how Clare settled practical questions; by a sentiment which had nothing to do with them. They decided to go immediately after the wedding, and remain for a fortnight, instead of journeying to towns and inns.

'Then we will start off to examine some farms on the other side of London that I have heard of,' he said, 'and by March or April we will pay a visit to my father and mother.'

Questions of procedure such as these arose and passed, and the day, the incredible day, on which she was to become his, loomed large in the near future. The thirty-first of December, New Year's Eve, was the date. His wife, she said to herself. Could it ever be? Their two selves together, nothing to divide them, every incident shared by them; why not? And yet why?

One Sunday morning Izz Huett returned from church, and spoke privately to Tess.

'You was not called home* this morning.'

'What?'

'It should ha' been the first time of asking today,' she answered, looking quietly at Tess. 'You meant to be married New Year's Eve, deary?'

The other returned a quick affirmative.

'And there must be three times of asking. And now there be only two Sundays left between.'

Tess felt her cheek paling; Izz was right; of course there must be three. Perhaps he had forgotten! If so, there must be a week's postponement, and that was unlucky. How could she remind her lover? She who had been so backward was suddenly fired with impatience and alarm lest she should lose her dear prize.

A natural incident relieved her anxiety. Izz mentioned the omission of the banns to Mrs Crick, and Mrs Crick assumed a matron's privilege of speaking to Angel on the point.

'Have ye forgot 'em, Mr Clare? The banns, I mean.'

'No, I have not forgot 'em,' says Clare.

As soon as he caught Tess alone he assured her:

'Don't let them tease you about the banns. A licence will be quieter for us, and I have decided on a licence without consulting you. So if you go to church on Sunday morning you will not hear your own name, if you wished to.'

'I didn't wish to hear it, dearest,' she said proudly.

But to know that things were in train was an immense relief to Tess notwithstanding, who had well-nigh feared that somebody would stand up and forbid the banns on the ground of her history. How events were favouring her!

'I don't quite feel easy,' she said to herself. 'All this good fortune may be scourged out of me afterwards by a lot of ill. That's how Heaven mostly does. I wish I could have had common banns!'

But everything went smoothly. She wondered whether he would like her to be married in her present best white frock, or if she ought to buy a new one. The question was set at rest by his forethought, disclosed by the arrival of some large packages addressed to her. Inside them she found a whole stock of clothing, from bonnet to shoes, including a perfect morning costume, such as would well suit the simple wedding they planned. He entered the house shortly after the arrival of the packages, and heard her upstairs undoing them.

* 'Called home' – local phrase for publication of banns.

A minute later she came down with a flush on her face and tears in her eyes.

'How thoughtful you've been!' she murmured, her cheek upon his shoulder. 'Even to the gloves and handkerchief! My own love – how good, how kind!'

'No, no, Tess; just an order to a tradeswoman in London – nothing more.

And to divert her from thinking too highly of him he told her to go upstairs, and take her time, and see if it all fitted, and, if not, to get the village sempstress to make a few alterations.

She did return upstairs, and put on the gown. Alone, she stood for a moment before the glass looking at the effect of her silk attire; and then there came into her head her mother's ballad of the mystic robe –

That never would become that wife
That had once done amiss,

which Mrs Durbeyfield had used to sing to her as a child, so blithely and so archly, her foot on the cradle, which she rocked to the tune. Suppose this robe should betray her by changing colour, as her robe had betrayed Queen Guénever. Since she had been at the dairy she had not once thought of the lines till now.

## *Chapter 33*

Angel felt that he would like to spend a day with her before the wedding, somewhere away from the dairy, as a last jaunt in her company while they were yet mere lover and mistress; a romantic day, in circumstances that would never be repeated; with that other and greater day beaming close ahead of them. During the preceding week, therefore, he suggested making a few purchases in the nearest town, and they started together.

Clare's life at the dairy had been that of a recluse in respect to the world of his own class. For months he had never gone near a town, and, requiring no vehicle, had never kept one, hiring the dairyman's cob or gig if he rode or drove. They went in the gig that day.

And then for the first time in their lives they shopped as partners in one concern. It was Christmas Eve, with its loads of holly and mistletoe, and the town was very full of strangers who had come in from all parts of the country on account of the day. Tess paid the penalty of walking about with happiness super-added to beauty on her countenance by being much stared at as she moved amid them on his arm.

In the evening they returned to the inn at which they had put up, and Tess waited in the entry while Angel went to see the horse and gig brought to the door. The general sitting-room was full of guests, who were continually going in and out. As the door opened and shut each time for the passage of these, the light within the parlour fell full upon Tess's face. Two men came out and passed by her among the rest. One of them had stared her up and down in surprise, and she fancied he was a Trantridge man, though that village lay so many miles off that Trantridge folk were rarities here.

'A comely maid that,' said the other.

'True, comely enough. But unless I make a great mistake – ' And he negatived the remainder of the definition forthwith.

Clare had just returned from the stable-yard, and, confronting the man on the threshold, heard the words, and saw the shrinking of Tess. The insult to her stung him to the quick, and before he had considered anything at all he struck the man on the chin with the full force of his fist, sending him staggering backwards into the passage.

The man recovered himself, and seemed inclined to come on, and Clare, stepping outside the door, put himself in a posture of defence. But his opponent began to think better of the matter. He looked anew at Tess as he passed her, and said to Clare – 'I beg pardon, sir; 'twas a complete mistake. I thought she was another woman, forty miles from here.'

Clare, feeling then that he had been too hasty, and that he was, moreover, to blame for leaving her standing in an inn-passage, did what he usually did in such cases, gave the man five shillings to plaster the blow; and thus they parted, bidding each other a pacific good-night. As soon as Clare had taken the reins from the ostler, and the young couple had driven off, the two men went in the other direction.

'And was it a mistake?' said the second one.

'Not a bit of it. But I didn't want to hurt the gentleman's feelings – not I.'

In the meantime the lovers were driving onward.

'Could we put off our wedding till a little later?' Tess asked in a dry dull voice. 'I mean if we wished?'

'No, my love. Calm yourself. Do you mean that the fellow may have time to summon me for assault?' he asked good-humouredly.

'No – I only meant – if it should have to be put off.'

What she meant was not very clear, and he directed her to dismiss such fancies from her mind, which she obediently did as well as she could. But she was grave, very grave, all the way home; till she thought, 'We shall go away, a very long distance, hundreds of miles from these parts, and such as this can never happen again, and no ghost of the past reach there.'

They parted tenderly that night on the landing, and Clare ascended to his attic. Tess sat up getting on with some little requisites, lest the few remaining days should not afford sufficient time. While she sat she heard a noise in Angel's room overhead, a sound of thumping and struggling. Everybody else in the house was asleep, and in her anxiety lest Clare should be ill she ran up and knocked at his door, and asked him what was the matter.

'Oh, nothing, dear,' he said from within. 'I am so sorry I disturbed you! But the reason is rather an amusing one: I fell asleep and dreamt that I was fighting that fellow again who insulted you and the noise you heard was my pummelling away with my fists at my portmanteau, which I pulled out today for packing. I am occasionally liable to these freaks in my sleep. Go to bed and think of it no more.'

This was the last drachm required to turn the scale of her indecision. Declare the past to him by word of mouth she could not; but there was another way. She sat down and wrote on the four pages of a note-sheet a succinct narrative of those events of three or four years ago, put it into an envelope, and directed it to Clare. Then, lest the flesh should again be weak, she crept upstairs without any shoes and slipped the note under his door.

Her night was a broken one, as it well might be, and she listened for the first faint noise overhead. It came, as usual; he descended, as usual. She descended. He met her at the bottom of the stairs and kissed her. Surely it was as warmly as ever!

He looked a little disturbed and worn, she thought. But he said not a word to her about her revelation, even when they were alone. Could he have had it? Unless he began the subject she felt that she could say nothing. So the day passed, and it was evident that whatever he thought he meant to keep to himself. Yet he was frank and affectionate as before. Could it be that her doubts were childish? that he forgave her; that he loved her for what she was, just as she was, and smiled at her disquiet as at a foolish nightmare? Had he really received her note? She glanced into his room, and could see nothing of it. It might be that he forgave her. But even if he had not received it she had a sudden enthusiastic trust that he surely would forgive her.

Every morning and night he was the same, and thus New Year's Eve broke – the wedding-day.

The lovers did not rise at milking-time, having through the whole of this last week of their sojourn at the dairy been accorded something of the position of guests, Tess being honoured with a room of her own. When they arrived downstairs at breakfast-time they were surprised to see what effects had been produced in the large kitchen for their glory since they had last beheld it. At some unnatural hour of the morning the dairyman had caused the yawning chimney-corner to be whitened, and the brick hearth reddened, and a blazing yellow damask blower to be hung across the arch in place of the old grimy blue cotton one with a black sprig pattern which had formerly done duty there. This renovated aspect of what was the focus indeed of the room on a dull winter morning, threw a smiling demeanour over the whole apartment.

'I was determined to do summat in honour o't,' said the dairyman. 'And as you wouldn't hear of my gieing a rattling good randy wi' fiddles and bass-viols complete, as we should ha' done in old times, this was all I could think o' as a noiseless thing.'

Tess's friends lived so far off that none could conveniently have been present at the ceremony, even had any been asked; but as a fact nobody was invited from Marlott. As for Angel's family, he had written and duly informed them of the time, and assured them that he would be glad to see one at least of them there for the day if he would like to come. His brothers had not replied at all, seeming to be indignant with him; while his father and mother had written a rather sad letter, deploring his precipitancy in rushing into marriage, but making the best of the matter by saying that, though a dairywoman was the last daughter-in-law they could have expected, their son had arrived at an age at which he might be supposed to be the best judge.

This coolness in his relations distressed Clare less than it would have done had he been without the grand card with which he meant to surprise them ere long. To produce Tess, fresh from the dairy, as a d'Urberville and a lady, he had felt to be temerarious and risky; hence he had concealed her lineage till such time as, familiarised with worldly ways by a few months' travel and reading with him, he could take her on a visit to his parents, and impart the knowledge while triumphantly producing her as worthy of such an ancient line. It was a pretty lover's dream, if no more. Perhaps Tess's lineage had more value for himself than for anybody in the world besides.

Her perception that Angel's bearing towards her still remained in no whit altered by her own communication rendered Tess guiltily doubtful if he could have received it. She rose from breakfast before he had finished, and hastened upstairs. It had occurred to her to look once more into the queer gaunt room which had been Clare's den, or rather eyrie, for so long and climbing the ladder she stood at the open door of the apartment, regarding and pondering. She stooped to the threshold of the doorway, where she had pushed in the note two or three days earlier in such excitement. The carpet reached close to the sill, and under the edge of the carpet she discerned the faint white margin of the envelope containing her letter to him, which he obviously had never seen, owing to her having in her haste thrust it beneath the carpet as well as beneath the door.

With a feeling of faintness she withdrew the letter. There it was – sealed up, just as it had left her hands. The mountain had not yet been removed. She could not let him read it now, the house being in full bustle of preparation; and descending to her own room she destroyed the letter there.

She was so pale when he saw her again that he felt quite anxious. The incident of the misplaced letter she had jumped at as if it prevented a confession; but she knew in her conscience that it need not; there was still time. Yet everything was in a stir; there was coming and going; all had to dress, the dairyman and Mrs Crick having been asked to accompany them as witnesses; and reflection or deliberate talk was wellnigh impossible. The only minute Tess could get to be alone with Clare was when they met upon the landing.

'I am so anxious to talk to you – I want to confess all my faults and blunders!' she said with attempted lightness.

'No, no – we can't have faults talked of – you must be deemed perfect today at least, my Sweet!' he cried. 'We shall have plenty of time, hereafter, I hope, to talk over our failings. I will confess mine at the same time.'

'But it would be better for me to do it now, I think, so that you could not say – '

'Well, my quixotic one, you shall tell me anything – say, as soon as we are settled in our lodging; not now. I, too, will tell you my faults then. But do not let us spoil the day with them; they will be excellent matter for a dull time.'

'Then you don't wish me to, dearest?'

'I do not, Tessy, really.'

The hurry of dressing and starting left no time for more than this. Those words of his seemed to reassure her on further reflection. She was whirled onward through the next couple of critical hours by the mastering tide of her devotion to him, which closed up further meditation. Her one desire, so long resisted, to make herself his, to call him her lord, her own – then, if necessary, to die – had at last lifted her up from her plodding reflective pathway. In dressing, she moved about in a mental cloud of many-coloured idealities, which eclipsed all sinister contingencies by its brightness.

The church was a long way off, and they were obliged to drive, particularly as it was winter. A close carriage was ordered from a roadside inn, a vehicle which had been kept there ever since the old days of post-chaise travelling. It had stout wheel-spokes, and heavy felloes, a great curved bed, immense straps and springs, and a pole like a battering-ram. The postilion was a venerable 'boy' of sixty – a martyr to rheumatic gout, the result of excessive exposure in youth, counteracted by strong liquors – who had stood at inn-doors doing nothing for the whole five-and-twenty years that had elapsed since he had no longer been required to ride professionally, as if expecting the old times to come back again. He had a permanent running wound on the outside of his right leg, originated by the constant bruisings of aristocratic carriage-poles during the many years that he had been in regular employ at the King's Arms, Casterbridge.

Inside this cumbrous and creaking structure, and behind this decayed conductor, the *partie carrée* took their seats – the bride and bridegroom and Mr and Mrs Crick. Angel would have liked one at least of his brothers to be present as groomsman, but their silence after his gentle hint to that effect by letter had signified that they did not care to come. They disapproved of the marriage, and could not be expected to countenance it. Perhaps it was as well that they could not be present. They were not worldly young fellows, but fraternising with dairy-folk would have struck unpleasantly upon their biassed niceness, apart from their views of the match.

Upheld by the momentum of the time Tess knew nothing of this; did not see anything; did not know the road they were taking to the church. She knew that Angel was close to her; all the rest was a luminous mist. She was a sort of celestial person, who owed her being to poetry – one of those classical divinities Clare was accustomed to talk to her about when they took their walks together.

The marriage being by licence there were only a dozen or so of people in the church; had there been a thousand they would have produced no more effect upon her. They were at stellar distances from her present world. In the ecstatic solemnity with which she swore her faith to him the ordinary sensibilities of sex seemed a flippancy. At a pause in the service, while they were kneeling together, she unconsciously inclined herself towards him, so that her shoulder touched his arm; she had been frightened by a passing thought, and the movement had been automatic, to assure herself that he was really there, and to fortify her belief that his fidelity would be proof against all things.

Clare knew that she loved him – every curve of her form showed that – but he did not know at that time the full depth of her devotion, its single-mindedess, its meekness; what long-suffering it guaranteed, what honesty, what endurance, what good faith.

As they came out of church the ringers swung the bells off their rests, and a modest peal of three notes broke forth – that limited amount of expression having been deemed sufficient by the church builders for the joys of such a small parish. Passing by the tower with her husband on the path to the gate she could feel the vibrant air humming round them from the louvred belfry in a circle of sound, and it matched the highly-charged mental atmosphere in which she was living.

This condition of mind, wherein she felt glorified by an irradiation not her own, like the angel whom St John saw in the sun, lasted till the sound of the church bells had died away, and the emotions of the wedding-service had calmed down. Her eyes could dwell upon details more clearly now, and Mr and Mrs Crick having directed their own gig to be sent for them, to leave the carriage to the young couple, she observed the build and character of that conveyance for the first time. Sitting in silence she regarded it long.

'I fancy you seem oppressed, Tessy,' said Clare.

'Yes,' she answered, putting her hand to her brow. 'I tremble at many things. It is all so serious, Angel. Among other things I seem to have seen this carriage before, to be very well acquainted with it. It is very odd – I must have seen it in a dream.'

'Oh – you have heard the legend of the d'Urberville Coach – that well-known superstition of this county about your family when they were very popular here; and this lumbering old thing reminds you of it.'

'I have never heard of it to my knowledge,' said she. 'What is the legend – may I know it?'

'Well – I would rather not tell it in detail just now. A certain d'Urberville of the sixteenth or seventeenth century committed a dreadful crime in his family coach; and since that time members of the family see or hear the old coach whenever – But I'll tell you another day – it is rather gloomy. Evidently some dim knowledge of it has been brought back to your mind by the sight of this venerable caravan.'

'I don't remember hearing it before,' she murmured. 'Is it when we are going to die, Angel, that members of my family see it, or is it when we have committed a crime?'

'Now, Tess!'

He silenced her by a kiss.

By the time they reached home she was contrite and spiritless. She was Mrs Angel Clare, indeed, but had she any moral right to the name? Was she not more truly Mrs Alexander d'Urberville? Could intensity of love justify what might be considered in upright souls as culpable reticence? She knew not what was expected of women in such cases; and she had no counsellor.

However, when she found herself alone in her room for a few minutes – the last day this on which she was ever to enter it – she knelt down and prayed. She tried to pray to God, but it was her husband who really had her supplication. Her idolatry of this man was such that she herself almost feared it to be ill-omened. She was conscious of the notion expressed by Friar Laurence: 'These violent delights have violent ends.' It might be too desperate for human conditions – too rank, too wild, too deadly.

'O my love, my love, why do I love you so!' she whispered there alone; 'for she you love is not my real self, but one in my image; the one I might have been!'

Afternoon came, and with it the hour for departure. They had decided to fulfil the plan of going for a few days to the lodgings in the old farmhouse near Wellbridge Mill, at which he meant to reside during his investigation of flour processes. At two o'clock there was nothing left to do but to start. All the servantry of the dairy were standing in the red-brick entry to see them go out, the dairyman and his wife following to the door. Tess saw her three chamber-mates in a row against the wall, pensively inclining their heads. She had much questioned if they would appear at the parting moment; but there they were, stoical and staunch to the last. She knew why the delicate Retty looked so fragile, and Izz so tragically sorrowful, and Marian so blank; and she forgot her own dogging shadow for a moment in contemplating theirs.

She impulsively whispered to him – 'Will you kiss 'em all, once, poor things, for the first and last time?'

Clare had not the least objection to such a farewell formality – which was all that it was to him – and as he passed them he kissed them in succession where they stood, saying 'Goodbye' to each as he did so. When they reached the door Tess femininely glanced back to discern the effect of that kiss of charity; there was no triumph in her glance, as there might have been. If there had it would have disappeared when she saw how moved the girls all were. The kiss had obviously done harm by awakening feelings they were trying to subdue.

Of all this Clare was unconscious. Passing on to the wicket-gate he shook hands with the dairyman and his wife, and expressed his last thanks to them for their attentions; after which there was a moment of silence before they had moved off. It was interrupted by the crowing of a cock. The white one with the rose comb had come and settled on the palings in front of the house, within a few yards of them, and his notes thrilled their ears through, dwindling away like echoes down a valley of rocks.

'Oh?' said Mrs Crick. 'An afternoon crow!'

Two men were standing by the yard gate, holding it open.

'That's bad,' one murmured to the other, not thinking that the words could be heard by the group at the door-wicket.

The cock crew again – straight towards Clare.

'Well!' said the dairyman.

'I don't like to hear him!' said Tess to her husband. 'Tell the man to drive on. Goodbye, goodbye!'

The cock crew again.

'Hoosh! Just you be off, sir, or I'll twist your neck!' said the dairyman with some irritation, turning to the bird and driving him away. And to his wife as they went indoors: 'Now, to think o' that just today! I've not heard his crow of an afternoon all the year afore.'

'It only means a change in the weather,' said she; 'not what you think: 'tis impossible!'

## *Chapter 34*

They drove by the level road along the valley to a distance of a few miles, and, reaching Wellbridge, turned away from the village to the left, and over the great Elizabethan bridge which gives the place half its name. Immediately behind it stood the house wherein they had engaged lodgings, whose exterior features are so well known to all travellers through the Froom Valley; once portion of a fine manorial residence, and the property and seat of a d'Urberville, but since its partial demolition a farmhouse.

'Welcome to one of your ancestral mansions!' said Clare as he handed her down. But he regretted the pleasantry; it was too near a satire.

On entering they found that, though they had only engaged a couple of rooms, the farmer had taken advantage of their proposed presence during the coming days to pay a New Year's visit to some friends, leaving a woman from a neighbouring cottage to minister to their few wants. The absoluteness of possession pleased them, and they realised it as the first moment of their experience under their own exclusive roof-tree.

But he found that the mouldy old habitation somewhat depressed his bride. When the carriage was gone they ascended the stairs to wash their hands, the charwoman showing the way. On the landing Tess stopped and started.

'What's the matter?' said he.

'Those horrid women!' she answered, with a smile. 'How they frightened me.'

He looked up, and perceived two life-size portraits on panels built into the masonry. As all visitors to the mansion are aware, these paintings represent women of middle age, of a date some two hundred years ago, whose lineaments once seen can never be forgotten. The long pointed features, narrow eye, and smirk of the one, so suggestive of merciless treachery; the bill-hook nose, large teeth, and bold eye of the other, suggesting arrogance to the point of ferocity, haunt the beholder afterwards in his dreams.

'Whose portraits are those?' asked Clare of the charwoman.

'I have been told by old folk that they were ladies of the d'Urberville family, the ancient lords of this manor,' she said. 'Owing to their being builded into the wall they can't be moved away.'

The unpleasantness of the matter was that, in addition to their effect upon Tess, her fine features were unquestionably traceable in these exaggerated forms. He said nothing of this, however, and, regretting that he had gone out of his way to choose the house for their bridal time, went on into the adjoining room. The place having been rather hastily prepared for them they washed their hands in one basin. Clare touched hers under the water.

'Which are my fingers and which are yours?' he said, looking up. 'They are very much mixed.'

'They are all yours,' said she, very prettily, and endeavoured to be gayer than she was. He had not been displeased with her thoughtfulness on such an occasion; it was what every sensible woman would show: but Tess knew that she had been thoughtful to excess, and struggled against it.

The sun was so low on that short last afternoon of the year that it shone in through a small opening and formed a golden staff which stretched across to her skirt, where it made a spot like a paint-mark set upon her. They went into the ancient parlour to tea, and here they shared their first common meal alone. Such was their childishness, or rather his, that he found it interesting to use the same bread-and-butter plate as herself, and to brush crumbs from her lips with his own. He wondered a little that she did not enter into these frivolities with his own zest.

Looking at her silently for a long time, 'She is a dear dear Tess,' he thought to himself, as one deciding on the true construction of a difficult passage. 'Do I realise solemnly enough how utterly and irretrievably this little womanly thing is the creature of my good or bad faith and fortune? I think not. I think I could not, unless I were a woman myself. What I am in worldly estate, she is. What I become, she must become. What I cannot be, she cannot be. And shall I ever neglect her, or hurt her, or even forget to consider her? God forbid such a crime!'

They sat on over the tea-table waiting for their luggage, which the dairyman had promised to send before it grew dark. But evening began to close in, and the luggage did not arrive, and they had brought nothing more than they stood in. With the departure of the sun the calm mood of the winter day changed. Out of doors there began noises as of silk smartly rubbed; the restful dead leaves of the preceding autumn were stirred to irritated resurrection, and whirled about unwillingly, and tapped against the shutters. It soon began to rain.

'That cock knew the weather was going to change,' said Clare.

The woman who had attended upon them had gone home for the night, but she had placed candles upon the table, and now they lit them. Each candle-flame drew towards the fireplace.

'These old houses are so draughty,' continued Angel, looking at the flames, and at the grease guttering down the sides. 'I wonder where that luggage is. We haven't even a brush and comb.'

'I don't know,' she answered, absent-minded.

'Tess, you are not a bit cheerful this evening – not at all as you used to be. Those harridans on the panels upstairs have unsettled you. I am sorry I brought you here. I wonder if you really love me, after all?'

He knew that she did, and the words had no serious intent; but she was surcharged with emotion, and winced like a wounded animal. Though she tried not to shed tears she could not help showing one or two.

'I did not mean it!' said he, sorry. 'You are worried at not having your things, I know. I cannot think why old Jonathan has not come with them. Why, it is seven o'clock? Ah, there he is!'

A knock had come to the door, and, there being nobody else to answer it, Clare went out. He returned to the room with a small package in his hand.

'It is not Jonathan, after all,' he said.

'How vexing!' said Tess.

The packet had been brought by a special messenger, who had arrived at Talbothays from Emminster Vicarage immediately after the departure of the married couple, and had followed them hither, being under injunction to deliver it into nobody's hands but theirs. Clare brought it to the light. It was less than a foot long, sewed up in canvas, sealed in red wax with his father's seal, and directed in his father's hand to 'Mrs Angel Clare'.

'It is a little wedding-present for you, Tess,' said he, handing it to her. 'How thoughtful they are!'

Tess looked a little flustered as she took it.

'I think I would rather have you open it, dearest,' said she, turning over the parcel. 'I don't like to break those great seals; they look so serious. Please open it for me!'

He undid the parcel. Inside was a case of morocco leather, on the top of which lay a note and a key.

The note was for Clare, in the following words:

> My Dear Son – Possibly you have forgotten that on the death of your godmother, Mrs Pitney, when you were a lad, she – vain kind woman that she was – left to me a portion of the contents of her jewel-case in trust for your wife, if you should ever have one, as a mark of her affection for you and whomsoever you should choose. This trust I have fulfilled, and the diamonds have been locked up at my banker's ever since. Though I feel it to be a somewhat incongruous act in the circumstances, I am, as you will see, bound to hand over the articles to the woman to whom the use of them for her lifetime will now rightly belong, and they are therefore promptly sent. They become, I believe, heirlooms, strictly speaking, according to the terms of your godmother's will. The precise words of the clause that refers to this matter are enclosed.

'I do remember,' said Clare; 'but I had quite forgotten.'

Unlocking the case, they found it to contain a necklace, with pendant, bracelets, and ear-rings; and also some other small ornaments.

Tess seemed afraid to touch them at first, but her eyes sparkled for a moment as much as the stones when Clare spread out the set.

'Are they mine?' she asked incredulously.

'They are, certainly,' said he.

He looked into the fire. He remembered how, when he was a lad of fifteen, his godmother, the Squire's wife – the only rich person with whom he had ever come in contact – had pinned her faith to his success; had prophesied a wondrous career for him. There had seemed nothing at all out of keeping with such a conjectured career in the storing up of these showy ornaments for his wife and the wives of her descendants. They gleamed somewhat ironically now.

'Yet why?' he asked himself. It was but a question of vanity throughout; and if that were admitted into one side of the equation it should be admitted into the other. His wife was a d'Urberville: whom could they become better than her?

Suddenly he said with enthusiasm – 'Tess, put them on – put them on!' And he turned from the fire to help her.

But as if by magic she had already donned them – necklace, ear-rings, bracelets, and all.

'But the gown isn't right, Tess,' said Clare. 'It ought to be a low one for a set of brilliants like that.'

'Ought it?' said Tess.

'Yes,' said he.

He suggested to her how to tuck in the upper edge of her bodice, so as to make it roughly approximate to the cut for evening wear; and when she had done this, and the pendant to the necklace hung isolated amid the whiteness of her throat, as it was designed to do, he stepped back to survey her.

'My heavens,' said Clare, 'how beautiful you are!'

As everybody knows, fine feathers make fine birds; a peasant girl but very moderately prepossessing to the casual observer in her simple condition and attire, will bloom as an amazing beauty if clothed as a woman of fashion with the aids that Art can render; while the beauty of the midnight crush would often cut but a sorry figure if placed inside the field-woman's wrapper upon a monotonous acreage of turnips on a dull day. He had never till now estimated the artistic excellence of Tess's limbs and features.

'If you were only to appear in a ballroom!' he said. 'But no – no, dearest; I think I love you best in the wing-bonnet and cotton-frock – yes, better than in this, well as you support these dignities.'

Tess's sense of her striking appearance had given her a flush of excitement, which was yet not happiness.

'I'll take them off,' she said, 'in case Jonathan should see me. They are not fit for me, are they? They must be sold, I suppose?'

'Let them stay a few minutes longer. Sell them? Never. It would be a breach of faith.'

Influenced by a second thought she readily obeyed. She had something to tell, and there might be help in these. She sat down with the jewels upon her; and they again indulged in conjectures as to where Jonathan could possibly be with their baggage. The ale they had poured out for his consumption when he came had gone flat with long standing.

Shortly after this they began supper, which was already laid on a side-table. Ere they had finished there was a jerk in the fire-smoke, the rising skein of which bulged out into the room, as if some giant had laid his hand on the chimney-top for a moment. It had been caused by the opening of the outer door. A heavy step was now heard in the passage, and Angel went out.

'I couldn' make nobody hear at all by knocking,' apologised Jonathan Kail, for it was he at last; 'and as't was raining out I opened the door. I've brought the things, sir.'

'I am very glad to see them. But you are very late.'

'Well, yes, sir.'

There was something subdued in Jonathan Kail's tone which had not been there in the day, and lines of concern were ploughed upon his forehead in addition to the lines of years. He continued – 'We've all been gallied at the dairy at what might ha' been a most terrible affliction since you and your Mis'ess – so to name her now – left us this a'ternoon. Perhaps you ha'nt forgot the cock's afternoon crow?'

'Dear me; – what – '

'Well, some says it do mane one thing, and some another; but what's happened is that poor little Retty Priddle hev tried to drown herself.'

'No! Really! Why, she bade us goodbye with the rest – '

'Yes. Well, sir, when you and your Mis'ess – so to name what she lawful is – when you two drove away, as I say, Retty and Marian put on their bonnets and went out; and as there is not much doing now, being New Year's Eve, and folks mops and brooms from what's inside 'em, nobody took much notice. They went on to Lew-Everard, where they had summut to drink, and then on they vamped to Dree-armed Cross, and there they seemed to have parted, Retty striking across the water-meads as if for home, and Marian going on to the next village, where there's another public-house. Nothing more was zeed or heard o' Retty till the waterman, on his way home, noticed something by the Great Pool; 'twas her bonnet and shawl packed up. In the water he found her. He and another man brought her home, thinking 'a was dead; but she fetched round by degrees.'

Angel, suddenly recollecting that Tess was overhearing this gloomy tale, went to shut the door between the passage and the ante-room to the inner parlour where she was; but his wife, flinging a shawl round her, had come to the outer room and was listening to the man's narrative, her eyes resting absently on the luggage and the drops of rain glistening upon it.

'And, more than this, there's Marian; she's been found dead drunk by the withy-bed – a girl who hev never been known to touch anything before except shilling ale; though, to be sure, 'a was always a good trencher-woman, as her face showed. It seems as if the maids had all gone out o' their minds!'

'And Izz?' asked Tess.

'Izz is about house as usual; but 'a do say 'a can guess how it happened; and she seems to be very low in mind about it, poor maid, as well she mid be. And so you see, sir, as all this happened just when we was packing your few traps and your Mis'ess's night-rail and dressing things into the cart, why, it belated me.'

'Yes. Well, Jonathan, will you get the trunks upstairs, and drink a cup of ale, and hasten back as soon as you can, in case you should be wanted?'

Tess had gone back to the inner parlour, and sat down by the fire, looking wistfully into it. She heard Jonathan Kail's heavy footsteps up and down the stairs till he had done placing the luggage, and heard him express his thanks for the ale her husband took out to him, and for the gratuity he received. Jonathan's footsteps then died from the door, and his cart creaked away.

Angel slid forward the massive oak bar which secured the door, and coming in to where she sat over the hearth, pressed her cheeks between his hands from behind. He expected her to jump up gaily and unpack the toilet-gear that she had been so anxious about, but as she did not rise he sat down with her in the firelight, the candles on the supper-table being too thin and glimmering to interfere with its glow.

'I am so sorry you should have heard this sad story about the girls,' he said. 'Still, don't let it depress you. Retty was naturally morbid, you know.'

'Without the least cause,' said Tess. 'While they who have cause to be, hide it, and pretend they are not.'

This incident had turned the scale for her. They were simple and innocent girls on whom the unhappiness of unrequited love had fallen; they had deserved better at the hands of Fate. She had deserved worse – yet she was the chosen one. It was wicked of her to take all without paying. She would pay to the uttermost farthing; she would tell, there and then. This final determination she came to when she looked into the fire, he holding her hand.

A steady glare from the now flameless embers painted the sides and back of the fireplace with its colour, and the well-polished andirons, and the old brass tongs that would not meet. The underside of the mantel-shelf was flushed with the high-coloured light, and the legs of the table nearest the fire. Tess's face and neck reflected the same warmth, which each gem turned into an Aldebaran or a Sirius – a constellation of white, red, and green flashes, that interchanged their hues with her every pulsation.

'Do you remember what we said to each other this morning about telling our faults?' he asked abruptly, finding that she still remained immovable. 'We spoke lightly perhaps, and you may well have done so. But for me it was no light promise. I want to make a confession to you, Love.'

This, from him, so unexpectedly apposite, had the effect upon her of a Providential interposition.

'You have to confess something?' she said quickly, and even with gladness and relief.

'You did not expect it? Ah – you thought too highly of me. Now listen. Put your head there, because I want you to forgive me, and not to be indignant with me for not telling you before, as perhaps I ought to have done.'

How strange it was! He seemed to be her double. She did not speak, and Clare went on – 'I did not mention it because I was afraid of endangering my chance of you, darling, the great prize of my life – my Fellowship I call you. My brother's Fellowship was won at his college, mine at Talbothays Dairy. Well, I would not risk it. I was going to tell you a month ago – at the time you agreed to be mine, but I could not; I thought it might frighten you away from me. I put it off; then I thought I would tell you yesterday, to give you a chance at least of escaping me. But I did not. And I did not this morning, when you proposed our confessing our faults on the landing – the sinner that I was! But I must, now I see you sitting there so solemnly. I wonder if you will forgive me?'

'O yes! I am sure that – '

'Well, I hope so. But wait a minute. You don't know. To begin at the beginning. Though I imagine my poor father fears that I am one of the eternally lost for my doctrines, I am of course, a believer in good morals, Tess, as much as you. I used to wish to be a teacher of men, and it was a great disappointment to me when I found I could not enter the Church. I admired spotlessness, even though I could lay no claim to it, and hated impurity, as I hope I do now. Whatever one may think of plenary inspiration, one must heartily subscribe to these words of Paul: "Be thou an example – in word, in conversation, in charity, in spirit, in faith, in purity." It is the only safeguard for us poor human beings. "Integer vitae", says a Roman poet, who is strange company for St Paul –

> The man of upright life, from frailties free,
> Stands not in need of Moorish spear or bow.

Well, a certain place is paved with good intentions, and having felt all that so strongly, you will see what a terrible remorse it bred in me when, in the midst of my fine aims for other people, I myself fell.'

He then told her of that time of his life to which allusion has been made when, tossed about by doubts and difficulties in London, like a cork on the waves, he plunged into eight-and-forty hours' dissipation with a stranger.

'Happily I awoke almost immediately to a sense of my folly,' he continued. 'I would have no more to say to her, and I came home. I have never repeated the offence. But I felt I should like to treat you with perfect frankness and honour, and I could not do so without telling this. Do you forgive me?'

She pressed his hand tightly for an answer.

'Then we will dismiss it at once and for ever! – too painful as it is for the occasion – and talk of something lighter.'

'O, Angel – I am almost glad – because now *you* can forgive *me*! I have not made my confession. I have a confession, too – remember, I said so.'

'Ah, to be sure! Now then for it, wicked little one.'

'Perhaps, although you smile, it is as serious as yours, or more so.'

'It can hardly be more serious, dearest.'

'It cannot – O no, it cannot!' She jumped up joyfully at the hope. 'No, it cannot be more serious, certainly,' she cried, 'because 'tis just the same! I will tell you now.'

She sat down again.

Their hands were still joined. The ashes under the grate were lit by the fire vertically, like a torrid waste. Imagination might have beheld a Last Day luridness in this red-coaled glow, which fell on his face and hand, and on hers, peering into the loose hair about her brow, and firing the delicate skin underneath. A large shadow of her shape rose upon the wall and ceiling. She bent forward, at which each diamond on her neck gave a sinister wink like a toad's; and pressing her forehead against his temple she entered on her story of her acquaintance with Alec d'Urberville and its results, murmuring the words without flinching, and with her eyelids drooping down.

END OF PHASE THE FOURTH

# PHASE THE FIFTH

## *The Woman Pays*

# *Chapter 35*

Her narrative ended; even its reassertions and secondary explanations were done. Tess's voice throughout had hardly risen higher than its opening tone; there had been no exculpatory phrase of any kind, and she had not wept.

But the complexion even of external things seemed to suffer transmutation as her announcement progressed. The fire in the grate looked impish – demonaically funny, as if it did not care in the least about her strait. The fender grinned idly, as if it too did not care. The light from the water-bottle was merely engaged in a chromatic problem. All material objects around announced their irresponsibility with terrible iteration. And yet nothing had changed since the moments when he had been kissing her; or rather, nothing in the substance of things. But the essence of things had changed.

When she ceased the auricular impressions from their previous endearments seemed to hustle away into the corner of their brains, repeating themselves as echoes from a time of supremely purblind foolishness.

Clare performed the irrelevant act of stirring the fire; the intelligence had not even yet got to the bottom of him. After stirring the embers he rose to his feet; all the force of her disclosure had imparted itself now. His face had withered. In the strenuousness of his concentration he treadled fitfully on the floor. He could not, by any contrivance, think closely enough; that was the meaning of his vague movement. When he spoke it was in the most inadequate, commonplace voice of the many varied tones she had heard from him.

'Tess!'

'Yes, dearest.'

'Am I to believe this? From your manner I am to take it as true. O you cannot be out of your mind! You ought to be! Yet you are not . . . My wife, my Tess – nothing in you warrants such a supposition as that?'

'I am not out of my mind,' she said.

'And yet – ' He looked vacantly at her, to resume with dazed senses: 'Why didn't you tell me before? Ah, yes, you would have told me, in a way – but I hindered you, I remember!'

These and other of his words were nothing but the perfunctory babble of the surface while the depths remained paralysed. He turned away, and bent over a chair. Tess followed him to the middle of the room where he was, and stood there staring at him with eyes that did not weep. Presently she slid down upon her knees beside his foot, and from this position she crouched in a heap.

'In the name of our love, forgive me!' she whispered with a dry mouth. 'I have forgiven you for the same!'

And, as he did not answer, she said again – 'Forgive me as you are forgiven! *I* forgive *you*, Angel.'

'You – yes, you do.'

'But you do not forgive me?'

'O Tess, forgiveness does not apply to the case! You were one person; now you are another. My God – how can forgiveness meet such a grotesque prestidigitation as that!'

He paused, contemplating this definition; then suddenly broke into horrible laughter – as unnatural and ghastly as a laugh in hell.

'Don't – don't! It kills me quite, that!' she shrieked. 'O have mercy upon me – have mercy!'

He did not answer; and, sickly white, she jumped up.

'Angel, Angel! what do you mean by that laugh?' she cried out. 'Do you know what this is to me?'

He shook his head.

'I have been hoping, longing, praying, to make you happy! I have thought what joy it will be to do it, what an unworthy wife I shall be if I do not! That's what I have felt, Angel!'

'I know that.'

'I thought, Angel, that you loved me – me, my very self! If it is I you do love, O how can it be that you look and speak so? It frightens me! Having begun to love you, I love you for ever – in all changes, in all disgraces, because you are yourself. I ask no more. Then how can you, O my own husband, stop loving me?'

'I repeat, the woman I have been loving is not you.'

'But who?'

'Another woman in your shape.'

She perceived in his words the realisation of her own apprehensive foreboding in former times. He looked upon her as a species of impostor; a guilty woman in the guise of an innocent one. Terror was upon her white face as she saw it; her cheek was flaccid, and her mouth had almost the aspect of a round little hole. The horrible sense of his view of her so deadened her that she staggered; and he stepped forward, thinking she was going to fall.

'Sit down, sit down,' he said gently. 'You are ill; and it is natural that you should be.'

She did sit down, without knowing where she was, that strained look still upon her face, and her eyes such as to make his flesh creep.

'I don't belong to you any more, then; do I, Angel?' she asked helplessly. 'It is not me, but another woman like me that he loved, he says.'

The image raised caused her to take pity upon herself as one who was ill-used. Her eyes filled as she regarded her position further; she turned round and burst into a flood of self-sympathetic tears.

Clare was relieved at this change, for the effect on her of what had happened was beginning to be a trouble to him only less than the woe of the disclosure itself. He waited patiently, apathetically, till the violence of her grief had worn itself out, and her rush of weeping had lessened to a catching gasp at intervals.

'Angel,' she said suddenly, in her natural tones, the insane, dry voice of terror having left her now. 'Angel, am I too wicked for you and me to live together?'

'I have not been able to think what we can do.'

'I shan't ask you to let me live with you, Angel, because I have no right to! I shall not write to mother and sisters to say we be married, as I said I would do; and I shan't finish the good-hussif' I cut out and meant to make while we were in lodgings.'

'Shan't you?'

'No, I shan't do anything, unless you order me to; and if you go away from me I shall not follow 'ee; and if you never speak to me any more I shall not ask why, unless you tell me I may.'

'And if I order you to do anything?'

'I will obey you like your wretched slave, even if it is to lie down and die.'

'You are very good. But it strikes me that there is a want of harmony between your present mood of self-sacrifice and your past mood of self-preservation.'

These were the first words of antagonism. To fling elaborate sarcasms at Tess, however, was much like flinging them at a dog or cat. The charms of their subtlety passed by her unappreciated, and she only received them as inimical sounds which meant that anger ruled. She remained mute, not knowing that he was smothering his affection for her. She hardly observed that a tear descended slowly upon his cheek, a tear so large that it magnified the pores of the skin over which it rolled, like the object lens of a microscope. Meanwhile reillumination as to the terrible and total change that her confession had wrought in his life, in his universe, returned to him, and he tried desperately to advance among the new conditions in which he stood. Some consequent action was necessary; yet what?

'Tess,' he said, as gently as he could speak, 'I cannot stay – in this room – just now. I will walk out a little way.'

He quietly left the room, and the two glasses of wine that he had poured out for their supper – one for her, one for him – remained on the table untasted. This was what their *Agape* had come to. At tea, two or three hours earlier, they had, in the freakishness of affection, drunk from one cup.

The closing of the door behind him, gently as it had been pulled to, roused Tess from her stupor. He was gone; she could not stay. Hastily flinging her cloak around her she opened the door and followed, putting out the candles as if she were never coming back. The rain was over and the night was now clear.

She was soon close at his heels, for Clare walked slowly and without purpose. His form beside her light grey figure looked black, sinister, and forbidding, and she felt as sarcasm the touch of the jewels of which she had been momentarily so proud. Clare turned at hearing her footsteps, but his recognition of her presence seemed to make no difference to him, and he went on over the five yawning arches of the great bridge in front of the house.

The cow and horse tracks in the road were full of water, the rain having been enough to charge them, but not enough to wash them away. Across these minute pools the reflected stars flitted in a quick transit as she passed; she would not have known they were shining overhead if she had not seen them there – the vastest things of the universe imaged in objects so mean.

The place to which they had travelled today was in the same valley as

Talbothays, but some miles lower down the river; and the surroundings being open she kept easily in sight of him. Away from the house the road wound through the meads, and along these she followed Clare without any attempt to come up with him or to attract him, but with dumb and vacant fidelity.

At last, however, her listless walk brought her up alongside him, and still he said nothing. The cruelty of fooled honesty is often great after enlightenment, and it was mighty in Clare now. The outdoor air had apparently taken away from him all tendency to act on impulse; she knew that he saw her without irradiation – in all her bareness; that Time was chanting his satiric psalm at her then –

> Behold, when thy face is made bare, he that loved thee shall hate;
> Thy face shall be no more fair at the fall of thy fate.
> For thy life shall fall as a leaf and be shed as the rain;
> And the veil of thine head shall be grief, and the crown shall be pain.

He was still intently thinking, and her companionship had now insufficient power to break or divert the strain of thought. What a weak thing her presence must have become to him! She could not help addressing Clare.

'What have I done – what *have* I done! I have not told of anything that interferes with or belies my love for you. You don't think I planned it, do you? It is in your own mind what you are angry at, Angel; it is not in me. O, it is not in me, and I am not that deceitful woman you think me!'

'H'm – well. Not deceitful, my wife; but not the same. No, not the same. But do not make me reproach you. I have sworn that I will not; and I will do everything to avoid it.'

But she went on pleading in her distraction; and perhaps said things that would have been better left to silence.

'Angel! – Angel! I was a child – a child when it happened! I knew nothing of men.'

'You were more sinned against than sinning, that I admit.'

'Then will you not forgive me?'

'I do forgive you, but forgiveness is not all.'

'And love me?'

To this question he did not answer.

'O Angel – my mother says that it sometimes happens so! – she knows several cases where they were worse than I, and the husband has not minded it much – has got over it at least. And yet the woman has not loved him as I do you!'

'Don't, Tess; don't argue. Different societies, different manners. You almost make me say you are an unapprehending peasant woman, who have never been initiated into the proportions of social things. You don't know what you say.'

'I am only a peasant by position, not by nature!'

She spoke with an impulse to anger, but it went as it came.

'So much the worse for you. I think that parson who unearthed your pedigree would have done better if he had held his tongue. I cannot help associating your decline as a family with this other fact – of your want of firmness. Decrepit families imply decrepit wills, decrepit conduct. Heaven, why did you give me a handle for despising you more by informing me of your descent! Here was I thinking you a new-sprung child of nature; there were you, the belated seedling of an effete aristocracy!'

'Lots of families are as bad as mine in that! Retty's family were once large landowners, and so were Dairyman Billett's. And the Debbyhouses, who now are carters, were once the De Bayeux family. You find such as I everywhere; 'tis a feature of our county, and I can't help it.'

'So much the worse for the county.'

She took these reproaches in their bulk simply, not in their particulars; he did not love her as he had loved her hitherto, and to all else she was indifferent.

They wandered on again in silence. It was said afterwards that a cottager of Wellbridge, who went out late that night for a doctor, met two lovers in the pastures, walking very slowly, without converse, one behind the other, as in a funeral procession, and the glimpse that he obtained of their faces seemed to denote that they were anxious and sad. Returning later, he passed them again in the same field, progressing just as slowly, and as regardless of the hour and of the cheerless night as before. It was only on account of his preoccupation with his own affairs, and the illness in his house, that he did not bear in mind the curious incident, which, however, he recalled a long while after.

During the interval of the cottager's going and coming, she had said to her husband – 'I don't see how I can help being the cause of much misery to you all your life. The river is down there. I can put an end to myself in it. I am not afraid.'

'I don't wish to add murder to my other follies,' he said.

'I will leave something to show that I did it myself – on account of my shame. They will not blame you then.'

'Don't speak so absurdly – I wish not to hear it. It is nonsense to have such thoughts in this kind of case, which is rather one for satirical laughter than for tragedy. You don't in the least understand the quality of the mishap. It would be viewed in the light of a joke by nine-tenths of the world if it were known. Please oblige me by returning to the house, and going to bed.'

'I will,' said she dutifully.

They had rambled round by a road which led to the well-known ruins of the Cistercian abbey behind the mill, the latter having, in centuries past, been attached to the monastic establishment. The mill still worked on, food being a perennial necessity; the abbey had perished, creeds being transient. One continually sees the ministration of the temporary outlasting the ministration of the eternal. Their walk having been circuitous they were still not far from the house, and in obeying his direction she only had to reach the large stone bridge across the main river, and follow the road for a few yards. When she got back everything remained as she had left it, the fire being still burning. She did not stay downstairs for more than a minute, but proceeded to her chamber, whither the luggage had been taken. Here she sat down on the edge of the bed, looking blankly around, and presently began to undress. In removing the light towards the bedstead its rays fell upon the tester of white dimity; something was hanging beneath it, and she lifted the candle to see what it was. A bough of mistletoe. Angel had put it there; she knew that in an instant. This was the explanation of that mysterious parcel which it had been so difficult to pack and bring; whose contents he would not explain to her, saying that time would soon show her the purpose thereof. In his zest and his gaiety he had hung it there. How foolish and inopportune that mistletoe looked now.

Having nothing more to fear, having scarce anything to hope, for that he would relent there seemed no promise whatever, she lay down dully. When sorrow ceases to be speculative sleep sees her opportunity. Among so many happier moods which forbid repose this was a mood which welcomed it, and in a few minutes the lonely Tess forgot existence, surrounded by the aromatic stillness of the chamber that had once, possibly, been the bride-chamber of her own ancestry.

Later on that night Clare also retraced his steps to the house. Entering softly to the sitting-room he obtained a light, and with the manner of one who had considered his course he spread his rugs upon the old horsehair sofa which stood there, and roughly shaped it to a sleeping-couch. Before lying down he crept shoeless upstairs, and listened at the door of her apartment. Her measured breathing told that she was sleeping profoundly.

'Thank God!' murmured Clare; and yet he was conscious of a pang of bitterness at the thought – approximately true, though not wholly so – that having shifted the burden of her life to his shoulders she was now reposing without care.

He turned away to descend; then, irresolute, faced round to her door again. In the act he caught sight of one of the d'Urberville dames, whose portrait was immediately over the entrance to Tess's bedchamber. In the candlelight the painting was more than unpleasant. Sinister design lurked in the woman's features, a concentrated purpose of revenge on the other sex – so it seemed to him then. The Caroline bodice of the portrait was low – precisely as Tess's had been when he tucked it in to show the necklace; and again he experienced the distressing sensation of a resemblance between them.

The check was sufficient. He resumed his retreat and descended.

His air remained calm and cold, his small compressed mouth indexing his powers of self-control; his face wearing still that terribly sterile expression which had spread thereon since her disclosure. It was the face of a man who was no longer passion's slave, yet who found no advantage in his enfranchisement. He was simply regarding the harrowing contingencies of human experience, the unexpectedness of things. Nothing so pure, so sweet, so virginal as Tess had seemed possible all the long while that he had adored her, up to an hour ago; but, 'The little less, and what worlds away!

He argued erroneously when he said to himself that her heart was not indexed in the honest freshness of her face; but Tess had no advocate to set him right. Could it be possible, he continued, that eyes which as they gazed never expressed any divergence from what the tongue was telling, were yet ever seeing another world behind her ostensible one, discordant and contrasting?

He reclined on his couch in the sitting-room, and extinguished the light. The night came in, and took up its place there, unconcerned and indifferent; the night which had already swallowed up his happiness, and was now digesting it listlessly; and was ready to swallow up the happiness of a thousand other people with as little disturbance or change of mien.

## *Chapter 36*

Clare arose in the light of a dawn that was ashy and furtive, as though associated with crime. The fireplace confronted him with its extinct embers; the spread supper-table, whereon stood the two full glasses of untasted wine, now flat and filmy; her vacated seat and his own; the other articles of furniture, with their eternal look of not being able to help it, their intolerable enquiry what was to be done? From above there was no sound; but in a few minutes there came a knock at the door. He remembered that it would be the neighbouring cottager's wife, who was to minister to their wants while they remained here.

The presence of a third person in the house would be extremely awkward just now, and, being already dressed, he opened the window and informed her that they could manage to shift for themselves that morning. She had a milk-can in her hand, which he told her to leave at the door. When the dame had gone away he searched in the back quarters of the house for fuel, and speedily lit a fire. There was plenty of eggs, butter, bread, and so on in the larder, and Clare soon had breakfast laid, his experiences at the dairy having rendered him facile in domestic preparations. The smoke of the kindled wood rose from the chimney without like a lotus-headed column; local people who were passing by saw it, and thought of the newly-married couple, and envied their happiness.

Angel cast a final glance round, and then going to the foot of the stairs, called in a conventional voice – 'Breakfast is ready!'

He opened the front door, and took a few steps in the morning air. When, after a short space, he came back she was already in the sitting-room mechanically readjusting the breakfast things. As she was fully attired, and the interval since his calling her had been but two or three minutes, she must have been dressed or nearly so before he went to summon her. Her hair was twisted up in a large round mass at the back of her head, and she had put on one of the new frocks – a pale blue woollen garment with neck-frillings of white. Her hands and face appeared to be cold, and she had possibly been sitting dressed in the bedroom a long time without any fire. The marked civility of Clare's tone in calling her seemed to have inspired her, for the moment, with a new glimmer of hope. But it soon died when she looked at him.

The pair were, in truth, but the ashes of their former fires. To the hot sorrow of the previous night had succeeded heaviness; it seemed as if nothing could kindle either of them to fervour of sensation any more.

He spoke gently to her, and she replied with a like undemonstrativeness. At last she came up to him, looking in his sharply-defined face as one who had no consciousness that her own formed a visible object also.

'Angel!' she said, and paused, touching him with her fingers lightly as a breeze, as though she could hardly believe to be there in the flesh the man who was once her lover. Her eyes were bright, her pale cheek still showed its wonted roundness though half-dried tears had left glistening traces thereon; and the usually ripe red mouth was almost as pale as her cheek. Throbbingly alive as she was still, under the stress of her mental grief the life beat so brokenly, that a little further pull upon it would cause real illness, dull her characteristic eyes, and make her mouth thin.

She looked absolutely pure. Nature, in her fantastic trickery, had set such a seal of maidenhood upon Tess's countenance that he gazed at her with a stupefied air.

'Tess! Say it is not true! No, it is not true!'

'It is true.'

'Every word?'

'Every word.'

He looked at her imploringly, as if he would willingly have taken a lie from her lips, knowing it to be one, and have made of it, by some sort of sophistry, a valid denial. However, she only repeated – 'It is true.'

'Is he living?' Angel then asked.

'The baby died.'

'But the man?'

'He is alive.'

A last despair passed over Clare's face.

'Is he in England?'

'Yes.'

He took a few vague steps.

'My position – is this,' he said abruptly. 'I thought – any man would have thought – that by giving up all ambition to win a wife with social standing, with fortune, with knowledge of the world, I should secure rustic innocence as surely as I should secure pink cheeks; but – However, I am no man to reproach you, and I will not.'

Tess felt his position so entirely that the remainder had not been needed. Therein lay just the distress of it; she saw that he had lost all round.

'Angel – I should not have let it go on to marriage with you if I had not known that, after all, there was a last way out of it for you; though I hoped you would never – ' Her voice grew husky.

'A last way?'

'I mean, to get rid of me. You *can* get rid of me.'

'How?'

'By divorcing me.'

'Good heavens – how can you be so simple! How can I divorce you?'

'Can't you – now I have told you? I thought my confession would give you grounds for that.'

'O Tess – you are too, too – childish – unformed – crude, I suppose! I don't know what you are. You don't understand the law – you don't understand!'

'What – you cannot?'

'Indeed I cannot.'

A quick shame mixed with the misery upon his listener's face.

'I thought – I thought,' she whispered. 'O, now I see how wicked I seem to you! Believe me – believe me, on my soul, I never thought but that you could! I hoped you would not; yet I believed, without a doubt, that you could cast me off if you were determined, and didn't love me at – at – all!'

'You were mistaken,' he said.

'O, then I ought to have done it, to have done it last night! But I hadn't the courage. That's just like me!'

'The courage to do what?'

As she did not answer he took her by the hand.

'What were you thinking of doing?' he enquired.

'Of putting an end to myself.'

'When?'

She writhed under this enquisitorial manner of his. 'Last night,' she answered.

'Where?'

'Under your mistletoe.'

'My good – ! How?' he asked sternly.

'I'll tell you, if you won't be angry with me!' she said, shrinking. 'It was with the cord of my box. But I could not – do the last thing! I was afraid that it might cause a scandal to your name.'

The unexpected quality of this confession, wrung from her, and not volunteered, shook him perceptibly. But he still held her, and, letting his glance fall from her face downwards, he said,

'Now, listen to this. You must not dare to think of such a horrible thing! How could you! You will promise me as your husband to attempt that no more.'

'I am ready to promise. I saw how wicked it was.'

'Wicked! The idea was unworthy of you beyond description.'

'But, Angel,' she pleaded, enlarging her eyes in calm unconcern upon him, 'it was thought of entirely on your account – to set you free without the scandal of the divorce that I thought you would have to get. I should never have dreamt of doing it on mine. However, to do it with my own hand is too good for me, after all. It is you, my ruined husband, who ought to strike the blow. I think I should love you more, if that were possible, if you could bring yourself to do it, since there's no other way of escape for 'ee. I feel I am so utterly worthless! So very greatly in the way!'

'Ssh!'

'Well, since you say no, I won't. I have no wish opposed to yours.'

He knew this to be true enough. Since the desperation of the night her activities had dropped to zero, and there was no further rashness to be feared.

Tess tried to busy herself again over the breakfast-table with more or less success, and they sat down both on the same side, so that their glances did not meet. There was at first something awkward in hearing each other eat and drink, but this could not be escaped; moreover, the amount of eating done was small on both sides. Breakfast over he rose, and telling her the hour at which he might be expected to dinner, went off to the miller's in a mechanical pursuance of the plan of studying that business, which had been his only practical reason for coming here.

When he was gone Tess stood at the window, and presently saw his form crossing the great stone bridge which conducted to the mill premises. He sank behind it, crossed the railway beyond, and disappeared. Then, without a sigh, she turned her attention to the room, and began clearing the table and setting it in order.

The charwoman soon came. Her presence was at first a strain upon Tess, but afterwards an alleviation. At half-past twelve she left her assistant alone in the kitchen, and, returning to the sitting-room, waited for the reappearance of Angel's form behind the bridge.

About one he showed himself. Her face flushed, although he was a quarter of a mile off. She ran to the kitchen to get the dinner served by the time he should enter. He went first to the room where they had washed their hands together the day before, and as he entered the sitting-room the dish-covers rose from the dishes as if by his own motion.

'How punctual!' he said.

'Yes. I saw you coming over the bridge,' said she.

The meal was passed in commonplace talk of what he had been doing during the morning at the Abbey Mill, of the methods of bolting and the old-fashioned machinery, which he feared would not enlighten him greatly on modern improved methods, some of it seeming to have been in use ever since the days it ground for the monks in the adjoining conventual buildings – now a heap of ruins. He left the house again in the course of an hour, coming home at dusk, and occupying himself through the evening with his papers. She feared she was in the way, and, when the old woman was gone, retired to the kitchen, where she made herself busy as well as she could for more than an hour.

Clare's shape appeared at the door.

'You must not work like this,' he said. 'You are not my servant; you are my wife.'

She raised her eyes, and brightened somewhat. 'I may think myself that – indeed?' she murmured, in piteous raillery. 'You mean in name! Well, I don't want to be anything more.'

'You *may* think so, Tess! You are. What do you mean?'

'I don't know,' she said hastily, with tears in her accents. 'I thought I – because I am not respectable, I mean. I told you I thought I was not respectable enough long ago – and on that account I didn't want to marry you, only – only you urged me!'

She broke into sobs, and turned her back to him. It would almost have won round any man but Angel Clare. Within the remote depths of his constitution, so gentle and affectionate as he was in general, there lay hidden a hard logical deposit, like a vein of metal in a soft loam, which turned the edge of everything that attempted to traverse it. It had blocked his acceptance of the Church; it blocked his acceptance of Tess. Moreover, his affection itself was less fire than radiance, and, with regard to the other sex, when he ceased to believe he ceased to follow: contrasting in this with many impressionable natures, who remain sensuously infatuated with what they intellectually despise. He waited till her sobbing ceased.

'I wish half the women in England were as respectable as you,' he said, in an ebullition of bitterness against womankind in general. 'It isn't a question of respectability, but one of principle!'

He spoke such things as these and more of a kindred sort to her, being still swayed by the antipathetic wave which warps direct souls with such persistence when once their vision finds itself mocked by appearances. There was, it is true, underneath, a back current of sympathy through which a woman of the world might have conquered him. But Tess did not think of this; she took everything as her deserts, and hardly opened her mouth. The firmness of her devotion to him was indeed almost pitiful; quick-tempered as she naturally was, nothing that he could say made her unseemly; she sought not her own; was not provoked; thought no evil of his treatment of her. She might just now have been Apostolic Charity herself returned to a self-seeking modern world.

This evening, night, and morning were passed precisely as the preceding ones had been passed. On one, and only one, occasion did she – the formerly free and independent Tess – venture to make any advances. It was on the third occasion of his starting after a meal to go out to the flour-mill. As he was leaving the table he said 'Goodbye,' and she replied in the same words, at the same time inclining her mouth in the way of his. He did not avail himself of the invitation, saying, as he turned hastily aside – 'I shall be home punctually.'

Tess shrank into herself as if she had been struck. Often enough had he tried to reach those lips against her consent – often had he said gaily that her mouth and breath tasted of the butter and eggs and milk and honey on which she mainly lived, that he drew sustenance from them, and other follies of that sort. But he did not care for them now. He observed her sudden shrinking, and said gently – 'You know, I have to think of a course. It was imperative that we should stay together a little while, to avoid the scandal to you that would have resulted from our immediate parting. But you must see it is only for form's sake.'

'Yes,' said Tess absently.

He went out, and on his way to the mill stood still, and wished for a moment that he had responded yet more kindly and kissed her once at least.

Thus they lived through this despairing day or two; in the same house, truly; but more widely apart than before they were lovers. It was evident to her that he was, as he had said, living with paralysed activities, in his endeavour to think of a plan of procedure. She was awe-stricken to discover such determination under such apparent flexibility. His consistency was, indeed, too cruel. She no longer expected forgiveness now. More than once she thought of going away from him during his absence at the mill; but she feared that this, instead of benefiting him, might be the means of hampering and humiliating him yet more if it should become known.

Meanwhile Clare was meditating, verily. His thought had been unsuspended; he was becoming ill with thinking; eaten out with thinking, withered by thinking; scourged out of all his former pulsating flexuous domesticity. He walked about saying to himself, 'What's to be done – what's to be done?' and by chance she overheard him. It caused her to break the reserve about their future which had hitherto prevailed.

'I suppose – you are not going to live with me – long, are you, Angel?' she asked, the sunk corners of her mouth betraying how purely mechanical were the means by which she retained that expression of chastened calm upon her face.

'I cannot,' he said, 'without despising myself, and what is worse, perhaps, despising you. I mean, of course, cannot live with you in the ordinary sense. At present, whatever I feel, I do not despise you. And, let me speak plainly, or you may not see all my difficulties. How can we live together while that man lives? – he being your husband in nature, and not I. If he were dead it might be different . . . Besides, that's not all the difficulty; it lies in another consideration – one bearing upon the future of other people than ourselves. Think of years to come, and children being born to us, and this past matter getting known – for it must get known. There is not an uttermost part of the earth but somebody comes from it or goes to it from elsewhere. Well, think of wretches of our flesh and blood growing up under a taunt which they will gradually get to feel the full force of with their expanding years. What an awakening for them! What a prospect! Can you honestly say Remain, after contemplating this contingency? Don't you think we had better endure the ills we have than fly to others?'

Her eyelids, weighted with trouble, continued drooping as before.

'I cannot say Remain,' she answered. 'I cannot; I had not thought so far.'

Tess's feminine hope – shall we confess it? – had been so obstinately recuperative as to revive in her surreptitious visions of a domiciliary intimacy continued long enough to break down his coldness even against his judgment. Though unsophisticated in the usual sense, she was not incomplete; and it would have denoted deficiency of womanhood if she had not instinctively known what an argument lies in propinquity. Nothing else would serve her, she knew, if this failed. It was wrong to hope in what was of the nature of strategy, she said to herself: yet that sort of hope she could not extinguish. His last representation had now been made, and it was, as she said, a new view. She had truly never thought so far as that, and his lucid picture of possible offspring who would scorn her was one that brought deadly conviction to an honest heart which was humanitarian to its centre. Sheer experience had already taught her that, in some circumstances, there was one thing better than to lead a good life, and that was to be saved from leading any life whatever. Like all who have been previsioned by suffering, she could, in the words of M. Sully-Prudhomme, hear a penal sentence in the fiat, 'You shall be born,' particularly if addressed to potential issue of hers.

Yet such is the vulpine slyness of Dame Nature, that, till now, Tess had been hoodwinked by her love for Clare into forgetting it might result in vitalisations that would inflict upon others what she had bewailed as misfortune to herself.

She therefore could not withstand his argument. But with the self-combating proclivity of the supersensitive, an answer thereto arose in Clare's own mind, and he almost feared it. It was based on her exceptional physical nature; and she might have used it promisingly. She might have added besides: 'On an Australian upland or Texan plain, who is to know or care about my misfortunes, or to reproach me or you?' Yet, like the majority of women, she accepted the momentary presentment as if it were the inevitable. And she may have been right. The intuitive heart of woman knoweth not only its own bitterness, but its husband's, and even if these assumed reproaches were not likely to be addressed to him or to his by strangers, they might have reached his ears from his own fastidious brain.

It was the third day of the estrangement. Some might risk the odd paradox that with more animalism he would have been the nobler man. We do not say it. Yet Clare's love was doubtless ethereal to a fault, imaginative to impracticability. With these natures, corporeal presence is something less appealing than corporeal absence; the latter creating an ideal presence that conveniently drops the defects of the real. She found that her personality did not plead her cause so forcibly as she had anticipated. The figurative phrase was true: she was another woman than the one who had excited his desire.

'I have thought over what you say,' she remarked to him moving her forefinger over the tablecloth, her other hand, which bore the ring that mocked them both, supporting her forehead. 'It is quite true all of it; it must be. You must go away from me.'

'But what can you do?'

'I can go home.'

Clare had not thought of that.

'Are you sure?' he enquired.

'Quite sure. We ought to part, and we may as well get it past and done. You once said that I was apt to win men against their better judgment; and if I am constantly before your eyes I may cause you to change your plans in opposition to your reason and wish; and afterwards your repentance and my sorrow will be terrible.'

'And you would like to go home?' he asked.

'I want to leave you, and go home.'

'Then it shall be so.'

Though she did not look up at him, she started. There was a difference between the proposition and the convenant, which she had felt only too quickly.

'I feared it would come to this,' she murmured, her countenance meekly fixed. 'I don't complain, Angel. I – I think it best. What you said has quite convinced me. Yes, though nobody else should reproach me if we should stay together, yet somewhen, years hence, you might get angry with me for any ordinary matter, and knowing what you do of my bygones you yourself might be tempted to say words, and they might be overheard, perhaps by my own children. O, what only hurts me now would torture and kill me then! I will go tomorrow.'

'And I shall not stay here. Though I didn't like to initiate it, I have seen that it was advisable we should part – at least for a while, till I can better see the shape that things have taken, and can write to you.'

Tess stole a glance at her husband. He was pale, even tremulous; but, as before, she was appalled by the determination revealed in the depths of this gentle being she had married – the will to subdue the grosser to the subtler emotion, the substance to the conception, the flesh to the spirit. Propensities, tendencies, habits, were as dead leaves upon the tyrannous wind of his imaginative ascendency.

He may have observed her look, for he explained – 'I think of people more kindly when I am away from them'; adding cynically, 'God knows; perhaps we shall shake down together someday, for weariness; thousands have done it!'

That day he began to pack up, and she went upstairs and began to pack also. Both knew that it was in their two minds that they might part the next morning for ever, despite the gloss of assuaging conjectures thrown over their proceeding because they were of the sort to whom any parting which has an air of finality is a torture. He knew, and she knew, that, though the fascination which each had exercised over the other – on her part independently of accomplishments – would probably in the first days of their separation be even more potent than ever, time must attenuate that effect; the practical arguments against accepting her as a housemate might pronounce themselves more strongly in the boreal light of a remoter view. Moreover, when two people are once parted – have abandoned a common domicile and a common environment – new growths insensibly bud upward to fill each vacated place; unforeseen accidents hinder intentions, and old plans are forgotten.

## *Chapter 37*

Midnight came and passed silently, for there was nothing to announce it in the Valley of the Froom.

Not long after one o'clock there was a slight creak in the darkened farmhouse once the mansion of the d'Urbervilles. Tess, who used the upper chamber, heard it and awoke. It had come from the corner step of the staircase, which, as usual, was loosely nailed. She saw the door of her bedroom open, and the figure of her husband crossed the stream of moonlight with a curiously careful tread. He was in his shirt and trousers only, and her first flush of joy died when she perceived that his eyes were fixed in an unnatural stare on vacancy. When he reached the middle of the room he stood still and murmured in tones of indescribable sadness – 'Dead! dead! dead!'

Under the influence of any strongly-disturbing force Clare would occasionally walk in his sleep, and even perform strange feats, such as he had done on the night of their return from market just before their marriage, when he re-enacted in his bedroom his combat with the man who had insulted her. Tess saw that continued mental distress had wrought him into that somnambulistic state now.

Her loyal confidence in him lay so deep down in her heart, that, awake or asleep, he inspired her with no sort of personal fear. If he had entered with a pistol in his hand he would scarcely have disturbed her trust in his protectiveness.

Clare came close, and bent over her. 'Dead, dead, dead!' he murmured.

After fixedly regarding her for some moments with the same gaze of unmeasurable woe he bent lower, enclosed her in his arms, and rolled her in the sheet as in a shroud. Then lifting her from the bed with as much respect as one would show to a dead body, he carried her across the room, murmuring – 'My poor, poor Tess – my dearest, darling Tess! So sweet, so good, so true!'

The words of endearment, withheld so severely in his waking hours, were inexpressibly sweet to her forlorn and hungry heart. If it had been to save her weary life she would not, by moving or struggling, have put an end to the position she found herself in. Thus she lay in absolute stillness, scarcely venturing to breathe, and, wondering what he was going to do with her, suffered herself to be borne out upon the landing.

'My wife – dead, dead!' he said.

He paused in his labours for a moment to lean with her against the banister. Was he going to throw her down? Self-solicitude was near extinction in her, and in the knowledge that he had planned to depart on the morrow, possibly for always, she lay in his arms in this precarious position with a sense rather of luxury than of terror. If they could only fall together, and both be dashed to pieces, how fit, how desirable.

However, he did not let her fall, but took advantage of the support of the handrail to imprint a kiss upon her lips – lips in the daytime scorned. Then he clasped her with a renewed firmness of hold, and descended the staircase. The creak of the loose stair did not awaken him, and they reached the ground-floor safely. Freeing one of his hands from his grasp of her for a moment, he slid back the door-bar and passed out, slightly striking his stockinged toe against the edge of the door. But this he seemed not to mind, and, having room for extension in the open air, he lifted her against his shoulder, so that he could carry her with ease, the absence of clothes taking much from his burden. Thus he bore her off the premises in the direction of the river a few yards distant.

His ultimate intention, if he had any, she had not yet divined; and she found herself conjecturing on the matter as a third person might have done. So easefully had she delivered her whole being up to him that it pleased her to think he was regarding her as his absolute possession, to dispose of as he should choose. It was consoling, under the hovering terror of tomorrow's separation, to feel that he really recognised her now as his wife Tess, and did not cast her off, even if in that recognition he went so far as to arrogate to himself the right of harming her.

Ah! now she knew what he was dreaming of – that Sunday morning when he had borne her along through the water with the other dairymaids, who had loved him nearly as much as she, if that were possible, which Tess could hardly admit. Clare did not cross the bridge with her, but proceeding several paces on the same side towards the adjoining mill, at length stood still on the brink of the river.

Its waters, in creeping down these miles of meadowland, frequently divided, serpentining in purposeless curves, looping themselves around little islands that had no name, returning and re-embodying themselves as a broad main stream further on. Opposite the spot to which he had brought her was such a general confluence, and the river was proportionately voluminous and deep. Across it was a narrow footbridge; but now the autumn flood had washed the handrail away, leaving the bare plank only, which, lying a few inches above the speeding current, formed a giddy pathway for even steady heads; and Tess had noticed from the window of the house in the daytime young men walking across upon it as a feat in balancing. Her husband had possibly observed the same performance; anyhow, he now mounted the plank, and, sliding one foot forward, advanced along it.

Was he going to drown her? Probably he was. The spot was lonely, the river deep and wide enough to make such a purpose easy of accomplishment. He might drown her if he would; it would be better than parting tomorrow to lead severed lives.

The swift stream raced and gyrated under them, tossing, distorting, and splitting the moon's reflected face. Spots of froth travelled past, and intercepted weeds waved behind the piles. If they could both fall together into the current now, their arms would be so tightly clasped together that they could not be saved; they would go out of the world almost painlessly, and there would be no more reproach to her, or to him for marrying her. His last half-hour with her would have been a loving one, while if they lived till he awoke his daytime aversion would return, and this hour would remain to be contemplated only as a transient dream.

The impulse stirred in her, yet she dared not indulge it, to make a movement that would have precipitated them both into the gulf. How she valued her own life had been proved; but his – she had no right to tamper with it. He reached the other side with her in safety.

Here they were within a plantation which formed the Abbey grounds, and taking a new hold of her he went onward a few steps till they reached the ruined choir of the Abbey-church. Against the north wall was the empty stone coffin of an abbot, in which every tourist with a turn for grim humour was accustomed to stretch himself. In this Clare carefully laid Tess. Having kissed her lips a second time he breathed deeply, as if a greatly desired end were attained. Clare then lay down on the ground alongside, when he immediately fell into the deep dead slumber of exhaustion, and remained motionless as a log. The spurt of mental excitement which had produced the effort was now over.

Tess sat up in the coffin. The night, though dry and mild for the season, was more than sufficiently cold to make it dangerous for him to remain here long, in his half-clothed state. If he were left to himself he would in all probability stay there till the morning, and be chilled to certain death. She had heard of such deaths after sleep-walking. But how could she dare to awaken him, and let him know what he had been doing, when it would mortify him to discover his folly in respect of her? Tess, however, stepping out of her stone confine, shook him slightly, but was unable to arouse him without being violent. It was indispensable to do something, for she was beginning to shiver, the sheet being but a poor protection. Her excitement had in a measure kept her warm during the few minutes' adventure; but that beatific interval was over.

It suddenly occurred to her to try persuasion; and accordingly she whispered in his ear, with as much firmness and decision as she could summon – 'Let us walk on, darling,' at the same time taking him suggestively by the arm. To her relief, he unresistingly acquiesced; her words had apparently thrown him back into his dream which thenceforward seemed to enter on a new phase, wherein he fancied she had risen as a spirit, and was leading him to Heaven. Thus she conducted him by the arm to the stone bridge in front of their residence, crossing which they stood at the manor-house door. Tess's feet were quite bare, and the stones hurt her, and chilled her to the bone; but Clare was in his woollen stockings, and appeared to feel no discomfort.

There was no further difficulty. She induced him to lie down on his own sofa bed, and covered him up warmly, lighting a temporary fire of wood, to dry any dampness out of him. The noise of these attentions she thought might awaken him, and secretly wished that they might. But the exhaustion of his mind and body was such that he remained undisturbed.

As soon as they met the next morning Tess divined that Angel knew little or nothing of how far she had been concerned in the night's excursion, though, as regarded himself, he may have been aware that he had not lain still. In truth, he had awakened that morning from a sleep deep as annihilation; and during those first few moments in which the brain, like a Samson shaking himself, is trying its strength, he had some dim notion of an unusual nocturnal proceeding. But the realities of his situation soon displaced conjecture on the other subject.

He waited in expectancy to discern some mental pointing; he knew that if any intention of his, concluded overnight, did not vanish in the light of morning, it stood on a basis approximating to one of pure reason, even if initiated by impulse of feeling; that it was so far, therefore, to be trusted. He thus beheld in the pale morning light the resolve to separate from her; not as a hot and indignant instinct, but denuded of the passionateness which had made it scorch and burn; standing in its bones; nothing but a skeleton, but none the less there. Clare no longer hesitated.

At breakfast, and while they were packing the few remaining articles, he showed his weariness from the night's effort so unmistakably that Tess was on the point of revealing all that had happened; but the reflection that it would anger him, grieve him, stultify him, to know that he had instinctively manifested a fondness for her of which his common-sense did not approve; that his inclination had compromised his dignity when reason slept, again deterred her. It was too much like laughing at a man when sober for his erratic deeds during intoxication.

It just crossed her mind, too, that he might have a faint recollection of his tender vagary, and was disinclined to allude to it from a conviction that she would take amatory advantage of the opportunity it gave her of appealing to him anew not to go.

He had ordered by letter a vehicle from the nearest town, and soon after breakfast it arrived. She saw in it the beginning of the end – the temporary end, at least, for the revelation of his tenderness by the incident of the night raised dreams of a possible future with him. The luggage was put on the top, and the man drove them off, the miller and the old waiting-woman expressing some surprise at their precipitate departure, which Clare attributed to his discovery that the mill-work was not of the modern kind which he wished to investigate, a statement that was true so far as it went. Beyond this there was nothing in the manner of their leaving to suggest a *fiasco*, or that they were not going together to visit friends.

Their route lay near the dairy from which they had started with such solemn joy in each other a few days back, and as Clare wished to wind up his business with Mr Crick, Tess could hardly avoid paying Mrs Crick a call at the same time, unless she would excite suspicion of their unhappy state.

To make the call as unobtrusive as possible they left the carriage by the wicket leading down from the high road to the dairy-house, and descended the track on foot, side by side. The withy-bed had been cut, and they could see over the stumps the spot to which Clare had followed her when he pressed her to be his wife; to the left the enclosure in which she had been fascinated by his harp; and far away behind the cow stalls the mead which had been the scene of their first embrace. The gold of the summer picture was now grey, the colours mean, the rich soil mud, and the river cold.

Over the barton-gate the dairyman saw them, and came forward, throwing into his face the kind of jocularity deemed appropriate in Talbothays and its vicinity on the re-appearance of the newly-married. Then Mrs Crick emerged from the house, and several others of their old acquaintance, though Marian and Retty did not seem to be there.

Tess valiantly bore their sly attacks and friendly humours, which affected her far otherwise than they supposed. In the tacit agreement of husband and wife to keep their estrangement a secret they behaved as would have been ordinary. And then, although she would rather there had been no word spoken on the subject, Tess had to hear in detail the story of Marian and Retty. The latter had gone home to her father's, and Marian had left to look for employment elsewhere. They feared she would come to no good.

To dissipate the sadness of this recital Tess went and bade all her favourite cows goodbye, touching each of them with her hand, and as she and Clare stood side by side at leaving, as if united body and soul, there would have been something peculiarly sorry in their aspect to one who should have seen it truly; two limbs of one life, as they outwardly were, his arm touching hers, her skirts touching him, facing one way, as against all the dairy facing the other, speaking in their adieux as 'we', and yet sundered like the poles. Perhaps something unusually stiff and embarrassed in their attitude, some awkwardness in acting up to their profession of unity, different from the natural shyness of young couples, may have been apparent, for when they were gone Mrs Crick said to her husband – 'How unnatural the brightness of her eyes did seem, and how they stood like waxen images and talked as if they were in a dream! Didn't it strike 'ee that 'twas so? Tess had always sommat strange in her, and she's not now quite like the proud young bride of a well-be-doing man.'

They re-entered the vehicle, and were driven along the roads towards Weatherbury and Stagfoot Lane, till they reached the Lane inn, where Clare dismissed the fly and man. They rested here a while, and entering the Vale were next driven onward towards her home by a stranger who did not know their relations. At a midway point, when Nuttlebury had been passed, and where there were crossroads, Clare stopped the conveyance and said to Tess that if she meant to return to her mother's house it was here that he would leave her. As they could not talk with freedom in the driver's presence he asked her to accompany him for a few steps on foot along one of the branch roads; she assented, and directing the man to wait a few minutes they strolled away.

'Now, let us understand each other,' he said gently. 'There is no anger between us, though there is that which I cannot endure at present. I will try to bring myself to endure it. I will let you know where I go to as soon as I know myself. And if I can bring myself to bear it – if it is desirable, possible – I will come to you. But until I come to you it will be better that you should not try to come to me.'

The severity of the decree seemed deadly to Tess; she saw his view of her clearly enough; he could regard her in no other light than that of one who had practised gross deceit upon him. Yet could a woman who had done even what she had done deserve all this? But she could contest the point with him no further. She simply repeated after him his own words.

'Until you come to me I must not try to come to you?'

'Just so.'

'May I write to you?'

'O yes – if you are ill, or want anything at all. I hope that will not be the case; so that it may happen that I write first to you.'

'I agree to the conditions, Angel; because you know best what my punishment ought to be; only – only – don't make it more than I can bear!'

That was all she said on the matter. If Tess had been artful, had she made a scene, fainted, wept hysterically, in that lonely lane, notwithstanding the fury of fastidiousness with which he was possessed, he would probably not have withstood her. But her mood of long-suffering made his way easy for him, and she herself was his best advocate. Pride, too, entered into her submission – which perhaps was a symptom of that reckless acquiescence in chance too apparent in the whole d'Urberville family – and the many effective chords which she could have stirred by an appeal were left untouched.

The remainder of their discourse was on practical matters only. He now handed her a packet containing a fairly good sum of money, which he had obtained from his bankers for the purpose. The brilliants, the interest in which seemed to be Tess's for her life only (if he understood the wording of the will), he advised her to let him send to a bank for safety; and to this she readily agreed.

These things arranged he walked with Tess back to the carriage, and handed her in. The coachman was paid and told where to drive her. Taking next his own bag and umbrella – the sole articles he had brought with him hitherwards – he bade her goodbye; and they parted there and then.

The fly moved creepingly up a hill, and Clare watched it go with an unpremeditated hope that Tess would look out of the window for one moment. But that she never thought of doing, would not have ventured to do, lying in a half-dead faint inside. Thus he beheld her recede, and in the anguish of his heart quoted a line from a poet, with peculiar emendations of his own; 'God's *not* in his heaven: all's *wrong* with the world!'

When Tess had passed over the crest of the hill he turned to go his own way, and hardly knew that he loved her still.

## *Chapter 38*

As she drove on through Blackmoor Vale, and the landscape of her youth began to open around her, Tess aroused herself from her stupor. Her first thought was how would she be able to face her parents?

She reached a turnpike-gate which stood upon the highway to the village. It was thrown open by a stranger, not by the old man who had kept it for many years, and to whom she had been known; he had probably left on New Year's Day, the date when such changes were made. Having received no intelligence lately from her home, she asked the turnpike-keeper for news.

'Oh – nothing, miss,' he answered. 'Marlott is Marlott still. Folks have died and that. John Durbeyfield, too, hev had a daughter married this week to a gentleman-farmer; not from John's own house, you know; they was married elsewhere; the gentleman being of that high standing that John's own folk was not considered well-be-doing enough to have any part in it, the bridegroom seeming not to know how't have been discovered that John is a old and ancient nobleman himself by blood, with family skillentons in their own vaults to this day, but done out of his property in the time o' the Romans. However, Sir John, as we call 'n now, kept up the wedding-day as well as he could, and stood treat to everybody in the parish; and John's wife sung songs at the Pure Drop till past eleven o'clock.'

Hearing this, Tess felt so sick at heart that she could not decide to go home publicly in the fly with her luggage and belongings. She asked the turnpike-keeper if she might deposit her things at his house for a while, and, on his offering no objection, she dismissed her carriage, and went on to the village alone by a back lane.

At sight of her father's chimney she asked herself how she could possibly enter the house? Inside that cottage her relations were calmly supposing her far away on a wedding-tour with a comparatively rich man, who was to conduct her to bouncing prosperity; while here she was, friendless, creeping up to the old door quite by herself, with no better place to go to in the world.

She did not reach the house unobserved. Just by the garden hedge she was met by a girl who knew her – one of the two or three with whom she had been intimate at school. After making a few enquiries as to how Tess came there, her friend, unheeding her tragic look, interrupted with; 'But where's thy gentleman, Tess?'

Tess hastily explained that he had been called away on business, and, leaving her interlocutor, clambered over the garden hedge, and thus made her way to the house.

As she went up the garden-path she heard her mother singing by the back door, coming in sight of which she perceived Mrs Durbeyfield on the doorstep in the act of wringing a sheet. Having performed this without observing Tess, she went indoors, and her daughter followed her.

The washing-tub stood in the same old place on the same old quarter-hogshead, and her mother, having thrown the sheet aside, was about to plunge her arms in anew.

'Why – Tess! – my chil' – I thought you was married! – married really and truly this time – we sent the cider – '

'Yes, mother; so I am.'

'Going to be?'

'No – I am married.'

'Married! Then where's thy husband?'

'Oh, he's gone away for a time.'

'Gone away! When was you married, then? The day you said?'

'Yes, Tuesday, mother.'

'And now 'tis on'y Saturday, and he gone away?'

'Yes, he's gone.'

'What's the meaning o' that? 'Nation seize such husbands as you seem to get, say I!'

'Mother!' Tess went across to Joan Durbeyfield, laid her face upon the matron's bosom, and burst into sobs. 'I don't know how to tell 'ee, mother! You said to me, and wrote to me, that I was not to tell him. But I did tell him – I couldn't help it – and he went away!'

'O you little fool – you little fool!' burst out Mrs Durbeyfield, splashing Tess and herself in her agitation. 'My good God! that ever I should ha' lived to say it, but I say it again, you little fool!'

Tess was convulsed with weeping, the tension of so many days having relaxed at last.

'I know it – I know – I know!' she gasped through her sobs. 'But, O my mother, I could not help it! He was so good – and I felt the wickedness of trying to blind him as to what had happened! If – if – it were to be done again – I should do the same. I could not – I dared not – so sin – against him!'

'But you sinned enough to marry him first!'

'Yes, yes; that's where my misery do lie! But I thought he could get rid o' me by law if he were determined not to overlook it. And O, if you knew – if you could only half know how I loved him – how anxious I was to have him – and how wrung I was between caring so much for him and my wish to be fair to him!'

Tess was so shaken that she could get no further, and sank a helpless thing into a chair.

'Well, well; what's done can't be undone! I'm sure I don't know why children o' my bringing forth should all be bigger simpletons than other people's – not to know better than to blab such a thing as that, when he couldn't ha' found it out till too late!' Here Mrs Durbeyfield began shedding tears on her own account as a mother to be pitied. 'What your father will say I don't know,' she continued; 'for he's been talking about the wedding up at Rolliver's and the Pure Drop every day since, and about his family getting back to their rightful position through you – poor silly man! – and now you've made this mess of it! The Lord-a-Lord!'

As if to bring matters to a focus, Tess's father was heard approaching at that moment. He did not, however, enter immediately, and Mrs Durbeyfield said that she would break the bad news to him herself, Tess keeping out of sight for the present. After her first burst of disappointment Joan began to take the mishap as she had taken Tess's original trouble, as she would have taken a wet holiday or failure in the potato-crop; as a thing which had come upon them irrespective of desert or folly; a chance external impingement to be borne with; not a lesson.

Tess retreated upstairs and beheld casually that the beds had been shifted, and new arrangements made. Her old bed had been adapted for two younger children. There was no place here for her now.

The room below being unceiled she could hear most of what went on there. Presently her father entered, apparently carrying a live hen. He was a foot-haggler now, having been obliged to sell his second horse, and he travelled with his basket on his arm. The hen had been carried about this morning as it was often carried, to show people that he was in his work, though it had lain, with its legs tied, under the table at Rolliver's for more than an hour.

'We've just had up a story about – ' Durbeyfield began, and thereupon related in detail to his wife a discussion which had arisen at the inn about the clergy, originated by the fact of his daughter having married into a clerical family. 'They was formerly styled "sir", like my own ancestry,' he said, 'though nowadays their true style, strictly speaking, is "clerk" only.' As Tess had wished that no great publicity should be given to the event, he had mentioned no particulars. He hoped she would remove that prohibition soon. He proposed that the couple should take Tess's own name, d'Urberville, as uncorrupted. It was better than her husband's. He asked if any letter had come from her that day.

Then Mrs Durbeyfield informed him that no letter had come, but Tess unfortunately had come herself.

When at length the collapse was explained to him a sullen mortification, not usual with Durbeyfield, overpowered the influence of the cheering glass. Yet the intrinsic quality of the event moved his touchy sensitiveness less than its conjectured effect upon the minds of others.

'To think, now, that this was to be the end o't!' said Sir John. 'And I with a family vault under that there church of Kingsbere as big as Squire Jollard's ale-cellar, and my folk lying there in sixes and sevens, as genuine county bones and marrow as any recorded in history. And now to be sure what they fellers at Rolliver's and the Pure Drop will say to me! How they'll squint and glane, and say, "This is yer mighty match is it; this is yer getting back to the true level of yer forefathers in King Norman's time!" I feel this is too much, Joan; I shall put an end to myself, title and all – I can bear it no longer! . . . But she can make him keep her if he's married her?'

'Why, yes. But she won't think o' doing that.'

'D'ye think he really have married her? – or is it like the first – '

Poor Tess, who had heard as far as this, could not bear to hear more. The perception that her word could be doubted even here, in her own parental house, set her mind against the spot as nothing else could have done. How unexpected were the attacks of destiny! And if her father doubted her a little, would not neighbours and acquaintance doubt her much? O, she could not live long at home!

A few days, accordingly, were all that she allowed herself here, at the end of which time she received a short note from Clare, informing her that he had gone to the North of England to look at a farm. In her craving for the lustre of her true position as his wife, and to hide from her parents the vast extent of the division between them, she made use of this letter as her reason for again departing, leaving them under the impression that she was setting out to join him. Still further to screen her husband from any imputation of unkindness to her, she took twenty-five of the fifty pounds Clare had given her, and handed the sum over to her mother, as if the wife of a man like Angel Clare could well afford it, saying that it was a slight return for the trouble and humiliation she had brought upon them in years past. With this assertion of her dignity she bade them farewell; and after that there were lively doings in the Durbeyfield household for some time on the strength of Tess's bounty, her mother saying, and, indeed, believing, that the rupture which had arisen between the young husband and wife had adjusted itself under their strong feeling that they could not live apart from each other.

## *Chapter 39*

It was three weeks after the marriage that Clare found himself descending the hill which led to the well-known parsonage of his father. With his downward course the tower of the church rose into the evening sky in a manner of enquiry as to why he had come; and no living person in the twilighted town seemed to notice him, still less to expect him. He was arriving like a ghost, and the sound of his own footsteps was almost an encumbrance to be got rid of.

The picture of life had changed for him. Before this time he had known it but speculatively; now he thought he knew it as a practical man; though perhaps he did not, even yet. Nevertheless humanity stood before him no longer in the pensive sweetness of Italian art, but in the staring and ghastly attitudes of a Wiertz Museum, and with the leer of a study by Van Beers.

His conduct during these first weeks had been desultory beyond description. After mechanically attempting to pursue his agricultural plans as though nothing unusual had happened, in the manner recommended by the great and wise men of all ages, he concluded that very few of those great and wise men had ever gone so far outside themselves as to test the feasibility of their counsel. 'This is the chief thing: be not perturbed,' said the Pagan moralist. That was just Clare's own opinion. But he was perturbed. 'Let not your heart be troubled, neither let it be afraid,' said the Nazarene. Clare chimed in cordially; but his heart was troubled all the same. How he would have liked to confront those two great thinkers, and earnestly appeal to them as fellow-man to fellow-men, and ask them to tell him their method!

His mood transmuted itself into a dogged indifference till at length he fancied he was looking on his own existence with the passive interest of an outsider.

He was embittered by the conviction that all this desolation had been brought about by the accident of her being a d'Urberville. When he found that Tess came of that exhausted ancient line, and was not of the new tribes from below, as he had fondly dreamed, why had he not stoically abandoned her, in fidelity to his principles? This was what he had got by apostasy, and his punishment was deserved.

Then he became weary and anxious, and his anxiety increased. He wondered if he had treated her unfairly. He ate without knowing that he ate, and drank without tasting. As the hours dropped past, as the motive of each act in the long series of bygone days presented itself to his view, he perceived how intimately the notion of having Tess as a dear possession was mixed up with all his schemes and words and ways.

In going hither and thither he observed in the outskirts of a small town a red-and-blue placard setting forth the great advantages of the Empire of Brazil as a field for the emigrating agriculturist. Land was offered there on exceptionally advantageous terms. Brazil somewhat attracted him as a new idea. Tess could eventually join him there, and perhaps in that country of contrasting scenes and notions and habits the conventions would not be so operative which made life with her seem impracticable to him here. In brief he was strongly inclined to try Brazil, especially as the season for going thither was just at hand.

With this view he was returning to Emminster to disclose his plan to his parents, and to make the best explanation he could make of arriving without Tess, short of revealing what had actually separated them. As he reached the door the new moon shone upon his face, just as the old one had done in the small hours of that morning when he had carried his wife in his arms across the river to the graveyard of the monks; but his face was thinner now.

Clare had given his parents no warning of his visit, and his arrival stirred the atmosphere of the vicarage as the dive of the kingfisher stirs a quiet pool. His father and mother were both in the drawing-room, but neither of his brothers was now at home. Angel entered, and closed the door quietly behind him.

'But – where's your wife, dear Angel?' cried his mother. 'How you surprise us!'

'She is at her mother's – temporarily. I have come home rather in a hurry because I've decided to go to Brazil.'

'Brazil! Why they are all Roman Catholics there surely!'

'Are they? I hadn't thought of that.'

But even the novelty and painfulness of his going to a Papistical land could not displace for long Mr and Mrs Clare's natural interest in their son's marriage.

'We had your brief note three weeks ago announcing that it had taken place,' said Mrs Clare, 'and your father sent your godmother's gift to her, as you know. Of course it was best that none of us should be present, especially as you preferred to marry her from the dairy, and not at her home, wherever that may be. It would have embarrassed you, and given us no pleasure. Your brothers felt that very strongly. Now it is done we do not complain, particularly if she suits you for the business you have chosen to follow instead of the ministry of the Gospel . . . Yet I wish I could have seen her first, Angel, or have known a little more about her. We sent her no present of our own, not knowing what would best give her pleasure, but you must suppose it only delayed. Angel, there is no irritation in my mind or your father's against you for this marriage; but we have thought it much better to reserve our liking for your wife till we could see her. And now you have not brought her. It seems strange. What has happened?'

He replied that it had been thought best by them that she should go to her parents' home for the present, whilst he came there.

'I don't mind telling you, dear mother,' he said, 'that I always meant to keep her away from this house till I should feel she could come with credit to you. But this idea of Brazil is quite a recent one. If I do go it will be unadvisable for me to take her on this my first journey. She will remain at her mother's till I come back.'

'And I shall not see her before you start?'

He was afraid they would not. His original plan had been, as he had said, to refrain from bringing her there for some little while – not to wound their prejudices – feelings – in any way; and for other reasons he had adhered to it. He would have to visit home in the course of a year, if he went out at once; and it would be possible for them to see her before he started a second time – with her.

A hastily prepared supper was brought in, and Clare made further exposition of his plans. His mother's disappointment at not seeing the bride still remained with her. Clare's late enthusiasm for Tess had infected her through her maternal sympathies, till she had almost fancied that a good thing could come out of Nazareth – a charming woman out of Talbothays Dairy. She watched her son as he ate.

'Cannot you describe her? I am sure she is very pretty, Angel.'

'Of that there can be no question!' he said, with a zest which covered its bitterness.

'And that she is pure and virtuous goes without question?'

'Pure and virtuous, of course, she is.'

'I can see her quite distinctly. You said the other day that she was fine in figure; roundly built; had deep red lips like Cupid's bow; dark eyelashes and brows, an immense rope of hair like a ship's cable; and large eyes violety-bluey-blackish.'

'I did, mother.'

'I quite see her. And living in such seclusion she naturally had scarce ever seen any young man from the world without till she saw you.'

'Scarcely.'

'You were her first love?'

'Of course.'

'There are worse wives than these simple, rosy-mouthed, robust girls of the farm. Certainly I could have wished – well, since my son is to be an agriculturist, it is perhaps but proper that his wife should have been accustomed to an outdoor life.'

His father was less inquisitive; but when the time came for the chapter from the Bible which was always read before evening prayers, the vicar observed to Mrs Clare – 'I think, since Angel has come, that it will be more appropriate to read the thirty-first of Proverbs than the chapter which we should have had in the usual course of our reading?'

'Yes, certainly,' said Mrs Clare. 'The words of King Lemuel' (she could cite chapter and verse as well as her husband). 'My dear son, your father has decided to read us the chapter in Proverbs in praise of a virtuous wife. We shall not need to be reminded to apply the words to the absent one. May Heaven shield her in all her ways!'

A lump rose in Clare's throat. The portable lectern was taken out from the corner and set in the middle of the fireplace, the two old servants came in, and Angel's father began to read at the tenth verse of the aforesaid chapter – ' "Who can find a virtuous woman? for her price is far above rubies. She riseth while it is yet night, and giveth meat to her household. She girdeth her loins with strength and strengtheneth her arms. She perceiveth that her merchandise is good; her candle goeth not out by night. She looketh well to the ways of her household, and eateth not the bread of idleness. Her children arise up and call her blessed; her husband also, and he praiseth her. Many daughters have done virtuously, but thou excellest them all." '

When prayers were over, his mother said – 'I could not help thinking how very aptly that chapter your dear father read applied, in some of its particulars, to the woman you have chosen. The perfect woman, you see, was a working woman; not an idler; not a fine lady; but one who used her hands and her head and her heart for the good of others. "Her children arise up and call her blessed; her husband also, and he praiseth her. Many daughters have done virtuously, but she excelleth them all." Well, I wish I could have seen her, Angel. Since she is pure and chaste she would have been refined enough for me.'

Clare could bear this no longer. His eyes were full of tears, which seemed like drops of molten lead. He bade a quick good-night to these sincere and simple souls whom he loved so well; who knew neither the world, the flesh, nor the devil in their own hearts; only as something vague and external to themselves. He went to his own chamber.

His mother followed him, and tapped at his door. Clare opened it to discover her standing without, with anxious eyes.

'Angel,' she asked, 'is there something wrong that you go away so soon? I am quite sure you are not yourself.'

'I am not, quite, mother,' said he.

'About her? Now, my son, I know it is that – I know it is about her! Have you quarrelled in these three weeks?'

'We have not exactly quarrelled,' he said. 'But we have had a difference – '

'Angel – is she a young woman whose history will bear investigation?'

With a mother's instinct Mrs Clare had put her finger on the kind of trouble that would cause such a disquiet as seemed to agitate her son.

'She is spotless!' he replied; and felt that if it had sent him to eternal hell there and then he would have told that lie.

'Then never mind the rest. After all, there are few purer things in nature than an unsullied country maid. Any crudeness of manner which may offend your more educated sense at first, will, I am sure, disappear under the influence of your companionship and tuition.'

Such terrible sarcasm of blind magnanimity brought home to Clare the secondary perception that he had utterly wrecked his career by this marriage, which had not been among his early thoughts after the disclosure. True, on his own account he cared very little about his career; but he had wished to make it at least a respectable one on account of his parents and brothers. And now as he looked into the candle its flame dumbly expressed to him that it was made to shine on sensible people, and that it abhorred lighting the face of a dupe and a failure.

When his agitation had cooled he would be at moments incensed with his poor wife for causing a situation in which he was obliged to practise deception on his parents. He almost talked to her in his anger, as if she had been in the room. And then her cooing voice, plaintive in expostulation, disturbed the darkness, the velvet touch of her lips passed over his brow, and he could distinguish in the air the warmth of her breath.

This night the woman of his belittling deprecations was thinking how great and good her husband was. But over them both there hung a deeper shade than the shade which Angel Clare perceived, namely, the shade of his own limitations. With all his attempted independence of judgment this advanced and well-meaning young man, a sample product of the last five-and-twenty years, was yet the slave to custom and conventionality when surprised back into his early teachings. No prophet had told him, and he was not prophet enough to tell himself, that essentially this young wife of his was as deserving of the praise of King Lemuel as any other woman endowed with the same dislike of evil, her moral value having to be reckoned not by achievement but by tendency. Moreover, the figure near at hand suffers on such occasions, because it shows up its sorriness without shade; while vague figures afar off are honoured, in that their distance makes artistic virtues of their stains. In considering what Tess was not, he overlooked what she was, and forgot that the defective can be more than the entire.

## *Chapter 40*

At breakfast Brazil was the topic, and all endeavoured to take a hopeful view of Clare's proposed experiment with that country's soil, notwithstanding the discouraging reports of some farm-labourers who had emigrated thither and returned home within the twelve months. After breakfast Clare went into the little town to wind up such trifling matters as he was concerned with there, and to get from the local bank all the money he possessed. On his way back he encountered Miss Mercy Chant by the church, from whose walls she seemed to be a sort of emanation. She was carrying an armful of Bibles for her class, and such was her view of life that events which produced heartache in others wrought beatific smiles upon her – an enviable result, although, in the opinion of Angel, it was obtained by a curiously unnatural sacrifice of humanity to mysticism.

She had learnt that he was about to leave England, and observed what an excellent and promising scheme it seemed to be.

'Yes; it is a likely scheme enough in a commercial sense, no doubt,' he replied. 'But, my dear Mercy, it snaps the continuity of existence. Perhaps a cloister would be preferable.'

'A cloister! O, Angel Clare!'

'Well?'

'Why, you wicked man, a cloister implies a monk, and a monk Roman Catholicism.'

'And Roman Catholicism sin, and sin damnation. Thou art in a parlous state, Angel Clare.'

'*I* glory in my Protestantism!' she said severely.

Then Clare, thrown by sheer misery into one of the demoniacal moods in which a man does despite to his true principles, called her close to him, and fiendishly whispered in her ear the most heterodox ideas he could think of. His momentary laughter at the horror which appeared on her fair face ceased when it merged in pain and anxiety for his welfare.

'Dear Mercy,' he said, 'you must forgive me. I think I am going crazy!'

She thought that he was; and thus the interview ended, and Clare re-entered the vicarage. With the local banker he deposited the jewels till happier days should arise. He also paid into the bank thirty pounds – to be sent to Tess in a few months, as she might require; and wrote to her at her parents' home in Blackmoor Vale to inform her of what he had done. This amount, with the sum he had already placed in her hands – about fifty pounds – he hoped would be amply sufficient for her wants just at present, particularly as in an emergency she had been directed to apply to his father.

He deemed it best not to put his parents into communication with her by informing them of her address; and, being unaware of what had really happened to estrange the two, neither his father nor his mother suggested that he should do so. During the day he left the parsonage, for what he had to complete he wished to get done quickly.

As the last duty before leaving this part of England it was necessary for him to call at the Wellbridge farmhouse, in which he had spent with Tess the first three days of their marriage, the trifle of rent having to be paid, the key given up of the rooms they had occupied, and two or three small articles fetched away that they had left behind. It was under this roof that the deepest shadow ever thrown upon his life had stretched its gloom over him. Yet when he had unlocked the door of the sitting-room and looked into it, the memory which returned first upon him was that of their happy arrival on a similar afternoon, the first fresh sense of sharing a habitation conjointly, the first meal together, the chatting by the fire with joined hands.

The farmer and his wife were in the field at the moment of his visit, and Clare was in the rooms alone for some time. Inwardly swollen with a renewal of sentiment that he had not quite reckoned with, he went upstairs to her chamber, which had never been his. The bed was smooth as she had made it with her own hands on the morning of leaving. The mistletoe hung under the tester just as he had placed it. Having been there three or four weeks it was turning colour, and the leaves and berries were wrinkled. Angel took it down and crushed it into the grate. Standing there he for the first time doubted whether his course in this conjuncture had been a wise, much less a generous, one. But had he not been cruelly blinded? In the incoherent multitude of his emotions he knelt down at the bedside wet-eyed. 'O Tess! If you had only told me sooner, I would have forgiven you!' he mourned.

Hearing a footstep below he rose and went to the top of the stairs. At the bottom of the flight he saw a woman standing, and on her turning up her face recognised the pale, dark-eyed Izz Huett.

'Mr Clare,' she said, 'I've called to see you and Mrs Clare, and to enquire if ye be well. I thought you might be back here again.'

This was a girl whose secret he had guessed, but who had not yet guessed his; an honest girl who loved him – one who would have made as good, or nearly as good, a practical farmer's wife as Tess.

'I am here alone,' he said; 'we are not living here now.' Explaining why he had come, he asked, 'Which way are you going home, Izz?'

'I have no home at Talbothays Dairy now, sir,' she said.

'Why is that?'

Izz looked down.

'It was so dismal there that I left! I am staying out this way.' She pointed in a contrary direction, the direction in which he was journeying.

'Well – are you going there now? I can take you if you wish for a lift.'

Her olive complexion grew richer in hue.

'Thank 'ee, Mr Clare,' she said.

He soon found the farmer, and settled the account for his rent and the few other items which had to be considered by reason of the sudden abandonment of the lodgings. On Clare's return to his horse and gig Izz jumped up beside him.

'I am going to leave England, Izz,' he said, as they drove on. 'Going to Brazil.'

'And do Mrs Clare like the notion of such a journey?' she asked.

'She is not going at present – say for a year or so. I am going out to reconnoitre – to see what life there is like.'

They sped along eastward for some considerable distance, Izz making no observation.

'How are the others?' he enquired. 'How is Retty?'

'She was in a sort of nervous state when I zid her last; and so thin and hollow-cheeked that 'a do seem in a decline. Nobody will ever fall in love wi' her any more,' said Izz absently.

'And Marian?'

Izz lowered her voice.

'Marian drinks.'

'Indeed!'

'Yes. The dairyman has got rid of her.'

'And you!'

'I don't drink, and I bain't in a decline. But – I am no great things at singing afore breakfast now!'

'How is that? Do you remember how neatly you used to turn " 'Twas down in Cupid's Gardens" and "The Tailor's Breeches" at morning milking?'

'Ah, yes! When you first came, sir, that was. Not when you had been there a bit.'

'Why was that falling-off?'

Her black eyes flashed up to his face for one moment by way of answer.

'Izz! – how weak of you – for such as I!' he said, and fell into reverie. 'Then – suppose I had asked you to marry me?'

'If you had I should have said "Yes," and you would have married a woman who loved 'ee!'

'Really!'

'Down to the ground!' she whispered vehemently. 'O my God! did you never guess it till now!'

By and by they reached a branch road to a village.

'I must get down. I live out there,' said Izz abruptly, never having spoken since her avowal.

Clare slowed the horse. He was incensed against his fate, bitterly disposed towards social ordinances; for they had cooped him up in a corner, out of which there was no legitimate pathway. Why not be revenged on society by shaping his future domesticities loosely, instead of kissing the pedagogic rod of convention in this ensnaring manner?

'I am going to Brazil alone, Izz,' said he. 'I have separated from my wife for personal, not voyaging, reasons. I may never live with her again. I may not be able to love you; but – will you go with me instead of her?'

'You truly wish me to go?'

'I do. I have been badly used enough to wish for relief. And you at least love me disinterestedly.'

'Yes – I will go,' said Izz, after a pause.

'You will? You know what it means, Izz?'

'It means that I shall live with you for the time you are over there – that's good enough for me.'

'Remember, you are not to trust me in morals now. But I ought to remind you that it will be wrong-doing in the eyes of civilisation – Western civilisation, that is to say.'

'I don't mind that; no woman do when it comes to agony-point, and there's no other way!'

'Then don't get down, but sit where you are.'

He drove past the crossroads, one mile, two miles, without showing any signs of affection.

'You love me very, very much, Izz?' he suddenly asked.

'I do – I have said I do! I loved you all the time we was at the dairy together!'

'More than Tess?'

She shook her head.

'No,' she murmured, 'not more than she.'

'How's that?'

'Because nobody could love 'ee more than Tess did! . . . She would have laid down her life for 'ee. I could do no more.'

Like the prophet on the top of Peor Izz Huett would fain have spoken perversely at such a moment, but the fascination exercised over her rougher nature by Tess's character compelled her to grace.

Clare was silent; his heart had risen at these straightforward words from such an unexpected unimpeachable quarter. In his throat was something as if a sob had solidified there. His ears repeated, '*She would have laid down her life for 'ee. I could do no more!*'

'Forget our idle talk, Izz,' he said, turning the horse's head suddenly. 'I don't know what I've been saying! I will now drive you back to where your lane branches off.'

'So much for honesty towards 'ee! O – how can I bear it – how can I – how can I!'

Izz Huett burst into wild tears, and beat her forehead as she saw what she had done.

'Do you regret that poor little act of justice to an absent one? O, Izz, don't spoil it by regret!'

She stilled herself by degrees.

'Very well, sir. Perhaps I didn't know what I was saying, either, wh – when I agreed to go! I wish – what cannot be!'

'Because I have a loving wife already.'

'Yes, yes! You have.'

They reached the corner of the lane which they had passed half an hour earlier, and she hopped down.

'Izz – please, please forget my momentary levity!' he cried. 'It was so ill-considered, so ill-advised!'

'Forget it? Never, never! O, it was no levity to me!'

He felt how richly he deserved the reproach that the wounded cry conveyed, and, in a sorrow that was inexpressible, leapt down and took her hand.

'Well, but, Izz, we'll part friends, anyhow? You don't know what I've had to bear!'

She was a really generous girl, and allowed no further bitterness to mar their adieux.

'I forgive 'ee, sir!' she said.

'Now, Izz,' he said, while she stood beside him there, forcing himself to the mentor's part he was far from feeling; 'I want you to tell Marian when you see her that she is to be a good woman, and not to give way to folly. Promise that, and tell Retty that there are more worthy men than I in the world, that for my sake she is to act wisely and well – remember the words – wisely and well – for my sake. I send this message to them as a dying man to the dying; for I shall never see them again. And you, Izzy, you have saved me by your honest words about my wife from an incredible impulse towards folly and treachery. Women may be bad, but they are not so bad as men in these things! On that one account I can never forget you. Be always the good and sincere girl you have hitherto been; and think of me as a worthless lover, but a faithful friend. Promise.'

She gave the promise.

'Heaven bless and keep you, sir. Goodbye!'

He drove on; but no sooner had Izz turned into the lane, and Clare was out of sight, than she flung herself down on the bank in a fit of racking anguish; and it was with a strained unnatural face that she entered her mother's cottage late that night. Nobody ever was told how Izz spent the dark hours that intervened between Angel Clare's parting from her and her arrival home.

Clare, too, after bidding the girl farewell, was wrought to aching thoughts and quivering lips. But his sorrow was not for Izz. That evening he was within a featherweights turn of abandoning his road to the nearest station, and driving across that elevated dorsal line of South Wessex which divided him from his Tess's home. It was neither a contempt for her nature, nor the probable state of her heart, which deterred him.

No; it was a sense that, despite her love, as corroborated by Izz's admission, the facts had not changed. If he was right at first, he was right now. And the momentum of the course on which he had embarked tended to keep him going in it, unless diverted by a stronger, more sustained force than had played upon him this afternoon. He could soon come back to her. He took the train that night for London, and five days after shook hands in farewell of his brothers at the port of embarkation.

## *Chapter 41*

From the foregoing events of the wintertime let us press on to an October day, more than eight months subsequent to the parting of Clare and Tess. We discover the latter in changed conditions; instead of a bride with boxes and trunks which others bore, we see her a lonely woman with a basket and a bundle in her own porterage, as at an earlier time when she was no bride; instead of the ample means that were projected by her husband for her comfort through this probationary period, she can produce only a flattened purse.

After again leaving Marlott, her home, she had got through the spring and summer without any great stress upon her physical powers, the time being mainly spent in rendering light irregular service at dairy-work near Port-Bredy to the west of the Blackmoor Valley, equally remote from her native place and from Talbothays. She preferred this to living on his allowance. Mentally she remained in utter stagnation, a condition which the mechanical occupation rather fostered than checked. Her consciousness was at that other dairy, at that other season, in the presence of the tender lover who had confronted her there – he who, the moment she had grasped him to keep for her own, had disappeared like a shape in a vision.

The dairy-work lasted only till the milk began to lessen, for she had not met with a second regular engagement as at Talbothays, but had done duty as a supernumerary only. However, as harvest was now beginning, she had simply to remove from the pasture to the stubble to find plenty of further occupation, and this continued till harvest was done.

Of the five-and-twenty pounds which had remained to her of Clare's allowance, after deducting the other half of the fifty as a contribution to her parents for the trouble and expense to which she had put them, she had as yet spent but little. But there now followed an unfortunate interval of wet weather during which she was obliged to fall back upon her sovereigns.

She could not bear to let them go. Angel had put them into her hand, had obtained them bright and new from his bank for her; his touch had consecrated them to souvenirs of himself – they appeared to have had as yet no other history than such as was created by his and her own experiences – and to disperse them was like giving away relics. But she had to do it, and one by one they left her hands.

She had been compelled to send her mother her address from time to time, but she concealed her circumstances. When her money had almost gone a letter from her mother reached her. Joan stated that they were in dreadful difficulty; the autumn rains had gone through the thatch of the house, which required entire renewal; but this could not be done because the previous thatching had never been paid for. New rafters and a new ceiling upstairs also were required, which, with the previous bill, would amount to a sum of twenty pounds. As her husband was a man of means, and had doubtless returned by this time, could she not send them the money?

Tess had thirty pounds coming to her almost immediately from Angel's bankers, and, the case being so deplorable, as soon as the sum was received she sent the twenty as requested. Part of the remainder she was obliged to expend in winter clothing, leaving only a nominal sum for the whole inclement season at hand. When the last pound had gone, a remark of Angel's that whenever she required further resources she was to apply to his father, remained to be considered.

But the more Tess thought of the step the more reluctant was she to take it. The same delicacy, pride, false shame, whatever it may be called, on Clare's account, which had led her to hide from her own parents the prolongation of the estrangement, hindered her in owning to his that she was in want after the fair allowance he had left her. They probably despised her already; how much more they would despise her in the character of a mendicant! The consequence was that by no effort could the parson's daughter-in-law bring herself to let him know her state.

Her reluctance to communicate with her husband's parents might, she thought, lessen with the lapse of time; but with her own the reverse obtained. On her leaving their house after the short visit subsequent to her marriage they were under the impression that she was ultimately going to join her husband; and from that time to the present she had done nothing to disturb their belief that she was awaiting his return in comfort, hoping against hope that his journey to Brazil would result in a short stay only, after which he would come to fetch her, or that he would write for her to join him; in any case that they would soon present a united front to their families and the world. This hope she still fostered. To let her parents know that she was a deserted wife, dependent, now that she had relieved their necessities, on her own hands for a living, after the *éclat* of a marriage which was to nullify the collapse of the first attempt, would be too much indeed.

The set of brilliants returned to her mind. Where Clare had deposited them she did not know, and it mattered little, if it were true that she could only use and not sell them. Even were they absolutely hers it would be passing mean to enrich herself by a legal title to them which was not essentially hers at all.

Meanwhile her husband's days had been by no means free from trial. At this moment he was lying ill of fever in the clay lands near Curitiba in Brazil, having been drenched with thunderstorms and persecuted by other hardships, in common with all the English farmers and farm-labourers who, just at this time, were deluded into going thither by the promises of the Brazilian Government, and by the baseless assumption that those frames which, ploughing and sowing on English uplands, had resisted all the weathers to whose moods they had been born, could resist equally well all the weathers by which they were surprised on Brazilian plains.

To return. Thus it happened that when the last of Tess's sovereigns had been spent she was unprovided with others to take their place, while on account of the season she found it increasingly difficult to get employment. Not being aware of the rarity of intelligence, energy, health, and willingness in any sphere of life, she refrained from seeking an indoor occupation; fearing towns, large houses, people of means and social sophistication, and of manners other than rural. From that direction of gentility Black Care had come. Society might be better than she supposed from her slight experience of it. But she had no proof of this, and her instinct in the circumstances was to avoid its purlieus.

The small dairies to the west, beyond Port-Bredy, in which she had served as supernumerary milkmaid during the spring and summer required no further aid. Room would probably have been made for her at Talbothays, if only out of sheer compassion; but comfortable as her life had been there she could not go back. The anti-climax would be too intolerable; and her return might bring reproach upon her idolised husband. She could not have borne their pity, and their whispered remarks to one another upon her strange situation; though she would almost have faced a knowledge of her circumstances by every individual there, so long as her story had remained isolated in the mind of each. It was the interchange of ideas about her that made her sensitiveness wince. Tess could not account for this distinction; she simply knew that she felt it.

She was now on her way to an upland farm in the centre of the county, to which she had been recommended by a wandering letter which had reached her from Marian. Marian had somehow heard that Tess was separated from her husband – probably through Izz Huett – and the good-natured and now tippling girl, deeming Tess in trouble, had hastened to notify to her former friend that she herself had gone to this upland spot after leaving the dairy, and would like to see her there, where there was room for other hands, if it was really true that she worked again as of old.

With the shortening of the days all hope of obtaining her husband's forgiveness began to leave her; and there was something of the habitude of the wild animal in the unreflecting instinct with which she rambled on – disconnecting herself by littles from her eventful past at every step, obliterating her identity, giving no thought to accidents or contingencies which might make a quick discovery of her whereabouts by others of importance to her own happiness, if not to theirs.

Among the difficulties of her lonely position not the least was the attention she excited by her appearance, a certain bearing of distinction, which she had caught from Clare, being super-added to her natural attractiveness. Whilst the clothes lasted which had been prepared for her marriage, these casual glances of interest caused her no inconvenience, but as soon as she was compelled to don the wrapper of a field-woman, rude words were addressed to her more than once; but nothing occurred to cause her bodily fear till a particular November afternoon.

She had preferred the country west of the River Brit to the upland farm for which she was now bound, because, for one thing, it was nearer to the home of her husband's father; and to hover about that region unrecognised, with the notion that she might decide to call at the vicarage some day, gave her pleasure. But having once decided to try the higher and drier levels, she pressed back eastward, marching afoot towards the village of Chalk-Newton, where she meant to pass the night.

The lane was long and unvaried, and, owing to the rapid shortening of the days, dusk came upon her before she was aware. She had reached the top of a hill down which the lane stretched its serpentine length in glimpses, when she heard footsteps behind her back, and in a few moments she was overtaken by a man. He stepped up alongside Tess and said – 'Good-night, my pretty maid': to which she civilly replied.

The light still remaining in the sky lit up her face, though the landscape was nearly dark. The man turned and stared hard at her.

'Why, surely, it is the young wench who was at Trantridge awhile – young Squire d'Urberville's friend? I was there at that time, though I don't live there now.'

She recognised in him the well-to-do boor whom Angel had knocked down at the inn for addressing her coarsely. A spasm of anguish shot through her, and she returned him no answer.

'Be honest enough to own it, and that what I said in the town was true, though your fancy-man was so up about it – hey, my sly one? You ought to beg my pardon for that blow of his, considering.'

Still no answer came from Tess. There seemed only one escape for her hunted soul. She suddenly took to her heels with the speed of the wind, and, without looking behind her, ran along the road till she came to a gate which opened directly into a plantation. Into this she plunged, and did not pause till she was deep enough in its shade to be safe against any possibility of discovery.

Under foot the leaves were dry, and the foliage of some holly bushes which grew among the deciduous trees was dense enough to keep off draughts. She scraped together the dead leaves till she had formed them into a large heap, making a sort of nest in the middle. Into this Tess crept.

Such sleep as she got was naturally fitful; she fancied she heard strange noises, but persuaded herself that they were caused by the breeze. She thought of her husband in some vague warm clime on the other side of the globe, while she was here in the cold. Was there another such a wretched being as she in the world? Tess asked herself; and, thinking of her wasted life, said, 'All is vanity.' She repeated the words mechanically, till she reflected that this was a most inadequate thought for modern days. Solomon had thought as far as that more than two thousand years ago; she herself, though not in the van of thinkers, had got much further. If all were only vanity, who would mind it? All was, alas, worse than vanity – injustice, punishment, exaction, death. The wife of Angel Clare put her hand to her brow, and felt its curve, and the edges of her eye-sockets perceptible under the soft skin, and thought as she did so that a time would come when that bone would be bare. 'I wish it were now,' she said.

In the midst of these whimsical fancies she heard a new strange sound among the leaves. It might be the wind; yet there was scarcely any wind. Sometimes it was a palpitation, sometimes a flutter; sometimes it was a sort of gasp or gurgle. Soon she was certain that the noises came from wild creatures of some kind, the more so when, originating in the boughs overhead, they were followed by the fall of a heavy body upon the ground. Had she been ensconced here under other and more pleasant conditions she would have become alarmed; but, outside humanity, she had at present no fear.

Day at length broke in the sky. When it had been day aloft for some little while it became day in the wood.

Directly the assuring and prosaic light of the world's active hours had grown strong she crept from under her hillock of leaves, and looked around boldly. Then she perceived what had been going on to disturb her. The plantation wherein she had taken shelter ran down at this spot into a peak, which ended it hitherward, outside the hedge being arable ground. Under the trees several pheasants lay about, their rich plumage dabbled with blood; some were dead, some feebly twitching a wing, some staring up at the sky, some pulsating quickly, some contorted, some stretched out – all of them writhing in agony, except the fortunate ones whose tortures had ended during the night by the inability of nature to bear more.

Tess guessed at once the meaning of this. The birds had been driven down into this corner the day before by some shooting-party; and while those that had dropped dead under the shot, or had died before nightfall, had been searched for and carried off, many badly wounded birds had escaped and hidden themselves away, or risen among the thick boughs, where they had maintained their position till they grew weaker with loss of blood in the night-time, when they had fallen one by one as she had heard them.

She had occasionally caught glimpses of these men in girlhood, looking over hedges, or peeping through bushes, and pointing their guns, strangely accoutred, a bloodthirsty light in their eyes. She had been told that, rough and brutal as they seemed just then, they were not like this all the year round, but were, in fact, quite civil persons save during certain weeks of autumn and winter, when, like the inhabitants of the Malay Peninsula, they ran amuck, and made it their purpose to destroy life – in this case harmless feathered creatures, brought into being by artificial means solely to gratify these propensities – at once so unmannerly and so unchivalrous towards their weaker fellows in Nature's teeming family.

With the impulse of a soul who could feel for kindred sufferers as much as for herself, Tess's first thought was to put the still living birds out of their torture, and to this end with her own hands she broke the necks of as many as she could find, leaving them to lie where she had found them till the gamekeepers should come – as they probably would come – to look for them a second time.

'Poor darlings – to suppose myself the most miserable being on earth in the sight o' such misery as yours!' she exclaimed, her tears running down as she killed the birds tenderly. 'And not a twinge of bodily pain about me! I be not mangled, and I be not bleeding, and I have two hands to feed and clothe me.' She was ashamed of herself for her gloom of the night, based on nothing more tangible than a sense of condemnation under an arbitrary law of society which had no foundation in Nature.

## *Chapter 42*

It was now broad day, and she started again, emerging cautiously upon the highway. But there was no need for caution; not a soul was at hand, and Tess went onward with fortitude, her recollection of the birds' silent endurance of their night of agony impressing upon her the relativity of sorrows and the tolerable nature of her own, if she could once rise high enough to despise opinion. But that she could not do so long as it was held by Clare.

She reached Chalk-Newton, and breakfasted at an inn, where several young men were troublesomely complimentary to her good looks. Somehow she felt hopeful, for was it not possible that her husband also might say these same things to her even yet? She was bound to take care of herself on the chance of it, and keep off these casual lovers. To this end Tess resolved to run no further risks from her appearance. As soon as she got out of the village she entered a thicket and took from her basket one of the oldest field-gowns, which she had never put on even at the dairy – never since she had worked among the stubble at Marlott. She also, by a felicitous thought, took a handkerchief from her bundle and tied it round her face under her bonnet, covering her chin and half her checks and temples, as if she were suffering from toothache. Then with her little scissors, by the aid of a pocket looking-glass, she mercilessly nipped her eyebrows off, and thus insured against aggressive admiration she went on her uneven way.

'What a mommet of a maid!' said the next man who met her to a companion.

Tears came into her eyes for very pity of herself as she heard him.

'But I don't care!' she said. 'O no – I don't care! I'll always be ugly now, because Angel is not here, and I have nobody to take care of me. My husband that was is gone away, and never will love me any more; but I love him just the same, and hate all other men, and like to make 'em think scornfully of me!'

Thus Tess walks on; a figure which is part of the landscape; a field-woman pure and simple, in winter guise; a grey serge cape, a red woollen cravat, a stuff skirt covered by a whitey-brown rough wrapper, and buff-leather gloves. Every thread of that old attire has become faded and thin under the stroke of rain-drops, the burn of sunbeams, and the stress of winds. There is no sign of young passion in her now –

The maiden's mouth is cold
. . .
Fold over simple fold
Binding her head.

Inside this exterior, over which the eye might have roved as over a thing scarcely percipient, almost inorganic, there was the record of a pulsing life which had learnt too well, for its years, of the dust and ashes of things, of the cruelty of lust and the fragility of love.

Next day the weather was bad, but she trudged on, the honesty, directness, and impartiality of elemental enmity disconcerting her but little. Her object being a winter's occupation and a winter's home, there was no time to lose. Her experience of short hirings had been such that she was determined to accept no more.

Thus she went forward from farm to farm in the direction of the place whence Marian had written to her, which she determined to make use of as a last shift only, its rumoured stringencies being the reverse of tempting. First she enquired for the lighter kinds of employment, and, as acceptance in any variety of these grew hopeless, applied next for the less light, till, beginning with the dairy and poultry tendance that she liked best, she ended with the heavy and coarse pursuits which she liked least – work on arable land: work of such roughness, indeed, as she would never have deliberately volunteered for.

Towards the second evening she reached the irregular chalk table-land or plateau, bosomed with semi-globular tumuli – as if Cybele the Many-breasted were supinely extended there – which stretched between the valley of her birth and the valley of her love.

Here the air was dry and cold, and the long cart-roads were blown white and dusty within a few hours after rain. There were few trees, or none, those that would have grown in the hedges being mercilessly plashed down with the quickset by the tenant-farmers, the natural enemies of tree, bush, and brake. In the middle distance ahead of her she could see the summits of Bulbarrow and of Nettlecombe Tout, and they seemed friendly. They had a low and unassuming aspect from this upland, though as approached on the other side from Blackmoor in her childhood they were as lofty bastions against the sky. Southerly, at many miles' distance, and over the hills and ridges coastward, she could discern a surface like polished steel: it was the English Channel at a point far out towards France.

Before her, in a slight depression, were the remains of a village. She had, in fact, reached Flintcomb-Ash, the place of Marian's sojourn. There seemed to be no help for it; hither she was doomed to come. The stubborn soil around her showed plainly enough that the kind of labour in demand here was of the roughest kind; but it was time to rest from searching, and she resolved to stay, particularly as it began to rain. At the entrance to the village was a cottage whose gable jutted into the road, and before applying for a lodging she stood under its shelter, and watched the evening close in.

'Who would think I was Mrs Angel Clare!' she said.

The wall felt warm to her back and shoulders, and she found that immediately within the gable was the cottage fireplace, the heat of which came through the bricks. She warmed her hands upon them, and also put her cheek – red and moist with the drizzle – against their comforting surface. The wall seemed to be the only friend she had. She had so little wish to leave it that she could have stayed there all night.

Tess could hear the occupants of the cottage – gathered together after their day's labour – talking to each other within, and the rattle of their supper-plates was also audible. But in the village-street she had seen no soul as yet. The solitude was at last broken by the approach of one feminine figure, who, though the evening was cold, wore the print gown and the tilt-bonnet of summer time. Tess instinctively thought it might be Marian, and when she came near enough to be distinguishable in the gloom surely enough it was she. Marian was even stouter and redder in the face than formerly, and decidedly shabbier in attire. At any previous period of her existence Tess would hardly have cared to renew the acquaintance in such conditions; but her loneliness was excessive, and she responded readily to Marian's greeting.

Marian was quite respectful in her enquiries, but seemed much moved by the fact that Tess should still continue in no better condition than at first; though she had dimly heard of the separation.

'Tess – Mrs Clare – the dear wife of dear he! And is it really so bad as this, my child? Why is your comely face tied up in such a way? Anybody been beating 'ee? Not *he*?'

'No, no, no! I merely did it not to be clipsed or colled, Marian.'

She pulled off in disgust a bandage which could suggest such wild thoughts.

'And you've got no collar on' (Tess had been accustomed to wear a little white collar at the dairy).

'I know it, Marian.'

'You've lost it travelling.'

'I've not lost it. The truth is, I don't care anything about my looks; and so I didn't put it on.'

'And you don't wear your wedding-ring?'

'Yes, I do; but not in public. I wear it round my neck on a ribbon. I don't wish people to think who I am by marriage, or that I am married at all; it would be so awkward while I lead my present life.'

Marian paused.

'But you *be* a gentleman's wife; and it seems hardly fair that you should live like this!'

'O yes it is, quite fair; though I am very unhappy.'

'Well, well. *He* married you – and you can be unhappy!'

'Wives are unhappy sometimes; from no fault of their husbands – from their own.'

'You've no faults, deary; that I'm sure of. And he's none. So it must be something outside ye both.'

'Marian, dear Marian, will you do me a good turn without asking questions? My husband has gone abroad, and somehow I have overrun my allowance, so that I have to fall back upon my old work for a time. Do not call me Mrs Clare, but Tess, as before. Do they want a hand here?'

'O yes; they'll take one always, because few care to come. 'Tis a starve-acre place. Corn and swedes are all they grow. Though I be here myself, I feel 'tis a pity for such as you to come.'

'But you used to be as good a dairywoman as I.'

'Yes; but I've got out o' that since I took to drink. Lord, that's the only comfort I've got now! If you engage, you'll be set swede-hacking. That's what I be doing; but you won't like it.'

'O – anything! Will you speak for me?'

'You will do better by speaking for yourself.'

'Very well. Now, Marian, remember – nothing about *him*, if I get the place. I don't wish to bring his name down to the dirt.'

Marian, who was really a trustworthy girl though of coarser grain than Tess, promised anything she asked.

'This is pay-night,' she said, 'and if you were to come with me you would know at once. I be real sorry that you are not happy; but 'tis because he's away, I know. You couldn't be unhappy if he were here, even if he gie'd ye no money – even if he used you like a drudge.'

'That's true; I could not!'

They walked on together, and soon reached the farmhouse, which was almost sublime in its dreariness. There was not a tree within sight; there was not, at this season, a green pasture – nothing but fallow and turnips everywhere; in large fields divided by hedges plashed to unrelieved levels.

Tess waited outside the door of the farmhouse till the group of workfolk had received their wages, and then Marian introduced her. The farmer himself, it appeared, was not at home, but his wife, who represented him this evening, made no objection to hiring Tess, on her agreeing to remain till Old Lady-Day. Female field-labour was seldom offered now, and its cheapness made it profitable for tasks which women could perform as readily as men.

Having signed the agreement, there was nothing more for Tess to do at present than to get a lodging, and she found one in the house at whose gable-wall she had warmed herself. It was a poor subsistence that she had ensured, but it would afford a shelter for the winter at any rate.

That night she wrote to inform her parents of her new address, in case a letter should arrive at Marlott from her husband. But she did not tell them of the sorriness of her situation: it might have brought reproach upon him.

## *Chapter 43*

There was no exaggeration in Marian's definition of Flintcomb-Ash farm as a starve-acre place. The single fat thing on the soil was Marian herself; and she was an importation. Of the three classes of village, the village cared for by its lord, the village cared for by itself, and the village uncared for either by itself or by its lord (in other words, the village of a resident squire's tenantry, the village of free or copy-holders, and the absentee-owner's village, farmed with the land) this place, Flintcomb-Ash, was the third.

But Tess set to work. Patience, that blending of moral courage with physical timidity, was now no longer a minor feature in Mrs Angel Clare; and it sustained her.

The swede-field in which she and her companion were set hacking was a stretch of a hundred odd acres, in one patch, on the highest ground of the farm, rising above stony lanchets or lynchets – the outcrop of siliceous veins in the chalk formation, composed of myriads of loose white flints in bulbous, cusped, and phallic shapes. The upper half of each turnip had been eaten off by the livestock, and it was the business of the two women to grub up the lower or earthy half of the root with a hooked fork called a hacker, that it might be eaten also. Every leaf of the vegetable having already been consumed, the whole field was in colour a desolate drab; it was a complexion without features, as if a face, from chin to brow, should be only an expanse of skin. The sky wore, in another colour, the same likeness; a white vacuity of countenance with the lineaments gone. So these two upper and nether visages confronted each other all day long, the white face looking down on the brown face, and the brown face looking up at the white face, without anything standing between them but the two girls crawling over the surface of the former like flies.

Nobody came near them, and their movements showed a mechanical regularity; their forms standing enshrouded in Hessian 'wroppers' – sleeved brown pinafores, tied behind to the bottom, to keep their gowns from blowing about – scant skirts revealing boots that reached high up the ankles, and yellow sheepskin gloves with gauntlets. The pensive character which the curtained hood lent to their bent heads would have reminded the observer of some early Italian conception of the two Marys.

They worked on hour after hour, unconscious of the forlorn aspect they bore in the landscape, not thinking of the justice or injustice of their lot. Even in such a position as theirs it was possible to exist in a dream. In the afternoon the rain came on again, and Marian said that they need not work any more. But if they did not work they would not be paid; so they worked on. It was so high a situation, this field, that the rain had no occasion to fall, but raced along horizontally upon the yelling wind, sticking into them like glass splinters till they were wet through. Tess had not known till now what was really meant by that. There are degrees of dampness, and a very little is called being wet through in common talk. But to stand working slowly in a field, and feel the creep of rainwater, first in legs and shoulders, then on hips and head, then at back, front, and sides, and yet to work on till the leaden light diminishes and marks that the sun is down, demands a distinct modicum of stoicism, even of valour.

Yet they did not feel the wetness so much as might be supposed. They were both young, and they were talking of the time when they lived and loved together at Talbothays Dairy, that happy green tract of land where summer had been liberal in her gifts; in substance to all, emotionally to these. Tess would fain not have conversed with Marian of the man who was legally, if not actually, her husband; but the irresistible fascination of the subject betrayed her into reciprocating Marian's remarks. And thus, as has been said, though the damp curtains of their bonnets flapped smartly into their faces, and their wrappers clung about them to wearisomeness, they lived all this afternoon in memories of green, sunny, romantic Talbothays.

'You can see a gleam of a hill within a few miles o' Froom Valley from here when 'tis fine,' said Marian.

'Ah! Can you?' said Tess, awake to the new value of this locality.

So the two forces were at work here as everywhere, the inherent will to enjoy, and the circumstantial will against enjoyment. Marian's will had a method of assisting itself by taking from her pocket as the afternoon wore on a pint bottle corked with white rag, from which she invited Tess to drink. Tess's unassisted power of dreaming, however, being enough for her sublimation at present, she declined except the merest sip, and then Marian took a pull herself from the spirits.

'I've got used to it,' she said, 'and can't leave it off now. 'Tis my only comfort – You see I lost him: you didn't; and you can do without it perhaps.'

Tess thought her loss as great as Marian's, but upheld by the dignity of being Angel's wife, in the letter at least, she accepted Marian's differentiation.

Amid this scene Tess slaved in the morning frosts and in the afternoon rains. When it was not swede-grubbing it was swede-trimming, in which process they sliced off the earth and the fibres with a bill-hook before storing the roots for future use. At this occupation they could shelter themselves by a thatched hurdle if it rained; but if it was frosty even their thick leather gloves could not prevent the frozen masses they handled from biting their fingers. Still Tess hoped. She had a conviction that sooner or later the magnanimity which she persisted in reckoning as a chief ingredient of Clare's character would lead him to rejoin her.

Marian, primed to a humorous mood, would discover the queer-shaped flints aforesaid, and shriek with laughter, Tess remaining severely obtuse. They often looked across the country to where the Var or Froom was known to stretch, even though they might not be able to see it; and, fixing their eyes on the cloaking grey mist, imagined the old times they had spent out there.

'Ah,' said Marian, 'how I should like another or two of our old set to come here! Then we could bring up Talbothays every day here afield, and talk of he, and of what nice times we had there, and o' the old things we used to know, and make it all come back again a'most, in seeming!' Marian's eyes softened, and her voice grew vague as the visions returned. 'I'll write to Izz Huett,' she said. 'She's biding at home doing nothing now, I know, and I'll tell her we be here, and ask her to come; and perhaps Retty is well enough now.'

Tess had nothing to say against the proposal, and the next she heard of this plan for importing old Talbothays' joys was two or three days later, when Marian informed her that Izz had replied to her enquiry, and had promised to come if she could.

There had not been such a winter for years. It came on in stealthy and measured glides, like the moves of a chess-player. One morning the few lonely trees and the thorns of the hedgerows appeared as if they had put off a vegetable for an animal integument. Every twig was covered with a white nap as of fur grown from the rind during the night, giving it four times its usual stoutness; the whole bush or tree forming a staring sketch in white lines on the mournful grey of the sky and horizon. Cobwebs revealed their presence on sheds and walls where none had ever been observed till brought out into visibility by the crystallising atmosphere, hanging like loops of white worsted from salient points of the out-houses, posts, and gates.

After this season of congealed dampness came a spell of dry frost, when strange birds from behind the North Pole began to arrive silently on the upland of Flintcomb-Ash; gaunt spectral creatures with tragical eyes – eyes which had witnessed scenes of cataclysmal horror in inaccessible polar regions of a magnitude such as no human being had ever conceived, in curdling temperatures that no man could endure; which had beheld the crash of ice-bergs and the slide of snow-hills by the shooting light of the Aurora; been half blinded by the whirl of colossal storms and terraqueous distortions; and retained the expression of feature that such scenes had engendered. These nameless birds came quite near to Tess and Marian, but of all they had seen which humanity would never see, they brought no account. The traveller's ambition to tell was not theirs, and, with dumb impassivity, they dismissed experiences which they did not value for the immediate incidents of this homely upland – the trivial movements of the two girls in disturbing the clods with their hackers so as to uncover something or other that these visitants relished as food.

Then one day a peculiar quality invaded the air of this open country. There came a moisture which was not of rain, and a cold which was not of frost. It chilled the eyeballs of the twain, made their brows ache, penetrated to their skeletons, affecting the surface of the body less than its core. They knew that it meant snow, and in the night the snow came. Tess, who continued to live at the cottage with the warm gable that cheered any lonely pedestrian who paused beside it, awoke in the night, and heard above the thatch noises which seemed to signify that the roof had turned itself into a gymnasium of all the winds. When she lit her lamp to get up in the morning she found that the snow had blown through a chink in the casement, forming a white cone of the finest powder against the inside, and had also come down the chimney, so that it lay sole-deep upon the floor, on which her shoes left tracks when she moved about. Without, the storm drove so fast as to create a snow-mist in the kitchen; but as yet it was too dark out-of-doors to see anything.

Tess knew that it was impossible to go on with the swedes; and by the time she had finished breakfast beside the solitary little lamp, Marian arrived to tell her that they were to join the rest of the women at reed-drawing in the barn till the weather changed. As soon, therefore, as the uniform cloak of darkness without began to turn to a disordered medley of greys, they blew out the lamp, wrapped themselves up in their thickest pinners, tied their woollen cravats round their necks and across their chests, and started for the barn. The snow had followed the birds from the polar basin as a white pillar of a cloud, and individual flakes could not be seen. The blast smelt of icebergs, arctic seas, whales, and white bears, carrying the snow so that it licked the land but did not deepen on it. They trudged onwards with slanted bodies through the flossy fields, keeping as well as they could in the shelter of hedges, which, however, acted as strainers rather than screens. The air, afflicted to pallor with the hoary multitudes that infested it, twisted and spun them eccentrically, suggesting an achromatic chaos of things. But both the young women were fairly cheerful; such weather on a dry upland is not in itself dispiriting.

'Ha-ha! the cunning northern birds knew this was coming,' said Marian. 'Depend upon't, they keep just in front o't all the way from the North Star. Your husband, my dear, is, I make no doubt, having scorching weather all this time. Lord, if he could only see his pretty wife now! Not that this weather hurts your beauty at all – in fact, it rather does it good.'

'You mustn't talk about him to me, Marian,' said Tess severely.

'Well, but – surely you care for 'n! Do you?'

Instead of answering, Tess, with tears in her eyes, impulsively faced in the direction in which she imagined South America to lie, and, putting up her lips, blew out a passionate kiss upon the snowy wind.

'Well, well, I know you do. But 'pon my body, it is a rum life for a married couple! There – I won't say another word! Well, as for the weather, it won't hurt us in the wheat-barn; but reed-drawing is fearful hard work – worse than swede-hacking. I can stand it because I'm stout; but you be slimmer than I. I can't think why maister should have set 'ee at it.'

They reached the wheat-barn and entered it. One end of the long structure was full of corn; the middle was where the reed-drawing was carried on, and there had already been placed in the reed-press the evening before as many sheaves of wheat as would be sufficient for the women to draw from during the day.

'Why, here's Izz!' said Marian.

Izz it was, and she came forward. She had walked all the way from her mother's home on the previous afternoon, and, not deeming the distance so great, had been belated, arriving, however, just before the snow began, and sleeping at the alehouse. The farmer had agreed with her mother at market to take her on if she came today, and she had been afraid to disappoint him by delay.

In addition to Tess, Marian, and Izz, there were two women from a neighbouring village; two Amazonian sisters, whom Tess with a start remembered as Dark Car the Queen of Spades and her junior the Queen of Diamonds – those who had tried to fight with her in the midnight quarrel at Trantridge. They showed no recognition of her, and possibly had none, for they had been under the influence of liquor on that occasion, and were only temporary sojourners there as here. They did all kinds of men's work by preference, including well-sinking, hedging, ditching, and excavating, without any sense of fatigue. Noted reed-drawers were they too, and looked round upon the other three with some superciliousness.

Putting on their gloves all set to work in a row in front of the press, an erection formed of two posts connected by a cross-beam, under which the sheaves to be drawn from were laid ears outward, the beam being pegged down by pins in the uprights, and lowered as the sheaves diminished.

The day hardened in colour, the light coming in at the barn-doors upwards from the snow instead of downwards from the sky. The girls pulled handful after handful from the press; but by reason of the presence of the strange women, who were recounting scandals, Marian and Izz could not at first talk of old times as they wished to do. Presently they heard the muffled tread of a horse, and the farmer rode up to the barn-door. When he had dismounted he came close to Tess, and remained looking musingly at the side of her face. She had not turned at first, but his fixed attitude led her to look round, when she perceived that her employer was the native of Trantridge from whom she had taken flight on the highroad because of his allusion to her history.

He waited till she had carried the drawn bundles to the pile outside, when he said, 'So you be the young woman who took my civility in such ill part? Be drowned if I didn't think you might be as soon as I heard of your being hired! Well, you thought you had got the better of me the first time at the inn with your fancy-man, and the second time on the road, when you bolted; but now I think I've got the better of you.' He concluded with a hard laugh.

Tess, between the Amazons and the farmer like a bird caught in a clap-net, returned no answer, continuing to pull the straw. She could read character sufficiently well to know by this time that she had nothing to fear from her employer's gallantry; it was rather the tyranny induced by his mortification at Clare's treatment of him. Upon the whole she preferred that sentiment in man and felt brave enough to endure it.

'You thought I was in love with 'ee I suppose? Some women are such fools, to take every look as serious earnest. But there's nothing like a winter afield for taking that nonsense out o' young wenches' heads; and you've signed and agreed till Lady-Day. Now, are you going to beg my pardon?'

'I think you ought to beg mine.'

'Very well – as you like. But we'll see which is master here. Be they all the sheaves you've done today?'

'Yes, sir.'

' 'Tis a very poor show. Just see what they've done over there' (pointing to the two stalwart women). 'The rest, too, have done better than you.'

'They've all practised it before, and I have not. And I thought it made no difference to you as it is task work, and we are only paid for what we do.'

'Oh, but it does. I want the barn cleared.'

'I am going to work all the afternoon instead of leaving at two as the others will do.'

He looked sullenly at her and went away. Tess felt that she could not have come to a much worse place; but anything was better than gallantry. When two o'clock arrived the professional reed-drawers tossed off the last half-pint in their flagon, put down their hooks, tied their last sheaves, and went away. Marian and

Izz would have done likewise, but on hearing that Tess meant to stay, to make up by longer hours for her lack of skill, they would not leave her. Looking out at the snow, which still fell, Marian exclaimed, 'Now, we've got it all to ourselves.' And so at last the conversation turned to their old experiences at the dairy; and, of course, the incidents of their affection for Angel Clare.

'Izz and Marian,' said Mrs Angel Clare, with a dignity which was extremely touching, seeing how very little of a wife she was: 'I can't join in talk with you now, as I used to do, about Mr Clare; you will see that I cannot; because, although he is gone away from me for the present, he is my husband.'

Izz was by nature the sauciest and most caustic of all the four girls who had loved Clare. 'He was a very splendid lover, no doubt,' she said; 'but I don't think he is a too fond husband to go away from you so soon.'

'He had to go – he was obliged to go, to see about the land over there!' pleaded Tess.

'He might have tided 'ee over the winter.'

'Ah – that's owing to an accident – a misunderstanding; and we won't argue it,' Tess answered, with tearfulness in her words. 'Perhaps there's a good deal to be said for him! He did not go away, like some husbands, without telling me; and I can always find out where he is.'

After this they continued for some long time in a reverie, as they went on seizing the ears of corn, drawing out the straw, gathering it under their arms, and cutting off the ears with their bill-hooks, nothing sounding in the barn but the swish of the straw and the crunch of the hook. Then Tess suddenly flagged, and sank down upon the heap of wheat-ears at her feet.

'I knew you wouldn't be able to stand it!' cried Marian. 'It wants harder flesh than yours for this work.'

Just then the farmer entered. 'Oh, that's how you get on when I am away,' he said to her.

'But it is my own loss,' she pleaded. 'Not yours.'

'I want it finished,' he said doggedly, as he crossed the barn and went out at the other door.

'Don't 'ee mind him, there's a dear,' said Marian. 'I've worked here before. Now you go and lie down there, and Izz and I will make up your number.'

'I don't like to let you do that. I'm taller than you, too.'

However, she was so overcome that she consented to lie down awhile, and reclined on a heap of pull-tails – the refuse after the straight straw had been drawn – thrown up at the further side of the barn. Her succumbing had been as largely owing to agitation at re-opening the subject of her separation from her husband as to the hard work. She lay in a state of percipience without volition, and the rustle of the straw and the cutting of the ears by the others had the weight of bodily touches.

She could hear from her corner, in addition to these noises, the murmur of their voices. She felt certain that they were continuing the subject already broached, but their voices were so low that she could not catch the words. At last Tess grew more and more anxious to know what they were saying, and, persuading herself that she felt better, she got up and resumed work.

Then Izz Huett broke down. She had walked more than a dozen miles the previous evening, had gone to bed at midnight, and had risen again at five o'clock. Marian alone, thanks to her bottle of liquor and her stoutness of build, stood the strain upon back and arms without suffering. Tess urged Izz to leave off, agreeing, as she felt better, to finish the day without her, and make equal division of the number of sheaves.

Izz accepted the offer gratefully, and disappeared through the great door into the snowy track to her lodging. Marian, as was the case every afternoon at this time on account of the bottle, began to feel in a romantic vein.

'I should not have thought it of him – never!' she said in a dreamy tone. 'And I loved him so! I didn't mind his having you. But this about Izz is too bad!'

Tess, in her start at the words, narrowly missed cutting off a finger with the bill-hook.

'Is it about my husband?' she stammered.

'Well, yes. Izz said, "Don't 'ee tell her"; but I am sure I can't help it! It was what he wanted Izz to do. He wanted her to go off to Brazil with him.'

Tess's face faded as white as the scene without, and its curves straightened. 'And did Izz refuse to go?' she asked.

'I don't know. Anyhow he changed his mind.'

'Pooh – then he didn't mean it! 'Twas just a man's jest!'

'Yes he did; for he drove her a good-ways towards the station.'

'He didn't take her!'

They pulled on in silence till Tess, without any premonitory symptoms, burst out crying.

'There!' said Marian. 'Now I wish I hadn't told 'ee!'

'No. It is a very good thing that you have done! I have been living on in a thirtover, lackaday way, and have not seen what it may lead to! I ought to have sent him a letter oftener. He said I could not go to him, but he didn't say I was not to write as often as I liked. I won't dally like this any longer! I have been very wrong and neglectful in leaving everything to be done by him!'

The dim light in the barn grew dimmer, and they could see to work no longer. When Tess had reached home that evening, and had entered into the privacy of her little whitewashed chamber, she began impetuously writing a letter to Clare. But falling into doubt she could not finish it. Afterwards she took the ring from the ribbon on which she wore it next her heart, and retained it on her finger all night, as if to fortify herself in the sensation that she was really the wife of this elusive lover of hers, who could propose that Izz should go with him abroad, so shortly after he had left her. Knowing that, how could she write entreaties to him, or show that she cared for him any more?

## *Chapter 44*

By the disclosure in the barn her thoughts were led anew in the direction which they had taken more than once of late – to the distant Emminster Vicarage. It was through her husband's parents that she had been charged to send a letter to Clare if she desired; and to write to them direct if in difficulty. But that sense of her having morally no claim upon him had always led Tess to suspend her impulse to send these notes; and to the family at the vicarage, therefore, as to her own parents since her marriage, she was virtually non-existent. This self-effacement in both directions had been quite in consonance with her independent character of desiring nothing by way of favour or pity to which she was not entitled on a fair consideration of her deserts. She had set herself to stand or fall by her qualities, and to waive such merely technical claims upon a strange family as had been established for her by the flimsy fact of a member of that family, in a season of impulse, writing his name in a church-book beside hers.

But now that she was stung to a fever by Izz's tale there was a limit to her powers of renunciation. Why had her husband not written to her? He had distinctly implied that he would at least let her know of the locality to which he had journeyed; but he had not sent a line to notify his address. Was he really indifferent? But was he ill? Was it for her to make some advance? Surely she might summon the courage of solicitude, call at the vicarage for intelligence, and express her grief at his silence. If Angel's father were the good man she had heard him represented to be, he would be able to enter into her heart-starved situation. Her social hardships she could conceal.

To leave the farm on a weekday was not in her power. Sunday was the only possible opportunity. Flintcomb-Ash being in the middle of the cretaceous tableland over which no railway had climbed as yet, it would be necessary to walk. And the distance being fifteen miles each way she would have to allow herself a long day for the undertaking by rising early.

A fortnight later, when the snow had gone, and had been followed by a hard black frost, she took advantage of the state of the roads to try the experiment. At four o'clock that Sunday morning she came downstairs and stepped out into the starlight. The weather was still favourable, the ground ringing under her feet like an anvil.

Marian and Izz were much interested in her excursion, knowing that the journey concerned her husband. Their lodgings were in a cottage a little further along the lane, but they came and assisted Tess in her departure, and argued that she should dress up in her very prettiest guise to captivate the hearts of her parents-in-law; though she, knowing of the austere and Calvinistic tenets of old Mr Clare, was indifferent, and even doubtful. A year had now elapsed since her sad marriage, but she had preserved sufficient draperies from the wreck of her then full wardrobe to clothe her very charmingly as a simple country girl with no pretensions to recent fashion; a soft grey woollen gown, with white crepe quilling against the pink skin of her face and neck, and a black velvet jacket and hat.

' 'Tis a thousand pities your husband can't see 'ee now – you do look a real beauty!' said Izz Huett, regarding Tess as she stood on the threshold between the steely starlight without and the yellow candlelight within. Izz spoke with a magnanimous abandonment of herself to the situation; she could not be – no woman with a heart bigger than a hazelnut could be – antagonistic to Tess in her presence, the influence which she exercised over those of her own sex being of a warmth and strength quite unusual, curiously overpowering the less worthy feminine feelings of spite and rivalry.

With a final tug and touch here, and a slight brush there, they let her go; and she was absorbed into the pearly air of the fore-dawn. They heard her footsteps tap along the hard road as she stepped out to her full pace. Even Izz hoped she would win, and, though without any particular respect for her own virtue, felt glad that she had been prevented wronging her friend when momentarily tempted by Clare.

It was a year ago, all but a day, that Clare had married Tess, and only a few days less than a year that he had been absent from her. Still, to start on a brisk walk, and on such an errand as hers, on a dry clear wintry morning, through the rarefied air of these chalky hogs'-backs, was not depressing; and there is no doubt that her dream at starting was to win the heart of her mother-in-law, tell her whole history to that lady, enlist her on her side, and so gain back the truant.

In time she reached the edge of the vast escarpment below which stretched the loamy Vale of Blackmoor, now lying misty and still in the dawn. Instead of the colourless air of the uplands the atmosphere down there was a deep blue. Instead of the great enclosures of a hundred acres in which she was now accustomed to toil there were little fields below her of less than half a dozen acres, so numerous that they looked from this height like the meshes of a net. Here the landscape was whitey-brown; down there, as in Froom Valley, it was always green. Yet it was in that vale that her sorrow had taken shape, and she did not love it as formerly. Beauty to her, as to all who have felt, lay not in the thing, but in what the thing symbolised.

Keeping the Vale on her right she steered steadily westward; passing above the Hintocks, crossing at right-angles the highroad from Sherton-Abbas to Casterbridge, and skirting Dogbury Hill and High-Stoy, with the dell between them called 'The Devil's Kitchen'. Still following the elevated way she reached Cross-in-Hand, where the stone pillar stands desolate and silent, to mark the site of a miracle, or murder, or both. Three miles further she cut across the straight and deserted Roman road called Long-Ash Lane; leaving which as soon as she reached it she dipped down a hill by a transverse lane into the small town or village of Evershead, being now about halfway over the distance. She made a halt here, and breakfasted a second time, heartily enough – not at the Sow-and-Acorn, for she avoided inns, but at a cottage by the church.

The second half of her journey was through a more gentle country, by way of Benvill Lane. But as the mileage lessened between her and the spot of her pilgrimage, so did Tess's confidence decrease, and her enterprise loom out more formidably. She saw her purpose in such staring lines, and the landscape so faintly, that she was sometimes in danger of losing her way. However, about noon she paused by a gate on the edge of the basin in which Emminster and its vicarage lay.

The square tower, beneath which she knew that at that moment the vicar and his congregation were gathered, had a severe look in her eyes. She wished that she had somehow contrived to come on a weekday. Such a good man might be prejudiced against a woman who had chosen Sunday, never realising the necessities of her case. But it was incumbent upon her to go on now. She took off the thick boots in which she had walked thus far, put on her pretty thin ones of patent leather, and, stuffing the former into the hedge by the gatepost where she might readily find them again, descended the hill; the freshness of colour she had derived from the keen air thinning away in spite of her as she drew near the parsonage.

Tess hoped for some accident that might favour her, but nothing favoured her. The shrubs on the vicarage lawn rustled uncomfortably in the frosty breeze; she could not feel by any stretch of imagination, dressed to her highest as she was, that the house was the residence of near relations; and yet nothing essential, in nature or emotion, divided her from them: in pains, pleasures, thoughts, birth, death, and after-death, they were the same.

She nerved herself by an effort, entered the swing-gate, and rang the door-bell. The thing was done; there could be no retreat. No; the thing was not done. Nobody answered to her ringing. The effort had to be risen to and made again. She rang a second time, and the agitation of the act, coupled with her weariness after the fifteen miles' walk, led her to support herself while she waited by resting her hand on her hip, and her elbow against the wall of the porch. The wind was so nipping that the ivy-leaves had become wizened and grey, each tapping incessantly upon its neighbour with a disquieting stir of her nerves. A piece of blood-stained paper, caught up from some meat-buyer's dust-heap, beat up and down the road without the gate; too flimsy to rest, too heavy to fly away; and a few straws kept it company.

The second peal had been louder, and still nobody came. Then she walked out of the porch, opened the gate, and passed through. And though she looked dubiously at the house-front as if inclined to return, it was with a breath of relief that she closed the gate. A feeling haunted her that she might have been recognised (though how she could not tell), and orders been given not to admit her.

Tess went as far as the corner. She had done all she could do; but determined not to escape present trepidation at the expense of future distress, she walked back again quite past the house, looking up at all the windows.

Ah – the explanation was that they were all at church, every one. She remembered her husband saying that his father always insisted upon the household, servants included, going to morning-service, and, as a consequence, eating cold food when they came home. It was, therefore, only necessary to wait till the service was over. She would not make herself conspicuous by waiting on the spot, and she started to get past the church into the lane. But as she reached the churchyard-gate the people began pouring out, and Tess found herself in the midst of them.

The Emminster congregation looked at her as only a congregation of small country-townsfolk walking home at its leisure can look at a woman out of the common whom it perceives to be a stranger. She quickened her pace, and ascended the road by which she had come, to find a retreat between its hedges till the Vicar's family should have lunched, and it might be convenient for them to receive her. She soon distanced the churchgoers, except two youngish men, who linked arm in arm, were beating up behind her at a quick step.

As they drew nearer she could hear their voices engaged in earnest discourse, and, with the natural quickness of a woman in her situation, did not fail to recognise in those voices the quality of her husband's tones. The pedestrians were his two brothers. Forgetting all her plans, Tess's one dread was lest they should overtake her now, in her disorganised condition, before she was prepared to confront them; for though she felt that they could not identify her she instinctively dreaded their scrutiny. The more briskly they walked the more briskly walked she. They were plainly bent upon taking a short quick stroll before going indoors to lunch or dinner, to restore warmth to limbs chilled with sitting through a long service.

Only one person had preceded Tess up the hill – a ladylike young woman, somewhat interesting, though, perhaps, a trifle *guindée* and prudish. Tess had nearly overtaken her when the speed of her brothers-in-law brought them so nearly behind her back that she could hear every word of their conversation. They said nothing, however, which particularly interested her till, observing the young lady still further in front, one of them remarked, 'There is Mercy Chant. Let us overtake her.'

Tess knew the name. It was the woman who had been destined for Angel's life-companion by his and her parents, and whom he probably would have married but for her intrusive self. She would have known as much without previous information if she had waited a moment, for one of the brothers proceeded to say: 'Ah! poor Angel, poor Angel! I never see that nice girl without more and more regretting his precipitancy in throwing himself away upon a dairymaid, or whatever she may be. It is a queer business, apparently. Whether she has joined him yet or not I don't know; but she had not done so some months ago when I heard from him.'

'I can't say. He never tells me anything nowadays. His ill-considered marriage seems to have completed that estrangement from me which was begun by his extraordinary opinions.'

Tess beat up the long hill still faster; but she could not outwalk them without exciting notice. At last they outsped her altogether, and passed her by. The young lady still further ahead heard their footsteps and turned. Then there was a greeting and a shaking of hands, and the three went on together.

They soon reached the summit of the hill, and, evidently intending this point to be the limit of their promenade, slackened pace and turned all three aside to the gate whereat Tess had paused an hour before that time to reconnoitre the town before descending into it. During their discourse one of the clerical brothers probed the hedge carefully with his umbrella, and dragged something to light.

'Here's a pair of old boots,' he said. 'Thrown away, I suppose, by some tramp or other.'

'Some impostor who wished to come into the town barefoot, perhaps, and so excite our sympathies,' said Miss Chant. 'Yes, it must have been, for they are excellent walking-boots – by no means worn out. What a wicked thing to do! I'll carry them home for some poor person.'

Cuthbert Clare, who had been the one to find them, picked them up for her with the crook of his stick; and Tess's boots were appropriated.

She, who had heard this, walked past under the screen of her woollen veil, till, presently looking back, she perceived that the church party had left the gate with her boots and retreated down the hill.

Thereupon our heroine resumed her walk. Tears, blinding tears, were running down her face. She knew that it was all sentiment, all baseless impressibility, which had caused her to read the scene as her own condemnation; nevertheless she could not get over it; she could not contravene in her own defenceless person all these untoward omens. It was impossible to think of returning to the vicarage. Angel's wife felt almost as if she had been hounded up that hill like a scorned thing by those – to her – superfine clerics. Innocently as the slight had been inflicted, it was somewhat unfortunate that she had encountered the sons and not the father, who, despite his narrowness, was far less starched and ironed than they, and had to the full the gift of charity. As she again thought of her dusty boots she almost pitied those habiliments for the quizzing to which they had been subjected, and felt how hopeless life was for their owner.

'Ah!' she said, still sighing in pity of herself, '*they* didn't know that I wore those over the roughest part of the road to save these pretty ones *he* bought for me – no – they did not know it! And they didn't think that *he* chose the colour o' my pretty frock – no – how could they? If they had known perhaps they would not have cared, for they don't care much for him, poor thing!'

Then she grieved for the beloved man whose conventional standard of judgment had caused her all these latter sorrows; and she went her way without knowing that the greatest misfortune of her life was this feminine loss of courage at the last and critical moment through her estimating her father-in-law by his sons. Her present condition was precisely one which would have enlisted the sympathies of old Mr and Mrs Clare. Their hearts went out of them at a bound towards extreme cases, when the subtle mental troubles of the less desperate among mankind failed to win their interest or regard. In jumping at Publicans and Sinners they would forget that a word might be said for the worries of Scribes and Pharisees; and this defect or limitation might have recommended their own daughter-in-law to them at this moment as a fairly choice sort of lost person for their love.

Thereupon she began to plod back along the road by which she had come not altogether full of hope, but full of a conviction that a crisis in her life was approaching. No crisis, apparently, had supervened; and there was nothing left for her to do but to continue upon that starve-acre farm till she could again summon courage to face the Vicarage. She did, indeed, take sufficient interest in herself to throw up her veil on this return journey, as if to let the world see that she could at least exhibit a face such as Mercy Chant could not show. But it was done with a sorry shake of the head. 'It is nothing – it is nothing!' she said. 'Nobody loves it; nobody sees it. Who cares about the looks of a castaway like me!'

Her journey back was rather a meander than a march. It had no sprightliness, no purpose; only a tendency. Along the tedious length of Benvill Lane she began to grow tired, and she leant upon gates and paused by milestones.

She did not enter any house till, at the seventh or eighth mile, she descended the steep long hill below which lay the village or townlet of Evershead, where in the morning she had breakfasted with such contrasting expectations. The cottage by the church, in which she again sat down, was almost the first at that end of the village, and while the woman fetched her some milk from the pantry, Tess, looking down the street, perceived that the place seemed quite deserted.

'The people are gone to afternoon service, I suppose?' she said.

'No, my dear,' said the old woman. ' 'Tis too soon for that; the bells hain't strook out yet. They be all gone to hear the preaching in yonder barn. A ranter preaches there between the services – an excellent, fiery, Christian man, they say. But, Lord, I don't go to hear'n! What comes in the regular way over the pulpit is hot enough for I.'

Tess soon went onward into the village, her footsteps echoing against the houses as though it were a place of the dead. Nearing the central part her echoes were intruded on by other sounds; and seeing the barn not far off the road, she guessed these to be the utterances of the preacher.

His voice became so distinct in the still clear air that she could soon catch his sentences, though she was on the closed side of the barn. The sermon, as might be expected, was of the extremest antinomian type; on justification by faith, as expounded in the theology of St Paul. This fixed idea of the rhapsodist was delivered with animated enthusiasm, in a manner entirely declamatory, for he had plainly no skill as a dialectician. Although Tess had not heard the beginning of the address, she learnt what the text had been from its constant iteration – 'O foolish Galatians, who hath bewitched you, that ye should not obey the truth, before whose eyes Jesus Christ hath been evidently set forth, crucified among you?'

Tess was all the more interested, as she stood listening behind, in finding that the preacher's doctrine was a vehement form of the views of Angel's father, and her interest intensified when the speaker began to detail his own spiritual experiences of how he had come by those views. He had, he said, been the greatest of sinners. He had scoffed; he had wantonly associated with the reckless and the lewd. But a day of awakening had come, and, in a human sense, it had been brought about mainly by the influence of a certain clergyman, whom he had at first grossly insulted; but whose parting words had sunk into his heart, and had remained there, till by the grace of Heaven they had worked this change in him, and made him what they saw him.

But more startling to Tess than the doctrine had been the voice, which, impossible as it seemed, was precisely that of Alec d'Urberville. Her face fixed in painful suspense, she came round to the font of the barn, and passed before it. The low winter sun beamed directly upon the great double-doored entrance on this side; one of the doors being open, so that the rays stretched far in over the threshing-floor to the preacher and his audience, all snugly sheltered from the northern breeze. The listeners were entirely villagers, among them being the man whom she had seen carrying the red paint-pot on a former memorable occasion. But her attention was given to the central figure, who stood upon some sacks of corn, facing the people and the door. The three o'clock sun shone full upon him, and the strange enervating conviction that her seducer confronted her, which had been gaining ground in Tess ever since she had heard his words distinctly, was at last established as a fact indeed.

END OF PHASE THE FIFTH

# PHASE THE SIXTH

## *The Convert*

# *Chapter 45*

Till this moment she had never seen or heard from d'Urberville since her departure from Trantridge.

The encounter came at a heavy moment, one of all moments calculated to permit its impact with the least emotional shock. But such was unreasoning memory that, though he stood there openly and palpably a converted man, who was sorrowing for his past irregularities, a fear overcame her, paralysing her movement so that she neither retreated nor advanced.

To think of what emanated from that countenance when she saw it last, and to behold it now! . . . There was the same handsome unpleasantness of mien, but now he wore neatly trimmed, old-fashioned whiskers, the sable moustache having disappeared; and his dress was half-clerical, a modification which had changed his expression sufficiently to abstract the dandyism from his features, and to hinder for a second her belief in his identity.

To Tess's sense there was, just at first, a ghastly *bizarrerie*, a grim incongruity, in the march of these solemn words of Scripture out of such a mouth. This too familiar intonation, less than four years earlier, had brought to her ears expressions of such divergent purpose that her heart became quite sick at the irony of the contrast.

It was less a reform than a transfiguration. The former curves of sensuousness were now modulated to lines of devotional passion. The lip-shapes that had meant seductiveness were now made to express supplication; the glow on the cheek that yesterday could be translated as riotousness was evangelised today into the splendour of pious rhetoric; animalism had become fanaticism; Paganism Paulinism; the bold rolling eye that had flashed upon her form in the old time with such mastery now beamed with the rude energy of a theolatry that was almost ferocious. Those black angularities which his face had used to put on when his wishes were thwarted now did duty in picturing the incorrigible backslider who would insist upon turning again to his wallowing in the mire.

The lineaments, as such, seemed to complain. They had been diverted from their hereditary connotation to signify impressions for which Nature did not intend them. Strange that their very elevation was a misapplication, that to raise seemed to falsify.

Yet could it be so? She would admit the ungenerous sentiment no longer. D'Urberville was not the first wicked man who had turned away from his wickedness to save his soul alive, and why should she deem it unnatural in him? It was but the usage of thought which had been jarred in her at hearing good new words in bad old notes. The greater the sinner the greater the saint; it was not necessary to dive far into Christian history to discover that.

Such impressions as these moved her vaguely, and without strict definiteness. As soon as the nerveless pause of her surprise would allow her to stir, her impulse was to pass on out of his sight. He had obviously not discerned her yet in her position against the sun.

But the moment that she moved again he recognised her. The effect upon her old lover was electric, far stronger than the effect of his presence upon her. His fire, the tumultuous ring of his eloquence, seemed to go out of him. His lip struggled and trembled under the words that lay upon it; but deliver them it could not as long as she faced him. His eyes, after their first glance upon her face, hung confusedly in every other direction but hers, but came back in a desperate leap every few seconds. This paralysis lasted, however, but a short time; for Tess's energies returned with the atrophy of his, and she walked as fast as she was able past the barn and onward.

As soon as she could reflect it appalled her, this change in their relative platforms. He who had wrought her undoing was now on the side of the Spirit, while she remained unregenerate. And, as in the legend, it had resulted that her Cyprian image had suddenly appeared upon his altar, whereby the fire of the priest had been wellnigh extinguished.

She went on without turning her head. Her back seemed to be endowed with a sensitiveness to ocular beams – even her clothing – so alive was she to a fancied gaze which might be resting upon her from the outside of that barn. All the way along to this point her heart had been heavy with an inactive sorrow; now there was a change in the quality of its trouble. That hunger for affection too long withheld was for the time displaced by an almost physical sense of an implacable past which still engirdled her. It intensified her consciousness of error to a practical despair; the break of continuity between her earlier and present existence, which she had hoped for, had not, after all, taken place. Bygones would never be complete bygones till she was a bygone herself.

Thus absorbed she recrossed the northern part of Long-Ash Lane at right angles, and presently saw before her the road ascending whitely to the upland along whose margin the remainder of her journey lay. Its dry pale surface stretched severely onward, unbroken by a single figure, vehicle, or mark, save some occasional brown horse-droppings which dotted its cold aridity here and there. While slowly breasting this ascent Tess became conscious of footsteps behind her, and turning she saw approaching that well-known form – so strangely accoutred as the Methodist – the one personage in all the world she wished not to encounter alone on this side of the grave.

There was not much time, however, for thought or elusion, and she yielded as calmly as she could to the necessity of letting him overtake her. She saw that he was excited, less by the speed of his walk than by the feelings within him.

'Tess!' he said.

She slackened speed without looking round.

'Tess!' he repeated. 'It is I – Alec d'Urberville.'

She then looked back at him, and he came up.

'I see it is,' she answered coldly.

'Well – is that all? Yet I deserve no more! Of course,' he added, with a slight laugh, 'there is something of the ridiculous to your eyes in seeing me like this.

But – I must put up with that . . . I heard you had gone away, nobody knew where. Tess, you wonder why I have followed you?'

'I do, rather; and I would that you had not, with all my heart!'

'Yes – you may well say it,' he returned grimly, as they moved onward together, she with unwilling tread. 'But don't mistake me; I beg this because you may have been led to do so in noticing – if you did notice it – how your sudden appearance unnerved me down there. It was but a momentary faltering; and considering what you had been to me, it was natural enough. But will helped me through it – though perhaps you think me a humbug for saying it – and immediately afterwards I felt that of all persons in the world whom it was my duty and desire to save from the wrath to come – sneer if you like – the woman whom I had so grievously wronged was that person. I have come with that sole purpose in view – nothing more.'

There was the smallest vein of scorn in her words of rejoinder: 'Have you saved yourself? Charity begins at home, they say.'

'*I* have done nothing!' said he indifferently. 'Heaven, as I have been telling my hearers, has done all. No amount of contempt that you can pour upon me, Tess, will equal what I have poured upon myself – the old Adam of my former years! Well, it is a strange story; believe it or not; but I can tell you the means by which my conversion was brought about, and I hope you will be interested enough at least to listen. Have you ever heard the name of the parson of Emminster – you must have done so? – old Mr Clare; one of the most earnest of his school; one of the few intense men left in the Church; not so intense as the extreme wing of Christian believers with which I have thrown in my lot, but quite an exception among the Established clergy, the younger of whom are gradually attenuating the true doctrines by their sophistries, till they are but the shadow of what they were. I only differ from him on the question of Church and State – the interpretation of the text, "Come out from among them and be ye separate, saith the Lord" – that's all. He is one who, I firmly believe, has been the humble means of saving more souls in this country than any other man you can name. You have heard of him?'

'I have,' she said.

'He came to Trantridge two or three years ago to preach on behalf of some missionary society; and I, wretched fellow that I was, insulted him when, in his disinterestedness, he tried to reason with me and show me the way. He did not resent my conduct, he simply said that someday I should receive the first-fruits of the Spirit – that those who came to scoff sometimes remained to pray. There was a strange magic in his words. They sank into my mind. But the loss of my mother hit me most; and by degrees I was brought to see daylight. Since then my one desire has been to hand on the true view to others, and that is what I was trying to do today; though it is only lately that I have preached hereabout. The first months of my ministry have been spent in the North of England among strangers, where I preferred to make my earliest clumsy attempts, so as to acquire courage before undergoing that severest of all tests of one's sincerity, addressing those who have known one, and have been one's companions in the days of darkness. If you could only know, Tess, the pleasure of having a good slap at yourself, I am sure – '

'Don't go on with it!' she cried passionately, as she turned away from him to a stile by the wayside, on which she bent herself. 'I can't believe in such sudden things! I feel indignant with you for talking to me like this, when you know – when you know what harm you've done me! You, and those like you, take your fill of pleasure on earth by making the life of such as me bitter and black with sorrow; and then it is a fine thing, when you have had enough of that, to think of securing your pleasure in heaven by becoming converted! Out upon such – I don't believe in you – I hate it!'

'Tess,' he insisted; 'don't speak so! It came to me like a jolly new idea! And you don't believe me? What don't you believe?'

'Your conversion. Your scheme of religion.'

'Why?'

She dropped her voice. 'Because a better man than you does not believe in such.'

'What a woman's reason! Who is this better man?'

'I cannot tell you.'

'Well,' he declared, a resentment beneath his words seeming ready to spring out at a moment's notice, 'God forbid that I should say I am a good man – and you know I don't say any such thing. I am new to goodness, truly; but new comers see furthest sometimes.'

'Yes,' she replied sadly. 'But I cannot believe in your conversion to a new spirit. Such flashes as you feel, Alec, I fear don't last!'

Thus speaking she turned from the stile over which she had been leaning, and faced him; whereupon his eyes, falling casually upon the familiar countenance and form, remained contemplating her. The inferior man was quiet in him now; but it was surely not extracted, nor even entirely subdued.

'Don't look at me like that!' he said abruptly.

Tess, who had been quite unconscious of her action and mien, instantly withdrew the large dark gaze of her eyes, stammering with a flush, 'I beg your pardon!' And there was revived in her the wretched sentiment which had often come to her before, that in inhabiting the fleshly tabernacle with which Nature had endowed her she was somehow doing wrong.

'No, no! Don't beg my pardon. But since you wear a veil to hide your good looks, why don't you keep it down?'

She pulled down the veil, saying hastily, 'It was mostly to keep off the wind.'

'It may seem harsh of me to dictate like this,' he went on; 'but it is better that I should not look too often on you. It might be dangerous.'

'Ssh!' said Tess.

'Well, women's faces have had too much power over me already for me not to fear them! An evangelist has nothing to do with such as they; and it reminds me of the old times that I would forget!'

After this their conversation dwindled to a casual remark now and then as they rambled onward, Tess inwardly wondering how far he was going with her, and not liking to send him back by positive mandate. Frequently when they came to a gate or stile they found painted thereon in red or blue letters some text of Scripture, and she asked him if he knew who had been at the pains to blazon these announcements. He told her that the man was employed by himself and others who were working with him in that district, to paint these reminders that no means might be left untried which might move the hearts of a wicked generation.

At length the road touched the spot called 'Cross-in-Hand'. Of all spots on the bleached and desolate upland this was the most forlorn. It was so far removed from the charm which is sought in landscape by artists and view-lovers as to reach a new kind of beauty, a negative beauty of tragic tone. The place took its name from a stone pillar which stood there, a strange rude monolith, from a stratum unknown in any local quarry, on which was roughly carved a human hand. Differing accounts were given of its history and purport. Some authorities stated that a devotional cross had once formed the complete erection thereon, of which the present relic was but the stump; others that the stone as it stood was entire, and that it had been fixed there to mark a boundary or place of meeting. Anyhow, whatever the origin of the relic, there was and is something sinister, or solemn, according to mood, in the scene amid which it stands; something tending to impress the most phlegmatic passer-by.

'I think I must leave you now,' he remarked, as they drew near to this spot. 'I have to preach at Abbot's Cernel at six this evening, and my way lies across to the right from here. And you upset me somewhat too, Tessy – I cannot, will not, say why. I must go away and get strength . . . How is it that you speak so fluently now? Who has taught you such good English?'

'I have learnt things in my troubles,' she said evasively.

'What troubles have you had?'

She told him of the first one – the only one that related to him.

D'Urberville was struck mute. 'I knew nothing of this till now!' he next murmured. 'Why didn't you write to me when you felt your trouble coming on?'

She did not reply; and he broke the silence by adding: 'Well – you will see me again.'

'No,' she answered. 'Do not again come near me!'

'I will think. But before we part come here.' He stepped up to the pillar. 'This was once a Holy Cross. Relics are not in my creed; but I fear you at moments – far more than you need fear me at present; and to lessen my fear, put your hand upon that stone hand, and swear that you will never tempt me – by your charms or ways.'

'Good God – how can you ask what is so unnecessary! All that is furthest from my thought!'

'Yes – but swear it.'

Tess, half frightened, gave way to his importunity; placed her hand upon the stone and swore.

'I am sorry you are not a believer,' he continued; 'that some unbeliever should have got hold of you and unsettled your mind. But no more now. At home at least I can pray for you; and I will; and who knows what may not happen? I'm off. Goodbye!'

He turned to a hunting-gate in the hedge, and without letting his eyes again rest upon her leapt over, and struck out across the down in the direction of Abbot's Cernel. As he walked his pace showed perturbation, and by and by, as if instigated by a former thought, he drew from his pocket a small book, between the leaves of which was folded a letter, worn and soiled, as from much re-reading. D'Urberville opened the letter. It was dated several months before this time, and was signed by Parson Clare.

The letter began by expressing the writer's unfeigned joy at d'Urberville's conversion, and thanked him for his kindness in communicating with the parson on the subject. It expressed Mr Clare's warm assurance of forgiveness for d'Urberville's former conduct, and his interest in the young man's plans for the future. He, Mr Clare, would much have liked to see d'Urberville in the Church to whose ministry he had devoted so many years of his own life, and would have helped him to enter a theological college to that end; but since his correspondent had possibly not cared to do this on account of the delay it would have entailed, he was not the man to insist upon its paramount importance. Every man must work as he could best work, and in the method towards which he felt impelled by the Spirit.

D'Urberville read and re-read this letter, and seemed to quiz himself cynically. He also read some passages from memoranda as he walked till his face assumed a calm, and apparently the image of Tess no longer troubled his mind.

She meanwhile had kept along the edge of the hill by which lay her nearest way home. Within the distance of a mile she met a solitary shepherd.

'What is the meaning of that old stone I have passed?' she asked of him. 'Was it ever a Holy Cross?'

'Cross – no; 'twer not a cross! 'Tis a thing of ill-omen, Miss. It was put up in wuld times by the relations of a malefactor who was tortured there by nailing his hand to a post and afterwards hung. The bones lie underneath. They say he sold his soul to the devil, and that he walks at times.'

She felt the *petite mort* at this unexpectedly gruesome information, and left the solitary man behind her. It was dusk when she drew near to Flintcomb-Ash, and in the lane at the entrance to the hamlet she approached a girl and her lover without their observing her. They were talking no secrets, and the clear unconcerned voice of the young woman, in response to the warmer accents of the man, spread into the chilly air as the one soothing thing within the dusky horizon, full of a stagnant obscurity upon which nothing else intruded. For a moment the voices cheered the heart of Tess, till she reasoned that this interview had its origin, on one side or the other, in the same attraction which had been the prelude to her own tribulation. When she came close the girl turned serenely and recognised her, the young man walking off in embarrassment. The woman was Izz Huett, whose interest in Tess's excursion immediately superseded her own proceedings. Tess did not explain very clearly its results, and Izz, who was a girl of tact, began to speak of her own little affair, a phase of which Tess had just witnessed.

'He is Amby Seedling, the chap who used to sometimes come and help at Talbothays,' she explained indifferently. 'He actually enquired and found out that I had come here, and has followed me. He says he's been in love wi' me these two years. But I've hardly answered him.'

## *Chapter 46*

Several days had passed since her futile journey, and Tess was afield. The dry winter wind still blew, but a screen of thatched hurdles erected in the eye of the blast kept its force away from her. On the sheltered side was a turnip-slicing machine, whose bright blue hue of new paint seemed almost vocal in the otherwise subdued scene. Opposite its front was a long mound or 'grave,' in which the roots had been preserved since early winter. Tess was standing at the uncovered end, chopping off with a bill-hook the fibres and earth from each root, and throwing it after the operation into the slicer. A man was turning the handle of the machine, and from its trough came the newly-cut swedes, the fresh smell of whose yellow chips was accompanied by the sounds of the snuffling wind, the smart swish of the slicing-blades, and the choppings of the hook in Tess's leather-gloved hand.

The wide acreage of blank agricultural brownness, apparent where the swedes had been pulled, was beginning to be striped in wales of darker brown, gradually broadening to ribands. Along the edge of each of these something crept upon ten legs, moving without haste and without rest up and down the whole length of the field; it was two horses and a man, the plough going between them, turning up the cleared ground for a spring sowing.

For hours nothing relieved the joyless monotony of things. Then, far beyond the ploughing-teams, a black speck was seen. It had come from the corner of a fence, where there was a gap, and its tendency was up the incline, towards the swede-cutters. From the proportions of a mere point it advanced to the shape of a ninepin, and was soon perceived to be a man in black, arriving from the direction of Flintcomb-Ash. The man at the slicer, having nothing else to do with his eyes, continually observed the comer, but Tess, who was occupied, did not perceive him till her companion directed her attention to his approach.

It was not her hard taskmaster, Farmer Groby; it was one in a semi-clerical costume, who now represented what had once been the free and easy Alec d'Urberville. Not being hot at his preaching there was less enthusiasm about him now, and the presence of the grinder seemed to embarrass him. A pale distress was already on Tess's face, and she pulled her curtained hood further over it.

D'Urberville came up and said quietly – 'I want to speak to you, Tess.'

'You have refused my last request, not to come near me!' said she.

'Yes, but I have a good reason.'

'Well, tell it.'

'It is more serious than you may think.'

He glanced round to see if he were overheard. They were at some distance from the man who turned the slicer, and the movement of the machine, too, sufficiently prevented Alec's words reaching other ears. D'Urberville placed himself so as to screen Tess from the labourer, turning his back to the latter.

'It is this,' he continued, with capricious compunction. 'In thinking of your soul and mine when we last met, I neglected to enquire as to your worldly condition. You were well dressed, and I did not think of it. But I see now that it is hard – harder than it used to be when I – knew you – harder than you deserve. Perhaps a good deal of it is owing to me!'

She did not answer, and he watched her enquiringly, as, with bent head, her face completely screened by the hood, she resumed her trimming of the swedes. By going on with her work she felt better able to keep him outside her emotions.

'Tess,' he added, with a sigh of discontent – 'yours was the very worst case I ever was concerned in! I had no idea of what had resulted till you told me. Scamp that I was to foul that innocent life! The whole blame was mine – the whole unconventional business of our time at Trantridge. You, too, the real blood of which I am but the base imitation, what a blind young thing you were as to possibilities! I say in all earnestness that it is a shame for parents to bring up their girls in such dangerous ignorance of the gins and nets that the wicked may set for them, whether their motive be a good one or the result of simple indifference.'

Tess still did no more than listen, throwing down one globular root and taking up another with automatic regularity, the pensive contour of the mere field-woman alone marking her.

'But it is not that I came to say,' d'Urberville went on. 'My circumstances are these. I have lost my mother since you were at Trantridge, and the place is my own. But I intend to sell it, and devote myself to missionary work in Africa. A devil of a poor hand I shall make at the trade, no doubt. However, what I want to ask you is, will you put it in my power to do my duty – to make the only reparation I can make for the trick played you: that is, will you be my wife, and go with me? . . . I have already obtained this precious document. It was my old mother's dying wish.'

He drew a piece of parchment from his pocket, with a slight fumbling of embarrassment.

'What is it?' said she.

'A marriage licence.'

'O no, sir – no!' she said quickly, starting back.

'You will not? Why is that?'

And as he asked the question a disappointment which was not entirely the disappointment of thwarted duty crossed d'Urberville's face. It was unmistakably a symptom that something of his old passion for her had been revived; duty and desire ran hand in hand.

'Surely,' he began again, in more impetuous tones, and then looked round at the labourer who turned the slicer.

Tess, too, felt that the argument could not be ended there. Informing the man that a gentleman had come to see her, with whom she wished to walk a little way, she moved off with d'Urberville across the zebra-striped field. When they reached the first newly-ploughed section he held out his hand to help her over it; but she stepped forward on the summits of the earth-rolls as if she did not see him.

'You will not marry me, Tess, and make me a self-respecting man?' he repeated, as soon as they were over the furrows.

'I cannot.'

'But why?'

'You know I have no affection for you.'

'But you would get to feel that in time, perhaps – as soon as you really could forgive me?'

'Never!'

'Why so positive?'

'I love somebody else.'

The words seemed to astonish him.

'You do?' he cried. 'Somebody else? But has not a sense of what is morally right and proper any weight with you?'

'No, no, no – don't say that!'

'Anyhow, then, your love for this other man may be only a passing feeling which you will overcome – '

'No – no.'

'Yes, yes! Why not?'

'I cannot tell you.'

'You must in honour!'

'Well then . . . I have married him.'

'Ah!' he exclaimed; and he stopped dead and gazed at her. 'I did not wish to tell – I did not mean to!' she pleaded. 'It is a secret here, or at any rate but dimly known. So will you, *please* will you, keep from questioning me? You must remember that we are now strangers.'

'Strangers – are we? Strangers!'

For a moment a flash of his old irony marked his face; but he determinedly chastened it down.

'Is that man your husband?' he asked mechanically, denoting by a sign the labourer who turned the machine.

'That man!' she said proudly. 'I should think not!'

'Who, then?'

'Do not ask what I do not wish to tell!' she begged, and flashed her appeal to him from her upturned face and lash-shadowed eyes.

D'Urberville was disturbed.

'But I only asked for your sake!' he retorted hotly. 'Angels of heaven! – God forgive me for such an expression – I came here, I swear, as I thought for your good. Tess – don't look at me so – I cannot stand your looks! There never were such eyes, surely, before Christianity or since! There – I won't lose my head; I dare not. I own that the sight of you has waked up my love for you, which, I believed, was extinguished with all such feelings. But I thought that our marriage might be a sanctification for us both. "The unbelieving husband is sanctified by the wife, and the unbelieving wife is sanctified by the husband," I said to myself. But my plan is dashed from me; and I must bear the disappointment!'

He moodily reflected with his eyes on the ground.

'Married. Married! . . . Well, that being so,' he added, quite calmly, tearing the licence slowly into halves and putting them in his pocket; 'that being prevented, I should like to do some good to you and your husband, whoever he may be. There are many questions that I am tempted to ask, but I will not do so, of course, in opposition to your wishes. Though, if I could know your husband, I might more easily benefit him and you. Is he on this farm?'

'No,' she murmured. 'He is far away.'

'Far away? From *you?* What sort of husband can he be?'

'O, do not speak against him! It was through you! He found out – '

'Ah, is it so! . . . That's sad, Tess!'

'Yes.'

'But to stay away from you – to leave you to work like this!'

'He does not leave me to work!' she cried, springing to the defence of the absent one with all her fervour. 'He don't know it! It is by my own arrangement.'

'Then, does he write?'

'I – I cannot tell you. There are things which are private to ourselves.'

'Of course that means that he does not. You are a deserted wife, my fair Tess!'

In an impulse he turned suddenly to take her hand; the buff-glove was on it, and he seized only the rough leather fingers which did not express the life or shape of those within.

'You must not – you must not!' she cried fearfully, slipping her hand from the glove as from a pocket, and leaving it in his grasp. 'O, will you go away – for the sake of me and my husband – go, in the name of your own Christianity!'

'Yes, yes; I will,' he said abruptly, and thrusting the glove back to her he turned to leave. Facing round, however, he said, 'Tess, as God is my judge, I meant no humbug in taking your hand!'

A pattering of hoofs on the soil of the field, which they had not noticed in their pre-occupation, ceased close behind them; and a voice reached her ear:

'What the devil are you doing away from your work at this time o' day?'

Farmer Groby had espied the two figures from the distance, and had inquisitively ridden across, to learn what was their business in his field.

'Don't speak like that to her!' said d'Urberville, his face blackening with something that was not Christianity.

'Indeed, Mister! And what mid Methodist pa'sons have to do with she?'

'Who is the fellow?' asked d'Urberville, turning to Tess.

She went close up to him.

'Go – I do beg you!' she said.

'What! And leave you to that tyrant? I can see in his face what a churl he is.'

'He won't hurt me. *He's* not in love with me. I can leave at Lady-Day.'

'Well, I have no right but to obey, I suppose. But – well, goodbye!'

Her defender, whom she dreaded more than her assailant, having reluctantly disappeared, the farmer continued his reprimand, which Tess took with the greatest coolness, that sort of attack being independent of sex. To have as a master this man of stone, who would have cuffed her if he had dared, was almost a relief after her former experiences. She silently walked back towards the summit of the field that was the scene of her labour, so absorbed in the interview which had just taken place that she was hardly aware that the nose of Groby's horse almost touched her shoulders.

'If so be you make an agreement to work for me till Lady-Day, I'll see that you carry it out,' he growled. ' 'Od rot the women – now 'tis one thing, and then 'tis another. But I'll put up with it no longer!'

Knowing very well that he did not harass the other women of the farm as he harassed her out of spite for the flooring he had once received, she did for one moment picture what might have been the result if she had been free to accept the offer just made her of being the monied Alec's wife. It would have lifted her completely out of subjection, not only to her present oppressive employer, but to a whole world who seemed to despise her. 'But no, no!' she said breathlessly; 'I could not have married him now! He is so unpleasant to me.'

That very night she began an appealing letter to Clare, concealing from him her hardships, and assuring him of her undying affection. Anyone who had been in a position to read between the lines would have seen that at the back of her great love was some monstrous fear – almost a desperation – as to some secret contingencies which were not disclosed. But again she did not finish her effusion; he had asked Izz to go with him, and perhaps he did not care for her at all. She put the letter in her box, and wondered if it would ever reach Angel's hands.

After this her daily tasks were gone through heavily enough, and brought on the day which was of great import to agriculturists – the day of the Candlemas Fair. It was at this fair that new engagements were entered into for the twelve months following the ensuing Lady-Day, and those of the farming population who thought of changing their places duly attended at the county-town where the fair was held. Nearly all the labourers on Flintcomb-Ash farm intended flight, and early in the morning there was a general exodus in the direction of the town, which lay at a distance of from ten to a dozen miles over hilly country. Though Tess also meant to leave at the quarter-day she was one of the few who did not go to the fair, having a vaguely-shaped hope that something would happen to render another outdoor engagement unnecessary.

It was a peaceful February day, of wonderful softness for the time, and one would almost have thought that winter was over. She had hardly finished her dinner when d'Urberville's figure darkened the window of the cottage wherein she was a lodger, which she had all to herself today.

Tess jumped up, but her visitor had knocked at the door, and she could hardly in reason run away. D'Urberville's knock, his walk up to the door, had some indescribable quality of difference from his air when she last saw him. They seemed to be acts of which the doer was ashamed. She thought that she would not open the door; but, as there was no sense in that either, she arose, and having lifted the latch stepped back quickly. He came in, saw her, and flung himself down into a chair before speaking.

'Tess – I couldn't help it!' he began desperately, as he wiped his heated face, which had also a superimposed flush of excitement. 'I felt that I must call at least to ask how you are. I assure you I had not been thinking of you at all till I saw you that Sunday; now I cannot get rid of your image, try how I may! It is hard that a good woman should do harm to a bad man; yet so it is. If you would only pray for me, Tess!'

The suppressed discontent of his manner was almost pitiable, and yet Tess did not pity him.

'How can I pray for you,' she said, 'when I am forbidden to believe that the great Power who moves the world would alter His plans on my account?'

'You really think that?'

'Yes. I have been cured of the presumption of thinking otherwise.'

'Cured? By whom?'

'By my husband, if I must tell.'

'Ah – your husband – your husband! How strange it seems! I remember you hinted something of the sort the other day. What do you really believe in these matters, Tess?' he asked. 'You seem to have no religion – perhaps owing to me.'

'But I have. Though I don't believe in anything supernatural.'

D'Urberville looked at her with misgiving.

'Then do you think that the line I take is all wrong?'

'A good deal of it.'

'H'm – and yet I've felt so sure about it,' he said uneasily.

'I believe in the *spirit* of the Sermon on the Mount, and so did my dear husband . . . But I don't believe – '

Here she gave her negations.

'The fact is,' said d'Urberville drily, 'whatever your dear husband believed you accept, and whatever he rejected you reject, without the least enquiry or reasoning on your own part. That's just like you women. Your mind is enslaved to his.'

'Ah, because he knew everything!' said she, with a triumphant simplicity of faith in Angel Clare that the most perfect man could hardly have deserved, much less her husband.

'Yes, but you should not take negative opinions wholesale from another person like that. A pretty fellow he must be to teach you such scepticism!'

'He never forced my judgment! He would never argue on the subject with me! But I looked at it in this way; what he believed, after enquiring deep into doctrines, was much more likely to be right than what I might believe, who hadn't looked into doctrines at all.'

'What used he to say? He must have said something?'

She reflected; and with her acute memory for the letter of Angel Clare's remarks, even when she did not comprehend their spirit, she recalled a merciless polemical syllogism that she had heard him use when, as it occasionally happened, he indulged in a species of thinking aloud with her at his side. In delivering it she gave also Clare's accent and manner with reverential faithfulness.

'Say that again,' asked d'Urberville, who had listened with the greatest attention.

She repeated the argument, and d'Urberville thoughtfully murmured the words after her.

'Anything else?' he presently asked.

'He said at another time something like this'; and she gave another, which might possibly have been paralleled in many a work of the pedigree ranging from the *Dictionnaire Philosophique* to Huxley's *Essays.*

'Ah – ha! How do you remember them?'

'I wanted to believe what he believed, though he didn't wish me to; and I managed to coax him to tell me a few of his thoughts. I can't say I quite understand that one; but I know it is right.'

'H'm. Fancy your being able to teach me what you don't know yourself!'

He fell into thought.

'And so I threw in my spiritual lot with his,' she resumed. 'I didn't wish it to be different. What's good enough for him is good enough for me.'

'Does he know that you are as big an infidel as he?'

'No – I never told him – if I am an infidel.'

'Well – you are better off today than I am, Tess, after all! You don't believe that you ought to preach my doctrine, and, therefore, do no despite to your conscience in abstaining. I do believe I ought to preach it, but like the devils I believe and tremble, for I suddenly leave off preaching it, and give way to my passion for you.'

'How?'

'Why,' he said aridly; 'I have come all the way here to see you today! But I started from home to go to Casterbridge Fair, where I have undertaken to preach the Word from a waggon at half-past two this afternoon, and where all the brethren are expecting me this minute. Here's the announcement.'

He drew from his breast-pocket a poster whereon was printed the day, hour, and place of meeting, at which he, d'Urberville, would preach the Gospel as aforesaid.

'But how can you get there?' said Tess, looking at the clock.

'I cannot get there! I have come here.'

'What, you have really arranged to preach, and – '

I have arranged to preach, and I shall not be there – by reason of my burning desire to see a woman whom I once despised! – No, by my word and truth, I never despised you; if I had I should not love you now! Why I did not despise you was on account of your being unsmirched in spite of all; you withdrew yourself from me so quickly and resolutely when you saw the situation; you did not remain at my pleasure; so there was one petticoat in the world for whom I had no contempt, and you are she. But you may well despise me now! I thought I worshipped on the mountains, but I find I still serve in the groves! Ha! ha!'

'O Alec d'Urberville! what does this mean? What have I done!'

'Done?' he said, with a soulless sneer in the word. 'Nothing intentionally. But you have been the means – the innocent means – of my backsliding, as they call it. I ask myself, am I, indeed, one of those "servants of corruption" who, "after they have escaped the pollutions of the world, are again entangled therein and overcome" – whose latter end is worse than their beginning?' He laid his hand on her shoulder. 'Tess, my girl, I was on the way to, at least, social salvation till I saw you again!' he said freakishly shaking her, as if she were a child. 'And why then have you tempted me? I was firm as a man could be till I saw those eyes and that mouth again – surely there never was such a maddening mouth since Eve's!' His voice sank, and a hot archness shot from his own black eyes. 'You temptress, Tess; you dear damned witch of Babylon – I could not resist you as soon as I met you again!'

'I couldn't help your seeing me again!' said Tess, recoiling.

'I know it – I repeat that I do not blame you. But the fact remains. When I saw you ill-used on the farm that day I was nearly mad to think that I had no legal right to protect you – that I could not have it; whilst he who has it seems to neglect you utterly!'

'Don't speak against him – he is absent!' she cried in much excitement. 'Treat him honourably – he has never wronged you! O leave his wife before any scandal spreads that may do harm to his honest name!'

'I will – I will,' he said, like a man awakening from a luring dream. 'I have broken my engagement to preach to those poor drunken boobies at the fair – it is the first time I have played such a practical joke. A month ago I should have been horrified at such a possibility. I'll go away – to swear – and – ah, can I! to keep away.' Then, suddenly: 'One clasp, Tessy – one! Only for old friendship – '

'I am without defence, Alec! A good man's honour is in my keeping – think – be ashamed!'

'Pooh! Well, yes – yes!'

He clenched his lips, mortified with himself for his weakness. His eyes were equally barren of worldly and religious faith. The corpses of those old fitful passions which had lain inanimate amid the lines of his face ever since his reformation seemed to wake and come together as in a resurrection. He went out indeterminately.

Though d'Urberville had declared that this breach of his engagement today was the simple backsliding of a believer, Tess's words, as echoed from Angel Clare, had made a deep impression upon him, and continued to do so after he had left her. He moved on in silence, as if his energies were benumbed by the hitherto undreamt-of possibility that his position was untenable. Reason had

had nothing to do with his whimsical conversion, which was perhaps the mere freak of a careless man in search of a new sensation, and temporarily impressed by his mother's death.

The drops of logic Tess had let fall into the sea of his enthusiasm served to chill its effervescence to stagnation. He said to himself, as he pondered again and again over the crystallised phrases that she had handed on to him, 'That clever fellow little thought that, by telling her those things, he might be paving my way back to her!'

## *Chapter 47*

It is the threshing of the last wheat-rick at Flintcomb-Ash farm. The dawn of the March morning is singularly inexpressive, and there is nothing to show where the eastern horizon lies. Against the twilight rises the trapezoidal top of the stack, which has stood forlornly here through the washing and bleaching of the wintry weather.

When Izz Huett and Tess arrived at the scene of operations only a rustling denoted that others had preceded them; to which, as the light increased, there were presently added the silhouettes of two men on the summit. They were busily 'unhaling' the rick, that is, stripping off the thatch before beginning to throw down the sheaves; and while this was in progress Izz and Tess, with the other women-workers, in their whitey-brown pinners, stood waiting and shivering, Farmer Groby having insisted upon their being on the spot thus early to get the job over if possible by the end of the day. Close under the eaves of the stack, and as yet barely visible, was the red tyrant that the women had come to serve – a timber-framed construction, with straps and wheels appertaining – the threshing-machine which, whilst it was going, kept up a despotic demand upon the endurance of their muscles and nerves.

A little way off there was another indistinct figure; this one black, with a sustained hiss that spoke of strength very much in reserve. The long chimney running up beside an ash tree, and the warmth which radiated from the spot, explained without the necessity of much daylight that here was the engine which was to act as the *primum mobile* of this little world. By the engine stood a dark motionless being, a sooty and grimy embodiment of tallness, in a sort of trance, with a heap of coals by his side: it was the engineman. The isolation of his manner and colour lent him the appearance of a creature from Tophet, who had strayed into the pellucid smokelessness of this region of yellow grain and pale soil, with which he had nothing in common, to amaze and to discompose its aborigines.

What he looked he felt. He was in the agricultural world, but not of it. He served fire and smoke; these denizens of the fields served vegetation, weather, frost, and sun. He travelled with his engine from farm to farm, from county to county, for as yet the steam threshing-machine was itinerant in this part of

Wessex. He spoke in a strange northern accent; his thoughts being turned inwards upon himself, his eye on his iron charge, hardly perceiving the scenes around him, and caring for them not at all: holding only strictly necessary intercourse with the natives, as if some ancient doom compelled him to wander here against his will in the service of his Plutonic master. The long strap which ran from the driving-wheel of his engine to the red thresher under the rick was the sole tie-line between agriculture and him.

While they uncovered the sheaves he stood apathetic beside his portable repository of force, round whose hot blackness the morning air quivered. He had nothing to do with preparatory labour. His fire was waiting incandescent, his steam was at high pressure, in a few seconds he could make the long strap move at an invisible velocity. Beyond its extent the environment might be corn, straw, or chaos; it was all the same to him. If any of the autochthonous idlers asked him what he called himself, he replied shortly, 'an engineer'.

The rick was unhaled by full daylight; the men then took their places, the women mounted, and the work began. Farmer Groby – or, as they called him, 'he' – had arrived ere this, and by his orders Tess was placed on the platform of the machine, close to the man who fed it, her business being to untie every sheaf of corn handed on to her by Izz Huett, who stood next, but on the rick; so that the feeder could seize it and spread it over the revolving drum, which whisked out every grain in one moment.

They were soon in full progress, after a preparatory hitch or two, which rejoiced the hearts of those who hated machinery.

The work sped on till breakfast-time, when the thresher was stopped for half an hour; and on starting again after the meal the whole supplementary strength of the farm was thrown into the labour of constructing the straw-rick, which began to grow beside the stack of corn. A hasty lunch was eaten as they stood, without leaving their positions, and then another couple of hours brought them near to dinner-time; the inexorable wheels continuing to spin, and the penetrating hum of the thresher to thrill to the very marrow all who were near the revolving wire-cage.

The old men on the rising straw-rick talked of the past days when they had been accustomed to thresh with flails on the oaken barn-floor; when everything, even to winnowing, was effected by hand-labour, which, to their thinking, though slow, produced better results. Those, too, on the corn-rick talked a little; but the perspiring ones at the machine, including Tess, could not lighten their duties by the exchange of many words. It was the ceaselessness of the work which tried her so severely, and began to make her wish that she had never come to Flintcomb-Ash. The women on the corn-rick – Marian, who was one of them, in particular – could stop to drink ale or cold tea from the flagon now and then, or to exchange a few gossiping remarks while they wiped their faces or cleared the fragments of straw and husk from their clothing; but for Tess there was no respite; for, as the drum never stopped, the man who fed it could not stop, and she, who had to supply the man with untied sheaves, could not stop either, unless Marian changed places with her, which she sometimes did for half an hour in spite of Groby's objection that she was too slow-handed for a feeder.

For some probably economical reason it was usually a woman who was chosen for this particular duty, and Groby gave as his motive in selecting Tess that she was one of those who best combined strength with quickness in untying, and both with staying power, and this may have been true. The hum of the thresher, which prevented speech, increased to a raving whenever the supply of corn fell short of the regular quantity. As Tess and the man who fed could never turn their heads she did not know that just before the dinner-hour a person had come silently into the field by the gate, and had been standing under a second rick watching the scene, and Tess in particular. He was dressed in a tweed suit of fashionable pattern, and he twirled a gay walking-cane.

'Who is that?' said Izz Huett to Marian. She had at first addressed the enquiry to Tess, but the latter could not hear it.

'Somebody's fancy-man, I s'pose,' said Marian laconically.

'I'll lay a guinea he's after Tess.'

'O no. 'Tis a ranter pa'son who's been sniffing after her lately; not a dandy like this.'

'Well – this is the same man.'

'The same man as the preacher? But he's quite different!'

'He hev left off his black coat and white neckercher, and hev cut off his whiskers; but he's the same man for all that.'

'D'ye really think so? Then I'll tell her,' said Marian.

'Don't. She'll see him soon enough, good-now.'

'Well, I don't think it at all right for him to join his preaching to courting a married woman, even though her husband mid be abroad, and she, in a sense, a widow.'

'Oh – he can do her no harm,' said Izz drily. 'Her mind can no more be heaved from that one place where it do bide than a stooded waggon from the hole he's in. Lord love 'ee, neither court-paying, nor preaching, nor the seven thunders themselves, can wean a woman when 'twould be better for her that she should be weaned.'

Dinner-time came, and the whirling ceased; whereupon Tess left her post, her knees trembling so wretchedly with the shaking of the machine that she could scarcely walk.

'You ought to het a quart o' drink into 'ee, as I've done,' said Marian. 'You wouldn't look so white then. Why, souls above us, your face is as if you'd been hagrode!'

It occurred to the good-natured Marian that, as Tess was so tired, her discovery of her visitor's presence might have the bad effect of taking away her appetite; and Marian was thinking of inducing Tess to descend by a ladder on the further side of the stack when the gentleman came forward and looked up.

Tess uttered a short little 'Oh!' And a moment after she said, quickly, 'I shall eat my dinner here – right on the rick.'

Sometimes, when they were so far from their cottages, they all did this; but as there was rather a keen wind going today, Marian and the rest descended, and sat under the straw-stack.

The newcomer was, indeed, Alec d'Urberville, the late Evangelist, despite his changed attire and aspect. It was obvious at a glance that the original *Weltlust* had come back; that he had restored himself, as nearly as a man could do who had grown three or four years older, to the old jaunty, slapdash guise under which Tess had first known her admirer, and cousin so-called. Having decided to remain where she was, Tess sat down among the bundles, out of sight of the ground, and began her meal; till, by and by, she heard footsteps on the ladder, and immediately after Alec appeared upon the stack – now an oblong and level platform of sheaves. He strode across them, and sat down opposite to her without a word.

Tess continued to eat her modest dinner, a slice of thick pancake which she had brought with her. The other workfolk were by this time all gathered under the rick, where the loose straw formed a comfortable retreat.

'I am here again, as you see,' said d'Urberville.

'Why do you trouble me so!' she cried, reproach flashing from her very finger-ends.

'*I* trouble *you?* I think I may ask, why do you trouble me?'

'Sure, I don't trouble you any-when!'

'You say you don't? But you do! You haunt me. Those very eyes that you turned upon me with such a bitter flash a moment ago, they come to me just as you showed them then, in the night and in the day! Tess, ever since you told me of that child of ours, it is just as if my feelings, which have been flowing in a strong puritanical stream, had suddenly found a way open in the direction of you, and had all at once gushed through. The religious channel is left dry forthwith; and it is you who have done it!'

She gazed in silence.

'What – you have given up your preaching entirely?' she asked.

She had gathered from Angel sufficient of the incredulity of modern thought to despise flash enthusiasms; but, as a woman, she was somewhat appalled.

In affected severity d'Urberville continued – 'Entirely. I have broken every engagement since that afternoon I was to address the drunkards at Casterbridge Fair. The deuce only knows what I am thought of by the brethren. Ah-ha! The brethren! No doubt they pray for me – weep for me; for they are kind people in their way. But what do I care? How could I go on with the thing when I had lost my faith in it? – it would have been hypocrisy of the basest kind! Among them I should have stood like Hymenaeus and Alexander, who were delivered over to Satan that they might learn not to blaspheme. What a grand revenge you have taken! I saw you innocent, and I deceived you. Four years after, you find me a Christian enthusiast; you then work upon me, perhaps to my complete perdition! But Tess, my coz, as I used to call you, this is only my way of talking, and you must not look so horribly concerned. Of course you have done nothing except retain your pretty face and shapely figure. I saw it on the rick before you saw me – that tight pinafore-thing sets it off, and that wing-bonnet – you field-girls should never wear those bonnets if you wish to keep out of danger.' He regarded her silently for a few moments, and with a short cynical laugh resumed: 'I believe that if the bachelor-apostle, whose deputy I thought I was, had been tempted by such a pretty face, he would have let go the plough for her sake as I do!'

Tess attempted to expostulate, but at this juncture all her fluency failed her, and without heeding he added:

'Well, this paradise that you supply is perhaps as good as any other, after all. But to speak seriously, Tess.' D'Urberville rose and came nearer, reclining sideways amid the sheaves, and resting upon his elbow. 'Since I last saw you I have been thinking of what you said that *he* said. I have come to the conclusion that there does seem rather a want of common-sense in these threadbare old propositions; how I could have been so fired by poor Parson Clare's enthusiasm, and have gone so madly to work, transcending even him, I cannot make out! As for what you said last time, on the strength of your wonderful husband's intelligence – whose name you have never told me – about having what they call an ethical system without any dogma, I don't see my way to that at all.'

'Why, you can have the religion of loving-kindness and purity at least, if you can't have – what do you call it – dogma.'

'O no! I'm a different sort of fellow from that! If there's nobody to say, "Do this, and it will be a good thing for you after you are dead; do that, and it will be a bad thing for you," I can't warm up. Hang it, I am not going to feel responsible for my deeds and passions if there's nobody to be responsible to; and if I were you, my dear, I wouldn't either!'

She tried to argue, and tell him that he had mixed in his dull brain two matters, theology and morals, which in the primitive days of mankind had been quite distinct. But owing to Angel Clare's reticence, to her absolute want of training, and to her being a vessel of emotions rather than reasons, she could not get on.

'Well, never mind,' he resumed. 'Here I am, my love, as in the old times!'

'Not as then – never as then – 'tis different!' she entreated. 'And there was never warmth with me! O why didn't you keep your faith, if the loss of it has brought you to speak to me like this!'

'Because you've knocked it out of me; so the evil be upon your sweet head! Your husband little thought how his teaching would recoil upon him! Ha-ha – I'm awfully glad you have made an apostate of me all the same! Tess, I am more taken with you than ever, and I pity you too. For all your closeness, I see you are in a bad way – neglected by one who ought to cherish you.'

She could not get her morsels of food down her throat; her lips were dry, and she was ready to choke. The voices and laughs of the workfolk eating and drinking under the rick came to her as if they were a quarter of a mile off.

'It is cruelty to me!' she said. 'How – how can you treat me to this talk, if you care ever so little for me?'

'True, true,' he said, wincing a little. 'I did not come to reproach you for my deeds. I came, Tess, to say that I don't like you to be working like this, and I have come on purpose for you. You say you have a husband who is not I. Well, perhaps you have; but I've never seen him, and you've not told me his name; and altogether he seems rather a mythological personage. However, even if you have one, I think I am nearer to you than he is. I, at any rate, try to help you out of trouble, but he does not, bless his invisible face! The words of the stern prophet Hosea that I used to read come back to me. Don't you know them, Tess? – "And she shall follow after her lover, but she shall not overtake him; and she shall seek him, but shall not find him; then shall she say, I will go and return to my first husband; for then was it better with me than now!" . . . Tess, my trap is waiting just under the hill, and – darling mine, not his! – you know the rest.'

Her face had been rising to a dull crimson fire while he spoke; but she did not answer.

'You have been the cause of my backsliding,' he continued, stretching his arm towards her waist; 'you should be willing to share it, and leave that mule you call husband for ever.'

One of her leather gloves, which she had taken off to eat her skimmer-cake, lay in her lap, and without the slightest warning she passionately swung the glove by the gauntlet directly in his face. It was heavy and thick as a warrior's, and it struck him flat on the mouth. Fancy might have regarded the act as the recrudescence of a trick in which her armed progenitors were not unpractised. Alec fiercely started up from his reclining position. A scarlet oozing appeared where her blow had alighted, and in a moment the blood began dropping from his mouth upon the straw. But he soon controlled himself, calmly drew his handkerchief from his pocket, and mopped his bleeding lips.

She too had sprung up, but she sank down again.

'Now, punish me!' she said, turning up her eyes to him with the hopeless defiance of the sparrow's gaze before its captor twists its neck. 'Whip me, crush me; you need not mind those people under the rick! I shall not cry out. Once victim, always victim – that's the law!'

'O no, no, Tess,' he said blandly. 'I can make full allowance for this. Yet you most unjustly forget one thing, that I would have married you if you had not put it out of my power to do so. Did I not ask you flatly to be my wife – hey? Answer me.'

'You did.'

'And you cannot be. But remember one thing!' His voice hardened as his temper got the better of him with the recollection of his sincerity in asking her and her present ingratitude, and he stepped across to her side and held her by the shoulders, so that she shook under his grasp. 'Remember, my lady, I was your master once! I will be your master again. If you are any man's wife you are mine!'

The threshers now began to stir below.

'So much for our quarrel,' he said, letting her go. 'Now I shall leave you, and shall come again for your answer during the afternoon. You don't know me yet! But I know you.'

She had not spoken again, remaining as if stunned. D'Urberville retreated over the sheaves, and descended the ladder, while the workers below rose and stretched their arms, and shook down the beer they had drunk. Then the threshing-machine started afresh; and amid the renewed rustle of the straw Tess resumed her position by the buzzing drum as one in a dream, untying sheaf after sheaf in endless succession.

## *Chapter 48*

In the afternoon the farmer made it known that the rick was to be finished that night, since there was a moon by which they could see to work, and the man with the engine was engaged for another farm on the morrow. Hence the twanging and humming and rustling proceeded with even less intermission than usual.

It was not till 'nammet'-time, about three o'clock, that Tess raised her eyes and gave a momentary glance round. She felt but little surprise at seeing that Alec d'Urberville had come back, and was standing under the hedge by the gate. He had seen her lift her eyes, and waved his hand urbanely to her, while he blew her a kiss. It meant that their quarrel was over. Tess looked down again, and carefully abstained from gazing in that direction.

Thus the afternoon dragged on. The wheat-rick shrank lower, and the straw-rick grew higher, and the corn-sacks were carted away. At six o'clock the wheat-rick was about shoulder-high from the ground. But the unthreshed sheaves remaining untouched seemed countless still, notwithstanding the enormous numbers that had been gulped down by the insatiable swallower, fed by the man and Tess, through whose two young hands the greater part of them had passed. And the immense stack of straw where in the morning there had been nothing, appeared as the *faeces* of the same buzzing red glutton. From the west sky a wrathful shine – all that wild March could afford in the way of sunset – had burst forth after the cloudy day, flooding the tired and sticky faces of the threshers, and dyeing them with a coppery light, as also the flapping garments of the women, which clung to them like dull flames.

A panting ache ran through the rick. The man who fed was weary, and Tess could see that the red nape of his neck was encrusted with dirt and husks. She still stood at her post, her flushed and perspiring face coated with the corn-dust, and her white bonnet embrowned by it. She was the only woman whose place was upon the machine so as to be shaken bodily by its spinning, and the decrease of the stack now separated her from Marian and Izz, and prevented their changing duties with her as they had done. The incessant quivering, in which every fibre of her frame participated, had thrown her into a stupefied reverie in which her arms worked on independently of her consciousness. She hardly knew where she was, and did not hear Izz Huett tell her from below that her hair was tumbling down.

By degrees the freshest among them began to grow cadaverous and saucer-eyed. Whenever Tess lifted her head she beheld always the great upgrown straw-stack, with the men in shirt-sleeves upon it, against the grey north sky; in front of it the long red elevator like a Jacob's ladder, on which a perpetual stream of threshed straw ascended, a yellow river running uphill, and spouting out on the top of the rick.

She knew that Alec d'Urberville was still on the scene, observing her from some point or other, though she could not say where. There was an excuse for his remaining, for when the threshed rick drew near its final sheaves a little ratting was always done, and men unconnected with the threshing sometimes dropped in for that performance – sporting characters of all descriptions, gents with terriers and facetious pipes, roughs with sticks and stones.

But there was another hour's work before the layer of live rats at the base of the stack would be reached; and as the evening light in the direction of the Giant's Hill by Abbot's Cernel dissolved away, the white-faced moon of the season arose from the horizon that lay towards Middleton Abbey and Shottsford on the other side. For the last hour or two Marian had felt uneasy about Tess, whom she could not get near enough to speak to, the other women having kept up their strength by drinking ale, and Tess having done without it through traditionary dread, owing to its results at her home in childhood. But Tess still kept going: if she could not fill her part she would have to leave; and this contingency, which she would have regarded with equanimity and even with relief a month or two earlier, had become a terror since d'Urberville had begun to hover round her.

The sheaf-pitchers and feeders had now worked the rick so low that people on the ground could talk to them. To Tess's surprise Farmer Groby came up on the machine to her, and said that if she desired to join her friend he did not wish her to keep on any longer, and would send somebody else to take her place. The 'friend' was d'Urberville, she knew, and also that this concession had been granted in obedience to the request of that friend, or enemy. She shook her head and toiled on.

The time for the rat-catching arrived at last, and the hunt began. The creatures had crept downwards with the subsidence of the rick till they were all together at the bottom, and being now uncovered from their last refuge they ran across the open ground in all directions, a loud shriek from the by-this-time half-tipsy Marian informing her companions that one of the rats had invaded her person – a terror which the rest of the women had guarded against by various schemes of skirt-tucking and self-elevation. The rat was at last dislodged, and, amid the barking of dogs, masculine shouts, feminine screams, oaths, stampings, and confusion as of Pandemonium, Tess untied her last sheaf; the drum slowed, the whizzing ceased, and she stepped from the machine to the ground.

Her lover, who had only looked on at the rat-catching, was promptly at her side.

'What – after all – my insulting slap, too!' said she in an underbreath. She was so utterly exhausted that she had not strength to speak louder.

'I should indeed be foolish to feel offended at anything you say or do,' he answered, in the seductive voice of the Trantridge time. 'How the little limbs tremble! You are as weak as a bled calf, you know you are; and yet you need have done nothing since I arrived. How could you be so obstinate? However, I have told the farmer that he has no right to employ women at steam-threshing. It is not proper work for them; and on all the better class of farms it has been given up, as he knows very well. I will walk with you as far as your home.'

'O yes,' she answered with a jaded gait. 'Walk wi' me if you will! I do bear in mind that you came to marry me before you knew o' my state. Perhaps – perhaps you are a little better and kinder than I have been thinking you were. Whatever is meant as kindness I am grateful for; whatever is meant in any other way I am angered at. I cannot sense your meaning sometimes.'

'If I cannot legitimise our former relations at least I can assist you. And I will do it with much more regard for your feelings than I formerly showed. My religious mania, or whatever it was, is over. But I retain a little good nature; I hope I do. Now, Tess, by all that's tender and strong between man and woman, trust me! I have enough and more than enough to put you out of anxiety, both for yourself and your parents and sisters. I can make them all comfortable if you will only show confidence in me.'

'Have you seen 'em lately?' she quickly enquired.

'Yes. They didn't know where you were. It was only by chance that I found you here.'

The cold moon looked aslant upon Tess's fagged face between the twigs of the garden hedge as she paused outside the cottage which was her temporary home, d'Urberville pausing beside her.

'Don't mention my little brothers and sisters – don't make me break down quite!' she said. 'If you want to help them – God knows they need it – do it without telling me. But no, no!' she cried. 'I will take nothing from you, either for them or for me!'

He did not accompany her further, since, as she lived with the household, all was public indoors. No sooner had she herself entered, laved herself in a washing-tub, and shared supper with the family than she fell into thought, and withdrawing to the table under the wall, by the light of her own little lamp wrote in a passionate mood –

> MY OWN HUSBAND – Let me call you so – I must – even if it makes you angry to think of such an unworthy wife as I. I must cry to you in my trouble – I have no one else! I am so exposed to temptation, Angel. I fear to say who it is, and I do not like to write about it at all. But I cling to you in a way you cannot think! Can you not come to me now, at once, before anything terrible happens? O, I know you cannot, because you are so far away! I think I must die if you do not come soon, or tell me to come to you. The punishment you have measured out to me is deserved – I do know that – well deserved – and you are right and just to be angry with me. But, Angel, please, please, not to be just – only a little kind to me, even if I do not deserve it, and come to me! If you would come, I could die in your arms! I would be well content to do that if so be you had forgiven me!

Angel, I live entirely for you. I love you too much to blame you for going away, and I know it was necessary you should find a farm. Do not think I shall say a word of sting or bitterness. Only come back to me. I am desolate without you, my darling, O, so desolate! I do not mind having to work: but if you will send me one little line, and say, '*I am coming soon*,' I will bide on, Angel – O, so cheerfully!

It has been so much my religion ever since we were married to be faithful to you in every thought and look, that even when a man speaks a compliment to me before I am aware, it seems wronging you. Have you never felt one little bit of what you used to feel when we were at the dairy? If you have, how can you keep away from me? I am the same woman, Angel, as you fell in love with; yes, the very same! – not the one you disliked but never saw. What was the past to me as soon as I met you? It was a dead thing altogether. I became another woman, filled full of new life from you. How could I be the early one? Why do you not see this? Dear, if you would only be a little more conceited, and believe in yourself so far as to see that you were strong enough to work this change in me, you would perhaps be in a mind to come to me, your poor wife.

How silly I was in my happiness when I thought I could trust you always to love me! I ought to have known that such as that was not for poor me. But I am sick at heart, not only for old times, but for the present. Think – think how it do hurt my heart not to see you ever – ever! Ah, if I could only make your dear heart ache one little minute of each day as mine does every day and all day long, it might lead you to show pity to your poor lonely one.

People still say that I am rather pretty, Angel (handsome is the word they use, since I wish to be truthful). Perhaps I am what they say. But I do not value my good looks; I only like to have them because they belong to you, my dear, and that there may be at least one thing about me worth your having. So much have I felt this, that when I met with annoyance on account of the same I tied up my face in a bandage as long as people would believe in it. O Angel, I tell you all this not from vanity – you will certainly know I do not – but only that you may come to me!

If you really cannot come to me will you let me come to you? I am, as I say, worried, pressed to do what I will not do. It cannot be that I shall yield one inch, yet I am in terror as to what an accident might lead to, and I so defenceless on account of my first error. I cannot say more about this – it makes me too miserable. But if I break down by falling into some fearful snare, my last state will be worse than my first. O God, I cannot think of it! Let me come at once, or at once come to me!

I would be content, ay, glad, to live with you as your servant, if I may not as your wife; so that I could only be near you, and get glimpses of you, and think of you as mine.

The daylight has nothing to show me, since you are not here, and I don't like to see the rooks and starlings in the fields, because I grieve and grieve to miss you who used to see them with me. I long for only one thing in heaven or earth or under the earth, to meet you, my own dear! Come to me – come to me, and save me from what threatens me! – Your faithful heartbroken

TESS

## *Chapter 49*

The appeal duly found its way to the breakfast-table of the quiet vicarage to the westward, in that valley where the air is so soft and the soil so rich that the effort of growth requires but superficial aid by comparison with the tillage at Flintcomb-Ash, and where to Tess the human world seemed so different (though it was much the same). It was purely for security that she had been requested by Angel to send her communications through his father, whom he kept pretty well informed of his changing addresses in the country he had gone to exploit for himself with a heavy heart.

'Now,' said old Mr Clare to his wife, when he had read the envelope, 'if Angel proposes leaving Rio for a visit home at the end of next month, as he told us that he hoped to do, I think this may hasten his plans; for I believe it to be from his wife.' He breathed deeply at the thought of her; and the letter was redirected to be promptly sent on to Angel.

'Dear fellow, I hope he will get home safely,' murmured Mrs Clare. 'To my dying day I shall feel that he has been ill-used. You should have sent him to Cambridge in spite of his want of faith, and given him the same chance as the other boys had. He would have grown out of it under proper influence, and perhaps would have taken orders after all. Church or no Church, it would have been fairer to him.'

This was the only wail with which Mrs Clare ever disturbed her husband's peace in respect of their sons. And she did not vent this often; for she was as considerate as she was devout, and knew that his mind too was troubled by doubts as to his justice in this matter. Only too often had she heard him lying awake at night, stifling sighs for Angel with prayers. But the uncompromising Evangelical did not even now hold that he would have been justified in giving his son, an unbeliever, the same academic advantages that he had given to the two others, when it was possible, if not probable, that those very advantages might have been used to decry the doctrines which he had made it his life's mission and desire to propagate, and the mission of his ordained sons likewise. To put with one hand a pedestal under the feet of the two faithful ones, and with the other to exalt the unfaithful by the same artificial means, he deemed to be alike inconsistent with his convictions, his position, and his hopes. Nevertheless, he loved his misnamed Angel, and in secret mourned over this treatment of him as Abraham might have mourned over the doomed Isaac while they went up the hill together. His silent self-generated regrets were far bitterer than the reproaches which his wife rendered audible.

They blamed themselves for this unlucky marriage. If Angel had never been destined for a farmer he would never have been thrown with agricultural girls. They did not distinctly know what had separated him and his wife, nor the date on which the separation had taken place. At first they had supposed it must be something of the nature of a serious aversion. But in his later letters he occasionally alluded to the intention of coming home to fetch her; from which expressions they hoped the division might not owe its origin to anything so hopelessly permanent as that. He had told them that she was with her relatives, and in their doubts they had decided not to intrude into a situation which they knew no way of bettering.

The eyes for which Tess's letter was intended were gazing at this time on a limitless expanse of country from the back of a mule which was bearing him from the interior of the South-American Continent towards the coast. His experiences of this strange land had been sad. The severe illness from which he had suffered shortly after his arrival had never wholly left him, and he had by degrees almost decided to relinquish his hope of farming here, though, as long as the bare possibility existed of his remaining, he kept this change of view a secret from his parents.

The crowds of agricultural labourers who had come out to the country in his wake, dazzled by representations of easy independence, had suffered, died, and wasted away. He would see mothers from English farms trudging along with their infants in their arms, when the child would be stricken with fever and would die; the mother would pause to dig a hole in the loose earth with her bare hands, would bury the babe therein with the same natural grave-tools, shed one tear, and again trudge on.

Angel's original intention had not been emigration to Brazil, but a northern or eastern farm in his own country. He had come to this place in a fit of desperation, the Brazil movement among the English agriculturists having by chance coincided with his desire to escape from his past existence.

During this time of absence he had mentally aged a dozen years. What arrested him now as of value in life was less its beauty than its pathos. Having long discredited the old systems of mysticism, he now began to discredit the old appraisements of morality. He thought they wanted readjusting. Who was the moral man? Still more pertinently, who was the moral woman? The beauty or ugliness of a character lay not only in its achievements, but in its aims and impulses; its true history lay, not among things done, but among things willed.

How, then, about Tess?

Viewing her in these lights, a regret for his hasty judgment began to oppress him. Did he reject her eternally, or did he not? He could no longer say that he would always reject her, and not to say that was in spirit to accept her now.

This growing fondness for her memory coincided in point of time with her residence at Flintcomb-Ash, but it was before she had felt herself at liberty to trouble him with a word about her circumstances or her feelings. He was greatly perplexed; and in his perplexity as to her motives in withholding intelligence he did not enquire. Thus her silence of docility was misinterpreted. How much it really said if he had understood! – that she adhered with literal exactness to orders which he had given and forgotten; that despite her natural fearlessness she asserted no rights, admitted his judgment to be in every respect the true one, and bent her head dumbly thereto.

In the before-mentioned journey by mules through the interior of the country, another man rode beside him. Angel's companion was also an Englishman, bent on the same errand, though he came from another part of the island. They were both in a state of mental depression, and they spoke of home affairs. Confidence begat confidence. With that curious tendency evinced by men, more especially when in distant lands, to entrust to strangers details of their lives which they would on no account mention to friends, Angel admitted to this man as they rode along the sorrowful facts of his marriage.

The stranger had sojourned in many more lands and among many more peoples than Angel; to his cosmopolitan mind such deviations from the social norm, so immense to domesticity, were no more than are the irregularities of vale and mountain-chain to the whole terrestrial curve. He viewed the matter in quite a different light from Angel; thought that what Tess had been was of no importance beside what she would be, and plainly told Clare that he was wrong in coming away from her.

The next day they were drenched in a thunderstorm. Angel's companion was struck down with fever, and died by the week's end. Clare waited a few hours to bury him, and then went on his way.

The cursory remarks of the large-minded stranger, of whom he knew absolutely nothing beyond a commonplace name, were sublimed by his death, and influenced Clare more than all the reasoned ethics of the philosophers. His own parochialism made him ashamed by its contrast. His inconsistencies rushed upon him in a flood. He had persistently elevated Hellenic Paganism at the expense of Christianity; yet in that civilisation an illegal surrender was not certain disesteem. Surely then he might have regarded that abhorrence of the un-intact state, which he had inherited with the creed of mysticism, as at least open to correction when the result was due to treachery. A remorse struck into him. The words of Izz Huett, never quite stilled in his memory, came back to him. He had asked Izz if she loved him, and she had replied in the affirmative. Did she love him more than Tess did? No, she had replied; Tess would lay down her life for him, and she herself could do no more.

He thought of Tess as she had appeared on the day of the wedding. How her eyes had lingered upon him; how she had hung upon his words as if they were a god's! And during the terrible evening over the hearth, when her simple soul uncovered itself to his, how pitiful her face had looked by the rays of the fire, in her inability to realise that his love and protection could possibly be withdrawn.

Thus from being her critic he grew to be her advocate. Cynical things he had uttered to himself about her; but no man can be always a cynic and live; and he withdrew them. The mistake of expressing them had arisen from his allowing himself to be influenced by general principles to the disregard of the particular instance.

But the reasoning is somewhat musty; lovers and husbands have gone over the ground before today. Clare had been harsh towards her; there is no doubt of it. Men are too often harsh with women they love or have loved; women with men. And yet these harshnesses are tenderness itself when compared with the universal harshness out of which they grow; the harshness of the position towards the temperament, of the means towards the aims, of today towards yesterday, of hereafter towards today.

The historic interest of her family – that masterful line of d'Urbervilles – whom he had despised as a spent force, touched his sentiments now. Why had he not known the difference between the political value and the imaginative value of these things? In the latter aspect her d'Urberville descent was a fact of great dimensions; worthless to economics, it was a most useful ingredient to the dreamer, to the moraliser on declines and falls. It was a fact that would soon be forgotten – that bit of distinction in poor Tess's blood and name, and oblivion would fall upon her hereditary link with the marble monuments and leaded skeletons at Kingsbere. So does Time ruthlessly destroy his own romances. In recalling her face again and again, he thought now that he could see therein a flash of the dignity which must have graced her grand-dames; and the vision sent that *aura* through his veins which he had formerly felt, and which left behind it a sense of sickness.

Despite her not inviolate past, what still abode in such a woman as Tess outvalued the freshness of her fellows. Was not the gleaning of the grapes of Ephraim better than the vintage of Abiezer?

So spoke love renascent, preparing the way for Tess's devoted outpouring, which was then just being forwarded to him by his father; though owing to his distance inland it was to be a long time in reaching him.

Meanwhile the writer's expectation that Angel would come in response to the entreaty was alternately great and small. What lessened it was that the facts of her life which had led to the parting had not changed – could never change; and that, if her presence had not attenuated them, her absence could not. Nevertheless she addressed her mind to the tender question of what she could do to please him best if he should arrive. Sighs were expended on the wish that she had taken more notice of the tunes he played on his harp, that she had enquired more curiously of him which were his favourite ballads among those the country-girls sang. She indirectly enquired of Amby Seedling, who had followed Izz from Talbothays, and by chance Amby remembered that, amongst the snatches of melody in which they had indulged at the dairyman's, to induce the cows to let down their milk, Clare had seemed to like 'Cupid's Gardens,' 'I have parks, I have hounds,' and 'The break o' the day'; and had seemed not to care for 'The Tailor's Breeches,' and 'Such a beauty I did grow,' excellent ditties as they were.

To perfect the ballads was now her whimsical desire. She practised them privately at odd moments, especially 'The break o' the day' –

Arise, arise, arise!

And pick your love a posy,
All o' the sweetest flowers
That in the garden grow.
The turtle doves and sma' birds
In every bough a-building,
So early in the Maytime
At the break o' the day!

It would have melted the heart of a stone to hear her singing these ditties, whenever she worked apart from the rest of the girls in this cold dry time; the tears running down her cheeks all the while at the thought that perhaps he would not, after all, come to hear her, and the simple silly words of the songs resounding in painful mockery of the aching heart of the singer.

Tess was so wrapped up in this fanciful dream that she seemed not to know how the season was advancing; that the days had lengthened, that Lady-Day was at hand, and would soon be followed by Old Lady-Day, the end of her term here.

But before the quarter-day had quite come something happened which made Tess think of far different matters. She was at her lodging as usual one evening, sitting in the downstairs room with the rest of the family, when somebody knocked at the door and enquired for Tess. Through the doorway she saw against the declining light a figure with the height of a woman and the breadth of a child, a tall, thin, girlish creature whom she did not recognise in the twilight till the girl said 'Tess!'

'What – is it 'Liza-Lu?' asked Tess, in startled accents. Her sister, whom a little over a year ago she had left at home as a child, had sprung up by a sudden shoot to a form of this presentation, of which as yet Lu seemed herself scarce able to understand the meaning. Her thin legs, visible below her once long frock, now short by her growing, and her uncomfortable hands and arms, revealed her youth and inexperience.

'Yes I have been traipsing about all day, Tess,' said Lu, with unemotional gravity, 'a-trying to find 'ee; and I'm very tired.'

'What is the matter at home?'

'Mother is took very bad, and the doctor says she's dying, and as father is not very well neither, and says 'tis wrong for a man of such a high family as his to slave and drave at common labouring work, we don't know what to do.'

Tess stood in reverie a long time before she thought of asking 'Liza-Lu to come in and sit down. When she had done so, and 'Liza-Lu was having some tea, she came to a decision. It was imperative that she should go home. Her agreement did not end till Old Lady-Day, the sixth of April, but as the interval thereto was not a long one she resolved to run the risk of starting at once.

To go that night would be a gain of twelve hours; but her sister was too tired to undertake such a distance till the morrow. Tess ran down to where Marian and Izz lived, informed them of what had happened, and begged them to make the best of her case to the farmer. Returning, she got Lu a supper, and after that, having tucked the younger into her own bed, packed up as many of her belongings as would go into a withy basket, and started, directing Lu to follow her next morning.

## *Chapter 50*

She plunged into the chilly equinoctial darkness as the clock struck ten, for her fifteen miles' walk under the steely stars. In lonely districts night is a protection rather than a danger to a noiseless pedestrian, and knowing this Tess pursued the nearest course along by-lanes that she would almost have feared in the daytime; but marauders were wanting now, and spectral fears were driven out of her mind by thoughts of her mother. Thus she proceeded mile after mile, ascending and descending till she came to Bulbarrow, and about midnight looked from that height into the abyss of chaotic shade which was all that revealed itself of the vale on whose further side she was born. Having already traversed about five miles on the upland she had now some ten or eleven in the lowland before her journey would be finished. The winding road downwards became just visible to her under the wan starlight as she followed it, and soon she paced a soil so contrasting with that above it that the difference was perceptible to the tread and to the smell. It was the heavy clay land of Blackmoor Vale, and a part of the Vale to which turnpike-roads had never penetrated. Superstitions linger longest on these heavy soils. Having once been forest, at this shadowy time it seemed to assert something of its old character, the far and the near being blended, and every tree and tall hedge making the most of its presence. The harts that had been hunted here, the witches that had been pricked and ducked, the green-spangled fairies that 'whickered' at you as you passed; – the place teemed with beliefs in them still, and they formed an impish multitude now.

At Nuttlebury she passed the village inn, whose sign creaked in response to the greeting of her footsteps, which not a human soul heard but herself. Under the thatched roofs her mind's eye beheld relaxed tendons and flaccid muscles, spread out in the darkness beneath coverlets made of little purple patchwork squares, and undergoing a bracing process at the hands of sleep for renewed labour on the morrow, as soon as a hint of pink nebulosity appeared on Hambledon Hill.

At three she turned the last corner of the maze of lanes she had threaded, and entered Marlott, passing the field in which, as a club-girl, she had first seen Angel Clare, when he had not danced with her; the sense of disappointment remained with her yet. In the direction of her mother's house she saw a light. It came from the bedroom window, and a branch waved in front of it and made it wink at her. As soon as she could discern the outline of the house – newly thatched with her money – it had all its old effect upon Tess's imagination. Part of her body and life it ever seemed to be; the slope of its dormers, the finish of its gables, the broken courses of brick which topped the chimney, all had something in common with her personal character. A stupefaction had come into these features, to her regard; it meant the illness of her mother.

She opened the door so softly as to disturb nobody; the lower room was vacant, but the neighbour who was sitting up with her mother came to the top of the stairs, and whispered that Mrs Durbeyfield was no better, though she was sleeping just then. Tess prepared herself a breakfast, and then took her place as nurse in her mother's chamber.

In the morning, when she contemplated the children, they had all a curiously elongated look; although she had been away little more than a year their growth was astounding; and the necessity of applying herself heart and soul to their needs took her out of her own cares.

Her father's ill-health was of the same indefinite kind, and he sat in his chair as usual. But the day after her arrival he was unusually bright. He had a rational scheme for living, and Tess asked him what it was.

'I'm thinking of sending round to all the old antiqueerians in this part of England,' he said, 'asking them to subscribe to a fund to maintain me. I'm sure they'd see it as a romantical, artistical, and proper thing to do. They spend lots o' money in keeping up old ruins, and finding the bones o' things, and such like; and living remains must be more interesting to 'em still, if they only knowed of me. Would that somebody would go round and tell 'em what there is living among 'em, and they thinking nothing of him! If Pa'son Tringham, who discovered me, had lived, he'd ha' done it, I'm sure.'

Tess postponed her arguments on this high project till she had grappled with pressing matters in hand, which seemed little improved by her remittances. When indoor necessities had been eased she turned her attention to external things. It was now the season for planting and sowing; many gardens and allotments of the villagers had already received their spring tillage; but the garden and the allotment of the Durbeyfields were behindhand. She found, to her dismay, that this was owing to their having eaten all the seed potatoes, – that last lapse of the improvident. At the earliest moment she obtained what others she could procure, and in a few days her father was well enough to see to the garden, under Tess's persuasive efforts: while she herself undertook the allotment-plot which they rented in a field a couple of hundred yards out of the village.

She liked doing it after the confinement of the sick chamber, where she was not now required by reason of her mother's improvement. Violent motion relieved thought. The plot of ground was in a high, dry, open enclosure, where there were forty or fifty such pieces, and where labour was at its briskest when the hired labour of the day had ended. Digging began usually at six o'clock, and extended indefinitely into the dusk or moonlight. Just now heaps of dead weeds and refuse were burning on many of the plots, the dry weather favouring their combustion.

One fine day Tess and 'Liza-Lu worked on here with their neighbours till the last rays of the sun smote flat upon the white pegs that divided the plots. As soon as twilight succeeded to sunset the flare of the couch-grass and cabbage-stalk fires began to light up the allotments fitfully, their outlines appearing and disappearing under the dense smoke as wafted by the wind. When a fire glowed, banks of smoke, blown level along the ground, would themselves become illuminated to an opaque lustre, screening the workpeople from one another; and the meaning of the 'pillar of a cloud', which was a wall by day and a light by night, could be understood.

As evening thickened some of the gardening men and women gave over for the night, but the greater number remained to get their planting done, Tess being among them, though she sent her sister home. It was on one of the couch-burning plots that she laboured with her fork, its four shining prongs resounding against the stones and dry clods in little clicks. Sometimes she was completely involved in the smoke of her fire; then it would leave her figure free, irradiated by the brassy glare from the heap. She was oddly dressed tonight, and presented a somewhat staring aspect, her attire being a gown bleached by many washings, with a short black jacket over it, the effect of the whole being that of a wedding and funeral guest in one. The women further back wore white aprons, which, with their pale faces, were all that could be seen of them in the gloom, except when at moments they caught a flash from the flames.

Westward, the wiry boughs of the bare thorn hedge which formed the boundary of the field rose against the pale opalescence of the lower sky. Above, Jupiter hung like a full-blown jonquil, so bright as almost to throw a shade. A few small nondescript stars were appearing elsewhere. In the distance a dog barked, and wheels occasionally rattled along the dry road.

Still the prongs continued to click assiduously, for it was not late; and though the air was fresh and keen there was a whisper of spring in it that cheered the workers on. Something in the place, the hour, the crackling fires, the fantastic mysteries of light and shade, made others as well as Tess enjoy being there. Nightfall, which in the frost of winter comes as a fiend and in the warmth of summer as a lover, came as a tranquilliser on this March day.

Nobody looked at his or her companions. The eyes of all were on the soil as its turned surface was revealed by the fires. Hence as Tess stirred the clods, and sang her foolish little songs with scarce now a hope that Clare would ever hear them, she did not for a long time notice the person who worked nearest to her – a man in a long smockfrock who, she found, was forking the same plot as herself, and whom she supposed her father had sent there to advance the work. She became more conscious of him when the direction of his digging brought him closer. Sometimes the smoke divided them; then it swerved, and the two were visible to each other but divided from all the rest.

Tess did not speak to her fellow-worker, nor did he speak to her. Nor did she think of him further than to recollect that he had not been there when it was broad daylight, and that she did not know him as any one of the Marlott labourers, which was no wonder, her absences having been so long and frequent of late years. By and by he dug so close to her that the fire-beams were reflected as distinctly from the steel prongs of his fork as from her own.

On going up to the fire to throw a pitch of dead weeds upon it, she found that he did the same on the other side. The fire flared up, and she beheld the face of d'Urberville.

The unexpectedness of his presence, the grotesqueness of his appearance in a gathered smockfrock, such as was now worn only by the most old-fashioned of the labourers, had a ghastly comicality that chilled her as to its bearing. D'Urberville emitted a low long laugh.

'If I were inclined to joke I should say, How much this seems like Paradise!' he remarked whimsically, looking at her with an inclined head.

'What do you say?' she weakly asked.

'A jester might say this is just like Paradise. You are Eve, and I am the old Other One come to tempt you in the disguise of an inferior animal. I used to be quite up in that scene of Milton's when I was theological. Some of it goes –

> "Empress, the way is ready, and not long,
> Beyond a row of myrtles . . . . . . If thou accept
> My conduct, I can bring thee thither soon."
> "Lead then," said Eve.

And so on. My dear, dear Tess, I am only putting this to you as a thing that you might have supposed or said quite untruly, because you think so badly of me.'

'I never said you were Satan, or thought it. I don't think of you in that way at all. My thoughts of you are quite cold, except when you affront me. What, did you come digging here entirely because of me?'

'Entirely. To see you; nothing more. The smockfrock, which I saw hanging for sale as I came along, was an afterthought, that I mightn't be noticed. I come to protest against your working like this.'

'But I like doing it – it is for my father.'

'Your engagement at the other place is ended?'

'Yes.'

'Where are you going to next? To join your dear husband?'

She could not bear the humiliating reminder.

'O – I don't know!' she said bitterly. 'I have no husband!'

'It is quite true – in the sense you mean. But you have a friend, and I have determined that you shall be comfortable in spite of yourself. When you get down to your house you will see what I have sent there for you.'

'O, Alec, I wish you wouldn't give me anything at all! I cannot take it from you! I don't like – it is not right!'

'It *is* right!' he cried lightly. 'I am not going to see a woman whom I feel so tenderly for as I do for you, in trouble without trying to help her.'

'But I am very well off! I am only in trouble about – about – not about living at all!'

She turned, and desperately resumed her digging, tears dripping upon the fork-handle and upon the clods.

'About the children – your brothers and sisters,' he resumed. 'I've been thinking of them.'

Tess's heart quivered – he was touching her in a weak place. He had divined her chief anxiety. Since returning home her soul had gone out to those children with an affection that was passionate.

'If your mother does not recover, somebody ought to do something for them; since your father will not be able to do much, I suppose?'

'He can with my assistance. He must!'

'And with mine.'

'No, sir!'

'How damned foolish this is!' burst out d'Urberville. 'Why, he thinks we are the same family; and will be quite satisfied!'

'He don't. I've undeceived him.'

'The more fool you!'

D'Urberville in anger retreated from her to the hedge, where he pulled off the long smockfrock which had disguised him; and rolling it up and pushing it into the couch-fire, went away.

Tess could not get on with her digging after this; she felt restless; she wondered if he had gone back to her father's house; and taking the fork in her hand proceeded homewards.

Some twenty yards from the house she was met by one of her sisters.

'O, Tessy – what do you think! 'Liza-Lu is a-crying, and there's a lot of folk in the house, and mother is a good deal better, but they think father is dead!'

The child realised the grandeur of the news; but not as yet its sadness; and stood looking at Tess with round-eyed importance, till, beholding the effect produced upon her, she said – 'What, Tess, shan't we talk to father never no more?'

'But father was only a little bit ill!' exclaimed Tess distractedly.

'Liza-Lu came up.

'He dropped down just now, and the doctor who was there for mother said there was no chance for him, because his heart was growed in.'

Yes; the Durbeyfield couple had changed places; the dying one was out of danger, and the indisposed one was dead. The news meant even more than it sounded. Her father's life had a value apart from his personal achievements, or perhaps it would not have had much. It was the last of the three lives for whose duration the house and premises were held under a lease; and it had long been coveted by the tenant-farmer for his regular labourers, who were stinted in cottage accommodation. Moreover, 'liviers' were disapproved of in villages almost as much as little freeholders, because of their independence of manner, and when a lease determined it was never renewed.

Thus the Durbeyfields, once d'Urbervilles, saw descending upon them the destiny which, no doubt, when they were among the Olympians of the county, they had caused to descend many a time, and severely enough, upon the heads of such landless ones as they themselves were now. So do flux and reflux – the rhythm of change – alternate and persist in everything under the sky.

## *Chapter 51*

At length it was the eve of Old Lady-Day, and the agricultural world was in a fever of mobility such as only occurs at that particular date of the year. It is a day of fulfilment; agreements for outdoor service during the ensuing year, entered into at Candlemas, are to be now carried out. The labourers – or 'workfolk,' as they used to call themselves immemorially till the other word was introduced from without – who wish to remain no longer in old places are removing to the new farms. These annual migrations from farm to farm were on the increase here. When Tess's mother was a child the majority of the field-folk about Marlott had remained all their lives on one farm, which had been the home also of their fathers and grandfathers; but latterly the desire for yearly removal had risen to a high pitch. With the younger families it was a pleasant excitement which might possibly be an advantage. The Egypt of one family was the Land of Promise to the family who saw it from a distance, till by residence there it became in turn their Egypt also; and so they changed and changed.

However, all the mutations so increasingly discernible in village life did not originate entirely in the agricultural unrest. A depopulation was also going on. The village had formerly contained, side by side with the agricultural labourers, an interesting and better-informed class, ranking distinctly above the former – the class to which Tess's father and mother had belonged – and including the carpenter, the smith, the shoemaker, the huckster, together with nondescript workers other than farm-labourers; a set of people who owed a certain stability of aim and conduct to the fact of their being life-holders like Tess's father, or copyholders, or, occasionally, small freeholders. But as the long holdings fell in they were seldom again let to similar tenants, and were mostly pulled down, if not absolutely required by the farmer for his hands. Cottagers who were not directly employed on the land were looked upon with disfavour, and the banishment of some starved the trade of others, who were thus obliged to follow. These families, who had formed the backbone of the village life in the past, who were the depositaries of the village traditions, had to seek refuge in the large centres; the process, humorously designated by statisticians as 'the tendency of the rural population towards the large towns', being really the tendency of water to flow uphill when forced by machinery.

The cottage accommodation at Marlott having been in this manner considerably curtailed by demolitions, every house which remained standing was required by the agriculturist for his work-people. Ever since the occurrence of the event which had cast such a shadow over Tess's life, the Durbeyfield family (whose descent was not credited) had been tacitly looked on as one which would have to go when their lease ended, if only in the interests of morality. It was, indeed, quite true that the household had not been shining examples either of temperance, soberness, or chastity. The father, and even the mother, had got drunk at times, the younger children seldom had gone to church, and the eldest daughter had made queer unions. By some means the village had to be kept pure. So on this, the first Lady-Day on which the Durbeyfields were expellable, the house, being roomy, was required for a carter with a large family; and Widow Joan, her daughters Tess and 'Liza-Lu, the boy Abraham and the younger children, had to go elsewhere.

On the evening preceding their removal it was getting dark betimes by reason of a drizzling rain which blurred the sky. As it was the last night they would spend in the village which had been their home and birthplace, Mrs Durbeyfield, 'Liza-Lu, and Abraham had gone out to bid some friends goodbye, and Tess was keeping house till they should return.

She was kneeling in the window-bench, her face close to the casement, where an outer pane of rainwater was sliding down the inner pane of glass. Her eyes rested on the web of a spider, probably starved long ago, which had been mistakenly placed in a corner where no flies ever came, and shivered in the slight draught through the casement. Tess was reflecting on the position of the household, in which she perceived her own evil influence. Had she not come home her mother and the children might probably have been allowed to stay on as weekly tenants. But she had been observed almost immediately on her return by some people of scrupulous character and great influence: they had seen her idling in the churchyard, restoring as well as she could with a little trowel a baby's obliterated grave. By this means they had found that she was living here again; her mother was scolded for 'harbouring' her; sharp retorts had ensued from Joan, who had independently offered to leave at once; she had been taken at her word; and here was the result.

'I ought never to have come home,' said Tess to herself, bitterly.

She was so intent upon these thoughts that she hardly at first took note of a man in a white mackintosh whom she saw riding down the street. Possibly it was owing to her face being near to the pane that he saw her so quickly, and directed his horse so close to the cottage-front that his hoofs were almost upon the narrow border for plants growing under the wall. It was not till he touched the window with his riding-crop that she observed him. The rain had nearly ceased, and she opened the casement in obedience to his gesture.

'Didn't you see me?' asked d'Urberville.

'I was not attending,' she said. 'I heard you, I believe, though I fancied it was a carriage and horses. I was in a sort of dream.'

'Ah! you heard the d'Urberville Coach, perhaps. You know the legend, I suppose?'

'No. My – somebody was going to tell it me once, but didn't.'

'If you are a genuine d'Urberville I ought not to tell you either, I suppose. As for me, I'm a sham one, so it doesn't matter. It is rather dismal. It is that this sound of a non-existent coach can only be heard by one of d'Urberville blood, and it is held to be of ill-omen to the one who hears it. It has to do with a murder, committed by one of the family centuries ago.'

'Now you have begun it, finish it.'

'Very well. One of the family is said to have abducted some beautiful woman, who tried to escape from the coach in which he was carrying her off, and in the struggle he killed her – or she killed him – I forget which. Such is one version of the tale . . . I see that your tubs and buckets are packed. Going away, aren't you?'

'Yes, tomorrow – old Lady-Day.'

'I heard you were, but could hardly believe it; it seems so sudden. Why is it?'

'Father's was the last life on the property, and when that dropped we had no further right to stay. Though we might, perhaps, have stayed as weekly tenants – if it had not been for me.'

'What about you?'

'I am not a – proper woman.'

D'Urberville's face flushed.

'What a blasted shame! Miserable snobs! May their dirty souls be burnt to cinders!' he exclaimed in tones of ironic resentment. 'That's why you are going, is it? Turned out?'

'We are not turned out exactly; but as they said we should have to go soon, it was best to go now everybody was moving, because there are better chances.'

'Where are you going to?'

'Kingsbere. We have taken rooms there. Mother is so foolish about father's people that she will go there.'

'But your mother's family are not fit for lodgings, and in a little hole of a town like that. Now why not come to my garden-house at Trantridge? There are hardly any poultry now, since my mother's death; but there's the house, as you know it, and the garden. It can be whitewashed in a day, and your mother can live there quite comfortably; and I will put the children to a good school. Really I ought to do something for you!'

'But we have already taken the rooms at Kingsbere!' she declared. 'And we can wait there – '

'Wait – what for? For that nice husband, no doubt. Now look here, Tess, I know what men are, and, bearing in mind the *grounds* of your separation, I am quite positive he will never make it up with you. Now, though I have been your enemy, I am your friend, even if you won't believe it. Come to this cottage of mine. We'll get up a regular colony of fowls, and your mother can attend to them excellently; and the children can go to school.'

Tess breathed more and more quickly, and at length she said – 'How do I know that you would do all this? Your views may change – and then – we should be – my mother would be – homeless again.'

'O no – no. I would guarantee you against such as that in writing, if necessary. Think it over.'

Tess shook her head. But d'Urberville persisted; she had seldom seen him so determined; he would not take a negative.

'Please just tell your mother,' he said, in emphatic tones. 'It is her business to judge – not yours. I shall get the house swept out and whitened tomorrow morning, and fires lit; and it will be dry by the evening, so that you can come straight there. Now mind, I shall expect you.'

Tess again shook her head; her throat swelling with complicated emotion. She could not look up at d'Urberville.

'I owe you something for the past, you know,' he resumed. 'And you cured me, too, of that craze; so I am glad – '

'I would rather you had kept the craze, so that you had kept the practice which went with it!'

'I am glad of this opportunity of repaying you a little. Tomorrow I shall expect to hear your mother's goods unloading . . . Give me your hand on it now – dear, beautiful Tess!'

With the last sentence he had dropped his voice to a murmur, and put his hand in at the half-open casement. With stormy eyes she pulled the stay-bar quickly, and, in doing so, caught his arm between the casement and the stone mullion.

'Damnation – you are very cruel!' he said, snatching out his arm. 'No, no! – I know you didn't do it on purpose. Well, I shall expect you, or your mother and the children at least.'

'I shall not come – I have plenty of money!' she cried.

'Where?'

'At my father-in-law's, if I ask for it.'

'*If* you ask for it. But you won't, Tess; I know you; you'll never ask for it – you'll starve first!'

With these words he rode off. Just at the corner of the street he met the man with the paint-pot, who asked him if he had deserted the brethren.

'You go to the devil!' said d'Urberville.

Tess remained where she was a long while, till a sudden rebellious sense of injustice caused the region of her eyes to swell with the rush of hot tears thither. Her husband, Angel Clare himself, had, like others, dealt out hard measure to her, surely he had! She had never before admitted such a thought; but he had surely! Never in her life – she could swear it from the bottom of her soul – had she ever intended to do wrong; yet these hard judgments had come. Whatever her sins, they were not sins of intention, but of inadvertence, and why should she have been punished so persistently?

She passionately seized the first piece of paper that came to hand, and scribbled the following lines:

> O why have you treated me so monstrously, Angel! I do not deserve it. I have thought it all over carefully, and I can never, never forgive you! You know that I did not intend to wrong you – why have you so wronged me? You are cruel, cruel indeed! I will try to forget you. It is all injustice I have received at your hands!
>
> T

She watched till the postman passed by, ran out to him with her epistle, and then again took her listless place inside the window-panes.

It was just as well to write like that as to write tenderly. How could he give way to entreaty? The facts had not changed: there was no new event to alter his opinion.

It grew darker, the firelight shining over the room. The two biggest of the younger children had gone out with their mother; the four smallest, their ages ranging from three and a half years to eleven, all in black frocks, were gathered round the hearth babbling their own little subjects. Tess at length joined them, without lighting a candle.

'This is the last night that we shall sleep here, dears, in the house where we were born,' she said quickly. 'We ought to think of it, oughtn't we?'

They all became silent; with the impressibility of their age they were ready to burst into tears at the picture of finality she had conjured up, though all the day hitherto they had been rejoicing in the idea of a new place. Tess changed the subject.

'Sing to me, dears,' she said.

'What shall we sing?'

'Anything you know; I don't mind.'

There was a momentary pause; it was broken, first, by one little tentative note; then a second voice strengthened it, and a third and a fourth chimed in in unison, with words they had learnt at the Sunday-school –

Here we suffer grief and pain,
Here we meet to part again;
In Heaven we part no more.

The four sang on with the phlegmatic passivity of persons who had long ago settled the question, and there being no mistake about it, felt that further thought was not required. With features strained hard to enunciate the syllables they continued to regard the centre of the flickering fire, the notes of the youngest straying over into the pauses of the rest.

Tess turned from them, and went to the window again. Darkness had now fallen without, but she put her face to the pane as though to peer into the gloom. It was really to hide her tears. If she could only believe what the children were singing; if she were only sure, how different all would now be; how confidently she would leave them to Providence and their future kingdom! But, in default of that, it behoved her to do something; to be their Providence; for to Tess, as to not a few millions of others, there was ghastly satire in the poet's lines –

Not in utter nakedness
But trailing clouds of glory do we come.

To her and her like, birth itself was an ordeal of degrading personal compulsion, whose gratuitousness nothing in the result seemed to justify, and at best could only palliate.

In the shades of the wet road she soon discerned her mother with tall 'Liza-Lu and Abraham. Mrs Durbeyfield's pattens clicked up to the door, and Tess opened it.

'I see the tracks of a horse outside the window,' said Joan. 'Hev somebody called?'

'No,' said Tess.

The children by the fire looked gravely at her, and one murmured – 'Why, Tess, the gentleman a-horseback!'

'He didn't call,' said Tess. 'He spoke to me in passing.'

'Who was the gentleman?' asked her mother. 'Your husband?'

'No. He'll never, never come,' answered Tess in stony hopelessness.

'Then who was it?'

'Oh, you needn't ask. You've seen him before, and so have I.'

'Ah! What did he say?' said Joan curiously.

'I will tell you when we are settled in our lodgings at Kingsbere tomorrow – every word.'

It was not her husband, she had said. Yet a consciousness that in a physical sense this man alone was her husband seemed to weigh on her more and more.

## *Chapter 52*

During the small hours of the next morning, while it was still dark, dwellers near the highways were conscious of a disturbance of their night's rest by rumbling noises, intermittently continuing till daylight – noises as certain to recur in this particular first week of the month as the voice of the cuckoo in the third week of the same. They were the preliminaries of the general removal, the passing of the empty waggons and teams to fetch the goods of the migrating families; for it was always by the vehicle of the farmer who required his services that the hired man was conveyed to his destination. That this might be accomplished within the day was the explanation of the reverberation occurring so soon after midnight, the aim of the carters being to reach the door of the outgoing households by six o'clock, when the loading of their movables at once began.

But to Tess and her mother's household no such anxious farmer sent his team. They were only women; they were not regular labourers; they were not particularly required anywhere; hence they had to hire a waggon at their own expense, and got nothing sent gratuitously.

It was a relief to Tess, when she looked out of the window that morning, to find that though the weather was windy and louring, it did not rain, and that the waggon had come. A wet Lady-Day was a spectre which removing families never forgot; damp furniture, damp bedding, damp clothing accompanied it, and left a train of ills.

Her mother, 'Liza-Lu, and Abraham were also awake, but the younger children were let sleep on. The four breakfasted by the thin light, and the 'house-ridding' was taken in hand.

It proceeded with some cheerfulness, a friendly neighbour or two assisting. When the large articles of furniture had been packed in position a circular nest was made of the beds and bedding, in which Joan Durbeyfield and the young children were to sit through the journey. After loading there was a long delay before the horses were brought, these having been unharnessed during the ridding; but at length, about two o'clock, the whole was under way, the cooking-pot swinging from the axle of the waggon, Mrs Durbeyfield and family at the top, the matron having in her lap, to prevent injury to its works, the head of the clock, which, at any exceptional lurch of the waggon, struck one, or one and a half, in hurt tones. Tess and the next eldest girl walked alongside till they were out of the village.

They had called on a few neighbours that morning and the previous evening, and some came to see them off, all wishing them well, though, in their secret hearts, hardly expecting welfare possible to such a family, harmless as the Durbeyfields were to all except themselves. Soon the equipage began to ascend to higher ground, and the wind grew keener with the change of level and soil.

The day being the sixth of April, the Durbeyfield waggon met many other waggons with families on the summit of the load, which was built on a wellnigh unvarying principle, as peculiar, probably, to the rural labourer as the hexagon to the bee. The groundwork of the arrangement was the family dresser, which, with its shining handles, and fingermarks, and domestic evidences thick upon it, stood importantly in front, over the tails of the shaft-horses, in its erect and natural position, like some Ark of the Covenant that they were bound to carry reverently.

Some of the households were lively, some mournful; some were stopping at the doors of wayside inns; where, in due time, the Durbeyfield menagerie also drew up to bait horses and refresh the travellers.

During the halt Tess's eyes fell upon a three-pint blue mug, which was ascending and descending through the air to and from the feminine section of a household, sitting on the summit of a load that had also drawn up at a little distance from the same inn. She followed one of the mug's journeys upward, and perceived it to be clasped by hands whose owner she well knew. Tess went towards the waggon.

'Marian and Izz!' she cried to the girls, for it was they, sitting with the moving family at whose house they had lodged. 'Are you house-ridding today, like everybody else?'

They were, they said. It had been too rough a life for them at Flintcomb-Ash, and they had come away, almost without notice, leaving Groby to prosecute them if he chose. They told Tess their destination, and Tess told them hers.

Marian leant over the load, and lowered her voice. 'Do you know that the gentleman who follows 'ee – you'll guess who I mean – came to ask for 'ee at Flintcomb after you had gone? We didn't tell'n where you was, knowing you wouldn't wish to see him.'

'Ah – but I did see him!' Tess murmured. 'He found me.'

'And do he know where you be going?'

'I think so.'

'Husband come back?'

'No.'

She bade her acquaintance goodbye – for the respective carters had now come out from the inn – and the two waggons resumed their journey in opposite directions; the vehicle whereon sat Marian, Izz, and the ploughman's family with whom they had thrown in their lot, being brightly painted, and drawn by three powerful horses with shining brass ornaments on their harness; while the waggon on which Mrs Durbeyfield and her family rode was a creaking erection that would scarcely bear the weight of the superincumbent load; one which had known no paint since it was made, and drawn by two horses only. The contrast well marked the difference between being fetched by a thriving farmer and conveying oneself whither no hirer waited one's coming.

The distance was great – too great for a day's journey – and it was with the utmost difficulty that the horses performed it. Though they had started so early it was quite late in the afternoon when they turned the flank of an eminence which formed part of the upland called Greenhill. While the horses stood to stale and breathe themselves Tess looked around. Under the hill, and just ahead of them, was the half-dead townlet of their pilgrimage, Kingsbere, where lay those ancestors of whom her father had spoken and sung to painfulness: Kingsbere, the spot of all spots in the world which could be considered the d'Urbervilles' home, since they had resided there for full five hundred years.

A man could be seen advancing from the outskirts towards them, and when he beheld the nature of their waggon-load he quickened his steps.

'You be the woman they call Mrs Durbeyfield, I reckon?' he said to Tess's mother, who had descended to walk the remainder of the way.

She nodded. 'Though widow of the late Sir John d'Urberville, poor nobleman, if I cared for my rights; and returning to the domain of his forefathers.'

'Oh? Well, I know nothing about that; but if you be Mrs Durbeyfield, I am sent to tell 'ee that the rooms you wanted be let. We didn't know that you was coming till we got your letter this morning – when 'twas too late. But no doubt you can get other lodgings somewhere.'

The man had noticed the face of Tess, which had become ash-pale at his intelligence. Her mother looked hopelessly at fault. 'What shall we do now, Tess?' she said bitterly. 'Here's a welcome to your ancestors' lands! However, let's try further.'

They moved on into the town, and tried with all their might, Tess remaining with the waggon to take care of the children whilst her mother and 'Liza-Lu made enquiries. At the last return of Joan to the vehicle, an hour later, when her search for accommodation had still been fruitless, the driver of the waggon said the goods must be unloaded, as the horses were half-dead, and he was bound to return part of the way at least that night.

'Very well – unload it here,' said Joan recklessly. 'I'll get shelter somewhere.'

The waggon had drawn up under the churchyard wall, in a spot screened from view, and the driver, nothing loth, soon hauled down the poor heap of household goods. This done she paid him, reducing herself to almost her last shilling thereby, and he moved off and left them, only too glad to get out of further dealings with such a family. It was a dry night, and he guessed that they would come to no harm.

Tess gazed desperately at the pile of furniture. The cold sunlight of this spring evening peered invidiously upon the crocks and kettles, upon the bunches of dried herbs shivering in the breeze, upon the brass handles of the dresser, upon the wicker-cradle they had all been rocked in, and upon the well-rubbed clock-case, all of which gave out the reproachful gleam of indoor articles abandoned to the vicissitudes of a roofless exposure for which they were never made. Round about were deparked hills and slopes – now cut up into little paddocks – and the green foundations that showed where the d'Urberville mansion once had stood; also an outlying stretch of Egdon Heath that had always belonged to the estate. Hard by, the aisle of the church called the d'Urberville Aisle looked on imperturbably.

'Isn't your family vault your own freehold?' said Tess's mother, as she returned from a reconnoitre of the church and graveyard. 'Why, of course 'tis, and that's where we will camp, girls, till the place of your ancestors finds us a roof! Now, Tess and 'Liza and Abraham, you help me. We'll make a nest for these children, and then we'll have another look round.'

Tess listlessly lent a hand, and in a quarter of an hour the old four-post bedstead was dissociated from the heap of goods, and erected under the south wall of the church, the part of the building known as the d'Urberville Aisle, beneath which the huge vaults lay. Over the tester of the bedstead was a beautifully traceried window, of many lights, its date being the fifteenth century. It was called the d'Urberville Window, and in the upper part could be discerned heraldic emblems like those on Durbeyfield's old seal and spoon.

Joan drew the curtains round the bed so as to make an excellent tent of it, and put the smaller children inside. 'If it comes to the worst we can sleep there too, for one night,' she said. 'But let us try further on, and get something for the dears to eat! O, Tess, what's the use of your playing at marrying gentlemen, if it leaves us like this!'

Accompanied by 'Liza-Lu and the boy she again ascended the little lane which secluded the church from the townlet. As soon as they got into the street they beheld a man on horseback gazing up and down. 'Ah – I'm looking for you!' he said, riding up to them. 'This is indeed a family gathering on the historic spot!'

It was Alec d'Urberville. 'Where is Tess?' he asked.

Personally Joan had no liking for Alec. She cursorily signified the direction of the church, and went on, d'Urberville saying that he would see them again, in case they should be still unsuccessful in their search for shelter, of which he had just heard. When they had gone d'Urberville rode to the inn, and shortly after came out on foot.

In the interim Tess, left with the children inside the bedstead, remained talking with them awhile, till, seeing that no more could be done to make them comfortable just then, she walked about the churchyard, now beginning to be embrowned by the shades of nightfall. The door of the church was unfastened, and she entered it for the first time in her life.

Within the window under which the bedstead stood were the tombs of the family, covering in their dates several centuries. They were canopied, altar-shaped, and plain; their carvings being defaced and broken; their brasses torn from the matrices, the rivet-holes remaining like martin-holes in a sand-cliff. Of all the reminders that she had ever received that her people were socially extinct there was none so forcible as this spoliation.

She drew near to a dark stone on which was inscribed:

Ostium sepulchri antiquae familiae d'Urberville.

Tess did not read Church-Latin like a Cardinal, but she knew that this was the door of her ancestral sepulchre, and that the tall knights of whom her father had chanted in his cups lay inside.

She musingly turned to withdraw, passing near an altar-tomb, the oldest of them all, on which was a recumbent figure. In the dusk she had not noticed it before, and would hardly have noticed it now but for an odd fancy that the effigy moved. As soon as she drew close to it she discovered all in a moment that the figure was a living person; and the shock to her sense of not having been alone was so violent that she was quite overcome, and sank down nigh to fainting, not, however, till she had recognised Alec d'Urberville in the form.

He leapt off the slab and supported her.

'I saw you come in,' he said smiling, 'and got up there not to interrupt your meditations. A family gathering, is it not, with these old fellows under us here? Listen.'

He stamped with his heel heavily on the floor; whereupon there arose a hollow echo from below.

'That shook them a bit, I'll warrant!' he continued. 'And you thought I was the mere stone reproduction of one of them. But no. The old order changeth. The little finger of the sham d'Urberville can do more for you than the whole dynasty of the real underneath . . . Now command me. What shall I do?'

'Go away!' she murmured.

'I will – I'll look for your mother,' said he blandly. But in passing her he whispered: 'Mind this; you'll be civil yet!'

When he was gone she bent down upon the entrance to the vaults, and said – 'Why am I on the wrong side of this door!'

In the meantime Marian and Izz Huett had journeyed onward with the chattels of the ploughman in the direction of their land of Canaan – the Egypt of some other family who had left it only that morning. But the girls did not for a long time think of where they were going. Their talk was of Angel Clare and Tess, and Tess's persistent lover, whose connection with her previous history they had partly heard and partly guessed ere this.

' 'Tisn't as though she had never known him afore,' said Marian. 'His having won her once makes all the difference in the world. 'Twould be a thousand pities if he were to tole her away again. Mr Clare can never be anything to us, Izz; and why should we grudge him to her, and not try to mend this quarrel? If he could on'y know what straits she's put to, and what's hovering round, he might come to take care of his own.'

'Could we let him know?'

They thought of this all the way to their destination; but the bustle of re-establishment in their new place took up all their attention then. But when they were settled, a month later, they heard of Clare's approaching return, though they had learnt nothing more of Tess. Upon that, agitated anew by their attachment to him, yet honourably disposed to her, Marian uncorked the penny ink-bottle they shared, and a few lines were concocted between the two girls.

> HONOUR'D SIR – Look to your Wife if you do love her as much as she do love you. For she is sore put to by an Enemy in the shape of a Friend. Sir, there is one near her who ought to be Away. A woman should not be try'd beyond her Strength, and continual dropping will wear away a Stone – ay, more – a Diamond. FROM TWO WELL-WISHERS

This was addressed to Angel Clare at the only place they had ever heard him to be connected with, Emminster Vicarage; after which they continued in a mood of emotional exaltation at their own generosity, which made them sing in hysterical snatches and weep at the same time.

END OF PHASE THE SIXTH

# PHASE THE SEVENTH

## *Fulfilment*

## *Chapter 53*

It was evening at Emminster Vicarage. The two customary candles were burning under their green shades in the Vicar's study, but he had not been sitting there. Occasionally he came in, stirred the small fire which sufficed for the increasing mildness of the spring, and went out again; sometimes pausing at the front door, going on to the drawing-room, then returning again to the front door.

It faced westward, and though gloom prevailed inside, there was still light enough without to see with distinctness. Mrs Clare, who had been sitting in the drawing-room, followed him hither.

'Plenty of time yet,' said the vicar. 'He doesn't reach Chalk-Newton till six, even if the train should be punctual, and ten miles of country-road, five of them in Crimmercrock Lane, are not jogged over in a hurry by our old horse.'

'But he has done it in an hour with us, my dear.'

'Years ago.'

Thus they passed the minutes, each well knowing that this was only waste of breath, the one essential being simply to wait.

At length there was a slight noise in the lane, and the old pony-chaise appeared indeed outside the railings. They saw alight therefrom a form which they affected to recognise, but would actually have passed by in the street without identifying had he not got out of their carriage at the particular moment when a particular person was due.

Mrs Clare rushed through the dark passage to the door, and her husband came more slowly after her.

The new arrival, who was just about to enter, saw their anxious faces in the doorway and the gleam of the west in their spectacles because they confronted the last rays of day; but they could only see his shape against the light.

'O, my boy, my boy – home again at last!' cried Mrs Clare, who cared no more at that moment for the stains of heterodoxy which had caused all this separation than for the dust upon his clothes. What woman, indeed, among the most faithful adherents of the truth, believes the promises and threats of the Word in the sense in which she believes in her own children, or would not throw her theology to the wind if weighed against their happiness? As soon as they reached the room where the candles were lighted she looked at his face.

'O, it is not Angel – not my son – the Angel who went away!' she cried in all the irony of sorrow, as she turned herself aside.

His father, too, was shocked to see him, so reduced was that figure from its former contours by worry and the bad season that Clare had experienced, in the climate to which he had so rashly hurried in his first aversion to the mockery of events at home. You could see the skeleton behind the man, and almost the ghost behind the skeleton. He matched Chrivelli's dead *Christus*. His sunken eye-pits were of morbid hue, and the light in his eyes had waned. The angular hollows and lines of his aged ancestors had succeeded to their reign in his face twenty years before their time.

'I was ill over there, you know,' he said. 'I am all right now.'

As if, however, to falsify this assertion, his legs seemed to give way, and he suddenly sat down to save himself from falling. It was only a slight attack of faintness, resulting from the tedious day's journey, and the excitement of arrival.

'Has any letter come for me lately?' he asked. 'I received the last you sent on by the merest chance, and after considerable delay through being inland; or I might have come sooner.'

'It was from your wife, we supposed?'

'It was.'

Only one other had recently come. They had not sent it on to him, knowing he would start for home so soon.

He hastily opened the letter produced, and was much disturbed to read in Tess's handwriting the sentiments expressed in her last hurried scrawl to him.

> O why have you treated me so monstrously, Angel! I do not deserve it. I have thought it all over carefully, and I can never, never forgive you! You know that I did not intend to wrong you – why have you so wronged me? You are cruel, cruel indeed! I will try to forget you. It is all injustice I have received at your hands.
>
> T

'It is quite true!' said Angel, throwing down the letter. 'Perhaps she will never be reconciled to me!'

'Don't, Angel, be so anxious about a mere child of the soil!' said his mother.

'Child of the soil! Well, we all are children of the soil. I wish she were so in the sense you mean; but let me now explain to you what I have never explained before, that her father is a descendant in the male line of one of the oldest Norman houses, like a good many others who lead obscure agricultural lives in our villages, and are dubbed "sons of the soil".'

He soon retired to bed; and the next morning, feeling exceedingly unwell, he remained in his room pondering. The circumstances amid which he had left Tess were such that though, while on the south of the Equator and just in receipt of her loving epistle, it had seemed the easiest thing in the world to rush back into her arms the moment he chose to forgive her, now that he had arrived it was not so easy as it had seemed. She was passionate, and her present letter, showing that her estimate of him had changed under his delay – too justly changed, he sadly owned, – made him ask himself if it would be wise to confront her unannounced in the presence of her parents. Supposing that her love had indeed turned to dislike during the last weeks of separation, a sudden meeting might lead to bitter words.

Clare therefore thought it would be best to prepare Tess and her family by sending a line to Marlott announcing his return, and his hope that she was still living with them there, as he had arranged for her to do when he left England.

He despatched the enquiry that very day, and before the week was out there came a short reply from Mrs Durbeyfield which did not remove his embarrassment, for it bore no address, though to his surprise it was not written from Marlott.

> SIR – J write these few lines to say that my Daughter is away from me at present, and J am not sure when she will return, but J will let you know as Soon as she do. J do not feel at liberty to tell you Where she is temperly biding. J should say that me and my Family have left Marlott for some Time. – Yours,
>
> J. DURBEYFIELD

It was such a relief to Clare to learn that Tess was at least apparently well that her mother's stiff reticence as to her whereabouts did not long distress him. They were all angry with him, evidently. He would wait till Mrs Durbeyfield could inform him of Tess's return, which her letter implied to be soon. He deserved no more. His had been a love 'which alters when it alteration finds'. He had undergone some strange experiences in his absence; he had seen the virtual Faustina in the literal Cornelia, a spiritual Lucretia in a corporeal Phryne; he had thought of the woman taken and set in the midst as one deserving to be stoned, and of the wife of Uriah being made a queen; and he had asked himself why he had not judged Tess constructively rather than biographically, by the will rather than by the deed?

A day or two passed while he waited at his father's house for the promised second note from Joan Durbeyfield, and indirectly to recover a little more strength. The strength showed signs of coming back, but there was no sign of Joan's letter. Then he hunted up the old letter sent on to him in Brazil, which Tess had written from Flintcomb-Ash, and re-read it. The sentences touched him now as much as when he had first perused them.

> I must cry to you in my trouble – I have no one else . . . I think I must die if you do not come soon, or tell me to come to you . . . Please, please, not to be just – only a little kind to me! . . . If you would come, I could die in your arms! I would be well content to do that if so be you had forgiven me! . . . If you will send me one little line and say, '*I am coming soon*,' I will bide on, Angel – O so cheerfully! . . . Think how it do hurt my heart not to see you ever – ever! Ah, if I could only make your dear heart ache one little minute of each day as mine does every day and all day long, it might lead you to show pity to your poor lonely one . . . I would be content, ay, glad, to live with you as your servant, if I may not as your wife; so that I could only be near you, and get glimpses of you, and think of you as mine . . . I long for only one thing in heaven or earth or under the earth, to meet you, my own dear! Come to me – come to me, and save me from what threatens me.

Clare determined that he would no longer believe in her more recent and severer regard of him; but would go and find her immediately. He asked his father if she had applied for any money during his absence. His father returned a negative, and then for the first time it occurred to Angel that her pride had stood in her way, and that she had suffered privation. From his remarks his parents now gathered the real reason of the separation; and their Christianity was such that, reprobates being their especial care, the tenderness towards Tess which her blood, her simplicity, even her poverty, had not engendered, was instantly excited by her sin.

Whilst he was hastily packing together a few articles for his journey he glanced over a poor plain missive also lately come to hand – the one from Marian and Izz Huett, beginning – 'Honour'd sir – Look to your Wife if you do love her as much as she do love you,' and signed, 'From Two Well-Wishers.'

## *Chapter 54*

In a quarter of an hour Clare was leaving the house, whence his mother watched his thin figure as it disappeared into the street. He had declined to borrow his father's old mare, well knowing of its necessity to the household. He went to the inn, where he hired a trap, and could hardly wait during the harnessing. In a very few minutes after he was driving up the hill out of the town which, three or four months earlier in the year, Tess had descended with such hopes and ascended with such shattered purposes.

Benvill Lane soon stretched before him, its hedges and trees purple with buds; but he was looking at other things, and only recalled himself to the scene sufficiently to enable him to keep the way. In something less than an hour and a half he had skirted the south of the King's Hintock estates and ascended to the untoward solitude of Cross-in-Hand, the unholy stone whereon Tess had been compelled by Alec d'Urberville, in his whim of reformation, to swear the strange oath that she would never wilfully tempt him again. The pale and blasted nettle-stems of the preceding year even now lingered nakedly in the banks, young green nettles of the present spring growing from their roots.

Thence he went along the verge of the upland overhanging the other Hintocks, and, turning to the right, plunged into the bracing calcareous region of Flintcomb-Ash, the address from which she had written to him in one of the letters, and which he supposed to be the place of sojourn referred to by her mother. Here, of course, he did not find her; and what added to his depression was the discovery that no 'Mrs Clare' had ever been heard of by the cottagers or by the farmer himself, though Tess was remembered well enough by her Christian name. His name she had obviously never used during their separation, and her dignified sense of their total severance was shown not much less by this abstention than by the hardships she had chosen to undergo (of which he now learnt for the first time) rather than apply to his father for more funds.

From this place they told him Tess Durbeyfield had gone, without due notice, to the home of her parents on the other side of Blackmoor, and it therefore became necessary to find Mrs Durbeyfield. She had told him she was not now at Marlott, but had been curiously reticent as to her actual address, and the only course was to go to Marlott and enquire for it. The farmer who had been so churlish with Tess was quite smooth-tongued to Clare, and lent him a horse and man to drive him towards Marlott, the gig he had arrived in being sent back to Emminster; for the limit of a day's journey with that horse was reached.

Clare would not accept the loan of the farmer's vehicle for a further distance than to the outskirts of the Vale, and, sending it back with the man who had driven him, he put up at an inn, and next day entered on foot the region wherein was the spot of his dear Tess's birth. It was as yet too early in the year for much colour to appear in the gardens and foliage; the so-called spring was but winter overlaid with a thin coat of greenness, and it was of a parcel with his expectations.

The house in which Tess had passed the years of her childhood was now inhabited by another family who had never known her. The new residents were in the garden, taking as much interest in their own doings as if the homestead had never passed its primal time in conjunction with the histories of others, beside which the histories of these were but as a tale told by an idiot. They walked about the garden paths with thoughts of their own concerns entirely uppermost, bringing their actions at every moment into jarring collision with the dim ghosts behind them, talking as though the time when Tess lived there were not one whit intenser in story than now. Even the spring birds sang over their heads as if they thought there was nobody missing in particular.

On enquiry of these precious innocents, to whom even the name of their predecessors was a failing memory, Clare learned that John Durbeyfield was dead; that his widow and children had left Marlott, declaring that they were going to live at Kingsbere, but instead of doing so had gone on to another place they mentioned. By this time Clare abhorred the house for ceasing to contain Tess, and hastened away from its hated presence without once looking back.

His way was by the field in which he had first beheld her at the dance. It was as bad as the house – even worse. He passed on through the churchyard, where, amongst the new headstones, he saw one of a somewhat superior design to the rest. The inscription ran thus:

In memory of JOHN DURBEYFIELD, rightly d'Urberville, of the once powerful family of that Name, and Direct Descendant through an illustrious Line from Sir Pagan d'Urberville, one of the Knights of the Conqueror. Died March 10th, 18—
HOW ARE THE MIGHTY FALLEN

Some man, apparently the sexton, had observed Clare standing there, and drew nigh. 'Ah, sir, now that's a man who didn't want to lie here, but wished to be carried to Kingsbere, where his ancestors be.'

'And why didn't they respect his wish?'

'Oh – no money. Bless your soul, sir, why – there, I wouldn't wish to say it everywhere, but – even this headstone, for all the flourish wrote upon en, is not paid for.'

'Ah, who put it up?'

The man told the name of a mason in the village, and, on leaving the churchyard, Clare called at the mason's house. He found that the statement was true, and paid the bill. This done he turned in the direction of the migrants.

The distance was too long for a walk, but Clare felt such a strong desire for isolation that at first he would neither hire a conveyance nor go to a circuitous line of railway by which he might eventually reach the place. At Shaston, however, he found he must hire; but the way was such that he did not enter Joan's place till about seven o'clock in the evening, having traversed a distance of over twenty miles since leaving Marlott.

The village being small he had little difficulty in finding Mrs Durbeyfield's tenement, which was a house in a walled garden, remote from the main road, where she had stowed away her clumsy old furniture as best she could. It was plain that for some reason or other she had not wished him to visit her, and he felt his call to be somewhat of an intrusion. She came to the door herself, and the light from the evening sky fell upon her face.

This was the first time that Clare had ever met her, but he was too preoccupied to observe more than that she was still a handsome woman, in the garb of a respectable widow. He was obliged to explain that he was Tess's husband, and his object in coming there, and he did it awkwardly enough. 'I want to see her at once,' he added. 'You said you would write to me again, but you have not done so.'

'Because she've not come home,' said Joan.

'Do you know if she is well?'

'I don't. But you ought to, sir,' said she.

'I admit it. Where is she staying?'

From the beginning of the interview Joan had disclosed her embarrassment by keeping her hand to the side of her cheek.

'I – don't know exactly where she is staying,' she answered. 'She was – but – '

'Where was she?'

'Well, she is not there now.'

In her evasiveness she paused again, and the younger children had by this time crept to the door, where, pulling at his mother's skirts, the youngest murmured: 'Is this the gentleman who is going to marry Tess?'

'He has married her,' Joan whispered. 'Go inside.'

Clare saw her efforts for reticence, and asked: 'Do you think Tess would wish me to try and find her? If not, of course – '

'I don't think she would.'

'Are you sure?'

'I am sure she wouldn't.'

He was turning away; and then he thought of Tess's tender letter.

'I am sure she would!' he retorted passionately. 'I know her better than you do.'

'That's very likely, sir; for I have never really known her.'

'Please tell me her address, Mrs Durbeyfield, in kindness to a lonely wretched man!'

Tess's mother again restlessly swept her cheek with her vertical hand, and seeing that he suffered, she at last said, in a low voice: 'She is at Sandbourne.'

'Ah – where there? Sandbourne has become a large place, they say.'

'I don't know more particularly than I have said – Sandbourne. For myself, I was never there.'

It was apparent that Joan spoke the truth in this, and he pressed her no further.

'Are you in want of anything?' he said gently.

'No, sir,' she replied. 'We are fairly well provided for.'

Without entering the house Clare turned away. There was a station three miles ahead, and paying off his coachman, he walked thither. The last train to Sandbourne left shortly after, and it bore Clare on its wheels.

## *Chapter 55*

At eleven o'clock that night, having secured a bed at one of the hotels and telegraphed his address to his father immediately on his arrival, he walked out into the streets of Sandbourne. It was too late to call on or enquire for anyone, and he reluctantly postponed his purpose till the morning. But he could not retire to rest just yet.

This fashionable watering-place, with its eastern and its western stations, its piers, its groves of pines, its promenades, and its covered gardens, was, to Angel Clare, like a fairy place suddenly created by the stroke of a wand, and allowed to get a little dusty. An outlying eastern tract of the enormous Egdon Waste was close at hand, yet on the very verge of that tawny piece of antiquity such a glittering novelty as this pleasure city had chosen to spring up. Within the space of a mile from its outskirts every irregularity of the soil was prehistoric, every channel an undisturbed British trackway; not a sod having been turned there since the days of the Caesars. Yet the exotic had grown here, suddenly as the prophet's gourd; and had drawn hither Tess.

By the midnight lamps he went up and down the winding way of this new world in an old one, and could discern between the trees and against the stars the lofty roofs, chimneys, gazebos, and towers of the numerous fanciful residences of which the place was composed. It was a city of detached mansions; a Mediterranean lounging-place on the English Channel; and as seen now by night it seemed even more imposing than it was.

The sea was near at hand, but not intrusive; it murmured, and he thought it was the pines; the pines murmured in precisely the same tones, and he thought they were the sea.

Where could Tess possibly be, a cottage-girl, his young wife, amidst all this wealth and fashion? The more he pondered the more was he puzzled. Were there any cows to milk here? There certainly were no fields to till. She was most probably engaged to do something in one of these large houses; and he sauntered along, looking at the chamber-windows and their lights going out one by one; and wondered which of them might be hers.

Conjecture was useless, and just after twelve o'clock he entered and went to bed. Before putting out his light he reread Tess's impassioned letter. Sleep, however, he could not, – so near her, yet so far from her – and he continually lifted the window-blind and regarded the backs of the opposite houses, and wondered behind which of the sashes she reposed at that moment.

He might almost as well have sat up all night. In the morning he arose at seven, and shortly after went out, taking the direction of the chief post-office. At the door he met an intelligent postman coming out with letters for the morning delivery.

'Do you know the address of a Mrs Clare?' asked Angel.

The postman shook his head.

Then, remembering that she would have been likely to continue the use of her maiden name, Clare said – 'Or a Miss Durbeyfield?'

'Durbeyfield?'

This also was strange to the postman addressed.

'There's visitors coming and going every day, as you know, sir,' he said; 'and without the name of the house 'tis impossible to find 'em.'

One of his comrades hastening out at that moment, the name was repeated to him.

'I know no name of Durbeyfield; but there is the name of d'Urberville at The Herons,' said the second.

'That's it!' cried Clare, pleased to think that she had reverted to the real pronunciation. 'What place is The Herons?'

'A stylish lodging-house. 'Tis all lodging-houses here, bless 'ee.'

Clare received directions how to find the house, and hastened thither, arriving with the milkman. The Herons, though an ordinary villa, stood in its own grounds, and was certainly the last place in which one would have expected to find lodgings, so private was its appearance. If poor Tess was a servant here, as he feared, she would go to the backdoor to that milkman, and he was inclined to go thither also. However, in his doubts he turned to the front, and rang.

The hour being early the landlady herself opened the door. Clare enquired for Teresa d'Urberville or Durbeyfield.

'Mrs d'Urberville?'

'Yes.'

Tess, then, passed as a married woman, and he felt glad, even though she had not adopted his name.

'Will you kindly tell her that a relative is anxious to see her?'

'It is rather early. What name shall I give, sir?'

'Angel.'

'Mr Angel?'

'No; Angel. It is my Christian name. She'll understand.'

'I'll see if she is awake.'

He was shown into the front room – the dining-room – and looked out through the spring curtains at the little lawn, and the rhododendrons and other shrubs upon it. Obviously her position was by no means so bad as he had feared, and it crossed his mind that she must somehow have claimed and sold the jewels to attain it. He did not blame her for one moment. Soon his sharpened ear detected footsteps upon the stairs, at which his heart thumped so painfully that he could hardly stand firm. 'Dear me! what will she think of me, so altered as I am!' he said to himself; and the door opened.

Tess appeared on the threshold – not at all as he had expected to see her – bewilderingly otherwise, indeed. Her great natural beauty was, if not heightened, rendered more obvious by her attire. She was loosely wrapped in a cashmere dressing-gown of grey-white, embroidered in half-mourning tints, and she wore slippers of the same hue. Her neck rose out of a frill of down, and her well-remembered cable of dark-brown hair was partially coiled up in a mass at the back of her head and partly hanging on her shoulder – the evident result of haste.

He had held out his arms, but they had fallen again to his side; for she had not come forward, remaining still in the opening of the doorway. Mere yellow skeleton that he was now he felt the contrast between them, and thought his appearance distasteful to her.

'Tess!' he said huskily, 'can you forgive me for going away? Can't you – come to me? How do you get to be – like this?'

'It is too late,' said she, her voice sounding hard through the room, her eyes shining unnaturally.

'I did not think rightly of you – I did not see you as you were!' he continued to plead. 'I have learnt to since, dearest Tessy mine!'

'Too late, too late!' she said, waving her hand in the impatience of a person whose tortures cause every instant to seem an hour. 'Don't come close to me, Angel! No – you must not. Keep away.'

'But don't you love me, my dear wife, because I have been so pulled down by illness? You are not so fickle – I am come on purpose for you – my mother and father will welcome you now!'

'Yes – O, yes, yes! But I say, I say it is too late.'

She seemed to feel like a fugitive in a dream, who tries to move away, but cannot. 'Don't you know all – don't you know it? Yet how do you come here if you do not know?'

'I enquired here and there, and I found the way.'

'I waited and waited for you,' she went on, her tones suddenly resuming their old fluty pathos. 'But you did not come! And I wrote to you, and you did not come! He kept on saying you would never come any more, and that I was a foolish woman. He was very kind to me, and to mother, and to all of us after father's death. He – '

'I don't understand.'

'He has won me back to him.'

Clare looked at her keenly, then, gathering her meaning, flagged like one plague-stricken, and his glance sank; it fell on her hands, which, once rosy, were now white and more delicate.

She continued – 'He is upstairs. I hate him now, because he told me a lie – that you would not come again; and you *have* come! These clothes are what he's put upon me: I didn't care what he did wi' me! But – will you go away, Angel, please, and never come any more?'

They stood fixed, their baffled hearts looking out of their eyes with a joylessness pitiful to see. Both seemed to implore something to shelter them from reality.

'Ah – it is my fault!' said Clare.

But he could not get on. Speech was as inexpressive as silence. But he had a vague consciousness of one thing, though it was not clear to him till later; that his original Tess had spiritually ceased to recognise the body before him as hers – allowing it to drift, like a corpse upon the current, in a direction dissociated from its living will.

A few instants passed, and he found that Tess was gone. His face grew colder and more shrunken as he stood concentrated on the moment, and a minute or two after he found himself in the street, walking along he did not know whither.

## *Chapter 56*

Mrs Brooks, the lady who was the householder at The Herons, and owner of all the handsome furniture, was not a person of an unusually curious turn of mind. She was too deeply materialised, poor woman, by her long and enforced bondage to that arithmetical demon Profit and Loss, to retain much curiosity for its own sake, and apart from possible lodgers' pockets. Nevertheless, the visit of Angel Clare to her well-paying tenants, Mr and Mrs d'Urberville, as she deemed them, was sufficiently exceptional in point of time and manner to reinvigorate the feminine proclivity which had been stifled down as useless save in its bearings to the letting trade.

Tess had spoken to her husband from the doorway, without entering the dining-room, and Mrs Brooks, who stood within the partly-closed door of her own sitting-room at the back of the passage, could hear fragments of the conversation – if conversation it could be called – between those two wretched souls. She heard Tess re-ascend the stairs to the first floor, and the departure of Clare, and the closing of the front door behind him. Then the door of the room above was shut, and Mrs Brooks knew that Tess had re-entered her apartment. As the young lady was not fully dressed, Mrs Brooks knew that she would not emerge again for some time.

She accordingly ascended the stairs softly, and stood at the door of the front room – a drawing-room, connected with the room immediately behind it (which was a bedroom) by folding-doors in the common manner. This first floor, containing Mrs Brooks's best apartments, had been taken by the week by the d'Urbervilles. The back room was now in silence; but from the drawing-room there came sounds.

All that she could at first distinguish of them was one syllable, continually repeated in a low note of moaning, as if it came from a soul bound to some Ixionian wheel – 'O – O – O!'

Then a silence, then a heavy sigh, and again – 'O – O – O!'

The landlady looked through the keyhole. Only a small space of the room inside was visible, but within that space came a corner of the breakfast table, which was already spread for the meal, and also a chair beside. Over the seat of the chair Tess's face was bowed, her posture being a kneeling one in front of it; her hands were clasped over her head, the skirts of her dressing-gown and the embroidery of her nightgown flowed upon the floor behind her, and her stockingless feet, from which the slippers had fallen, protruded upon the carpet. It was from her lips that came the murmur of unspeakable despair.

Then a man's voice from the adjoining bedroom – 'What's the matter?'

She did not answer, but went on, in a tone which was a soliloquy rather than an exclamation, and a dirge rather than a soliloquy. Mrs Brooks could only catch a portion:

'And then my dear, dear husband came home to me . . . and I did not know it! . . . And you had used your cruel persuasion upon me . . . you did not stop using it – no – you did not stop! My little sisters and brothers and my mother's needs – they were the things you moved me by . . . and you said my husband would never come back – never; and you taunted me, and said what a simpleton I was to expect him! . . . And at last I believed you and gave way! . . . And then he came back! Now he is gone. Gone a second time, and I have lost him now for ever . . . and he will not love me the littlest bit ever any more – only hate me! . . . O yes, I have lost him now – again because of – you!' In writhing, with her head on the chair, she turned her face towards the door, and Mrs Brooks could see the pain upon it; and that her lips were bleeding from the clench of her teeth upon them, and that the long lashes of her closed eyes stuck in wet tags to her cheeks. She continued: 'And he is dying – he looks as if he is dying! . . . And my sin will kill him and not kill me! . . . O, you have torn my life all to pieces . . . made me be what I prayed you in pity not to make me be again! . . . My own true husband will never, never – O God – I can't bear this! – I cannot!'

There were more and sharper words from the man; then a sudden rustle; she had sprung to her feet. Mrs Brooks, thinking that the speaker was coming to rush out of the door, hastily retreated down the stairs.

She need not have done so, however, for the door of the sitting-room was not opened. But Mrs Brooks felt it unsafe to watch on the landing again, and entered her own parlour below.

She could hear nothing through the floor, although she listened intently, and thereupon went to the kitchen to finish her interrupted breakfast. Coming up presently to the front room on the ground floor she took up some sewing, waiting for her lodgers to ring that she might take away the breakfast, which she meant to do herself, to discover what was the matter if possible. Overhead, as she sat, she could now hear the floorboards slightly creak, as if someone were walking about, and presently the movement was explained by the rustle of garments against the banisters, the opening and the closing of the front door, and the form of Tess passing to the gate on her way into the street. She was fully dressed now in the walking costume of a well-to-do young lady in which she had arrived, with the sole addition that over her hat and black feathers a veil was drawn.

Mrs Brooks had not been able to catch any word of farewell, temporary or otherwise, between her tenants at the door above. They might have quarrelled, or Mr d'Urberville might still be asleep, for he was not an early riser.

She went into the back room which was more especially her own apartment, and continued her sewing there. The lady lodger did not return, nor did the gentleman ring his bell. Mrs Brooks pondered on the delay, and on what probable relation the visitor who had called so early bore to the couple upstairs. In reflecting she leant back in her chair.

As she did so her eyes glanced casually over the ceiling till they were arrested by a spot in the middle of its white surface which she had never noticed there before. It was about the size of a wafer when she first observed it, but it speedily grew as large as the palm of her hand, and then she could perceive that it was red. The oblong white ceiling, with this scarlet blot in the midst, had the appearance of a gigantic ace of hearts.

Mrs Brooks had strange qualms of misgiving. She got upon the table, and touched the spot in the ceiling with her fingers. It was damp, and she fancied that it was a blood stain.

Descending from the table, she left the parlour, and went upstairs, intending to enter the room overhead, which was the bedchamber at the back of the drawing-room. But, nerveless woman as she had now become, she could not bring herself to attempt the handle. She listened. The dead silence within was broken only by a regular beat.

Drip, drip, drip.

Mrs Brooks hastened downstairs, opened the front door, and ran into the street. A man she knew, one of the workmen employed at an adjoining villa, was passing by, and she begged him to come in and go upstairs with her; she feared something had happened to one of her lodgers. The workman assented, and followed her to the landing.

She opened the door of the drawing-room, and stood back for him to pass in, entering herself behind him. The room was empty; the breakfast – a substantial repast of coffee, eggs, and a cold ham – lay spread upon the table untouched, as when she had taken it up, excepting that the carving-knife was missing. She asked the man to go through the folding-doors into the adjoining room.

He opened the doors, entered a step or two, and came back almost instantly with a rigid face. 'My good God, the gentleman in bed is dead! I think he has been hurt with a knife – a lot of blood has run down upon the floor!'

The alarm was soon given, and the house which had lately been so quiet resounded with the tramp of many footsteps, a surgeon among the rest. The wound was small, but the point of the blade had touched the heart of the victim, who lay on his back, pale, fixed, dead, as if he had scarcely moved after the infliction of the blow. In a quarter of an hour the news that a gentleman who was a temporary visitor to the town had been stabbed in his bed, spread through every street and villa of the popular watering-place.

## *Chapter 57*

Meanwhile Angel Clare had walked automatically along the way by which he had come, and, entering his hotel, sat down over the breakfast, staring at nothingness. He went on eating and drinking unconsciously till on a sudden he demanded his bill; having paid which he took his dressing-bag in his hand, the only luggage he had brought with him, and went out.

At the moment of his departure a telegram was handed to him – a few words from his mother, stating that they were glad to know his address, and informing him that his brother Cuthbert had proposed to and been accepted by Mercy Chant.

Clare crumpled up the paper, and followed the route to the station; reaching it, he found that there would be no train leaving for an hour and more. He sat down to wait, and having waited a quarter of an hour felt that he could wait there no longer. Broken in heart and numbed, he had nothing to hurry for; but he wished to get out of a town which had been the scene of such an experience, and turned to walk to the first station onward, and let the train pick him up there.

The highway that he followed was open, and at a little distance dipped into a valley, across which it could be seen running from edge to edge. He had traversed the greater part of this depression, and was climbing the western acclivity, when, pausing for breath, he unconsciously looked back. Why he did so he could not say, but something seemed to impel him to the act. The tape-like surface of the road diminished in his rear as far as he could see, and as he gazed a moving spot intruded on the white vacuity of its perspective.

It was a human figure running. Clare waited, with a dim sense that somebody was trying to overtake him.

The form descending the incline was a woman's, yet so entirely was his mind blinded to the idea of his wife's following him that even when she came nearer he did not recognise her under the totally changed attire in which he now beheld her. It was not till she was quite close that he could believe her to be Tess.

'I saw you – turn away from the station – just before I got there – and I have been following you all this way!'

She was so pale, so breathless, so quivering in every muscle, that he did not ask her a single question, but seizing her hand, and pulling it within his arm, he led her along. To avoid meeting any possible wayfarers he left the high road, and took a footpath under some fir trees. When they were deep among the moaning boughs he stopped and looked at her enquiringly.

'Angel,' she said, as if waiting for this, 'do you know what I have been running after you for? To tell you that I have killed him!' A pitiful white smile lit her face as she spoke.

'What!' said he, thinking from the strangeness of her manner that she was in some delirium.

'I have done it – I don't know how,' she continued. 'Still, I owed it to you, and to myself, Angel. I feared long ago, when I struck him on the mouth with my glove, that I might do it someday for the trap he set for me in my simple youth, and his wrong to you through me. He has come between us and ruined us, and now he can never do it any more. I never loved him at all, Angel, as I loved you. You know it, don't you? You believe it? You didn't come back to me, and I was obliged to go back to him. Why did you go away – why did you – when I loved you so? I can't think why you did it. But I don't blame you; only, Angel, will you forgive me my sin against you, now I have killed him? I thought as I ran along that you would be sure to forgive me now I have done that. It came to me as a shining light that I should get you back that way. I could not bear the loss of you any longer – you don't know how entirely I was unable to bear your not loving me! Say you do now, dear, dear husband; say you do, now I have killed him!'

'I do love you, Tess – O, I do – it is all come back!' he said, tightening his arms round her with fervid pressure. 'But how do you mean – you have killed him?'

'I mean that I have,' she murmured in a reverie.

'What, bodily? Is he dead?'

'Yes. He heard me crying about you, and he bitterly taunted me; and called you by a foul name; and then I did it. My heart could not bear it. He had nagged me about you before. And then I dressed myself and came away to find you.'

By degrees he was inclined to believe that she had faintly attempted, at least, what she said she had done; and his horror at her impulse was mixed with amazement at the strength of her affection for himself, and at the strangeness of its quality, which had apparently extinguished her moral sense altogether. Unable to realise the gravity of her conduct she seemed at last content; and he looked at her as she lay upon his shoulder, weeping with happiness, and wondered what obscure strain in the d'Urberville blood had led to this aberration – if it were an aberration. There momentarily flashed through his mind that the family tradition of the coach and murder might have arisen because the d'Urbervilles had been known to do these things. As well as his confused and excited ideas could reason, he supposed that in the moment of mad grief of which she spoke her mind had lost its balance, and plunged her into this abyss.

It was very terrible if true; if a temporary hallucination, sad. But, anyhow, here was this deserted wife of his, this passionately-fond woman, clinging to him without a suspicion that he would be anything to her but a protector. He saw that for him to be otherwise was not, in her mind, within the region of the possible. Tenderness was absolutely dominant in Clare at last. He kissed her endlessly with his white lips, and held her hand, and said – 'I will not desert you! I will protect you by every means in my power, dearest love, whatever you may have done or not have done!'

They then walked on under the trees, Tess turning her head every now and then to look at him. Worn and unhandsome as he had become, it was plain that she did not discern the least fault in his appearance. To her he was, as of old, all that was perfection, personally and mentally. He was still her Antinous, her Apollo even; his sickly face was beautiful as the morning to her affectionate regard on this day no less than when she first beheld him; for was it not the face of the one man on earth who had loved her purely, and who had believed in her as pure!

With an instinct as to possibilities he did not now, as he had intended, make for the first station beyond the town, but plunged still farther under the firs, which here abounded for miles. Each clasping the other round the waist they promenaded over the dry bed of fir-needles, thrown into a vague intoxicating atmosphere at the consciousness of being together at last, with no living soul between them; ignoring that there was a corpse. Thus they proceeded for several miles till Tess, arousing herself, looked about her, and said, timidly –

'Are we going anywhere in particular?'

'I don't know, dearest. Why?'

'I don't know.'

'Well, we might walk a few miles further, and when it is evening find lodgings somewhere or other – in a lonely cottage, perhaps. Can you walk well, Tessy?'

'O yes! I could walk for ever and ever with your arm round me!'

Upon the whole it seemed a good thing to do. Thereupon they quickened their pace, avoiding high roads, and following obscure paths tending more or less northward. But there was an unpractical vagueness in their movements throughout the day; neither one of them seemed to consider any question of effectual escape, disguise, or long concealment. Their every idea was temporary and unforfending, like the plans of two children.

At midday they drew near to a roadside inn, and Tess would have entered it with him to get something to eat, but he persuaded her to remain among the trees and bushes of this half-woodland, half-moorland part of the country, till he should come back. Her clothes were of recent fashion; even the ivory-handled parasol that she carried was of a shape unknown in the retired spot to which they had now wandered; and the cut of such articles would have attracted attention in the settle of a tavern. He soon returned, with food enough for half a dozen people and two bottles of wine – enough to last them for a day or more, should any emergency arise.

They sat down upon some dead boughs and shared their meal. Between one and two o'clock they packed up the remainder and went on again.

'I feel strong enough to walk any distance,' said she.

'I think we may as well steer in a general way towards the interior of the country, where we can hide for a time, and are less likely to be looked for than anywhere near the coast,' Clare remarked. 'Later on, when they have forgotten us, we can make for some port.'

She made no reply to this beyond that of grasping him more tightly, and straight inland they went. Though the season was an English May the weather was serenely bright, and during the afternoon it was quite warm. Through the latter miles of their walk their footpath had taken them into the depths of the New Forest, and towards evening, turning the corner of a lane, they perceived behind a brook and bridge a large board on which was painted in white letters, 'This desirable Mansion to be Let Furnished'; particulars following, with directions to apply to some London agents. Passing through the gate they could see the house, an old brick building of regular design and large accommodation.

'I know it,' said Clare. 'It is Bramshurst Court. You can see that it is shut up, and grass is growing on the drive.'

'Some of the windows are open,' said Tess.

'Just to air the rooms, I suppose.'

'All these rooms empty, and we without a roof to our heads!'

'You are getting tired, my Tess!' he said. 'We'll stop soon.' And kissing her sad mouth he again led her onwards.

He was growing weary likewise, for they had wandered a dozen or fifteen miles, and it became necessary to consider what they should do for rest. They looked from afar at isolated cottages and little inns, and were inclined to approach one of the latter, when their hearts failed them, and they sheered off. At length their gait dragged, and they stood still.

'Could we sleep under the trees?' she asked.

He thought the season insufficiently advanced.

'I have been thinking of that empty mansion we passed,' he said. 'Let us go back towards it again.'

They retraced their steps, but it was half an hour before they stood without the entrance-gate as earlier. He then requested her to stay where she was, whilst he went to see who was within.

She sat down among the bushes within the gate, and Clare crept towards the house. His absence lasted some considerable time, and when he returned Tess was wildly anxious, not for herself, but for him. He had found out from a boy that there was only an old woman in charge as caretaker, and she only came there on fine days, from the hamlet near, to open and shut the windows. She would come to shut them at sunset. 'Now, we can get in through one of the lower windows, and rest there,' said he.

Under his escort she went tardily forward to the main front, whose shuttered windows, like sightless eyeballs, excluded the possibility of watchers. The door was reached a few steps further, and one of the windows beside it was open. Clare clambered in, and pulled Tess in after him.

Except the hall the rooms were all in darkness, and they ascended the staircase. Up here also the shutters were tightly closed, the ventilation being perfunctorily done, for this day at least, by opening the hall-window in front and an upper window behind. Clare unlatched the door of a large chamber, felt his way across it, and parted the shutters to the width of two or three inches. A shaft of dazzling sunlight glanced into the room, revealing heavy, old-fashioned furniture, crimson damask hangings, and an enormous four-post bedstead, along the head of which were carved running figures, apparently Atalanta's race.

'Rest at last!' said he, setting down his bag and the parcel of viands.

They remained in great quietness till the caretaker should have come to shut the windows: as a precaution, putting themselves in total darkness by barring the shutters as before, lest the woman should open the door of their chamber for any casual reason. Between six and seven o'clock she came, but did not approach the wing they were in. They heard her close the windows, fasten them, lock the door, and go away. Then Clare again stole a chink of light from the window, and they shared another meal, till by and by they were enveloped in the shades of night which they had no candle to disperse.

## *Chapter 58*

The night was strangely solemn and still. In the small hours she whispered to him the whole story of how he had walked in his sleep with her in his arms across the Froom stream, at the imminent risk of both their lives, and laid her down in the stone coffin at the ruined abbey. He had never known of that till now.

'Why didn't you tell me next day?' he said. 'It might have prevented much misunderstanding and woe.'

'Don't think of what's past!' said she. 'I am not going to think outside of now. Why should we! Who knows what tomorrow has in store?'

But it apparently had no sorrow. The morning was wet and foggy, and Clare, rightly informed that the caretaker only opened the windows on fine days, ventured to creep out of their chamber, and explore the house, leaving Tess asleep. There was no food on the premises, but there was water, and he took advantage of the fog to emerge from the mansion, and fetch tea, bread, and butter from a shop in a little place two miles beyond, as also a small tin kettle and spirit-lamp, that they might get fire without smoke. His re-entry awoke her; and they breakfasted on what he had brought.

They were indisposed to stir abroad, and the day passed, and the night following, and the next, and next; till, almost without their being aware, five days had slipped by in absolute seclusion, not a sight or sound of a human being disturbing their peacefulness, such as it was. The changes of the weather were their only events, the birds of the New Forest their only company. By tacit consent they hardly once spoke of any incident of the past subsequent to their wedding-day. The gloomy intervening time seemed to sink into chaos, over which the present and prior times closed as if it never had been. Whenever he suggested that they should leave their shelter, and go forwards towards Southampton or London, she showed a strange unwillingness to move.

'Why should we put an end to all that's sweet and lovely!' she deprecated. 'What must come will come.' And, looking through the shutter-chink: 'All is trouble outside there; inside here content.'

He peeped out also. It was quite true; within was affection, union, error forgiven: outside was the inexorable.

'And – and,' she said, pressing her cheek against his, 'I fear that what you think of me now may not last. I do not wish to outlive your present feeling for me. I would rather not. I would rather be dead and buried when the time comes for you to despise me, so that it may never be known to me that you despised me.'

'I cannot ever despise you.'

'I also hope that. But considering what my life has been I cannot see why any man should, sooner or later, be able to help despising me . . . How wickedly mad I was! Yet formerly I never could bear to hurt a fly or a worm, and the sight of a bird in a cage used often to make me cry.'

They remained yet another day. In the night the dull sky cleared, and the result was that the old caretaker at the cottage awoke early. The brilliant sunrise made her unusually brisk; she decided to open the contiguous mansion immediately, and to air it thoroughly on such a day. Thus it occurred that, having arrived and opened the lower rooms before six o'clock, she ascended to the bedchambers, and was about to turn the handle of the one wherein they lay. At that moment she fancied she could hear the breathing of persons within. Her slippers and her antiquity had rendered her progress a noiseless one so far, and she made for instant retreat; then, deeming that her hearing might have deceived her, she turned anew to the door and softly tried the handle. The lock was out of order, but a piece of furniture had been moved forward on the inside, which prevented her opening the door more than an inch or two. A stream of morning light through the shutter-chink fell upon the faces of the pair, wrapped in profound slumber, Tess's lips being parted like a half-opened flower near his cheek. The caretaker was so struck with their innocent appearance, and with the elegance of Tess's gown hanging across a chair, her silk stockings beside it, the pretty parasol, and the other habits in which she had arrived because she had none else, that her first indignation at the effrontery of tramps and vagabonds gave way to a momentary sentimentality over this genteel elopement, as it seemed. She closed the door, and withdrew as softly as she had come, to go and consult with her neighbours on the odd discovery.

Not more than a minute had elapsed after her withdrawal when Tess woke, and then Clare. Both had a sense that something had disturbed them, though they could not say what; and the uneasy feeling which it engendered grew stronger. As soon as he was dressed he narrowly scanned the lawn through the two or three inches of shutter-chink.

'I think we will leave at once,' said he. 'It is a fine day. And I cannot help fancying somebody is about the house. At any rate, the woman will be sure to come today.'

She passively assented, and putting the room in order they took up the few articles that belonged to them, and departed noiselessly. When they had got into the Forest she turned to take a last look at the house.

'Ah, happy house – goodbye!' she said. 'My life can only be a question of a few weeks. Why should we not have stayed there?'

'Don't say it, Tess! We shall soon get out of this district altogether. We'll continue our course as we've begun it, and keep straight north. Nobody will think of looking for us there. We shall be looked for at the Wessex ports if we are sought at all. When we are in the north we will get to a port and away.'

Having thus persuaded her the plan was pursued, and they kept a bee-line northward. Their long repose at the manor-house lent them walking power now; and towards midday they found that they were approaching the steepled city of Melchester, which lay directly in their way. He decided to rest her in a clump of trees during the afternoon, and push onward under cover of darkness. At dusk Clare purchased food as usual, and their night march began, the boundary between Upper and Mid-Wessex being crossed about eight o'clock.

To walk across country without much regard to roads was not new to Tess, and she showed her old agility in the performance. The intercepting city, ancient Melchester, they were obliged to pass through in order to take advantage of the town bridge for crossing a large river that obstructed them. It was about midnight when they went along the deserted streets, lighted fitfully by the few lamps, keeping off the pavement that it might not echo their footsteps. The graceful pile of cathedral architecture rose dimly on their left hand, but it was lost upon them now. Once out of the town they followed the turnpike-road, which after a few miles plunged across an open plain.

Though the sky was dense with cloud a diffused light from some fragment of a moon had hitherto helped them a little. But the moon had now sunk, the clouds seemed to settle almost on their heads, and the night grew as dark as a cave. However, they found their way along, keeping as much on the turf as possible that their tread might not resound, which it was easy to do, there being no hedge or fence of any kind. All around was open loneliness and black solitude, over which a stiff breeze blew.

They had proceeded thus gropingly two or three miles further when on a sudden Clare became conscious of some vast erection close in his front, rising sheer from the grass. They had almost struck themselves against it.

'What monstrous place is this?' said Angel.

'It hums,' said she. 'Hearken!'

He listened. The wind, playing upon the edifice, produced a booming tune, like the note of some gigantic one-stringed harp. No other sound came from it, and lifting his hand and advancing a step or two, Clare felt the vertical surface of the structure. It seemed to be of solid stone, without joint or moulding. Carrying his fingers onward he found that what he had come in contact with was a colossal rectangular pillar; by stretching out his left hand he could feel a similar one adjoining. At an indefinite height overhead something made the black sky blacker, which had the semblance of a vast architrave uniting the pillars horizontally. They carefully entered beneath and between; the surfaces echoed their soft rustle; but they seemed to be still out of doors. The place was roofless. Tess drew her breath fearfully, and Angel, perplexed, said – 'What can it be?'

Feeling sideways they encountered another tower-like pillar, square and uncompromising as the first; beyond it another and another. The place was all doors and pillars, some connected above by continuous architraves.

'A very Temple of the Winds,' he said.

The next pillar was isolated; others composed a trilithon; others were prostrate, their flanks forming a causeway wide enough for a carriage; and it was soon obvious that they made up a forest of monoliths grouped upon the grassy expanse of the plain. The couple advanced further into this pavilion of the night till they stood in its midst.

'It is Stonehenge!' said Clare.

'The heathen temple, you mean?'

'Yes. Older than the centuries; older than the d'Urbervilles! Well, what shall we do, darling? We may find shelter further on.'

But Tess, really tired by this time, flung herself upon an oblong slab that lay close at hand, and was sheltered from the wind by a pillar. Owing to the action of the sun during the preceding day the stone was warm and dry, in comforting contrast to the rough and chill grass around, which had damped her skirts and shoes.

'I don't want to go any further, Angel,' she said, stretching out her hand for his. 'Can't we bide here?'

'I fear not. This spot is visible for miles by day, although it does not seem so now.'

'One of my mother's people was a shepherd hereabouts, now I think of it. And you used to say at Talbothays that I was a heathen. So now I am at home.'

He knelt down beside her outstretched form, and put his lips upon hers.

'Sleepy are you, dear? I think you are lying on an altar.'

'I like very much to be here,' she murmured. 'It is so solemn and lonely – after my great happiness – with nothing but the sky above my face. It seems as if there were no folk in the world but we two; and I wish there were not – except 'Liza-Lu.'

Clare thought she might as well rest here till it should get a little lighter, and he flung his overcoat upon her, and sat down by her side.

'Angel, if anything happens to me, will you watch over 'Liza-Lu for my sake?' she asked, when they had listened a long time to the wind among the pillars.

'I will.'

'She is so good and simple and pure. O, Angel – I wish you would marry her if you lose me, as you will do shortly. O, if you would!'

'If I lose you I lose all! And she is my sister-in-law.'

'That's nothing, dearest. People marry sister-in-laws continually about Marlott; and 'Liza-Lu is so gentle and sweet, and she is growing so beautiful. O, I could share you with her willingly when we are spirits! If you would train her and teach her, Angel, and bring her up for your own self! . . . She has all the best of me without the bad of me; and if she were to become yours it would almost seem as if death had not divided us . . . Well, I have said it. I won't mention it again.'

She ceased, and he fell into thought. In the far north-east sky he could see between the pillars a level streak of light. The uniform concavity of black cloud was lifting bodily like the lid of a pot, letting in at the earth's edge the coming day, against which the towering monoliths and trilithons began to be blackly defined.

'Did they sacrifice to God here?' asked she.

'No,' said he.

'Who to?'

'I believe to the sun. That lofty stone set away by itself is in the direction of the sun, which will presently rise behind it.'

'This reminds me, dear,' she said. 'You remember you never would interfere with any belief of mine before we were married? But I knew your mind all the same, and I thought as you thought – not from any reasons of my own, but because you thought so. Tell me now, Angel, do you think we shall meet again after we are dead? I want to know.'

He kissed her to avoid a reply at such a time.

'O, Angel – I fear that means no!' said she, with a suppressed sob. 'And I wanted so to see you again – so much, so much! What – not even you and I, Angel, who love each other so well?'

Like a greater than himself, to the critical question at the critical time he did not answer; and they were again silent. In a minute or two her breathing became more regular, her clasp of his hand relaxed, and she fell asleep. The band of silver paleness along the east horizon made even the distant parts of the Great Plain appear dark and near; and the whole enormous landscape bore that impress of reserve, taciturnity, and hesitation which is usual just before day. The eastward pillars and their architraves stood up blackly against the light, and the great flame-shaped Sun-stone beyond them; and the Stone of Sacrifice midway. Presently the night wind died out, and the quivering little pools in the cup-like hollows of the stones lay still. At the same time something seemed to move on the verge of the dip eastward – a mere dot. It was the head of a man approaching them from the hollow beyond the Sun-stone. Clare wished they had gone onward, but in the circumstances decided to remain quiet. The figure came straight towards the circle of pillars in which they were.

He heard something behind him, the brush of feet. Turning, he saw over the prostrate columns another figure; then before he was aware, another was at hand on the right, under a trilithon, and another on the left. The dawn shone full on the front of the man westward, and Clare could discern from this that he was tall, and walked as if trained. They all closed in with evident purpose. Her story then was true! Springing to his feet, he looked around for a weapon, loose stone, means of escape, anything. By this time the nearest man was upon him.

'It is no use, sir,' he said. 'There are sixteen of us on the Plain, and the whole country is reared.'

'Let her finish her sleep!' he implored in a whisper of the men as they gathered round.

When they saw where she lay, which they had not done till then, they showed no objection, and stood watching her, as still as the pillars around. He went to the stone and bent over her, holding one poor little hand; her breathing now was quick and small, like that of a lesser creature than a woman. All waited in the growing light, their faces and hands as if they were silvered, the remainder of their figures dark, the stones glistening green-grey, the Plain still a mass of shade. Soon the light was strong, and a ray shone upon her unconscious form, peering under her eyelids and waking her.

'What is it, Angel?' she said, starting up. 'Have they come for me?'

'Yes, dearest,' he said. 'They have come.'

'It is as it should be,' she murmured. 'Angel, I am almost glad – yes, glad! This happiness could not have lasted. It was too much. I have had enough; and now I shall not live for you to despise me!'

She stood up, shook herself, and went forward, neither of the men having moved.

'I am ready,' she said quietly.

## *Chapter 59*

The city of Wintoncester, that fine old city, aforetime capital of Wessex, lay amidst its convex and concave downlands in all the brightness and warmth of a July morning. The gabled brick, tile, and freestone houses had almost dried off for the season their integument of lichen, the streams in the meadows were low, and in the sloping High Street, from the West Gateway to the medieval cross, and from the medieval cross to the bridge, that leisurely dusting and sweeping was in progress which usually ushers in an old-fashioned market-day.

From the western gate aforesaid the highway, as every Wintoncestrian knows, ascends a long and regular incline of the exact length of a measured mile, leaving the houses gradually behind. Up this road from the precincts of the city two persons were walking rapidly, as if unconscious of the trying ascent – unconscious through preoccupation and not through buoyancy. They had emerged upon this road through a narrow barred wicket in a high wall a little lower down. They seemed anxious to get out of the sight of the houses and of their kind, and this road appeared to offer the quickest means of doing so. Though they were young they walked with bowed heads, which gait of grief the sun's rays smiled on pitilessly.

One of the pair was Angel Clare, the other a tall budding creature – half girl, half woman – a spiritualised image of Tess, slighter than she, but with the same beautiful eyes – Clare's sister-in-law, 'Liza-Lu. Their pale faces seemed to have shrunk to half their natural size. They moved on hand in hand, and never spoke a word, the drooping of their heads being that of Giotto's 'Two Apostles'.

When they had nearly reached the top of the great West Hill the clocks in the town struck eight. Each gave a start at the notes, and, walking onward yet a few steps, they reached the first milestone, standing whitely on the green margin of the grass, and backed by the down, which here was open to the road. They entered upon the turf, and, impelled by a force that seemed to overrule their will, suddenly stood still, turned, and waited in paralysed suspense beside the stone.

The prospect from this summit was almost unlimited. In the valley beneath lay the city they had just left, its more prominent buildings showing as in an isometric drawing – among them the broad cathedral tower, with its Norman windows and immense length of aisle and nave, the spires of St Thomas's, the pinnacled tower of the College, and, more to the right, the tower and gables of the ancient hospice, where to this day the pilgrim may receive his dole of bread and ale. Behind the city swept the rotund upland of St Catherine's Hill; further off, landscape beyond landscape, till the horizon was lost in the radiance of the sun hanging above it.

Against these far stretches of country rose, in front of the other city edifices, a large red-brick building, with level grey roofs, and rows of short barred windows bespeaking captivity, the whole contrasting greatly by its formalism with the quaint irregularities of the Gothic erections. It was somewhat disguised from the road in passing it by yews and evergreen oaks, but it was visible enough up here. The wicket from which the pair had lately emerged was in the wall of this structure. From the middle of the building an ugly flat-topped octagonal tower ascended against the east horizon, and viewed from this spot, on its shady side and against the light, it seemed the one blot on the city's beauty. Yet it was with this blot, and not with the beauty, that the two gazers were concerned.

Upon the cornice of the tower a tall staff was fixed. Their eyes were riveted on it. A few minutes after the hour had struck something moved slowly up the staff, and extended itself upon the breeze. It was a black flag.

'Justice' was done, and the President of the Immortals, in Aeschylean phrase, had ended his sport with Tess. And the d'Urberville knights and dames slept on in their tombs unknowing. The two speechless gazers bent themselves down to the earth, as if in prayer, and remained thus a long time, absolutely motionless: the flag continued to wave silently. As soon as they had strength they arose, joined hands again, and went on.